SIR ARTHUR CONAN DOYLE

THE HISTORICAL NOVELS

VOLUME TWO

Micah Clarke
The Refugees
Rodney Stone

by
Sir Arthur Conan Doyle

New Orchard Editions
Poole · New York · Sydney

Copyright © 1986 New Orchard Editions Ltd

This edition first published 1986 by
New Orchard Editions Ltd
Robert Rogers House
New Orchard
Poole, Dorset, BH15 1LU

ISBN: 1 85079 041 8 Vol. One
      1 85079 042 6 Vol. Two
      1 85079 045 0 Two Volume Set

Printed in Great Britain by
The Bath Press, Avon

CONTENTS

MICAH CLARKE

HIS STATEMENT

1. *Of Cornet Joseph Clarke of the Ironsides*

IT may be, my dear grandchildren, that at one time or another I have told you nearly all the incidents which have occurred during my adventurous life. To your father and to your mother, at least, I know that none of them are unfamiliar. Yet when I consider that time wears on, and that a grey head is apt to contain a failing memory, I am prompted to use these long winter evenings in putting it all before you from the beginning, that you may have it as one clear story in your minds, and pass it on as such to those who come after you. For now that the house of Brunswick is firmly established upon the throne and that peace prevails in the land, it will become less easy for you every year to understand how men felt when Englishmen were in arms against Englishmen, and when he who should have been the shield and the protector of his subjects had no thought but to force upon them what they most abhorred and detested.

My story is one which you may well treasure up in your memories, and tell again to others, for it is not likely that in this whole county of Hampshire, or even perhaps in all England, there is another left alive who is so well able to speak from his own knowledge of these events, or who has played a more forward part in them. All that I know I shall endeavour soberly and in due order to put before you. I shall try to make these dead men quicken into life for your behoof, and to call back out of the mists of the past those scenes which were brisk enough in the acting, though they read so dully and so heavily in the pages of the worthy men who have set themselves to record them. Perchance my words, too, might, in the ears of strangers,

3

seem to be but an old man's gossip. To you, however, who know that these eyes which are looking at you looked also at the things which I describe, and that this hand has struck in for a good cause, it will, I know, be different. Bear in mind as you listen that it was your quarrel as well as our own in which we fought, and that if now you grow up to be free men in a free land, privileged to think or to pray as your consciences shall direct, you may thank God that you are reaping the harvest which your fathers sowed in blood and suffering when the Stuarts were on the throne.

I was born then in the year 1664, at Havant, which is a flourishing village a few miles from Portsmouth off the main London road, and there it was that I spent the greater part of my youth. It is now as it was then, a pleasant, healthy spot, with a hundred or more brick cottages scattered along in a single irregular street, each with its little garden in front, and maybe a fruit tree or two at the back. In the middle of the village stood the old church with the square tower and the great sun-dial like a wrinkle upon its grey weather-blotched face. On the outskirts the Presbyterians had their chapel; but when the Act of Uniformity was passed, their good minister, Master Breckinridge, whose discourses had often crowded his rude benches while the comfortable pews of the church were empty, was cast into gaol, and his flock dispersed. As to the Independents, of whom my father was one, they also were under the ban of the law, but they attended conventicle at Emsworth, whither we would trudge, rain or shine, on every Sabbath morning. These meetings were broken up more than once, but the congregation was composed of such harmless folk, so well beloved and respected by their neighbours, that the peace officers came after a time to ignore them, and to let them worship in their own fashion. There were Papists, too, amongst us, who were compelled to go as far as Portsmouth for their Mass. Thus, you see, small as was our village, we were a fair miniature of the whole country, for

we had our sects and our factions, which were all the more bitter for being confined in so narrow a compass.

My father, Joseph Clarke, was better known over the countryside by the name of Ironside Joe, for he had served in his youth in the Yaxley troop of Oliver Cromwell's famous regiment of horse, and had preached so lustily and fought so stoutly that old Noll himself called him out of the ranks after the fight at Dunbar, and raised him to a cornetcy. It chanced, however, that having some little time later fallen into an argument with one of his troopers concerning the mystery of the Trinity, the man, who was a half-crazy zealot, smote my father across the face, a favour which he returned by a thrust from his broadsword, which sent his adversary to test in person the truth of his beliefs. In most armies it would have been conceded that my father was within his rights in punishing promptly so rank an act of mutiny, but the soldiers of Cromwell had so high a notion of their own importance and privileges, that they resented this summary justice upon their companion. A court-martial sat upon my father, and it is likely that he would have been offered up as a sacrifice to appease the angry soldiery, had not the Lord Protector interfered, and limited the punishment to dismissal from the army. Cornet Clarke was accordingly stripped of his buff coat and steel cap, and wandered down to Havant, where he settled into business as a leather merchant and tanner, thereby depriving Parliament of as trusty a soldier as ever drew blade in its service. Finding that he prospered in trade, he took as wife Mary Shepstone, a young Churchwoman, and I, Micah Clarke, was the first pledge of their union.

My father, as I remember him first, was tall and straight, with a great spread of shoulder and a mighty chest. His face was craggy and stern, with large harsh features, shaggy overhanging brows, high-bridged fleshy nose, and a full-lipped mouth which tightened and set when he was angry. His grey eyes were piercing and soldier-like, yet I have seen them lighten up into a kindly and merry

twinkle. His voice was the most tremendous and awe-inspiring that I have ever listened to. I can well believe what I have heard, that when he chanted the Hundredth Psalm as he rode down among the blue bonnets at Dunbar, the sound of him rose above the blare of trumpets and the crash of guns, like the deep roll of a breaking wave. Yet though he possessed every quality which was needed to raise him to distinction as an officer, he had thrown off his military habits when he returned to civil life. As he prospered and grew rich he might well have worn a sword, but instead he would ever bear a small copy of the Scriptures bound to his girdle, where other men hung their weapons. He was sober and measured in his speech, and it was seldom, even in the bosom of his own family, that he would speak of the scenes which he had taken part in, or of the great men, Fleetwood and Harrison, Blake and Ireton, Desborough and Lambert, some of whom had been simple troopers like himself when the troubles broke out. He was frugal in his eating, backward in drinking, and allowed himself no pleasures save three pipes a day of Oronooko tobacco, which he kept ever in a brown jar by the great wooden chair on the left-hand side of the mantelshelf.

Yet for all his self-restraint the old leaven would at times begin to work in him, and bring on fits of what his enemies would call fanaticism and his friends piety, though it must be confessed that this piety was prone to take a fierce and fiery shape. As I look back, one or two instances of that stand out so hard and clear in my recollection that they might be scenes which I had seen of late in the playhouse, instead of memories of my childhood more than threescore years ago, when the second Charles was on the throne.

The first of these occurred when I was so young that I can remember neither what went before nor what immediately after it. It stuck in my infant mind when other things slipped through it. We were all in the house one sultry summer evening, when there came a

6

rattle of kettledrums and a clatter of hoofs, which brought my mother and my father to the door, she with me in her arms that I might have the better view. It was a regiment of horse on their way from Chichester to Portsmouth, with colours flying and band playing, making the bravest show that ever my youthful eyes had rested upon. With what wonder and admiration did I gaze at the sleek prancing steeds, the steel morions, the plumed hats of the officers, the scarfs and bandoliers. Never, I thought, had such a gallant company assembled, and I clapped my hands and cried out in my delight. My father smiled gravely, and took me from my mother's arms. " Nay, lad," he said, " thou art a soldier's son, and should have more judgment than to commend such a rabble as this. Canst thou not, child as thou art, see that their arms are ill-found, their stirrup-irons rusted, and their ranks without order or cohesion ? Neither have they thrown out a troop in advance, as should even in times of peace be done, and their rear is straggling from here to Bed-hampton. Yea," he continued, suddenly shaking his long arm at the troopers, and calling out to them, " ye are corn ripe for the sickle and waiting only for the reapers ! " Several of them reined up at this sudden out-flame. " Hit the crop-eared rascal over the pate, Jack ! " cried one to another, wheeling his horse round ; but there was that in my father's face which caused him to fall back into the ranks again with his purpose unfulfilled. The regiment jingled on down the road, and my mother laid her thin hands upon my father's arm, and lulled with her pretty coaxing ways the sleeping devil which had stirred within him.

On another occasion which I can remember, about my seventh or eighth year, his wrath burst out with more dangerous effect. I was playing about him as he worked in the tanning yard one spring afternoon, when in through the open doorway strutted two stately gentlemen, with gold facings to their coats and smart cockades at the side of their three-cornered hats. They were, as I afterwards

understood, officers of the fleet who were passing through Havant, and seeing us at work in the yard, designed to ask us some question as to their route. The younger of the pair accosted my father and began his speech by a great clatter of words which were all High Dutch to me, though I now see that they were a string of such oaths as are common in the mouth of a sailor ; though why the very men who are in most danger of appearing before the Almighty should go out of their way to insult Him, hath ever been a mystery to me. My father in a rough stern voice bade him speak with more reverence of sacred things, on which the pair of them gave tongue together, swearing tenfold worse than before, and calling my father a canting rogue and a smug-faced Presbytery Jack. What more they might have said I know not, for my father picked up the great roller wherewith he smoothed the leather, and dashing at them he brought it down on the side of one of their heads with such a swashing blow, that had it not been for his stiff hat the man would never have uttered oath again. As it was, he dropped like a log upon the stones of the yard, while his companion whipped out his rapier and made a vicious thrust ; but my father, who was as active as he was strong, sprang aside, and bringing his cudgel down upon the out-stretched arm of the officer, cracked it like the stem of a tobacco-pipe. This affair made no little stir, for it occurred at the time when those arch-liars, Oates, Bedloe and Carstairs, were disturbing the public mind by their rumours of plots, and a rising of some sort was expected throughout the country. Within a few days all Hampshire was ringing with an account of the malcontent tanner of Havant, who had broken the head and the arm of two of his Majesty's servants. An inquiry showed, however, that there was no treasonable meaning in the matter, and the officers having confessed that the first words came from them, the Justices contented themselves with imposing a fine upon my father, and binding him over to keep the peace for a period of six months.

8

I tell you these incidents that you may have an idea of the fierce and earnest religion which filled not only your own ancestor, but most of those men who were trained in the parliamentary armies. In many ways they were more like those fanatic Saracens, who believe in conversion by the sword, than the followers of a Christian creed. Yet they have this great merit, that their own lives were for the most part clean and commendable, for they rigidly adhered themselves to those laws which they would gladly have forced at the sword's point upon others. It is true that among so many there were some whose piety was a shell for their ambition, and others who practised in secret what they denounced in public, but no cause, however good, is free from such hypocritical parasites. That the greater part of the saints, as they termed themselves, were men of sober and God-fearing lives, may be shown by the fact that, after the disbanding of the army of the Commonwealth, the old soldiers flocked into trade throughout the country, and made their mark wherever they went by their industry and worth. There is many a wealthy business house now in England which can trace its rise to the thrift and honesty of some simple pikeman of Ireton or Cromwell.

But that I may help you to understand the character of your great-grandfather, I shall give an incident which shows how fervent and real were the emotions which prompted the violent moods which I have described. I was about twelve at the time, my brothers Hosea and Ephraim were respectively nine and seven, while little Ruth could scarce have been more than four. It chanced that a few days before a wandering preacher of the Independents had put up at our house, and his religious ministrations had left my father moody and excitable. One night I had gone to bed as usual, and was sound asleep with my two brothers beside me, when we were roused and ordered to come downstairs. Huddling on our clothes we followed him into the kitchen, where my mother was sitting pale and scared with Ruth upon her knee.

9

" Gather round me, my children," he said, in a deep reverent voice, " that we may all appear before the throne together. The kingdom of the Lord is at hand—oh, be ye ready to receive Him! This very night, my loved ones, ye shall see Him in His splendour, with the angels and the archangels in their might and their glory. At the third hour shall He come—that very third hour which is now drawing upon us."

" Dear Joe," said my mother, in soothing tones, " thou art scaring thyself and the children to no avail. If the Son of Man be indeed coming, what matters it whether we be abed or afoot ? "

" Peace, woman," he answered sternly ; " has He not said that He will come like a thief in the night, and that it is for us to await Him ? Join with me, then, in prayerful outpourings that we may be found as those in bridal array. Let us offer up thanks that He has graciously vouchsafed to warn us through the words of His servant. Oh, great Lord, look down upon this small flock and lead it to the sheepfold ! Mix not the little wheat with the great world of chaff. Oh, merciful Father ! look graciously upon my wife, and forgive her the sin of Erastianism, she being but a woman and little fitted to cast off the bonds of antichrist wherein she was born. And these too, my little ones, Micah and Hosea, Ephraim and Ruth, all named after Thy faithful servants of old, oh let them stand upon Thy right hand this night ! " Thus he prayed on in a wild rush of burning, pleading words, writhing prostrate upon the floor in the vehemence of his supplication, while we, poor trembling mites, huddled round our mother's skirts and gazed with terror at the contorted figure seen by the dim light of the simple oil lamp. On a sudden the clang of the new church clock told that the hour had come. My father sprang from the floor, and rushing to the casement, stared up with wild expectant eyes at the starry heavens. Whether he conjured up some vision in his excited brain, or whether the rush of feeling on finding that his expectations

were in vain, was too much for him, it is certain that he threw his long arms upwards, uttered a hoarse scream, and tumbled backwards with foaming lips and twitching limbs upon the ground. For an hour or more my poor mother and I did what we could to soothe him, while the children whimpered in a corner, until at last he staggered slowly to his feet, and in brief broken words ordered us to our rooms. From that time I have never heard him allude to the matter, nor did he ever give us any reason why he should so confidently have expected the second coming upon that particular night. I have learned since, however, that the preacher who visited us was what was called in those days a fifth-monarchy man, and that this particular sect was very liable to these premonitions. I have no doubt that something which he had said had put the thought into my father's head, and that the fiery nature of the man had done the rest.

So much for your great-grandfather, Ironside Joe. I have preferred to put these passages before you, for on the principle that actions speak louder than words, I find that in describing a man's character it is better to give examples of his ways than to speak in broad and general terms. Had I said that he was fierce in his religion and subject to strange fits of piety, the words might have made little impression upon you ; but when I tell you of his attack upon the officers in the tanning-yard, and his summoning us down in the dead of the night to await the second coming, you can judge for yourselves the lengths to which his belief would carry him. For the rest, he was an excellent man of business, fair and even generous in his dealings, respected by all and loved by few, for his nature was too self-contained to admit of much affection. To us he was a stern and rigid father, punishing us heavily for whatever he regarded as amiss in our conduct. He had a store of such proverbs as " Give a child its will and a whelp its fill, and neither will strive," or " Children are certain cares and uncertain comforts," wherewith he would temper my mother's

more kindly impulses. He could not bear that we should play trick-track upon the green, or dance with the other children upon the Saturday night.

As to my mother, dear soul, it was her calm, peaceful influence which kept my father within bounds, and softened his austere rule. Seldom indeed, even in his darkest moods, did the touch of her gentle hand and the sound of her voice fail to soothe his fiery spirit. She came of a Church stock, and held to her religion with a quiet grip which was proof against every attempt to turn her from it. I imagine that at one time her husband had argued much with her upon Arminianism and the sin of simony, but finding his exhortations useless, he had abandoned the subject save on very rare occasions. In spite of her Episcopacy, however, she remained a staunch Whig, and never allowed her loyalty to the throne to cloud her judgment as to the doings of the monarch who sat upon it.

Women were good housekeepers fifty years ago, but she was conspicuous among the best. To see her spotless cuffs and snowy kirtle one would scarce credit how hard she laboured. It was only the well-ordered house and the dustless rooms which proclaimed her constant industry. She made salves and eyewaters, powders and confects, cordials and persico, orangeflower water and cherry brandy, each in its due season, and all of the best. She was wise, too, in herbs and simples. The villagers and the farm labourers would rather any day have her advice upon their ailments than that of Dr. Jackson of Purbrook, who never mixed a draught under a silver crown. Over the whole countryside there was no woman more deservedly respected and more esteemed both by those above her and by those beneath.

Such were my parents as I remember them in my childhood. As to myself, I shall let my story explain the growth of my own nature. My brothers and my sister were all brown-faced, sturdy little country children, with no very marked traits save a love of mischief controlled

by the fear of their father. These, with Martha the serving-maid, formed our whole household during those boyish years when the pliant soul of the child is hardening into the settled character of the man. How these influences affected me I shall leave for a future sitting, and if I weary you by recording them, you must remember that I am telling these things rather for your profit than for your amusement ; that it may assist you in your journey through life to know how another has picked out the path before you.

2. *Of my Going to School and of my Coming Thence*

WITH the home influences which I have described, it may be readily imagined that my young mind turned very much upon the subject of religion, the more so as my father and mother took different views upon it. The old Puritan soldier held that the Bible alone contained all things essential to salvation, and that though it might be advisable that those who were gifted with wisdom or eloquence should expound the Scriptures to their brethren, it was by no means necessary, but rather hurtful and degrading, that any organised body of ministers or of bishops should claim special prerogatives, or take the place of mediators between the creature and the Creator. For the wealthy dignitaries of the Church, rolling in their carriages to their cathedrals, in order to preach the doctrines of their Master, who wore His sandals out in tramping over the countryside, he professed the most bitter contempt ; nor was he more lenient to those poorer members of the clergy who winked at the vices of their patrons that they might secure a seat at their table, and who would sit through a long evening of profanity rather than bid good-bye to the cheesecakes and the wine flask. That such men represented religious truth was abhorrent to his mind, nor would he even

give his adhesion to that form of church government dear to the Presbyterians, where a general council of the ministers directed the affairs of their church. Every man was, in his opinion, equal in the eyes of the Almighty, and none had a right to claim any precedence over his neighbour in matters of religion. The Book was written for all, and all were equally able to read it, provided that their minds were enlightened by the Holy Spirit.

My mother, on the other hand, held that the very essence of a church was that it should have a hierarchy and a graduated government within itself, with the king at the apex, the archbishops beneath him, the bishops under their control, and so down through the ministry to the common folk. Such was, in her opinion, the Church as established in the beginning, and no religion without these characteristics could lay any claim to being the true one. Ritual was to her of as great importance as morality, and if every tradesman and farmer were allowed to invent prayers, and change the service as the fancy seized him, it would be impossible to preserve the purity of the Christian creed. She agreed that religion was based upon the Bible, but the Bible was a book which contained much that was obscure, and unless that obscurity were cleared away by a duly elected and consecrated servant of God, a lineal descendant of the Disciples, all human wisdom might not serve to interpret it aright. That was my mother's position, and neither argument nor entreaty could move her from it. The only question of belief on which my two parents were equally ardent was their mutual dislike and distrust of the Roman Catholic forms of worship, and in this the Churchwoman was every whit as decided as the fanatical Independent.

It may seem strange to you in these days of tolerance, that the adherents of this venerable creed should have met with such universal ill-will from successive generations of Englishmen. We recognise now that there are no more useful or loyal citizens in the state than our Catholic brethren, and Mr. Alexander Pope or any other leading

Papist is no more looked down upon for his religion than was Mr. William Penn for his Quakerism in the reign of King James. We can scarce credit how noblemen like Lord Stafford, ecclesiastics like Archbishop Plunkett, and commoners like Langhorne and Pickering, were dragged to death on the testimony of the vilest of the vile, without a voice being raised in their behalf ; or how it could be considered a patriotic act on the part of an English Protestant to carry a flail loaded with lead beneath his cloak as a menace against his harmless neighbours who differed from him on points of doctrine. It was a long madness which has now happily passed off, or at least shows itself in a milder and rarer form.

Foolish as it appears to us, there were some solid reasons to account for it. You have read doubtless how, a century before I was born, the great kingdom of Spain waxed and prospered. Her ships covered every sea. Her troops were victorious wherever they appeared. In letters, in learning, in all the arts of war and peace they were the foremost nation in Europe. You have heard also of the ill-blood which existed between this great nation and ourselves ; how our adventurers harried their possessions across the Atlantic, while they retorted by burning such of our seamen as they could catch by their devilish Inquisition, and by threatening our coasts both from Cadiz and from their provinces in the Netherlands. At last so hot became the quarrel that the other nations stood off, as I have seen the folk clear a space for the sword-players at Hockley-in-the-Hole, so that the Spanish giant and tough little England were left face to face to fight the matter out. Throughout all that business it was as the emissary of the Pope, and as the avenger of the dishonoured Roman Church, that King Philip professed to come. It is true that Lord Howard and many another gentleman of the old religion fought stoutly against the Dons, but the people could never forget that the reformed faith had been the flag under which they had conquered, and that the blessing of the Pontiff had rested with their

15

opponents. Then came the cruel and foolish attempt of Mary to force upon them a creed for which they had no sympathy, and at the heels of it another great Roman Catholic power menaced our liberty from the Continent. The growing strength of France promoted a corresponding distrust of Papistry in England, which reached a head when, at about the time of which I write, Louis XIV threatened us with invasion at the very moment when, by the revocation of the Edict of Nantes, he showed his intolerant spirit towards the faith which we held dear. The narrow Protestantism of England was less a religious sentiment than a patriotic reply to the aggressive bigotry of her enemies. Our Catholic countrymen were unpopular, not so much because they believed in Transubstantiation, as because they were unjustly suspected of sympathising with the Emperor or with the King of France. Now that our military successes have secured us against all fear of attack, we have happily lost that bitter religious hatred but for which Oates and Dangerfield would have lied in vain.

In the days when I was young, special causes had inflamed this dislike and made it all the more bitter because there was a spice of fear mingled with it. As long as the Catholics were only an obscure faction they might be ignored, but when, towards the close of the reign of the second Charles, it appeared to be absolutely certain that a Catholic dynasty was about to fill the throne, and that Catholicism was to be the court religion and the stepping-stone to preferment, it was felt that a day of vengeance might be at hand for those who had trampled upon it when it was defenceless. There was alarm and uneasiness amongst all classes. The Church of England, which depends upon the monarch as an arch depends upon the keystone ; the nobility, whose estates and coffers had been enriched by the plunder of the abbeys ; the mob, whose ideas of Papistry were mixed up with thumbscrews and Fox's Martyrology, were all equally disturbed. Nor was the prospect a hopeful one for their cause. Charles

was a very lukewarm Protestant, and indeed showed upon his deathbed that he was no Protestant at all. There was no longer any chance of his having legitimate offspring. The Duke of York, his younger brother, was therefore heir to the throne, and he was known to be an austere and narrow Papist, while his spouse, Mary of Modena, was as bigoted as himself. Should they have children, there could be no question but that they would be brought up in the faith of their parents, and that a line of Catholic monarchs would occupy the throne of England. To the Church, as represented by my mother, and to Nonconformity, in the person of my father, this was an equally intolerable prospect.

I have been telling you all this old history because you will find, as I go on, that this state of things caused in the end such a seething and fermenting throughout the nation that even I, a simple village lad, was dragged into the whirl and had my whole life influenced by it. If I did not make the course of events clear to you, you would hardly understand the influences which had such an effect upon my whole history. In the meantime, I wish you to remember that when King James II ascended the throne he did so amid a sullen silence on the part of a large class of his subjects, and that both my father and my mother were among those who were zealous for a Protestant succession.

My childhood was, as I have already said, a gloomy one. Now and again when there chanced to be a fair at Portsdown Hill, or when a passing raree showman set up his booth in the village, my dear mother would slip a penny or two from her housekeeping money into my hand, and with a warning finger upon her lip would send me off to see the sights. These treats were, however, rare events, and made such a mark upon my mind, that when I was sixteen years of age I could have checked off upon my fingers all that I had ever seen. There was William Harker the strong man, who lifted Farmer Alcott's roan mare ; and there was Tubby Lawson the dwarf, who

could fit himself into a pickle jar—these two I well remember from the wonder wherewith they struck my youthful soul. Then there was the show of the playing dolls, and that of the enchanted island and Mynheer Munster from the Lowlands, who could turn himself round upon a tight-rope while playing most sweetly upon a virginal. Last, but far the best in my estimation, was the grand play at the Portsdown Fair, entitled " The true and ancient story of Maudlin, the merchant's daughter of Bristol, and of her lover Antonio. How they were cast away upon the shores of Barbary, where the mermaids are seen floating upon the sea and singing in the rocks, foretelling their danger." This little piece gave me keener pleasure than ever in after years I received from the grandest comedies of Mr. Congreve and of Mr. Dryden, though acted by Kynaston, Betterton and the whole strength of the King's own company. At Chichester once I remember that I paid a penny to see the left shoe of the youngest sister of Potiphar's wife, but as it looked much like any other old shoe, and was just about the size to have fitted the show-woman, I have often feared that my penny fell into the hands of rogues.

There were other shows, however, which I might see for nothing, and yet were more real and every whit as interesting as any for which I paid. Now and again upon a holiday I was permitted to walk down to Portsmouth—once I was even taken in front of my father upon his pad nag, and there I wandered with him through the streets with wondering eyes, marvelling over the strange sights around me. The walls and the moats, the gates and the sentinels, the long High Street with the great government buildings, and the constant rattle of drums and blare of trumpets ; they made my little heart beat quicker beneath my sagathy stuff jacket. Here was the house in which some thirty years before the proud Duke of Buckingham had been struck down by the assassin's dagger. There, too, was the Governor's dwelling, and I remember that even as I looked he came

riding up to it, red-faced and choleric, with a nose such as a Governor should have, and his breast all slashed with gold. " Is he not a fine man ? " I said, looking up at my father. He laughed and drew his hat down over his brows. " It is the first time that I have seen Sir Ralph Lingard's face," said he, " but I saw his back at Preston fight. Ah, lad, proud as he looks, if he did but see old Noll coming in through the door he would not think it beneath him to climb out through the window ! " The clank of steel or the sight of a buff-coat would always serve to stir up the old Roundhead bitterness in my father's breast.

But there were other sights in Portsmouth besides the red-coats and their Governor. The yard was the second in the kingdom, after Chatham, and there was ever some new warship ready upon the slips. Then there was a squadron of King's ships, and sometimes the whole fleet at Spithead, when the streets would be full of sailors, with their faces as brown as mahogany and pigtails as stiff and hard as their cutlasses. To watch their rolling gait, and to hear their strange, quaint talk, and their tales of the Dutch wars, was a rare treat to me ; and I have sometimes when I was alone fastened myself on to a group of them, and passed the day in wandering from tavern to tavern. It chanced one day, however, that one of them insisted upon my sharing his glass of Canary wine, and afterwards out of roguishness persuaded me to take a second, with the result that I was sent home speechless in the carrier's cart, and was never again allowed to go into Portsmouth alone. My father was less shocked at the incident than I should have expected, and reminded my mother that Noah had been overtaken in a similar manner. He also narrated how a certain field-chaplain Grant, of Desborough's regiment, having after a hot and dusty day drunk sundry flagons of mum, had thereafter sung certain ungodly songs, and danced in a manner unbecoming to his sacred profession. Also, how he had afterwards explained that such backslidings were not to be regarded

19

as faults of the individual, but rather as actual obsessions of the evil one, who contrived in this manner to give scandal to the faithful, and selected the most godly for his evil purpose. This ingenious defence of the field-chaplain was the saving of my back, for my father, who was a believer in Solomon's axiom, had a stout ash stick and a strong arm for whatever seemed to him to be a falling away from the true path.

From the day that I first learned my letters from the hornbook at my mother's knee I was always hungry to increase my knowledge, and never a piece of print came in my way that I did not eagerly master. My father pushed the sectarian hatred of learning to such a length that he was averse to having any worldly books within his doors.[1] I was dependent therefore for my supply upon one or two of my friends in the village, who lent me a volume at a time from their small libraries. These I would carry inside my shirt, and would only dare to produce when I could slip away into the fields, and lie hid among the long grass, or at night when the rushlight was still burning, and my father's snoring assured me that there was no danger of his detecting me. In this way I worked up from Don Bellianis of Greece and the *Seven Champions*, through Tarleton's *Jests* and other such books, until I could take pleasure in the poetry of Waller and of Herrick, or in the plays of Massinger and Shakespeare. How sweet were the hours when I could lay aside all thought of freewill and of predestination, to lie with my heels in the air among the scented clover, and listen to old Chaucer telling the sweet story of Grisel the patient, or to weep for the chaste Desdemona, and mourn over the untimely end of her gallant spouse. There were times as I rose up with my mind full of the noble poetry, and glanced over the fair slope of the countryside, with the gleaming sea beyond it, and the purple outline of the Isle of Wight upon the horizon ; when it would be borne in upon me that the Being who created all this, and who

[1] Note A, Appendix.

gave man the power of pouring out these beautiful thoughts, was not the possession of one sect or another, or of this nation or that, but was the kindly Father of every one of the little children whom He had let loose on this fair playground. It grieved me then, and it grieves me now, that a man of such sincerity and lofty purpose as your great-grandfather should have been so tied down by iron doctrines, and should imagine his Creator to be so niggard of His mercy as to withhold it from nine-and-ninety in the hundred. Well, a man is as he is trained, and if my father bore a narrow mind upon his broad shoulders, he has at least the credit that he was ready to do and to suffer all things for what he conceived to be the truth. If you, my dears, have more enlightened views, take heed that they bring you to lead a more enlightened life.

When I was fourteen years of age, a yellow-haired, brown-faced lad, I was packed off to a small private school at Petersfield, and there I remained for a year, returning home for the last Saturday in each month. I took with me only a scanty outfit of schoolbooks, with Lilly's *Latin Grammar*, and Rosse's *View of all the Religions in the World from the Creation down to our own Times*, which was shoved into my hands by my good mother as a parting present. With this small stock of letters I might have fared badly, had it not happened that my master, Mr. Thomas Chillingfoot, had himself a good library, and took a pleasure in lending his books to any of his scholars who showed a desire to improve themselves. Under this good old man's care I not only picked up some smattering of Latin and Greek, but I found means to read good English translations of many of the classics, and to acquire a knowledge of the history of my own and other countries. I was rapidly growing in mind as well as in body, when my school career was cut short by no less an event than my summary and ignominious expulsion. How this unlooked-for ending to my studies came about I must now set before you.

Petersfield had always been a great stronghold of the
Church, having hardly a Nonconformist within its bounds.
The reason of this was that most of the house property
was owned by zealous Churchmen, who refused to allow
anyone who differed from the Established Church to
settle there. The Vicar, whose name was Pinfold,
possessed in this manner great power in the town, and
as he was a man with a high inflamed countenance and a
pompous manner, he inspired no little awe among the
quiet inhabitants. I can see him now with his beaked
nose, his rounded waistcoat, and his bandy legs, which
looked as if they had given way beneath the load of
learning which they were compelled to carry. Walking
slowly with right hand stiffly extended, tapping the
pavement at every step with his metal-headed stick, he
would pause as each person passed him, and wait to see
that he was given the salute which he thought due to his
dignity. This courtesy he never dreamed of returning,
save in the case of some of his richer parishioners ; but if
by chance it were omitted, he would hurry after the
culprit, and, shaking his stick in his face, insist upon his
doffing his cap to him. We youngsters, if we met him
on our walks, would scuttle by him like a brood of chickens
passing an old turkey cock, and even our worthy master
showed a disposition to turn down a side-street when the
portly figure of the Vicar was seen rolling in our direction.
This proud priest made a point of knowing the history of
everyone within his parish, and having learnt that I was
the son of an Independent, he spoke severely to Mr.
Chillingfoot upon the indiscretion which he had shown
in admitting me to his school. Indeed, nothing but my
mother's good name for orthodoxy prevented him from
insisting upon my dismissal.

At the other end of the village there was a large day-
school. A constant feud prevailed between the scholars
who attended it and the lads who studied under our
master. No one could tell how the war broke out, but
for many years there had been a standing quarrel between

the two, which resulted in skirmishes, sallies and ambuscades, with now and then a pitched battle. No great
harm was done in these encounters, for the weapons were
usually snowballs in winter and pine-cones or clods of
earth in the summer. Even when the contest got closer
and we came to fisticuffs, a few bruises and a little blood
was the worst that could come of it. Our opponents were
more numerous than we, but we had the advantage of
being always together and of having a secure asylum upon
which to retreat, while they, living in scattered houses all
over the parish, had no common rallying-point. A
stream, crossed by two bridges, ran through the centre
of the town, and this was the boundary which separated
our territories from those of our enemies. The boy who
crossed the bridge found himself in hostile country.

It chanced that in the first conflict which occurred after
my arrival at the school I distinguished myself by singling
out the most redoubtable of our foemen, and smiting him
such a blow that he was knocked helpless and was carried
off by our party as a prisoner. This feat of arms established my good name as a warrior, so I came at last to be
regarded as the leader of our forces, and to be looked up
to by bigger boys than myself. This promotion tickled
my fancy so much, that I set to work to prove that I
deserved it by devising fresh and ingenious schemes for
the defeat of our enemies.

One winter's evening news reached us that our rivals
were about to make a raid upon us under cover of night,
and that they proposed coming by the little-used plank
bridge, so as to escape our notice. This bridge lay
almost out of the town, and consisted of a single broad
piece of wood without a rail, erected for the good of the
town clerk, who lived just opposite to it. We proposed
to hide ourselves amongst the bushes on our side of the
stream, and make an unexpected attack upon the in-
vaders as they crossed. As we started, however, I
bethought me of an ingenious stratagem which I had read
of as being practised in the German wars, and having

expounded it to the great delight of my companions, we took Mr. Chillingfoot's saw, and set off for the seat of action.

On reaching the bridge all was quiet and still. It was quite dark and very cold, for Christmas was approaching. There were no signs of our opponents. We exchanged a few whispers as to who should do the daring deed, but as the others shrank from it, and as I was too proud to propose what I dare not execute, I gripped the saw, and sitting astraddle upon the plank set to work upon the very centre of it.

My purpose was to weaken it in such a way that, though it would bear the weight of one, it would collapse when the main body of our foemen were upon it, and so precipitate them into the ice-cold stream. The water was but a couple of feet deep at the place, so that there was nothing for them but a fright and a ducking. So cool a reception ought to deter them from ever invading us again, and confirm my reputation as a daring leader. Reuben Lockarby, my lieutenant, son of old John Lockarby of the Wheatsheaf, marshalled our forces behind the hedgerow, whilst I sawed vigorously at the plank until I had nearly severed it across. I had no compunction about the destruction of the bridge, for I knew enough of carpentry to see that a skilful joiner could in an hour's work make it stronger than ever by putting a prop beneath the point where I had divided it. When at last I felt by the yielding of the plank that I had done enough, and that the least strain would snap it, I crawled quietly off, and taking up my position with my schoolfellows, awaited the coming of the enemy.

I had scarce concealed myself when we heard the steps of someone approaching down the footpath which led to the bridge. We crouched behind the cover, convinced that the sound must come from some scout whom our foemen had sent on in front—a big boy evidently, for his step was heavy and slow, with a clinking noise mingling with it, of which we could make nothing. Nearer came

the sound and nearer, until a shadowy figure loomed out of the darkness upon the other side, and after pausing and peering for a moment, came straight for the bridge. It was only as he was setting foot upon the plank and beginning gingerly to pick his way across it, that we discerned the outlines of the familiar form, and realised the dreadful truth that the stranger whom we had taken for the advance guard of our enemy was in truth none other than Vicar Pinfold, and that it was the rhythmic pat of his stick which we heard mingling with his footfalls. Fascinated by the sight, we lay bereft of all power to warn him—a line of staring eyeballs. One step, two steps, three steps did the haughty Churchman take, when there was a rending crack, and he vanished with a mighty splash into the swift-flowing stream. He must have fallen upon his back, for we could see the curved outline of his portly figure standing out above the surface as he struggled desperately to regain his feet. At last he managed to get erect, and came spluttering for the bank with such a mixture of godly ejaculations and of profane oaths that, even in our terror, we could not keep from laughter. Rising from under his feet like a covey of wild-fowl, we scurried off across the fields and so back to the school, where, as you may imagine, we said nothing to our good master of what had occurred.

The matter was too serious, however, to be hushed up. The sudden chill set up some manner of disturbance in the bottle of sack which the Vicar had just been drinking with the town clerk, and an attack of gout set in which laid him on his back for a fortnight. Meanwhile an examination of the bridge had shown that it had been sawn across, and an inquiry traced the matter to Mr. Chillingfoot's boarders. To save a wholesale expulsion of the school from the town, I was forced to acknowledge myself as both the inventor and perpetrator of the deed. Chillingfoot was entirely in the power of the Vicar, so he was forced to read me a long homily in public—which he balanced by an affectionate leave-taking in private—and

to expel me solemnly from the school. I never saw my old master again, for he died not many years afterwards ; but I hear that his second son William is still carrying on the business, which is larger and more prosperous than of old. His eldest son turned Quaker and went out to Penn's settlement, where he is reported to have been slain by the savages.

This adventure shocked my dear mother, but it found great favour in the eyes of my father, who laughed until the whole village resounded with his stentorian merriment. It reminded him, he said, of a similar stratagem executed at Market Drayton by that God-fearing soldier Colonel Pride, whereby a captain and three troopers of Lunsford's own regiment of horse had been drowned, and many others precipitated into a river, to the great glory of the true Church and to the satisfaction of the chosen people. Even of the Church folk many were secretly glad at the misfortune which had overtaken the Vicar, for his pretensions and his pride had made him hated throughout the district.

By this time I had grown into a sturdy, broad-shouldered lad, and every month added to my strength and my stature. When I was sixteen I could carry a bag of wheat or a cask of beer against any man in the village, and I could throw the fifteen-pound putting-stone to a distance of thirty-six feet, which was four feet farther than could Ted Dawson, the blacksmith. Once when my father was unable to carry a bale of skins out of the yard, I whipped it up and bare it away upon my shoulders. The old man would often look gravely at me from under his heavy thatched eyebrows, and shake his grizzled head as he sat in his arm-chair puffing his pipe. " You grow too big for the nest, lad," he would say. " I doubt some of these days you'll find your wings and away ! " In my heart I longed that the time would come, for I was weary of the quiet life of the village, and was anxious to see the great world of which I had heard and read so much. I could not look southward without my spirit stirring within me as my

eyes fell upon those dark waves, the white crests of which are like a fluttering signal ever waving to an English youth and beckoning him to some unknown but glorious goal.

3. *Of Two Friends of my Youth*

I FEAR, my children, that you will think that the prologue is overlong for the play ; but the foundations must be laid before the building is erected, and a statement of this sort is a sorry and a barren thing unless you have a knowledge of the folk concerned. Be patient, then, while I speak to you of the old friends of my youth, some of whom you may hear more of hereafter, while others remained behind in the country hamlet, and yet left traces of our early intercourse upon my character which might still be discerned there.

Foremost for good amongst all whom I knew was Zachary Palmer, the village carpenter, a man whose aged and labour-warped body contained the simplest and purest of spirits. Yet his simplicity was by no means the result of ignorance, for from the teachings of Plato to those of Hobbes there were few systems ever thought out by man which he had not studied and weighed. Books were far dearer in my boyhood than they are now, and carpenters were less well paid, but old Palmer had neither wife nor child, and spent little on food or raiment. Thus it came about that on the shelf over his bed he had a more choice collection of books—few as they were in number —than the squire or the parson, and these books he had read until he not only understood them himself, but could impart them to others.

This white-bearded and venerable village philosopher would sit by his cabin door upon a summer evening, and was never so pleased as when some of the young fellows would slip away from their bowls and their quoit-playing in order to lie in the grass at his feet, and ask him questions about the great men of old, their words and their deeds.

But of all the youths I and Reuben Lockarby, the inn-keeper's son, were his two favourites, for we would come the earliest and stop the latest to hear the old man talk. No father could have loved his children better than he did us, and he would spare no pains to get at our callow thoughts, and to throw light upon whatever perplexed or troubled us. Like all growing things, we had run our heads against the problem of the universe. We had peeped and pryed with our boyish eyes into those pro-found depths in which the keenest-sighted of the human race had seen no bottom. Yet when we looked around us in our own village world, and saw the bitterness and rancour which pervaded every sect, we could not but think that a tree which bore such fruit must have some-thing amiss with it. This was one of the thoughts unspoken to our parents which we carried to good old Zachary, and on which he had much to say which cheered and comforted us.

" These janglings and wranglings," said he, " are but on the surface, and spring from the infinite variety of the human mind, which will ever adapt a creed to suit its own turn of thought. It is the solid core that underlies every Christian creed which is of importance. Could you but live among the Romans or the Greeks, in the days before this new doctrine was preached, you would then know the change that it has wrought in the world. How this or that text should be construed is a matter of no moment, however warm men may get over it. What is of the very greatest moment is, that every man should have a good and solid reason for living a simple, cleanly life. This the Christian creed has given us."

" I would not have you be virtuous out of fear," he said upon another occasion. " The experience of a long life has taught me, however, that sin is always punished in this world, whatever may come in the next. There is always some penalty in health, in comfort or in peace of mind to be paid for every wrong. It is with nations as it is with individuals. A book of history is a book of

sermons. See how the luxurious Babylonians were destroyed by the frugal Persians, and how these same Persians when they learned the vices of prosperity were put to the sword by the Greeks. Read on and mark how the sensual Greeks were trodden down by the more robust and hardier Romans, and finally how the Romans, having lost their manly virtues, were subdued by the nations of the north. Vice and destruction came ever hand in hand. Thus did Providence use each in turn as a scourge wherewith to chastise the follies of the other. These things do not come by chance. They are part of a great system which is at work in your own lives. The longer you live the more you will see that sin and sadness are never far apart, and that no true prosperity can exist away from virtue."

A very different teacher was the sea-dog Solomon Sprent, who lived in the second last cottage on the left-hand side of the main street of the village. He was one of the old tarpaulin breed, who had fought under the red cross ensign against Frenchman, Don, Dutchman and Moor, until a round shot carried off his foot and put an end to his battles for ever. In person he was thin, and hard, and brown, as lithe and active as a cat, with a short body and very long arms, each ending in a great hand which was ever half closed as though shutting upon a rope. From head to foot he was covered with the most marvellous tattooings, done in blue, red and green, beginning with the Creation upon his neck and winding up with the Ascension upon his left ankle. Never have I seen such a walking work of art. He was wont to say that had he been drowned and his body cast up upon some savage land, the natives might have learned the whole of the blessed gospel from a contemplation of his carcass. Yet with sorrow I must say that the seaman's religion appeared to have all worked into his skin, so that very little was left for inner use. It had broken out upon the surface, like the spotted fever, but his system was clear of it elsewhere. He could swear in eleven languages and three-and-twenty

29

dialects, nor did he ever let his great powers rust for want of practice. He would swear when he was happy or when he was sad, when he was angry or when he was loving, but this swearing was so mere a trick of speech, without malice or bitterness, that even my father could hardly deal harshly with the sinner. As time passed, however, the old man grew more sober and more thoughtful, until in his latter days he went back to the simple beliefs of his childhood, and learned to fight the devil with the same steady courage with which he had faced the enemies of his country.

Old Solomon was a never-failing source of amusement and of interest to my friend Lockarby and myself. On gala days he would have us in to dine with him, when he would regale us with lobscouse and salmagundi, or perhaps with an outland dish, a pillaw or olla podrida, or fish broiled after the fashion of the Azores, for he had a famous trick of cooking, and could produce the delicacies of all nations. And all the time that we were with him he would tell us the most marvellous stories of Rupert, under whom he served ; how he would shout from the poop to his squadron to wheel to the right, or to charge, or to halt, as the case might be, as if he were still with his regiment of horse. Of Blake, too, he had many stories to tell. But even the name of Blake was not so dear to our old sailor as was that of Sir Christopher Mings. Solomon had at one time been his coxswain, and could talk by the hour of those gallant deeds which had distinguished him from the day that he entered the navy as a cabin boy until he fell upon his own quarter-deck, a full admiral of the red, and was borne by his weeping ship's company to his grave in Chatham churchyard. " If so be as there's a jasper sea up aloft," said the old seaman, " I'll wager that Sir Christopher will see that the English flag has proper respect paid to it upon it, and that we are not fooled by foreigners. I've served under him in this world, and I ask nothing better than to be his coxswain in the next— if so be as he should chance to have a vacancy for such."

These remembrances would always end in the brewing of an extra bowl of punch, and the drinking of a solemn bumper to the memory of the departed hero.

Stirring as were Solomon Sprent's accounts of his old commanders, their effect upon us was not so great as when, about his second or third glass, the floodgates of his memory would be opened, and he would pour out long tales of the lands which he had visited, and the peoples which he had seen. Leaning forward in our seats with our chins resting upon our hands, we two youngsters would sit for hours, with our eyes fixed upon the old adventurer, drinking in his words, while he, pleased at the interest which he excited, would puff slowly at his pipe and reel off story after story of what he had seen or done. In those days, my dears, there was no Defoe to tell us the wonders of the world, no *Spectator* to lie upon our breakfast table, no Gulliver to satisfy our love of adventure by telling us of such adventures as never were. Not once in a month did a common newsletter fall into our hands. Personal hazards, therefore, were of more value then than they are now, and the talk of a man like old Solomon was a library in itself. To us it was all real. His husky tones and ill-chosen words were as the voice of an angel, and our eager minds filled in the details and supplied all that was wanting in his narratives. In one evening we have engaged a Sallee rover off the Pillars of Hercules ; we have coasted down the shores of the African continent, and seen the great breakers of the Spanish Main foaming upon the yellow sand ; we have passed the black-ivory merchants with their human cargoes ; we have faced the terrible storms which blow ever around the Cape de Boa Esperanza ; and finally, we have sailed away out over the great ocean beyond, amid the palm-clad coral islands, with the knowledge that the realms of Prester John lie somewhere behind the golden haze which shimmers upon the horizon. After such a flight as that we would feel, as we came back to the Hampshire village and the dull realities of country life,

like wild birds who had been snared by the fowler and clapped into narrow cages. Then it was that the words of my father, " You will find your wings some day and fly away," would come back to me, and set up such a restlessness as all the wise words of Zachary Palmer could not allay.

4. *Of the Strange Fish that we Caught at Spithead*

ONE evening in the month of May 1685, about the end of the first week of the month, my friend Reuben Lockarby and I borrowed Ned Marley's pleasure boat, and went a-fishing out of Langston Bay. At that time I was close on one-and-twenty years of age, while my companion was one year younger. A great intimacy had sprung up between us, founded on mutual esteem, for he being a little undergrown man was proud of my strength and stature, while my melancholy and somewhat heavy spirit took a pleasure in the energy and joviality which never deserted him, and in the wit which gleamed as bright and as innocent as summer lightning through all that he said. In person he was short and broad, round-faced, ruddy-cheeked, and in truth a little inclined to be fat, though he would never confess to more than a pleasing plumpness, which was held, he said, to be the acme of manly beauty amongst the ancients. The stern test of common danger and mutual hardship entitle me to say that no man could have desired a stauncher or more trusty comrade. As he was destined to be with me in the sequel, it was but fitting that he should have been at my side on that May evening which was the starting-point of our adventures.

We pulled out beyond the Warner Sands to a place half-way between them and the Nab, where we usually found bass in plenty. There we cast the heavy stone which served us as an anchor overboard, and proceeded to set

32

our lines. The sun sinking slowly behind a fog-bank had slashed the whole western sky with scarlet streaks, against which the wooded slopes of the Isle of Wight stood out vaporous and purple. A fresh breeze was blowing from the south-east, flecking the long green waves with crests of foam, and filling our eyes and lips with the smack of the salt spray. Over near St. Helen's Point a King's ship was making her way down the channel, while a single large brig was tacking about a quarter of a mile or less from where we lay. So near were we that we could catch a glimpse of the figures upon her deck as she heeled over to the breeze, and could hear the creaking of her yards and the flapping of her weather-stained canvas as she prepared to go about.

" Look ye, Micah," said my companion, looking up from his fishing-line. " That is a most weak-minded ship—a ship which will make no way in the world. See how she hangs in the wind, neither keeping on her course nor tacking. She is a trimmer of the seas—the Lord Halifax of the ocean."

" Why, there is something amiss with her," I replied, staring across with hand-shaded eyes. " She yaws about as though there were no one at the helm. Her main-yard goes aback ! Now it is forward again ! The folk on her deck seem to me to be either fighting or dancing. Up with the anchor, Reuben, and let us pull to her."

" Up with the anchor and let us get out of her way," he answered, still gazing at the stranger. " Why will you ever run that meddlesome head of yours into danger's way ? She flies Dutch colours, but who can say whence she really comes ? A pretty thing if we were snapped up by a buccaneer and sold in the Plantations ! "

" A buccaneer in the Solent ! " cried I derisively. " We shall be seeing the black flag in Emsworth Creek next. But hark ! What is that ? "

The crack of a musket sounded from aboard the brig. Then came a moment's silence and another musket shot rang out, followed by a chorus of shouts and cries. Simul-

33

taneously the yards swung round into position, the sails caught the breeze once more, and the vessel darted away on a course which would take her past Bembridge Point out to the English Channel. As she flew along her helm was put hard down, a puff of smoke shot out from her quarter, and a cannon ball came hopping and splashing over the waves, passing within a hundred yards of where we lay. With this farewell greeting she came up into the wind again and continued her course to the southward.

" Heart o' grace ! " ejaculated Reuben in loose-lipped astonishment. " The murdering villains ! "

" I would to the Lord that King's ship would snap them up ! " cried I savagely, for the attack was so unprovoked that it stirred my bile. " What could the rogues have meant ? They are surely drunk or mad ! "

" Pull at the anchor, man, pull at the anchor ! " my companion shouted, springing up from the seat. " I understand it ! Pull at the anchor ! "

" What then ? " I asked, helping him to haul the great stone up, hand over hand, until it came dripping over the side.

" They were not firing at us, lad. They were aiming at someone in the water between us and them. Pull, Micah ! Put your back into it ! Some poor fellow may be drowning."

" Why, I declare ! " said I, looking over my shoulder as I rowed, " there is his head upon the crest of a wave. Easy, or we shall be over him ! Two more strokes and be ready to seize him ! Keep up, friend ! There's help at hand ! "

" Take help to those who need help," said a voice out of the sea. " Zounds, man, keep a guard on your oar ! I fear a pat from it very much more than I do the water."

These words were delivered in so calm and self-possessed a tone that all concern for the swimmer was set at rest. Drawing in our oars we faced round to have a look at him. The drift of the boat had brought us so

close that he could have grasped the gunwale had he been so minded.

" Sapperment ! " he cried in a peevish voice ; " to think of my brother Nonus serving me such a trick ! What would our blessed mother have said could she have seen it ? My whole kit gone, to say nothing of my venture in the voyage ! And now I have kicked off a pair of new jack-boots that cost sixteen rix-dollars at Vanseddar's at Amsterdam. I can't swim in jack-boots, nor can I walk without them."

" Won't you come in out of the wet, sir ? " asked Reuben, who could scarce keep serious at the stranger's appearance and address. A pair of long arms shot out of the water, and in a moment, with a lithe, snake-like motion, the man wound himself into the boat and coiled his great length upon the stern-sheets. Very lanky he was and very thin, with a craggy hard face, clean-shaven and sunburned, with a thousand little wrinkles inter-secting it in every direction. He had lost his hat, and his short wiry hair, slightly flecked with grey, stood up in a bristle all over his head. It was hard to guess at his age, but he could scarce have been under his fiftieth year, though the ease with which he had boarded our boat proved that his strength and energy were unimpaired. Of all his characteristics, however, nothing attracted my attention so much as his eyes, which were almost covered by their drooping lids, and yet looked out through the thin slits which remained with marvellous brightness and keenness. A passing glance might give the idea that he was languid and half asleep, but a closer one would reveal those glittering, shifting lines of light, and warn the prudent man not to trust too much to his first impressions.

" I could swim to Portsmouth," he remarked, rum-maging in the pockets of his sodden jacket ; " I could swim well-nigh anywhere. I once swam from Gran on the Danube to Buda, while a hundred thousand janissaries danced with rage on the nether bank. I did, by the keys of St. Peter ! Wessenburg's Pandours would tell you

whether Decimus Saxon could swim. Take my advice, young men, and always carry your tobacco in a watertight metal box."

As he spoke he drew a flat box from his pocket, and several wooden tubes, which he screwed together to form a long pipe. This he stuffed with tobacco, and having lit it by means of a flint and steel with a piece of touch-paper from the inside of his box, he curled his legs under him in Eastern fashion, and settled down to enjoy a smoke. There was something so peculiar about the whole incident, and so preposterous about the man's appearance and actions, that we both broke into a roar of laughter, which lasted until for very exhaustion we were compelled to stop. He neither joined in our merriment nor expressed offence at it, but continued to suck away at his long wooden tube with a perfectly stolid and impassive face, save that the half-covered eyes glinted rapidly backwards and forwards from one to the other of us.

" You will excuse our laughter, sir," I said at last ; " my friend and I are unused to such adventures, and are merry at the happy ending of it. May we ask whom it is that we have picked up ? "

" Decimus Saxon is my name," the stranger answered ; " I am the tenth child of a worthy father, as the Latin implies. There are but nine betwixt me and an inheritance. Who knows ? Small-pox might do it, or the plague ! "

" We heard a shot aboard of the brig," said Reuben.

" That was my brother Nonus shooting at me," the stranger observed, shaking his head sadly.

" But there was a second shot."

" Ah, that was me shooting at my brother Nonus."

" Good lack ! " I cried. " I trust that thou hast done him no hurt."

" But a flesh wound, at the most," he answered. " I thought it best to come away, however, lest the affair grow into a quarrel. I am sure that it was he who trained the nine-pounder on me when I was in the water.

It came near enough to part my hair. He was always a good shot with a falconet or a mortar-piece. He could not have been hurt, however, to get down from the poop to the main-deck in the time."

There was a pause after this, while the stranger drew a long knife from his belt, and cleaned out his pipe with it. Reuben and I took up our oars, and having pulled up our tangled fishing-lines, which had been streaming behind the boat, we proceeded to pull in towards the land.

"The question now is," said the stranger, "where we are to go to?"

"We are going down Langston Bay," I answered.

"Oh, we are, are we?" he cried, in a mocking voice; "you are sure of it—eh? You are certain we are not going to France? We have a mast and sail there, I see, and water in the beaker. All we want are a few fish, which I hear are plentiful in these waters, and we might make a push for Barfleur."

"We are going down Langston Bay," I repeated coldly.

"You see might is right upon the waters," he explained, with a smile which broke his whole face up into crinkles. "I am an old soldier, a tough fighting man, and you are two raw lads. I have a knife, and you are unarmed. D'ye see the line of argument? The question now is, Where are we to go?"

I faced round upon him with the oar in my hand. "You boasted that you could swim to Portsmouth," said I, "and so you shall. Into the water with you, you sea-viper, or I'll push you in as sure as my name is Micah Clarke."

"Throw your knife down, or I'll drive the boat-hook through you," cried Reuben, pushing it forward to within a few inches of the man's throat.

"Sink me, but this is most commendable!" he said, sheathing his weapon, and laughing softly to himself. "I love to draw spirit out of the young fellows. I am the steel, d'ye see, which knocks the valour out of your flint. A notable simile, and one in every way worthy of

that most witty of mankind, Samuel Butler. This," he continued, tapping a protuberance which I had remarked over his chest, " is not a natural deformity, but is a copy of that inestimable *Hudibras*, which combines the light touch of Horace with the broader mirth of Catullus. Heh ! what think you of the criticism ? "

" Give up that knife," said I sternly.

" Certainly," he replied, handing it over to me with a polite bow. " Is there any other reasonable matter in which I can oblige ye ?   I will give up anything to do ye pleasure—save only my good name and soldierly repute, or this same copy of *Hudibras*, which, together with a Latin treatise upon the usages of war, written by a Fleming and printed at Liège in the Lowlands, I do ever bear in my bosom."

I sat down beside him with the knife in my hand. " You pull both oars," I said to Reuben ; " I'll keep guard over the fellow and see that he plays us no trick. I believe that you are right, and that he is nothing better than a pirate. He shall be given over to the justices when we get to Havant."

I thought that our passenger's coolness deserted him for a moment, and that a look of annoyance passed over his face.

" Wait a bit ! " he said ; " your name, I gather, is Clarke, and your home is Havant. Are you a kinsman of Joseph Clarke, the old Roundhead of that town ? "

" He is my father," I answered.

" Hark to that, now ! " he cried, with a throb of laughter ; " I have a trick of falling on my feet. Look at this, lad ! Look at this ! " He drew a packet of letters from his inside pocket, wrapped in a bit of tarred cloth, and opening it he picked one out and placed it upon my knee. " Read ! " said he, pointing at it with his long thin finger.

It was inscribed in large plain characters, " To Joseph Clarke, leather merchant of Havant, by the hand of Master Decimus Saxon, part-owner of the ship *Providence*,

from Amsterdam to Portsmouth." At each side it was sealed with a massive red seal, and was additionally secured with a broad band of silk.

" I have three-and-twenty of them to deliver in the neighbourhood," he remarked. " That shows what folk think of Decimus Saxon. Three-and-twenty lives and liberties are in my hands. Ah, lad, invoices and bills of lading are not done up in that fashion. It is not a cargo of Flemish skins that is coming for the old man. The skins have good English hearts in them ; aye, and English swords in their fists to strike out for freedom and for conscience. I risk my life in carrying this letter to your father ; and you, his son, threaten to hand me over to the justices ! For shame ! For shame ! I blush for you ! "

" I don't know what you are hinting at," I answered. " You must speak plainer if I am to understand you."

" Can we trust him ? " he asked, jerking his head in the direction of Reuben.

" As myself."

" How very charming ! " said he, with something between a smile and a sneer. " David and Jonathan—or, to be more classical and less scriptural, Damon and Pythias—eh ? These papers, then, are from the faithful abroad, the exiles in Holland, ye understand, who are thinking of making a move and of coming over to see King James in his own country with their swords strapped on their thighs. The letters are to those from whom they expect sympathy, and notify when and where they will make a landing. Now, my dear lad, you will perceive that instead of my being in your power, you are so completely in mine that it needs but a word from me to destroy your whole family. Decimus Saxon is staunch, though, and that word shall never be spoken."

" If all this be true," said I, " and if your mission is indeed as you have said, why did you even now propose to make for France ? "

" Aptly asked, and yet the answer is clear enough," he replied ; " sweet and ingenuous as are your faces, I could

not read upon them that ye would prove to be Whigs and friends of the good old cause. Ye might have taken me to where excisemen or others would have wanted to pry and peep, and so endangered my commission. Better a voyage to France in an open boat than that."

" I will take you to my father," said I, after a few moments' thought. " You can deliver your letter and make good your story to him. If you are indeed a true man, you will meet with a warm welcome ; but should you prove, as I shrewdly suspect, to be a rogue, you need expect no mercy."

" Bless the youngster ! He speaks like the Lord High Chancellor of England ! What is it the old man says ?

> ' He could not ope
> His mouth, but out there fell a trope.'

But it should be a threat, which is the ware in which you are fond of dealing,

> ' He could not let
> A minute pass without a threat.'

How's that, eh ? Waller himself could not have capped the couplet neater."

All this time Reuben had been swinging away at his oars, and we had made our way into Langston Bay, down the sheltered waters of which we were rapidly shooting. Sitting in the sheets, I turned over in my mind all that this waif had said. I had glanced over his shoulder at the addresses of some of the letters—Steadman of Basingstoke, Wintle of Alresford, Fortescue of Bognor, all well-known leaders of the Dissenters. If they were what he represented them to be it was no exaggeration to say that he held the fortunes and fates of these men entirely in his hands. Government would be only too glad to have a valid reason for striking hard at the men whom they feared. On the whole it was well to tread carefully in the matter, so I restored our prisoner's knife to him, and treated him with increased consideration. It was well-nigh dark when we beached the boat, and entirely so before we reached

Havant, which was fortunate, as the bootless and hatless state of our dripping companion could not have failed to set tongues wagging, and perhaps to excite the inquiries of the authorities. As it was, we scarce met a soul before reaching my father's door.

5. *Of the Man with the Drooping Lids*

MY mother and my father were sitting in their high-backed chairs on either side of the empty fire-place when we arrived, he smoking his evening pipe of Oronooko, and she working at her embroidery. The moment that I opened the door the man whom I had brought stepped briskly in, and bowing to the old people began to make glib excuses for the lateness of his visit, and to explain the manner in which we had picked up him. I could not help smiling at the utter amazement expressed upon my mother's face as she gazed at him, for the loss of his jack-boots exposed a pair of interminable spindle-shanks which were in ludicrous contrast to the baggy low country knee-breeches which surmounted them. His tunic was made of coarse sad-coloured kersey stuff with flat new gilded brass buttons, beneath which was a whitish callamanca vest edged with silver. Round the neck of his coat was a broad white collar after the Dutch fashion, out of which his long scraggy throat shot upwards with his round head and bristle of hair balanced upon the top of it, like the turnip on a stick at which we used to throw at the fairs. In this guise he stood blinking and winking in the glare of light, and pattering out his excuses with as many bows and scrapes as Sir Peter Witling in the play. I was in the act of following him into the room, when Reuben plucked at my sleeve to detain me.

"Nay, I won't come in with you, Micah," said he; "there's mischief likely to come of all this. My father may grumble over his beer jugs, but he's a Churchman and a Tantivy for all that. I'd best keep out of it."

41

" You are right," I answered. " There is no need for you to meddle in the business. Be mum as to all that you have heard."

" Mum as a mouse," said he, and pressing my hand turned away into the darkness. When I returned to the sitting-room I found that my mother had hurried into the kitchen, where the crackling of sticks showed that she was busy in building a fire. Decimus Saxon was seated at the edge of the iron-bound oak chest at the side of my father, and was watching him keenly with his little twinkling eyes, while the old man was fixing his horn glasses and breaking the seals of the packet which his strange visitor had just handed to him.

I saw that when my father looked at the signature at the end of the long, closely written letter he gave a whiff of surprise and sat motionless for a moment or so staring at it. Then he turned to the commencement and read it very carefully through, after which he turned it over and read it again. Clearly it brought no unwelcome news, for his eyes sparkled with joy when he looked up from his reading, and more than once he laughed aloud. Finally he asked the man Saxon how it had come into his possession, and whether he was aware of its contents.

" Why, as to that," said the messenger, " it was handed to me by no less a person than Dicky Rumbold himself, and in the presence of others whom it's not for me to name. As to the contents, your own sense will tell you that I would scarce risk my neck by bearing a message without I knew what the message was. I am no chicken at the trade, sir. Cartels, *pronunciamientos*, challenges, flags of truce, and proposals for waffenstillstands, as the Deutschers call it—they've all gone through my hands, and never one gone awry."

" Indeed ! " quoth my father. " You are yourself one of the faithful ? "

" I trust that I am one of those who are on the narrow and thorny track," said he, speaking through his nose, as was the habit of the extreme sectaries.

" A track upon which no prelate can guide us," said my father.

" Where man is nought and the Lord is all," rejoined Saxon.

" Good ! good ! " cried my father. " Micah, you shall take this worthy man to my room, and see that he hath dry linen, and my second-best suit of Utrecht velvet. It may serve until his own are dried. My boots, too, may perchance be useful—my riding ones of untanned leather. A hat with silver braiding hangs above them in the cupboard. See that he lacks for nothing which the house can furnish. Supper will be ready when he hath changed his attire. I beg that you will go at once, good Master Saxon, lest you take a chill."

" There is but one thing that we have omitted," said our visitor, solemnly rising up from his chair and clasping his long nervous hands together. " Let us delay no longer to send up a word of praise to the Almighty for His manifold blessings, and for the mercy wherewith He plucked me and my letters out of the deep, even as Jonah was saved from the violence of the wicked ones who hurled him overboard, and it may be fired falconets at him, though we are not so informed in Holy Writ. Let us pray, my friends ! " Then in a high-toned chanting voice he offered up a long prayer of thanksgiving, winding up with a petition for grace and enlightenment for the house and all its inmates. Having concluded by a sonorous amen, he at last suffered himself to be led upstairs ; while my mother, who had slipped in and listened with much edification to his words, hurried away to prepare him a bumper of green usquebaugh with ten drops of Daffy's Elixir therein, which was her sovereign recipe against the effects of a soaking. There was no event in life, from a christening to a marriage, but had some appropriate food or drink in my mother's vocabulary, and no ailment for which she had not some pleasant cure in her well-stocked cupboards.

Master Decimus Saxon in my father's black Utrecht velvet and untanned riding boots looked a very different

man to the bedraggled castaway who had crawled like a conger eel into our fishing-boat. It seemed as if he had cast off his manner with his raiment, for he behaved to my mother during supper with an air of demure gallantry which sat upon him better than the pert and flippant carriage which he had shown towards us in the boat. Truth to say, if he was now more reserved, there was a very good reason for it, for he played such havoc amongst the eatables that there was little time for talk. At last, after passing from the round of cold beef to a capon pasty, and topping up with a two-pound perch, washed down by a great jug of ale, he smiled upon us all and told us that his fleshly necessities were satisfied for the nonce. " It is my rule," he remarked, " to obey the wise precept which advises a man to rise from table feeling that he could yet eat as much as he has partaken of."

" I gather from your words, sir, that you have yourself seen hard service," my father remarked when the board had been cleared and my mother had retired for the night.

" I am an old fighting man," our visitor answered, screwing his pipe together, " a lean old dog of the holdfast breed. This body of mine bears the mark of many a cut and slash received for the most part in the service of the Protestant faith, though some few were caught for the sake of Christendom in general when warring against the Turk. There is blood of mine, sir, spotted all over the map of Europe. Some of it, I confess, was spilled in no public cause, but for the protection of mine own honour in the private duello or holmgang, as it was called among the nations of the north. It is necessary that a cavaliero of fortune, being for the greater part a stranger in a strange land, should be somewhat nice in matters of the sort, since he stands, as it were, as the representative of his country, whose good name should be more dear to him than his own."

" Your weapon on such occasions was, I suppose, the sword ? " my father asked, shifting uneasily in his seat, as he would do when his old instincts were waking up.

" Broadsword, rapier, Toledo, spontoon, battle-axe, pike or half-pike, morgenstiern and halbert. I speak with all due modesty, but with backsword, sword and dagger, sword and buckler, single falchion, case of falchions or any other such exercise, I will hold mine own against any man that ever wore neat's leather, save only my elder brother Quartus."

" By my faith," said my father with his eyes shining, " were I twenty years younger I should have at you ! My backsword play hath been thought well of by stout men of war. God forgive me that my heart should still turn to such vanities."

" I have heard godly men speak well of it," remarked Saxon. " Master Richard Rumbold himself spake of your deeds of arms to the Duke of Argyle. Was there not a Scotsman, one Storr or Stour ? "

" Aye, aye ! Storr of Drumlithie. I cut him nigh to the saddle-bow in a skirmish on the eve of Dunbar. So Dicky Rumbold had not forgotten it, eh ? He was a hard one both at praying and at fighting. We have ridden knee to knee in the field, and we have sought truth together in the chamber. So, Dick will be in harness once again ! He could not be still if a blow were to be struck for the trampled faith. If the tide of war set in this direction, I too—who knows ? who knows ? "

" And here is a stout man-at-arms," said Saxon, passing his hand down my arm. " He hath thew and sinew, and can use proud words too upon occasion, as I have good cause to know, even in our short acquaintance. Might it not be that he too should strike in in this quarrel ? "

" We shall discuss it," my father answered, looking thoughtfully at me from under his heavy brows. " But I pray you, friend Saxon, to give us some further account upon these matters. My son Micah, as I understand, hath picked you out of the waves. How came you there ? "

Decimus Saxon puffed at his pipe for a minute or more in silence, as one who is marshalling facts each in its due order.

45

" It came about in this wise," he said at last. " When John of Poland chased the Turk from the gates of Vienna, peace broke out in the Principalities, and many a wandering cavaliero like myself found his occupation gone. There was no war waging save only some petty Italian skirmish, in which a soldier could scarce expect to reap either dollars or repute, so I wandered across the Continent, much cast down at the strange peace which prevailed in every quarter. At last, however, on reaching the Lowlands, I chanced to hear that the *Providence*, owned and commanded by my two brothers, Nonus and Quartus, was about to start from Amsterdam for an adventure to the Guinea coast. I proposed to them that I should join them, and was accordingly taken into partnership on condition that I paid one-third of the cost of the cargo. While waiting at the port I chanced to come across some of the exiles, who, having heard of my devotion to the Protestant cause, brought me to the Duke and to Master Rumbold, who committed these letters to my charge. This makes it clear how they came into my possession."

" But not how you and they came into the water," my father suggested.

" Why, that was but the veriest chance," the adventurer answered with some little confusion of manner. " It was the *fortuna belli*, or more properly *pacis*. I had asked my brothers to put into Portsmouth that I might get rid of these letters, on which they replied in a boorish and unmannerly fashion that they were still waiting for the thousand guineas which represented my share of the venture. To this I answered with brotherly familiarity that it was a small thing, and should be paid for out of the profits of our enterprise. Their reply was that I had promised to pay the money down, and that money down they must have. I then proceeded to prove, both by the Aristotelian and by the Platonic or deductive method, that having no guineas in my possession it was impossible for me to produce a thousand of them, at the same time pointing out that the association of an honest man in the business

was in itself an ample return for the money, since their own reputations had been somewhat blown on. I further offered in the same frank and friendly spirit to meet either of them with sword or with pistol, a proposal which should have satisfied any honour-loving cavaliero. Their base mercantile souls prompted them, however, to catch up two muskets, one of which Nonus discharged at me, and it is likely that Quartus would have followed suit had I not plucked the gun from his hand and unloaded it to prevent further mischief. In unloading it I fear that one of the slugs blew a hole in brother Nonus. Seeing that there was a chance of further disagreements aboard the vessel, I at once decided to leave her, in doing which I was forced to kick off my beautiful jack-boots, which were said by Vanseddars himself to be the finest pair that ever went out of his shop, square-toes, double-soled—alas ! alas ! "

" Strange that you should have been picked up by the son of the very man to whom you had a letter."

" The working of Providence," Saxon answered. " I have two-and-twenty other letters which must all be delivered by hand. If you will permit me to use your house for a while, I shall make it my headquarters."

" Use it as though it were your own," said my father.

" Your most grateful servant, sir," he cried, jumping up and bowing with his hand over his heart. " This is indeed a haven of rest after the ungodly and profane company of my brothers. Shall we then put up a hymn, and retire from the business of the day ? "

My father willingly agreed, and we sang " Oh, happy land ! " after which our visitor followed me to his room, bearing with him the unfinished bottle of usquebaugh which my mother had left on the table. He took it with him, he explained, as a precaution against Persian ague, contracted while battling against the Ottoman, and liable to recur at strange moments. I left him in our best spare bedroom, and returned to my father, who was still seated, heavy with thought, in his old corner.

" What think you of my find, dad ? " I asked.

" A man of parts and of piety," he answered ; " but in truth he has brought me news so much after my heart, that he could not be unwelcome were he the Pope of Rome."

" What news, then ? "

" This, this ! " he cried joyously, plucking the letter out of his bosom. " I will read it to you, lad. Nay, perhaps I had best sleep the night upon it, and read it to-morrow when our heads are clearer. May the Lord guide my path, and confound the tyrant ! Pray for light, boy, for my life and yours may be equally at stake."

6. *Of the Letter that came from the Lowlands*

IN the morning I was up betimes, and went forthwith, after the country fashion, to our guest's room to see if there was aught in which I could serve him. On pushing at his door, I found that it was fastened, which surprised me the more as I knew that there was neither key nor bolt upon the inside. On my pressing against it, however, it began to yield, and I could see then that a heavy chest which was used to stand near the window had been pulled round in order to shut out any intrusion. This precaution, taken under my father's roof, as though he were in a den of thieves, angered me, and I gave a butt with my shoulder which cleared the box out of the way, and enabled me to enter the room.

The man Saxon was sitting up in bed, staring about him as though he were not very certain for the moment where he was. He had tied a white kerchief round his head by way of night bonnet, and his hard-visaged, clean-shaven face, looking out through this, together with his bony figure, gave him some resemblance to a gigantic old woman. The bottle of usquebaugh stood empty by his bedside. Clearly his fears had been realised, and he had had an attack of the Persian ague.

" Ah, my young friend ! " he said at last. " Is it, then,

the custom of this part of the country to carry your visitor's rooms by storm or escalado in the early hours of the morning ? "

" Is it the custom," I answered sternly, " to barricade up your door when you are sleeping under the roof-tree of an honest man ? What did you fear, that you should take such a precaution ? "

" Nay, you are indeed a spitfire," he replied, sinking back upon the pillow, and drawing the clothes round him, " a feuerkopf as the Germans call it, or sometimes tollkopf, which in its literal significance meaneth a fool's head. Your father was, as I have heard, a strong and a fierce man when the blood of youth ran in his veins ; but you, I should judge, are in no way behind him. Know, then, that the bearer of papers of import, *documenta preciosa sed periculosa*, is bound to leave nought to chance, but to guard in every way the charge which hath been committed to him. True it is that I am in the house of an honest man, but I know not who come or who may go during the hours of the night. Indeed, for the matter of that—but enough is said. I shall be with you anon."

" Your clothes are dry and are ready for you," I remarked.

" Enough ! enough ! " he answered. " I have no quarrel with the suit which your father has lent me. It may be that I have been used to better, but they will serve my turn. The camp is not the court."

It was evident to me that my father's suit was infinitely better, both in texture and material, than that which our visitor had brought with him. As he had withdrawn his head, however, entirely beneath the bedclothes, there was nothing more to be said, so I descended to the lower room, where I found my father busily engaged fastening a new buckle to his sword-belt while my mother and the maid were preparing the morning meal.

" Come into the yard with me, Micah," quoth my father ; " I would have a word with you." The workmen had not yet come to their work, so we strolled out

into the sweet morning air, and seated ourselves on the low stone bankment on which the skins are dressed.

" I have been out here this morning trying my hand at the broadsword exercise," said he ; " I find that I am as quick as ever on a thrust, but my cuts are sadly stiff. I might be of use at a pinch, but, alas ! I am not the same swordsman who led the left troop of the finest horse regiment that ever followed a kettledrum. The Lord hath given, and the Lord hath taken away ! Yet, if I am old and worn, there is the fruit of my loins to stand in my place and to wield the same sword in the same cause. You shall go in my place, Micah."

" Go ! Go whither ? "

" Hush, lad, and listen ! Let not your mother know too much, for the hearts of women are soft. When Abraham offered up his eldest born, I trow that he said little to Sarah on the matter. Here is the letter. Know you who this Dicky Rumbold is ? "

" Surely I have heard you speak of him as an old companion of yours."

" The same—a staunch man and true. So faithful was he—faithful even to slaying—that when the army of the righteous dispersed, he did not lay aside his zeal with his buff-coat. He took to business as a maltster at Hoddesdon, and in his house was planned the famous Rye House Plot, in which so many good men were involved."

" Was it not a foul assassination plot ? " I asked.

" Nay, nay, be not led away by terms ! It is a vile invention of the malignants that these men planned assassination. What they would do they purposed doing in broad daylight, thirty of them against fifty of the Royal Guard, when Charles and James passed on their way to Newmarket. If the royal brothers got pistol-bullet or sword-stab, it would be in open fight, and at the risk of their attackers. It was give and take, and no murder."

He paused and looked inquiringly at me ; but I could not truthfully say that I was satisfied, for an attack upon the lives of unarmed and unsuspecting men, even though

surrounded by a bodyguard, could not, to my mind, be justified.

" When the plot failed," my father continued, " Rumbold had to fly for his life, but he succeeded in giving his pursuers the slip and in making his way to the Lowlands. There he found that many enemies of the Government had gathered together. Repeated messages from England, especially from the western counties and from London, assured them that if they would but attempt an invasion they might rely upon help both in men and in money. They were, however, at fault for some time for want of a leader of sufficient weight to carry through so large a project ; but now at last they have one, who is the best that could have been singled out—none other than the well-beloved Protestant chieftain James, Duke of Monmouth, son of Charles II."

" Illegitimate son," I remarked.

" That may or may not be. There are those who say that Lucy Walters was a lawful wife. Bastard or no, he holds the sound principles of the true Church, and he is beloved by the people. Let him appear in the West, and soldiers will rise up like the flowers in the spring time."

He paused, and led me away to the farther end of the yard, for the workmen had begun to arrive and to cluster round the dipping trough.

" Monmouth is coming over," he continued, " and he expects every brave Protestant man to rally to his standard. The Duke of Argyle is to command a separate expedition, which will set the Highlands of Scotland in a blaze. Between them they hope to bring the persecutor of the faithful on his knees. But I hear the voice of the man Saxon, and I must not let him say that I have treated him in a churlish fashion. Here is the letter, lad. Read it with care, and remember that when brave men are striving for their rights it is fitting that one of the old rebel house of Clarke should be among them."

I took the letter, and wandering off into the fields, I settled myself under a convenient tree, and set myself to

read it. This yellow sheet which I now hold in my hand is the very one which was brought by Decimus Saxon, and read by me that bright May morning under the hawthorn shade. I give it to you as it stands :

" To my friend and companion in the cause of the Lord, Joseph Clarke.—Know, friend, that aid and delivery is coming upon Israel, and that the wicked king and those who uphold him shall be smitten and entirely cast down, until their place in the land shall know them no more. Hasten, then, to testify to thy own faith, that in the day of trouble ye be not found wanting.

" It has chanced from time to time that many of the suffering Church, both from our own land and from among the Scots, have assembled in this good Lutheran town of Amsterdam, until enough are gathered together to take a good work in hand. For amongst our own folk there are my Lord Grey of Wark, Wade, Dare of Taunton, Ayloffe, Holmes, Hollis, Goodenough and others whom thou shalt know. Of the Scots there are the Duke of Argyle, who has suffered sorely for the Covenant, Sir Patrick Hume, Fletcher of Saltoun, Sir John Cochrane, Dr. Ferguson, Major Elphinstone and others. To these we would fain have added Locke and old Hal Ludlow, but they are, as those of the Laodicean Church, neither cold nor warm.

" It has now come to pass, however, that Monmouth, who has long lived in dalliance with the Midianitish woman known by the name of Wentworth, has at last turned him to higher things, and has consented to make a bid for the crown. It was found that the Scots preferred to follow a chieftain of their own, and it has therefore been determined that Argyle—M'Callum More, as the breechless savages of Inverary call him—shall command a separate expedition landing upon the western coast of Scotland. There he hopes to raise five thousand Campbells, and to be joined by all the Covenanters and Western Whigs, men who would make troops of the old

breed had they but God-fearing officers with an experience of the chance of fields and the usages of war. With such a following he should be able to hold Glasgow, and to draw away the King's force to the north. Ayloffe and I go with Argyle. It is likely that our feet may be upon Scottish ground before thy eyes read these words.

" The stronger expedition starts with Monmouth, and lands at a fitting place in the West, where we are assured that we have many friends. I cannot name the spot lest this letter miscarry, but thou shalt hear anon. I have written to all good men along the coast, bidding them to be prepared to support the rising. The King is weak, and hated by the greater part of his subjects. It doth but need one good stroke to bring his crown in the dust. Monmouth will start in a few weeks, when his equipment is finished and the weather favourable. If thou canst come, mine old comrade, I know well that thou will need no bidding of mine to bring thee to our banner. Should perchance a peaceful life and waning strength forbid thy attendance, I trust that thou wilt wrestle for us in prayer, even as the holy prophet of old ; and perchance, since I hear that thou hast prospered according to the things of this world, thou mayst be able to fit out a pikeman or two, or to send a gift towards the military chest, which will be none too plentifully lined. We trust not to gold, but to steel and to our own good cause, yet gold will be welcome none the less. Should we fall, we fall like men and Christians. Should we succeed, we shall see how the perjured James, the persecutor of the saints with the heart like a nether millstone, the man who smiled when the thumbs of the faithful were wrenched out of their sockets at Edinburgh—we shall see how manfully he can bear adversity when it falls to his lot. May the hand of the Almighty be over us !

" I know little of the bearer of this, save that he professes to be of the elect. Shouldst thou go to Monmouth's camp, see that thou take him with thee, for I hear that he hath had good experience in the German,

Swedish and Ottoman wars.—Yours in the faith of Christ, RICHARD RUMBOLD.

"Present my services to thy spouse. Let her read Timothy, chapter two, ninth to fifteenth verses."

This long letter I read very carefully, and then putting it in my pocket returned indoors to my breakfast. My father looked at me, as I entered, with questioning eyes, but I had no answer to return him, for my own mind was clouded and uncertain.

That day Decimus Saxon left us, intending to make a round of the country and to deliver his letters, but promising to be back again ere long. We had a small mishap ere he went, for as we were talking of his journey my brother Hosea must needs start playing with my father's powder-flask, which in some way went off with a sudden fluff, spattering the walls with fragments of metal. So unexpected and loud was the explosion, that both my father and I sprang to our feet ; but Saxon, whose back was turned to my brother, sat four-square in his chair without a glance behind him or a shade of change in his rugged face. As luck would have it, no one was injured, not even Hosea, but the incident made me think more highly of our new acquaintance. As he started off down the village street, his long stringy figure and strange gnarled visage, with my father's silver-braided hat cocked over his eye, attracted rather more attention than I cared to see, considering the importance of the missives which he bore, and the certainty of their discovery should he be arrested as a masterless man. Fortunately, however, the curiosity of the country folk did but lead them to cluster round their doors and windows, staring open-eyed, while he, pleased at the attention which he excited, strode along with his head in the air and a cudgel of mine twirling in his hand. He had left golden opinions behind him. My father's good wishes had been won by his piety and by the sacrifices which he claimed to have made for the

faith. My mother he had taught how wimples are worn amongst the Serbs, and had also demonstrated to her a new method of curing marigolds in use in some parts of Lithuania. For myself, I confess that I retained a vague distrust of the man, and was determined to avoid putting faith in him more than was needful. At present, however, we had no choice but to treat him as an ambassador from friends.

And I ? What was I to do ? Should I follow my father's wishes, and draw my maiden sword on behalf of the insurgents, or should I stand aside and see how events shaped themselves ? It was more fitting that I should go than he. But, on the other hand, I was no keen religious zealot. Papistry, Church, Dissent, I believed that there was good in all of them, but that not one was worth the spilling of human blood. James might be a perjurer and a villain, but he was, as far as I could see, the rightful king of England, and no tales of secret marriages or black boxes could alter the fact that his rival was apparently an illegitimate son, and as such ineligible to the throne. Who could say what evil act upon the part of a monarch justified his people in setting him aside ? Who was the judge in such a case ? Yet, on the other hand, the man had notoriously broken his own pledges, and that surely should absolve his subjects from their allegiance. It was a weighty question for a country-bred lad to have to settle, and yet settled it must be, and that speedily. I took up my hat and wandered away down the village street, turning the matter over in my head.

But it was no easy thing for me to think seriously of anything in the hamlet ; for I was in some way, my dear children, though I say it myself, a favourite with the young and with the old, so that I could not walk ten paces without some greeting or address. There were my own brothers trailing behind me, Baker Mitford's children tugging at my skirts, and the millwright's two little maidens one on either hand. Then, when I had persuaded these young rompers to leave me, out came Dame Fullar-

ton the widow, with a sad tale about how her grindstone had fallen out of its frame, and neither she nor her household could lift it in again. That matter I set straight and proceeded on my way ; but I could not pass the sign of the Wheatsheaf without John Lockarby, Reuben's father, plunging out at me and insisting upon my coming in with him for a morning cup.

" The best glass of mead in the countryside, and brewed under my own roof," said he proudly, as he poured it into the flagon. " Why, bless you, Master Micah, a man with a frame like yours wants store o' good malt to keep it up wi'."

" And malt like this is worthy of a good frame to contain it," quoth Reuben, who was at work among the flasks.

" What think ye, Micah ? " said the landlord. " There was the Squire o' Milton over here yester morning wi' Johnny Ferneley o' the Bank side, and they will have it that there's a man in Fareham who could wrestle you, the best of three, and find your own grip, for a good round stake."

" Tut ! tut ! " I answered ; " you would have me like a prize mastiff, showing my teeth to the whole countryside. What matter if the man can throw me, or I him ? "

" What matter ? Why, the honour of Havant," quoth he. " Is that no matter ? But you are right," he continued, draining off his horn. " What is all this village life with its small successes to such as you ? You are as much out of your place as a vintage wine at a harvest supper. The whole of broad England, and not the streets of Havant, is the fit stage for a man of your kidney. What have you to do with the beating of skins and the tanning of leather ? "

" My father would have you go forth as a knight-errant, Micah," said Reuben, laughing. " You might chance to get your own skin beaten and your own leather tanned."

" Who ever knew so long a tongue in so short a body ? " cried the innkeeper. " But in good sooth, Master Micah, I am in sober earnest when I say that you are indeed

wasting the years of your youth, when life is sparkling and clear, and that you will regret it when you have come to the flat and flavourless dregs of old age."

" There spoke the brewer," said Reuben ; " but indeed, Micah, my father is right, for all that he hath such a hops-and-water manner of putting it."

" I will think over it," I answered, and with a nod to the kindly couple proceeded on my way.

Zachariah Palmer was planing a plank as I passed. Looking up he bade me good-morrow.

" I have a book for you, lad," he said.

" I have but now finished the *Comus*," I answered, for he had lent me John Milton's poem. " But what is this new book, daddy ? "

" It is by the learned Locke, and treateth of states and statecraft. It is but a small thing, but if wisdom could show in the scales it would weigh down many a library. You shall have it when I have finished it, to-morrow may-hap or the day after. A good man is Master Locke. Is he not at this moment a wanderer in the Lowlands, rather than bow his knee to what his conscience approved not of ? "

" There are many good men among the exiles, are there not ? " said I.

" The pick of the country," he answered. " Ill fares the land that drives the highest and bravest of its citizens away from it. The day is coming, I fear, when every man will have to choose betwixt his beliefs and his freedom. I am an old man, Micah boy, but I may live long enough to see strange things in this once Protestant kingdom."

" But if these exiles had their way," I objected, " they would place Monmouth upon the throne, and so unjustly alter the succession."

" Nay, nay," old Zachary answered, laying down his plane. " If they use Monmouth's name, it is but to strengthen their cause, and to show that they have a leader of repute. Were James driven from the throne,

the Commons of England in Parliament assembled would be called upon to name his successor. There are men at Monmouth's back who would not stir unless this were so."

" Then, daddy," said I, " since I can trust you, and since you will tell me what you do really think, would it be well, if Monmouth's standard be raised, that I should join it ? "

The carpenter stroked his white beard and pondered for a while. " It is a pregnant question," he said at last, " and yet methinks that there is but one answer to it, especially for your father's son. Should an end be put to James's rule, it is not too late to preserve the nation in its old faith ; but if the disease is allowed to spread, it may be that even the tyrant's removal would not prevent his evil seed from sprouting. I hold, therefore, that should the exiles make such an attempt, it is the duty of every man who values liberty of conscience to rally round them. And you, my son, the pride of the village, what better use could you make of your strength than to devote it to helping to relieve your country of this insupportable yoke ? It is treasonable and dangerous counsel—counsel which might lead to a short shrift and a bloody death— but, as the Lord liveth, if you were child of mine I should say the same."

So spoke the old carpenter with a voice which trembled with earnestness, and went to work upon his plank once more, while I, with a few words of gratitude, went on my way pondering over what he had said to me. I had not gone far, however, before the hoarse voice of Solomon Sprent broke in upon my meditations.

" Hoy there ! Ahoy ! " he bellowed, though his mouth was but a few yards from my ear. " Would ye come across my hawse without slacking weigh ? Clew up, d'ye see, clew up ! "

" Why, Captain," I said, " I did not see you. I was lost in thought."

" All adrift and without look-outs," quoth he, pushing

his way through the break in the garden hedge. " Od's niggars, man ! friends are not so plentiful, d'ye see, that ye need pass 'em by without a dip o' the ensign. So help me, if I had had a barker I'd have fired a shot across your bows."

" No offence, Captain," said I, for the veteran appeared to be nettled ; " I have much to think of this morning."

" And so have I, mate," he answered, in a softer voice. "What think ye of my rig, eh ? " He turned himself slowly round in the sunlight as he spoke, and I perceived that he was dressed with unusual care. He had a blue suit of broad-cloth trimmed with eight rows of buttons, and breeches of the same material with great bunches of ribbon at the knee. His vest was of lighter blue picked out with anchors in silver, and edged with a finger's-breadth of lace. His boot was so wide that he might have had his foot in a bucket, and he wore a cutlass at his side suspended from a buff belt, which passed over his right shoulder.

" I've had a new coat o' paint all over," said he, with a wink. " Carramba ! the old ship is water-tight yet. What would ye say, now, were I about to sling my hawser over a little scow, and take her in tow ? "

" A cow ! " I cried.

" A cow ! what d'ye take me for ? A wench, man, and as tight a little craft as ever sailed into the port of wedlock."

" I have heard no better news for many a long day," said I ; " I did not even know that you were betrothed. When then is the wedding to be ? "

" Go slow, friend—go slow, and heave your lead-line ! You have got out of your channel, and are in shoal water. I never said as how I was betrothed."

" What then ? " I asked.

" I am getting up anchor now, to run down to her and summon her. Look ye, lad," he continued, plucking off his cap and scratching his ragged locks ; " I've had to do wi' wenches enow from the Levant to the Antilles—

wenches such as a sailorman meets, who are all paint and pocket. It's but the heaving of a hand grenade, and they strike their colours. This is a craft of another guess build, and unless I steer wi' care she may put one in between wind and water before I so much as know that I am engaged. What think ye, heh ? Should I lay myself boldly alongside, d'ye see, and ply her with small arms, or should I work myself clear and try a long-range action ? I am none of your slippery, grease-tongued, long-shore lawyers, but if so be as she's willing for a mate, I'll stand by her in wind and weather while my planks hold out."

" I can scarce give advice in such a case," said I, " for my experience is less than yours. I should say though that you had best speak to her from your heart, in plain sailor language."

" Aye, aye, she can take it or leave it. Phœbe Dawson it is, the sister of the blacksmith. Let us work back and have a drop of the right Nants before we go. I have an anker newly come, which never paid the King a groat."

" Nay, you had best leave it alone," I answered.

" Say you so ? Well, mayhap you are right. Throw off your moorings, then, and clap on sail, for we must go."

" But I am not concerned," said I.

" Not concerned ! Not——" he was too much over-come to go on, and could but look at me with a face full of reproach. " I thought better of you, Micah. Would you let this crazy old hulk go into action, and not stand by to fire a broadside ? "

" What would you have me do then ? "

" Why, I would have you help me as the occasion may arise. If I start to board her, I would have you work across the bows so as to rake her. Should I range up on the larboard quarter, do you lie on the starboard. If I get crippled, do you draw her fire until I refit. What, man, you would not desert me ! "

The old seaman's tropes and maritime conceits were not always intelligible to me, but it was clear that he had set his heart upon my accompanying him, which I was

equally determined not to do. At last by much reasoning I made him understand that my presence would be more hindrance than help, and would probably be fatal to his chances of success.

" Well, well," he grumbled at last, " I've been concerned in no such expedition before. An it be the custom for single ships to engage, I'll stand to it alone. You shall come with me as consort, though, and stand to and fro in the offing, or sink me if I stir a step."

My mind was full of my father's plans and of the courses which lay before me. There seemed to be no choice, however, as old Solomon was in dead earnest, but to lay the matter aside for the moment and see the upshot of this adventure.

" Mind, Solomon," said I, " I don't cross the threshold."

" Aye, aye, mate. You can please yourself. We have to beat up against the wind all the way. She's on the look-out, for I hailed her yesternight, and let her know as how I should bear down on her about seven bells of the morning watch."

I was thinking as we trudged down the road that Phœbe would need to be learned in sea terms to make out the old man's meaning, when he pulled up short and clapped his hands to his pockets.

" Zounds ! " he cried, " I have forgot to bring a pistol."

" In Heaven's name ! " I said in amazement, " what could you want with a pistol ? "

" Why, to make signals with," said he. " Odds me that I should have forgot it ! How is one's consort to know what is going forward when the flagship carries no artillery ? Had the lass been kind I should have fired one gun, that you might know it."

" Why," I answered, " if you come not out I shall judge that all is well. If things go amiss I shall see you soon."

" Aye—or stay ! I'll hoist a white jack at the port-hole. A white jack means that she hath hauled down her colours.

Nombre de Dios, when I was a powder-boy in the old ship *Lion*, the day that we engaged the *Spiritus Sanctus* of two tier o' guns—the first time that ever I heard the screech of ball—my heart never thumped as it does now. What say ye if we run back with a fair wind and broach that anker of Nants ? "

" Nay, stand to it, man," said I ; for by this time we had come to the ivy-clad cottage behind which was the village smithy. " What, Solomon ! an English seaman never feared a foe, either with petticoats or without them."

" No, curse me if he did ! " quoth Solomon, squaring his shoulders, " never a one, Don, Devil or Dutchman ; so here goes for her ! " So saying he made his way into the cottage, leaving me standing by the garden wicket, half amused and half annoyed at this interruption to my musings.

As it proved, the sailor had no very great difficulty with his suit, and soon managed to capture his prize, to use his own language. I heard from the garden the growling of his gruff voice, and a good deal of shrill laughter ending in a small squeak, which meant, I suppose, that he was coming to close quarters. Then there was silence for a little while, and at last I saw a white kerchief waving from the window, and perceived, moreover, that it was Phœbe herself who was fluttering it. Well, she was a smart, kindly-hearted lass, and I was glad in my heart that the old seaman should have such a one to look after him.

Here, then, was one good friend settled down finally for life. Another warned me that I was wasting my best years in the hamlet. A third, the most respected of all, advised me openly to throw in my lot with the insurgents, should the occasion arise. If I refused, I should have the shame of seeing my aged father setting off for the wars, whilst I lingered at home. And why should I refuse ? Had it not long been the secret wish of my heart to see something of the great world, and what fairer chance could present itself ? My wishes, my friend's advice and my father's hopes all pointed in the one direction.

"Father," said I, when I returned home, "I am ready to go where you will."

"May the Lord be glorified!" he cried solemnly. "May He watch over your young life, and keep your heart steadfast to the cause which is assuredly His!"

And so, my dear grandsons, the great resolution was taken, and I found myself committed to one side in the national quarrel.

7. Of the Horseman who rode from the West

MY father set to work forthwith preparing for our equipment, furnishing Saxon out as well as myself on the most liberal scale, for he was determined that the wealth of his age should be as devoted to the cause as was the strength of his youth. These arrangements had to be carried out with the most extreme caution, for there were many Prelatists in the village, and in the present disturbed state of the public mind any activity on the part of so well known a man would have at once attracted attention. So carefully did the wary old soldier manage matters, however, that we soon found ourselves in a position to start at an hour's notice, without any of our neighbours being a whit the wiser.

His first move was to purchase through an agent two suitable horses at Chichester fair, which were conveyed to the stables of a trusty Whig farmer living near Portchester, who was ordered to keep them until they were called for. Of these animals one was a mottled grey, of great mettle and power, standing seventeen and a half hands high, and well up to my weight, for in those days, my dears, I had not laid on flesh, and weighed a little under sixteen stone for all my height and strength. A critic might have said that Covenant, for so I named my steed, was a trifle heavy about the head and neck, but I found him a trusty, willing brute, with great power and endurance. Saxon, who when fully accoutred could scarce have weighed more

than twelve stone, had a light bay Spanish jennet, of great speed and spirit. This mare he named Chloe, " after a godly maiden of his acquaintance," though, as my father remarked, there was a somewhat ungodly and heathenish smack about the appellation. These horses and their harness were bought and held ready without my father appearing in the matter in any way.

This important point having been settled, there was the further question of arms to be discussed, which gave rise to much weighty controversy between Decimus Saxon and my father, each citing many instances from their own experiences where the presence or absence of some taslet or arm-guard had been of the deepest import to the wearer. Your great-grandfather had set his heart upon my wearing the breastplate which still bore the dints of the Scottish spears at Dunbar, but on trying it on we found it was too small for me. I confess that this was a surprise, for when I looked back at the awe with which I had regarded my father's huge proportions, it was marvellous to me to have this convincing proof that I had outgrown him. By ripping down the side-leather and piercing holes through which a lace could be passed, my mother managed to arrange it so that I could wear it without discomfort. A pair of taslets or thigh-pieces, with guards for the upper arm and gauntlets, were all borrowed from the old Parliamentary equipment, together with the heavy straight sword and pair of horse-pistols which formed the usual weapons of a cavalier. My father had chosen me a headpiece in Portsmouth, fluted, with good barrets, padded inside with soft leather, very light and yet very strong. When fully equipped, both Saxon and my father agreed that I had all that was requisite for a well-appointed soldier. Saxon had purchased a buff-coat, a steel cap and a pair of jack-boots, so that with the rapier and pistols which my father had presented him with, he was ready to take the field at any time.

There would, we hoped, be no great difficulty in our reaching Monmouth's forces when the hour came. In

those troublous times the main roads were so infested by highwaymen and footpads, that it was usual for travellers to carry weapons and even armour for their protection. There was no reason therefore why our appearance should excite suspicion. Should questions be asked, Saxon had a long story prepared, to the effect that we were travelling to join Henry Somerset, Duke of Beaufort, to whose household we belonged. This invention he explained to me, with many points of corroboration which I was to furnish, but when I said positively that I should rather be hanged as a rebel than speak a falsehood, he looked at me open-eyed, and shook his head as one much shocked. A few weeks of campaigning, he said, would soon cure me of my squeamishness. For himself, no more truthful child had ever carried a horn-book, but he had learned to lie upon the Danube, and looked upon it as a necessary part of the soldier's upbringing. " For what are all stratagems, ambuscades and outfalls but lying upon a large scale ? " he argued. " What is an adroit commander but one who hath a facility for disguising the truth ? When, at the battle of Senlac, William the Norman ordered his men to feign flight in order that they might break his enemy's array, a wile much practised both by the Scythians of old and by the Croats of our own day, pray what is it but the acting of a lie ? Or when Hannibal, having tied torches to the horns of great droves of oxen, caused the Roman Consuls to imagine that his army was in retreat, was it not a deception or infraction of the truth ?—a point well brought out by a soldier of repute in the treatise ' An in bello dolo uti liceat ; an apud hostes falsiloquio uti liceat.' And so if, after these great models, I in order to gain mine ends do announce that we are bound to Beaufort when we are in truth making for Monmouth, is it not in accord with the usages of war and the customs of great commanders ? " All which specious argument I made no attempt to answer, beyond repeating that he might avail himself of the usage, but that he must not look to me for corroboration. On the

other hand, I promised to hold my speech and to say nothing which might hamper him, with which pledge he was forced to be contented.

And now at last, my patient listeners, I shall be able to carry you out of the humble life of the village, and to cease my gossip of the men who were old when I was young, and who are now lying this many a year in the Bedhampton churchyard. You shall come with me now, and you shall see England as it was in those days, and you shall hear of how we set forth to the wars, and of all the adventures which overtook us. And if what I tell you should ever chance to differ from what you have read in the book of Mr. Coke or of Mr. Oldmixon, or of anyone else who has set these matters down in print, do ye bear in mind that I am telling of what I saw with these very eyes, and that I have helped to make history, which is a higher thing than to write it.

It was, then, towards nightfall upon the twelfth day of June, 1685, that the news reached our part of the country that Monmouth had landed the day before at Lyme, a small seaport on the boundary between Dorsetshire and Devonshire. A great beacon blaze upon Portsdown Hill was the first news that we had of it, and then came a rattling and a drumming from Portsmouth, where the troops were assembled under arms. Mounted messengers clattered through the village street with their heads low on their horses' necks, for the great tidings must be carried to London, that the Governor of Portsmouth might know how to act.[1] We were standing at our doorway in the gloaming, watching the coming and the going, and the line of beacon fires which were lengthening away to the eastward, when a little man galloped up to the door and pulled his panting horse up.

" Is Joseph Clarke here ? " he asked.

" I am he," said my father.

" Are these men true ? " he whispered, pointing with his whip at Saxon and myself. " Then the trysting-place

---

[1] Note B, Appendix.

is Taunton. Pass it on to all whom ye know. Give my horse a bait and a drink, I beg of ye, for I must get on my way."

My young brother Hosea looked to the tired creature, while we brought the rider inside and drew him a stoup of beer. A wiry, sharp-faced man he was, with a birth-mark upon his temple. His face and clothes were caked with dust, and his limbs were so stiff from the saddle that he could scarce put one foot before another.

" One horse hath died under me," he said, " and this can scarce last another twenty miles. I must be in London by morning, for we hope that Danvers and Wild-man may be able to raise the city. Yester evening I left Monmouth's camp. His blue flag floats over Lyme."

" What force hath he ? " my father asked anxiously.

" He hath but brought over leaders. The force must come from you folk at home. He has with him Lord Grey of Wark, with Wade, the German Buyse, and eighty or a hundred more. Alas ! that two who came are already lost to us. It is an evil, evil omen."

" What is amiss, then ? "

" Dare, the goldsmith of Taunton, hath been slain by Fletcher of Saltoun in some child's quarrel about a horse. The peasants cried out for the blood of the Scot, and he was forced to fly aboard the ships. A sad mishap it is, for he was a skilful leader and a veteran soldier."

" Aye, aye," cried Saxon impatiently, " there will be some more skilful leaders and veteran soldiers in the West presently to take his place. But if he knew the usages of war, how came it that he should fight upon a private quarrel at such a time ? " He drew a flat brown book from his bosom, and ran his long thin finger down the table of contents. " Subsectio nona—here is the very case set forth, ' An in bello publico provocatus ad duellum privatæ amicitiæ causâ declinare possit,' in which the learned Fleming layeth it down that a man's private honour must give way to the good of the cause. Did it not happen in my own case that, on the eve of the raising

of the Anlagerung of Vienna, we stranger officers having
been invited to the tent of the General, it chanced that a
red-headed Irisher, one O'Daffy, an ancient in the regiment of Pappenheimer, did claim precedence of me on
the ground of superiority of blood ? On this I drew my
glove across his face, not, mark ye, in anger, but as showing that I differed in some degree from his opinion. At
which dissent he did at once offer to sustain his contention,
but I, having read this subsection to him, did make it clear
to him that we could not in honour settle the point until
the Turk was chased from the city. So after the onfall——"

"Nay, sir, I may hear the narrative some future day,"
said the messenger, staggering to his feet. "I hope to
find a relay at Chichester, and time presses. Work for
the cause now, or be slaves for ever. Farewell!" He
clambered into his saddle, and we heard the clatter of his
hoofs dying away down the London road.

"The time hath come for you to go, Micah," said my
father solemnly. "Nay, wife, do not weep, but rather
hearten the lad on his way by a blithe word and a merry
face. I need not tell you to fight manfully and fearlessly
in this quarrel. Should the tide of war set in this direction, you may find your old father riding by your side.
Let us now bow down and implore the favour of the
Almighty upon this expedition."

We all knelt down in the low-roofed, heavy-raftered
room while the old man offered up an earnest, strenuous
prayer for our success. Even now, as I speak to ye, that
group rises up before mine eyes. I see once again your
ancestor's stern, rugged face, with his brows knitted and
his corded hands writhed together in the fervour of his
supplication. My mother kneels beside him with the
tears trickling down her sweet, placid face, stifling her
sobs lest the sound of them make my leave-taking more
bitter. The children are in the sleeping-room upstairs,
and we hear the patter of their bare feet upon the floor.
The man Saxon sprawls across one of the oaken chairs,

half kneeling, half reclining, with his long legs trailing out behind, and his face buried in his hands. All round in the flickering light of the hanging lamp I see the objects which have been so familiar to me from childhood—the settle by the fireplace, the high-back stiff-elbowed chairs, the stuffed fox above the door, the picture of Christian viewing the Promised Land from the summit of the Delectable Mountains—all small trifles in themselves, but making up among them the marvellous thing we call home, the all-powerful loadstone which draws the wanderer's heart from the farther end of the earth. Should I ever see it again save in my dreams—I, who was leaving this sheltered cove to plunge into the heart of the storm ?

The prayer finished, we all rose with the exception of Saxon, who remained with his face buried in his hands for a minute or so before starting to his feet. I shrewdly suspect that he had been fast asleep, though he explained that he had paused to offer up an additional supplication. My father placed his hands upon my head and invoked the blessing of Heaven upon me. He then drew my companion aside, and I heard the jingling of coin, from which I judge that he was giving him something wherewith to start upon his travels. My mother clasped me to her heart, and slipped a small square of paper into my hand, saying that I was to look at it at my leisure, and that I should make her happy if I would but conform to the instructions contained in it. This I promised to do, and tearing myself away I set off down the darkened village street, with my long-limbed companion striding by my side.

It was close upon one in the morning, and all the country folk had been long abed. Passing the Wheatsheaf and the house of old Solomon, I could not but wonder what they would think of my martial garb were they afoot. I had scarce time to form the same thought before Zachary Palmer's cottage when his door flew open, and the carpenter came running out with his white hair streaming in the fresh night breeze.

" I have been awaiting you, Micah," he cried. " I had

heard that Monmouth was up, and I knew that you would not lose a night ere starting. God bless you, lad, God bless you ! Strong of arm and soft of heart, tender to the weak and stern to the oppressor, you have the prayers and the love of all who know you." I pressed his extended hands, and the last I saw of my native hamlet was the shadowy figure of the carpenter as he waved his good wishes to me through the darkness.

We made our way across the fields to the house of Whittier, the Whig farmer, where Saxon got into his war harness. We found our horses ready saddled and bridled, for my father had at the first alarm sent a message across that we should need them. By two in the morning we were breasting Portsdown Hill, armed, mounted and fairly started on our journey to the rebel camp.

8. *Of our Start for the Wars*

ALL along the ridge of Portsdown Hill we had the lights of Portsmouth and of the harbour ships twinkling beneath us on the left, while on the right the Forest of Bere was ablaze with the signal fires which proclaimed the landing of the invader. One great beacon throbbed upon the summit of Butser, while beyond that, as far as eye could reach, twinkling sparks of light showed how the tidings were being carried north into Berkshire and eastward into Sussex. Of these fires, some were composed of faggots piled into heaps, and others of tar barrels set upon poles. We passed one of these last just opposite to Porchester, and the watchers around it, hearing the tramp of our horses and the clank of our arms, set up a loud huzza, thinking doubtless that we were King's officers bound for the West.

Master Decimus Saxon had flung to the winds the precise demeanour which he had assumed in the presence of my father, and rattled away with many a jest and scrap of rhyme or song as we galloped through the darkness.

" Gadzooks ! " said he frankly, " it is good to be able to speak freely without being expected to tag every sentence with a hallelujah or an amen."

" You were ever the leader in those pious exercises," I remarked drily.

" Aye, indeed. You have nicked it there ! If a thing must be done, then take a lead in it, whatever it may be. A plaguy good precept, which has stood me in excellent stead before now. I cannot bear in mind whether I told you how I was at one time taken prisoner by the Turks and conveyed to Stamboul. There were a hundred of us or more, but the others either perished under the bastinado, or are to this day chained to an oar in the Imperial Ottoman galleys, where they are like to remain until they die under the lash, or until some Venetian or Genoese bullet finds its way into their wretched carcasses. I alone came off with freedom."

" And pray, how did you make your escape ? " I asked.

" By the use of the wit wherewith Providence hath endowed me," he answered complacently ; " for, seeing that their accursed religion is the blind side of these infidels, I did set myself to work upon it. To this end I observed the fashion in which our guard performed their morning and evening exercises, and having transformed my doublet into a praying cloth, I did imitate them, save only that I prayed at greater length and with more fervour."

" What ! " I cried in horror. " You did pretend to be a Mussulman ? "

" Nay, there was no pretence. I became a Mussulman. That, however, betwixt ourselves, as it might not stand me in very good stead with some Reverend Aminadab Fount-of-Grace in the rebel camp, who is no admirer of Mahmoud."

I was so astounded at the impudence of this confession, coming from the mouth of one who had been leading the exercises of a pious Christian family, that I was fairly

bereft of speech. Decimus Saxon whistled a few bars of a sprightly tune, and then continued—

" My perseverance in these exercises soon led to my being singled out from among the other prisoners, until I so prevailed upon my gaolers that the doors were opened for me, and I was allowed out on condition of presenting myself at the prison gates once a day. What use, think ye, did I make of my freedom ? "

" Nay, you are capable of anything," said I.

" I set off forthwith to their chief mosque—that of St. Sophia. When the doors opened and the muezzin called, I was ever the first to hurry in to devotions and the last to leave them. Did I see a Mussulman strike his head upon the pavement I would strike mine twice. Did I see him bend and bow, I was ready to prostrate myself. In this way ere long the piety of the converted Giaour became the talk of the city, and I was provided with a hut in which to make my sacred meditations. Here I might have done well, and indeed I had well-nigh made up my mind to set up as a prophet and write an extra chapter to the Koran, when some foolish trifle made the faithful suspicious of my honesty. It was but some nonsense of a wench being found in my hut by some who came to consult me upon a point of faith, but it was enough to set their heathen tongues wagging ; so I thought it wisest to give them the slip in a Levantine coaster and leave the Koran uncompleted. It is perhaps as well, for it would be a sore trial to have to give up Christian women and pork, for their garlic-breathing houris and accursed kybobs of sheep's flesh."

We had passed through Fareham and Botley during this conversation, and were now making our way down the Bishopstoke road. The soil changes about here from chalk to sand, so that our horses' hoofs did but make a dull subdued rattle, which was no bar to our talk—or rather to my companion's, for I did little more than listen. In truth, my mind was so full of anticipations of what was before us, and of thoughts of the home behind, that I was

in no humour for sprightly chatter. The sky was somewhat clouded, but the moon glinted out between the rifts, showing us the long road which wound away in front of us. On either side were scattered houses with gardens sloping down towards the road. The heavy, sickly scent of strawberries was in the air.

" Hast ever slain a man in anger ? " asked Saxon, as we galloped along.

" Never," I answered.

" Ha ! You will find that when you hear the clink of steel against steel, and see your foeman's eyes, you will straightway forget all rules, maxims and precepts of the fence which your father or others may have taught you."

" I have learned little of the sort," said I. " My father did but teach me to strike an honest downright blow. This sword can shear through a square inch of iron bar."

" Scanderbeg's sword must have Scanderbeg's arm," he remarked. " I have observed that it is a fine piece of steel. One of the real old text-compellers and psalm-expounders which the faithful drew in the days of yore, when they would

> ' Prove their religion orthodox,
> By Apostolic blows and knocks.'

You have not fenced much, then ? "

" Scarce at all," said I.

" It is as well. With an old and tried swordsman like myself, knowledge of the use of his weapon is everything ; but with a young Hotspur of your temper, strength and energy go for much. I have oft remarked that those who are most skilled at the shooting of the popinjay, the cleaving of the Turk's head, and other such sports, are ever laggards in the field. Had the popinjay a crossbow as well, and an arrow on the string, or had the Turk a fist as well as a head, our young gallant's nerves would scarce be as steady over the business. I make no doubt, Master

Clarke, that we shall make trusty comrades. What saith old Butler ?

> ' Never did trusty squire with knight,
> Or knight with squire e'er jump more right.'

I have scarce dared to quote *Hudibras* for these weeks past, lest I should set the Covenant fermenting in the old man's veins."

" If we are indeed to be comrades," said I sternly, " you must learn to speak with more reverence and less flippancy of my father, who would assuredly never have harboured you had he heard the tale which you have told me even now."

" Belike not," the adventurer answered, chuckling to himself. " It is a long stride from a mosque to a conventicle. But be not so hot-headed, my friend. You lack that repose of character which will come to you, no doubt, in your more mature years. What, man ! within five minutes of seeing me you would have smitten me on the head with an oar, and ever since you have been like a bandog at my heels, ready to bark if I do but set my foot over what you regard as the straight line. Remember that you go now among men who fight on small occasion of quarrel. A word awry may mean a rapier thrust."

" Do you bear the same in mind," I answered hotly ; " my temper is peaceful, but covert threats and veiled menace I shall not abide."

" Od's mercy ! " he cried. " I see that you will start carving me anon, and take me to Monmouth's camp in sections. Nay, nay, we shall have fighting enow without falling out among ourselves. What houses are those on the left ? "

" The village of Swathling," I replied. " The lights of Bishopstoke lie to the right, in the hollow."

" Then we are fifteen miles on our way, and methinks there is already some faint flush of dawn in the east. Hullo, what have we here ? Beds must be scarce if folks sleep on the highways."

A dark blur which I had remarked upon the roadway in front of us had resolved itself as we approached into the figure of a man, stretched at full length, with his face downwards, and his head resting upon his crossed arms.

" Some reveller, mayhap, from the village inn," I remarked.

" There's blood in the air," said Saxon, raising up his beak-like nose like a vulture which scents carrion. " Methinks he sleeps the sleep which knows no waking."

He sprang down from his saddle, and turned the figure over upon his back. The cold pale light of the early dawn shimmering upon his staring eyes and colourless face showed that the old soldier's instinct was correct, and that he had indeed drawn his last breath.

" Here's a pretty piece of work," said Saxon, kneeling by the dead man's side and passing his hands over his pockets. " Footpads, doubtless. Not a stiver in his pockets, nor as much as a sleeve-link to help pay for the burial."

" How was he slain ? " I asked in horror, looking down at the poor vacant face, the empty house from which the tenant had departed.

" A stab from behind and a tap on the head from the butt of a pistol. He cannot have been dead long, and yet every groat is gone. A man of position, too, I should judge from his dress—broadcloth coat by the feel, satin breeches, and silver buckles on his shoes. The rogues must have had some plunder with him. Could we but run across them, Clarke, it would be a great and grand thing."

" It would indeed," said I heartily. " What greater privilege than to execute justice upon such cowardly murderers ! "

" Pooh ! pooh ! " he cried. " Justice is a slippery dame, and hath a two-edged sword in her hand. We may have enough of justice in our character as rebels to give us a surfeit of it. I would fain overtake these robbers that we may relieve them of their *spolia opima*, together with

any other wealth which they may have unlawfully amassed. My learned friend the Fleming layeth it down that it is no robbery to rob a robber. But where shall we conceal this body ? "

" Wherefore should we conceal it ? " I asked.

" Why, man, unused to war or the precautions of a warrior, you must yet see that should this body be found here, there will be a hue and cry through the country, and that strangers like ourselves will be arrested on suspicion. Should we clear ourselves, which is no very easy matter, the justice will at least want to know whence we come and whither we go, which may lead to inquiries that may bode us little good. I shall therefore take the liberty, mine unknown and silent friend, of dragging you into yon bushes, where for a day or two at least you are like to lie unobserved, and so bring no harm upon honest men."

" For God's sake do not treat it so unkindly," I cried, springing down from my horse and laying my hand upon my companion's arm. " There is no need to trail it in so unseemly a fashion. If it must be moved hence, I shall carry it with all due reverence." So saying, I picked the body up in my arms, and bearing it to a wayside clump of yellow gorse bushes, I laid it solemnly down and drew the branches over it to conceal it.

" You have the thews of an ox and the heart of a woman," muttered my companion. " By the Mass, that old white-headed psalm-singer was right ; for if my memory serves me, he said words to that effect. A few handfuls of dust will hide the stains. Now we may jog upon our way without any fear of being called upon to answer for another man's sins. Let me but get my girth tightened and we may soon be out of danger's way.

" I have had to do," said Saxon, as we rode onwards, " with many gentry of this sort, with Albanian brigands, the banditti of Piedmont, the Lanzknechte and Freiritter of the Rhine, Algerine picaroons, and other such folk. Yet I cannot call to mind one who hath ever been able to retire in his old age on a sufficient competence. It is but

a precarious trade, and must end sooner or later in a dance on nothing in a tight cravat, with some kind friend tugging at your legs to ease you of any breath that you might have left."

" Nor does that end all," I remarked.

" No. There is Tophet behind and the flames of hell. So our good friends the parsons tell us. Well, if a man is to make no money in this world, be hanged at the end of it, and finally burn for ever, he hath assuredly wandered on to a thorny track. If, on the other hand, one could always lay one's hands on a well-lined purse, as these rogues have done to-night, one might be content to risk something in the world to come."

" But what can the well-filled purse do for them ? " said I. " What will the few score pieces which these bloodthirsty wretches have filched from this poor creature avail them when their own hour of death comes round ? "

" True," said Saxon drily ; " they may, however, prove useful in the meantime. This you say is Bishopstoke. What are the lights over yonder ? "

" They come, I think, from Bishop's Waltham," I answered.

" We must press on, for I would fain be in Salisbury before it is broad day. There we shall put our horses up until evening and have some rest, for there is nothing gained by man or beast coming jaded to the wars. All this day the western roads will be crowded with couriers, and mayhap patrolled by cavalry as well, so that we cannot show our faces upon it without a risk of being stopped and examined. Now if we lie by all day, and push on at dusk, keeping off the main road and making our way across Salisbury Plain and the Somersetshire downs, we shall be less likely to come to harm."

" But what if Monmouth be engaged before we come up to him ? " I asked.

" Then we shall have missed a chance of getting our throats cut. Why, man, supposing that he has been routed and entirely dispersed, would it not be a merry

ccnceit for us to appear upon the scene as two loyal
yeomen, who had ridden all the way from Hampshire to
strike in against the King's enemies ? We might chance
to get some reward in money or in land for our zeal.
Nay, frown not, for I was but jesting. Breathe our
horses by walking them up this hill. My jennet is as
fresh as when we started, but those great limbs of thine
are telling upon the grey."

The patch of light in the east had increased and
broadened, and the sky was mottled with little pink
feathers of cloud. As we passed over the low hills by
Chandler's Ford and Romsey we could see the smoke of
Southampton to the south-east, and the broad dark
expanse of the New Forest with the haze of morning
hanging over it. A few horsemen passed us, pricking
along, too much engrossed in their own errand to inquire
ours. A couple of carts and a long string of pack-horses,
laden principally with bales of wool, came straggling
along a by-road, and the drivers waved their broad hats
to us and wished us Godspeed. At Dunbridge the folk
were just stirring, and paused in taking down the cottage
shutters to come to the garden railings and watch us pass.
As we entered Dean, the great red sun pushed its rosy
rim over the edge of the horizon, and the air was filled
with the buzz of insects and the sweet scent of the
morning. We dismounted at this latter village, and had
a cup of ale while resting and watering the horses. The
landlord could tell us nothing about the insurgents, and
indeed seemed to care very little about the matter one
way or the other. " As long as brandy pays a duty of
six shillings and eightpence a gallon, and freight and
leakage comes to half a crown, while I am expected to sell
it at twelve shillings, it matters little to me who is King
of England. Give me a king that will prevent the hop-
blight and I am his man." Those were the landlord's
politics, and I dare say a good many more were of his
way of thinking.

From Dean to Salisbury is all straight road with moor,

morass and fenland on either side, broken only by the single hamlet of Aldersbury, just over the Wiltshire border. Our horses, refreshed by the short rest, stepped out gallantly, and the brisk motion, with the sunlight and the beauty of the morning, combined to raise our spirits and cheer us after the depression of the long ride through the darkness, and the incident of the murdered traveller. Wild duck, widgeon and snipe flapped up from either side of the road at the sound of the horses' hoofs, and once a herd of red deer sprang to their feet from among the ferns and scampered away in the direction of the forest. Once, too, when passing a dense clump of trees, we saw a shadowy white creature half hidden by the trunks, which must, I fancy, have been one of those wild cattle of which I have heard the peasants speak, who dwell in the recesses of the southern woods, and are so fierce and intractable that none dare approach them. The breadth of the view, the keenness of the air, and the novelty of the sense of having great work to do, all combined to send a flush of life through my veins such as the quiet village existence had never been able to give. My more experienced companion felt the influence too, for he lifted up a cracked voice and broke into a droning chant, which he assured me was an Eastern ode which had been taught him by the second sister of the Hospodar of Wallachia.

" Anent Monmouth," he remarked, coming back suddenly to the realities of our position. " It is unlikely that he can take the field for some days, though much depends upon his striking a blow soon, and so raising the courage of his followers before the King's troops can come down upon him. He has, mark ye, not only his troops to find, but their weapons, which is like to prove a more difficult matter. Suppose he can raise five thousand men—and he cannot stir with less—he will not have one musket in five, so the rest must do as they can with pikes and bills, or such other rude arms as they can find. All this takes time, and though there may be skirmishes, there can scarce be any engagement of import before we arrive."

" He will have been landed three or four days ere we reach him," said I.

" Hardly time for him with his small staff of officers to enrol his men and divide them into regiments. I scarce expect to find him at Taunton, though we were so directed. Hast ever heard whether there are any rich Papists in those parts ? "

" I know not," I replied.

" If so there might be plate chests and silver chargers, to say nothing of my lady's jewels and other such trifles to reward a faithful soldier. What would war be without plunder ! A bottle without the wine—a shell without the oyster. See the house yonder that peeps through the trees. I warrant there is a store of all good things under that roof, which you and I might have for the asking, did we but ask with our swords in our grip. You are my witness that your father did give and not lend me this horse." '

" Why say you that, then ? "

" Lest he claim a half of whatever booty I may chance to gain. What saith my learned Fleming under the heading ' an qui militi equum præbuit, prædæ ab eo captæ particeps esse debeat ? ' which signifieth ' whether he who lendeth a horse hath a claim on the plunder of him who borroweth it.' In this discourse he cites a case wherein a Spanish commander having lent a steed to one of his captains, and the said captain having captured the general of the enemy, the commander did sue him for a half share of the twenty thousand crowns which formed the ransom of the prisoner. A like case is noted by the famous Petrinus Bellus in his book *De Re Militari*, much read by leaders of repute." [1]

" I can promise you," I answered, " that no such claim shall ever be made by my father upon you. See yonder, over the brow of the hill, how the sun shines upon the high cathedral tower, which points upwards with its great stone finger to the road that every man must travel."

[1] Note C, Appendix.

" There is good store of silver and plate in these same churches," quoth my companion. " I remember that at Leipsic, when I was serving my first campaign, I got a candlestick, which I was forced to sell to a Jew broker for a fourth of its value ; yet even at his price it sufficed to fill my haversack with broad pieces."

It chanced that Saxon's mare had gained a stride or two upon mine whilst he spoke, so that I was able to get a good view of him without turning my head. I had scarce had light during our ride to see how his harness sat upon him, but now I was amazed on looking at him to mark the change which it had wrought in the man. In his civil dress his lankiness and length of limb gave him an awkward appearance, but on horseback, with his lean, gaunt face looking out from his steel cap, his breast-plate and buff jacket filling out his figure, and his high boots of untanned leather reaching to the centre of his thighs, he looked the veteran man-at-arms which he purported to be. The ease with which he sat his horse, the high, bold expression upon his face, and the great length of his arms, all marked him as one who could give a good account of himself in a fray. In his words alone I could have placed little trust, but there was that in his bearing which assured even a novice like myself that he was indeed a trained man of war.

" That is the Avon which glitters amongst the trees," I remarked. " We are about three miles from Salisbury town."

" It is a noble spire," said he, glancing at the great stone spire in front of us. " The men of old would seem to have spent all their days in piling stones upon stones. And yet we read of tough battles and shrewd blows struck, showing that they had some time for soldierly relaxation, and were not always at this mason work."

" The Church was rich in those days," I answered, shaking my bridle, for Covenant was beginning to show signs of laziness. " But here comes one who might perhaps tell us something of the war."

A horseman who bore traces of having ridden long and hard was rapidly approaching us. Both rider and steed were grey with dust and splashed with mire, yet he galloped with loosened rein and bent body, as one to whom every extra stride is of value.

" What ho, friend ! " cried Saxon, reining his mare across the road so as to bar the man's passage. " What news from the West ? "

" I must not tarry," the messenger gasped, slackening his speed for an instant. " I bear papers of import from Gregory Alford, Mayor of Lyme, to his Majesty's Council. The rebels make great head, and gather together like bees in the swarming time. There are some thousands in arms already, and all Devonshire is on the move. The rebel horse under Lord Grey hath been beaten back from Bridport by the red militia of Dorset, but every prickeared Whig from the Channel to the Severn is making his way to Monmouth." With this brief summary of the news he pushed his way past us and clattered on in a cloud of dust upon his mission.

" The broth is fairly on the fire, then," quoth Decimus Saxon, as we rode onwards. " Now that skins have been slit the rebels may draw their swords and fling away their scabbards, for it's either victory for them or their quarters will be dangling in every market town of the county. Heh, lad ? we throw a main for a brave stake."

" Marked ye that Lord Grey had met with a check," said I.

" Pshaw ! it is of no import. A cavalry skirmish at the most, for it is impossible that Monmouth could have brought his main forces to Bridport ; nor would he if he could, for it is out of his track. It was one of those three-shots-and-a-gallop affrays, where each side runs away and each claims the victory. But here we are in the streets of Salisbury. Now leave the talking to me, or your wrong-headed truthfulness may lay us by the heels before our time."

Passing down the broad High Street we dismounted in front of the Blue Boar inn, and handed our tired horses over to the ostler, to whom Saxon, in a loud voice, and with many rough military oaths, gave strict injunctions as to their treatment. He then clanked into the inn parlour, and throwing himself into one chair with his feet upon another, he summoned the landlord up before him, and explained our needs in a tone and manner which should give him a due sense of our quality.

" Of your best, and at once," quoth he. " Have your largest double-couched chamber ready with your softest lavender-scented sheets, for we have had a weary ride and must rest. And hark ye, landlord, no palming off your stale, musty goods as fresh, or of your washy French wines for the true Hainault vintage. I would have you to understand that my friend here and I are men who meet with some consideration in the world, though we care not to speak our names to every underling. Deserve well of us, therefore, or it may be the worse for you."

This speech, combined with my companion's haughty manner and fierce face, had such an effect upon the landlord that he straightway sent us in the breakfast which had been prepared for three officers of the Blues, who were waiting for it in the next apartment. This kept them fasting for another half-hour, and we could hear their oaths and complaints through the partition while we were devouring their capon and venison pie. Having eaten a hearty meal and washed it down with a bottle of Burgundy we sought our room, and throwing our tired limbs upon the bed, were soon in a deep slumber.

9. *Of a Passage of Arms at the Blue Boar*

I HAD slept several hours when I was suddenly aroused by a prodigious crash, followed by the clash of arms and shrill cries from the lower floor. Springing to my feet I found that the bed upon which my

comrade had lain was vacant, and that the door of the apartment was opened. As the uproar still continued, and as I seemed to discern his voice in the midst of it, I caught up my sword, and without waiting to put on either headpiece, steel-breast or arm-plates, I hurried to the scene of the commotion.

The hall and passage were filled with silly maids and staring drawers, attracted, like myself, by the uproar. Through these I pushed my way into the apartment where we had breakfasted in the morning, which was a scene of the wildest disorder. The round table in the centre had been tilted over upon its side, and three broken bottles of wine, with apples, pears, nuts and the fragments of the dishes containing them, were littered over the floor. A couple of packs of cards and a dice-box lay amongst the scattered feast. Close by the door stood Decimus Saxon, with his drawn rapier in his hand and a second one beneath his feet, while facing him there was a young officer in a blue uniform, whose face was reddened with shame and anger, and who looked wildly about the room as though in search of some weapon to replace that of which he had been deprived. He might have served Cibber or Gibbons as a model for a statue of impotent rage. Two other officers dressed in the same blue uniform stood by their comrade, and as I observed that they had laid their hands upon the hilts of their swords, I took my place by Saxon's side, and stood ready to strike in should the occasion arise.

" What would the maitre d'armes say—the maitre d'escrime ? " cried my companion. " Methinks he should lose his place for not teaching you to make a better show. Out on him ! Is this the way that he teaches the officers of his Majesty's guard to use their weapons ? "

" This raillery, sir," said the elder of the three, a squat, brown, heavy-faced man, " is not undeserved, and yet might perchance be dispensed with. I am free to say that our friend attacked you somewhat hastily, and that a

little more deference should have been shown by so young a soldier to a cavalier of your experience."

The other officer, who was a fine-looking, noble-featured man, expressed himself in much the same manner. "If this apology will serve," said he, "I am prepared to join in it. If, however, more is required, I shall be happy to take the quarrel upon myself."

"Nay, nay, take your bradawl!" Saxon answered good-humouredly, kicking the sword towards his youthful opponent. "But, mark you! when you would lunge, direct your point upwards rather than down, for otherwise you must throw your wrist open to your antagonist, who can scarce fail to disarm you. In quarte, tierce or saccoon the same holds good."

The youth sheathed his sword, but was so overcome by his own easy defeat and the contemptuous way in which his opponent had dismissed him, that he turned and hurried out of the room. Meanwhile Decimus Saxon and the two officers set to work getting the table upon its legs and restoring the room to some sort of order, in which I did what I could to assist them.

"I held three queens for the first time to-day," grumbled the soldier of fortune. "I was about to declare them when this young bantam flew at my throat. He hath likewise been the cause of our losing three flasks of most excellent muscadine. When he hath drunk as much bad wine as I have been forced to do, he will not be so hasty in wasting the good."

"He is a hot-headed youngster," the older officer replied, "and a little solitary reflection added to the lesson which you have taught him may bring him profit. As for the muscadine, that loss will soon be repaired, the more gladly as your friend here will help us to drink it."

"I was roused by the crash of weapons," said I, "and I scarce know now what has occurred."

"Why, a mere tavern brawl, which your friend's skill and judgment prevented from becoming serious. I prythee take the rush-bottomed chair, and do you, Jack,

order the wine. If our comrade hath spilled the last it is
for us to furnish this, and the best the cellars contain.
We have been having a hand at basset, which Mr. Saxon
here playeth as skilfully as he wields the small-sword.
It chanced that the luck ran against young Horsford,
which doubtless made him prone to be quick in taking
offence. Your friend in conversation, when discoursing
of his experiences in foreign countries, remarked that the
French household troops were to his mind brought to a
higher state of discipline than any of our own regiments,
on which Horsford fired up, and after a hot word or two
they found themselves, as you have seen, at drawn bilbo.
The boy hath seen no service, and is therefore over-
eager to give proof of his valour."

" Wherein," said the tall officer, " he showed a want of
thought towards me, for had the words been offensive it
was for me, who am a senior captain and brevet-major,
to take it up, and not for a slip of a cornet, who scarce
knows enough to put his troop through the exercise."

" You say right, Ogilvy," said the other, resuming his
seat by the table and wiping the cards which had been
splashed by the wine. " Had the comparison been made
by an officer of Louis's guard for the purpose of contumely and braggadocio, it would then indeed have
become us to venture a passado. But when spoken by
an Englishman of ripe experience it becomes a matter
of instructive criticism, which should profit rather than
annoy."

" True, Ambrose," the other answered. " Without
such criticism a force would become stagnant, and could
never hope to keep level with those continental armies,
which are ever striving amongst themselves for increased
efficacy."

So pleased was I at these sensible remarks on the part
of the strangers, that I was right glad to have the opportunity of making their closer acquaintance over a flask of
excellent wine. My father's prejudices had led me to
believe that a King's officer was ever a compound of the

coxcomb and the bully, but I found on testing it that this idea, like most others which a man takes upon trust, had very little foundation upon truth. As a matter of fact, had they been dressed in less warlike garb and deprived of their swords and jack-boots, they would have passed as particularly mild-mannered men, for their conversation ran in the learned channels, and they discussed Boyle's researches in chemistry and the ponderation of air with much gravity and show of knowledge. At the same time, their brisk bearing and manly carriage showed that in cultivating the scholar they had not sacrificed the soldier.

" May I ask, sir," said one of them, addressing Saxon, " whether in your wide experiences you have ever met with any of those sages and philosophers who have con- ferred such honour and fame upon France and Germany ? "

My companion looked ill at ease, as one who feels that he has been taken off his ground. " There was indeed one such at Nurnberg," he answered, " one Gervinus or Gervanus, who, the folk said, could turn an ingot of iron into an ingot of gold as easily as I turn this tobacco into ashes. Old Pappenheimer shut him up with a ton of metal, and threatened to put the thumbikins upon him unless he changed it into gold pieces. I can vouch for it that there was not a yellow-boy there, for I was captain of the guard and searched the whole dungeon through. To my sorrow I say it, for I had myself added a small iron brazier to the heap, thinking that if there should be any such change it would be as well that I should have some small share in the experiment."

" Alchemy, transmutation of metals and the like have been set aside by true science," remarked the taller officer. " Even old Sir Thomas Browne of Norwich, who is ever ready to plead the cause of the ancients, can find nothing to say in favour of it. From Trismegistus downwards through Albertus Magnus, Aquinas, Raymond Lullius, Basil Valentine, Paracelsus and the rest, there is not one who has left more than a cloud of words behind him."

" Nor did the rogue I mention," said Saxon. " There was another, Van Helstatt, who was a man of learning, and cast horoscopes in consideration of some small fee or honorarium. I have never met so wise a man, for he would talk of the planets and constellations as though he kept them all in his own backyard. He made no more of a comet than if it were a mouldy china orange, and he explained their nature to us, saying that they were but common stars which had had a hole knocked in them, so that their insides or viscera protruded. He was indeed a philosopher ! "

" And did you ever put his skill to the test ? " asked one of the officers, with a smile.

" Not I, forsooth, for I have ever kept myself clear of black magic or diablerie of the sort. My comrade Pierce Scotton, who was an Oberst in the Imperial cavalry brigade, did pay him a rose noble to have his future expounded. If I remember aright, the stars said that he was over-fond of wine and women—he had a wicked eye and a nose like a carbuncle. They foretold also that he would attain a marshal's baton and die at a ripe age, which might well have come true had he not been unhorsed a month later at Ober-Graustock, and slain by the hoofs of his own troop. Neither the planets nor even the experienced farrier of the regiment could have told that the brute would have foundered so completely."

The officers laughed heartily at my companion's views, and rose from their chairs, for the bottle was empty and the evening beginning to draw in. " We have work to do here," said the one addressed as Ogilvy. " Besides, we must find this foolish boy of ours, and tell him that it is no disgrace to be disarmed by so expert a swordsman. We have to prepare the quarters for the regiment, who will be up to join Churchill's forces not later than to-night. Ye are yourselves bound for the West, I understand ? "

" We belong to the Duke of Beaufort's household," said Saxon.

" Indeed ! I thought ye might belong to Portman's

yellow regiment of militia. I trust that the Duke will muster every man he can, and make play until the royal forces come up."

" How many will Churchill bring ? " asked my companion carelessly.

" Eight hundred horse at the most, but my Lord Feversham will follow after with close on four thousand foot."

" We may meet on the field of battle, if not before," said I, and we bade our friendly enemies a very cordial adieu.

" A skilful equivoque that last of yours, Master Micah," quoth Decimus Saxon, " though smacking of double dealing in a truth-lover like yourself. If we meet them in battle I trust that it may be with cheváux-de-frise of pikes and morgenstierns before us, and a litter of caltrops in front of them, for Monmouth has no cavalry that could stand for a moment against the Royal Guards."

" How came you to make their acquaintance ? " I asked.

" I slept a few hours, but I have learned in camps to do with little rest. Finding you in sound slumber, and hearing the rattle of the dice-box below, I came softly down and found means to join their party—whereby I am a richer man by fifteen guineas, and might have had more had that young fool not lugged out at me, or had the talk not turned afterwards upon such unseemly subjects as the laws of chemistry and the like. Prithee, what have the Horse Guards Blue to do with the laws of chemistry ? Wessenburg of the Pandours would, even at his own mess table, suffer much free talk—more perhaps than fits in with the dignity of a leader. Had his officers ventured upon such matter as this, however, there would have been a drum-head court-martial, or a cashiering at the least."

Without stopping to dispute either Master Saxon's judgment or that of Wessenburg of the Pandours, I proposed that we should order an evening meal, and should employ the remaining hour or two of daylight in looking over the city. The principal sight is of course the noble cathedral, which is built in such exact proportion

89

that one would fail to understand its great size did one not actually enter it and pace round the long dim aisles. So solemn were its sweeping arches and the long shafts of coloured light which shone through the stained-glass windows, throwing strange shadows amongst the pillars, that even my companion, albeit not readily impressed, was silent and subdued. It was a great prayer in stone.

On our way back to the inn we passed the town lock-up, with a railed space in front of it, in which three great black-muzzled bloodhounds were stalking about, with fierce crimsoned eyes and red tongues lolling out of their mouths. They were used, a bystander told us, for the hunting down of criminals upon Salisbury Plain, which had been a refuge for rogues and thieves, until this means had been adopted for following them to their hiding-places. It was well-nigh dark before we returned to the hostel, and entirely so by the time that we had eaten our suppers, paid our reckoning, and got ready for the road.

Before we set off I bethought me of the paper which my mother had slipped into my hand on parting, and drawing it from my pouch I read it by the rushlight in our chamber. It still bore the splotches of the tears which she had dropped on it, poor soul, and ran in this wise :

" Instructions from Mistress Mary Clarke to her son Micah, on the twelfth day of June in the year of our Lord sixteen hundred and eighty-five.

" On occasion of his going forth, like David of old, to do battle with the Goliath of Papistry, which hath over-shadowed and thrown into disrepute that true and reverent regard for ritual which should exist in the real Church of England, as ordained by law.

" Let these points be observed by him, namely, to wit :

" 1. Change your hosen when the occasion serves. You have two pairs in your saddle-bag, and can buy more, for the wool work is good in the West.

" 2. A hare's foot suspended round the neck driveth away colic.

" 3. Say the Lord's Prayer night and morning. Also read the scriptures, especially Job, the Psalms and the Gospel according to St. Matthew.

" 4. Daffy's elixir possesses extraordinary powers in purifying the blood and working off all phlegms, humours, vapours or rheums. The dose is five drops. A small phial of it will be found in the barrel of your left pistol, with wadding around it lest it come to harm.

" 5. Ten golden pieces are sewn into the hem of your under doublet. Touch them not, save as a last resource.

" 6. Fight stoutly for the Lord, and yet I pray you, Micah, be not too forward in battle, but let others do their turn also. Press not into the heart of the fray, and yet flinch not from the standard of the Protestant faith.

" And oh, Micah, my own bright boy, come back safe to your mother, or my very heart will break !

" And the deponent will ever pray."

The sudden gush of tenderness in the last few lines made the tears spring to my eyes, and yet I could scarce forbear from smiling at the whole composition, for my dear mother had little time to cultivate the graces of style, and it was evidently her thought that in order to make her instructions binding it was needful to express them in some sort of legal form. I had little time to think over her advice, however, for I had scarce finished reading it before the voice of Decimus Saxon, and the clink of the horses' hoofs upon the cobble-stones of the yard, informed me that all was ready for our departure.

10. *Of our Perilous Adventure on the Plain*

WE were not half a mile from the town before the roll of kettle drums and the blare of bugles swelling up musically through the darkness announced the arrival of the regiment of horse which our friends at the inn had been expecting.

" It is as well, perhaps," said Saxon, " that we gave them the slip, for that young springald might have smelled a rat and played us some ill-turn. Have you chanced to see my silken kerchief ? "

" Not I," I answered.

" Nay, then, it must have fallen from my bosom during our ruffle. I can ill afford to leave it, for I travel light in such matters. Eight hundred men, quoth the major, and three thousand to follow. Should I meet this same Oglethorpe or Ogilvy when the little business is over, I shall read him a lesson on thinking less of chemistry and more of the need of preserving military precautions. It is well always to be courteous to strangers and to give them information, but it is well also that the information should be false."

" As his may have been," I suggested.

" Nay, nay, the words came too glibly from his tongue. So ho, Chloe, so ho ! She is full of oats and would fain gallop, but it is so plaguy dark that we can scarce see where we are going."

We had been trotting down the broad high-road skimmering vaguely white in the gloom, with the shadowy trees dancing past us on either side, scarce outlined against the dark background of cloud. We were now coming upon the eastern edge of the great plain, which extends forty miles one way and twenty the other, over the greater part of Wiltshire and past the boundaries of Somersetshire. The main road to the West skirts this wilderness, but we had agreed to follow a less important track, which would lead us to our goal, though in a more tedious manner. Its insignificance would, we hoped, prevent it from being guarded by the King's horse. We had come to the point where this by-road branches off from the main highway when we heard the clatter of horses' hoofs behind us.

" Here comes someone who is not afraid to gallop," I remarked.

" Halt here in the shadow ! " cried Saxon, in a short,

quick whisper. " Have your blade loose in the scabbard. He must have a set errand who rides so fast o' nights."

Looking down the road we could make out through the darkness a shadowy blur which soon resolved itself into man and horse. The rider was well-nigh abreast of us before he was aware of our presence, when he pulled up his steed in a strange, awkward fashion, and faced round in our direction.

" Is Micah Clarke there ? " he said, in a voice which was strangely familiar to my ears.

" I am Micah Clarke," said I.

" And I am Reuben Lockarby," cried our pursuer, in a mock heroic voice. " Ah, Micah lad, I'd embrace you were it not that I should assuredly fall out of the saddle if I attempted it, and perchance drag you along. That sudden pull up well-nigh landed me on the roadway. I have been sliding off and clambering on ever since I bade good-bye to Havant. Sure, such a horse for slipping from under one was never bestridden by man."

" Good Heavens, Reuben ! " I cried in amazement, " what brings you all this way from home ? "

" The very same cause which brings you, Micah, and also Don Decimo Saxon, late of the Solent, whom methinks I see in the shadow behind you. How fares it, oh illustrious one ? "

" It is you, then, young cock of the woods ! " growled Saxon, in no very overjoyed voice.

" No less a person," said Reuben. " And now, my gay cavalieros, round with your horses and trot on your way, for there is no time to be lost. We ought all to be at Taunton to-morrow."

" But, my dear Reuben," said I, " it cannot be that you are coming with us to join Monmouth. What would your father say ? This is no holiday jaunt, but one that may have a sad and stern ending. At the best, victory can only come through much bloodshed and danger. At the worst, we are as like to wind up upon a scaffold as not."

" Forwards, lads, forwards ! " cried he, spurring on his

horse, " it is all arranged and settled. I am about to offer my august person, together with a sword which I borrowed and a horse which I stole, to his most Protestant highness, James, Duke of Monmouth."

" But how comes it all ? " I asked, as we rode on together. " It warms my very heart to see you, but you were never concerned either in religion or in politics. Whence, then, this sudden resolution ? "

" Well, truth to tell," he replied, " I am neither a king's man nor a duke's man, nor would I give a button which sat upon the throne. I do not suppose that either one or the other would increase the custom of the Wheatsheaf, or want Reuben Lockarby for a councillor. I am a Micah Clarke man, though, from the crown of my head to the soles of my feet ; and if he rides to the wars, may the plague strike me if I don't stick to his elbow ! " He raised his hand excitedly as he spoke, and instantly losing his balance, he shot into a dense clump of bushes by the roadside whence his legs flapped helplessly in the darkness.

" That makes the tenth," said he, scrambling out and clambering into his saddle once more. " My father used to tell me not to sit a horse too closely. ' A gentle rise and fall,' said the old man. Egad, there is more fall than rise, and it is anything but gentle."

" Od's truth ! " exclaimed Saxon. " How in the name of all the saints in the calendar do you expect to keep your seat in the presence of an enemy if you lose it on a peaceful high-road ? "

" I can but try, my illustrious," he answered, rearranging his ruffled clothing. " Perchance the sudden and unexpected character of my movements may disconcert the said enemy."

" Well, well, there may be more truth in that than you are aware of," quoth Saxon, riding upon Lockarby's bridle arm, so that there was scarce room for him to fall between us. " I had sooner fight a man like that young fool at the inn, who knew a little of the use of his weapon,

than one like Micah here, or yourself, who know nothing. You can tell what the one is after, but the other will invent a system of his own which will serve his turn for the nonce. Ober-hauptmann Muller was reckoned to be the finest player at the small-sword in the Kaiser's army, and could for a wager snick any button from an opponent's vest without cutting the cloth. Yet was he slain in an encounter with Fahnführer Zollner, who was a cornet in our own Pandour corps, and who knew as much of the rapier as you do of horsemanship. For the rapier, be it understood, is designed to thrust and not to cut, so that no man wielding it ever thinks of guarding a side-stroke. But Zollner, being a long-armed man, smote his antagonist across the face with his weapon as though it had been a cane, and then, ere he had time to recover himself, fairly pinked him. Doubtless if the matter were to do again, the Ober-hauptmann would have got his thrust in sooner, but as it was, no explanation or excuse could get over the fact that the man was dead."

" If want of knowledge maketh a dangerous swordsman," quoth Reuben, " then am I even more deadly than the unpronounceable gentleman whom you have mentioned. To continue my story, however, which I broke off in order to step down from my horse, I found out early in the morning that ye were gone, and Zachary Palmer was able to tell me whither. I made up my mind, therefore, that I would out into the world also. To this end I borrowed a sword from Solomon Sprent, and my father having gone to Gosport, I helped myself to the best nag in his stables—for I have too much respect for the old man to allow one of his flesh and blood to go ill-provided to the wars. All day I have ridden, since early morning, being twice stopped on suspicion of being ill-affected, but having the good luck to get away each time. I knew that I was close at your heels, for I found them searching for you at the Salisbury Inn."

Decimus whistled. " Searching for us ? " said he.

" Yes. It seems that they had some notion that ye

were not what ye professed to be, so the inn was surrounded as I passed, but none knew which road ye had
taken."

" Said I not so ? " cried Saxon. " That young viper
hath stirred up the regiment against us. We must push
on, for they may send a party on our track."

" We are off the main road now," I remarked ; " even
should they pursue us, they would be unlikely to follow
this side track."

" Yet it would be wise to show them a clean pair of
heels," said Saxon, spurring his mare into a gallop.
Lockarby and I followed his example, and we all three
rode swiftly along the rough moorland track.

We passed through scattered belts of pinewood, where
the wild cat howled and the owl screeched, and across
broad stretches of fenland and moor, where the silence
was only broken by the booming cry of the bittern or the
fluttering of wild duck far above our heads. The road
was in parts overgrown with brambles, and was so
deeply rutted and so studded with sharp and dangerous
hollows, that our horses came more than once upon their
knees. In one place the wooden bridge which led over
a stream had broken down, and no attempt had been
made to repair it, so that we were compelled to ride our
horses girth deep through the torrent. At first some
scattered lights had shown that we were in the neighbourhood of human habitations, but these became fewer
as we advanced, until the last died away and we found
ourselves upon the desolate moor which stretched away
in unbroken solitude to the shadowy horizon. The moon
had broken through the clouds and now shone hazily
through wreaths of mist, throwing a dim light over the
wild scene, and enabling us to keep to the track, which
was not fenced in in any way and could scarce be distinguished from the plain around it.

We had slackened our pace under the impression that
all fear of pursuit was at an end, and Reuben was amusing
us by an account of the excitement which had been caused

in Havant by our disappearance, when through the still-ness of the night a dull, muffled rat-tat-tat struck upon my ear. At the same moment Saxon sprang from his horse and listened intently with sidelong head.

" Boot and saddle ! " he cried, springing into his seat again. " They are after us as sure as fate. A dozen troopers by the sound. We must shake them off, or good-bye to Monmouth."

" Give them their heads," I answered, and striking spurs into our steeds, we thundered on through the darkness. Covenant and Chloe were as fresh as could be wished, and soon settled down into a long springy gallop. Our friend's horse, however, had been travelling all day, and its long-drawn, laboured breathing showed that it could not hold out for long. Through the clatter of our horses' hoofs I could still from time to time hear the ominous murmur from behind us.

" This will never do, Reuben," said I anxiously, as the weary creature stumbled, and the rider came perilously near to shooting over its head.

" The old horse is nearly foundered," he answered ruefully. " We are off the road now, and the rough ground is too much for her."

" Yes, we are off the track," cried Saxon over his shoulder—for he led us by a few paces. " Bear in mind that the Bluecoats have been on the march all day, so that their horses may also be blown. How in Himmel came they to know which road we took ? "

As if in answer to his ejaculation, there rose out of the still night behind us a single, clear, bell-like note, swelling and increasing in volume until it seemed to fill the whole air with its harmony.

" A bloodhound ! " cried Saxon.

A second sharper, keener note, ending in an un-mistakable howl, answered the first.

" Another of them," said he. " They have loosed the brutes that we saw near the Cathedral. Gad ! we little thought when we peered over the rails at them, a few

hours ago, that they would so soon be on our own track. Keep a firm knee and a steady seat, for a slip now would be your last."

" Holy mother ! " cried Reuben, " I had steeled myself to die in battle—but to be dog's-meat ! It is something outside the contract."

" They hold them in leash," said Saxon, between his teeth, " else they would outstrip the horses and be lost in the darkness. Could we but come on running water we might put them off our track."

" My horse cannot hold on at this pace for more than a very few minutes," Reuben cried. " If I break down, do ye go on, for ye must remember that they are upon your track and not mine. They have found cause for suspicion of the two strangers of the inn, but none of me."

" Nay, Reuben, we shall stand or fall together," said I sadly, for at every step his horse grew more and more feeble. " In this darkness they will make little distinction between persons."

" Keep a good heart," shouted the old soldier, who was now leading us by twenty yards or more. " We can hear them because the wind blows from that way, but it's odds whether they have heard us. Methinks they slacken in their pursuit."

" The sound of their horses has indeed grown fainter," said I joyfully.

" So faint that I can hear it no longer," my companion cried.

We reined up our panting steeds and strained our ears, but not a sound could we hear save the gentle murmur of the breeze amongst the whin-bushes, and the melancholy cry of the night-jar. Behind us the broad rolling plain, half light and half shadow, stretched away to the dim horizon without sign of life or movement.

" We have either outstripped them completely, or else they have given up the chase," said I. " What ails the horses that they should tremble and snort ? "

" My poor beast is nearly done for," Reuben remarked,

leaning forward and passing his hand down the creature's reeking neck.

" For all that we cannot rest," said Saxon. " We may not be out of danger yet. Another mile or two may shake us clear. But I like it not."

" Like not what ? "

" These horses and their terrors. The beasts can at times both see and hear more than we, as I could show by divers examples drawn from mine own experience on the Danube and in the Palatinate, were the time and place more fitting. Let us on, then, before we rest."

The weary horses responded bravely to the call, and struggled onwards over the broken ground for a considerable time. At last we were thinking of pulling up in good earnest, and of congratulating ourselves upon having tired out our pursuers, when of a sudden the bell-like baying broke upon our ears far louder than it had been before—so loud, indeed, that it was evident that the dogs were close upon our heels.

" The accursed hounds ! " cried Saxon, putting spurs to his horse and shooting ahead of us ; " I feared as much. They have freed them from the leash. There is no escape from the devils, but we can choose the spot where we shall make our stand."

" Come on, Reuben," I shouted. " We have only to reckon with the dogs now. Their masters have let them loose, and turned back for Salisbury."

" Pray heaven they break their necks before they get there ! " he cried. " They set dogs on us as though we were rats in a cock-pit. Yet they call England a Christian country ! It's no use, Micah. Poor Dido can't stir another step."

As he spoke, the sharp fierce bay of the hounds rose again, clear and stern on the night air, swelling up from a low hoarse growl to a high angry yelp. There seemed to be a ring of exultation in their wild cry, as though they knew that their quarry was almost run to earth.

" Not another step ! " said Reuben Lockarby, pulling

up and drawing his sword. " If I must fight, I shall fight here."

" There could be no better place," I replied. Two great jagged rocks rose before us, jutting abruptly out of the ground, and leaving a space of twelve or fifteen feet between them. Through this gap we rode, and I shouted loudly for Saxon to join us. His horse, however, had been steadily gaining upon ours, and at the renewed alarm had darted off again, so that he was already some hundred yards from us. It was useless to summon him, even could he hear our voices, for the hounds would be upon us before he could return.

" Never heed him," I said hurriedly. " Do you rein your steed behind that rock, and I behind this. They will serve to break the force of the attack. Dismount not, but strike down, and strike hard."

On either side in the shadow of the rock we waited in silence for our terrible pursuers. Looking back at it, my dear children, I cannot but think that it was a great trial on such young soldiers as Reuben and myself to be put, on the first occasion of drawing our swords, into such a position. For I have found, and others have confirmed my opinion, that of all dangers that a man is called upon to face, that arising from savage and determined animals is the most unnerving. For with men there is ever the chance that some trait of weakness or of want of courage may give you an advantage over them, but with fierce beasts there is no such hope. We knew that the creatures to whom we were opposed could never be turned from our throats while there was breath in their bodies. One feels in one's heart, too, that the combat is an unequal one, for your life is precious at least to your friends, while their lives, what are they ? All this and a great deal more passed swiftly through our minds as we sat with drawn swords, soothing our trembling horses as best we might, and waiting for the coming of the hounds.

Nor had we long to wait. Another long, deep, thunderous bay sounded in our ears, followed by a profound

silence, broken only by the quick shivering breathing of the horses. Then suddenly, and noiselessly, a great tawny brute, with its black muzzle to the earth, and its overhung cheeks flapping on either side, sprang into the band of moonlight between the rocks, and on into the shadow beyond. It never paused or swerved for an instant, but pursued its course straight onwards without a glance to right or to left. Close behind it came a second, and behind that a third, all of enormous size, and looking even larger and more terrible than they were in the dim shifting light. Like the first, they took no notice of our presence, but bounded on along the trail left by Decimus Saxon.

The first and second I let pass, for I hardly realised that they so completely overlooked us. When the third, however, sprang out into the moonlight, I drew my right-hand pistol from its holster, and resting its long barrel across my left forearm, I fired at it as it passed. The bullet struck the mark, for the brute gave a fierce howl of rage and pain, but true to the scent, it never turned or swerved. Lockarby fired also as it disappeared among the brushwood, but with no apparent effect. So swiftly and so noiselessly did the great hounds pass, that they might have been grim silent spirits of the night, the phantom dogs of Herne the hunter, but for that one fierce yelp which followed my shot.

" What brutes ! " my companion ejaculated ; " what shall we do, Micah ? "

" They have clearly been laid on Saxon's trail," said I. " We must follow them up, or they will be too many for him. Can you hear anything of our pursuers ? "

" Nothing."

" They have given up the chase, then, and let the dogs loose as a last resource. Doubtless the creatures are trained to return to the town. But we must push on, Reuben, if we are to help our companion."

" One more spurt, then, little Dido," cried Reuben ; " can you muster strength for one more ? Nay, I have

not the heart to put spurs to you. If you can do it, I know you will."

The brave mare snorted, as though she understood her rider's words, and stretched her weary limbs into a gallop. So stoutly did she answer the appeal that, though I pressed Covenant to his topmost speed, she was never more than a few strides behind him.

" He took this direction," said I, peering anxiously out into the darkness. " He can scarce have gone far, for he spoke of making a stand. Or, perhaps, finding that we are not with him, he may trust to the speed of his horse."

" What chance hath a horse of outstripping these brutes ? " Reuben answered. " They must run him to earth, and he knows it. Hullo ! what have we here ? "

A dark dim form lay stretched in the moonlight in front of us. It was the dead body of a hound—the one evidently at which I had fired.

" There is one of them disposed of," I cried joyously ; " we have but two to settle with now."

As I spoke we heard the crack of two pistol-shots some little distance to the left. Heading our steeds in that direction, we pressed on at the top of our speed. Presently out of the darkness in front of us there arose such a roaring and a yelping as sent the hearts into our mouths. It was not a single cry, such as the hounds had uttered when they were on the scent, but a continuous deep-mouthed uproar, so fierce and so prolonged, that we could not doubt that they had come to the end of their run.

" Pray God that they have not got him down ! " cried Reuben, in a faltering voice.

The same thought had crossed my own mind, for I have heard a similar though lesser din come from a pack of otter hounds when they had overtaken their prey and were tearing it to pieces. Sick at heart, I drew my sword with the determination that, if we were too late to save our companion, we should at least revenge him upon the four-footed fiends. Bursting through a thick belt of

scrub and tangled gorse bushes, we came upon a scene so unlike what we had expected that we pulled up our horses in astonishment.

A circular clearing lay in front of us, brightly illuminated by the silvery moonshine. In the centre of this rose a giant stone, one of those high dark columns which are found all over the plain, and especially in the parts round Stonehenge. It could not have been less than fifteen feet in height, and had doubtless been originally straight, but wind and weather, or the crumbling of the soil, had gradually suffered it to tilt over until it inclined at such an angle that an active man might clamber up to the summit. On the top of this ancient stone, cross-legged and motionless, like some strange carved idol of former days, sat Decimus Saxon, puffing sedately at the long pipe which was ever his comfort in moments of difficulty. Beneath him, at the base of the monolith, as our learned men call them, the two great bloodhounds were rearing and springing, clambering over each other's backs in their frenzied and futile eagerness to reach the impassive figure perched above them, while they gave vent to their rage and disappointment in the hideous uproar which had suggested such terrible thoughts to our mind.

We had little time, however, to gaze at this strange scene, for upon our appearance the hounds abandoned their helpless attempts to reach Saxon, and flew, with a fierce snarl of satisfaction, at Reuben and myself. One great brute, with flaring eyes and yawning mouth, his white fangs glistening in the moonlight, sprang at my horse's neck ; but I met him fair with a single sweeping cut, which shore away his muzzle, and left him wallowing and writhing in a pool of blood. Reuben, meanwhile, had spurred his horse forward to meet his assailant ; but the poor tired steed flinched at the sight of the fierce hound, and pulled up suddenly, with the result that her rider rolled headlong into the very jaws of the animal. It might have gone ill with Reuben had he been left to his own resources. At the most he could only have kept the cruel teeth from his

throat for a very few moments ; but seeing the mischance, I drew my remaining pistol, and springing from my horse, discharged it full into the creature's flank while it struggled with my friend. With a last yell of rage and pain it brought its fierce jaws together in one wild impotent snap, and then sank slowly over upon its side, while Reuben crawled from beneath it, scared and bruised, but none the worse otherwise for his perilous adventure.

" I owe you one for that, Micah," he said gratefully. " I may live to do as much for you."

" And I owe ye both one," said Saxon, who had scrambled down from his place of refuge. " I pay my debts, too, whether for good or evil. I might have stayed up there until I had eaten my jack-boots, for all the chance I had of ever getting down again. Sancta Maria ! but that was a shrewd blow of yours, Clarke ! The brute's head flew in halves like a rotten pumpkin. No wonder that they stuck to my track, for I have left both my spare girth and my kerchief behind me, which would serve to put them on Chloe's scent as well as mine own."

" And where is Chloe ? " I asked, wiping my sword.

" Chloe had to look out for herself. I found the brutes gaining on me, you see, and I let drive at them with my barkers ; but with a horse flying at twenty mile an hour, what chance is there for a single slug finding its way home ? Things looked black then, for I had no time to reload ; and the rapier, though the king of weapons in the duello, is scarce strong enough to rely upon on an occasion like this. As luck would have it, just as I was fairly puzzled, what should I come across but this handy stone, which the good priests of old did erect, as far as I can see, for no other purpose than to provide worthy cavalieros with an escape from such ignoble and scurvy enemies. I had no time to spare in clambering up it, for I had to tear my heel out of the mouth of the foremost of them, and might have been dragged down by it had he not found my spur too tough a morsel for his chewing. But

surely one of my bullets must have reached its mark."
Lighting the touch-paper in his tobacco-box, he passed
it over the body of the hound which had attacked me,
and then of the other.

" Why, this one is riddled like a sieve," he cried.
" What do you load your petronels with, good Master
Clarke ? "

" With two leaden slugs."

" Yet two leaden slugs have made a score of holes at
the least ! And of all things in this world, here is the
neck of a bottle stuck in the brute's hide ! "

" Good heavens ! " I exclaimed. " I remember. My
dear mother packed a bottle of Daffy's elixir in the barrel
of my pistol."

" And you have shot it into the bloodhound ! " roared
Reuben. " Ho ! ho ! When they hear that tale at the
tap of the Wheatsheaf, there will be some throats dry with
laughter. Saved my life by shooting a dog with a bottle
of Daffy's elixir ! "

" And a bullet as well, Reuben, though I dare warrant
the gossips will soon contrive to leave that detail out. It
is a mercy the pistol did not burst. But what do you
propose to do now, Master Saxon ? "

" Why, to recover my mare if it can anywise be done,"
said the adventurer. " Though on this vast moor, in the
dark, she will be as difficult to find as a Scotsman's
breeches or a flavourless line in *Hudibras*."

" And Reuben Lockarby's steed can go no further,"
I remarked. " But do mine eyes deceive me, or is there
a glimmer of light over yonder ? "

" A Will-o'-the-wisp," said Saxon.

" ' An *ignis fatuus* that bewitches,
And leads men into pools and ditches.'

Yet I confess that it burns steady and clear, as though it
came from lamp, candle, rushlight, lanthorn or other
human agency."

" Where there is light there is life," cried Reuben.

" Let us make for it, and see what chance of shelter we may find there."

" It cannot come from our dragoon friends," remarked Decimus. "A murrain on them ! how came they to guess our true character ; or was it on the score of some insult to the regiment that that young Fahnführer has set them on our track ? If I have him at my sword's point again, he shall not come off so free. Well, do ye lead your horses, and we shall explore this light, since no better course is open to us."

Picking our way across the moor, we directed our course for the bright point which twinkled in the distance ; and as we advanced we hazarded a thousand conjectures as to whence it could come. If it were a human dwelling, what sort of being could it be who, not content with living in the heart of this wilderness, had chosen a spot so far removed from the ordinary tracks which crossed it ? The roadway was miles behind us, and it was probable that no one save those driven by such a necessity as that which had overtaken us would ever find themselves in that desolate region. No hermit could have desired an abode more completely isolated from all communion with his kind.

As we approached we saw that the light did indeed come from a small cottage, which was built in a hollow, so as to be invisible from any quarter save that from which we approached it. In front of this humble dwelling a small patch of ground had been cleared of shrub, and in the centre of this little piece of sward our missing steed stood grazing at her leisure upon the scanty herbage. The same light which had attracted us had doubtless caught her eye, and drawn her towards it by hopes of oats and of water. With a grunt of satisfaction Saxon resumed possession of his lost property, and leading her by the bridle, approached the door of the solitary cottage.

11. *Of the Lonely Man and the Gold Chest*

THE strong yellow glare which had attracted us across the moor found its way out through a single narrow slit alongside the door which served the purpose of a rude window. As we advanced towards it the light changed suddenly to red, and that again to green, throwing a ghastly pallor over our faces, and especially heightening the cadaverous effect of Saxon's austere features. At the same time we became aware of a most subtle and noxious odour which poisoned the air all round the cottage. This combination of portents in so lonely a spot worked upon the old man-at-arms' superstitious feelings to such an extent that he paused and looked back at us inquiringly. Both Reuben and I were determined, however, to carry the adventure through, so he contented himself with falling a little behind us, and pattering to himself some exorcism appropriate to the occasion. Walking up to the door, I rapped upon it with the hilt of my sword and announced that we were weary travellers who were seeking a night's shelter.

The first result of my appeal was a sound as of someone bustling rapidly about, with the clinking of metal and noise of the turning of locks. This died away into a hush, and I was about to knock once more when a crackling voice greeted us from the other side of the door.

" There is little shelter here, gentlemen, and less provisions," it said. " It is but six miles to Amesbury, where at the Cecil Arms ye shall find, I doubt not, all that is needful for man and for beast."

" Nay, nay, mine invisible friend," quoth Saxon, who was much reassured by the sound of a human voice, " this is surely but a scurvy reception. One of our horses is completely foundered, and none of them are in very good plight, so that we could no more make for the Cecil Arms at Amesbury than for the Gruner Mann at Lubeck. I

prithee, therefore, that you will allow us to pass the remainder of the night under your roof."

At this appeal there was much creaking of locks and rasping of bolts, which ended in the door swinging slowly open, and disclosing the person who had addressed us.

By the strong light which shone out from behind him we could see that he was a man of venerable aspect, with snow-white hair and a countenance which bespoke a thoughtful and yet fiery nature. The high pensive brow and flowing beard smacked of the philosopher, but the keen sparkling eye, the curved aquiline nose, and the lithe upright figure which the weight of years had been unable to bend, were all suggestive of the soldier. His lofty bearing, and his rich though severe costume of black velvet, were at strange variance with the humble nature of the abode which he had chosen for his dwelling-place.

" Ho ! " said he, looking keenly at us. " Two of ye unused to war, and the other an old soldier. Ye have been pursued, I see ! "

" How did you know that, then ? " asked Decimus Saxon.

" Ah, my friend, I too have served in my time. My eyes are not so old but that they can tell when horses have been spurred to the utmost, nor is it difficult to see that this young giant's sword hath been employed in something less innocent than toasting bacon. Your story, however, can keep. Every true soldier thinks first of his horse, so I pray that you will tether yours without, since I have neither ostler nor serving man to whom I may entrust them."

The strange dwelling into which we presently entered had been prolonged into the side of the little hill against which it had been built, so as to form a very long narrow hall. The ends of this great room, as we entered, were wrapped in shadow, but in the centre was a bright glare from a brazier full of coals, over which a brass pipkin was

suspended. Beside the fire a long wooden table was plentifully covered with curved glass flasks, basins, tubings and other instruments of which I knew neither the name nor the purpose. A long row of bottles containing various coloured liquids and powders were arranged along a shelf, whilst above it another shelf bore a goodly array of brown volumes. For the rest there was a second rough-hewn table, a pair of cupboards, three or four wooden settles, and several large screens pinned to the walls and covered all over with figures and symbols, of which I could make nothing. The vile smell which had greeted us outside was very much worse within the chamber, and arose apparently from the fumes of the boiling, bubbling contents of the brazen pot.

" Ye behold in me," said our host, bowing courteously to us, " the last of an ancient family. I am Sir Jacob Clancing of Snellaby Hall."

" Smellaby it should be, methinks," whispered Reuben, in a voice which fortunately did not reach the ears of the old knight.

" I pray that ye be seated," he continued, " and that ye lay aside your plates and headpieces, and remove your boots. Consider this to be your inn, and behave as freely. Ye will hold me excused if for a moment I turn my attention from you to this operation on which I am engaged, which will not brook delay."

Saxon began forthwith to undo his buckles and to pull off his harness, while Reuben, throwing himself into a chair, appeared to be too weary to do more than unfasten his sword-belt. For my own part, I was glad to throw off my gear, but I kept my attention all the while upon the movements of our host, whose graceful manners and learned appearance had aroused my curiosity and admiration.

He approached the evil-smelling pot, and stirred it up with a face which indicated so much anxiety that it was clear that he had pushed his courtesy to us so far as to risk the ruin of some important experiment. Dipping

his ladle into the compound, he scooped some up, and then poured it slowly back into the vessel, showing a yellow turbid fluid. The appearance of it evidently reassured him, for the look of anxiety cleared away from his features, and he uttered an exclamation of relief. Taking a handful of a whitish powder from a trencher at his side he threw it into the pipkin, the contents of which began immediately to seethe and froth over into the fire, causing the flames to assume the strange greenish hue which we had observed before entering. This treatment had the effect of clearing the fluid, for the chemist was enabled to pour off into a bottle a quantity of perfectly watery transparent liquid, while a brownish sediment remained in the vessel, and was emptied out upon a sheet of paper. This done, Sir Jacob Clancing pushed aside all his bottles, and turned towards us with a smiling face and a lighter air.

" We shall see what my poor larder can furnish forth," said he. " Meanwhile, this odour may be offensive to your untrained nostrils, so we shall away with it." He threw a few grains of some balsamic resin into the brazier, which at once filled the chamber with a most agreeable perfume. He then laid a white cloth upon the table, and taking from a cupboard a dish of cold trout and a large meat pasty, he placed them upon it, and invited us to draw up our settles and set to work.

" I would that I had more toothsome fare to offer ye," said he. " Were we at Snellaby Hall, ye should not be put off in this scurvy fashion, I promise ye. This may serve, however, for hungry men, and I can still lay my hands upon a brace of bottles of the old Alicant." So saying, he brought a pair of flasks out from a recess, and having seen us served and our glasses filled, he seated himself in a high-backed oaken chair and presided with old-fashioned courtesy over our feast. As we supped, I explained to him what our errand was, and narrated the adventures of the night, without making mention of our destination.

" You are bound for Monmouth's camp," he said quietly, when I had finished, looking me full in the face with his keen dark eyes. " I know it, but ye need not fear lest I betray you, even were it in my power. What chance, think ye, hath the Duke against the King's forces ? "

" As much chance as a farmyard fowl against a spurred gamecock, did he rely only on those whom he hath with him," Saxon answered. " He hath reason to think, however, that all England is like a powder magazine, and he hopes to be the spark to set it alight."

The old man shook his head sadly. " The King hath great resources," he remarked. " Where is Monmouth to get his trained soldiers ? "

" There is the militia," I suggested.

" And there are many of the old parliamentary breed, who are not too far gone to strike a blow for their belief," said Saxon. " Do you but get half-a-dozen broad-brimmed, snuffle-nosed preachers into a camp, and the whole Presbytery tribe will swarm round them like flies on a honey-pot. No recruiting sergeants will ever raise such an army as did Noll's preachers in the eastern counties, where the promise of a seat by the throne was thought of more value than a ten-pound bounty. I would I could pay mine own debts with these same promises."

" I should judge from your speech, sir," our host observed, " that you are not one of the sectaries. How comes it, then, that you are throwing the weight of your sword and your experience into the weaker scale ? "

" For the very reason that it is the weaker scale," said the soldier of fortune. " I should gladly have gone with my brother to the Guinea coast and had no say in the matter one way or the other, beyond delivering letters and such trifles. Since I must be doing something, I choose to fight for Protestantism and Monmouth. It is nothing to me whether James Stuart or James Walters sits upon the throne, but the court and army of the King

are already made up. Now, since Monmouth hath both courtiers and soldiers to find, it may well happen that he may be glad of my services and reward them with honourable preferment."

"Your logic is sound," said our host, " save only that you have omitted the very great chance which you will incur of losing your head if the Duke's party are borne down by the odds against them."

"A man cannot throw a main without putting a stake on the board," said Saxon.

"And you, young sir," the old man asked, " what has caused you to take a hand in so dangerous a game ? "

"I come of a Roundhead stock," I answered, " and my folk have always fought for the liberty of the people and the humbling of tyranny. I come in the place of my father."

"And you, sir ? " our questioner continued, looking at Reuben.

"I have come to see something of the world, and to be with my friend and companion here," he replied.

"And I have stronger reasons than any of ye," Sir Jacob cried, " for appearing in arms against any man who bears the name of Stuart. Had I not a mission here which cannot be neglected, I might myself be tempted to hie westward with ye, and put these grey hairs of mine once more into the rough clasp of a steel headpiece. For where now is the noble castle of Snellaby, and where those glades and woods amidst which the Clancings have grown up, and lived and died, ere ever Norman William set his foot on English soil ? A man of trade—a man who, by the sweat of his half-starved workers, had laid by ill-gotten wealth, is now the owner of all that fair property. Should I, the last of the Clancings, show my face upon it, I might be handed over to the village beadle as a trespasser, or scourged off it perhaps by the bowstrings of insolent huntsmen."

"And how comes so sudden a reverse of fortune ? " I asked.

" Fill up your glasses ! " cried the old man, suiting the action to the word. " Here's a toast for you ! Perdition to all faithless princes ! How came it about, ye ask ? Why, when the troubles came upon the first Charles, I stood by him as though he had been mine own brother. At Edgehill, at Naseby, in twenty skirmishes and battles, I fought stoutly in his cause, maintaining a troop of horse at my own expense, formed from among my own gardeners, grooms and attendants. Then the military chest ran low, and money must be had to carry on the contest. My silver chargers and candlesticks were thrown into the melting-pot, as were those of many another cavalier. They went in metal and they came out as troopers and pikemen. So we tided over a few months until again the purse was empty, and again we filled it amongst us. This time it was the home farm and the oak trees that went. Then came Marston Moor, and every penny and man was needed to repair that great disaster. I flinched not, but gave everything. This boiler of soap, a prudent, fat-cheeked man, had kept himself free from civil broils, and had long had a covetous eye upon the castle. It was his ambition, poor worm, to be a gentleman, as though a gabled roof and a crumbling house could ever make him that. I let him have his way, however, and threw the sum received, every guinea of it, into the King's coffers. And so I held out until the final ruin of Worcester, when I covered the retreat of the young prince, and may indeed say that save in the Isle of Man I was the last Royalist who upheld the authority of the crown. The Commonwealth had set a price upon my head as a dangerous malignant, so I was forced to take my passage in a Harwich ketch, and arrived in the Lowlands with nothing save my sword and a few broad pieces in my pocket."

" A cavalier might do well even then," remarked Saxon. " There are ever wars in Germany where a man is worth his hire. When the North Germans are not in arms against the Swedes or French, the South Germans are sure to be having a turn with the janissaries."

" I did indeed take arms for a time in the employ of the United Provinces, by which means I came face to face once more with mine old foes, the Roundheads. Oliver had lent Reynolds's brigade to the French, and right glad was Louis to have the service of such seasoned troops. 'Fore God, I stood on the counterscarp at Dunkirk, and I found myself, when I should have been helping the defence, actually cheering on the attack. My very heart rose when I saw the bull-dog fellows clambering up the breach with their pikes at the trail, and never quavering in their psalm-tune, though the bullets sung around them as thick as bees in the hiving time. And when they did come to close hugs with the Flemings, I tell you they set up such a rough cry of soldierly joy that my pride in them as Englishmen overtopped my hatred of them as foes. However, my soldiering was of no great duration, for peace was soon declared, and I then pursued the study of chemistry, for which I had a strong turn, first with Vorhaager of Leyden, and later with De Huy of Strasburg, though I fear that these weighty names are but sounds to your ears."

" Truly," said Saxon, " there seemeth to be some fatal attraction in this same chemistry, for we met two officers of the Blue Guards in Salisbury, who, though they were stout soldierly men in other respects, had also a weakness in that direction."

" Ha ! " cried Sir Jacob, with interest. " To what school did they belong ? "

" Nay, I know nothing of the matter," Saxon answered, " save that they denied that Gervinus of Nurnberg, whom I guarded in prison, or any other man, could transmute metals."

" For Gervinus I cannot answer," said our host, " but for the possibility of it I can pledge my knightly word. However, of that anon. The time came at last when the second Charles was invited back to his throne, and all of us, from Jeffrey Hudson, the court dwarf, up to my Lord Clarendon, were in high feather at the hope of

regaining our own once more. For my own claim, I let it stand for some time, thinking that it would be a more graceful act for the King to help a poor cavalier who had ruined himself for the sake of his family without solicitation on his part. I waited and waited, but no word came, so at last I betook myself to the levée and was duly presented to him. 'Ah,' said he, greeting me with the cordiality which he could assume so well, 'you are, if I mistake not, Sir Jasper Killigrew ? ' ' Nay, your Majesty,' I answered, ' I am Sir Jacob Clancing, formerly of Snellaby Hall, in Staffordshire ' ; and with that I reminded him of Worcester fight and of many passages which had occurred to us in common. ' Od's fish ! ' he cried, ' how could I be so forgetful ! And how are all at Snellaby ? ' I then explained to him that the Hall had passed out of my hands, and told him in a few words the state to which I had been reduced. His face clouded over and his manner chilled to me at once. ' They are all on to me for money and for places,' he said, ' and truly the Commons are so niggardly to me that I can scarce be generous to others. However, Sir Jacob, we shall see what can be done for thee,' and with that he dismissed me. That same night the secretary of my Lord Clarendon came to me, and announced with much form and show that, in consideration of my long devotion and the losses which I had sustained, the King was graciously pleased to make me a lottery cavalier."

" And pray, sir, what is a lottery cavalier ? " I asked.

" It is nothing else than a licensed keeper of a gambling-house. This was his reward to me. I was to be allowed to have a den in the piazza of Covent Garden, and there to decoy the young sparks of the town and fleece them at ombre. To restore my own fortunes I was to ruin others. My honour, my family, my reputation, they were all to weigh for nothing so long as I had the means of bubbling a few fools out of their guineas."

" I have heard that some of the lottery cavaliers did well," remarked Saxon reflectively.

" Well or ill, it was no employment for me. I waited upon the King and implored that his bounty would take another form. His only reply was that for one so poor I was strangely fastidious. For weeks I hung about the court—I and other poor cavaliers like myself—watching the royal brothers squandering upon their gaming and their harlots sums which would have restored us to our patrimonies. I have seen Charles put upon one turn of a card as much as would have satisfied the most exacting of us. In the parks of St. James, or in the Gallery at Whitehall, I still endeavoured to keep myself before his eyes, in the hope that some provision would be made for me. At last I received a second message from him. It was that unless I could dress more in the mode he could dispense with my attendance. That was his message to the old broken soldier who had sacrificed health, wealth, position, everything in the service of his father and himself."

" Shameful ! " we cried, all three.

" Can you wonder, then, that I cursed the whole Stuart race, false-hearted, lecherous and cruel ? For the Hall, I could buy it back to-morrow if I chose, but why should I do so when I have no heir ? "

" Ho, you have prospered then ! " said Decimus Saxon, with one of his shrewd sidelong looks. " Perhaps you have yourself found out how to convert pots and pans into gold in the way you have spoken of. But that cannot be, for I see iron and brass in this room which would hardly remain there could you convert it to gold."

" Gold has its uses, and iron has its uses," said Sir Jacob oracularly. " The one can never supplant the other."

" Yet these officers," I remarked, " did declare to us that it was but a superstition of the vulgar."

" Then these officers did show that their knowledge was less than their prejudice. Alexander Setonius, a Scot, was first of the moderns to achieve it. In the month of March 1602 he did change a bar of lead into gold in the house of a certain Hansen, at Rotterdam, who hath testi-

fied to it. He then not only repeated the same process before three learned men sent by the Kaiser Rudolph, but he taught Johann Wolfgang Dienheim of Freibourg, and Gustenhofer of Strasburg, which latter taught it to my own illustrious master——"

"Who in turn taught it to you," cried Saxon triumphantly. "I have no great store of metal with me, good sir, but there are my headpiece, back and breastplate, taslets and thigh-pieces, together with my sword, spurs and the buckles of my harness. I pray you to use your most excellent and praiseworthy art upon these, and I will promise within a few days to bring round a mass of metal which shall be more worthy of your skill."

"Nay, nay," said the alchemist, smiling and shaking his head. "It can indeed be done, but only slowly and in order, small pieces at a time, and with much expenditure of work and patience. For a man to enrich himself at it he must labour hard and long ; yet in the end I will not deny that he may compass it. And now, since the flasks are empty and your young comrade is nodding in his chair, it will perhaps be as well for you to spend as much of the night as is left in repose." He drew several blankets and rugs from a corner and scattered them over the floor. "It is a soldier's couch," he remarked ; "but ye may sleep on worse before ye put Monmouth on the English throne. For myself, it is my custom to sleep in an inside chamber, which is hollowed out of the hill." With a few last words and precautions for our comfort he withdrew with the lamp, passing through a door which had escaped our notice at the further end of the apartment.

Reuben, having had no rest since he left Havant, had already dropped upon the rugs, and was fast asleep, with a saddle for a pillow. Saxon and I sat for a few minutes longer by the light of the burning brazier.

"One might do worse than take to this same chemical business," my companion remarked, knocking the ashes out of his pipe. "See you yon iron-bound chest in the corner ? "

" What of it ? "

" It is two-thirds full of gold, which this worthy gentleman hath manufactured."

" How know you that ? " I asked incredulously.

" When you did strike the door panel with the hilt of your sword, as though you would drive it in, you may have heard some scuttling about, and the turning of a lock. Well, thanks to my inches, I was able to look through yon slit in the wall, and I saw our friend throw something into the chest with a chink, and then lock it. It was but a glance at the contents, yet I could swear that that dull yellow light could come from no metal but gold. Let us see if it be indeed locked." Rising from his seat he walked over to the box and pulled vigorously at the lid.

" Forbear, Saxon, forbear ! " I cried angrily. " What would our host say, should he come upon you ? "

" Nay, then, he should not keep such things beneath his roof. With a chisel or a dagger now, this might be prised open."

" By Heaven ! " I whispered, " if you should attempt it I shall lay you on your back."

" Well, well, young Anak ! it was but a passing fancy to see the treasure again. Now, if he were but well favoured to the King, this would be fair prize of war. Marked ye not that he claimed to have been the last Royalist who drew sword in England ? and he confessed that he had been proscribed as a malignant. Your father, godly as he is, would have little compunction in despoiling such an Amalekite. Besides, bethink you, he can make more as easily as your good mother maketh cranberry dumplings."

" Enough said ! " I answered sternly. " It will not bear discussion. Get ye to your couch, lest I summon our host and tell him what manner of man he hath entertained."

With many grumbles Saxon consented at last to curl his long limbs up upon a mat, whilst I lay by his side and remained awake until the mellow light of morning

streamed through the chinks between the ill-covered rafters. Truth to tell, I feared to sleep, lest the free-booting habits of the soldier of fortune should be too strong for him, and he should disgrace us in the eyes of our kindly and habits entertainer. At last, however, his long-drawn breathing assured me that he was asleep, and I was able to settle down to a few hours of welcome rest.

12. *Of Certain Passages upon the Moor*

IN the morning, after a breakfast furnished by the remains of our supper, we looked to our horses and prepared for our departure. Ere we could mount, however, our kindly host came running out to us with a load of armour in his arms.

" Come hither," said he, beckoning to Reuben. " It is not meet, lad, that you should go bare-breasted against the enemy when your comrades are girt with steel. I have here mine own old breastplate and headpiece, which should, methinks, fit you, for if you have more flesh than I, I am a larger framework of a man. Ah, said I not so ! Were't measured for you by Silas Thomson, the court armourer, it could not grip better. Now on with the headpiece. A close fit again. You are now a cavalier whom Monmouth or any other leader might be proud to see ride beneath his banner."

Both helmet and body-plates were of the finest Milan steel, richly inlaid with silver and with gold, and carved all over in rare and curious devices. So stern and soldierly was the effect, that the ruddy, kindly visage of our friend staring out of such a panoply had an ill-matched and somewhat ludicrous appearance.

" Nay, nay," cried the old cavalier, seeing a smile upon our features, " it is but right that so precious a jewel as a faithful heart should have a fitting casket to protect it."

" I am truly beholden to you, sir," said Reuben ; " I can scarce find words to express my thanks. Holy

mother ! I have a mind to ride straight back to Havant, to show them how stout a man-at-arms hath been reared amongst them."

" It is steel of proof," Sir Jacob remarked ; " a pistol-bullet might glance from it. And you," he continued, turning to me, " here is a small gift by which you shall remember this meeting. I did observe that you did cast a wistful eye upon my bookshelf. It is Plutarch's lives of the ancient worthies, done into English by the ingenious Mr. Latimer. Carry this volume with you, and shape your life after the example of the giant men whose deeds are here set forth. In your saddle-bag I place a small but weighty packet, which I desire you to hand over to Monmouth upon the day of your arrival in his camp. As to you, sir," addressing Decimus Saxon, " here is a slug of virgin gold for you, which may fashion into a pin or such-like ornament. You may wear it with a quiet conscience, for it is fairly given to you and not filched from your entertainer whilst he slept."

Saxon and I shot a sharp glance of surprise at each other at this speech, which showed that our words of the night before were not unknown to him. Sir Jacob, how-ever, showed no signs of anger, but proceeded to point out our road and to advise us as to our journey.

" You must follow this sheep-track until you come on another and broader pathway which makes for the West," said he. " It is little used, and there is small chance of your falling in with any of your enemies upon it. This path will lead you between the villages of Fovant and Hindon, and so on to Mere, which is no great distance from Bruton, upon the Somersetshire border."

Thanking our venerable host for his great kindness towards us we gave rein to our horses, and left him once more to the strange solitary existence in which we had found him. So artfully had the site of his cottage been chosen, that when we looked back to give him a last greeting both he and his dwelling had disappeared al-ready from our view, nor could we, among the many

mounds and hollows, determine where the cottage lay which had given us such welcome shelter. In front of us and on either side the great uneven dun-coloured plain stretched away to the horizon, without a break in its barren gorse-covered surface. Over the whole expanse there was no sign of life, save for an occasional rabbit which whisked into its burrow on hearing our approach, or a few thin and hungry sheep, who could scarce sustain life by feeding on the coarse and wiry grass which sprang from the unfruitful soil.

The pathway was so narrow that only one of us could ride upon it at a time, but we presently abandoned it altogether, using it simply as a guide, and galloping along side by side over the rolling plain. We were all silent, Reuben meditating upon his new corslet, as I could see from his frequent glances at it ; while Saxon, with his eyes half closed, was brooding over some matter of his own. For my own part, my thoughts ran upon the ignominy of the old soldier's designs upon the gold chest, and the additional shame which rose from the knowledge that our host had in some way divined his intention. No good could come of an alliance with a man so devoid of all feelings of honour or of gratitude. So strongly did I feel upon it that I at last broke the silence by pointing to a cross path, which turned away from the one which we were pursuing, and recommending him to follow it, since he had proved that he was no fit company for honest men.

" By the living rood ! " he cried, laying his hand upon the hilt of his rapier, " have you taken leave of your senses ? These are words such as no honourable cavaliero can abide."

" They are none the less words of truth," I answered.

His blade flashed out in an instant, while his mare bounded twice her length under the sharp dig of his spurs.

" We have here," he cried, reining her round, with his fierce lean face all of a quiver with passion, " an excellent level stretch on which to discuss the matter. Out with your bilbo and maintain your words."

121

" I shall not stir a hair's-breadth to attack you," I answered. " Why should I, when I bear you no ill-will ? If you come against me, however, I will assuredly beat you out of your saddle, for all your tricky sword play." I drew my broadsword as I spoke, and stood upon my guard, for I guessed that with so old a soldier the onset would be sharp and sudden.

" By all the saints in heaven ! " cried Reuben, " which ever of ye strikes first at the other I'll snap this pistol at his head. None of your jokes, Don Decimo, for by the Lord I'll let drive at you if you were my own mother's son. Put up your sword, for the trigger falls easy, and my finger is a twitching."

" Curse you for a spoil-sport ! " growled Saxon, sulkily sheathing his weapon. " Nay, Clarke," he added, after a few moments of reflection, " this is but child's play, that two camarados with a purpose in view should fall out over such a trifle. I, who am old enough to be your father, should have known better than to have drawn upon you, for a boy's tongue wags on impulse and without due thought. Do but say that you have said more than you meant."

" My way of saying it may have been over-plain and rough," I answered, for I saw that he did but want a little salve where my short words had galled him. " At the same time, our ways differ from your ways, and that difference must be mended, or you can be no true comrade of ours."

" All right, Master Morality," quoth he, " I must e'en unlearn some of the tricks of my trade. Od's feet, man, if ye object to me, what the henker would ye think of some whom I have known ? However, let that pass. It is time that we were at the wars, for our good swords will not bide in their scabbards.

> ' The trenchant blade, Toledo trusty,
> For want of fighting was grown rusty,
> And ate into itself for lack
> Of somebody to hew and hack.'

You cannot think a thought but old Samuel hath been before you."

" Surely we shall be at the end of this dreary plain presently," Reuben cried. " Its insipid flatness is enough to set the best of friends by the ears. We might be in the deserts of Libya instead of his most graceless Majesty's county of Wiltshire."

" There is smoke over yonder, upon the side of that hill," said Saxon, pointing to the southward.

" Methinks I see one straight line of houses there," I observed, shading my eyes with my hand. " But it is distant, and the shimmer of the sun disturbs the sight."

" It must be the hamlet of Hindon," said Reuben. " Oh, the heat of this steel coat ! I wonder if it were very unsoldierly to slip it off and tie it about Dido's neck. I shall be baked alive else, like a crab in its shell. How say you, illustrious, is it contravened by any of those thirty-nine articles of war which you bear about in your bosom ? "

" The bearing of the weight of your harness, young man," Saxon answered gravely, " is one of the exercises of war, and as such only attainable by such practice as you are now undergoing. You have many things to learn, and one of them is not to present petronels too readily at folk's heads when you are on horseback. The jerk of your charger's movement even now might have drawn your trigger, and so deprived Monmouth of an old and tried soldier."

" There would be much weight in your contention," my friend answered, " were it not that I now bethink me that I had forgot to recharge my pistol since discharging it at that great yellow beast yesternight."

Decimus Saxon shook his head sadly. " I doubt we shall never make a soldier of you," he remarked. " You fall from your horse if the brute does but change his step, you show a levity which will not jump with the gravity of the true soldado, you present empty petronels as a menace, and finally, you crave permission to tie your armour— armour which the Cid himself might be proud to wear—

around the neck of your horse. Yet you have heart and mettle, I believe, else you would not be here."

" Gracias, Signor ! " cried Reuben, with a bow which nearly unhorsed him ; " the last remark makes up for all the rest, else had I been forced to cross blades with you, to maintain my soldierly repute."

" Touching that same incident last night," said Saxon, " of the chest filled, as I surmise, with gold, which I was inclined to take as lawful plunder, I am now ready to admit that I may have shown an undue haste and pre-cipitance, considering that the old man treated us fairly."

" Say no more of it," I answered, " if you will but guard against such impulses for the future."

" They do not properly come from me," he replied, " but from Will Spotterbridge, who was a man of no character at all."

" And how comes he to be mixed up in the matter ? " I asked curiously.

" Why, marry, in this wise. My father married the daughter of this same Will Spotterbridge, and so weakened a good old stock by an unhealthy strain. Will was a rake-hell of Fleet Street in the days of James, a chosen light of Alsatia, the home of bullies and of brawlers. His blood hath through his daughter been transmitted to the ten of us, though I rejoice to say that I, being the tenth, it had by that time lost much of its virulence, and indeed amounts to little more than a proper pride, and a laudable desire to prosper."

" How, then, has it affected the race ? " I asked.

" Why," he answered, " the Saxons of old were a round-faced, contented generation, with their ledgers in their hands for six days and their bibles on the seventh. If my father did but drink a cup of small beer more than his wont, or did break out upon provocation into any fond oath, as ' Od's niggers ! ' or ' Heart alive ! ' he would mourn over it as though it were the seven deadly sins. Was this a man, think ye, in the ordinary course of nature to beget ten long lanky children, nine of whom might

have been first cousins of Lucifer, and foster-brothers of Beelzebub ? "

" It was hard upon him," remarked Reuben.

" On him ! Nay, the hardship was all with us. If he with his eyes open chose to marry the daughter of an incarnate devil like Will Spotterbridge, because she chanced to be powdered and patched to his liking, what reason hath he for complaint ? It is we, who have the blood of this Hector of the taverns grafted upon our own good honest stream, who have most reason to lift up our voices."

" Faith, by the same chain of reasoning," said Reuben, " one of my ancestors must have married a woman with a plaguy dry throat, for both my father and I are much troubled with the complaint."

" You have assuredly inherited a plaguy pert tongue," growled Saxon. " From what I have told you, you will see that our whole life is a conflict between our natural Saxon virtue and the ungodly impulses of the Spotterbridge taint. That of which you have had cause to complain yesternight is but an example of the evil to which I am subjected."

" And your brothers and sisters ? " I asked ; " how hath this circumstance affected them ? " The road was bleak and long, so that the old soldier's gossip was a welcome break to the tedium of the journey.

" They have all succumbed," said Saxon, with a groan. " Alas, alas ! they were a goodly company could they have turned their talents to better uses. Prima was our eldest born. She did well until she attained womanhood. Secundus was a stout seaman, and owned his own vessel when he was yet a young man. It was remarked, however, that he started on a voyage in a schooner and came back in a brig, which gave rise to some inquiry. It may be, as he said, that he found it drifting about in the North Sea, and abandoned his own vessel in favour of it, but they hung him before he could prove it. Tertia ran away with a north-country drover, and hath been on the run ever

since. Quartus and Nonus have been long engaged in busying themselves over the rescue of the black folk from their own benighted and heathen country, conveying them over by the shipload to the plantations, where they may learn the beauties of the Christian religion. They are, however, men of violent temper and profane speech, who cherish no affection for their younger brother. Quintus was a lad of promise, but he found a hogshead of rumbo which was thrown up from a wreck, and he died soon afterwards. Sextus might have done well, for he became clerk to Johnny Tranter the attorney ; but he was of an enterprising turn, and he shifted the whole business, papers, cash and all, to the Lowlands, to the no small inconvenience of his employer, who hath never been able to lay hands either on one or the other from that day to this. Septimus died young. As to Octavius, Will Spotterbridge broke out early in him, and he was slain in a quarrel over some dice, which were said by his enemies to be so weighted that the six must ever come upwards. Let this moving recital be a warning to ye, if ye are fools enough to saddle yourselves with a wife, to see that she hath no vice in her, for a fair face is a sorry make-weight against a foul mind."

Reuben and I could not but laugh over this frank family confession, which our companion delivered without a sign of shame or embarrassment. " Ye have paid a heavy price for your father's want of discretion," I remarked. " But what in the name of fate is this upon our left ? "

" A gibbet, by the look of it," said Saxon, peering across at the gaunt framework of wood, which rose up from a little knoll. " Let us ride past it, for it is little out of our way. They are rare things in England, though by my faith there were more gallows than milestones when Turenne was in the Palatinate. What between the spies and traitors who were bred by the war, the rascally Schwartzritter and Lanzknechte, the Bohemian vagabonds, and an occasional countryman who was put out of the

way lest he do something amiss, there was never such a brave time for the crows."

As we approached this lonely gibbet we saw that a dried-up wisp of a thing which could hardly be recognised as having once been a human being was dangling from the centre of it. This wretched relic of mortality was secured to the cross-bar by an iron chain, and flapped drearily backwards and forwards in the summer breeze. We had pulled up our horses, and were gazing in silence at this sign-post of death, when what had seemed to us to be a bundle of rags thrown down at the foot of the gallows began suddenly to move, and turned towards us the wizened face of an aged woman, so marked with evil passions and so malignant in its expression that it inspired us with even more horror than the unclean thing which dangled above her head.

" Gott in Himmel ! " cried Saxon, " it is ever thus ! A gibbet draws witches as a magnet draws needles. All the hexerei of the countryside will sit round one, like cats round a milk-pail. Beware of her ! she hath the evil eye!''

" Poor soul ! It is the evil stomach that she hath," said Reuben, walking his horse up to her. " Whoever saw such a bag of bones ! I warrant that she is pining away for want of a crust of bread."

The creature whined, and thrust out two skinny claws to grab the piece of silver which our friend had thrown down to her. Her fierce dark eyes and beak-like nose, with the gaunt bones over which the yellow parchment-like skin was stretched tightly, gave her a fear-inspiring aspect, like some foul bird of prey, or one of those vampires of whom the story-tellers write.

" What use is money in the wilderness ? " I remarked ; " she cannot feed herself upon a silver piece."

She tied the coin hurriedly into the corner of her rags, as though she feared that I might try to wrest it from her. " It will buy bread," she croaked.

" But who is there to sell it, good mistress ? " I asked.

127

" They sell it at Fovant, and they sell it at Hindon," she answered. " I bide here o' days, but I travel at night."

" I warrant she does, and on a broomstick," quoth Saxon ; " but tell us, mother, who is it who hangs above your head ? "

" It is he who slew my youngest born," cried the old woman, casting a malignant look at the mummy above her, and shaking a clenched hand at it which was hardly more fleshy than its own. " It is he who slew my bonny boy. Out here upon the wide moor he met him, and he took his young life from him when no kind hand was near to stop the blow. On that ground there my lad's blood was shed, and from that watering hath grown this goodly gallows-tree with its fine ripe fruit upon it. And here, come rain, come shine, shall I, his mother, sit while two bones hang together of the man who slew my heart's darling." She nestled down in her rags as she spoke, and leaning her chin upon her hands stared up with an intensity of hatred at the hideous remnant.

" Come away, Reuben," I cried, for the sight was enough to make one loathe one's kind. " She is a ghoul, not a woman."

" Pah ! it gives one a foul taste in the mouth," quoth Saxon. " Who is for a fresh gallop over the Downs ? Away with care and carrion !

> ' Sir John got on his bonny brown steed,
>   To Monmouth for to ride—a.
> A brave buff-coat upon his back,
>   A broadsword by his side—a.
> Ha, ha, young man, we rebels can
>   Pull down King James's pride—a ! '

Hark away, lads, with a loose rein and a bloody heel ! "

We spurred our steeds and galloped from the unholy spot as fast as our brave beasts could carry us. To all of us the air had a purer flavour and the heath a sweeter scent by contrast with the grim couple whom we had left behind us. What a sweet world would this be, my children, were it not for man and his cruel ways !

When we at last pulled up we had set some three or four miles between the gibbet and ourselves. Right over against us, on the side of a gentle slope, stood a bright little village, with a red-roofed church rising up from amidst a clump of trees. To our eyes, after the dull sward of the plain, it was a glad sight to see the green spread of the branches and the pleasant gardens which girt the hamlet round. All morning we had seen no sight of a human being, save the old hag upon the moor and a few peat-cutters in the distance. Our belts, too, were beginning to be loose upon us, and the remembrance of our breakfast more faint.

" This," said I, " must be the village of Mere, which we were to pass before coming to Bruton. We shall soon be over the Somersetshire border."

" I trust that we shall soon be over a dish of beef-steaks," groaned Reuben. " I am well-nigh famished. So fair a village must needs have a passable inn, though I have not seen one yet upon my travels which would compare with the old Wheatsheaf."

" Neither inn nor dinner for us just yet," said Saxon. " Look yonder to the north, and tell me what you see."

On the extreme horizon there was visible a long line of gleaming, glittering points, which shone and sparkled like a string of diamonds. These brilliant specks were all in rapid motion, and yet kept their positions to each other.

" What is it, then ? " we both cried.

" Horse upon the march," quoth Saxon. " It may be our friends of Salisbury, who have made a long day's journey ; or, as I am inclined to think, it may be some other body of the King's horse. They are far distant, and what we see is but the sun shining on their casques ; yet they are bound for this very village, if I mistake not. It would be wisest to avoid entering it, lest the rustics set them upon our track. Let us skirt it and push on for Bruton, where we may spare time for bite and sup."

" Alas, alas ! for our dinners ! " cried Reuben ruefully. " I have fallen away until my body rattles about, inside

this shell of armour, like a pea in a pod. However, lads, it is all for the Protestant faith."

" One more good stretch to Bruton, and we may rest in peace," said Saxon. " It is ill dining when a dragoon may be served up as a grace after meat. Our horses are still fresh, and we should be there in little over an hour."

We pushed on our way accordingly, passing at a safe distance from Mere, which is the village where the second Charles did conceal himself after the battle of Worcester. The road beyond was much crowded by peasants, who were making their way out of Somersetshire, and by farmers' waggons, which were taking loads of food to the West, ready to turn a few guineas either from the King's men or from the rebels. We questioned many as to the news from the war, but though we were now on the outskirts of the disturbed country, we could gain no clear account of how matters stood, save that all agreed that the rising was on the increase. The country through which we rode was a beautiful one, consisting of low swelling hills, well tilled and watered by numerous streamlets. Crossing over the River Brue by a good stone bridge, we at last reached the small country town for which we had been making, which lies embowered in the midst of a broad expanse of fertile meadows, orchards, and sheep-walks. From the rising ground by the town we looked back over the plain without seeing any traces of the troopers. We learned, too, from an old woman of the place, that though a troop of the Wiltshire Yeomanry had passed through the day before, there were no soldiers quartered at present in the neighbourhood. Thus assured we rode boldly into the town, and soon found our way to the principal inn. I have some dim remembrance of an ancient church upon an eminence, and of a quaint stone cross within the market-place, but assuredly, of all the recollections which I retain of Bruton there is none so pleasing as that of the buxom landlady's face, and of the steaming dishes which she lost no time in setting before us.

13. *Of Sir Gervas Jerome, Knight Banneret of the County of Surrey*

THE inn was very full of company, being occupied not only by many Government agents and couriers on their way to and from the seat of the rising, but also by all the local gossips, who gathered there to exchange news and consume Dame Hobson the landlady's home-brewed. In spite, however, of this stress of custom and the consequent uproar, the hostess conducted us into her own private room, where we could consume her excellent cheer in peace and quietness. This favour was due, I think, to a little sly manœuvring and a few whispered words from Saxon, who amongst other accomplishments which he had picked up during his chequered career had a pleasing knack of establishing friendly relations with the fair sex, irrespective of age, size, or character. Gentle and simple, Church and Dissent, Whig and Tory, if they did but wear a petticoat our comrade never failed, in spite of his fifty years, to make his way into their good graces by the help of his voluble tongue and assured manner.

" We are your grateful servants, mistress," said he, when the smoking joint and the batter pudding had been placed upon the table. " We have robbed you of your room. Will you not honour us so far as to sit down with us and share our repast ? "

" Nay, kind sir," said the portly dame, much flattered by the proposal ; " it is not for me to sit with gentles like yourselves."

" Beauty has a claim which persons of quality, and above all cavalieros of the sword, are the first to acknowledge," cried Saxon, with his little twinkling eyes fixed in admiration upon her buxom countenance. " Nay, by my troth, you shall not leave us. I shall lock the door first. If you will not eat, you shall at least drink a cup of Alicant with me."

" Nay, sir, it is too much honour," cried Dame Hobson, with a simper. " I shall go down into the cellars and bring a flask of the best."

" Nay, by my manhood, you shall not," said Saxon, springing up from his seat. " What are all these infernal lazy drawers here for if you are to descend to menial offices ? " Handing the widow to a chair he clanked away into the tap-room, where we heard him swearing at the men-servants, and cursing them for a droning set of rascals who had taken advantage of the angelic good-ness of their mistress and her incomparable sweetness of temper.

" Here is the wine, fair mistress," said he, returning presently with a bottle in either hand. " Let me fill your glass. Ha ! it flows clear and yellow like a prime vintage. These rogues can stir their limbs when they find that there is a man to command them."

" Would that there were ever such," said the widow meaningly, with a languishing look at our companion. " Here is to you, sir—and to ye, too, young sirs," she added, sipping at her wine. " May there be a speedy end to the insurrection, for I judge, from your gallant equipment, that ye be serving the King."

" His business takes us to the West," said Reuben, " and we have every reason to hope that there will be a speedy end to the insurrection."

" Aye, aye, though blood will be shed first," she said, shaking her head. " They tell me that the rebels are as many as seven thousand, and that they swear to give an' take no quarter, the murderous villains ! Alas ! how any gentleman can fall to such bloody work when he might have a clean honourable occupation, such as innkeeping or the like, is more than my poor mind can understand. There is a sad difference betwixt the man who lieth on the cold ground, not knowing how long it may be before he is three feet deep in it, and he who passeth his nights upon a warm feather bed, with mayhap a cellar beneath it stocked with even such wines as we are now drinking."

132

She again looked hard at Saxon as she spoke, while Reuben and I nudged each other beneath the table.

" This business hath doubtless increased your trade, fair mistress," quoth Saxon.

" Aye, and in the way that payeth best," said she. " The few kilderkins of beer which are drunk by the common folk make little difference one way or the other. But now, when we have lieutenants of counties, officers, mayors, and gentry spurring it for very life down the highways, I have sold more of my rare old wines in three days than ever I did before in a calendar month. It is not ale, or strong waters, I promise you, that these gentles drink, but Priniac, Languedoc, Tent, Muscadine, Chiante, and Tokay—never a flask under the half-guinea."

" So indeed ! " quoth Saxon thoughtfully. " A snug home and a steady income."

" Would that my poor Peter had lived to share it with me," said Dame Hobson, laying down her glass, and rubbing her eyes with a corner of her kerchief. " He was a good man, poor soul, though in very truth and between friends he did at last become as broad and as thick as one of his own puncheons. Ah well, the heart is the thing ! Marry come up ! if a woman were ever to wait until her own fancy came her way, there would be more maids than mothers in the land."

" Prithee, good dame, how runs your own fancy ? " asked Reuben mischievously.

" Not in the direction of fat, young man," she answered smartly, with a merry glance at our plump companion.

" She has hit you there, Reuben," said I.

" I would have no pert young springald," she continued, " but one who hath knowledge of the world, and ripe experience. Tall he should be, and of sinewy build, free of speech that he might lighten the weary hours, and help entertain the gentles when they crack a flagon of wine. Of business habits he must be, too, forsooth, for is there not a busy hostel and two hundred good pounds

a year to pass through his fingers ? If Jane Hobson is to be led to the altar again it must be by such a man as this."

Saxon had listened with much attention to the widow's words, and had just opened his mouth to make some reply to her when a clattering and bustle outside announced the arrival of some traveller. Our hostess drank off her wine and pricked up her ears, but when a loud authoritative voice was heard in the passage, demanding a private room and a draught of sack, her call to duty overcame her private concerns, and she bustled off with a few words of apology to take the measure of the newcomer.

" Body o' me, lads ! " quoth Decimus Saxon the moment that she disappeared, " ye can see how the land lies. I have half a mind to let Monmouth carve his own road, and to pitch my tent in this quiet English township."

" Your tent, indeed ! " cried Reuben ; " it is a brave tent that is furnished with cellars of such wine as we are drinking. And as to the quiet, my illustrious, if you take up your residence here I'll warrant that the quiet soon comes to an end."

" You have seen the woman," said Saxon, with his brow all in a wrinkle with thought. " She hath much to commend her. A man must look to himself. Two hundred pounds a year are not to be picked off the roadside every June morning. It is not princely, but it is something for an old soldier of fortune who hath been in the wars for five-and-thirty years, and foresees the time when his limbs will grow stiff in his harness. What sayeth our learned Fleming—' an mulier—— ' but what in the name of the devil have we here ? "

Our companion's ejaculation was called forth by a noise as of a slight scuffle outside the door, with a smothered " Oh, sir ! " and " What will the maids think ? " The contest was terminated by the door being opened, and Dame Hobson re-entering the room with her face in a glow, and a slim young man dressed in the height of fashion at her heels.

134

" I am sure, good gentlemen," said she, " that ye will
not object to this young nobleman drinking his wine in
the same room with ye, since all the others are filled with
the townsfolk and commonalty."

" Faith ! I must needs be mine own usher," said the
stranger, sticking his gold-laced cap under his left arm
and laying his hand upon his heart, while he bowed until
his forehead nearly struck the edge of the table. " Your
very humble servant, gentlemen, Sir Gervas Jerome,
knight banneret of his Majesty's county of Surrey, and
at one time custos rotulorum of the district of Beacham
Ford."

" Welcome, sir," quoth Reuben, with a merry twinkle
in his eye. " You have before you Don Decimo Saxon
of the Spanish nobility, together with Sir Micah Clarke
and Sir Reuben Lockarby, both of his Majesty's county
of Hampshire."

" Proud and glad to meet ye, gentlemen ! " cried the
newcomer, with a flourish. " But what is this upon the
table ? Alicant ? Fie, fie, it is a drink for boys. Let us
have some good sack with plenty of body in it. Claret
for youth, say I, sack for maturity, and strong waters in
old age. Fly, my sweetest, move those dainty feet of
thine, for egad ! my throat is like leather. Od's 'oons, I
drank deep last night, and yet it is clear that I could not
have drunk enough, for I was as dry as a concordance
when I awoke."

Saxon sat silently at the table, looking so viciously at
the stranger out of his half-closed glittering eyes that I
feared that we should have another such brawl as occurred
at Salisbury, with perhaps a more unpleasant ending.
Finally, however, his ill-humour at the gallant's free and
easy attention to our hostess spent itself in a few muttered
oaths, and he lit his long pipe, the never-failing remedy
of a ruffled spirit. As to Reuben and myself, we watched
our new companion half in wonder and half in amusement,
for his appearance and manners were novel enough to raise
the interest of inexperienced youngsters like ourselves.

135

I have said that he was dressed in the height of fashion, and such indeed was the impression which a glance would give. His face was thin and aristocratic, with a well-marked nose, delicate features, and gay careless expression. Some little paleness of the cheeks and darkness under the eyes, the result of hard travel or dissipation, did but add a chastening grace to his appearance. His white periwig, velvet and silver riding-coat, lavender vest, and red satin knee-breeches were all of the best style and cut, but when looked at closely, each and all of these articles of attire bore evidence of having seen better days. Beside the dust and stains of travel, there was a shininess or a fading of colour here and there which scarce accorded with the costliness of their material or the bearing of their wearer. His long riding-boots had a gaping seam in the side of one of them, whilst his toe was pushing its way through the end of the other. For the rest, he wore a handsome silver-hilted rapier at his side, and had a frilled cambric shirt somewhat the worse for wear and open at the front, as was the mode with the gallants of those days. All the time he was speaking he mumbled a toothpick, which together with his constant habit of pronouncing his o's as a's made his conversation sound strange to our ears.[1] Whilst we were noting these peculiarities he was reclining upon Dame Hobson's best taffetta-covered settee, tranquilly combing his wig with a delicate ivory comb which he had taken from a small satin bag which hung upon the right of his sword-belt.

" Lard preserve us from country inns ! " he remarked. " What with the boors that swarm in every chamber, and the want of mirrors, and jasmine water, and other ne-cessaries, blister me if one has not to do one's toilet in the common room. 'Oons ! I'd as soon travel in the land of the Great Mogul ! "

" When you shall come to be my age, young sir," Saxon answered, " you may know better than to decry a comfortable country hostel."

[1] Note D, Appendix.

" Very like, sir, very like ! " the gallant answered, with a careless laugh. " For all that, being mine own age, I feel the wilds of Wiltshire and the inns of Bruton to be a sorry change after the Mall, and the fare of Pontack's or the Coca Tree. Ah, Lud ! here comes the sack ! Open it, my pretty Hebe, and send a drawer with fresh glasses, for these gentlemen must do me the honour of drinking with me. A pinch of snuff, sirs ? Aye, ye may well look hard at the box. A pretty little thing, sirs, from a certain lady of title, who shall be nameless ; though, if I were to say that her title begins with a D and her name with a C, a gentleman of the Court might hazard a guess."

Our hostess, having brought fresh glasses, withdrew, and Decimus Saxon soon found an opportunity for following her. Sir Gervas Jerome continued, however, to chatter freely to Reuben and myself over the wine, rattling along as gaily and airily as though we were old acquaintances.

" Sink me, if I have not frighted your comrade away ! " he remarked. " Or is it possible that he hath gone on the slot of the plump widow ? Methought he looked in no very good temper when I kissed her at the door. Yet it is a civility which I seldom refuse to anything which wears a cap. Your friend's appearance smacked more of Mars than of Venus, though, indeed, those who worship the god are wont to be on good terms with the goddess. A hardy old soldier, I should judge, from his feature and attire."

" One who hath seen much service abroad," I answered.

" Ha ! ye are lucky to ride to the wars in the company of so accomplished a cavalier. For I presume that it is to the wars that ye are riding, since ye are all so armed and accoutred."

" We are indeed bound for the West," I replied, with some reserve, for in Saxon's absence I did not care to be too loose-tongued.

" And in what capacity ? " he persisted. " Will ye risk your crowns in defence of King James's one, or will

ye strike in, hit or miss, with these rogues of Devon and Somerset ? Stop my vital breath, if I would not as soon side with the clown as with the crown, with all due respect to your own principles ! "

" You are a daring man," said I, " if you air your opinions thus in every inn parlour. Dost not know that a word of what you have said, whispered to the nearest justice of the peace, might mean your liberty, if not your life ? "

" I don't care the rind of a rotten orange for life or liberty either," cried our acquaintance, snapping his finger and thumb. " Burn me if it wouldn't be a new sensation to bandy words with some heavy-chopped country justice, with the Popish plot still stuck in his gizzard, and be thereafter consigned to a dungeon, like the hero in John Dryden's latest. I have been round-housed many a time by the watch in the old Hawkubite days ; but this would be a more dramatic matter, with high treason, block, and axe all looming in the background."

" And rack and pincers for a prologue," said Reuben. " This ambition is the strangest that I have ever heard tell of."

" Anything for a change," cried Sir Gervas, filling up a bumper. " Here's to the maid that's next our heart, and here's to the heart that loves the maids ! War, wine, and women, 'twould be a dull world without them. But you have not answered my question."

" Why truly, sir," said I, " frank as you have been with us, I can scarce be equally so with you, without the permission of the gentlemen who has just left the room. He is the leader of our party. Pleasant as our short intercourse has been, these are parlous times, and hasty confidences are apt to lead to repentance."

" A Daniel come to judgment ! " cried our new acquaintance. " What ancient, ancient words from so young a head ! You are, I'll warrant, five years younger than a scatterbrain like myself, and yet you talk like the seven wise men of Greece. Wilt take me as a valet ? "

" A valet ! " I exclaimed.

" Aye, a valet, a man-servant. I have been waited upon so long that it is my turn to wait now, and I would not wish a more likely master. By the Lard ! I must, in applying for a place, give an account of my character and a list of my accomplishments. So my rascals ever did with me, though in good truth I seldom listened to their recital. Honesty—there I score a trick. Sober—Ananias himself could scarce say that I am that. Trustworthy—indifferently so. Steady—hum ! about as much so as Garraway's weathercock. Hang it, man, I am choke full of good resolutions, but a sparkling glass or a roguish eye will deflect me, as the mariners say of the compass. So much for my weaknesses. Now let me see what qualifications I can produce. A steady nerve, save only when I have my morning qualms, and a cheerful heart ; I score two on that. I can dance saraband, minuet, or corranto ; fence, ride, and sing French chansons. Good Lard ! who ever heard a valet urge such accomplishments ? I can play the best game of piquet in London. So said Sir George Etherege when I won a cool thousand off him at the Groom Parter. But that won't advance me much, either. What is there, then, to commend me ? Why, marry, I can brew a bowl of punch, and I can broil a devilled fowl. It is not much, but I can do it well."

" Truly, good sir," I said, with a smile, " neither of these accomplishments is like to prove of much use to us on our present errand. You do, however, but jest, no doubt, when you talk of descending to such a position."

" Not a whit ! not a whit ! " he replied earnestly. " ' To such base uses do we come,' as Will Shakespeare has it. If you would be able to say that you have in your service Sir Gervas Jerome, knight banneret, and sole owner of Beacham Ford Park, with a rent-roll of four thousand good pounds a year, he is now up for sale, and will be knocked down to the bidder who pleases him best. Say but the word, and we'll have another flagon of sack to clinch the bargain."

" But," said I, " if you are indeed owner of this fair property, why should you descend to so menial an occupation ? "

" The Jews, the Jews, oh most astute and yet most slow-witted master ! The ten tribes have been upon me, and I have been harried and wasted, bound, ravished, and despoiled. Never was Agag, king of Amalek, more completely in the hands of the chosen, and the sole difference is that they have hewed into pieces mine estate instead of myself."

" Have you lost all, then ? " Reuben asked, open-eyed.

" Why no—not all—by no means all ! " he answered, with a merry laugh ; " I have a gold Jacobus and a guinea or two in my purse. 'Twill serve for a flask or so yet. There is my silver-hilted rapier, my rings, my gold snuff-box, and my watch by Tompion at the sign of the Three Crowns. It was never bought under a hundred, I'll warrant. Then there are such relics of grandeur as you see upon my person, though they begin to look as frail and worn as a waiting-woman's virtue. In this bag, too, I retain the means for preserving that niceness and elegance of person which made me, though I say it, as well groomed a man as ever set foot in St. James's Park. Here are French scissors, eyebrow brush, toothpick case, patch-box, powder-bag, comb, puff, and my pair of red-heeled shoes. What could a man wish for more ? These, with a dry throat, a cheerful heart, and a ready hand, are my whole stock in trade."

Reuben and I could not forbear from laughing at the curious inventory of articles which Sir Gervas had saved from the wreck of his fortunes. He upon seeing our mirth was so tickled at his own misfortunes, that he laughed in a high treble key until the whole house resounded with his merriment. " By the Mass," he cried at last, " I have never had so much honest amusement out of my prosperity as hath been caused in me by my downfall. Fill up your glasses ! "

"We have still some distance to travel this evening, and must not drink more," I observed, for prudence told me that it was dangerous work for two sober country lads to keep pace with an experienced toper.

"So!" said he in surprise. "I should have thought that would be a ' raison de plus,' as the French say. But I wish your long-legged friend would come back, even if he were intent upon slitting my weazand for my attention to the widow. He is not a man to flinch from his liquor, I'll warrant. Curse this Wiltshire dust that clings to my periwig!"

"Until my comrade returns, Sir Gervas," said I, "you might, since the subject does not appear to be a painful one to you, let us know how these evil times, which you bear with such philosophy, came upon you."

"The old story!" he answered, flicking away a few grains of snuff with his deeply-laced cambric handkerchief. "The old, old story! My father, a good, easy country baronet, finding the family purse somewhat full, must needs carry me up to town to make a man of me. There as a young lad I was presented at Court, and being a slim active youngster with a pert tongue and assured manner, I caught the notice of the Queen, who made me one of her pages of honour. This post I held until I grew out of it, when I withdrew from town, but egad! I found I must get back to it again, for Beacham Ford Park was as dull as a monastery after the life which I had been living. In town I stayed then with such boon companions as Tommy Lawson, my Lord Halifax, Sir Jasper Lemarck, little Geordie Chichester, aye, and old Sidney Godolphin of the Treasury ; for with all his staid ways and long-winded budgets he could drain a cup with the best of us, and was as keen on a main of cocks as on a committee of ways and means. Well, it was rare sport while it lasted, and sink me if I wouldn't do the same again if I had my time once more. It is like sliding down a greased plank though, for at first a man goes slow enough, and thinks he can pull himself up, but presently

he goes faster and faster, until he comes with a crash on to the rocks of ruin at the bottom."

" And did you run through four thousand pounds a year ? " I exclaimed.

" Od's bodikins, man, you speak as if this paltry sum were all the wealth of the Indies. Why, from Ormonde or Buckingham, with their twenty thousand, down to ranting Dicky Talbot, there was not one of my set who could not have bought me out. Yet I must have my coach and four, my town house, my liveried servants, and my stable full of horses. To be in the mode I must have my poet, and throw him a handful of guineas for his dedication. Well, poor devil, he is one who will miss me. I warrant his heart was as heavy as his verses when he found me gone, though perchance he has turned a few guineas by this time by writing a satire upon me. It would have a ready sale among my friends. Gad's life ! I wonder how my levées get on, and whom all my suitors have fastened on to now. There they were morning after morning, the French pimp, the English bully, the needy man o' letters, the neglected inventor—I never thought to have got rid of them, but indeed I have shaken them off very effectually now. When the honey-pot is broken it is farewell to the flies."

" And your noble friends ? " I asked. " Did none of them stand by you in your adversity ? "

" Well, well, I have nought to complain of ! " exclaimed Sir Gervas. " They were brave-hearted boys for the most part. I might have had their names on my bills as long as their fingers could hold a pen, but slit me if I like bleeding my own companions. They might have found a place for me, too, had I consented to play second-fiddle where I had been used to lead the band. I' faith, I care not what I turn my hand to amongst strangers, but I would fain leave my memory sweet in town."

" As to what you proposed, of serving us as a valet," said I, " it is not to be thought of. We are, in spite of my friend's waggishness, but two plain blunt countrymen,

and have no more need of a valet than one of those poets which you have spoken of. On the other hand, if you should care to attach yourself to our party, we shall take you where you will see service which shall be more to your taste than the curling of periwigs or the brushing of eyebrows."

"Nay, nay, my friend. Speak not with unseemly levity of the mysteries of the toilet," he cried. "Ye would yourselves be none the worse for a touch of mine ivory comb, and a closer acquaintance with the famous skin-purifying wash of Murphy which I am myself in the habit of using."

"I am beholden to you, sir," said Reuben, "but the famous spring water wash by Providence is quite good enough for the purpose."

"And Dame Nature hath placed a wig of her own upon me," I added, "which I should be very loth to change."

"Goths! Perfect Goths!" cried the exquisite, throwing up his white hands. "But here comes a heavy tread and the clink of armour in the passage. 'Tis our friend the knight of the wrathful countenance, if I mistake not."

It was indeed Saxon, who strode into the room to tell us that our horses were at the door, and that all was ready for our departure. Taking him aside I explained to him in a whisper what had passed between the stranger and ourselves, with the circumstances which had led me to suggest that he should join our party. The old soldier frowned at the news.

"What have we to do with such a coxcomb?" he said. "We have hard fare and harder blows before us. He is not fit for the work."

"You said yourself that Monmouth will be weak in horse," I answered. "Here is a well-appointed cavalier, who is to all appearance a desperate man and ready for anything. Why should we not enrol him?"

"I fear," said Saxon, "that his body may prove to be like the bran of a fine cushion, of value only for what it has around it. However, it is perhaps for the best. The

handle to his name may make him welcome in the camp, for from what I hear there is some dissatisfaction at the way in which the gentry stand aloof from the enterprise."

" I had feared," I remarked, still speaking in a whisper, " that we were about to lose one of our party instead of gaining one in this Bruton inn."

" I have thought better of it," he answered, with a smile. " Nay, I'll tell you of it anon. Well, Sir Gervas Jerome," he added aloud, turning to our new associate, " I hear that you are coming with us. For a day you must be content to follow without question or remark. Is that agreed ? "

" With all my heart," cried Sir Gervas.

" Then here's a bumper to our better acquaintance," cried Saxon, raising his glass.

" I pledge ye all," quoth the gallant. " Here's to a fair fight, and may the best men win."

" Donnerblitz, man ! " said Saxon. " I believe there's mettle in you for all your gay plumes. I do conceive a liking for you. Give me your hand ! "

The soldier of fortune's great brown grip enclosed the delicate hand of our new friend in a pledge of comradeship. Then, having paid our reckoning and bade a cordial adieu to Dame Hobson, who glanced methought somewhat reproachfully or expectantly at Saxon, we sprang on our steeds and continued our journey amidst a crowd of staring villagers, who huzzaed lustily as we rode out from amongst them.

14. *Of the Stiff-legged Parson and his Flock*

OUR road lay through Castle Carey and Somerton, which are small towns lying in the midst of a most beautiful pastoral country, well wooded and watered by many streams. The valleys along the centre of which the road lies are rich and luxuriant, sheltered from the winds by long rolling hills, which are themselves highly

cultivated. Here and there we passed the ivy-clad turret of an old castle or the peaked gables of a rambling country house, protruding from amongst the trees and marking the country seat of some family of repute. More than once, when these mansions were not far from the road, we were able to perceive the unrepaired dints and fractures on the walls received during the stormy period of the civil troubles. Fairfax it seems had been down that way, and had left abundant traces of his visit. I have no doubt that my father would have had much to say of these signs of Puritan wrath had he been riding at our side.

The road was crowded with peasants who were travelling in two strong currents, the one setting from east to west, and the other from west to east. The latter consisted principally of aged people and of children, who were being sent out of harm's way to reside in the less disturbed counties until the troubles should be over. Many of these poor folk were pushing barrows in front of them, in which a few bedclothes and some cracked utensils represented the whole of their worldly goods. Others more prosperous had small carts, drawn by the wild shaggy colts which are bred on the Somerset moors. What with the spirit of the half-tamed beasts and the feebleness of the drivers, accidents were not uncommon, and we passed several unhappy groups who had been tumbled with their property into a ditch, or who were standing in anxious debate round a cracked shaft or a broken axle.

The countrymen who were making for the West were upon the other hand men in the prime of life, with little or no baggage. Their brown faces, heavy boots, and smockfrocks proclaimed most of them to be mere hinds, though here and there we overtook men who, by their top-boots and corduroys, may have been small farmers or yeomen. These fellows walked in gangs, and were armed for the most part with stout oak cudgels, which were carried as an aid to their journey, but which in the hands of powerful men might become formidable weapons.

From time to time one of these travellers would strike up a psalm tune, when all the others within earshot would join in, until the melody rippled away down the road. As we passed some scowled angrily at us, while others whispered together and shook their heads, in evident doubt as to our character and aims. Now and again among the people we marked the tall broad-brimmed hat and Geneva mantle which were the badges of the Puritan clergy.

" We are in Monmouth's country at last," said Saxon to me, for Reuben Lockarby and Sir Gervas Jerome had ridden on ahead. " This is the raw material which we shall have to lick into soldiership."

" And no bad material either," I replied, taking note of the sturdy figures and bold, hearty faces of the men. " Think ye that they are bound for Monmouth's camp, then ? "

" Aye, are they. See you yon long-limbed parson on the left—him with the pent-house hat. Markest thou not the stiffness wherewith he moves his left leg ? "

" Why, yes ; he is travel-worn doubtless."

" Ho ! ho ! " laughed my companion. " I have seen such a stiffness before now. The man hath a straight sword within the leg of his breeches. A regular Parliamentary tuck, I'll warrant. When he is on safe ground he will produce it, aye, and use it too, but until he is out of all danger of falling in with the King's horse he is shy of strapping it to his belt. He is one of the old breed by his cut, who

> ' Call fire and sword and desolation,
> A godly thorough reformation.'

Old Samuel hath them to a penstroke ! There is another ahead of him there, with the head of a scythe inside his smock. Can you not see the outline ? I warrant there is not one of the rascals but hath a pikehead or sickle-blade concealed somewhere about him. I begin to feel the breath of war once more, and to grow

younger with it. Hark ye, lad! I am glad that I did not tarry at the inn."

" You seemed to be in two minds about it," said I.

" Aye, aye. She was a fine woman, and the quarters were comfortable. I do not gainsay it. But marriage, d'ye see, is a citadel that it is plaguy easy to find one's way into, but once in old Tilly himself could not bring one out again with credit. I have known such a device on the Danube, where at the first onfall the Mamelukes have abandoned the breach for the very purpose of ensnaring the Imperial troops in the narrow streets beyond, from which few ever returned. Old birds are not caught with such wiles. I did succeed in gaining the ear of one of the gossips, and asking him what he could tell me of the good dame and her inn. It seemeth that she is somewhat of a shrew upon occasion, and that her tongue had more to do with her husband's death than the dropsy which the leech put it down to. Again, a new inn hath been started in the village, which is well-managed, and is like to draw the custom from her. It is, too, as you have said, a dull, sleepy spot. All these reasons weighed with me, and I decided that it would be best to raise my siege of the widow, and to retreat whilst I could yet do so with the credit and honours of war."

" 'Tis best so," said I ; " you could not have settled down to a life of toping and ease. But our new comrade, what think you of him ? "

" Faith ! " Saxon answered, " we shall extend into a troop of horse if we add to our number every gallant who is in want of a job. As to this Sir Gervas, however, I think, as I said at the inn, that he hath more mettle in him than one would judge at first sight. These young sprigs of the gentry will always fight, but I doubt if he is hardened enough or hath constancy enough for such a campaign as this is like to be. His appearance, too, will be against him in the eyes of the saints ; and though Monmouth is a man of easy virtue, the saints are like to have the chief voice in his councils. Now do but look at

him as he reins up that showy grey stallion and gazes back at us. Mark his riding-hat tilted over his eye, his open bosom, his whip dangling from his button-hole, his hand on his hip, and as many oaths in his mouth as there are ribbons to his doublet. Above all, mark the air with which he looks down upon the peasants beside him. He will have to change his style if he is to fight by the side of the fanatics. But hark ! I am much mistaken if they have not already got themselves into trouble."

Our friends had pulled up their horses to await our coming. They had scarce halted, however, before the stream of peasants who had been moving along abreast of them slackened their pace, and gathered round them with a deep ominous murmur and threatening gestures. Other rustics, seeing that there was something afoot, hurried up to help their companions. Saxon and I put spurs to our horses, and pushing through the throng, which was becoming every instant larger and more menacing, made our way to the aid of our friends, who were hemmed in on every side by the rabble. Reuben had laid his hand upon the hilt of his sword, while Sir Gervas was placidly chewing his toothpick and looking down at the angry mob with an air of amused contempt.

" A flask or two of scent amongst them would not be amiss," he remarked ; " I would I had a casting bottle."

" Stand on your guard, but do not draw," cried Saxon. " What the henker hath come over the chaw-bacons ? They mean mischief. How now, friends, why this uproar ? "

This question instead of allaying the tumult appeared to make it tenfold worse. All round us twenty deep were savage faces and angry eyes, with the glint here and there of a weapon half drawn from its place of concealment. The uproar, which had been a mere hoarse growl, began to take shape and form. " Down with the Papists ! " was the cry. " Down with the Prelatists ! " " Smite the Erastian butchers ! " " Smite the Philistine horsemen ! " " Down with them ! "

A stone or two had already whistled past our ears, and we had been forced in self-defence to draw our swords, when the tall minister whom we had already observed shoved his way through the crowd, and by dint of his lofty stature and commanding voice prevailed upon them to be silent.

" How say ye," he asked, turning upon us, " fight ye for Baal or for the Lord ? He who is not with us is against us."

" Which is the side of Baal, most reverend sir, and which of the Lord ? " asked Sir Gervas Jerome. " Methinks if you were to speak plain English instead of Hebrew we might come to an understanding sooner."

" This is no time for light words," the minister cried, with a flush of anger upon his face. " If ye would keep your skins whole, tell me, are ye for the bloody usurper James Stuart, or are ye for his most Protestant Majesty King Monmouth ? "

" What ! He hath come to the title already ! " exclaimed Saxon. " Know then that we are four unworthy vessels upon our way to offer our services to the Protestant cause."

" He lies, good Master Pettigrue, he lies most foully," shouted a burly fellow from the edge of the crowd. " Who ever saw a good Protestant in such a Punchinello dress as yonder ? Is not Amalekite written upon his raiment ? Is he not attired as becometh the bridegroom of the harlot of Rome ? Why then should we not smite him ? "

" I thank you, my worthy friend," said Sir Gervas, whose attire had moved this champion's wrath. " If I were nearer I should give you some return for the notice which you have taken of me."

" What proof have we that ye are not in the pay of the usurper, and on your way to oppress the faithful ? " asked the Puritan divine.

" I tell you, man," said Saxon impatiently, " that we have travelled all the way from Hampshire to fight

against James Stuart. We will ride with ye to Monmouth's camp, and what better proof could ye desire than that ? "

" It may be that ye do but seek an opportunity of escaping from our bondage," the minister observed, after conferring with one or two of the leading peasants. " It is our opinion, therefore, that before coming with us ye must deliver unto us your swords, pistols, and other carnal weapons."

" Nay, good sir, that cannot be," our leader answered. " A cavalier may not with honour surrender his blade or his liberty in the manner ye demand. Keep close to my bridle-arm, Clarke, and strike home at any rogue who lays hands on you."

A hum of anger rose from the crowd, and a score of sticks and scythe-blades were raised against us, when the minister again interposed and silenced his noisy following.

" Did I hear aright ? " he asked. " Is your name Clarke ? "

" It is," I answered.

" Your Christian name ? "

" Micah."

" Living at ? "

" Havant."

The clergyman conferred for a few moments with a grizzly-bearded, harsh-faced man dressed in black buckram who stood at his elbow.

" If you are really Micah Clarke of Havant," quoth he, " you will be able to tell us the name of an old soldier, skilled in the German wars, who was to have come with ye to the camp of the faithful."

" Why, this is he," I answered ; " Decimus Saxon is his name."

" Aye, aye, Master Pettigrue," cried the old man. " The very name given by Dicky Rumbold. He said that either the old Roundhead Clarke or his son would go with him. But who are these ? "

" This is Master Reuben Lockarby, also of Havant, and

Sir Gervas Jerome of Surrey," I replied. " They are both here as volunteers desiring to serve under the Duke of Monmouth."

" Right glad I am to see ye, then," said the stalwart minister heartily. " Friends, I can answer for these gentlemen that they favour the honest folk and the old cause."

At these words the rage of the mob turned in an instant into the most extravagant adulation and delight. They crowded round us, patting our riding-boots, pulling at the skirts of our dress, pressing our hands and calling down blessings upon our heads, until their pastor succeeded at last in rescuing us from their attentions and in persuading them to resume their journey. We walked our horses in the midst of them whilst the clergyman strode along betwixt Saxon and myself. He was, as Reuben remarked, well fitted to be an intermediary between us, for he was taller though not so broad as I was, and broader though not so tall as the adventurer. His face was long, thin, and hollow-cheeked, with a pair of great thatched eyebrows and deep-sunken melancholy eyes, which lit up upon occasion with a sudden quick flash of fiery enthusiasm.

" Joshua Pettigrue is my name, gentlemen," said he ; " I am an unworthy worker in the Lord's vineyard, testifying with voice and with arm to His holy covenant. These are my faithful flock, whom I am bringing westward that they may be ready for the reaping when it pleases the Almighty to gather them in."

" And why have you not brought them into some show of order or formation ? " asked Saxon. " They are straggling along the road like a line of geese upon a common when Michaelmas is nigh. Have you no fears ? Is it not written that your calamity cometh suddenly— suddenly shall you be broken down without remedy ? "

" Aye, friend, but is it not also written, ' Trust in the Lord with all thine heart, and lean not unto thine own understanding ' ? Mark ye, if I were to draw up my men

151

in military fashion it would invite attention and attack from any of James Stuart's horse who may come our way. It is my desire to bring my flock to the camp and obtain pieces for them before exposing them to so unequal a contest."

" Truly, sir, it is a wise resolution," said Saxon grimly, " for if a troop of horse came down upon these good people the pastor would find himself without his flock."

" Nay, that could never be ! " cried Master Pettigrue with fervour. " Say rather that pastor, flock, and all would find their way along the thorny track of martyrdom to the new Jerusalem. Know, friend, that I have come from Monmouth in order to conduct these men to his standard. I received from him, or rather from Master Ferguson, instruction to be on the look-out for ye and for several others of the faithful we expect to join us from the East. By what route came ye ? "

" Over Salisbury Plain and so through Bruton."

" And saw ye or met ye any of our people upon the way ? "

" None," Saxon answered. " We left the Blue Guards at Salisbury, however, and we saw either them or some other horse regiment near this side of the Plain at the village of Mere."

" Ah, there is a gathering of the eagles," cried Master Joshua Pettigrue, shaking his head. " They are men of fine raiment, with war-horses and chariots and trappings, like the Assyrians of old, yet shall the angel of the Lord breathe upon them in the night. Yea, He shall cut them off utterly in His wrath, and they shall be destroyed."

" Amen ! Amen ! " cried as many of the peasants as were within earshot.

" They have elevated their horn, Master Pettigrue," said the grizzly-haired Puritan. " They have set up their candlestick on high—the candlestick of a perverse ritual and of an idolatrous service. Shall it not be dashed down by the hands of the righteous ? "

" Lo, this same candle waxed big and burned sooty,

even as an offence to the nostrils, in the days of our fathers," cried a burly red-faced man, whose dress proclaimed him to be one of the yeoman class. " So was it when Old Noll did get his snuffing shears to work upon it. It is a wick which can only be trimmed by the sword of the faithful." A grim laugh from the whole party proclaimed their appreciation of the pious waggery of their companion.

" Ah, Brother Sandcroft," cried the pastor, " there is much sweetness and manna hidden in thy conversation. But the way is long and dreary. Shall we not lighten it by a song of praise ? Where is Brother Thistlethwaite, whose voice is as the cymbal, the tabor, and the dulcimer?"

" Lo, most pious Master Pettigrue," said Saxon, " I have myself at times ventured to lift up my voice before the Lord." Without any further apology he broke out in stentorian tones into the following hymn, the refrain of which was caught up by pastor and congregation.

> The Lord He is a morion
> That guards me from all wound ;
> The Lord He is a coat of mail
> That circles me all round.
> Who then fears to draw the sword,
> And fight the battle of the Lord ?
>
> The Lord He is the buckler true
> That swings on my left arm ;
> The Lord He is the plate of proof
> That shieldeth me from harm.
> Who then fears to draw the sword,
> And fight the battle of the Lord ?
>
> Who then dreads the violent,
> Or fears the man of pride ?
> Or shall I flee from two or three
> If He be by my side ?
> Who then fears to draw the sword,
> And fight the battle of the Lord ?
>
> My faith is like a citadel
> Girt round with moat and wall,
> No mine, or sap, or breach, or gap
> Can e'er prevail at all.
> Who then fears to draw the sword,
> And fight the battle of the Lord ?

Saxon ceased, but the Reverend Joshua Pettigrue waved his long arms and repeated the refrain, which was taken up again and again by the long column of marching peasants.

" It is a godly hymn," said our companion, who had, to my disgust and to the evident astonishment of Reuben and Sir Gervas, resumed the snuffling, whining voice which he had used in the presence of my father. " It hath availed much on the field of battle."

" Truly," returned the clergyman, " if your comrades are of as sweet a savour as yourself, ye will be worth a brigade of pikes to the faithful," a sentiment which raised a murmur of assent from the Puritans around. " Since, sir," he continued, " you have had much experience in the wiles of war, I shall be glad to hand over to you the command of this small body of the faithful, until such time as we reach the army."

" It is time, too, in good faith, that ye had a soldier at your head," Decimus Saxon answered quietly. " My eyes deceive me strangely if I do not see the gleam of sword and cuirass upon the brow of yonder declivity. Methinks our pious exercises have brought the enemy upon us."

15. *Of our Brush with the King's Dragoons*

SOME little distance from us a branch road ran into that along which we and our motley assemblage of companions-in-arms were travelling. This road curved down the side of a well-wooded hill, and then over the level for a quarter of a mile or so before opening on the other. Just at the brow of the rising ground there stood a thick bristle of trees, amid the trunks of which there came and went a bright shimmer of sparkling steel, which proclaimed the presence of armed men. Farther back, where the road took a sudden turn and ran along the ridge of the hill, several horsemen could be plainly seen outlined against the evening sky. So peaceful, however,

was the long sweep of countryside, mellowed by the golden light of the setting sun, with a score of village steeples and manor-houses peeping out from amongst the woods, that it was hard to think that the thundercloud of war was really lowering over that fair valley, and that at any instant the lightning might break from it.

The country folk, however, appeared to have no difficulty at all in understanding the danger to which they were exposed. The fugitives from the West gave a yell of consternation, and ran wildly down the road or whipped up their beasts of burden in the endeavour to place as safe a distance as possible between themselves and the threatened attack. The chorus of shrill cries and shouts, with the cracking of whips, creaking of wheels, and the occasional crash when some cart-load of goods came to grief, made up a most deafening uproar, above which our leader's voice resounded in sharp, eager exhortation and command. When, however, the loud brazen shriek from a bugle broke from the wood, and the head of a troop of horse began to descend the slope, the panic became greater still, and it was difficult for us to preserve any order at all amidst the wild rush of the terrified fugitives.

" Stop that cart, Clarke," cried Saxon vehemently, pointing with his sword to an old waggon, piled high with furniture and bedding, which was lumbering along drawn by two raw-boned colts. At the same moment I saw him drive his horse into the crowd and catch at the reins of another similar one. Giving Covenant's bridle a shake I was soon abreast of the cart which he had indicated, and managed to bring the furious young horses to a standstill.

" Bring it up ! " cried our leader, working with the coolness which only a long apprenticeship to war can give. " Now, friends, cut the traces ! " A dozen knives were at work in a moment, and the kicking struggling animals scampered off, leaving their burdens behind them. Saxon sprang off his horse and set the example in dragging the waggon across the roadway, while some of the peasants, under the direction of Reuben Lockarby and of Master

Joshua Pettigrue, arranged a couple of other carts to block the way fifty yards further down. The latter precaution was to guard against the chance of the royal horse riding through the fields and attacking us from behind. So speedily was the scheme conceived and carried out, that within a very few minutes of the first alarm we found our-selves protected front and rear by a lofty barricade, while within this improvised fortress was a garrison of a hundred and fifty men.

" What firearms have we amongst us ? " asked Saxon hurriedly.

" A dozen pistols at the most," replied the elderly Puritan, who was addressed by his companions as Hope-above Williams. " John Rodway, the coachman, hath his blunderbuss. There are also two godly men from Hungerford, who are keepers of game, and who have brought their pieces with them."

" They are here, sir," cried another, pointing to two stout, bearded fellows, who were ramming charges into their long-barrelled muskets. " Their names are Wat and Nat Millman."

" Two who can hit their mark are worth a battalion who shoot wide," our leader remarked. " Get under the waggon, my friends, and rest your pieces upon the spokes. Never draw trigger until the sons of Belial are within three pikes' length of ye."

" My brother and I," quoth one of them, " can hit a running doe at two hundred paces. Our lives are in the hands of the Lord, but two, at least, of these hired butchers we shall send before us."

" As gladly as ever we slew stoat or wild-cat," cried the other, slipping under the waggon. " We are keeping the Lord's preserves now, brother Wat, and truly these are some of the vermin that infest them."

" Let all who have pistols line the waggon," said Saxon, tying his mare to the hedge—an example which we all followed. " Clarke, do you take charge upon the right with Sir Gervas, while Lockarby assists Master

Pettigrue upon the left. Ye others shall stand behind
with stones. Should they break through our barricades
slash at the horses with your scythes. Once down, the
riders are no match for ye."

A low sullen murmur of determined resolution rose
from the peasants, mingled with pious ejaculations and
little scraps of hymn or of prayer. They had all produced
from under their smocks rustic weapons of some sort.
Ten or twelve had petronels, which, from their antique
look and rusty condition, threatened to be more dangerous
to their possessors than to the enemy. Others had sickles,
scythe-blades, flails, half-pikes, or hammers, while the
remainder carried long knives and oaken clubs. Simple as
were these weapons, history has proved that in the hands
of men who are deeply stirred by religious fanaticism
they are by no means to be despised. One had but to
look at the stern, set faces of our followers, and the gleam
of exultation and expectancy which shone from their eyes,
to see that they were not the men to quail, either from
superior numbers or equipment.

" By the Mass ! " whispered Sir Gervas, " it is magnificent ! An hour of this is worth a year in the Mall. The
old Puritan bull is fairly at bay. Let us see what sort of
sport the bull-pups make in the baiting of him ! I'll lay
five pieces to four on the chaw-bacons ! "

" Nay, it's no matter for idle betting," said I shortly,
for his light-hearted chatter annoyed me at so solemn a
moment.

" Five to four on the soldiers, then ! " he persisted.
" It is too good a match not to have a stake on it one way
or the other."

" Our lives are the stake," said I.

" Faith, I had forgot it ! " he replied, still mumbling
his toothpick. " ' To be or not to be ? ' as Will of Strat-
ford says. Kynaston was great on the passage. But here
is the bell that rings the curtain up."

Whilst we had been making our dispositions the troop
of horse—for there appeared to be but one—had trotted

down the cross-road, and had drawn up across the main highway. They numbered, as far as I could judge, about ninety troopers, and it was evident from their three-cornered hats, steel plates, red sleeves, and bandoliers, that they were dragoons of the regular army. The main body halted a quarter of a mile from us, while three officers rode to the front and held a short consultation, which ended in one of them setting spurs to his horse and cantering down in our direction. A bugler followed a few paces behind him, waving a white kerchief and blowing an occasional blast upon his trumpet.

"Here comes an envoy," cried Saxon, who was standing up in the waggon. "Now, my brethren, we have neither kettledrum nor tinkling brass, but we have the instrument wherewith Providence hath endowed us. Let us show the red-coats that we know how to use it.

> ' Who then dreads the violent,
> Or fears the man of pride ?
> Or shall I flee from two or three
> If He be by my side ? '

Seven score voices broke in, in a hoarse roar, upon the chorus—

> " Who then fears to draw the sword,
> And fight the battle of the Lord ? "

I could well believe at that moment that the Spartans had found the lame singer Tyrtæus the most successful of their generals, for the sound of their own voices increased the confidence of the country folk, while the martial words of the old hymn roused the dogged spirit in their breasts. So high did their courage run that they broke off their song with a loud warlike shout, waving their weapons above their heads, and ready I verily believe to march out from their barricades and make straight for the horsemen. In the midst of this clamour and turmoil the young dragoon officer, a handsome, olive-faced lad, rode fearlessly up to the barrier, and pulling up his beautiful roan steed, held up his hand with an imperious gesture which demanded silence.

" Who is the leader of this conventicle ? " he asked.

" Address your message to me, sir," said our leader from the top of the waggon, " but understand that your white flag will only protect you whilst you use such language as may come from one courteous adversary to another. Say your say or retire."

" Courtesy and honour," said the officer, with a sneer, " are not extended to rebels who are in arms against their lawful sovereign. If you are the leader of this rabble, I warn you if they are not dispersed within five minutes by this watch "—he pulled out an elegant gold time-piece— " we shall ride down upon them and cut them to pieces."

" The Lord can protect His own," Saxon answered, amid a fierce hum of approval from the crowd. " Is this all thy message ? "

" It is all, and you will find it enough, you Presbyterian traitor," cried the dragoon cornet. " Listen to me, misguided fools," he continued, standing up upon his stirrups and speaking to the peasants at the other side of the waggon. " What chance have ye with your whittles and cheese-scrapers ? Ye may yet save your skins if ye will but deliver up your leaders, throw down what ye are pleased to call your arms, and trust to the King's mercy."

" This exceedeth the limitations of your privileges," said Saxon, drawing a pistol from his belt and cocking it. " If you say another word to seduce these people from their allegiance, I fire."

" Hope not to benefit Monmouth," cried the young officer, disregarding the threat, and still addressing his words to the peasants. " The whole royal army is drawing round him and——"

" Have a care ! " shouted our leader, in a deep harsh voice.

" His head within a month shall roll upon the scaffold."

" But you shall never live to see it," said Saxon, and stooping over he fired straight at the cornet's head. At the flash of the pistol the trumpeter wheeled round and galloped for his life, while the roan horse turned and followed with its master still seated firmly in the saddle.

" Verily you have missed the Midianite ! " cried Hope-above Williams.

" He is dead," said our leader, pouring a fresh charge into his pistol. " It is the law of war, Clarke," he added, looking round at me. " He hath chosen to break it, and must pay forfeit."

As he spoke I saw the young officer lean gradually over in his saddle, until, when about half-way back to his friends, he lost his balance and fell heavily in the roadway, turning over two or three times with the force of his fall, and lying at last still and motionless, a dust-coloured heap. A loud yell of rage broke from the troopers at the sight, which was answered by a shout of defiance from the Puritan peasantry.

" Down on your faces ! " cried Saxon ; " they are about to fire."

The crackle of musketry and a storm of bullets, pinging on the hard ground, or cutting twigs from the hedges on either side of us, lent emphasis to our leader's order. Many of the peasants crouched behind the feather beds and tables which had been pulled out of the cart. Some lay in the waggon itself, and some sheltered themselves behind or underneath it. Others again lined the ditches on either side or lay flat upon the roadway, while a few showed their belief in the workings of Providence by standing upright without flinching from the bullets. Amongst these latter were Saxon and Sir Gervas, the former to set an example to his raw troops, and the latter out of pure laziness and indifference. Reuben and I sat together in the ditch, and I can assure you, my dear grandchildren, that we felt very much inclined to bob our heads when we heard the bullets piping all around them. If any soldier ever told you that he did not the first time that he was under fire, then that soldier is not a man to trust. After sitting rigid and silent, however, as if we had both stiff necks, for a very few minutes, the feeling passed completely away, and from that day to this it has never returned to me. You see familiarity breeds con-

tempt with bullets as with other things, and though it is
no easy matter to come to like them, like the King of
Sweden or my Lord Cutts, it is not so very hard to become
indifferent to them.

The cornet's death did not remain long unavenged. A
little old man with a sickle, who had been standing near
Sir Gervas, gave a sudden sharp cry, and springing up
into the air with a loud " Glory to God ! " fell flat upon
his face dead. A bullet had struck him just over the right
eye. Almost at the same moment one of the peasants in
the waggon was shot through the chest, and sat up cough-
ing blood all over the wheel. I saw Master Joshua Pettigrue catch him in his long arms, and settle some bedding
under his head, so that he lay breathing heavily and pattering forth prayers. The minister showed himself a man
that day, for amid the fierce carbine fire he walked boldly
up and down, with a drawn rapier in his left hand—for
he was a left-handed man—and his Bible in the other.
" This is what you are dying for, dear brothers," he cried
continually, holding the brown volume up in the air ;
" are ye not ready to die for this ? " And every time he
asked the question a low eager murmur of assent rose from
the ditches, the waggon, and the road.

" They aim like yokels at a Wappenschaw," said Saxon,
seating himself on the side of the waggon. " Like all
young soldiers they fire too high. When I was an adjutant
it was my custom to press down the barrels of the muskets
until my eye told me that they were level. These rogues
think that they have done their part if they do but let the
gun off, though they are as like to hit the plovers above
us as ourselves."

" Five of the faithful have fallen," said Hope-above
Williams. " Shall we not sally forth and do battle with
the children of Antichrist ? Are we to lie here like so
many popinjays at a fair for the troopers to practise
upon ? "

" There is a stone barn over yonder on the hillside," I
remarked. " If we who have horses, and a few others,

were to keep the dragoons in play, the people might be able to reach it, and so be sheltered from the fire."

" At least let my brother and me have a shot or two back at them," cried one of the marksmen beside the wheel.

To all our entreaties and suggestions, however, our leader only replied by a shake of the head, and continued to swing his long legs over the side of the waggon with his eyes fixed intently upon the horsemen, many of whom had dismounted and were leaning their carbines over the cruppers of their chargers.

" This cannot go on, sir," said the pastor, in a low earnest voice ; " two more men have just been hit."

" If fifty more men are hit we must wait until they charge," Saxon answered. " What would you do, man ? If you leave this shelter you will be cut off and utterly destroyed. When you have seen as much of war as I have done, you will learn to put up quietly with what is not to be avoided. I remember on such another occasion when the rearguard or nachhut of the Imperial troops was followed by Croats, who were in the pay of the Grand Turk, I lost half my company before the mercenary renegades came to close fighting. Ha, my brave boys, they are mounting ! We shall not have to wait long now."

The dragoons were indeed climbing into their saddles again, and forming across the road, with the evident intention of charging down upon us. At the same time about thirty men detached themselves from the main body and trotted away into the fields upon our right. Saxon growled a hearty oath under his breath as he observed them.

" They have some knowledge of warfare after all," said he. " They mean to charge us flank and front. Master Joshua, see that your scythesmen line the quickset hedge upon the right. Stand up well, my brothers, and flinch not from the horses. You men with the sickles, lie in the ditch there, and cut at the legs of the brutes. A line of stone throwers behind that. A heavy stone is as sure as a

bullet at close quarters. If ye would see your wives and children again, make that hedge good against the horsemen. Now for the front attack. Let the men who carry petronels come into the waggon. Two of yours, Clarke, and two of yours, Lockarby. I can spare one also. That makes five. Now here are ten others of a sort and three muskets. Twenty shots in all. Have you no pistols, Sir Gervas ? "

" No, but I can get a pair," said our companion, and springing upon his horse he forced his way through the ditch, past the barrier, and so down the road in the direction of the dragoons.

The movement was so sudden and so unexpected that there was a dead silence for a few seconds, which was broken by a general howl of hatred and execration from the peasants. " Shoot upon him ! Shoot down the false Amalekite ! " they shrieked. " He hath gone to join his kind ! He hath delivered us up into the hands of the enemy ! Judas ! Judas ! " As to the horsemen, who were still forming up for a charge and waiting for the flanking party to get into position, they sat still and silent, not knowing what to make of the gaily-dressed cavalier who was speeding towards them.

We were not left long in doubt, however. He had no sooner reached the spot where the cornet had fallen than he sprang from his horse and helped himself to the dead man's pistols, and to the belt which contained his powder and ball. Mounting at his leisure, amid a shower of bullets which puffed up the white dust all around him, he rode onwards towards the dragoons and discharged one of his pistols at them. Wheeling round he politely raised his cap, and galloped back to us, none the worse for his adventure, though a ball had grazed his horse's fetlock and another had left a hole in the skirt of his riding-coat. The peasants raised a shout of jubilation as he rode in, and from that day forward our friend was permitted to wear his gay trappings and to bear himself as he would, without being suspected of having mounted the livery of

Satan or of being wanting in zeal for the cause of the saints.

" They are coming," cried Saxon. " Let no man draw trigger until he sees me shoot. If any does, I shall send a bullet through him, though it was my last shot and the troopers were amongst us."

As our leader uttered this threat and looked grimly round upon us with an evident intention of executing it, a shrill blare of a bugle burst from the horsemen in front of us, and was answered by those upon our flank. At the signal both bodies set spurs to their horses and dashed down upon us at the top of their speed. Those in the field were delayed for a few moments, and thrown into some disorder, by finding that the ground immediately in front of them was soft and boggy, but having made their way through it they re-formed upon the other side and rode gallantly at the hedge. Our own opponents, having a clear course before them, never slackened for an instant, but came thundering down with a jingling of harness and a tempest of oaths upon our rude barricades.

Ah, my children ! when a man in his age tries to describe such things as these, and to make others see what he has seen, it is only then that he understands what a small stock of language a plain man keeps by him for his ordinary use in the world, and how unfit it is to meet any call upon it. For though at this very moment I can myself see that white Somersetshire road, with the wild whirling charge of the horsemen, the red angry faces of the men, and the gaping nostrils of the horses all wreathed and framed in clouds of dust, I cannot hope to make it clear to your young eyes, which never have looked, and, I trust, never shall look, upon such a scene. When, too, I think of the sound, a mere rattle and jingle at first, but growing in strength and volume with every step, until it came upon us with a thunderous rush and roar which gave the impression of irresistible power, I feel that that too is beyond the power of my feeble words to express. To inexperienced soldiers like ourselves it seemed impossible

that our frail defence and our feeble weapons could check for an instant the impetus and weight of the dragoons. To right and left I saw white set faces, open-eyed and rigid, unflinching, with a stubbornness which rose less from hope than from despair. All round rose exclamations and prayers. " Lord, save Thy people ! " " Mercy, Lord, mercy ! " " Be with us this day ! " " Receive our souls, O merciful Father ! " Saxon lay across the waggon with his eyes glinting like diamonds and his petronel presented at the full length of his rigid arm. Following his example we all took aim as steadily as possible at the first rank of the enemy. Our only hope of safety lay in making that one discharge so deadly that our opponents should be too much shaken to continue their attack.

Would the man never fire ? They could not be more than ten paces from us. I could see the buckles of the men's plates and the powder charges in their bandoliers. One more stride yet, and at last our leader's pistol flashed and we poured in a close volley, supported by a shower of heavy stones from the sturdy peasants behind. I could hear them splintering against casque and cuirass like hail upon a casement. The cloud of smoke veiling for an instant the line of galloping steeds and gallant riders drifted slowly aside to show a very different scene. A dozen men and horses were rolling in one wild blood-spurting heap, the unwounded falling over those whom our balls and stones had brought down. Struggling, snorting chargers, iron-shod feet, staggering figures rising and falling, wild, hatless, bewildered men half stunned by a fall, and not knowing which way to turn—that was the foreground of the picture, while behind them the remainder of the troop were riding furiously back, wounded and hale, all driven by the one desire of getting to a place of safety where they might rally their shattered formation. A great shout of praise and thanksgiving rose from the delighted peasants, and surging over the barricade they struck down or secured the few uninjured troopers who

had been unable or unwilling to join their companions in their flight. The carbines, swords, and bandoliers were eagerly pounced upon by the victors, some of whom had served in the militia, and knew well how to handle the weapons which they had won.

The victory, however, was by no means completed. The flanking squadron had ridden boldly at the hedge, and a dozen or more had forced their way through, in spite of the showers of stones and the desperate thrusts of the pikemen and scythemen. Once amongst the peasants, the long swords and the armour of the dragoons gave them a great advantage, and though the sickles brought several of the horses to the ground the soldiers continued to lay about them freely, and to beat back the fierce but ill-armed resistance of their opponents. A dragoon sergeant, a man of great resolution and of prodigious strength, appeared to be the leader of the party, and encouraged his followers both by word and example. A stab from a half-pike brought his horse to the ground, but he sprang from the saddle as it fell, and avenged its death by a sweeping back-handed cut from his broadsword. Waving his hat in his left hand he continued to rally his men, and to strike down every Puritan who came against him, until a blow from a hatchet brought him on his knees and a flail stroke broke his sword close by the hilt. At the fall of their leader his comrades turned and fled through the hedge, but the gallant fellow, wounded and bleeding, still showed fight, and would assuredly have been knocked upon the head for his pains had I not picked him up and thrown him into the waggon, where he had the good sense to lie quiet until the skirmish was at an end. Of the dozen who broke through, not more than four escaped, and several others lay dead or wounded upon the other side of the hedge, impaled by scythe-blades or knocked off their horses by stones. Altogether nine of the dragoons were slain and fourteen wounded, while we retained seven unscathed prisoners, ten horses fit for service, and a score or so of carbines, with good store of match, powder, and

ball. The remainder of the troop fired a single, straggling, irregular volley, and then galloped away down the cross-road, disappearing amongst the trees from which they had emerged.

All this, however, had not been accomplished without severe loss upon our side. Three men had been killed and six wounded, one of them very seriously, by the musketry fire. Five had been cut down when the flanking party broke their way in, and only one of these could be expected to recover. In addition to this, one man had lost his life through the bursting of an ancient petronel, and another had his arm broken by the kick of a horse. Our total losses, therefore, were eight killed and the same wounded, which could not but be regarded as a very moderate number when we consider the fierceness of the skirmish, and the superiority of our enemy both in discipline and in equipment.

So elated were the peasants by their victory, that those who had secured horses were clamorous to be allowed to follow the dragoons, the more so as Sir Gervas Jerome and Reuben were both eager to lead them. Decimus Saxon refused, however, to listen to any such scheme, nor did he show more favour to the Reverend Joshua Pettigrue's proposal, that he should in his capacity as pastor mount immediately upon the waggon, and improve the occasion by a few words of healing and unction.

" It is true, good Master Pettigrue, that we owe much praise and much outpouring, and much sweet and holy contending, for this blessing which hath come upon Israel," said he, " but the time hath not yet arrived. There is an hour for prayer and an hour for labour. Hark ye, friend "—to one of the prisoners—" to what regiment do you belong ? "

" It is not for me to reply to your questions," the man answered sulkily.

" Nay, then, we'll try if a string round your scalp and a few twists of a drumstick will make you find your tongue," said Saxon, pushing his face up to that of the prisoner, and

staring into his eyes with so savage an expression that the man shrank away affrighted.

" It is a troop of the second dragoon regiment," he said.

" Where is the regiment itself ? "

" We left it on the Ilchester and Langport road."

" You hear," said our leader. " We have not a moment to spare, or we may have the whole crew about our ears. Put our dead and wounded in the carts, and we can harness two of these chargers to them. We shall not be in safety until we are in Taunton town."

Even Master Joshua saw that the matter was too pressing to permit of any spiritual exercises. The wounded men were lifted into the waggon and laid upon the bedding, while our dead were placed in the cart which had defended our rear. The peasants who owned these, far from making any objection to this disposal of their property, assisted us in every way, tightening girths and buckling traces. Within an hour of the ending of the skirmish we found ourselves pursuing our way once more, and looking back through the twilight at the scattered black dots upon the white road, where the bodies of the dragoons marked the scene of our victory.

16. *Of our Coming to Taunton*

THE purple shadows of evening had fallen over the countryside, and the sun had sunk behind the distant Quantock and Brendon Hills, as our rude column of rustic infantry plodded through Curry Rivell, Wrantage, and Henlade. At every wayside cottage and red-tiled farmhouse the people swarmed out as we passed, with jugs full of milk or beer, shaking hands with our yokels, and pressing food and drink upon them. In the little villages old and young came buzzing to greet us, and cheered long and loud for King Monmouth and the Protestant cause. The stay-at-homes were mostly elderly folks and children, but here and there a young labourer, whom hesitation or duties had kept back, was so

carried away by our martial appearance, and by the visible trophies of our victory, that he snatched up a weapon and joined our ranks.

The skirmish had reduced our numbers, but it had done much to turn our rabble of peasants into a real military force. The leadership of Saxon, and his stern, short words of praise or of censure, had done even more. The men kept some sort of formation, and stepped together briskly in a compact body. The old soldier and I rode at the head of the column, with Master Pettigrue still walking between us. Then came the cartful of our dead, whom we were carrying with us to ensure their decent burial. Behind this walked twoscore of scythe and sickle men, with their rude weapons over their shoulders, preceding the waggon in which the wounded were carried. This was followed by the main body of the peasants, and the rear was brought up by ten or twelve men under the command of Lockarby and Sir Gervas, mounted upon captured chargers, and wearing the breastplates, swords, and carbines of the dragoons.

I observed that Saxon rode with his chin upon his shoulder, casting continual uneasy glances behind him, and halting at every piece of rising ground to make sure that there were no pursuers at our heels. It was not until, after many weary miles of marching, the lights of Taunton could be seen twinkling far off in the valley beneath us that he at last heaved a deep sigh of relief, and expressed his belief that all danger was over.

" I am not prone to be fearful upon small occasion," he remarked, " but hampered as we are with wounded men and prisoners, it might have puzzled Petrinus himself to know what we should have done had the cavalry overtaken us. I can now, Master Pettigrue, smoke my pipe in peace, without pricking up my ears at every chance rumble of a wheel or shout of a village roisterer."

"Even had they pursued us," said the minister stoutly, " as long as the hand of the Lord shall shield us, why should we fear them ? "

" Aye, aye ! " Saxon answered impatiently, " but the devil prevaileth at times. Were not the chosen people themselves overthrown and led into captivity ? How say you, Clarke ? "

" One such skirmish is enough for a day," I remarked. " Faith ! if instead of charging us they had continued that carbine fire, we must either have come forth or been shot where we lay."

" For that reason I forbade our friends with the muskets to answer it," said Saxon. " Our silence led them to think that we had but a pistol or two among us, and so brought them to charge us. Thus our volley became the more terrifying since it was unexpected. I'll wager there was not a man amongst them who did not feel that he had been led into a trap. Mark you how the rogues wheeled and fled with one accord, as though it had been part of their daily drill ! "

" The peasants stood to it like men," I remarked.

" There is nothing like a tincture of Calvinism for stiffening a line of battle," said Saxon. " Look at the Swede when he is at home. What more honest, simple-hearted fellow could you find with no single soldierly virtue, save that he could put away more spruce beer than you would care to pay for. Yet if you do but cram him with a few strong, homely texts, place a pike in his hand, and give him a Gustavus to lead him, there is no infantry in the world that can stand against him. On the other hand, I have seen young Turks, untrained to arms, strike in on behalf of the Koran as lustily as these brave fellows behind us did for the Bible which Master Pettigrue held up in front of them."

" I trust, sir," said the minister gravely, " that you do not, by these remarks, intend to institute any comparison between our sacred scriptures and the writings of the impostor Mahomet, or to infer that there is any similarity between the devil-inspired fury of the infidel Saracens and the Christian fortitude of the struggling faithful ! "

" By no means," Saxon answered, grinning at me over the minister's head. " I was but showing how closely the Evil One can imitate the workings of the Spirit."

" Too true, Master Saxon, too true ! " the clergyman answered sadly. " Amid the conflict and discord it is hard to pick out the true path. But I marvel much that amidst the snares and temptations that beset a soldier's life you have kept yourself unsullied, with your heart still set upon the true faith."

" It was through no strength of mine own," said Saxon piously.

" In very truth, such men as you are much needed in Monmouth's army," Master Joshua exclaimed. " They have there several, as I understand, from Holland, Brandenburg, and Scotland, who have been trained in arms, but who care so little for the cause which we uphold that they curse and swear in a manner that affrights the peasants, and threatens to call down a judgment upon the army. Others there are who cling close to the true faith, and have been born again among the righteous ; but alas ! they have had no experience of camps and fields. Our blessed Master can work by means of weak instruments, yet the fact remains that a man may be a chosen light in a pulpit, and yet be of little avail in an onslaught such as we have seen this day. I can myself arrange my discourse to the satisfaction of my flock, so that they grieve when the sand is run out ; [1] but I am aware that this power would stand me in little stead when it came to the raising of barricades and the use of carnal weapons. In this way it comes about, in the army of the faithful, that those who are fit to lead are hateful to the people, while those to whose words the people will hearken know little of war. Now we have this day seen that you are ready of head and of hand, of much experience of battle, and yet of demure and sober life, full of yearnings after the word and strivings against Apollyon. I therefore repeat that you shall be as a very Joshua amongst them, or as a Samson, destined

[1] Note E, Appendix—Hour-glasses in pulpits.

to tear down the twin pillars of Prelacy and Popery, so as to bury this corrupt government in its fall."

Decimus Saxon's only reply to this eulogy was one of those groans which were supposed, among the zealots, to be the symbol of intense inner conflict and emotion. So austere and holy was his expression, so solemn his demeanour, and so frequent the upturnings of his eyes, clasping of his hands, and other signs which marked the extreme sectary, that I could not but marvel at the depths and completeness of the hypocrisy which had cast so complete a cloak over his rapacious self. For very mischief's sake I could not refrain from reminding him that there was one at least who valued his professions at their real value.

" Have you told the worthy minister," said I, " of your captivity amongst the Mussulmans, and of the noble way in which you did uphold the Christian faith at Stamboul ? "

" Nay," cried our companion, " I would fain hear the tale. I marvel much that one so faithful and unbending as thyself was ever let loose by the unclean and bloodthirsty followers of Mahomet."

" It does not become me to tell the tale," Saxon answered with great presence of mind, casting at the same time a most venomous sidelong glance at me. " It is for my comrades in misfortune and not for me to describe what I endured for the faith. I have little doubt, Master Pettigrue, that you would have done as much had you been there. The town of Taunton lies very quiet beneath us, and there are few lights for so early an hour, seeing that it has not yet gone ten. It is clear that Monmouth's forces have not reached it yet, else had there been some show of camp-fires in the valley ; for though it is warm enough to lie out in the open, the men must have fires to cook their victual."

" The army could scarce have come so far," said the pastor. " They have, I hear, been much delayed by the want of arms and by the need of discipline. Bethink ye,

it was on the eleventh day of the month that Monmouth landed at Lyme, and it is now but the night of the fourteenth. There was much to be done in the time."

" Four whole days ! " growled the old soldier. " Yet I expected no better, seeing that they have, so far as I can hear, no tried soldiers amongst them. By my sword, Tilly or Wallenstein would not have taken four days to come from Lyme to Taunton, though all James Stuart's cavalry barred the way. Great enterprises are not pushed through in this halting fashion. The blow should be sharp and sudden. But tell me, worthy sir, all that you know about the matter, for we have heard little upon the road save rumour and surmise. Was there not some fashion of onfall at Bridport ? "

" There was indeed some shedding of blood at that place. The first two days were consumed, as I understand, in the enrolling of the faithful and the search for arms wherewith to equip them. You may well shake your head, for the hours were precious. At last five hundred men were broken into some sort of order, and marched along the coast under command of Lord Grey of Wark and Wade the lawyer. At Bridport they were opposed by the red Dorset militia and part of Portman's yellow coats. If all be true that is said, neither side had much to boast of. Grey and his cavalry never tightened bridle until they were back in Lyme once more, though it is said their flight had more to do with the hard mouths of their horses than with the soft hearts of the riders. Wade and his footmen did bravely, and had the best of it against the King's troops. There was much outcry against Grey in the camp, but Monmouth can scarce afford to be severe upon the only nobleman who hath ioined his standard."

" Pshaw ! " cried Saxon peevishly. " There was no great stock of noblemen in Cromwell's army, I trow, and yet they held their own against the King, who had as many lords by him as there are haws in a thicket. If ye have the people on your side, why should ye crave for

these bewigged fine gentlemen, whose white hands and delicate rapiers are of as much service as so many ladies' bodkins ? "

" Faith ! " said I, " if all the fops are as careless for their lives as our friend Sir Gervas, I could wish no better comrades in the field."

" In good sooth, yes ! " cried Master Pettigrue heartily. " What though he be clothed in a Joseph's coat of many colours, and hath strange turns of speech !   No man could have fought more stoutly or shown a bolder front against the enemies of Israel.   Surely the youth hath good in his heart, and will become a seat of grace and a vessel of the Spirit, though at present he be entangled in the net of worldly follies and carnal vanities."

" It is to be hoped so," quoth Saxon devoutly.   " And what else can you tell us of the revolt, worthy sir ? "

" Very little, save that the peasants have flocked in in such numbers that many have had to be turned away for want of arms.   Every tithing-man in Somersetshire is searching for axes and scythes.   There is not a blacksmith but is at his forge from morn to night at work upon pike-heads.   There are six thousand men of a sort in the camp, but not one in five carries a musket.   They have advanced, I hear, upon Axminster, where they must meet the Duke of Albemarle, who hath set out from Exeter with four thousand of the train bands."

" Then we shall be too late, after all," I exclaimed.

" You will have enough of battles before Monmouth exchanges his riding-hat for a crown, and his laced roquelaure for the royal purple," quoth Saxon.   " Should our worthy friend here be correctly informed and such an engagement take place, it will but be the prologue to the play.   When Feversham and Churchill come up with the King's own troops it is then that Monmouth takes the last spring, that lands him either on the throne or the scaffold."

Whilst this conversation had been proceeding we had been walking our horses down the winding track which

leads along the eastern slope of Taunton Deane. For some time past we had been able to see in the valley beneath us the lights of Taunton town and the long silver strip of the river Tone. The moon was shining brightly in a cloudless heaven, throwing a still and peaceful radiance over the fairest and richest of English valleys. Lordly manorial houses, pinnacled towers, clusters of nestling thatch-roofed cottages, broad silent stretches of cornland, dark groves with the glint of lamp-lit windows shining from their recesses—it all lay around us like the shadowy, voiceless landscapes which stretch before us in our dreams. So calm and so beautiful was the scene that we reined up our horses at the bend of the pathway, the tired and foot-sore peasants came to a halt, while even the wounded raised themselves in the waggon in order to feast their eyes upon this land of promise. Suddenly, in the still-ness, a strong fervent voice was heard calling upon the source of all life to guard and preserve that which He had created. It was Joshua Pettigrue, who had flung himself upon his knees, and who, while asking for future guidance, was returning thanks for the safe deliverance which his flock had experienced from the many perils which had beset them upon their journey. I would, my children, that I had one of those magic crystals of which we have read, that I might show you that scene. The dark figures of the horsemen, the grave, earnest bearing of the rustics as they knelt in prayer or leaned upon their rude weapons, the half-cowed, half-sneering expression of the captive dragoons, the line of white pain-drawn faces that peeped over the side of the waggon, and the chorus of groans, cries, and ejaculations which broke in upon the steady earnest voice of the pastor. Above us the brilliant heavens, beneath us the beautiful sloping valley, stretch-ing away in the white moonlight as far as the eye could reach. Could I but paint such a scene with the brush of a Verrio or Laguerre, I should have no need to describe it in these halting and feeble words.

Master Pettigrue had concluded his thanksgiving, and

was in the act of rising to his feet, when the musical peal of a bell rose up from the sleeping town before us. For a minute or more it rose and fell in its sweet clear cadence. Then a second with a deeper, harsher note joined in, and then a third, until the air was filled with the merry jangling. At the same time a buzz of shouting or huzzaing could be heard, which increased and spread until it swelled into a mighty uproar. Lights flashed in the windows, drums beat, and the whole place was astir. These sudden signs of rejoicing coming at the heels of the minister's prayer were seized upon as a happy omen by the superstitious peasants, who set up a glad cry, and pushing onwards were soon within the outskirts of the town.

The footpaths and causeway were black with throngs of the townsfolk, men, women and children, many of whom were bearing torches and lanthorns, all flocking in the same direction. Following them we found ourselves in the market-place, where crowds of apprentice lads were piling up faggots for a bonfire, while others were broaching two or three great puncheons of ale. The cause of this sudden outbreak of rejoicing was, we learned, that news had just come in that Albemarle's Devonshire militia had partly deserted and partly been defeated at Axminster that very morning. On hearing of our own successful skirmish the joy of the people became more tumultuous than ever. They rushed in amongst us, pouring blessings on our heads, in their strange burring west-country speech, and embracing our horses as well as ourselves. Preparations were soon made for our weary companions. A long empty wool warehouse, thickly littered with straw, was put at their disposal, with a tub of ale and a plentiful supply of cold meats and wheaten bread. For our own part we made our way down East Street through the clamorous hand-shaking crowd to the White Hart Inn, where after a hasty meal we were right glad to seek our couches. Late into the night, however, our slumbers were disturbed by the rejoicings of the mob, who, having

burned the effigies of Lord Sunderland and of Gregory Alford, Mayor of Lyme, continued to sing west-country songs and Puritan hymns into the small hours of the morning.

17. *Of the Gathering in the Market-square*

THE fair town in which we now found ourselves was, although Monmouth had not yet reached it, the real centre of the rebellion. It was a prosperous place, with a great woollen and kersey trade, which gave occupation to as many as seven thousand inhabitants. It stood high, therefore, amongst English boroughs, being inferior only to Bristol, Norwich, Bath, Exeter, York, Worcester and Nottingham amongst the country towns. Taunton had long been famous not only for its own resources and for the spirit of its inhabitants, but also for the beautiful and highly cultivated country which spread around it, and gave rise to a gallant breed of yeomen. From time immemorial the town had been a rallying-point for the party of liberty, and for many years it had leaned to the side of Republicanism in politics and of Puritanism in religion. No place in the kingdom had fought more stoutly for the Parliament, and though it had been twice besieged by Goring, the burghers, headed by the brave Robert Blake, had fought so desperately, that the Royalists had been compelled each time to retire discomfited. On the second occasion the garrison had been reduced to dog's-flesh and horseflesh, but no word of surrender had come either from them or their heroic commander, who was the same Blake under whom the old seaman Solomon Sprent had fought against the Dutch. After the Restoration the Privy Council had shown their recollection of the part played by the Somersetshire town, by issuing a special order that the battlements which fenced round the maiden stronghold should be destroyed. Thus, at the time of which I speak, nothing but a line of ruins and

a few unsightly mounds represented the massive line of
wall which had been so bravely defended by the last
generation of townsmen. There were not wanting, however, many other relics of those stormy times. The
houses on the outskirts were still scarred and splintered
from the effects of the bombs and grenades of the Cavaliers.
Indeed, the whole town bore a grimly martial appearance, as though she were a veteran among boroughs who
had served in the past, and was not averse to seeing the
flash of guns and hearing the screech of shot once more.

Charles's Council might destroy the battlements which
his soldiers had been unable to take, but no royal edict
could do away with the resolute spirit and strong opinions
of the burghers. Many of them, born and bred amidst
the clash of civil strife, had been fired from their infancy
by the tales of the old war, and by reminiscences of the
great assault when Lunsford's babe-eaters were hurled
down the main breach by the strong arms of their fathers.
In this way there was bred in Taunton a fiercer and more
soldierly spirit that is usual in an English country town,
and this flame was fanned by the unwearied ministerings
of a chosen band of Nonconformist clergymen, amongst
whom Joseph Alleine was the most conspicuous. No
better focus for a revolt could have been chosen, for no
city valued so highly those liberties and that creed which
was in jeopardy.

A large body of the burghers had already set out to join
the rebel army, but a good number had remained behind
to guard the city, and these were reinforced by gangs of
peasants, like the one to which we had attached ourselves,
who had trooped in from the surrounding country, and
now divided their time between listening to their favourite
preachers and learning to step in line and to handle their
weapons. In yard, street and market-square there was
marching and drilling, night, morning and noon. As
we rode out after breakfast the whole town was ringing
with the shouting of orders and the clatter of arms. Our
own friends of yesterday marched into the market-place

at the moment we entered it, and no sooner did they catch sight of us than they plucked off their hats and cheered lustily, nor would they desist until we cantered over to them and took our places at their head.

"They have vowed that none other should lead them," said the minister, standing by Saxon's stirrup.

"I could not wish to lead stouter fellows," said he. "Let them deploy into double line in front of the town hall. So, so, smartly there, rear rank!" he shouted, facing his horse towards them. "Now swing round into position. Keep your ground, left flank, and let the others pivot upon you. So—as hard and as straight as an Andrea Ferrara. I prithee, friend, do not carry your pike as though it were a hoe, though I trust you will do some weeding in the Lord's vineyard with it. And you, sir, your musquetoon should be sloped upon your shoulder, and not borne under your arm like a dandy's cane. Did ever an unhappy soldier find himself called upon to make order among so motley a crew! Even my good friend the Fleming cannot so avail here, nor does Petrinus, in his 'De re militari,' lay down any injunctions as to the method of drilling a man who is armed with a sickle or a scythe."

"Shoulder scythe, port scythe, present scythe—mow!" whispered Reuben to Sir Gervas, and the pair began to laugh, heedless of the angry frowns of Saxon.

"Let us divide them," he said, "into three companies of eighty men. Or stay—how many musqueteers have we in all? Five-and-fifty. Let them stand forward, and form the first line or company. Sir Gervas Jerome, you have officered the militia of your county, and have doubtless some knowledge of the manual exercise. If I am commandment of this force I hand over the captaincy of this company to you. It shall be the first line in battle, a position which I know you will not be averse to."

"Gad, they'll have to powder their heads," said Sir Gervas, with decision.

"You shall have the entire ordering of them," Saxon

answered. " Let the first company take six paces to the front—so ! Now let the pikeman stand out. Eighty-seven, a serviceable company ! Lockarby, do you take these men in hand, and never forget that the German wars have proved that the best of horse has no more chance against steady pikemen than the waves against a crag. Take the captaincy of the second company, and ride at their head."

" Faith ! If they don't fight better than their captain rides," whispered Reuben, " it will be an evil business. I trust they will be firmer in the field than I am in the saddle."

" The third company of scythesmen I commit to your charge, Captain Micah Clarke," continued Saxon. " Good Master Joshua Pettigrue will be our field-chaplain. Shall not his voice and his presence be to us as manna in the wilderness, and as springs of water in dry places ? The under-officers I see that you have your-selves chosen, and your captains shall have power to add to the number from those who smite boldly and spare not. Now one thing I have to say to you, and I speak it that all may hear, and that none may hereafter complain that the rules he serves under were not made clear to him. For I tell you now that when the evening bugle calls, and the helm and pike are laid aside, I am as you and you as I, fellow-workers in the same field, and drinkers from the same wells of life. Lo, I will pray with you, or preach with you, or hearken with you, or expound to you, or do aught that may become a brother pilgrim upon the weary road. But hark you, friends ! when we are in arms and the good work is to be done, on the march, in the field, or on parade, then let your bearing be strict, soldierly and scrupulous, quick to hear and alert to obey, for I shall have no sluggards or laggards, and if there be any such my hand shall be heavy upon them, yea, even to the cutting of them off. I say there shall be no mercy for such," here he paused and surveyed his force with a set face and his eyelids drawn low over his glinting, shift-

ing eyes. " If, then," he continued, " there is any man among you who fears to serve under a hard discipline, let him stand forth now, and let him betake him to some easier leader, for I say to you that whilst I command this corps, Saxon's regiment of Wiltshire foot shall be worthy to testify in this great and soul-raising cause."

The Colonel stopped and sat silent upon his mare. The long lines of rustic faces looked up, some stolidly, some admiringly, some with an expression of fear at his stern, gaunt face and baneful eyes. None moved, however, so he continued.

" Worthy Master Timewell, the Mayor of this fair town of Taunton, who has been a tower of strength to the faithful during these long and spirit-trying times, is about to inspect us when the others shall have assembled. Captains, to your companies then ! Close up there on the musqueteers, with three paces between each line. Scythesmen, take ground to your left. Let the under-officers stand on the flanks and rear. So ! 'tis smartly done for a first venture, though a good adjutant with a prugel after the Imperial fashion might find work to do."

Whilst we were thus rapidly and effectively organising ourselves into a regiment, other bodies of peasantry more or less disciplined had marched into the market-square, and had taken up their position there. Those on our right had come from Frome and Radstock, in the north of Somersetshire, and were a mere rabble armed with flails, hammers and other such weapons, with no common sign of order or cohesion save the green boughs which waved in their hat-bands. The body upon our left, who bore a banner amongst them announcing that they were men of Dorset, were fewer in number but better equipped, having a front rank, like our own, entirely armed with muskets.

The good townsmen of Taunton, with their wives and their daughters, had meanwhile been assembling on the balconies and at the windows which overlooked the square, whence they might have a view of the pageant. The

grave, square-bearded, broadclothed burghers, and their portly dames in velvet and three-piled taffeta, looked down from every post of vantage, while here and there a pretty, timid face peeping out from a Puritan coif made good the old claim, that Taunton excelled in beautiful women as well as in gallant men. The side-walks were crowded with the commoner folk—old white-bearded wool-workers, stern-faced matrons, country lasses with their shawls over their heads, and swarms of children, who cried out with their treble voices for King Monmouth and the Protestant succession.

" By my faith ! " said Sir Gervas, reining back his steed until he was abreast of me, " our square-toed friends need not be in such post-haste to get to heaven when they have so many angels among them on earth. Gad's wounds, are they not beautiful ? Never a patch or a diamond amongst them, and yet what would not our faded belles of the Mall or the Piazza give for their innocence and freshness ? "

"Nay, for Heaven's sake do not smile and bow at them," said I. " These courtesies may pass in London, but they may be misunderstood among simple Somerset maidens and their hot-headed, hard-handed kinsfolk."

I had hardly spoken before the folding-doors of the town-hall were thrown open, and a procession of the city fathers emerged into the market-place. Two trumpeters in parti-coloured jerkins preceded them, who blew a flourish upon their instruments as they advanced. Behind came the aldermen and councilmen, grave and reverend elders, clad in their sweeping gowns of black silk, trimmed and tippeted with costly furs. In rear of these walked a pursy little red-faced man, the town clerk, bearing a staff of office in his hand, while the line of dignitaries was closed by the tall and stately figure of Stephen Timewell, Mayor of Taunton.

There was much in this magistrate's appearance to attract attention, for all the characteristics of the Puritan party to which he belonged were embodied and exaggerated

in his person. Of great height he was and very thin, with a long-drawn, heavy-eyelidded expression, which spoke of fasts and vigils. The bent shoulders and the head sunk upon the breast proclaimed the advances of age, but his bright steel-grey eyes and the animation of his eager face showed how the enthusiasm of religion could rise superior to bodily weakness. A peaked, straggling grey beard descended half-way to his waist, and his long snow-white hairs fluttered out from under a velvet skull-cap. The latter was drawn tightly down upon his head, so as to make his ears protrude in an unnatural manner on either side, a custom which had earned for his party the title of " prickeared," so often applied to them by their opponents. His attire was of studious plainness and sombre in colour, consisting of his black mantle, dark velvet breeches and silk hosen, with velvet bows upon his shoes instead of the silver buckles then in vogue. A broad chain of gold around his neck formed the badge of his office. In front of him strutted the fat red-vested town clerk, one hand upon his hip, the other extended and bearing his wand of office, looking pompously to right and left, and occasionally bowing as though the plaudits were entirely on his own behalf. This little man had tied a huge broadsword to his girdle, which clanked along the cobblestones when he walked and occasionally inserted itself between his legs, when he would gravely cock his foot over it again and walk on without any abatement of his dignity. At last, finding these interruptions become rather too frequent he depressed the hilt of his great sword in order to elevate the point, and so strutted onwards like a bantam cock with a single straight feather in its tail.

Having passed round the front and rear of the various bodies, and inspected them with a minuteness and attention which showed that his years had not dulled his soldier's faculties, the Mayor faced round with the evident intention of addressing us. His clerk instantly darted in front of him, and waving his arms began to shout, " Silence, good people ! Silence for his most worshipful

the Mayor of Taunton! Silence for the worthy Master Stephen Timewell!" until in the midst of his gesticulations and cries he got entangled once more with his overgrown weapon, and went sprawling on his hands and knees in the kennel.

"Silence yourself, Master Tetheridge," said the chief magistrate severely. "If your sword and your tongue were both clipped, it would be as well for yourself and us. Shall I not speak a few words in season to these good people but you must interrupt with your discordant bellowings?"

The busybody gathered himself together and slunk behind the group of councilmen, while the Mayor slowly ascended the steps of the market cross. From this position he addressed us, speaking in a high piping voice which gathered strength as he proceeded, until it was audible at the remotest corners of the square.

"Friends in the faith," he said, "I thank the Lord that I have been spared in my old age to look down upon this goodly assembly. For we of Taunton have ever kept the flame of the Covenant burning amongst us, obscured it may be at times by time-servers and Laodiceans, but none the less burning in the hearts of our people. All round us, however, there was a worse than Egyptian darkness, where Popery and Prelacy, Arminianism, Erastianism and Simony might rage and riot unchecked and unconfined. But what do I see now? Do I see the faithful cowering in their hiding-places and straining their ears for the sound of the horsehoofs of their oppressors? Do I see a time-serving generation, with lies on their lips and truth buried in their hearts? No! I see before me godly men, not from this fair city only, but from the broad country round, and from Dorset, and from Wiltshire, and some even as I hear from Hampshire, all ready and eager to do mighty work in the cause of the Lord. And when I see these faithful men, and when I think that every broad piece in the strong boxes of my townsmen is ready to support them, and when I know that the

persecuted remnant throughout the country is wrestling hard in prayer for us, then a voice speaks within me and tells me that we shall tear down the idols of Dagon, and build up in this England of ours such a temple of the true faith that not Popery, nor Prelacy, nor idolatry, nor any other device of the Evil One shall ever prevail against it."

A deep irrepressible hum of approval burst from the close ranks of the insurgent infantry, with a clang of arms as musquetoon or pike was grounded upon the stone pavement. Saxon half-turned his fierce face, raising an impatient hand, and the hoarse murmur died away among our men, though our less-disciplined companions to right and left continued to wave their green boughs and to clatter their arms. The Taunton men opposite stood grim and silent, but their set faces and bent brows showed that their townsman's oratory had stirred the deep fanatic spirit which distinguished them.

" In my hands," continued the Mayor, drawing a roll of paper from his bosom, " is the proclamation which our royal leader hath sent in advance of him. In his great goodness and self-abnegation he had, in his early declaration given forth at Lyme, declared that he should leave the choice of a monarch to the Commons of England, but having found that his enemies did most scandalously and basely make use of this his self-denial, and did assert that he had so little confidence in his own cause that he dared not take publicly the title which is due to him, he hath determined that this should have an end. Know, therefore, that it is hereby proclaimed that James, Duke of Monmouth, is now and henceforth rightful King of England ; that James Stuart, the Papist and fratricide, is a wicked usurper, upon whose head, dead or alive, a price of five thousand guineas is affixed ; and that the assembly now sitting at Westminster, and calling itself the Commons of England, is an illegal assembly, and its acts are null and void in the sight of the law. God bless King Monmouth and the Protestant religion ! "

The trumpeters struck up a flourish and the people

huzzaed, but the Mayor raised his thin white hands as a signal for silence. " A messenger hath reached me this morning from the King," he continued. " He sends a greeting to all his faithful Protestant subjects, and having halted at Axminster to rest after his victory, he will advance presently and be with ye in two days at the latest.

" Ye will grieve to hear that good Alderman Rider was struck down in the thick of the fray. He hath died like a man and a Christian, leaving all his worldly goods, together with his cloth works and household property, to the carrying on of the war. Of the other slain there are not more than ten of Taunton birth. Two gallant young brothers have been cut off, Oliver and Ephraim Hollis, whose poor mother——"

" Grieve not for me, good Master Timewell," cried a female voice from the crowd. " I have three others as stout, who shall all be offered in the same quarrel."

" You are a worthy woman, Mistress Hollis," the Mayor answered, " and your children shall not be lost to you. The next name upon my list is Jesse Trefail, then come Joseph Millar, and Aminadab Holt——"

An elderly musqueteer in the first line of the Taunton foot pulled his hat down over his brows and cried out in a loud steady voice, " The Lord hath given and the Lord hath taken away. Blessed be the name of the Lord."

" It is your only son, Master Holt," said the Mayor, " but the Lord also sacrificed His only Son that you and I might drink the waters of eternal life. The others are Path of Light Regan, James Fletcher, Salvation Smith and Robert Johnstone."

The old Puritan gravely rolled up his papers, and having stood for a few moments with his hands folded across his breast in silent prayer, he descended from the market cross, and moved off, followed by the aldermen and councilmen. The crowd began likewise to disperse in sedate and sober fashion, with grave earnest faces and downcast eyes. A large number of the countryfolk, however, more curious or less devout than the citizens,

gathered round our regiment to see the men who had beaten off the dragoons.

" See the mon wi' a face like a gerfalcon," cried one, pointing to Saxon ; " 'tis he that slew the Philistine officer yestreen, an' brought the faithful off victorious."

" Mark ye yon other one," cried an old dame, " him wi' the white face an' the clothes like a prince. He's one o' the Quality, what's come a' the way froe Lunnon to testify to the Protestant creed. He's a main pious gentlemen, he is, an' if he had bided in the wicked city they'd ha' had his head off, like they did the good Lord Roossell, or put him in chains wi' the worthy Maister Baxter."

" Marry come up, gossip," cried a third. " The girt mun on the grey horse is the soldier for me. He has the smooth cheeks o' a wench, an' limbs like Goliath o' Gath. I'll war'nt he could pick up my old gaffer Jones an' awa' wi' him at his saddle-bow, as easy as Towser does a rotten ! But here's good Master Tetheridge, the clark, and on great business too, for he's a mun that spares ne time ne trooble in the great cause."

" Room, good people, room ! " cried the little clerk, bustling up with an air of authority. " Hinder not the high officials of the Corporation in the discharge of their functions. Neither should ye hamper the flanks of fighting men, seeing that you thereby prevent that deploying and extending of the line which is now advocated by many high commanders. I prithee, who commands this cohort, or legion rather, seeing that you have auxiliary horse attached to it ? "

" 'Tis a regiment, sirrah," said Saxon sternly. " Colonel Saxon's regiment of Wiltshire foot, which I have the honour to command."

" I beg your Colonelship's pardon," cried the clerk nervously, edging away from the swarthy-faced soldier. " I have heard speak of your Colonelship, and of your doings in the German wars. I have myself trailed a pike in my youth and have broken a head or two, aye, and a heart or two also, when I wore buff and bandolier."

" Discharge your message," said our Colonel shortly.

" 'Tis from his most worshipful the Mayor, and is addressed to yourself and to your captains, who are doubtless these tall cavaliers whom I see on either side of me. Pretty fellows, by my faith ! but you and I know well, Colonel, that a little trick of fence will set the smallest of us on a level with the brawniest. Now I warrant that you and I, being old soldiers, could, back to back, make it good against these three gallants."

" Speak, fellow," snarled Saxon, and reaching out a long sinewy arm he seized the loquacious clerk by the lappet of his gown, and shook him until his long sword clattered again.

" How, Colonel, how ? " cried Master Tetheridge, while his vest seemed to acquire a deeper tint from the sudden pallor of his face. " Would you lay an angry hand upon the Mayor's representative ? I wear a bilbo by my side, as you can see. I am also somewhat quick and choleric, and warn you therefore not to do aught which I might perchance construe into a personal slight. As to my message, it was that his most worshipful the Mayor did desire to have word with you and your captains in the town-hall."

" We shall be there anon," said Saxon, and turning to the regiment he set himself to explain some of the simpler movements and exercises, teaching his officers as well as his men, for though Sir Gervas knew something of the manual, Lockarby and I brought little but our good-will to the task. When the order to dismiss was at last given, our companies marched back to their barracks in the wool warehouse, while we handed over our horses to the grooms from the White Hart, and set off to pay our respects to the Mayor.

18. *Of Master Stephen Timewell, Mayor of Taunton*

WITHIN the town-hall all was bustle and turmoil. At one side behind a low table covered with green baize sat two scriveners with great rolls of paper in front of them. A long line of citizens passed slowly before them, each in turn putting down a roll or bag of coins which was duly noted by the receivers. A square iron-bound chest stood by their side, into which the money was thrown, and we noted as we passed that it was half full of gold pieces. We could not but mark that many of the givers were men whose threadbare doublets and pinched faces showed that the wealth which they were dashing down so readily must have been hoarded up for such a purpose, at the cost of scanty fare and hard living. Most of them accompanied their gift by a few words of prayer, or by some pithy text anent the treasure which rusteth not, or the lending to the Lord. The town clerk stood by the table giving forth the vouchers for each sum, and the constant clack of his tongue filled the hall, as he read aloud the names and amounts, with his own remarks between.

" Abraham Willis," he shouted as we entered ; " put him down twenty-six pounds and ten shillings. You shall receive ten per centum upon this earth, Master Willis, and I warrant that it shall not be forgotten hereafter. John Standish, two pounds. William Simons, two guineas. Stand-fast Healing, forty-five pounds. That is a rare blow which you have struck into the ribs of Prelacy, good Master Healing. Solomon Warren, five guineas. James White, five shillings—the widow's mite, James ! Thomas Bakewell, ten pounds. Nay, Master Bakewell, surely out of three farms on the banks of Tone, and grazing land in the fattest part of Athelney, you can spare more than this for the good cause. We shall doubtless see you again. Alderman Smithson, ninety

pounds. Aha! There is a slap for the scarlet woman! A few more such and her throne shall be a ducking-stool. We shall break her down, worthy Master Smithson, even as Jehu, the son of Nimshi, broke down the house of Baal." So he babbled on with praise, precept and rebuke, though the grave and solemn burghers took little notice of his empty clamour.

At the other side of the hall were several long wooden drinking-troughs, which were used for the storing of pikes and scythes. Special messengers and tithing-men had been sent out to scour the country for arms, who, as they returned, placed their prizes here under the care of the armourer-general. Besides the common weapons of the peasants there was a puncheon half full of pistols and petronels, together with a good number of muskets, screw-guns, snaphances, birding-pieces and carbines, with a dozen bell-mouthed brass blunderbusses, and a few old-fashioned wall-pieces, such as sakers and culverins taken from the manor-houses of the county. From the walls and the lumber-rooms of these old dwellings many other arms had been brought to light which were doubtless esteemed as things of price by our forefathers, but which would seem strange to your eyes in these days, when a musket may be fired once in every two minutes, and will carry a ball to a distance of four hundred paces. There were halberds, battle-axes, morning stars, brown bills, maces and ancient coats of chain mail, which might even now save a man from sword stroke or pike thrust.

In the midst of the coming and the going stood Master Timewell, the Mayor, ordering all things like a skilful and provident commander. I could understand the trust and love which his townsmen had for him, as I watched him labouring with all the wisdom of an old man and the blithesomeness of a young one. He was hard at work as we approached in trying the lock of a falconet ; but per-ceiving us, he came forward and saluted us with much kindliness.

" I have heard much of ye," said he ; " how ye caused

the faithful to gather to a head, and so beat off the horsemen of the usurper. It will not be the last time, I trust,
that ye shall see their backs. I hear, Colonel Saxon, that
ye have seen much service abroad."

"I have been the humble tool of Providence in much
good work," said Saxon, with a bow. "I have fought
with the Swedes against the Brandenburgers, and again
with the Brandenburgers against the Swedes, my time
and conditions with the latter having been duly carried
out. I have afterwards in the Bavarian service fought
against Swedes and Brandenburgers combined, besides
having undergone the great wars on the Danube against
the Turk, and two campaigns with the Messieurs in the
Palatinate, which latter might be better termed holiday
making than fighting."

"A soldierly record in very truth," cried the Mayor,
stroking his white beard. "I hear that you are also
powerfully borne onwards in prayer and song. You are,
I perceive, one of the old breed of '44, Colonel—the men
who were in the saddle all day, and on their knees half the
night. When shall we see the like of them again ? A
few such broken wrecks as I are left, with the fire of our
youth all burned out and nought left but the ashes of
lethargy and lukewarmness."

"Nay, nay," said Saxon, "your position and present
business will scarce jump with the modesty of your words.
But here are young men who will find the fire if their
elders bring the brains. This is Captain Micah Clarke,
and Captain Lockarby, and Captain the Honourable
Sir Gervas Jerome, who have all come far to draw their
swords for the downtrodden faith."

"Taunton welcomes ye, young sirs," said the Mayor,
looking a trifle askance, as I thought, at the baronet, who
had drawn out his pocket-mirror, and was engaged in the
brushing of his eyebrows. "I trust that during your
stay in this town ye will all four take up your abode with
me. 'Tis a homely roof, and simple fare, but a soldier's
wants are few. And now, Colonel, I would fain have your

advice as to these three drakes, whether if rehooped they may be deemed fit for service ; and also as to these demi-cannons, which were used in the old Parliamentary days, and may yet have a word to say in the people's cause."

The old soldier and the Puritan instantly plunged into a deep and learned disquisition upon the merits of wall-pieces, drakes, demi-culverins, sakers, minions, mortar-pieces, falcons and pattereroes, concerning all which pieces of ordnance Saxon had strong opinions to offer, fortified by many personal hazards and experiences. He then dwelt upon the merits of fire-arrows and fire-pikes in the attack or defence of places of strength, and had finally begun to descant upon sconces, "directis lateribus," and upon works, semilunar, rectilineal, horizontal or orbicular, with so many references to his Imperial Majesty's lines at Gran, that it seemed that his discourse would never find an end. We slipped away at last, leaving him still discussing the effects produced by the Austrian grenadoes upon a Bavarian brigade of pikes at the battle of Ober-Graustock.

" Curse me if I like accepting this old fellow's offer," said Sir Gervas, in an undertone. " I have heard of these Puritan households. Much grace to little sack, and texts flying about as hard and as jagged as flint stones. To bed at sundown, and a sermon ready if ye do but look kindly at the waiting-wench or hum the refrain of a ditty."

" His home may be larger, but it could scarce be stricter than that of my own father," I remarked.

" I'll warrant that," cried Reuben. " When we have been a-morris-dancing, or having a Saturday night game of ' kiss-in-the-ring,' or ' parson-has-lost-his-coat,' I have seen Ironside Joe stride past us, and cast a glance at us which hath frozen the smile upon our lips. I warrant that he would have aided Colonel Pride to shoot the bears and hack down the maypoles."

" 'Twere fratricide for such a man to shoot a bear," quoth Sir Gervas, " with all respect, friend Clarke, for your honoured progenitor."

" No more than for you to shoot at a popinjay," I
answered, laughing ; " but as to the Mayor's offer, we
can but go to meat with him now, and should it prove
irksome it will be easy for you to plead some excuse, and
so get honourably quit of it. But bear in mind, Sir
Gervas, that such households are in very truth different
to any with which you are acquainted, so curb your tongue
or offence may come of it. Should I cry ' hem ! ' or
cough, it will be a sign to you that you had best beware."

" Agreed, young Solomon ! " cried he. " It is, indeed,
well to have a pilot like yourself who knows these godly
waters. For my own part, I should never know how near
I was to the shoals. But our friends have finished the
battle of Ober what's its name, and are coming towards us.
I trust, worthy Mr. Mayor, that your difficulties have been
resolved ? "

" They are, sir," replied the Puritan. " I have been
much edified by your Colonel's discourse, and I have
little doubt that by serving under him ye will profit much
by his ripe experience."

" Very like, sir, very like," said Sir Gervas carelessly.

" But it is nigh one o'clock," the Mayor continued,
" our frail flesh cries aloud for meat and drink. I beg
that ye will do me the favour to accompany me to my
humble dwelling, where we shall find the household board
already dressed."

With these words he led the way out of the hall and
paced slowly down Fore Street, the people falling back
to right and to left as he passed, and raising their caps
to do him reverence. Here and there, as he pointed out
to us, arrangements had been made for barring the road
with strong chains to prevent any sudden rush of cavalry.
In places, too, at the corner of a house, a hole had been
knocked in the masonry through which peeped the dark
muzzle of a carronade or wall-piece. These precautions
were the more necessary as several bodies of the Royal
Horse, besides the one which we had repulsed, were
known to be within the Deane, and the town, deprived of

193

its ramparts, was open to an incursion from any daring commander.

The chief magistrate's house was a squat square-faced stone building within a court which opened on to East Street. The peaked oak door, spangled with broad iron nails, had a gloomy and surly aspect, but the hall within was lightful and airy, with a bright polished cedar planking, and high panelling of some dark-grained wood which gave forth a pleasant smell as of violets. A broad flight of steps rose up from the farther end of the hall, down which as we entered a young sweet-faced maid came tripping, with an old dame behind her, who bore in her hands a pile of fresh napery. At the sight of us the elder one retreated up the stairs again, whilst the younger came flying down three steps at a time, threw her arms round the old Mayor's neck, and kissed him fondly, looking hard into his face the while, as a mother gazes into that of a child with whom she fears that aught may have gone amiss.

" Weary again, daddy, weary again," she said, shaking her head anxiously with a small white hand upon each of his shoulders. " Indeed, and indeed, thy spirit is greater than thy strength."

" Nay, nay, lass," said he, passing his hand fondly over her rich brown hair. " The workman must toil until the hour of rest is rung. This, gentlemen, is my granddaughter Ruth, the sole relic of my family and the light of mine old age. The whole grove hath been cut down, and only the oldest oak and the youngest sapling left. These cavaliers, little one, have come from afar to serve the cause, and they have done us the honour to accept of our poor hospitality."

" Ye are come in good time, gentlemen," she answered, looking us straight in the eyes with a kindly smile as a sister might greet her brothers. " The household is gathered round the table and the meal is ready."

" But not more ready than we," cried the stout old burgher. " Do thou conduct our guests to their places,

whilst I seek my room and doff these robes of office, with my chain and tippet, ere I break my fast."

Following our fair guide we passed into a very large and lofty room, the walls of which were wainscoted with carved oak, and hung at either end with tapestry. The floor was tessellated after the French fashion, and plentifully strewn with skins and rugs. At one end of the apartment stood a great white marble fireplace, like a small room in itself, fitted up, as was the ancient custom, with an iron stand in the centre, and with broad stone benches in the recess on either side. Lines of hooks above the chimneypiece had been used, as I surmise, to support arms, for the wealthy merchants of England were wont to keep enough in their houses to at least equip their apprentices and craftsmen. They had now, however, been removed, nor was there any token of the troublous times save a single heap of pikes and halberds piled together in a corner.

Down the centre of this room there ran a long and massive table, which was surrounded by thirty or forty people, the greater part of whom were men. They were on their feet as we entered, and a grave-faced man at the farther end was drawling forth an interminable grace, which began as a thanksgiving for food, but wandered away into questions of Church and State, and finally ended in a supplication for Israel now in arms to do battle for the Lord. While this was proceeding we stood in a group by the door with our caps doffed, and spent our time in observing the company more closely than we could have done with courtesy had their eyes not been cast down and their thoughts elsewhere.

They were of all ages, from greybeards down to lads scarce out of their teens, all with the same solemn and austere expression of countenance, and clad in the same homely and sombre garb. Save their wide white collars and cuffs, not a string of any colour lessened the sad severity of their attire. Their black coats and doublets were cut straight and close, and their cordovan leather

195

shoes, which in the days of our youth were usually the seat of some little ornament, were uniformly square-toed and tied with sad-coloured ribbon. Most of them wore plain sword-belts of untanned hide, but the weapons themselves, with their broad felt hats and black cloaks, were laid under the benches or placed upon the settles which lined the walls. They stood with their hands clasped and their heads bent, listening to the untimely address, and occasionally by some groan or exclamation testifying that the preacher's words had moved them.

The overgrown grace came at last to an end, when the company sat silently down, and proceeded without pause or ceremony to attack the great joints which smoked before them. Our young hostess led us to the end of the table, where a high carved chair with a black cushion upon it marked the position of the master of the house. Mistress Timewell seated herself upon the right of the Mayor's place, with Sir Gervas beside her, while the post of honour upon the left was assigned to Saxon. On my left sat Lockarby, whose eyes I observed had been fixed in undisguised and all-absorbing admiration upon the Puritan maiden from the first moment that he had seen her. The table was of no great breadth, so that we could talk across in spite of the clatter of plates and dishes, the bustle of servants, and the deep murmur of voices.

"This is my father's household," said our hostess, addressing herself to Saxon. "There is not one of them who is not in his employ. He hath many apprentices in the wool trade. We sit down forty to meat every day in the year."

"And to right good fare, too," quoth Saxon, glancing down the table. "Salmon, ribs of beef, loin of mutton, veal, pasties—what could man wish for more? Plenty of good home-brewed, too, to wash it down. If worthy Master Timewell can arrange that the army be victualled after the same fashion, I for one shall be beholden to him. A cup of dirty water and a charred morsel cooked on a

ramrod over the camp fire are like to take the place of these toothsome dainties."

" Is it not best to have faith ? " said the Puritan maiden. " Shall not the Almighty feed His soldiers even as Elisha was fed in the wilderness and Hagar in the desert ? "

" Aye," exclaimed a lanky-haired, swarthy young man who sat upon the right of Sir Gervas, " He will provide for us, even as the stream of water gushed forth out of dry places, even as the quails and the manna lay thick upon barren soil."

" So I trust, young sir," quoth Saxon, " but we must none the less arrange a victual-train, with a staff of wains, duly numbered, and an intendant over each, after the German fashion. Such things should not be left to chance."

Pretty Mistress Timewell glanced up with a half-startled look at this remark, as though shocked at the want of faith implied in it. Her thoughts might have taken the form of words had not her father entered the room at the moment, the whole company rising and bowing to him as he advanced to his seat.

" Be seated, friends," said he, with a wave of his hand ; " we are a homely folk, Colonel Saxon, and the old-time virtue of respect for our elders has not entirely forsaken us. I trust, Ruth," he continued, " that thou hast seen to the wants of our guests."

We all protested that we had never received such attention and hospitality.

" 'Tis well, 'tis well," said the good wool-worker. " But your plates are clear and your glasses empty. William, look to it ! A good workman is ever a good trencherman. If a 'prentice of mine cannot clean his platter, I know that I shall get little from him with carder and teazel. Thew and sinew need building up. A slice from that round of beef, William ! Touching that same battle of Ober-Graustock, Colonel, what part was played in the fray by that regiment of Pandour horse, in which, as I understand, thou didst hold a commission ? "

This was a question on which, as may be imagined, Saxon had much to say, and the pair were soon involved in a heated discussion, in which the experiences of Roundway Down and Marston Moor were balanced against the results of a score of unpronounceable fights in the Styrian Alps and along the Danube. Stephen Timewell in his lusty youth had led first a troop and then a regiment through the wars of the Parliament, from Chalgrove Field to the final battle at Worcester, so that his warlike passages, though less varied and extensive than those of our companion, were enough to enable him to form and hold strong opinions. These were in the main the same as those of the soldier of fortune, but when their ideas differed upon any point, there arose forthwith such a cross-fire of military jargon, such speech of estacados and palisados, such comparisons of light horse and heavy, of pikemen and musqueteers, of Lanzknechte, Leaguers and on-falls, that the unused ear became bewildered with the babble. At last, on some question of fortification, the Mayor drew his outworks with the spoons and knives, on which Saxon opened his parallels with lines of bread, and pushing them rapidly up with traverses and covered ways, he established himself upon the re-entering angle of the Mayor's redoubt. This opened up a fresh question as to counter-mines, with the result that the dispute raged with renewed vigour.

Whilst this friendly strife was proceeding between the elders, Sir Gervas Jerome and Mistress Ruth had fallen into conversation at the other side of the table. I have seldom seen, my dear children, so beautiful a face as that of this Puritan damsel ; and it was beautiful with that sort of modest and maidenly comeliness where the features derive their sweetness from the sweet soul which shines through them. The perfectly-moulded body appeared to be but the outer expression of the perfect spirit within. Her dark-brown hair swept back from a broad and white forehead, which surmounted a pair of well-marked eyebrows and large blue thoughtful eyes. The whole cast of

her features was gentle and dove-like, yet there was a firmness in the mouth and delicate prominence of the chin which might indicate that in times of trouble and danger the little maid would prove to be no unworthy descendant of the Roundhead soldier and Puritan magistrate. I doubt not that where more loud-tongued and assertive dames might be cowed, the Mayor's soft-voiced daughter would begin to cast off her gentler disposition, and to show the stronger nature which underlay it. It amused me much to listen to the efforts which Sir Gervas made to converse with her, for the damsel and he lived so entirely in two different worlds, that it took all his gallantry and ready wit to keep on ground which would be intelligible to her.

" No doubt you spend much of your time in reading, Mistress Ruth," he remarked. " It puzzles me to think what else you can do so far from town ? "

" Town ! " said she in surprise. " What is Taunton but a town ? "

" Heaven forbid that I should deny it," replied Sir Gervas, " more especially in the presence of so many worthy burghers, who have the name of being somewhat jealous of the honour of their native city. Yet the fact remains, fair mistress, that the town of London so far transcends all other towns that it is called, even as I called it just now, *the* town."

" Is it so very large, then ? " she cried, with pretty wonder. " But new houses are building in Taunton, outside the old walls, and beyond Shuttern, and some even at the other side of the river. Perhaps in time it may be as large."

" If all the folks in Taunton were to be added to London," said Sir Gervas, " no one there would observe that there had been any increase."

" Nay, there you are laughing at me. That is against all reason," cried the country maiden.

" Your grandfather will bear out my words," said Sir Gervas. " But to return to your reading, I'll warrant

that there is not a page of Scudéry and her *Grand Cyprus*
which you have not read. You are familiar, doubtless,
with every sentiment in Cowley, or Waller, or Dryden ? ''

" Who are these ? " she asked. " At what church do
they preach ? "

" Faith ! " cried the baronet, with a laugh, " honest
John preaches at the church of Will Unwin, commonly
known as Will's, where many a time it is two in the morning before he comes to the end of his sermon. But why
this question ? Do you think that no one may put pen
to paper unless they have also a right to wear a gown
and climb up to a pulpit ? I had thought that all of your
sex had read Dryden. Pray, what are your own favourite
books ? "

" There is Alleine's *Alarm to the Unconverted*," said
she. " It is a stirring work, and one which hath wrought
much good. Hast thou not found it to fructify within
thee ? "

" I have not read the book you name," Sir Gervas
confessed.

" Not read it ? " she cried, with raised eyebrows.
" Truly I had thought that everyone had read the
Alarm. What dost thou think, then, of *Faithful Con-
tendings* ? "

" I have not read it."

" Or of Baxter's Sermons ? " she asked.

" I have not read them."

" Of Bull's *Spirit Cordial*, then ? "

" I have not read it."

Mistress Ruth Timewell stared at him in undisguised
wonder. " You may think me ill-bred to say it, sir,"
she remarked, " but I cannot but marvel where you have
been, or what you have done all your life. Why, the very
children in the street have read these books."

" In truth, such works come little in our way in
London," Sir Gervas answered. " A play of George
Etherege's, or a jingle of Sir John Suckling's is lighter,
though mayhap less wholesome food for the mind. A

man in London may keep pace with the world of letters without much reading, for what with the gossip of the coffee-houses and the news-letters that fall in his way, and the babble of poets or wits at the assemblies, with mayhap an evening or two in the week at the playhouse, with Vanbrugh or Farquhar, one can never part company for long with the muses. Then, after the play, if a man is in no humour for a turn of luck at the green table at the Groom Porter's, he may stroll down to the Coca Tree if he be a Tory, or to St. James's if he be a Whig, and it is ten to one if the talk turn not upon the turning of alcaics, or the contest between blank verse or rhyme. Then one may, after an arrière supper, drop into Will's or Slaughter's and find Old John, with Tickell and Congreve and the rest of them, hard at work on the dramatic unities, or poetical justice, or some such matter. I confess that my own tastes lay little in that line, for about that hour I was likely to be worse employed with wine-flask, dice-box or——"

" Hem ! hem ! " cried I warningly, for several of the Puritans were listening with faces which expressed anything but approval.

" What you say of London is of much interest to me," said the Puritan maiden, " though these names and places have little meaning to my ignorant ears. You did speak, however, of the playhouse. Surely no worthy man goes near those sinks of iniquity, the baited traps of the Evil One ? Has not the good and sanctified Master Bull declared from the pulpit that they are the gathering-place of the froward, the chosen haunts of the perverse Assyrians, as dangerous to the soul as any of those Papal steeple-houses wherein the creature is sacrilegiously confounded with the Creator ? "

" Well and truly spoken, Mistress Timewell," cried the lean young Puritan upon the right, who had been an attentive listener to the whole conversation. " There is more evil in such houses than ever in the cities of the plain. I doubt not that the wrath of the Lord will

descend upon them, and destroy them, and wreck them utterly, together with the dissolute men and abandoned women who frequent them."

" Your strong opinions, friend," said Sir Gervas quietly, " are borne out doubtless by your full knowledge of the subject. How often, prithee, have you been in these playhouses which you are so ready to decry ? "

" I thank the Lord that I have never been so far tempted from the straight path as to set foot within one," the Puritan answered, " nor have I ever been in that great sewer which is called London. I trust, however, that I with others of the faithful may find our way thither with our tucks at our sides ere this business is finished, when we shall not be content, I'll warrant, with shutting these homes of vice, as Cromwell did, but we shall not leave one stone upon another, and shall sow the spot with salt, that it may be a hissing and a byword amongst the people."

" You are right, John Derrick," said the Mayor, who had overheard the latter part of his remarks. " Yet methinks that a lower tone and a more backward manner would become you better when you are speaking with your master's guests. Touching these same playhouses, Colonel, when we have carried the upper hand this time, we shall not allow the old tares to check the new wheat. We know what fruit these places have borne in the days of Charles, the Gwynnes, the Palmers and the whole base crew of foul lecherous parasites. Have you ever been in London, Captain Clarke ? "

" Nay, sir ; I am country born and bred."

" The better man you," said our host. " I have been there twice. The first time was in the days of the Rump, when Lambert brought in his division to overawe the Commons. I was then quartered at the sign of the Four Crosses in Southwark, then kept by a worthy man, one John Dolman, with whom I had much edifying speech concerning predestination. All was quiet and sober then, I promise you, and you might have walked from West-

minster to the Tower in the dead of the night without hearing aught save the murmur of prayer and the chanting of hymns. Not a ruffler or a wench was in the streets after dark, nor anyone save staid citizens upon their business, or the halberdiers of the watch. The second visit which I made was over this business of the levelling of the ramparts, when I and neighbour Foster, the glover, were sent at the head of a deputation from this town to the Privy Council of Charles. Who could have credited that a few years would have made such a change ? Every evil thing that had been stamped underground had spawned and festered until its vermin brood flooded the streets, and the godly were themselves driven to shun the light of day. Apollyon had indeed triumphed for awhile. A quiet man could not walk the highways without being elbowed into the kennel by swaggering swashbucklers, or accosted by painted hussies. Padders and michers, laced cloaks, jingling spurs, slashed boots, tall plumes, bullies and pimps, oaths and blasphemies—I promise you hell was waxing fat. Even in the solitude of one's coach one was not free from the robber."

" How that, sir ? " asked Reuben.

" Why, marry, in this wise. As I was the sufferer I have best right to tell the tale. Ye must know that after our reception—which was cold enough, for we were about as welcome to the Privy Council as the hearth-tax man is to the village housewife—we were asked, more as I guess from derision than from courtesy, to the evening levée at Buckingham Palace. We would both fain have been excused from going, but we feared that our refusal might give undue offence, and so hinder the success of our mission. My homespun garments were somewhat rough for such an occasion, yet I determined to appear in them, with the addition of a new black baize waistcoat faced with silk, and a good periwig, for which I gave three pounds ten shillings in the Haymarket."

The young Puritan opposite turned up his eyes and murmured something about " sacrificing to Dagon,"

which fortunately for him was inaudible to the high-spirited old man.

" It was but a worldly vanity," quoth the Mayor ; " for, with all deference, Sir Gervas Jerome, a man's own hair arranged with some taste, and with perhaps a sprinkling of powder, is to my mind the fittest ornament to his head. It is the contents and not the case which availeth. Having donned this frippery, good Master Foster and I hired a calash and drove to the Palace. We were deep in grave and, I trust, profitable converse speeding through the endless streets, when of a sudden I felt a sharp tug at my head, and my hat fluttered down on to my knees. I raised my hands, and lo ! they came upon my bare pate. The wig had vanished. We were rolling down Fleet Street at the moment, and there was no one in the calash save neighbour Foster, who sat as astounded as I. We looked high and low, on the seats and beneath them, but not a sign of the periwig was there. It was gone utterly and without a trace."

" Whither then ? " we asked with one voice.

" That was the question which we set ourselves to solve. For a moment I do assure ye that we bethought us that it might be a judgment upon us for our attention to such carnal follies. Then it crossed my mind that it might be the doing of some malicious sprite, as the Drummer of Tedworth, or those who occasioned the disturbances no very long time since at the old Gast House at Little Burton here in Somersetshire.[1] With this thought we hallooed to the coachman, and told him what had occurred to us. The fellow came down from his perch, and having heard our story, he burst straightway into much foul language, and walking round to the back of his calash, showed us that a slit had been made in the leather wherewith it was fashioned. Through this the thief had thrust his hand and had drawn my wig through the hole, resting the while on the crossbar of the coach. It was no uncommon thing, he said, and the

[1] Note F, Appendix.—Disturbances in the Little Gast House.

wig-snatchers were a numerous body who waited beside the peruke-makers' shops, and when they saw a customer come forth with a purchase which was worth their pains they would follow him, and, should he chance to drive, deprive him of it in this fashion. Be that as it may, I never saw my wig again, and had to purchase another before I could venture into the royal presence."

" A strange adventure truly," exclaimed Saxon. " How fared it with you for the remainder of the evening ? "

" But scurvily, for Charles's face, which was black enough at all times, was blackest of all to us ; nor was his brother the Papist more complaisant. They had but brought us there that they might dazzle us with their glitter and gee-gaws, in order that we might bear a fine report of them back to the West with us. There were supple-backed courtiers, and strutting nobles, and hussies with their shoulders bare, who should for all their high birth have been sent to Bridewell as readily as any poor girl who ever walked at the cart's tail. Then there were the gentlemen of the chamber, with cinnamon and plum-coloured coats, and a brave show of gold lace and silk and ostrich feather. Neighbour Foster and I felt as two crows might do who have wandered among the peacocks. Yet we bare in mind in whose image we were fashioned, and we carried ourselves, I trust, as independent English burghers. His Grace of Buckingham had his flout at us, and Rochester sneered, and the women simpered ; but we stood four square, my friend and I, discussing, as I well remember, the most precious doctrines of election and reprobation, without giving much heed either to those who mocked us, or to the gamesters upon our left, or to the dancers upon our right. So we stood throughout the evening, until, finding that they could get little sport from us, my Lord Clarendon, the Chancellor, gave us the word to retire, which we did at our leisure after saluting the King and the company."

" Nay, that I should never have done ! " cried the young Puritan, who had listened intently to his elder's narrative.

" Would it not have been more fitting to have raised up your hands and called down vengeance upon them, as the holy man of old did upon the wicked cities ? "

" More fitting, quotha ! " said the Mayor impatiently. " It is most fitting that youth should be silent until his opinion is asked on such matters. God's wrath comes with leaden feet, but it strikes with iron hands. In His own good time He has judged when the cup of these men's iniquities is overflowing. It is not for us to instruct Him. Curses have, as the wise man said, a habit of coming home to roost. Bear that in mind, Master John Derrick, and be not too liberal with them."

The young apprentice, for such he was, bowed his head sullenly to the rebuke, whilst the Mayor, after a short pause, resumed his story.

" Being a fine night," said he, " we chose to walk back to our lodgings ; but never shall I forget the wicked scenes wherewith we were encountered on the way. Good Master Bunyan, of Elstow, might have added some pages to his account of Vanity Fair had he been with us. The women, be-patched, be-ruddled and brazen ; the men swaggering, roistering, cursing—the brawling, the drabbing and the drunkenness ! It was a fit kingdom to be ruled over by such a court. At last we had made our way to more quiet streets, and were hoping that our adventures were at an end, when of a sudden there came a rush of half-drunken cavaliers from a side street, who set upon the passers-by with their swords, as though we had fallen into an ambuscade of savages in some Paynim country. They were, as I surmise, of the same breed as those of whom the excellent John Milton wrote : ' The sons of Belial, flown with insolence and wine.' Alas ! my memory is not what it was, for at one time I could say by rote whole books of that noble and godly poem."

" And pray, how fared ye with these rufflers, sir ? " I asked.

" They beset us, and some few other honest citizens who were wending their ways homewards, and waving

their naked swords they called upon us to lay down our arms and pay homage. ' To whom ? ' I asked. They pointed to one of their number who was more gaudily dressed and somewhat drunker than the rest. ' This is our most sovereign liege,' they cried. ' Sovereign over whom ? ' I asked. ' Over the Tityre Tus,' they answered. ' Oh, most barbarous and cuckoldy citizen, do you not recognise that you have fallen into the hands of that most noble order ? ' ' This is not your real monarch,' said I, ' for he is down beneath us chained in the pit, where some day he will gather his dutiful subjects around him.' ' Lo, he hath spoken treason ! ' they cried, on which, without much more ado, they set upon us with sword and dagger. Neighbour Foster and I placed our backs against a wall, and with our cloaks round our left arms we made play with our tucks, and managed to put in one or two of the old Wigan Lane raspers. In particular, friend Foster pinked the King in such wise that his Majesty ran howling down the street like a gored bull-pup. We were beset by numbers, however, and might have ended our mission then and there had not the watch appeared upon the scene, struck up our weapons with their halberds, and so arrested the whole party. Whilst the fray lasted the burghers from the adjoining houses were pouring water upon us, as though we were cats on the tiles, which, though it did not cool our ardour in the fight, left us in a scurvy and unsavoury condition. In this guise we were dragged to the round-house, where we spent the night amidst bullies, thieves and orange wenches, to whom I am proud to say that both neighbour Foster and myself spoke some words of joy and comfort. In the morning we were released, and forthwith shook the dust of London from our feet ; nor do I ever wish to return thither, unless it be at the head of our Somersetshire regiments, to see King Monmouth don the crown which he had wrested in fair fight from the Popish perverter."

As Master Stephen Timewell ended his tale a general shuffling and rising announced the conclusion of the meal.

The company filed slowly out in order of seniority, all wearing the same gloomy and earnest expression, with grave gait and downcast eyes. These Puritan ways were, it is true, familiar to me from childhood, yet I had never before seen a large household conforming to them, or marked their effect upon so many young men.

" You shall bide behind for a while," said the Mayor, as we were about to follow the others. " William, do you bring a flask of the old green-sealed sack. These creature comforts I do not produce before my lads, for beef and honest malt is the fittest food for such. On occasion, however, I am of Paul's opinion, that a flagon of wine among friends is no bad thing for mind or for body. You can away now, sweetheart, if you have aught to engage you."

" Do you go out again ? " asked Mistress Ruth.

" Presently, to the town-hall. The survey of arms is not yet complete."

" I shall have your robes ready, and also the rooms of our guests," she answered, and so, with a bright smile to us, tripped away upon her duty.

" I would that I could order our town as that maiden orders this house," said the Mayor. " There is not a want that is not supplied before it is felt. She reads my thoughts and acts upon them ere my lips have time to form them. If I have still strength to spend in the public service, it is because my private life is full of restful peace. Do not fear the sack, sirs. It cometh from Brooke and Hellier's of Abchurch Lane, and may be relied upon."

" Which showeth that one good thing cometh out of London," remarked Sir Gervas.

" Aye, truly," said the old man, smiling. " But what think ye of my young men, sir ? They must needs be of a very different class to any with whom you are acquainted, if, as I understand, you have frequented court circles."

" Why, marry, they are good enough young men, no doubt," Sir Gervas answered lightly. " Methinks, how-

ever, that there is a want of sap about them. It is not blood, but sour butter-milk that flows in their veins."

" Nay, nay," the Mayor responded warmly. " There you do them an injustice. Their passions and feelings are under control, as the skilful rider keeps his horse in hand ; but they are as surely there as is the speed and endurance of the animal. Did you observe the godly youth who sat upon your right, whom I had occasion to reprove more than once for over-zeal ? He is a fit example of how a man may take the upper hand of his feelings, and keep them in control."

" And how has he done so ? " I asked.

" Why, between friends," quoth the Mayor, " it was but last Lady-day that he asked the hand of my grand-daughter Ruth in marriage. His time is nearly served, and his father, Sam Derrick, is an honourable craftsman, so that the match would have been no unfitting one. The maiden turned against him, however—young girls will have their fancies—and the matter came to an end. Yet here he dwells under the same roof-tree, at her elbow from morn to night, with never a sign of that passion which can scarce have died out so soon. Twice my wool warehouse hath been nigh burned to the ground since then, and twice he hath headed those who fought the flames. There are not many whose suit hath been rejected who would bear themselves in so resigned and patient a fashion."

" I am prepared to find that your judgment is the correct one," said Sir Gervas Jerome. " I have learned to distrust too hasty dislikes, and bear in mind that couplet of John Dryden—

' Errors, like straws, upon the surface flow.
He who would search for pearls must dive below.' "

" Or worthy Dr. Samuel Butler," said Saxon, " who, in his immortal poem of *Hudibras*, says—

' The fool can only see the skin :
The wise man tries to peep within.' "

" I wonder, Colonel Saxon," said our host severely, " that you should speak favourably of that licentious poem, which is composed, as I have heard, for the sole purpose of casting ridicule upon the godly. I should as soon have expected to hear you praise the wicked and foolish work of Hobbes, with his mischievous thesis, *A Deo rex, a rege lex.*"

" It is true that I contemn and despise the use which Butler hath made of his satire," said Saxon adroitly ; " yet I may admire the satire itself, just as one may admire a damascened blade without approving of the quarrel in which it is drawn."

" These distinctions are, I fear, too subtle for my old brain," said the stout old Puritan. " This England of ours is divided into two camps, that of God and that of Antichrist. He who is not with us is against us, nor shall any who serve under the devil's banner have anything from me save my scorn and the sharp edge of my sword."

" Well, well," said Saxon, filling up his glass, " I am no Laodicean or time-server. The cause shall not find me wanting with tongue or with sword."

" Of that I am well convinced, my worthy friend," the Mayor answered, " and if I have spoken over sharply you will hold me excused. But I regret to have evil tidings to announce to you. I have not told the commonalty lest it cast them down, but I know that adversity will be but the whet-stone to give your ardour a finer edge. Argyle's rising has failed, and he and his companions are prisoners in the hands of the man who never knew what pity was."

We all started in our chairs at this, and looked at one another aghast, save only Sir Gervas Jerome, whose natural serenity was, I am well convinced, proof against any disturbance. For you may remember, my children, that I stated when I first took it in hand to narrate to you these passages of my life, that the hopes of Monmouth's party rested very much upon the raid which Argyle and the Scottish exiles had made upon Ayrshire, where it was hoped that they would create such a disturbance as

would divert a good share of King James's forces, and so make our march to London less difficult. This was the more confidently expected since Argyle's own estates lay upon that side of Scotland, where he could raise five thousand swordsmen among his own clansmen. The western counties abounded, too, in fierce zealots who were ready to assert the cause of the Covenant, and who had proved themselves in many a skirmish to be valiant warriors. With the help of the Highlanders and of the Covenanters it seemed certain that Argyle would be able to hold his own, the more so since he took with him to Scotland the English Puritan Rumbold, and many others skilled in warfare. This sudden news of his total defeat and downfall was therefore a heavy blow, since it turned the whole forces of the Government upon ourselves.

" Have you the news from a trusty source ? " asked Decimus Saxon, after a long silence.

" It is beyond all doubt or question," Master Stephen Timewell answered. " Yet I can well understand your surprise, for the Duke had trusty councillors with him. There was Sir Patrick Hume of Polwarth——"

" All talk and no fight," said Saxon.

" And Richard Rumbold."

" All fight and no talk," quoth our companion. " He should, methinks, have rendered a better account of himself."

" Then there was Major Elphinstone."

" A bragging fool ! " cried Saxon.

" And Sir John Cochrane."

" A captious, long-tongued, short-witted sluggard," said the soldier of fortune. " The expedition was doomed from the first with such men at its head. Yet I had thought that could they have done nought else, they might at least have flung themselves into the mountain country, where these bare-legged caterans could have held their own amid their native clouds and mists. All taken, you say ! It is a lesson and a warning to us. I tell you that

unless Monmouth infuses more energy into his councils, and thrusts straight for the heart instead of fencing and foining at the extremities, we shall find ourselves as Argyle and Rumbold. What mean these two days wasted at Axminster at a time when every hour is of import ? Is he, every time that he brushes a party of militia aside, to stop forty-eight hours and chant ' Te Deums ' when Churchill and Feversham are, as I know, pushing for the West with every available man, and the Dutch grenadiers are swarming over like rats into a granary ? "

" You are very right, Colonel Saxon," the Mayor answered. " And I trust that when the King comes here we may stir him up to more prompt action. He has much need of more soldierly advisers, for since Fletcher hath gone there is hardly a man about him who hath been trained to arms."

" Well," said Saxon moodily, " now that Argyle hath gone under we are face to face with James, with nothing but our own good swords to trust to."

" To them and to the justice of our cause. How like ye the news, young sirs ? Has the wine lost its smack on account of it ? Are ye disposed to flinch from the standard of the Lord ? "

" For my own part I shall see the matter through," said I.

" And I shall bide where Micah Clarke bides," quoth Reuben Lockarby.

" And to me," said Sir Gervas, " it is a matter of indifference, so long as I am in good company and there is something stirring."

" In that case," said the Mayor, " we had best each turn to his own work, and have all ready for the King's arrival. Until then I trust that ye will honour my humble roof."

" I fear that I cannot accept your kindness," Saxon answered. " When I am in harness I come and go early and late. I shall therefore take up my quarters in the inn, which is not very well furnished with victual, and yet can

supply me with the simple fare which, with a black Jack of October and a pipe of Trinidado, is all I require."

As Saxon was firm in this resolution the Mayor forbore to press it upon him, but my two friends gladly joined with me in accepting the worthy wool-worker's offer, and took up our quarters for the time under his hospitable roof.

19. *Of a Brawl in the Night*

DECIMUS SAXON refused to avail himself of Master Timewell's house and table for the reason, as I afterwards learned, that, the Mayor being a firm Presbyterian, he thought it might stand him in ill stead with the Independents and other zealots were he to allow too great an intimacy to spring up between them. Indeed, my dears, from this time onward this cunning man framed his whole life and actions in such a way as to make friends of the sectaries, and to cause them to look upon him as their leader. For he had a firm belief that in all such outbreaks as that in which we were engaged, the most extreme party is sure in the end to gain the upper hand. " Fanatics," he said to me one day, " mean fervour, and fervour means hard work, and hard work means power." That was the centre point of all his plotting and scheming.

And first of all he set himself to show how excellent a soldier he was, and he spared neither time nor work to make this apparent. From morn till midday, and from afternoon till night, we drilled and drilled until in very truth the shouting of the orders and the clatter of the arms became wearisome to our ears. The good burghers may well have thought that Colonel Saxon's Wiltshire foot were as much part of the market-place as the town cross or the parish stocks. There was much to be done in very little time, so much that many would have thought it hopeless to attempt it. Not only was there the general muster of the regiment, but we had each to practise our

own companies in their several drills, and to learn as best we could the names and the wants of the men. Yet our work was made easier to us by the assurance that it was not thrown away, for at every gathering our bumpkins stood more erect, and handled their weapons more deftly. From cock-crow to sun-down the streets resounded with " Poise your muskets ! Order your muskets ! Rest your muskets ! Handle your primers ! " and all the other orders of the old manual exercise.

As we became more soldierly we increased in numbers, for our smart appearance drew the pick of the new-comers into our ranks. My own company swelled until it had to be divided, and the others enlarged in proportion. The baronet's musqueteers mustered a full hundred, skilled for the most part in the use of the gun. Altogether we sprang from three hundred to four hundred and fifty, and our drill improved until we received praise from all sides on the state of our men.

Late in the evening I was riding slowly back to the house of Master Timewell when Reuben clattered after me, and besought me to turn back with him to see a note-worthy sight. Though feeling little in the mood for such things, I turned Covenant and rode with him down the length of High Street, and into the suburb which is known as Shuttern, where my companion pulled up at a bare barn-like building, and bade me look in through the window.

The interior, which consisted of a single great hall, the empty warehouse in which wool had used to be stored, was all alight with lamps and candles. A great throng of men, whom I recognised as belonging to my own company, or that of my companion, lay about on either side, some smoking, some praying, and some burnishing their arms. Down the middle a line of benches had been drawn up, on which there were seated astraddle the whole hundred of the baronet's musqueteers, each engaged in plaiting into a queue the hair of the man who sat in front of him. A boy walked up and down with a pot of grease,

by the aid of which with some whipcord the work was going forward merrily. Sir Gervas himself with a great flour dredger sat perched upon a bale of wool at the head of the line, and as quickly as any queue was finished he examined it through his quizzing glass, and if it found favour in his eyes, daintily powdered it from his dredger, with as much care and reverence as though it were some service of the Church. No cook seasoning a dish could have added his spices with more nicety of judgment than our friend displayed in whitening the pates of his company. Glancing up from his labours he saw our two smiling faces looking in at him through the window, but his work was too engrossing to allow him to leave it, and we rode off at last without having speech with him.

By this time the town was very quiet and still, for the folk in those parts were early bed-goers, save when some special occasion kept them afoot. We rode slowly together through the silent streets, our horses' hoofs ringing out sharp against the cobble stones, talking about such light matters as engage the mind of youth. The moon was shining very brightly above us, silvering the broad streets, and casting a fretwork of shadows from the peaks and pinnacles of the churches. At Master Timewell's courtyard I sprang from my saddle, but Reuben, attracted by the peace and beauty of the scene, rode onwards with the intention of going as far as the town gate.

I was still at work upon my girth buckles, undoing my harness, when of a sudden there came from the street a shouting and a rushing, with the clinking of blades, and my comrade's voice calling upon me for help. Drawing my sword I ran out. Some little way down there was a clear space, white with the moonshine, in the centre of which I caught a glimpse of the sturdy figure of my friend springing about with an activity for which I had never given him credit, and exchanging sword thrusts with three or four men who were pressing him closely. On the ground there lay a dark figure, and behind the struggling group Reuben's mare reared and plunged in sympathy

with her master's peril. As I rushed down, shouting and waving my sword, the assailants took flight down a side street, save one, a tall sinewy swordsman, who rushed in upon Reuben, stabbing furiously at him, and cursing him the while for a spoil-sport. To my horror I saw, as I ran, the fellow's blade slip inside my friend's guard, who threw up his arms and fell prostrate, while the other with a final thrust dashed off down one of the narrow winding lanes which led from East Street to the banks of the Tone.

" For Heaven's sake where are you hurt ? " I cried, throwing myself upon my knees beside his prostrate body. " Where is your injury, Reuben ? "

" In the wind, mostly," quoth he, blowing like a smithy bellows ; " likewise on the back of my pate. Give me your hand, I pray."

" And are you indeed scathless ? " I cried, with a great lightening of the heart as I helped him to his feet. " I thought that the villain had stabbed you."

" As well stab a Warsash crab with a bodkin," said he. " Thanks to good Sir Jacob Clancing, once of Snellaby Hall and now of Salisbury Plain, their rapiers did no more than scratch my plate of proof. But how is it with the maid ? "

" The maid ? " said I.

" Aye, it was to save her that I drew. She was beset by these night walkers. See, she rises ! They threw her down when I set upon them."

" How is it with you, mistress ? " I asked ; for the prostrate figure had arisen and taken the form of a woman, young and graceful to all appearance, with her face muffled in a mantle. " I trust that you have met with no hurt."

" None, sir," she answered, in a low, sweet voice, " but that I have escaped is due to the ready valour of your friend, and the guiding wisdom of Him who confutes the plots of the wicked. Doubtless a true man would have rendered this help to any damsel in distress, and yet it may add to your satisfaction to know that she whom you

have served is no stranger to you." With these words she dropped her mantle and turned her face towards us in the moonlight.

"Good lack! it is Mistress Timewell!" I cried, in amazement.

"Let us homewards," she said, in firm, quick tones. "The neighbours are alarmed, and there will be a rabble collected anon. Let us escape from the babblement."

Windows had indeed begun to clatter up in every direction, and loud voices to demand what was amiss. Far away down the street we could see the glint of lanthorns swinging to and fro as the watch hurried thitherwards. We slipped along in the shadow, however, and found ourselves safe within the Mayor's courtyard, without let or hindrance.

"I trust, sir, that you have really met with no hurt," said the maiden to my companion.

Reuben had said not a word since she had uncovered her face, and bore the face of a man who finds himself in some pleasant dream and is vexed only by the fear lest he wake up from it. "Nay, I am not hurt," he answered, "but I would that you could tell us who these roving blades may be, and where they may be found."

"Nay, nay," said she, with uplifted finger, "you shall not follow the matter further. As to the men, I cannot say with certainty who they may have been. I had gone forth to visit Dame Clatworthy, who hath the tertian ague, and they did beset me on my return. Perchance they are some who are not of my grandfather's way of thinking in affairs of State, and who struck at him through me. But ye have both been so kind that ye will not refuse me one other favour which I shall ask ye?"

We protested that we could not, with our hands upon our sword-hilts.

"Nay, keep them for the Lord's quarrel," said she, smiling at the action. "All that I ask is that ye will say nothing of this matter to my grandsire. He is choleric, and a little matter doth set him in a flame, so old as he is.

I would not have his mind turned from the public needs to a private trifle of this sort. Have I your promises ? "

" Mine," said I, bowing.

" And mine," said Lockarby.

" Thanks, good friends. Alack ! I have dropped my gauntlet in the street. But it is of no import. I thank God that no harm has come to anyone. My thanks once more, and may pleasant dreams await ye." She sprang up the steps and was gone in an instant.

Reuben and I unharnessed our horses and saw them cared for in silence. We then entered the house and ascended to our chambers, still without a word. Outside his room door my friend paused.

" I have heard that long man's voice before, Micah," said he.

" And so have I," I answered. " The old man must beware of his 'prentices. I have half a mind to go back for the little maiden's gauntlet."

A merry twinkle shot through the cloud which had gathered on Reuben's brow. He opened his left hand and showed me the doe-skin glove crumpled up in his palm.

" I would not barter it for all the gold in her grandsire's coffers," said he, with a sudden outflame, and then half-laughing, half-blushing at his own heat, he whisked in and left me to my thoughts.

And so I learned for the first time, my dears, that my good comrade had been struck by the little god's arrows. When a man's years number one score, love springs up in him, as the gourd grew in the Scriptures, in a single night. I have told my story ill if I have not made you understand that my friend was a frank, warm-hearted lad of impulse, whose reason seldom stood sentry over his inclinations. Such a man can no more draw away from a winning maid than the needle can shun the magnet. He loves as the mavis sings or the kitten plays. Now, a slow-witted, heavy fellow like myself, in whose veins the blood has always flowed somewhat coolly and temperately, may go

into love as a horse goes into a shelving stream, step by step, but a man like Reuben is kicking his heels upon the bank one moment, and is over ears in the deepest pool the next.

Heaven only knows what match it was that had set the tow alight. I can but say that from that day on my comrade was sad and cloudy one hour, gay and blithesome the next. His even flow of good spirits had deserted him, and he became as dismal as a moulting chicken, which has ever seemed to me to be one of the strangest outcomes of what poets have called the joyous state of love. But, indeed, pain and pleasure are so very nearly akin in this world, that it is as if they were tethered in neighbouring stalls, and a kick would at any time bring down the partition. Here is a man who is as full of sighs as a grenade is of powder, his face is sad, his brow is downcast, his wits are wandering ; yet if you remark to him that it is an ill thing that he should be in this state, he will answer you, as like as not, that he would not exchange it for all the powers and principalities. Tears to him are golden, and laughter is but base coin. Well, my dears, it is useless for me to expound to you that which I cannot myself understand. If, as I have heard, it is impossible to get the thumb-marks of any two men to be alike, how can we expect their inmost thoughts and feelings to tally ? Yet this I can say with all truth, that when I asked your grandmother's hand I did not demean myself as if I were chief mourner at a funeral. She will bear me out that I walked up to her with a smile upon my face, though mayhap there was a little flutter at my heart, and I took her hand and I said—but, lack-a-day, whither have I wandered ? What has all this to do with Taunton town and the rising of 1685 ?

On the night of Wednesday, June 17, we learned that the King, as Monmouth was called throughout the West, was lying less than ten miles off with his forces, and that he would make his entry into the loyal town of Taunton the next morning. Every effort was made, as ye may well

guess, to give him a welcome which should be worthy of the most Whiggish and Protestant town in England. An arch of evergreens had already been built up at the western gate, bearing the motto, " Welcome to King Monmouth ! " and another spanned the entrance to the market-place from the upper window of the White Hart Inn, with " Hail to the Protestant Chief ! " in great scarlet letters. A third, if I remember right, bridged the entrance to the Castle yard, but the motto on it has escaped me. The cloth and wool industry is, as I have told you, the staple trade of the town, and the merchants had no mercy on their wares, but used them freely to beautify the streets. Rich tapestries, glossy velvets and costly brocades fluttered from the windows or lined the balconies. East Street, High Street and Fore Street were draped from garret to basement with rare and beautiful fabrics, while gay flags hung from the roofs on either side, or fluttered in long festoons from house to house. The royal banner of England floated from the lofty tower of St. Mary Magdalene, while the blue ensign of Monmouth waved from the sister turret of St. James. Late into the night there was planning and hammering, working and devising, until when the sun rose upon Thursday, June 18, it shone on as brave a show of bunting and evergreen as ever graced a town. Taunton had changed as by magic from a city into a flower garden.

Master Stephen Timewell had busied himself in these preparations, but he had borne in mind at the same time that the most welcome sight which he could present to Monmouth's eyes was the large body of armed men who were prepared to follow his fortunes. There were sixteen hundred in the town, two hundred of which were horse, mostly well armed and equipped. These were disposed in such a way that the King should pass them in his progress. The townsmen lined the market-place three deep from the Castle gate to the entrance to the High Street ; from thence to Shuttern, Dorsetshire and Frome peasants were drawn up on either side of the street ;

while our own regiment was stationed at the western
gate. With arms well burnished, serried ranks and fresh
sprigs of green in every bonnet, no leader could desire a
better addition to his army. When all were in their
places, and the burghers and their wives had arrayed
themselves in their holiday gear, with gladsome faces and
baskets of new-cut flowers, all was ready for the royal
visitor's reception.

"My orders are," said Saxon, riding up to us as we
sat our horses beside our companions, "that I and my
captains should fall in with the King's escort as he passes,
and so accompany him to the market-place. Your men
shall present arms, and shall then stand their ground
until we return."

We all three drew our swords and saluted.

"If ye will come with me, gentlemen, and take position
to the right of the gate here," said he, "I may be able to
tell ye something of these folk as they pass. Thirty
years of war in many climes should give me the master
craftsman's right to expound to his apprentices."

We all very gladly followed his advice, and passed out
through the gate, which was now nothing more than a
broad gap amongst the mounds which marked the lines
of the old walls. "There is no sign of them yet," I
remarked, as we pulled up upon a convenient hillock.
"I suppose that they must come by this road which winds
through the valley before us."

"There are two sorts of bad general," quoth Saxon,
"the man who is too fast and the man who is too slow.
His Majesty's advisers will never be accused of the former
failing, whatever other mistakes they may fall into. There
was old Marshal Grunberg, with whom I did twenty-six
months' soldiering in Bohemia. He would fly through
the country pell-mell, horse, foot and artillery, as if the
devil were at his heels. He might make fifty blunders,
but the enemy had never time to take advantage. I call
to mind a raid which we made into Silesia, when, after two
days or so of mountain roads, his Oberhauptmann of the

staff told him that it was impossible for the artillery to
keep up. ' Lass es hinter ! ' says he. So the guns were
left, and by the evening of the next day the foot were
dead-beat. ' They cannot walk another mile ! ' says the
Oberhauptmann. ' Lassen Sie hinter ! ' says he. So on
we went with the horse—I was in his Pandour regiment,
worse luck ! But after a skirmish or two, what with the
roads and what with the enemy, our horses were foundered
and useless. ' The horses are used up ! ' says the Ober-
hauptmann. ' Lassen Sie hinter ! ' he cries ; and I
warrant that he would have pushed on to Prague with his
staff, had they allowed him. ' General Hinterlassen ' we
called him after that."

" A dashing commander, too," cried Sir Gervas. " I
would fain have served under him."

" Aye, and he had a way of knocking his recruits into
shape which would scarce be relished by our good friends
here in the west country," said Saxon. " I remember
that after the leaguer of Salzburg, when we had taken
the castle or fortalice of that name, we were joined by
some thousand untrained foot, which had been raised in
Dalmatia in the Emperor's employ. As they approached
our lines with waving of hands and blowing of bugles, old
Marshal Hinterlassen discharged a volley of all the cannon
upon the walls at them, killing threescore and striking
great panic into the others. ' The rogues must get used
to standing fire sooner or later,' said he, ' so they may as
well commence their education at once.' "

" He was a rough schoolmaster," I remarked. " He
might have left that part of the drill to the enemy."

" Yet his soldiers loved him," said Saxon. " He was
not a man, when a city had been forced, to inquire into
every squawk of a woman, or give ear to every burgess who
chanced to find his strong-box a trifle the lighter. But as
to the slow commanders, I have known none to equal
Brigadier Baumgarten, also of the Imperial service. He
would break up his winter-quarters and sit down before
some place of strength, where he would raise a sconce

here, and sink a sap there, until his soldiers were sick of
the very sight of the place. So he would play with it, as
a cat with a mouse, until at last it was about to open its
gates, when, as like as not, he would raise the leaguer and
march back into his winter-quarters. I served two campaigns under him without honour, sack, plunder or
emolument, save a beggarly stipend of three gulden a day,
paid in clipped money, six months in arrear. But mark
ye the folk upon yonder tower! They are waving their
kerchiefs as though something were visible to them."

" I can see nothing," I answered, shading my eyes and
gazing down the tree-sprinkled valley which rose slowly
in green uplands to the grassy Blackdown hills.

" Those on the housetops are waving and pointing,"
said Reuben. " Methinks I can myself see the flash of
steel among yonder woods."

" There it is," cried Saxon, extending his gauntleted
hand, " on the western bank of the Tone, hard by the
wooden bridge. Follow my finger, Clarke, and see if you
cannot distinguish it."

" Yes, truly," I exclaimed, " I see a bright shimmer
coming and going. And there to the left, where the
road curves over the hill, mark you that dense mass of
men! Ha! the head of the column begins to emerge
from the trees."

There was not a cloud in the sky, but the great heat
had caused a haze to overlie the valley, gathering thickly
along the winding course of the river, and hanging in
little sprays and feathers over the woodlands which clothe
its banks. Through this filmy vapour there broke from
time to time fierce sparkles of brilliant light as the sun's
rays fell upon breastplate or headpiece. Now and again
the gentle summer breeze wafted up sudden pulses of
martial music to our ears, with the blare of trumpets and
the long deep snarl of the drums. As we gazed, the van
of the army began to roll out from the cover of the trees
and to darken the white dusty roads. The long line
slowly extended itself, writhing out of the forest land like

a dark snake with sparkling scales, until the whole rebel army—horse, foot and ordnance—were visible beneath us. The gleam of the weapons, the waving of numerous banners, the plumes of the leaders, and the deep columns of marching men, made up a picture which stirred the very hearts of the citizens, who, from the housetops and from the ruinous summit of the dismantled walls, were enabled to gaze down upon the champions of their faith. If the mere sight of a passing regiment will cause a thrill in your bosoms, you can fancy how it is when the soldiers upon whom you look are in actual arms for your own dearest and most cherished interests, and have just come out victorious from a bloody struggle. If every other man's hand was against us, these at last were on our side, and our hearts went out to them as to friends and brothers. Of all the ties that unite men in this world, that of a common danger is the strongest.

It all appeared to be most warlike and most imposing to my inexperienced eyes, and I thought as I looked at the long array that our cause was as good as won. To my surprise, however, Saxon pished and pshawed under his breath, until at last, unable to contain his impatience, he broke out in hot discontent.

" Do but look at that vanguard as they breast the slope," he cried. " Where is the advance party, or Vorreiter, as the Germans call them ? Where, too, is the space which should be left between the fore-guard and the main battle ? By the sword of Scanderbeg, they remind me more of a drove of pilgrims, as I have seen them approaching the shrine of St. Sebaldus of Nürnberg with their banners and streamers. There in the centre, amid that cavalcade of cavaliers, rides our new monarch doubtless. Pity he hath not a man by him who can put this swarm of peasants into something like campaign order. Now do but look at those four pieces of ordnance trailing along like lame sheep behind the flock. Caracco, I would that I were a young King's officer with a troop of light horse on the ridge yonder ! My faith, how I should sweep

down yon cross-road like a kestrel on a brood of young plover ! Then heh for cut and thrust, down with the skulking cannoniers, a carbine fire to cover us, round with the horses, and away go the rebel guns in a cloud of dust ! How's that, Sir Gervas ? "

" Good sport, Colonel," said the baronet, with a touch of colour in his white cheeks. " I warrant that you did keep your Pandours on the trot."

" Aye, the rogues had to work or hang—one or t'other. But methinks our friends here are scarce as numerous as reported. I reckon them to be a thousand horse, and mayhap five thousand two hundred foot. I have been thought a good tally-man on such occasions. With fifteen hundred in the town that would bring us to close on eight thousand men, which is no great force to invade a kingdom and dispute a crown."

" If the West can give eight thousand, how many can all the counties of England afford ? " I asked. " Is not that the fairer way to look at it ? "

" Monmouth's popularity lies mostly in the West," Saxon answered. " It was the memory of that which prompted him to raise his standard in these counties."

" His standards, rather," quoth Reuben. " Why, it looks as though they had hung their linen up to dry all down the line."

" True ! They have more ensigns than ever I saw with so small a force," Saxon answered, rising in his stirrups. " One or two are blue, and the rest, as far as I can see for the sun shining upon them, are white, with some motto or device."

Whilst we had been conversing, the body of horse which formed the vanguard of the Protestant army had approached within a quarter of a mile or less of the town, when a loud, clear bugle-call brought them to a halt. In each successive regiment or squadron the signal was repeated, so that the sound passed swiftly down the long array until it died away in the distance. As the coil of men formed up upon the white road, with just a tremulous

shifting motion along the curved and undulating line, its likeness to a giant serpent occurred again to my mind.

" I could fancy it a great boa," I remarked, " which was drawing its coils round the town."

" A rattlesnake, rather," said Reuben, pointing to the guns in the rear. " It keeps all its noise in its tail."

" Here comes its head, if I mistake not," quoth Saxon. " It were best perhaps that we stand at the side of the gate."

As he spoke a group of gaily dressed cavaliers broke away from the main body and rode straight for the town. Their leader was a tall, slim, elegant young man, who sat his horse with the grace of a skilled rider, and who was remarkable amongst those around him for the gallantry of his bearing and the richness of his trappings. As he galloped towards the gate a roar of welcome burst from the assembled multitude, which was taken up and prolonged by the crowds behind, who, though unable to see what was going forward, gathered from the shouting that the King was approaching.

20. *Of the Muster of the Men of the West*

MONMOUTH was at that time in his thirty-sixth year, and was remarkable for those superficial graces which please the multitude and fit a man to lead in a popular cause. He was young, well-spoken, witty and skilled in all martial and manly exercises. On his progress in the West he had not thought it beneath him to kiss the village maidens, to offer prizes at the rural sports, and to run races in his boots against the fleetest of the barefooted countrymen.[1] His nature was vain and prodigal, but he excelled in that showy magnificence and careless generosity which wins the hearts of the people. Both on the Continent and at Bothwell Bridge, in Scotland, he had led armies with success, and his kindness and

[1] Note G, Appendix.—Monmouth's Progress.

mercy to the Covenanters after his victory had caused him
to be as much esteemed amongst the Whigs as Dalzell
and Claverhouse were hated. As he reined up his beautiful black horse at the gate of the city, and raised his plumed
montero cap to the shouting crowd, the grace and dignity
of his bearing were such as might befit the knight-errant
in a Romance who is fighting at long odds for a crown
which a tyrant has filched from him.

He was reckoned well-favoured, but I cannot say that
I found him so. His face was, I thought, too long and
white for comeliness, yet his features were high and noble,
with well-marked nose and clear, searching eyes. In his
mouth might perchance be noticed some trace of that
weakness which marred his character, though the expression was sweet and amiable. He wore a dark purple
roquelaure, riding-jacket, faced and lapelled with gold
lace, through the open front of which shone a silver breastplate. A velvet suit of a lighter shade than the jacket, a
pair of high yellow Cordovan boots, with a gold-hilted
rapier on one side, and a poniard of Parma on the other,
each hung from the morocco-leather sword-belt, completed
his attire. A broad collar of Mechlin lace flowed over his
shoulders, while wristbands of the same costly material
dangled from his sleeves. Again and again he raised his
cap and bent to the saddle-bow in response to the storm
of cheering. " A Monmouth ! A Monmouth ! " cried
the people ; " Hail to the Protestant chief ! " " Long
live the noble King Monmouth ! " while from every
window, and roof, and balcony fluttering kerchief or
waving hat brightened the joyous scene. The rebel van
caught fire at the sight and raised a great deep-chested
shout, which was taken up again and again by the rest of
the army, until the whole countryside was sonorous.

In the meanwhile the city elders, headed by our friend
the Mayor, advanced from the gate in all the dignity of
silk and fur to pay homage to the King. Sinking upon
one knee by Monmouth's stirrup, he kissed the hand which
was graciously extended to him.

" Nay, good Master Mayor," said the King, in a clear, strong voice, " it is for my enemies to sink before me, and not for my friends. Prithee, what is this scroll which you do unroll ? "

" It is an address of welcome and of allegiance, your Majesty, from your loyal town of Taunton."

" I need no such address," said King Monmouth, looking round. " It is written all around me in fairer characters than ever found themselves upon parchment. My good friends have made me feel that I was welcome without the aid of clerk or scrivener. Your name, good Master Mayor, is Stephen Timewell, as I understand ? "

" The same, your Majesty."

" Too curt a name for so trusty a man," said the King, drawing his sword and touching him upon the shoulder with it. " I shall make it longer by three letters. Rise up, Sir Stephen, and may I find that there are many other knights in my dominions as loyal and as stout."

Amidst the huzzas which broke out afresh at this honour done to the town, the Mayor withdrew with the councilmen to the left side of the gate, whilst Monmouth with his staff gathered upon the right. At a signal a trumpeter blew a fanfare, the drums struck up a point of war, and the insurgent army, with serried ranks and waving banners, resumed its advance upon the town. As it approached, Saxon pointed out to us the various leaders and men of note who surrounded the King, giving us their names and some few words as to their characters.

" That is Lord Grey of Wark," said he ; " the little middle-aged lean man at the King's bridle-arm. He hath been in the Tower once for treason. 'Twas he who fled with the Lady Henrietta Berkeley, his wife's sister. A fine leader truly for a godly cause ! The man upon his left, with the red swollen face and the white feather in his cap, is Colonel Holmes. I trust that he will never show the white feather save on his head. The other upon the high chestnut horse is a lawyer, though, by my soul, he is a better man at ordering a battalion than at drawing a bill

of costs. He is the republican Wade who led the foot at the skirmish at Bridport, and brought them off with safety. The tall heavy-faced soldier in the steel bonnet is Anthony Buyse, the Brandenburger, a soldado of fortune, and a man of high heart, as are most of his countrymen. I have fought both with him and against him ere now."

"Mark ye the long thin man behind him?" cried Reuben. "He hath drawn his sword, and waves it over his head. 'Tis a strange time and place for the broadsword exercise. He is surely mad."

"Perhaps you are not far amiss," said Saxon. "Yet, by my hilt, were it not for that man there would be no Protestant army advancing upon us down yonder road. 'Tis he who by dangling the crown before Monmouth's eyes beguiled him away from his snug retreat in Brabant. There is not one of these men whom he hath not tempted into this affair by some bait or other. With Grey it was a dukedom, with Wade the woolsack, with Buyse the plunder of Cheapside. Every one hath his own motive, but the clues to them all are in the hands of yonder crazy fanatic, who makes the puppets dance as he will. He hath plotted more, lied more, and suffered less than any Whig in the party."

"It must be that Dr. Robert Ferguson of whom I have heard my father speak," said I.

"You are right. 'Tis he. I have but seen him once in Amsterdam, and yet I know him by his shock wig and crooked shoulders. It is whispered that of late his overweening conceit hath unseated his reason. See, the German places his hand upon his shoulder and persuades him to sheathe his weapon. King Monmouth glances round too, and smiles as though he were the Court buffoon with a Geneva cloak instead of the motley. But the van is upon us. To your companies, and mind that ye raise your swords to the salute while the colours of each troop go by."

Whilst our companion had been talking the whole Protestant army had been streaming towards the town,

and the head of the fore-guard was abreast with the gateway. Four troops of horse led the way, badly equipped and mounted, with ropes instead of bridles, and in some cases squares of sacking in place of saddles. The men were armed for the most part with sword and pistol, while a few had the buff-coats, plates and headpieces taken at Axminster, still stained sometimes with the blood of the last wearer. In the midst of them rode a banner-bearer, who carried a great square ensign hung upon a pole, which was supported upon a socket let into the side of the girth. Upon it was printed in golden letters the legend, " Pro libertate et religione nostrâ." These horse-soldiers were made up of yeomen's and farmers' sons, unused to discipline, and having a high regard for themselves as volunteers, which caused them to cavil and argue over every order. For this cause, though not wanting in natural courage, they did little service during the war, and were a hindrance rather than a help to the army.

Behind the horse came the foot, walking six abreast, divided into companies of varying size, each company bearing a banner which gave the name of the town or village from which it had been raised. This manner of arranging the troops had been chosen because it had been found to be impossible to separate men who were akin and neighbours to each other. They would fight, they said, side by side, or they would not fight at all. For my own part, I think that it is no bad plan, for when it comes to push of pike, a man stands all the faster when he knows that he hath old and tried friends on either side of him. Many of these country places I came to know afterwards from the talk of the men, and many others I have travelled through so that the names upon the banners have come to have a real meaning with me. Homer hath, I remember, a chapter or book wherein he records the names of all the Grecian chiefs and whence they came, and how many men they brought to the common muster. It is a pity that there is not some Western Homer who could record the names of these brave peasants and artisans,

and recount what each did or suffered in upholding a noble though disastrous cause. Their places of birth at least shall not be lost as far as mine own feeble memory can carry me.

The first foot regiment, if so rudely formed a band could be so called, consisted of men of the sea, fishers and coastmen, clad in the heavy blue jerkins and rude garb of their class. They were bronzed, weather-beaten tarpaulins, with hard mahogany faces, variously armed with birding pieces, cutlasses or pistols. I have a notion that it was not the first time that those weapons had been turned against King James's servants, for the Somerset and Devon coasts were famous breeding-places for smugglers, and many a saucy lugger was doubtless lying up in creek or in bay whilst her crew had gone a-soldiering to Taunton. As to discipline, they had no notion of it, but rolled along in true blue-water style, with many a shout and halloo to each other or to the crowd. From Star Point to Portland Roads there would be few nets for many weeks to come, and fish would swim the narrow seas which should have been heaped on Lyme Cobb or exposed for sale in Plymouth market. Each group, or band, of these men of the sea bore with it its own banner, that of Lyme in the front, followed by Topsham, Colyford, Bridport, Sidmouth, Otterton, Abbotsbury and Charmouth, all southern towns, which are on or near the coast. So they trooped past us, rough and careless, with caps cocked, and the reek of their tobacco rising up from them like the steam from a tired horse. In number they may have been four hundred or thereabouts.

The peasants of Rockbere, with flail and scythe, led the next column, followed by the banner of Honiton, which was supported by two hundred stout lacemakers from the banks of the Otter. These men showed by the colour of their faces that their work kept them within four walls, yet they excelled their peasant companions in their alert and soldierly bearing. Indeed, with all the troops, we observed that, though the countrymen were the stouter

and heartier, the craftsmen were the most ready to catch the air and spirit of the camp. Behind the men of Honiton came the Puritan clothworkers of Wellington, with their mayor upon a white horse beside their standard-bearer, and a band of twenty instruments before him. Grim-visaged, thoughtful, sober men, they were for the most part clad in grey suits and wearing broad-brimmed hats. "For God and faith" was the motto of a streamer which floated from amongst them. The clothworkers formed three strong companies, and the whole regiment may have numbered close on six hundred men.

The third regiment was headed by five hundred foot from Taunton, men of peaceful and industrious life, but deeply imbued with those great principles of civil and religious liberty which were three years later to carry all before them in England. As they passed the gates they were greeted by a thunderous welcome from their townsmen upon the walls and at the windows. Their steady, solid ranks, and broad, honest burgher faces, seemed to me to smack of discipline and of work well done. Behind them came the musters of Winterbourne, Ilminster, Chard, Yeovil and Collumpton, a hundred or more pikesmen to each, bringing the tally of the regiment to a thousand men.

A squadron of horse trotted by, closely followed by the fourth regiment, bearing in its van the standards of Beaminster, Crewkerne, Langport and Chidiock, all quiet Somersetshire villages, which had sent out their manhood to strike a blow for the old cause. Puritan ministers, with their steeple hats and Geneva gowns, once black, but now white with dust, marched sturdily along beside their flocks. Then came a strong company of wild half-armed shepherds from the great plains which extend from the Blackdowns on the south to the Mendips on the north—very different fellows, I promise you, from the Corydons and Strephons of Master Waller or Master Dryden, who have depicted the shepherd as ever shedding tears of love, and tootling upon a plaintive pipe. I fear that Chloë or

Phyllis would have met with rough wooing at the hands of these Western savages. Behind them were musqueteers from Dorchester, pikemen from Newton Poppleford, and a body of stout infantry from among the serge workers of Ottery St. Mary. This fourth regiment numbered rather better than eight hundred, but was inferior in arms and in discipline to that which preceded it.

The fifth regiment was headed by a column of fen men from the dreary marches which stretch round Athelney. These men, in their sad and sordid dwellings, had retained the same free and bold spirit which had made them in past days the last resource of the good King Alfred and the protectors of the Western shires from the inroads of the Danes, who were never able to force their way into their watery strongholds. Two companies of them, towsy-headed and bare-legged, but loud in hymn and prayer, had come out from their fastnesses to help the Protestant cause. At their heels came the woodmen and lumberers of Bishop's Lidiard, big, sturdy men in green jerkins, and the white-smocked villagers of Huish Champflower. The rear of the regiment was formed by four hundred men in scarlet coats, with white cross-belts and well-burnished muskets. These were deserters from the Devonshire Militia, who had marched with Albemarle from Exeter, and who had come over to Monmouth on the field at Axminster. These kept together in a body, but there were many other militiamen, both in red and in yellow coats, amongst the various bodies which I have set forth. This regiment may have numbered seven hundred men.

The sixth and last column of foot was headed by a body of peasants bearing " Minehead " upon their banner, and the ensign of the three wool-bales and the sailing ship, which is the sign of that ancient borough. They had come for the most part from the wild country which lies to the north of Dunster Castle and skirts the shores of the Bristol Channel. Behind them were the poachers and

huntsmen of Porlock Quay, who had left the red deer of Exmoor to graze in peace whilst they followed a nobler quarry. They were followed by men from Dulverton, men from Milverton, men from Wiveliscombe and the sunny slopes of the Quantocks, swart, fierce men from the bleak moors of Dunkerry Beacon, and tall, stalwart pony rearers and graziers from Bampton. The banners of Bridgewater, of Shepton Mallet and of Nether Stowey swept past us, with that of the fishers of Clovelly and the quarreymen of the Blackdowns. In the rear were three companies of strange men, giants in stature, though some-what bowed with labour, with long tangled beards, and unkempt hair hanging over their eyes. These were the miners from the Mendip hills and from the Oare and Bagworthy valleys, rough, half-savage men, whose eyes rolled up at the velvets and brocades of the shouting citizens, or fixed themselves upon their smiling dames with a fierce intensity which scared the peaceful burghers. So the long line rolled in until three squadrons of horse and four small cannon, with the blue-coated Dutch cannoniers as stiff as their own ramrods, brought up the rear. A long train of carts and of waggons which had followed the army were led into the fields outside the walls and there quartered.

When the last soldier had passed through the Shuttern Gate, Monmouth and his leaders rode slowly in, the Mayor walking by the King's charger. As we saluted they all faced round to us, and I saw a quick flush of surprise and pleasure come over Monmouth's pale face as he noted our close lines and soldierly bearing.

" By my faith, gentlemen," he said, glancing round at his staff, " our worthy friend the Mayor must have inherited Cadmus's dragon teeth. Where raised ye this pretty crop, Sir Stephen ? How came ye to bring them to such perfection too, even, I declare, to the hair powder of the grenadiers ? "

" I have fifteen hundred in the town," the old wool-worker answered proudly ; " though some are scarce as disciplined. These men come from Wiltshire, and the

officers from Hampshire. As to their order, the credit is due not to me, but to the old soldier, Colonel Decimus Saxon, whom they have chosen as their commander, as well as to the captains who serve under him."

" My thanks are due to you, Colonel," said the King, turning to Saxon, who bowed and sank the point of his sword to the earth, " and to you also, gentlemen. I shall not forget the warm loyalty which brought you from Hampshire in so short a time. Would that I could find the same virtue in higher places ! But, Colonel Saxon, you have, I gather, seen much service abroad. What think you of the army which hath just passed before you ? "

" If it please your Majesty," Saxon answered, "it is like so much uncarded wool, which is rough enough in itself, and yet may in time come to be woven into a noble garment."

" Hem ! There is not much leisure for the weaving," said Monmouth. " But they fight well. You should have seen them fall on at Axminster ! We hope to see you and to hear your views at the council table. But how is this ? Have I not seen this gentleman's face before ? "

" It is the Honourable Sir Gervas Jerome of the county of Surrey," quoth Saxon.

" Your Majesty may have seen me at St. James's," said the baronet, raising his hat, " or in the balcony at White-hall. I was much at Court during the latter years of the late king."

" Yes, yes. I remember the name as well as the face," cried Monmouth. " You see, gentlemen," he continued, turning to his staff, " the courtiers begin to come in at last. Were you not the man who did fight Sir Thomas Killigrew behind Dunkirk House ? I thought as much. Will you not attach yourself to my personal attendants ? "

" If it please your Majesty," Sir Gervas answered, " I am of opinion that I could do your royal cause better service at the head of my musqueteers."

" So be it ! So be it ! " said King Monmouth. Setting spurs to his horse, he raised his hat in response to the cheers of the troops and cantered down the High Street

under a rain of flowers, which showered from roof and window upon him, his staff and his escort. We had joined in his train, as commanded, so that we came in for our share of this merry crossfire. One rose as it fluttered down was caught by Reuben, who, I observed, pressed it to his lips, and then pushed it inside his breastplate. Glancing up, I caught sight of the smiling face of our host's daughter peeping down at us from a casement.

" Well caught, Reuben ! " I whispered. " At trick-track or trap and ball you were ever our best player."

" Ah, Micah," said he, " I bless the day that ever I followed you to the wars. I would not change places with Monmouth this day."

" Has it gone so far then ! " I exclaimed. " Why, lad, I thought that you were but opening your trenches, and you speak as though you had carried the city."

" Perhaps I am over-hopeful," he cried, turning from hot to cold, as a man doth when he is in love, or hath the tertian ague, or other bodily trouble. " God knows that I am little worthy of her, and yet——"

" Set not your heart too firmly upon that which may prove to be beyond your reach," said I. " The old man is rich, and will look higher."

" I would he were poor ! " sighed Reuben, with all the selfishness of a lover. " If this war last I may win myself some honour or title. Who knows ? Others have done it, and why not I ? "

" Of our three from Havant," I remarked, " one is spurred onwards by ambition, and one by love. Now, what am I to do who care neither for high office nor for the face of a maid ? What is to carry me into the fight ? "

" Our motives come and go, but yours is ever with you," said Reuben. " Honour and duty are the two stars, Micah, by which you have ever steered your course."

" Faith, Mistress Ruth has taught you to make pretty speeches," said I, " but methinks she ought to be here amid the beauty of Taunton."

As I spoke we were riding into the market-place, which

was now crowded with our troops. Round the cross were grouped a score of maidens clad in white muslin dresses with blue scarfs around their waists. As the King approached, these little maids, with much pretty nervousness, advanced to meet him, and handed him a banner which they had worked for him, and also a dainty gold-clasped Bible. Monmouth handed the flag to one of his captains, but he raised the book above his head, exclaiming that he had come there to defend the truths contained within it, at which the cheerings and acclamations broke forth with redoubled vigour. It had been expected that he might address the people from the cross, but he contented himself with waiting while the heralds proclaimed his titles to the Crown, when he gave the word to disperse, and the troops marched off to the different centres where food had been provided for them. The King and his chief officers took up their quarters in the Castle, while the Mayor and richer burgesses found bed and board for the rest. As to the common soldiers, many were billeted among the townsfolk, many others encamped in the streets and Castle grounds, while the remainder took up their dwelling among the waggons in the fields outside the city, where they lit up great fires, and had sheep roasting and beer flowing as merrily as though a march on London were but a holiday outing.

21. *Of my Hand-grips with the Brandenburger*

KING MONMOUTH had called a council meeting for the evening, and summoned Colonel Decimus Saxon to attend it, with whom I went, bearing with me the small package which Sir Jacob Clancing had given over to my keeping. On arriving at the Castle we found that the King had not yet come out from his chamber, but we were shown into the great hall to await him, a fine room with lofty windows and a noble ceiling of carved

woodwork. At the further end the royal arms had been erected without the bar sinister which Monmouth had formerly worn. Here were assembled the principal chiefs of the army, with many of the inferior commanders, town officers, and others who had petitions to offer. Lord Grey of Wark stood silently by the window, looking out over the countryside with a gloomy face. Wade and Holmes shook their heads and whispered in a corner. Ferguson strode about with his wig awry, shouting out exhortations and prayers in a broad Scottish accent. A few of the more gaily dressed gathered round the empty fireplace, and listened to a tale from one of their number which appeared to be shrouded in many oaths, and which was greeted with shouts of laughter. In another corner a numerous group of zealots, clad in black or russet gowns, with broad white bands and hanging mantles, stood round some favourite preacher, and discussed in an undertone Calvinistic philosophy and its relation to statecraft. A few plain, homely soldiers, who were neither sectaries nor courtiers, wandered up and down, or stared out through the windows at the busy encampment upon the Castle Green. To one of these, remarkable for his great size and breadth of shoulder, Saxon led me, and touching him on the sleeve, he held out his hand as to an old friend.

" Mein Gott ! " cried the German soldier of fortune, for it was the same man whom my companion had pointed out in the morning, " I thought it was you, Saxon, when I saw you by the gate, though you are even thinner than of old. How a man could suck up so much good Bavarian beer as you have done, and yet make so little flesh upon it, is more than I can verstehen. How have all things gone with you ? "

" As of old," said Saxon. " More blows than thalers, and greater need of a surgeon than of a strong-box. When did I see you last, friend ? Was it not at the onfall at Nürnberg, when I led the right and you the left wing of the heavy horse ? "

" Nay," said Buyse. " I have met you in the way of

business since then. Have you forgot the skirmish on the Rhine bank, when you did flash your snapphahn at me? Sapperment! Had some rascally schelm not stabbed my horse I should have swept your head off as a boy cuts thistles mit a stick."

" Aye, aye," Saxon answered composedly, " I had forgot it. You were taken, if I remember aright, but did afterwards brain the sentry with your fetters, and swam the Rhine under the fire of a regiment. Yet, I think that we did offer you the same terms that you were having with the others."

" Some such base offer was indeed made me," said the German sternly. " To which I answered that, though I sold my sword, I did not sell my honour. It is well that cavaliers of fortune should show that an engagement is with them—how do ye say it?—unbreakable until the war is over. Then by all means let him change his pay-master. Warum nicht?"

" True, friend, true!" replied Saxon. " These beggarly Italians and Swiss have made such a trade of the matter, and sold themselves so freely, body and soul, to the longest purse, that it is well that we should be nice upon points of honour. But you remember the old hand-grip which no man in the Palatinate could exchange with you? Here is my captain, Micah Clarke. Let him see how warm a North German welcome may be."

The Brandenburger showed his white teeth in a grin as he held out his broad brown hand to me. The instant that mine was enclosed in it he suddenly bent his whole strength upon it, and squeezed my fingers together until the blood tingled in the nails, and the whole hand was limp and powerless.

" Donnerwetter!" he cried, laughing heartily at my start of pain and surprise. " It is a rough Prussian game, and the English lads have not much stomach for it."

" Truly, sir," said I, " it is the first time that I have seen the pastime, and I would fain practise it under so able a master."

" What, another ! " he cried. " Why, you must be still pringling from the first. Nay, if you will I shall not refuse you, though I fear it may weaken your hold upon your sword-hilt."

He held out his hand as he spoke, and I grasped it firmly, thumb to thumb, keeping my elbow high so as to bear all my force upon it. His own trick was, as I observed, to gain command of the other hand by a great output of strength at the onset. This I prevented by myself putting out all my power. For a minute or more we stood motionless, gazing into each other's faces. Then I saw a bead of sweat trickle down his forehead, and I knew that he was beaten. Slowly his grip relaxed, and his hand grew limp and slack while my own tightened ever upon it, until he was forced in a surly, muttering voice to request that I should unhand him.

" Teufel und hexerei ! " he cried, wiping away the blood which oozed from under his nails, " I might as well put my fingers in a rat-trap. You are the first man that ever yet exchanged fair hand-grips with Anthony Buyse."

" We breed brawn in England as well as in Brandenburg," said Saxon, who was shaking with laughter over the German soldier's discomfiture. " Why, I have seen that lad pick up a full-size sergeant of dragoons and throw him into a cart as though he had been a clod of earth."

" Strong he is," grumbled Buyse, still wringing his injured hand, " strong as old Gotz mit de iron grip. But what good is strength alone in the handling of a weapon ? It is not the force of a blow, but the way in which it is geschlagen, that makes the effect. Your sword now is heavier than mine, by the look of it, and yet my blade would bite deeper. Eh ? Is not that a more soldierly sport than kinderspiel such as hand-grasping and the like ? "

" He is a modest youth," said Saxon. " Yet I would match his stroke against yours."

" For what ? " snarled the German.

" For as much wine as we can take at a sitting."

" No small amount, either," said Buyse ; " a brace of gallons at the least. Well, be it so. Do you accept the contest ? "

" I shall do what I may," I answered, " though I can scarce hope to strike as heavy a blow as so old and tried a soldier."

" Henker take your compliments," he cried gruffly. " It was with sweet words that you did coax my fingers into that fool-catcher of yours. Now, here is my old headpiece of Spanish steel. It has, as you can see, one or two dints of blows, and a fresh one will not hurt it. I place it here upon this oaken stool high enough to be within fair sword-sweep. Have at it, Junker, and let us see if you can leave your mark upon it ! "

" Do you strike first, sir," said I, " since the challenge is yours."

" I must bruise my own headpiece to regain my soldierly credit," he grumbled. " Well, well, it has stood a cut or two in its day." Drawing his broadsword, he waved back the crowd who had gathered around us, while he swung the great weapon with tremendous force round his head, and brought it down with a full, clean sweep on to the smooth cap of steel. The headpiece sprang high into the air and then clattered down upon the oaken floor with a long, deep line bitten into the solid metal.

" Well struck ! " " A brave stroke ! " cried the spectators. " It is proof steel thrice welded, and warranted to turn a sword-blade," one remarked, raising up the helmet to examine it, and then replacing it upon the stool.

" I have seen my father cut through proof steel with this very sword," said I, drawing the fifty-year-old weapon. " He put rather more of his weight into it than you have done. I have heard him say that a good stroke should come from the back and loins rather than from the mere muscles of the arm."

" It is not a lecture we want, but a beispiel or example," sneered the German. " It is with your stroke that we have to do, and not with the teaching of your father."

" My stroke," said I, " is in accordance with his teaching " ; and, whistling round the sword, I brought it down
with all my might and strength upon the German's
helmet. The good old Commonwealth blade shore
through the plate of steel, cut the stool asunder and
buried its point two inches deep in the oaken floor. " It
is but a trick," I explained. " I have practised it in the
winter evenings at home."

" It is not a trick that I should care to have played upon
me," said Lord Grey, amid a general murmur of applause
and surprise. " Od's bud, man, you have lived two
centuries too late. What would not your thews have been
worth before gunpowder put all men upon a level ! "

" Wunderbar ! " growled Buyse, " wunderbar ! I am
past my prime, young sir, and may well resign the palm
of strength to you. It was a right noble stroke. It hath
cost me a runlet or two of canary, and a good old helmet ;
but I grudge it not, for it was fairly done. I am thankful
that my head was not darin. Saxon, here, used to show
us some brave schwertspielerei, but he hath not the
weight for such smashing blows as this."

" My eye is still true and my hand firm, though both
are perhaps a trifle the worse for want of use," said Saxon,
only too glad at the chance of drawing the eyes of the
chiefs upon him. " At backsword, sword and dagger,
sword and buckler, single falchion and case of falchions,
mine old challenge still holds good against any comer,
save only my brother Quartus, who plays as well as I do,
but hath an extra half-inch in reach which gives him the
vantage."

" I studied sword-play under Signor Contarini of
Paris," said Lord Grey. " Who was your master ? "

" I have studied, my lord, under Signor Stern Necessity
of Europe," quoth Saxon. " For five-and-thirty years
my life has depended from day to day upon being able to
cover myself with this slip of steel. Here is a small trick
which showeth some nicety of eye : to throw this ring to
the ceiling and catch it upon a rapier point. It seems

simple, perchance, and yet is only to be attained by some practice."

"Simple!" cried Wade the lawyer, a square-faced, bold-eyed man. "Why, the ring is but the girth of your little finger. A man might do it once by good luck, but none could ensure it."

"I will lay a guinea a thrust on it," said Saxon; and tossing the little gold circlet up into the air, he flashed out his rapier and made a pass at it. The ring rasped down the steel blade and tinkled against the hilt, fairly impaled. By a sharp motion of the wrist he shot it up to the ceiling again, where it struck a carved rafter and altered its course; but again, with a quick step forward, he got beneath it and received it on his sword-point. "Surely there is some cavalier present who is as apt at the trick as I am," he said, replacing the ring upon his finger.

"I think, Colonel, that I could venture upon it," said a voice; and looking round, we found that Monmouth had entered the room and was standing quietly on the outskirts of the throng, unperceived in the general interest which our contention had excited. "Nay, nay, gentlemen," he continued pleasantly, as we uncovered and bowed with some little embarrassment; "how could my faithful followers be better employed than by breathing themselves in a little sword-play? I prithee lend me your rapier, Colonel." He drew a diamond ring from his finger, and spinning it up into the air, he transfixed it as deftly as Saxon had done. "I practised the trick at The Hague, where, by my faith, I had only too many hours to devote to such trifles. But how come these steel links and splinters of wood to be littered over the floor?"

"A son of Anak hath appeared amang us," said Ferguson, turning his face, all scarred and reddened with the king's evil, in my direction. "A Goliath o' Gath, wha hath a stroke like untae a weaver's beam. Hath he no the smooth face o' a bairn and the thews o' Behemoth?"

"A shrewd blow indeed," King Monmouth remarked,

243

picking up half the stool. " How is our champion named ? "

" He is my captain, your Majesty," Saxon answered, resheathing the sword which the King had handed to him ; " Micah Clarke, a man of Hampshire birth."

" They breed a good old English stock in those parts," said Monmouth ; " but how comes it that you are here, sir ? I summoned this meeting for my own immediate household, and for the colonels of the regiments. If every captain is to be admitted into our councils, we must hold our meetings on the Castle Green, for no apartment could contain us."

" I ventured to come here, your Majesty," I replied, " because on my way hither I received a commission, which was that I should deliver this small but weighty package into your hands. I therefore thought it my duty to lose no time in fulfilling my errand."

" What is in it ? " he asked.

" I know not," I answered.

Doctor Ferguson whispered a few words into the King's ear, who laughed and held out his hand for the packet.

" Tut ! tut ! " said he. " The days of the Borgias and the Medicis are over, Doctor. Besides, the lad is no Italian conspirator, but hath honest blue eyes and flaxen hair as Nature's certificate to his character. This is passing heavy—an ingot of lead, by the feel. Lend me your dagger, Colonel Holmes. It is stitched round with packthread. Ha ! it is a bar of gold—solid virgin gold by all that is wonderful. Take charge of it, Wade, and see that it is added to the common fund. This little piece of metal may furnish ten pikemen. What have we here ? A letter and an enclosure. ' To James, Duke of Monmouth '—hum ! It was written before we assumed our royal state. ' Sir Jacob Clancing, late of Snellaby Hall, sends greeting and a pledge of affection. Carry out the good work. A hundred more such ingots await you when you have crossed Salisbury Plain.' Bravely promised, Sir Jacob ! I would that you had sent them.

Well, gentlemen, ye see how support and tokens of good-will come pouring in upon us. Is not the tide upon the turn? Can the usurper hope to hold his own? Will his men stand by him? Within a month or less I shall see ye all gathered round me at Westminster, and no duty will then be so pleasing to me as to see that ye are all, from the highest to the lowest, rewarded for your loyalty to your monarch in this the hour of his darkness and his danger."

A murmur of thanks rose up from the courtiers at this gracious speech, but the German plucked at Saxon's sleeve and whispered, " He hath his warm fit upon him. You shall see him cold anon."

" Fifteen hundred men have joined me here where I did but expect a thousand at the most," the King continued. " If we had high hopes when we landed at Lyme Cobb with eighty at our back, what should we think now when we find ourselves in the chief city of Somerset with eight thousand brave men around us? 'Tis but one other affair like that at Axminster, and my uncle's power will go down like a house of cards. But gather round the table, gentlemen, and we shall discuss matters in due form."

" There is yet a scrap of paper which you have not read, sire," said Wade, picking up a little slip which had been enclosed in the note.

" It is a rhyming catch or the posy of a ring," said Monmouth, glancing at it. " What are we to make of this?

' When thy star is in trine,
Between darkness and shine,
Duke Monmouth, Duke Monmouth,
Beware of the Rhine ! '

Thy star in trine ! What tomfoolery is this? "

" If it please your Majesty," said I, " I have reason to believe that the man who sent you this message is one of those who are deeply skilled in the arts of divination, and who pretend from the motions of the celestial bodies to foretell the fates of men."

" This gentleman is right, sir," remarked Lord Grey.
" ' Thy star in trine ' is an astrological term, which signifieth when your natal planet shall be in a certain quarter
of the heavens. The verse is of the nature of a prophecy.
The Chaldeans and Egyptians of old are said to have
attained much skill in the art, but I confess that I have
no great opinion of those latter-day prophets who busy
themselves in answering the foolish questions of every
housewife."

> " And tell by Venus and the moon,
> Who stole a thimble or a spoon,"

muttered Saxon, quoting from his favourite poem.

" Why, here are our Colonels catching the rhyming
complaint," said the King, laughing. " We shall be
dropping the sword and taking to the harp anon, as
Alfred did in these very parts. Or I shall become a king
of bards and trouveurs, like good King René of Provence.
But, gentlemen, if this be indeed a prophecy, it should,
methinks, bode well for our enterprise. It is true that
I am warned against the Rhine, but there is little prospect
of our fighting this quarrel upon its banks."

" Worse luck ! " murmured the German, under his
breath.

" We may, therefore, thank this Sir Jacob and his giant
messenger for his forecast as well as for his gold. But
here comes the worthy Mayor of Taunton, the oldest of
our councillors and the youngest of our knights. Captain
Clarke, I desire you to stand at the inside of the door and
to prevent intrusion. What passes amongst us will, I am
well convinced, be safe in your keeping."

I bowed and took up my post as ordered, while the
councilmen and commanders gathered round the great
oaken table which ran down the centre of the hall. The
mellow evening light was streaming through the three
western windows, while the distant babble of the soldiers
upon the Castle Green sounded like the sleepy drone of
insects. Monmouth paced with quick uneasy steps up

and down the further end of the room until all were seated, when he turned towards them and addressed them.

" You will have surmised, gentlemen," he said, " that I have called you together to-day that I might have the benefit of your collective wisdom in determining what our next steps should be. We have now marched some forty miles into our kingdom, and we have met wherever we have gone with the warm welcome which we expected. Close upon eight thousand men follow our standards, and as many more have been turned away for want of arms. We have twice met the enemy, with the effect that we have armed ourselves with their muskets and field-pieces. From first to last there hath been nothing which has not prospered with us. We must look to it that the future be as successful as the past. To ensure this I have called ye together, and I now ask ye to give me your opinions of our situation, leaving me after I have listened to your views to form our plan of action. There are statesmen among ye, and there are soldiers among ye, and there are godly men among ye who may chance to get a flash of light when statesman and soldier are in the dark. Speak fearlessly, then, and let me know what is in your minds."

From my central post by the door I could see the lines of faces on either side of the board, the solemn close-shaven Puritans, sunburned soldiers and white-wigged moustachioed courtiers. My eyes rested particularly upon Ferguson's scorbutic features, Saxon's hard aquiline profile, the German's burly face, and the peaky thoughtful countenance of the Lord of Wark.

" If naebody else will gie an opeenion," cried the fanatical Doctor, " I'll een speak mysel' as led by the inward voice. For have I no worked in the cause and slaved in it, much enduring and suffering mony things at the honds o' the froward, whereby my ain speerit hath plentifully fructified ? Have I no been bruised as in a wine-press, and cast oot wi' hissing and scorning into waste places ? "

" We know your merits and your sufferings, Doctor,"

said the King. " The question before us is as to our course of action."

" Was there no a voice heard in the East ? " cried the old Whig. " Was there no a soond as o' a great crying, the crying for a broken covenant and a sinful generation ? Whence came the cry ? Wha's was the voice ? Was it no that o' the man Robert Ferguson, wha raised himsel' up against the great ones in the land, and wouldna be appeased ? "

" Aye, aye, Doctor," said Monmouth impatiently. " Speak to the point, or give place to another."

" I shall mak' mysel' clear, your Majesty. Have we no heard that Argyle is cutten off ? And why was he cutten off ? Because he hadna due faith in the workings o' the Almighty, and must needs reject the help o' the children o' light in favour o' the bare-legged spawn o' Prelacy, wha are half Pagan, half Popish. Had he walked in the path o' the Lord he wudna be lying in the Tolbooth o' Edinburgh wi' the tow or the axe before him. Why did he no gird up his loins and march straight onwards wi' the banner o' light, instead o' dallying here and biding there like a half-hairted Didymus ? And the same or waur will fa' upon us if we dinna march on intae the land and plant our ensigns afore the wicked toun o' London—the toun where the Lord's wark is tae be done, and the tares tae be separated frae the wheat, and piled up for the burning."

" Your advice, in short, is that we march on ? " said Monmouth.

" That we march on, your Majesty, and that we prepare oorselves tae be the vessels o' grace, and forbear frae polluting the cause o' the Gospel by wearing the livery o' the devil "—here he glared at a gaily attired cavalier at the other side of the table—" or by the playing o' cairds, the singing o' profane songs and the swearing o' oaths, all which are nichtly done by members o' this army, wi' the effect o' giving much scandal tae God's ain folk."

A hum of assent and approval rose up from the more Puritan members of the council at this expression of

opinion, while the courtiers glanced at each other and curled their lips in derision. Monmouth took two or three turns and then called for another opinion.

" You, Lord Grey," he said, " are a soldier and a man of experience. What is your advice ? Should we halt here or push forward towards London ? "

" To advance to the East would, in my humble judgment, be fatal to us," Grey answered, speaking slowly, with the manner of a man who has thought long and deeply before delivering an opinion. " James Stuart is strong in horse, and we have none. We can hold our own amongst hedgerows or in broken country, but what chance could we have in the middle of Salisbury Plain ? With the dragoons round us we should be like a flock of sheep amid a pack of wolves. Again, every step which we take towards London removes us from our natural vantage ground, and from the fertile country which supplies our necessities, while it strengthens our enemy by shortening the distance he has to convey his troops and his victuals. Unless, therefore, we hear of some great outbreak elsewhere, or of some general movement in London in our favour, we would do best to hold our ground and wait an attack."

" You argue shrewdly and well, my Lord Grey," said the King. " But how long are we to wait for this outbreak which never comes, and for this support which is ever promised and never provided ? We have now been seven long days in England, and during that time of all the House of Commons no single man hath come over to us, and of the lords none save my Lord Grey, who was himself an exile. Not a baron or an earl, and only one baronet, hath taken up arms for me. Where are the men whom Danvers and Wildman promised me from London ? Where are the brisk boys of the City who were said to be longing for me ? Where are the breakings out from Berwick to Portland which they foretold ? Not a man hath moved save only these good peasants. I have been deluded, ensnared, trapped—trapped by vile agents who

have led me into the shambles." He paced up and down, wringing his hands and biting his lips, with despair stamped upon his face. I observed that Buyse smiled and whispered something to Saxon—a hint, I suppose, that this was the cold fit of which he spoke.

" Tell me, Colonel Buyse," said the King, mastering his emotion by a strong effort. " Do you, as a soldier, agree with my Lord Grey ? "

" Ask Saxon, your Majesty," the German answered. " My opinion in a Raths-Versammling is, I have observed, ever the same as his."

" Then we turn to you, Colonel Saxon," said Monmouth. " We have in this council a party who are in favour of an advance and a party who wish to stand their ground. Their weight and numbers are, methinks, nearly equal. If you had the casting vote how would you decide ? " All eyes were bent upon our leader, for his martial bearing, and the respect shown to him by the veteran Buyse, made it likely that his opinion might really turn the scale. He sat for a few moments in silence with his hands before his face.

" I will give my opinion, your Majesty," he said at last. " Feversham and Churchill are making for Salisbury with three thousand foot, and they have pushed on eight hundred of the Blue Guards, and two or three dragoon regiments. We should, therefore, as Lord Grey says, have to fight on Salisbury Plain, and our foot armed with a medley of weapons could scarce make head against their horse. All is possible to the Lord, as Dr. Ferguson wisely says. We are as grains of dust in the hollow of His hand. Yet He hath given us brains wherewith to choose the better course, and if we neglect it we must suffer the consequence of our folly."

Ferguson laughed contemptuously, and breathed out a prayer, but many of the other Puritans nodded their heads to acknowledge that this was not an unreasonable view to take of it.

" On the other hand, sire," Saxon continued, " it

appears to me that to remain here is equally impossible. Your Majesty's friends throughout England would lose all heart if the army lay motionless and struck no blow. The rustics would flock off to their wives and homes. Such an example is catching. I have seen a great army thaw away like an icicle in the sunshine. Once gone, it is no easy matter to collect them again. To keep them we must employ them. Never let them have an idle minute. Drill them. March them. Exercise them. Work them. Preach to them. Make them obey God and their Colonel. This cannot be done in snug quarters. They must travel. We cannot hope to end this business until we get to London. London, then, must be our goal. But there are many ways of reaching it. You have, sire, as I have heard, many friends at Bristol and in the Midlands. If I might advise, I should say let us march round in that direction. Every day that passes will serve to swell your forces and improve your troops, while all will feel something is astirring. Should we take Bristol—and I hear that the works are not very strong—it would give us a very good command of shipping, and a rare centre from which to act. If all goes well with us, we could make our way to London through Gloucestershire and Worcestershire. In the meantime I might suggest that a day of fast and humiliation be called to bring down a blessing on the cause."

This address, skilfully compounded of worldly wisdom and of spiritual zeal, won the applause of the whole council, and especially that of King Monmouth, whose melancholy vanished as if by magic.

" By my faith, Colonel," said he, " you make it all as clear as day. Of course, if we make ourselves strong in the West, and my uncle is threatened with disaffection elsewhere, he will have no chance to hold out against us. Should he wish to fight us upon our own ground, he must needs drain his troops from north, south and east, which is not to be thought of. We may very well march to London by way of Bristol."

" I think that the advice is good," Lord Grey observed ;

" but I should like to ask Colonel Saxon what warrant he
hath for saying that Churchill and Feversham are on their
way, with three thousand regular foot and several regiments of horse ? "

" The word of an officer of the Blues with whom I
conversed at Salisbury," Saxon answered. " He confided in me, believing me to be one of the Duke of
Beaufort's household. As to the horse, one party pursued
us on Salisbury Plain with bloodhounds, and another
attacked us not twenty miles from here and lost a score of
troopers and a cornet."

" We heard something of the brush," said the King.
" It was bravely done. But if these men are so close we
have no great time for preparation."

" Their foot cannot be here before a week," said the
Mayor. " By that time we might be behind the walls of
Bristol."

" There is one point which might be urged," observed
Wade the lawyer. " We have, as your Majesty most
truly says, met with heavy discouragement in the fact that
no noblemen and few commoners of repute have declared
for us. The reason is, I opine, that each doth wait for
his neighbour to make a move. Should one or two come
over the others would soon follow. How, then, are we
to bring a duke or two to our standards ? "

" There's the question, Master Wade," said Monmouth,
shaking his head despondently.

" I think that it might be done," continued the Whig
lawyer. " Mere proclamations addressed to the commonalty will not catch these gold fish. They are not to
be angled for with a naked hook. I should recommend
that some form of summons or writ be served upon each
of them calling upon them to appear in our camp within
a certain date under pain of high treason."

" There spake the legal mind," quoth King Monmouth,
with a laugh. " But you have omitted to tell us how the
said writ or summons is to be conveyed to these same
delinquents."

" There is the Duke of Beaufort," continued Wade, disregarding the King's objection. " He is President of Wales, and he is, as your Majesty knows, lieutenant of four English counties. His influence overshadows the whole West. He hath two hundred horses in his stables at Badminton, and a thousand men, as I have heard, sit down at his tables every day. Why should not a special effort be made to gain over such a one, the more so as we intend to march in his direction ? "

" Henry, Duke of Beaufort, is unfortunately already in arms against his sovereign," said Monmouth gloomily.

" He is, sire, but he may be induced to turn in your favour the weapon which he hath raised against you. He is a Protestant. He is said to be a Whig. Why should we not send a message to him ? Flatter his pride. Appeal to his religion. Coax and threaten him. Who knows ? He may have private grievances of which we know nothing, and may be ripe for such a move."

" Your counsel is good, Wade," said Lord Grey, " but methinks his Majesty hath asked a pertinent question. Your messenger would, I fear, find himself swinging upon one of the Badminton oaks if the Duke desired to show his loyalty to James Stuart. Where are to we find a man who is wary enough and bold enough for such a mission, without risking one of our leaders, who could be ill-spared at such a time ? "

" It is true," said the King. " It were better not to venture it at all than to do it in a clumsy and halting fashion. Beaufort would think that it was a plot not to gain him over, but to throw discredit upon him. But what means our giant at the door by signing to us ? "

" If it please your Majesty," I asked, " have I permission to speak ? "

" We would fain hear you, Captain," he answered graciously. " If your understanding is in any degree correspondent to your strength, your opinion should be of weight."

" Then, your Majesty," said I, " I would offer myself

as a fitting messenger in this matter. My father bid me spare neither life nor limb in this quarrel, and if this honourable council thinks that the Duke may be gained over, I am ready to guarantee that the message shall be conveyed to him if man and horse can do it."

" I'll warrant that no better herald could be found," cried Saxon. " The lad hath a cool head and a staunch heart."

" Then, young sir, we shall accept your loyal and gallant offer," said Monmouth. " Are ye all agreed, gentlemen, upon the point ? "

A murmur of assent rose from the company.

" You shall draw up the paper, Wade. Offer him money, a seniority amongst the dukes, the perpetual Presidentship of Wales—what you will, if you can but shake him. If not, sequestration, exile and everlasting infamy. And, hark ye ! you can enclose a copy of the papers drawn up by Van Brunow, which prove the marriage of my mother, together with the attestations of the witnesses. Have them ready by to-morrow at daybreak, when the messenger may start." [1]

" They shall be ready, your Majesty," said Wade.

" In that case, gentlemen," continued King Monmouth, " I may now dismiss ye to your posts. Should anything fresh arise I shall summon ye again, that I may profit by your wisdom. Here we shall stay, if Sir Stephen Timewell will have us, until the men are refreshed and the recruits enrolled. We shall then make our way Bristolwards, and see what luck awaits us in the North. If Beaufort comes over all will be well. Farewell, my kind friends ! I need not tell ye to be diligent and faithful."

The council rose at the King's salutation, and bowing to him they began to file out of the Castle hall. Several of the members clustered round me with hints for my journey or suggestions as to my conduct.

" He is a proud, froward man," said one. " Speak

[1] Note H, Appendix.—Monmouth's Contention of Legitimacy.

humbly to him or he will never hearken to your message, but will order you to be scourged out of his presence."

" Nay, nay ! " cried another. " He is hot, but he loves a man that is a man. Speak boldly and honestly to him, and he is more like to listen to reason."

" Speak as the Lord shall direct you," said a Puritan. " It is His message which you bear as well as the King's."

" Entice him out alone upon some excuse," said Buyse, " then up and away mit him upon your crupper. Hagel-sturm ! that would be a proper game."

" Leave him alone," cried Saxon. " The lad hath as much sense as any of ye. He will see which way the cat jumps. Come, friend, let us make our way back to our men."

" I am sorry, indeed, to lose you," he said, as we threaded our way through the throng of peasants and soldiers upon the Castle Green. " Your company will miss you sorely. Lockarby must see to the two. If all goes well you should be back in three or four days. I need not tell you that there is a real danger. If the Duke wishes to prove to James that he would not allow himself to be tampered with, he can only do it by punishing the messenger, which as lieutenant of a county he hath power to do in times of civil commotion. He is a hard man if all reports be true. On the other hand, if you should chance to succeed it may lay the foundations of your fortunes and be the means of saving Monmouth. He needs help, by the Lord Harry ! Never have I seen such a rabble as this army of his. Buyse says that they fought lustily at this ruffle at Axminster, but he is of one mind with me, that a few whiffs of shot and cavalry charges would scatter them over the countryside. Have you any message to leave ? "

" None, save my love to my mother," said I.

" It is well. Should you fall in any unfair way, I shall not forget his Grace of Beaufort, and the next of his gentlemen who comes in my way shall hang as high as Haman. And now you had best make for your chamber,

and have as good a slumber as you may, since to-morrow at cock-crow begins your new mission."

22. *Of the News from Havant*

HAVING given my orders that Covenant should be saddled and bridled by daybreak, I had gone to my room and was preparing for a long night's rest, when Sir Gervas, who slept in the same apartment, came dancing in with a bundle of papers waving over his head.

" Three guesses, Clarke ! " he cried. " What would you most desire ? "

" Letters from Havant," said I eagerly.

" Right," he answered, throwing them into my lap. " Three of them, and not a woman's hand among them. Sink me, if I can understand what you have been doing all your life.

> ' How can youthful heart resign
> Lovely woman, sparkling wine ? '

But you are so lost in your news that you have not observed my transformation."

" Why, wherever did you get these ? " I asked in astonishment, for he was attired in a delicate plum-coloured suit with gold buttons and trimmings, set off by silken hosen and Spanish leather shoes with roses on the instep.

" It smacks more of the court than of the camp," quoth Sir Gervas, rubbing his hands and glancing down at himself with some satisfaction. " I am also revictualled in the matter of ratafia and orange-flower water, together with two new wigs, a bob and a court, a pound of the Imperial snuff from the sign of the Black Man, a box of De Crepigny's hair powder, my foxskin muff and several other necessaries. But I hinder you in your reading."

" I have seen enough to tell me that all is well at home,"

I answered, glancing over my father's letter. " But how came these things ? "

" Some horsemen have come in from Petersfield, bearing them with them. As to my little box, which a fair friend of mine in town packed for me, it was to be forwarded to Bristol, where I am now supposed to be, and should be were it not for my good fortune in meeting your party. It chanced to find its way, however, to the Bruton inn, and the good woman there, whom I had conciliated, found means to send it after me. It is a good rule to go upon, Clarke, in this earthly pilgrimage, always to kiss the landlady. It may seem a small thing, and yet life is made up of small things. I have few fixed principles, I fear, but two there are which I can say from my heart that I never transgress. I always carry a corkscrew, and I never forget to kiss the landlady."

" From what I have seen of you," said I, laughing, " I could be warranty that those two duties are ever fulfilled."

" I have letters, too," said he, sitting on the side of the bed and turning over a sheaf of papers. " ' Your brokenhearted Araminta.' Hum ! The wench cannot know that I am ruined or her heart would speedily be restored. What's this ? A challenge to match my bird Julius against my Lord Dorchester's cockerel for a hundred guineas. Faith ! I am too busy backing the Monmouth rooster for the champion stakes. Another asking me to chase the stag at Epping. Zounds ! had I not cleared off I should have been run down myself, with a pack of bandog bailiffs at my heels. A dunning letter from my clothier. He can afford to lose this bill. He hath had many a long one out of me. An offer of three thousand from little Dicky Chichester. No, no, Dicky, it won't do. A gentleman can't live upon his friends. None the less grateful. How now ? From Mrs. Butterworth ! No money for three weeks ! Bailiffs in the house ! Now, curse me, if this is not too bad ! "

" What is the matter ? " I asked, glancing up from my own letters. The baronet's pale face had taken a tinge of

red, and he was striding furiously up and down the bedroom with a letter crumpled up in his hand.

" It is a burning shame, Clarke," he cried. " Hang it, she shall have my watch. It is by Tompion, of the sign of the Three Crowns in Paul's Yard, and cost a hundred when new. It should keep her for a few months. Mortimer shall measure swords with me for this. I shall write villain upon him with my rapier's point."

" I have never seen you ruffled before," said I.

" No," he answered, laughing. " Many have lived with me for years and would give me a certificate for temper. But this is too much. Sir Edward Mortimer is my mother's younger brother, Clarke, but he is not many years older than myself. A proper, strait-laced, soft-voiced lad he has ever been, and, as a consequence, he throve in the world, and joined land to land after the scriptural fashion. I had befriended him from my purse in the old days, but he soon came to be a richer man than I, for all that he gained he kept, whereas all I got—well, it went off like the smoke of the pipe which you are lighting. When I found that all was up with me I received from Mortimer an advance, which was sufficient to take me according to my wish over to Virginia, together with a horse and a personal outfit. There was some chance, Clarke, of the Jerome acres going to him should aught befall me, so that he was not averse to helping me off to a land of fevers and scalping knives. Nay, never shake your head, my dear country lad, you little know the wiles of the world."

" Give him credit for the best until the worst is proved," said I, sitting up in bed smoking, with my letters littered about in front of me.

" The worst *is* proved," said Sir Gervas, with a darkening face. " I have, as I said, done Mortimer some turns which he might remember, though it did not become me to remind him of them. This Mistress Butterworth is mine old wet-nurse, and it hath been the custom of the family to provide for her. I could not bear the thought

that in the ruin of my fortune she should lose the paltry guinea or so a week which stood between her and hunger. My only request to Mortimer, therefore, made on the score of old friendship, was that he should continue this pittance, I promising that should I prosper I would return whatever he should disburse. The mean-hearted villain wrung my hand and swore that it should be so. How vile a thing is human nature, Clarke ! For the sake of this paltry sum, he, a rich man, hath broken his pledge, and left this poor woman to starve. But he shall answer to me for it. He thinks that I am on the Atlantic. If I march back to London with these brave boys I shall disturb the tenor of his sainted existence. Meanwhile I shall trust to sun-dials, and off goes my watch to Mother Butterworth. Bless her ample bosoms ! I have tried many liquors, but I dare bet that the first was the most healthy. But how of your own letters ? You have been frowning and smiling like an April day."

" There is one from my father, with a few words attached from my mother," said I. " The second is from an old friend of mine, Zachariah Palmer, the village carpenter. The third is from Solomon Sprent, a retired seaman, for whom I have an affection and respect."

" You have a rare trio of newsmen. I would I knew your father, Clarke. He must, from what you say, be a stout bit of British oak. I spoke even now of your knowing little of the world, but indeed it may be that in your village you can see mankind without the varnish, and so come to learn more of the good of human nature. Varnish or none, the bad will ever peep through. Now this carpenter and seaman show themselves no doubt for what they are. A man might know my friends of the court for a lifetime, and never come upon their real selves, nor would it perhaps repay the search when you had come across it. Sink me, but I wax philosophical, which is the old refuge of the ruined man. Give me a tub, and I shall set up in the Piazza of Covent Garden, and be the

Diogenes of London. I would not be wealthy again, Micah! How goes the old lilt?—

> ' Our money shall never indite us
> Or drag us to Goldsmith Hall,
> No pirates or wrecks can affright us.
> We that have no estates
> Fear no plunder or rates,
> Nor care to lock gates.
> He that lies on the ground cannot fall!'

That last would make a good motto for an almshouse."

" You will have Sir Stephen up," said I warningly, for he was carolling away at the pitch of his lungs.

" Never fear! He and his 'prentices were all at the broadsword exercise in the hall as I came by. It is worth something to see the old fellow stamp, and swing his sword, and cry, ' Ha!' on the down-cut. Mistress Ruth and friend Lockarby are in the tapestried room, she spinning and he reading aloud one of those entertaining volumes which she would have me read. Methinks she hath taken his conversion in hand, which may end in his converting her from a maid into a wife. And so you go to the Duke of Beaufort! Well, I would that I could travel with you, but Saxon will not hear of it, and my musqueteers must be my first care. God send you safe back! Where is my jasmine powder and the patch-box? Read me your letters if there be aught in them of interest. I have been splitting a flask with our gallant Colonel at his inn, and he hath told me enough of your home at Havant to make me wish to know more."

" This one is somewhat grave," said I.

" Nay, I am in the humour for grave things. Have at it, if it contain the whole Platonic philosophy."

" 'Tis from the venerable carpenter who hath for many years been my adviser and friend. He is one who is religious without being sectarian, philosophic without being a partisan, and loving without being weak."

" A paragon, truly!" exclaimed Sir Gervas, who was busy with his eyebrow brush.

" This is what he saith," I continued, and proceeded to read the very letter which I now read to you.

" ' Having heard from your father, my dear lad, that there was some chance of being able to send a letter to you, I have written this, and am now sending it under the charge of the worthy John Packingham, of Chichester, who is bound for the West. I trust that you are now safe with Monmouth's army, and that you have received honourable appointment therein. I doubt not that you will find among your comrades some who are extreme sectaries, and others who are scoffers and disbelievers. Be advised by me, friend, and avoid both the one and the other. For the zealot is a man who not only defends his own right of worship, wherein he hath justice, but wishes to impose upon the consciences of others, by which he falls into the very error against which he fights. The mere brainless scoffer is, on the other hand, lower than the beast of the field, since he lacks the animal's self-respect and humble resignation.' "

" My faith ! " cried the Baronet, " the old gentleman hath a rough side to his tongue."

" ' Let us take religion upon its broadest base, for the truth must be broader than aught which we can conceive. The presence of a table doth prove the existence of a carpenter, and so the presence of a universe proves the existence of a universe Maker, call Him by what name you will. So far the ground is very firm beneath us, without either inspiration, teaching or any aid whatever. Since, then, there *must* be a world Maker, let us judge of His nature by His work. We cannot observe the glories of the firmament, its infinite extent, its beauty and the Divine skill wherewith every plant and animal hath its wants cared for, without seeing that He is full of wisdom, intelligence and power. We are still, you will perceive, upon solid ground, without having to call to our aid aught save pure reason.

" ' Having got so far, let us inquire to what end the universe was made, and we put upon it. The teaching

of all nature shows that it must be to the end of improvement and upward growth, the increase in real virtue, in knowledge and in wisdom. Nature is a silent preacher which holds forth upon week-days as on Sabbaths. We see the acorn grow into the oak, the egg into the bird, the maggot into the butterfly. Shall we doubt, then, that the human soul, the most precious of all things, is also upon the upward path ? And how can the soul progress save through the cultivation of virtue and self-mastery ? What other way is there ? There is none. We may say with confidence, then, that we are placed here to increase in knowledge and in virtue.

" ' This is the core of all religion, and this much needs no faith in the acceptance. It is as true and as capable of proof as one of those exercises of Euclid which we have gone over together. On this common ground men have raised many different buildings. Christianity, the creed of Mahomet, the creed of the Easterns, have all the same essence. The difference lies in the forms and the details. Let us hold to our own Christian creed, the beautiful, often-professed, and seldom-practised doctrine of love, but let us not despise our fellow-men, for we are all branches from the common root of truth.

" ' Man comes out of darkness into light. He tarries awhile and then passes into darkness again. Micah, lad, the days are passing, mine as well as thine. Let them not be wasted. They are few in number. What says Petrarch ? " To him that enters, life seems infinite ; to him that departs, nothing." Let every day, every hour, be spent in furthering the Creator's end—in getting out whatever power for good there is in you. What is pain, or work, or trouble ? The cloud that passes over the sun. But the result of work well done is everything. It is eternal. It lives and waxes stronger through the centuries. Pause not for rest. The rest will come when the hour of work is past.

" ' May God protect and guard you ! There is no great news. The Portsmouth garrison hath marched to

the West. Sir John Lawson, the magistrate, hath been down here threatening your father and others, but he can do little for want of proofs. Church and Dissent are at each other's throats as ever. Truly the stern law of Moses is more enduring than the sweet words of Christ. Adieu, my dear lad ! All good wishes from your grey-headed friend, ZACHARIAH PALMER.' "

" Od's fish ! " cried Sir Gervas, as I folded up the letter, " I have heard Stillingfleet and Tenison, but I never listened to a better sermon. This is a bishop disguised as a carpenter. The crozier would suit his hand better than the plane. But how of our seaman friend ? Is he a tarpaulin theologian—a divine among the tarry-breeks ? "

" Solomon Sprent is a very different man, though good enough in his way," said I. " But you shall judge him from his letter."

" ' Master Clarke. Sir,—When last we was in company I had run in under the batteries on cutting-out service, while you did stand on and off in the channel and wait signals. Having stopped to refit and to overhaul my prize, which proved to be in proper trim alow and aloft——' "

" What the devil doth he mean ? " asked Sir Gervas.

" It is a maid of whom he talks—Phœbe Dawson, the sister of the blacksmith. He hath scarce put foot on land for nigh forty years, and can as a consequence only speak in this sea jargon, though he fancies that he uses as pure King's English as any man in Hampshire."

" Proceed, then," quoth the Baronet.

" ' Having also read her the articles of war, I explained to her the conditions under which we were to sail in company on life's voyage, namely :

" ' First. She to obey signals without question as soon as received.

" ' Second. She to steer by my reckoning.

" ' Third. She to stand by me as true consort in foul weather, battle or shipwreck.

" ' Fourth. She to run under my guns if assailed by picaroons, privateeros or garda-costas.

" ' Fifth. Me to keep her in due repair, dry-dock her at intervals, and see that she hath her allowance of coats of paint, streamers and bunting, as befits a saucy pleasure boat.

" ' Sixth. Me to take no other craft in tow, and if any be now attached, to cut their hawsers.

" ' Seventh. Me to revictual her day by day.

" ' Eighth. Should she chance to spring a leak, or be blown on her beam ends by the winds of misfortune, to stand by her and see her pumped out or righted.

" ' Ninth. To fly the Protestant ensign at the peak during life's voyage, and to lay our course for the great harbour, in the hope that moorings and ground to swing may be found for two British-built crafts when laid up for eternity.

" ' 'Twas close on eight-bells before these articles were signed and sealed. When I headed after you I could not so much as catch a glimpse of your topsail. Soon after I heard as you had gone a-soldiering, together with that lean, rakish, long-sparred, picaroon-like craft which I have seen of late in the village. I take it unkind of you that you have not so much as dipped ensign to me on leaving. But perchance the tide was favourable, and you could not tarry. Had I not been jury-rigged, with one of my spars shot away, I should have dearly loved to have strapped on my hanger and come with you to smell gun-powder once more. I would do it now, timber-toe and all, were it not for my consort, who might claim it as a breach of the articles, and so sheer off. I must follow the light on her poop until we are fairly joined.

" ' Farewell, mate ! In action, take an old sailor's advice. Keep the weather-gauge and board ! Tell that to your admiral on the day of battle. Whisper it in his ear. Say to him, ' Keep the weather-gauge and board ! ' Tell him also to strike quick, strike hard and keep on striking. That's the word of Christopher Mings, and

a better man has not been launched, though he did climb in through the hawse-pipe.—Yours to command, SOLOMON SPRENT.' "

Sir Gervas had been chuckling to himself during the reading of this epistle, but at the last part we both broke out a-laughing.

" Land or sea, he will have it that battles are fought in ships," said the Baronet. " You should have had that sage piece of advice for Monmouth's council to-day. Should he ever ask your opinion it must be, ' Keep the weather-gauge and board ! ' "

" I must to sleep," said I, laying aside my pipe. " I should be on the road by daybreak."

" Nay, I prithee, complete your kindness by letting me have a glimpse of your respected parent, the Roundhead."

" 'Tis but a few lines," I answered. " He was ever short of speech. But if they interest you, you shall hear them. ' I am sending this by a godly man, my dear son, to say that I trust that you are bearing yourself as becomes you. In all danger and difficulty trust not to yourself, but ask help from on high. If you are in authority, teach your men to sing psalms when they fall on, as is the good old custom. In action give point rather than edge. A thrust must beat a cut. Your mother and the others send their affection to you. Sir John Lawson hath been down here like a ravening wolf, but could find no proof against me. John Marchbank, of Bedhampton, is cast into prison. Truly Antichrist reigns in the land, but the kingdom of light is at hand. Strike lustily for truth and conscience.—Your loving father, JOSEPH CLARKE.

" ' Postscriptum [from my mother].—I trust that you will remember what I have said concerning your hosen and also the broad linen collars, which you will find in the bag. It is little over a week since you left, yet it seems a year. When cold or wet, take ten drops of Daffy's elixir in a small glass of strong waters. Should your feet chafe, rub tallow on the inside of your boots. Commend me to Master Saxon and to Master Lockarby,

if he be with you. His father was mad at his going, for he hath a great brewing going forward, and none to mind the mash-tub. Ruth hath baked a cake, but the oven hath played her false, and it is lumpy in the inside. A thousand kisses, dear heart, from your loving mother, M. C.' "

" A right sensible couple," quoth Sir Gervas, who, having completed his toilet, had betaken him to his couch. " I now begin to understand your manufacture, Clarke. I see the threads that are used in the weaving of you. Your father looks to your spiritual wants. Your mother concerns herself with the material. Yet the old carpenter's preaching is, methinks, more to your taste. You are a rank latitudinarian, man. Sir Stephen would cry fie upon you, and Joshua Pettigrue abjure you ! Well, out with the light, for we should both be stirring at cock-crow. That is our religion at present."

" Early Christians," I suggested, and we both laughed as we settled down to sleep.

23. *Of the Snare on the Weston Road*

JUST after sunrise I was awoke by one of the Mayor's servants, who brought word that the Honourable Master Wade was awaiting me downstairs. Having dressed and descended, I found him seated by the table in the sitting-room with papers and wafer-box, sealing up the missive which I was to carry. He was a small, worn, grey-faced man, very erect in his bearing and sudden in his speech, with more of the soldier than of the lawyer in his appearance.

" So," said he, pressing his seal above the fastening of the string, " I see that your horse is ready for you outside. You had best make your way round by Nether Stowey and the Bristol Channel, for we have heard that the enemy's horse guard the roads on the far side of Wells. Here is your packet."

I bowed and placed it in the inside of my tunic.

" It is a written order as suggested in the council. The Duke's reply may be written, or it may be by word of mouth. In either case guard it well. This packet contains also a copy of the depositions of the clergyman at The Hague, and of the other witnesses who saw Charles of England marry Lucy Walters, the mother of his Majesty. Your mission is one of such importance that the whole success of our enterprise may turn upon it. See that you serve the paper upon Beaufort in person, and not through any intermediary, or it might not stand in a court of law."

I promised to do so if possible.

" I should advise you also," he continued, " to carry sword and pistol as a protection against the chance dangers of the road, but to discard your headpiece and steel-front as giving you too warlike an aspect for a peaceful messenger."

" I had already come to that resolve," said I.

" There is nothing more to be said, Captain," said the lawyer, giving me his hand. " May all good fortune go with you. Keep a still tongue and a quick ear. Watch keenly how all things go. Mark whose face is gloomy and whose content. The Duke may be at Bristol, but you had best make for his seat at Badminton. Our sign of the day is Tewkesbury."

Thanking my instructor for his advice I went out and mounted Covenant, who pawed and champed at his bit in his delight at getting started once more. Few of the townsmen were stirring, though here and there a night-bonneted head stared out at me through a casement. I took the precaution of walking the horse very quietly until we were some distance from the house, for I had told Reuben nothing of my intended journey, and I was convinced that if he knew of it neither discipline, nor even his new ties of love, would prevent him from coming with me. Covenant's iron-shod feet rang sharply, in spite of my care, upon the cobble-stones, but looking back I

saw that the blinds of my faithful friend's room were undrawn, and that all seemed quiet in the house. I shook my bridle, therefore, and rode at a brisk trot through the silent streets, which were still strewn with faded flowers and gay with streamers. At the north gate a guard of half a company was stationed, who let me pass upon hearing the word. Once beyond the old walls I found myself out on the countryside, with my face to the north and a clear road in front of me.

It was a blithesome morning. The sun was rising over the distant hills, and heaven and earth were ruddy and golden. The trees in the wayside orchards were full of swarms of birds, who chattered and sang until the air was full of their piping. There was lightsomeness and gladness in every breath. The wistful-eyed red Somerset kine stood along by the hedgerows, casting great shadows down the fields and gazing at me as I passed. Farm horses leaned over wooden gates, and snorted a word of greeting to their glossy-coated brother. A great herd of snowy-fleeced sheep streamed towards us over the hillside and frisked and gambolled in the sunshine. All was innocent life, from the lark which sang on high to the little shrew-mouse which ran amongst the ripening corn, or the martin which dashed away at the sound of my approach. All alive and all innocent. What are we to think, my dear children, when we see the beasts of the field full of kindness and virtue and gratitude ? Where is this superiority of which we talk ?

From the high ground to the north I looked back upon the sleeping town, with the broad edging of tents and waggons, which showed how suddenly its population had outgrown it. The Royal Standard still fluttered from the tower of St. Mary Magdalene, while close by its beautiful brother-turret of St. James bore aloft the blue flag of Monmouth. As I gazed the quick petulant roll of a drum rose up on the still morning air, with the clear ringing call of the bugles summoning the troops from their slumbers. Beyond the town, and on either side of it, stretched a

glorious view of the Somersetshire downs, rolling away to the distant sea, with town and hamlet, castle turret and church tower, wooded coombe and stretch of grain-land —as fair a scene as the eye could wish to rest upon. As I wheeled my horse and sped upon my way I felt, my dears, that this was a land worth fighting for, and that a man's life was a small thing if he could but aid, in however trifling a degree, in working out its freedom and its happiness. At a little village over the hill I fell in with an outpost of horse, the commander of which rode some distance with me, and set me on my road to Nether Stowey. It seemed strange to my Hampshire eyes to note that the earth is all red in these parts—very different to the chalk and gravel of Havant. The cows, too, are mostly red. The cottages are built neither of brick nor of wood, but of some form of plaster, which they call cob, which is strong and smooth so long as no water comes near it. They shelter the walls from the rain, therefore, by great overhanging thatches. There is scarcely a steeple in the whole countryside, which also seems strange to a man from any other part of England. Every church hath a square tower, with pinnacles upon the top, and they are mostly very large, with fine peals of bells.

My course ran along by the foot of the beautiful Quantock Hills, where heavy-wooded coombes are scattered over the broad heathery downs, deep with bracken and whortlebushes. On either side of the track steep winding glens sloped downwards, lined with yellow gorse, which blazed out from the deep-red soil like a flame from embers. Peat-coloured streams splashed down these valleys and over the road, through which Covenant ploughed fetlock deep, and shied to see the broad-backed trout darting from between his fore feet.

All day I rode through this beautiful country, meeting few folk, for I kept away from the main roads. A few shepherds and farmers, a long-legged clergyman, a packman with his mule, and a horseman with a great bag,

whom I took to be a buyer of hair, are all that I can recall. A black jack of ale and the heel of a loaf at a wayside inn were all my refreshments. Near Combwich, Covenant cast a shoe, and two hours were wasted before I found a smithy in the town and had the matter set right. It was not until evening that I at last came out upon the banks of the Bristol Channel, at a place called Shurton Bars, where the muddy Parret makes its way into the sea. At this point the channel is so broad that the Welsh mountains can scarcely be distinguished. The shore is flat and black and oozy, flecked over with white patches of sea-birds, but further to the east there rises a line of hills, very wild and rugged, rising in places into steep precipices. These cliffs run out into the sea, and numerous little harbours and bays are formed in their broken surface, which are dry half the day, but can float a good-sized boat at half-tide. The road wound over these bleak and rocky hills, which are sparsely inhabited by a wild race of fishermen, or shepherds, who came to their cabin doors on hearing the clatter of my horse's hoofs, and shot some rough West-country jest at me as I passed. As the night drew in the country became bleaker and more deserted. An occasional light twinkling in the distance from some lonely hillside cottage was the only sign of the presence of man. The rough track still skirted the sea, and high as it was, the spray from the breakers drifted across it. The salt prinkled on my lips, and the air was filled with the hoarse roar of the surge and the thin piping of curlews, who flitted past in the darkness like white, shadowy, sad-voiced creatures from some other world. The wind blew in short, quick, angry puffs from the westward, and far out on the black waters a single glimmer of light rising and falling, tossing up, and then sinking out of sight, showed how fierce a sea had risen in the channel.

Riding through the gloaming in this strange wild scenery my mind naturally turned towards the past. I thought of my father and my mother, of the old carpenter

and of Solomon Sprent. Then I pondered over Decimus Saxon, his many-faced character having in it so much to be admired and so much to be abhorred. Did I like him or no ? It was more than I could say. From him I wandered off to my faithful Reuben, and to his love passage with the pretty Puritan, which in turn brought me to Sir Gervas and the wreck of his fortunes. My mind then wandered to the state of the army and the prospects of the rising, which led me to my present mission with its perils and its difficulties. Having turned over all these things in my mind I began to doze upon my horse's back, overcome by the fatigue of the journey and the drowsy lullaby of the waves. I had just fallen into a dream in which I saw Reuben Lockarby crowned King of England by Mistress Ruth Timewell, while Decimus Saxon endeavoured to shoot him with a bottle of Daffy's elixir, when in an instant, without warning, I was dashed violently from my horse, and left lying half-conscious on the stony track.

So stunned and shaken was I by the sudden fall, that though I had a dim knowledge of shadowy figures bending over me, and of hoarse laughter sounding in my ears, I could not tell for a few minutes where I was nor what had befallen me. When at last I did make an attempt to recover my feet I found that a loop of rope had been slipped round my arms and my legs so as to secure them. With a hard struggle I got one hand free, and dashed it in the face of one of the men who were holding me down ; but the whole gang of a dozen or more set upon me at once, and while some thumped and kicked at me, others tied a fresh cord round my elbows, and deftly fastened it in such a way as to pinion me completely. Finding that in my weak and dazed state all efforts were of no avail, I lay sullen and watchful, taking no heed of the random blows which were still showered upon me. So dark was it that I could neither see the faces of my attackers, nor form any guess as to who they might be, or how they had hurled me from my saddle. The champing and stamping

of a horse hard by showed me that Covenant was a prisoner as well as his master.

" Dutch Pete's got as much as he can carry," said a rough, harsh voice. " He lies on the track as limp as a conger."

" Ah, poor Pete ! " muttered another. " He'll never deal a card or drain a glass of the right Cognac again."

" There you lie, mine goot vriend," said the injured man, in weak, quavering tones. " And I will prove that you lie if you have a flaschen in your pocket."

" If Pete were dead and buried," the first speaker said, " a word about strong waters would bring him to. Give him a sup from your bottle, Dicon."

There was a great gurgling and sucking in the darkness, followed by a gasp from the drinker. " Gott sei gelobt," he exclaimed in a stronger voice, " I have seen more stars than ever were made. Had my kopf not been well hooped he would have knocked it in like an ill-staved cask. He shlags like the kick of a horse."

As he spoke the edge of the moon peeped over a cliff and threw a flood of cold clear light upon the scene. Looking up I saw that a strong rope had been tied across the road from one tree trunk to another about eight feet above the ground. This could not be seen by me, even had I been fully awake, in the dusk ; but catching me across the breast as Covenant trotted under it, it had swept me off and dashed me with great force to the ground. Either the fall or the blows which I had received had cut me badly, for I could feel the blood trickling in a warm stream past my ear and down my neck. I made no attempt to move, however, but waited in silence to find out who these men were into whose hands I had fallen. My one fear was lest my letters should be taken away from me, and my mission rendered of no avail. That in this, my first trust, I should be disarmed without a blow and lose the papers which had been confided to me, was a chance which made me flush and tingle with shame at the very thought.

The gang who had seized me were rough-bearded fellows in fur caps and fustian jackets, with buff belts round their waists, from which hung short straight whinyards. Their dark sun-dried faces and their great boots marked them as fishermen or seamen, as might be guessed from their rude sailor speech. A pair knelt on either side with their hands upon my arms, a third stood behind with a cocked pistol pointed at my head, while the others, seven or eight in number, were helping to his feet the man whom I had struck, who was bleeding freely from a cut over the eye.

" Take the horse up to Daddy Mycroft's," said a stout, black-bearded man, who seemed to be their leader. " It is no mere dragooner hack,[1] but a comely, full-blooded brute, which will fetch sixty pieces at the least. Your share of that, Peter, will buy salve and plaster for your cut."

" Ha, houndsfoot ! " cried the Dutchman, shaking his fist at me. " You would strike Peter, would you ? You would draw Peter's blood, would you ? Tausend Teufel, man ! if you and I were together upon the hillside we should see vich vas the petter man."

" Slack your jaw tackle, Pete," growled one of his comrades. " This fellow is a limb of Satan for sure, and doth follow a calling that none but a mean, snivelling, baseborn son of a gun would take to. Yet I warrant, from the look of him, that he could truss you like a woodcock if he had his great hands upon you. And you would howl for help as you did last Martinmas, when you did mistake Cooper Dick's wife for a gauger."

" Truss me, would he ? Todt und Hölle ! " cried the other, whom the blow and the brandy had driven to madness. " We shall see. Take that, thou deyvil's spawn, take that ! " He ran at me, and kicked me as hard as he could with his heavy sea-boots.

Some of the gang laughed, but the man who had spoken before gave the Dutchman a shove that sent him whirling.

[1] Note I, Appendix.—Dragooners and Chargers.

" None of that," he said sternly. " We'll have British fair-play on British soil, and none of your cursed long-shore tricks. I won't stand by and see an Englishman kicked, d'ye see, by a tub-bellied, round-starned, schnapps-swilling, chicken-hearted son of an Amsterdam lust-vrouw. Hang him, if the skipper likes. That's all above-board, but by thunder, if it's a fight that you will have, touch that man again."

" All right, Dicon," said their leader soothingly. " We all know that Pete's not a fighting man, but he's the best cooper on the coast, eh, Pete ? There is not his equal at staving, hooping and bumping. He'll take a plank of wood and turn it into a keg while another man would be thinking of it."

" Oh, you remember that, Captain Murgatroyd," said the Dutchman sulkily. " But see you me knocked about and shlagged, and bullied, and called names, and what help have I ? So help me, when the *Maria* is in the Texel next, I'll take to my old trade, I will, and never set foot on her again."

" No fear," the Captain answered, laughing. " While the *Maria* brings in five thousand good pieces a year, and can show her heels to any cutter on the coast, there is no fear of greedy Pete losing his share of her. Why, man, at this rate you may have a lust-haus of your own in a year or two, with a trimmed lawn, and the trees all clipped like peacocks, and the flowers in pattern, and a canal by the door, and a great bouncing housewife just like any Burgomeister. There's many such a fortune been made out of Mechlin and Cognac."

" Aye, and there's many a broken kopf got over Mechlin and Cognac," grumbled my enemy. " Donner ! There are other things beside lust-houses and flower-beds. There are lee-shores and nor'-westers, beaks and pre-ventives."

" And there's where the smart seaman has the pull over the herring buss, or the skulking coaster that works from Christmas to Christmas with all the danger and none of

the little pickings. But enough said! Up with the prisoner, and let us get him safely into the bilboes."

I was raised to my feet and half-carried, half dragged along in the midst of the gang. My horse had already been led away in the opposite direction. Our course lay off the road, down a very rocky and rugged ravine which sloped away towards the sea. There seemed to be no trace of a path, and I could only stumble along over rocks and bushes as best I might in my fettered and crippled state. The blood, however, had dried over my wounds, and the cool sea breeze playing upon my forehead refreshed me, and helped me to take a clearer view of my position.

It was plain from their talk that these men were smugglers. As such, they were not likely to have any great love for the Government, or desire to uphold King James in any way. On the contrary, their goodwill would probably be with Monmouth, for had I not seen the day before a whole regiment of foot in his army, raised from among the coaster folk? On the other hand, their greed might be stronger than their loyalty, and might lead them to hand me over to justice in the hope of reward. On the whole it would be best, I thought, to say nothing of my mission, and to keep my papers secret as long as possible.

But I could not but wonder, as I was dragged along, what had led these men to lie in wait for me as they had done. The road along which I had travelled was a lonely one, and yet a fair number of travellers bound from the West through Weston to Bristol must use it. The gang could not lie in perpetual guard over it. Why had they set a trap on this particular night, then? The smugglers were a lawless and desperate body, but they did not, as a rule, descend to foot-paddery or robbery. As long as no one interfered with them they were seldom the first to break the peace. Then, why had they lain in wait for me, who had never injured them? Could it possibly be that I had been betrayed? I was still turning over these questions in my mind when we all came to a

halt, and the Captain blew a shrill note on a whistle which hung round his neck.

The place where we found ourselves was the darkest and most rugged spot in the whole wild gorge. On either side great cliffs shot up, which arched over our heads, with a fringe of ferns and bracken on either lip, so that the dark sky and the few twinkling stars were well-nigh hid. Great black rocks loomed vaguely out in the shadowy light, while in front a high tangle of what seemed to be brushwood barred our road. At a second whistle, however, a glint of light was seen through the branches, and the whole mass was swung to one side as though it moved upon a hinge. Beyond it a dark winding passage opened into the side of the hill, down which we went with our backs bowed, for the rock ceiling was of no great height. On every side of us sounded the throbbing of the sea.

Passing through the entrance, which must have been dug with great labour through the solid rock, we came out into a lofty and roomy cave, lit up by a fire at one end, and by several torches. By their smoky yellow glare I could see that the roof was, at least, fifty feet above us, and was hung by long lime-crystals, which sparkled and gleamed with great brightness. The floor of the cave was formed of fine sand, as soft and velvety as a Wilton carpet, sloping down in a way which showed that the cave must at its mouth open upon the sea, which was confirmed by the booming and splashing of the waves, and by the fresh salt air which filled the whole cavern. No water could be seen, however, as a sharp turn cut off our view of the outlet.

In this rock-girt space, which may have been sixty paces long and thirty across, there were gathered great piles of casks, kegs and cases ; muskets, cutlasses, staves, cudgels and straw were littered about upon the floor. At one end a high wood fire blazed merrily, casting strange shadows along the walls, and sparkling like a thousand diamonds among the crystals on the roof. The smoke was carried away through a great cleft in the rocks.

Seated on boxes, or stretched on the sand round the fire, there were seven or eight more of the band, who sprang to their feet and ran eagerly towards us as we entered.

"Have ye got him?" they cried. "Did he indeed come? Had he attendants?"

"He is here, and he is alone," the Captain answered. "Our hawser fetched him off his horse as neatly as ever a gull was netted by a cragsman. What have ye done in our absence, Silas?"

"We have the packs ready for carriage," said the man addressed, a sturdy, weather-beaten seaman of middle age. "The silk and lace are done in these squares covered over with sacking. The one I have marked 'yarn' and the other 'jute'—a thousand of Mechlin to a hundred of the shiny. They will sling over a mule's back. Brandy, schnapps, Schiedam and Hamburg Goldwasser are all set out in due order. The 'baccy is in the flat cases over by the Black Drop there. A plaguy job we had carrying it all out, but here it is ship-shape at last, and the lugger floats like a skimming dish, with scarce ballast enough to stand up to a five-knot breeze."

"Any signs of the *Fairy Queen*?" asked the smuggler.

"None. Long John is down at the water's edge looking out for her flash-light. This wind should bring her up if she has rounded Combe-Martin Point. There was a sail about ten miles to the east-nor'-east at sundown. She might have been a Bristol schooner, or she might have been a King's fly-boat."

"A King's crawl-boat," said Captain Murgatroyd, with a sneer. "We cannot hang the gauger until Venables brings up the *Fairy Queen*, for after all it was one of his hands that was snackled. Let him do his own dirty work."

"Tausend Blitzen!" cried the ruffian Dutchman, "would it not be a kindly gruss to Captain Venables to chuck the gauger down the Black Drop ere he come? He may have such another job to do for us some day."

"Zounds, man, are you in command or am I?" said

the leader angrily. " Bring the prisoner forward to the
fire ! Now, hark ye, dog of a land-shark ; you are as
surely a dead man as though you were laid out with the
tapers burning. See here "—he lifted a torch, and showed
by its red light a great crack in the floor across the far end
of the cave—" you can judge of the Black Drop's depth ! "
he said, raising an empty keg and tossing it over into the
yawning gulf. For ten seconds we stood silent before a
dull distant clatter told that it had at last reached the
bottom.

" It will carry him half-way to hell before the breath
leaves him," said one.

" It's an easier death than the Devizes gallows ! " cried
a second.

" Nay, he shall have the gallows first ! " a third shouted.
" It is but his burial that we are arranging."

" He hath not opened his mouth since we took him,"
said the man who was called Dicon. " Is he a mute,
then ? Find your tongue, my fine fellow, and let us
hear what your name is. It would have been well for
you if you had been born dumb, so that you could not
have sworn our comrade's life away."

" I have been waiting for a civil question after all this
brawling and brabbling," said I. " My name is Micah
Clarke. Now, pray inform me who ye may be, and by
what warrant ye stop peaceful travellers upon the public
highway ? "

" This is our warrant," Murgatroyd answered, touching the hilt of his cutlass. " As to who we are, ye know
that well enough. Your name is not Clarke, but Westhouse, or Waterhouse, and you are the same cursed
exciseman who snackled our poor comrade, Cooper Dick,
and swore away his life at Ilchester."

" I swear that you are mistaken," I replied. " I have
never in my life been in these parts before."

" Fine words ! Fine words ! " cried another smuggler.
" Gauger or no, you must jump for it, since you know the
secret of our cave."

" Your secret is safe with me," I answered. " But if ye wish to murder me, I shall meet my fate as a soldier should. I should have chosen to die on the field of battle, rather than to lie at the mercy of such a pack of water-rats in their burrow."

" My faith ! " said Murgatroyd. " This is too tall talk for a gauger. He bears himself like a soldier, too. It is possible that in snaring the owl we have caught the falcon. Yet we had certain token that he would come this way, and on such another horse."

" Call up Long John," suggested the Dutchman. " I vould not give a plug of Trinidado for the Schelm's word. Long John was with Cooper Dick when he was taken."

" Aye," growled the mate Silas. " He got a wipe over the arm from the gauger's whinyard. He'll know his face, if any will."

" Call him, then," said Murgatroyd, and presently a long, loose-limbed seaman came up from the mouth of the cave, where he had been on watch. He wore a red kerchief round his forehead, and a blue jerkin, the sleeve of which he slowly rolled up as he came nigh.

" Where is Gauger Westhouse ? " he cried ; " he has left his mark on my arm. Rat me, if the scar is healed yet. The sun is on our side of the wall now, gauger. But hullo, mates ! who be this that ye have clapped into irons ? This is not our man ! "

" Not our man ! " they cried, with a volley of curses.

" Why, this fellow would make two of the gauger, and leave enough over to fashion a magistrate's clerk. Ye may hang him to make sure, but still he's not the man."

" Yes, hang him ! " said Dutch Pete. " Sapperment ! is our cave to be the talk of all the country ? Vere is the pretty *Maria* to go then, vid her silks and her satins, her kegs and her cases ? Are we to risk our cave for the sake of this fellow ? Besides, has he not schlagged my kopf— schlagged your cooper's kopf—as if he had hit me mit mine own mallet ? Is that not vorth a hemp cravat ? "

" Worth a jorum of rumbo," cried Dicon. " By your

279

leave, Captain, I would say that we are not a gang of
padders and michers, but a crew of honest seamen, who
harm none but those who harm us. Exciseman Westhouse hath slain Cooper Dick, and it is just that he should
die for it ; but as to taking this young soldier's life, I'd
as soon think of scuttling the saucy *Maria*, or of mounting
the Jolly Roger at her peak."

What answer would have been given to this speech I
cannot tell, for at that moment a shrill whistle resounded
outside the cave, and two smugglers appeared bearing
between them the body of a man. It hung so limp that
I thought at first that he might be dead, but when they
threw him on the sand he moved, and at last sat up like
one who is but half awoken from a swoon. He was a
square dogged-faced fellow, with a long white scar down
his cheek, and a close-fitting blue coat with brass buttons.

" It's Gauger Westhouse ! " cried a chorus of voices.

" Yes, it is Gauger Westhouse," said the man calmly,
giving his neck a wriggle as though he were in pain.
" I represent the King's law, and in its name I arrest ye
all, and declare all the contraband goods which I see
around me to be confiscate and forfeited, according to the
second section of the first clause of the statute upon illegal
dealing. If there are any honest men in this company,
they will assist me in the execution of my duty." He
staggered to his feet as he spoke, but his spirit was greater
than his strength, and he sank back upon the sand amid
a roar of laughter from the rough seamen.

" We found him lying on the road when we came from
Daddy Mycroft's," said one of the newcomers, who were
the same men who had led away my horse. " He must
have passed just after you left, and the rope caught him
under the chin and threw him a dozen paces. We saw
the revenue button on his coat, so we brought him down.
Body o' me, but he kicked and plunged for all that he was
three-quarters stunned."

" Have ye slacked the hawser ? " the Captain asked.

" We cast one end loose and let it hang."

" 'Tis well. We must keep him for Captain Venables. But now, as to our other prisoner : we must overhaul him and examine his papers, for so many craft are sailing under false colours that we must needs be careful. Hark ye, Mister Soldier ! What brings you to these parts, and what king do you serve ! for I hear there's a mutiny broke out, and two skippers claim equal rating in the old British ship."

" I am serving under King Monmouth," I answered, seeing that the proposed search must end in the finding of my papers.

" Under King Monmouth ! " cried the smuggler. " Nay, friend, that rings somewhat false. The good King hath, I hear, too much need of his friends in the south to let an able soldier go wandering along the sea-coast like a Cornish wrecker in a sou'-wester."

" I bear despatches," said I, " from the King's own hand to Henry Duke of Beaufort, at his castle at Badminton. Ye can find them in my inner pocket, but I pray ye not to break the seal, lest it bring discredit upon my mission."

" Sir," cried the gauger, rising himself upon his elbow, " I do hereby arrest you on the charge of being a traitor, a promoter of treason, a vagrant and a masterless man within the meaning of the fourth statute of the Act. As an officer of the law I call upon you to submit to my warrant."

" Brace up his jaw with your scarf, Jim," said Murgatroyd. " When Venables comes he will soon find a way to check his gab. Yes," he continued, looking at the back of my papers, " it is marked, as you say, ' From James the Second of England, known lately as the Duke of Monmouth, to Henry Duke of Beaufort, President of Wales, by the hand of Captain Micah Clarke, of Saxon's regiment of Wiltshire foot.' Cast off the lashings, Dicon. So, Captain, you are a free man once more, and I grieve that we should have unwittingly harmed you. We are good Lutherans to a man, and would rather speed you than hinder you on this mission."

" Could we not indeed help him on his way ? " said the mate Silas. " For myself, I don't fear a wet jacket or a tarry hand for the cause, and I doubt not ye are all of my way of thinking. Now with this breeze we could run up to Bristol and drop the Captain by morning, which would save him from being snapped up by any land-sharks on the road."

" Aye, aye," cried Long John. " The King's horse are out beyond Weston, but he could give them the slip if he had the *Maria* under him."

" Well," said Murgatroyd, " we could get back by three long tacks. Venables will need a day or so to get his goods ashore. If we are to sail back in company we shall have time on our hands. How would the plan suit you, Captain ? "

" My horse ! " I objected.

" It need not stop us. I can rig up a handy horse-stall with my spare spars and the grating. The wind has died down. The lugger could be brought to Dead Man's Edge, and the horse led down to it. Run up to Daddy's, Jim ; and you, Silas, see to the boat. Here is some cold junk and biscuit—seaman's fare, Captain—and a glass o' the real Jamaica to wash it down, an thy stomach be not too dainty for rough living."

I seated myself on a barrel by the fire, and stretched my limbs, which were cramped and stiffened by their confinement, while one of the seamen bathed the cut on my head with a wet kerchief, and another laid out some food on a case in front of me. The rest of the gang had trooped away to the mouth of the cave to prepare the lugger, save only two or three who stood on guard round the ill-fated gauger. He lay with his back resting against the wall of the cave, and his arms crossed over his breast, glancing round from time to time at the smugglers with menacing eyes, as a staunch old hound might gaze at a pack of wolves who had overmatched him. I was turning it over in my own mind whether aught could be done to help him, when Murgatroyd came over, and dipping a

tin pannikin into the open rum tub, drained it to the success of my mission.

" I shall send Silas Bolitho with you," said he, " while I bide here to meet Venables, who commands my consort. If there is aught that I can do to repay you for your ill usage——"

" There is but one thing, Captain," I broke in eagerly. " It is as much, or more, for your own sake than mine that I ask it. Do not allow this unhappy man to be murdered."

Murgatroyd's face flushed with anger. " You are a plain speaker, Captain Clarke," said he. " This is no murder. It is justice. What harm do we here ? There is not an old housewife over the whole countryside who does not bless us. Where is she to buy her souchong, or her strong waters, except from us ? We charge little, and force our goods on no one. We are peaceful traders. Yet this man and his fellows are ever yelping at our heels, like so many dogfish on a cod bank. We have been harried, and chivied, and shot at until we are driven into such dens as this. A month ago, four of our men were bearing a keg up the hillside to Farmer Black, who hath dealt with us these five years back. Of a sudden, down came half a score of horse, led by this gauger, hacked and slashed with their broadswords, cut Long John's arm open, and took Cooper Dick prisoner. Dick was haled to Ilchester Gaol, and hung up after the assizes like a stoat on a gamekeeper's door. This night we had news that this very gauger was coming this way, little knowing that we should be on the look-out for him. Is it a wonder that we should lay a trap for him, and that, having caught him, we should give him the same justice as he gave our comrades ? "

" He is but a servant," I argued. " He hath not made the law. It is his duty to enforce it. It is with the law itself that your quarrel is."

" You are right," said the smuggler gloomily. " It is with Judge Moorcroft that we have our chief account to

square. He may pass this road upon his circuit. Heaven send he does ! But we shall hang the gauger too. He knows our cave now, and it would be madness to let him go."

I saw that it was useless to argue longer, so I contented myself with dropping my pocket-knife on the sand within reach of the prisoner, in the hope that it might prove to be of some service to him. His guards were laughing and joking together, and giving little heed to their charge, but the gauger was keen enough, for I saw his hand close over it.

I had walked and smoked for an hour or more, when Silas the mate appeared, and said that the lugger was ready and the horse aboard. Bidding Murgatroyd fare-well, I ventured a few more words in favour of the gauger, which were received with a frown and an angry shake of the head. A boat was drawn up on the sand, inside the cave, at the water's edge. Into this I stepped, as directed, with my sword and pistols, which had been given back to me, while the crew pushed her off and sprang in as she glided into deep water.

I could see by the dim light of the single torch which Murgatroyd held upon the margin, that the roof of the cave sloped sheer down upon us as we sculled slowly out towards the entrance. So low did it come at last that there was only a space of a few feet between it and the water, and we had to bend our heads to avoid the rocks above us. The boatmen gave two strong strokes, and we shot out from under the overhanging ledge, and found ourselves in the open with the stars shining murkily above us, and the moon showing herself dimly and cloudily through a gathering haze. Right in front of us was a dark blur, which, as we pulled towards it, took the outline of a larger lugger rising and falling with the pulse of the sea. Her tall thin spars and delicate network of cordage towered above us as we glided under the counter, while the creak-ing of blocks and rattle of ropes showed that she was all ready to glide off upon her journey. Lightly and daintily

she rode upon the waters, like some giant seafowl, spreading one white pinion after another in preparation for her flight. The boatmen ran us alongside and steadied the dingy while I climbed over the bulwarks on to the deck.

She was a roomy vessel, very broad in the beam, with a graceful curve in her bows, and masts which were taller than any that I had seen on such a boat on the Solent. She was decked over in front, but very deep in the after part, with ropes fixed all round the sides to secure kegs when the hold should be full. In the midst of this after-deck the mariners had built a strong stall, in which my good steed was standing, with a bucket full of oats in front of him. My old friend shoved his nose against my face as I came aboard, and neighed his pleasure at finding his master once more. We were still exchanging caresses when the grizzled head of Silas Bolitho the mate popped out of the cabin hatchway.

" We are fairly on our way now, Captain Clarke," said he. " The breeze has fallen away to nothing, as you can see, and we may be some time in running down to our port. Are you not aweary ? "

" I am a little tired," I confessed. " My head is throbbing from the crack I got when that hawser of yours dashed me from my saddle."

" An hour or two of sleep will make you as fresh as a Mother Carey's chicken," said the smuggler. " Your horse is well cared for, and you can leave him without fear. I will set a man to tend him, though, truth to say, the rogues know more about studding-sails and halliards than they do of steeds and their requirements. Yet no harm can come to him, so you had best come down and turn in."

I descended the steep stairs which led down into the low-roofed cabin of the lugger. On either side a recess in the wall had been fitted up as a couch.

" This is your bed," said he, pointing to one of them. " We shall call you if there be aught to report." I needed no second invitation, but flinging myself down without undressing, I sank in a few minutes into a dream-

less sleep, which neither the gentle motion of the boat nor the clank of feet above my head could break off.

24. *Of the Welcome that Met me at Badminton*

WHEN I opened my eyes I had some ado to recall where I was, but on sitting up it was brought home to me by my head striking the low ceiling with a sharp rap. On the other side of the cabin Silas Bolitho was stretched at full length with a red woollen nightcap upon his head, fast asleep and snoring. In the centre of the cabin hung a swing-table, much worn, and stained all over with the marks of countless glasses and pannikins. A wooden bench, screwed to the floor, completed the furniture, with the exception of a stand of muskets along one side. Above and below the berths in which we lay were rows of lockers, in which, doubtless, some of the more choice laces and silks were stowed. The vessel was rising and falling with a gentle motion, but from the flapping of canvas I judged that there was a little wind. Slipping quietly from my couch, so as not to wake the mate, I stole upon deck.

We were, I found, not only becalmed, but hemmed in by a dense fog-bank which rolled in thick, choking wreaths all round us, and hid the very water beneath us. We might have been a ship of the air riding upon a white cloud-bank. Now and anon a little puff of breeze caught the foresail and bellied it out for a moment, only to let it flap back against the mast, limp and slack, once more. A sunbeam would at times break through the dense cloud, and would spangle the dead grey wall with a streak of rainbow colour, but the haze would gather in again and shut off the bright invader. Covenant was staring right and left with great questioning eyes. The crew were gathered along the bulwarks and smoking their pipes while they peered out into the dense fog.

" God den, Captain," said Dicon, touching his fur cap. " We have had a rare run while the breeze lasted, and the mate reckoned before he turned in that we were not many miles from Bristol town."

" In that case, my good fellow," I answered, " ye can set me ashore, for I have not far to go."

" We must e'en wait till the fog lifts," said Long John. " There's only one place along here, d'ye see, where we can land cargoes unquestioned. When it clears we shall turn her head for it, but until we can take our bearings it is anxious work wi' the sands under our lee."

" Keep a look-out there, Tom Baldock ! " cried Dicon to a man in the bows. " We are in the track of every Bristol ship, and though there's so little wind, a high-sparred craft might catch a breeze which we miss."

" Sh ! " said Long John suddenly, holding up his hand in warning. " Sh ! "

We listened with all our ears, but there was no sound, save the gentle wash of the unseen waves against our sides.

" Call the mate ! " whispered the seaman. " There's a craft close by us. I heard the rattle of a rope upon her deck."

Silas Bolitho was up in an instant, and we all stood straining our ears, and peering through the dense fog-bank. We had well-nigh made up our minds that it was a false alarm, and the mate was turning back in no very good humour, when a clear loud bell sounded seven times quite close to us, followed by a shrill whistle and a confused shouting and stamping.

" It's a King's ship," growled the mate. " That's seven bells, and the bo'sun is turning out the watch below."

" It was on our quarter," whispered one.

" Nay, I think it was on our larboard bow," said another. The mate held up his hand, and we all listened for some fresh sign of the whereabouts of our scurvy neighbour. The wind had freshened a little, and we were slipping through the water at four or five knots an hour. Of a sudden a hoarse voice was heard roaring at our very side.

" 'Bout ship ! " it shouted. " Bear a hand on the lee-braces, there ! Stand by the halliards ! Bear a hand, ye lazy rogues, or I'll be among ye with my cane, with a wannion to ye ! "

" It is a King's ship, sure enough, and she lies just there," said Long John, pointing out over the quarter. " Merchant adventurers have civil tongues. It's your blue-coated, gold-braided, swivel-eyed quarter-deckers that talk of canes. Ha ! did I not tell ye ? "

As he spoke, the white screen of vapour rolled up like the curtain in a playhouse, and uncovered a stately war-ship, lying so close that we could have thrown a biscuit aboard. Her long, lean, black hull rose and fell with a slow, graceful rhythm, while her beautiful spars and snow-white sails shot aloft until they were lost in the wreaths of fog which still hung around her. Nine bright brass cannons peeped out at us from her portholes. Above the line of hammocks, which hung like carded wool along her bulwarks, we could see the heads of the seamen staring down at us, and pointing us out to each other. On the high poop stood an elderly officer with cocked hat and trim white wig, who at once whipped up his glass and gazed at us through it.

" Ahoy, there ! " he shouted, leaning over the taffrail. " What lugger is that ? "

" The *Lucy*," answered the mate, " bound from Por-lock Quay to Bristol with hides and tallow. Stand ready to tack ! " he added in a lower voice, " the fog is coming down again."

" Ye have one of the hides with the horse still in it," cried the officer. " Run down under our counter. We must have a closer look at ye."

" Aye, aye, sir ! " said the mate, and putting his helm hard down the boom swung across, and the *Maria* darted off like a scared seabird into the fog. Looking back there was nothing but a dim loom to show where we had left the great vessel. We could hear, however, the hoarse shouting of orders and the bustle of men.

" Look out for squalls, lads ! " cried the mate. " He'll let us have it now."

He had scarcely spoken before there were half-a-dozen throbs of flame in the mist behind, and as many balls sung among our rigging. One cut away the end of the yard, and left it dangling ; another grazed the bowsprit, and sent a puff of white splinters into the air.

" Warm work, Captain, eh ? " said old Silas, rubbing his hands. " Zounds, they shoot better in the dark than ever they did in the light. There have been more shots fired at this lugger than she could carry were she loaded with them. And yet they never so much as knocked the paint off her before. There they go again ! "

A fresh discharge burst from the man-of-war, but this time they had lost all trace of us, and were firing by guess.

" That is their last bark, sir," said Dixon.

" No fear. They'll blaze away for the rest of the day," growled another of the smugglers. " Why, Lor' bless ye, it's good exercise for the crew, and the 'munition is the King's, so it don't cost nobody a groat."

" It's well the breeze freshened," said Long John. " I heard the creak o' davits just after the first discharge. She was lowering her boats, or I'm a Dutchman."

" The petter for you if you vas, you seven-foot stock-fish," cried my enemy the cooper, whose aspect was not improved by a great strip of plaster over his eye. " You might have learned something petter than to pull on a rope, or to swab decks like a vrouw all your life."

" I'll set you adrift in one of your own barrels, you skin of lard," said the seaman. " How often are we to trounce you before we knock the sauce out of you ? "

" The fog lifts a little towards the land," Silas remarked. " Methinks I see the loom of St. Austin's Point. It rises there upon the starboard bow."

" There it is, sure enough, sir ! " cried one of the sea-men, pointing to a dark cape which cut into the mist.

" Steer for the three-fathom creek then," said the mate.

" When we are on the other side of the point, Captain Clarke, we shall be able to land your horse and yourself. You will then be within a few hours' ride of your destination."

I led the old seaman aside, and having thanked him for the kindness which he had shown me, I spoke to him of the gauger, and implored him to use his influence to save the man.

" It rests with Captain Venables," said he gloomily. " If we let him go what becomes of our cave ? "

" Is there no way of ensuring his silence ? " I asked.

" Well, we might ship him to the Plantations," said the mate. " We could take him to the Texel with us, and get Captain Donders or some other to give him a lift across the western ocean."

" Do so," said I, " and I shall take care that King Monmouth shall hear of the help which ye have given his messenger."

" Well, we shall be there in a brace of shakes," he remarked. " Let us go below and load your ground tier, for there is nothing like starting well trimmed with plenty of ballast in the hold."

Following the sailor's advice I went down with him and enjoyed a rude but plentiful meal. By the time that we had finished, the lugger had been run into a narrow creek, with shelving sandy banks on either side. The district was wild and marshy, with few signs of any inhabitants. With much coaxing and pushing Covenant was induced to take to the water, and swam easily ashore, while I followed in the smugglers' dingy. A few words of rough, kindly leave-taking were shouted after me ; I saw the dingy return, and the beautiful craft glided out to sea and faded away once more into the mists which still hung over the face of the waters.

Truly Providence works in strange ways, my children, and until a man comes to the autumn of his days he can scarce say what hath been ill-luck and what hath been good. For of all the seeming misfortunes which have befallen

me during my wandering life, there is not one which I have not come to look upon as a blessing. And if you once take this into your hearts, it is a mighty help in enabling you to meet all troubles with a stiff lip ; for why should a man grieve when he hath not yet determined whether what hath chanced may not prove to be a cause of rejoicing ? Now here ye will perceive that I began by being dashed upon a stony road, beaten, kicked and finally well-nigh put to death in mistake for another. Yet it ended in my being safely carried to my journey's end, whereas, had I gone by land, it is more than likely that I should have been cut off at Weston ; for, as I heard afterwards, a troop of horse were making themselves very active in those parts by blocking the roads and seizing all who came that way.

Being now alone, my first care was to bathe my face and hands in a stream which ran down to the sea, and to wipe away any trace of my adventures of the night before. My cut was but a small one, and was concealed by my hair. Having reduced myself to some sort of order I next rubbed down my horse as best I could, and rearranged his girth and his saddle. I then led him by the bridle to the top of a sand-hill hard by, whence I might gain some idea as to my position.

The fog lay thick upon the Channel, but all inland was very clear and bright. Along the coast the country was dreary and marshy, but at the other side a goodly extent of fertile plain lay before me, well tilled and cared for. A range of lofty hills, which I guessed to be the Mendips, bordered the whole skyline, and further north there lay a second chain in the blue distance. The glittering Avon wound its way over the countryside like a silver snake in a flower-bed. Close to its mouth, and not more than two leagues from where I stood, rose the spires and towers of stately Bristol, the Queen of the West, which was and still may be the second city in the kingdom. The forests of masts which shot up like a pinegrove above the roofs of the houses bore witness to the great trade both with

Ireland and with the Plantations which had built up so flourishing a city.

As I knew that the Duke's seat was miles on the Gloucestershire side of the city, and as I feared lest I might be arrested and examined should I attempt to pass the gates, I struck inland with intent to ride round the walls and so avoid the peril. The path which I followed led me into a country lane, which in turn opened into a broad highway crowded with travellers, both on horseback and on foot. As the troublous times required that a man should journey with his arms, there was nought in my outfit to excite remark, and I was able to jog on among the other horsemen without question or suspicion. From their appearance they were, I judged, country farmers or squires for the most part, who were riding into Bristol to hear the news, and to store away their things of price in a place of safety.

" By your leave, zur ! " said a burly, heavy-faced man in a velveteen jacket, riding up upon my bridle-arm. " Can you tell me whether his Grace of Beaufort is in Bristol or at his house o' Badminton ? "

I answered that I could not tell, but that I was myself bound for his presence.

" He was in Bristol yestreen a-drilling o' the train-bands," said the stranger ; " but, indeed, his Grace be that loyal, and works that hard for his Majesty's cause, that he's a' ower the country, and it is but chance work for to try and to catch him. But if you are about to zeek him, whither shall you go ? "

" I will to Badminton," I answered, " and await him there. Can you tell me the way ? "

" What ! Not know the way to Badminton ! " he cried with a blank stare of wonder. " Whoy, I thought all the warld knew that. You're not fra Wales or the border counties, zur, that be very clear."

" I am a Hampshire man," said I. " I have come some distance to see the Duke."

" Aye, so I should think ! " he cried, laughing loudly.

" If you doan't know the way to Badminton you doan't know much ! But I'll go with you, danged if I doan't, and I'll show you your road, and run my chance o' finding the Duke there. What be your name ? "

" Micah Clarke is my name."

" And Vairmer Brown is mine—John Brown by the register, but better knowed as the Vairmer. Tak' this turn to the right off the high-road. Now we can trot our beasts and not be smothered in other folk's dust. And what be you going to Beaufort for ? "

" On private matters which will not brook discussion," I answered.

" Lor', now ! Affairs o' State belike," said he, with a whistle. " Well, a still tongue saves many a neck. I'm a cautious man myself, and these be times when I wouldna whisper some o' my thoughts—not, not into the ears o' my old brown mare here—for fear I'd see her some day standing over against me in the witness-box."

" They seem very busy over there," I remarked, for we were now in full sight of the walls of Bristol, where gangs of men were working hard with pick and shovel improving the defences.

" Aye, they be busy sure enough, makin' ready in case the rebels come this road. Cromwell and his tawnies found it a rasper in my vather's time, and Monmouth is like to do the same."

" It hath a strong garrison, too," said I, bethinking me of Saxon's advice at Salisbury. " I see two or three regiments out yonder on the bare open space."

" They have four thousand foot and a thousand horse," the farmer answered. " But the foot are only train-bands, and there's no trusting them after Axminster. They say up here that the rebels run to nigh twenty thousand, and that they give no quarter. Well, if we must have civil war, I hope it may be hot and sudden, not spun out for a dozen years like the last one. If our throats are to be cut, let it be with a shairp knife, and not with a blunt hedge shears."

" What say you to a stoup of cider ? " I asked, for we were passing an ivy-clad inn, with " The Beaufort Arms " printed upon the sign.

" With all my heart, lad," my companion answered. " Ho, there ! two pints of the old hard-brewed ! That will serve to wash the dust down. The real Beaufort Arms is up yonder at Badminton, for at the buttery hatch one may call for what one will in reason and never put hand to pocket."

" You speak of the house as though you knew it well," said I.

" And who should know it better ? " asked the sturdy farmer, wiping his lips, as we resumed our journey. " Why, it seems but yesterday that I played hide-and-seek wi' my brothers in the old Boteler Castle, that stood where the new house o' Badminton, or Acton Turville, as some calls it, now stands. The Duke hath built it but a few years, and, indeed, his Dukedom itself is scarce older. There are some who think that he would have done better to stick by the old name that his forebears bore."

" What manner of man is the Duke ? " I asked.

" Hot and hasty, like all of his blood. Yet when he hath time to think, and hath cooled down, he is just in the main. Your horse hath been in the water this morning, vriend."

" Yes," said I shortly, " he hath had a bath."

" I am going to his Grace on the business of a horse," quoth my companion. " His officers have pressed my piebald four-year-old, and taken it without a ' With your leave,' or ' By your leave,' for the use of the King. I would have them know that there is something higher than the Duke, or even than the King. There is the English law, which will preserve a man's goods and his chattels. I would do aught in reason for King James's service, but my piebald four-year-old is too much."

" I fear that the needs of the public service will override your objection," said I.

" Why, it is enough to make a man a Whig," he cried.

" Even the Roundheads always paid their vair penny for every pennyworth they had, though they wanted a vair pennyworth for each penny. I have heard my father say that trade was never so brisk as in 'forty-six, when they were down this way. Old Noll had a noose of hemp ready for horse-stealers, were they for King or for Parliament. But here comes his Grace's carriage, if I mistake not."

As he spoke a great heavy yellow coach, drawn by six cream-coloured Flemish mares, dashed down the road, and came swiftly towards us. Two mounted lackeys galloped in front, and two others all in light blue and silver liveries rode on either side.

" His Grace is not within, else there had been an escort behind," said the farmer, as we reined our horses aside to let the carriage pass. As they swept by he shouted out a question as to whether the Duke was at Badminton, and received a nod from the stately bewigged coachman in reply.

" We are in luck to catch him," said Farmer Brown. " He's as hard to find these days as a crake in a wheatfield. We should be there in an hour or less. I must thank you that I did not take a fruitless journey into Bristol. What did you say your errand was ? "

I was again compelled to assure him that the matter was not one of which I could speak with a stranger, on which he appeared to be huffed, and rode for some miles without opening his mouth. Groves of trees lined the road on either side, and the sweet smell of pines was in our nostrils. Far away the musical pealing of a bell rose and fell on the hot, close summer air. The shelter of the branches was pleasant, for the sun was very strong, blazing down out of a cloudless heaven, and raising a haze from the fields and valleys.

" 'Tis the bell from Chipping Sodbury," said my companion at last, wiping his ruddy face. " That's Sodbury Church yonder over the brow of the hill, and here on the right is the entrance of Badminton Park."

High iron gates, with the leopard and griffin, which are

the supporters of the Beaufort arms, fixed on the pillars which flanked them, opened into a beautiful domain of lawn and grass land with clumps of trees scattered over it, and broad sheets of water, thick with wild fowl. At every turn as we rode up the winding avenue some new beauty caught our eyes, all of which were pointed out and expounded by Farmer Brown, who seemed to take as much pride in the place as though it belonged to him. Here it was a rockery where a thousand bright-coloured stones shone out through the ferns and creepers which had been trained over them. There it was a pretty prattling brook, the channel of which had been turned so as to make it come foaming down over a steep ledge of rocks. Or perhaps it was some statue of nymph or sylvan god, or some artfully built arbour overgrown with roses or honeysuckle. I have never seen grounds so tastefully laid out, and it was done, as all good work in art must be done, by following Nature so closely that it only differed from her handiwork in its profusion in so narrow a compass. A few years later our healthy English taste was spoiled by the pedant gardening of the Dutch with their straight flat ponds, and their trees all clipped and in a line like vegetable grenadiers. In truth, I think that the Prince of Orange and Sir William Temple had much to answer for in working this change, but things have now come round again, I understand, and we have ceased to be wiser than Nature in our pleasure-grounds.

As we drew near the house we came on a large extent of level sward on which a troop of horse were exercising, who were raised, as my companion informed me, entirely from the Duke's own personal attendants. Passing them we rode through a grove of rare trees and came out on a broad space of gravel which lay in front of the house. The building itself was of great extent, built after the new Italian fashion, rather for comfort than for defence ; but on one wing there remained, as my companion pointed out, a portion of the old keep and battlements of the feudal castle of the Botelers, looking as out of place as a

farthingale of Queen Elizabeth joined to a court dress fresh from Paris. The main doorway was led up to by lines of columns and a broad flight of marble steps, on which stood a group of footmen and grooms, who took our horses when we dismounted. A grey-haired steward or major-domo inquired our business, and on learning that we wished to see the Duke in person, he told us that his Grace would give audience to strangers in the afternoon at half after three by the clock. In the meantime he said that the guests' dinner had just been laid in the hall, and it was his master's wish that none who came to Badminton should depart hungry. My companion and I were but too glad to accept the steward's invitation, so having visited the bathroom and attended to the needs of the toilet, we followed a footman, who ushered us into a great room where the company had already assembled.

The guests may have numbered fifty or sixty, old and young, gentle and simple, of the most varied types and appearance. I observed that many of them cast haughty and inquiring glances round them, in the pauses between the dishes, as though each marvelled how he came to be a member of so motley a crew. Their only common feature appeared to be the devotion which they showed to the platter and the wine flagon. There was little talking, for there were few who knew their neighbours. Some were soldiers who had come to offer their swords and their services to the King's lieutenant ; others were merchants from Bristol, with some proposal or suggestion anent the safety of their property. There were two or three officials of the city, who had come out to receive instructions as to its defence, while here and there I marked the child of Israel, who had found his way there in the hope that in times of trouble he might find high interest and noble borrowers. Horse-dealers, saddlers, armourers, surgeons and clergymen completed the company, who were waited upon by a staff of powdered and liveried servants, who brought and removed the dishes with the silence and deftness of long training.

The room was a contrast to the bare plainness of Sir Stephen Timewell's dining-hall at Taunton, for it was richly panelled and highly decorated all round. The floor was formed of black and white marble, set in squares, and the walls were of polished oak, and bore a long line of paintings of the Somerset family, from John of Gaunt downwards. The ceiling, too, was tastefully painted with flowers and nymphs, so that a man's neck was stiff ere he had done admiring it. At the further end of the hall yawned a great fireplace of white marble, with the lions and lilies of the Somerset arms carved in oak above it, and a long gilt scroll bearing the family motto, " Mutare vel timere sperno." The massive tables at which we sat were loaded with silver chargers and candelabra, and bright with the rich plate for which Badminton was famous. I could not but think that, if Saxon could clap eyes upon it, he would not be long in urging that the war be carried on in this direction.

After dinner we were all shown into a small ante-chamber, set round with velvet settees, where we were to wait till the Duke was ready to see us. In the centre of this room there stood several cases, glass-topped and lined with silk, wherein were little steel and iron rods, with brass tubes and divers other things, very bright and ingenious, though I could not devise for what end they had been put together. A gentleman in waiting came round with paper and ink-horn, making notes of our names and of our business. Him I asked whether it might not be possible for me to have an entirely private audience.

" His Grace never sees in private," he replied. " He has ever his chosen councillors and officers in attendance."

" But the business is one which is only fit for his own ear," I urged.

" His Grace holds that there is no business fit only for his own ear," said the gentleman. " You must arrange matters as best you can when you are shown in to him. I will promise, however, that your request be carried to him, though I warn you that it cannot be granted."

I thanked him for his good offices, and turned away with the farmer to look at the strange little engines within the cases.

" What is it ? " I asked. " I have never seen aught that was like it."

" It is the work of the mad Marquis of Worcester," quoth he. " He was the Duke's grandfather. He was ever making and devising such toys, but they were never of any service to himself or to others. Now, look ye here ! This wi' the wheels were called the water-engine, and it was his crazy thought that, by heating the water in that 'ere kettle, ye might make the wheels go round, and thereby travel along iron bars quicker nor a horse could run. 'Oons ! I'd match my old brown mare against all such contrivances to the end o' time. But to our places, for the Duke is coming."

We had scarce taken our seats with the other suitors, when the folding-doors were flung open, and a stout, thick, short man of fifty, or thereabouts, came bustling into the room, and strode down it between two lines of bowing clients. He had large projecting blue eyes, with great pouches of skin beneath them, and a yellow, sallow visage. At his heels walked a dozen officers and men of rank, with flowing wigs and clanking swords. They had hardly passed through the opposite door into the Duke's own room, when the gentleman with the list called out a name, and the guests began one after the other to file into the great man's presence.

" Methinks his Grace is in no very gentle temper," quoth Farmer Brown. " Did you not mark how he gnawed his nether lip as he passed ? "

" He seemed a quiet gentleman enough," I answered, " it would try Job himself to see all these folk of an afternoon."

" Hark at that ! " he whispered, raising his finger. As he spoke the sound of the Duke's voice in a storm of wrath was heard from the inner chamber, and a little sharp-faced man came out and flew through the ante-chamber as though fright had turned his head.

" He is an armourer of Bristol," whispered one of my neighbours. " It is likely that the Duke cannot come to terms with him over a contract."

" Nay," said another. " He supplied Sir Marmaduke Hyson's troop with sabres, and it is said that the blades will bend as though they were lead. Once used they can never be fitted back into the scabbard again."

" The tall man who goes in now is an inventor," quoth the first. " He hath the secret of some very grievous fire, such as hath been used by the Greeks against the Turks in the Levant, which he desires to sell for the better fortifying of Bristol."

The Greek fire seemed to be in no great request with the Duke, for the inventor came out presently with his face as red as though it had been touched by his own compound. The next upon the list was my honest friend the farmer. The angry tones which greeted him promised badly for the fate of the four-year-old, but a lull ensued, and the farmer came out and resumed his seat, rubbing his great red hands with satisfaction.

" Ecod ! " he whispered. " He was plaguy hot at first, but he soon came round, and he hath promised that if I pay for the hire of a dragooner as long as the war shall last I shall have back the piebald."

I had been sitting all this time wondering how in the world I was to conduct my business amid the swarm of suppliants and the crowd of officers who were attending the Duke. Had there been any likelihood of my gaining audience with him in any other way I should gladly have adopted it, but all my endeavours to that end had been useless. Unless I took this occasion I might never come face to face with him at all. But how could he give due thought or discussion to such a matter before others ? What chance was there of his weighing it as it should be weighed ? Even if his feelings inclined him that way, he dared not show any sign of wavering when so many eyes were upon him. I was tempted to feign some other reason for my coming, and trust to fortune to give me

some more favourable chance for handing him my papers. But then that chance might never arrive, and time was pressing. It was said that he would return to Bristol next morning. On the whole, it seemed best that I should make the fittest use I could of my present position in the hope that the Duke's own discretion and self-command might, when he saw the address upon my despatches, lead to a more private interview.

I had just come to this resolution when my name was read out, on which I rose and advanced into the inner chamber. It was a small but lofty room, hung in blue silk with a broad gold cornice. In the centre was a square table littered over with piles of papers, and behind this sat his Grace with full-bottomed wig rolling down to his shoulders, very stately and imposing. He had the same subtle air of the court which I had observed both in Monmouth and in Sir Gervas, which, with his high bold features and large piercing eyes, marked him as a leader of men. His private scrivener sat beside him, taking notes of his directions, while the others stood behind in a half circle, or took snuff together in the deep recess of the window.

" Make a note of Smithson's order," he said, as I entered. " A hundred pots and as many fronts and backs to be ready by Tuesday ; also sixscore snaphances for the musqueteers, and two hundred extra spades for the workers. Mark that the order be declared null and void unless fulfilled within the time appointed."

" It is so marked, your Grace."

" Captain Micah Clarke," said the Duke, reading from the list in front of him. " What is your wish, Captain ? "

" One which it would be better if I could deliver privately to your Grace," I answered.

" Ah, you are he who desired private audience ? Well Captain, these are my council and they are as myself. So we may look upon ourselves as alone. What I may hear they may hear. Zounds, man, never stammer and boggle, but out with it ! "

301

My request had roused the interest of the company, and those who were in the window came over to the table. Nothing could have been worse for the success of my mission, and yet there was no help for it but to deliver my despatches. I can say with a clear conscience, without any vainglory, that I had no fears for myself. The doing of my duty was the one thought in my mind. And here I may say once for all, my dear children, that I am speaking of myself all through this statement with the same freedom as though it were another man. In very truth the strong active lad of one-and-twenty *was* another man from the grey-headed old fellow who sits in the chimney corner and can do nought better than tell old tales to the youngsters. Shallow water gives a great splash, and so a braggart has ever been contemptible in my eyes. I trust, therefore, that ye will never think that your grandad is singing his own praises, or setting himself up as better than his neighbours. I do but lay the facts, as far I can recall them, before ye with all freedom and with all truth.

My short delay and hesitation had sent a hot flush of anger into the Duke's face, so I drew the packet of papers from my inner pocket and handed them to him with a respectful bow. As his eyes fell upon the superscription, he gave a sudden start of surprise and agitation, making a motion as though to hide them in his bosom. If this were his impulse he overcame it, and sat lost in thought for a minute or more with the papers in his hand. Then with a quick toss of the head, like a man who hath formed his resolution, he broke the seals and cast his eyes over the contents, which he then threw down upon the table with a bitter laugh.

" What think ye, gentlemen ? " he cried, looking round with scornful eyes ; " what think ye this private message hath proved to be ? It is a letter from the traitor Monmouth, calling upon me to resign the allegiance of my natural sovereign and to draw my sword in his behalf ! If I do this I am to have his gracious favour and protec-

tion. If not, I incur sequestration, banishment and ruin. He thinks Beaufort's loyalty is to be bought like a packman's ware, or bullied out of him by ruffling words. The descendant of John of Gaunt is to render fealty to the brat of a wandering playwoman ! "

Several of the company sprang to their feet, and a general buzz of surprise and anger greeted the Duke's words. He sat with bent brows, beating his foot against the ground, and turning over the papers upon the table.

" What hath raised his hopes to such mad heights ? " he cried. " How doth he presume to send such a missive to one of my quality ? Is it because he hath seen the backs of a parcel of rascally militiamen, and because he hath drawn a few hundred chaw-bacons from the plough's tail to his standard, that he ventures to hold such language to the President of Wales ? But ye will be my witnesses as to the spirit in which I received it ? "

" We can preserve your Grace from all danger of slander on that point," said an elderly officer, while a murmur of assent from the others greeted the remark.

" And you ! " cried Beaufort, raising his voice and turning his flashing eyes upon me ; " who are you that dare to bring such a message to Badminton ? You had surely taken leave of your senses ere you did set out upon such an errand ! "

" I am in the hands of God here as elsewhere," I answered, with some flash of my father's fatalism. " I have done what I promised to do, and the rest is no concern of mine."

" You shall find it a very close concern of thine," he shouted, springing from his chair and pacing up and down the room ; " so close as to put an end to all thy other concerns in this life. Call in the halberdiers from the outer hall ! Now, fellow, what have you to say for yourself ? "

" There is nought to be said," I answered.

" But something to be done," he retorted in a fury. " Seize this man and secure his hands ! "

Four halberdiers who had answered the summons

closed in upon me and laid hands on me. Resistance would have been folly, for I had no wish to harm the men in the doing of their duty. I had come to take my chance, and if that chance should prove to be death, as seemed likely enough at present, it must be met as a thing foreseen. I thought of those old-time lines which Master Chillingfoot, of Petersfield, had ever held up to our admiration—

> Non civium ardor prava jubentium
> Non vultus instantis tyranni
> Mente quatit solidâ.

Here was the " vultus instantis tyranni," in this stout, bewigged, lace-covered, yellow-faced man in front of me. I had obeyed the poet in so far that my courage had not been shaken. I confess that this spinning dust-heap of a world has never had such attractions for me that it would be a pang to leave it. Never, at least, until my marriage —and that, you will find, alters your thoughts about the value of your life, and many other of your thoughts as well. This being so, I stood erect, with my eyes fixed upon the angry nobleman, while his soldiers were putting the gyves about my wrists.

25. *Of Strange Doings in the Boteler Dungeon*

" TAKE down this fellow's statement," said the Duke to his scrivener. " Now, sirrah, it may not be known to you that his gracious Majesty the King hath conferred plenary powers upon me during these troubled times, and that I have his warrant to deal with all traitors without either jury or judge. You do bear a commission, I understand, in the rebellious body which is here described as Saxon's regiment of Wiltshire Foot ? Speak the truth for your neck's sake."

" I will speak the truth for the sake of something higher than that, your Grace," I answered. " I command a company in that regiment."

" And who is this Saxon ? "

" I will answer all that I may concerning myself," said I, " but not a word which may reflect upon others."

" Ha ! " he roared, hot with anger. " Our pretty gentleman must needs stand upon the niceties of honour after taking up arms against his King. I tell you, sir, that your honour is in such a parlous state already that you may well throw it over and look to your safety. The sun is sinking in the west. Ere it set your life, too, may have set for ever."

" I am the keeper of my own honour, your Grace," I answered. " As to my life, I should not be standing here this moment if I had any great dread of losing it. It is right that I should tell you that my Colonel hath sworn to exact a return for any evil that may befall me, on you or any of your household who may come into his power. This I say, not as a threat, but as a warning, for I know him to be a man who is like to be as good as his word."

" Your Colonel, as you call him, may find it hard enough to save himself soon," the Duke answered with a sneer. " How many men hath Monmouth with him ? "

I smiled and shook my head.

" How shall we make this traitor find his tongue ? " he asked furiously, turning to his council.

" I should clap on the thumbkins," said one fierce-faced old soldier.

" I have known a lighted match between the fingers work wonders," another suggested. " Sir Thomas Dalzell hath in the Scottish war been able to win over several of that most stubborn and hardened race, the Western Covenanters, by such persuasion."

" Sir Thomas Dalzell," said a grey-haired gentleman, clad in black velvet, " hath studied the art of war among the Muscovites, in their barbarous and bloody encounters with the Turks. God forbid that we Christians of England should seek our examples among the skin-clad idolaters of a savage country."

" Sir William would like to see war carried out on truly

courteous principles," said the first speaker. " A battle should be like a stately minuet, with no loss of dignity or of etiquette."

" Sir," the other answered hotly, " I have been in battles when you were in your baby linen, and I handled a battoon when you could scarce shake a rattle. In leaguer or onfall a soldier's work is sharp and stern, but I say that the use of torture, which the law of England hath abolished, should also be laid aside by the law of nations."

" Enough, gentlemen, enough ! " cried the Duke, seeing that the dispute was like to wax warm. " Your opinion, Sir William, hath much weight with us, and yours also, Colonel Hearn. We shall discuss this at greater length in privacy. Halberdiers, remove the prisoner, and let a clergyman be sent to look to his spiritual needs ! "

" Shall we take him to the strong room, your Grace ? " asked the Captain of the guard.

" No, to the old Boteler dungeon," he replied ; and I heard the next name upon the list called out, while I was led through a side door with a guard in front and behind me. We passed through endless passages and corridors, with heavy step and clank of arms, until we reached the ancient wing. Here, in the corner turret, was a small, bare room, mouldy and damp, with a high, arched roof, and a single long slit in the outer wall to admit light. A small wooden couch and a rude chair formed the whole of the furniture. Into this I was shown by the Captain, who stationed a guard at the door, and then came in after me and loosened my wrists. He was a sad-faced man, with solemn sunken eyes and a dreary expression, which matched ill with his bright trappings and gay sword-knot.

" Keep your heart up, friend," said he, in a hollow voice. " It is but a choke and a struggle. A day or two since we had the same job to do, and the man scarcely groaned. Old Spender, the Duke's marshal, hath as sure a trick of tying and as good judgment in arranging a drop as hath Dun of Tyburn. Be of good heart, therefore, for you shall not fall into the hands of a bungler."

" I would that I could let Monmouth know that his letters were delivered," I exclaimed, seating myself on the side of the bed.

" I' faith, they were delivered. Had you been the penny postman of Mr. Robert Murray, of whom we heard so much in London last spring, you could not have handed it in more directly. Why did you not talk the Duke fair ? He is a gracious nobleman, and kind of heart, save when he is thwarted or angered. Some little talk as to the rebels' numbers and dispositions might have saved you."

" I wonder that you, as a soldier, should speak or think of such a thing," said I coldly.

" Well, well ! Your neck is your own. If it please you to take a leap into nothing it were pity to thwart you. But his Grace commanded that you should have the chaplain. I must away to him."

" I prithee do not bring him," said I. " I am one of a dissenting stock, and I see that there is a Bible in yonder recess. No man can aid me in making my peace with God."

" It is well," he answered, " for Dean Hewby hath come over from Chippenham, and he is discoursing with our good chaplain on the need of self-denial, moistening his throat the while with a flask of the prime tokay. At dinner I heard him put up thanks for what he was to receive, and in the same breath ask the butler how he dared to serve a deacon of the Church with a pullet without truffle dressing. But, perhaps, you would desire Dean Hewby's spiritual help ? No ? Well, what I can do for you in reason shall be done, since you will not be long upon our hands. Above all, keep a cheery heart."

He left the cell, but presently unlocked the door and pushed his dismal face round the corner. " I am Captain Sinclair, of the Duke's household," he said, " should you have occasion to ask for me. You had best have spiritual help, for I do assure you that there hath been something worse than either warder or prisoner in this cell."

" What then ? " I asked.

307

" Why, marry, nothing less than the Devil," he answered, coming in and closing the door. " It was in this way," he went on, sinking his voice : " Two years agone Hector Marot, the highwayman, was shut up in this very Boteler dungeon. I was myself on guard in the corridor that night, and saw the prisoner at ten o'clock sitting on that bed even as you are now. At twelve I had occasion to look in, as my custom is, with the hope of cheering his lonely hours, when, lo he was gone ! Yes, you may well stare. Mine eyes had never been off the door, and you can judge what chance there was of his getting through the windows. Walls and floor are both solid stone, which might be solid rock for the thickness. When I entered there was a plaguy smell of brimstone, and the flame of my lanthorn burned blue. Nay, it is no smiling matter. If the Devil did not run away with Hector Marot, pray who did ? for sure I am that no angel of grace could come to him as to Peter of old. Perchance the Evil One may desire a second bird out of the same cage, and so I tell you this that you may be on your guard against his assaults."

" Nay, I fear him not," I answered.

" It is well," croaked the Captain. " Be not cast down ! " His head vanished, and the key turned in the creaking lock. So thick were the walls that I could hear no sound after the door was closed. Save for the sighing of the wind in the branches of the trees outside the narrow window, all was as silent as the grave within the dungeon.

Thus left to myself I tried to follow Captain Sinclair's advice as to the keeping up of my heart, though his talk was far from being of a cheering nature. In my young days, more particularly among the sectaries with whom I had been brought most in contact, a belief in the occasional appearance of the Prince of Darkness, and his interference in bodily form with the affairs of men, was widespread and unquestioning. Philosophers in their own quiet chambers may argue learnedly on the absurdity of such things, but in a dim-lit dungeon, cut off from the world,

with the grey gloaming creeping down, and one's own
fate hanging in the balance, it becomes a very different
matter. The escape, if the Captain's story were true,
appeared to border upon the miraculous. I examined
the walls of the cell very carefully. They were formed of
great square stones cunningly fitted together. The thin
slit or window was cut through the centre of a single
large block. All over, as high as the hand could reach,
the face of the walls was covered with letters and legends
cut by many generations of captives. The floor was
composed of old foot-worn slabs, firmly cemented together.
The closest search failed to show any hole or cranny where
a rat could have escaped, far less a man.

It is a very strange thing, my dears, to sit down in cold
blood, and think that the chances are that within a few
hours your pulses will have given their last throb, and
your soul have sped away upon its final errand. Strange
and very awesome ! The man who rideth down into the
press of the battle with his jaw set and his grip tight upon
reign and sword-hilt cannot feel this, for the human mind
is such that one emotion will ever push out another.
Neither can the man who draws slow and catching breaths
upon the bed of deadly sickness be said to have experience
of it, for the mind weakened with disease can but submit
without examining too closely that which it submits to.
When, however, a young and hale man sits alone in quiet,
and sees present death hanging over him, he hath such
food for thought that, should he survive and live to be
grey-headed, his whole life will be marked and altered by
those solemn hours, as a stream is changed in its course
by some rough bank against which it hath struck. Every
little fault and blemish stands out clear in the presence of
death, as the dust specks appear when the sunbeam shines
into the darkened room. I noted them then, and I have,
I trust, noted them ever since.

I was seated with my head bowed upon my breast,
deeply buried in this solemn train of thoughts, when I
was startled by hearing a sharp click, such as a man might

give who wished to attract attention. I sprang to my feet and gazed round in the gathering gloom without being able to tell whence it came. I had well-nigh persuaded myself that my senses had deceived me, when the sound was repeated louder than before, and casting my eyes upwards I saw a face peering in at me through the slit, or part of a face rather, for I could but see the eye and corner of the cheek. Standing on my chair I made out that it was none other than the farmer who had been my companion upon the road.

" Hush, lad ! " he whispered, with a warning fore-finger pushed through the narrow crack. " Speak low, or the guard may chance to hear. What can I do for you ? "

" How did you come to know where I was ? " I asked in astonishment.

" Whoy, mun," he answered, " I know as much of this 'ere house as Beaufort does himsel'. Afore Badminton was built, me and my brothers has spent many a day in climbing over the old Boteler tower. It's not the first time that I have spoke through this window. But, quick ; what can I do for you ? "

" I am much beholden to you, sir," I answered, " but I fear that there is no help which you can give me, unless, indeed, you could convey news to my friends in the army of what hath befallen me."

" I might do that," whispered Farmer Brown. " Hark ye in your ear, lad, what I never breathed to man yet. Mine own conscience pricks me at times over this bolster-ing up of a Papist to rule over a Protestant nation. Let like rule like, say I. At the 'lections I rode to Sudbury, and I put in my vote for Maister Evans, of Turnford, who was in favour o' the Exclusionists. Sure enough, if that same Bill had been carried, the Duke would be sitting on his father's throne. The law would have said yes. Now, it says nay. A wonderful thing is the law with its yea, yea, and nay, nay, like Barclay, the Quaker man, that came down here in a leather suit, and ca'd the parson a steepleman. There's the law. It's no use shootin' at it,

or passin' pikes through it, no, nor chargin' at it wi' a troop of horse. If it begins by saying ' nay ' it will say ' nay ' to the end of the chapter. Ye might as well fight wi' the book o' Genesis. Let Monmouth get the law changed, and it will do more for him than all the dukes in England. For all that he's a Protestant, and I would do what I might to serve him."

" There is a Captain Lockarby, who is serving in Colonel Saxon's regiment, in Monmouth's army," said I. " Should things go wrong with me, I would take it as a great kindness if you would bear him my love, and ask him to break it gently, by word or by letter, to those at Havant. If I were sure that this would be done, it would be a great ease to my mind."

" It shall be done, lad," said the good farmer. " I shall send my best man and fleetest horse this very night, that they may know the straits in which you are. I have a file here if it would help you."

" Nay," I answered, " human aid can do little to help me here."

" There used to be a hole in the roof. Look up and see if you can see aught of it."

" It arches high above my head," I answered, looking upwards ; " but there is no sign of any opening."

" There was one," he repeated. " My brother Roger hath swung himself down wi' a rope. In the old time the prisoners were put in so, like Joseph into the pit. The door is but a new thing."

" Hole or no hole, it cannot help me," I answered. " I have no means of climbing to it. Do not wait longer, kind friend, or you may find yourself in trouble."

" Good-bye then, my brave heart," he whispered, and the honest grey eye and corner of ruddy cheek disappeared from the casement. Many a time during the course of the long evening I glanced up with some wild hope that he might return, and every creak of the branches outside brought me on to the chair, but it was the last that I saw of Farmer Brown.

This kindly visit, short as it was, relieved my mind greatly, for I had a trusty man's word that, come what might, my friends should, at least, have some news of my fate. It was now quite dark, and I was pacing up and down the little chamber, when the key turned in the door, and the Captain entered with a rushlight and a great bowl of bread and milk.

" Here is your supper, friend," said he. " Take it down, appetite or no, for it will give you strength to play the man at the time ye wot of. They say it was beautiful to see my Lord Russell die upon Tower Hill. Be of good cheer ! Folk may say as much of you. His Grace is in a terrible way. He walketh up and down, and biteth his lip, and clencheth his hands like one who can scarce contain his wrath. It may not be against you, but I know not what else can have angered him."

I made no answer to this Job's comforter, so he presently left me, placing the bowl upon the chair, with the rushlight beside it. I finished the food, and feeling the better for it, stretched myself upon the couch, and fell into a heavy and dreamless sleep. This may have lasted three or four hours, when I was suddenly awoken by a sound like the creaking of hinges. Sitting up on the pallet I gazed around me. The rushlight had burned out and the cell was impenetrably dark. A greyish glimmer at one end showed dimly the position of the aperture, but all else was thick and black. I strained my ears, but no further sound fell upon them. Yet I was certain that I had not been deceived, and that the noise which had aroused me was within my very chamber. I rose and felt my way slowly round the room, passing my hand over the walls and door. Then I paced backwards and forwards to test the flooring. Neither around me nor beneath me was there any change. Whence did the sound come from, then ? I sat down upon the side of the bed and waited patiently in the hope of hearing it once again.

Presently it was repeated, a low groaning and creaking

as though a door or shutter long disused was being
slowly and stealthily opened. At the same time a dull
yellow light streamed down from above, issuing from a
thin slit in the centre of the arched roof above me.
Slowly as I watched it this slit widened and extended as
if a sliding panel were being pulled out, until a good-
sized hole was left, through which I saw a head, looking
down at me, outlined against the misty light behind it.
The knotted end of a rope was passed through this
aperture, and came dangling down to the dungeon floor.
It was a good stout piece of hemp, strong enough to bear
the weight of a heavy man, and I found, upon pulling at
it, that it was firmly secured above. Clearly it was the
desire of my unknown benefactor that I should ascend
by it, so I went up hand over hand, and after some
difficulty in squeezing my shoulders through the hole I
succeeded in reaching the room above. While I was still
rubbing my eyes after the sudden change from darkness
into light, the rope was swiftly whisked up and the sliding
shutter closed once more. To those who were not in the
secret there was nothing to throw light upon my disappearance.

I found myself in the presence of a stout short man
clad in a rude jerkin and leather breeches, which gave
him somewhat the appearance of a groom. He wore a
broad felt hat drawn down very low over his eyes, while
the lower part of his face was swathed round with a
broad cravat. In his hand he bore a horn lanthorn, by
the light of which I saw that the room in which we were
was of the same size as the dungeon beneath, and differed
from it only in having a broad casement which looked
out upon the park. There was no furniture in the chamber, but a great beam ran across it, to which the rope had
been fastened by which I ascended.

" Speak low, friend," said the stranger. " The walls
are thick and the doors are close, yet I would not have
your guardians know by what means you have been
spirited away."

" Truly, sir," I answered, " I can scarce credit that it
is other than a dream. It is wondrous that my dungeon
should be so easily broken into, and more wondrous
still that I should find a friend who would be willing to
risk so much for my sake."

" Look there ! " quoth he, holding down his lanthorn
so as to cast its light on the part of the floor where the
panel was fitted. " Can you not see how old and crumbled
is the stonework which surrounds it ? This opening in
the roof is as old as the dungeon itself, and older far than
the door by which you were led into it. For this was one
of those bottle-shaped cells or oubliettes which hard
men of old devised for the safe keeping of their captives.
Once lowered through this hole into the stone-girt pit a
man might eat his heart out, for his fate was sealed.
Yet you see that the very device which once hindered
escape has now brought freedom within your reach."

" Thanks to your clemency, your Grace," I answered,
looking keenly at my companion.

" Now out on these disguises ! " he cried, peevishly
pushing back the broad-edged hat and disclosing, as I
expected, the features of the Duke. " Even a blunt
soldier lad can see through my attempts at concealment.
I fear, Captain, that I should make a bad plotter, for my
nature is as open—well, as thine is. I cannot better the
simile."

" Your Grace's voice once heard is not easily forgot,"
said I.

" Especially when it talks of hemp and dungeons," he
answered, with a smile. " But if I clapped you into
prison, you must confess that I have made you amends by
pulling you out again at the end of my line, like a minnow
out of a bottle. But how came you to deliver such papers
in the presence of my council ? "

" I did what I could to deliver them in private,"
said I. " I sent you a message to that effect."

" It is true," he answered ; " but such messages come
in to me from every soldier who wishes to sell his sword,

and every inventor who hath a long tongue and a short purse. How could I tell that the matter was of real import ? "

" I feared to let the chance slip lest it might never return," said I. " I hear that your Grace hath little leisure during these times."

" I cannot blame you," he answered, pacing up and down the room. " But it was untoward. I might have hid the despatches, yet it would have roused suspicions. Your errand would have leaked out. There are many who envy my lofty fortunes and who would seize upon a chance of injuring me with King James. Sunderland or Somers would either of them blow the least rumour into a flame which might prove unquenchable. There was nought for it, therefore, but to show the papers and to turn a harsh face on the messenger. The most venomous tongue could not find fault in my conduct. What course would you have advised under such circumstances ? "

" The most direct," I answered.

" Aye, aye, Sir Honesty. Public men have, however, to pick their steps as best they may, for the straight path would lead too often to the cliff-edge. The Tower would be too scanty for its guests were we all to wear our hearts upon our sleeves. But to you in this privacy I can tell my real thoughts without fear of betrayal or misconstruction. On paper I will not write one word. Your memory must be the sheet which bears my answer to Monmouth. And first of all, erase from it all that you have heard me say in the council-room. Let it be as though it never were spoken. Is that done ? "

" I understand that it did not really represent your Grace's thoughts."

" Very far from it, Captain. But prithee tell me what expectation of success is there among the rebels themselves ? You must have heard your Colonel and others discuss the question, or noted by their bearing which way their thoughts lay. Have they good hopes of holding out against the King's troops ? "

"'They have met with nought but success hitherto," I answered.

" Against the militia. But they will find it another thing when they have trained troops to deal with. And yet—and yet ! . . . One thing I know, that any defeat of Feversham's army would cause a general rising throughout the country. On the other hand, the King's party are active. Every post brings news of some fresh levy. Albemarle still holds the militia together in the west. The Earl of Pembroke is in arms in Wiltshire. Lord Lumley is moving from the east with the Sussex forces. The Earl of Abingdon is up in Oxfordshire. At the university the caps and gowns are all turning into headpieces and steel fronts. James's Dutch regiments have sailed from Amsterdam. Yet Monmouth hath gained two fights, and why not a third ? They are troubled waters—troubled waters ! " The Duke paced backwards and forwards with brows drawn down, muttering all this to himself rather than to me, and shaking his head like one in the sorest perplexity.

" I would have you tell Monmouth," he said at last, " that I thank him for the papers which he hath sent me, and that I will duly read and weigh them. Tell him also that I wish him well in his enterprise, and would help him were it not that I am hemmed in by those who watch me closely, and who would denounce me were I to show my true thoughts. Tell him that, should he move his army into these parts, I may then openly declare myself ; but to do so now would be to ruin the fortunes of my house, without in any way helping him. Can you bear him that message ? "

" I shall do so, your Grace."

" Tell me," he asked, " how doth Monmouth bear himself in this enterprise ? "

" Like a wise and gallant leader," I answered.

" Strange," he murmured ; " it was ever the jest at court that he had scarce energy or constancy enough to finish a game at ball, but would ever throw his racquet

down ere the winning point was scored. His plans were like a weather-vane, altered by every breeze. He was constant only in his inconstancy. It is true that he led the King's troops in Scotland, but all men knew that Claverhouse and Dalzell were the real conquerors at Bothwell Bridge. Methinks he resembles that Brutus in Roman history who feigned weakness of mind as a cover to his ambitions."

The Duke was once again conversing with himself rather than with me, so that I made no remark, save to observe that Monmouth had won the hearts of the lower people.

"There lies his strength," said Beaufort. "The blood of his mother runs in his veins. He doth not think it beneath him to shake the dirty paw of Jerry the tinker, or to run a race against a bumpkin on the village green. Well, events have shown that he hath been right. These same bumpkins have stood by him when nobler friends have held aloof. I would I could see into the future. But you have my message, Captain, and I trust that, if you change it in the delivery, it will be in the direction of greater warmth and kindliness. It is time now that you depart, for within three hours the guard is changed, and your escape will be discovered."

"But how depart?" I asked.

"Through here," he answered, pushing open the casement, and sliding the rope along the beam in that direction. "The rope may be a foot or two short, but you have extra inches to make matters even. When you have reached the ground, take the gravel path which turns to the right, and follow it until it leads you to the high trees which skirt the park. The seventh of these hath a bough which shoots over the boundary wall. Climb along the bough, drop over upon the other side, and you will find my own valet waiting with your horse. Up with you, and ride, haste, haste, post-haste, for the south. By morn you should be well out of danger's way."

"My sword?" I asked.

" All your property is there. Tell Monmouth what I have said, and let him know that I have used you as kindly as was possible."

" But what will your Grace's council say when they find that I am gone ? " I asked.

" Pshaw, man ! Never fret about that ! I will off to Bristol at daybreak, and give my council enough to think of without their having time to devote to your fate. The soldiers will but have another instance of the working of the Father of Evil, who hath long been thought to have a weakness for that cell beneath us. Faith, if all we hear be true, there have been horrors enough acted there to call up every devil out of the pit. But time presses. Gently through the casement ! So ! Remember the message."

" Adieu, your Grace ! " I answered, and seizing the rope slipped rapidly and noiselessly to the ground, upon which he drew it up and closed the casement. As I looked round, my eye fell upon the dark narrow slit which opened into my cell, and through which honest Farmer Brown had held converse with me. Half-an-hour ago I had been stretched upon the prison pallet without a hope or a thought of escape. Now I was out in the open with no hand to stay me, breathing the air of freedom with the prison and the gallows cast off from me, as the waking man casts off his evil dreams. Such changes shake a man's soul, my children. The heart that can steel itself against death is softened by the assurance of safety. So I have known a worthy trader bear up manfully when convinced that his fortunes had been engulfed in the ocean, but lose all philosophy on finding that the alarm was false, and that they had come safely through the danger. For my own part believing as I do that there is nothing of chance in the affairs of this world, I felt that I had been exposed to this trial in order to dispose me to serious thought, and that I had been saved that I might put those thoughts into effect. As an earnest of my endeavour to do so I knelt down on the green sward, in the shadow of the Boteler turret, and I

prayed that I might come to be of use on the earth, and that I might be helped to rise above my own wants and interests, to aid forward whatever of good or noble might be stirring in my days. It is well-nigh fifty years, my dears, since I bowed my spirit before the Great Unknown in the moon-tinted park of Badminton, but I can truly say that from that day to this the aims which I laid down for myself have served me as a compass over the dark waters of life—a compass which I may perchance not always follow—for flesh is weak and frail, but which hath, at least, been ever present, that I might turn to it in seasons of doubt and of danger.

The path to the right led through groves and past carp ponds for a mile or more, until I reached the line of trees which skirted the boundary wall. Not a living thing did I see upon my way, save a herd of fallow-deer, which scudded away like swift shadows through the shimmering moonshine. Looking back, the high turrets and gables of the Boteler wing stood out dark and threatening against the starlit sky. Having reached the seventh tree, I clambered along the projecting bough which shot over the park wall, and dropped down upon the other side, where I found my good old dapple-grey awaiting me in the charge of a groom. Springing to my saddle, I strapped my sword once more to my side, and galloped off as fast as the four willing feet could carry me on my return journey.

All that night I rode hard without drawing bridle, through sleeping hamlets, by moon-bathed farmhouses, past shining stealthy rivers, and over birch-clad hills. When the eastern sky deepened from pink into scarlet, and the great sun pushed his rim over the blue north Somerset hills, I was already far upon my journey. It was a Sabbath morning, and from every village rose the sweet tinkling and calling of the bells. I bore no dangerous papers with me now, and might therefore be more careless as to my route. At one point I was questioned by a keen-eyed toll-keeper as to whence I came, but my

reply that I was riding direct from his Grace of Beaufort put an end to his suspicions. Further down, near Axbridge, I overtook a grazier who was jogging into Wells upon his sleek cob. With him I rode for some time, and learned that the whole of North Somerset, as well as south, was now in open revolt, and that Wells, Shepton Mallet and Glastonbury were held by armed volunteers for King Monmouth. The royal forces had all retired west, or east, until help should come. As I rode through the villages I marked the blue flag upon the church towers, and the rustics drilling upon the green, without any sign of trooper or dragoon to uphold the authority of the Stuarts.

My road lay through Shepton Mallet, Piper's Inn, Bridgewater and North Petherton, until in the cool of the evening I pulled up my weary horse at the Cross Hands, and saw the towers of Taunton in the valley beneath me. A flagon of beer for the rider, and a sieveful of oats for the steed, put fresh mettle into both of us, and we were jogging on our way once more, when there came galloping down the side of the hill about forty cavaliers, as hard as their horses could carry them. So wild was their riding that I pulled up, uncertain whether they were friend or foe, until, as they came whirling towards me, I recognised that the two officers who rode in front of them were none other than Reuben Lockarby and Sir Gervas Jerome. At the sight of me they flung up their hands, and Reuben shot on to his horse's neck, where he sat for a moment astride of the mane, until the brute tossed him back into the saddle.

" It's Micah ! It's Micah ! " he gasped, with his mouth open, and the tears hopping down his honest face.

" Od's pitlikins, man, how did you come here ? " asked Sir Gervas, poking me with his forefinger as though to see if I were really of flesh and blood. " We were leading a forlorn of horse into Beaufort's country to beat him up, and to burn his fine house about his ears if you had come to harm. There has just come a groom from

some farmer in those parts who hath brought us news
that you were under sentence of death, on which I came
away with my wig half frizzled, and found that friend
Lockarby had leave from Lord Grey to go north with
these troopers. But how have you fared ? "

" Well and ill," I answered, wringing their kindly
hands. " I had not thought last night to see another sun
rise, and yet ye see that I am here, sound in life and
limb. But all these things will take some time in the
telling."

" Aye, and King Monmouth will be on thorns to see
you. Right about, my lads, and back for the camp.
Never was errand so rapidly and happily finished as this
of ours. It would have fared ill with Badminton had you
been hurt."

The troopers turned their horses and trotted slowly
back to Taunton, while I rode behind them between my
two faithful friends, hearing from them all that had
occurred in my absence, and telling my own adventures
in return. The night had fallen ere we rode through the
gates, where I handed Covenant over to the Mayor's
groom, and went direct to the castle to deliver an account
of my mission.

26. *Of the Strife in the Council*

KING MONMOUTH'S council was assembled at
the time of my coming, and my entrance caused
the utmost surprise and joy, as they had just heard
news of my sore danger. Even the royal presence could
not prevent several members, among whom were the old
Mayor and the two soldiers of fortune, from springing
to their feet and shaking me warmly by the hand.
Monmouth himself said a few gracious words, and
requested that I should be seated at the board with the
others.

" You have earned the right to be of our council," said

he ; " and lest there should be a jealousy amongst other captains that you should come among us, I do hereby confer upon you the special title of Scout-master, which, though it entail few if any duties in the present state of our force, will yet give you precedence over your fellows. We had heard that your greeting from Beaufort was of the roughest, and that you were in sore straits in his dungeons. But you have happily come yourself on the very heels of him who bore the tidings. Tell us then from the beginning how things have fared with you."

I should have wished to have limited my story to Beaufort and his message, but as the council seemed to be intent upon hearing a full account of my journey, I told in as short and simple speech as I could the various passages which had befallen me—the ambuscado of the smugglers, the cave, the capture of the gauger, the journey in the lugger, the acquaintance with Farmer Brown, my being cast into prison, with the manner of my release and the message wherewith I had been commissioned. To all of this the council hearkened with the uttermost attention, while a muttered oath ever and anon from a courtier or a groan and prayer from a Puritan showed how keenly they followed the various phases of my fortunes. Above all, they gave the greatest heed to Beaufort's words, and stopped me more than once when I appeared to be passing over any saying or event before they had due time to weigh it. When I at last finished they all sat speechless, looking into each other's faces and waiting for an expression of opinion.

" On my word," said Monmouth at last, " this is a young Ulysses, though his Odyssey doth but take three days in the acting. Scudéry might not be so dull were she to take a hint from these smugglers' caves and sliding panels. How say you, Grey ? "

" He hath indeed had his share of adventure," the nobleman answered, " and hath also performed his mission like a fearless and zealous messenger. You say that Beaufort gave you nought in writing ? "

" Not a word, my lord," I replied.

" And his private message was that he wished us well and would join us if we were in his country ? "

" That was the effect, my lord."

" Yet in his council, as I understand, he did utter bitter things against us, putting affronts upon the King, and making light of his just claims upon the fealty of his nobility ? "

" He did," I answered.

" He would fain stand upon both sides of the hedge at once," said King Monmouth. " Such a man is very like to find himself on neither side, but in the very heart of the briars. It may be as well, however, that we should move his way, so as to give him the chance of declaring himself."

" In any case, as your Majesty remembers," said Saxon, " we had determined to march Bristolwards and attempt the town."

" The works are being strengthened," said I, " and there are five thousand of the Gloucestershire train-bands assembled within. I saw the labourers at work upon the ramparts as I passed."

" If we gain Beaufort we shall gain the town," quoth Sir Stephen Timewell. " There are already a strong body of godly and honest folk therein, who would rejoice to see a Protestant army within their gates. Should we have to beleaguer it we may count upon some help from within."

" Hegel und blitzen ! " exclaimed the German soldier, with an impatience which even the presence of the King could not keep in bounds ; " how can we talk of sieges and leaguers when we have not a breaching-piece in the army ? "

" The Lard will find us the breaching-pieces," cried Ferguson, in his strange, nasal voice. " Did the Lard no breach the too'ers o' Jericho withoot the aid o' gun-pooder ? Did the Lard no raise up the man Robert Ferguson and presairve him through five-and-thairty

indictments and twa-and-twenty proclamations o' the godless ? What is there He canna do ? Hosannah ! Hosannah ! "

" The Doctor is right," said a square-faced, leather-skinned English Independent. " We talk too much o' carnal means and worldly chances, without leaning upon that heavenly goodwill which should be to us as a staff on stony and broken paths. Yes, gentlemen," he continued, raising his voice and glancing across the table at some of the courtiers, " ye may sneer at words of piety, but I say that it is you and those like you who will bring down God's anger upon this army."

" And I say so too," cried another sectary fiercely.

" And I," " And I," shouted several, with Saxon, I think, among them.

" Is it your wish, your Majesty, that we should be insulted at your very council board ? " cried one of the courtiers, springing to his feet with a flushed face. " How long are we to be subject to this insolence because we have the religion of a gentleman, and prefer to practise it in the privacy of our hearts rather than at the street corners with these pharisees ? "

" Speak not against God's saints," cried a Puritan, in a loud, stern voice. " There is a voice within me which tells me that it were better to strike thee dead—yea, even in the presence of the King—than to allow thee to revile those who have been born again."

Several had sprung to their feet on either side. Hands were laid upon sword-hilts, and glances as stern and as deadly as rapier thrusts were flashing backwards and forwards ; but the more neutral and reasonable members of the council succeeded in restoring peace, and in persuading the angry disputants to resume their seats.

" How now, gentlemen ? " cried the King, his face dark with anger, when silence was at last restored. " Is this the extent of my authority that ye should babble and brawl as though my council-chamber were a Fleet Street pot-house ? Is this your respect for my person ? I tell ye

that I would forfeit my just claims for ever, and return to Holland, or devote my sword to the cause of Christianity against the Turk, rather than submit to such indignity. If any man be proved to have stirred up strife amongst the soldiers or commonalty on the score of religion I shall know how to deal with him. Let each preach to his own, but let him not interfere with the flock of his neighbour. As to you, Mr. Bramwell, and you, Mr. Joyce, and you also, Sir Henry Nuttall, we shall hold ye excused from attending these meetings until ye have further notice from us. Ye may now separate, each to your quarters, and to-morrow morning we shall, with the blessing of God, start for the north to see what luck may await our enterprise in those parts."

The King bowed as a sign that the formal meeting was over, and taking Lord Grey aside, he conversed with him anxiously in a recess. The courtiers, who numbered in their party several English and foreign gentlemen, who had come over together with some Devonshire and Somerset country squires, swaggered out of the room in a body, with much clinking of spurs and clanking of swords. The Puritans drew gravely together and followed after them, walking not with demure and downcast looks, as was their common use, but with grim faces and knitted brows, as the Jews of old may have appeared when, "To your tents, O Israel!" was still ringing in their ears.

Indeed, religious dissension and sectarian heat were in the very air. Outside, on the Castle Green, the voices of preachers rose up like the drone of insects. Every waggon or barrel or chance provision case had been converted into a pulpit, each with its own orator and little knot of eager hearkeners. Here was a russet-coated Taunton volunteer in jackboots and bandolier, holding forth on the justification by works. Further on a grenadier of the militia, with blazing red coat and white crossbelt, was deep in the mystery of the Trinity. In one or two places, where the rude pulpits were too near to each other, the

sermons had changed into a hot discussion between the two preachers, in which the audience took part by hums or groans, each applauding the champion whose creed was most in accordance with his own. Through this wild scene, made more striking by the ruddy flickering glare of the camp-fires, I picked my way with a weight at my heart, for I felt how vain it must be to hope for success where such division reigned. Saxon looked on, however, with glistening eyes, and rubbed his hands with satisfaction.

" The leaven is working," quoth he. " Something will come of all this ferment."

" I see not what can come of it save disorder and weakness," I answered.

" Good soldiers will come of it, lad," said he. " They are all sharpening themselves, each after his own fashion, on the whetstone of religion. This arguing breedeth fanatics, and fanatics are the stuff out of which conquerors are fashioned. Have you not heard how Old Noll's army divided into Presbyterians, Independents, Ranters, Anabaptists, Fifth Monarchy men, Brownists and a score of other sects, out of whose strife rose the finest regiments that ever formed line upon a field of battle ?

> ' Such as do build their faith upon
> The holy text of sword and gun.'

You know old Samuel's couplet. I tell you, I would rather see them thus employed than at their drill, for all their wrangling and jangling."

" But how of this split in the council ? " I asked.

" Ah, that is indeed a graver matter. All creeds may be welded together, but the Puritan and the scoffer are like oil and water. Yet the Puritan is the oil, for he will be ever atop. These courtiers do but stand for themselves, while the others are backed up by the pith and marrow of the army. It is well that we are afoot tomorrow. The King's troops are, I hear, pouring across Salisbury Plain, but their ordnance and stores are delaying

them, for they know well that they must bring all they need, since they can expect little from the goodwill of the country folk. Ah, friend Buyse, wie geht es ? "

" Ganz gut," said the big German, looming up before us through the darkness. " But, sapperment, what a cawing and croaking, like a rookery at sunset ! You English are a strange people—yes, donnerwetter, a very strange people ! There are no two of you who think alike upon any subject under Himmel ! The Cavalier will have his gay coat and his loose word. The Puritan will cut your throat rather than give up his sad-coloured dress and his Bible. " King James ! " cry some, " King Monmouth ! " say the peasants. " King Jesus ! " says the Fifth Monarchy man. " No King at all ! " cry Master Wade and a few others who are for a Commonwealth. Since I set foot on the Helderenbergh at Amsterdam, my head hath been in a whirl with trying to understand what it is that ye desire, for before I have got to the end of one man's tale, and begin to see a little through the finsterniss, another will come with another story, and I am in as evil a case as ever. But, my young Hercules, I am right glad to see you back in safety. I am half in fear to give you my hand now, after your recent treatment of it. I trust that you are none the worse for the danger that you have gone through."

" Mine eyelids are in truth a little heavy," I answered. " Save for an hour or two aboard the lugger, and about as long on a prison couch, I have not closed eye since I left the camp."

" We shall fall in at the second bugle call, about eight of the clock," said Saxon. " We shall leave you, therefore, that you may restore yourself after your fatigues." With a parting nod the two old soldiers strode off together down the crowded Fore Street, while I made the best of my way back to the Mayor's hospitable dwelling, where I had to repeat my story all over again to the assembled household before I was at last suffered to seek my room.

27. *Of the Affair near Keynsham Bridge*

MONDAY, June 21, 1685, broke very dark and windy, with dull clouds moving heavily across the sky and a constant sputter of rain. Yet a little after daybreak Monmouth's bugles were blowing in every quarter of the town, from Tone Bridge to Shuttern, and by the hour appointed the regiments had mustered, the roll had been called, and the vanguard was marching briskly out through the eastern gate. It went forth in the same order as it entered, our own regiment and the Taunton burghers bringing up the rear. Mayor Timewell and Saxon had the ordering of this part of the army between them, and being men who had seen much service, they drew the ordnance into a less hazardous position, and placed a strong guard of horse, a cannon's shot in the rear, to meet any attempt of the Royal dragoons.

It was remarked on all sides that the army had improved in order and discipline during the three days' halt, owing perchance to the example of our own unceasing drill and soldierly bearing. In numbers it had increased to nigh eight thousand, and the men were well fed and light of heart. With sturdy close-locked ranks they splashed their way through mud and puddle, with many a rough country joke and many a lusty stave from song or hymn. Sir Gervas rode at the head of his musqueteers, whose befloured tails hung limp and lank with the water dripping from them. Lockarby's pikemen and my own company of scythesmen were mostly labourers from the country, who were hardened against all weathers, and plodded patiently along with the rain-drops glistening upon their ruddy faces. In front were the Taunton foot ; behind, the lumbering train of baggage waggons, with the horse in the rear of them. So the long line wound its way over the hills.

At the summit, where the road begins to dip down upon

the other side, a halt was called to enable the regiments to close up, and we looked back at the fair town which many of us were never to see again. From the dark walls and house roofs we could still mark the flapping and flutter of white kerchiefs from those whom we left behind. Reuben sat his horse beside me, with his spare shirt streaming in the wind and his great pikemen all agrin behind him, though his thoughts and his eyes were too far away to note them. As we gazed, a long thin quiver of sunshine slipped out between two cloud banks and gilded the summit of the Magdalene tower, with the Royal standard which still waved from it. The incident was hailed as a happy augury, and a great shout spread from rank to rank at the sight of it, with a waving of hats and a clattering of weapons. Then the bugles blew a fanfare, the drums struck up a point of war, Reuben thrust his shirt into his haversack, and on we marched through mud and slush, with the dreary clouds bending low over us, and buttressed by the no less dreary hills on either side. A seeker for omens might have said that the heavens were weeping over our ill-fated venture.

All day we trudged along roads which were quagmires, over our ankles in mud, until in the evening we made our way to Bridgewater, where we gained some recruits, and also some hundred pounds for our military chest, for it was a well-to-do place, with a thriving coast trade carried on down the river Parret. After a night in snug quarters we set off again in even worse weather than before. The country in these parts is a quagmire in the driest season, but the heavy rains had caused the fens to overflow, and turned them into broad lakes on either side of the road. This may have been to some degree in our favour, as shielding us from the raids of the King's cavalry, but it made our march very slow. All day it was splashing and swashing through mud and mire, the rain-drops shining on the gun-barrels and dripping from the heavy-footed horses. Past the swollen Parret, through Eastover, by the peaceful village of Bawdrip, and over Polden Hill

we made our way, until the bugles sounded a halt under the groves of Ashcot, and a rude meal was served out to the men. Then on again, through the pitiless rain, past the wooded park of Piper's Inn, through Walton, where the floods were threatening the cottages, past the orchards of Street, and so in the dusk of the evening into the grey old town of Glastonbury, where the good folk did their best by the warmth of their welcome to atone for the bitterness of the weather.

The next morning was wet still and inclement, so the army made a short march to Wells, which is a good-sized town, well laid out, with a fine cathedral, which hath a great number of figures carved in stone and placed in niches on the outer side, like that which we saw at Salisbury. The townsfolk were strong for the Protestant cause, and the army was so well received that their victual cost little from the military chest. On this march we first began to come into touch with the Royal horse. More than once when the rain mist cleared we saw the gleam of arms upon the low hills which overlook the road, and our scouts came in with reports of strong bodies of dragoons on either flank. At one time they massed heavily upon our rear, as though planning a descent upon the baggage. Saxon, however, planted a regiment of pikes on either side, so that they broke up again and glinted off over the hills.

From Wells we marched upon the twenty-fourth to Shepton Mallet, with the ominous sabres and helmet still twinkling behind and on either side of us.

That evening we were at Keynsham Bridge, less than two leagues from Bristol as the crow flies, and some of our horse forded the river and pushed on almost to the walls.

By morning the rainclouds had at last cleared, so Reuben and I rode slowly up one of the sloping green hills which rose behind the camp, in the hope of gaining some sight of the enemy. Our men we left littered about upon the grass, trying to light fires with the damp sticks,

or laying out their clothes to dry in the sunshine. A strange-looking band they were, coated and splashed with mud from head to heel, their hats all limp and draggled, their arms rusted, and their boots so worn that many walked barefoot, and others had swathed their kerchiefs round their feet. Yet their short spell of soldiering had changed them from honest-faced yokels into fierce-eyed, half-shaven, gaunt-cheeked fellows, who could carry arms or port pikes as though they had done nought else since childhood.

The plight of the officers was no better than that of the men, nor should an officer, my dears, when he is upon service, ever demean himself by partaking of any comfort which all cannot share with him. Let him lie by a soldier's fire and eat a soldier's fare, or let him hence, for he is a hindrance and a stumbling-block. Our clothes were pulp, our steel fronts red with rust, and our chargers as stained and splashed as though they had rolled in the mire. Our very swords and pistols were in such a plight that we could scarce draw the one or snap the other. Sir Gervas alone succeeded in keeping his attire and his person as neat and as dainty as ever. What he did in the watches of the night, and how he gained his sleep, hath ever been a mystery to me, for day after day he turned out at the bugle call, washed, scented, brushed, with wig in order, and clothes from which every speck of mud had been carefully removed. At his saddle-bow he bore with him the great flour dredger which we saw him use at Taunton, and his honest musqueteers had their heads duly dusted every morning, though in an hour their tails would be as brown as nature made them, while the flour would be trickling in little milky streams down their broad backs, or forming in cakes upon the skirts of their coats. It was a long contest between the weather and the Baronet, but our comrade proved the victor.

" There was a time when I was called plump Reuben," quoth my friend, as we rode together up the winding track. " What with too little that is solid and too much

that is liquid I am like to be skeleton Reuben ere I see Havant again. I am as full of rain-water as my father's casks are of October. I would, Micah, that you would wring me out and hang me to dry upon one of these bushes."

" If we are wet, King James's men must be wetter," said I, " for at least we have had such shelter as there was."

" It is poor comfort when you are starved to know that another is in the same plight. I give you my word, Micah, I took in one hole of my sword-belt on Monday, two on Tuesday, one yesterday, and one to-day. I tell you, I am thawing like an icicle in the sun."

" If you should chance to dwindle to nought," said I, laughing, " what account are we to give of you in Taunton? Since you have donned armour and taken to winning the hearts of fair maidens, you have outstripped us all in importance, and become a man of weight and substance."

" I had more substance and weight ere I began trailing over the countryside like a Hambledon packman," quoth he. " But in very truth and with all gravity, Micah, it is a strange thing to feel that the whole world for you, your hopes, your ambitions, your all, are gathered into so small a compass that a hood might cover it, and two little pattens support it. I feel as if she were my own higher self, my loftier part, and that I, should I be torn from her, would remain for ever an incomplete and half-formed being. With her, I ask nothing else. Without her, all else is nothing."

" But have you spoken to the old man ? " I asked. " Are you indeed betrothed ? "

" I have spoken to him," my friend answered, " but he was so busy in filling ammunition cases that I could not gain his attention. When I tried once more he was counting the spare pikes in the Castle armoury with a tally and an ink-horn. I told him that I had come to crave his granddaughter's hand, on which he turned to me and asked, ' which hand ? ' with so blank a stare that

it was clear that his mind was elsewhere. On the third trial, though, the day that you did come back from Badminton, I did at last prefer my request, but he flashed out at me that this was no time for such fooleries, and he bade me wait until King Monmouth was on the throne, when I might ask him again. I warrant that he did not call such things fooleries fifty years ago, when he went a-courting himself."

" At least he did not refuse you," said I. " It is as good as a promise that ; should the cause be successful, you shall be so too."

" By my faith," cried Reuben, " if a man could by his own single blade bring that about, there is none who hath so strong an interest in it as I. No, not Monmouth himself ! The apprentice Derrick hath for a long time raised his eyes to his master's daughter, and the old man was ready to have him as a son, so much was he taken by his godliness and zeal. Yet I have learned from a side-wind that he is but a debauched and low-living man, though he covers his pleasures with a mask of piety. I thought as you did think that he was at the head of the roisterers who tried to bear Mistress Ruth away, though, i' faith, I can scarce think harshly of them, since they did me the greatest service that ever men did yet. Meanwhile I have taken occasion, ere we left Wells two nights ago, to speak to Master Derrick on the matter, and to warn him as he loved his life to plan no treachery against her."

" And how took he this mild intimation ? " I asked.

" As a rat takes a rat trap. Snarled out some few words of godly hatred, and so slunk away."

" On my life, lad," said I, " you have been having as many adventures in your own way as I in mine. But here we are upon the hill-top, with as fair an outlook as man could wish to have."

Just beneath us ran the Avon, curving in long bends through the woodlands, with the gleam of the sun striking back from it here and there, as though a row of baby suns

had been set upon a silver string. On the further side
the peaceful, many-hued country, rising and falling in a
swell of cornfields and orchards, swept away to break in
a fringe of forest upon the distant Malverns. On our
right were the green hills near Bath and on our left the
rugged Mendips, with queenly Bristol crouching behind
her forts, and the grey channel behind flecked with snow-
white sails. At our very feet lay Keynsham Bridge, and
our army spotted in dark patches over the green fields,
the smoke of their fires and the babble of their voices
floating up in the still summer air.

A road ran along the Somersetshire bank of the Avon,
and down this two troops of our horse were advancing,
with intent to establish outposts upon our eastern flank.
As they jangled past in somewhat loose order, their course
lay through a pine-wood, into which the road takes a
sharp bend. We were gazing down at the scene when,
like lightning from a cloud, a troop of the Horse Guards
wheeled out into the open, and breaking from trot to
canter, and from canter to gallop, dashed down in a
whirlwind of blue and steel upon our unprepared squadrons. A crackle of hastily unslung carbines broke from
the leading ranks, but in an instant the Guards burst
through them and plunged on into the second troop.
For a space the gallant rustics held their own, and the
dense mass of men and horses swayed backwards and
forwards, with the swirling sword-blades playing above
them in flashes of angry light. Then blue coats began
to break from among the russet, the fight rolled wildly
back for a hundred paces, the dense throng was split
asunder, and the Royal Guards came pouring through
the rent, and swerved off to right and left through hedges
and over ditches, stabbing and hacking at the fleeing
horsemen. The whole scene, with the stamping horses,
tossing manes, shouts of triumph or despair, gasping of
hard-drawn breath and musical clink and clatter of steel,
was to us upon the hill like some wild vision, so swiftly
did it come and so swiftly go. A sharp, stern bugle-call

summoned the Blues back into the road, where they formed up and trotted slowly away before fresh squadrons could come up from the camp. The sun gleamed and the river rippled as ever, and there was nothing save the long litter of men and horses to mark the course of the hell blast which had broken so suddenly upon us.

As the Blues retired we observed that a single officer brought up the rear, riding very slowly, as though it went much against his mood to turn his back even to an army. The space betwixt the troop and him was steadily growing greater, yet he made no effort to quicken his pace, but jogged quietly on, looking back from time to time to see if he were followed. The same thought sprang into my comrade's mind and my own at the same instant, and we read it in each other's faces.

" This path," cried he eagerly. " It brings us out beyond the grove, and is in the hollow all the way."

" Lead the horses until we get on better ground," I answered. " We may just cut him off if we are lucky."

There was no time for another word, for we hurried off down the uneven track, sliding and slipping on the rain-soaked turf. Springing into our saddles we dashed down the gorge, through the grove, and so out on to the road in time to see the troop disappear in the distance, and to meet the solitary officer face to face.

He was a sun-burned, high-featured man, with black moustachios, mounted on a great raw-boned chestnut charger. As we broke out on to the road he pulled up to have a good look at us. Then, having fully made up his mind as to our hostile intent, he drew his sword, plucked a pistol out of his holster with his left hand, and gripping the bridle between his teeth, dug his spurs into his horse's flanks and charged down upon us at the top of his speed. As we dashed at him, Reuben on his bridle-arm and I on the other, he cut fiercely at me, and at the same moment fired at my companion. The ball grazed Reuben's cheek, leaving a red weal behind it like a lash from a whip, and blackening his face with the pow-

der. His cut, however, fell short, and throwing my arm round his waist as the two horses dashed past each other, I plucked him from the saddle and drew him face upwards across my saddlebow. Brave Covenant lumbered on with his double burden, and before the Guards had learned that they had lost their officer, we had brought him safe, in spite of his struggles and writhings, to within sight of Monmouth's camp.

"A narrow shave, friend," quoth Reuben, with his hand to his cheek. "He hath tattooed my face with powder until I shall be taken for Solomon Sprent's younger brother."

"Thank God that you are unhurt," said I. "See, our horse are advancing along the upper road. Lord Grey himself rides at their head. We had best take our prisoner into camp, since we can do nought here."

"For Christ's sake, either slay me or set me down!" he cried. "I cannot bear to be carried in this plight, like a half-weaned infant, through your campful of grinning yokels."

"I would not make sport of a brave man," I answered. "If you will give your word to stay with us, you shall walk between us."

"Willingly," said he, scrambling down and arranging his ruffled attire. "By my faith, sirs, ye have taught me a lesson not to think too meanly of mine enemies. I should have ridden with my troop had I thought that there was a chance of falling in with outposts or videttes."

"We were upon the hill before we cut you off," quoth Reuben. "Had that pistol ball been a thought straighter it is I that should have been truly the cut-off one. Zounds, Micah! I was grumbling even now that I had fallen away, but had my cheek been as round as of old the slug had been through it."

"Where have I seen you before?" asked our captive, bending his dark eyes upon me. "Aye, I have it! It was in the inn at Salisbury, where my light-headed comrade Horsford did draw upon an old soldier who was

riding with you. Mine own name is Ogilvy—Major
Ogilvy of the Horse Guards Blue. I was right glad that
ye did come off safely from the hounds. Some word had
come of your errand after your departure, so this same
Horsford with the Mayor and one or two other Tantivies,
whose zeal methinks outran their humanity, slipped the
dogs upon your trail."

" I remember you well," I answered. " You will find
Colonel Decimus Saxon, my former companion, in the
camp. No doubt you will be shortly exchanged for
some prisoner of ours."

" Much more likely to have my throat cut," said he,
with a smile. " I fear that Feversham in his present
temper will scarce pause to make prisoners, and Monmouth may be tempted to pay him back in his own coin.
Yet it is the fortune of war, and I should pay for my want
of all soldierly caution. Truth to tell, my mind was far
from battles and ruses at the moment, for it had wandered
away to aqua regia and its action upon the metals, until
your appearance brought me back to soldiership."

" The horse are out of sight," said Reuben, looking
backwards, " ours as well as theirs. Yet I see a clump of
men over yonder at the other side of the Avon, and there
on the hillside can you not see the gleam of steel ? "

" There are foot there," I answered, puckering my
eyes. " It seems to me that I can discern four or five
regiments and as many colours of horse. King Monmouth should know of this with all speed."

" He does know of it," said Reuben. " Yonder he
stands under the trees with his council about him. See,
one of them rides this way ! "

A trooper had indeed detached himself from the group
and galloped towards us. " If you are Captain Clarke,
sir," he said, with a salute, " the King orders you to
join his council."

" Then I leave the Major in your keeping, Reuben," I
cried. " See that he hath what our means allow." So
saying I spurred my horse, and soon joined the group

who were gathered round the King. There were Grey, Wade, Buyse, Ferguson, Saxon, Hollis, and a score more, all looking very grave, and peering down the valley with their glasses. Monmouth himself had dismounted, and was leaning against the trunk of a tree, with his arms folded upon his breast, and a look of white despair upon his face. Behind the tree a lacquey paced up and down leading his glossy black charger, who pranced and tossed his lordly mane, a very king among horses.

" You see, friends," said Monmouth, turning lacklustre eyes from one leader to another, " Providence would seem to be against us. Some new mishap is ever at our heels."

" Not Providence, your Majesty, but our own negligence," cried Saxon boldly. " Had we advanced on Bristol last night, we might have been on the right side of the ramparts by now."

" But we had no thought that the enemy's foot was so near ! " exclaimed Wade.

" I told ye what would come of it, and so did Oberst Buyse and the worthy Mayor of Taunton," Saxon answered. " However, there is nought to be gained by mourning over a broken pipkin. We must e'en piece it together as best we may."

" Let us advance on Bristol, and put oor trust in the Highest," quoth Ferguson. " If it be His mighty wull that we should tak' it, then shall we enter into it, yea, though drakes and sakers lay as thick as cobblestanes in the streets."

" Aye ! aye ! On to Bristol ! God with us ! " cried several of the Puritans excitedly.

" But it is madness—dummheit—utter foolishness," Buyse broke in hotly. " You have the chance and you will not take it. Now the chance is gone and you are all eager to go. Here is an army of, as near as I can judge, five thousand men on the right side of the river. We are on the wrong side, and yet you talk of crossing and making a beleaguering of Bristol without breaching-pieces

or spades, and with this force in our rear. Will the town make terms when they can see from their ramparts the van of the army which comes to help them ? Or does it assist us in fighting the army to have a strong town beside us, from which horse and foot can make an outfall upon our flank ? I say again that it is madness."

What the German soldier said was so clearly the truth that even the fanatics were silenced. Away in the east the long shimmering lines of steel, and the patches of scarlet upon the green hillside, were arguments which the most thoughtless could not overlook.

" What would you advise, then ? " asked Monmouth moodily, tapping his jewelled riding-whip against his high boots.

" To cross the river and come to hand-grips with them ere they can get help from the town," the burly German answered bluntly. " I cannot understand what we are here for if it be not to fight. If we win, the town must fall. If we lose, we have had a bold stroke for it, and can do no more."

" Is that your opinion, too, Colonel Saxon ? " the King asked.

" Assuredly, your Majesty, if we can fight to advantage. We can scarce do that, however, by crossing the river on a single narrow bridge in the face of such a force. I should advise that we destroy this Keynsham Bridge, and march down this southern bank in the hope of forcing a fight in a position which we may choose."

" We have not yet summoned Bath," said Wade. "Let us do as Colonel Saxon proposes, and let us in the meantime march in that direction and send a trumpet to the governor."

" There is yet another plan," quoth Sir Stephen Timewell, " which is to hasten to Gloucester, to cross the Severn there, and so march through Worcestershire into Shropshire and Cheshire. Your Majesty has many friends in those parts."

Monmouth paced up and down with his hand to his

forehead like one distrait. " What am I to do," he cried
at last, " in the midst of all this conflicting advice, when
I know that not only my own success but the lives of these
poor faithful peasants and craftsmen depend upon my
resolution ? "

" With all humbleness, your Majesty," said Lord Grey,
who had just returned with the horse, " I should suggest,
since there are only a few troops of their cavalry on this
side of the Avon, that we blow up the bridge and move
onwards to Bath, whence we can pass into Wiltshire,
which we know to be friendly."

" So be it ! " cried the King, with the reckless air of
one who accepts a plan, not because it is the best, but
because he feels that all are equally hopeless. " What
think you, gentlemen ? " he added, with a bitter smile.
" I have heard news from London this morning, that my
uncle has clapped two hundred merchants and others who
are suspected of being true to their creed into the Tower
and the Fleet. He will have one-half of the nation
mounting guard over the other half ere long."

" Or the whole, your Majesty, mounting guard over
him," suggested Wade. " He may himself see the
Traitor's Gate some of these mornings."

" Ha, há ! Think ye so ? think ye so ? " cried Mon-
mouth, rubbing his hands and brightening into a smile.
" Well, mayhap you have nicked the truth. Who knows ?
Henry's cause seemed a losing one until Bosworth Field
settled the contention. To your charges, gentlemen.
We shall march in half-an-hour. Colonel Saxon and you,
Sir Stephen, shall cover the rear and guard the baggage—a
service of honour with this fringe of horse upon our skirts."

The council broke up forthwith, every man riding off
to his own regiment. The whole camp was in a stir,
bugles blowing and drums rattling, until in a very short
time the army was drawn up in order, and the forlorn of
cavalry had already started along the road which leads to
Bath. Five hundred horse with the Devonshire militiamen were in the van. After them in order came the

sailor regiment, the North Somerset men, the first Taunton regiment of burghers, the Mendip and Bagworthy miners, the lace- and wool-workers of Honiton, Wellington and Ottery St. Mary ; the woodmen, the graziers, the marshmen and the men from the Quantock district. Behind were the guns and the baggage, with our own brigade and four colours of horse as a rearguard. On our march we could see the red-coats of Feversham keeping pace with us upon the other side of the Avon. A large body of his horse and dragoons had forded the stream and hovered upon our skirts, but Saxon and Sir Stephen covered the baggage so skilfully, and faced round so fiercely with such a snarl of musketry whenever they came too nigh, that they never ventured to charge home.

28. *Of the Fight in Wells Cathedral*

I AM fairly tied to the chariot-wheels of history now, my dear children, and must follow on with name and place and date, whether my tale suffer by it or no. With such a drama as this afoot it were impertinent to speak of myself, save in so far as I saw or heard what may make these old scenes more vivid to you. It is no pleasant matter for me to dwell upon, yet, convinced as I am that there is no such thing as chance either in the great or the little things of this world, I am very sure that the sacrifices of these brave men were not thrown away, and that their strivings were not as profitless as might at first sight appear. If the perfidious race of Stuart is not now seated upon the throne, and if religion in England is still a thing of free growth, we may, to my thinking, thank these Somerset yokels for it, who first showed how small a thing would shake the throne of an unpopular monarch. Monmouth's army was but the vanguard of that which marched three years later into London, when James and his cruel ministers were flying as outcasts over the face of the earth.

On the night of June 27, or rather early in the morning of June 28, we reached the town of Frome, very wet and miserable, for the rain had come on again, and all the roads were quagmires. From this next day we pushed on once more to Wells, where we spent the night and the whole of the next day, to give the men time to get their clothes dry, and to recover themselves after their privations.

In the forenoon a parade of our Wiltshire regiment was held in the Cathedral Close, when Monmouth praised it, as it well deserved, for the soldierly progress made in so short a time.

As we returned to our quarters after dismissing our men we came upon a great throng of the rough Bagworthy and Oare miners, who were assembled in the open space in front of the Cathedral, listening to one of their own number, who was addressing them from a cart. The wild and frenzied gestures of the man showed us that he was one of those extreme sectaries whose religion runs perilously near to madness. The hums and groans which rose from the crowd proved, however, that his fiery words were well suited to his hearers, so we halted on the verge of the multitude and hearkened to his address. A red-bearded, fierce-faced man he was, with tangled shaggy hair tumbling over his gleaming eyes, and a hoarse voice which resounded over the whole square.

" What shall we not do for the Lord ? " he cried ; " what shall we not do for the Holy of Holies ? Why is it that His hand is heavy upon us ? Why is it that we have not freed this land, even as Judith freed Bethulia ? Behold, we have looked for peace but no good came, and for a time of health, and behold trouble ! Why is this, I say ? Truly, brothers, it is because we have slighted the Lord, because we have not been whole-hearted towards Him. Lo ! we have praised Him with our breath, but in our deeds we have been cold towards Him. Ye know well that Prelacy is an accursed thing—a hissing and an abomination in the eyes of the Almighty ! Yet what

have we, His servants, wrought for Him in this matter ?
Have we not seen Prelatist churches, churches of form
and of show, where the creature is confounded with the
Creator—have we not seen them, I say, and have we not
forborne to sweep them away, and so lent our sanction to
them ?   There is the sin of a lukewarm and backsliding
generation !   There is the cause why the Lord should
look coldly upon His people !   Lo ! at Shepton and at
Frome we have left such churches behind us.   At
Glastonbury, too, we have spared those wicked walls
which were reared by idolatrous hands of old.   Woe
unto ye, if, after having put your hands to God's plough,
ye turn back from the work !   See there ! " he howled,
facing round to the beautiful Cathedral, " what means
this great heap of stones ?   Is it not an altar of Baal ?
Is it not built for man-worship rather than God-worship ?
Is it not there that the man Ken, tricked out in his foolish
rochet and baubles, may preach his soulless and lying
doctrines, which are but the old dish of Popery served
up under a new cover ?   And shall we suffer this thing ?
Shall we, the chosen children of the Great One, allow
this plague-spot to remain ?   Can we expect the Almighty
to help us when we will not stretch out a hand to help
Him ?   We have left the other temples of Prelacy behind
us.   Shall we leave this one, too, my brothers ? "

" No, no ! " yelled the crowd, tossing and swaying.

" Shall we pluck it down, then, until no one stone is
left upon another ? "

" Yes, yes ! " they shouted.

" Now, at once ? "

" Yes, yes ! "

" Then to work ! " he cried, and springing from the
cart he rushed towards the Cathedral, with the whole
mob of wild fanatics at his heels.   Some crowded in,
shouting and yelling, through the open doors, while
others swarmed up the pillars and pedestals of the front,
hacking at the sculptured ornaments, and tugging at the
grey old images which filled every niche.

"This must be stopped," said Saxon curtly. "We cannot afford to insult and estray the whole Church of England to please a few hot-headed ranters. The pillage of this Cathedral would do our cause more harm than a pitched battle lost. Do you bring up your company, Sir Gervas, and we shall do what we can to hold them in check until they come."

"Hi, Masterton!" cried the Baronet, spying one of his under-officers among the crowd who were looking on, neither assisting nor opposing the rioters. "Do you hasten to the quarters, and tell Barker to bring up the company with their matches burning. I may be of use here."

"Ha, here is Buyse!" cried Saxon joyously, as the huge German ploughed his way through the crowd. "And Lord Grey, too! We must save the Cathedral, my lord! They would sack and burn it."

"This way, gentlemen," cried an old grey-haired man, running out towards us with hands outspread, and a bunch of keys clanking at his girdle. "Oh hasten, gentlemen, if ye can indeed prevail over these lawless men! They have pulled down Saint Peter, and they will have Paul down too unless help comes. There will not be an apostle left. The east window is broken. They have brought a hogshead of beer, and are broaching it upon the high altar. Oh, alas, alas! that such things should be in a Christian land!" He sobbed aloud and stamped about in a very frenzy of grief.

"It is the verger, sirs," said one of the townsfolk. "He hath grown grey in the Cathedral."

"This way to the vestry door, my lords and gentlemen," cried the old man, pushing a way strenuously through the crowd. "Now, lack-a-day, the sainted Paul hath gone too!"

As he spoke a splintering crash from inside the Cathedral announced some fresh outrage on the part of the zealots. Our guide hastened on with renewed speed, until he came to a low oaken door heavily arched, which

he unlocked with much rasping of wards and creaking of hinges. Through this we sidled as best we might, and hurried after the old man down a stone-flagged corridor, which led through a wicket into the Cathedral close by the high altar.

The great building was full of the rioters, who were rushing hither and thither, destroying and breaking everything which they could lay their hands on. A good number of these were genuine zealots, the followers of the preacher whom we had listened to outside. Others, however, were on the face of them mere rogues and thieves such as gather round every army upon the march. While the former were tearing down images from the walls, or hurling the books of common prayer through the stained-glass windows, the others were rooting up the massive brass candlesticks, and carrying away everything which promised to be of value. One ragged fellow was in the pulpit, tearing off the crimson velvet and hurling it down among the crowd. Another had upset the reading-desk, and was busily engaged in wrenching off the brazen fastenings. In the centre of the side aisle a small group had a rope round the neck of Mark the Evangelist, and were dragging lustily upon it, until, even as we entered, the statue, after tottering for a few moments, came crashing down upon the marble floor. The shouts which greeted every fresh outrage, with the splintering of woodwork, the smashing of windows, and the clatter of falling masonry, made up a most deafening uproar, which was increased by the droning of the organ, until some of the rioters silenced it by slitting up the bellows.

What more immediately concerned ourselves was the scene which was being enacted just in front of us at the high altar. A barrel of beer had been placed upon it, and a dozen ruffians gathered round it, one of whom with many ribald jests had climbed up, and was engaged in knocking in the top of the cask with a hatchet. As we entered he had just succeeded in broaching it, and the brown mead was foaming over, while the mob with roars

of laughter were passing up their dippers and pannikins. The German soldier rapped out a rough jagged oath at this spectacle, and shouldering his way through the roisterers he sprang upon the altar. The ringleader was bending over his cask, black-jack in hand, when the soldier's iron grip fell upon his collar, and in a moment his heels were flapping in the air, and his head three feet deep in the cask, while the beer splashed and foamed in every direction. With a mighty heave Buyse picked up the barrel with the half-drowned miner inside, and hurled it clattering down the broad marble steps which led from the body of the church. At the same time, with the aid of a dozen of our men who had followed us into the Cathedral, we drove back the fellow's comrades, and thrust them out beyond the rails which divided the choir from the nave.

Our inroad had the effect of checking the riot, but it simply did so by turning the fury of the zealots from the walls and windows to ourselves. Images, stone-work and wood-carvings were all abandoned, and the whole swarm came rushing up with a hoarse buzz of rage, all discipline and order completely lost in their religious frenzy. " Smite the Prelatists ! " they howled. " Down with the friends of Antichrist ! Cut them off even at the horns of the altar ! Down with them ! " On either side they massed, a wild, half-demented crowd, some with arms and some without, but filled to a man with the very spirit of murder.

" This is a civil war within a civil war," said Lord Grey, with a quiet smile. " We had best draw, gentle-men, and defend the gap in the rails, if we may hold it good until help arrives." He flashed out his rapier as he spoke, and took his stand on the top of the steps, with Saxon and Sir Gervas upon one side of him, Buyse, Reuben and myself upon the other. There was only room for six to wield their weapons with effect, so our scanty band of followers scattered themselves along the line of the rails, which were luckily so high and strong

as to make an escalado difficult in the face of any opposition.

The riot had now changed into open mutiny among these marshmen and miners. Pikes, scythes and knives glimmered through the dim light, while their wild cries re-echoed from the high arched roof like the howling of a pack of wolves. " Go forward, my brothers," cried the fanatic preacher who had been the cause of the outbreak —" go forward against them ! What though they be in high places ! There is One who is higher than they. Shall we shrink from His work because of a naked sword ? Shall we suffer the Prelatist altar to be preserved by these sons of Amalek ? On, on ! In the name of the Lord ! "

" In the name of the Lord ! " cried the crowd, with a sort of hissing gasp, like one who is about to plunge into an icy bath. " In the name of the Lord ! " From either side they came on, gathering speed and volume, until at last with a wild cry they surged right down upon our sword-points.

I can say nothing of what took place to right or left of me during the ruffle, for indeed there were so many pressing upon us, and the fight was so hot, that it was all that each of us could do to hold our own. The very number of our assailants was in our favour, by hampering their sword-arms. One burly miner cut fiercely at me with his scythe, but missing me he swung half round with the force of the blow, and I passed my sword through his body before he could recover himself. It was the first time that I had ever slain a man in anger, my dear children, and I shall never forget his white startled face as he looked over his shoulder at me ere he fell. Another closed in with me before I could get my weapon disengaged, but I struck him out with my left hand, and then brought the flat of my sword upon his head, laying him senseless upon the pavement. God knows, I did not wish to take the lives of the misguided and ignorant zealots, but our own were at stake. A marshman, looking more like a shaggy wild beast than a

human being, darted under my weapon and caught me round the knees, while another brought a flail down upon my headpiece, from which it glanced on to my shoulder. A third thrust at me with a pike, and pricked me on the thigh, but I shore his weapon in two with one blow, and split his head with the next. The man with the flail gave back at sight of this, and a kick freed me from the unarmed ape-like creature at my feet, so that I found myself clear of my assailants, and none the worse for my encounter, save for a touch on the leg and some stiffness of the neck and shoulder.

Looking round I found that my comrades had also beaten off those who were opposed to them. Saxon was holding his bloody rapier in his left hand, while the blood was trickling from a slight wound upon his right. Two miners lay across each other in front of him, but at the feet of Sir Gervas Jerome no fewer than four bodies were piled together. He had plucked out his snuff-box as I glanced at him, and was offering it with a bow and a flourish to Lord Grey, as unconcernedly as though he were back once more in his London coffee-house. Buyse leaned upon his long broadsword, and looked gloomily at a headless trunk in front of him, which I recognised from the dress as being that of the preacher. As to Reuben, he was unhurt himself, but in sore distress over my own trifling scar, though I assured the faithful lad that it was a less thing than many a tear from branch or thorn which we had had when blackberrying together.

The fanatics, though driven back, were not men to be content with a single repulse. They had lost ten of their number, including their leader, without being able to break our line, but the failure only served to increase their fury. For a minute or so they gathered panting in the aisle. Then with a mad yell they dashed in once more, and made a desperate effort to cut a way through to the altar. It was a fiercer and more prolonged struggle than before. One of our followers was stabbed to the heart over the rails, and fell without a groan. Another was

stunned by a mass of masonry hurled at him by a giant cragsman. Reuben was felled by a club, and would have been dragged out and hacked to pieces had I not stood over him and beaten off his assailants. Sir Gervas was borne off his legs by the rush, but lay like a wounded wildcat, striking out furiously at everything which came within his reach. Buyse and Saxon, back to back, stood firm amidst the seething, rushing crowd, cutting down every man within sweep of their swords. Yet in such a struggle numbers must in the end prevail, and I confess that I for one had begun to have fears for the upshot of our contest, when the heavy tramp of disciplined feet rang through the Cathedral, and the Baronet's musketeers came at a quick run up the central aisle. The fanatics did not await their charge, but darted off over benches and pews, followed by our allies, who were furious on seeing their beloved Captain upon the ground. There was a wild minute or two, with confused shuffling of feet, stabs, groans and the clatter of musket butts on the marble floor. Of the rioters some were slain, but the greater part threw down their arms and were arrested at the command of Lord Grey, while a strong guard was placed at the gates to prevent any fresh outburst of sectarian fury.

When at last the Cathedral was cleared and order restored, we had time to look around us and to reckon our own injuries. In all my wanderings, and the many wars in which I afterwards fought—wars compared to which this affair of Monmouth's was but the merest skirmish—I have never seen a stranger or more impressive scene. In the dim, solemn light the pile of bodies in front of the rails, with their twisted limbs and white-set faces, had a most sad and ghost-like aspect. The evening light, shining through one of the few unbroken stained-glass windows, cast great splotches of vivid crimson and of sickly green upon the heap of motionless figures. A few wounded men sat about in the front pews or lay upon the steps moaning for water. Of our own small company

not one had escaped unscathed. Three of our followers had been slain outright, while a fourth was lying stunned from a blow. Buyse and Sir Gervas were much bruised. Saxon was cut on the right arm. Reuben had been felled by a bludgeon stroke, and would certainly have been slain but for the fine temper of Sir Jacob Clancing's breastplate, which had turned a fierce pike-thrust. As to myself it is scarce worth the mention, but my head sang for some hours like a good wife's kettle, and my boot was full of blood, which may have been a blessing in disguise, for Sneckson, our Havant barber, was ever dinning into my ears how much the better I should be for a phlebotomy.

In the meantime all the troops had assembled and the mutiny been swiftly stamped out. There were doubtless many among the Puritans who had no love for the Prelatists, but none save the most crack-brained fanatics could fail to see that the sacking of the Cathedral would set the whole Church of England in arms, and ruin the cause for which they were fighting. As it was, much damage had been done ; for whilst the gang within had been smashing all which they could lay their hands upon, others outside had chipped off cornices and gargoyles, and had even dragged the lead covering from the roof and hurled it down in great sheets to their companions beneath. This last led to some profit, for the army had no great store of ammunition, so the lead was gathered up by Monmouth's orders and recast into bullets. The prisoners were held in custody for a time, but it was deemed unwise to punish them, so that they were finally pardoned and dismissed from the army.

A parade of our whole force was held in the fields outside the town upon the second day of our stay at Wells, the weather having at last become warm and sunny. The foot was then found to muster six regiments of nine hundred men, or five thousand four hundred in all. Of these fifteen hundred were musketeers, two thousand were pikemen, and the rest were scythesmen or peasants with flails and hammers. A few bodies, such as our own

or those from Taunton, might fairly lay claim to be soldiers, but the most of them were still labourers and craftsmen with weapons in their hands. Yet, ill-armed and ill-drilled as they were, they were still strong robust Englishmen, full of native courage and of religious zeal. The light and fickle Monmouth began to take heart once more at the sight of their sturdy bearing, and at the sound of their hearty cheers. I heard him as I sat my horse beside his staff speak exultantly to those around him, and ask whether these fine fellows could possibly be beaten by mercenary half-hearted hirelings.

" What say you, Wade ? " he cried. " Are we never to see a smile on that sad face of yours ? Do you not see a woolsack in store for you as you look upon these brave fellows ? "

" God forbid that I should say a word to damp your Majesty's ardour," the lawyer answered ; " yet I cannot but remember that there was a time when your Majesty, at the head of these same hirelings, did drive men as brave as these in headlong rout from Bothwell Bridge."

" True, true ! " said the King, passing his hand over his forehead—a favourite motion when he was worried and annoyed. " They were bold men, the western Covenanters, yet they could not stand against the rush of our battalions. But they had had no training, whereas these can fight in line and fire a platoon as well as one would wish to see."

" If we hadna a gun nor a patronal among us," said Ferguson, " if we hadna sae muckle as a sword, but just oor ain honds, yet would the Lard gie us the victory, if it seemed good in His a'-seeing een."

" All battles are but chance work, your Majesty," remarked Saxon, whose sword-arm was bound round with his kerchief. " Some lucky turn, some slip or chance which none can foresee, is ever likely to turn the scale. I have lost when I have looked to win, and I have won when I have looked to lose. It is an uncertain game, and one never knows the finish till the last card is played."

" Not till the stakes are drawn," said Buyse, in his deep guttural voice. " There is many a leader that wins what you call the trick, and yet loses the game."

" The trick being the battle and the game the campaign," quoth the King, with a smile. " Our German friend is a master of camp-fire metaphors. But methinks our poor horses are in a sorry state. What would cousin William over at The Hague, with his spruce guards, think of such a show as this ? "

During this talk the long column of foot had tramped past, still bearing the banners which they had brought with them to the wars, though much the worse for wind and weather. Monmouth's remarks had been drawn forth by the aspect of the ten troops of horse which followed. The chargers had been sadly worn by the continued work and constant rain, while the riders, having allowed their caps and fronts to get coated with rust, appeared to be in as bad a plight as their steeds. It was clear to the least experienced of us that if we were to hold our own it was upon our foot that we must rely. On the tops of the low hills all round the frequent shimmer of arms, glancing here and there when the sun's rays struck upon them, showed how strong our enemies were in the very point in which we were so weak. Yet in the main this Wells review was cheering to us, as showing that the men kept in good heart, and that there was no ill-feeling at the rough handling of the zealots upon the day before.

The enemy's horse hovered about us during these days, but the foot had been delayed through the heavy weather and the swollen streams. On the last day of June we marched out of Wells, and made our way across flat sedgy plains and over the low Polden Hills to Bridgewater, where we found some few recruits awaiting us. Here Monmouth had some thoughts of making a stand, and even set to work raising earthworks, but it was pointed out to him that, even could he hold the town, there was not more than a few days' provisions within it, while the

country round had been already swept so bare that little more could be expected from it. The works were therefore abandoned, and, fairly driven to bay, without a loophole of escape left, we awaited the approach of the enemy.

29. *Of the Great Cry from the Lonely House*

AND so our weary marching and counter-marching came at last to an end, and we found ourselves with our backs fairly against the wall, and the whole strength of the Government turned against us. Not a word came to us of a rising or movement in our favour in any part of England. Everywhere the Dissenters were cast into prison and the Church dominant. From north and east and west the militia of the counties was on its march against us. In London six regiments of Dutch troops had arrived as a loan from the Prince of Orange. Others were said to be on their way. The City had enrolled ten thousand men. Everywhere there was mustering and marching to succour the flower of the English army, which was already in Somersetshire. And all for the purpose of crushing some five or six thousand clodhoppers and fishermen, half-armed and penniless, who were ready to throw their lives away for a man and for an idea.

But this idea, my dear children, was a noble one, and one which a man might very well sacrifice all for, and yet feel that all was well spent. For though these poor peasants, in their dumb, blundering fashion, would have found it hard to give all their reasons in words, yet in the inmost heart of them they knew and felt that it was England's cause which they were fighting for, and that they were upholding their country's true self against those who would alter the old systems under which she had led the nations. Three more years made all this very plain, and showed that our simple unlettered followers had seen and judged the signs of the times more correctly than

those who called themselves their betters. There are, to my thinking, stages of human progress for which the Church of Rome is admirably suited. Where the mind of a nation is young, it may be best that it should not concern itself with spiritual affairs, but should lean upon the øld staff of custom and authority. But England had cast off her swaddling-clothes, and was a nursery of strong, thinking men, who would bow to no authority save that which their reason and conscience approved. It was hopeless, useless, foolish, to try to drive such men back into a creed which they had outgrown. Such an attempt was, however, being made, backed by all the weight of a bigoted king with a powerful and wealthy Church as his ally. In three years the nation would understand it, and the King would be flying from his angry people ; but at present, sunk in a torpor after the long civil wars and the corrupt reign of Charles, they failed to see what was at stake, and turned against those who would warn them, as a hasty man turns on the messenger who is the bearer of evil tidings. Is it not strange, my dears, how quickly a mere shadowy thought comes to take living form, and grow into a very tragic reality ? At one end of the chain is a king brooding over a point of doctrine ; at the other are six thousand desperate men, chivied and chased from shire to shire, standing to bay at last amid the bleak Bridgewater marshes, with their hearts as bitter and as hopeless as those of hunted beasts of prey. A king's theology is a dangerous thing for his subjects.

But if the idea for which these poor men fought was a worthy one, what shall we say of the man who had been chosen as the champion of their cause ? Alas, that such men should have had such a leader ! Swinging from the heights of confidence to the depths of despair, choosing his future council of state one day and proposing to fly from the army on the next, he appeared from the start to be possessed by the very spirit of fickleness. Yet he had borne a fair name before this enterprise. In Scotland he had won golden opinions, not only for his success, but

for the moderation and mercy with which he treated the vanquished. On the Continent he had commanded an English brigade in a way that earned praise from old soldiers of Louis and the Empire. Yet now, when his own head and his own fortunes were at stake, he was feeble, irresolute, and cowardly. In my father's phrase, " all the virtue had gone out of him." I declare when I have seen him riding among his troops, with his head bowed upon his breast and a face like a mute at a burying, casting an air of gloom and of despair all round him, I have felt that, even in case of success, such a man could never wear the crown of the Tudors and the Plantagenets, but that some stronger hand, were it that of one of his own generals, would wrest it from him.

I will do Monmouth the justice to say that from the time when it was at last decided to fight—for the very good reason that no other course was open—he showed up in a more soldierly and manlier spirit. For the first few days in July no means were neglected to hearten our troops and to nerve them for the coming battle. From morning to night we were at work, teaching our foot how to form up in dense groups to meet the charge of horse, and how to depend upon each other, and look to their officers for orders. At night the streets of the little town from the Castle Field to the Parret Bridge resounded with the praying and the preaching. There was no need for the officers to quell irregularities, for the troops punished them amongst themselves. One man who came out on the streets hot with wine was well-nigh hanged by his companions, who finally cast him out of the town as being unworthy to fight in what they looked upon as a sacred quarrel. As to their courage, there was no occasion to quicken that, for they were as fearless as lions, and the only danger was lest their fiery daring should lead them into foolhardiness. Their desire was to hurl themselves upon the enemy like a horde of Moslem fanatics, and it was no easy matter to drill such hot-headed fellows into the steadiness and caution which war demands.

Provisions ran low upon the third day of our stay in Bridgewater, which was due to our having exhausted that part of the country before, and also to the vigilance of the Royal Horse, who scoured the district round and cut off our supplies. Lord Grey determined, therefore, to send out two troops of horse under cover of night, to do what they could to refill the larder. The command of the small expedition was given over to Major Martin Hooker, an old Lifeguardsman of rough speech and curt manners, who had done good service in drilling the headstrong farmers and yeomen into some sort of order. Sir Gervas Jerome and I asked leave from Lord Grey to join the foray—a favour which was readily granted, since there was little stirring in the town.

It was about eleven o'clock on a moonless night that we sallied out of Bridgewater, intending to explore the country in the direction of Boroughbridge and Athelney. We had word that there was no large body of the enemy in that quarter, and it was a fertile district where good store of supplies might be hoped for. We took with us four empty waggons, to carry whatever we might have the luck to find. Our commander arranged that one troop should ride before these and one behind, while a small advance party, under the charge of Sir Gervas, kept some hundreds of paces in front. In this order we clattered out of the town, just as the late bugles were blowing, and swept away down the quiet shadowy roads, bringing anxious peering faces to the casements of the wayside cottages as we whirled past in the darkness.

That ride comes very clearly before me as I think of it. The dark loom of the club-headed willows flitting by us, the moaning of the breeze among the withies, the vague, blurred figures of the troopers, the dull thud of the hoofs, and the jingling of scabbard against stirrup—eye and ear can both conjure up those old-time memories. The Baronet and I rode in front, knee against knee, and his light-hearted chatter of life in town, with his little snatches of verse or song from Cowley or Waller, were

a very balm of Gilead to my sombre and somewhat heavy spirit.

" Life is indeed life on such a night as this," quoth he, as we breathed in the fresh country air with the reeks of crops and of kine. " Rabbit me ! but you are to be envied, Clarke, for having been born and bred in the country ! What pleasures has the town to offer compared to the free gifts of nature, provided always that there be a perruquier's and a snuff merchant's, and a scent vendor's, and one or two tolerable outfitters within reach ? With these and a good coffee-house and a playhouse, I think I could make shift to lead a simple pastoral life for some months."

" In the country," said I, laughing, " we have ever the feeling that the true life of mankind, with the growth of knowledge and wisdom, are being wrought out in the towns."

" Ventre Saint-Gris ! It was little knowledge or wisdom that I acquired there," he answered. " Truth to tell, I have lived more and learned more during these few weeks that we have been sliding about in the rain with our ragged lads, than ever I did when I was page of the court, with the ball of fortune at my feet. It is a sorry thing for a man's mind to have nothing higher to dwell upon than the turning of a compliment or the dancing of a corranto. Zounds, lad ! I have your friend the carpenter to thank for much. As he says in his letter, unless a man can get the good that is in him out, he is of less value in the world than one of those fowls that we hear cackling, for they at least fulfil their mission, if it be only to lay eggs. Ged, it is a new creed for me to be preaching ! "

" But," said I, " when you were a wealthy man you must have been of service to someone, for how could one spend so much money and yet none be the better ? "

" You dear bucolic Micah ! " he cried, with a gay laugh. " You will ever speak of my poor fortune with bated breath and in an awestruck voice, as though it were the wealth of the Indies. You cannot think, lad, how easy

it is for a money-bag to take unto itself wings and fly. It is true that the man who spends it doth not consume the money, but passes it on to someone who profits thereby. Yet the fault lies in the fact that it was to the wrong folk that we passed our money, thereby breeding a useless and debauched class at the expense of honest callings. Od's fish, lad! when I think of the swarms of needy beggars, the lecherous pimps, the nose-slitting bullies, the toadies and the flatterers who were reared by us, I feel that in hatching such a poisonous brood our money hath done what no money can undo. Have I not seen them thirty deep of a morning when I have held my levée, cringing up to my bedside——"

" Your bedside ! " I exclaimed.

" Aye ! it was the mode to receive in bed, attired in laced cambric shirt and periwig, though afterwards it was permitted to sit up in your chamber, but dressed *à la négligence*, in gown and slippers. The mode is a terrible tyrant, Clarke, though its arm may not extend as far as Havant. The idle man of the town must have some rule of life, so he becomes a slave to the law of the fashions. No man in London was more subject to it than myself. I was regular in my irregularities, and orderly in my disorders. At eleven o'clock to the stroke, up came my valet with the morning cup of hippocras, an excellent thing for the qualms, and some slight refection, as the breast of an ortolan or wing of a widgeon. Then came the levée, twenty, thirty or forty of the class I have spoken of, though now and then perhaps there might be some honest case of want among them, some needy man-of-letters in quest of a guinea, or pupil-less pedant with much ancient leaning in his head and very little modern coinage in his pocket. It was not only that I had some power of mine own, but I was known to have the ear of my Lord Halifax, Sidney Godolphin, Lawrence Hyde and others whose will might make or mar a man. Mark you those lights upon the left ! Would it not be well to see if there is not something to be had there ? "

" Hooker hath orders to proceed to a certain farm," I answered. " This we could take upon our return should we still have space. We shall be back here before morning."

" We must get supplies, if I have to ride back to Surrey for them," said he. " Rat me, if I dare look my musqueteers in the face again unless I bring them something to toast upon the end of their ramrods ! They had little more savoury than their own bullets to put in their mouths when I left them. But I was speaking of old days in London. Our time was well filled. Should a man of quality incline to sport there was ever something to attract him. He might see sword-playing at Hockley, or cocking at Shoe Lane, or baiting at Southwark, or shooting at Tothill Fields. Again, he might walk in the physic gardens of St. James's, or go down the river with the ebb tide to the cherry orchards at Rotherhithe, or drive to Islington to drink the cream, or, above all, walk in the Park, which is most modish for a gentleman who dresses in the fashion. You see, Clarke, that we were active in our idleness, and that there was no lack of employment. Then as evening came on there were the playhouses to draw us, Dorset Gardens, Lincoln's Inn, Drury Lane and the Queen's—among the four there was ever some amusement to be found."

" There, at least, your time was well employed," said I ; " you could not hearken to the grand thoughts or lofty words of Shakespeare or of Massinger without feeling some image of them in your own soul."

Sir Gervas chuckled quietly. " You are as fresh to me, Micah, as this sweet country air," said he. " Know, thou dear babe, that it was not to see the play that we frequented the playhouse."

" Then, why, in Heaven's name ? " I asked.

" To see each other," he answered. " It was the mode, I assure you, for a man of fashion to stand with his back turned to the stage from the rise of the curtain to the fall of it. There were the orange wenches to quiz—plaguy sharp of tongue the hussies are, too—and there were the

vizards of the pit, whose little black masks did invite inquiry, and there were the beauties of the town and the toasts of the Court, all fair mark for our quizzing-glasses. Play, indeed ! S'bud, we had something better to do than to listen to alexandrines or weigh the merits of hexameters ! 'Tis true that if La Jeune were dancing, or if Mrs. Bracegirdle or Mrs. Oldfield came upon the boards, we would hum and clap, but it was the fine woman that we applauded rather than the actress."

" And when the play was over you went doubtless to supper and so to bed ? "

" To supper, certainly. Sometimes to the Rhenish House, sometimes to Pontack's in Abchurch Lane. Everyone had his own taste in that matter. Then there were dice and cards at the Groom Porter's or under the arches at Covent Garden, piquet, passage, hazard, primero —what you choose. After that you could find all the world at the coffee-houses, where an arrière supper was often served with devilled bones and prunes, to drive the fumes of wine from the head. Zounds, Micah ! if the Jews should relax their pressure, or if this war brings us any luck, you shall come to town with me and shall see all these things for yourself."

" Truth to tell, it doth not tempt me much," I answered. " Slow and solemn I am by nature, and in such scenes as you have described I should feel a very death's head at a banquet."

Sir Gervas was about to reply, when of a sudden out of the silence of the night there rose a long-drawn piercing scream, which thrilled through every nerve of our bodies. I have never heard such a wail of despair. We pulled up our horses, as did the troopers behind us, and strained our ears for some sign as to whence the sound proceeded, for some were of opinion that it came from our right and some from our left. The main body with the waggons had come up, and we all listened intently for any return of the terrible cry. Presently it broke upon us again, wild, shrill and agonised : the scream of a woman in mortal distress.

" 'Tis over there, Major Hooker," cried Sir Gervas,

standing up in his stirrups and peering through the darkness. " There is a house about two fields off. I can see some glimmer, as from a window with the blind drawn."

" Shall we not make for it at once ? " I asked impatiently, for our commander sat stolidly upon his horse as though by no means sure what course he should pursue.

" I am here, Captain Clarke," said he, " to convey supplies to the army, and I am by no means justified in turning from my course to pursue other adventures."

" Death, man ! there is a woman in distress," cried Sir Gervas. " Why, Major, you would not ride past and let her call in vain for help ? Hark, there she is again ! " As he spoke the wild scream rang out once more from the lonely house.

" Nay, I can abide this no longer," I cried, my blood boiling in my veins ; " do you go on your errand, Major Hooker, and my friend and I shall leave you here. We shall know how to justify our action to the King. Come, Sir Gervas ! "

" Mark ye, this is flat mutiny, Captain Clarke," said Hooker ; " you are under my orders, and should you desert me you do so at your peril."

" In such a case I care not a groat for thy orders," I answered hotly. Turning Covenant I spurred down a narrow, deeply-rutted lane which led towards the house, followed by Sir Gervas and two or three of the troopers. At the same moment I heard a sharp word of command from Hooker and the creaking of wheels, showing that he had indeed abandoned us and proceeded on his mission.

" He is right," quoth the Baronet, as we rode down the lane ; " Saxon or any other old soldier would commend his discipline."

" There are things which are higher than discipline," I muttered. " I could not pass on and leave this poor soul in her distress. But see—what have we here ? "

A dark mass loomed in front of us, which proved as we approached to be four horses fastened by their bridles to the hedge.

" Cavalry horses, Captain Clarke ! " cried one of the troopers who had sprung down to examine them. " They have the Government saddle and holsters. Here is a wooden gate which opens on a pathway leading to the house."

" We had best dismount, then," said Sir Gervas, jumping down and tying his horse beside the others. " Do you, lads, stay by the horses, and if we call for ye come to our aid. Sergeant Holloway, you can come with us. Bring your pistols with you ! "

30. *Of the Swordsman with the Brown Jacket*

THE sergeant, who was a great raw-boned west-countryman, pushed the gate open, and we were advancing up the winding pathway, when a stream of yellow light flooded out from a suddenly opened door, and we saw a dark squat figure dart through it into the inside of the house. At the same moment there rose up a babel of sounds, followed by two pistol shots, and a roaring, gasping hubbub, with clash of swords and storm of oaths. At this sudden uproar we all three ran at our topmost speed up the pathway and peered in through the open door, where we saw a scene such as I shall never forget while this old memory of mine can conjure up any picture of the past.

The room was large and lofty, with long rows of hams and salted meats dangling from the smoke-browned rafters, as is usual in Somersetshire farmhouses. A high black clock ticked in a corner, and a rude table, with plates and dishes laid out as for a meal, stood in the centre. Right in front of the door a great fire of wood faggots was blazing, and before this, to our unutterable horror, there hung a man head downwards, suspended by a rope which was knotted round his ankles, and which, passing over a hook in a beam, had been made fast to a ring in the floor. The struggles of this unhappy man had caused the rope

to whirl round, so that he was spinning in front of the blaze like a joint of meat. Across the threshold lay a woman, the one whose cries had attracted us, but her rigid face and twisted body showed that our aid had come too late to save her from the fate which she had seen impending. Close by her two swarthy dragoons in the glaring red coats of the Royal army lay stretched across each other upon the floor, dark and scowling even in death. In the centre of the room two other dragoons were cutting and stabbing with their broadswords at a thick, short, heavy-shouldered man, clad in coarse brown kersey stuff, who sprang about among the chairs and round the table with a long basket-hilted rapier in his hand, parrying or dodging their blows with wonderful adroitness, and every now and then putting in a thrust in return. Hard pressed as he was, his set resolute face, firm mouth, and bright well-opened eyes spoke of a bold spirit within, while the blood which dripped from the sleeve of one of his opponents proved that the contest was not so unequal as it might appear. Even as we gazed he sprang back to avoid a fierce rush of the furious soldiers, and by a quick sharp side-stroke he severed the rope by which the victim was hung. The body fell with a heavy thud upon the brick floor, while the little swordsman danced off in a moment into another quarter of the room, still stopping or avoiding with the utmost ease and skill the shower of blows which rained upon him.

This strange scene held us spell-bound for a few seconds, but there was no time for delay, for a slip or trip would prove fatal to the gallant stranger. Rushing into the chamber, sword in hand, we fell upon the dragoons, who, outnumbered as they were, backed into a corner and struck out fiercely, knowing that they need expect no mercy after the devil's work in which they had been engaged. Holloway, our sergeant of horse, springing furiously in, laid himself open to a thrust which stretched him dead upon the ground. Before the dragoon could disengage his weapon, Sir Gervas cut him down, while at

the same moment the stranger got past the guard of his antagonist, and wounded him mortally in the throat. Of the four red-coats not one escaped alive, while the bodies of our sergeant and of the old couple who had been the first victims increased the horror of the scene.

" Poor Holloway is gone," said I, placing my hand over his heart. " Who ever saw such a shambles ? I feel sick and ill."

" Here is eau-de-vie, if I mistake not," cried the stranger, clambering up on a chair and reaching a bottle from the shelf. " Good, too, by the smell. Take a sup, for you are as white as a new-bleached sheet."

" Honest warfare I can abide, but scenes like this make my blood run cold," I answered, taking a gulp from the flask. I was a very young soldier then, my dears, but I confess that to the end of my campaigns any form of cruelty had the same effect upon me. I give you my word that when I went to London last fall the sight of an overworked, raw-backed cart-horse straining with its load, and flogged for not doing that which it could not do, gave me greater qualms than did the field of Sedgemoor, or that greater day when ten thousand of the flower of France lay stretched before the earthworks of Landen.

" The woman is dead," said Sir Gervas, " and the man is also, I fear, past recovery. He is not burned, but suffers, I should judge, poor devil ! from the rush of blood to the head."

" If that be all it may well be cured," remarked the stranger ; and taking a small knife from his pocket, he rolled up the old man's sleeve and opened one of his veins. At first only a few sluggish black drops oozed from the wound, but presently the blood began to flow more freely, and the injured man showed signs of returning sense.

" He will live," said the little swordsman, putting his lancet back in his pocket. " And now, who may you be to whom I owe this interference which shortened the affair, though mayhap the result would have been the same had you left us to settle it amongst ourselves ? "

" We are from Monmouth's army," I answered. " He lies at Bridgewater, and we are scouting and seeking supplies."

" And who are you ? " asked Sir Gervas. " And how came you into this ruffle ? S'bud, you are a game little rooster to fight four such great cockerels ! "

" My name is Hector Marot," the man answered, cleaning out his empty pistols and very carefully reloading them. " As to who I am, it is a matter of small moment. Suffice it that I have helped to lessen Kirke's horse by four of his rogues. Mark their faces, so dusky and sun-dried even in death. These men have learned warfare fighting against the heathen in Africa, and now they practise on poor harmless English folk the devil's tricks which they have picked up amongst the savages. The Lord help Monmouth's men should they be beaten ! These vermin are more to be feared than hangman's cord or headsman's axe."

" But how did you chance upon the spot at the very nick of time ? " I asked.

" Why, marry, I was jogging down the road on my mare when I heard the clatter of hoofs behind me, and concealing myself in a field, as a prudent man would while the country is in its present state, I saw these four rogues gallop past. They made their way up to the farmhouse here, and presently from cries and other tokens I knew what manner of hell-fire business they had on hand. On that I left my mare in the field and ran up, when I saw them through the casement, tricing the good man up in front of his fire to make him confess where his wealth lay hidden, though indeed it is my own belief that neither he nor any other farmer in these parts hath any wealth left to hide, after two armies have been quartered in turn upon them. Finding that his mouth remained closed, they ran him up, as you saw, and would assuredly have toasted him like a snipe, had I not stepped in and winged two of them with my barkers. The others set upon me, but I pinked one through the forearm, and should doubt-

less have given a good account of both of them but for your incoming."

" Right gallantly done ! " I exclaimed. " But where have I heard your name before, Mr. Hector Marot ? "

" Nay," he answered, with a sharp, sidelong look, " I cannot tell that."

" It is familiar to mine ear," said I.

He shrugged his broad shoulders, and continued to look to the priming of his pistols, with a half-defiant and half-uneasy expression. He was a very sturdy, deep-chested man, with a stern, square-jawed face, and a white seam across his bronzed forehead as from a slash with a knife. He wore a gold-edged riding-cap, a jacket of brown sad-coloured stuff much stained by the weather, a pair of high rusty jack-boots, and a small bob-wig.

Sir Gervas, who had been staring very hard at the man, suddenly gave a start, and slapped his hand against his leg.

" Of course ! " he cried. " Sink me, if I could remember where I had seen your face, but now it comes back to me very clearly."

The man glanced doggedly from under his bent brows at each of us in turn. " It seems that I have fallen among acquaintances," he said gruffly ; " yet I have no memory of ye. Methinks, young sirs, that your fancy doth play ye false."

" Not a whit," the Baronet answered quietly, and, bending forward, he whispered a few words into the man's ear, which caused him to spring from his seat and take a couple of quick strides forward, as though to escape from the house.

" Nay, nay ! " cried Sir Gervas, springing between him and the door, " you shall not run away from us. Pshaw, man ! never lay your hand upon your sword. We have had bloody work enough for one night. Besides, we would not harm you."

" What mean ye, then ? What would ye have ? " he asked, glancing about like some fierce wild beast in a trap.

" I have a most kindly feeling to you, man, after this

night's work," cried Sir Gervas. " What is it to me how ye pick up a living, as long as you are a true man at heart ? Let me perish if I ever forget a face which I have once seen, and your bonne mine, with the trade-mark upon your forehead, is especially hard to overlook."

" Suppose I be the same ? What then ? " the man asked suddenly.

" There is no suppose in the matter. I could swear to you. But I would not, lad—not if I caught you red-handed. You must know, Clarke, since there is none to overhear us, that in the old days I was a Justice of the Peace in Surrey, and that our friend here was brought up before me on a charge of riding somewhat late o' night, and of being plaguy short with travellers. You will understand me. He was referred to assizes, but got away in the meanwhile, and so saved his neck. Right glad I am of it, for you will agree with me that he is too proper a man to give a tight-rope dance at Tyburn."

" And I remember well now where I have heard your name," said I. " Were you not a captive in the Duke of Beaufort's prison at Badminton, and did you not succeed in escaping from the old Boteler dungeon ? "

" Nay, gentlemen," he replied, seating himself on the edge of the table, and carelessly swinging his legs, " since ye know so much it would be folly for me to attempt to deceive ye. I am indeed the same Hector Marot who hath made his name a terror on the great Western road, and who hath seen the inside of more prisons than any man in the south. With truth, however, I can say that though I have been ten years upon the roads, I have never yet taken a groat from the poor, or injured any man who did not wish to injure me. On the contrary, I have often risked life and limb to save those who were in trouble."

" We can bear you out in that," I answered, " for if these four red-coat devils have paid the price of their crimes, it is your doing rather than ours."

" Nay, I can take little credit for that," our new acquaintance answered. " Indeed, I had other scores to

settle with Colonel Kirke's horse, and was but too glad to have this breather with them."

Whilst we were talking the men whom we had left with the horses had come up, together with some of the neighbouring farmers and cottagers, who were aghast at the scene of slaughter, and much troubled in their minds over the vengeance which might be exacted by the Royal troops next day.

" For Christ's zake, zur," cried one of them, an old ruddy-faced countryman, " move the bodies o' these soldier rogues into the road, and let it zeem as how they have perished in a chance fight wi' your own troopers loike. Should it be known as they have met their end within a varmhouse, there will not be a thatch left un-lighted over t' whole countryside ; as it is, us can scarce keep these murthering Tangiers devils from oor throats."

" His request is in reason," said the highwayman bluntly. " We have no right to have our fun, and then go our way leaving others to pay the score."

" Well, hark ye," said Sir Gervas, turning to the group of frightened rustics. " I'll strike a bargain with ye over the matter. We have come out for supplies, and can scarce go back empty-handed. If ye will among ye provide us with a cart, filling it with such breadstuffs and greens as ye may, with a dozen bullocks as well, we shall not only screen ye in this matter, but I shall promise payment at fair market rates if ye will come to the Pro-testant camp for the money."

" I'll spare the bullocks," quoth the old man whom we had rescued, who was now sufficiently recovered to sit up. " Zince my poor dame is foully murthered it matters little to me what becomes o' the stock. I shall zee her laid in Durston graveyard, and shall then vollow you to t' camp, where I shall die happy if I can but rid the earth o' one more o' these incarnate devils."

" You say well, gaffer ! " cried Hector Marot ; " you show the true spirit. Methinks I see an old birding-piece on yonder hooks, which, with a brace of slugs in it and a

bold man behind it, might bring down one of these fine
birds for all their gay feathers."

" Her's been a true mate to me for mor'n thirty year,"
said the old man, the tears coursing down his wrinkled
cheeks. " Thirty zeed-toimes and thirty harvests we've
worked together. But this is a zeed-toime which shall
have a harvest o' blood if my right hand can compass
it."

" If you go to t' wars, Gaffer Swain, we'll look to your
homestead," said the farmer who had spoken before.
" As to t' green stuffs as this gentleman asks for he shall
have not one wainload but three, if he will but gi' us
half-an-hour to fill them up. If he does not take them t'
others will, so we had raither that they go to the good
cause. Here, Miles, do you wak the labourers, and zee
that they throw the potato store wi' the spinach and the
dried meats into the waggons wi' all speed."

" Then we had best set about our part of the contract,"
said Hector Marot. With the aid of our troopers he
carried out the four dragoons and our dead sergeant, and
laid them on the ground some way down the lane, leading
the horses all round and between their bodies, so as to
trample the earth, and bear out the idea of a cavalry
skirmish. While this was doing, some of the labourers
had washed down the brick floor of the kitchen and removed all traces of the tragedy. The murdered woman
had been carried up to her own chamber, so that nothing
was left to recall what had occurred, save the unhappy
farmer, who sat moodily in the same place, with his chin
resting upon his stringy work-worn hands, staring out in
front of him with a stony, empty gaze, unconscious
apparently of all that was going on around him.

The loading of the waggons had been quickly accomplished, and the little drove of oxen gathered from a
neighbouring field. We were just starting upon our
return journey when a young countryman rode up, with
the news that a troop of the Royal Horse were between
the camp and ourselves. This was grave tidings, for we

were but seven all told, and our pace was necessarily slow whilst we were hampered with the supplies.

" How about Hooker ? " I suggested. " Should we not send after him and give him warning ? "

" I'll goo at once," said the countryman. " I'm bound to zee him if he be on the Athelney road." So saying he set spurs to his horse and galloped off through the darkness.

" While we have such volunteer scouts as this," I remarked, " it is easy to see which side the country folk have in their hearts. Hooker hath still the better part of two troops with him, so surely he can hold his own. But how are we to make our way back ? "

" Zounds, Clarke ! let us extemporise a fortress," suggested Sir Gervas. " We could hold this farmhouse against all comers until Hooker returns, and then join our forces to his. Now would our redoubtable Colonel be in his glory, to have a chance of devising cross-fires, and flanking-fires, with all the other refinements of a well-conducted leaguer."

" Nay," I answered, " after leaving Major Hooker in a somewhat cavalier fashion, it would be a bitter thing to have to ask his help now that there is danger."

" Ho, ho ! " cried the Baronet. " It does not take a very deep lead-line to come to the bottom of your stoical philosophy, friend Micah. For all your cold-blooded stolidity you are keen enough where pride or honour is concerned. Shall we then ride onwards, and chance it ? I'll lay an even crown that we never so much as see a red-coat."

" If you will take my advice, gentlemen," said the highwayman, trotting up upon a beautiful bay mare, " I should say that your best course is to allow me to act as guide to you as far as the camp. It will be strange if I cannot find roads which shall baffle these blundering soldiers."

" A very wise and seasonable proposition," cried Sir Gervas. " Master Marot, a pinch from my snuff-box, which is ever a covenant of friendship with its owner. Adslidikins, man ! though our acquaintance at present is limited to my having nearly hanged you on one occasion,

yet I have a kindly feeling towards you, though I wish you had some more savoury trade."

" So do many who ride o' night," Marot answered, with a chuckle. " But we had best start, for the east is whitening, and it will be daylight ere we come to Bridgewater."

Leaving the ill-omened farmhouse behind us we set off with all military precautions, Marot riding with me some distance in front, while two of the troopers covered the rear. It was still very dark, though a thin grey line on the horizon showed that the dawn was not far off. In spite of the gloom, however, our new acquaintance guided us without a moment's halt or hesitation through a network of lanes and bypaths, across fields and over bogs, where the waggons were sometimes up to their axles in bog, and sometimes were groaning and straining over rocks and stones. So frequent were our turnings, and so often did we change the direction of our advance, that I feared more than once that our guide was at fault ; yet, when at last the first rays of the sun brightened the landscape we saw the steeple of Bridgewater parish church shooting up right in front of us.

" Zounds, man ! you must have something of the cat in you to pick your way so in the dark," cried Sir Gervas, riding up to us. " I am right glad to see the town, for my poor waggons have been creaking and straining until my ears are weary with listening for the snap of the axle-bar. Master Marot, we owe you something for this."

" Is this your own particular district ? " I asked, " or have you a like knowledge of every part of the south ? "

" My range," said he, lighting his short, black pipe, " is from Kent to Cornwall, though never north of the Thames or Bristol Channel. Through that district there is no road which is not familiar to me, nor as much as a break of the hedge which I could not find in blackest midnight. It is my calling. But the trade is not what it was. If I had a son I should not bring him up to it. It hath been spoiled by the armed guards to the mail-coaches, and by the accursed goldsmiths, who have opened their

banks and so taken the hard money into their strong boxes, giving out instead slips of paper, which are as useless to us as an old newsletter. I give ye my word that only a week gone last Friday I stopped a grazier coming from Blandford fair, and I took seven hundred guineas off him in these paper cheques, as they call them—enough, had it been in gold, to have lasted me for a three-month rouse. Truly the country is coming to a pretty pass when such trash as that is allowed to take the place of the King's coinage."

" Why should you persevere in such a trade ? " said I. " Your own knowledge must tell you that it can only lead to ruin and the gallows. Have you ever known one who has thriven at it ? "

" That have I," he answered readily. " There was Kingston Jones, who worked Hounslow for many a year. He took ten thousand yellow boys on one job, and like a wise man, he vowed never to risk his neck again. He went into Cheshire, with some tale of having newly arrived from the Indies, bought an estate, and is now a flourishing country gentleman of good repute, and a Justice of the Peace into the bargain. Zounds, man ! to see him on the bench, condemning some poor devil for stealing a dozen eggs, is as good as a comedy in the playhouse."

" Nay ! but," I persisted, " you are a man, judging from what we have seen of your courage and skill in the use of your weapons, who would gain speedy preferment in any army. Surely it were better to use your gifts to the gaining of honour and credit, than to make them a stepping-stone to disgrace and the gallows ? "

" For the gallows I care not a clipped shilling," the highwayman answered, sending up thick blue curls of smoke into the morning air. " We have all to pay nature's debt, and whether I do it in my boots or on a feather bed, in one year or in ten, matters little to me as to any soldier among you. As to disgrace it is a matter of opinion. I see no shame myself in taking a toll upon the wealth of the rich, since I freely expose my own skin in the doing of it."

" There is a right and there is a wrong," I answered,
" which no words can do away with, and it is a dangerous
and unprofitable trick to juggle with them."

" Besides, even if what you have said were true as to
property," Sir Gervas remarked, " it would not hold you
excused for that recklessness of human life which your
trade begets."

" Nay! it is but hunting, save that your quarry may at
any time turn round upon you, and become in turn the
hunter. It is, as you say, a dangerous game, but two can
play at it, and each has an equal chance. There is no
loading of the dice, or throwing of fulhams. Now it was
but a few days back that, riding down the high-road, I
perceived three jolly farmers at full gallop across the
fields with a leash of dogs yelping in front of them, and
all in pursuit of one little harmless bunny. It was a bare
and unpeopled countryside on the border of Exmoor, so
I bethought me that I could not employ my leisure better
than by chasing the chasers. Od's wouns! it was a
proper hunt. Away went my gentlemen, whooping like
madmen, with their coat skirts flapping in the breeze,
chivying on the dogs, and having a rare morning's sport.
They never marked the quiet horseman who rode behind
them, and who without a ' yoick! ' or ' hark-a-way! '
was relishing his chase with the loudest of them. It
needed but a posse of peace officers at my heels to make
up a brave string of us, catch-who-catch-can, like the
game the lads play on the village green."

" And what came of it ? " I asked, for our new acquaintance was laughing silently to himself.

" Well, my three friends ran down their hare, and
pulled out their flasks, as men who had done a good stroke
of work. They were still hobnobbing and laughing over
the slaughtered bunny, and one had dismounted to cut
off its ears as the prize of their chase, when I came up at
a hand-gallop. ' Good-morrow, gentlemen,' said I, ' we
have had rare sport.' They looked at me blankly enough,
I promise you, and one of them asked me what the devil

I did there, and how I dared to join in a private sport. 'Nay, I was not chasing your hare, gentlemen,' said I. 'What then, fellow?' asked one of them. 'Why, marry, I was chasing you,' I answered, 'and a better run I have not had for years.' With that I lugged out my persuaders, and made the thing clear in a few words, and I'll warrant you would have laughed could you have seen their faces as they slowly dragged the fat leather purses from their fobs. Seventy-one pounds was my prize that morning, which was better worth riding for than a hare's ears."

"Did they not raise the country on your track?" I asked.

"Nay! When Brown Alice is given her head she flies faster than the news. Rumour spreads quick, but the good mare's stride is quicker still."

"And here we are within our own outposts," quoth Sir Gervas. "Now, mine honest friend—for honest you have been to us, whatever others may say of you—will you not come with us, and strike in for a good cause? Zounds, man! you have many an ill deed to atone for, I'll warrant. Why not add one good one to your account, by risking your life for the reformed faith?"

"Not I," the highwayman answered, reining up his horse. "My own skin is nothing, but why should I risk my mare in such a fool's quarrel? Should she come to harm in the ruffle, where could I get such another? Besides, it matters nothing to her whether Papist or Protestant sits on the throne of England—does it, my beauty?"

"But you might chance to gain preferment," I said. "Our Colonel, Decimus Saxon, is one who loves a good swordsman, and his word hath power with King Monmouth and the council."

"Nay, nay!" cried Hector Marot gruffly. "Let every man stick to his own trade. Kirke's Horse I am ever ready to have a brush with, for a party of them hung old blind Jim Houston of Milverton, who was a friend of mine. I have sent seven of the red-handed rogues to their last account for it, and might work through the whole regiment had I time. But I will not fight against

King James, nor will I risk the mare, so let me hear no more of it. And now I must leave ye, for I have much to do. Farewell to you ! "

" Farewell, farewell ! " we cried, pressing his brown horny hands ; " our thanks to you for your guidance." Raising his hat, he shook his bridle and galloped off down the road in a rolling cloud of dust.

" Rat me, if I ever say a word against the thieves again !" said Sir Gervas. " I never saw a man wield sword more deftly in my life, and he must be a rare hand with a pistol to bring those two tall fellows down with two shots. But look over there, Clarke ! Can you not see bodies of red-coats ? "

" Surely I can," I answered, gazing out over the broad, reedy, dead-coloured plain, which extended from the other side of the winding Parret to the distant Polden Hills. " I can see them over yonder in the direction of Westonzoyland, as bright as the poppies among corn."

" There are more upon the left, near Chedzoy," quoth Sir Gervas. " One, two, three, and one yonder, and two others behind—six regiments of foot in all. Methinks I see breastplates of horse over there, and some sign of ordnance too ! Faith ! Monmouth must fight now, if he ever hopes to feel the gold rim upon his temples. The whole of King James's army hath closed upon him."

" We must get back to our command, then," I answered. " If I mistake not, I see the flutter of our standards in the market-place." We spurred our weary steeds forward, and made our way with our little party and the supplies which we had collected, until we found ourselves back in our quarters, where we were hailed by the lusty cheers of our hungry comrades. Before noon the drove of bullocks had been changed into joints and steaks, while our green stuff and other victuals had helped to furnish the last dinner which many of our men were ever destined to eat. Major Hooker came in shortly after with a good store of provisions, but in no very good case, for he had had a skirmish with the dragoons, and had lost eight or

ten of his men. He bore a complaint straightway to the council concerning the manner in which we had deserted him ; but great events were coming fast upon us now, and there was small time to inquire into petty matters of discipline. For myself, I freely confess, looking back on it, that as a soldier he was entirely in the right, and that from a strict military point of view our conduct was not to be excused. Yet I trust, my dears, even now, when years have weighed me down, that the scream of a woman in distress would be a signal which would draw me to her aid while these old limbs could bear me. For the duty which we owe to the weak overrides all other duties and is superior to all circumstances, and I for one cannot see why the coat of the soldier should harden the heart of the man.

31. *Of the Maid of the Marsh and the Bubble which rose from the Bog*

ALL Bridgewater was in a ferment as we rode in, for King James's forces were within four miles, on the Sedgemoor Plain, and it was likely that they would push on at once and storm the town. Some rude works had been thrown up on the Eastover side, behind which two brigades were drawn up in arms, while the rest of the army was held in reserve in the market-place and Castle Field. Towards afternoon, however, parties of our horse and peasants from the fen country came in with the news that there was no fear of an assault being attempted. The Royal troops had quartered themselves snugly in the little villages of the neighbourhood, and having levied contributions of cider and of beer from the farmers, they showed no sign of any wish to advance.

The town was full of women, the wives, mothers and sisters of our peasants, who had come in from far and near to see their loved once ones more. Fleet Street or Cheapside upon a busy day are not more crowded than were the narrow streets and lanes of the Somersetshire town. Jack-

booted, buff-coated troopers ; scarlet militiamen ; brown, stern-faced Tauntonians ; serge-clad pikemen ; wild, ragged miners ; smock-frocked yokels ; reckless, weather-tanned seamen ; gaunt cragsmen from the northern coast —all pushed and jostled each other in a thick, many-coloured crowd. Everywhere among them were the country women, straw-bonneted and loud-tongued, weep-ing, embracing and exhorting. Here and there amid the motley dresses and gleam of arms moved the dark, sombre figure of a Puritan minister, with sweeping sad-coloured mantle and penthouse hat, scattering abroad short fiery ejaculations and stern pithy texts of the old fighting order, which warmed the men's blood like liquor. Ever and anon a sharp fierce shout would rise from the people, like the yelp of a high-spirited hound which is straining at its leash and hot to be at the throat of its enemy.

Our regiment had been taken off duty whenever it was clear that Feversham did not mean to advance, and they were now busy upon the victuals which our night foray had furnished. It was a Sunday, fresh and warm, with a clear unclouded sky, and a gentle breeze, sweet with the smack of the country. All day the bells of the neighbour-ing villages rang out their alarm, pealing their music over the sunlit countryside. The upper windows and red-tiled roofs of the houses were crowded with pale-faced women and children, who peered out to eastward, where the splotches of crimson upon the dun-coloured moor marked the position of our enemies.

At four o'clock Monmouth held a last council of war upon the square tower out of which springs the steeple of Bridgewater parish church, whence a good view can be obtained of all the country round. Since my ride to Beaufort I had always been honoured with a summons to attend, in spite of my humble rank in the army There were some thirty councillors in all, as many as the space would hold, soldiers and courtiers, Cavaliers and Puritans, all drawn together now by the bond of a common danger. Indeed, the near approach of a crisis in their fortunes had

broken down much of the distinction of manner which had served to separate them. The sectary had lost something of his austerity and become flushed and eager at the prospect of battle, while the giddy man of fashion was hushed into unwonted gravity as he considered the danger of his position. Their old feuds were forgotten as they gathered on the parapet and gazed with set faces at the thick columns of smoke which rose along the skyline.

King Monmouth stood among his chiefs, pale and haggard, with the dishevelled, unkempt look of a man whose distress of mind has made him forgetful of the care of his person. He held a pair of ivory glasses, and as he raised them to his eyes his thin white hands shook and twitched until it was grievous to watch him. Lord Grey handed his own glasses to Saxon, who leaned his elbows upon the rough stone breastwork and stared long and earnestly at the enemy.

" They are the very men I have myself led," said Monmouth at last, in a low voice, as though uttering his thoughts aloud. " Over yonder at the right I see Dumbarton's foot. I know these men well. They will fight. Had we them with us all would be well."

" Nay, your Majesty," Lord Grey answered with spirit, " you do your brave followers an injustice. They too will fight to the last drop of their blood in your quarrel."

" Look down at them ! " said Monmouth sadly, pointing at the swarming streets beneath us. " Braver hearts never beat in English breasts, yet do but mark how they brabble and clamour like clowns on a Saturday night. Compare them with the stern, orderly array of the trained battalions. Alas ! that I should have dragged these honest souls from their little homes to fight so hopeless a battle !"

" Hark at that ! " cried Wade. " They do not think it hopeless, nor do we." As he spoke a wild shout rose from the dense crowd beneath, who were listening to a preacher who was holding forth from a window.

" It is worthy Doctor Ferguson," said Sir Stephen Timewell, who had just come up. " He is as one inspired,

powerfully borne onwards in his discourse. Verily he is even as one of the prophets of old. He has chosen for his text, ' The Lord God of gods he knoweth and Israel he shall know. If it be in rebellion or if in transgression against the Lord, save us not this day.' "

" Amen, amen ! " cried several of the Puritan soldiers devoutly, while another hoarse burst of shouting from below, with the clashing of scythe-blades and the clatter of arms, showed how deeply the people were moved by the burning words of the fanatic.

" They do indeed seem to be hot for battle," said Monmouth, with a more sprightly look. " It may be that one who has commanded regular troops, as I have done, is prone to lay too much weight upon the difference which discipline and training make. These brave lads seem high of heart. What think you of the enemy's dispositions, Colonel Saxon ? "

" By my faith, I think very little of them, your Majesty," Saxon answered bluntly. " I have seen armies drawn up in array in many different parts of the world and under many commanders. I have likewise read the section which treats of the matter in the ' De re militari ' of Petrinus Bellus, and in the works of a Fleming of repute, yet I have neither seen nor heard anything which can commend the arrangements which we see before us."

" How call you the hamlet on the left—that with the square ivy-clad church tower ? " asked Monmouth, turning to the Mayor of Bridgewater, a small, anxious-faced man, who was evidently far from easy at the prominence which his office had brought upon him.

" Westonzoyland, your Honour—that is, your Grace— I mean, your Majesty," he stammered. " The other, two miles farther off, is Middlezoy, and away to the left, just on the far side of the rhine, is Chedzoy."

" The rhine, sir ! What do you mean ? " asked the King, starting violently, and turning so fiercely upon the timid burgher, that he lost the little balance of wits which was left to him.

" Why, the rhine, your Grace, your Majesty," he quavered. " The rhine, which, as your Majesty's Grace cannot but perceive, is what the country folk call the rhine."

" It is a name, your Majesty, for the deep and broad ditches which drain off the water from the great morass of Sedgemoor," said Sir Stephen Timewell.

Monmouth turned white to his very lips, and several of the council exchanged significant glances, recalling the strange prophetic jingle which I had been the means of bringing to the camp. The silence was broken, however, by an old Cromwellian Major named Hollis, who had been drawing upon paper the position of the villages in which the enemy was quartered.

" If it please your Majesty, there is something in their order which recalls to my mind that of the army of the Scots upon the occasion of the battle of Dunbar. Cromwell lay in Dunbar even as we lie in Bridgewater. The ground around, which was boggy and treacherous, was held by the enemy. There was not a man in the army who would not own that, had old Leslie held his position, we should, as far as human wisdom could see, have had to betake us to our ships, leave our stores and ordnance, and so make the best of our way to Newcastle. He moved, however, through the blessing of Providence, in such a manner that a quagmire intervened between his right wing and the rest of his army, on which Cromwell fell upon that wing in the early dawn, and dashed it to pieces, with such effect that the whole army fled, and we had the execution of them to the very gates of Leith. Seven thousand Scots lost their lives, but not more than a hundred or so of the honest folk. Now, your Majesty will see through your glass that a mile of bogland intervenes between these villages, and that the nearest one, Chedzoy, as I think they call it, might be approached without ourselves entering the morass. Very sure I am that were the Lord-General with us now he would counsel us to venture some such attack."

" It is a bold thing with raw peasants to attack old

soldiers," quoth Sir Stephen Timewell. "Yet if it is to be done, I know well that there is not a man born within sound of the bells of St. Mary Magdalene who will flinch from it."

"You say well, Sir Stephen," said Monmouth. "At Dunbar Cromwell had veterans at his back, and was opposed to troops who had small experience of war."

"Yet there is much good sense in what Major Hollis has said," remarked Lord Grey. "We must either fall on, or be gradually girt round and starved out. That being so, why not take advantage at once of the chance which Feversham's ignorance or carelessness hath given us? To-morrow, if Churchill can prevail over his chief, I have little doubt that we shall find their camp rearranged, and so have cause to regret our lost opportunity."

"Their horse lie at Westonzoyland," said Wade. "The sun is so fierce now that we can scarce see for its glare and the haze which rises up from the marshes. Yet a little while ago I could make out through my glasses the long lines of horses picketed on the moor beyond the village. Behind, in Middlezoy, are two thousand militia, while in Chedzoy, where our attack would fall, there are five regiments of regular foot."

"If we could break those all would be well," cried Monmouth. "What is your advice, Colonel Buyse?"

"My advice is ever the same," the German answered. "We are here to fight, and the sooner we get to work at it the better."

"And yours, Colonel Saxon? Do you agree with the opinion of your friend?"

"I think with Major Hollis, your Majesty, that Feversham by his dispositions hath laid himself open to attack, and that we should take advantage of it forthwith. Yet, considering that trained men and a numerous horse have great advantage by daylight, I should be in favour of a camisado or night onfall."

"The same thought was in my mind," said Grey. "Our friends here know every inch of the ground, and

could guide us to Chedzoy as surely in the darkness as in the day."

" I have heard," said Saxon, " that much beer and cider, with wine and strong waters, have found their way into their camp. If this be so we may give them a rouse while their heads are still buzzing with the liquor, when they shall scarce know whether it is ourselves or the blue devils which have come upon them."

A general chorus of approval from the whole council showed that the prospect of at last coming to an engagement was welcome, after the weary marchings and delays of the last few weeks.

" Has any cavalier anything to say against this plan ? " asked the King.

We all looked from one to the other, but though many faces were doubtful or desponding, none had a word to say against the night attack, for it was clear that our action in any case must be hazardous, and this had at least the merit of promising a better chance of success than any other. Yet, my dears, I dare say the boldest of us felt a sinking at the heart as we looked at our downcast, sad-faced leader, and asked ourselves whether this was a likely man to bring so desperate an enterprise to a success.

" If all are agreed," said he, " let our word be ' Soho,' and let us come upon them as soon after midnight as may be. What remains to be settled as to the order of battle may be left for the meantime. You will now, gentlemen, return to your regiments, and you will remember that be the upshot of this what it may, whether Monmouth be the crowned King of England or a hunted fugitive, his heart, while it can still beat, will ever bear in memory the brave friends who stood at his side in the hour of his trouble."

At this simple and kindly speech a flush of devotion, mingled in my own case at least with a heart-whole pity for the poor, weak gentleman, swept over us. We pressed round him with our hands upon the hilts of our swords, swearing that we would stand by him, though all the world stood between him and his rights. Even the rigid

and impassive Puritans were moved to a show of loyalty ; while the courtiers, carried away by zeal, drew their rapiers and shouted until the crowd beneath caught the enthusiasm, and the air was full of the cheering. The light returned to Monmouth's eye and the colour to his cheek as he listened to the clamour. For a moment at least he looked like the King which he aspired to be.

" My thanks to ye, dear friends and subjects," he cried. " The issue rests with the Almighty, but what men can do will, I know well, be done by you this night. If Monmouth cannot have all England, six feet of her shall at least be his. Meanwhile, to your regiments, and may God defend the right ! "

" May God defend the right ! " cried the council solemnly, and separated, leaving the King with Grey to make the final dispositions for the attack.

" These popinjays of the Court are ready enough to wave their rapiers and shout when there are four good miles between them and the foe," said Saxon, as we made our way through the crowd. " I fear that they will scarce be as forward when there is a line of musqueteers to be faced, and a brigade of horse perhaps charging down upon their flank. But here comes friend Lockarby, with news written upon his face."

" I have a report to make, Colonel," said Reuben, hurrying breathlessly up to us. " You may remember that I and my company were placed on guard this day at the eastern gates ? "

Saxon nodded.

" Being desirous of seeing all that I could of the enemy, I clambered up a lofty tree which stands just without the town. From this post, by the aid of a glass, I was able to make out their lines and camp. Whilst I was gazing I chanced to observe a man slinking along under cover of the birch-trees half-way between their lines and the town. Watching him, I found that he was indeed moving in our direction. Presently he came so near that I was able to distinguish who it was—for it was one whom I know—

but instead of entering the town by my gate he walked round under cover of the peat cuttings, and so made his way doubtless to some other entrance. He is a man, however, who I have reason to believe has no true love for the cause, and it is my belief that he hath been to the Royal camp with news of our doings, and hath now come back for further information."

"Aye!" said Saxon, raising his eyebrows. "And what is the man's name?"

"His name is Derrick, one time chief apprentice to Master Timewell at Taunton, and now an officer in the Taunton Foot."

"What, the young springald who had his eye upon pretty Mistress Ruth! Now, out on love, if it is to turn a true man into a traitor! But methought he was one of the elect? I have heard him hold forth to the pikemen. How comes it that one of his kidney should lend help to the Prelatist cause?"

"Love again," quoth I. "This same love is a pretty flower when it grows unchecked, but a sorry weed if thwarted."

"He hath an ill-feeling towards many in the camp," said Reuben, "and he would ruin the army to avenge himself on them, as a rogue might sink a ship in the hope of drowning one enemy. Sir Stephen himself hath incurred his hatred for refusing to force his daughter into accepting his suit. He has now returned into the camp, and I have reported the matter to you, that you may judge whether it would not be well to send a file of pikemen and lay him by the heels lest he play the spy once more."

"Perhaps it would be best so," Saxon answered, full of thought, "and yet no doubt the fellow would have some tale prepared which would outweigh our mere suspicions. Could we not take him in the very act?"

A thought slipped into my head. I had observed from the tower that there was a single lonely cottage about a third of the way to the enemy's camp, standing by the road at a place where there were marshes on either side.

Anyone journeying that way must pass it. If Derrick tried to carry our plans to Feversham he might be cut off at this point by a party placed to lie in wait for him.

" Most excellent ! " Saxon exclaimed, when I had explained the project. " My learned Fleming himself could not have devised a better rusus belli. Do ye convey as many files as ye may think fit to this point, and I shall see that Master Derrick is primed up with some fresh news for my Lord Feversham."

" Nay, a body of troops marching out would set tongues wagging," said Reuben. " Why should not Micah and I go ourselves ? "

" That would indeed be better," Saxon answered. " But ye must pledge your words, come what may, to be back at sundown, for your companies must stand to arms an hour before the advance."

We both gladly gave the desired promise ; and having learned for certain that Derrick had indeed returned to the camp, Saxon undertook to let drop in his presence some words as to the plans for the night, while we set off at once for our post. Our horses we left behind, and slipping out through the eastern gate we made our way over bog and moor, concealing ourselves as best we could, until we came out upon the lonely roadway, and found ourselves in front of the house.

It was a plain, whitewashed, thatch-roofed cottage, with a small board above the door, whereon was written a notice that the occupier sold milk and butter. No smoke reeked up from the chimney, and the shutters of the window were closed, from which we gathered that the folk who owned it had fled away from their perilous position. On either side the marsh extended, reedy and shallow at the edge, but deeper at a distance, with a bright green scum which covered its treacherous surface. We knocked at the weather-blotched door, but receiving, as we expected, no reply, I presently put my shoulder against it and forced the staple from its fastenings.

There was but a single chamber within, with a straight

ladder in the corner, leading through a square hole in the ceiling to the sleeping chamber under the roof. Three or four chairs and stools were scattered over the earthen floor, and at the side a deal table with the broad brown milk basins upon it. Green blotches upon the wall and a sinking in of one side of the cottage showed the effect of its damp, marsh-girt position.

To our surprise it had still one inmate within its walls. In the centre of the room, facing the door as we entered, stood a little bright, golden-haired maid, five or six years of age. She was clad in a clean white smock, with trim leather belt and shining buckle about her waist. Two plump little legs with socks and leathern boots peeped out from under the dress, stoutly planted with right foot in advance as one who was bent upon holding her ground. Her tiny head was thrown back, and her large blue eyes were full of mingled wonder and defiance. As we entered the little witch flapped her kerchief at us, and shooed as though we were two of the intrusive fowl whom she was wont to chevy out of the house. Reuben and I stood on the threshold, uncertain and awkward, like a pair of overgrown school lads, looking down at this fairy queen whose realms we had invaded, in two minds whether to beat a retreat or to appease her wrath by soft and coaxing words.

" Go 'way ! " she cried, still waving her hands and shaking her kerchief. " Go 'way ! Granny told me to tell anyone that came to go 'way ! "

" But if they would not go away, little mistress," asked Reuben, " what were you to do then ? "

" I was to drive them 'way," she answered, advancing boldly against us with many flaps. " You bad man ! " she continued, flashing out at me, " you have broken granny's bolt."

" Nay, I'll mend it again," I answered penitently, and catching up a stone I soon fastened the injured staple. " There, mistress, your grandam will never tell the difference."

386

" Ye must go 'way all the same," she persisted ; " this is granny's house, not yours."

What were we to do with this resolute little dame of the marshes ?   That we should stay in the house was a crying need, for there was no other cover or shelter among the dreary bogs where we could hide ourselves.   Yet she was bent upon driving us out with a decision and fearlessness which might have put Monmouth to shame.

" You sell milk," said Reuben.   " We are tired and thirsty, so we have come to have a horn of it."

" Nay," she cried, breaking into smiles, " will ye pay me just as the folk pay granny ?   Oh, heart alive ! but that will be fine ! "   She skipped up on to a stool and filled a pair of deep mugs from the basins upon the table. " A penny, please ! " said she.

It was strange to see the little wife hide the coin away in her smock, with pride and joy in her innocent face at this rare stroke of business which she had done for her absent granny.   We bore our milk away to the window, and having loosed the shutters we seated ourselves so as to have an outlook down the road.

" For the Lord's sake, drink slow ! " whispered Reuben, under his breath.   " We must keep on swilling milk or she will want to turn us out."

" We have paid toll now," I answered ; " surely she will let us bide."

" If you have done you must go 'way," said she firmly.

" Were ever two men-at-arms so tyrannised over by a little dolly like this ! " said I, laughing.   " Nay, little one, we shall compound with you by paying you this shilling, which will buy all your milk.   We can stay here and drink it at our ease."

" Jinny, the cow, is just across the marsh," quoth she. " It is nigh milking time, and I shall fetch her round if ye wish more."

" Now, God forbid ! " cried Reuben.   " It will end in our having to buy the cow.   Where is your granny, little maid ? "

" She hath gone into the town," the child answered. " There are bad men with red coats and guns coming to steal and to fight, but granny will soon make them go 'way. Granny has gone to set it all right."

" We are fighting against the men with the red coats, my chuck," said I ; " we shall take care of your house with you, and let no one steal anything."

" Nay, then ye may stay," quoth she, climbing up upon my knee as grave as a sparrow upon a bough. " What a great boy you are ! "

" And why not a man ? " I asked.

" Because you have no beard upon your face. Why, granny hath more hair upon her chin than you. Besides, only boys drink milk. Men drink cider."

" Then if I am a boy I shall be your sweetheart," said I.

" Nay, indeed ! " she cried, with a toss of her golden locks. " I have no mind to wed for a while, but Giles Martin of Gommatch is my sweetheart. What a pretty shining tin smock you have, and what a great sword ! Why should people have these things to harm each other with when they are in truth all brothers ? "

" Why are they all brothers, little mistress ? " asked Reuben.

" Because granny says that they are all the children of the great Father," she answered. " If they have all one father they must be brothers, mustn't they ? "

" Out of the mouths of babes and sucklings, Micah," quoth Reuben, staring out of the window.

" You are a rare little marsh flower," I said, as she clambered up to grasp at my steel cap. " Is it not strange to think, Reuben, that there should be thousands of Christian men upon either side of us, athirst for each other's lives, and here between them is a blue-eyed cherub who lisps out the blessed philosophy which would send us all to our homes with softened hearts and hale bodies ? "

" A day of this child would sicken me for ever of soldiering," Reuben answered. " The cavalier and the butcher become too near of kin, as I listen to her."

" Perhaps both are equally needful," said I, shrugging my shoulders. " We have put our hands to the plough. But methinks I see the man for whom we wait coming down under the shadow of yonder line of pollard willows."

" It is he, sure enough," cried Reuben, peeping through the diamond-paned window.

" Then, little one, you must sit here," said I, raising her up from my knee and placing her on a chair in a corner. " You must be a brave lass and sit still, whatever may chance. Will you do so ? "

She pursed up her rosy lips and nodded her head.

" He comes on apace, Micah," quoth my comrade, who was still standing by the casement. " Is he not like some treacherous fox or other beast of prey ? "

There was indeed something in his lean, black-clothed figure and swift furtive movements which was like some cruel and cunning animal. He stole along under shadow of the stunted trees and withies, with bent body and gliding gait, so that from Bridgewater it would be no easy matter for the most keen-sighted to see him. Indeed, he was so far from the town that he might safely have come out from his concealment and struck across the moor, but the deep morass on either side prevented him from leaving the road until he had passed the cottage.

As he came abreast of our ambush we both sprang out from the open door and barred his way. I have heard the Independent minister at Emsworth give an account of Satan's appearance, but if the worthy man had been with us that day, he need not have drawn upon his fancy. The man's dark face whitened into a sickly and mottled pallor, while he drew back with a long sharp intaking of the breath and a venomous flash from his black eyes, glancing swiftly from right to left for some means of escape. For an instant his hand shot towards his sword-hilt, but his reason told him that he could scarce expect to fight his way past us. Then he glanced round, but any retreat would lead him back to the men whom he had betrayed. So he stood sullen and stolid, with heavy, downcast face and

shifting, restless eye, the very type and symbol of treachery.

" We have waited some time for you, Master John Derrick," said I. " You must now return with us to the town."

" On what grounds do you arrest me ? " he asked, in hoarse, broken tones. " Where is your warranty ? Who hath given you a commission to molest travellers upon the King's highway ? "

" I have my Colonel's commission," I answered shortly. " You have been once already to Feversham's camp this morning."

" It is a lie," he snarled fiercely. " I do but take a stroll to enjoy the air."

" It is the truth," said Reuben. " I saw you myself on your return. Let us see that paper which peeps from your doublet."

" We all know why you should set this trap for me," Derrick cried bitterly. " You have set evil reports afloat against me, lest I stand in your light with the Mayor's daughter. What are you that you should dare to raise your eyes to her ? A mere vagrant and masterless man, coming none know whence. Why should you aspire to pluck the flower which has grown up amongst us ? What had you to do with her or with us ? Answer me ! "

" It is not a matter which I shall discuss, save at a more fitting time and place," Reuben answered quietly. " Do you give over your sword and come back with us. For my part, I promise to do what I can to save your life. Should we win this night, your poor efforts can do little to harm us. Should we lose, there may be few of us left to harm."

" I thank you for your kindly protection," he replied, in the same white, cold, bitter manner, unbuckling his sword as he spoke, and walking slowly up to my companion. " You can take this as a gift to Mistress Ruth," he said, presenting the weapon in his left hand, " and this ! " he added, plucking a knife from his belt and burying it in my poor friend's side.

It was done in an instant—so suddenly that I had neither time to spring between, nor to grasp his intention before the wounded man sank gasping on the ground, and the knife tinkled upon the pathway at my feet. The villain set up a shrill cry of triumph, and bounding back in time to avoid the savage sword thrust which I made at him, he turned and fled down the road at the top of his speed. He was a far lighter man than I, and more scantily clad, yet I had, from my long wind and length of limb, been the best runner of my district, and he soon learned by the sound of my feet that he had no chance of shaking me off. Twice he doubled as a hare does when the hound is upon him, and twice my sword passed within a foot of him, for in very truth I had no more thought of mercy than if he had been a poisonous snake who had fastened his fangs into my friend before my eyes. I never dreamed of giving nor did he of claiming it. At last, hearing my steps close upon him and my breathing at his very shoulder, he sprang wildly through the reeds and dashed into the treacherous morass. Ankle-deep, knee-deep, thigh-deep, waist-deep, we struggled and staggered, I still gaining upon him, until I was within arm's reach of him, and had whirled up my sword to strike. It had been ordained, however, my dear children, that he should die not the death of a man, but that of the reptile which he was, for even as I closed upon him he sank of a sudden with a gurgling sound, and the green marsh scum met above his head. No ripple was there and no splash to mark the spot. It was sudden and silent, as though some strange monster of the marshes had seized him and dragged him down into the depths. As I stood with upraised sword still gazing upon the spot, one single great bubble rose and burst upon the surface, and then all was still once more, and the dreary fens lay stretched before me, the very home of death and of desolation. I know not whether he had indeed come upon some sudden pit which had engulfed him, or whether in his despair he had cast himself down of set purpose. I do but know that there

in the great Sedgemoor morass are buried the bones of the traitor and the spy.

I made my way as best I could through the oozy clinging mud to the margin, and hastened back to where Reuben was lying. Bending over him I found that the knife had pierced through the side leather which connected his back and front plates, and that the blood was not only pouring out of the wound, but was trickling from the corner of his mouth. With trembling fingers I undid the straps and buckles, loosened the armour, and pressed my kerchief to his side to staunch the flow.

" I trust that you have not slain him, Micah," he said of a sudden, opening his eyes.

" A higher power than ours has judged him, Reuben," I answered.

" Poor devil ! He has had much to embitter him," he murmured, and straightway fainted again. As I knelt over him, marking the lad's white face and laboured breathing, and bethought me of his simple, kindly nature and of the affection which I had done so little to deserve, I am not ashamed to say, my dears, albeit I am a man somewhat backward in my emotions, that my tears were mingled with his blood.

As it chanced, Decimus Saxon had found time to ascend the church tower for the purpose of watching us through his glass and seeing how we fared. Noting that there was something amiss, he had hurried down for a skilled chirurgeon, whom he brought out to us under an escort of scythesmen. I was still kneeling by my senseless friend, doing what an ignorant man might to assist him, when the party arrived and helped me to bear him into the cottage, out of the glare of the sun. The minutes were as hours while the man of physic with a grave face examined and probed the wound.

" It will scarce prove fatal," he said at last, and I could have embraced him for the words. " The blade has glanced on a rib though the lung is slightly torn. We shall bear him back with us to the town."

" You hear what he says," said Saxon kindly. " He is a man whose opinion is of weight—

> ' A skilful leech is better far,
> Than half a hundred men of war.'

Cheer up, man ! You are as white as though it were your blood and not his which was drained away. Where is Derrick ? "

" Drowned in the marshes," I answered.

" 'Tis well ! It will save us six feet of good hemp. But our position here is somewhat exposed, since the Royal Horse might make a dash at us. Who is this little maid who sits so white and still in the corner ? "

" 'Tis the guardian of the house. Her granny has left her here."

" You had better come with us. There may be rough work here ere all is over."

" Nay, I must wait for granny," she answered, with the tears running down her cheeks.

" But how if I take you to granny, little one," said I. " We cannot leave you here." I held out my arms, and the child sprang into them and nestled up against my bosom, sobbing as though her heart would break. " Take me away," she cried ; " I'se frightened."

I soothed the little trembling thing as best I might, and bore her off with me upon my shoulder. The scythes- men had passed the handles of their long weapons through the sleeves of their jerkins in such a way as to form a couch or litter, upon which poor Reuben was laid. A slight dash of colour had come back to his cheeks in answer to some cordial given him by the chirurgeon, and he nodded and smiled at Saxon. Thus, pacing slowly, we returned to Bridgewater, where Reuben was carried to our quarters, and I bore the little maid of the marshes to kind townsfolk, who promised to restore her to her home when the troubles were over.

32. *Of the Onfall at Sedgemoor*

HOWEVER pressing our own private griefs and needs, we had little time now to dwell upon them, for the moment was at hand which was to decide for the time not only our own fates, but that of the Protestant cause in England. None of us made light of the danger. Nothing less than a miracle could preserve us from defeat, and most of us were of opinion that the days of the miracles were past. Others, however, thought otherwise. I believe that many of our Puritans, had they seen the heavens open that night, and the armies of the Seraphim and the Cherubim descending to our aid, would have looked upon it as by no means a wonderful or unexpected occurrence.

The whole town was loud with the preaching. Every troop or company had its own chosen orator, and sometimes more than one, who held forth and expounded. From barrels, from waggons, from windows, and even from housetops, they addressed the crowds beneath ; nor was their eloquence in vain. Hoarse, fierce shouts rose up from the streets, with broken prayers and ejaculations. Men were drunk with religion as with wine. Their faces were flushed, their speech thick, their gestures wild. Sir Stephen and Saxon smiled at each other as they watched them, for they knew, as old soldiers, that of all causes which make a man valiant in deed and careless of life, this religious fit is the strongest and the most enduring.

In the evening I found time to look in upon my wounded friend, and found him propped up with cushions upon his couch, breathing with some pain, but as bright and merry as ever. Our prisoner, Major Ogilvy, who had conceived a warm affection for us, sat by his side and read aloud to him out of an old book of plays.

" This wound hath come at an evil moment," said Reuben impatiently. " Is it not too much that a little prick like this should send my men captainless into battle,

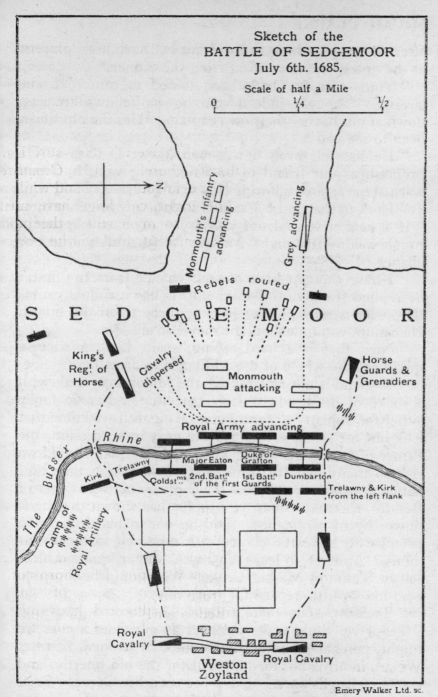

Sketch of the
BATTLE OF SEDGEMOOR
July 6th. 1685.

Scale of half a Mile

0   ¼   ½

Monmouth's Infantry advancing

Grey advancing

Rebels routed

S E D G E M O O R

King's Reg! of Horse

Cavalry dispersed

Monmouth attacking

Horse Guards & Grenadiers

Royal Army advancing

Rhine

The Bussex

Kirk   Trelawny   Coldstᵐˢ   Major Eaton   Duke of Grafton   Dumbarton

2nd. Battⁿ of the first Guards   1st. Battⁿ   Trelawny & Kirk from the left flank

Camp of Royal Artillery

Royal Cavalry

Weston Zoyland

Royal Cavalry

Emery Walker Ltd. sc.

(From Hale's *Fall of Stuarts*.)

395

after all our marching and drilling ? I have been present at the grace, and am cut off from the dinner."

" Your company hath been joined to mine," I answered, " though, indeed, the honest fellows are cast down at not having their own captain. Has the physician been to see you ? "

" He has left even now," said Major Ogilvy. " He pronounces our friend to be doing right well, but hath warned me against allowing him to talk."

" Hark to that, lad ! " said I, shaking my finger at him. " If I hear a word from you I go. You will escape a rough waking this night, Major. What think you of our chance ? "

" I have thought little of your chance from the first," he replied frankly. " Monmouth is like a ruined gamester, who is now putting his last piece upon the board. He cannot win much, and he may lose all."

" Nay, that is a hard saying," said I. " A success might set the whole of the Midlands in arms."

" England is not ripe for it," the Major answered, with a shake of his head. " It is true that it has no fancy either for Papistry or for a Papist King, but we know that it is but a passing evil, since the next in succession, the Prince of Orange, is a Protestant. Why, then, should we risk so many evils to bring that about which time and patience must, perforce, accomplish between them ? Besides, the man whom ye support has shown that he is unworthy of confidence. Did he not in his declaration promise to leave the choice of a monarch to the Commons ? And yet, in less than a week, he proclaimed himself at Taunton Market Cross ! Who could believe one who has so little regard for truth ? "

" Treason, Major, rank treason," I answered, laughing. " Yet if we could order a leader as one does a coat we might, perchance, have chosen one of a stronger texture. We are in arms not for him, but for the old liberties and rights of Englishmen. Have you seen Sir Gervas ? "

Major Ogilvy, and even Reuben, burst out laughing.

" You will find him in the room above," said our prisoner.
" Never did a famous toast prepare herself for a court ball
as he is preparing for his battle. If the King's troops
take him they will assuredly think that they have the
Duke. He hath been in here to consult us as to his patches,
hosen and I know not what beside. You had best go
up to him."

" Adieu, then, Reuben ! " I said, grasping his hand in
mine.

" Adieu, Micah ! God shield you from harm," said he.

" Can I speak to you aside, Major ? " I whispered. " I
think," I went on, as he followed me into the passage,
" that you will not say that your captivity hath been made
very harsh for you. May I ask, therefore, that you will
keep an eye upon my friend should we be indeed defeated
this night ? No doubt if Feversham gains the upper
hand there will be bloody work. The hale can look after
themselves, but he is helpless, and will need a friend."

The Major pressed my hand. " I swear to God," he
said, " that no harm shall befall him."

" You have taken a load from my heart," I answered ;
" I know that I leave him in safety. I can now ride to
battle with an easy mind." With a friendly smile the
soldier returned to the sick-room, whilst I ascended the
stair and entered the quarters of Sir Gervas Jerome.

He was standing before a table which was littered all
over with pots, brushes, boxes and a score of the like
trifles, which he had either bought or borrowed for the
occasion. A large hand-mirror was balanced against the
wall, with rushlights on either side of it. In front of this,
with a most solemn and serious expression upon his pale,
handsome face, the Baronet was arranging and rearranging a white berdash cravat. His riding-boots were
brightly polished, and the broken seam repaired. His
sword-sheath, breastplate and trappings were clear and
bright. He wore his gayest and newest suit, and above
all he had donned a most noble and impressive full-
bottomed periwig, which drooped down to his shoulders,

as white as powder could make it. From his dainty riding-hat to his shining spur there was no speck or stain upon him—a sad set-off to my own state, plastered as I was with a thick crust of the Sedgemoor mud, and disordered from having ridden and worked for two days without rest or repose.

" Split me, but you have come in good time ! " he exclaimed, as I entered. " I have even now sent down for a flask of canary. Ah, and here it comes ! " as a maid from the inn tripped upstairs with the bottle and glasses. " Here is a gold piece, my pretty dear, the very last that I have in the whole world. It is the only survivor of a goodly family. Pay mine host for the wine, little one, and keep the change for thyself, to buy ribbons for the next holiday. Now, curse me if I can get this cravat to fit unwrinkled ! "

" There is nought amiss with it," I answered. " How can such trifles occupy you at such a time ? "

" Trifles ! " he cried angrily. " Trifles ! Well, there, it boots not to argue with you. Your bucolic mind would never rise to the subtle import which may lie in such matters—the rest of mind which it is to have them right, and the plaguy uneasiness when aught is wrong. It comes, doubtless, from training, and it may be that I have it more than others of my class. I feel as a cat who would lick all day to take the least speck from her fur. Is not the patch over the eyebrow happily chosen ? Nay, you cannot even offer an opinion ; I would as soon ask friend Marot, the knight of the pistol. Fill up your glass ! "

" Your company awaits you by the church," I remarked ; " I saw them as I passed."

" How looked they ? " he asked. " Were they powdered and clean ? "

" Nay, I had little leisure to observe. I saw that they were cutting their matches and arranging their priming."

" I would that they had all snaphances," he answered, sprinkling himself with scented water ; " the matchlocks are slow and cumbersome. Have you had wine enough ? "

" I will take no more," I answered.

" Then mayhap the Major may care to finish it. It is not often I ask help with a bottle, but I would keep my head cool this night. Let us go down and see to our men."

It was ten o'clock when we descended into the street. The hubbub of the preachers and the shouting of the people had died away, for the regiments had fallen into their places, and stood silent and stern, with the faint light from the lamps and windows playing over their dark serried ranks. A cool, clear moon shone down upon us from amidst fleecy clouds, which drifted ever and anon across her face. Away in the north tremulous rays of light flickered up into the heavens, coming and going like long, quivering fingers. They were the northern lights, a sight rarely seen in the southland counties. It is little wonder that, coming at such a time, the fanatics should have pointed to them as signals from another world, and should have compared them to that pillar of fire which guided Israel through the dangers of the desert. The footpaths and the windows were crowded with women and children, who broke into shrill cries of fear or of wonder as the strange light waxed and waned.

" It is half after ten by St. Mary's clock," said Saxon, as we rode up to the regiment. " Have we nothing to give the men ? "

" There is a hogshead of Zoyland cider in the yard of yonder inn," said Sir Gervas. " Here, Dawson, do you take these gold sleeve links and give them to mine host in exchange. Broach the barrel, and let each man have his horn full. Sink me, if they shall fight with nought but cold water in them."

" They will feel the need of it ere morning," said Saxon, as a score of pikemen hastened off to the inn. " The marsh air is chilling to the blood."

" I feel cold already, and Covenant is stamping with it," said I. " Might we not, if we have time upon our hands, canter our horses down the line ? "

" Of a surety," Saxon answered gladly, " we could not do better " ; so shaking our bridles we rode off, our horses' hoofs striking fire from the flint-paved streets as we passed.

Behind the horse, in a long line which stretched from the Eastover gate, across the bridge, along the High Street, up the Cornhill, and so past the church to the Pig Cross, stood our foot, silent and grim, save when some woman's voice from the windows called forth a deep, short answer from the ranks. The fitful light gleamed on scythes-blade or gun-barrel, and showed up the lines of rugged, hard set faces, some of mere children with never a hair upon their cheeks, others of old men whose grey beards swept down to their cross-belts, but all bearing the same stamp of a dogged courage and a fierce self-contained resolution. Here were still the fisher folk of the south. Here, too, were the fierce men from the Mendips, the wild hunters from Porlock Quay and Minehead, the poachers of Exmoor, the shaggy marsh-men of Axbridge, the mountain men from the Quantocks, the serge- and wool-workers of Devonshire, the graziers of Bampton, the red-coats from the Militia, the stout burghers of Taunton, and then, as the very bone and sinew of all, the brave smock-frocked peasants of the plains, who had turned up their jackets to the elbow, and exposed their brown and corded arms, as was their wont when good work had to be done. As I speak to you, dear children, fifty years rolls by like a mist in the morning and I am riding once more down the winding street, and see again the serried ranks of my gallant companions. Brave hearts ! They showed to all time how little training it takes to turn an Englishman into a soldier, and what manner of men are bred in those quiet, peaceful hamlets which dot the sunny slopes of the Somerset and Devon downs. If ever it should be that England should be struck upon her knees, if those who fight her battles should have deserted her, and she should find herself unarmed in the presence of her enemy, let her take heart and re-member that every village in the realm is a barrack, and

that her real standing army is the hardy courage and simple virtue which stand ever in the breast of the humblest of her peasants.

As we rode down the long line a buzz of greeting and welcome rose now and again from the ranks as they recognised through the gloom Saxon's tall, gaunt figure. The clock was on the stroke of eleven as we returned to our own men, and at that very moment King Monmouth rode out from the inn where he was quartered, and trotted with his staff down the High Street. All cheering had been forbidden, but waving caps and brandished arms spoke the ardour of his devoted followers. No bugle was to sound the march, but as each received the word the one in its rear followed its movements. The clatter and shuffle of hundreds of moving feet came nearer and nearer, until the Frome men in front of us began to march, and we found ourselves fairly started upon the last journey which many of us were ever to take in this world.

Our road lay across the Parret, through Eastover, and so along the winding track past the spot where Derrick met his fate, and the lonely cottage of the little maid. At the other side of this the road becomes a mere pathway over the plain. A dense haze lay over the moor, gathering thickly in the hollows, and veiling both the town which we had left and the villages which we were approaching. Now and again it would lift for a few moments, and then I could see in the moonlight the long black writhing line of the army, with the shimmer of steel playing over it, and the rude white standards flapping in the night breeze. Far on the right a great fire was blazing—some farmhouse, doubtless, which the Tangiers devils had made spoil of. Very slow our march was, and very careful, for the plain was, as Sir Stephen Timewell had told us, cut across by great ditches or rhines, which could not be passed save at some few places. These ditches were cut for the purpose of draining the marshes, and were many feet deep of water and of mud, so that even the horse could not cross them. The bridges were

narrow, and some time passed before the army could get over. At last, however, the two main ones, the Black Ditch and the Langmoor Rhine, were safely traversed, and a halt was called while the foot was formed in line, for we had reason to believe that no other force lay between the Royal camp and ourselves. So far our enterprise had succeeded admirably. We were within half a mile of the camp without mistake or accident, and none of the enemy's scouts had shown sign of their presence. Clearly they held us in such contempt that it had never occurred to them that we might open the attack. If ever a general deserved a beating it was Feversham that night. As we drew up upon the moor the clock of Chedzoy struck one.

" Is it not glorious ! " whispered Sir Gervas, as we reined up upon the further side of the Langmoor Rhine. " What is there on earth to compare with the excitement of this ? "

" You speak as though it were a cocking-match or a bull-baiting," I answered, with some little coldness. " It is a solemn and a sad occasion. Win who will, English blood must soak the soil of England this night."

" The more room for those who are left," said he lightly. " Mark over yonder the glow of their camp-fires amidst the fog. What was it that your seaman friend did recommend ? Get the weather-gauge of them and board— eh ? Have you told that to the Colonel ? "

" Nay, this is no time for quips and cranks," I answered gravely ; " the chances are that few of us will ever see to-morrow's sun rise."

" I have no great curiosity to see it," he remarked, with a laugh. " It will be much as yesterday's. Zounds ! though I have never risen to see one in my life, I have looked on many a hundred ere I went to bed."

" I have told friend Reuben such few things as I should desire to be done in case I should fall," said I. " It has eased my mind much to know that I leave behind some word of farewell, and little remembrance to all whom I

have known. Is there no service of the sort which I can do for you ? "

" Hum ! " said he, musing. " If I go under, you can tell Araminta—nay, let the poor wench alone ! Why should I send her messages which may plague her ! Should you be in town, little Tommy Chichester would be glad to hear of the fun which we have had in Somerset. You will find him at the Coca Tree every day of the week between two and four of the clock. There is Mother Butterworth, too, whom I might commend to your notice. She was the queen of wet-nurses, but alas ! cruel time hath dried up her business, and she hath need of some little nursing herself."

" If I live and you should fall, I shall do what may be done for her," said I. " Have you aught else to say ? "

" Only that Hacker of Paul's Yard is the best for vests," he answered. " It is a small piece of knowledge, yet like most other knowledge it hath been bought and paid for. One other thing ! I have a trinket or two left which might serve as a gift for the pretty Puritan maid, should our friend lead her to the altar. Od's my life, but she will make him read some queer books ! How now, Colonel, why are we stuck out on the moor like a row of herons among the sedges ? "

" They are ordering the line for the attack," said Saxon, who had ridden up during our conversation. " Donnerblitz ! Who ever saw a camp so exposed to an onfall ? Oh for twelve hundred good horse—for an hour of Wessenburg's Pandours ! Would I not trample them down until their camp was like a field of young corn after a hail-storm ! "

" May not our horse advance ? " I asked.

The old soldier gave a deep snort of disdain. " If this fight is to be won it must be by our foot," said he ; " what can we hope for from such cavalry ? Keep your men well in hand, for we may have to bear the brunt of the King's dragoons. A flank attack would fall upon us, for we are in the post of honour."

" There are troops to the right of us," I answered, peering through the darkness.

" Aye ! the Taunton burghers and the Frome peasants. Our brigade covers the right flank. Next us are the Mendip miners, nor could I wish for better comrades, if their zeal do not outrun their discretion. They are on their knees in the mud at this moment."

" They will fight none the worse for that," I remarked ; " but surely the troops are advancing ! "

" Aye, aye ! " cried Saxon joyously, plucking out his sword, and tying his handkerchief round the handle to strengthen his grip. " The hour has come ! Forwards ! "

Very slowly and silently we crept on through the dense fog, our feet splashing and slipping in the sodden soil. With all the care which we could take, the advance of so great a number of men could not be conducted without a deep sonorous sound from the thousands of marching feet. Ahead of us were splotches of ruddy light twinkling through the fog which marked the Royal watch-fires. Immediately in front in a dense column our own horse moved forwards. Of a sudden out of the darkness there came a sharp challenge and a shout, with the discharge of a carbine and the sound of galloping hoofs. Away down the line we heard a ripple of shots. The first line of outposts had been reached. At the alarm our horse charged forward with a huzza, and we followed them as fast as our men could run. We had crossed two or three hundred yards of moor, and could hear the blowing of the Royal bugles quite close to us, when our horse came to a sudden halt, and our whole advance was at a standstill.

" Sancta Maria ! " cried Saxon, dashing forward with the rest of us to find out the cause of the delay. " We must on at any cost ! A halt now will ruin our camisado."

" Forwards, forwards ! " cried Sir Gervas and I, waving our swords.

" It is no use, gentlemen," cried a cornet of horse, wringing his hands ; " we are undone and betrayed.

There is a broad ditch without a ford in front of us, full twenty feet across ! "

" Give me room for my horse, and I shall show ye the way across ! " cried the Baronet, backing his steed. " Now, lads, who's for a jump ? "

" Nay, sir, for God's sake ! " said a trooper, laying his hand upon his bridle. " Sergeant Sexton hath sprung in even now, and horse and man have gone to the bottom ! "

" Let us see it, then ! " cried Saxon, pushing his way through the crowd of horsemen. We followed close at his heels, until we found ourselves on the borders of the vast trench which impeded our advance.

To this day I have never been able to make up my mind whether it was by chance or by treachery on the part of our guides that this fosse was overlooked until we stumbled upon it in the dark. There are some who say that the Bussex Rhine, as it is called, is not either deep or broad, and was, therefore, unmentioned by the moorsmen, but that the recent constant rains had swollen it to an extent never before known. Others say that the guides had been deceived by the fog, and taken a wrong course, whereas, had we followed another track, we might have been able to come upon the camp without crossing the ditch. However that may be, it is certain that we found it stretching in front of us, broad, black, and forbidding, full twenty feet from bank to bank, with the cap of the ill-fated sergeant just visible in the centre as a mute warning to all who might attempt to ford it.

" There must be a passage somewhere," cried Saxon furiously. " Every moment is worth a troop of horse to them. Where is my Lord Grey ? Hath the guide met with his deserts ? "

" Major Hollis hath hurled the guide into the ditch," the young cornet answered. " My Lord Grey hath ridden along the bank seeking for a ford."

I caught a pike out of a footman's hand, and probed into the black oozy mud, standing myself up to the waist in it, and holding Covenant's bridle in my left hand.

Nowhere could I touch bottom or find any hope of solid foothold.

" Here, fellow ! " cried Saxon, seizing a trooper by the arm. " Make for the rear ! Gallop as though the devil were behind you ! Bring up a pair of ammunition waggons, and we shall see whether we cannot bridge this infernal puddle."

" If a few of us could make a lodgment upon the other side we might make it good until help came," said Sir Gervas, as the horseman galloped off upon his mission.

All down the rebel line a fierce low roar of disappointment and rage showed that the whole army had met the same obstacle which hindered our attack. On the other side of the ditch the drums beat, the bugles screamed, and the shouts and oaths of the officers could be heard as they marshalled their men. Glancing lights in Chedzoy, Westonzoyland, and the other hamlets to left and right, showed how fast the alarm was extending. Decimus Saxon rode up and down the edge of the fosse, pattering forth foreign oaths, grinding his teeth in his fury, and rising now and again in his stirrups to shake his gauntleted hands at the enemy.

" For whom are ye ? " shouted a hoarse voice out of the haze.

" For the King ! " roared the peasants in answer.

" For which King ? " cried the voice.

" For King Monmouth ! "

" Let them have it, lads ! " and instantly a storm of musket bullets whistled and sung about our ears. As the sheet of flame sprang out of the darkness the maddened, half-broken horses dashed wildly away across the plain, resisting the efforts of the riders to pull them up. There are some, indeed, who say that those efforts were not very strong, and that our troopers, disheartened at the check at the ditch, were not sorry to show their heels to the enemy. As to my Lord Grey, I can say truly that I saw him in the dim light among the flying squadrons, doing all that a brave cavalier could do to bring them to a stand.

Away they went, however, thundering through the ranks of the foot and out over the moor, leaving their companions to bear the whole brunt of the battle.

" On to your faces, men ! " shouted Saxon, in a voice which rose high above the crash of the musketry and the cries of the wounded. The pikemen and scythesmen threw themselves down at his command, while the musqueteers knelt in front of them, loading and firing, with nothing to aim at save the turning matches of the enemy's pieces, which could be seen twinkling through the darkness. All along, both to the right and the left, a rolling fire had broken out, coming in short, quick volleys from the soldiers, and in a continuous confused rattle from the peasants. On the further wing our four guns had been brought into play, and we could hear their dull growling in the distance.

" Sing, brothers, sing ! " cried our stout-hearted chaplain, Master Joshua Pettigrue, bustling backwards and forwards among the prostrate ranks. " Let us call upon the Lord in our day of trial ! " The men raised a loud hymn of praise, which swelled into a great chorus as it was taken up by the Taunton burghers upon our right and the miners upon our left. At the sound the soldiers on the other side raised a fierce huzza, and the whole air was full of clamour.

Our musqueteers had been brought to the very edge of the Bussex Rhine, and the Royal troops had also advanced as far as they were able, so that there were not five pikes'-lengths between the lines. Yet that short distance was so impassable that, save for the more deadly fire, a quarter of a mile might have divided us. So near were we that the burning wads from the enemy's muskets flew in flakes of fire over our heads, and we felt upon our faces the hot, quick flush of their discharges. Yet though the air was alive with bullets the aim of the soldiers was too high for our kneeling ranks, and very few of the men were struck. For our part, we did what we could to keep the barrels of our muskets from inclining upwards. Saxon,

Sir Gervas, and I walked our horses up and down without ceasing, pushing them level with our sword-blades, and calling on the men to aim steadily and slowly. The groans and cries from the other side of the ditch showed that some, at least, of our bullets had not been fired in vain.

" We hold our own in this quarter," said I to Saxon. " It seems to me that their fire slackens."

" It is their horse that I fear," he answered. " They can avoid the ditch, since they come from the hamlets on the flank. They may be upon us at any time."

" Hullo, sir ! " shouted Sir Gervas, reining up his steed upon the very brink of the ditch, and raising his cap in salute to a mounted officer upon the other side. " Can you tell me if we have the honour to be opposed to the foot guards ? "

" We are Dumbarton's regiment, sir," cried the other. " We shall give ye good cause to remember having met us."

" We shall be across presently to make your further acquaintance," Sir Gervas answered, and at the same moment rolled, horse and all, into the ditch, amid a roar of exultation from the soldiers. Half-a-dozen of his musketeers sprang instantly, waist deep, into the mud, and dragged our friend out of danger, but the charger, which had been shot through the heart, sank without a struggle.

" There is no harm ! " cried the Baronet, springing to his feet, " I would rather fight on foot like my brave musketeers." The men broke out a-cheering at his words, and the fire on both sides became hotter than ever. It was a marvel to me, and to many more, to see these brave peasants with their mouths full of bullets, loading, priming, and firing as steadily as though they had been at it all their lives, and holding their own against a veteran regiment which has proved itself in other fields to be second to none in the army of England.

The grey light of morning was stealing over the moor,

and still the fight was undecided. The fog hung about us in feathery streaks, and the smoke from our guns drifted across in a dun-coloured cloud, through which the long lines of red-coats upon the other side of the rhine loomed up like a battalion of giants. My eyes ached and my lips pringled with the smack of the powder. On every side of me men were falling fast, for the increased light had improved the aim of the soldiers. Our good chaplain, in the very midst of a psalm, had uttered a great shout of praise and thanksgiving, and so passed on to join those of his parishioners who were scattered round him upon the moor. Hope-above William and Keeper Milson, under-officers, and among the stoutest men in the company, were both down, the one dead and the other sorely wounded, but still ramming down charges, and spitting bullets into his gun-barrel. The two Stukeleys of Somerton, twins, and lads of great promise, lay silently with grey faces turned to the grey sky, united in death as they had been in birth. Everywhere the dead lay thick amid the living. Yet no man flinched from his place, and Saxon still walked his horse among them with words of hope and praise, while his stern, deep-lined face and tall sinewy figure were a very beacon of hope to the simple rustics. Such of my scythesmen as could handle a musket were thrown forward into the fighting line, and furnished with the arms and pouches of those who had fallen.

Ever and anon as the light waxed I could note through the rifts in the smoke and the fog how the fight was progressing in other parts of the field. On the right the heath was brown with the Taunton and Frome men, who, like ourselves, were lying down to avoid the fire. Along the borders of the Bussex Rhine a deep fringe of their musketeers were exchanging murderous volleys, almost muzzle to muzzle, with the left wing of the same regiment with which we were engaged, which was supported by a second regiment in broad white facings, which I believe to have belonged to the Wiltshire Militia.

On either bank of the black trench a thick line of dead, brown on the one side, and scarlet on the other, served as a screen to their companions, who sheltered themselves behind them and rested their musket-barrels upon their prostrate bodies. To the left amongst the withies lay five hundred Mendip and Bagworthy miners, singing lustily, but so ill-armed that they had scarce one gun among ten wherewith to reply to the fire which was poured into them. They could not advance, and they would not retreat, so they sheltered themselves as best they might, and waited patiently until their leaders might decide what was to be done. Further down for half a mile or more the long rolling cloud of smoke, with petulant flashes of flame spurting out through it, showed that every one of our raw regiments was bearing its part manfully. The cannon on the left had ceased firing. The Dutch gunners had left the Islanders to settle their own quarrels, and were scampering back to Bridgewater, leaving their silent pieces to the Royal Horse.

The battle was in this state when there rose a cry of " The King, the King ! " and Monmouth rode through our ranks, bareheaded and wild-eyed, with Buyse, Wade and a dozen more beside him. They pulled up within a spear's-length of me, and Saxon, spurring forward to meet them, raised his sword to the salute. I could not but mark the contrast between the calm, grave face of the veteran, composed yet alert, and the half-frantic bearing of the man whom we were compelled to look upon as our leader.

" How think ye, Colonel Saxon ? " he cried wildly. " How goes the fight ? Is all well with ye ? What an error, alas ! what an error ! Shall we draw off, eh ? How say you ? "

" We hold our own here, your Majesty," Saxon answered. " Methinks had we something after the nature of palisados or stockados, after the Swedish fashion, we might even make it good against the horse."

" Ah, the horse ! " cried the unhappy Monmouth.

" If we get over this, my Lord Grey shall answer for it. They ran like a flock of sheep. What leader could do anything with such troops ? Oh, lack-a-day, lack-a-day ! Shall we not advance ? "

" There is no reason to advance, your Majesty, now that the surprise has failed," said Saxon. " I had sent for carts to bridge over the trench, according to the plan which is commended in the treatise, *De vallis et fossis*, but they are useless now. We can but fight it out as we are."

" To throw troops across would be to sacrifice them," said Wade. " We have lost heavily, Colonel Saxon, but I think from the look of yonder bank that ye have given a good account of the red-coats."

" Stand firm ! For God's sake, stand firm ! " cried Monmouth distractedly. " The horse have fled, and the cannoniers also. Oh ! what can I do with such men ? What shall I do ? Alas, alas ! " He set spurs to his horse and galloped off down the line, still wringing his hands and uttering his dismal wailings. Oh, my children, how small, how very small a thing is death when weighed in the balance with dishonour ! Had this man but borne his fate silently, as did the meanest footman who followed his banners, how proud and glad would we have been to have discoursed of him, our princely leader. But let him rest. The fears and agitations and petty fond emotions, which showed upon him as the breeze shows upon the water, are all stilled now for many a long year. Let us think of the kind heart and forget the feeble spirit.

As his escort trooped after him, the great German man-at-arms separated from them and turned back to us. " I am weary of trotting up and down like a lust-ritter at a fair," said he. " If I bide with ye I am like to have my share of any fighting which is going. So, steady, mein Liebchen. That ball grazed her tail, but she is too old a soldier to wince at trifles. Hullo, friend, where is your horse ? "

" At the bottom of the ditch," said Sir Gervas, scraping the mud of his dress with his sword-blade. " 'Tis now

half-past two," he continued, " and we have been at this
child's-play for an hour and more. With a line regiment
too ! It is not what I had looked forward to ! "

" You shall have something to console you anon,"
cried the German, with his eyes shining. " Mein Gott !
Is it not splendid ? Look to it, friend Saxon, look to it ! "

It was no light matter which had so roused the soldier's
admiration. Out of the haze which still lay thick upon our
right there twinkled here and there a bright gleam of
silvery light, while a dull, thundering noise broke upon
our ears like that of the surf upon a rocky shore. More
and more frequent came the fitful flashes of steel, louder
and yet louder grew the hoarse gathering tumult, until
of a sudden the fog was rent, and the long lines of the
Royal cavalry broke out from it, wave after wave, rich in
scarlet and blue and gold, as grand a sight as ever the eye
rested upon. There was something in the smooth,
steady sweep of so great a body of horsemen which gave
the feeling of irresistible power. Rank after rank, and
line after line, with waving standards, tossing manes, and
gleaming steel, they poured onwards, an army in themselves, with either flank still shrouded in the mist. As
they thundered along, knee to knee and bridle to bridle,
there came from them such a gust of deep-chested oaths
with the jangle of harness, the clash of steel, and the
measured beat of multitudinous hoofs, that no man who
hath not stood up against such a whirlwind, with nothing
but a seven-foot pike in his hand, can know how hard it
is to face it with a steady lip and a firm grip.

But wonderful as was the sight, there was, as ye may
guess, my dears, little time for us to gaze upon it. Saxon
and the German flung themselves among the pikemen and did all that men could do to thicken their
array. Sir Gervas and I did the same with the scythesmen, who had been trained to form a triple front after the
German fashion, one rank kneeling, one stooping, and
one standing erect, with weapons advanced. Close to
us the Taunton men had hardened into a dark sullen

ring, bristling with steel, in the centre of which might be seen and heard their venerable Mayor, his long beard fluttering in the breeze, and his strident voice clanging over the field. Louder and louder grew the roar of the horse. " Steady, my brave lads," cried Saxon, in trumpet tones. " Dig the pike-butt into the earth ! Rest it on the right foot ! Give not an inch ! Steady ! " A great shout went up from either side, and then the living wave broke over us.

What hope is there to describe such a scene as that— the crashing of wood, the sharp gasping cries, the snorting of horses, the jar when the push of pike met with the sweep of sword ! Who can hope to make another see that of which he himself carries away so vague and dim an impression ? One who has acted in such a scene gathers no general sense of the whole combat, such as might be gained by a mere onlooker, but he has stamped for ever upon his mind just the few incidents which may chance to occur before his own eyes. Thus my memories are confined to a swirl of smoke with steel caps and fierce, eager faces breaking through it, with the red gaping nostrils of horses and their pawing fore-feet as they re-coiled from the hedge of steel. I see, too, a young beard-less lad, an officer of dragoons, crawling on hands and knees under the scythes, and I hear his groan as one of the peasants pinned him to the ground. I see a bearded, broad-faced trooper riding a grey horse just outside the fringe of the scythes, seeking for some entrance, and screaming the while with rage. Small things imprint themselves upon a man's notice at such a time. I even marked the man's strong white teeth and pink gums. At the same time I see a white-faced, thin-lipped man leaning far forward over his horse's neck and driving at me with his sword point, cursing the while as only a dragoon can curse. All these images start up as I think of that fierce rally, during which I hacked and cut and thrust at man and horse without a thought of parry or of guard. All round rose a fierce babel of shouts and cries,

godly ejaculations from the peasants and oaths from the horsemen, with Saxon's voice above all imploring his pikemen to stand firm. Then the cloud of horsemen recoiled, circling off over the plain, and the shout of triumph from my comrades, and an open snuff-box thrust out in front of me, proclaimed that we had seen the back of as stout squadrons as ever followed a kettledrum.

But if we could claim it as a victory, the army in general could scarce say as much. None but the very pick of the troops could stand against the flood of heavy horses and steel-clad men. The Frome peasants were gone, swept utterly from the field. Many had been driven by pure weight and pressure into the fatal mud which had checked our advance. Many others, sorely cut and slashed, lay in ghastly heaps all over the ground which they had held. A few by joining our ranks had saved themselves from the fate of their companions. Further off the men of Taunton still stood fast, though in sadly diminished numbers. A long ridge of horses and cavaliers in front of them showed how stern had been the attack and how fierce the resistance. On our left the wild miners had been broken at the first rush, but had fought so savagely, throwing themselves upon the ground and stabbing upwards at the stomachs of the horses, that they had at last beaten off the dragoons. The Devonshire militiamen, however, had been scattered, and shared the fate of the men of Frome. During the whole of the struggle the foot upon the further bank of the Bussex Rhine were pouring in a hail of bullets, which our musqueteers, having to defend themselves against the horse, were unable to reply to.

It needed no great amount of soldierly experience to see that the battle was lost, and that Monmouth's cause was doomed. It was broad daylight now, though the sun had not yet risen. Our cavalry was gone, our ordnance was silent, our line was pierced in many places, and more than one of our regiments had been destroyed. On the right flank the Horse Guards Blue, the Tangiers

Horse and two dragoon regiments were forming up for a fresh attack. On the left the foot-guards had bridged the ditch and were fighting hand to hand with the men from North Somerset. In front a steady fire was being poured into us, to which our reply was feeble and uncertain, for the powder carts had gone astray in the dark, and many were calling hoarsely for ammunition, while others were loading with pebbles instead of ball. Add to this that the regiments which still held their ground had all been badly shaken by the charge, and had lost a third of their number. Yet the brave clowns sent up cheer after cheer, and shouted words of encouragement and homely jests to each other, as though a battle were but some rough game which must as a matter of course be played out while there was a player left to join in it.

"Is Captain Clarke there?" cried Decimus Saxon, riding up with his sword-arm flecked with blood. "Ride over to Sir Stephen Timewell and tell him to join his men to ours. Apart we shall be broken—together we may stand another charge."

Setting spurs to Covenant I rode over to our companions and delivered the message. Sir Stephen, who had been struck by a petronel bullet, and wore a crimsoned kerchief bound round his snow-white head, saw the wisdom of the advice, and moved his townsmen as directed. His musqueteers being better provided with powder than ours did good service by keeping down for a time the deadly fire from across the fosse.

"Who would have thought it of him?" cried Sir Stephen, with flashing eyes, as Buyse and Saxon rode out to meet him. "What think ye now of our noble monarch, our champion of the Protestant cause?"

"He is no very great Krieger," said Buyse. "Yet perhaps it may be from want of habit as much as from want of courage."

"Courage!" cried the old Mayor, in a voice of scorn. "Look over yonder and behold your King." He pointed out over the moor with a finger which shook as much

from anger as from age. There, far away, showing up against the dark peat-coloured soil, rode a gaily-dressed cavalier, followed by a knot of attendants, galloping as fast as his horse would carry him from the field of battle. There was no mistaking the fugitive. It was the recreant Monmouth.

" Hush ! " cried Saxon, as we all gave a cry of horror and execration ; " do not dishearten our brave lads ! Cowardice is catching and will run through an army like the putrid fever."

" Der Feigherzige ! " cried Buyse, grinding his teeth. " And the brave country folk ! It is too much."

" Stand to your pikes, men ! " roared Saxon, in a voice of thunder, and we had scarce time to form our square and throw ourselves inside of it, before the whirlwind of horse was upon us once more. When the Taunton men had joined us a weak spot had been left in our ranks, and through this in an instant the Blue Guards smashed their way, pouring through the opening, and cutting fiercely to right and left. The burghers on the one side and our own men on the other replied by savage stabs from their pikes and scythes, which emptied many a saddle, but while the struggle was at its hottest the King's cannon opened for the first time with a deafening roar upon the other side of the rhine, and a storm of balls ploughed their way through our dense ranks, leaving furrows of dead and wounded behind them. At the same moment a great cry of " Powder ! For Christ's sake, powder ! " arose from the musketeers whose last charge had been fired. Again the cannon roared, and again our men were mowed down as though Death himself with his scythe were amongst us. At last our ranks were breaking. In the very centre of the pikemen steel caps were gleaming, and broadswords rising and falling. The whole body was swept back two hundred paces or more, struggling furiously the while, and was there mixed with other like bodies which had been dashed out of all semblance of military order, and yet refused to fly. Men of Devon,

of Dorset, of Wiltshire and of Somerset, trodden down by horse, slashed by dragoons, dropping by scores under the rain of bullets, still fought on with a dogged, desperate courage for a ruined cause and a man who had deserted them. Everywhere as I glanced around me were set faces, clenched teeth, yells of rage and defiance, but never a sound of fear or of submission. Some clambered up upon the cruppers of the riders and dragged them backwards from their saddles. Others lay upon their faces and hamstrung the chargers with their scythe-blades, stabbing the horsemen before they could disengage themselves. Again and again the guards crashed through them from side to side, and yet the shattered ranks closed up behind them and continued the long-drawn struggle. So hopeless was it and so pitiable that I could have found it in my heart to wish that they would break and fly, were it not that on the broad moor there was no refuge which they could make for. And all this time, while they struggled and fought, blackened with powder and parched with thirst, spilling their blood as though it were water, the man who called himself their King was spurring over the countryside with a loose rein and a quaking heart, his thoughts centred upon saving his own neck, come what might to his gallant followers.

Large numbers of the foot fought to the death, neither giving nor receiving quarter; but at last, scattered, broken and without ammunition, the main body of the peasants dispersed and fled across the moor, closely followed by the horse. Saxon, Buyse and I had done all that we could to rally them once more, and had cut down some of the foremost of the pursuers, when my eye fell suddenly upon Sir Gervas, standing hatless with a few of his musketeers in the midst of a swarm of dragoons. Spurring our horses we cut a way to his rescue, and laid our swords about us until we had cleared off his assailants for the moment.

" Jump up behind me ! " I cried. " We can make good our escape."

He looked up smiling and shook his head. " I stay with my company," said he.

" Your company ! " Saxon cried. " Why, man, you are mad ! Your company is cut off to the last man."

" That's what I mean," he answered, flicking some dirt from his cravat. " Don't ye mind ! Look out for your-selves. Good-bye, Clarke ! Present my compliments to——" The dragoons charged down upon us again. We were all borne backwards, fighting desperately, and when we could look round the Baronet was gone for ever. We heard afterwards that the King's troops found upon the field a body which they mistook for that of Mon-mouth, on account of the effeminate grace of the features and richness of the attire. No doubt it was that of our undaunted friend, Sir Gervas Jerome, a name which shall ever be dear to my heart. When, ten years after-wards, we heard much of the gallantry of the young courtiers of the household of the French King, and of the sprightly courage with which they fought against us in the Lowlands at Steinkirk and elsewhere, I have always thought, from my recollection of Sir Gervas, that I knew what manner of men they were.

And now it was every man for himself. In no part of the field did the insurgents continue to resist. The first rays of the sun shining slantwise across the great dreary plain lit up the long line of the scarlet battalions, and glittered upon the cruel swords which rose and fell among the struggling drove of resistless fugitives. The German had become separated from us in the tumult, and we knew not whether he lived or was slain, though long after-wards we learned that he made good his escape, only to be captured with the ill-fated Duke of Monmouth. Grey, Wade, Ferguson and others had contrived also to save themselves, while Stephen Timewell lay in the midst of a stern ring of his hard-faced burghers, dying as he had lived, a gallant Puritan Englishman. All this we learned after-wards. At present we rode for our lives across the moor, followed by a few scattered bodies of horse, who soon

abandoned their pursuit in order to fasten upon some more easy prey.

We were passing a small clump of alder bushes when a loud manly voice raised in prayer attracted our attention. Pushing aside the branches, we came upon a man, seated with his back up against a great stone, cutting at his own arm with a broad-bladed knife, and giving forth the Lord's prayer the while, without a pause or a quiver in his tone. As he glanced up from his terrible task we both recognised him as one Hollis, whom I have mentioned as having been with Cromwell at Dunbar. His arm had been half severed by a cannon-ball, and he was quietly completing the separation in order to free himself from the dangling and useless limb. Even Saxon, used as he was to all the forms and incidents of war, stared open-eyed and aghast at this strange surgery ; but the man, with a short nod of recognition, went grimly forward with his task, until, even as we gazed, he separated the last shred which held it, and lay over with blanched lips which still murmured the prayer.[1] We could do little to help him, and indeed, might by our halt attract his pursuers to his hiding place ; so, throwing him down my flask half filled with water, we hastened on upon our way. Oh, war, my children, what a terrible thing it is ! How are men cozened and cheated by the rare trappings and prancing steeds, by the empty terms of honour and of glory, until they forget in the outward tinsel and show the real ghastly horror of the accursed thing ! Think not of the dazzling squadrons, nor of the spirit-stirring blare of the trumpets, but think of that lonely man under the shadow of the alders, and of what he was doing in a Christian age and a Christian land. Surely I, who have grown grey in harness, and who have seen as many fields as I have years of my life, should be the last to preach upon this subject, and yet I can clearly see that, in honesty, men must either give up war, or else they must confess that

---

[1] The incident is historically true, and may serve to show what sort of men they were who had learned their soldiering under Cromwell.

the words of the Redeemer are too lofty for them, and that there is no longer any use in pretending that His teaching can be reduced to practice. I have seen a Christian minister blessing a cannon which had just been founded, and another blessing a war-ship as it glided from the slips. They, the so-called representatives of Christ, blessed these engines of destruction which cruel man has devised to destroy and tear his fellow-worms. What would we say if we read in Holy Writ of our Lord having blessed the battering-rams and the catapults of the legions ? Would we think that it was in agreement with His teaching ? But there ! As long as the heads of the Church wander away so far from the spirit of its teaching as to live in palaces and drive in carriages, what wonder if, with such examples before them, the lower clergy overstep at times the lines laid down by their great Master ?

Looking back from the summit of the low hills which lie to the westward of the moor, we could see the cloud of horsemen streaming over the bridge of the Parret and into the town of Bridgewater, with the helpless drove of fugitives still flying in front of them. We had pulled up our horses, and were looking sadly and silently back at the fatal plain, when the thuds of hoofs fell upon our ears, and, turning round, we found two horsemen in the dress of the guards riding towards us. They had made a circuit to cut us off, for they were riding straight for us with drawn swords and eager gestures.

" More slaughter," I said wearily. " Why will they force us to it ? "

Saxon glanced keenly from beneath his drooping lids at the approaching horsemen, and a grim smile wreathed his face in a thousand lines and wrinkles.

" It is our friend who set the hounds upon our track at Salisbury," he said. " This is a happy meeting. I have a score to settle with him."

It was, indeed, the hot-headed young cornet whom we had met at the outset of our adventures. Some evil

chance had led him to recognise the tall figure of my companion as we rode from the field, and to follow him, in the hope of obtaining revenge for the humiliation which he had met with at his hands. The other was a lance-corporal, a man of square, soldierly build, riding a heavy black horse with a white blaze upon its forehead.

Saxon rode slowly towards the officer, while the trooper and I fixed our eyes upon each other.

" Well, boy," I heard my companion say, " I trust that you have learned to fence since we met last."

The young guardsman gave a snarl of rage at the taunt, and an instant afterwards the clink of their sword-blades showed that they had met. For my own part I dared not spare a glance upon them, for my opponent attacked me with such fury that it was all that I could do to keep him off. No pistol was drawn upon either side. It was an honest contest of steel against steel. So constant were the corporal's thrusts, now at my face, now at my body, that I had never an opening for one of the heavy cuts which might have ended the matter. Our horses spun round each other, biting and pawing, while we thrust and parried, until at last, coming together knee to knee, we found ourselves within sword-point, and grasped each other by the throat. He plucked a dagger from his belt and struck it into my left arm, but I dealt him a blow with my gauntleted hand, which smote him off his horse and stretched him speechless upon the plain. Almost at the same moment the cornet dropped from his horse, wounded in several places. Saxon sprang from his saddle, and picking the soldier's dagger from the ground, would have finished them both had I not jumped down also and restrained him. He flashed round upon me with so savage a face that I could see that the wild-beast nature within him was fairly roused.

" What hast thou to do ? " he snarled. " Let go ! "

" Nay, nay ! Blood enough hath been shed," said I. " Let them lie."

" What mercy would they have had upon us ? " he

cried passionately, struggling to get his wrist free. " They have lost, and must pay forfeit."

" Not in cold blood," I said firmly. " I shall not abide it."

" Indeed, your lordship," he sneered, with the devil peeping out through his eyss. With a violent wrench, he freed himself from my grasp, and springing back picked up the sword which he had dropped.

" What then ? " I asked, standing on my guard astride of the wounded man.

He stood for a minute or more looking at me from under his heavy-hung brows, with his whole face writhing with passion. Every instant I expected that he would fly at me, but at last, with a gulp in his throat, he sheathed his rapier with a sharp clang, and sprang back into the saddle.

" We part here," he said coldly. " I have twice been on the verge of slaying you, and the third time might be too much for my patience. You are no fit companion for a cavalier of fortune. Join the clergy, lad; it is your vocation."

" Is this Decimus Saxon who speaks, or is it Will Spotterbridge ? " I asked, remembering his jest concerning his ancestry, but no answering smile came upon his rugged face. Gathering up his bridle in his left hand, he shot one last malignant glance at the bleeding officer, and galloped off along one of the tracks which led to the southward. I stood gazing after him, but he never sent so much as a hand-wave back, riding on with a rigid neck until he vanished in a dip in the moor.

" There goes one friend," thought I sadly, " and all forsooth because I will not stand by and see a helpless man's throat cut. Another friend is dead on the field. A third, the oldest and dearest of all, lies wounded at Bridgewater, at the mercy of a brutal soldiery. If I return to my home I do but bring trouble and danger to those whom I love. Whither shall I turn ? " For some minutes I stood irresolute beside the prostrate guardsmen, while Covenant strolled slowly along cropping the scanty herbage, and turning his dark full eyes towards me from

time to time, as though to assure me that one friend at least was steadfast. Northward I looked at the Polden Hills, southwards at the Blackdowns, westward at the long blue range of the Quantocks, and eastward at the broad fen country ; but nowhere could I see any hope of safety. Truth to say I felt sick at heart and cared little for the time whether I escaped or no.

A muttered oath followed by a groan roused me from my meditations. The corporal was sitting up rubbing his head with a look of stupid astonishment upon his face, as though he were not very sure either of where he was or how he came there. The officer, too, had opened his eyes and showed other signs of returning consciousness. His wounds were clearly of no very serious nature. There was no danger of their pursuing me even should they wish to do so, for their horses had trotted off to join the numerous other riderless steeds who were wandering all over the moorlands. I mounted, therefore, and rode slowly away, saving my good charger as much as possible, for the morning's work had already told somewhat heavily upon him.

There were many scattered bodies of horse riding hither and thither over the marshes, but I was able to avoid them, and trotted onwards, keeping to the waste country until I found myself eight or ten miles from the battlefield. The few cottages and houses which I passed were deserted, and many of them bore signs of having been plundered. Not a peasant was to be seen. The evil fame of Kirke's lambs had chased away all those who had not actually taken arms. At last, after riding for three hours, I bethought me that I was far enough from the main line of pursuit to be free from danger, so I chose out a sheltered spot where a clump of bushes overhung a little brook. There, seated upon a bank of velvet moss, I rested my weary limbs, and tried to wash the stains of battle from my person.

It was only now when I could look quietly at my own attire that it was brought home to me how terrible the en-

counter must have been in which I had been engaged, and
how wonderful it was that I had come off so scathless.
Of the blows which I had struck in the fight I had faint
remembrance, yet they must have been many and terrible,
for my sword edge was as jagged and turned as though I
had hacked for an hour at an iron bar. From head to
foot I was splashed and crimsoned with blood, partly
my own, but mostly that of others. My headpiece was
dinted with blows. A petronel bullet had glanced off
my front plate, striking it at an angle, and had left a broad
groove across it. Two or three other cracks and stars
showed where the good sheet of proof steel had saved me.
My left arm was stiff and well-nigh powerless from the
corporal's stab, but on stripping off my doublet and
examining the place, I found that though there had been
much bleeding the wound was on the outer side of the
bone, and was therefore of no great import. A kerchief
dipped in water and bound tightly round it eased the
smart and stanched the blood. Beyond this scratch I
had no injuries, though from my own efforts I felt as stiff
and sore all over as though I had been well cudgelled,
and the slight wound got in Wells Cathedral had reopened
and was bleeding. With a little patience and cold water,
however, I was able to dress it and to tie myself up as well
as any chirurgeon in the kingdom.

Having seen to my injuries I had now to attend to my
appearance, for in truth I might have stood for one of
those gory giants with whom the worthy Don Bellianis
of Greece and other stout champions were wont to con-
tend. No woman or child but would have fled at the
sight of me, for I was as red as the parish butcher when
Martinmas is nigh. A good wash, however, in the brook
soon removed those traces of war, and I was able to get the
marks off my breastplate and boots. In the case of my
clothes, however, it was so hopeless to clean them that I
gave it up in despair. My good old horse had been never
so much as grazed by steel or bullet, so that with a little
watering and tending he was soon as fresh as ever, and we

turned our backs on the streamlet a better-favoured pair than we had approached it.

It was now going on to mid-day, and I began to feel very hungry, for I had tasted nothing since the evening before. Two or three houses stood in a cluster upon the moor, but the blackened walls and scorched thatch showed that it was hopeless to expect anything from them. Once or twice I spied folk in the fields or on the roadway ; but at sight of an armed horseman they ran for their lives, diving into the brushwood like wild animals. At one place, where a high oak tree marked the meeting of three roads, two bodies dangling from one of the branches showed that the fears of the villagers were based upon experience. These poor men had in all likelihood been hanged because the amount of their little hoardings had not come up to the expectations of their plunderers ; or because, having given all to one band of robbers, they had nothing with which to appease the next. At last, when I was fairly weary of my fruitless search for food, I espied a windmill standing upon a green hill at the other side of some fields. Judging from its appearance that it had escaped the general pillage, I took the pathway which branched away to it from the high-road.[1]

33. *Of my Perilous Adventure at the Mill*

AT the base of the mill there stood a shed which was evidently used to stall the horses which brought the farmers' grain. Some grass was heaped up inside it, so I loosened Covenant's girths and left him to have a hearty meal. The mill itself appeared to be silent and empty. I climbed the steep wood ladder, and pushing the door open, walked into a round stone-flagged room, from which a second ladder led to the loft above. On one side of this chamber was a long wooden box, and all round the walls were ranged rows of sacks full of flour.

[1] Note J, Appendix.—Battle of Sedgemoor.

In the fireplace stood a pile of faggots ready for lighting, so with the aid of my tinder-box I soon had a cheerful blaze. Taking a large handful of flour from the nearest bag I moistened it with water from a pitcher, and having rolled it out into a flat cake, proceeded to bake it, smiling the while to think of what my mother would say to such rough cookery. Very sure I am that Patrick Lamb himself, whose book, the *Complete Court Cook*, was ever in the dear soul's left hand while she stirred and basted with her right, could not have turned out a dish which was more to my taste at the moment, for I had not even patience to wait for the browning of it, but snapped it up and devoured it half hot. I then rolled a second one, and having placed it before the fire, and drawn my pipe from my pocket, I set myself to smoke, waiting with all the philosophy which I could muster until it should be ready.

I was lost in thought, brooding sadly over the blow which the news would be to my father, when I was startled by a loud sneeze, which sounded as though it were delivered in my very ear. I started to my feet and gazed all round me, but there was nothing save the solid wall behind and the empty chamber before. I had almost come to persuade myself that I had been the creature of some delusion, when again a crashing sneeze, louder and more prolonged than the last, broke upon the silence. Could someone be hid in one of the bags? Drawing my sword I walked round pricking the great flour sacks, but without being able to find cause for the sound. I was still marvelling over the matter when a most extraordinary chorus of gasps, snorts and whistles broke out, with cries of " Oh, holy mother ! " " Blessed Redeemer ! " and other such exclamations. This time there could be no doubt as to whence the uproar came. Rushing up to the great chest upon which I had been seated, I threw back the heavy lid and gazed in.

It was more than half full of flour, in the midst of which was floundering some creature, which was so coated and

caked with the white powder, that it would have been hard to say that it was human were it not for the pitiable cries which it was uttering. Stooping down I dragged the man from his hiding-place, when he dropped upon his knees upon the floor and yelled for mercy, raising such a cloud of dust from every wriggle of his body that I began to cough and to sneeze. As the skin of powder began to scale off from him, I saw to my surprise that he was no miller or peasant, but was a man-at-arms, with a huge sword girt to his side, looking at present not unlike a frosted icicle, and a great steel-faced breastplate. His steel cap had remained behind in the flour-bin, and his bright red hair, the only touch of colour about him, stood straight up in the air with terror, as he implored me to spare his life. Thinking that there was something familiar about his voice, I drew my hand across his face, which set him yelling as though I had slain him. There was no mistaking the heavy cheeks and the little greedy eyes. It was none other than Master Tetheridge, the noisy town-clerk of Taunton.

But how much changed from the town-clerk whom we had seen strutting, in all the pomp and bravery of his office, before the good Mayor on the day of our coming to Somersetshire! Where now was the ruddy colour like a pippin in September? Where was the assured manner and the manly port? As he knelt his great jack-boots clicked together with apprehension, and he poured forth in a piping voice, like that of a Lincoln's Inn mumper, a string of pleadings, excuses and entreaties, as though I were Feversham in person, and was about to order him to instant execution.

" I am but a poor scrivener man, your serene Highness," he bawled. " Indeed, I am a most unhappy clerk, your Honour, who has been driven into these courses by the tyranny of those above him. A more loyal man, your Grace, never wore neat's leather, but when the mayor says ' Yes,' can the clerk say ' No '? Spare me, your lordship ; spare a most penitent wretch,

whose only prayer is that he may be allowed to serve King James to the last drop of his blood ! "

" Do you renounce the Duke of Monmouth ? " I asked, in a stern voice.

" I do—from my heart ! " said he fervently.

" Then prepare to die ! " I roared, whipping out my sword, " for I am one of his officers."

At the sight of the steel the wretched clerk gave a perfect bellow of terror, and falling upon his face he wriggled and twisted, until looking up he perceived that I was laughing. On that he crawled up on to his knees once more, and from that to his feet, glancing at me askance, as though by no means assured of my intentions.

" You must remember me, Master Tetheridge," I said. " I am Captain Clarke, of Saxon's regiment of Wiltshire foot. I am surprised, indeed, that you should have fallen away from that allegiance to which you did not only swear yourself, but did administer the oath to so many others."

" Not a whit, Captain, not a whit ! " he answered, resuming his old bantam-cock manner as soon as he saw that there was no danger. " I am upon oath as true and as leal a man as ever I was."

" That I can fully believe," I answered.

" I did but dissimulate," he continued, brushing the flour from his person. " I did but practise that cunning of the serpent which should in every warrior accompany the courage of the lion. You have read your Homer, doubtless. Eh ? I too have had a touch of the humanities. I am no mere rough soldier, however stoutly I can hold mine own at sword-play. Master Ulysses is my type, even as thine, I take it, is Master Ajax."

" Methinks that Master Jack-in-the-box would fit you better," said I. " Wilt have a half of this cake ? How came you in the flour-bin ? "

" Why, marry, in this wise," he answered, with his mouth full of dough. " It was a wile or ruse, after the fashion of the greatest commanders, who have always been famous for concealing their movements, and lurking

428

where they were least expected. For when the fight was lost, and I had cut and hacked until my arm was weary and my edge blunted, I found that I was left alone alive of all the Taunton men. Were we on the field you could see where I had stood by the ring of slain which would be found within the sweep of my sword-arm. Finding that all was lost and that our rogues were fled, I mounted our worthy Mayor's charger, seeing that the gallant gentleman had no further need for it, and rode slowly from the field. I promise you that there was that in my eye and bearing which prevented their horse from making too close a pursuit of me. One trooper did indeed throw himself across my path, but mine old back-handed cut was too much for him. Alas, I have much upon my conscience ! I have made both widows and orphans. Why will they brave me when—God of mercy, what is that ? "

" 'Tis but my horse in the stall below," I answered.

" I thought it was the dragoons," quoth the clerk, wiping away the drops which had started out upon his brow. " You and I would have gone forth and smitten them."

" Or climbed into the flour-bin," said I.

" I have not yet made clear to you how I came there," he continued. " Having ridden, then, some leagues from the field, and noting this windmill, it did occur to me that a stout man might single-handed make it good against a troop of horse. We have no great love of flight, we Tetheridges. It may be mere empty pride, and yet the feeling runs strong in the family. We have a fighting strain in us ever since my kinsman followed Ireton's army as a sutler. I pulled up, therefore, and had dismounted to take my observations, when my brute of a charger gave the bridle a twitch, jerked itself free, and was off in an instant over hedges and ditches. I had, therefore, only my good sword left to trust to. I climbed up the ladder, and was engaged in planning how the defence could best be conducted, when I heard the clank of hoofs, and on the top of it you did ascend from below. I retired at once into ambush, from which I should assuredly have made a

sudden outfall or sally, had the flour not so choked my breathing that I felt as though I had a two-pound loaf stuck in my gizzard. For myself, I am glad that it has so come about, for in my blind wrath I might unwittingly have done you an injury. Hearing the clank of your sword as you did come up the ladder, I did opine that you were one of King James's minions, the captain, perchance, of some troop in the fields below."

" All very clear and explicit, Master Tetheridge," said I, relighting my pipe. " No doubt your demeanour when I did draw you from your hiding-place was also a mere cloak for your valour. But enough of that. It is to the future that we have to look. What are your intentions ? "

" To remain with you, Captain," said he.

" Nay, that you shall not," I answered ; " I have no great fancy for your companionship. Your overflowing valour may bring me into ruffles which I had otherwise avoided."

" Nay, nay ! I shall moderate my spirit," he cried. " In such troublous times you will find yourself none the worse for the company of a tried fighting man."

" Tried and found wanting," said I, weary of the man's braggart talk. " I tell you I will go alone."

" Nay, you need not be so hot about it," he exclaimed, shrinking away from me. " In any case, we had best stay here until nightfall, when we may make our way to the coast."

" That is the first mark of sense that you have shown," said I. " The King's horse will find enough to do with the Zoyland cider and the Bridgewater ale. If we can pass through, I have friends on the north coast who would give us a lift in their lugger as far as Holland. This help I will not refuse to give you, since you are my fellow in misfortune. I would that Saxon had stayed with me ! I fear he will be taken ! "

" If you mean Colonel Saxon," said the clerk, " I think that he also is one who hath much guile as well as valour. A stern, fierce soldier he was, as I know well, having fought back to back with him for forty minutes

430

by the clock, against a troop of Sarsfield's horse. Plain of speech he was, and perhaps a trifle inconsiderate of the honour of a cavalier, but in the field it would have been well for the army had they had more such commanders."

"You say truly," I answered; "but now that we have refreshed ourselves it is time that we bethought us of taking some rest, since we may have far to travel this night. I would that I could lay my hand upon a flagon of ale."

"I would gladly drink to our further acquaintanceship in the same," said my companion, "but as to the matter of slumber that may be readily arranged. If you ascend that ladder you will find in the loft a litter of empty sacks, upon which you can repose. For myself, I will stay down here for a while and cook myself another cake."

"Do you remain on watch for two hours, and then arouse me," I replied. "I shall then keep guard whilst you sleep." He touched the hilt of his sword as a sign that he would be true to his post, so not without some misgivings I climbed up into the loft, and throwing myself upon the rude couch was soon in a deep and dreamless slumber, lulled by the low, mournful groaning and creaking of the sails.

I was awoken by steps beside me, and found that the little clerk had come up the ladder and was bending over me. I asked him if the time had come for me to rouse, on which he answered in a strange quavering voice that I had yet an hour, and that he had come up to see if there was any service which he could render me. I was too weary to take much note of his slinking manner and pallid cheeks, so thanking him for his attention, I turned over and was soon asleep once more.

My next waking was a rougher and a sterner one. There came a sudden rush of heavy feet up the ladder, and a dozen red-coats swarmed into the room. Springing on to my feet I put out my hand for the sword which I had laid all ready by my side, but the trusty weapon had gone. It had been stolen whilst I slumbered. Unarmed and taken at a vantage, I was struck down and

pinioned in a moment. One held a pistol to my head, and swore that he would blow my brains out if I stirred, while the others wound a coil of rope round my body and arms, until Samson himself could scarce have got free. Feeling that my struggles were of no possible avail, I lay silent and waited for whatever was to come. Neither now nor at any time, dear children, have I laid great store upon my life, but far less then than now, for each of you are tiny tendrils which bind me to this world. Yet, when I think of the other dear ones who are waiting for me on the further shore, I do not think that even now death would seem an evil thing in my eyes. What a hopeless and empty thing would life be without it !

Having lashed my arms, the soldiers dragged me down the ladder, as though I had been a truss of hay, into the room beneath, which was also crowded with troopers. In one corner was the wretched scrivener, a picture of abject terror, with chattering teeth and trembling knees, only prevented from falling upon the floor by the grasp of a stalwart corporal. In front of him stood two officers, one a little hard brown man with dark twinkling eyes and an alert manner, the other tall and slender, with a long golden moustache, which drooped down half-way to his shoulders. The former had my sword in his hand, and they were both examining the blade curiously.

" It is a good bit of steel, Dick," said one, putting the point against the stone floor, and pressing down until he touched it with the handle. " See, with what a snap it rebounds ! No maker's name, but the date 1638 is stamped upon the pommel. Where did you get it, fellow ? " he asked, fixing his keen gaze upon my face.

" It was my father's before me," I answered.

" Then I trust that he drew it in a better quarrel than his son hath done," said the taller officer, with a sneer.

" In as good, though not in a better," I returned. " That sword hath always been drawn for the rights and liberties of Englishmen, and against the tyranny of kings and the bigotry of priests."

"What a tag for a playhouse, Dick," cried the officer. "How doth it run ? 'The bigotry of kings and the tyranny of priests.' Why, if well delivered by Betterton close up to the footlights, with one hand upon his heart and the other pointing to the sky, I warrant the pit would rise at it."

"Very like," said the other, twirling his moustache. "But we have no time for fine speeches now. What are we to do with the little one ? "

"Hang him," the other answered carelessly.

"No, no, your most gracious honours," howled Master Tetheridge, suddenly writhing out of the corporal's grip and flinging himself upon the floor at their feet. "Did I not tell ye where ye could find one of the stoutest soldiers of the rebel army ? Did not I guide ye to him ? Did not I even creep up and remove his sword lest any of the King's subjects be slain in the taking of him ? Surely, surely, ye would not use me so scurvily when I have done ye these services ? Have I not made good my words ? Is he not as I described him, a giant in stature and of wondrous strength ? The whole army will bear me out in it, that he was worth any two in single fight. I have given him over to ye. Surely ye will let me go ! "

"Very well delivered—plaguily so ! " quoth the little officer, clapping the palm of one hand softly against the back of the other. "The emphasis was just, and the enunciation clear. A little further back towards the wings, corporal, if you please. Thank you ! Now, Dick, it is your cue."

"Nay, John, you are too absurd ! " cried the other impatiently. "The mask and the buskins are well enough in their place, but you look upon the play as a reality and upon the reality as but a play. What this reptile hath said is true. We must keep faith with him if we wish that others of the country folk should give up the fugitives. There is no help for it ! "

"For myself I believe in Jeddart law," his companion answered. "I would hang the man first and then discuss

the question of our promise. However, pink me if I will obtrude my opinion on any man ! "

" Nay, it cannot be," the taller said. " Corporal, do you take him down. Henderson will go with you. Take from him that plate and sword, which his mother would wear with as good a grace. And hark ye, corporal, a few touches of thy stirrup leathers across his fat shoulders might not be amiss, as helping him to remember the King's dragoons."

My treacherous companion was dragged off, struggling and yelping, and presently a series of piercing howls, growing fainter and fainter as he fled before his tormentors, announced that the hint had been taken. The two officers rushed to the little window of the mill and roared with laughter, while the troopers, peeping furtively over their shoulders, could not restrain themselves from joining in their mirth, from which I gathered that Master Tetheridge, as, spurred on by fear, he hurled his fat body through hedges and into ditches, was a somewhat comical sight.

" And now for the other," said the little officer, turning away from the window and wiping the tears of laughter from his face. " That beam over yonder would serve our purpose. Where is Hangman Broderick, the Jack Ketch of the Royals ? "

" Here I am, sir," responded a sullen, heavy-faced trooper, shuffling forward ; " I have a rope here with a noose."

" Throw it over the beam, then. What is amiss with your hand, you clumsy rogue, that you should wear linen round it ? "

" May it please you, sir," the man answered, " it was all through an ungrateful, prick-eared Presbyterian knave whom I hung at Gommatch. I had done all that could be done for him. Had he been at Tyburn he could scarce have met with more attention. Yet when I did put my hand to his neck to see that all was as it should be, he did fix me with his teeth, and hath gnawed a great piece from my thumb."

" I am sorry for you," said the officer. " You know, no doubt, that the human bite under such circumstances is as deadly as that of the mad dog, so that you may find yourself snapping and barking one of these fine mornings. Nay, turn not pale ! I have heard you preach patience and courage to your victims. You are not afraid of death ? "

" Not of any Christian death, your Honour. Yet, ten shillings a week is scarce enough to pay a man for an end like that ! "

" Nay, it is all a lottery," remarked the Captain cheerily. " I have heard that in these cases a man is so drawn up that his heels do beat a tattoo against the back of his head. But, mayhap, it is not as painful as it would appear. Meanwhile, do you proceed to do your office."

Three or four troopers caught me by the arms, but I shook them off as best I might, and walked with, as I trust, a steady step and a cheerful face under the beam, which was a great smoke-blackened rafter passing from one side of the chamber to the other. The rope was thrown over this, and the noose placed round my neck with trembling fingers by the hangman, who took particular care to keep beyond the range of my teeth. Half-a-dozen dragoons seized the further end of the coil, and stood ready to swing me into eternity. Through all my adventurous life I have never been so close upon the threshold of death as at that moment, and yet I declare to you that, terrible as my position was, I could think of nothing but the tattoo marks upon old Solomon Sprent's arm, and the cunning fashion in which he had interwoven the red and the blue. Yet I was keenly alive to all that was going on around me. The scene of the bleak stone-floored room, the single narrow window, the two lounging elegant officers, the pile of arms in the corner, and even the texture of the coarse red serge and the patterns of the great brass buttons upon the sleeve of the man who held me, are all stamped clearly upon my mind.

" We must do our work with order," remarked the

435

taller Captain, taking a note-book from his pocket. " Colonel Sarsfield may desire some details. Let me see ! This is the seventeenth, is it not ? "

" Four at the farm and five at the cross-roads," the other answered, counting upon his fingers. " Then there was the one whom we shot in the hedge, and the wounded one who nearly saved himself by dying, and the two in the grove under the hill. I can remember no more, save those who were strung up in Bridgewater immediately after the action."

" It is well to do it in an orderly fashion," quoth the other, scribbling in his book. " It is very well for Kirke and his men, who are half Moors themselves, to hang and to slaughter without discrimination or ceremony, but we should set them a better example. What is your name, sirrah ? "

" My name is Captain Micah Clarke," I answered.

The two officers looked at each other, and the smaller one gave a long whistle. " It is the very man ! " said he. " This comes of asking questions ! Rat me, if I had not misgivings that it might prove to be so. They said that he was large of limb."

" Tell me, sirrah, have you ever known one Major Ogilvy of the Horse Guards Blue ? " asked the Captain.

" Seeing that I had the honour of taking him prisoner," I replied, " and seeing also that he hath shared soldier's fare and quarters with me ever since, I think I may fairly say that I do know him."

" Cast loose the cord ! " said the officer, and the hangman reluctantly slipped the cord over my head once more. " Young man, you are surely reserved for something great, for you will never be nearer your grave until you do actually step into it. This Major Ogilvy hath made great interest both for you and for a wounded comrade of yours who lies at Bridgewater. Your name hath been given to the commanders of horse, with orders to bring you in unscathed should you be taken. Yet it is but fair to tell you that though the Major's good word may

save you from martial law, it will stand you in small stead before a civil judge, before whom ye must in the end take your trial."

" I desire to share the same lot and fortune as has befallen my companions-in-arms," I answered.

" Nay, that is but a sullen way to take your deliverance," cried the smaller officer. " The situation is as flat as sutler's beer. Otway would have made a better thing of it. Can you not rise to the occasion? Where is she?"

" She! Who?" I asked.

" She. The she. The woman. Your wife, sweetheart, betrothed, what you will."

" There is none such," I answered.

" There now! What can be done in a case like that?" cried he despairingly. " She should have rushed in from the wings and thrown herself upon your bosom. I have seen such a situation earn three rounds from the pit. There is good material spoiling here for want of someone to work it up."

" We have something else to work up, Jack," exclaimed his companion impatiently. " Sergeant Gredder, do you with two troopers conduct the prisoner to Gommatch Church. It is time that we were once more upon our way, for in a few hours the darkness will hinder the pursuit."

At the word of command the troopers descended into the field where their horses were picketed, and were speedily on the march once more, the tall Captain leading them, and the stage-struck cornet bringing up the rear. The sergeant to whose care I had been committed—a great square-shouldered, dark-browed man—ordered my own horse to be brought out, and helped me to mount it. He removed the pistols from the holsters, however, and hung them with my sword at his own saddle-bow.

" Shall I tie his feet under the horse's belly?" asked one of the dragoons.

" Nay, the lad hath an honest face," the sergeant answered. " If he promises to be quiet we shall cast free his arms."

" I have no desire to escape," said I.

" Then untie the rope. A brave man in misfortune hath ever my goodwill, strike me dumb else ! Sergeant Gredder is my name, formerly of Mackay's and now of the Royals—as hard-worked and badly-paid a man as any in his Majesty's service. Right wheel, and down the pathway ! Do ye ride on either side, and I behind ! Our carbines are primed, friend, so stand true to your promise ! "

" Nay, you can rely upon it," I answered.

" Your little comrade did play you a scurvy trick," said the sergeant, " for seeing us ride down the road he did make across to us, and bargained with the Captain that his life should be spared, on condition that he should deliver into our hands what he described as one of the stoutest soldiers in the rebel army. Truly you have thews and sinews enough, though you are surely too young to have seen much service."

" This hath been my first campaign," I answered.

" And is like to be your last," he remarked, with soldierly frankness. " I hear that the Privy Council intend to make such an example as will take the heart out of the Whigs for twenty years to come. They have a lawyer coming from London whose wig is more to be feared than our helmets. He will slay more men in a day than a troop of horse in a ten-mile chase. Faith ! I would sooner they took this butcher-work into their own hands. See those bodies on yonder tree. It is an evil season when such acorns grow upon English oaks."

" It is an evil season," said I, " when men who call themselves Christians inflict such vengeance upon poor simple peasants, who have done no more than their conscience urged them. That the leaders and officers should suffer is but fair. They stood to win in case of success, and should pay forfeit now that they have lost. But it goes to my heart to see those poor godly country folk so treated."

" Aye, there is truth in that," said the sergeant. " Now

if it were some of these snuffle-nosed preachers, the old lank-haired bell-wethers who have led their flocks to the devil, it would be another thing. Why can they not conform to the Church, and be plagued to them ? It is good enough for the King, so surely it is good enough for them ; or are their souls so delicate that they cannot satisfy themselves with that on which every honest Englishman thrives ? The main road to Heaven is too common for them. They must needs have each a bypath of their own, and cry out against all who will not follow it."

"Why," said I, "there are pious men of all creeds. If a man lead a life of virtue, what matter what he believes ? "

" Let a man keep his virtue in his heart," quoth Sergeant Gredder. " Let him pack it deep in the knapsack of his soul. I suspect godliness which shows upon the surface, the snuffling talk, the rolling eyes, the groaning and the hawking. It is like the forged money, which can be told by its being more bright and more showy than the real."

" An apt comparison ! " said I. " But how comes it, sergeant, that you have given attention to these matters ? Unless they are much belied, the Royal Dragoons find other things to think of."

" I was one of Mackay's foot," he answered shortly.

" I have heard of him," said I. " A man, I believe, both of parts and of piety."

" That, indeed, he is," cried Sergeant Gredder warmly. " He is a man stern and soldierly to the outer eye, but with the heart of a saint within him. I promise you there was little need of the strapado in his regiment, for there was not a man who did not fear the look of sorrow in his Colonel's eyes far more than he did the provost-marshal."

During the whole of our long ride I found the worthy sergeant a true follower of the excellent Colonel Mackay, for he proved to be a man of more than ordinary intelligence, and of serious and thoughtful habit. As to the two troopers, they rode on either side of me as silent as statues ; for the common dragoons of those days could

but talk of wine and women, and were helpless and speechless when aught else was to the fore. When we at last rode into the little village of Gommatch, which overlooks the plain of Sedgemoor, it was with regret on each side that I bade my guardian adieu. As a parting favour I begged him to take charge of Covenant for me, promising to pay a certain sum by the month for his keep, and commissioning him to retain the horse for his own use should I fail to claim him within the year. It was a load off my mind when I saw my trusty companion led away, staring back at me with questioning eyes, as though unable to understand the separation. Come what might, I knew now that he was in the keeping of a good man who would see that no harm befell him.

34. *Of the Coming of Solomon Sprent*

THE church of Gommatch was a small ivy-clad building with a square Norman tower, standing in the centre of the hamlet of that name. Its great oaken doors, studded with iron, and high narrow windows, fitted it well for the use to which it was now turned. Two companies of Dumbarton's Foot had been quartered in the village, with a portly major at their head, to whom I was handed over by Sergeant Gredder, with some account of my capture, and of the reasons which had prevented my summary execution.

Night was now drawing in, but a few dim lamps, hung here and there upon the walls, cast an uncertain, flickering light over the scene. A hundred or more prisoners were scattered about upon the stone floor, many of them wounded, and some evidently dying. The hale had gathered in silent, subdued groups round their stricken friends, and were doing what they could to lessen their sufferings. Some had even removed the greater part of their clothing in order to furnish head-rests and pallets for the wounded. Here and there in the shadows dark

kneeling figures might be seen, and the measured sound of their prayers rang through the aisles, with a groan now and again, or a choking gasp as some poor sufferer battled for breath. The dim yellow light streaming over the earnest pain-drawn faces, and the tattered mud-coloured figures, would have made it a fitting study for any of those Low Country painters whose pictures I saw long afterwards at The Hague.

On Thursday morning, the third day after the battle, we were all conveyed into Bridgewater, where we were confined for the remainder of the week in St. Mary's Church, the very one from the tower of which Monmouth and his commanders had inspected Feversham's position. The more we heard of the fight from the soldiers and others, the more clear it became that, but for the most unfortunate accidents, there was every chance that our night attack might have succeeded. There was scarcely a fault which a General could commit which Feversham had not been guilty of. He had thought too lightly of his enemy, and left his camp entirely open to a surprise. When the firing broke out he sprang from his couch, but failing to find his wig, he had groped about his tent while the battle was being decided, and only came out when it was well-nigh over. All were agreed that had it not been for the chance of the Bussex Rhine having been over-looked by our guides and scouts, we should have been among the tents before the men could have been called to arms. Only this and the fiery energy of John Churchill, the second in command, afterwards better known under a higher name, both to French and to English history, prevented the Royal army from meeting with a reverse which might have altered the result of the campaign.[1] Should ye hear or read, then, my dear children, that Monmouth's rising was easily put down, or that it was hopeless from the first, remember that I, who was concerned in it, say confidently that it really trembled in the balance, and that this handful of resolute peasants

[1] Note K, Appendix.—Ferguson's Account.

with their pikes and their scythes were within an ace of altering the whole course of English history. The ferocity of the Privy Council, after the rebellion was quelled, arose from their knowledge of how very close it had been to success.

I do not wish to say too much of the cruelty and barbarity of the victors, for it is not good for your childish ears to hear of such doings. The sluggard Feversham and the brutal Kirke have earned themselves a name in the West, which is second only to that of the arch villain who came after them. As for their victims, when they had hanged and quartered and done their wicked worst upon them, at least they left their names in their own little villages, to be treasured up and handed from generation to generation, as brave men and true who had died for a noble cause. Go now to Milverton, or to Wiveliscombe, or to Minehead, or to Colyford, or to any village through the whole breadth and length of Somersetshire, and you will find that they have not forgotten what they proudly call their martyrs. But where now is Kirke and where is Feversham ? Their names are preserved, it is true, but preserved in a county's hatred. Who can fail to see now that these men in punishing others brought a far heavier punishment upon themselves ? Their sin hath indeed found them out.

They did all that wicked and callous-hearted men could do, knowing well that such deeds were acceptable to the cold-blooded, bigoted hypocrite who sat upon the throne. They worked to win his favour, and they won it. Men were hanged and cut down and hanged again. Every cross-road in the country was ghastly with gibbets. There was not an insult or a contumely which might make the pangs of death more unendurable, which was not heaped upon these long-suffering men ; yet it is proudly recounted in their native shire that of all the host of victims there was not one who did not meet his end with a firm lip, protesting that if the thing were to do again he was ready to do it.

At the end of a week or two news came of the fugitives. Monmouth, it seems, had been captured by Portman's yellow-coats when trying to make his way to the New Forest, whence he hoped to escape to the Continent. He was dragged, gaunt, unshaven and trembling, out of a bean-field in which he had taken refuge, and was carried to Ringwood, in Hampshire. Strange rumours reached us concerning his behaviour—rumours which came to our ears through the coarse jests of our guards. Some said that he had gone on his knees to the yokels who had seized him. Others that he had written to the King offering to do anything, even to throw over the Protestant cause, to save his head from the scaffold.[1] We laughed at these stories at the time, and set them down as inventions of our enemies. It seemed too impossible that, at a time when his supporters were so sternly and so loyally standing true to him, he, their leader, with the eyes of all men upon him, should be showing less courage than every little drummer-boy displays, who trips along at the head of his regiment upon the field of battle. Alas ! time showed that the stories were indeed true, and that there was no depth of infamy to which this unhappy man would not descend, in the hope of prolonging for a few years that existence which had proved a curse to so many who trusted him.

Of Saxon no news had come, good or bad, which encouraged me to hope that he had found a hiding-place for himself. Reuben was still confined to his couch by his wound, and was under the care and protection of Major Ogilvy. The good gentleman came to see me more than once, and endeavoured to add to my comfort, until I made him understand that it pained me to find myself upon a different footing to the brave fellows with whom I had shared the perils of the campaign. One great favour he did me in writing to my father, and informing him that I was well and in no pressing danger. In reply to this letter I had a stout Christian answer from

---

[1] Note L, Appendix.—Monmouth's attitude.

the old man, bidding me to be of good courage, and quoting largely from a sermon on patience by the Reverend Josiah Seaton of Petersfield. My mother, he said, was in deep distress at my position, but was held up by her confidence in the decrees of Providence. He enclosed a draft for Major Ogilvy, commissioning him to use it in whatever way I should suggest. This money, together with the small hoard which my mother had sewed into my collar, proved to be invaluable, for when the gaol fever broke out amongst us I was able to get fitting food for the sick, and also to pay for the services of physicians, so that the disease was stamped out ere it had time to spread.

Early in August we were brought from Bridgewater to Taunton, where we were thrown with hundreds of others into the same wool storehouse where our regiment had been quartered in the early days of the campaign. We gained little by the change, save that we found that our new guards were somewhat more satiated with cruelty than our old ones, and were therefore less exacting upon their prisoners. Not only were friends allowed in occasionally to see us, but books and papers could be obtained by the aid of a small present to the sergeant on duty. We were able, therefore, to spend our time with some degree of comfort during the month or more which passed before our trial.

One evening I was standing listlessly with my back against the wall, looking up at a thin slit of blue sky which showed itself through the narrow window, and fancying myself back in the meadows of Havant once more, when a voice fell upon my ear which did, indeed, recall me to my Hampshire home. Those deep, husky tones, rising at times into an angry roar, could belong to none other than my old friend the seaman. I approached the door from which the uproar came, and all doubt vanished as I listened to the conversation.

" Won't let me pass, won't ye ? " he was shouting. " Let me tell you I've held on my course when better

men than you have asked me to veil topsails. I tell you I have the admiral's permit, and I won't clew up for a bit of a red-painted cockboat ; so move from athwart my hawse, or I may chance to run you down."

" We don't know nothing about admirals here," said the sergeant of the guard. " The time for seeing prisoners is over for the day, and if you do not take your ill-favoured body out of this I may try the weight o' my halberd on your back."

" I have taken blows and given them ere you were ever thought of, you land-swab," roared old Solomon. " I was yardarm and yardarm with De Ruyter when you were learning to suck milk ; but, old as I am, I would have you know that I am not condemned yet, and that I am fit to exchange broadsides with any lobster-tailed piccaroon that ever was triced up to a triangle and had the King's diamonds cut in his back. If I tack back to Major Ogilvy and signal him the way that I have been welcomed, he'll make your hide redder than ever your coat was."

" Major Ogilvy ! " exclaimed the sergeant, in a more respectful voice. " If you had said that your permit was from Major Ogilvy it would have been another thing, but you did rave of admirals and commodores, and God knows what other outlandish talk ! "

" Shame on your parents that they should have reared you with so slight a knowledge o' the King's English ! " grumbled Solomon. " In truth, friend, it is a marvel to me why sailor men should be able to show a lead to those on shore in the matter of lingo. For out of seven hundred men in the ship *Worcester*—the same that sank in the Bay of Funchal—there was not so much as a powder-boy but could understand every word that I said, whereas on shore there is many a great jolterhead, like thyself, who might be a Portugee for all the English that he knows, and who stares at me like a pig in a hurricane if I do but ask him what he makes the reckoning, or how many bells have gone."

" Whom is it that you would see ? " asked the sergeant gruffly. " You have a most infernally long tongue."

" Aye, and a rough one, too, when I have fools to deal with," returned the seaman. " If I had you in my watch, lad, for a three years' cruise, I would make a man of you yet."

" Pass the old man through ! " cried the sergeant furiously, and the sailor came stumping in, with his bronzed face all screwed up and twisted, partly with amusement at his victory over the sergeant, and partly from a great chunk of tobacco which he was wont to stow within his cheek. Having glanced round without perceiving me, he put his hands to his mouth and bellowed out my name, with a string of " Ahoys ! " which rang through the building.

" Here I am, Solomon," said I, touching him on the shoulder.

" God bless you, lad ! God bless you ! " he cried, wringing my hand. " I could not see you, for my port eye is as foggy as the Newfoundland banks, and has been ever since Long Sue Williams of the Point hove a quart pot at it in the Tiger inn nigh thirty year agone. How are you ? All sound, alow and aloft ? "

" As well as might be," I answered. " I have little to complain of."

" None of your standing rigging shot away ? " said he. " No spars crippled ? No shots between wind and water, eh ? You have not been hulled, nor raked, nor laid aboard of ? "

" None of these things," said I, laughing.

" Faith ! you are leaner than of old, and have aged ten years in two months. You did go forth as smart and trim a fighting ship as ever answered helm, and now you are like the same ship when the battle and the storm have taken the gloss from her sides and torn the love-pennants from her peak. Yet am I right glad to see you sound in wind and limb."

" I have looked upon sights," said I, " which might well add ten years to a man's age."

" Aye, aye ! " he answered, with a hollow groan, shaking his head from side to side. " It is a most accursed affair. Yet, bad as the tempest is, the calm will ever come afterwards if you will but ride it out with your anchor placed deep in Providence. Ah, lad, that is good holding ground ! But if I know you aright, your grief is more for these poor wretches around you than for yourself."

" It is, indeed, a sore sight to see them suffer so patiently and uncomplainingly," I answered, " and for such a man, too ! "

" Aye, the chicken-livered swab ! " growled the seaman, grinding his teeth.

" How are my mother and my father," I asked, " and how came you so far from home ? "

" Nay, I should have grounded on my beef bones had I waited longer at my moorings. I cut my cable, therefore, and, making a northerly tack as far as Salisbury, I ran down with a fair wind. Thy father hath set his face hard, and goes about his work as usual, though much troubled by the Justices, who have twice had him up to Winchester for examination, but have found his papers all right and no charge to be brought against him. Your mother, poor soul, hath little time to mope or to pipe her eye, for she hath such a sense of duty that, were the ship to founder under her, it is a plate galleon to a china orange that she would stand fast in the caboose curing marigolds or rolling pastry. They have taken to prayer as some would to rum, and warm their hearts with it when the wind of misfortune blows chill. They were right glad that I should come down to you, and I gave them the word of a sailor that I would get you out of the bilboes if it might anyhow be done."

" Get me out, Solomon ! " said I ; " nay, that may be put outside the question. How could you get me out ? "

" There are many ways," he answered, sinking his voice to a whisper, and nodding his grizzled head as one

who talks upon what has cost him much time and thought.
" There is scuttling."

" Scuttling ? "

" Aye, lad ! When I was quartermaster of the galley
Providence in the second Dutch war, we were caught
betwixt a lee shore and Van Tromp's squadron, so that
after fighting until our sticks were shot away and our
scuppers were arun with blood, we were carried by
boarding- and sent as prisoners to the Texel. We were
stowed away in irons in the afterhold, amongst the bilge
water and the rats, with hatches battened down and
guards atop, but even then they could not keep us, for the
irons got adrift, and Will Adams, the carpenter's mate,
picked a hole in the seams so that the vessel nearly
foundered, and in the confusion we fell upon the prize
crew, and, using our fetters as cudgels, regained possession
of the vessel. But you smile, as though there were little
hopes from any such plan ! "

" If this wool-house were the galley *Providence* and
Taunton Deane were the Bay of Biscay, it might be
attempted," I said.

" I have indeed got out o' the channel," he answered,
with a wrinkled brow. " There is, however, another most
excellent plan which I have conceived, which is to blow
up the building."

" To blow it up ! " I cried.

" Aye ! A brace of kegs and a slow match would do it
any dark night. Then where would be these walls which
now shut ye in ? "

" Where would be the folk that are now inside them ? "
I asked. " Would you not blow them up as well ? "

" Plague take it, I had forgot that," cried Solomon.
" Nay, then, I leave it with you. What have you to
propose ? Do but give your sailing orders, and, with or
without a consort, you will find that I will steer by them
as long as this old hulk can answer to her helm."

" Then my advice is, my dear old friend," said I, " that
you leave matters to take their course, and hie back to

Havant with a message from me to those who know me,
telling them to be of good cheer, and to hope for the best.
Neither you nor any other man can help me now, for I
have thrown in my lot with these poor folk, and I would
not leave them if I could. Do what you can to cheer my
mother's heart, and commend me to Zachary Palmer.
Your visit hath been a joy to me, and your return will be
the same to them. You can serve me better so than by
biding here."

" Sink me if I like going back without a blow struck,"
he growled. " Yet if it is your will there is an end of the
matter. Tell me, lad. Has that lank-sparred, slab-
sided, herring-gutted friend of yours played you false ?
for if he has, by the eternal, old as I am, my hanger shall
scrape acquaintance with the longshore tuck which hangs
at his girdle. I know where he hath laid himself up,
moored stem and stern, all snug and shipshape, waiting
for the turn of the tide."

" What, Saxon ! " I cried. " Do you indeed know
where he is ? For God's sake speak low, for it would
mean a commission and five hundred good pounds to any
one of these soldiers could he lay hands upon him."

" They are scarce like to do that," said Solomon. " On
my journey hither I chanced to put into port at a place
called Bruton, where there is an inn that will compare
with most, and the skipper is a wench with a glib tongue
and a merry eye. I was drinking a glass of spiced ale, as
is my custom about six bells of the middle watch, when
I chanced to notice a great lanky carter, who was loading
up a waggon in the yard with a cargo o' beer casks. Looking closer it seemed to me that the man's nose, like the
beak of a goshawk, and his glinting eyes with the lids only
half-reefed, were known to me, but when I overheard him
swearing to himself in good High Dutch, then his figure-
head came back to me in a moment. I put out into the
yard, and touched him on the shoulder. Zounds, lad !
you should have seen him spring back and spit at me like a
wildcat with every hair of his head in a bristle. He

whipped a knife from under his smock, for he thought, doubtless, that I was about to earn the reward by handing him over to the red-coats. I told him that his secret was safe with me, and I asked him if he had heard that you were laid by the heels. He answered that he knew it, and that he would be answerable that no harm befell you, though in truth it seemed to me that he had his hands full in trimming his own sails, without acting as pilot to another. However, there I left him, and there I shall find him again if so be as he has done you an injury."

" Nay," I answered, " I am right glad that he has found this refuge. We did separate upon a difference of opinion, but I have no cause to complain of him. In many ways he hath shown me both kindness and good-will."

" He is as crafty as a purser's clerk," quoth Solomon. " I have seen Reuben Lockarby, who sends his love to you. He is still kept in his bunk from his wound, but he meets with good treatment. Major Ogilvy tells me that he has made such interest for him that there is every chance that he will gain his discharge, the more particularly since he was not present at the battle. Your own chance of pardon would, he thinks, be greater if you had fought less stoutly, but you have marked yourself as a dangerous man, more especially as you have the love of many of the common folk among the rebels."

The good old seaman stayed with me until late in the night, listening to my adventures, and narrating in return the simple gossip of the village, which is of more interest to the absent wanderer than the rise and fall of empires. Before he left he drew a great handful of silver pieces from his pouch, and went round amongst the prisoners, listening to their wants, and doing what he could with rough sailor talk and dropping coins to lighten their troubles. There is a language in the kindly eye and the honest brow which all men may understand ; and though the seaman's speeches might have been in Greek, for all that they conveyed to the Somersetshire peasants, yet

they crowded round him as he departed and called blessings upon his head. I felt as though he had brought a whiff of his own pure ocean breezes into our close and noisome prison, and left us the sweeter and the healthier.

Late in August the judges started from London upon that wicked journey which blighted the lives and the homes of so many, and hath left a memory in the counties through which they passed which shall never fade while a father can speak to a son. We heard reports of them from day to day, for the guards took pleasure in detailing them with many coarse and foul jests, that we might know what was in store for us, and lose none of what they called the pleasures of anticipation. At Winchester the sainted and honoured Lady Alice Lisle was sentenced by Chief Justice Jeffreys to be burned alive, and the exertions and prayers of her friends could scarce prevail upon him to allow her the small boon of the axe instead of the faggot. Her graceful head was hewn from her body amidst the groans and the cries of a weeping multitude in the market-place of the town. At Dorchester the slaughter was wholesale. Three hundred were condemned to death, and seventy-four were actually executed, until the most loyal and Tory of the country squires had to complain of the universal presence of the dangling bodies. Thence the judges proceeded to Exeter and thence to Taunton, which they reached in the first week of September, more like furious and ravenous beasts which have tasted blood and cannot quench their cravings for slaughter, than just-minded men, trained to distinguish the various degrees of guilt, or to pick out the innocent and screen him from injustice. A rare field was open for their cruelty, for in Taunton alone there lay a thousand hapless prisoners, many of whom were so little trained to express their thoughts, and so hampered by the strange dialect in which they spoke, that they might have been born dumb for all the chance they had of making either judge or counsel understand the pleadings which they wished to lay before them.

It was on a Monday evening that the Lord Chief Justice made his entry. From one of the windows of the room in which we were confined I saw him pass. First rode the dragoons with their standards and kettledrums, then the javelin-men with their halberds, and behind them the line of coaches full of the high dignitaries of the law. Last of all, drawn by six long-tailed Flemish mares, came a great open coach, thickly crusted with gold, in which, reclining amidst velvet cushions, sat the infamous Judge, wrapped in a cloak of crimson plush with a heavy white periwig upon his head, which was so long that it dropped down over his shoulders. They say that he wore scarlet in order to strike terror into the hearts of the people, and that his courts were for the same reason draped in the colour of blood. As for himself, it hath ever been the custom, since his wickedness hath come to be known to all men, to picture him as a man whose expression and features were as monstrous and as hideous as was the mind behind them. This is by no means the case. On the contrary, he was a man who, in his younger days, must have been remarkable for his extreme beauty.[1] He was not, it is true, very old, as years go, when I saw him, but debauchery and low living had left their traces upon his countenance, without, however, entirely destroying the regularity and the beauty of his features. He was dark, more like a Spaniard than an Englishman, with black eyes and olive complexion. His expression was lofty and noble, but his temper was so easily aflame that the slightest cross or annoyance would set him raving like a madman, with blazing eyes and foaming mouth. I have seen him myself with the froth upon his lips and his whole face twitching with passion, like one who hath the falling sickness. Yet his other emotions were under as little control, for I have heard say that a very little would cause him to sob and to weep, more especially

---

[1] The painting of Jeffreys in the National Portrait Gallery more than bears out Micah Clarke's remarks. He is the handsomest man in the collection.

when he had himself been slighted by those who were above him. He was, I believe, a man who had great powers either for good or for evil, but by pandering to the darker side of his nature and neglecting the other, he brought himself to be as near a fiend as it is possible for a man to be. It must indeed have been an evil government where so vile and foul-mouthed a wretch was chosen out to hold the scales of justice. As he drove past, a Tory gentleman riding by the side of his coach drew his attention to the faces of the prisoners looking out at him. He glanced up at them with a quick, malicious gleam of his white teeth, then settled down again amongst the cushions. I observed that as he passed not a hat was raised among the crowd, and that even the rude soldiers appeared to look upon him half in terror, half in disgust, as a lion might look upon some foul, blood-sucking bat which battened upon the prey which he had himself struck down.

35. *Of the Devil in Wig and Gown*

THERE was no delay in the work of slaughter. That very night the great gallows was erected outside the White Hart inn. Hour after hour we could hear the blows of mallets and the sawing of beams, mingled with the shoutings and the ribald choruses of the Chief Justice's suite, who were carousing with the officers of the Tangiers regiment in the front room, which overlooked the gibbet. Amongst the prisoners the night was passed in prayer and meditation, the stout-hearted holding forth to their weaker brethren, and exhorting them to play the man, and to go to their death in a fashion which should be an example to true Protestants throughout the world. The Puritan divines had been mostly strung up off-hand immediately after the battle, but a few were left to sustain the courage of their flocks, and to show them the way upon the scaffold. Never have I

seen anything so admirable as the cool and cheerful bravery wherewith these poor clowns faced their fate. Their courage on the battlefield paled before that which they showed in the shambles of the law. So amid the low murmur of prayer and appeals for mercy to God from tongues which never yet asked mercy from man, the morning broke, the last morning which many of us were to spend upon earth.

The court should have opened at nine, but my Lord Chief Justice was indisposed, having sat up somewhat late with Colonel Kirke. It was nearly eleven before the trumpeters and criers announced that he had taken his seat. One by one my fellow-prisoners were called out by name, the more prominent being chosen first. They went out from amongst us amid handshakings and blessings, but we saw and heard no more of them, save that a sudden fierce rattle of kettledrums would rise up now and again, which was, as our guards told us, to drown any dying words which might fall from the sufferers and bear fruit in the breasts of those who heard them. With firm steps and smiling faces the roll of marytrs went forth to their fate during the whole of that long autumn day, until the rough soldiers of the guard stood silent and awed in the presence of a courage which they could not but recognise as higher and nobler than their own. Folk may call it a trial that they received, and a trial it really was, but not in the sense that we Englishmen use it. It was but being haled before a Judge, and insulted before being dragged to the gibbet. The court-house was the thorny path which led to the scaffold. What use to put a witness up, when he was shouted down, cursed at, and threatened by the Chief Justice, who bellowed and swore until the frightened burghers in Fore Street could hear him ? I have heard from those who were there that day that he raved like a demoniac, and that his black eyes shone with a vivid vindictive brightness which was scarce human. The jury shrank from him as from a venomous thing when he turned his baleful glance upon

them. At times, as I have been told, his sternness gave place to a still more terrible merriment, and he would lean back in his seat of justice and laugh until the tears hopped down upon his ermine. Nearly a hundred were either executed or condemned to death upon that opening day.

I had expected to be amongst the first of those called, and no doubt I should have been so but for the exertions of Major Ogilvy. As it was, the second day passed, but I still found myself overlooked. On the third and fourth days the slaughter was slackened, not on account of any awakening grace on the part of the Judge, but because the great Tory landowners, and the chief supporters of the Government, had still some bowels of compassion, which revolted at this butchery of defenceless men. Had it not been for the influence which these gentlemen brought to bear upon the Judge, I have no doubt at all that Jeffreys would have hung the whole eleven hundred prisoners then confined in Taunton. As it was, two hundred and fifty fell victims to this accursed monster's thirst for human blood.

On the eighth day of the assizes there were but fifty of us left in the wool warehouse. For the last few days prisoners had been tried in batches of ten and twenty, but now the whole of us were taken in a drove, under escort, to the courthouse, where as many as could be squeezed in were ranged in the dock, while the rest were penned, like calves in the market, in the body of the hall. The Judge reclined in a high chair, with a scarlet daïs above him, while two other Judges, in less elevated seats, were stationed on either side of him. On the right hand was the jury-box, containing twelve carefully picked men— Tories of the old school—firm upholders of the doctrines of non-resistance and the divine right of kings. Much care had been taken by the Crown in the choice of these men, and there was not one of them but would have sentenced his own father had there been so much as a suspicion that he leaned to Presbyterianism or to Whig-

gery. Just under the Judge was a broad table, covered with green cloth and strewn with papers. On the right hand of this were a long array of Crown lawyers, grim, ferret-faced men, each with a sheaf of papers in his hands, which they sniffed through again and again, as though they were so many bloodhounds picking up the trail along which they were to hunt us down. On the other side of the table sat a single fresh-faced young man, in silk gown and wig, with a nervous, shuffling manner. This was the barrister, Master Helstrop, whom the Crown in its clemency had allowed us for our defence, lest any should be bold enough to say that we had not had every fairness in our trial. The remainder of the court was filled with the servants of the Justices' retinue and the soldiers of the garrison, who used the place as their common lounge, looking on the whole thing as a mighty cheap form of sport, and roaring with laughter at the rude banter and coarse pleasantries of his Lordship.

The clerk having gabbled through the usual form that we, the prisoners at the bar, having shaken off the fear of God, had unlawfully and traitorously assembled, and so onwards, the Lord Justice proceeded to take matters into his own hands, as was his wont.

" I trust that we shall come well out of this ! " he broke out. " I trust that no judgment will fall upon this building ! Was ever so much wickedness fitted into one court-house before ? Who ever saw such an array of villainous faces ? Ah, rogues, I see a rope ready for every one of ye ! Art not afraid of judgment ? Art not afraid of hell-fire ? You grey-bearded rascal in the corner, how comes it that you have not had more of the grace of God in you than to take up arms against your most gracious and loving sovereign ? "

" I have followed the guidance of my conscience, my Lord," said the venerable cloth-worker of Wellington, to whom he spoke.

" Ha, your conscience ! " howled Jeffreys. " A ranter with a conscience ! Where has your conscience been

456

these two months back, you villain and rogue ? Your conscience will stand you in little stead, sirrah, when you are dancing on nothing with a rope round your neck. Was ever such wickedness ? Who ever heard such effrontery ? And you, you great hulking rebel, have you not grace enough to cast your eyes down, but must needs look justice in the face as though you were an honest man ? Are you not afeard, sirrah ? Do you not see death close upon you ? "

" I have seen that before now, my Lord, and I was not afeard," I answered.

" Generation of vipers ! " he cried, throwing up his hands. " The best of fathers ! The kindest of kings ! See that my words are placed upon the record, clerk ! The most indulgent of parents ! But wayward children must, with all kindness, be flogged into obedience." Here he broke into a savage grin. " The King will save your own natural parents all further care on your account. If they had wished to keep ye, they should have brought ye up in better principles. Rogues, we shall be merciful to ye—oh, merciful, merciful ! How many are here, recorder ? "

" Fifty and one, my Lord."

" Oh, sink of villainy ! Fifty and one as arrant knaves as ever lay on a hurdle ! Oh, what a mass of corruption have we here ! Who defends the villains ? "

" I defend the prisoners, your Lordship," replied the young lawyer.

" Master Helstrop, Master Helstrop ! " cried Jeffreys, shaking his great wig until the powder flew out of it ; " you are in all these dirty cases, Master Helstrop. You might find yourself in a parlous condition, Master Helstrop. I think sometimes that I see you yourself in the dock, Master Helstrop. You may yourself soon need the help of a gentleman of the long robe, Master Helstrop. Oh, have a care ! Have a care ! "

" The brief is from the Crown, your Lordship," the lawyer answered, in a quavering voice.

" Must I be answered back, then ? " roared Jeffreys, his black eyes blazing with the rage of a demon. " Am I to be insulted in my own court ? Is every five-groat piece of a pleader, because he chance to have a wig and a gown, to browbeat the Lord Justice, and to fly in the face of the ruling of the Court ? Oh, Master Helstrop, I fear that I shall live to see some evil come upon you ! "

" I crave your Lordship's pardon ! " cried the faint-hearted barrister, with his face the colour of his brief.

" Keep a guard upon your words and upon your actions ! " Jeffreys answered, in a menacing voice. " See that you are not too zealous in the cause of the scum of the earth. How now, then ? What do these one and fifty villains desire to say for themselves ? What is their lie ? Gentlemen of the jury, I beg that ye will take particular notice of the cut-throat faces of these men. 'Tis well that Colonel Kirke hath afforded the Court a sufficient guard, for neither justice nor the Church is safe at their hands."

" Forty of them desire to plead guilty to the charge of taking up arms against the King," replied our barrister.

" Ah ! " roared the Judge. " Was ever such un-paralleled impudence ? Was there ever such brazen effrontery ? Guilty, quotha ! Have they expressed their repentance for this sin against a most kind and long-suffering monarch ? Put down those words on the record, clerk ! "

" They have refused to express repentance, your Lordship ! " replied the counsel for the defence.

" Oh, the parricides ! Oh, the shameless rogues ! " cried the Judge. " Put the forty together on this side of the enclosure. Oh, gentlemen, have ye ever seen such a concentration of vice ? See how baseness and wicked-ness can stand with head erect ! Oh, hardened monsters ! But the other eleven. How can they expect us to believe this transparent falsehood—this palpable device ? How can they foist it upon the Court ? "

" My Lord, their defence hath not yet been advanced ! " stammered Master Helstrop.

" I can sniff a lie before it is uttered," roared the Judge, by no means abashed. " I can read it as quick as ye can think it. Come, come, the Court's time is precious. Put forward a defence, or seat yourself, and let judgment be passed."

" These men, my Lord," said the counsel, who was trembling until the parchment rattled in his hand. " These eleven men, my Lord——"

" Eleven devils, my Lord," interrupted Jeffreys.

" They are innocent peasants, my Lord, who love God and the King, and have in no wise mingled themselves in this recent business. They have been dragged from their homes, my Lord, not because there was suspicion against them, but because they could not satisfy the greed of certain common soldiers who were balked of plunder in——"

" Oh, shame, shame ! " cried Jeffreys, in a voice of thunder. " Oh, threefold shame, Master Helstrop ! Are you not content with bolstering up rebels, but you must go out of your way to slander the King's troops ? What is the world coming to ? What, in a word, is the defence of these rogues ? "

" An alibi, your Lordship."

" Ha ! The common plea of every scoundrel. Have they witnesses ? "

" We have here a list of forty witnesses, your Lordship. They are waiting below, many of them having come great distances, and with much toil and trouble."

" Who are they ? What are they ? " cried Jeffreys.

" They are country folk, your Lordship. Cottagers and farmers, the neighbours of these poor men, who knew them well, and can speak as to their doings."

" Cottagers and farmers ! " the Judge shouted. " Why then, they are drawn from the very class from which these men come. Would you have us believe the oath of those who are themselves Whigs, Presbyterians, Somersetshire

ranters, the pothouse companions of the men whom we are trying ? I warrant they have arranged it all snugly over their beer—snugly, snugly, the rogues ! "

" Will you not hear the witnesses, your Lordship ? " cried our counsel, shamed into some little sense of manhood by this outrage.

" Not a word from them, sirrah," said Jeffreys. " It is a question whether my duty towards my kind master the King—write down ' kind master,' clerk—doth not warrant me in placing all your witnesses in the dock as the aiders and abetters of treason."

" If it please your Lordship," cried one of the prisoners, " I have for witnesses Mr. Johnson, of Nether Stowey, who is a good Tory, and also Mr. Shepperton, the clergyman."

" The more shame to them to appear in such a cause," replied Jeffreys. " What are we to say, gentlemen of the jury, when we see county gentry and the clergy of the Established Church supporting treason and rebellion in this fashion ? Surely the last days are at hand ! You are a most malignant and dangerous Whig to have so far drawn them from their duty."

" But hear me, my Lord ! " cried one of the prisoners.

" Hear you, you bellowing calf ! " shouted the Judge. " We can hear nought else. Do you think that you are back in your conventicle, that you should dare to raise your voice in such a fashion ? Hear you, quotha ! We shall hear you at the end of a rope, ere many days."

" We scarce think, your Lordship," said one of the Crown lawyers, springing to his feet amid a great rustling of papers, " we scarce think that it is necessary for the Crown to state any case. We have already heard the whole tale of this most damnable and execrable attempt many times over. The men in the dock before your Lordship have for the most part confessed to their guilt, and of those who hold out there is not one who has given us any reason to believe that he is innocent of the foul crime laid to his charge. The gentlemen of the long

robe are therefore unanimously of opinion that the jury may at once be required to pronounce a single verdict upon the whole of the prisoners."

" Which is——? " asked Jeffreys, glancing round at the foreman—

" Guilty, your Lordship," said he, with a grin, while his brother jurymen nodded their heads and laughed to one another.

" Of course, of course ! guilty as Judas Iscariot ! " cried the Judge, looking down with exultant eyes at the throng of peasants and burghers before him. " Move them a little forwards, ushers, that I may see them to more advantage. Oh, ye cunning ones ! Are ye not taken ? Are ye not compassed around ? Where now can ye fly ? Do ye not see hell opening at your feet ? Eh ? Are ye not afraid ? Oh, short, short shall be your shrift ! " The very devil seemed to be in the man, for as he spoke he writhed with unholy laughter, and drummed his hand upon the red cushion in front of him. I glanced round at my companions, but their faces were all as though they had been chiselled out of marble. If he had hoped to see a moist eye or a quivering lip, the satisfaction was denied him.

" Had I my way," said he, " there is not one of ye but should swing for it. Aye, and if I had my way, some of those whose stomachs are too nice for this work, and who profess to serve the King with their lips while they intercede for his worst enemies, should themselves have cause to remember Taunton assizes. Oh, most ungrateful rebels ! Have ye not heard how your most soft-hearted and compassionate monarch, the best of men— put it down in the record, clerk—on the intercession of that great and charitable statesman, Lord Sunderland— mark it down, clerk—hath had pity on ye ? Hath it not melted ye ? Hath it not made ye loathe yourselves ? I declare, when I think of it "—here, with a sudden catching of the breath, he burst out a-sobbing, the tears running down his cheeks—" when I think of it, the

Christian forbearance, the ineffable mercy, it doth bring forcibly to my mind that great Judge before whom all of us—even I—shall one day have to render an account. Shall I repeat it, clerk, or have you it down ? "

" I have it down, your Lordship."

" Then write ' sobs ' in the margin. 'Tis well that the King should know our opinion on such matters. Know, then, you most traitorous and unnatural rebels, that this good father whom ye have spurned has stepped in between yourselves and the laws which ye have offended. At his command we withhold from ye the chastisement which ye have merited. If ye can indeed pray, and if your soul-cursing conventicles have not driven all grace out of ye, drop on your knees and offer up thanks when I tell ye that he hath ordained that ye shall all have a free pardon." Here the Judge rose from his seat as though about to descend from the tribunal, and we gazed upon each other in the utmost astonishment at this most unlooked-for end to the trial. The soldiers and lawyers were equally amazed, while a hum of joy and applause rose up from the few country folk who had dared to venture within the accursed precincts.

" This pardon, however," continued Jeffreys, turning round with a malicious smile upon his face, " is coupled with certain conditions and limitations. Ye shall all be removed from here to Poole, in chains, where ye shall find a vessel awaiting ye. With others ye shall be stowed away in the hold of the said vessel, and conveyed at the King's expense to the Plantations, there to be sold as slaves. God send ye masters who will know by the free use of wood and leather to soften your stubborn thoughts and incline your mind to better things." He was again about to withdraw, when one of the Crown lawyers whispered something across to him.

" Well thought of, coz," cried the Judge. " I had forgot. Bring back the prisoners, ushers ! Perhaps ye think that by the Plantations I mean his Majesty's American dominions. Unhappily, there are too many of

your breed in that part already. Ye would fall among friends who might strengthen ye in your evil courses, and so risk your salvation. To send ye there would be to add one brand to another and yet hope to put out the fire. By the Plantations, therefore, I mean Barbadoes and the Indies, where ye shall live with the other slaves, whose skins may be blacker than yours, but I dare warrant that their souls are more white." With this concluding speech the trial ended, and we were led back through the crowded streets to the prison from which we had been brought. On either side of the street, as we passed, we could see the limbs of former companions dangling in the wind, and their heads grinning at us from the tops of poles and pikes. No savage country in the heart of heathen Africa could have presented a more dreadful sight than did the old English town of Taunton when Jeffreys and Kirke had the ordering of it. There was death in the air, and the townsfolk crept silently about, scarcely daring to wear black for those whom they had loved and lost, lest it should be twisted into an act of treason.

We were scarce back in the wool-house once more when a file of guards with a sergeant entered, escorting a long, pale-faced man with protruding teeth, whose bright blue coat and white silk breeches, gold-headed sword and glancing shoe-buckles, proclaimed him to be one of those London exquisites whom interest or curiosity had brought down to the scene of the rebellion. He tripped along upon his tiptoes like a French dancing-master, waving his scented kerchief in front of his thin high nose, and inhaling aromatic salts from a blue phial which he carried in his left hand.

" By the Lard !" he cried, " but the stench of these filthy wretches is enough to stap one's breath. It is, by the Lard ! Smite my vitals if I would venture among them if I were not a very rake hell. Is there a danger of prison fever, sergeant ? Heh ? "

" They are all sound as roaches, your honour," said the under-officer, touching his cap.

" Heh, heh ! " cried the exquisite, with a shrill treble laugh. " It is not often ye have a visit from a person of quality, I'll warrant. It is business, sergeant, business ! ' Auri sacra fames '—you remember what Virgilius Maro says, sergeant ? "

" Never heard the gentleman speak, sir—at least not to my knowledge, sir," said the sergeant.

" Heh, heh ! Never heard him speak, heh ? That will do for Slaughter's, sergeant. That will set them all in a titter at Slaughter's. Pink my soul ! but when I venture on a story the folk complain that they can't get served, for the drawers laugh until there is no work to be got out of them. Oh, lay me bleeding, but these are a filthy and most ungodly crew ! Let the musqueteers stand close, sergeant, lest they fly at me."

" We shall see to that, your honour."

" I have a grant of a dozen of them, and Captain Pogram hath offered me twelve pounds a head. But they must be brawny rogues—strong and brawny, for the voyage kills many, sergeant, and the climate doth also tell upon them. Now here is one whom I must have. Yes, in very truth he is a young man, and hath much life in him and much strength. Tick him off, sergeant, tick him off ! "

" His name is Clarke," said the soldier. " I have marked him down."

" If this is the clerk I would I had a parson to match him," cried the fop, sniffing at his bottle. " Do you see the pleasantry, sergeant. Heh, heh ! Does your sluggish mind rise to the occasion ? Strike me purple, but I am in excellent fettle ! There is yonder man with the brown face, you can mark him down. And the young man beside him, also. Tick him off. Ha, he waves his hand towards me ! Stand firm, sergeant ! Where are my salts ? What is it, man, what is it ? "

" If it plaize your han'r," said the young peasant, " if so be as you have chose me to be of a pairty, I trust that you will allow my vaither yander to go with us also."

" Pshaw, pshaw ! " cried the fop, " you are beyond reason, you are indeed ! Who ever heard of such a thing ? Honour forbids it ! How could I foist an old man upon mine honest friend, Captain Pogram. Fie, fie ! Split me asunder if he would not say that I had choused him ! There is yonder lusty fellow with the red head, sergeant ! The blacks will think he is a-fire. Those, and these six stout yokels, will make up my dozen."

" You have indeed the pick of them," said the sergeant.

" Aye, sink me, but I have a quick eye for horse, man or woman ! I'll pick the best of a batch with most. Twelve twelves, close on a hundred and fifty pieces, sergeant, and all for a few words, my friend, all for a few words. I did but send my wife, a demmed handsome woman, mark you, and dresses in the mode, to my good friend the secretary to ask for some rebels. ' How many ? ' says he. ' A dozen will do,' says she. It was all done in a penstroke. What a cursed fool she was not to have asked for a hundred ! But what is this, sergeant, what is this ? "

A small, brisk, pippin-faced fellow in a riding-coat and high boots had come clanking into the wool-house with much assurance and authority, with a great old-fashioned sword trailing behind him, and a riding-whip switching in his hand.

" Morning, sergeant ! " said he, in a loud, overbearing voice. " You may have heard my name ? I am Master John Wooton, of Langmere House, near Dulverton, who bestirred himself so for the King, and hath been termed by Mr. Godolphin, in the House of Commons, one of the local pillars of the State. Those were his words. Fine, were they not ? Pillars, mark ye, the conceit being that the State was, as it were, a palace or a temple, and the loyal men so many pillars, amongst whom I also was one. I am a local pillar. I have received a Royal permit, sergeant, to choose from amongst your prisoners ten sturdy rogues whom I may sell as a reward to me for my exertions. Draw them up, therefore, that I may make my choice ! "

" Then, sir, we are upon the same errand," quoth the Londoner, bowing with his hand over his heart, until his sword seemed to point straight up to the ceiling. " The Honourable George Dawnish, at your service ! Your very humble and devoted servant, sir ! Yours to command in any or all ways. It is a real joy and privilege to me, sir, to make your distinguished acquaintance. Hem ! "

The country squire appeared to be somewhat taken aback at this shower of London compliments. " Ahem, sir ! Yes, sir ! " said he, bobbing his head. " Glad to see you, sir ! Most damnably so ! But these men, sergeant ? Time presses, for to-morrow is Shepton market, and I would fain see my old twenty-score boar once more before he is sold. There is a beefy one. I'll have him."

" Ged, I've forestalled you," cried the courtier. " Sink me, but it gives me real pain. He is mine."

" Then this," said the other, pointing with his whip.

" He is mine, too. Heh, heh, heh ! Strike me stiff, but this is too funny ! "

" Od's wounds ! How many are yours ? " cried the Dulverton squire.

" A dozen. Heh, heh ! A round dozen. All those who stand upon this side. Pink me, but I have got the best of you there ! The early bird—you know the old saw ? "

" It is a disgrace," the squire cried hotly. " A shame and a disgrace. We must needs fight for the King and risk our skins, and then when all is done, down come a drove of lacqueys in waiting, and snap up the pickings before their betters are served."

" Lacqueys in waiting, sir ! " shrieked the exquisite. " S'death, sir ! This toucheth mine honour very nearly ! I have seen blood flow, yes, sir, and wounds gape on less provocation. Retract, sir, retract ! "

" Away, you clothes-pole ! " cried the other contemptuously. " You are come like the other birds of

carrion when the fight is o'er. Have you been named in full Parliament ? Are you a local pillar ? Away, away, you tailor's dummy ! "

" You insolent clodhopper ! " cried the fop. " You most foul-mouthed bumpkin ! The only local pillar that you have ever deserved to make acquaintance with is the whipping-post. Ha, sergeant, he lays his hand upon his sword ! Stop him, sergeant, stop him, or I may do him an injury."

" Nay, gentlemen," cried the under-officer. " This quarrel must not continue here. We must have no brawling within the prison. Yet there is a level turf without, and as fine elbow-room as a gentleman could wish for a breather."

This proposal did not appear to commend itself to either of the angry gentlemen, who proceeded to exchange the length of their swords, and to promise that each should hear from the other before sunset. Our owner, as I may call him, the fop, took his departure at last, and the country squire having chosen the next ten swaggered off, cursing the courtiers, the Londoners, the sergeant, the prisoners, and above all, the ingratitude of the Government which had made him so small a return for his exertions. This was but the first of many such scenes, for the Government, in endeavouring to satisfy the claims of its supporters, had promised many more than there were prisoners. I am grieved to say that I have seen not only men, but even my own countrywomen, and ladies of title to boot, wringing their hands and bewailing themselves because they were unable to get any of the poor Somersetshire folk to sell as slaves. Indeed, it was only with difficulty that they could be made to see that their claim upon Government did not give them the right of seizing any burgher or peasant who might come in their way, and shipping him right off for the Plantations.

Well, my dear grandchildren, from night to night through this long and weary winter I have taken you back with me into the past, and made you see scenes the

players in which are all beneath the turf, save that perhaps here and there some greybeard like myself may have a recollection of them. I understand that you, Joseph, have every morning set down upon paper that which I have narrated the night before. It is as well that you should do so, for your own children and your children's children may find it of interest, and even perhaps take a pride in hearing that their ancestors played a part in such scenes. But now the spring is coming, and the green is bare of snow, so that there are better things for you to do than to sit listening to the stories of a garrulous old man. Nay, nay, you shake your heads, but indeed those young limbs want exercising and strengthening and knitting together, which can never come from sitting toasting round the blaze. Besides, my story draws quickly to an end now, for I had never intended to tell you more than the events connected with the Western rising. If the closing part hath been of the dreariest, and if all doth not wind up with the ringing of bells and the joining of hands, like the tales in the chap-books, you must blame history and not me. For Truth is a stern mistress, and when one hath once started off with her one must follow on after the jade, though she lead in flat defiance of all the rules and conditions which would fain turn that tangled wilderness the world into the trim Dutch garden of the story-tellers.

Three days after our trial we were drawn up in North Street in front of the Castle with others from the other prisons who were to share our fate. We were placed four abreast, with a rope connecting each rank, and of these ranks I counted fifty, which would bring our total to two hundred. On each side of us rode dragoons, and in front and behind were companies of musqueteers to prevent any attempt at rescue or escape. In this order we set off upon the tenth day of September, amidst the weeping and wailing of the townsfolk, many of whom saw their sons or brothers marching off into exile without their being able to exchange a last word or embrace with

them. Some of these poor folk, doddering old men and wrinkled, decrepit women, toiled for miles after us down the high-road, until the rearguard of foot faced round upon them, and drove them away with curses and blows from their ramrods.

That day we made our way through Yeovil and Sherborne, and on the morrow proceeded over the North Downs as far as Blandford, where we were penned together like cattle and left for the night. On the third day we resumed our march through Wimbourne and a line of pretty Dorsetshire villages—the last English villages which most of us were destined to see for many a long year to come. Late in the afternoon the spars and rigging of the shipping in Poole Harbour rose up before us, and in another hour we had descended the steep and craggy path which leads to the town. Here we were drawn up upon the quay opposite the broad-decked, heavy-sparred brig which was destined to carry us into slavery. Through all this march we met with the greatest kindness from the common people, who flocked out from their cottages with fruit and with milk, which they divided amongst us. At other places, at the risk of their lives, Dissenting ministers came forth and stood by the wayside, blessing us as we passed, in spite of the rough jeers and oaths of the soldiers.

We were marched aboard and led below by the mate of the vessel, a tall red-faced seaman with ear-rings in his ears, while the captain stood on the poop with his legs apart and a pipe in his mouth, checking us off one by one by means of a list which he held in his hand. As he looked at the sturdy build and rustic health of the peasants, which even their long confinement had been unable to break down, his eyes glistened, and he rubbed his big red hands together with delight.

" Show them down, Jem ! " he kept shouting to the mate. " Stow them safe, Jem ! There's lodgings for a duchess down there, s'help me, there's lodgings for a duchess ! Pack 'em away ! "

One by one we passed before the delighted captain, and down the steep ladder which led into the hold. Here we were led along a narrow passage, on either side of which opened the stalls which were prepared for us. As each man came opposite to the one set aside for him he was thrown into it by the brawny mate, and fastened down with anklets of iron by the seaman and armourer in attendance. It was dark before we were all secured, but the captain came round with lanthorn to satisfy himself that all his property was really safe. I could hear the mate and him reckoning the value of each prisoner, and counting what he would fetch in the Barbadoes market.

" Have you served out their fodder, Jem ? " he asked, flashing his light into each stall in turn. " Have you seen that they had their rations ? "

" A rye bread loaf and a pint o' water," answered the mate.

" Fit for a duchess, s'help me ! " cried the captain. " Look to this one, Jem. He is a lusty rogue. Look to his great hands. He might work for years in the rice-swamps ere the land crabs have the picking of him."

" Aye, we'll have smart bidding amid the settlers for this lot. 'Cod, captain, but you have made a bargain of it ! Od's bud ! you have done these London fools to some purpose."

" What is this ? " roared the captain. " Here is one who hath not touched his allowance. How now, sirrah, art too dainty in the stomach to eat what your betters have eaten before you ? "

" I have no hairt for food, zur," the prisoner answered.

" What, you must have your whims and fancies ! You must pick and you must choose ! I tell you, sirrah, that you are mine, body and soul ! Twelve good pieces I paid for you, and now, forsooth, I am to be told that you will not eat ! Turn to it at this instant, you saucy rogue, or I shall have you triced to the triangles ! "

" Here is another," said the mate, " who sits ever with his head sunk upon his breast without spirit or life."

" Mutinous, obstinate dog ! " cried the captain.
" What ails you then ? Why have you a face like an
underwriter in a tempest ? "

" If it plaize you, zur," the prisoner answered, " Oi do
but think o' m' ould mother at Wellington, and woonder
who will kape her now that Oi'm gone ! "

" And what is that to me ? " shouted the brutal seaman. " How can you arrive at your journey's end sound
and hearty if you sit like a sick fowl upon a perch ? Laugh,
man, and be merry, or I will give you something to weep
for. Out on you, you chicken-hearted swab, to sulk and
fret like a babe new weaned ! Have you not all that heart
could desire ? Give him a touch with the rope's-end,
Jem, if ever you do observe him fretting. It is but to
spite us that he doth it."

" If it please your honour," said a seaman, coming
hurriedly down from the deck, " there is a stranger upon
the poop who will have speech with your honour."

" What manner of man, sirrah ? "

" Surely he is a person of quality, your honour. He is
as free wi' his words as though he were the captain o' the
ship. The boatswain did but jog against him, and he
swore so woundily at him and stared at him so, wi' een
like a tiger-cat, that Job Harrison says we have shipped
the devil himsel'. The men don't like the look of him,
your honour ! "

" Who the plague can this spark be ? " said the skipper.
" Go on deck, Jem, and tell him that I am counting my
live stock, and that I shall be with him anon."

" Nay, your honour ! There will trouble come of it
unless you come up. He swears that he will not bear to
be put off, and that he must see you on the instant."

" Curse his blood, whoever he be ! " growled the seaman. " Every cock on his own dunghill. What doth
the rogue mean ? Were he the Lord High Privy Seal, I
would have him to know that I am lord of my own quarter-
deck ! " So saying, with many snorts of indignation, the
mate and the captain withdrew together up the ladder,

471

banging the heavy hatchways down as they passed through.

A single oil-lamp swinging from a beam in the centre of the gangway which led between the rows of cells was the only light which was vouchsafed us. By its yellow, murky glimmer we could dimly see the great wooden ribs of the vessel, arching up on either side of us, and crossed by the huge beams which held the deck. A grievous stench from foul bilge water poisoned the close, heavy air. Every now and then, with a squeak and a clutter, a rat would dart across the little zone of light and vanish in the gloom upon the farther side. Heavy breathing all round me showed that my companions, wearied out by their journey and their sufferings, had dropped into a slumber. From time to time one could hear the dismal clank of fetters, and the start and incatching of the breath as some poor peasant, fresh from dreams of his humble homestead amid the groves of the Mendips, awoke of a sudden to see the great wooden coffin around him, and to breathe the venomous air of the prison ship.

I lay long awake full of thought both for myself and for the poor souls around me. At last, however, the measured swash of the water against the side of the vessel and the slight rise and fall had lulled me into a sleep, from which I was suddenly aroused by the flashing of a light in my eyes. Sitting up, I found several sailors gathered about me, and a tall man with a black cloak swathed round him swinging a lanthorn over me.

" That is the man," he said.

" Come, mate, you are to come on deck ! " said the seaman armourer. With a few blows from his hammer he knocked the irons from my feet.

" Follow me ! " said the tall stranger, and led the way up the hatchway ladder. It was heavenly to come out into the pure air once more. The stars were shining brightly overhead. A fresh breeze blew from the shore, and hummed a pleasant tune among the cordage. Close beside us the lights of the town gleamed yellow and

cheery. Beyond, the moon was peeping over the Bournemouth hills.

" This way, sir," said the sailor, " right aft into the cabin, sir."

Still following my guide, I found myself in the low cabin of the brig. A square shining table stood in the centre, with a bright swinging lamp above it. At the farther end in the glare of the light sat the captain—his face shining with greed and expectation. On the table stood a small pile of gold pieces, a rum-flask, glasses, a tobacco-box and two long pipes.

" My compliments to you, Captain Clarke," said the skipper, bobbing his round bristling head. " An honest seaman's compliments to you. It seems that we are not to be shipmates this voyage, after all."

" Captain Micah Clarke must do a voyage of his own," said the stranger.

At the sound of his voice I sprang round in amazement. " Good Heavens ! " I cried, " Saxon ! "

" You have nicked it," said he, throwing down his mantle and showing the well-known face and figure of the soldier of fortune. " Zounds, man ! if you can pick me out of the Solent, I suppose that I may pick you out of this accursed rat-trap in which I find you. Tie and tie, as we say at the green table. In truth, I was huffed with you when last we parted, but I have had you in my mind for all that."

" A seat and a glass, Captain Clarke," cried the skipper. " Od's bud ! I should think that you would be glad to raise your little finger and wet your whistle after what you have gone through."

I seated myself by the table with my brain in a whirl. " This is more than I can fathom," said I. " What is the meaning of it, and how comes it about ? "

" For my own part, the meaning is as clear as the glass of my binnacle," quoth the seaman. " Your good friend Colonel Saxon, as I understand his name to be, has offered me as much as I could hope to gain by selling you

in the Indies. Sink it, I may be rough and ready, but my heart is in the right place ! Aye, aye ! I would not maroon a man if I could set him free. But we have all to look for ourselves, and trade is dull."

" Then I am free ! " said I.

"You are free," he answered. "There is your purchase-money upon the table. You can go where you will, save only upon the land of England, where you are still an outlaw under sentence."

" How have you done this, Saxon ? " I asked. " Are you not afraid for yourself ? "

" Ho, ho ! " laughed the old soldier. " I am a free man, my lad ! I hold my pardon, and care not a maravedi for spy or informer. Who should I meet but Colonel Kirke a day or so back. Yes, lad ! I met him in the street, and I cocked my hat in his face. The villain laid his hand upon his hilt, and I should have out bilbo and sent his soul to hell had they not come between us. I care not the ashes of this pipe for Jeffreys or any other of them. I can snap this finger and thumb at them, so ! They would rather see Decimus Saxon's back than his face, I promise ye ! "

" But how comes this about ? " I asked.

" Why, marry, it is no mystery. Cunning old birds are not to be caught with chaff. When I left you I made for a certain inn where I could count upon finding a friend. There I lay by for a while, en cachette, as the Messieurs call it, while I could work out the plan that was in my head. Donner wetter ! but I got a fright from that old seaman friend of yours, who should be sold as a pic-ture, for he is of little use as a man. Well, I bethought me early in the affair of your visit to Badminton, and of the Duke of B. We shall mention no names, but you can follow my meaning. To him I sent a messenger, to the effect that I purposed to purchase my own pardon by letting out all that I knew concerning his double dealing with the rebels. The message was carried to him secretly, and his answer was that I should meet him at a certain

474

spot by night. I sent my messenger instead of myself, and he was found in the morning stiff and stark, with more holes in his doublet than ever the tailor made. On this I sent again, raising my demands, and insisting upon a speedy settlement. He asked my conditions. I replied, a free pardon and a command for myself. For you, money enough to land you safely in some foreign country where you can pursue the noble profession of arms. I got them both, though it was like drawing teeth from his head. His name hath much power at Court just now, and the King can refuse him nothing. I have my pardon and a command of troops in New England. For you I have two hundred pieces, of which thirty have been paid in ransom to the captain, while twenty are due to me for my disbursements over the matter. In this bag you will find the odd hundred and fifty, of which you will pay fifteen to the fishermen who have promised to see you safe to Flushing."

I was, as you may readily believe, my dear children, bewildered by this sudden and most unlooked-for turn which events had taken. When Saxon had ceased to speak I sat as one stunned, trying to realise what he had said to me. There came a thought into my head, how-ever, which chilled the glow of hope and of happiness which had sprung up in me at the thought of recovering my freedom. My presence had been a support and a comfort to my unhappy companions. Would it not be a cruel thing to leave them in their distress ? There was not one of them who did not look to me in his trouble, and to the best of my poor power I had befriended and consoled them. How could I desert them now ?

" I am much beholden to you, Saxon," I said at last, speaking slowly and with some difficulty, for the words were hard to utter. " But I fear that your pains have been thrown away. These poor country folk have none to look after or assist them. They are as simple as babes, and as little fitted to be landed in a strange country. I cannot find it in my heart to leave them ! "

Saxon burst out laughing, and leaned back in his seat with his long legs stretched straight out and his hands in his breeches pockets.

" This is too much ! " he said at last. " I saw many difficulties in my way, yet I did not foresee this one. You are in very truth the most contrary man that ever stood in neat's leather. You have ever some outlandish reason for jibbing and shying like a hot-blooded, half-broken colt. Yet I think that I can overcome these strange scruples of yours by a little persuasion."

" As to the prisoners, Captain Clarke," said the sea-man, " I'll be as good as a father to them. S'help me, I will, on the word of an honest sailor ! If you should choose to lay out a trifle of twenty pieces upon their comfort, I shall see that their food is such as mayhap many of them never got at their own tables. They shall come on deck, too, in watches, and have an hour or two o' fresh air in the day. I can't say fairer ! "

" A word or two with you on deck ! " said Saxon. He walked out of the cabin and I followed him to the far end of the poop, where we stood leaning against the bulwarks. One by one the lights had gone out in the town, until the black ocean beat against a blacker shore.

" You need not have any fear of the future of the prisoners," he said, in a low whisper. " They are not bound for the Barbadoes, nor will this skinflint of a captain have the selling of them, for all that he is so cocksure. If he can bring his own skin out of the business, it will be more than I expect. He hath a man aboard his ship who would think no more of giving him a tilt over the side than I should."

" What mean you, Saxon ? " I cried.

" Hast ever heard of a man named Marot ? "

" Hector Marot ! Yes, surely I knew him well. A highwayman he was, but a mighty stout man with a kind heart beneath a thief's jacket."

" The same. He is as you say a stout man and a reso-lute swordsman, though from what I have seen of his

play he is weak in stoccado, and perhaps somewhat too much attached to the edge, and doth not give prominence enough to the point, in which respect he neglects the advice and teaching of the most noteworthy fencers in Europe. Well, well, folk differ on this as on every other subject ! Yet it seems to me that I would sooner be carried off the field after using my weapon secundum artem, than walk off unscathed after breaking the laws d'escrime Quarte, tierce and saccoon, say I, and the devil take your estramacons and passados ! "

" But what of Marot ? " I asked impatiently.

" He is aboard," said Saxon. " It appears that he was much disturbed in his mind over the cruelties which were inflicted on the country folk after the battle at Bridgewater. Being a man of a somewhat stern and fierce turn of mind, his disapproval did vent itself in actions rather than words. Soldiers were found here and there over the countryside pistolled or stabbed, and no trace left of their assailant. A dozen of more were cut off in this way, and soon it came to be whispered about that Marot the highwayman was the man that did it, and the chase became hot at his heels."

" Well, and what then ? " I asked, for Saxon had stopped to light his pipe at the same old metal tinderbox which he had used when first I met him. When I pictured Saxon to myself it is usually of that moment that I think, when the red glow beat upon his hard, eager, hawk-like face, and showed up the thousand little seams and wrinkles which time and care had imprinted upon his brown, weather-beaten skin. Sometimes in my dreams that face in the darkness comes back to me, and his half-closed eyelids and shifting, blinky eyes are turned towards me in his sidelong fashion, until I find myself sitting up and holding out my hand into empty space, half expecting to feel another thin, sinewy hand close round it. A bad man he was in many ways, my dears, cunning and wily, with little scruple or conscience ; and yet so strange a thing is human nature, and so difficult

is it for us to control our feelings, that my heart warms when I think of him, and that fifty years have increased rather than weakened the kindliness which I bear to him.

" I had heard," quoth he, puffing slowly at his pipe, " that Marot was a man of this kidney, and also that he was so compassed round that he was in peril of capture. I sought him out, therefore, and held council with him. His mare, it seems, had been slain by some chance shot, and as he was much attached to the brute, the accident made him more savage and more dangerous than ever. He had no heart, he said, to continue in his old trade. Indeed, he was ripe for anything—the very stuff out of which useful tools are made. I found that in his youth he had had a training for the sea. When I heard that, I saw my way in the snap of a petronel."

" What then ? " I asked. " I am still in the dark."

" Nay, it is surely plain enough to you now. Marot's end was to baffle his pursuers and to benefit the exiles. How could he do this better than by engaging as a seaman aboard this brig, the *Dorothy Fox*, and sailing away from England in her ? There are but thirty of a crew. Below hatches are close on two hundred men, who, simple as they may be, are, as you and I know, second to none in the cut-and-thrust work, without order or discipline, which will be needed in such an affair. Marot has but to go down amongst them some dark night, knock off their anklets, and fit them up with a few stanchions or cudgels. Ho, ho, Micah ! what think you ? The planters may dig their plantations themselves for all the help they are like to get from West countrymen this bout."

" It is, indeed, a well-conceived plan," said I. " It is a pity, Saxon, that your ready wit and quick invention hath not had a fair field. You are, as I know well, as fit to command armies and to order campaigns as any man that ever bore a truncheon."

" Mark ye there ! " whispered Saxon, grasping me by the arm. " See where the moonlight falls beside the hatchway ! Do you not see that short squat seaman who

478

stands alone, lost in thought, with his head sunk upon his breast ? It is Marot ! I tell you that if I were Captain Pogram I would rather have the devil himself, horns, hoofs and tail, for my first mate and bunk companion, than have that man aboard my ship. You need not concern yourself about the prisoners, Micah. Their future is decided."

" Then, Saxon," I answered, " it only remains for me to thank you, and to accept the means of safety which you have placed within my reach."

" Spoken like a man," said he ; " is there aught which I may do for thee in England ? though, by the Mass, I may not be here very long myself, for, as I understand, I am to be entrusted with the command of an expedition that is fitting out against the Indians, who have ravaged the plantations of our settlers. It will be good to get to some profitable employment, for such a war, without either fighting or plunder, I have never seen. I give you my word that I have scarce fingered silver since the beginning of it. I would not for the sacking of London go through with it again."

" There is a friend whom Sir Gervas Jerome did commend to my care," I remarked ; " I have, however, already taken measures to have his wishes carried out. There is nought else save to assure all in Havant that a King who hath battened upon his subjects, as this one of ours hath done, is not one who is like to keep his seat very long upon the throne of England. When he falls I shall return, and perhaps it may be sooner than folk think."

" These doings in the West have indeed stirred up much ill-feeling all over the country," said my companion. " On all hands I hear that there is more hatred of the King and of his ministers than before the outbreak. What ho, Captain Pogram, this way ! We have settled the matter, and my friend is willing to go."

" I thought he would tack round," the captain said, staggering towards us with a gait which showed that he

had made the rum bottle his companion since we had left
him. " S'help me, I was sure of it ! Though, by the
Mass, I don't wonder that he thought twice before leaving
the *Dorothy Fox*, for she is fitted up fit for a duchess,
s'help me ! Where is your boat ? "

" Alongside," replied Saxon ; " my friend joins with
me in hoping that you, Captain Pogram, will have a
pleasant and profitable voyage."

" I am cursedly beholden to him," said the captain,
with a flourish of his three-cornered hat.

" Also that you will reach Barbadoes in safety."

" Little doubt of that ! " quoth the captain.

" And that you will dispose of your wares in a manner
which will repay you for your charity and humanity."

" Nay, these are handsome words," cried the captain.
" Sir, I am your debtor."

A fishing-boat was lying alongside the brig. By the
murky light of the poop lanterns I could see the figures
upon her deck, and the great brown sail all ready for
hoisting. I climbed the bulwark and set my foot upon
the rope-ladder which led down to her.

" Good-bye, Decimus ! " said I.

" Good-bye, my lad ! You have your pieces all safe ? "

" I have them."

" Then I have one other present to make you. It was
brought to me by a sergeant of the Royal Horse. It is
that, Micah, on which you must now depend for food,
lodging, raiment and all which you would have. It is
that to which a brave man can always look for his living.
It is the knife wherewith you can open the world's oyster.
See, lad, it is your sword ! "

" The old sword ! My father's sword ! " I cried in
delight, as Saxon drew from under his mantle and handed
to me the discoloured, old-fashioned leathern sheath with
the heavy brass hilt which I knew so well.

" You are now," said he, " one of the old and honourable guild of soldiers of fortune. While the Turk is still
snarling at the gates of Vienna there will ever be work for

strong arms and brave hearts. You will find that among these wandering, fighting men, drawn from all climes and nations, the name of Englishman stands high. Well I know that it will stand none the lower for your having joined the brotherhood. I would that I could come with you, but I am promised pay and position which it would be ill to set aside. Farewell, lad, and may fortune go with you ! "

I pressed the rough soldier's horny hand, and descended into the fishing-boat. The rope that held us was cast off, the sail mounted up, and the boat shot out across the bay. Onward she went and on, through the gathering gloom—a gloom as dark and impenetrable as the future towards which my life's bark was driving. Soon the long rise and fall told us that we were over the harbour bar and out in the open channel. On the land, scattered twinkling lights at long stretches marked the line of the coast. As I gazed backwards a cloud trailed off from the moon, and I saw the hard lines of the brig's rigging stand out against the white cold disk. By the shrouds stood the veteran, holding to a rope with one hand, and waving the other in farewell and encouragement. Another great cloud blurred out the light, and that lean sinewy figure with its long extended arm was the last which I saw for a weary time of the dear country where I was born and bred.

36. *Of the End of it All*

AND so, my dear children, I come to the end of the history of a failure—a brave failure and a noble one, but a failure none the less. In three more years England was to come to herself, to tear the fetters from her free limbs, and to send James and his poisonous brood flying from her shores even as I was flying then. We had made the error of being before our time. Yet there came days when folk thought kindly of the lads who had fought so stoutly in the West, and when their

limbs, gathered from many a hangman's pit and waste place, were borne amid the silent sorrow of a nation to the pretty country burial-grounds where they would have chosen to lie. There, within the sound of the bell which from infancy had called them to prayer, beneath the turf over which they had wandered, under the shadow of those Mendip and Quantock Hills which they loved so well, these brave hearts lie still and peaceful, like tired children in the bosom of their mother. *Requiescant— requiescant in pace !*

Not another word about myself, dear children. This narrative doth already bristle with I's, as though it were an Argus—which is a flash of wit, though I doubt if ye will understand it. I set myself to tell ye the tale of the war in the West, and that tale ye have heard, nor will I be coaxed or cajoled into one word farther. Ah ! ye know well how garrulous the old man is, and that if you could but get to Flushing with him he would take ye to the wars of the Empire, to William's Court, and to the second invasion of the West, which had a better outcome than the first. But not an inch farther will I budge. On to the green, ye young rogues ! Have ye not other limbs to exercise besides your ears, that ye should be so fond of squatting round grandad's chair ? If I am spared to next winter, and if the rheumatiz keeps away, it is like that I may take up once more the broken thread of my story.

Of the others I can only tell ye what I know. Some slipped out of my ken entirely. Of others I have heard vague and incomplete accounts. The leaders of the insurrection got off much more lightly than their followers, for they found that the passion of greed was even stronger than the passion of cruelty. Grey, Buyse, Wade and others bought themselves free at the price of all their possessions. Ferguson escaped. Monmouth was executed on Tower Hill, and showed in his last moments some faint traces of that spirit which spurted up now and again from his feeble nature, like the momentary flash of an expiring fire.

My father and my mother lived to see the Protestant religion regain its place once more, and to see England become the champion of the reformed faith upon the Continent. Three years later I found them in Havant much as I had left them, save that there were more silver hairs amongst the brown braided tresses of my mother, and that my father's great shoulders were a trifle bowed and his brow furrowed with the lines of care. Hand in hand they passed onwards down life's journey, the Puritan and the Church woman, and I have never despaired of the healing of religious feud in England since I have seen how easy it is for two folks to retain the strongest belief in their own creeds, and yet to bear the heartiest love and respect for the professor of another. The days may come when the Church and the Chapel may be as a younger and an elder brother, each working to one end, and each joying in the other's success. Let the contest between them be not with pike and pistol, not with court and prison ; but let the strife be which shall lead the higher life, which shall take the broader view, which shall boast the happiest and best cared-for poor. Then their rivalry shall be not a curse, but a blessing to this land of England.

Reuben Lockarby was ill for many months, but when he at last recovered he found a pardon awaiting him through the interest of Major Ogilvy. After a time, when the troubles were all blown over, he married the daughter of Mayor Timewell, and he still lives in Taunton, a well-to-do and prosperous citizen. Thirty years ago there was a little Micah Lockarby, and now I am told that there is another, the son of the first, who promises to be as arrant a little Roundhead as ever marched to the tuck of drum.

Of Saxon I have heard more than once. So skilfully did he use his hold over the Duke of Beaufort, that he was appointed through his interest to the command of an expedition which had been sent to chastise the savages of Virginia, who had wrought great cruelties upon the settlers. There he did so out-ambush their ambushes,

and out-trick their most cunning warriors, that he hath left a great name among them, and is still remembered there by an Indian word which signifieth " The long-legged wily one with the eye of a rat." Having at last driven the tribes far into the wilderness he was presented with a tract of country for his services, where he settled down. There he married, and spent the rest of his days in rearing tobacco and in teaching the principles of war to a long line of gaunt and slab-sided children. They tell me that a great nation of exceeding strength and of wondrous size promises some day to rise up on the other side of the water. If this should indeed come to pass, it may perhaps happen that these young Saxons or their children may have a hand in the building of it. God grant that they may never let their hearts harden to the little isle of the sea, which is and must ever be the cradle of their race.

Solomon Sprent married and lived for many years as happily as his friends could wish. I had a letter from him when I was abroad, in which he said that though his consort and he had started alone on the voyage of wedlock, they were now accompanied by a jolly-boat and a gig. One winter's night when the snow was on the ground he sent down for my father, who hurried up to his house. He found the old man sitting up in bed, with his flask of rumbo within reach, his tobacco-box beside him, and a great brown Bible balanced against his updrawn knees. He was breathing heavily, and was in sore distress.

" I've strained a plank, and have nine feet in the well," said he. " It comes in quicker than I can put it out. In truth, friend, I have not been seaworthy this many a day, and it is time that I was condemned and broken up."

My father shook his head sadly as he marked his dusky face and laboured breathing. " How of your soul ? " he asked.

" Aye ! " said Solomon, " that's a cargo that we carry under our hatches, though we can't see it, and had no hand in the stowing of it. I've been overhauling the sailing orders here, and the ten articles of war, but I can't

find that I've gone so far out of my course that I may not hope to come into the channel again."

" Trust not in yourself, but in Christ," said my father.

" He is the pilot, in course," replied the old seaman. " When I had a pilot aboard o' my ship, however, it was my way always to keep my own weather eye open, d'ye see, and so I'll do now. The pilot don't think none the worse of ye for it. So I'll throw my own lead line, though I hear as how there are no soundings in the ocean of God's mercy. Say, friend, d'ye think this very body, this same hull o' mine, will rise again ? "

" So we are taught," my father answered.

" I'd know it anywhere from the tattoo marks," said Solomon. " They was done when I was with Sir Christopher in the West Indies, and I'd be sorry to part with them. For myself, d'ye see, I've never borne ill-will to any one, not even to the Dutch lubbers, though I fought three wars wi' them, and they carried off one of my spars, and be hanged to them ! If I've let daylight into a few of them, d'ye see, it's all in good part and by way of duty. I've drunk my share—enough to sweeten my bilge-water—but there are few that have seen me cranky in the upper rigging or refusing to answer to my helm. I never drew pay or prize-money that my mate in distress was not welcome to the half of it. As to the Polls, the less said the better. I've been a true consort to my Phœbe since she agreed to look to me for signals. Those are my papers, all clear and aboveboard. If I'm summoned aft this very night by the great Lord High Admiral of all, I ain't afeard that He'll clap me into the bilboes, for though I'm only a poor sailor-man, I've got His promise in this here book, and I'm not afraid of His going back from it."

My father sat with the old man for some hours and did all that he could to comfort and assist him, for it was clear that he was sinking rapidly. When he at last left him, with his faithful wife beside him, he grasped the brown but wasted hand which lay above the clothes.

" I'll see you again soon," he said.

" Yes. In the latitude of heaven," replied the dying seaman.

His foreboding was right, for in the early hours of the morning his wife, bending over him, saw a bright smile upon his tanned, weather-beaten face. Raising himself upon his pillow he touched his forelock, as is the habit of sailor-men, and so sank slowly and peacefully back into the long sleep which wakes when the night has ceased to be.

You will ask me doubtless what became of Hector Marot and of the strange shipload which had set sail from Poole Harbour. There was never a word heard of them again, unless indeed a story which was spread some months afterwards by Captain Elias Hopkins, of the Bristol ship *Caroline*, may be taken as bearing upon their fate. For Captain Hopkins relates that, being on his homeward voyage from our settlements, he chanced to meet with thick fogs and a head wind in the neighbourhood of the great cod banks. One night as he was beating about, with the weather so thick that he could scarce see the truck of his own mast, a most strange passage befell him. For as he and others stood upon the deck, they heard to their astonishment the sound of many voices joined in a great chorus, which was at first faint and distant, but which presently waxed and increased until it appeared to pass within a stone-throw of his vessel, when it slowly died away once more and was lost in the distance. There were some among the crew who set the matter down as the doing of the evil one, but, as Captain Elias Hopkins was wont to remark, it was a strange thing that the foul fiend should choose West-country hymns for his nightly exercise, and stranger still that the dwellers in the pit should sing with a strong Somersetshire burr. For myself, I have little doubt that it was indeed the *Dorothy Fox* which had swept past in the fog, and that the prisoners, having won their freedom, were celebrating their delivery in true Puritan style. Whether they were

driven on to the rocky coast of Labrador, or whether they found a home in some desolate land whence no kingly cruelty could harry them, is what must remain for ever unknown.

Zachariah Palmer lived for many years, a venerable and honoured old man, before he, too, was called to his fathers. A sweet and simple village philosopher he was, with a child's heart in his aged breast. The véry thought of him is to me as the smell of violets ; for if in my views of life and in my hopes of the future I differ somewhat from the hard and gloomy teaching of my father, I know that I owe it to the wise words and kindly training of the carpenter. If, as he was himself wont to say, deeds are everything in this world and dogma is nothing, then his sinless, blameless life might be a pattern to you and to all. May the dust lie light upon him !

One word of another friend—the last mentioned, but not the least valued. When Dutch William had been ten years upon the English throne there was still to be seen in the field by my father's house a tall, strong-boned horse, whose grey skin was flecked with dashes of white. And it was ever observed that, should the soldiers be passing from Portsmouth, or should the clank of trumpet or the rattle of drum break upon his ear, he would arch his old neck, throw out his grey-streaked tail, and raise his stiff knees in a pompous and pedantic canter. The country folk would stop to watch these antics of the old horse, and then the chances are that one of them would tell the rest how that charger had borne one of their own village lads to the wars, and how, when the rider had to fly the country, a kindly sergeant in the King's troops had brought the steed as a remembrance of him to his father at home. So Covenant passed the last years of his life, a veteran among steeds, well fed and cared for, and much given, mayhap, to telling in equine language to all the poor, silly country steeds the wonderful passages which had befallen him in the West.

Appendix

NOTE A.—*Hatred of Learning among the Puritans.*

In spite of the presence in their ranks of such ripe scholars as John Milton, Colonel Hutchinson and others, there was among the Independents and Anabaptists a profound distrust of learning, which is commented upon by writers of all shades of politics. Dr. South in his sermons remarks that " All learning was cried down, so that with them the best preachers were such as could not read, and the best divines such as could not write. In all their preachments they so highly pretended to the Spirit, that some of them could hardly spell a letter. To be blind with them was a proper qualification of a spiritual guide, and to be book-learned, as they called it, and to be irreligious, were almost convertible terms. None save tradesmen and mechanics were allowed to have the Spirit, and those only were accounted like St. Paul who could work with their hands, and were able to make a pulpit before preaching in it."

In the collection of loyal ballads reprinted in 1731, the Royalist bard harps upon the same characteristic :

> " We'll down with universities
>   Where learning is professed,
> Because they practise and maintain
>   The language of the beast.
> We'll drive the doctors out of doors,
>   And parts, whate'er they be,
> We'll cry all parts and learning down,
>   And heigh, then up go we ! "

NOTE B.—*On the Speed of Couriers.*

It is difficult for us in these days of steam and electricity to realise how long it took to despatch a message in the seventeenth century, even when the occasion was most pressing. Thus, Monmouth landed at Lyme on the morning of Thursday, the 11th of June. Gregory Alford, the Tory mayor of Lyme, instantly fled to Honiton, whence he despatched a messenger to the Privy Council. Yet it was five o'clock in the morning of Saturday, the 13th, before the news reached London, though the distance is but 156 miles.

NOTE C.—*On the Claims of the Lender of a Horse.*

The difficulty touched upon by Decimus Saxon, as to the claim of the lender of a horse upon the booty gained by the rider, is one frequently discussed by writers of that date upon the usages of war. One distinguished authority says : Præfectus turmæ equitum Hispanorum, cum prœlio tuba caneret, unum ex equitibus suæ turmæ obvium habuit ; qui questus est quod paucis ante diebus equum suum in certamine amiserat, propter quod non poterat imminenti prœlio interesse ; unde jussit Præfectus ut unum ex suis equis conscenderet et ipsum comitaretur. Miles, equo conscenso, inter fugandum hostes, incidit in ipsum ducem hostilis exercitus. quem cepit et consignavit Duci

exercitus Hispani, qui a captivo vicena aureorum millia est conse-
quutus. Dicebat Præfectus partem pretii hujus redemptionis sibi
debere, quod miles equo suo dimicaverat, qui alias prœlio interesse
non potuit. Petrinus Bellus affirmat se, cum esset Bruxellis in curia
Hispaniarum Regis de hac quæstione consultum, et censuisse, pro
Præfecto facere æquitatem quæ præcipue respicitur inter milites, quo-
rum controversiæ ex æquo et bono dirimendæ sunt ; unde ultra con-
venta quis obligatur ad id quod alterum alteri præstare oportet." The
case, it appears, ultimately went against the horse-lending præfect.

Note D.—*On the Pronunciation of Exquisites.*

The substitution of the *a* for the *o* was a common affectation in
the speech of the fops of the period, as may be found in Vanbrugh's
Relapse. The notorious Titus Oates, in his efforts to be in the mode,
pushed this trick to excess, and his cries of " Oh Lard ! Oh Lard ! "
were familiar sounds in Westminster Hall at the time when the Sala-
manca doctor was at the flood of his fortune.

Note E.—*Hour-glasses in Pulpits.*

In those days it was customary to have an hour-glass stationed in a
frame of iron at the side of the pulpit, and visible to the whole congregation. It was turned up as soon as the text was announced, and a
minister earned a name as a lazy preacher if he did not hold out until
the sand had ceased to run. If, on the other hand, he exceeded that
limit, his audience would signify by gapes and yawns that they had
had as much spiritual food as they could digest. Sir Roger L'Estrange
(*Fables*, Part II. Fab. 262) tells of a notorious spin-text who, having
exhausted his glass and being half-way through a second one, was at
last arrested in his career by a valiant sexton, who rose and departed,
remarking as he did so, " Pray, sir, be pleased when you have done to
leave the key under the door."

Note F.—*Disturbances at the old Gast House of Little Burton.*

The circumstances referred to by the Mayor of Taunton in his allusion to the Drummer of Tedsworth are probably too well known to
require elucidation. The haunting of the old Gast House at Burton
would, however, be fresh at that time in the minds of Somersetshire
folk, occurring as it did in 1677. Some short account from documents
of that date may be of interest.

" The first night that I was there, with Hugh Mellmore and Edward
Smith, they heard as it were the washing of water over their heads.
Then, taking the candle and going up the stairs, there was a wet cloth
thrown at them, but it fell on the stairs. They going up further,
there was another thrown as before. And when they were come up
into the chamber there stood a bowl of water, looking white, as though
soap had been used in it. The bowl just before was in the kitchen,
and could not be carried up but through the room where they were.
The next thing was a terrible noise, like a clap of thunder, and shortly
afterwards they heard a great scratching about the bedstead, and
after that great knocking with a hammer against the bed's-head, so
that the two maids that were in bed cried out for help. Then they

ran up the stairs, and there lay the hammer on the bed, and on the bed's-head there were near a thousand prints of the hammer. The maids said that they were scratched and pinched with a hand which had exceeding long nails.

" The second night that James Sherring and Thomas Hillary were there, James Sherring sat down in the chimney to fill a pipe of tobacco. He used the tongs to lift a coal to light his pipe, and by-and-by the tongs were drawn up the stairs and were cast upon the bed. The same night one of the maids left her shoes by the fire, and they were carried up into the chamber, and the old man's brought down and set in their places. As they were going upstairs there were many things thrown at them which were just before in the low room, and when they went down the stairs the old man's breeches were thrown down after them.

" On another night a saddle did come into the house from a pin in the entry, and did hop about the place from table to table. It was very troublesome to them, until they broke it into small pieces and threw it out into the roadway. So for some weeks the haunting continued, with rappings, scratching, movements of heavy articles, and many other strange things, as are attested by all who were in the village, until at last they ceased as suddenly as they had begun."

NOTE G.—*Monmouth's Progress in the West.*

During his triumphal progress through the western shires, some years before the rebellion, Monmouth first ventured to exhibit upon his escutcheon the lions of England and the lilies of France, without the bâton sinister. A still more ominous sign was that he ventured to touch for the king's evil. The appended letter, extracted from the collection of tracts in the British Museum, may be of interest as first-hand evidence of the occasional efficacy of that curious ceremony.

" His Grace the Duke of Monmouth honoured in his progress in the West of England, in an account of an extraordinary cure of the king's evil.

" Given in a letter from Crewkhorn, in Somerset, from the minister of the parish and many others.

" We, whose names are underwritten, do certify the miraculous cure of a girl of this town, about twenty, by name Elizabeth Parcet, a poor widow's daughter, who hath languished under sad affliction from that distemper of the king's evil termed the joint evil, being said to be the worst evil. For about ten or twelve years' time she had in her right hand four running wounds, one on the inside, three on the back of her hand, as well as two more in the same arm, one above her hand-wrist, the other above the bending of her arm. She had betwixt her arm-pits a swollen bunch, which the doctors said fed those six running wounds. She had the same distemper also on her left eye, so she was almost blind. Her mother, despairing of preserving her sight, and being not of ability to send her to London to be touched by the king, being miserably poor, having many poor children, and this girl not being able to work, her mother, desirous to have her daughter cured, sent to the chirurgeons for help, who tampered with it for some time, but could do no good. She went likewise ten or eleven miles to a seventh

son, but all in vain. No visible hopes remained, and she expected nothing but the grave.

" But now, in this the girl's great extremity, God, the great physician, dictates to her, then languishing in her miserable, hopeless condition, what course to take and what to do for a cure, which was to go and touch the Duke of Monmouth. The girl told her mother that if she could but touch the Duke she would be well. The mother reproved her for her foolish conceit, but the girl did often persuade her mother to go to Lackington to the Duke, who then lay with Mr. Speaks. ' Certainly,' said she, ' I should be well if I could touch him.' The mother slighted these pressing requests, but the more she slighted and reproved, the more earnest the girl was for it. A few days after, the girl having noticed that Sir John Sydenham intended to treat the Duke at White Lodge in Henton Park, this girl with many of her neighbours went to the said park. She being there timely waited the Duke's coming. When first she observed the Duke she pressed in among a crowd of people and caught him by the hand, his glove being on, and she likewise having a glove to cover her wounds. She not being herewith satisfied at the first attempt of touching his glove only, but her mind was she must touch some part of his bare skin, she, weighing his coming forth, intended a second attempt. The poor girl, thus between hope and fear, waited his motion. On a sudden there was news of the Duke's coming, on which she to be prepared rent off her glove, that was clung to the sores, in such haste that she broke her glove, and brought away not only the sores but the skin. The Duke's glove, as Providence would have it, the upper part hung down, so that his hand-wrist was bare. She pressed on, and caught him by the bare hand-wrist with her running hand, crying, ' God bless your highness ! ' and the Duke said ' God bless you ! ' The girl, not a little transported at her good success, came and assured her friends that she would now be well. She came home to her mother in great joy, and told her that she had touched the Duke's hand. The mother, hearing what she had done, reproved her sharply for her boldness, asked how she durst do such a thing, and threatened to beat her for it. She cried out, ' Oh, mother, I shall be well again, and healed of my wounds ! ' And as God Almighty would have it, to the wonder and admiration of all, the six wounds were speedily dried up, the eye became perfectly well, and the girl was in good health. All which has been discovered to us by the mother and daughter, and by neighbours that know her.

" Henry Clark, minister ; Captain James Bale, &c. &c. Whoever doubts the truth of this relation may see the original under the hands of the persons mentioned at the Amsterdam Coffee House, Bartholomew Lane, Royal Exchange."

In spite of the uncouth verbiage of the old narrative, there is a touch of human pathos about it which makes it worthy of reproduction.

NOTE H.—*Monmouth's Contention of Legitimacy.*

Sir Patrick Hume, relating a talk with Monmouth before his expedition, says : " I urged if he considered himself as lawful son of King Charles, late deceased. He said he did. I asked him if he were able to make out and prove the marriage of his mother to King Charles,

and whether he intended to lay claim to the crown. He answered that he had been able lately to prove the marriage, and if some persons are not lately dead, of which he would inform himself, he would yet be able to prove it. As for his claiming the crown, he intended not to do it unless it were advised to be done by those who should concern themselves and join for the delivery of the nations."

It may be remarked that in Monmouth's commission to be general, dated April 1668, he is styled " our most entirely beloved and natural son." Again, in a commission for the government of Hull, April 1673, he is " our well-beloved natural son."

NOTE I.—*Dragooners and Chargers*.

The dragoons, being really mounted infantry, were provided with very inferior animals to the real cavalry. From a letter of Cromwell's (*Squire Correspondence*, April 3, 1643), it will be seen that a dragooner was worth twenty pieces, while a charger could not be obtained under sixty.

NOTE J.—*Battle of Sedgemoor*.

A curious little sidelight upon the battle is afforded by the two following letters exhibited to the Royal Archæological Institute by the Rev. C. W. Bingham.

" *To Mrs. Chaffin at Chettle House*.
" *Monday, about ye forenoon, July* 6, 1685.

" My dearest creature,—This morning about one o'clock the rebbells fell upon us whilest we were in our tents in King's Sedgemoor, with their whole army. . . . We have killed and taken at least 1000 of them. They are fled into Bridgewater. It is said that we have taken all their cannon, but sure it is that most are, if all be not. A coat with stars on 't is taken. 'Tis run through the back. By some 'tis thought that the Duke rebbell had it on and is killed, but most doe think that a servant wore it. I wish he were called, that the wars may be ended. It's thought he'll never be able to make his men fight again. I thank God I am very well without the least hurt, soe are our Dorsetshire friends. Prithee let Biddy know this by the first opportunity. I am thyne onely deare, TOSSEY."

BRIDGEWATER : *July* 7, 1685.

" We have totally routed the enemies of God and the King, and can't hear of fifty men together of the whole rebel army. We pick them up every houre in cornfields and ditches. Williams, the late Duke's valet de chambre, is taken, who gives a very ingenious account of the whole affair, which is too long to write. The last word that he said to him was at the time when his army fled, that he was undone and must shift for himself. We think to march with the General this day to Wells, on his way homeward. At present he is 2 miles off at the camp, soe I can't certainly tell whether he intends for Wells. I shall be home certainly on Saturday at farthest. I believe my deare Nan would for £500 that her Tossey had served the King to the end of the war. I am thyne, my deare childe, for ever."

NOTE K.—*Lord Grey and the Horse at Sedgemoor.*

It is only fair to state that Ferguson is held by many to have been as doughty a soldier as he was zealous in religion. His own account of Sedgemoor is interesting, as showing what was thought by those who were actually engaged on the causes of their failure.

" Now besides these two troops, whose officers though they had no great skill yet had courage enough to have done something honourably, had they not for want of a guide met with the aforesaid obstruction, there was no one of all the rest of our troops that ever advanced to charge or approached as near to the enemy as to give or receive a wound. Mr. Hacker, one of our captains, came no sooner within view of their camp than he villainously fired a pistol to give them notice of our approach, and then forsook his charge and rode off with all the speed he could, to take the benefit of a proclamation emitted by the King, offering pardon to all such as should return home within such a time. And this he pleaded at his tryal, but was answered by Jeffreys ' that he above all other men deserved to be hanged, and that for his treachery to Monmouth as well as his treason to the King.' And though no other of our officers acted so villainously, yet they were useless and unserviceable, as never once attempting to charge, nor so much as keeping their men in a body. And I dare affirm that if our horse had never fired a pistol, but only stood in a posture to have given jealousy and apprehension to the enemy, our foot alone would have carried the day and been triumphant. But our horse standing scattered and disunited, and flying upon every approach of a squadron of theirs, commanded by Oglethorpe, gave that body of their cavalry an advantage, after they had hovered up and down in the field without thinking it necessary to attack those whom their own fears had dispersed, to fall in at last in the rear of our battalions, and to wrest that victory out of their hands which they were grasping at, and stood almost possessed of. Nor was that party of their horse above three hundred at most, whereas we had more than enough had they had any courage, and been commanded by a gallant man, to have attacked them with ease both in front and flank. These things I can declare with more certainty, because I was a doleful spectator of them ; for having contrary to my custom left attending upon the Duke, who advanced with the foot, I betook myself to the horse, because the first of that morning's action was expected from them, which was to break in and disorder the enemy's camp. Against the time that our battalions should come up, I endeavoured whatsoever I was capable of performing, for I not only struck at several troopers who had forsaken their station, but upbraided divers of the captains for being wanting in their duty. But I spoke with great warmth to my Lord Grey, and conjured him to charge, and not suffer the victory, which our foot had in a manner taken hold of, to be ravished from us. But instead of hearkening, he not only as an unworthy man and cowardly poltroon deserted that part of the field and forsook his command, but rode with the utmost speed to the Duke, telling him that all was lost and it was more than time to shift for himself. Wherebye, as an addition to all the mischief he had been the occasion of before, he drew the easy and unfortunate gentleman to leave the battalions while they were courageously disputing on which side the victory should fall. And this fell

most unhappily out, while a certain person was endeavouring to find out the Duke to have begged of him to come and charge at the head of his own troops. However, this I dare affirm, that if the Duke had been but master of two hundred horse, well mounted, completely armed, personally valiant, and commanded by experienced officers, they would have been victorious. This is acknowledged by our enemies, who have often confessed they were ready to fly through the impressions made upon them by our foot, and must have been beaten had our horse done their part, and not tamely looked on till their cavalry retrieved the day by falling into the rear of our battalions. Nor was the fault in the private men, who had courage to have followed their leaders, but it was in those who led them, particularly my Lord Grey, in whom, if cowardice may be called treachery, we may safely charge him with betraying our cause."

Extract from MS. of Dr. Ferguson, quoted in *Ferguson the Plotter*, an interesting work by his immediate descendant, an advocate of Edinburgh.

NOTE L.—*Monmouth's Attitude after Capture.*

The following letter, written by Monmouth to the Queen from the Tower, is indicative of his abject state of mind.

" Madam,—I would not take the boldness of writing to your Majesty till I had shown the King how I do abhor the thing that I have done, and how much I desire to live to serve him. I hope, madam, by what I have said to the King to-day will satisfy how sincere I am, and how much I detest all those people who have brought me to this. Having done this, madam, I thought I was in a fitt condition to beg your intercession, which I am sure you never refuse to the distressed, and I am sure, madam, that I am an object of your pity, having been cousened and cheated into this horrid business. Did I wish, madam, to live for living sake I would never give you this trouble, but it is to have life to serve the King, which I am able to doe, and will doe beyond what I can express. Therefore, madam, upon such an account as that I may take the boldness to press you and beg of you to intersaid for me, for I am sure, madam, the King will hearken to you. Your prairs can never be refused, especially when it is begging for a life only to serve the King. I hope, madam, by the King's generosity and goodness, and your intercession, I may hope for my life, which if I have shall be ever employed in showing to your Majesty all the sense immadginable of grattitude, and in serving of the King like a true subject. And ever be your Majesty's most dutiful and obedient servant, MONMOUTH."

THE REFUGEES

1. The Man from America

IT was the sort of window which was common in Paris about the end of the seventeenth century. It was high-mullioned with a broad transom, and its casements stood the middle of three rooms...

PART I

IN THE OLD WORLD

1. The Man from America

IT was the sort of window which was common in Paris about the end of the seventeenth century. It was high, mullioned, with a broad transom across the centre, and above the middle of the transom a tiny coat of arms—three caltrops gules upon a field argent—let into the diamond-paned glass. Outside there projected a stout iron rod, from which hung a gilded miniature of a bale of wool which swung and squeaked with every puff of wind. Beyond that again were the houses of the other side, high, narrow and prim, slashed with diagonal wood-work in front, and topped with a bristle of sharp gables and corner turrets. Between were the cobble-stones of the Rue St. Martin and the clatter of innumerable feet.

Inside, the window was furnished with a broad bancal of brown stamped Spanish leather, where the family might recline and have an eye from behind the curtains on all that was going forward in the busy world beneath them. Two of them sat there now, a man and a woman, but their backs were turned to the spectacle, and their faces to the large and richly furnished room. From time to time they stole a glance at each other, and their eyes told that they needed no other sight to make them happy.

Nor was it to be wondered at, for they were a well-favoured pair. She was very young, twenty at the most, with a face which was pale, indeed, and yet of a brilliant pallor, which was so clear and fresh, and carried with it

such a suggestion of purity and innocence, that one would not wish its maiden grace to be marred by an intrusion of colour. Her features were delicate and sweet, and her blue-black hair and long dark eyelashes formed a piquant contrast to her dreamy grey eyes and her ivory skin. In her whole expression there was something quiet and sub-dued, which was accentuated by her simple dress of black taffeta, and by the little jet brooch and bracelet which were her sole ornaments. Such was Adèle Catinat, the only daughter of the famous Huguenot cloth-merchant.

But if her dress was sombre, it was atoned for by the magnificence of her companion. He was a man who might have been ten years her senior, with a keen soldier face, small well-marked features, a carefully trimmed black moustache, and a dark hazel eye which might harden to command a man, or soften to supplicate a woman, and be successful at either. His coat was of sky-blue, slashed across with silver braidings, and with broad silver shoulder straps on either side. A vest of white calamanca peeped out from beneath it, and knee-breeches of the same disappeared into high polished boots with gilt spurs upon the heels. A silver-hilted rapier and a plumed cap lying upon a settle beside him completed a costume which was a badge of honour to the wearer, for any Frenchman would have recognised it as being that of an officer in the famous Blue Guard of Louis the Fourteenth. A trim, dashing soldier he looked, with his curling black hair and well-poised head. Such he had proved himself before now in the field, too, until the name of Amory de Catinat had become conspicuous among the thousands of the valiant lesser *noblesse* who had flocked into the service of the king.

They were first cousins, these two, and there was just sufficient resemblance in the clear-cut features to recall the relationship. De Catinat was sprung from a noble Huguenot family, but having lost his parents early he had joined the army, and had worked his way without influence and against all odds to his present position. His father's

younger brother, however, finding every path to fortune barred to him through the persecution to which men of his faith were already subjected, had dropped the " de " which implied his noble descent, and had taken to trade in the city of Paris, with such success that he was now one of the richest and most prominent citizens of the town. It was under his roof that the guardsman now sat, and it was his only daughter whose white hand he held in his own.

" Tell me, Adèle," said he, " why do you look troubled ? "

" I am not troubled, Amory."

" Come, there is just one little line between those curving brows. Ah, I can read you, you see, as a shepherd reads the sky."

" It is nothing, Amory, but——"

" But what ? "

" You leave me this evening."

" But only to return to-morrow."

" And must you really, really go to-night ? "

" It would be as much as my commission is worth to be absent. Why, I am on duty to-morrow morning outside the king's bedroom ! After chapel-time Major de Brissac will take my place, and then I am free once more."

" Ah, Amory, when you talk of the king and the court and the grand ladies, you fill me with wonder."

" And why with wonder ? "

" To think that you who live amid such splendour should stoop to the humble room of a mercer."

" Ah, but what does the room contain ? "

" There is the greatest wonder of all. That you who pass your days amid such people, so beautiful, so witty, should think me worthy of your love, me, who am such a quiet little mouse, all alone in this great house, so shy and so backward ! It is wonderful ! "

" Every man has his own taste," said her cousin, stroking the tiny hand. " It is with women as with flowers. Some may prefer the great brilliant sunflower, or the rose, which is so bright and large that it must ever

catch the eye. But give me the little violet which hides among the mosses, and yet is so sweet to look upon, and sheds its fragrance round it. But still that line upon your brow, dearest."

" I was wishing that father would return."

" And why ? Are you so lonely, then ? "

Her pale face lit up with a quick smile. " I shall not be lonely until to-night. But I am always uneasy when he is away. One hears so much now of the persecution of our poor brethren."

" Tut ! my uncle can defy them."

" He has gone to the provost of the Mercer Guild about this notice of the quartering of the dragoons."

" Ah, you have not told me of that."

" Here it is." She rose and took up a slip of blue paper with a red seal dangling from it which lay upon the table. His strong, black brows knitted together as he glanced at it.

" Take notice," it ran, " that you, Théophile Catinat, cloth-mercer of the Rue St. Martin, are hereby required to give shelter and rations to twenty men of the Languedoc Blue Dragoons under Captain Dalbert, until such time as you receive a further notice. [Signed] De Beaupré (Commissioner of the King)."

De Catinat knew well how this method of annoying Huguenots had been practised all over France, but he had flattered himself that his own position at court would have ensured his kinsman from such an outrage. He threw the paper down with an exclamation of anger.

" When do they come ? "

" Father said to-night."

" Then they shall not be here long. To-morrow I shall have an order to remove them. But the sun has sunk behind St. Martin's Church, and I should already be upon my way."

" No, no ; you must not go yet."

" I would that I could give you into your father's charge first, for I fear you alone when these troopers may

500

come. And yet no excuse will avail me if I am not at Versailles. But see, a horseman has stopped before the door. He is not in uniform. Perhaps he is a messenger from your father."

The girl ran eagerly to the window, and peered out, with her hand resting upon her cousin's silver-corded shoulder.

" Ah ! " she cried, " I had forgotten. It is the man from America. Father said that he would come to-day."

" The man from America ! " repeated the soldier, in a tone of surprise, and they both craned their necks from the window. The horseman, a sturdy, broad-shouldered young man, clean-shaven and crop-haired, turned his long, swarthy face and his bold features in their direction as he ran his eyes over the front of the house. He had a soft-brimmed grey hat of a shape which was strange to Parisian eyes, but his sombre clothes and high boots were such as any citizen might have worn. Yet his general appearance was so unusual that a group of towns-folk had already assembled round him, staring with open mouth at his horse and himself. A battered gun with an extremely long barrel was fastened by the stock to his stirrup, while the muzzle stuck up into the air behind him. At each holster was a large dangling black bag, and a gaily coloured red-slashed blanket was rolled up at the back of his saddle. His horse, a strong-limbed dapple-grey, all shiny with sweat above, and all caked with mud beneath, bent its fore knees as it stood, as though it were overspent. The rider, however, having satisfied himself as to the house, sprang lightly out of his saddle and disengaging his gun, his blanket and his bags, pushed his way unconcernedly through the gaping crowd and knocked loudly at the door.

" Who is he, then ? " asked De Catinat. " A Canadian ? I am almost one myself. I had as many friends on one side of the sea as on the other. Perchance I know him. There are not so many white faces yonder, and in two years there was scarce one from the Saguenay to Nipissing that I had not seen."

"Nay, he is from the English provinces, Amory. But he speaks our tongue. His mother was of our blood."

"And his name?"

"Is Amos—Amos—ah, those names! Yes, Green, that was it—Amos Green. His father and mine have done much trade together, and now his son, who, as I understand, has lived ever in the woods, is sent here to see something of men and cities. Ah, my God! what can have happened now?"

A sudden chorus of screams and cries had broken out from the passage beneath, with the shouting of a man and the sound of rushing steps. In an instant De Catinat was half-way down the stairs, and was staring in amazement at the scene in the hall beneath.

Two maids stood, screaming at the pitch of their lungs, at either side. In the centre the aged man-servant Pierre, a stern old Calvinist, whose dignity had never before been shaken, was spinning round, waving his arms, and roaring so that he might have been heard at the Louvre. Attached to the grey worsted stocking which covered his fleshless calf was a fluffy black hairy ball, with one little red eye glancing up, and the gleam of two white teeth where it held its grip. At the shrieks, the young stranger, who had gone out to his horse, came rushing back, and plucking the creature off, he slapped it twice across the snout, and plunged it head-foremost back into the leather bag from which it had emerged.

"It is nothing," said he, speaking in excellent French; "it is only a bear."

"Ah, my God!" cried Pierre, wiping the drops from his brow. "Ah, it has aged me five years! I was at the door, bowing to monsieur, and in a moment it had me from behind."

"It was my fault for leaving the bag loose. The creature was but pupped the day we left New York, six weeks come Tuesday. Do I speak with my father's friend, Monsieur Catinat?"

"No, monsieur," said the guardsman, from the stair-

case. " My uncle is out, but I am Captain de Catinat, at your service, and here is Mademoiselle Catinat, who is your hostess."

The stranger ascended the stair, and paid his greetings to them both with the air of a man who was as shy as a wild deer, and yet who had steeled himself to carry a thing through. He walked with them to the sitting-room, and then in an instant was gone again, and they heard his feet thudding upon the stairs. Presently he was back, with a lovely glossy skin in his hands. " The bear is for your father, mademoiselle," said he. " This little skin I have brought from America for you. It is but a trifle, and yet it may serve to make a pair of mocassins or a pouch."

Adèle gave a cry of delight as her hands sank into the depths of its softness. She might well admire it, for no king in the world could have had a finer skin. " Ah, it is beautiful, monsieur," she cried ; " and what creature is it ; and where did it come from ? "

" It is a black fox. I shot it myself last fall up near the Iroquois villages at Lake Oneida."

She pressed it to her cheek, her white face showing up like marble against its absolute blackness. " I am sorry my father is not here to welcome you, monsieur," she said ; " but I do so very heartily in his place. Your room is above. Pierre will show you to it, if you wish."

" My room ? For what ? "

" Why, monsieur, to sleep in ! "

" And must I sleep in a room ? "

De Catinat laughed at the gloomy face of the American. " You shall not sleep there if you do not wish," said he.

The other brightened at once, and stepped across to the farther window, which looked down upon the court-yard. " Ah," he cried. " There is a beech-tree there, mademoiselle, and if I might take my blanket out yonder, I should like it better than any room. In winter, indeed, one must do it, but in summer I am smothered with a ceiling pressing down upon me."

" You are not from a town then ? " said De Catinat.

" My father lives in New York—two doors from the house of Peter Stuyvesant, of whom you must have heard. He is a very hardy man, and he can do it, but I—even a few days of Albany or of Schenectady are enough for me. My life has been in the woods."

" I am sure that my father would wish you to sleep where you like and to do what you like, as long as it makes you happy."

" I thank you, mademoiselle. Then I shall take my things out there, and I shall groom my horse."

" Nay, there is Pierre."

" I am used to doing it myself."

" Then I will come with you," said De Catinat, " for I would have a word with you. Until to-morrow, then, Adèle, farewell ! "

" Until to-morrow, Amory."

The two young men passed downstairs together, and the guardsman followed the American out into the yard.

" You have had a long journey," he said.

" Yes ; from Rouen."

" Are you tired ? "

" No ; I am seldom tired."

" Remain with the lady, then, until her father comes back."

" Why do you say that ? "

" Because I have to go, and she might need a protector."

The stranger said nothing, but he nodded, and throwing off his black coat, set to work vigorously rubbing down his travel-stained horse.

2. *A Monarch in Déshabille*

IT was the morning after the guardsman had returned to his duties. Eight o'clock had struck on the great clock of Versailles, and it was almost time for the monarch to rise. Through all the long corridors and

frescoed passages of the monster palace there was a subdued hum and rustle, with a low muffled stir of preparation, for the rising of the king was a great state function in which many had a part to play. A servant with a steaming silver saucer hurried past, bearing it to Monsieur de St. Quentin, the state barber. Others, with clothes thrown over their arms, bustled down the passage which led to the ante-chamber. The knot of guardsmen in their gorgeous blue and silver coats straightened themselves up and brought their halberds to attention, while the young officer, who had been looking wistfully out of the window at some courtiers who were laughing and chatting on the terraces, turned sharply upon his heel, and strode over to the white and gold door of the royal bedroom.

He had hardly taken his stand there before the handle was very gently turned from within, the door revolved noiselessly upon its hinges, and a man slid silently through the aperture, closing it again behind him.

" Hush ! " said he, with his finger to his thin, precise lips, while his whole clean-shaven face and high-arched brows were an entreaty and a warning. " The king still sleeps."

The words were whispered from one to another among the group who had assembled outside the door. The speaker, who was Monsieur Bontems, head *valet de chambre*, gave a sign to the officer of the guard, and led him into the window alcove from which he had lately come.

" Good-morning, Captain de Catinat," said he, with a mixture of familiarity and respect in his manner.

" Good-morning, Bontems. How has the king slept ? "

" Admirably."

" But it is his time."

" Hardly."

" You will not rouse him yet ? "

" In seven and a half minutes." The valet pulled out the little round watch which gave the law to the man

who *was* the law to twenty millions of people. " Who commands at the main guard ? "

" Major de Brissac."

" And you will be here ? "

" For four hours I attend the king."

" Very good. He gave me some instructions for the officer of the guard, when he was alone last night after the *petit coucher*. He bade me to say that Monsieur de Vivonne was not to be admitted to the *grand lever*. You are to tell him so."

" I shall do so."

" Then, should a note come from *her*—you understand me, the new one——"

" Madame de Maintenon ? "

" Precisely. But it is more discreet not to mention names. Should she send a note, you will take it and deliver it quietly when the king gives you an opportunity."

" It shall be done."

" But if the other should come, as is possible enough—the other, you understand me, the former——"

" Madame de Montespan."

" Ah, that soldierly tongue of yours, captain ! Should she come, I say, you will gently bar her way, with courteous words, you understand, but on no account is she to be permitted to enter the royal room."

" Very good, Bontems."

" And now we have but three minutes."

He strode through the rapidly increasing group of people in the corridor with an air of proud humility, as befitted a man who, if he was a valet, was at least the king of valets by being the valet of the king. Close by the door stood a line of footmen, resplendent in their powdered wigs, red plush coats and silver shoulder-knots.

" Is the officer of the oven here ? " asked Bontems.

" Yes, sir," replied a functionary who bore in front of him an enamelled tray heaped with pine shavings.

" The opener of the shutters ? "

" Here, sir."

' The remover of the taper ? "

" Here, sir."

" Be ready for the word." He turned the handle once more, and slipped into the darkened room.

It was a large square apartment, with two high windows upon the farther side, curtained across with priceless velvet hangings. Through the chinks the morning sun shot a few little gleams, which widened as they crossed the room to break in bright blurs of light upon the primrose-tinted wall. A large arm-chair stood by the side of the burned-out fire, shadowed over by the huge marble mantelpiece, the back of which was carried up, twining and curving into a thousand arabesque and armorial devices until it blended with the richly painted ceiling. In one corner a narrow couch with a rug thrown across it showed where the faithful Bontems had spent the night.

In the very centre of the chamber there stood a large four-post bed, with curtains of Gobelin tapestry looped back from the pillow. A square of polished rails surrounded it, leaving a space some five feet in width all round between the enclosure and the bedside. Within this enclosure, or *ruelle*, stood a small round table, covered over with a white napkin, upon which lay a silver platter and an enamelled cup, the one containing a little Frontiniac wine and water, the other bearing three slices of the breast of a chicken, in case the king should hunger during the night.

As Bontems passed noiselessly across the room, his feet sinking into the moss-like carpet, there was the heavy close smell of sleep in the air, and he could hear the long thin breathing of the sleeper. He passed through the opening in the rails, and stood, watch in hand, waiting for the exact instant when the iron routine of the court demanded that the monarch should be roused. Beneath him, from under the costly green coverlet of Oriental silk, half buried in the fluffy Valenciennes lace which edged the pillow, there protruded a round black bristle of close-cropped hair, with the profile of a curving nose

and petulant lip outlined against the white background.
The valet snapped his watch, and bent over the sleeper.

" I have the honour to inform your Majesty that it is
half-past eight," said he.

" Ah ! " The king slowly opened his large dark-brown
eyes, made the sign of the cross, and kissed a little dark
reliquary which he drew from under his night-dress.
Then he sat up in bed, and blinked about him with the
air of a man who is collecting his thoughts.

" Did you give my orders to the officer of the guard,
Bontems ? " he asked.

" Yes, sire."

" Who is on duty ? "

" Major de Brissac at the main guard, and Captain de
Catinat in the corridor."

" De Catinat ! Ah, the young man who stopped my
horse at Fontainebleau. I remember him. You may
give the signal, Bontems."

The chief valet walked swiftly across to the door and
threw it open. In rushed the officer of the ovens and
the four red-coated, white-wigged footmen, ready-handed,
silent-footed, each intent upon his own duties. The one
seized upon Bontems' rug and couch, and in an instant
had whipped them off into an ante-chamber ; another had
carried away the " en cas " meal and the silver taper-stand ;
while a third drew back the great curtains of stamped
velvet and let a flood of light into the apartment. Then,
as the flames were already flickering among the pine
shavings in the fireplace, the officer of the ovens placed
two round logs crosswise above them, for the morning
air was chilly, and withdrew with his fellow-servants.

They were hardly gone before a more august group
entered the bed-chamber. Two walked together in front,
the one a youth little over twenty years of age, middle-
sized, inclining to stoutness, with a slow, pompous bearing,
a well-turned leg, and a face which was comely enough in
a mask-like fashion, but which was devoid of any shadow
of expression, except perhaps of an occasional lurking

gleam of mischievous humour. He was richly clad in plum-coloured velvet, with a broad band of blue silk across his breast, and the glittering edge of the order of St. Louis protruding from under it. His companion was a man of forty, swarthy, dignified and solemn, in a plain but rich dress of black silk with slashes of gold at the neck and sleeves. As the pair faced the king there was sufficient resemblance between the three faces to show that they were of one blood, and to enable a stranger to guess that the older was Monsieur, the younger brother of the king, while the other was Louis the Dauphin, his only legitimate child, and heir to a throne to which in the strange workings of Providence neither he nor his sons were destined to ascend.

Strong as was the likeness between the three faces, each with the curving Bourbon nose, the large full eye, and the thick Hapsburg under-lip, their common heritage from Anne of Austria, there was still a vast difference of temperament and character stamped upon their features. The king was now in his six-and-fortieth year, and the cropped black head was already thinning a little on the top, and shading away to grey over the temples. He still, however, retained much of the beauty of his youth, tempered by the dignity and sternness which increased with his years. His dark eyes were full of expression, and his clear-cut features were the delight of the sculptor and the painter. His firm and yet sensitive mouth and his thick, well-arched brows gave an air of authority and power to his face, while the more subdued expression which was habitual to his brother marked the man whose whole life had been spent in one long exercise of deference and self-effacement. The dauphin, on the other hand, with a more regular face than his father, had none of that quick play of feature when excited, or that kingly serenity when composed, which had made a shrewd observer say that Louis, if he were not the greatest monarch that ever lived, was at least the best fitted to act the part.

Behind the king's son and the king's brother there entered a little group of notables and of officials whom duty had called to this daily ceremony. There was the grand master of the robes, the first lord of the bed-chamber, the Duc du Maine, a pale youth clad in black velvet, limping heavily with his left leg, and his little brother, the young Comte de Toulouse, both of them the illegitimate sons of Madame de Montespan and the king. Behind them, again, was the first valet of the wardrobe, followed by Fagon, the first physician, Telier, the head surgeon, and three pages in scarlet and gold who bore the royal clothes. Such were the partakers in the family entry, the highest honour which the court of France could aspire to.

Bontems had poured on the king's hands a few drops of spirits of wine, catching them again in a silver dish ; and the first lord of the bed-chamber had presented the bowl of holy water with which he made the sign of the cross, muttering to himself the short office of the Holy Ghost. Then, with a nod to his brother and a short word of greeting to the dauphin and to the Duc du Maine, he swung his legs over the side of the bed, and sat in his long silken night-dress, his little white feet dangling from beneath it—a perilous position for any man to assume, were it not that he had so heart-felt a sense of his own dignity that he could not realise that under any circumstances it might be compromised in the eyes of others. So he sat, the master of France, and yet the slave to every puff of wind, for a wandering draught had set him shivering and shaking. Monsieur de St. Quentin, the noble barber, flung purple dressing-gown over the royal shoulders, and placed a long many-curled court wig upon his head, while Bontems drew on his red stockings and laid before him his slippers of embroidered velvet. The monarch thrust his feet into them, tied his dressing-gown, and passed out to the fireplace, where he settled himself down in his easy-chair, holding out his thin delicate hands towards the blazing logs, while the others stood

round in a semicircle, waiting for the *grand lever* which was to follow.

" How is this, messieurs ? " the king asked suddenly, glancing round him with a petulant face. " I am conscious of a smell of scent. Surely none of you would venture to bring perfume into the presence, knowing, as you must all do, how offensive it is to me."

The little group glanced from one to the other with protestations of innocence. The faithful Bontems, however, with his stealthy step, had passed along behind them, and had detected the offender.

" My lord of Toulouse, the smell comes from you," he said.

The Comte de Toulouse, a little ruddy-cheeked lad, flushed up at the detection.

" If you please, sire, it is possible that Mademoiselle de Grammont may have wet my coat with her casting-bottle when we all played together at Marly yesterday," he stammered. " I had not observed it, but if it offends your Majesty——"

" Take it away ! take it away ! " cried the king. " Pah ! it chokes and stifles me ! Open the lower casement, Bontems. No ; never heed, now that he is gone. Monsieur de St. Quentin, is this not our shaving morning ? "

" Yes, sire ; all is ready."

" Then why not proceed ? It is three minutes after the accustomed time. To work, sir ; and you, Bontems, give word for the *grand lever*."

It was obvious that the king was not in a very good humour that morning. He darted little quick questioning glances at his brother and at his sons, but whatever complaint or sarcasm may have trembled upon his lips, was effectually stifled by De St. Quentin's ministrations. With the nonchalance born of long custom, the official covered the royal chin with soap, drew the razor swiftly round it, and sponged over the surface with spirits of wine. A nobleman then helped to draw on the king's

black velvet *haut-de-chausses*, a second assisted in arranging them, while a third drew the night-gown over the shoulders, and handed the royal shirt, which had been warming before the fire. His diamond-buckled shoes, his gaiters, and his scarlet inner vest were successively fastened by noble courtiers, each keenly jealous of his own privilege, and over the vest was placed the blue ribbon with the cross of the Holy Ghost in diamonds, and that of St. Louis tied with red. To one to whom the sight was new, it might have seemed strange to see the little man, listless, passive, with his eyes fixed thoughtfully on the burning logs, while this group of men, each with a historic name, bustled round him, adding a touch here and a touch there, like a knot of children with a favourite doll. The black undercoat was drawn on, the cravat of rich lace adjusted, the loose overcoat secured, two handkerchiefs of costly point carried forward upon an enamelled saucer, and thrust by separate officials into each side pocket, the silver and ebony cane laid to hand, and the monarch was ready for the labours of the day.

During the half-hour or so which had been occupied in this manner there had been a constant opening and closing of the chamber door, and a muttering of names from the captain of the guard to the attendant in charge, and from the attendant in charge to the first gentleman of the chamber, ending always in the admission of some new visitor. Each as he entered bowed profoundly three times, as a salute to majesty, and then attached himself to his own little clique or coterie, to gossip in a low voice over the news, the weather and the plans of the day. Gradually the numbers increased, until by the time the king's frugal first breakfast of bread and twice-watered wine had been carried in, the large square chamber was quite filled with a throng of men, many of whom had helped to make the epoch the most illustrious of French history. Here, close by the king, was the harsh but energetic Louvois, all-powerful now since the death of his rival Colbert, discussing a question of military

organisation with two officers, the one a tall and stately soldier, the other a strange little figure, undersized and misshapen, but bearing the insignia of a marshal of France, and owning a name which was of evil omen over the Dutch frontier, for Luxembourg was looked upon already as the successor of Condé, even as his companion Vauban was of Turenne. Beside them, a small white-haired clerical with a kindly face, Père la Chaise, confessor to the king, was whispering his views upon Jansenism to the portly Bossuet, the eloquent Bishop of Meaux, and to the tall thin young Abbé de Fénélon, who listened with a clouded brow, for it was suspected that his own opinions were tainted with the heresy in question. There, too, was Le Brun, the painter, discussing art in a small circle which contained his fellow-workers Verrio and Laguerre, the architects Blondel and Le Nôtre, and sculptors Girardon, Puget, Desjardins and Coysevox, whose works had done so much to beautify the new palace of the king. Close to the door, Racine, with his handsome face wreathed in smiles, was chatting with the poet Boileau and the architect Mansard, the three laughing and jesting with the freedom which was natural to the favourite servants of the king, the only subjects who might walk unannounced and without ceremony into and out of his chamber.

" What is amiss with him this morning ? " asked Boileau in a whisper, nodding his head in the direction of the royal group. " I fear that his sleep has not improved his temper."

" He becomes harder and harder to amuse," said Racine, shaking his head. " I am to be at Madame de Maintenon's room at three to see whether a page or two of the *Phèdre* may not work a change."

" My friend," said the architect, " do you not think that madame herself might be a better consoler than your *Phèdre* ? "

" Madame is a wonderful woman. She has brains, she has heart, she has tact—she is admirable."

513

" And yet she has one gift too many."

" And that is ? "

" Age."

" Pooh ! What matter her years when she can carry them like thirty ? What an eye ! What an arm ! And besides, my friends, he is not himself a boy any longer."

" Ah, but that is another thing."

" A man's age is an incident, a woman's a calamity."

" Very true. But a young man consults his eye, and an older man his ear. Over forty, it is the clever tongue which wins ; under it, the pretty face."

" Ah, you rascal ! Then you have made up your mind that five-and-forty years with tact will hold the field against nine-and-thirty with beauty. Well, when your lady has won, she will doubtless remember who were the first to pay court to her."

" But I think that you are wrong, Racine."

" Well, we shall see."

" And if you are wrong——"

" Well, what then ? "

" Then it may be a little serious for you."

" And why ? "

" The Marquise de Montespan has a memory."

" Her influence may soon be nothing more."

" Do not rely too much upon it, my friend. When the Fontanges came up from Provence, with her blue eyes and her copper hair, it was in every man's mouth that Montespan had had her day. Yet Fontanges is six feet under a church crypt, and the marquise spent two hours with the king last week. She has won once, and may again."

" Ah, but this is a very different rival. This is no slip of a country girl, but the cleverest woman in France."

" Pshaw, Racine, you know our good master well, or you should, for you seem to have been at his elbow since the days of the Fronde. Is he a man, think you, to be amused for ever by sermons, or to spend his days at the feet of a lady of that age, watching her at her tapestry-

work, and fondling her poodle, when all the fairest faces and brightest eyes of France are as thick in his *salons* as the tulips in a Dutch flower-bed ? No, no, it will be the Montespan, or if not she, some younger beauty."

" My dear Boileau, I say again that her sun is setting. Have you not heard the news ? "

" Not a word."

" Her brother, Monsieur de Vivonne, has been refused the *entrée*."

" Impossible ! "

" But it is a fact."

" And when ? "

" This very morning."

" From whom had you it ? "

" From De Catinat, the captain of the guard. He had his orders to bar the way to him."

" Ha ! then the king does indeed mean mischief. That is why his brow is so cloudy this morning, then. By my faith, if the marquise has the spirit with which folk credit her, he may find that it was easier to win her than to slight her."

" Aye ; the Mortemarts are no easy race to handle."

" Well, heaven send him a safe way out of it ! But who is this gentleman ? His face is somewhat grimmer than those to which the court is accustomed. Ha ! the king catches sight of him, and Louvois beckons to him to advance. By my faith, he is one who would be more at his ease in a tent than under a painted ceiling."

The stranger who had attracted Racine's attention was a tall thin man, with a high aquiline nose, stern fierce grey eyes, peeping out from under tufted brows, and a countenance so lined and marked by age, care and stress of weather that it stood out amid the prim courtier faces which surrounded it as an old hawk might in a cage of birds of gay plumage. He was clad in a sombre-coloured suit which had become usual at court since the king had put aside frivolity and Fontanges, but the sword which hung from his waist was no fancy rapier, but a good brass-

515

hilted blade in a stained leather-sheath, which showed every sign of having seen hard service. He had been standing near the door, his black-feathered beaver in his hand, glancing with a half-amused, half-disdainful expression at the groups of gossips around him, but at the sign from the minister of war he began to elbow his way forward, pushing aside in no very ceremonious fashion all who barred his passage.

Louis possessed in a high degree the royal faculty of recognition. " It is years since I have seen him, but I remember his face well," said he, turning to his minister. " It is the Comte de Frontenac, is it not ? "

" Yes, sire," answered Louvois ; " it is indeed Louis de Buade, Comte de Frontenac, and formerly governor of Canada."

" We are glad to see you once more at our *lever*," said the monarch, as the old nobleman stooped his head and kissed the white hand which was extended to him. " I hope that the cold of Canada has not chilled the warmth of your loyalty."

" Only death itself, sire, would be cold enough for that."

" Then I trust that it may remain to us for many long years. We would thank you for the care and pains which you have spent upon our province, and if we have recalled you, it is chiefly that we would fain hear from your own lips how all things go there. And first, as the affairs of God take precedence of those of France, how does the conversion of the heathen prosper ? "

" We cannot complain, sire. The good fathers, both Jesuits and Récollets, have done their best, though indeed they are both rather ready to abandon the affairs of the next world in order to meddle with those of this."

" What say you to that, father ? " asked Louis, glancing, with a twinkle of the eyes, at his Jesuit confessor.

" I say, sire, that when the affairs of this world have a bearing upon those of the next, it is indeed the duty of a good priest, as of every other good Catholic, to guide them right."

" That is very true, sire," said De Frontenac, with an angry flush upon his swarthy cheek ; " but as long as your Majesty did me the honour to intrust those affairs to my own guidance, I would brook no interference in the performance of my duties, whether the meddler were clad in coat or cassock."

" Enough, sir, enough ! " said Louis sharply. " I had asked you about the missions."

" They prosper, sire. There are Iroquois at the Sault and the mountain, Hurons at Lorette, and Algonquins along the whole river *côtes* from Tadousac in the East to Sault la Marie, and even the great plains of the Dakotas, who have all taken the cross as their token. Marquette has passed down the river of the West to preach among the Illinois, and Jesuits have carried the Gospel to the warriors of the Long House in their wigwams at Onondaga."

" I may add, your Majesty," said Père la Chaise, " that in leaving the truth there, they have too often left their lives with it."

"Yes, sire, it is very true,"cried De Frontenac cordially. " Your Majesty has many brave men within your domains, but none braver than these. They have come back up the Richelieu River, from the Iroquois villages with their nails gone, their fingers torn out, a cinder where their eye should be, and the scars of pine splinters as thick upon their bodies as the *fleurs-de-lis* on yonder curtain. Yet, with a month of nursing from the good Ursulines, they have used their remaining eye to guide them back to the Indian country once more, where even the dogs have been frightened at their haggled faces and twisted limbs."

" And you have suffered this ? " cried Louis hotly. " You allow these infamous assassins to live ? "

" I have asked for troops, sire."

" And I have sent some."

" One regiment."

" The Carignan-Salière. I have no better in my service."

517

" But more is needed, sire."

" There are the Canadians themselves. Have you not a militia ? Could you not raise force enough to punish these rascally murderers of God's priests ! I had always understood that you were a soldier."

De Frontenac's eyes flashed, and a quick answer seemed for an instant to tremble upon his lips, but with an effort the fiery old man restrained himself. " Your Majesty will learn best whether I am a soldier or not," said he, " by asking those who have seen me at Seneffe, Mulhausen, Salzbach and half a score of other places where I had the honour of upholding your Majesty's cause."

" Your services have not been forgotten."

" It is just because I am a soldier and have seen something of war that I know how hard it is to penetrate into a country much larger than the Lowlands, all thick with forest and bog, with a savage lurking behind every tree, who, if he has not learned to step in time or to form line, can at least bring down the running caribou at two hundred paces, and travel three leagues to your one. And then when you have at last reached their villages, and burned their empty wigwams and a few acres of maize fields, what the better are you then ? You can but travel back again to your own land with a cloud of unseen men lurking behind you, and a scalp-yell for every straggler. You are a soldier yourself, sire. I ask you if such a war is an easy task for a handful of soldiers, with a few *censitaires* straight from the plough, and a troop of *coureurs-de-bois* whose hearts all the time are with their traps and their beaver-skins."

" No, no ; I am sorry if I spoke too hastily," said Louis. " We shall look into the matter at our council."

" Then it warms my heart to hear you say so," cried the old governor. " There will be joy down the long St. Lawrence, in white hearts and in red, when it is known that their great father over the waters has turned his mind towards them."

" And yet you must not look for too much, for Canada has been a heavy cost to us, and we have many calls in Europe."

" Ah, sire, I would that you could see that great land. When your Majesty has won a campaign over here, what may come of it ? Glory, a few miles of land, Luxembourg, Strassburg, one more city in the kingdom ; but over there, with a tenth of the cost and a hundredth part of the force, there is a world ready to your hand. It is so vast, sire, so rich, so beautiful ! Where are there such hills, such forests, such rivers ! And it is all for us if we will but take it. Who is there to stand in our way ? A few nations of scattered Indians and a thin strip of English farmers and fishermen. Turn your thoughts there, sire, and in a few years you would be able to stand upon your citadel at Quebec, and to say there is one great empire here from the snows of the North to the warm Southern gulf, and from the waves of the ocean to the great plains beyond Marquette's river, and the name of this empire is France, and her king is Louis, and her flag is the *fleurs-de-lis*."

Louis's cheek had flushed at this ambitious picture, and he had leaned forward in his chair, with flashing eyes, but he sank back again as the governor concluded.

"On my word, count," said he, "you have caught something of this gift of Indian eloquence of which we have heard. But about these English folk. They are Huguenots, are they not ? "

" For the most part. Especially in the North."

" Then it might be a service to Holy Church to send them packing. They have a city there, I am told. New— New —— How do they call it ? "

" New York, sire. They took it from the Dutch."

" Ah, New York. And have I not heard of another ? Bos—Bos——"

" Boston, sire."

" That is the name. The harbours might be of service to us. Tell me, now, Frontenac," lowering his voice so that his words might be audible only to the count, Louvois

and the royal circle, " what force would you need to clear these people out ? One regiment, two regiments, and perhaps a frigate or two ? "

But the ex-governor shook his grizzled head. " You do not know them, sire," said he. " They are stern folk, these. We in Canada, with all your gracious help, have found it hard to hold our own. Yet these men have had no help, but only hindrance, with cold and disease, and barren lands, and Indian wars, but they have thriven and multiplied until the woods thin away in front of them like ice in the sun, and their church bells are heard where but yesterday the wolves were howling. They are peaceful folk, and slow to war, but when they have set their hands to it, though they may be slack to begin, they are slacker still to cease. To put New England into your Majesty's hands, I would ask fifteen thousand of your best troops and twenty ships of the line."

Louis sprang impatiently from his chair, and caught up his cane. " I wish," said he, " that you would imitate these people who seem to you to be so formidable, in their excellent habit of doing things for themselves. The matter may stand until our council. Reverend father, it has struck the hour of chapel, and all else may wait until we have paid our duties to heaven." Taking a missal from the hands of an attendant, he walked as fast as his very high heels would permit him, towards the door, the court forming a lane through which he might pass, and then closing up behind to follow him in order of precedence.

3. *The Holding of the Door*

WHILST Louis had been affording his court that which he had openly stated to be the highest of human pleasures—the sight of the royal face— the young officer of the guard outside had been very busy passing on the titles of the numerous applicants for

admission, and exchanging usually a smile or a few words of greeting with them, for his frank handsome face was a well-known one at the court. With his merry eyes and his brisk bearing, he looked like a man who was on good terms with fortune. Indeed, he had good cause to be so, for she had used him well. Three years ago he had been an unknown subaltern bushfighting with Algonquins and Iroquois in the wilds of Canada. An exchange had brought him back to France and into the regiment of Picardy, but the lucky chance of having seized the bridle of the king's horse one winter's day in Fontainebleau when the creature was plunging within a few yards of a deep gravel-pit had done for him what ten campaigns might have failed to accomplish. Now as a trusted officer of the king's guard, young, gallant and popular, his lot was indeed an enviable one. And yet, with the strange perversity of human nature, he was already surfeited with the dull if magnificent routine of the king's household and looked back with regret to the rougher and freer days of his early service. Even there at the royal door his mind had turned away from the frescoed passage and the groups of courtiers to the wild ravines and foaming rivers of the West, when suddenly his eyes lit upon a face which he had last seen among those very scenes.

" Ah, Monsieur de Frontenac ! " he cried. " You cannot have forgotten me."

" What ! De Catinat ! Ah, it is a joy indeed to see a face from over the water. But there is a long step between a subaltern in the Carignan and a captain in the guards. You have risen rapidly."

" Yes ; and yet I may be none the happier for it. There are times when I would give it all to be dancing down the Lachine Rapids in a birch canoe, or to see the red and the yellow on those hill-sides once more at the fall of the leaf."

" Aye," sighed De Frontenac. " You know that my fortunes have sunk as yours have risen. I have been recalled, and De la Barre is in my place. But there will be a storm there which such a man as he can never stand

against. With the Iroquois all dancing the scalp-dance, and Dongan behind them in New York to whoop them on, they will need me, and they will find me waiting when they send. I will see the king now, and try if I cannot rouse him to play the great monarch there as well as here. Had I but his power in my hands, I should change the world's history."

" Hush ! No treason to the captain of the guard," cried De Catinat, laughing, while the stern old soldier strode past him into the king's presence.

A gentleman very richly dressed in black and silver had come up during this short conversation, and advanced, as the door opened, with the assured air of a man whose rights are beyond dispute. Captain de Catinat, however, took a quick step forward, and barred him off from the door.

" I am very sorry, Monsieur de Vivonne," said he, " but you are forbidden the presence."

" Forbidden the presence ! I ? You are mad ! " He stepped back with grey face and staring eyes, one shaking hand half raised in protest.

" I assure you that it is his order."

" But it is incredible. It is a mistake."

" Very possibly."

" Then you will let me past."

" My orders leave me no discretion."

" If I could have one word with the king."

" Unfortunately, monsieur, it is impossible."

" Only one word."

" It really does not rest with me, monsieur."

The angry nobleman stamped his foot, and stared at the door as though he had some thoughts of forcing a passage. Then turning on his heel, he hastened away down the corridor with the air of a man who has come to a decision.

" There, now," grumbled De Catinat to himself, as he pulled at his thick dark moustache, " he is off to make some fresh mischief. I'll have his sister here presently, as like as not, and a pleasant little choice between breaking

my orders and making an enemy of her for life. I'd rather hold Fort Richelieu against the Iroquois than the king's door against an angry woman. By my faith, here *is* a lady, as I feared ! Ah, heaven be praised ! it is a friend, and not a foe. Good-morning, Mademoiselle Nanon."

" Good-morning, Captain de Catinat."

The new-comer was a tall, graceful brunette, her fresh face and sparkling black eyes the brighter in contrast with her plain dress.

" I am on guard, you see. I cannot talk with you."

" I cannot remember having asked monsieur to talk with me."

" Ah, but you must not pout in that pretty way, or else I cannot help talking to you," whispered the captain. " What is this in your hand, then ? "

" A note from Madame de Maintenon to the king. You will hand it to him, will you not ? "

" Certainly, mademoiselle. And how is madame, your mistress ? "

" Oh, her director has been with her all the morning, and his talk is very, very good ; but it is also very, very sad. We are not very cheerful when Monsieur Godet has been to see us. But I forget monsieur is a Huguenot, and knows nothing of directors."

" Oh, but I do not trouble about such differences. I let the Sorbonne and Geneva fight it out between them. Yet a man must stand by his family, you know."

" Ah ! if monsieur could talk to Madame de Maintenon a little ! She would convert him."

" I would rather talk to Mademoiselle Nanon, but if——"

" Oh ! " There was an exclamation, a whisk of dark skirts, and the soubrette had disappeared down a side passage.

Along the broad, lighted corridor was gliding a very stately and beautiful lady, tall, graceful and exceedingly haughty. She was richly clad in a bodice of gold-coloured camlet and a skirt of grey silk trimmed with gold and silver lace. A handkerchief of priceless Genoa point

half hid and half revealed her beautiful throat, and was fastened in front by a cluster of pearls, while a rope of the same, each one worth a bourgeois' income, was coiled in and out through her luxuriant hair. The lady was past her first youth, it is true, but the magnificent curves of her queenly figure, the purity of her complexion, the brightness of her deep-lashed blue eyes, and the clear regularity of her features enabled her still to claim to be the most handsome as well as the most sharp-tongued woman in the court of France. So beautiful was her bearing, the carriage of her dainty head upon her proud white neck, and the sweep of her stately walk, that the young officer's fears were overpowered in his admiration, and he found it hard, as he raised his hand in salute, to retain the firm countenance which his duties demanded.

" Ah, it is Captain de Catinat," said Madame de Montespan, with a smile which was more embarrassing to him than any frown could have been.

" Your humble servant, marquise."

" I am fortunate in finding a friend here, for there has been some ridiculous mistake this morning."

" I am concerned to hear it."

" It was about my brother, Monsieur de Vivonne. It is almost too laughable to mention, but he was actually refused admission to the *lever*."

" It was my misfortune to have to refuse him, madame."

" You, Captain de Catinat ? And by what right ? " She had drawn up her superb figure, and her large blue eyes were blazing with indignant astonishment.

" The king's order, madame."

" The king ! Is it likely that the king would cast a public slight upon my family ? From whom had you this preposterous order ? "

" Direct from the king through Bontems."

" Absurd ! Do you think that the king would venture to exclude a Mortemart through the mouth of a valet ? You have been dreaming, captain."

" I trust that it may prove so, madame."

"But such dreams are not very fortunate to the dreamer. Go, tell the king that I am here, and would have a word with him."

"Impossible, madame."

"And why?"

"I have been forbidden to carry a message."

"To carry any message?"

"Any from you, madame."

"Come, captain, you improve. It only needed this insult to make the thing complete. You may carry a message to the king from any adventuress, from any decayed governess"—she laughed shrilly at her description of her rival—"but none from Françoise de Morte-mart, Marquise de Montespan?"

"Such are my orders, madame. It pains me deeply to be compelled to carry them out."

"You may spare your protestations, captain. You may yet find that you have every reason to be deeply pained. For the last time, do you refuse to carry my message to the king?"

"I must, madame."

"Then I carry it myself."

She sprang forward at the door, but he slipped in front of her with outstretched arms.

"For God's sake, consider yourself, madame!" he entreated. "Other eyes are upon you."

"Pah! Canaille!" She glanced at the knot of Switzers, whose sergeant had drawn them off a few paces, and who stood open-eyed, staring at the scene. "I tell you that I *will* see the king."

"No lady has ever been at the morning *lever*."

"Then I shall be the first."

"You will ruin me if you pass."

"And none the less, I shall do so."

The matter looked serious. De Catinat was a man of resource, but for once he was at his wit's end. Madame de Montespan's resolution, as it was called in her presence, or effrontery, as it was termed behind her back, was

proverbial. If she attempted to force her way, would he venture to use violence upon one who only yesterday had held the fortunes of the whole court in the hollow of her hand, and who, with her beauty, her wit and her energy, might very well be in the same position to-morrow ? If she passed him, then his future was ruined with the king, who never brooked the smallest deviation from his orders. On the other hand, if he thrust her back, he did that which could never be forgiven, and which would entail some deadly vengeance should she return to power. It was an unpleasant dilemma. But a happy thought flashed into his mind at the very moment when she, with clenched hand and flashing eyes, was on the point of making a fresh attempt to pass him.

" If madame would deign to wait," said he soothingly, " the king will be on his way to the chapel in an instant."

" It is not yet time."

" I think the hour has just gone."

" And why should I wait like a lackey ? "

" It is but a moment, madame."

" No, I shall not wait." She took a step forward towards the door.

But the guardsman's quick ear had caught the sound of moving feet from within, and he knew that he was master of the situation.

" I will take madame's message," said he.

" Ah, you have recovered your senses ! Go, tell the king that I wish to speak with him."

He must gain a little time yet. " Shall I say it through the lord in waiting ? "

" No ; yourself."

" Publicly ? "

" No, no ; for his private ear."

" Shall I give a reason for your request ? "

" Oh, you madden me ! Say what I have told you, and at once."

But the young officer's dilemma was happily over. At that instant the double doors were swung open, and Louis

appeared in the opening, strutting forwards on his high-heeled shoes, his stick tapping, his broad skirts flapping, and his courtiers spreading out behind him. He stopped as he came out, and turned to the captain of the guard.

" You have a note for me ? "

" Yes, sire."

The monarch slipped it into the pocket of his scarlet undervest, and was advancing once more when his eyes fell upon Madame de Montespan standing very stiff and erect in the middle of the passage. A dark flush of anger shot to his brow, and he walked swiftly past her without a word ; but she turned and kept pace with him down the corridor.

" I had not expected this honour, madame," said he.

" Nor had I expected this insult, sire."

" An insult, madame ? You forget yourself."

" No ; it is you who have forgotten me, sire."

" You intrude upon me."

" I wished to hear my fate from your own lips," she whispered. " I can bear to be struck myself, sire, even by him who has my heart. But it is hard to hear that one's brother has been wounded through the mouths of valets and Huguenot soldiers for no fault of his, save that his sister has loved too fondly."

" It is no time to speak of such things."

" When can I see you, then, sire ? "

" In your chamber."

" At what hour ? "

" At four."

" Then I shall trouble your Majesty no further."

She swept him one of the graceful courtesies for which she was famous, and turned away down a side passage with triumph shining in her eyes. Her beauty and her spirit had never failed her yet, and now that she had the monarch's promise of an interview she never doubted that she could do as she had done before, and win back the heart of the man, however much against the conscience of the king.

4. *The Father of His People*

LOUIS had walked on to his devotions in no very charitable frame of mind, as was easily to be seen from his clouded brow and compressed lips. He knew his late favourite well, her impulsiveness, her audacity, her lack of all restraint when thwarted or opposed. She was capable of making a hideous scandal, of turning against him that bitter tongue which had so often made him laugh at the expense of others, perhaps even of making some public exposure which would leave him the butt and gossip of Europe. He shuddered at the thought. At all costs such a catastrophe must be averted. And yet how could he cut the tie which bound them ? He had broken other such bonds as these ; but the gentle La Vallière had shrunk into a convent at the very first glance which had told her of waning love. That was true affection. But this woman would struggle hard, fight to the bitter end, before she would quit the position which was so dear to her. She spoke of her wrongs. What were her wrongs ? In his intense selfishness, nurtured by the eternal flattery which was the very air he breathed, he could not see that the fifteen years of her life which he had absorbed, or the loss of the husband whom he had supplanted, gave her any claim upon him. In his view he had raised her to the highest position which a subject could occupy. Now he was weary of her, and it was her duty to retire with resignation, nay, even with gratitude for past favours. She should have a pension, and the children should be cared for. What could a reasonable woman ask for more ?

And then his motives for discarding her were so excellent. He turned them over in his mind as he knelt listening to the Archbishop of Paris reciting the mass, and the more he thought, the more he approved. His conception of the deity was as a larger Louis, and of heaven as a more gorgeous Versailles. If he exacted obedience from his twenty millions, then he must show it also to

this one who had a right to demand it of him. On the whole, his conscience acquitted him. But in this one matter he had been lax. From the first coming of his gentle and forgiving young wife from Spain, he had never once permitted her to be without a rival. Now that she was dead, the matter was no better. One favourite had succeeded another, and if De Montespan had held her own so long, it was rather from her audacity than from his affection. But now Father La Chaise and Bossuet were ever reminding him that he had topped the summit of his life, and was already upon that downward path which leads to the grave. His wild outburst over the unhappy Fontanges had represented the last flicker of his passions. The time had come for gravity and for calm, neither of which was to be expected in the company of Madame de Montespan.

But he had found out where they were to be enjoyed. From the day when De Montespan had introduced the stately and silent widow as a governess for his children, he had found a never-failing and ever-increasing pleasure in her society. In the early days of her coming he had sat for hours in the rooms of his favourite, watching the tact and sweetness of temper with which her dependent controlled the mutinous spirits of the petulant young Duc du Maine and the mischievous little Comte de Toulouse. He had been there nominally for the purpose of superintending the teaching, but he had confined himself to admiring the teacher. And then in time he too had been drawn into the attraction of that strong sweet nature, and had found himself consulting her upon points of conduct, and acting upon her advice with a docility which he had never shown before to minister or mistress. For a time he had thought that her piety and her talk of principle might be a mere mask, for he was accustomed to hypocrisy all round him. It was surely unlikely that a woman who was still beautiful, with as bright an eye and as graceful a figure as any in his court, could, after a life spent in the gayest circles, preserve the spirit of a nun.

But on this point he was soon undeceived, for when his own language had become warmer than that of friendship, he had been met by an iciness of manner and a brevity of speech which had shown him that there was one woman at least in his dominions who had a higher respect for herself than for him. And perhaps it was better so. The placid pleasures of friendship were very soothing after the storms of passion. To sit in her room every afternoon, to listen to talk which was not tainted with flattery, and to hear opinions which were not framed to please his ear, were the occupations now of his happiest hours. And then her influence over him was all so good ! She spoke of his kingly duties, of his example to his subjects, of his preparation for the world beyond, and of the need for an effort to snap the guilty ties which he had formed. She was as good as a confessor—a confessor with a lovely face and a perfect arm.

And now he knew that the time had come when he must choose between her and De Montespan. Their influences were antagonistic. They could not continue together. He stood between virtue and vice, and he must choose. Vice was very attractive too, very comely, very witty, and holding him by that chain of custom which is so hard to shake off. There were hours when his nature swayed strongly over to that side, and when he was tempted to fall back into his old life. But Bossuet and Père La Chaise were ever at his elbows to whisper encouragement, and, above all, there was Madame de Maintenon to remind him of what was due to his position and to his six-and-forty years. Now at last he had braced himself for a supreme effort. There was no safety for him while his old favourite was at court. He knew himself too well to have any faith in a lasting change so long as she was there ever waiting for his moment of weakness. She must be persuaded to leave Versailles, if without a scandal it could be done. He would be firm when he met her in the afternoon, and make her understand once for all that her reign was for ever over.

Such were the thoughts which ran through the king's head as he bent over the rich crimson cushion which topped his *prie-dieu* of carved oak. He knelt in his own enclosure to the right of the altar, with his guards and his immediate household around him, while the court, ladies and cavaliers, filled the chapel. Piety was a fashion now, like dark overcoats and lace cravats, and no courtier was so worldly-minded as not to have had a touch of grace since the king had taken to religion. Yet they looked very bored, these soldiers and seigneurs, yawning and blinking over the missals, while some who seemed more intent upon their devotions were really dipping into the latest romance of Scudéry or Calpernedi, cunningly bound up in a sombre cover. The ladies, indeed, were more devout, and were determined that all should see it, for each had lit a tiny taper, which she held in front of her on the plea of lighting up her missal, but really that her face might be visible to the king, and inform him that hers was a kindred spirit. A few there may have been, here and there, whose prayers rose from their hearts, and who were there of their own free will ; but the policy of Louis had changed his noblemen into courtiers and his men of the world into hypocrites, until the whole court was like one gigantic mirror which reflected his own likeness a hundredfold.

It was the habit of Louis, as he walked back from the chapel, to receive petitions or to listen to any tales of wrong which his subjects might bring to him. His way, as he returned to his rooms, lay partly across an open space, and here it was that the suppliants were wont to assemble. On this particular morning there were but two or three—a Parisian, who conceived himself injured by the provost of his guild, a peasant whose cow had been torn by a huntsman's dog, and a farmer who had had hard usage from his feudal lord. A few questions, and then a hurried order to his secretary disposed of each case, for if Louis was a tyrant himself, he had at least the merit that he insisted upon being the only one within his kingdom. He was about to resume his way again, when an elderly man, clad

in the garb of a respectable citizen, and with a strong deep-lined face which marked him as a man of character, darted forward, and threw himself down upon one knee in front of the monarch.

" Justice, sire, justice ! " he cried.

" What is this, then ? " asked Louis. " Who are you, and what is it that you want ? "

" I am a citizen of Paris, and I have been cruelly wronged."

" You seem a very worthy person. If you have indeed been wronged you shall have redress. What have you to complain of ? "

" Twenty of the Blue Dragoons of Languedoc are quartered in my house, with Captain Dalbert at their head. They have devoured my food, stolen my property, and beaten my servants, yet the magistrates will give me no redress."

" On my life, justice seems to be administered in a strange fashion in our city of Paris ! " exclaimed the king wrathfully.

" It is indeed a shameful case," said Bossuet.

" And yet there may be a very good reason for it," suggested Père La Chaise. " I would suggest that your Majesty should ask this man his name, his business and why it was that the dragoons were quartered upon him."

" You hear the reverend father's question."

" My name, sire, is Catinat, by trade I am a merchant in cloth, and I am treated in this fashion because I am of the Reformed Church."

" I thought as much ! " cried the confessor.

" That alters matters," said Bossuet.

The king shook his head and his brow darkened. " You have only yourself to thank, then. The remedy is in your hands."

" And how, sire ? "

" By embracing the only true faith."

" I am already a member of it, sire."

The king stamped his foot angrily. " I can see that

you are a very insolent heretic," said he. " There is but one Church in France, and that is my Church. If you are outside that, you cannot look to me for aid."

" My creed is that of my father, sire, and of my grandfather."

" If they have sinned it is no reason why you should. My own grandfather erred also before his eyes were opened."

" But he nobly atoned for his error," murmured the Jesuit.

" Then you will not help me, sire ? "

" You must first help yourself."

The old Huguenot stood up with a gesture of despair, while the king continued on his way, the two ecclesiastics, on either side of him, murmuring their approval into his ears.

" You have done nobly, sire."

" You are truly the first son of the Church."

" You are the worthy successor of St. Louis."

But the king bore the face of a man who was not absolutely satisfied with his own action.

" You do not think, then, that these people have too hard a measure ? " said he.

" Too hard ? Nay, your Majesty errs on the side of mercy."

" I hear that they are leaving my kingdom in great numbers."

" And surely it is better so, sire ; for what blessing can come upon a country which has such stubborn infidels within its boundaries ? "

" Those who are traitors to God can scarce be loyal to the king," remarked Bossuet. " Your Majesty's power would be greater if there were no temple, as they call their dens of heresy, within your dominions."

" My grandfather promised them protection. They are shielded, as you well know, by the edict which he gave at Nantes."

" But it lies with your Majesty to undo the mischief that has been done."

" And how ? "

" By recalling the edict."

" And driving into the open arms of my enemies two millions of my best artisans and of my bravest servants. No, no, father, I have, I trust, every zeal for Mother-Church, but there is some truth in what De Frontenac said this morning of the evil which comes from mixing the affairs of this world with those of the next. How say you, Louvois ? "

" With all respect to the Church, sire, I would say that the devil has given these men such cunning of hand and of brain that they are the best workers and traders in your Majesty's kingdom. I know not how the state coffers are to be filled if such tax-payers go from among us. Already many have left the country and taken their trades with them. If all were to go, it would be worse for us than a lost campaign."

" But," remarked Bossuet, " if it were once known that the king's will had been expressed, your Majesty may rest assured that even the worst of his subjects bear him such love that they would hasten to come within the pale of Holy Church. As long as the edict stands, it seems to them that the king is lukewarm and that they may abide in their error."

The king shook his head. " They have always been stubborn folk," said he.

" Perhaps," remarked Louvois, glancing maliciously at Bossuet, " were the bishops of France to make an offering to the state of the treasurers of their sees, we might then do without these Huguenot taxes."

" All that the Church has is at the king's service," answered Bossuet curtly.

" The kingdom is mine and all that is in it," remarked Louis, as they entered the *Grand Salon*, in which the court assembled after chapel, " yet I trust that it may be long before I have to claim the wealth of the Church."

" We trust so, sire," echoed the ecclesiastics.

" But we may reserve such topics for our council

chamber. Where is Mansard ? I must see his plans for the new wing at Marly." He crossed to a side table, and was buried in an instant in his favourite pursuit, inspecting the gigantic plans of the great architect, and inquiring eagerly as to the progress of the work.

" I think," said Père La Chaise, drawing Bossuet aside, " that your Grace has made some impression upon the king's mind."

" With your powerful assistance, father."

" Oh, you may rest assured that I shall lose no opportunity of pushing on the good work."

" If you take it in hand, it is done."

" But there is another who has more weight than I."

" The favourite, De Montespan ? "

" No, no ; her day is gone. It is Madame de Maintenon."

" I hear that she is very devout."

" Very. But she has no love for my Order. She is a Sulpitian. Yet we may all work to one end. Now if you were to speak to her, your Grace."

" With all my heart."

" Show her how good a service it would be could she bring about the banishment of the Huguenots."

" I shall do so."

" And offer her in return that we will promote——" he bent forward and whispered into the prelate's ear.

" What ! He would not do it ! "

" And why ? The queen is dead."

" The widow of the poet Scarron ! "

" She is of good birth. Her grandfather and his were dear friends."

" It is impossible ! "

" But I know his heart, and I say it is possible."

" You certainly know his heart, father, if any can. But such a thought had never entered my head."

" Then let it enter and remain there. If she will serve the Church, the Church will serve her. But the king beckons, and I must go."

The thin dark figure hastened off through the throng of courtiers, and the great Bishop of Meaux remained standing with his chin upon his breast, sunk in reflection.

By this time all the court was assembled in the *Grand Salon* and the huge room was gay from end to end with the silks, the velvets and the brocades of the ladies, the glitter of jewels, the flirt of painted fans, and the sweep of plume or aigrette. The greys, blacks and browns of the men's coats toned down the mass of colour, for all must be dark, when the king was dark, and only the blues of the officers' uniforms, and the pearl and grey of the musketeers of the guard, remained to call back those early days of the reign when the men had vied with the women in the costliness and brilliancy of their wardrobes. And if dresses had changed, manners had done so even more. The old levity and the old passions lay doubtless very near the surface, but grave faces and serious talk were the fashion of the hour. It was no longer the lucky *coup* at the lansquenet table, the last comedy of Molière, or the new opera of Lully about which they gossiped, but it was on the evils of Jansenism, on the expulsion of Arnauld from the Sorbonne, on the insolence of Pascal, or on the comparative merits of two such popular preachers as Bourdaloue and Massilon. So, under a radiant ceiling and over a many-coloured floor, surrounded by immortal paintings, set thickly in gold and ornament, there moved these nobles and ladies of France, all moulding themselves upon the one little dark figure in their midst, who was himself so far from being his own master that he hung balanced even now between two rival women, who were playing a game in which the future of France and his own destiny were the stakes.

5. *Children of Belial*

THE elderly Huguenot had stood silent after his repulse by the king, with his eyes cast moodily downwards, and a face in which doubt, sorrow and anger contended for the mastery. He was a very large, gaunt man, rawboned and haggard, with a wide forehead, a large, fleshy nose, and a powerful chin. He wore neither wig nor powder, but Nature had put her own silvering upon his thick grizzled locks, and the thousand puckers which clustered round the edges of his eyes, or drew at the corners of his mouth, gave a set gravity to his face which needed no device of the barber to increase it. Yet, in spite of his mature years, the swift anger with which he had sprung up when the king refused his plaint, and the keen fiery glance which he had shot at the royal court as they filed past him with many a scornful smile and whispered gibe at his expense, all showed that he had still preserved something of the strength and of the spirit of his youth. He was dressed as became his rank, plainly and yet well, in a sad-coloured brown kersey coat with silver-plated buttons, knee-breeches of the same, and white woollen stockings, ending in broad-toed black leather shoes cut across with a great steel buckle. In one hand he carried his low felt hat, trimmed with gold edging, and in the other a little cylinder of paper containing a recital of his wrongs, which he had hoped to leave in the hands of the king's secretary.

His doubts as to what his next step should be were soon resolved for him in a very summary fashion. These were days when, if the Huguenot was not absolutely forbidden in France, he was at least looked upon as a man who existed upon sufferance, and who was unshielded by the laws which protected his Catholic fellow-subjects. For twenty years the stringency of the persecution had increased until there was no weapon which bigotry could employ, short of absolute expulsion, which had not been

537

turned against him. He was impeded in his business, elbowed out of all public employment, his house filled with troops, his children encouraged to rebel against him, and all redress refused him for the insults and assaults to which he was subjected. Every rascal who wished to gratify his personal spite, or to gain favour with his bigoted superiors, might do his worst upon him without fear of the law. Yet, in spite of all, these men clung to the land which disowned them, and, full of the love for their native soil which lies so deep in a Frenchman's heart, preferred insult and contumely at home to the welcome which would await them beyond the seas. Already, however, the shadow of those days was falling upon them when the choice should no longer be theirs.

Two of the king's big blue-coated guardsmen were on duty at that side of the palace, and had been witnesses to his unsuccessful appeal. Now they tramped across together to where he was standing, and broke brutally into the current of his thoughts.

" Now, Hymn-books," said one gruffly, " get off again about your business."

" You're not a very pretty ornament to the king's pathway," cried the other, with a hideous oath. " Who are you, to turn up your nose at the king's religion, curse you ? "

The old Huguenot shot a glance of anger and contempt at them, and was turning to go, when one of them thrust at his ribs with the butt end of his halberd.

" Take that, you dog ! " he cried. " Would you dare to look like that at the king's guard ! "

" Children of Belial," cried the old man, with his hand pressed to his side, " were I twenty years younger you would not have dared to use me so."

" Ha ! you would still spit your venom, would you ? That is enough, André ! He has threatened the king's guard. Let us seize him and drag him to the guardroom."

The two soldiers dropped their halberds and rushed

upon the old man, but, tall and strong as they were, they found it no easy matter to secure him. With his long sinewy arms and his wiry frame, he shook himself clear of them again and again, and it was only when his breath had failed him that the two, torn and panting, were able to twist round his wrists, and so secure him. They had hardly won their pitiful victory, however, before a stern voice and a sword flashing before their eyes, compelled them to release their prisoner once more.

It was Captain de Catinat, who, his morning duties over, had strolled out on to the terrace and had come upon this sudden scene of outrage. At the sight of the old man's face he gave a violent start, and drawing his sword, had rushed forward with such fury that the two guardsmen not only dropped their victim, but, staggering back from the threatening sword point, one of them slipped and the other rolled over him, a revolving mass of blue coat and white kersey.

" Villains ! " roared De Catinat. " What is the meaning of this ? "

The two had stumbled on to their feet again, very shamefaced and ruffled.

" If you please, captain," said one, saluting, " this is a Huguenot who abused the royal guard."

" His petition had been rejected by the king, captain, and yet he refused to go."

De Catinat was white with fury. " And so, when a French citizen has come to have a word with the great master of his country, he must be harassed by two Swiss dogs like you ? " he cried. " By my faith, we shall soon see about that ! "

He drew a little silver whistle from his pocket, and at the shrill summons an old sergeant and half a dozen soldiers came running from the guard-room.

" Your names ? " asked the captain sternly.

" André Meunier."

" And yours ? "

" Nicholas Klopper."

" Sergeant, you will arrest these men, Meunier and Klopper."

" Certainly, captain," said the sergeant, a dark grizzled old soldier of Condé and Turenne.

" See that they are tried to-day."

" And on what charge, captain ? "

" For assaulting an aged and respected citizen who had come on business to the king."

" He was a Huguenot on his own confession," cried the culprits together.

" Hum ! " The sergeant pulled doubtfully at his long moustache. " Shall we put the charge in that form, captain ? Just as the captain pleases." He gave a little shrug of his epauletted shoulders to signify his doubt whether any good could arise from it.

" No," said De Catinat, with a sudden happy thought. " I charge them with laying their halberds down while on duty, and with having their uniforms dirty and disarranged."

" That is better," answered the sergeant, with the freedom of a privileged veteran. " Thunder of God, but you have disgraced the guards ! An hour on the wooden horse with a musket at either foot may teach you that halberds were made for a soldier's hand, and not for the king's grassplot. Seize them ! Attention ! Right half turn ! March ! "

And away went the little clump of guardsmen with the sergeant in the rear.

The Huguenot had stood in the background, grave and composed, without any sign of exultation, during this sudden reversal of fortune ; but when the soldiers were gone, he and the young officer turned warmly upon each other.

" Amory, I had not hoped to see you ! "

" Nor I you, uncle. What, in the name of wonder, brings you to Versailles ? "

" My wrongs, Amory. The hand of the wicked is heavy upon us, and whom can we turn to, save only the king ? "

The young officer shook his head. " The king is at heart a good man," said he. " But he can only see the world through the glasses which are held before him. You have nothing to hope from him."

" He spurned me from his presence."

" Did he ask your name ? "

" He did, and I gave it."

The young guardsman whistled. " Let us walk to the gate," said he. " By my faith, if my kinsmen are to come and bandy arguments with the king, it may not be long before my company finds itself without its captain."

" The king would not couple us together. But indeed, nephew, it is strange to me how you can live in this house of Baal and yet bow down to no false gods."

" I keep my belief in my own heart."

The older man shook his head gravely.

" Your ways lie along a very narrow path," said he, " with temptation and danger ever at your feet. It is hard for you to walk with the Lord, Amory, and yet go hand in hand with the persecutors of His people."

" Tut, uncle ! " said the young man impatiently. " I am a soldier of the king's, and I am willing to let the black gown and the white surplice settle these matters between them. Let me live in honour and die in my duty, and I am content to wait to know the rest."

" Content, too, to live in palaces, and eat from fine linen," said the Huguenot bitterly, " when the hands of the wicked are heavy upon your kinsfolk, and there is a breaking of phials, and a pouring forth of tribulation, and a wailing and a weeping through the land."

" What is amiss, then ? " asked the young soldier, who was somewhat mystified by the scriptural language in use among the French Calvinists of the day.

" Twenty men of Moab have been quartered upon me with one Dalbert, their captain, who has long been a scourge to Israel."

" Captain Claude Dalbert, of the Languedoc Dragoons ? I have already some small score to settle with him."

" Aye, and the scattered remnant has also a score against this murderous dog and self-seeking Ziphite."

" What has he done, then ? "

" His men are over my house like moths in a cloth bale. No place is free from them. He sits in the room which should be mine, his great boots on my Spanish-leather chairs, his pipe in his mouth, his wine-pot at his elbow, and his talk a hissing and an abomination. He has beaten old Pierre of the warehouse."

" Ha ! "

" And thrust me into the cellar."

" Ha ! "

" Because I have dragged him back when in his drunken love he would have thrown his arms about your cousin Adèle."

" Oh ! " The young man's colour had been rising and his brows knitted at each successive charge, but at this last his anger boiled over, and he hurried forward with fury in his face, dragging his elderly companion by the elbow. They had been passing through one of those winding paths, bordered by high hedges, which thinned away every here and there to give a glimpse of some prowling faun or weary nymph who slumbered in marble amid the foliage. The few courtiers who met them gazed with surprise at so ill-assorted a pair of companions. But the young soldier was too full of his own plans to waste a thought upon their speculations. Still hurrying on, he followed a crescent path which led past a dozen stone dolphins shooting water out of their mouths over a group of Tritons, and so through an avenue of great trees which looked as if they had grown there for centuries, and yet had in truth been carried over that very year by incredible labour from St. Germain and Fontainebleau. Beyond this point a small gate led out of the grounds, and it was through it that the two passed, the elder man puffing and panting with this unusual haste.

" How did you come, uncle ? "

" In a calèche."

" Where is it ? "

" That is it, beyond the auberge."

" Come, let us make for it."

" And you, Amory, are you coming ? "

" My faith, it is time that I came, from what you tell me. There is room for a man with a sword at his side in this establishment of yours."

" But what would you do ? "

" I would have a word with this Captain Dalbert."

" Then I have wronged you, nephew, when I said even now that you were not whole-hearted towards Israel."

" I know not about Israel," cried De Catinat impatiently. " I only know that if my Adèle chose to worship the thunder like an Abenaqui squaw, or turned her innocent prayers to the Mitche Manitou, I should like to set eyes upon the man who would dare to lay a hand upon her. Ha, here comes our calèche ! Whip up, driver, and five livres to you if you pass the gate of the Invalides within the hour."

It was no light matter to drive fast in an age of springless carriages and deeply rutted roads, but the driver lashed at his two rough unclipped horses, and the calèche jolted and clattered upon its way. As they sped on, with the road-side trees dancing past the narrow windows, and the white dust streaming behind them, the guardsman drummed his fingers upon his knees, and fidgeted in his seat with impatience, shooting an occasional question across at his grim companion.

" When was all this, then ? "

" It was yesterday night."

" And where is Adèle now ? "

" She is at home."

" And this Dalbert ? "

" Oh, he is there also ! "

" What ! you have left her in his power while you came away to Versailles ? "

" She is locked in her room."

" Pah ! what is a lock ? " The young man raved with his hands in the air at the thought of his own impotence.

" And Pierre is there."

" He is useless."

" And Amos Green."

" Ah, that is better. He is a man, by the look of him."

" His mother was one of our own folk from Staten Island, near Manhattan. She was one of those scattered lambs who fled early before the wolves, when first it was seen that the king's hand waxed heavy upon Israel. He speaks French, and yet he is neither French to the eye, nor are his ways like our ways."

" He has chosen an evil time for his visit."

" Some wise purpose may lie hid in it."

" And you have left him in the house ? "

" Yes ; he was sat with this Dalbert, smoking with him, and telling him strange tales."

" What guard could he be ? He is a stranger in a strange land. You did ill to leave Adèle thus, uncle."

" She is in God's hands, Amory."

" I trust so. Oh, I am on fire to be there ! "

He thrust his head through the cloud of dust which rose from the wheels, and craned his neck to look upon the long curving river and broad-spread city, which was already visible before them, half hid by a thin blue haze, through which shot the double tower of Notre Dame, with the high spire of St. Jacques and a forest of other steeples and minarets, the monuments of eight hundred years of devotion. Soon, as the road curved down to the river-bank, the city wall grew nearer and nearer, until they had passed the southern gate, and were rattling over the stony causeway, leaving the broad Luxembourg upon their right, and Colbert's last work, the Invalides, upon their left. A sharp turn brought them on to the river quays, and crossing over the Pont Neuf, they skirted the stately Louvre, and plunged into the labyrinth of narrow but important streets which extended to the northward. The young officer had his head still thrust out of the

window, but his view was obscured by a broad gilded carriage which lumbered heavily along in front of them. As the road broadened, however, it swerved to one side, and he was able to catch a glimpse of the house to which they were making.

It was surrounded on every side by an immense crowd.

6. *A House of Strife*

THE house of the Huguenot merchant was a tall, narrow building standing at the corner of the Rue St. Martin and the Rue de Biron. It was four stories in height, grim and grave like its owner, with high peaked roof, long diamond-paned windows, a frame-work of black wood, with grey plaster filling the interstices, and five stone steps which led up to the narrow and sombre door. The upper story was but a warehouse in which the trader kept his stock, but the second and third were furnished with balconies edged with stout wooden balustrades. As the uncle and the nephew sprang out of the calèche, they found themselves upon the outskirts of a dense crowd of people, who were swaying and tossing with excitement, their chins all thrown forwards and their gaze directed upwards. Following their eyes, the young officer saw a sight which left him standing bereft of every sensation save amazement.

From the upper balcony there was hanging head downwards a man clad in the bright blue coat and white breeches of one of the king's dragoons His hat and wig had dropped off, and his close-cropped head swung slowly backwards and forwards a good fifty feet above the pavement. His face was turned towards the street, and was of a deadly whiteness, while his eyes were screwed up as though he dared not open them upon the horror which faced them. His voice, however, resounded over the whole place until the air was filled with his screams for mercy.

Above him, at the corner of the balcony, there stood a young man who leaned with a bent back over the balustrades, and who held the dangling dragoon by either ankle. His face, however, was not directed towards his victim, but was half turned over his shoulder to confront a group of soldiers who were clustering at the long, open window which led out into the balcony. His head, as he glanced at them, was poised with a proud air of defiance, while they surged and oscillated in the opening, uncertain whether to rush on or to retire.

Suddenly the crowd gave a groan of excitement. The young man had released his grip upon one of the ankles, and the dragoon hung now by one only, his other leg flapping helplessly in the air. He grabbed aimlessly with his hands at the wall and the wood-work behind him, still yelling at the pitch of his lungs.

" Pull me up, son of the devil, pull me up ! " he screamed. " Would you murder me, then ? Help, good people, help ! "

" Do you want to come up, captain ? " said the strong clear voice of the young man above him, speaking excellent French, but in an accent which fell strangely upon the ears of the crowd beneath.

" Yes, sacred name of God, yes ! "

" Order off your men, then."

" Away, you dolts, you imbeciles ! Do you wish to see me dashed to pieces ? Away, I say ! Off with you ! "

" That is better," said the youth, when the soldiers had vanished from the window. He gave a tug at the dragoon's leg as he spoke, which jerked him up so far that he could twist round and catch hold of the lower edge of the balcony. " How do you find yourself now ? " he asked.

" Hold me, for heaven's·sake, hold me ! "

" I have you quite secure."

" Then pull me up ! "

" Not so fast, captain. You can talk very well where you are."

" Let me up, sir, let me up ! "

" All in good time.   I fear that it is inconvenient to you
to talk with your heels in the air."

" Ah, you would murder me ! "

" On the contrary, I am going to pull you up."

" Heaven bless you ! "

" But only on conditions."

" Oh, they are granted ! I am slipping ! "

" You will leave this house—you and your men.   You
will not trouble this old man or this young girl any further.
Do you promise ? "

" Oh yes ; we shall go."

" Word of honour ? "

" Certainly.   Only pull me up ! "

" Not so fast.   It may be easier to talk to you like this.
I do not know how the laws are over here.   Maybe this
sort of thing is not permitted.   You will promise me that
I shall have no trouble over the matter."

" None, none.   Only pull me up ! "

" Very good.   Come along ! "

He dragged at the dragoon's leg while the other gripped
his way up the balustrade until, amid a buzz of congratulation from the crowd, he tumbled all in a heap over the rail
on to the balcony, where he lay for a few moments as he
had fallen.   Then staggering to his feet, without a glance
at his opponent, he rushed, with a bellow of rage, through
the open window.

While this little drama had been enacted overhead, the
young guardsman had shaken off his first stupor of amazement, and had pushed his way through the crowd with
such vigour that he and his companion had nearly reached
the bottom of the steps.   The uniform of the king's guard
was in itself a passport anywhere, and the face of old Catinat was so well known in the district that everyone drew
back to clear a path for him towards his house.   The door
was flung open for them, and an old servant stood wringing his hands in the dark passage.

" Oh,   master ! Oh,   master ! " he   cried.   " Such
doings, such infamy ! They will murder him ! "

" Whom, then ? "

" This brave monsieur from America. Oh, my God, hark to them now ! "

As he spoke, a clatter and shouting which had burst out again upstairs ended suddenly in a tremendous crash, with volleys of oaths and a prolonged bumping and smashing, which shook the old house to its foundations. The soldier and the Huguenot rushed swiftly up the first flight of stairs, and were about to ascend the second one, from the head of which the uproar seemed to proceed, when a great eight-day clock came hurtling down, springing four steps at a time, and ending with a leap across the landing and a crash against the wall, which left it a shattered heap of metal wheels and wooden splinters. An instant afterwards four men, so locked together that they formed but one rolling bundle, came thudding down amid a debris of splintered stair-rails, and writhed and struggled upon the landing, staggering up, falling down and all breathing together like a wind in a chimney. So twisted and twined were they that it was hard to pick one from the other, save that the innermost was clad in black Flemish cloth, while the three who clung to him were soldiers of the king. Yet so strong and vigorous was the man whom they tried to hold that as often as he could find his feet he dragged them after him from end to end of the passage, as a boar might pull the curs which had fastened on to his haunches. An officer, who had rushed down at the heels of the brawlers, thrust his hands in to catch the civilian by the throat, but he whipped them back again with an oath as the man's strong white teeth met in his left thumb. Clapping the wound to his mouth, he flashed out his sword and was about to drive it through the body of his unarmed opponent, when De Catinat sprang forward and caught him by the wrist.

" You villain, Dalbert ! " he cried.

The sudden appearance of one of the king's own body-guard had a magic effect upon the brawlers. Dalbert sprang back, with his thumb still in his mouth, and his

sword drooping, scowling darkly at the new-comer. His long sallow face was distorted with anger, and his small black eyes blazed with passion and with the hell-fire light of unsatisfied vengeance. His troopers had released their victim, and stood panting in a line, while the young man leaned against the wall, brushing the dust from his black coat, and looking from his rescuer to his antagonists.

" I had a little account to settle with you before, Dalbert," said De Catinat, unsheathing his rapier.

" I am on the king's errand," snarled the other.

" No doubt. On guard, sir ! "

" I am here on duty, I tell you ! "

" Very good. Your sword, sir ! "

" I have no quarrel with you."

" No ? " De Catinat stepped forward and struck him across the face with his open hand. " It seems to me that you have one now," said he.

" Hell and furies ! " screamed the captain. " To your arms, men ! Holà, there, from above ! Cut down this fellow, and seize your prisoner ! Holà ! in the king's name ! "

At his call a dozen more troopers came hurrying down the stairs, while the three upon the landing advanced upon their former antagonist. He slipped by them, however, and caught out of the old merchant's hand the thick oak stick which he carried.

" I am with you, sir," said he, taking his place beside the guardsman.

" Call off your canaille, and fight me like a gentleman," cried De Catinat.

" A gentleman ! Hark to the bourgeois Huguenot, whose family peddles cloth ! "

" You coward ! I will write liar on you with my sword point ! "

He sprang forward, and sent in a thrust which might have found its way to Dalbert's heart had the heavy sabre of a dragoon not descended from the side and shorn his more delicate weapon short off close to the hilt. With a

shout of triumph, his enemy sprang furiously upon him with his rapier shortened, but was met by a sharp blow from the cudgel of the young stranger which sent his weapon tinkling on to the ground. A trooper, however, on the stair had pulled out a pistol, and clapping it within a foot of the guardsman's head, was about to settle the combat, once and for ever, when a little old gentleman, who had quietly ascended from the street, and who had been looking on with an amused and interested smile at this fiery sequence of events, took a sudden step forward, and ordered all parties to drop their weapons with a voice so decided, so stern, and so full of authority, that the sabre points all clinked down together upon the parquet flooring as though it were a part of their daily drill.

" Upon my word, gentlemen, upon my word ! " said he, looking sternly from one to the other. He was a very small, dapper man, as thin as a herring, with projecting teeth and a huge drooping many-curled wig, which cut off the line of his skinny neck and the slope of his narrow shoulders. His dress was a long overcoat of mouse-coloured velvet slashed with gold, beneath which were high leather boots, which, with his little gold-laced, three-cornered hat, gave a military tinge to his appearance. In his gait and bearing he had a dainty strut and backward cock of the head, which, taken with his sharp black eyes, his high thin features, and his assured manner, would impress a stranger with the feeling that this was a man of power. And, indeed, in France or out of it there were few to whom this man's name was not familiar, for in all France the only figure which loomed up as large as that of the king was this very little gentleman who stood now, with gold snuff-box in one hand, and deep-laced handkerchief in the other, upon the landing of the Huguenot's house. For, who was there who did not know the last of the great French nobles, the bravest of French captains, the beloved Condé, victor of Recroy and hero of the Fronde ? At the sight of his pinched, sallow face the

dragoons and their leader had stood staring, while De Catinat raised the stump of his sword in a salute.

" Heh, heh ! " cried the old soldier, peering at him. " You were with me on the Rhine—heh ? I know your face, captain. But the household was with Turenne."

" I was in the regiment of Picardy, your Highness. De Catinat is my name."

" Yes, yes. But you, sir, who the devil are you ? "

" Captain Dalbert, your Highness, of the Languedoc Blue Dragoons."

" Heh ! I was passing in my carriage, and I saw you standing on your head in the air. The young man let you up on conditions, as I understood."

" He swore he would go from the house," cried the young stranger. " Yet when I had let him up, he set his men upon me, and we all came downstairs together."

" My faith, you seem to have left little behind you," said Condé, smiling, as he glanced at the litter which was strewed all over the floor. " And so you broke your parole, Captain Dalbert ? "

" I could not hold treaty with a Huguenot and an enemy of the king," said the dragoon sulkily.

" You could hold treaty, it appears, but not keep it. And why did you let him go, sir, when you had him at such a vantage ? "

" I believed his promise."

" You must be of a trusting nature."

" I have been used to deal with Indians."

" Heh ! And you think an Indian's word is better than that of an officer in the king's dragoons ? "

" I did not think so an hour ago."

" Hem ! " Condé took a large pinch of snuff, and brushed the wandering grains from his velvet coat with his handkerchief of point.

" You are very strong, monsieur," said he, glancing keenly at the broad shoulders and arching chest of the young stranger. " You are from Canada, I presume ? "

" I have been there, sir. But I am from New York."

Condé shook his head. " An island ? "

" No sir ; a town."

" In what province ? "

" The province of New York."

" The chief town, then ? "

" Nay ; Albany is the chief town."

" And how came you to speak French ? "

" My mother was of French blood."

" And how long have you been in Paris ? "

" A day."

" Heh ! And you already begin to throw your mother's country-folk out of windows ! "

" He was annoying a young maid, sir, and I asked him to stop, whereon he whipped out his sword, and would have slain me had I not closed with him, upon which he called upon his fellows to aid him. To keep them off, I swore that I would drop him over if they moved a step. Yet when I let him go, they set upon me again, and I know not what the end might have been had this gentleman not stood my friend."

" Hem ! You did very well. You are young, but you have resource."

" I was reared in the woods, sir."

" If there are many of your kidney, you may give my friend De Frontenac some work ere he found this empire of which he talks. But how is this, Captain Dalbert ? What have you to say ? "

" The king's orders, your Highness."

" Heh ! Did he order you to molest the girl ? I have never yet heard that his Majesty erred by being too *harsh* with a woman." He gave a little dry chuckle in his throat, and took another pinch of snuff.

" The orders are, your Highness, to use every means which may drive these people into the true Church."

" On my word, you look a very fine apostle and a pretty champion for a holy cause," said Condé, glancing sardonically out of his twinkling black eyes at the brutal face of the dragoon. " Take your men out of this, sir, and

never venture to set your foot again across this threshold."

" But the king's command, your Highness."

" I will tell the king when I see him that I left soldiers and that I find brigands. Not a word, sir ! Away ! You take your shame with you, and you leave your honour behind." He had turned in an instant from the sneering, strutting old beau to the fierce soldier with set face and eye of fire. Dalbert shrank back from his baleful gaze, and muttering an order to his men, they filed off down the stair with clattering feet and clank of sabres.

" Your Highness," said the old Huguenot, coming forward and throwing open one of the doors which led from the landing, " you have indeed been a saviour of Israel and a stumbling-block to the froward this day. Will you not deign to rest under my roof, and even to take a cup of wine ere you go onwards ? "

Condé raised his thick eyebrows at the scriptural fashion of the merchant's speech, but he bowed courteously to the invitation, and entered the chamber, looking around him in surprise and admiration at its magnificence. With its panelling of dark shining oak, its polished floor, its stately marble chimney-piece, and its beautifully moulded ceiling, it was indeed a room which might have graced a palace.

" My carriage waits below," said he, " and I must not delay longer. It is not often that I leave my castle of Chantilly to come to Paris, and it was a fortunate chance which made me pass in time to be of service to honest men. When a house hangs out such a sign as an officer of dragoons with his heels in the air, it is hard to drive past without a question. But I fear that as long as you are a Huguenot, there will be no peace for you in France, monsieur."

" The law is indeed heavy upon us."

" And will be heavier if what I hear from court is correct. I wonder that you do not fly the country."

" My business and my duty lie here."

" Well, every man knows his own affairs best. Would it not be wise to bend to the storm, heh ? "

The Huguenot gave a gesture of horror.

" Well, well, I meant no harm. And where is this fair maid who has been the cause of the broil ? "

" Where is Adèle, Pierre ? " asked the merchant of the old servant, who had carried in the silver tray with a squat flask and tinted Venetian glasses.

" I locked her in my room, master."

" And where is she now ? "

" I am here, father." The young girl sprang into the room, and threw her arms round the old merchant's neck. " Oh, I trust these wicked men have not hurt you, love ! "

" No, no, dear child ; none of us have been hurt, thanks to his Highness the Prince of Condé here."

Adèle raised her eyes, and quickly drooped them again before the keen questioning gaze of the old soldier. " May God reward your Highness ! " she stammered. In her confusion the blood rushed to her face, which was perfect in feature and expression. With her sweetly delicate contour, her large grey eyes, and the sweep of the lustrous hair, setting off with its rich tint the little shell-like ears and the alabaster whiteness of the neck and throat, even Condé, who had seen all the beauties of three courts and of sixty years defile before him, stood staring in admiration at the Huguenot maiden.

" Hey ! On my word, mademoiselle, you make me wish that I could wipe forty years from my account." He bowed, and sighed in the fashion that was in vogue when Buckingham came to the wooing of Anne of Austria, and the dynasty of cardinals was at its height.

" France could ill spare those forty years, your Highness."

" Heh, heh ! So quick of tongue too ? Your daughter has a courtly wit, monsieur."

" God forbid, your Highness ! She is as pure and good——"

" Nay, that is but a sorry compliment to the court. Surely, mademoiselle, you would love to go out into the great world, to hear sweet music, see all that is lovely, and

wear all that is costly, rather than look out ever upon the Rue St. Martin, and bide in this great dark house until the roses wither upon your cheeks."

" Where my father is, I am happy at his side," said she, putting her two hands upon his sleeve. " I ask nothing more than I have got."

" And I think it best that you go up to your room again," said the old merchant shortly, for the prince, in spite of his age, bore an evil name among women. He had come close to her as he spoke, and had even placed one yellow hand upon her shrinking arm, while his little dark eyes twinkled with an ominous light.

" Tut, tut ! " said he, as she hastened to obey. " You need not fear for your little dove. This hawk, at least, is far past the stoop, however tempting the quarry. But indeed, I can see that she is as good as she is fair, and one could not say more than that if she were from heaven direct. My carriage waits, gentlemen, and I wish you all a very good day ! " He inclined his bewigged head, and strutted off in his dainty, dandified fashion. From the window De Catinat could see him step into the same gilded chariot which had stood in his way as he drove from Versailles.

" By my faith," said he, turning to the young American, " we all owe thanks to the prince, but it seems to me, sir, that we are your debtors even more. You have risked your life for my cousin, and but for your cudgel, Dalbert would have had his blade through me when he had me at a vantage. Your hand, sir ! These are things which a man cannot forget."

" Aye, you may well thank him, Amory," broke in the old Huguenot, who had returned after escorting his illustrious guest to the carriage. " He has been raised up as a champion for the afflicted, and as a helper for those who are in need. An old man's blessing upon you, Amos Green, for my own son could not have done for me more than you, a stranger."

But their young visitor appeared to be more embar-

rassed by their thanks than by any of his preceding adventures. The blood flushed to his weather-tanned, clear-cut face, as smooth as that of a boy, and yet marked by a firmness of lip and a shrewdness in the keen blue eyes which spoke of a strong and self-reliant nature.

" I have a mother and two sisters over the water," said he diffidently.

" And you honour women for their sake ? "

" We always honour women over there. Perhaps it is that we have so few. Over in these old countries you have not learned what it is to be without them. I have been away up the lakes for furs, living for months on end the life of a savage among the wigwams of the Sacs and the Foxes, foul livers and foul talkers, ever squatting like toads around their fires. Then when I have come back to Albany where my folk then dwelt, and have heard my sisters play upon the spinet and sing, and my mother talk to us of the France of her younger days and of her child-hood, and of all that they had suffered for what they thought was right, then I have felt what a good woman is, and how, like the sunshine, she draws out of one's soul all that is purest and best."

" Indeed, the ladies should be very much obliged to monsieur, who is as eloquent as he is brave," said Adèle Catinat, who, standing in the open door, had listened to the latter part of his remarks.

He had forgotten himself for the instant, and had spoken freely and with energy. At the sight of the girl, however, he coloured up again, and cast down his eyes.

" Much of my life has been spent in the woods," said he, " and one speaks so little there that one comes to forget how to do it. It was for this that my father wished me to stay some time in France, for he would not have me grow up a mere trapper and trader."

" And how long do you stop in Paris ? " asked the guardsman.

" Until Ephraim Savage comes for me."

" And who is he ? "

" The master of the *Golden Rod*."

" And that is your ship ? "

" My father's ship. She has been to Bristol, is now at Rouen, and then must go to Bristol again. When she comes back once more, Ephraim comes to Paris for me, and it will be time for me to go."

" And how like you Paris ? "

The young man smiled. " They told me ere I came that it was a very lively place, and truly from the little that I have seen this morning, I think that it is the liveliest place that I have seen."

" By my faith," said De Catinat, " you came down those stairs in a very lively fashion, four of you together, with a Dutch clock as an *avant-courier*, and a whole train of wood-work at your heels. And you have not seen the city yet ? "

" Only as I journeyed through it yester-evening on my way to this house. It is a wondrous place, but I was pent in for lack of air as I passed through it. New York is a great city. There are said to be as many as three thousand folk living there, and they say that they could send out four hundred fighting-men, though I can scarce bring myself to believe it. Yet from all parts of the city one may see something of God's handiwork—the trees, the green of the grass, and the shine of the sun upon the bay and the rivers. But here it is stone and wood, and wood and stone, look where you will. In truth, you must be very hardy people to keep your health in such a place."

" And to us it is you who seem so hardy, with your life in the forest and on the river," cried the young girl. " And then the wonder that you can find your path through those great wildernesses, where there is nought to guide you."

" Well, there again ! I marvel how you can find your way among these thousands of houses. For myself, I trust that it will be a clear night to-night."

" And why ? "

" That I may see the stars."

" But you will find no change in them."

" That is it. If I can but see the stars, it will be easy for me to know how to walk when I would find this house again. In the daytime I can carry a knife and notch the door-posts as I pass, for it might be hard to pick up one's trail again, with so many folk ever passing over it."

De Catinat burst out laughing again. " By my faith, you will find Paris livelier than ever," said he, " if you blaze your way through on the door-posts as you would on the trees of a forest. But perchance it would be as well that you should have a guide at first ; so, if you have two horses ready in your stables, uncle, our friend and I might shortly ride back to Versailles together, for I have a spell of guard again before many hours are over. Then for some days he might bide with me there, if he will share a soldier's quarters, and so see more than the Rue St. Martin can offer. How would that suit you, Monsieur Green ? "

" I should be right glad to come out with you, if we may leave all here in safety."

" Oh, fear not for that," said the Huguenot. " The order of the Prince of Condé will be as a shield and a buckler to us for many a day. I will order Pierre to saddle the horses."

"And I must use the little time I have," said the guardsman, as he turned away to where Adèle waited for him in the window.

7. *The New World and the Old*

THE young American was soon ready for the expedition, but De Catinat lingered until the last possible minute. When at last he was able to tear himself away, he adjusted his cravat, brushed his brilliant coat, and looked very critically over the sombre suit of his companion.

" Where got you those ? " he asked.

" In New York, ere I left."

" Hem ! There is nought amiss with the cloth, and indeed the sombre colour is the mode, but the cut is strange to our eyes."

" I only know that I wish that I had my fringed hunting tunic and leggings on once more."

" This hat, now. We do not wear our brims flat like that. See if I cannot mend it." He took the beaver, and looping up one side of the brim, he fastened it with a golden brooch taken from his own shirt front. " There is a martial cock," said he, laughing, " and would do credit to the King's Own Musketeers. The black broadcloth and silk hose will pass, but why have you not a sword at your side ? "

" I carry a gun when I ride out."

" *Mon Dieu*, you will be laid by the heels as a bandit ? "

" I have a knife, too."

" Worse and worse ! Well, we must dispense with the sword, and with the gun too, I pray ! Let me re-tie your cravat. So ! Now if you are in the mood for a ten-mile gallop, I am at your service."

They were indeed a singular contrast as they walked their horses together through the narrow and crowded causeways of the Parisian streets. De Catinat, who was the older by five years, with his delicate small-featured face, his sharply trimmed moustache, his small but well-set and dainty figure, and his brilliant dress, looked the very type of the great nation to which he belonged.

His companion, however, large-limbed and strong, turning his bold and yet thoughtful face from side to side, and eagerly taking in all the strange, new life amidst which he found himself, was also a type, unfinished it is true, but bidding fair to be the higher of the two. His close yellow hair, blue eyes and heavy build showed that it was the blood of his father, rather than that of his mother, which ran in his veins ; and even the sombre coat and swordless belt, if less pleasing to the eye, were true badges of a race which found its fiercest battles and its most

glorious victories in bending nature to its will upon the seas and in the waste places of the earth.

"What is yonder great building?" he asked, as they emerged into a broader square.

"It is the Louvre, one of the palaces of the king."

"And is he there?"

"Nay; he lives at Versailles."

"What! Fancy that a man should have two such houses!"

"Two! He has many more—St. Germain, Marly, Fontainebleau, Clugny."

"But to what end? A man can but live at one at a time."

"Nay; he can now come or go as the fancy takes him."

"It is a wondrous building. I have seen the Seminary of St. Sulpice at Montreal, and thought that it was the greatest of all houses, and yet what is it beside this?"

"You have been to Montreal, then? You remember the fort?"

"Yes, and the Hôtel Dieu, and the wooden houses in a row, and eastward the great mill with the wall; but what do you know of Montreal?"

"I have soldiered there, and at Quebec, too. Why, my friend, you are not the only man of the woods in Paris, for I give you my word that I have worn the caribou mocassins, the leather jacket, and the fur cap with the eagle feather for six months at a stretch, and I care not how soon I do it again."

Amos Green's eyes shone with delight at finding that his companion and he had so much in common, and he plunged into a series of questions which lasted until they had crossed the river and reached the south-westerly gate of the city. By the moat and walls long lines of men were busy at their drill.

"Who are those, then?" he asked, gazing at them with curiosity.

"They are some of the king's soldiers."

" But why so many of them ? Do they await some enemy ? "

" Nay ; we are at peace with all the world. Worse luck ! "

" At peace. Why, then, all these men ? "

" That they may be ready."

The young man shook his head in bewilderment. " They might be as ready in their own homes surely. In our country every man has his musket in his chimney corner, and is ready enough, yet he does not waste his time when all is at peace."

" Our king is very great, and he has many enemies."

" And who made the enemies ? "

" Why, the king, to be sure."

" Then would it not be better to be without him ? "

The guardsman shrugged his epaulettes in despair. " We shall both wind up in the Bastille or Vincennes at this rate," said he. " You must know that it is in serving the country that he has made these enemies. It is but five years since he made a peace at Nimeguen, by which he tore away sixteen fortresses from the Spanish Lowlands. Then, also, he had laid his hands upon Strassburg and upon Luxembourg, and has chastised the Genoans, so that there are many who would fall upon him if they thought that he was weak."

" And why has he done all this ? "

" Because he is a great king, and for the glory of France."

The stranger pondered over this answer for some time as they rode on between the high, thin poplars, which threw bars across the sunlit road.

" There was a great man in Schenectady once," said he at last. " They are simple folk up yonder, and they all had great trust in each other. But after this man came among them they began to miss—one a beaver-skin and one a bag of ginseng, and one a belt of wampum, until at last old Pete Hendricks lost his chestnut three-year-old. Then there was a search and a fuss until they found all that had been lost in the stable of the new-comer, so we

took him, I and some others, and we hung him up on a tree, without ever thinking what a great man he had been."

De Catinat shot an angry glance at his companion. " Your parable, my friend, is scarce polite," said he. " If you and I are to travel in peace you must keep a closer guard upon your tongue."

" I would not give you offence, and it may be that I am wrong," answered the American, " but I speak as the matter seems to me, and it is the right of a free man to do that."

De Catinat's frown relaxed as the other turned his earnest blue eyes upon him. " By my soul, where would the court be if every man did that ? " said he. " But what in the name of heaven is amiss now ? "

His companion had hurled himself off his horse, and was stooping low over the ground, with his eyes bent upon the dust. Then, with quick, noiseless steps, he zigzagged along the road, ran swiftly across a grassy bank, and stood peering at the gap of a fence, with his nostrils dilated, his eyes shining and his whole face aglow with eagerness.

" The fellow's brain is gone," muttered De Catinat, as he caught at the bridle of the riderless horse. " The sight of Paris has shaken his wits. What in the name of the devil ails you, that you should stand glaring there ? "

" A deer has passed," whispered the other, pointing down at the grass. " Its trail lies along there and into the wood. It could not have been long ago, and there is no slur to the track, so that it was not going fast. Had we but fetched my gun, we might have followed it, and brought the old man back a side of venison."

" For God's sake get on your horse again ? " cried De Catinat distractedly. " I fear that some evil will come upon you ere I get you safe to the Rue St. Martin again ! "

" And what is wrong now ? " asked Amos Green, swinging himself into the saddle.

" Why, man, these woods are the king's preserves, and you speak as coolly of slaying his deer as though you were on the shores of Michigan ! "

" Preserves ! They are tame deer ! " An expression of deep disgust passed over his face, and spurring his horse, he galloped onwards at such a pace that De Catinat, after vainly endeavouring to keep up, had to shriek to him to stop.

" It is not usual in this country to ride so madly along the roads," he panted.

" It is a very strange country," cried the stranger, in perplexity. " Maybe it would be easier for me to re-remember what *is* allowed. It was but this morning that I took my gun to shoot a pigeon that was flying over the roofs in yonder street, and old Pierre caught my arm with a face as though it were the minister that I was aiming at. And then there is that old man—why, they will not even let him say his prayers."

De Catinat laughed. " You will come to know our ways soon," said he. " This is a crowded land, and if all men rode and shot as they listed, much harm would come from it. But let us talk rather of your own country. You have lived much in the woods from what you tell me."

" I was but ten when first I journeyed with my uncle to Sault la Marie, where the three great lakes meet, to trade with the Chippewas and the tribes of the west."

" I know not what La Salle or De Frontenac would have said to that. The trade in those parts belongs to France."

" We were taken prisoners, and so it was that I came to see Montreal and afterwards Quebec. In the end we were sent back because they did not know what they could do with us."

" It was a good journey for a first."

" And ever since I have been trading—first, on the Kennebec with the Abenaquis, in the great forests of Maine, and with the Micmac fish-eaters over the Penobscot. Then later with the Iroquois, as far west as the country of the Senecas. At Albany and Schenectady we stored our pelts, and so on to New York, where my father shipped them over the sea."

" But he could ill spare you, surely ? "

" Very ill. But as he was rich, he thought it best that I should learn some things that are not to be found in the woods. And so he sent me in the *Golden Rod*, under the care of Ephraim Savage."

" Who is also of New York ? "

" Nay ; he is the first man that ever was born at Boston."

" I cannot remember the names of all these villages."

" And yet there may come a day when their names shall be as well known as that of Paris."

De Catinat laughed heartily. " The woods may have given you much, but not the gift of prophecy, my friend. Well, my heart is often over the water even as yours is, and I would ask nothing better than to see the palisades of Point Levi again, even if all the Five Nations were raving upon the other side of them. But now, if you will look there in the gap of the tree, you will see the king's new palace."

The two young men pulled up their horses, and looked down at the widespreading building in all the beauty of its dazzling whiteness, and at the lovely grounds, dotted with fountain and with statue, and barred with hedge and with walk, stretching away to the dense woods which clustered round them. It amused De Catinat to watch the swift play of wonder and admiration which flashed over his companion's features.

" Well, what do you think of it ? " he asked at last.

" I think that God's best work is in America, and man's in Europe."

" Aye, and in all Europe there is no such palace as that, even as there is no such king as he who dwells within it."

" Can I see him, think you ? "

" Who, the king ? No, no ; I fear that you are scarce made for a court."

" Nay, I should show him all honour."

" How, then ? What greeting would you give him ? "

" I would shake him respectfully by the hand, and ask as to his health and that of his family."

" On my word, I think that such a greeting might please him more than the bent knee and the rounded back, and yet, I think, my son of the woods, that it were best not to lead you into paths where you would be lost, as would any of the courtiers if you dropped them in the gorge of the Saguenay. But holà ! what comes here ? It looks like one of the carriages of the court."

A white cloud of dust, which had rolled towards them down the road, was now so near that the glint of gilding and the red coat of the coachman could be seen breaking out through it. As the two cavaliers reined their horses aside to leave the roadway clear, the coach rumbled heavily past them, drawn by two dapple greys, and the horsemen caught a glimpse, as it passed, of a beautiful but haughty face which looked out at them. An instant afterwards a sharp cry had caused the driver to pull up his horses, and a white hand beckoned to them through the carriage window.

" It is Madame de Montespan, the proudest woman in France," whispered De Catinat. " She would speak with us, so do as I do."

He touched his horse with the spur, gave a *gambade* which took him across to the carriage, and then, sweeping off his hat, he bowed to his horse's neck ; a salute in which he was imitated, though in a somewhat ungainly fashion, by his companion.

" Ha, captain ! " said the lady, with no very pleasant face, " we meet again."

" Fortune has ever been good to me, madame."

" It was not so this morning."

" You say truly. It gave me a hateful duty to perform."

" And you performed it in a hateful fashion."

" Nay, madame, what could I do more ? "

The lady sneered, and her beautiful face turned as bitter as it could upon occasion.

" You thought that I had no more power with the king.

You thought that my day was past. No doubt it seemed to you that you might reap favour with the new by being the first to cast a slight upon the old."

" But, madame——"

" You may spare your protestations. I am one who judges by deeds and not by words. Did you, then, think that my charm had so faded, that any beauty which I ever have had is so withered ? "

" Nay, madame, I were blind to think that."

" Blind as a noontide owl," said Amos Green with emphasis.

Madame de Montespan arched her eyebrows and glanced at her singular admirer. " Your friend at least speaks that which he really feels," said she. " At four o'clock to-day we shall see whether others are of the same mind ; and if they are, then it may be ill for those who mistook what was but a passing shadow for a lasting cloud." She cast another vindictive glance at the young guardsman, and rattled on once more upon her way.

" Come on ! " cried De Catinat curtly, for his companion was staring open-mouthed after the carriage. " Have you never seen a woman before ? "

" Never such a one as that."

" Never one with so railing a tongue, I dare swear," said De Catinat.

" Never one with so lovely a face. And yet there is a lovely face at the Rue St. Martin also."

" You seem to have a nice taste in beauty, for all your woodland training."

" Yes, for I have been cut away from women so much that when I stand before one I feel that she is something tender and sweet and holy."

" You may find dames at the court who are both tender and sweet, but you will long look, my friend, before you find the holy one. This one would ruin me if she can, and only because I have done what it was my duty to do. To keep oneself in this court is like coming down the La

Chine Rapids where there is a rock to right, and a rock to left, and another perchance in front, and if you so much as graze one, where are you and your birch canoe ? But our rocks are women, and in our canoe we bear all our worldly fortunes. Now here is another who would sway me over to her side, and indeed I think it may prove to be the better side too."

They had passed through the gateway of the palace, and the broad sweeping drive lay in front of them, dotted with carriages and horsemen. On the gravel walks were many gaily dressed ladies, who strolled among the flower-beds or watched the fountains with the sunlight glinting upon their high water sprays. One of these, who had kept her eyes turned upon the gate, came hastening forward the instant that De Catinat appeared. It was Mademoiselle Nanon, the *confidante* of Madame de Maintenon.

" I am so pleased to see you, captain," she cried, " and I have waited so patiently. Madame would speak with you. The king comes to her at three, and we have but twenty minutes. I heard that you had gone to Paris, and so I stationed myself here. Madame has something which she would ask you."

" Then I will come at once. Ah, De Brissac, it is well met ! "

A tall, burly officer was passing in the same uniform which De Catinat wore. He turned at once, and came smiling towards his comrade.

" Ah, Amory, you have covered a league or two from the dust on your coat ! "

" We are fresh from Paris. But I am called on business. This is my friend, Monsieur Amos Green. I leave him in your hands, for he is a stranger from America, and would fain see all that you can show. He stays with me at my quarters. And my horse, too, De Brissac. You can give it to the groom."

Throwing the bridle to his brother officer, and pressing the hand of Amos Green, De Catinat sprang from his

horse, and followed at the top of his speed in the direction which the young lady had already taken.

8. *The Rising Sun*

THE rooms which were inhabited by the lady who had already taken so marked a position at the court of France were as humble as were her fortunes at the time when they were allotted to her, but with that rare tact and self-restraint which were the leading features in her remarkable character, she had made no change in her living with the increase of her prosperity, and forbore from provoking envy and jealousy by any display of wealth or of power. In a side wing of the palace, far from the central *salons*, and only to be reached by long corridors and stairs, were the two or three small chambers upon which the eyes, first of the court, then of France, and finally of the world, were destined to be turned. In such rooms had the destitute widow of the poet Scarron been housed when she had first been brought to court by Madame de Montespan as the governess of the royal children, and in such rooms she still dwelt, now that she had added to her maiden Françoise d'Aubigny the title of Marquise de Maintenon, with the pension and estate which the king's favour had awarded her. Here it was that every day the king would lounge, finding in the conversation of a clever and virtuous woman a charm and a pleasure which none of the professed wits of his sparkling court had ever been able to give to him, and here, too, the more sagacious of the courtiers were beginning to understand, was the point, formerly to be found in the magnificent *salons* of De Montespan, whence flowed those impulses and tendencies which were so eagerly studied, and so keenly followed up by all who wished to keep the favour of the king. It was a simple creed, that of the court. Were the king pious, then let all turn to their missals and their rosaries. Were

he rakish, then who so rakish as his devoted followers ? But woe to the man who was rakish when he should be praying, or who pulled a long face when the king wore a laughing one ! And thus it was that keen eyes were ever fixed upon him, and upon every influence that came near him, so that the wary courtier, watching the first subtle signs of a coming change, might so order his conduct as to seem to lead rather than to follow.

The young guardsman had scarce ever exchanged a word with this powerful lady, for it was her taste to isolate herself, and to appear with the court only at the hours of devotion. It was therefore with some feelings both of nervousness and of curiosity that he followed his guide down the gorgeous corridors, where art and wealth had been strewn with so lavish a hand. The lady paused in front of the chamber door, and turned to her companion.

" Madame wishes to speak to you of what occurred this morning," said she. " I should advise you to say nothing to madame about your creed, for it is the only thing upon which her heart can be hard." She raised her finger to emphasise the warning, and tapping at the door, she pushed it open. " I have brought Captain de Catinat, madame," said she.

" Then let the captain step in." The voice was firm, and yet sweetly musical.

Obeying the command, De Catinat found himself in a room which was no larger and but little better furnished than that which was allotted to his own use. Yet, though simple, everything in the chamber was scrupulously neat and clean, betraying the dainty taste of a refined woman. The stamped-leather furniture, the La Savonnière carpet, the pictures of sacred subjects, exquisite from an artist's point of view, the plain but tasteful curtains, all left an impression half religious and half feminine but wholly soothing. Indeed, the soft light, the high white statue of the Virgin in a canopied niche, with a perfumed red lamp burning before it, and the wooden *prie-dieu* with the red-edged prayer-book upon the top of it, made the

apartment look more like a private chapel than a fair lady's boudoir.

On each side of the empty fireplace was a little green-covered arm-chair, the one for madame and the other reserved for the use of the king. A small three-legged stool between them was heaped with her work-basket and her tapestry. On the chair which was furthest from the door, with her back turned to the light, madame was sitting as the young officer entered. It was her favourite position, and yet there were few women of her years who had so little reason to fear the sun, for a healthy life and active habits had left her with a clear skin and delicate bloom which any young beauty of the court might have envied. Her figure was graceful and queenly, her gestures and pose full of a natural dignity, and her voice, as he had already remarked, most sweet and melodious. Her face was handsome rather than beautiful, set in a statuesque classical mould, with broad white forehead, firm, delicately sensitive mouth, and a pair of large serene grey eyes, earnest and placid in repose, but capable of reflecting the whole play of her soul, from the merry gleam of humour to the quick flash of righteous anger. An elevating serenity was, however, the leading expression of her features, and in that she presented the strongest contrast to her rival, whose beautiful face was ever swept by the emotion of the moment, and who gleamed one hour and shadowed over the next like a corn-field in the wind. In wit and quickness of tongue it is true that De Montespan had the advantage, but the strong common-sense and the deeper nature of the elder woman might prove in the end to be the better weapon. De Catinat, at the moment, without having time to notice details, was simply conscious that he was in the presence of a very handsome woman, and that her large pensive eyes were fixed critically upon him, and seemed to be reading his thoughts as they had never been read before.

" I think that I have already seen you, sir, have I not ? "

" Yes, madame, I have once or twice had the honour

of attending upon you, though it may not have been my good fortune to address you."

" My life is so quiet and retired that I fear that much of what is best and worthiest at the court is unknown to me. It is the curse of such places that evil flaunts itself before the eye and cannot be overlooked, while the good retires in its modesty, so that at times we scarce dare hope that it is there. You have served, monsieur ? "

" Yes, madame. In the Lowlands, on the Rhine and in Canada."

" In Canada ! Ah ! What nobler ambition could woman have than to be a member of that sweet sisterhood which was founded by the holy Marie de l'Incarnation and the sainted Jeanne le Ber at Montreal ? It was but the other day that I had an account of them from Father Godet des Marais. What joy to be one of such a body, and to turn from the blessed work of converting the heathen to the even more precious task of nursing back health and strength into those of God's warriors who have been struck down in the fight with Satan ! "

It was strange to De Catinat, who knew well the sordid and dreadful existence led by these same sisters threatened ever with misery, hunger and the scalping-knife, to hear this lady, at whose feet lay all the good things of this earth, speaking enviously of their lot.

" They are very good women," said he shortly, remembering Mademoiselle Nanon's warning and fearing to trench upon the dangerous subject.

" And doubtless you have had the privilege also of seeing the holy Bishop Laval ? "

" Yes, madame, I have seen Bishop Laval."

" And I trust that the Sulpitians still hold their own against the Jesuits ? "

" I have heard, madame, that the Jesuits are the stronger at Quebec, and the others at Montreal."

" And who is your own director, monsieur ? "

De Catinat felt that the worst had come upon him. " I have none, madame."

" Ah, it is too common to dispense with a director, and yet I know not how I could guide my steps in the difficult path which I tread if it were not for mine. Who is your confessor, then ? "

" I have none. I am of the Reformed Church, madame."

The lady gave a gesture of horror, and a sudden hardening showed itself in mouth and eye. " What, in the court itself," she cried, " and in the neighbourhood of the king's own person ! "

De Catinat was lax enough in matters of faith, and held his creed rather as a family tradition than from any strong conviction, but it hurt his self-esteem to see himself regarded as though he had confessed to something that was loathsome and unclean. " You will find, madame," said he sternly, " that members of my faith have not only stood around the throne of France, but have even seated themselves upon it."

" God has for His own all-wise purposes permitted it, and none should know it better than I, whose grandsire, Théodore d'Aubigny, did so much to place a crown upon the head of the great Henry. But Henry's eyes were opened ere his end came, and I pray—oh, from my heart I pray—that yours may be also."

She rose, and throwing herself down upon the *prie-dieu*, sunk her face in her hands for some few minutes, during which the object of her devotions stood in some perplexity in the middle of the room, hardly knowing whether such an attention should be regarded as an insult or as a favour. A tap at the door brought the lady back to this world again, and her devoted attendant answered her summons to enter.

" The king is in the Hall of Victories, madame," said she. " He will be here in five minutes."

" Very well. Stand outside, and let me know when he comes. Now, sir," she continued, when they were alone once more, " you gave a note of mine to the king this morning ? "

572

" I did, madame."

" And, as I understand, Madame de Montespan was refused admittance to the *grand lever* ? "

" She was, madame."

" But she waited for the king in the passage ? "

" She did."

" And wrung from him a promise that he would see her to-day ? "

" Yes, madame."

" I would not have you tell me that which it may seem to you a breach of your duty to tell. But I am fighting now against a terrible foe, and for a great stake. Do you understand me ? "

De Catinat bowed.

" Then what do I mean ? "

" I presume that what madame means is that she is fighting for the king's favour with the lady you mentioned."

" As heaven is my judge, I have no thought of myself. I am fighting with the devil for the king's soul."

" 'Tis the same thing, madame."

The lady smiled. " If the king's body were in peril, I could call on the aid of his faithful guards, and not less so now, surely, when so much more is at stake. Tell me, then, at what hour was the king to meet the marquise in her room ? "

" At four, madame."

" I thank you. You have done me a service, and I shall not forget it."

" The king comes, madame," said Mademoiselle Nanon, again protruding her head.

" Then you must go, captain. Pass through the other room, and so into the outer passage. And take this. It is Bossuet's statement of the Catholic faith. It has softened the hearts of others, and may yours. Now, adieu ! "

De Catinat passed out through another door, and as he did so he glanced back. The lady had her back to him, and her hand was raised to the mantelpiece. At the

instant that he looked she moved her neck, and he could see what she was doing. She was pushing back the long hand of the clock.

9. *Le Roi s'Amuse*

CAPTAIN DE CATINAT had hardly vanished through the one door before the other was thrown open by Mademoiselle Nanon, and the king entered the room. Madame de Maintenon rose with a pleasant smile and courtesied deeply, but there was no answering light upon her visitor's face, and he threw himself down upon the vacant arm-chair with a pouting lip and a frown upon his forehead.

" Nay, now this is a very bad compliment," she cried, with the gaiety which she could assume whenever it was necessary to draw the king from his blacker humours. " My poor little dark room has already cast a shadow over you."

" Nay ; it is Father La Chaise and the Bishop of Meaux who have been after me all day like two hounds on a stag, with talk of my duty and my position and my sins, with judgment and hell-fire ever at the end of their exhortations."

" And what would they have your Majesty do ? "

" Break the promise which I made when I came upon the throne, and which my grandfather made before me. They wish me to recall the Edict of Nantes, and drive the Huguenots from the kingdom."

" Oh, but your Majesty must not trouble your mind about such matters."

" You would not have me to do it, madame ? "

" Not if it is to be a grief to your Majesty."

" You have, perchance, some soft feeling for the religion of your youth ? "

" Nay, sire ; I have nothing but hatred for heresy."

" And yet you would not have them thrust out ? "

" Bethink you, sire, that the Almighty can Himself incline their hearts to better things if He is so minded, even as mine was inclined. May you not leave it in His hands ? "

" On my word," said Louis, brightening, " it is well put. I shall see if Father La Chaise can find an answer to that. It is hard to be threatened with eternal flames because one will not ruin one's kingdom. Eternal torment ! I have seen the face of a man who had been in the Bastille for fifteen years. It was like a dreadful book with a scar or a wrinkle to mark every hour of that death in life. But Eternity ! " He shuddered, and his eyes were filled with the horror of his thought. The higher motives had but little power over his soul, as those about him had long discovered, but he was ever ready to wince at the image of the terrors to come.

" Why should you think of such things, sire ? " said the lady, in her rich, soothing voice. " What have you to fear, you who have been the first son of the Church ! "

" You think that I am safe, then ! "

" Surely, sire."

" But I have erred, and erred deeply. You have yourself said as much."

" But that is all over, sire. Who is there who is without stain ? You have turned away from temptation. Surely, then, you have earned your forgiveness."

" I would that the queen were living once more. She would find me a better man."

" I would that she were, sire."

" And she should know that it was to you that she owed the change. Oh, Françoise, you are surely my guardian angel, who has taken bodily form ! How can I thank you for what you have done for me ! " He leaned forward and took her hand, but at the touch a sudden fire sprang into his eyes, and he would have passed his other arm round her had she not risen hurriedly to avoid the embrace.

" Sire ! " said she, with a rigid face and one finger upraised.

" You are right, you are right, Françoise. Sit down
and I will control myself. Still at the same tapestry, then !
My workers at the Gobelins must look to their laurels."
He raised one border of the glossy roll, while she, having
reseated herself, though not without a quick questioning
glance at her companion, took the other end into her lap
and continued her work.

" Yes, sire. It is a hunting scene in your forests at
Fontainebleau. A stag of ten tines, you see, and the
hounds in full cry, and a gallant band of cavaliers and
ladies. Has your Majesty ridden to-day ? "

" No. How is it, Françoise, that you have such a
heart of ice ? "

" I would it were so, sire. Perhaps you have hawked,
then ? "

" No. But surely no man's love has ever stirred you !
And yet you have been a wife."

" A nurse, sire, but never a wife. See the lady in the
park ! It is surely mademoiselle. I did not know that
she had come up from Choisy."

But the king was not to be distracted from his subject.

" You did not love this Scarron, then ? " he persisted.
" He was old, I have heard, and as lame as some of his
verses."

" Do not speak lightly of him, sire. I was grateful to
him ; I honoured him ; I liked him."

" But you did not love him."

" Why should you seek to read the secrets of a woman's
heart ? "

" You did not love him, Françoise ? "

" At least, I did my duty towards him."

" Has that nun's heart never yet been touched by love
then ? "

" Sire, do not question me."

" Has it never—— "

" Spare me, sire, I beg of you ! "

" But I must ask, for my own peace hangs upon your
answer."

" Your words pain me to the soul."

" Have you never, Françoise, felt in your heart some
ittle flicker of the love which glows in mine ? "   He rose
vith his hands outstretched, a pleading monarch, but she,
vith half-turned head, still shrank away from him.

" Be assured of one thing, sire," said she, " that even
f I loved you as no woman ever loved a man yet, I should
·ather spring from that window on to the stone terraces
>eneath than ever by word or sign confess as much to
·ou."

" And why, Françoise ? "

" Because, sire, it is my highest hope upon earth that I
1ave been chosen to lift up your mind towards loftier
hings—that mind the greatness and nobility of which
1one know more than I."

" And is my love so base, then ? "

" You have wasted too much of your life and of your
houghts upon woman's love. And now, sire, the years
·teal on and the day is coming when even you will be called
1pon to give an account of your actions, and of the inner-
nost thoughts if your heart. I would see you spend the
ime that is left to you, sire, in building up the Church, in
·howing a noble example to your subjects, and in repairing
1ny evil which that example may have done in the past."

The king sank back into his chair with a groan. " For
·ver the same," said he. " Why, you are worse than
Father La Chaise and Bossuet."

" Nay, nay," said she gaily, with the quick tact in which
·he never failed. " I have wearied you, when you have
·tooped to honour my little room with your presence.
That is indeed ingratitude, and it were a just punishment
f you were to leave me in solitude to-morrow, and so cut
>ff all the light of my day. But tell me, sire, how go the
vorks at Marly ? I am all on fire to know whether the
;reat fountain will work."

" Yes, the fountain plays well, but Mansard has thrown
he right wing too far back. I have made him a good
1rchitect, but I have still much to teach him. I showed

577

him his fault on the plan this morning, and he promised
to amend it."

" And what will the change cost, sire ? "

" Some millions of livres, but then the view will be
much improved from the south side. I have taken in
another mile of ground in that direction, for there were a
number of poor folk living there, and their hovels were
far from pretty."

" And why have you not ridden to-day, sire ? "

" Pah ! it brings me no pleasure. There was a time
when my blood was stirred by the blare of the horn and
the rush of the hoofs, but now it is all wearisome to me.'

" And hawking too ? "

" Yes ; I shall hawk no more."

" But, sire, you must have amusement."

" What is so dull as an amusement which has ceased to
amuse ? I know not how it is. When I was but a lad
and my mother and I were driven from place to place
with the Fronde at war with us and Paris in revolt, with
our throne and even our lives in danger, all life seemed to
be so bright, so new and so full of interest. Now that
there is no shadow, and that my voice is the first in
France, as France's is in Europe, all is dull and lacking
in flavour. What use is it to have all pleasure before
me, when it turns to wormwood when it is tasted ? "

" True pleasure, sire, lies rather in the inward life
the serene mind, the easy conscience. And then, as we
grow older, is it not natural that our minds should take
a graver bent ? We might well reproach ourselves if i
were not so, for it would show that we had not learned
the lesson of life."

" It may be so, and yet it is sad and weary when nothing
amuses. But who is there ? "

" It is my companion knocking. What is it, made
moiselle ? "

" Monsieur Corneille, to read to the king," said the
young lady, opening the door.

" Ah, yes, sire ; I know how foolish is a woman'

tongue, and so I have brought a wiser one than mine here to charm you. Monsieur Racine was to have come, but I hear that he has had a fall from his horse and he sends his friend in his place. Shall I admit him ? "

" Oh, as you like, madame, as you like," said the king listlessly. At a sign from Mademoiselle Nanon a little peaky man with a shrewd petulant face, and long grey hair falling back over his shoulders, entered the room. He bowed profoundly three times, and then seated himself nervously on the very edge of the stool, from which the lady had removed her work-basket. She smiled and nodded to encourage the poet, while the monarch leaned back in his chair with an air of resignation.

" Shall it be a comedy, or a tragedy, or a burlesque pastoral ? " Corneille asked timidly.

" Not the burlesque pastoral," said the king with decision. " Such things may be played, but cannot be read, since they are for the eye rather than the ear."

The poet bowed his acquiescence.

" And not the tragedy, monsieur," said Madame de Maintenon, glancing up from her tapestry. " The king has enough that is serious in his graver hours, and so I trust that you will use your talent to amuse him."

" Aye, let it be a comedy," said Louis ; " I have not had a good laugh since poor Molière passed away."

" Ah, your Majesty has indeed a fine taste," cried the courtier poet. " Had you condescended to turn your own attention to poetry, where should we all have been then ? "

Louis smiled, for no flattery was too gross to please him.

" Even as you have taught our generals war and our builders art, so you would have set your poor singers a loftier strain. But Mars would hardly deign to share the humbler laurels of Apollo."

" I have sometimes thought that I had some such power," answered the king complacently ; " though amid my toils and the burdens of state I have had, as you say, little time for the softer arts."

" But you have encouraged others to do what you could so well have done yourself, sire. You have brought out poets as the sun brings out flowers. How many have we not seen—Molière, Boileau, Racine, one greater than the other. And the others, too, the smaller ones—Scarron, so scurrilous and yet so witty—— Oh, holy Virgin ! what have I said ? "

Madame had laid down her tapestry, and was staring in intense indignation at the poet, who writhed on his stool under the stern rebuke of those cold grey eyes.

" I think, Monsieur Corneille, that you had better go on with your reading," said the king dryly.

" Assuredly, sire. Shall I read my play about Darius ? "

" And who was Darius ? " asked the king, whose education had been so neglected by the crafty policy of Cardinal Mazarin that he was ignorant of everything save what had come under his own personal observation.

" Darius was King of Persia, sire."

" And where is Persia ? "

" It is a kingdom of Asia."

" Is Darius still king there ? "

" Nay, sire ; he fought against Alexander the Great."

" Ah, I have heard of Alexander. He was a famous king and general, was he not ? "

" Like your Majesty, he both ruled wisely and led his armies victoriously."

" And was King of Persia, you say ? "

" No, sire ; of Macedonia. It was Darius who was King of Persia."

The king frowned, for the slightest correction was offensive to him.

" You do not seem very clear about the matter, and I confess that it does not interest me deeply," said he. " Pray turn to something else."

" There is my *Pretended Astrologer*."

" Yes, that will do."

Corneille commenced to read his comedy, while Madame de Maintenon's white and delicate fingers

picked among the many-coloured silks which she was weaving into her tapestry. From time to time she glanced across, first at the clock and then at the king, who was leaning back, with his lace handkerchief thrown over his face. It was twenty minutes to four now, but she knew that she had put it back half an hour, and that the true time was ten minutes past.

" Tut ! tut ! " cried the king suddenly. " There is something amiss there. The second last line has a limp in it, surely." It was one of his foibles to pose as a critic, and the wise poet would fall in with his corrections, however unreasonable they might be.

" Which line, sire ? It is indeed an advantage to have one's faults made clear."

" Read the passage again."

> " Et si, quand je lui dis le secret de mon âme,
> Avec moins de rigueur elle eût traité ma flamme,
> Dans ma façon de vivre, et suivant mon humeur,
> Une autre eût eu bientôt le présent de mon cœur."

" Yes, the third line has a foot too many. Do you not remark it, madame ? "

" No ; but I fear that I should make a poor critic."

" Your Majesty is perfectly right," said Corneille unblushingly. " I shall mark the passage, and see that it is corrected."

" I thought that it was wrong. If I do not write myself, you can see that I have at least got the correct ear. A false quantity jars upon me. It is the same in music. Although I know little of the matter I can tell a discord where Lully himself would miss it. I have often shown him errors of the sort in his operas, and I have always convinced him that I was right."

" I can readily believe it, your Majesty." Corneille had picked up his book again, and was about to resume his reading when there came a sharp tap at the door.

" It is his Highness the minister, Monsieur de Louvois," said Mademoiselle Nanon.

" Admit him," answered Louis. " Monsieur Corneille, I am obliged to you for what you have read, and I regret that an affair of state will now interrupt your comedy. Some other day perhaps I may have the pleasure of hearing the rest of it." He smiled in the gracious fashion which made all who came within his personal influence forget his faults and remember him only as the impersonation of dignity and of courtesy.

The poet, with his book under his arm, slipped out, while the famous minister, tall, heavily wigged, eagle-nosed and commanding, came bowing into the little room. His manner was that of exaggerated politeness, but his haughty face marked only too plainly his contempt for such a chamber and for the lady who dwelt there. She was well aware of the feeling with which he regarded her, but her perfect self-command prevented her from ever by word or look returning his dislike.

" My apartments are indeed honoured to-day," said she, rising with outstretched hand. " Can monsieur condescend to a stool, since I have no fitter seat to offer you in this little doll's house ? But perhaps I am in the way, if you wish to talk of state affairs to the king. I can easily withdraw into my boudoir."

" No, no, nothing of the kind, madame," cried Louis. " It is my wish that you should remain here. What is it, Louvois ? "

" A messenger arrived from England with despatches, your Majesty," answered the minister, his ponderous figure balanced upon the three-legged stool. " There is very ill feeling there, and there is some talk of a rising. The letter from Lord Sunderland wished to know whether, in case the Dutch took the side of the malcontents, the king might look to France for help. Of course, knowing your Majesty's mind, I answered unhesitatingly that he might."

" You did what ! "

" I answered, sire, that he might."

King Louis flushed with anger, and he caught up the

tongs from the grate with a motion as though he would have struck his minister with them. Madame sprang from her chair, and laid her hand upon his arm with a soothing gesture. He threw down the tongs again, but his eyes still flashed with passion as he turned them upon Louvois.

" How dared you ! " he cried.

" But, sire——"

" How dared you, I say ! What ! You venture to answer such a message without consulting me ! How often am I to tell you that I am the state—I alone ; that all is to come from me ; and that I am answerable to God only ! What are you ? My instrument ! my tool ! And you venture to act without my authority ! "

" I thought that I knew your wishes, sire," stammered Louvois, whose haughty manner had quite deserted him, and whose face was as white as the ruffles of his shirt.

" You are not there to think about my wishes, sir. You are there to consult them and to obey them. Why is it that I have turned away from my old nobility, and have committed the affairs of my kingdom to men whose names have never been heard of in the history of France, such men as Colbert and yourself ? I have been blamed for it. There was the Duc de St. Simon, who said, the last time that he was at the court, that it was a bourgeois government. So it is. But I wished it to be so, because I knew that the nobles have a way of thinking for themselves, and I ask for no thought but mine in the governing of France. But if my bourgeois are to receive messages and give answers to embassies, then indeed I am to be pitied. I have marked you of late, Louvois. You have grown beyond your station. You take too much upon yourself. See to it that I have not again to complain to you upon this matter."

The humiliated minister sat as one crushed, with his chin sunk upon his breast. The king muttered and frowned for a few minutes, but the cloud cleared gradually

from his face, for his fits of anger were usually as short as they were fierce and sudden.

" You will detain that messenger, Louvois," he said at last, in a calm voice.

" Yes, sire."

" And we shall see at the council meeting to-morrow that a fitting reply be sent to Lord Sunderland. It would be best perhaps not to be too free with our promises in the matter. These English have ever been a thorn in our sides. If we could leave them among their own fogs with such a quarrel as would keep them busy for a few years, then indeed we might crush this Dutch prince at our leisure. Their last civil war lasted ten years, and their next may do as much. We could carry our frontier to the Rhine long ere that. Eh, Louvois ? "

" Your armies are ready, sire, on the day that you give the word."

" But war is a costly business. I do not wish to have to sell the court plate, as we did the other day. How are the public funds ? "

" We are not very rich, sire. But there is one way in which money may very readily be gained. There was some talk this morning about the Huguenots, and whether they should dwell any longer in this Catholic kingdom. Now, if they are driven out, and if their property were taken by the state, then indeed your Majesty would at once become the richest monarch in Christendom."

" But you were against it this morning, Louvois ? "

" I had not had time to think of it, sire."

" You mean that Father La Chaise and the bishop had not had time to get at you," said Louis sharply. " Ah, Louvois, I have not lived with a court round me all these years without learning how things are done. It is a word to him, and so on to another, and so to a third, and so to the king. When my good fathers of the Church have set themselves to bring anything to pass, I see traces of them at every turn, as one traces a mole by the dirt which it has thrown up. But I will not be moved against my own

reason to do wrong to those who, however mistaken they may be, are still the subjects whom God has given me."

" I would not have you do so, sire," cried Louvois in confusion. The king's accusation had been so true that he had been unable at the moment even to protest.

" I know but one person," continued Louis, glancing across at Madame de Maintenon, " who has no ambitions, who desires neither wealth nor preferment, and who can therefore never be bribed to sacrifice my interests. That is why I value that person's opinion so highly." He smiled at the lady as he spoke, while his minister cast a glance at her which showed the jealousy which ate into his soul.

" It was my duty to point this out to you, sire, not as a suggestion, but as a possibility," said he, rising. " I fear that I have already taken up too much of your Majesty's time, and I shall now withdraw." Bowing slightly to the lady, and profoundly to the monarch, he walked from the room.

" Louvois grows intolerable," said the king. " I know not where his insolence will end. Were it not that he is an excellent servant, I should have sent him from the court before this. He has his own opinions upon everything. It was but the other day that he would have it that I was wrong when I said that one of the windows in the Trianon was smaller than any of the others. It was the same size, said he. I brought Le Nôtre with his measures, and of course the window was, as I had said, too small. But I see by your clock that it is four o'clock. I must go."

" My clock, sire, is half an hour slow."

" Half an hour ! " The king look dismayed for an instant, and then began to laugh. " Nay, in that case," said he, " I had best remain where I am, for it is too late to go, and I can say with a clear conscience that it was the clock's fault rather than mine."

" I trust that it was nothing of very great importance, sire," said the lady, with a look of demure triumph in her eyes.

" By no means."

" No state affair ? "

" No, no ; it was only that it was the hour at which I had intended to rebuke the conduct of a presumptuous person. But perhaps it is better as it is. My absence will in itself convey my message, and in such a sort that I trust I may never see that person's face more at my court. But, ah, what is this ? "

The door had been flung open, and Madame de Montespan, beautiful and furious, was standing before them.

10. *An Eclipse at Versailles*

MADAME DE MAINTENON was a woman who was always full of self-restraint and of cool resource. She had risen in an instant, with an air as if she had at last seen the welcome guest for whom she had pined in vain. With a frank smile of greeting, she advanced with outstretched hand.

" This is indeed a pleasure," said she.

But Madame de Montespan was very angry, so angry that she was evidently making strong efforts to keep herself within control, and to avoid breaking into a furious outburst. Her face was very pale, her lips compressed, and her blue eyes had the set stare and the cold glitter of a furious woman. So for an instant they faced each other, the one frowning, the other smiling, two of the most beautiful and queenly women in France. Then De Montespan, disregarding her rival's outstretched hand, turned towards the king, who had been looking at her with a darkening face.

" I fear that I intrude, sire."

" Your entrance, madame, is certainly somewhat abrupt."

" I must crave pardon if it is so. Since this lady has been the governess of my children I have been in the habit of coming into her room unannounced."

" As far as I am concerned, you are most welcome to
do so," said her rival, with perfect composure.

" I confess that I had not even thought it necessary to
ask your permission, madame," the other answered coldly.

" Then you shall certainly do so in the future, madame,"
said the king sternly. " It is my express order to you
that every possible respect is to be shown in every way
to this lady."

" Oh, to *this* lady ! " with a wave of her hand in her
direction. " Your Majesty's commands are of course
our laws. But I must remember that it *is* this lady, for
sometimes one may get confused as to which name it is
that your Majesty has picked out for honour. To-day
it is De Maintenon ; yesterday it was Fontanges ; to-
morrow—— Ah, well, who can say who it may be to-
morrow ? "

She was superb in her pride and her fearlessness as she
stood, with her sparkling blue eyes and her heaving bosom,
looking down upon her royal lover. Angry as he was, his
gaze lost something of its sternness as it rested upon her
round full throat and the delicate lines of her shapely
shoulders. There was something very becoming in her
passion, in the defiant pose of her dainty head, and the
magnificent scorn with which she glanced at her rival.

" There is nothing to be gained, madame, by being insolent," said he.

" Nor is it my custom, sire."

" And yet I find your words so."

" Truth is always mistaken for insolence, sire, at the
court of France."

" We have had enough of this."

" A very little truth is enough."

" You forget yourself, madame. I beg that you will
leave the room."

" I must first remind your Majesty that I was so far
honoured as to have an appointment this afternoon. At
four o'clock I had your royal promise that you would
come to me. I cannot doubt that your Majesty will keep

that promise in spite of the fascinations which you may find here."

" I should have come, madame, but the clock, as you may observe, is half an hour slow, and the time had passed before I was aware of it."

" I beg, sire, that you will not let that distress you. I am returning to my chamber, and five o'clock will suit me as well as four."

" I thank you, madame, but I have not found this interview so pleasant that I should seek another."

" Then your Majesty will not come ? "

" I should prefer not."

" In spite of your promise ! "

" Madame ! "

" You will break your word ! "

" Silence, madame ; this is intolerable."

" It is indeed intolerable ! " cried the angry lady, throwing all discretion to the winds. " Oh, I am not afraid of you, sire. I have loved you, but I have never feared you. I leave you here. I leave you with your conscience and your—your lady confessor. But one word of truth you shall hear before I go. You have been false to your wife, and you have been false to your mistress, but it is only now that I find that you can be false also to your word." She swept him an indignant courtesy, and glided, with head erect, out of the room.

The king sprang from his chair as if he had been stung. Accustomed as he was to his gentle little wife, and the even gentler La Vallière, such language as this had never before intruded itself upon the royal ears. It was like a physical blow to him. He felt stunned, humiliated, bewildered, by so unwonted a sensation. What odour was this which mingled for the first time with the incense amid which he lived ? And then his whole soul rose up in anger at her, at the woman who had dared to raise her voice against him. That she should be jealous of and insult another woman, that was excusable. It was, in fact, an indirect compliment to himself. But that she should turn upon *him*,

as if they were merely man and woman, instead of monarch and subject, that was too much. He gave an inarticulate cry of rage, and rushed to the door.

" Sire ! " Madame de Maintenon, who had watched keenly the swift play of his emotions over his expressive face, took two quick steps forward, and laid her hand upon his arm.

" I will go after her."

" And why, sire ? "

" To forbid her the court."

" But, sire—— "

" You heard her ! It is infamous ! I shall go."

" But, sire, could you not write ? "

" No, no ; I shall see her." He pulled open the door.

" Oh, sire, be firm, then ! " It was with an anxious face that she watched him start off, walking rapidly, with angry gestures, down the corridor. Then she turned back, and dropping upon her knees on the *prie-dieu*, bowed her head in prayer for the king, for herself and for France.

De Catinat, the guardsman, had employed himself in showing his young friend from over the water all the wonders of the great palace, which the other had examined keenly, and had criticised or admired with an independence of judgment and a native correctness of taste natural to a man whose life had been spent in freedom amid the noblest works of nature. Grand as were the mighty fountains and the artificial cascades, they had no overwhelming effect on one who had travelled up from Erie to Ontario, and had seen the Niagara River hurl itself over its precipice, nor were the long level swards so very large to eyes which had rested upon the great plains of the Dakotas. The building itself, however, its extent, its height and the beauty of its stone, filled him with astonishment.

" I must bring Ephraim Savage here," he kept repeating. " He would never believe else that there was one

house in the world which would weigh more than all Boston and New York put together."

De Catinat had arranged that the American should remain with his friend Major de Brissac, as the time had come round for his own second turn of guard. He had hardly stationed himself in the corridor when he was astonished to see the king, without escort or attendants, walking swiftly down the passage. His delicate face was disfigured with anger, and his mouth was set grimly, like that of a man who had taken a momentous resolution.

" Officer of the guard," said he shortly.

" Yes, sire."

" What ! You again, Captain de Catinat ? You have not been on duty since morning ? "

" No, sire. It is my second guard."

" Very good. I wish your assistance."

" I am at your command, sire."

" Is there a subaltern here ? "

" Lieutenant de la Tremouille is at the side guard."

" Very well. You will place him in command."

" Yes, sire."

" You will yourself go to Monsieur de Vivonne. You know his apartments ? "

" Yes, sire."

" If he is not there, you must go and seek him. Wherever he is, you must find him within the hour."

" Yes, sire."

" You will give him an order from me. At six o'clock he is to be in his carriage at the east gate of the palace. His sister, Madame de Montespan, will await him there, and he is charged by me to drive her to the Château of Petit Bourg. You will tell him that he is answerable to me for her arrival there."

" Yes, sire." De Catinat raised his sword in salute, and started upon his mission.

The king passed on down the corridor, and opened a door which led him into a magnificent anteroom, all one blaze of mirrors and gold, furnished to a marvel with the

most delicate ebony and silver suite, on a deep red carpet of Aleppo, as soft and yielding as the moss of a forest. In keeping with the furniture was the sole occupant of this stately chamber—a little negro boy in a livery of velvet picked out with silver tinsel, who stood as motionless as a small swart statuette against the door which faced that through which the king entered.

" Is your mistress there ? "

" She has just returned, sire."

" I wish to see her."

" Pardon, sire, but she——"

" Is everyone to thwart me to-day ? " snarled the king, and taking the little page by his velvet collar, he hurled him to the other side of the room. Then, without knocking, he opened the door, and passed on into the lady's boudoir.

It was a large and lofty room, very different to that from which he had just come. Three long windows from ceiling to floor took up one side, and through the delicate pink-tinted blinds the evening sun cast a subdued and dainty light. Great gold candelabra glittered between the mirrors upon the wall, and Le Brun had expended all his wealth of colouring upon the ceiling, where Louis himself, in the character of Jove, hurled down his thunderbolts upon a writhing heap of Dutch and Palatine Titans. Pink was the prevailing tone in tapestry, carpet and furniture, so that the whole room seemed to shine with the sweet tints of the inner side of a shell, and when lit up, as it was then, formed such a chamber as some fairy hero might have built up for his princess. At the further side, prone upon an ottoman, her face buried in the cushion, her beautiful white arms thrown over it, the rich coils of her brown hair hanging in disorder across the long curve of her ivory neck, lay, like a drooping flower, the woman whom he had come to discard.

At the sound of the closing door she had glanced up, and then, at the sight of the king, she sprang to her feet and ran towards him, her hands out, her blue eyes be-

dimmed with tears, her whole beautiful figure softening into womanliness and humility.

" Ah, sire," she cried, with a pretty little sunburst of joy through her tears, " then I have wronged you ! I have wronged you cruelly ! You have kept your promise. You were but trying my faith ! Oh, how could I have said such words to you—how could I pain that noble heart ! But you have come after me to tell me that you have forgiven me ! " She put her arms forward with the trusting air of a pretty child who claims an embrace as her due, but the king stepped swiftly back from her, and warned her away from him with an angry gesture.

" All is over for ever between us," he cried harshly. " Your brother will await you at the east gate at six o'clock, and it is my command that you wait there until you receive my further orders."

She staggered back as if he had struck her.

" Leave you ! " she cried.

" You must leave the court."

" The court ! Aye, willingly, this instant ! But you ! Ah, sire, you ask what is impossible."

" I do not ask, madame ; I order. Since you have learned to abuse your position, your presence has become intolerable. The united kings of Europe have never dared to speak to me as you have spoken to-day. You have insulted me in my own palace—me, Louis, the king. Such things are not done twice, madame. Your insolence has carried you too far this time. You thought that because I was forbearing, I was therefore weak. It appeared to you that if you only humoured me one moment, you might treat me as if I were your equal the next, for that this poor puppet of a king could always be bent this way or that. You see your mistake now. At six o'clock you leave Versailles for ever." His eyes flashed, and his small upright figure seemed to swell in the violence of his indignation, while she leaned away from him, one hand across her eyes and one thrown forward, as if to screen her from that angry gaze.

" Oh, I have been wicked ! " she cried. " I know it, I know it ! "

" I am glad, madame, that you have the grace to acknowledge it."

" How could I speak to you so ! How could I ! Oh, that some blight may come upon this unhappy tongue ! I, who have had nothing but good from you ! I to insult you, who are the author of all my happiness ! Oh, sire, forgive me, forgive me ! for pity's sake forgive me ! "

Louis was by nature a kind-hearted man. His feelings were touched, and his pride also was flattered by the abasement of this beautiful and haughty woman. His other favourites had been amiable to all, but this one was so proud, so unyielding, until she felt his master-hand. His face softened somewhat in its expression as he glanced at her, but he shook his head, and his voice was as firm as ever as he answered.

" It is useless, madame," said he. " I have thought this matter over for a long time, and your madness to-day has only hurried what must in any case have taken place. You must leave the palace."

" I will leave the palace. Say only that you forgive me. Oh, sire, I cannot bear your anger. It crushes me down. I am not strong enough. It is not banishment, it is death to which you sentence me. Think of our long years of love, sire, and say that you forgive me. I have given up all for your sake—husband, honour, everything. Oh, will you not give your anger up for mine ? My God, he weeps ! Oh, I am saved, I am saved ! "

" No, no, madame," cried the king, dashing his hand across his eyes. " You see the weakness of the man, but you shall also see the firmness of the king. As to your insults to-day, I forgive them freely, if that will make you more happy in your retirement. But I owe a duty to my subjects also, and that duty is to set them an example. We have thought too little of such things. But a time has come when it is necessary to review our past life, and to prepare for that which is to come."

" Ah, sire, you pain me. You are not yet in the prime of your years, and you speak as though old age were upon you. In a score of years from now it may be time for folk to say that age has made a change in your life."

The king winced. " Who says so ? " he cried angrily.

" Oh, sire, it slipped from me unawares. Think no more of it. Nobody says so. Nobody."

" You are hiding something from me. Who is it who says this ? "

" Oh, do not ask me, sire."

" You said that it was reported that I had changed my life not through religion, but through stress of years. Who said so ? "

" Oh, sire, it was but foolish court gossip, all unworthy of your attention. It was but the empty common talk of cavaliers who had nothing else to say to gain a smile from their ladies."

" The common talk ? " Louis flushed crimson. " Have I, then, grown so aged ? You have known me for nearly twenty years. Do you see such changes in me ? "

" To me, sire, you are as pleasing and as gracious as when you first won the heart of Mademoiselle Tonnay-Charente."

The king smiled as he looked at the beautiful woman before him.

" In very truth," said he, " I can say that there has been no such great change in Mademoiselle Tonnay-Charente either. But still it is best that we should part, Françoise."

" If it will add aught to your happiness, sire, I shall go through it, be it to my death."

" Now that is the proper spirit."

" You have but to name the place, sire—Petit Bourg, Chargny or my own convent of St. Joseph in the Faubourg St. Germain. What matter where the flower withers, when once the sun has for ever turned from it ? At least, the past is my own, and I shall live in the remembrance of the days when none had come between us, and when your sweet love was all my own. Be happy, sire, be happy,

and think no more of what I said about the foolish gossip, of the court. Your life lies in the future. Mine is in the past. Adieu, dear sire, adieu ! " She threw forward her hands, her eyes dimmed over, and she would have fallen had Louis not sprung forward and caught her in his arms. Her beautiful head drooped upon his shoulder, her breath was warm upon his cheek, and the subtle scent of her hair was in his nostrils. His arm, as he held her, rose and fell with her bosom and he felt her heart, beneath his hand, fluttering like a caged bird. Her broad white throat was thrown back, her eyes almost closed, her lips just parted enough to show the line of pearly teeth, her beautiful face not three inches from his own. And then suddenly the eyelids quivered, and the great blue eyes looked up at him, lovingly, appealingly, half deprecating, half challenging, her whole soul in a glance. Did he move ? or was it she ? Who could tell ? But their lips had met in a long kiss, and then in another, and plans and resolutions were streaming away from Louis like autumn leaves in the west wind.

" Then I am not to go ? You would not have the heart to send me away, would you ? "

" No, no ; but you must not annoy me, Françoise."

" I had rather die than cause you an instant of grief. Oh, sire, I have seen so little of you lately ! And I love you so ! It has maddened me. And then that dreadful woman——"

" Who, then ? "

" Oh, I must not speak against her. I will be civil for your sake even to her, the widow of old Scarron."

" Yes, yes, you must be civil. I cannot have any unpleasantness."

" But you will stay with me, sire ? " Her supple arms coiled themselves round his neck. Then she held him for an instant at arm's length to feast her eyes upon his face, and then drew him once more towards her. " You will not leave me, dear sire. It is so long since you have been here."

The sweet face, the pink glow in the room, the hush of the evening, all seemed to join in their sensuous influence. Louis sank down upon the settee.

" I will stay," said he.

" And that carriage, dear sire, at the east door ? "

" I have been very harsh with you, Françoise. You will forgive me. Have you paper and pencil, that I may countermand the order ? "

" They are here, sire, upon the side table. I have also a note which, if I may leave you for an instant, I will write in the anteroom."

She swept out with triumph in her eyes. It had been a terrible fight, but all the greater the credit of her victory. She took a little pink slip of paper from an inlaid desk, and dashed off a few words upon it. They were : " Should Madame de Maintenon have any message for his Majesty, he will be for the next few hours in the room of Madame de Montespan." This she addressed to her rival, and it was sent on the spot, together with the king's order, by the hands of the little black page.

11. *The Sun Reappears*

FOR nearly a week the king was constant to his new humour. The routine of his life remained un-changed, save that it was the room of the frail beauty, rather than of Madame de Maintenon, which attracted him in the afternoon. And in sympathy with this sudden relapse into his old life, his coats lost something of their sombre hue, and fawn-colour, buff-colour and lilac began to replace the blacks and the blues. A little gold lace budded out upon his hats also and at the trimmings of his pockets, while for three days on end his *prie-dieu* at the royal chapel had been unoccupied. His walk was brisker, and he gave a youthful flourish to his cane as a defiance to those who had seen in his reformation the first symptoms of age. Madame had known her man well when she threw out that artful insinuation.

And as the king brightened, so all the great court brightened too. The *salons* began to resume their former splendour, and gay coats and glittering embroidery which had lain in drawers for years were seen once more in the halls of the palace. In the chapel, Bourdaloue preached in vain to empty benches, but a ballet in the grounds was attended by the whole court, and received with a frenzy of enthusiasm. The Montespan anteroom was crowded every morning with men and women who had some suit to be urged, while her rival's chambers were as deserted as they had been before the king first turned a gracious look upon her. Faces which had been long banished the court began to reappear in the corridors and gardens unchecked and unrebuked, while the black cassock of the Jesuit and the purple soutane of the bishop were less frequent colours in the royal circle.

But the Church party, who, if they were the champions of bigotry, were also those of virtue, were never seriously alarmed at this relapse. The grave eyes of priest or of prelate followed Louis in his escapade as wary huntsmen might watch a young deer which gambols about in the meadow under the impression that it is masterless, when every gap and path is netted, and it is in truth as much in their hands as though it were lying bound before them. They knew how short a time it would be before some ache, some pain, some chance word, would bring his mortality home to him again, and envelop him once more in those superstitious terrors which took the place of religion in his mind. They waited, therefore, and they silently planned how the prodigal might best be dealt with on his return.

To this end it was that his confessor, Père La Chaise, and Bossuet, the great Bishop of Meaux, waited one morning upon Madame de Maintenon in her chamber. With a globe beside her, she was endeavouring to teach geography to the lame Duc du Maine and the mischievous little Comte de Toulouse, who had enough of their

father's disposition to make them averse to learning, and of their mother's to cause them to hate any discipline or restraint. Her wonderful tact, however, and her unwearying patience had won the love and confidence even of these little perverse princes, and it was one of Madame de Montespan's most bitter griefs that not only her royal lover, but even her own children, turned away from the brilliancy and riches of her *salon* to pass their time in the modest apartment of her rival.

Madame de Maintenon dismissed her two pupils, and received the ecclesiastics with the mixture of affection and respect which was due to those who were not only personal friends, but great lights of the Gallican Church. She had suffered the minister Louvois to sit upon a stool in her presence, but the two chairs were allotted to the priests now, and she insisted upon reserving the humbler seat for herself. The last few days had cast a pallor over her face which spiritualised and refined the features, but she wore unimpaired the expression of sweet serenity which was habitual to her.

" I see, my dear daughter, that you have sorrowed," said Bossuet, glancing at her with a kindly and yet searching eye.

" I have indeed, your Grace. All last night I spent in prayer that this trial may pass away from us."

" And yet you have no need for fear, madame—none, I assure you. Others may think that your influence has ceased ; but we, who know the king's heart, we think otherwise. A few days may pass, a few weeks at the most, and once more it will be upon your rising fortunes that every eye in France will turn."

The lady's brow clouded, and she glanced at the prelate as though his speech were not altogether to her taste. " I trust that pride does not lead me astray," she said. " But if I can read my own soul aright, there is no thought of myself in the grief which now tears my heart. What is power to me ? What do I desire ? A little room, leisure for my devotions, a pittance to save me from want—what more

can I ask for ? Why, then, should I covet power ? If I am sore at heart, it is not for any poor loss which I have sustained. I think no more of it than of the snapping of one of the threads on yonder tapestry frame. It is for the king I grieve—for the noble heart, the kindly soul, which might rise so high, and which is dragged so low, like a royal eagle with some foul weight which ever hampers its flight. It is for him and for France that my days are spent in sorrow and my nights upon my knees."

" For all that, my daughter, you are ambitious."

It was the Jesuit who had spoken. His voice was clear and cold, and his piercing grey eyes seemed to read into the depths of her soul.

" You may be right, father. God guard me from self-esteem. And yet I do not think that I am. The king, in his goodness, has offered me titles—I have refused them ; money—I have returned it. He has deigned to ask my advice in matter of state, and I have withheld it. Where, then, is my ambition ? "

" In your heart, my daughter. But it is not a sinful ambition. It is not an ambition of this world. Would you not love to turn the king towards good ? "

" I would give my life for it."

" And there is your ambition. Ah, can I not read your noble soul ? Would you not love to see the Church reign pure and serene over all this realm—to see the poor housed, the needy helped, the wicked turned from their ways, and the king ever the leader in all that is noble and good ? Would you not love that, my daughter ? "

Her cheeks had flushed, and her eyes shone as she looked at the grey face of the Jesuit, and saw the picture which his words had conjured up before her. " Ah, that would be joy indeed ? " she cried.

" And greater joy still to know, not from the mouths of the people, but from the voice of your own heart in the privacy of your chamber, that you had been the cause of it, that your influence had brought this blessing upon the king and upon the country."

" I would die to do it."

" We wish you to do what may be harder. We wish you to live to do it."

" Ah ! " She glanced from one to the other with questioning eyes.

" My daughter," said Bossuet solemnly, leaning forward with his broad white hand outstretched and his purple pastoral ring sparkling in the sunlight, " it is time for plain speaking. It is in the interests of the Church that we do it. None hear, and none shall ever hear, what passes between us now. Regard us, if you will, as two confessors, with whom your secret is inviolable. I call it a secret, and yet it is none to us, for it is our mission to read the human heart. You love the king."

" Your Grace ! " She started, and a warm blush, mantling up in her pale cheeks, deepened and spread until it tinted her white forehead and her queenly neck.

" You love the king."

" Your Grace—father ! " She turned in confusion from one to the other.

" There is no shame in loving, my daughter. The shame lies only in yielding to love. I say again that you love the king."

" At least I have never told him so," she faltered.

" And will you never ? "

" May heaven wither my tongue first ! "

" But consider, my daughter. Such love in a soul like yours is heaven's gift, and sent for some wise purpose. This human love is too often but a noxious weed which blights the soil it grows in, but here it is a gracious flower, all fragrant with humility and virtue."

" Alas ! I have tried to tear it from my heart."

" Nay ; rather hold it firmly rooted there. Did the king but meet with some tenderness from you, some sign that his own affection met with an answer from your heart, it might be that this ambition which you profess would be secured, and that Louis, strengthened by the intimate companionship of your noble nature, might live in the

600

spirit as well as in the forms of the Church. All this might spring from the love which you hide away as though it bore the brand of shame."

The lady half rose, glancing from the prelate to the priest with eyes which had a lurking horror in their depths.

"Can I have understood you!" she gasped. "What meaning lies behind these words? You cannot counsel me to——"

The Jesuit had risen, and his spare figure towered above her.

"My daughter, we give no counsel which is unworthy of our office. We speak for the interests of Holy Church, and those interests demand that you should marry the king."

"Marry the king!" The little room swam round her. "Marry the king!"

"There lies the best hope for the future. We see in you a second Jeanne d'Arc, who will save both France and France's king."

Madame sat silent for a few moments. Her face had regained its composure, and her eyes were bent vacantly upon her tapestry frame as she turned over in her mind all that was involved in the suggestion.

"But surely—surely this could never be," she said at last. "Why should we plan that which can never come to pass?"

"And why?"

"What King of France has married a subject? See how every princess of Europe stretches out her hand to him. The Queen of France must be of queenly blood, even as the last was."

"All this may be overcome."

"And then there are the reasons of state. If the king marry, it should be to form a powerful alliance, to cement a friendship with a neighbour nation, or to gain some province which may be the bride's dowry. What is my dowry? A widow's pension and a work-box." She

laughed bitterly, and yet glanced eagerly at her companions, as one who wished to be confuted.

" Your dowry, my daughter, would be those gifts of body and of mind with which heaven has endowed you. The king has money enough, and the king has provinces enough. As to the state, how can the state be better served than by the assurance that the king will be saved in future from such sights as are to be seen in this palace to-day ? "

" Oh, if it could be so ! But think, father, think of those about him—the dauphin, monsieur his brother, his ministers. You know how little this would please them, and how easy it is for them to sway his mind. No, no ; it is a dream, father, and it can never be."

The faces of the two ecclesiastics, who had dismissed her other objections with a smile and a wave, clouded over at this, as though she had at last touched upon the real obstacle.

" My daughter," said the Jesuit gravely, " that is a matter which you may leave to the Church. It may be that we, too, have some power over the king's mind, and that we may lead him in the right path, even though those of his own blood would fain have it otherwise. The future only can show with whom the power lies. But you ? Love and duty both draw you one way now, and the Church may count upon you."

" To my last breath, father."

" And you upon the Church. It will serve you, if you in turn will but serve it."

" What higher wish could I have ? "

" You will be our daughter, our queen, our champion, and you will heal the wounds of the suffering Church."

" Ah ! if I could ! "

" But you can. While there is heresy within the land there can be no peace or rest for the faithful. It is the speck of mould which will in time, if it be not pared off, corrupt the whole fruit."

" What would you have, then, father ? "

" The Huguenots must go. They must be driven forth. The goats must be divided from the sheep. The king is already in two minds. Louvois is our friend now. If you are with us, then all will be well."

" But, father, think how many there are ! "

" The more reason that they should be dealt with."

" And think, too, of their sufferings should they be driven forth."

" Their cure lies in their own hands."

" That is true. And yet my heart softens for them."

Père La Chaise and the bishop shook their heads. Nature had made them both kind and charitable men, but the heart turns to flint when the blessing of religion is changed to the curse of sect.

" You would befriend God's enemies, then ? "

" No, no ; not if they are indeed so."

" Can you doubt it ? Is it possible that your heart still turns towards the heresy of your youth ? "

" No, father ; but it is not in nature to forget that my father and my grandfather——"

" Nay, they have answered for their own sins. Is it possible that the Church has been mistaken in you ? Do you then refuse the first favour which she asks of you ? You would accept her aid, and yet you would give none in return."

Madame de Maintenon rose with the air of one who has made her resolution. " You are wiser than I," said she, " and to you have been committed the interests of the Church. I will do what you advise."

" You promise it ? "

" I do."

Her two visitors threw up their hands together. " It is a blessed day," they cried, " and generations yet unborn will learn to deem it so."

She sat half stunned by the prospect which was opening out in front of her. Ambitious she had, as the Jesuit had surmised, always been—ambitious for the power which would enable her to leave the world better than she found

it. And this ambition she had already to some extent been able to satisfy, for more than once she had swayed both king and kingdom. But to marry the king—to marry the man for whom she would gladly lay down her life, whom in the depths of her heart she loved in as pure and as noble a fashion as woman ever yet loved man—that was indeed a thing above her utmost hopes. She knew her own mind, and she knew his. Once his wife, she could hold him to good, and keep every evil influence away from him. She was sure of it. She should be no weak Maria Theresa, but rather, as the priest had said, a new Jeanne d'Arc, come to lead France and France's king into better ways. And if, to gain this aim, she had to harden her heart against the Huguenots, at least the fault, if there were one, lay with those who made this condition rather than with herself. The king's wife! The heart of the woman and the soul of the enthusiast both leaped at the thought.

But close at the heels of her joy there came a sudden revulsion to doubt and despondency. Was not all this fine prospect a mere day dream? and how could these men be so sure that they held the king in the hollow of their hand? The Jesuit read the fears which dulled the sparkle of her eyes, and answered her thoughts before she had time to put them into words.

" The Church redeems its pledges swiftly," said he. " And you, my daughter, you must be as prompt when your own turn comes."

" I have promised, father."

" Then it is for us to perform. You will remain in your room all evening."

" Yes, father."

" The king already hesitates. I spoke with him this morning, and his mind was full of blackness and despair. His better self turns in disgust from his sins, and it is now when the first hot fit of repentance is just coming upon him that he may best be moulded to our ends. I have to see and speak with him once more, and I go from

your room to his. And when I have spoken, he will come from his room to yours, or I have studied his heart for twenty years in vain. We leave you now, and you will not see us, but you will see the effects of what we do, and you will remember your pledge to us." They bowed low to her both together, and left her to her thoughts.

An hour passed, and then a second one, as she sat in her *fauteuil*, her tapestry before her, but her hands listless upon her lap, waiting for her fate. Her life's future was now being settled for her, and she was powerless to turn it in one way or the other. Daylight turned to the pearly light of evening, and that again to dusk, but she still sat waiting in the shadow. Sometimes as a step passed in the corridor she would glance expectantly towards the door, and the light of welcome would spring up in her grey eyes, only to die away again into disappointment. At last, however, there came a quick sharp tread, crisp and authoritative, which brought her to her feet with flushed cheeks and her heart beating wildly. The door opened, and she saw outlined against the grey light of the outer passage the erect and graceful figure of the king.

"Sire! One instant, and mademoiselle will light the lamp."

"Do not call her." He entered and closed the door behind him. "Françoise, the dusk is welcome to me, because it screens me from the reproaches which must lie in your glance, even if your tongue be too kindly to speak them."

"Reproaches, sire! God forbid that I should utter them!"

"When I last left you, Françoise, it was with a good resolution in my mind. I tried to carry it out, and I failed—I failed. I remember that you warned me. Fool that I was not to follow your advice!"

"We are all weak and mortal, sire. Who has not fallen? Nay, sire, it goes to my heart to see you thus."

He was standing by the fireplace, his face buried in his hands, and she could tell by the catch of his breath that he

was weeping. All the pity of her woman's nature went out to that silent and repenting figure dimly seen in the failing light. She put out her hand with a gesture of sympathy, and it rested for an instant upon his velvet sleeve. The next he had clasped it between his own, and she made no effort to release it.

" I cannot do without you, Françoise," he cried. " I am the loneliest man in all this world, like one who lives on a great mountain-peak, with none to bear him company. Who have I for a friend ? Whom can I rely upon ? Some are for the Church ; some are for their families ; most are for themselves. But who of them all is single-minded ? You are my better self, Françoise ; you are my guardian angel. What the good father says is true, and the nearer I am to you the further am I from all that is evil. Tell me, Françoise, do you love me ? "

" I have loved you for years, sire." Her voice was low but clear—the voice of a woman to whom coquetry was abhorrent.

" I had hoped it, Françoise, and yet it thrills me to hear you say it. I know that wealth and title have no attraction for you, and that your heart turns rather towards the convent than the palace. Yet I ask you to remain in the palace, and to reign there. Will you be my wife, Françoise ? "

And so the moment had in very truth come. She paused for an instant, only an instant, before taking this last great step ; but even that was too long for the patience of the king.

" Will you not, Françoise ? " he cried, with a ring of fear in his voice.

" May God make me worthy of such an honour, sire ! " said she. " And here I swear that if heaven double my life, every hour shall be spent in the one endeavour to make you a happier man ! "

She had knelt down, and the king, still holding her hand, knelt down beside her.

" And I swear too," he cried, " that if my days also are

606

doubled, you will now and for ever be the one and only woman for me."

And so their double oath was taken, an oath which was to be tested in the future, for each did live almost double their years, and yet neither broke the promise made hand in hand on that evening in the shadow-girt chamber.

12. *The King Receives*

IT may have been that Mademoiselle Nanon, the faithful *confidante* of Madame de Maintenon, had learned something of this interview, or it may be that Père La Chaise, with the shrewdness for which his Order is famous, had come to the conclusion that publicity was the best means of holding the king to his present intention; but whatever the source, it was known all over the court next day that the old favourite was again in disgrace, and that there was talk of a marriage between the king and the governess of his children. It was whispered at the *petit lever*, confirmed at the *grand entrée*, and was common gossip by the time that the king had returned from chapel. Back into wardrobe and drawer went the flaring silks and the feathered hats, and out once more came the sombre coat and the matronly dress. Scudéry and Calpernedi gave place to the missal and St. Thomas à Kempis, while Bourdaloue, after preaching for a week to empty benches, found his chapel packed to the last seat with weary gentlemen and taper-bearing ladies. By midday there was none in the court who had not heard the tidings, save only Madame de Montespan, who, alarmed by her lover's absence, had remained in haughty seclusion in her room, and knew nothing of what had passed. Many there were who would have loved to carry her the tidings ; but the king's changes had been frequent of late, and who would dare to make a mortal enemy of one who might ere many weeks were past have the lives and fortunes of the whole court in the hollow of her hand ?

Louis, in his innate selfishness, had been so accustomed

to regard every event entirely from the side of how it would affect himself, that it had never struck him that his long-suffering family, who had always yielded to him the absolute obedience which he claimed as his right, would venture to offer any opposition to his new resolution. He was surprised, therefore, when his brother demanded a private interview that afternoon, and entered his presence without the complaisant smile and humble air with which he was wont to appear before him.

Monsieur was a curious travesty of his elder brother. He was shorter, but he wore enormously high boot-heels, which brought him to a fair stature. In figure he had none of that grace which marked the king, nor had he the elegant hand and foot which had been the delight of sculptors. He was fat, waddled somewhat in his walk, and wore an enormous black wig, which' rolled down in rows and rows of curls over his shoulders. His face was longer and darker than the king's, and his nose more prominent, though he shared with his brother the large brown eyes which each had inherited from Anne of Austria. He had none of the simple and yet stately taste which marked the dress of the monarch, but his clothes were all tagged over with fluttering ribbons, which rustled behind him as he walked, and clustered so thickly over his feet as to conceal them from view. Crosses, stars, jewels, and insignia were scattered-broadcast over his person, and the broad blue ribbon of the Order of the Holy Ghost was slashed across his coat, and was gathered at the end into a great bow, which formed the incongruous support of a diamond-hilted sword. Such was the figure which rolled towards the king, bearing in his right hand his many-feathered beaver, and appearing in his person, as he was in his mind, an absurd burlesque of the monarch.

" Why, monsieur, you seem less gay than usual to-day," said the king, with a smile. " Your dress, indeed, is bright, but your brow is clouded. I trust that all is well with madame and with the Duc de Chartres ? "

" Yes, sire, they are well ; but they are sad like myself, and from the same cause."

" Indeed ! and why ? "

" Have I ever failed in my duty as your younger brother, sire ? "

" Never, Philippe, never ! " said the king, laying his hand affectionately upon the other's shoulder. " You have set an excellent example to my subjects."

" Then why set a slight upon me ? "

" Philippe ! "

" Yes, sire, I say it is a slight. We are of royal blood, and our wives are of royal blood also. You married the Princess of Spain ; I married the Princess of Bavaria. It was a condescension, but still I did it. My first wife was the Princess of England. How can we admit into a house which has formed such alliances as these a woman who is the widow of a hunchback singer, a mere lampooner, a man whose name is a byword through Europe ? "

The king had stared in amazement at his brother, but his anger now overcame his astonishment.

" Upon my word ! " he cried ; " upon my word ! I have said just now that you have been an excellent brother, but I fear that I spoke a little prematurely. And so you take upon yourself to object to the lady whom I select as my wife ! "

" I do, sire."

" And by what right ? "

" By the right of the family honour, sire, which is as much mine as yours."

" Man," cried the king furiously, " have you not yet learned that within this kingdom I am the fountain of honour, and that whomsoever I may honour becomes by that very fact honourable ? Were I to take a cinder-wench out of the Rue Poissonnière, I could at my will raise her up until the highest in France would be proud to bow down before her. Do you not know this ? "

" No, I do not," cried his brother, with all the obstinacy of a weak man who has at last been driven to bay. " I

look upon it as a slight upon me and a slight upon my wife."

"Your wife! I have every respect for Charlotte Elizabeth of Bavaria, but how is she superior to one whose grandfather was the dear friend and comrade in arms of Henry the Great? Enough! I will not condescend to argue such a matter with you! Begone, and do not return to my presence until you have learned not to interfere in my affairs."

"For all that, my wife shall not know her!" snarled monsieur; and then, as his brother took a fiery step or two towards him, he turned and scuttled out of the room as fast as his awkward gait and high heels would allow him.

But the king was to have no quiet that day. If Madame de Maintenon's friends had rallied to her yesterday, her enemies were active to-day. Monsieur had hardly disappeared before there rushed into the room a youth who bore upon his rich attire every sign of having just arrived from a dusty journey. He was pale-faced and auburn-haired, with features which would have been strikingly like the king's if it were not that his nose had been disfigured in his youth. The king's face had lighted up at the sight of him, but it darkened again as he hurried forward and threw himself down at his feet.

"Oh, sire," he cried, "spare us this grief!—spare us this humiliation! I implore you to pause before you do what will bring dishonour upon yourself and upon us!"

The king started back from him, and paced angrily up and down the room.

"This is intolerable!" he cried. "It was bad from my brother, but worse from my son. You are in a conspiracy with him, Louis. Monsieur has told you to act this part."

The dauphin rose to his feet and looked steadfastly at his angry father.

"I have not seen my uncle," he said. "I was at Meudon when I heard this news—this dreadful news— and I sprang upon my horse, sire, and galloped over to

implore you to think again before you drag our royal house so low."

" You are insolent, Louis."

" I do not mean to be so, sire. But consider, sire, that my mother was a queen, and that it would be strange indeed if for a step-mother I had a——"

The king raised his hand with a gesture of authority which checked the word upon his lips.

" Silence ! " he cried, " or you may say that which would for ever set a gulf between us. Am I to be treated worse than my humblest subject, who is allowed to follow his own bent in his private affairs ? "

" This is not your own private affair, sire ; all that you do reflects upon your family. The great deeds of your reign have given a new glory to the name of Bourbon. Oh, do not mar it now, sire ! I implore it of you upon my bended knees ! "

" You talk like a fool ! " cried his father roughly. " I propose to marry a virtuous and charming lady of one of the oldest noble families of France, and you talk as if I were doing something degrading and unheard-of. What is your objection to this lady ? "

" That she is the daughter of a man whose vices were well known, that her brother is of the worst repute, that she has led the life of an adventuress, is the widow of a deformed scribbler, and that she occupies a menial position in the palace."

The king had stamped with his foot upon the carpet more than once during this frank address, but his anger blazed into a fury at its conclusion.

" Do you dare," he cried, with flashing eyes, " to call the charge of my children a menial position ? I say that there is no higher in the kingdom. Go back to Meudon, sir, this instant, and never dare to open your mouth again on the subject. Away, I say ! When, in God's good time, you are king of this country, you may claim your own way, but until then do not venture to cross the plans of one who is both your parent and your monarch."

611

The young man bowed low, and walked with dignity from the chamber ; but he turned with his hand upon the door.

" The Abbé Fénélon came with me, sire. Is it your pleasure to see him ? "

" Away ! away ! " cried the king furiously, still striding up and down the room with angry face and flashing eyes. The dauphin left the cabinet, and was instantly succeeded by a tall thin priest, some forty years of age, strikingly handsome, with a pale refined face, large well-marked features, and the easy deferential bearing of one who has had a long training in courts. The king turned sharply upon him, and looked hard at him with a distrustful eye.

" Good-day, Abbé Fénélon," said he. " May I ask what the object of this interview is ? "

" You have had the condescension, sire, on more than one occasion, to ask my humble advice, and even to express yourself afterwards as being pleased that you had acted upon it."

" Well ? Well ? Well ? " growled the monarch.

" If rumour says truly, sire, you are now at a crisis when a word of impartial counsel might be of value to you. Need I say that it would——"

" Tut ! tut ! Why all these words ? " cried the king. " You have been sent here by others to try and influence me against Madame de Maintenon."

" Sire, I have had nothing but kindness from that lady, I esteem and honour her more than any lady in France."

" In that case, abbé, you will, I am sure, be glad to hear that I am about to marry her. Good-day, abbé. I regret that I have not longer time to devote to this very interesting conversation."

" But, sire——"

" When my mind is in doubt, abbé, I value your advice very highly. On this occasion, my mind is happily *not* in doubt. I have the honour to wish you a very good-day."

The king's first hot anger had died away by now, and had left behind it a cold, bitter spirit which was even

more formidable to his antagonists. The abbé, glib of tongue and fertile of resource as he was, felt himself to be silenced and overmatched. He walked backwards, with three long bows, as was the custom of the court, and departed.

But the king had little breathing-space. His assailants knew that with persistence they had bent his will before, and they trusted that they might do so again. It was Louvois, the minister, now who entered the room, with his majestic port, his lofty bearing, his huge wig and his aristocratic face, which, however, showed some signs of trepidation as it met the baleful eye of the king.

" Well, Louvois, what now ? " he asked impatiently. " Has some new state matter arisen ? "

" There is but one new state matter which has arisen, sire, but it is of such importance as to banish all others from our mind."

" What then ? "

" Your marriage, sire."

" You disapprove of it ? "

" Oh, sire, can I help it ? "

" Out of my room, sir ! Am I to be tormented to death by your importunities ? What ! You dare to linger when I order you to go ! " The king advanced angrily upon the minister, but Louvois suddenly flashed out his rapier. Louis sprang back with alarm and amazement upon his face, but it was the hilt and not the point which was presented to him.

" Pass it through my heart, sire ! " the minister cried, falling upon his knees, his whole great frame in a quiver with emotion. " I will not live to see your glory fade ! "

" Great heaven ! " shrieked Louis, throwing the sword down upon the ground, and raising his hands to his temples, " I believe that this is a conspiracy to drive me mad. Was ever a man so tormented in this life ? This will be a private marriage, man, and it will not affect the state in the least degree. Do you hear me ? Have you understood me ? What more do you want ? "

Louvois gathered himself up, and shot his rapier back into its sheath.

" Your Majesty is determined ? " he said.

" Absolutely."

" Then I say no more. I have done my duty." He bowed his head as one in deep dejection when he departed, but in truth his heart was lightened within him, for he had the king's assurance that the woman whom he hated would, even though his wife, not sit on the throne of the Queens of France.

These repeated attacks, if they had not shaken the king's resolution, had at least irritated and exasperated him to the utmost. Such a blast of opposition was a new thing to a man whose will had been the one law of the land. It left him ruffled and disturbed, and without regretting his resolution, he still, with unreasoning petulance, felt inclined to visit the inconvenience to which he had been put upon those whose advice he had followed. He wore accordingly no very cordial face when the usher in attendance admitted the venerable figure of Father La Chaise, his confessor.

" I wish you all happiness, sire," said the Jesuit, " and I congratulate you from my heart that you have taken the great step which must lead ᵗᵒ content both in this world and the next."

" I have had neither happiness nor contentment yet, father," answered the king peevishly. " I have never been so pestered in my life. The whole court has been on its knees to me to entreat me to change my intention."

The Jesuit looked at him anxiously out of his keen grey eyes.

" Fortunately, your Majesty is a man of strong will," said he, " and not to be so easily swayed as they think."

" No, no, I did not give an inch. But still, it must be confessed that it is very unpleasant to have so many against one. I think that most men would have been shaken."

" Now is the time to stand firm, sire ; Satan rages to see you passing out of his power, and he stirs up all his friends and sends all his emissaries to endeavour to detain you."

But the king was not in a humour to be easily consoled.

" Upon my word, father," said he, " you do not seem to have much respect for my family. My brother and my son, with the Abbé Fénélon and the minister of war, are the emissaries to whom you allude."

" Then there is the more credit to your Majesty for having resisted them. You have done nobly, sire. You have earned the praise and blessing of Holy Church."

" I trust that what I have done is right, father," said the king gravely. " I should be glad to see you again later in the evening, but at present I desire a little leisure for solitary thought."

Father La Chaise left the cabinet with a deep distrust of the king's intentions. It was obvious that the powerful appeals which had been made to him had shaken if they had failed to alter his resolution. What would be the result if more were made ? And more would be made ; that was as certain as that darkness follows light. Some master-card must be played now which would bring the matter to a crisis at once, for every day of delay was in favour of their opponents. To hesitate was to lose. All must be staked upon one final throw.

The Bishop of Meaux was waiting in the anteroom, and Father La Chaise in a few brief words let him see the danger of the situation, and the means by which they should meet it. Together they sought Madame de Maintenon in her room. She had discarded the sombre widow's dress which she had chosen since her first coming to court, and wore now, as more in keeping with her lofty prospects, a rich yet simple costume of white satin with bows of silver serge. A single diamond sparkled in the thick coils of her dark tresses. The change had taken years from a face and figure which had always looked much younger than her age, and as the two plotters looked upon her perfect complexion, her regular features, so calm and yet so full of refinement, and the exquisite grace of her figure and bearing, they could not but feel that if they failed in their ends, it was not for want of having a perfect tool at their command.

She had risen at their entrance, and her expression showed that she had read upon their faces something of the anxiety which filled their minds.

" You have evil news ! " she cried.

" No, no, my daughter." It was the bishop who spoke. " But we must be on our guard against our enemies, who would turn the king away from you if they could."

Her face shone at the mention of her lover.

" Ah, you do not know ! " she cried. " He has made a vow. I would trust him as I would trust myself. I know that he will be true."

But the Jesuit's intellect was arrayed against the intuition of the woman.

" Our opponents are many and strong," said he, shaking his head. " Even if the king remain firm, he will be annoyed at every turn, so that he will feel his life is darker instead of lighter, save, of course, madame, for that brightness which you cannot fail to bring with you. We must bring the matter to an end."

" And how, father ? "

" The marriage must be at once ! "

" At once ! "

" Yes. This very night, if possible."

" Oh, father, you ask too much. The king would never consent to such a proposal."

" It is he that will propose it."

" And why ? "

" Because we shall force him to. It is only thus that all the opposition can be stopped. When it is done, the court will accept it. Until it is done, they will resist it."

" What would you have me do, then, father ? "

" Resign the king."

" Resign him ! " She turned as pale as a lily, and looked at him in bewilderment.

" It is the best course, madame."

" Ah, father, I might have done it last month, last week, even yesterday morning. But now—oh, it would break my heart ! "

" Fear not, madame. We advise you for the best. Go to the king now, at once. Say to him that you have heard that he has been subjected to much annoyance upon your account, that you cannot bear to think that you should be a cause of dissension in his own family, and therefore you will release him from his promise, and will withdraw yourself from the court for ever."

" Go now ? At once ? "

" Yes, without loss of an instant."

She cast a light mantle about her shoulders.

" I follow your advice," she said. "I believe that you are wiser than I. But, oh, if he should take me at my word."

" He will not take you at your word."

" It is a terrible risk."

" But such an end as this cannot be gained without risks. Go, my child, and may heaven's blessing go with you ! "

13. *The King has Ideas*

THE king had remained alone in his cabinet, wrapped in somewhat gloomy thoughts, and pondering over the means by which he might carry out his purpose and yet smooth away the opposition which seemed to be so strenuous and so universal. Suddenly there came a gentle tap at the door, and there was the woman who was in his thoughts, standing in the twilight before him. He sprang to his feet and held out his hands with a smile which would have reassured her had she doubted his constancy.

" Françoise ! You here ! Then I have at last a welcome visitor, and it is the first one to-day."

" Sire, I fear that you have been troubled."

" I have indeed, Françoise."

" But I have a remedy for it."

" And what is that ? "

" I shall leave the court, sire, and you shall think no

more of what has passed between us. I have brought discord where I meant to bring peace. Let me retire to St. Cyr, or to the Abbey of Fontevrault, and you will no longer be called upon to make such sacrifices for my sake."

The king turned deathly pale, and clutched at her shawl with a trembling hand, as though he feared that she was about to put her resolution into effect that very instant. For years his mind had accustomed itself to lean upon hers. He had turned to her whenever he needed support, and even when, as in the last week, he had broken away from her for a time, it was still all-important to him to know that she was there, the faithful friend, ever forgiving, ever soothing, waiting for him with her ready counsel and sympathy. But that she should leave him now, leave him altogether, such a thought had never occurred to him, and it struck him with a chill of surprised alarm.

" You cannot mean it, Françoise," he cried, in a trembling voice. " No, no, it is impossible that you are in earnest."

" It would break my heart to leave you, sire, but it breaks it also to think that for my sake you are estranged from your own family and ministers."

" Tut ! Am I not the king ? Shall I not take my own course without heed to them ? No, no, Françoise, you must not leave me ! You must stay with me and be my wife." He could hardly speak for agitation, and he still grasped at her dress to detain her. She had been precious to him before, but was far more so now that there seemed to be a possibility of losing her. She felt the strength of her position, and used it to the utmost.

" Some time must elapse before our wedding, sire. Yet during all that interval you will be exposed to these annoyances. How can I be happy when I feel that I have brought upon you so long a period of discomfort ? "

" And why should it be so long, Françoise ? "

" A day would be too long, sire, for you to be unhappy through my fault. It is a misery to me to think of it. Believe me, it would be better that I should leave you."

" Never ! You shall not ! Why should we even wait a day, Françoise ? I am ready. You are ready. Why should we not be married now ? "

" At once ! Oh, sire ! "

" We shall. It is my wish. It is my order. That is my answer to those who would drive me. They shall know nothing of it until it is done, and then let us see which of them will dare to treat my wife with anything but respect. Let it be done secretly, Françoise. I will send in a trusty messenger this very night for the Archbishop of Paris, and I swear that, if all France stand in the way, he shall make us man and wife before he departs."

" Is it your will, sire ? "

" It is ; and ah, I can see by your eyes that it is yours also ! We shall not lose a moment, Françoise. What a blessed thought of mine, which will silence their tongues for ever ! When it is ready they may know, but not before. To your room, then, dearest of friends and truest of women ! When we meet again, it will be to form a band which all this court and all this kingdom shall not be able to loose."

The king was all on fire with the excitement of this new resolution. He had lost his air of doubt and discontent, and he paced swiftly about the room with a smiling face and shining eyes. Then he touched a small gold bell, which summoned Bontems, his private body-servant.

" What o'clock is it, Bontems ? "

" It is nearly six, sire."

" Hum ! " The king considered for some moments. " Do you know where Captain de Catinat is, Bontems ? "

" He was in the grounds, sire, but I heard that he would ride back to Paris to-night."

" Does he ride alone ? "

" He has one friend with him."

" Who is this friend ? An officer of the guards ? "

" No, sire ; it is a stranger from over the seas, from America, as I understand, who has stayed with him of late, and to whom Monsieur de Catinat has been showing the wonders of your Majesty's palace."

" A stranger ! So much the better. Go, Bontems, and bring them both to me."

" I trust that they have not started, sire. I will see." He hurried off, and was back in ten minutes in the cabinet once more.

" Well ? "

" I have been fortunate, sire. Their horses had been led out and their feet were in the stirrups when I reached them."

" Where are they, then ? "

" They await your Majesty's orders in the anteroom."

" Show them in, Bontems, and give admission to none, not even to the minister, until they have left me."

To De Catinat an audience with the monarch was a common incident of his duties, but it was with profound astonishment that he learned from Bontems that his friend and companion was included in the order. He was eagerly endeavouring to whisper into the young American's ear some precepts and warnings as to what to do and what to avoid, when Bontems reappeared and ushered them into the presence.

It was with a feeling of curiosity, not unmixed with awe, that Amos Green, to whom Governor Dongan, of New York, had been the highest embodiment of human power, entered the private chamber of the greatest monarch in Christendom. The magnificence of the antechamber in which he had waited, the velvets, the paintings, the gild- ings, with the throng of gaily dressed officials and of magnificent guardsmen, had all impressed his imagination, and had prepared him for some wondrous figure robed and crowned, a fit centre for such a scene. As his eyes fell upon a quietly dressed, bright-eyed man, half a head shorter than himself, with a trim dapper figure and an erect carriage, he could not help glancing round the room to see if this were indeed the monarch, or if it were some other of those endless officials who interposed them- selves between him and the other world. The reverent salute of his companion, however, showed him that this

must indeed be the king, so he bowed and then drew himself erect with the simple dignity of a man who has been trained in Nature's school.

" Good-evening, Captain de Catinat," said the king, with a pleasant smile. " Your friend, as I understand, is a stranger to this country. I trust, sir, that you have found something here to interest and to amuse you ? "

" Yes, your Majesty. I have seen your great city, and it is a wonderful one. And my friend has shown me this palace, with its woods and its grounds. When I go back to my own country I will have much to say of what I have seen in your beautiful land."

" You speak French, and yet you are not a Canadian."

" No, sire ; I am from the English provinces."

The king looked with interest at the powerful figure, the bold features and the free bearing of the young foreigner, and his mind flashed back to the dangers which the Comte de Frontenac had foretold from these same colonies. If this were indeed a type of his race, they must in truth be a people whom it would be better to have as friends than as enemies. His mind, however, ran at present on other things than statecraft, and he hastened to give De Catinat his orders for the night.

" You will ride into Paris on my service. Your friend can go with you. Two are safer than one when they bear a message of state. I wish you, however, to wait until nightfall before you start."

" Yes, sire."

" Let none know your errand, and see that none follow you. You know the house of Archbishop Harlay, prelate of Paris ? "

" Yes, sire."

" You will bid him drive out hither and be at the north-west side postern by midnight. Let nothing hold him back. Storm or fine, he must be here to-night. It is of the first importance."

" He shall have your order, sire."

" Very good. Adieu, captain. Adieu, monsieur. I

621

trust that your stay in France may be a pleasant one." He waved his hand, smiling with the fascinating grace which had won so many hearts, and so dismissed the two friends to their new mission.

14. *The Last Card*

MADAME DE MONTESPAN still kept her rooms, uneasy in mind at the king's disappearance, but unwilling to show her anxiety to the court by appearing among them, or by making any inquiry as to what had occurred. While she thus remained in ignorance of the sudden and complete collapse of her fortunes, she had one active and energetic agent who had lost no incident of what had occurred, and who watched her interests with as much zeal as if they were his own. And indeed they were his own ; for her brother, Monsieur de Vivonne, had gained everything for which he yearned, money, lands and preferment, through his sister's notoriety, and he well knew that the fall of her fortunes must be very rapidly followed by that of his own. By nature bold, unscrupulous and resourceful, he was not a man to lose the game without playing it out to the very end with all the energy and cunning of which he was capable. Keenly alert to all that passed, he had, from the time that he first heard the rumour of the king's intention, haunted the antechamber and drawn his own conclusions from what he had seen. Nothing had escaped him—the disconsolate faces of monsieur and of the dauphin, the visit of Père La Chaise and Bossuet to the lady's room, her return, the triumph which shone in her eyes as she came away from the interview. He had seen Bontems hurry off and summon the guardsman and his friend. He had heard them order their horses to be brought out in a couple of hours' time, and finally, from a spy whom he employed among the servants, he learned that an unwonted bustle was going forward in Madame de Maintenon's room, that

Mademoiselle Nanon was half wild with excitement, and that two court milliners had been hastily summoned to madame's apartment. It was only, however, when he heard from the same servant that a chamber was to be prepared for the reception that night of the Archbishop of Paris that he understood how urgent was the danger.

Madame de Montespan had spent the evening stretched upon a sofa, in the worst possible humour with everyone around her. She had read, but had tossed aside the book. She had written, but had torn up the paper. A thousand fears and suspicions chased each other through her head. What had become of the king, then? He had seemed cold yesterday, and his eyes had been for ever sliding round to the clock. And to-day he had not come at all. Was it his gout, perhaps? Or was it possible that she was again losing her hold upon him? Surely it could not be that! She turned upon her couch and faced the mirror which flanked the door. The candles had just been lit in her chamber, two score of them, each with silver backs which reflected their light until the room was as bright as day. There in the mirror was the brilliant chamber, the deep red ottoman, and the single figure in its gauzy dress of white and silver. She leaned upon her elbow, admiring the deep tint of her own eyes with their long dark lashes, the white curve of her throat, and the perfect oval of her face. She examined it all carefully, keenly, as though it were her rival that lay before her, but nowhere could she see a scratch of Time's malicious nails. She still had her beauty, then. And if it had once won the king, why should it not suffice to hold him? Of course it would do so. She reproached herself for her fears. Doubtless he was indisposed, or perhaps he would come still. Ha! there was the sound of an opening door and of a quick step in her anteroom. Was it he, or at least his messenger with a note from him?

But no, it was her brother, with the haggard eyes and drawn face of a man who is weighed down with his own evil tidings. He turned as he entered, fastened the door,

and then, striding across the room, locked the other one which led to her boudoir.

"We are safe from interruption," he panted. "I have hastened here, for every second may be invaluable. Have you heard anything from the king?"

"Nothing." She had sprung to her feet, and was gazing at him with a face which was as pale as his own.

"The hour has come for action, Françoise. It is the hour at which the Mortemarts have always shown at their best. Do not yield to the blow, then, but gather yourself to meet it."

"What is it?" She tried to speak in her natural tone, but only a whisper came to her dry lips.

"The king is about to marry Madame de Maintenon."

"The *gouvernante!* The widow Scarron! It is impossible!"

"It is certain."

"To marry? Did you say to marry?"

"Yes, he will marry her."

The woman flung out her hands in a gesture of contempt, and laughed loud and bitterly.

"You are easily frightened, brother," said she. "Ah, you do not know your little sister. Perchance if you were not my brother you might rate my powers more highly. Give me a day, only one little day, and you will see Louis, the proud Louis, down at the hem of my dress to ask my pardon for this slight. I tell you that he cannot break the bonds that hold him. One day is all I ask to bring him back."

"But you cannot have it."

"What?"

"The marriage is to-night."

"You are mad, Charles."

"I am certain of it." In a few broken sentences he shot out all that he had seen and heard. She listened with a grim face, and hands which closed ever tighter and tighter as he proceeded. But he had said the truth about the Mortemarts. They came of a contentious blood, and were

ever at their best at a moment of action. Hate rather than
dismay filled her heart as she listened, and the whole
energy of her nature gathered and quickened to meet the
crisis.

" I shall go and see him," she cried, sweeping towards
the door.

" No, no, Françoise. Believe me you will ruin everything if you do. Strict orders have been given to the
guard to admit no one to the king."

" But I shall insist upon passing them."

" Believe me, sister, it is worse than useless. I have
spoken with the officer of the guard, and the command is a
stringent one."

" Ah, I shall manage."

" No, you shall not." He put his back against the door.
" I know that it is useless, and I will not have my sister
make herself the laughing-stock of the court, trying to
force her way into the room of a man who repulses her."

His sister's cheeks flushed at the words, and she paused
irresolute.

" Had I only a day, Charles, I am sure that I could bring
him back to me. There has been some other influence
here, that meddlesome Jesuit or the pompous Bossuet,
perhaps. Only one day to counteract their wiles ! Can I
not see them waving hell-fire before his foolish eyes, as
one swings a torch before a bull to turn it ? Oh, if I could
but baulk them to-night ! That woman ! that cursed
woman ! The foul viper which I nursed in my bosom !
Oh, I had rather see Louis in his grave than married to her !
Charles, Charles, it must be stopped ; I say it must be
stopped ! I will give anything, everything, to prevent it ! "

" What will you give, my sister ? "

She looked at him aghast. " What ! you do not wish
me to buy you ? " she said.

" No ; but I wish to buy others."

" Ha ! You see a chance, then ! "

" One, and one only. But time presses. I want money."

" How much ? "

" I cannot have too much. All that you can spare."

With hands which trembled with eagerness she unlocked a secret cupboard in the wall in which she concealed her valuables. A blaze of jewellery met her brother's eyes as he peered over her shoulder. Great rubies, costly emeralds, deep ruddy beryls, glimmering diamonds, were scattered there in one brilliant shimmering many-coloured heap, the harvest which she had reaped from the king's generosity during more than fifteen years. At one side were three drawers, the one over the other. She drew out the lowest one. It was full to the brim of glittering *louis d'ors*.

" Take what you will ! " she said. " And now your plan ! Quick ! "

He stuffed the money in handfuls into the side pockets of his coat. Coins slipped between his fingers and tinkled and wheeled over the floor, but neither cast a glance at them.

" Your plan ? " she repeated.

" We must prevent the archbishop from arriving here. Then the marriage would be postponed until to-morrow night, and you would have time to act."

" But how prevent it ? "

" There are a dozen good rapiers about the court which are to be bought for less than I carry in one pocket. There is De la Touche, young Turberville, old Major Despard, Raymond de Carnac and the four Latours. I will gather them together, and wait on the road."

" And waylay the archbishop ? "

" No ; the messengers."

" Oh, excellent ! You are a prince of brothers ! If no message reach Paris, we are saved. Go ; go ; do not lose a moment, my dear Charles."

" It is very well, Françoise ; but what are we to do with them when we get them ? We may lose our heads over the matter, it seems to me. After all, they are the king's messengers, and we can scarce pass our swords through them."

" No ? "

" There would be no forgiveness for that."

" But consider that before the matter is looked into I shall have regained my influence with the king."

" All very fine, my little sister, but how long is your influence to last ? A pleasant life for us if at every change of favour we have to fly the country ! No, no, Françoise ; the most that we can do is to detain the messengers."

" Where can you detain them ? "

" I have an idea. There is the castle of the Marquis de Montespan at Portillac."

" Of my husband ! "

" Precisely."

" Of my most bitter enemy ! Oh ! Charles, you are not serious."

" On the contrary, I was never more so. The marquis was away in Paris yesterday, and has not yet returned. Where is the ring with his arms ? "

She hunted among her jewels and picked out a gold ring with a broad engraved face.

" This will be our key. When good Marceau, the steward, sees it, every dungeon in the castle will be at our disposal. It is that or nothing. There is no other place where we can hold them safe."

" But when my husband returns ? "

" Ah, he may be a little puzzled as to his captives. And the complaisant Marceau may have an evil quarter of an hour. But that may not be for a week, and by that time, my little sister, I have confidence enough in you to think that you really may have finished the campaign. Not another word, for every moment is of value. Adieu, Françoise ! We shall not be conquered without a struggle. I will send a message to you to-night to let you know how fortune uses us." He took her fondly in his arms, kissed her, and then hurried from the room.

For hours after his departure she paced up and down with noiseless steps upon the deep soft carpet, her hands still clenched, her eyes flaming, her whole soul wrapped and consumed with jealousy and hatred of her rival. Ten

struck, and eleven, and midnight, but still she waited, fierce and eager, straining her ears for every foot-fall which might be the herald of news. At last it came. She heard the quick step in the passage, the tap at the anteroom door, and the whispering of her black page. Quivering with impatience, she rushed in and took the note herself from the dusty cavalier who had brought it. It was but six words scrawled roughly upon a wisp of dirty paper, but it brought the colour back to her cheeks and the smile to her lips. It was her brother's writing, and it ran, " The archbishop will not come to-night."

15. *The Midnight Mission*

DE CATINAT in the meanwhile was perfectly aware of the importance of the mission which had been assigned to him. The secrecy which had been enjoined by the king, his evident excitement, and the nature of his orders, all confirmed the rumours which were already beginning to buzz round the court. He knew enough of the intrigues and antagonisms with which the court was full to understand that every precaution was necessary in carrying out his instructions. He waited, therefore, until night had fallen before ordering his soldier-servant to bring round the two horses to one of the less public gates of the grounds. As he and his friend walked together to the spot, he gave the young American a rapid sketch of the situation at the court, and of the chance that this nocturnal ride might be an event which would affect the future history of France.

" I like your king," said Amos Green, " and I am glad to ride in his service. He is a slip of a man to be the head of a great nation, but he has the eye of a chief. If one met him alone in a Maine forest, one would know him as a man who was different to his fellows. Well, I am glad that he is going to marry again, though it's a great house for any woman to have to look after."

De Catinat smiled at his comrade's idea of a queen's duties.

" Are you armed ? " he asked. " You have no sword or pistols ? "

" No ; if I may not carry my gun, I had rather not be troubled by tools that I have never learned to use. I have my knife. But why do you ask ? "

" Because there may be danger."

" And how ? "

" Many have an interest in stopping this marriage. All the first men of the kingdom are bitterly against it. If they could stop *us*, they would stop *it*, for to-night at least."

" But I thought it was a secret ? "

" There is no such thing at a court. There is the dauphin, or the king's brother, either of them, or any of their friends, would be right glad that we should be in the Seine before we reach the archbishop's house this night. But who is this ? "

A burly figure had loomed up through the gloom on the path upon which they were going. As it approached, a coloured lamp dangling from one of the trees shone upon the blue and silver of an officer of the guards. It was Major de Brissac, of De Catinat's own regiment.

" Hullo ! Whither away ? " he asked.

" To Paris, major."

" I go there myself within an hour. Will you not wait, that we may go together ? "

" I am sorry, but I ride on a matter of urgency. I must not lose a minute."

" Very good. Good-night, and a pleasant ride."

" Is he a trusty man, our friend the major ? " asked Amos Green, glancing back.

" True as steel."

" Then I would have a word with him." The American hurried back along the way they had come, while De Catinat stood chafing at this unnecessary delay. It was a full five minutes before his companion joined him, and the

fiery blood of the French soldier was hot with impatience and anger.

" I think that perhaps you had best ride into Paris at your leisure, my friend," said he. " If I go upon the king's service I cannot be delayed whenever the whim takes you."

" I am sorry," answered the other quietly. " I had something to say to your major, and I thought that maybe I might not see him again."

" Well, here are the horses," said the guardsman as he pushed open the postern-gate. " Have you fed and watered them, Jacques ? "

" Yes, my captain," answered the man who stood at their head.

" Boot and saddle, then, friend Green, and we shall not draw rein again until we see the lights of Paris in front of us."

The soldier-groom peered through the darkness after them with a sardonic smile upon his face. " You won't draw rein, won't you ? " he muttered as he turned away. " Well, we shall see about that, my captain ; we shall see about that."

For a mile or more the comrades galloped along, neck to neck and knee to knee. A wind had sprung up from the westward, and the heavens were covered with heavy grey clouds, which drifted swiftly across, a crescent moon peeping fitfully from time to time between the rifts. Even during these moments of brightness the road, shadowed as it was by heavy trees, was very dark, but when the light was shut off it was hard, but for the loom upon either side, to tell where it lay. De Catinat at least found it so, and he peered anxiously over his horse's ears, and stooped his face to the mane in his efforts to see his way.

" What do you make of the road ? " he asked at last.

" It looks as if a good many carriage wheels had passed over it to-day."

" What ! *Mon Dieu !* Do you mean to say that you can see carriage wheels there ? "

" Certainly. Why not ? "

" Why, man, I cannot see the road at all."

Amos Green laughed heartily. " When you have travelled in the woods by night as often as I have," said he, " when to show a light may mean to lose your hair, one comes to learn to use one's eyes."

" Then you had best ride on, and I shall keep just behind you. So ! Holà ! What is the matter now ? "

There had been the sudden sharp snap of something breaking, and the American had reeled for an instant in the saddle.

" It's one of my stirrup leathers. It has fallen."

" Can you find it ? "

" Yes ; but I can ride as well without it. Let us push on."

" Very good. I can just see you now."

They had galloped for about five minutes in this fashion, De Catinat's horse's head within a few feet of the other's tail, when there was a second snap, and the guardsman rolled out of the saddle on to the ground. He kept his grip of the reins, however, and was up in an instant at his horse's head, sputtering out oaths as only an angry Frenchman can.

" A thousand thunders of heaven ! " he cried. " What was it that happened then ? "

" Your leather has gone too."

" Two stirrup leathers in five minutes ? It is not possible."

" It is not possible that it should be chance," said the American gravely, swinging himself off his horse. " Why, what is this ? My other leather is cut, and hangs only by a thread."

" And so does mine. I can feel it when I pass my hand along. Have you a tinder-box ? Let us strike a light."

" No, no ; the man who is in the dark is in safety. I let the other folk strike lights. We can see all that is needful to us."

" My rein is cut also."

" And so is mine."

" And the girth of my saddle."

" It is a wonder that we came so far with whole bones. Now, who has played us this little trick ? "

" Who could it be but that rogue, Jacques ! He has had the horses in his charge. By my faith, he shall know what the strappado means when I see Versailles again."

" But why should he do it ? "

" Ah, he has been set on to it. He has been a tool in the hands of those who wished to hinder our journey."

" Very like. But they must have had some reason behind. They knew well that to cut our straps would not prevent us from reaching Paris, since we could ride bareback, or, for that matter, could run it if need be."

" They hoped to break our necks."

" One neck they might break, but scarce those of two, since the fate of the one would warn the other."

"Well, then, what do you think that they meant? " cried De Catinat impatiently. " For heaven's sake, let us come to some conclusion, for every minute is of importance."

But the other was not to be hurried out of his cool, methodical fashion of speech and of thought.

" They could not have thought to stop us," said he. "What did they mean, then? They could only have meant to delay us. And why should they wish to delay us ? What could it matter to them if we gave our message an hour or two sooner or an hour or two later ? It could not matter."

" For heaven's sake——" broke in De Catinat impetuously.

But Amos Green went on hammering the matter slowly out.

" Why should they wish to delay us, then ? There's only one reason that I can see. In order to give other folk time to get in front of us and stop us. That is it, captain. I'd lay you a beaver-skin to a rabbit-pelt that I'm on the track. There's been a party of a dozen horsemen along this ground since the dew began to fall. If we were delayed, they would have time to form their plans before we came."

" By my faith, you may be right," said De Catinat thoughtfully, " What would you propose ? "

" That we ride back, and go by some less direct way."

" It is impossible. We should have to ride back to Meudon cross-roads, and then it would add ten miles to our journey."

" It is better to get there an hour later than not to get there at all."

" Pshaw ! we are surely not to be turned from our path by a mere guess. There is the St. Germain cross-road about a mile below. When we reach it we can strike to the right along the south side of the river, and so change our course."

" But we may not reach it."

" If anyone bars our way we shall know how to treat with them."

" You would fight, then ? "

" Yes."

" What ! with a dozen of them ? "

" A hundred, if we are on the king's errand."

Amos Green shrugged his shoulders.

" You are surely not afraid ? "

" Yes, I am, mighty afraid. Fighting's good enough when there's no help for it. But I call it a fool's plan to ride stright into a trap when you might go round it."

" You may do what you like," said De Catinat angrily. " My father was a gentleman, the owner of a thousand arpents of land, and his son is not going to flinch in the king's service."

" My father," answered Amos Green, "was a merchant, the owner of a thousand skunk-skins, and his son knows a fool when he sees one."

" You are insolent, sir," cried the guardsman. " We can settle this matter at some more fitting opportunity. At present I continue my mission, and you are very welcome to turn back to Versailles if you are so inclined." He raised his hat with punctilious politeness, sprang on to his horse, and rode on down the road.

Amos Green hesitated a little, and then mounting, he soon overtook his companion. The latter, however, was still in no very sweet temper, and rode with a rigid neck without a glance or a word for his comrade. Suddenly his eyes caught something in the gloom which brought a smile back to his face. Away in front of them, between two dark tree clumps, lay a vast number of shimmering, glittering yellow points, as thick as flowers in a garden. They were the lights of Paris.

" See ! " he cried, pointing. " There is the city, and close here must be the St. Germain road. We shall take it, so as to avoid any danger."

" Very good ! But you should not ride too fast, when your girth may break at any moment."

" Nay, come on ; we are close to our journey's end. The St. Germain road opens just round this corner, and then we shall see our way, for the lights will guide us."

He cut his horse with his whip, and they galloped together round the curve. Next instant they were both down in one wild heap of tossing heads and struggling hoofs, De Catinat partly covered by his horse, and his comrade hurled twenty paces, where he lay silent and motionless in the centre of the road.

16. " *When the Devil Drives* "

MONSIEUR DE VIVONNE had laid his ambuscade with discretion. With a closed carriage and a band of chosen ruffians he had left the palace a good half-hour before the king's messengers and by the aid of his sister's gold he had managed that their journey should not be a very rapid one. On reaching the branch road he had ordered the coachman to drive some little distance along it, and had tethered all the horses to a fence under his charge. He had then stationed one of the band as a sentinel some distance up the main highway to flash a light when the two couriers were approaching. A stout

cord had been fastened eighteen inches from the ground to the trunk of a wayside sapling, and on receiving the signal the other end was tied to a gate-post upon the further side. The two cavaliers could not possibly see it, coming as it did at the very curve of the road, and as a consequence their horses fell heavily to the ground, and brought them down with them. In an instant the dozen ruffians, who had lurked in the shadow of the trees, sprang out upon them, sword in hand ; but there was no movement from either of their victims. De Catinat lay breathing heavily, one leg under his horse's neck, and the blood trickling in a thin stream down his pale face, and falling, drop by drop, on to his silver shoulder-straps. Amos Green was unwounded, but his injured girth had given way in the fall, and he had been hurled from his horse on to the hard road with a violence which had driven every particle of breath from his body.

Monsieur de Vivonne lit a lantern, and flashed it upon the faces of the two unconscious men. " This is a bad business, Major Despard," said he to the man next him. " I believe that they are both gone."

"Tut! tut! By my soul, men did not die like that when I was young ! " answered the other, leaning forward his fierce grizzled face into the light of the lantern. " I've been cast from my horse as often as there are tags to my doublet, but, save for the snap of a bone or two, I never had any harm from it. Pass your rapier under the third rib of the horses, De la Touche ; they will never be fit to set hoof to ground again." Two sobbing gasps, and the thud of their straining necks falling back to earth told that the two steeds had come to the end of their troubles.

" Where is Latour ? " asked Monsieur de Vivonne. " Achille Latour has studied medicine at Montpellier. Where is he ? "

"Here I am, your excellency. It is not for me to boast, but I am as handy a man with a lancet as with a rapier, and it was an evil day for some sick folk when I first took to buff and bandolier. Which would you have me look to ? "

" This one in the road."

The trooper bent over Amos Green. " He is not long for this world," said he. " I can tell it by the catch of his breath."

" And what is his injury ? "

" A subluxation of the epigastrium. Ah, the words of learning will still come to my tongue, but it is hard to put into common terms. Methinks that it were well for me to pass my dagger through his throat, for his end is very near."

"Not for your life ! " cried the leader. " If he die without wound, they cannot lay it to our charge. Turn now to the other."

The man bent over De Catinat, and placed his hand upon his heart. As he did so the soldier heaved a long sigh, opened his eyes, and gazed about him with the face of one who knows neither where he is nor how he came there. De Vivonne, who had drawn his hat down over his eyes, and muffled the lower part of his face in his mantle, took out his flask, and poured a little of the contents down the injured man's throat. In an instant a dash of colour had come back into the guardsman's bloodless cheeks, and the light of memory into his eyes. He struggled up on to his feet, and strove furiously to push away those who held him. But his head still swam, and he could scarce hold himself erect.

" I must to Paris ! " he gasped ; " I must to Paris ! It is the king's mission. You stop me at your peril ! "

" He has no hurt save a scratch," said the ex-doctor.

" Then hold him fast. And first carry the dying man to the carriage."

The lantern threw but a small ring of yellow light, so that when it had been carried over to De Catinat, Amos Green was left lying in the shadow. Now they brought the light back to where the young man lay. But there was no sign of him. He was gone.

For a moment the little group of ruffians stood staring, the light of their lantern streaming up upon their plumed

hats, their fierce eyes and savage faces. Then a burst of oaths broke from them, and De Vivonne caught the false doctor by the throat, and hurling him down, would have choked him upon the spot, had the others not dragged them apart.

" You lying dog ! " he cried. " Is this your skill ? The man has fled, and we are ruined ! "

" He has done it in his death-struggle," gasped the other hoarsely, sitting up and rubbing his throat. " I tell you that he was *in extremis*. He cannot be far off."

" That is true. He cannot be far off," cried De Vivonne. " He has neither horse nor arms. You, Despard and Raymond de Carnac, guard the other, that he play us no trick. Do you, Latour, and you, Turberville, ride down the road, and wait by the south gate. If he enter Paris at all, he must come in that way. If you get him, tie him before you on your horse, and bring him to the rendezvous. In any case, it matters little, for he is a stranger, this fellow, and only here by chance. Now lead the other to the carriage, and we shall get away before an alarm is given."

The two horsemen rode off in pursuit of the fugitive, and De Catinat, still struggling desperately to escape, was dragged down the St. Germain road and thrust into the carriage, which had waited at some distance while these incidents were being enacted. Three of the horsemen rode ahead, the coachman was curtly ordered to follow them, and De Vivonne, having despatched one of the band with a note to his sister, followed after the coach with the remainder of his desperadoes.

The unfortunate guardsman had now entirely recovered his senses, and found himself with a strap round his ankles, and another round his wrists, a captive inside a moving prison which lumbered heavily along the country road. He had been stunned by the shock of his fall, and his leg was badly bruised by the weight of his horse ; but the cut on his forehead was a mere trifle, and the bleeding had already ceased. His mind, however, pained him more

than his body. He sank his head into his piniloned hands, and stamped madly with his feet, rocking himself to and fro in his despair. What a fool, a treble fool, he had been! He, an old soldier who had seen something of war, to walk with open eyes into such a trap! The king had chosen him, of all men, as a trusty messenger, and yet he had failed him—and failed him so ignominiously, without shot fired or sword drawn. He was warned, too, warned by a young man who knew nothing of court intrigue, and who was guided only by the wits which Nature had given him. De Catinat dashed himself down upon the leather cushion in the agony of his thoughts.

But then came a return of that common-sense which lies so very closely beneath the impetuosity of the Celt. The matter was done now, and he must see if it could not be mended. Amos Green had escaped. That was one grand point in his favour. And Amos Green had heard the king's message, and realised its importance. It was true that he knew nothing of Paris, but surely a man who could pick his way at night through the forests of Maine would not be baulked in finding so well known a house as that of the Archbishop of Paris. But then there came a sudden thought which turned De Catinat's heart to lead. The city gates were locked at eight o'clock in the evening. It was now nearly nine. It would have been easy for him, whose uniform was a voucher for his message, to gain his way through. But how could Amos Green, a foreigner and a civilian, hope to pass? It was impossible, clearly impossible. And yet, somehow, in spite of the impossibility, he still clung to a vague hope that a man so full of energy and resource might find some way out of the difficulty.

And then the thought of escape occurred to his mind. Might he not even now be in time, perhaps, to carry his own message? Who were these men who had seized him? They had said nothing to give him a hint as to whose tools they were. Monsieur and the dauphin occurred to his mind. Probably one or the other. He had only recognised one of them, old Major Despard, a man who fre-

quented the low wine-shops of Versailles, and whose sword was ever at the disposal of the longest purse. And where were these people taking him to ? It might be to his death. But if they wished to do away with him, why should they have brought him back to consciousness ? and why this carriage and drive ? Full of curiosity, he peered out of the windows.

A horseman was riding close up on either side ; but there was glass in front of the carriage, and through this he could gain some idea as to his whereabouts. The clouds had cleared now, and the moon was shining brightly, bathing the whole wide landscape in its shimmering light. To the right lay the open country, broad plains with clumps of woodland, and the towers of castles pricking out from above the groves. A heavy bell was ringing in some monastery, and its dull booming came and went with the breeze. On the left, but far away, lay the glimmer of Paris. They were leaving it rapidly behind. Whatever his destination, it was neither the capital nor Versailles. Then he began to count the chances of escape. His sword had been removed, and his pistols were still in the holsters beside his unfortunate horse. He was unarmed, then, even if he could free himself, and his captors were at least a dozen in number. There were three on ahead, riding abreast along the white, moonlit road. Then there was one on each side, and he should judge by the clatter of hoofs that there could not be fewer than half a dozen behind. That would make exactly twelve, including the coachman, too many, surely, for an unarmed man to hope to baffle. At the thought of the coachman he had glanced through the glass front at the broad back of the man, and he had suddenly, in the glimmer of the carriage lamp, observed something which struck him with horror.

The man was evidently desperately wounded. It was strange indeed that he could still sit there and flick his whip with so terrible an injury. In the back of his great red coat, just under the left shoulder-blade, was a gash in the cloth, where some weapon had passed, and all round was a

wide patch of dark scarlet which told its own tale. Nor was this all. As he raised his whip, the moonlight shone upon his hand, and De Catinat saw with a shudder that it also was splashed and clogged with blood. The guardsman craned his neck to catch a glimpse of the man's face ; but his broad-brimmed hat was drawn low, and the high collar of his driving-coat was raised, so that his features were in the shadow. This silent man in front of him, with the horrible marks upon his person, sent a chill to De Catinat's valiant heart, and he muttered over one of Marot's Huguenot psalms ; for who but the foul fiend himself would drive a coach with those crimsoned hands and with a sword driven through his body ?

And now they had come to a spot where the main road ran onwards, but a smaller side track wound away down the steep slope of a hill, and so in the direction of the Seine. The advance-guard had kept to the main road, and the two horsemen on either side were trotting in the same direction, when, to De Catinat's amazement, the carriage suddenly swerved to one side, and in an instant plunged down the steep incline, the two stout horses galloping at their topmost speed, the coachman standing up and lashing furiously at them, and the clumsy old vehicle bounding along in a way which threw him backwards and forwards from one seat to the other. Behind him he could hear a shout of consternation from the escort, and then the rush of galloping hoofs. Away they flew, the roadside poplars dancing past at either window, the horses thundering along with their 'stomachs to the earth, and that demon driver still waving those horrible red hands in the moonlight and screaming out to the maddened steeds. Sometimes the carriage jolted one way, sometimes another, swaying furiously, and running on two side wheels as though it must every instant go over. And yet, fast as they went, their pursuers went faster still. The rattle of their hoofs was at their very backs, and suddenly at one of the windows there came into view the red, distended nostrils of a horse. Slowly it drew for-

ward, the muzzle, the eye, the ears, the mane, coming into sight as the rider still gained upon them, and then above them the fierce face of Despard and the gleam of a brass pistol barrel.

"At the horse, Despard, at the horse!" cried an authoritative voice from behind.

The pistol flashed, and the coach lurched over as one of the horses gave a convulsive spring. But the driver still shrieked and lashed with his whip, while the carriage bounded onwards.

But now the road turned a sudden curve, and there, right in front of them, not a hundred paces away, was the Seine, running cold and still in the moonshine. The bank on either side of the highway ran straight down without any break to the water's edge. There was no sign of a bridge, and a black shadow in the centre of the stream showed where the ferry boat was returning after conveying some belated travellers across. The driver never hesitated, but gathering up the reins, he urged the frightened creatures into the river. They hesitated, however, when they first felt the cold water about their hocks, and even as they did so one of them, with a low moan, fell over upon her side. Despard's bullet had found its mark. Like a flash the coachman hurled himself from the box and plunged into the stream; but the pursuing horsemen were all round him before this, and half a dozen hands had seized him ere he could reach deep water, and had dragged him to the bank. His broad hat had been struck off in the struggle, and De Catinat saw his face in the moonshine. Great heavens! It was Amos Green.

17. *The Dungeon of Portillac*

THE desperadoes were as much astonished as was De Catinat when they found that they had re-captured in this extraordinary manner the messenger whom they had given up for lost. A volley of

oaths and exclamations broke from them, as, in tearing off the huge red coat of the coachman, they disclosed the sombre dress of the young American.

" A thousand thunders ! " cried one. " And this is the man whom that devil's brat Latour would make out to be dead ! "

" And how came he here ? "

" And where is Étienne Arnaud ? "

" He has stabbed Étienne. See the great cut in the coat ! "

" Aye ; and see the colour of his hand ! He has stabbed him, and taken his coat and hat."

" What ! while we were all within stone's cast ! "

" Aye ; there is no other way out of it."

" By my soul ! " cried old Despard, " I had never much love for old Étienne, but I have emptied a cup of wine with him before now, and I shall see that he has justice. Let us cast these reins round the fellow's neck and hang him upon this tree."

Several pairs of hands were already unbuckling the harness of the dead horse, when De Vivonne pushed his way into the little group, and with a few curt words checked their intended violence.

" It is as much as your lives are worth to touch him," said he.

" But he has slain Étienne Arnaud."

" That score may be settled afterwards. To-night he is the king's messenger. Is the other all safe ? "

" Yes, he is here."

" Tie this man, and put him in beside him. Unbuckle the traces of the dead horse. So ! Now, De Carnac, put your own into the harness. You can mount the box and drive, for we have not very far to go."

The changes were rapidly made ; Amos Green was thrust in beside De Catinat, and the carriage was soon toiling up the steep incline which it had come down so precipitately. The American had said not a word since his capture, and had remained absolutely stolid, with

his hands crossed over his chest whilst his fate was under
discussion. Now that he was alone once more with his
comrade, however, he frowned and muttered like a man
who feels that fortune has used him badly.

" Those infernal horses ! " he grumbled. " Why, an
American horse would have taken to the water like a duck.
Many a time have I swum my old stallion Sagamore
across the Hudson. Once over the river, we should have
had a clear lead to Paris."

"My dear friend,"cried De Catinat, laying his manacled
hands upon those of his comrade, " can you forgive me for
speaking as I did upon the way from Versailles ? "

" Tut, man ! I never gave it a thought."

" You were right a thousand times, and I was, as you
said, a fool—a blind, obstinate fool. How nobly you
have stood by me ! But how came you there ? Never
in my life have I been so astonished as when I saw your
face."

Amos Green chuckled to himself. " I thought that
maybe it would be a surprise to you if you knew who was
driving you," said he. " When I was thrown from my
horse I lay quiet, partly because I wanted to get a grip
of my breath, and partly because it seemed to me to be
more healthy to lie than to stand with all those swords
clinking in my ears. Then they all got round you, and
I rolled into the ditch, crept along it, got on the cross-
road in the shadow of the trees, and was beside the carriage
before ever they knew that I was gone. I saw in a flash
that there was only one way by which I could be of use
to you. The coachman was leaning round with his head
turned to see what was going on behind him. I out with
my knife, sprang up on the front wheel and stopped his
tongue for ever."

" What ! without a sound ! "

" I have not lived among the Indians for nothing."

" And then ? "

" I pulled him down into the ditch, and I got into his
coat and his hat. I did not scalp him."

" Scalp him ? Great heavens ! Such things are only done among savages."

" Ah ! I thought that maybe it was not the custom of the country. I am glad now that I did not do it. I had hardly got the reins before they were all back and bundled you into the coach. I was not afraid of their seeing me, but I was scared lest I should not know which road to take, and so set them on the trail. But they made it easy to me by sending some of their riders in front, so I did well until I saw that by-track and made a run for it. We'd have got away, too, if that rogue hadn't shot the horse, and if the beasts had faced the water."

The guardsman again pressed his comrade's hands. " You have been as true to me as hilt to blade," said he. " It was a bold thought and a bold deed."

" And what now ? " asked the American.

" I do not know who these men are, and I do not know whither they are taking us."

" To their villages, likely, to burn us."

De Catinat laughed in spite of his anxiety. " You will have it that we are back in America again," said he. " They don't do things in that way in France."

" They seem free enough with hanging in France. I tell you, I felt like a smoked-out 'coon when that trace was round my neck."

" I fancy that they are taking us to some place where they can shut us up until this business blows over."

" Well, they'll need to be smart about it."

" Why ? "

" Else maybe they won't find us when they want us."

" What do you mean ? "

For answer, the American, with a twist and a wriggle, drew his two hands apart, and held them in front of his comrade's face.

" Bless you, it is the first thing they teach the papooses in an Indian wigwam. I've got out of a Huron's thongs of raw hide before now, and it ain't very likely that a stiff

stirrup leather will hold me. Put your hands out." With
a few dexterous twists he loosened De Catinat's bonds,
until he also was able to slip his hands free. " Now
for your feet, if you'll put them up. They'll find that
we are easier to catch than to hold."

But at that moment the carriage began to slow down,
and the clank of the hoofs of the riders in front of them
died suddenly away. Peeping through the windows, the
prisoners saw a huge dark building stretching in front of
them, so high and so broad that the night shrouded it in
upon every side. A great archway hung above them, and
the lamps shone on the rude wooden gate, studded with
ponderous clamps and nails. In the upper part of the
door was a small square iron grating, and through this
they could catch a glimpse of the gleam of a lantern and
of a bearded face which looked out at th m. De Vivonne,
standing in his stirrups, craned his ' ad up towards the
grating, so that the two men mos⁺ iterested could hear
little of the conversation which ollowed. They saw
only that the horseman held a gold ring up in the air,
and that the face above, which had begun by shaking
and frowning, was now nodding and smiling. An instant
later the head disappeared, the door swung open upon
screaming hinges, and the carriage drove on into the
courtyard beyond, leaving the escort, with the exception
of De Vivonne, outside. As the horses pulled up, a
knot of rough fellows clustered round, and the two
prisoners were dragged roughly out. In the light of the
torches which flared around them they could see that they
were hemmed in by high turreted walls upon every side.
A bulky man with a bearded face, the same whom they
had seen at the grating, was standing in the centre of the
group of armed men issuing his orders.

" To the upper dungeon, Simon ! " he cried. " And
see that they have two bundles of straw and a loaf of
bread until we learn our master's will."

" I know not who your master may be," said De
Catinat, " but I would ask you by what warrant he dares

to stop two messengers of the king while travelling in his service ? "

" By St. Denis, if my master play the king a trick, it will be but tie and tie," the stout man answered, with a grin. " But no more talk ! Away with them, Simon, and you answer to me for their safe-keeping."

It was in vain that De Catinat raved and threatened, invoking the most terrible menaces upon all who were concerned in detaining him. Two stout knaves thrusting him from behind and one dragging in front forced him through a narrow gate and along a stone-flagged passage, a small man in black buckram with a bunch of keys in one hand and a swinging lantern in the other leading the way. Their ankles had been so tied that they could but take steps of a foot in length. Shuffling along, they made their way down three successive corridors and through three doors, each which was locked and barred behind them. Then they ascended a winding stone stair, hollowed out in the centre by the feet of generations of prisoners and of jailers, and finally they were thrust into a small square dungeon, and two trusses of straw were thrown in after them. An instant later a heavy key turned in the lock, and they were left to their own meditations.

Very grim and dark those meditations were in the case of De Catinat. A stroke of good luck had made him at court, and now this other of ill fortune had destroyed him. It would be in vain that he should plead his own powerlessness. He knew his royal master well. He was a man who was munificent when his orders were obeyed, and inexorable when they miscarried. No excuse availed with him. An unlucky man was as abhorrent to him as a negligent one. In this great crisis the king had trusted him with an all-important message, and that message had not been delivered. What could save him now from disgrace and from ruin ? He cared nothing for the dim dungeon in which he found himself, nor for the uncertain fate which hung over his head, but his heart turned to lead when he thought of his blasted career, and of the

triumph of those whose jealousy had been aroused by his rapid promotion. There were his people in Paris, too —his sweet Adèle, his old uncle, who had been as good as a father to him. What protector would they have in their troubles now that he had lost the power that might have shielded them ? How long would it be before they were exposed once more to the brutalities of Dalbert and his dragoons ? He clenched his teeth at the thought, and threw himself down with a groan upon the litter of straw dimly visible in the faint light which streamed through the single window.

But his energetic comrade had yielded to no feeling of despondency. The instant that the clang of the prison door had assured him that he was safe from interruption he had slipped off the bonds which held him and had felt all round the walls and flooring to see what manner of place this might be. His search had ended in the discovery of a small fireplace at one corner, and of two great clumsy billets of wood, which seemed to have been left there to serve as pillows for the prisoners. Having satisfied himself that the chimney was so small that it was utterly impossible to pass even his head up it, he drew the two blocks of wood over to the window, and was able, by placing one above the other and standing on tiptoe on the highest, to reach the bars which guarded it. Drawing himself up, and fixing one toe in an inequality of the wall, he managed to look out on to the courtyard which they had just quitted. The carriage and De Vivonne were passing out through the gate as he looked, and he heard a moment later the slam of the heavy door and the clatter of hoofs from the troop of horsemen outside. The seneschal and his retainers had disappeared ; the torches, too, were gone, and, save for the measured tread of a pair of sentinels in the yard twenty feet beneath him, all was silent throughout the great castle.

And a very great castle it was. Even as he hung there with straining hands his eyes were running in admiration and amazement over the huge wall in front of him, with its

fringe of turrets and pinnacles and battlements all lying so still and cold in the moonlight. Strange thoughts will slip into a man's head at the most unlikely moments. He remembered suddenly a bright summer day over the water when first he had come down from Albany, and how his father had met him on the wharf by the Hudson, and had taken him through the water-gate to see Peter Stuyvesant's house, as a sign of how great this city was which had passed from the Dutch to the English. Why, Peter Stuyvesant's house and Peter Stuyvesant's bowery villa put together would not make one wing of this huge pile, which was itself a mere dog-kennel beside the mighty palace at Versailles. He would that his father were here now ; and then, on second thoughts, he would not, for it came back to him that he was a prisoner in a far land, and that his sight-seeing was being done through the bars of a dungeon window.

The window was large enough to pass his body through if it were not for those bars. He shook them and hung his weight upon them, but they were as thick as his thumb and firmly welded. Then, getting some strong hold for his other foot, he supported himself by one hand while he picked with his knife at the setting of the iron. It was cement, as smooth as glass and as hard as marble. His knife turned when he tried to loosen it. But there was still the stone. It was sandstone, not so very hard. If he could cut grooves in it, he might be able to draw out bars, cement and all. He sprang down to the floor again, and was thinking how he should best set to work, when a groan drew his attention to his companion.

" You seem sick, friend," said he.

" Sick in mind," moaned the other. " Oh, the cursed fool that I have been ! It maddens me ! "

" Something on your mind ? " said Amos Green, sitting down upon his billets of wood. "What was it, then ? "

The guardsman made a movement of impatience. " What was it ? How can you ask me, when you know as well as I do the wretched failure of my mission. It was

648

the king's wish that the archbishop should marry them. The king's wish is the law. It must be the archbishop or none. He should have been at the palace by now. Ah, my God! I can see the king's cabinet, I can see him waiting, I can see madame waiting, I can hear them speak of the unhappy De Catinat——" He buried his face in his hands once more.

" I see all that," said the American stolidly, " and I see something more."

" What then ? "

" I see the archbishop tying them up together."

" The archbishop !   You are raving."

" Maybe.   But I see him."

" He could not be at the palace."

" On the contrary, he reached the palace about half an hour ago."

De Catinat sprang to his feet. " At the palace ! " he screamed. " Then who gave him the message ? "

" I did," said Amos Green.

18. *A Night of Surprises*

IF the American had expected to surprise or delight his companion by this curt announcement he was woefully disappointed, for De Catinat approached him with a face which was full of sympathy and trouble, and laid his hand caressingly upon his shoulder.

" My dear friend," said he, " I have been selfish and thoughtless. I have made too much of my own little troubles and too little of what you have gone through for me. That fall from your house has shaken you more than you think. Lie down upon this straw, and see if a little sleep may not——"

" I tell you that the bishop is there ! " cried Amos Green impatiently.

" Quite so.   There is water in this jug, and if I dip my scarf into it and tie it round your brow——"

" Man alive ! Don't you hear me ! The bishop is there."

" He is, he is," said De Catinat soothingly. " He is most certainly there. I trust that you have no pain ? "

The American waved in the air with his knotted fists. " You think that I'm crazed," he cried, " and, by the eternal, you are enough to make me so ! When I say that I sent the bishop, I mean that I saw to the job. You remember when I stepped back to your friend the major ? "

It was the soldier's turn to grow excited now. " Well ? " he cried, gripping the other's arm.

" Well, when we send a scout into the woods, if the matter is worth it, we send a second one at another hour, and so one or other comes back with his hair on. That's the Iroquois fashion, and a good fashion too."

" My God ! I believe that you have saved me ! "

" You needn't grip on to my arm like a fish-eagle on a trout ! I went back to the major, then, and I asked him when he was in Paris to pass by the archbishop's door."

" Well ? Well ? "

" I showed him this lump of chalk. ' If we've been there,' said I, ' you'll see a great cross on the left side of the doorpost. If there's no cross, then pull the latch and ask the bishop if he'll come up to the palace as quick as his horses can bring him.' The major started an hour after us ; he would be in Paris by half-past ten ; the bishop would be in his carriage by eleven, and he would reach Versailles half an hour ago, that is to say, about half-past twelve. By the Lord, I think I've driven him off his head ! "

It was no wonder that the young woodsman was alarmed at the effect of his own announcement. His slow and steady nature was incapable of the quick, violent variations of the fiery Frenchman. De Catinat, who had thrown off his bonds before he had lain down, spun round the cell now, waving his arms and his legs, with his shadow capering up the wall behind him, all distorted

in the moonlight. Finally he threw himself into his comrade's arms with a torrent of thanks and ejaculations and praises and promises, patting him with his hands and hugging him to his breast.

"Oh, if I could but do something for you!" he exclaimed. "If I could do something for you!"

"You can, then. Lie down on that straw and go to sleep."

"And to think that I sneered at you! I! Oh, you have had your revenge!"

"For the Lord's sake, lie down and go to sleep!" By persuasions and a little pushing he got his delighted companion on to his couch again, and heaped the straw over him to serve as a blanket. De Catinat was wearied out by the excitements of the day, and this last great reaction seemed to have absorbed all his remaining strength. His lids drooped heavily over his eyes, his head sank deeper into the soft straw, and his last remembrance was that the tireless American was seated cross-legged in the moonlight, working furiously with his long knife upon one of the billets of wood.

So weary was the young guardsman that it was long past noon, and the sun was shining out of a cloudless blue sky, before he awoke. For a moment, enveloped as he was in straw, and with the rude arch of the dungeon meeting in four rough-hewn groinings above his head, he stared about him in bewilderment. Then in an instant the doings of the day before, his mission, the ambuscade, his imprisonment, all flashed back to him, and he sprang to his feet. His comrade, who had been dozing in the corner, jumped up also at the first movement, with his hand on his knife, and a sinister glance directed towards the door.

"Oh, it's you, is it?" said he. "I thought it was the man."

"Has someone been in, then?"

"Yes; they brought those two loaves and a jug of water, just about dawn, when I was settling down for a rest."

" And did he say anything ? "

" No ; it was the little black one."

" Simon, they called him."

" The same. He laid the things down and was gone. I thought that maybe if he came again we might get him to stop."

" How, then ? "

"Maybe if we get these stirrup leathers round his ankles he would not get them off quite as easy as we have done."

" And what then ? "

" Well, he would tell us where we are, and what is to be done with us."

" Pshaw ! what does it matter, since our mission is done ? "

" It may not matter to you—there's no accounting for tastes—but it matters a good deal to me. I'm not used to sitting in a hole, like a bear in a trap, waiting for what other folks choose to do with me. It's new to me. I found Paris a pretty close sort of place, but it's a prairie compared to this. It don't suit a man of my habits, and I am going to come out of it."

" There's no help but patience, my friend."

" I don't know that. I'd get more help out of a bar and a few pegs." He opened his coat, and took out a short piece of rusted iron, and three small thick pieces of wood, sharpened at one end.

" Where did you get those, then ? "

" These are my night's work. The bar is the top one of the grate. I had a job to loosen it, but there it is. The pegs I whittled out of that log."

" And what are they for ? "

" Well, you see, peg number one goes in here, where I have picked a hole between the stones. Then I've made this other log into a mallet, and with two cracks there it is firm fixed, so that you can put your weight on it. Now these two go in the same way into the holes above here. So ! Now, you see, you can stand up there and look out

of that window without asking too much of your toe joint. Try it."

De Catinat sprang up and looked eagerly out between the bars.

" I do not know the place," said he, shaking his head. " It may be any one of thirty castles which lie upon the south side of Paris, and within six or seven leagues of it. Which can it be ? And who has any interest in treating us so ? I would that I could see a coat of arms, which might help us. Ah ! there is one yonder in the centre of the mullion of the window. But I can scarce read it at the distance. I warrant that your eyes are better than mine, Amos, and that you can read what is on yonder escutcheon."

" On what ? "

" On the stone slab in the centre window."

" Yes, I see it plain enough. It looks to me like three turkey-buzzards sitting on a barrel of molasses."

" Three allurions in chief over a tower proper, maybe. Those are the arms of the Provence De Hautevilles. But it cannot be that. They have no château within a hundred leagues. No, I cannot tell where we are."

He was dropping back to the floor, and put his weight upon the bar. To his amazement, it came away in his hand.

" Look, Amos, look ! " he cried.

" Ah, you've found it out ! Well, I did that during the night."

" And how ? With your knife ? "

" No ; I could make no way with my knife ; but when I got the bar out of the grate, I managed faster. I'll put this one back now, or some of those folks down below may notice that we have got it loose."

" Are they all loose ? "

" Only the one at present, but we'll get the other two out during the night. You can take that bar out and work with it, while I use my own picker at the other. You see, the stone is soft, and by grinding it you soon make a

groove along which you can slip the bar. It will be mighty queer if we can't clear a road for ourselves before morning."

" Well, but even if we could get out into the court-yard, where could we turn to then ? "

" One thing at a time, friend. You might as well stick at the Kennebec because you could not see how you would cross the Penobscot. Anyway, there is more air in the yard than in here, and when the window is clear we shall soon plan out the rest."

The two comrades did not dare to do any work during the day, for fear they should be surprised by the jailer, or observed from without. No one came near them, but they ate their loaves and drank their water with the appetite of men who had often known what it was to be without even such simple food as that. The instant that night fell they were both up upon the pegs, grinding away at the hard stone and tugging at the bars. It was a rainy night, and there was a sharp thunder-storm, but they could see very well, while the shadow of the arched window prevented their being seen. Before midnight they had loosened one bar and the other was just beginning to give, when some slight noise made them turn their heads, and there was their jailer standing, open-mouthed, in the middle of the cell, staring up at them.

It was De Catinat who observed him first, and he sprang down at him in an instant with his bar ; but at his movement the man rushed for the door, and drew it after him just as the American's tool whizzed past his ear and down the passage. As the door slammed, the two com-rades looked at each other. The guardsman shrugged his shoulders and the other whistled.

" It is scarce worth while to go on," said De Catinat.

" We may as well be doing that as anything else. If my picker had been an inch lower I'd have had him. Well, maybe he'll get a stroke, or break his neck down those stairs. I've nothing to work with now, but a few rubs

with your bar will finish the job. Ah, dear ! You are right, and we are fairly treed ! "

A great bell had begun to ring in the château, and there was a loud buzz of voices and a clatter of feet upon the stones. Hoarse orders were shouted, and there was the sound of turning keys. All this coming suddenly in the midst of the stillness of the night showed only too certainly that the alarm had been given. Amos Green threw himself down in the straw, with his hands in his pockets, and De Catinat leaned sulkily against the wall, waiting for whatever might come to him. Five minutes passed, however, and yet another five minutes, without anyone appearing. The hubbub in the courtyard continued, but there was no sound in the corridor which led to their cell.

" Well, I'll have that bar out, after all," said the American at last, rising and stepping over to the window. " Anyhow, we'll see what all this caterwauling is about." He climbed up on his pegs as he spoke, and peeped out.

" Come up ! " he cried excitedly to his comrade. " They've got some other game going on here, and they are all a deal too busy to bother their heads about us."

De Catinat clambered up beside him, and the two stood staring down into the courtyard. A brazier had been lit at each corner, and the place was thronged with men, many of whom carried torches. The yellow glare played fitfully over the grim grey walls, flickering up sometimes until the highest turrets shone golden against the black sky, and then, as the wind caught them, dying away until they scarce threw a glow upon the cheek of their bearer. The main gate was open, and a carriage, which had apparently just driven in, was standing at a small door immediately in front of their window. The wheels and sides were brown with mud and the two horses were reeking and heavy-headed, as though their journey had been both swift and long. A man wearing a plumed hat and enveloped in a riding-coat had stepped from the carriage, and then, turning round, had dragged a second

person out after him. There was a scuffle, a cry, a push, and the two figures had vanished through the door. As it closed, the carriage drove away, the torches and braziers were extinguished, the main gate was closed once more, and all was as quiet as before this sudden interruption.

" Well ! " gasped De Catinat. " Is this another king's messenger they've got ? "

" There will be lodgings for two more here in a short time," said Amos Green. " If they only leave us alone, this cell won't hold us long."

" I wonder where that jailer has gone ? "

" He may go where he likes, as long as he keeps away from here. Give me your bar again. This thing is giving. It won't take us long to have it out." He set to work furiously trying to deepen the groove in the stone, through which he hoped to drag the staple. Suddenly he ceased, and strained his ears.

" By thunder ! " said he, " there's someone working on the other side."

They both stood listening. There were the thud of hammers, the rasping of a saw, and the clatter of wood from the other side of the wall.

" What can they be doing ? "

" I can't think."

" Can you see them ? "

" They are too near the wall."

" I think I can manage," said De Catinat. " I am slighter than you." He pushed his head and neck and half of one shoulder through the gap between the bars, and there he remained until his friend thought that perhaps he had stuck, and pulled at his legs to extricate him. He writhed back, however, without any difficulty.

" They are building something," he whispered.

" Building ! "

" Yes ; there are four of them, with a lantern."

" What can they be building, then ? "

" It's a shed, I think. I can see four sockets in the ground, and they are fixing four uprights into them."

" Well, we can't get away as long as there are four men just under our window."

" Impossible."

" But we may as well finish our work, for all that."

The gentle scrapings of his iron were drowned amid the noise which swelled ever louder from without. The bar loosened at the end, and he drew it slowly towards him. At that instant, however, just as he was disengaging it, a round head appeared between him and the moonlight, a head with a great shock of tangled hair and a woollen cap upon the top of it. So astonished was Amos Green at the sudden apparition that he let go his grip upon the bar, which, falling outwards, toppled over the edge of the window-sill.

" You great fool ! " shrieked a voice from below, " are your fingers ever to be thumbs, then, that you should fumble your tools so ? A thousand thunders of heaven ! You have broken my shoulder."

" What is it, then ? " cried the other. " My faith, Pierre, if your fingers went as fast as your tongue, you would be the first joiner in France."

" What is it, you ape ! You have dropped your tool upon me."

. " I ! I have dropped nothing."

" Idiot ! Would you have me believe that iron falls from the sky ? I say that you have struck me, you foolish, clumsy-fingered lout."

" I have not struck you yet," cried the other, " but, by the Virgin, if I have more of this I will come down the ladder to you ! "

" Silence, you good-for-noughts ! " said a third voice sternly. " If the work be not done by daybreak, there will be a heavy reckoning for somebody."

And again the steady hammering and sawing went forward. The head still passed and repassed, its owner walking apparently upon some platform which they had constructed beneath their window, but never giving a glance or a thought to the black square opening beside

him. It was early morning, and the first cold light was beginning to steal over the courtyard before the work was at last finished and the workmen had left. Then at last the prisoners dared to climb up and to see what it was which had been constructed during the night. It gave them a catch of the breath as they looked at it. It was a scaffold.

There it lay, the ill-omened platform of dark greasy boards newly fastened together, but evidently used often before for the same purpose. It was buttressed up against their wall, and extended a clear twenty feet out, with a broad wooden stair leading down from the further side. In the centre stood a headsman's block, all haggled at the top, and smeared with rust-coloured stains.

" I think it is time that we left," said Amos Green.

" Our work is all in vain, Amos," said De Catinat sadly. " Whatever our fate may be—and this looks ill enough—we can but submit to it like brave men."

" Tut, man ; the window is clear ! Let us make a rush for it."

" It is useless. I can see a line of armed men along the further side of the yard."

" A line ! At this hour ! "

" Yes ; and here come more. See, at the centre gate. Now what in the name of heaven is this ? "

As he spoke the door which faced them opened, and a singular procession filed out. First came two dozen footmen, walking in pairs, all carrying halberds, and clad in the same maroon-coloured liveries. After them a huge bearded man, with his tunic off, and the sleeves of his coarse shirt rolled up over his elbows, strode along with a great axe over his left shoulder. Behind him, a priest with an open missal pattered forth prayers, and in his shadow was a woman, clad in black, her neck bared, and a black shawl cast over her head and drooping in front of her bowed face. Within grip of her walked a tall, thin, fierce-faced man, with harsh red features, and a great jutting nose. He wore a flat velvet cap with a single

eagle feather fastened into it by a diamond clasp, which gleamed in the morning light. But bright as was his gem, his dark eyes were brighter still, and sparkled from under his bushy brows with a mad brilliancy which bore with it something of menace and of terror. His limbs jerked as he walked, his features twisted, and he carried himself like a man who strives hard to hold himself in when his whole soul is aflame with exultation. Behind him again twelve more maroon-clad retainers brought up the rear of this singular procession.

The woman had faltered at the foot of the scaffold, but the man behind her had thrust her forward with such force that she stumbled over the lower step, and would have fallen had she not clutched at the arm of the priest. At the top of the ladder her eyes met the dreadful block, and she burst into a scream, and shrunk backwards. But again the man thrust her on, and two of the followers caught her by either wrist and dragged her forwards.

" Oh, Maurice ! Maurice ! " she screamed. " I am not fit to die ! Oh, forgive me, Maurice, as you hope for forgiveness yourself ! Maurice ! Maurice ! " She strove to get towards him, to clutch at his wrist, at his sleeve, but he stood with his hand on his sword, gazing at her with a face which was all wreathed and contorted with merriment. At the sight of that dreadful mocking face the prayers froze upon her lips. As well pray for mercy to the dropping stone or to the rushing stream. She turned away, and threw back the mantle which had shrouded her features.

" Ah, sire ! " she cried. " Sire ! If you could see me now ! "

And at the cry and at the sight of that fair pale face, De Catinat, looking down from the window, was stricken as though by a dagger ; for there standing beside the headsman's block was she who had been the most powerful, as well as the wittiest and the fairest, of the women of France—none other than Françoise de Montespan, so lately the favourite of the king.

19. *In the King's Cabinet*

ON the night upon which such strange chances had befallen his messengers, the king sat alone in his cabinet. Over his head a perfumed lamp, held up by four little flying Cupids of crystal, who dangled by golden chains from the painted ceiling, cast a brilliant light upon the chamber, which was flashed back twenty-fold by the mirrors upon the wall. The ebony and silver furniture, the dainty carpet of La Savonnière, the silks of Tours, the tapestries of the Gobelins, the gold-work and the delicate chinaware of Sèvres—the best of all that France could produce was centred between these four walls. Nothing had ever passed through that door which was not a masterpiece of its kind. And amid all this brillance the master of it sat, his chin resting upon his hands, his elbows upon the table, with eyes which stared vacantly at the wall, a moody and a solemn man.

But though his dark eyes were fixed upon the wall, they saw nothing of it. They looked rather down the long vista of his own life, away to those early years when what we dream and what we do shade so mistily into one another. Was it a dream or was it a fact, those two men who used to stoop over his baby crib, the one with the dark coat and the star upon his breast, whom he had been taught to call father, and the other one with the long red gown and the little twinkling eyes? Even now, after more than forty years, that wicked, astute, powerful face flashed up, and he saw once more old Richelieu, the great unanointed king of France. And then the other cardinal, the long lean one who had taken his pocket-money, and had grudged him his food, and had dressed him in old clothes. How well he could recall the day when Mazarin had rouged himself for the last time, and how the court had danced with joy at the news that he was no more! And his mother, too, how beautiful she was, and how masterful! Could he not remember how bravely she had borne her-

self during that war in which the power of the great nobles had been broken, and how she had at last lain down to die, imploring the priests not to stain her cap-strings with their holy oils ! And then he thought of what he had done himself, how he had shorn down his great subjects until, instead of being like a tree among saplings, he had been alone, far above all others, with his shadow covering the whole land. Then there were his wars and his laws and his treaties. Under his care France had overflowed her frontiers both on the north and on the east, and yet had been so welded together internally that she had but one voice, with which she spoke through him. And then there was that line of beautiful faces which wavered up in front of him. There was Olympe de Mancini, whose Italian eyes had first taught him that there is a power which can rule over a king ; her sister, too, Marie de Mancini ; his wife, with her dark little sun-browned face ; Henrietta of England, whose death had first shown him the horrors which lie in life ; La Vallière, Montespan, Fontanges. Some were dead ; some were in convents. Some who had been wicked and beautiful were now only wicked. And what had been the outcome of all this troubled, striving life of his ? He was already at the outer verge of his middle years ; he had lost his taste for the pleasures of his youth ; gout and vertigo were ever at his foot and at his head to remind him that between them lay a kingdom which he could not hope to govern. And after all these years he had not won a single true friend, not one, in his family, in his court, in his country, save only this woman whom he was to wed that night. And she, how patient she was, how good, how lofty ! With her he might hope to wipe off by the true glory of his remaining years all the sin and the folly of the past. Would that the archbishop might come, that he might feel that she was indeed his, that he held her with hooks of steel which would bind them as long as life should last !

There came a tap at the door. He sprang up eagerly,

thinking that the ecclesiastic might have arrived. It was, however, only his personal attendant, to say that Louvois would crave an interview. Close at his heels came the minister himself, high-nosed and heavy-chinned. Two leather bags were dangling from his hand.

" Sire," said he, when Bontems had retired, " I trust that I do not intrude upon you."

" No, no, Louvois. My thoughts were in truth beginning to be very indifferent company, and I am glad to be rid of them."

" Your Majesty's thoughts can never, I am sure, be anything but pleasant," said the courtier. " But I have brought you here something which I trust may make them even more so."

" Ah ! What is that ? "

"When so many of our young nobles went into Germany and Hungary, you were pleased in your wisdom to say that you would like well to see what reports they sent home to their friends ; also what news was sent out from the court to them."

" Yes."

" I have them here—all that the courier has brought in, and all that are gathered to go out, each in its own bag. The wax has been softened in spirit, the fastenings have been steamed, and they are now open."

The king took out a handful of the letters and glanced at the addresses.

" I should indeed like to read the hearts of these people," said he. " Thus only can I tell the true thoughts of those who bow and simper before my face. I suppose," with a sudden flash of suspicion from his eyes, " that you have not yourself looked into these ? "

" Oh, sire, I had rather die ! "

" You swear it ? "

" As I hope for salvation ! "

" Hum ! There is one among these which I see is from your own son."

Louvois changed colour, and stammered as he looked at

the envelope. " Your Majesty will find that he is as loyal out of your presence as in it, else he is no son of mine," said he.

" Then we shall begin with his. Ha ! it is but ten lines long. ' Dearest Achille, how I long for you to come back ! The court is as dull as a cloister now that you are gone. My ridiculous father still struts about like a turkey-cock, as if all his medals and crosses could cover the fact that he is but a head lackey, with no more real power than I have. He wheedles a good deal out of the king, but what he does with it I cannot imagine, for little comes my way. I still owe those ten thousand livres to the man in the Rue Orfévre. Unless I have some luck at lansquenet, I shall have to come out soon and join you.' Hem ! I did you an injustice, Louvois. I see that you have *not* looked over these letters."

The minister had sat with a face which was the colour of beetroot, and eyes which projected from his head, while this epistle was being read. It was with relief that he came to the end of it, for at least there was nothing which compromised him seriously with the king ; but every nerve in his great body tingled with rage as he thought of the way in which his young scapegrace had alluded to him. " The viper ! " he cried. " Oh, the foul snake in the grass ! I will make him curse the day that he was born."

" Tut, tut, Louvois ! " said the king. " You are a man who has seen much of life, and you should be a philosopher. Hot-headed youth says ever more than it means. Think no more of the matter. But what have we here ? A letter from my dearest girl to her husband, the Prince de Conti. I would pick her writing out of a thousand. Ah, dear soul, she little thought that my eyes would see her artless prattle ! Why should I read it, since I already know every thought of her innocent heart ? " He unfolded the sheet of pink scented paper with a fond smile upon his face, but it faded away as his eyes glanced down the page, and he sprang to his feet

with a snarl of anger, his hand over his heart and his eyes still glued to the paper. " Minx ! " he cried, in a choking voice. " Impertinent, heartless minx ! Louvois, you know what I have done for the princess. You know she has been the apple of my eye. What have I ever grudged her ? What have I ever denied her ? "

" You have been goodness itself, sire," said Louvois, whose own wounds smarted less now that he saw his master writhing.

" Hear what she says of me : ' Old Father Grumpy is much as usual, save that he gives a little at the knees. You remember how we used to laugh at his airs and graces ! Well, he has given up all that, and though he stills struts about on great high heels, like a Landes peasant on his stilts, he has no brightness at all in his clothes. Of course, all the court follow his example, so you can imagine what a nightmare-place this is. Then this woman still keeps in favour, and her frocks are as dismal as Grumpy's coats ; so when you come back we shall go into the country together, and you shall dress in red velvet, and I shall wear blue silk, and we shall have a little coloured court of our own in spite of my majestic papa.' "

Louis sank his face in his hands.

" You hear how she speaks of me, Louvois."

" It is infamous, sire ; infamous ! "

" She calls me names—me, Louvois ! "

" Atrocious, sire."

" And my knees ! One would think that I was an old man ! "

" Scandalous. But, sire, I would beg to say that it is a case in which your Majesty's philosophy may well soften your anger. Youth is ever hot-headed, and says more than it means. Think no more of the matter."

" You speak like a fool, Louvois. The child that I have loved turns upon me, and you ask me to think no more of it. Ah, it is one more lesson that a king can trust least of all those who have his own blood in their veins. What writing is this ? It is the good Cardinal de

Bouillon. One may not have faith in one's own kin, but this sainted man loves me, not only because I have placed him where he is, but because it is his nature to look up to and love those whom God has placed above him. I will read you his letter, Louvois, to show you that there is still such a thing as loyalty and gratitude in France. 'My dear Prince de la Roche-sur-Yon.' Ah, it is to him he writes. 'I promised when you left that I would let you know from time to time how things were going at court, as you consulted me about bringing your daughter up from Anjou, in the hope that she might catch the king's fancy.' What! What! Louvois! What villainy is this? 'The sultan goes from bad to worse. The Fontanges was at least the prettiest woman in France, though between ourselves there was just a shade too much of the red in her hair—an excellent colour in a cardinal's gown, my dear duke, but nothing brighter than chestnut is permissible in a lady. The Montespan, too, was a fine woman in her day, but fancy his picking up now with a widow who is older than himself, a woman, too, who does not even try to make herself attractive, but kneels at her *prie-dieu* or works at her tapestry from morning to night. They say that December and May make a bad match, but my own opinion is that two Novembers make an even worse one.' Louvois! Louvois! I can read no more! Have you a *lettre de cachet?* "

" There is one here, sire."

" For the Bastille ? "

" No ; for Vincennes."·

" That will do very well. Fill it up, Louvois! Put this villain's name in it ! Let him be arrested to-night, and taken there in his own calèche. The shameless, ungrateful, foul-mouthed villain ! Why did you bring me these letters, Louvois ? Oh, why did you yield to my foolish whim ? My God, is there no truth, or honour, or loyalty in the world ! " He stamped his feet, and shook his clenched hands in the air in the frenzy of his anger and disappointment.

" Shall I, then, put back the others ? " asked Louvois eagerly. He had been on thorns since the king had begun to read them, not knowing what disclosures might come next.

" Put them back, but keep the bag."

" Both bags ? "

" Ah ! I had forgot the other one. Perhaps if I have hypocrites around me, I have at least some honest subjects at a distance. Let us take one haphazard. Who is this from ? Ah ! it is from the Duc de la Rochefoucauld. He has ever seemed to be a modest and dutiful young man. What has he to say ? The Danube—Belgrade—the grand vizier—— Ah ! " He gave a cry as if he had been stabbed.

" What, then, sire ? " The minister had taken a step forward, for he was frightened by the expression upon the king's face.

" Take them away, Louvois ! Take them away ! " he cried, pushing the pile of papers away from him. " I would that I had never seen them ! I will look at them no more ! He gibes even at my courage, I who was in the trenches when he was in his cradle ! ' This war would not suit the king,' he says. ' For there are battles, and none of the nice little safe sieges which are so dear to him.' By God, he shall pay to me with his head for that jest ! Aye, Louvois, it will be a dear gibe to him. But take them away. I have seen as much as I can bear."

The minister was thrusting them back into the bag when suddenly his eye caught the bold, clear writing of Madame de Maintenon upon one of the letters. Some demon whispered to him that here was a weapon which had been placed in his hands, with which he might strike one whose very name filled him with jealousy and hatred. Had she been guilty of some indiscretion in this note, then he might even now, at this last hour, turn the king's heart against her. He was an astute man, and in an instant he had seen his chance and grasped it.

" Ha ! " said he, " it was hardly necessary to open this one."

" Which, Louvois ? Whose is it ? "

The minister pushed forward the letter, and Louis started as his eyes fell upon it.

" Madame's writing ! " he gasped.

" Yes ; it is to her nephew in Germany."

Louis took it in his hand. Then, with a sudden motion, he threw it down among the others, and then yet again his hand stole towards it. His face was grey and haggard, and beads of moisture had broken out upon his brow. If this too were to prove to be as the others ! He was shaken to the soul at the very thought. Twice he tried to pluck it out, and twice his trembling fingers fumbled with the paper. Then he tossed it over to Louvois. " Read it to me," said he.

The minister opened the letter out and flattened it upon the table, with a malicious light dancing in his eyes, which might have cost him his position had the king but read it aright.

" ' My dear nephew,' " he read, " ' what you ask me in your last is absolutely impossible. I have never abused the king's favour so far as to ask for any profit for myself, and I should be equally sorry to solicit any advance for my relatives. No one would rejoice more than I to see you rise to be major in your regiment, but your valour and your loyalty must be the cause, and you must not hope to do it through any word of mine. To serve such a man as the king is its own reward, and I am sure that whether you remain a cornet or rise to some higher rank, you will be equally zealous in his cause. He is surrounded, unhappily, by many base parasites. Some of these are mere fools, like Lauzun ; others are knaves, like the late Fouquet ; and some seem to be both fools and knaves, like Louvois, the minister of war.' " Here the reader choked with rage, and sat gurgling and drumming his fingers upon the table.

" Go on, Louvois, go on," said Louis, smiling up at the ceiling.

" ' These are the clouds which surround the sun, my

dear nephew ; but the sun is, believe me, shining brightly behind them. For years I have known that noble nature as few others can know it, and I can tell you that his virtues are his own, but that if ever his glory is for an instant dimmed over, it is because his kindness of heart has allowed him to be swayed by those who are about him. We hope soon to see you back at Versailles, staggering under the weight of your laurels. Meanwhile accept my love and every wish for your speedy promotion, although it cannot be obtained in the way which you suggest.' "

" Ah," cried the king, his love shining in his eyes, " how could I for an instant doubt her ! And yet I had been so shaken by the others ! Françoise is as true as steel. Was it not a beautiful letter, Louvois ? "

" Madame is a very clever woman," said the minister evasively.

" And such a reader of hearts ! Has she not seen my character aright ? "

" At least she has not read mine, sire."

There was a tap at the door, and Bontems peeped in. " The archbishop has arrived, sire."

" Very well, Bontems. Ask madame to be so good as to step this way. And order the witnesses to assemble in the anteroom."

As the valet hastened away, Louis turned to his minister : " I wish you to be one of the witnesses, Louvois."

" To what, sire ? "

" To my marriage."

The minister started. " What, sire ! Already ? "

" Now, Louvois ; within five minutes."

" Very good, sire." The unhappy courtier strove hard to assume a more festive manner ; but the night had been full of vexation to him, and to be condemned to assist in making this woman the king's wife was the most bitter drop of all.

" Put these letters away, Louvois. The last one has made up for all the rest. But these rascals shall smart

for it, all the same. By-the-way, there is that young nephew to whom madame wrote. Gérard d'Aubigny is his name, is it not ? "

" Yes, sire."

" Make him out a colonel's commission, and give him the next vacancy, Louvois."

" A colonel, sire ! Why, he is not yet twenty."

" Aye, Louvois. Pray, am I the chief of the army, or are you ? Take care, Louvois ! I have warned you once before. I tell you, man, that if I choose to promote one of my jack-boots to be the head of a brigade, you shall not hesitate to make out the papers. Now go into the ante-room, and wait with the other witnesses until you are wanted."

There had meanwhile been busy goings-on in the small room where the red lamp burned in front of the Virgin. Françoise de Maintenon stood in the centre, a little flush of excitement on her cheeks, and an unwonted light in her placid grey eyes. She was clad in a dress of shining white brocade, trimmed and slashed with silver serge, and fringed at the throat and arms with costly point-lace. Three women, grouped around her, rose and stooped and swayed, putting a touch here and a touch there, gathering in, looping up and altering until all was to their taste.

" There ! " said the head dressmaker, giving a final pat to a rosette of grey silk ; " I think that will do, your Majes—that is to say, madame."

The lady smiled at the adroit slip of the courtier dress-maker.

" My tastes lean little towards dress," said she, " yet I would fain look as he would wish me to look."

" Ah, it is easy to dress madame. Madame has a figure. Madame has a carriage. What costume would not look well with such a neck and waist and arm to set it off ? But, ah, madame, what are we to do when we have to make the figure as well as the dress ? There was the Princess Charlotte Elizabeth. It was but yesterday that we cut her gown. She was short, madame, but

thick. Oh, it is incredible how thick she was ! She uses more cloth than madame, though she is two hand-breadths shorter. Ah, I am sure that the good God never meant people to be as thick as that. But then, of course, she is Bavarian and not French."

But madame was paying little heed to the gossip of the dressmaker. Her eyes were fixed upon the statue in the corner, and her lips were moving in prayer—prayer that she might be worthy of this great destiny which had come so suddenly upon her, a poor governess ; that she might walk straight among the pitfalls which surrounded her upon every side ; that this night's work might bring a blessing upon France and upon the man whom she loved. There came a discreet tap at the door to break in upon her prayer.

" It is Bontems, madame," said Mademoiselle Nanon. " He says that the king is ready."

" Then we shall not keep him waiting. Come, mademoiselle, and may God shed His blessing upon what we are about to do ! "

The little party assembled in the king's anteroom, and started from there to the private chapel. In front walked the portly bishop, clad in a green vestment, puffed out with the importance of the function, his missal in his hand, and his fingers between the pages at the service *de matrimoniis*. Beside him strode his almoner, and two little servitors of the court in crimson cassocks bearing lighted torches. The king and Madame de Maintenon walked side by side, she quiet and composed, with gentle bearing and downcast eyes, he with a flush on his dark cheeks, and a nervous, furtive look in his eyes, like a man who knows that he is in the midst of one of the great crises of his life. Behind them, in solemn silence, followed a little group of chosen witnesses, the lean, silent Père La Chaise, Louvois, scowling heavily at the bride, the Marquis de Charmarante, Bontems and Mademoiselle Nanon.

The torches shed a strong yellow light upon this small

band as they advanced slowly through the corridors and *salons* which led to the chapel, and they threw a garish glare upon the painted walls and ceilings, flashing back from gold-work and from mirror, but leaving long trailing shadows in the corners. The king glanced nervously at these black recesses, and at the portraits of his ancestors and relations which lined the walls. As he passed that of his late queen, Maria Theresa, he started and gasped with horror.

" My God ! " he whispered ; " she frowned and spat at me ! "

Madame laid her cool hand upon his wrist. " It is nothing, sire," she murmured, in her soothing voice. " It was but the light flickering over the picture."

Her words had their usual effect upon him. The startled look died away from his eyes, and taking her hand in his he walked resolutely forwards. A minute later they were before the altar, and the words were being read which should bind them for ever together. As they turned away again, her new ring blazing upon her finger, there was a buzz of congratulation around her. The king only said nothing, but he looked at her, and she had no wish that he should say more. She was still calm and pale, but the blood throbbed in her temples. " You are Queen of France, now," it seemed to be humming— " queen, queen, queen ! "

But a sudden shadow had fallen across her, and a low voice was in her ear. " Remember your promise to the Church," it whispered. She started, and turned to see the pale, eager face of the Jesuit beside her.

" Your hand has turned cold, Françoise," said Louis. " Let us go, dearest. We have been too long in this dismal church."

20. *The Two Françoises*

MADAME DE MONTESPAN had retired to rest, easy in her mind, after receiving the message from her brother. She knew Louis as few others knew him, and she was well aware of that obstinacy in trifles which was one of his characteristics. If he had said that he would be married by the archbishop, then the archbishop it must be ; to-night, at least, there should be no marriage. To-morrow was a new day, and if it did not shake the king's plans, then indeed she must have lost her wit as well as her beauty.

She dressed herself with care in the morning, putting on her powder, her little touch of rouge, her one patch near the dimple of her cheek, her loose robe of violet velvet, and her casconet of pearls with all the solicitude of a warrior who is bracing on his arms for a life and death contest. No news had come to her of the great event of the previous night, although the court already rang with it, for her haughtiness and her bitter tongue had left her without a friend or intimate. She rose, therefore, in the best of spirits, with her mind set on the one question as to how best she should gain an audience with the king.

She was still in her boudoir putting the last touches to her toilet when her page announced to her that the king was waiting in her *salon*. Madame de Montespan could hardly believe in such good fortune. She had racked her brain all morning as to how she should win her way to him, and here he was waiting for her. With a last glance at the mirror, she hastened to meet him.

He was standing with his back turned, looking up at one of Snyders's paintings, when she entered ; but as she closed the door, he turned and took two steps towards her. She had run forward with a pretty little cry of joy, her white arms outstretched, and love shining on her face ; but he put out his hand, gently and yet with decision, with a gesture which checked her approach. Her hands

dropped to her side, her lip trembled, and she stood looking at him with her grief and her fears all speaking loudly from her eyes. There was a look upon his features which she had never seen before, and already something was whispering at the back of her soul that to-day at least his spirit was stronger than her own.

" You are angry with me again," she cried.

He had come with every intention of beginning the interview by telling her bluntly of his marriage ; but now, as he looked upon her beauty and her love, he felt that it would have been less brutal to strike her down at his feet. Let someone else tell her, then. She would know soon enough. Besides, there would be less chance then of a scene, which was a thing abhorrent to his soul. His task was, in any case, quite difficult enough. All this ran swiftly through his mind, and she as swiftly read it off in the brown eyes which gazed at her.

" You have something you came to say, and now you have not the heart to say it. God bless the kindly heart which checks the cruel tongue ! "

" No, no, madame," said Louis ; " I would not be cruel. I cannot forget that my life has been brightened and my court made brilliant during all these years by your wit and your beauty. But times change, madame, and I owe a duty to the world which overrides my own personal inclinations. For every reason I think that it is best that we should arrange in the way which we discussed the other day, and that you should withdraw yourself from the court."

" Withdraw, sire ! For how long ? "

" It must be a permanent withdrawal, madame."

She stood with clenched hands and a pale face staring at him.

" I need not say that I shall make your retirement a happy one as far as in me lies. Your allowance shall be fixed by yourself ; a palace shall be erected for you in whatever part of France you may prefer, provided that it is twenty miles from Paris. An estate also——"

" Oh, sire, how can you think that such things as these would compensate me for the loss of your love ? " Her heart had turned to lead within her breast. Had he spoken hotly and angrily she might have hoped to turn him as she had done before ; but this gentle and yet firm bearing was new to him, and she felt that all her arts were vain against it. His coolness enraged her, and yet she strove to choke down her passion and to preserve the humble attitude which was least natural to her haughty and vehement spirit ; but soon the effort became too much for her.

" Madame," said he, " I have thought well over this matter, and it must be as I say. There is no other way at all. Since we must part, the parting had best be short and sharp. Believe me, it is no pleasant matter for me either. I have ordered your brother to have his carriage at the postern at nine o'clock, for I thought that perhaps you would wish to retire after nightfall."

" To hide my shame from a laughing court ! It was thoughtful of you, sire. And yet, perhaps, this too was a duty, since we hear so much of duties nowadays, for who was it but you——"

" I know, madame, I know. I confess it. I have wronged you deeply. Believe me that every atonement which is in my power shall be made. Nay, do not look so angrily at me, I beg. Let our last sight of each other be one which may leave a pleasant memory behind it."

" A pleasant memory ! " All the gentleness and humility had fallen from her now, and her voice had the hard ring of contempt and of anger. " A pleasant memory ! It may well be pleasant to you, who are released from the woman whom you ruined, who can turn now to another without any pale face to be seen within the *salons* of your court to remind you of your perfidy. But to me, pining in some lonely country house, spurned by my husband, despised by my family, the scorn and jest of France, far from all which gave a charm to life, far from the man for whose love I have

sacrificed everything—this will be a very pleasant memory to me, you may be sure ! "

The king's eyes had caught the angry gleam which shot from hers, and yet he strove hard to set a curb upon his temper. When such a matter had to be discussed between the proudest man and the haughtiest woman in all France, one or the other must yield a point He felt that it was for him to do so, and yet it did not come kindly to his imperious nature.

" There is nothing to be gained, madame," said he, " by using words which are neither seemly for your tongue nor for my ears. You will do me the justice to confess that where I might command I am now entreating, and that instead of ordering you as my subject, I am persuading you as my friend."

" Oh, you show too much consideration, sire ! Our relations of twenty years or so can scarce suffice to explain such forbearance from you. I should indeed be grateful that you have not set your archers of the guard upon me, or marched me from the palace between a file of your mousqueteers. Sire, how can I thank you for this forbearance ? " She courtesied low, with her face set in a mocking smile.

" Your words are bitter, madame."

" My heart is bitter, sire."

" Nay, Françoise, be reasonable, I implore you. We have both left our youth behind."

" The allusion to my years comes gracefully from your lips."

" Ah, you distort my words. Then I shall say no more. You may not see me again, madame. Is there no question which you would wish to ask me before I go ? "

" Good God ! " she cried ; " is this a man ? Has it a heart ? Are these the lips which have told me so often that he loved me ? Are these the eyes which have looked so fondly into mine ? Can you then thrust away a woman whose life has been yours as you put away the St. Germain palace when a more showy one was ready

for you ? And this is the end of all those vows, those sweet whispers, those persuasions, those promises——This ! "

" Nay, madame, this is painful to both of us."

" Pain ! Where is the pain in your face ? I see anger in it because I have dared to speak truth ; I see joy in it because you feel that your vile task is done. But where is the pain ? Ah, when I am gone all will be so easy to you —will it not ? You can go back then to your governess——"

" Madame ! "

" Yes, yes, you cannot frighten me ! What do I care for all that you can do ? But I know all. Do not think that I am blind. And so you would even have married her ! You, the descendant of St. Louis, and she the Scarron widow, the poor drudge whom in charity I took into my household ! Ah, how your courtiers will smile ! how the little poets will scribble ! how the wits will whisper ! You do not hear of these things, of course, but they are a little painful for your friends."

" My patience can bear no more," cried the king furiously. " I leave you, madame, and for ever."

But her fury had swept all fear and discretion from her mind. She stepped between the door and him, her face flushed, her eyes blazing, her face thrust a little forward, one small white satin slipper tapping upon the carpet.

" You are in haste, sire ! She is waiting for you, doubtless."

" Let me pass, madame."

" But it was a disappointment last night, was it not, my poor sire ? Ah, and for the governess, what a blow ! Great heaven, what a blow ! No archbishop ! No marriage ! All the pretty plan gone wrong ! Was it not cruel ? "

Louis gazed at the beautiful furious face in bewilderment, and it flashed across his mind that perhaps her grief had turned her brain. What else could be the meaning of this wild talk of the archbishop and the dis-

appointment ? It would be unworthy of him to speak harshly to one who was so afflicted. He must soothe her, and, above all, he must get away from her.

" You have had the keeping of a good many of my family jewels," said he. " I beg that you will still retain them as a small sign of my regard."

He had hoped to please her and to calm her, but in an instant she was over at her treasure-cupboard hurling double handfuls of precious stones down at his feet. They clinked and rattled, the little pellets of red and yellow and green, rolling, glinting over the floor and rapping up against the oak panels at the base of the walls.

" They will do for the governess if the archbishop comes at last," she cried.

He was more convinced than ever that she had lost her wits. A thought struck him by which he might appeal to all that was softer and more gentle in her nature. He stepped swiftly to the door, pushed it half open, and gave a whispered order. A youth with long golden hair waving down over his black velvet doublet entered the room. It was her youngest son, the Count of Toulouse.

" I thought that you would wish to bid him farewell," said Louis.

She stood staring as though unable to realise the significance of his words. Then it was borne suddenly in upon her that her children as well as her lover were to be taken from her, that this other woman should see them and speak with them and win their love while she was far away. All that was evil and bitter in the woman flashed suddenly up in her, until for the instant she was what the king had thought her. If her son was not for her, then he should be for none. A jewelled knife lay among her treasures, ready to her hand. She caught it up and rushed at the cowering lad. Louis screamed and ran forward to stop her ; but another had been swifter than he. A woman had darted through the open door, and had caught the upraised wrist. There was a moment's struggle, two queenly figures swayed and strained, and

677

the knife dropped between their feet. The frightened Louis caught it up, and seizing his little son by the wrist, he rushed from the apartment. Françoise de Montespan staggered back against the ottoman to find herself confronted by the steady eyes and set face of that other Françoise, the woman whose presence fell like a shadow at every turn of her life.

" I have saved you, madame, from doing that which you would have been the first to bewail."

" Saved me ! It is you who have driven me to this ! "

The fallen favourite leaned against the high back of the ottoman, her hands resting behind her upon the curve of the velvet. Her lids were half closed on her flashing eyes, and her lips just parted to show a gleam of her white teeth. Here was the true Françoise de Montespan, a feline creature crouching for a spring, very far from that humble and soft-spoken Françoise who had won the king back by her gentle words. Madame de Maintenon's hand had been cut in the struggle, and the blood was dripping down from the end of her fingers, but neither woman had time to spare a thought upon that. Her firm grey eyes were fixed upon her former rival as one fixes them upon some weak and treacherous creature who may be dominated by a stronger will.

" Yes, it is you who have driven me to this—you, whom I picked up when you were hard pressed for a crust of bread or a cup of sour wine. What had you ? You had nothing—nothing except a name which was a laughing-stock. And what did I give you ? I gave you everything. You know that I gave you everything. Money, position, the entrance to the court. You had them all from me. And now you mock me ! "

" Madame, I do not mock you. I pity you from the bottom of my heart."

" Pity ? Ha ! ha ! A Mortemart is pitied by the widow Scarron ! Your pity may go where your gratitude is, and where your character is. We shall be troubled with it no longer then."

" Your words do not pain me."

" I can believe that you are not sensitive."

" Not when my conscience is at ease."

" Ah ! it has not troubled you, then ? "

" Not upon this point, madame."

" My God ! How terrible must those other points have been ! "

" I have never had an evil thought towards you."

" None towards me ? Oh, woman, woman ! "

" What have I done, then ? The king came to my room to see the children taught. He stayed. He talked. He asked my opinion on this and that. Could I be silent ? or could I say other than what I thought ? "

" You turned him against me ! "

" I should be proud indeed if I thought that I had turned him to virtue."

" The word comes well from your lips."

" I would that I heard it upon yours."

" And so, by your own confession, you stole the king's love from me, most virtuous of widows ! "

" I had all gratitude and kindly thought for you. You have, as you have so often reminded me, been my benefactress. It was not necessary for you to say it, for I had never for an instant forgotten it. Yet if the king has asked me what I thought, I will not deny to you that I have said that sin is sin, and that he would be a worthier man if he shook off the guilty bonds which held him."

" Or exchanged them for others."

" For those of duty."

" Pah ! Your hypocrisy sickens me ! If you pretend to be a nun, why are you not where the nuns are ? You would have the best of two worlds—would you not ?— have all that the court can give, and yet ape the manners of the cloister. But you need not do it with me ! I know you as your inmost heart knows you. I was honest, and what I did, I did before the world. You, behind your priests and your directors and your *prie-dieus* and

your missals—do you think that you deceive me, as you deceive others ? "

Her antagonist's grey eyes sparkled for the first time, and she took a quick step forward, with one white hand half lifted in rebuke.

" You may speak as you will of me," said she. " To me it is no more than the foolish paroquet that chatters in your anteroom. But do not touch upon things which are sacred. Ah, if you would but raise your own thoughts to such things—if you would but turn them inwards, and see, before it is too late, how vile and foul is this life which you have led ! What might you not have done ? His soul was in your hands like clay for the potter. If you had raised him up, if you had led him on the higher path, if you had brought out all that was noble and good within him, how your name would have been loved and blessed, from the château to the cottage ! But no ; you dragged him down ; you wasted his youth ; you drew him from his wife ; you marred his manhood. A crime in one so high begets a thousand others in those who look to him for an example ; and all, all are upon your soul. Take heed, madame, for God's sake take heed ere it be too late ! For all your beauty, there can be for you, as for me, a few short years of life. Then, when that brown hair is white, when that white cheek is sunken, when that bright eye is dimmed—ah, then God pity the sin-stained soul of Françoise de Montespan ! "

Her rival had sunk her head for the moment before the solemn words and the beautiful eyes. For an instant she stood silent, cowed for the first time in all her life ; but then the mocking, defiant spirit came back to her, and she glanced up with a curling lip.

" I am already provided with a spiritual director, thank you," said she. " Oh, madame, you must not think to throw dust in my eyes ! I know you, and know you well ! "

" On the contrary, you seem to know less than I had expected. If you know me so well, pray what am I ? "

All her rival's bitterness and hatred rang in the tones of her answer. "You are," said she, "the governess of my children, and the secret mistress of the king."

"You are mistaken," answered Madame de Maintenon serenely. "I am the governess of your children, and I am the king's wife."

21. *The Man in the Calèche*

OFTEN had De Montespan feigned a faint in the days when she wished to disarm the anger of the king. So she had drawn his arms round her, and won the pity which is the twin sister of love. But now she knew what it was to have the senses struck out of her by a word. She could not doubt the truth of what she heard. There was that in her rival's face, in her steady eye, in her quiet voice, which carried absolute conviction with it. She stood stunned for an instant, panting, her outstretched hands feeling at the air, her defiant eyes dulling and glazing. Then, with a short sharp cry, the wail of one who has fought hard and yet knows that she can fight no more, her proud head drooped, and she fell forward senseless at the feet of her rival.

Madame de Maintenon stooped and raised her up in her strong white arms. There was true grief and pity in her eyes as she looked down at the snow-pale face which lay against her bosom, all the bitterness and pride gone out of it, and nothing left save the tear which sparkled under the dark lashes, and the petulant droop of the lip, like that of a child which had wept itself to sleep. She laid her on the ottoman and placed a silken cushion under her head. Then she gathered together and put back into the open cupboard all the jewels which were scattered about the carpet. Having locked it, and placed the key on a table where its owner's eye would readily fall upon it, she struck a gong, which summoned the little black page.

"Your mistress is indisposed," said she. "Go and

bring her maids to her." And so, having done all that lay with her to do, she turned away from the great silent room, where, amid the velvet and the gilding, her beautiful rival lay like a crushed flower, helpless and hopeless.

Helpless enough, for what could she do ? and hopeless too, for how could fortune aid her ? The instant that her senses had come back to her she had sent away her waiting-women, and lay with clasped hands and a drawn face planning out her own weary future. She must go ; that was certain. Not merely because it was the king's order, but because only misery and mockery remained for her now in the palace where she had reigned supreme. It was true that she had held her position against the queen before, but all her hatred could not blind her to the fact that her rival was a very different woman to poor meek little Maria Theresa. No ; her spirit was broken at last. She must accept defeat, and she must go.

She rose from the couch, feeling that she had aged ten years in an hour. There was much to be done, and little time in which to do it. She had cast down her jewels when the king had spoken as though they would atone for the loss of his love ; but now that the love was gone, there was no reason why the jewels should be lost too. If she had ceased to be the most powerful, she might still be the richest woman in France. There was her pension, of course. That would be a munificent one, for Louis was always generous. And then there was all the spoil which she had collected during these long years, the jewels, the pearls, the gold, the vases, the pictures, the crucifixes, the watches, the trinkets—together they represented many millions of livres. With her own hands she packed away the more precious and portable of them, while she arranged with her brother for the safe-keeping of the others. All day she was at work in a mood of feverish energy, doing anything and everything which might distract her thoughts from her own defeat and her rival's victory. By evening all was ready, and she had arranged

that her property should be sent after her to Petit Bourg, to which castle she intended to retire.

It wanted half an hour of the time fixed for her departure, when a young cavalier, whose face was strange to her, was ushered into the room.

He came with a message from her brother.

" Monsieur de Vivonne regrets, madame, that the rumour of your departure has got abroad among the court."

" What do I care for that, monsieur ? " she retorted, with all her old spirit.

" He says, madame, that the courtiers may assemble at the west gate to see you go ; that Madame de Neuilly will be there, and the Duchesse de Chambord, and Mademoiselle de Rohan, and——"

The lady shrank with horror at the thought of such an ordeal. To drive away from the palace, where she had been more than queen, under the scornful eyes and bitter gibes of so many personal enemies ! After all the humiliations of the day, that would be the crowning cup of sorrow. Her nerve was broken. She could not face it.

" Tell my brother, monsieur, that I should be much obliged if he would make fresh arrangements, by which my departure might be private."

" He bade me say that he had done so, madame."

" Ah ! at what hour, then ? "

" Now. As soon as possible."

" I am ready. At the west gate, then ? "

" No ; at the east. The carriage waits."

" And where is my brother ? "

" We are to pick him up at the park gate."

" And why that ? "

" Because he is watched ; and were he seen beside the carriage, all would be known."

" Very good. Then, monsieur, if you will take my cloak and this casket we may start at once."

They made their way by a circuitous route through the less-used corridors, she hurrying on like a guilty creature,

a hood drawn over her face, and her heart in a flutter at every stray footfall. But fortune stood her friend. She met no one, and soon found herself at the eastern postern-gate. A couple of phlegmatic Swiss guardsmen leaned upon their muskets upon either side, and the lamp above shone upon the carriage which awaited her. The door was open, and a tall cavalier swathed in a black cloak handed her into it. He then took the seat opposite to her, slammed the door, and the calèche rattled away down the main drive.

It had not surprised her that this man should join her inside the coach, for it was usual to have a guard there, and he was doubtless taking the place which her brother would afterwards occupy. That was all natural enough. But when ten minutes passed by, and he had neither moved nor spoken, she peered at him through the gloom with some curiosity. In the glance which she had of him, as he handed her in, she had seen that he was dressed like a gentleman, and there was that in his bow and wave as he did it which told her experienced senses that he was a man of courtly manners. But courtiers, as she had known them, were gallant and garrulous, and this man was so very quiet and still. Again she strained her eyes through the gloom. His hat was pulled down and his cloak was still drawn across his mouth, but from out of the shadow she seemed to get a glimpse of two eyes which peered at her even as she did at him.

At last the silence impressed her with a vague uneasiness. It was time to bring it to an end.

" Surely, monsieur, we have passed the park gate where we were to pick up my brother."

Her companion neither answered nor moved. She thought that perhaps the rumble of the heavy calèche had drowned her voice.

" I say, monsieur," she repeated, leaning forward, " that we have passed the place where we were to meet Monsieur de Vivonne."

He took no notice.

" Monsieur," she cried, " I again remark that we have passed the gates."

There was no answer.

A thrill ran through her nerves. Who or what could he be, this silent man ? Then suddenly it struck her that he might be dumb.

" Perhaps monsieur is afflicted," she said. " Perhaps monsieur cannot speak. If that be the cause of your silence, will you raise your hand, and I shall understand." He sat rigid and silent.

Then a sudden mad fear came upon her, shut up in the dark with this dreadful voiceless thing. She screamed in her terror, and strove to pull down the window and open the door. But a grip of steel closed suddenly round her wrist and forced her back into her seat. And yet the man's body had not moved, and there was no sound save the lurching and rasping of the carriage and the clatter of the flying horses. They were already out on the country roads far beyond Versailles. It was darker than before, heavy clouds had banked over the heavens, and the rumbling of thunder was heard low down on the horizon.

The lady lay back panting upon the leather cushions of the carriage. She was a brave woman, and yet this sudden strange horror coming upon her at the moment when she was weakest had shaken her to the soul. She crouched in the corner, staring across with eyes which were dilated with terror at the figure on the other side. If he would but say something ! Any revelation, any menace, was better than this silence. It was so dark now that she could hardly see his vague outline, and every instant, as the storm gathered, it became still darker. The wind was blowing in little short angry puffs, and still there was that far-off rattle and rumble. Again the strain of the silence was unbearable. She must break it at any cost.

" Sir," said she, " there is some mistake here. I do not know by what right you prevent me from pulling down the window and giving my directions to the coachman."

He said nothing.

685

" I repeat, sir, that there is some mistake. This is the carriage of my brother, Monsieur de Vivonne, and he is not a man who will allow his sister to be treated uncourteously."

A few heavy drops of rain splashed against one window. The clouds were lower and denser. She had quite lost sight of that motionless figure, but it was all the more terrible to her now that it was unseen. She screamed with sheer terror, but her scream availed no more than her words.

" Sir," she cried, clutching forward with her hands and grasping his sleeve, " you frighten me. You terrify me. I have never harmed you. Why should you wish to hurt an unfortunate woman? Oh, speak to me; for God's sake, speak!"

Still the patter of rain upon the window, and no other sound save her own sharp breathing.

" Perhaps you do not know who I am!" she continued, endeavouring to assume her usual tone of command, and talking now to an absolute and impenetrable darkness. " You may learn when it is too late that you have chosen the wrong person for this pleasantry. I am the Marquise de Montespan, and I am not one who forgets a slight. If you know anything of the court, you must know that my word has some weight with the king. You may carry me away in this carriage, but I am not a person who can disappear without speedy inquiry, and speedy vengeance if I have been wronged. If you would—— Oh, Jesus! Have mercy!"

A livid flash of lightning had burst from the heart of the cloud, and, for an instant, the whole countryside and the interior of the calèche were as light as day. The man's face was within a hand's breadth of her own, his mouth wide open, his eyes mere shining slits, convulsed with silent merriment. Every detail flashed out clear in that vivid light—his red quivering tongue, the lighter pink beneath it, the broad white teeth, the short brown beard cut into a peak and bristling forward.

But it was not the sudden flash, it was not the laughing, cruel face, which shot an ice-cold shudder through Françoise de Montespan. It was that, of all men upon earth, this was he whom she most dreaded, and whom she had least thought to see.

" Maurice ! " she screamed. " Maurice ! it is you ! "

" Yes, little wifie, it is I. We are restored to each other's arms, you see, after this interval."

" Oh, Maurice, how you have frightened me ! How could you be so cruel ? Why would you not speak to me ? "

" Because it was so sweet to sit in silence and to think that I really had you to myself after all these years, with none to come between. Ah, little wifie, I have often longed for this hour."

" I have wronged you, Maurice ; I have wronged you ! Forgive me ! "

" We do not forgive in our family, my darling Françoise. Is it not like old days to find ourselves driving together ? And in this carriage, too. It is the very one which bore us back from the cathedral where you made your vows so prettily. I sat as I sit now, and you sat there, and I took your hand like this, and I pressed it, and——"

" Oh, villain, you have twisted my wrist ! You have broken my arm ! "

" Oh, surely not, my little wifie ! And then you remember that, as you told me how truly you would love me, I leaned forward to your lips, and——"

" Oh, help ! Brute, you have cut my mouth ! You have struck me with your ring."

" Struck you ! Now who would have thought that spring day when we planned out our futures, that this also was in the future waiting for me and you ? And this ! and this ! "

He struck savagely at her face in the darkness. She threw herself down, her head pressed against the cushions. With the strength and fury of a maniac he showered his blows above her, thudding upon the leather or crashing

upon the wood-work, heedless of his own splintered hands.

" So I have silenced you," said he at last. " I have stopped your words with my kisses before now. But the world goes on, Françoise, and times change, and women grow false, and men grow stern."

" You may kill me if you will," she moaned.

" I will," said he simply.

Still the carriage flew along, jolting and staggering in the deeply-rutted country roads. The storm had passed, but the growl of the thunder and the far-off glint of a lightning-flash were to be heard and seen on the other side of the heavens. The moon shone out with its clear-cold light, silvering the broad, hedgeless, poplar-fringed plains, and shining through the window of the carriage upon the crouching figure and her terrible companion. He leaned back now, his arms folded upon his chest, his eyes gloating upon the abject misery of the woman who had wronged him.

" Where are you taking me ? " she asked at last.

" To Portillac, my little wifie."

" And why there ? What would you do to me ? "

" I would silence that little lying tongue for ever. It shall deceive no more men."

" You would murder me ? "

" If you call it that."

" You have a stone for a heart."

" My other was given to a woman."

" Oh, my sins are indeed punished."

" Rest assured that they will be."

" Can I do nothing to atone ? "

" I will see that you atone."

" You have a sword by your side, Maurice. Why do you not kill me, then, if you are so bitter against me ? Why do you not pass it through my heart ? "

" Rest assured that I would have done so had I not an excellent reason."

" Why, then ? "

" I will tell you. At Portillac I have the right of the high justice, the middle and the low. I am seigneur there, and can try, condemn and execute. It is my lawful privilege. This pitiful king will not even know how to avenge you, for the right is mine, and he cannot gainsay it without making an enemy of every seigneur in France."

He opened his mouth again and laughed at his own device, while she, shivering in every limb, turned away from his cruel face and glowing eyes, and buried her face in her hands. Once more she prayed to God to forgive her for her poor sinful life. So they whirled through the night behind the clattering horses, the husband and the wife, saying nothing, but with hatred and fear raging in their hearts, until a brazier fire shone down upon them from the angle of a keep, and the shadow of the huge pile loomed vaguely up in front of them in the darkness. It was the Castle of Portillac.

22. *The Scaffold of Portillac*

AND thus it was that Amory de Catinat and Amos Green saw from their dungeon window the midnight carriage which discharged its prisoner before their eyes. Hence, too, came that ominous planking and that strange procession in the early morning. And thus it also happened that they found themselves looking down upon Françoise de Montespan as she was led to her death, and that they heard that last piteous cry for aid at the instant when the heavy hand of the ruffian with the axe fell upon her shoulder, and she was forced down upon her knees beside the block. She shrank screaming from the dreadful, red-stained, greasy billet of wood, but the butcher heaved up his weapon, and the seigneur had taken a step forward with hand outstretched to seize the long auburn hair and to drag the dainty head down with it when suddenly he was struck motionless with astonishment, and stood with his foot advanced and his hand still

out, his mouth half open, and his eyes fixed in front of him.

And, indeed, what he had seen was enough to fill any man with amazement. Out of the small square window which faced him a man had suddenly shot head-foremost, pitching on to his outstretched hands and then bounding to his feet. Within a foot of his heels came the head of a second one, who fell more heavily than the first, and yet recovered himself as quickly. The one wore the blue coat with silver facings of the king's guard ; the second had the dark coat and clean-shaven face of a man of peace ; but each carried a short rusty iron bar in his hand. Not a word did either of them say, but the soldier took two quick steps forward and struck at the headsman while he was still poising himself for a blow at the victim. There was a thud, with a crackle like a breaking egg, and the bar flew into pieces. The headsman gave a dreadful cry, and dropped his axe, clapped his two hands to his head, and running zigzag across the scaffold, fell over, a dead man, into the courtyard beneath.

Quick as a flash De Catinat had caught up the axe, and faced De Montespan with the heavy weapon slung over his shoulder and a challenge in his eyes.

" Now ! " said he.

The seigneur had for the instant been too astounded to speak. Now he understood at least that these strangers had come between him and his prey.

" Seize these men ! " he shrieked, turning to his followers.

" One moment ! " cried De Catinat, with a voice and manner which commanded attention. " You see by my coat what I am. I am the body-servant of the king. Who touches me touches him. Have a care to yourselves. It is a dangerous game ! "

" On, you cowards ! " roared De Montespan.

But the men-at-arms hesitated, for the fear of the king was as a great shadow which hung over all France. De Catinat saw their indecision, and he followed up his advantage.

" This woman," he cried, " is the king's own favourite, and if any harm come to a lock of her hair, I tell you that there is not a living soul within this porticullis who will not die a death of torture. Fools, will you gasp out your lives upon the rack, or writhe in boiling oil, at the bidding of this madman ? "

" Who are these men, Marceau ? " cried the seigneur furiously.

" They are prisoners, your excellency."

" Prisoners ! Whose prisoners ? "

" Yours, your excellency."

" Who ordered you to detain them ? "

" You did. The escort brought your signet-ring."

" I never saw the men. There is devilry in this. But they shall not beard me in my own castle, nor stand between me and my own wife. No, *par dieu !* they shall not and live ! You men, Marceau, Étienne, Gilbert, Jean, Pierre, all you who have eaten my bread, on to them, I say ! "

He glanced round with furious eyes, but they fell only upon hung heads and averted faces. With a hideous curse he flashed out his sword and rushed at his wife, who knelt half insensible beside the block. De Catinat sprang between them to protect her ; but Marceau, the bearded seneschal, had already seized his master round the waist. With the strength of a maniac, his teeth clenched and the foam churning from the corners of his lips, De Montespan writhed round in the man's grasp, and shortening his sword, he thrust it through the brown beard and deep into the throat behind it. Marceau fell back with a choking cry, the blood bubbling from his mouth and his wound ; but before his murderer could disengage his weapon, De Catinat and the American, aided by a dozen of the retainers, had dragged him down on to the scaffold, and Amos Green had pinioned him so securely that he could but move his eyes and his lips, with which he lay glaring and spitting at them. So savage were his own followers against him—for Marceau was

691

well loved amongst them—that, with axe and block so ready, justice might very swiftly have had her way, had not a long clear bugle call, rising and falling in a thousand little twirls and flourishes, clanged out suddenly in the still morning air. De Catinat pricked up his ears at the sound of it like a hound at the huntsman's call.

" Did you hear, Amos ? "

" It was a trumpet."

" It was the guards' bugle call. You, there, hasten to the gate ! Throw up the portcullis and drop the draw-bridge ! Stir yourselves, or even now you may suffer for your master's sins ! It has been a narrow escape, Amos ! "

" You may say so, friend. I saw him put out his hand to her hair, even as you sprang from the window. An-other instant and he would have had her scalped. But she is a fair woman, the fairest that ever my eyes rested upon, and it is not fit that she should kneel here upon these boards." He dragged her husband's long black cloak from him, and made a pillow for the senseless woman with a tenderness and delicacy which came strangely from a man of his build and bearing.

He was still stooping over her when there came the clang of the falling bridge, and an instant later the clatter of the hoofs of a troop of cavalry, who swept with wave of plumes, toss of manes and jingle of steel into the courtyard. At the head was a tall horseman in the full dress of the guards, with a curling feather in his hat, high buff gloves, and his sword gleaming in the sunlight. He cantered forward towards the scaffold, his keen dark eyes taking in every detail of the group which awaited him there. De Catinat's face brightened at the sight of him, and he was down in an instant beside his stirrup.

" De Brissac ! "

" De Catinat ! Now where in the name of wonder did you come from ? "

" I have been a prisoner. Tell me, De Brissac, did you leave the message in Paris ? "

" Certainly I did."

" And the archbishop came ? "

" He did."

" And the marriage ? "

" Took place as arranged. That is why this poor woman whom I see yonder has had to leave the palace."

" I thought as much."

" I trust that no harm has come to her ? "

" My friend and I were just in time to save her. Her husband lies there. He is a fiend, De Brissac."

" Very likely ; but an angel might have grown bitter had he had the same treatment."

" We have him pinioned here. He has slain a man, and I have slain another."

" On my word, you have been busy."

" How did you know that we were here ? "

" Nay, that is an unexpected pleasure."

" You did not come for us, then ? "

" No ; we came for the lady."

" And how did this fellow get hold of her ? "

" Her brother was to have taken her in his carriage. Her husband learned it, and by a lying message he coaxed her into his own, which was at another door. When De Vivonne found that she did not come, and that her rooms were empty, he made inquiries, and soon learned how she had gone. De Montespan's arms had been seen on the panel, and so the king sent me here with my troop as fast as we could gallop."

" Ah, and you would have come too late had a strange chance not brought us here. I know not who it was who waylaid us, for this man seemed to know nothing of the matter. However, all that will be clearer afterwards. What is to be done now ? "

" I have my own orders. Madame is to be sent to Petit Bourg, and any who are concerned in offering her violence are to be kept until the king's pleasure is known. The castle, too, must be held for the king. But you, De Catinat, you have nothing to do now ? "

" Nothing, save that I would like well to ride into Paris to see that all is right with my uncle and his daughter."

" Ah, that sweet little cousin of thine ! By my soul, I do not wonder that the folk know you well in the Rue St. Martin. Well, I have carried a message for you once, and you shall do as much for me now."

" With all my heart. And whither ? "

" To Versailles. The king will be on fire to know how we have fared. You have the best right to tell him, since without you and your friend yonder it would have been but a sorry tale."

" I will be there in two hours."

" Have you horses ? "

" Ours were slain."

" You will find some in the stables here. Pick the best, since you have lost your own in the king's service."

The advice was too good to be overlooked. De Catinat, beckoning to Amos Green, hurried away with him to the stables, while De Brissac, with a few short sharp orders, disarmed the retainers, stationed his guardsmen all over the castle, and arranged for the removal of the lady and for the custody of her husband. An hour later the two friends were riding swiftly down the country road, inhaling the sweet air, which seemed the fresher for their late experience of the dank foul vapours of their dungeon. Far behind them a little dark pinnacle jutting over a grove of trees marked the château which they had left, while on the extreme horizon to the west there came a quick shimmer and sparkle where the level rays of the early sun gleamed upon the magnificent palace which was their goal.

23. *The Fall of the Catinats*

TWO days after Madame de Maintenon's marriage to the king there was held within the humble walls of her little room a meeting which was destined to cause untold misery to many hundreds of thousands

of people, and yet, in the wisdom of Providence, to be an instrument in carrying French arts and French ingenuity and French sprightliness among those heavier Teutonic peoples who have been the stronger and the better ever since for the leaven which which they then received. For in history great evils have sometimes arisen from a virtue, and most beneficent results have often followed hard upon a crime.

The time had come when the Church was to claim her promise from madame, and her pale cheek and sad eyes showed how vain it had been for her to try and drown the pleadings of her tender heart by the arguments of the bigots around her. She knew the Huguenots of France. Who could know them better, seeing that she was herself from their stock, and had been brought up in their faith ? She knew their patience, their nobility, their independence, their tenacity. What chance was there that they would conform to the king's wish ? A few great nobles might, but the others would laugh at the galleys, the jail or even the gallows when the faith of their fathers was at stake. If their creed were no longer tolerated, then, and if they remained true to it, they must either fly from the country or spend a living death tugging at an oar or working in a chain-gang upon the roads. It was a dreadful alternative to present to a people who were so numerous that they made a small nation in themselves. And most dreadful of all that she who was of their own blood should cast her voice against them. And yet her promise had been given, and now the time had come when it must be redeemed.

The eloquent Bishop Bossuet was there, with Louvois, the minister of war, and the famous Jesuit, Father La Chaise, each piling argument upon argument to overcome the reluctance of the king. Beside them stood another priest, so thin and so pale that he might have risen from his bed of death, but with a fierce light burning in his large dark eyes, and with a terrible resolution in his drawn brows and in the set of his grim, lanky jaw. Madame

bent over her tapestry and weaved her coloured silks in silence, while the king leaned upon his hand and listened with the face of a man who knows that he is driven, and yet can hardly turn against the goads. On the low table lay a paper, with pen and ink beside it. It was the order for the revocation, and it only needed the king's signature to make it the law of the land.

" And so, father, you are of opinion that if I stamp out heresy in this fashion I shall assure my own salvation in the next world ? " he asked.

" You will have merited a reward."

" And you think so too, Monsieur Bishop ? "

" Assuredly, sire."

" And you, Abbé du Chayla ? "

The emaciated priest spoke for the first time, a tinge of colour creeping into his corpse-like cheeks, and a more lurid light in his deep-set eyes.

" I know not about assuring your salvation, sire. I think it would take very much more to do that. But there cannot be a doubt as to your damnation if you do not do it."

The king started angrily, and frowned at the speaker.

" Your words are somewhat more curt than I am accustomed to," he remarked.

" In such a matter it were cruel indeed to leave you in doubt. I say again that your soul's fate hangs upon the balance. Heresy is a mortal sin. Thousands of heretics would turn to the Church if you did but give the word. Therefore these thousands of mortal sins are all upon your soul. What hope for it then, if you do not amend ? "

" My father and my grandfather tolerated them."

" Then, without some special extension of the grace of God, your father and your grandfather are burning in hell."

" Insolent ! " The king sprang from his seat.

" Sire, I will say what I hold to be the truth were you fifty times a king. What care I for any man when I know that I speak for the King of kings ? See ; are these the limbs of one who would shrink from testifying to truth ? "

With a sudden movement he threw back the long sleeves of his gown and shot out his white fleshless arms. The bones were all knotted and bent and screwed into the most fantastic shapes. Even Louvois, the hardened man of the court, and his two brother priests, shuddered at the sight of those dreadful limbs. He raised them above his head and turned his burning eyes upwards.

" Heaven has chosen me to testify for the faith before now," said he. " I heard that blood was wanted to nourish the young Church of Siam, and so to Siam I journeyed. They tore me open ; they crucified me ; they wrenched and split my bones. I was left as a dead man, yet God has breathed the breath of life back into me that I may help in this great work of the regeneration of France."

" Your sufferings, father," said Louis, resuming his seat, " give you every claim, both upon the Church and upon me, who am its special champion and protector. What would you counsel, then, father, in the case of those Huguenots who refuse to change ? "

" They would change," cried Du Chayla, with a drawn smile upon his ghastly face. " They must bend or they must break. What matter if they be ground to powder, if we can but build up a complete Church in the land ? " His deep-set eyes glowed with ferocity, and he shook one bony hand in savage wrath above his head.

" The cruelty with which you have been used, then, has not taught you to be more tender to others."

" Tender ! To heretics ! No, sire, my own pains have taught me that the world and the flesh are as nothing, and that the truest charity to another is to capture his soul at all risks to his vile body. I should have these Huguenot souls, sire, though I turned France into a shambles to gain them."

Louis was evidently deeply inpressed by the fearless words and the wild earnestness of the speaker. He leaned his head upon his hand for a little time, and remained sunk in the deepest thought.

" Besides, sire," said Père La Chaise softly, " there would be little need for these stronger measures of which the good abbé speaks. As I have already remarked to you, you are so beloved in your kingdom that the mere assurance that you had expressed your will upon the subject would be enough to turn them all to the true faith."

" I wish that I could think so, father, I wish that I could think so. But what is this ? "

It was his valet who had half opened the door.

" Captain de Catinat is here, who desires to see you at once, sire."

" Ask the captain to enter. Ah ! " A happy thought seemed to have struck him. " We shall see what love for me will do in such a matter, for if it is anywhere to be found it must be among my own body-servants."

The guardsman had arrived that instant from his long ride, and leaving Amos Green with the horses, he had come on at once, all dusty and travel-stained, to carry his message to the king. He entered now, and stood with the quiet ease of a man who is used to such scenes, his hand raised in a salute.

" What news, captain ? "

" Major de Brissac bade me tell you, sire, that he held the Castle of Portillac, that the lady is safe, and that her husband is a prisoner."

Louis and his wife exchanged a quick glance of relief.

" That is well," said he. " By the way, captain, you have served me in many ways of late, and always with success. I hear, Louvois, that De la Salle is dead of the small-pox."

" He died yesterday, sire."

" Then I desire that you make out the vacant commission of major to Monsieur de Catinat. Let me be the first to congratulate you, major, upon your promotion, though you will need to exchange the blue coat for the pearl and grey of the mousquetaires. We cannot spare you from the household, you see."

De Catinat kissed the hand which the monarch held out to him.

" May I be worthy of your kindness, sire ! "

" You would do what you could to serve me, would you not ? "

" My life is yours, sire."

" Very good. Then I shall put your fidelity to the proof."

" I am ready for any proof."

" It is not a very severe one. You see this paper upon the table. It is an order that all the Huguenots in my dominions shall give up their errors, under pain of banishment or captivity. Now I have hopes that there are many of my faithful subjects who are at fault in this matter, but who will abjure it when they learn that it is my clearly expressed wish that they should do so. It would be a great joy to me to find that it was so, for it would be a pain to me to use force against any man who bears the name of Frenchman. Do you follow me ? "

" Yes, sire." The young man had turned deadly pale, and he shifted his feet, and opened and clasped his hands. He had faced death a dozen times and under many different forms, but never had he felt such a sinking of the heart as came over him now.

" You are yourself a Huguenot, I understand. I would gladly have you, then, as the first fruit of this great measure. Let us hear from your own lips that you, for one, are ready to follow the lead of your king in this as in other things."

The young guardsman still hesitated, though his doubts were rather as to how he should frame his reply than as to what its substance should be. He felt that in an instant Fortune had wiped out all the good turns which she had done him during his past life, and that now, far from being in her debt, he held a heavy score against her. The king arched his eyebrows and drummed his fingers impatiently as he glanced at the downcast face and dejected bearing.

" Why all this thought ? " he cried. " You are a man

whom I have raised and whom I will raise. He who has a major's epaulettes at thirty may carry a marshal's bâton at fifty. Your past is mine and your future shall be no less so. What other hopes have you ? "

" I have none, sire, outside your service."

" Why this silence, then ? Why do you not give the assurance which I demand ? "

" I cannot do it, sire."

" You cannot do it ! "

" It is impossible. I should have no more peace in my mind, or respect for myself, if I knew that for the sake of position or wealth I had given up the faith of my fathers."

" Man, you are surely mad ! There is all that a man could covet upon one side, and what is there upon the other ? "

" There is my honour."

" And is it, then, a dishonour to embrace my religion ? "

" It would be a dishonour to me to embrace it for the sake of gain without believing in it."

" Then believe it."

" Alas, sire, a man cannot force himself to believe. Belief is a thing which must come to him, not he to it."

" On my word, father," said Louis, glancing with a bitter smile at his Jesuit confessor, " I shall have to pick the cadets of the household from your seminary, since my officers have turned casuists and theologians. So, for the last time, you refuse to obey my request ? "

" Oh, sire—— " De Catinat took a step forward with outstretched hands and tears in his eyes.

But the king checked him with a gesture. " I desire no protestations," said he. " I judge a man by his acts. Do you abjure or not ? "

" I cannot, sire."

" You see," said Louis, turning again to the Jesuit, " it will not be as easy as you think."

" This man is obstinate, it is true, but many others will be more yielding."

The king shook his head. " I would that I knew what

to do," said he. " Madame, I know that you, at least, will ever give me the best advice. You have heard all that has been said. What do you recommend ? "

She kept her eyes still fixed upon her tapestry, but her voice was firm and clear as she answered :

" You have yourself said that you are the eldest son of the Church. If the eldest son desert her, then who will do her bidding ? And there is truth, too, in what the holy abbé has said. You may imperil your own soul by condoning this sin of heresy. It grows and flourishes, and if it be not rooted out now, it may choke the truth as weeds and briers choke the wheat."

" There are districts in France now," said Bossuet, " where a church is not to be seen in a day's journey, and where all the folk, from the nobles to the peasants, are of the same accursed faith. So it is in the Cévennes, where the people are as fierce and rugged as their own mountains. Heaven guard the priests who have to bring them back from their errors."

" Whom should I send on so perilous a task ? " asked Louis.

The Abbé du Chayla was down in an instant upon his knees with his gaunt hands outstretched. "Send me, sire ! Me ! " he cried. " I have never asked a favour of you, and never will again. But I am the man who could break this people. Send me with your message to the people of the Cévennes."

" God help the people of the Cévennes ! " muttered Louis as he looked with mingled respect and loathing at the emaciated face and fiery eyes of the fanatic. " Very well, abbé," he added aloud ; " you shall go to the Cévennes."

Perhaps for an instant there came upon the stern priest some premonition of that dreadful morning when, as he crouched in a corner of his burning home, fifty daggers were to rasp against each other in his body. He sunk his face in his hands, and a shudder passed over his gaunt frame. Then he rose, and folding his arms, he resumed

his impassive attitude. Louis took up the pen from the table, and drew the paper towards him.

" I have the same counsel, then, from all of you," said he, " from you, bishop ; from you, father ; from you, madame ; from you, abbé ; and from you, Louvois. Well, if ill come from it, may it not be visited upon me ! But what is this ? "

De Catinat had taken a step forward with his hand outstretched. His ardent, impetuous nature had suddenly broken down all the barriers of caution, and he seemed for the instant to see that countless throng of men, women, and children of his own faith, all unable to say a word for themselves, and all looking to him as their champion and spokesman. He had thought little of such matters when all was well, but now, when danger threatened, the deeper side of his nature was moved, and he felt how light a thing is life and fortune when weighed against a great abiding cause and principle.

" Do not sign it, sire," he cried. " You will live to wish that your hand had withered ere it grasped that pen. I know it, sire ; I am sure of it. Consider all these helpless folk—the little children, the young girls, the old and the feeble. Their creed is themselves. As well ask the leaves to change the twigs on which they grow. They could not change. At most you could but hope to turn them from honest folk into hypocrites. And why should you do it ? They honour you. They love you. They harm none. They are proud to serve in your armies, to fight for you, to work for you, to build up the greatness of your kingdom. I implore you, sire, to think again before you sign an order which will bring misery and desolation to so many."

For a moment the king had hesitated as he listened to the short abrupt sentences in which the soldier pleaded for his fellows, but his face hardened again as he remembered how even his own personal entreaty had been unable to prevail with this young dandy of the court.

" France's religion should be that of France's king,"

702

said he, " and if my own guardsmen thwart me in such a matter, I must find others who will be more faithful. That major's commission in the mousquetaires must go to Captain de Belmont, Louvois."

" Very good, sire."

" And De Catinat's commission may be transferred to Lieutenant Labadoyère."

" Very good, sire."

" And I am to serve you no longer ? "

" You are too dainty for my service."

De Catinat's arms fell listlessly to his side, and his head sunk forward upon his breast. Then, as he realised the ruin of all the hopes of his life, and the cruel injustice with which he had been treated, he broke into a cry of despair, and rushed from the room with the hot tears of impotent anger running down his face. So, sobbing, gesticulating, with coat unbuttoned and hat awry, he burst into the stable where placid Amos Green was smoking his pipe and watching with critical eyes the grooming of the horses.

" What in thunder is the matter now ? " he asked, holding his pipe by the bowl, while the blue wreaths curled up from his lips.

" This sword," cried the Frenchman—— " I have no right to wear it ! I shall break it ! "

" Well, and I'll break my knife too if it will hearten you up."

" And these," cried De Catinat, tugging at his silver shoulder-straps, " they must go."

" Ah, you draw ahead of me there, for I never had any. But come, friend, let me know the trouble, that I may see if it may not be mended."

" To Paris ! to Paris ! " shouted the guardsman, frantic-ally. " If I am ruined, I may yet be in time to save them. The horses, quick ! "

It was clear to the American that some sudden calamity had befallen, so he aided his comrade and the grooms to saddle and bridle.

Five minutes later they were flying on their way and in little more than an hour their steeds, all reeking and foam-flecked, were pulled up outside the high house in the Rue St. Martin. De Catinat sprang from his saddle and rushed upstairs, while Amos followed in his own leisurely fashion.

The old Huguenot and his beautiful daughter were seated at one side of the great fireplace, her hand in his, and they sprang up together, she to throw herself with a glad cry into the arms of her lover, and he to grasp the hand which his nephew held out to him.

At the other side of the fireplace, with a very long pipe in his mouth and a cup of wine upon a settle beside him, sat a strange-looking man, with grizzled hair and beard, a fleshy red projecting nose, and two little grey eyes, which twinkled out from under huge brindled brows. His long thin face was laced and seamed with wrinkles, crossing and recrossing everywhere, but fanning out in hundreds from the corners of his eyes. It was set in an unchanging expression, and as it was of the same colour all over, as dark as the darkest walnut, it might have been some quaint figure-head cut out of a coarse-grained wood. He was clad in a blue serge jacket, a pair of red breeches smeared at the knees with tar, clean grey worsted stockings, large steel buckles over his coarse square-toed shoes, and beside him, balanced upon the top of a thick oaken cudgel, was a weather-stained silver-laced hat. His grey-shot hair was gathered up behind into a short stiff tail, and a seaman's hanger, with a brass handle, was girded to his waist by a tarnished leather belt.

De Catinat had been too occupied to take notice of this singular individual, but Amos Green gave a shout of delight at the sight of him, and ran forward to greet him. The other's wooden face relaxed so far as to show two tobacco-stained fangs, and, without rising, he held out a great red hand, of the size and shape of a moderate spade.

" Why, Captain Ephraim," cried Amos in English, " who ever would have thought of finding you here ?

De Catinat, this is my old friend Ephraim Savage, under
whose charge I came here."

" Anchor's apeak, lad, and the hatches down," said the
stranger, in the peculiar drawling voice which the New
Englanders had retained from their ancestors, the English
Puritans.

" And when do you sail ? "

" As soon as your foot is on her deck, if Providence
serve us with wind and tide. And how has all gone
with thee, Amos ? "

" Right well. I have much to tell you of."

" I trust that you have held yourself apart from all
their popish devilry."

" Yes, yes, Ephraim."

" And have had no truck with the scarlet woman."

" No, no ; but what is it now ? "

The grizzled hair was bristling with rage, and the little
grey eyes were gleaming from under the heavy tufts.
Amos, following their gaze, saw that De Catinat was
seated with his arm round Adèle, while her head rested
upon his shoulder.

" Ah, if I but knew their snip-snap, lippetty-chippetty
lingo ! Saw one ever such a sight ! Amos, lad, what is
the French for a ' shameless hussy ' ? "

" Nay, nay, Ephraim. Surely one may see such a
sight, and think no harm of it, on our side of the water."

" Never, Amos. In no godly country."

" Tut ! I have seen folks courting in New York."

" Ah, New York ! I said in no godly country. I
cannot answer for New York or Virginia. South of
Cape Cod, or of New Haven at the furthest, there is no
saying what folk will do. Very sure I am that in Boston
or Salem or Plymouth she would see the bridewell and
he the stocks for half as much. Ah ! " He shook his
head and bent his brows at the guilty couple.

But they and their old relative were far too engrossed
with their own affairs to give a thought to the Puritan
seaman. De Catinat had told his tale in a few short,

bitter sentences, the injustice that had been done to him, his dismissal from the king's service, and the ruin which had come upon the Huguenots of France. Adèle, as is the angel instinct of woman, thought only of her lover and his misfortunes as she listened to his story, but the old merchant tottered to his feet when he heard of the revocation of the edict, and stood with shaking limbs, staring about him in bewilderment.

" What am I to do ? " he cried. " What am I to do ? I am too old to begin my life again."

" Never fear, uncle," said De Catinat heartily. " There are other lands beyond France."

" But not for me. No, no ; I am too old. Lord, but Thy hand is heavy upon Thy servants. Now is the vial opened, and the carved work of the sanctuary thrown down. Ah, what shall I do, and whither shall I turn ? " He wrung his hands in his perplexity.

" What is amiss with him, then, Amos ? " asked the seaman. " Though I know nothing of what he says, yet I can see that he flies a distress signal."

" He and his must leave the country, Ephraim."

" And why ? "

" Because they are Protestants, and the king will not abide their creed."

Ephraim Savage was across the room in an instant, and had enclosed the old merchant's thin hand in his own great knotted fist. There was a brotherly sympathy in his strong grip and rugged weather-stained face which held up the other's courage as no words could have done.

" What is the French for ' the scarlet woman,' Amos ? " he asked, glancing over his shoulder. " Tell this man that we shall see him through. Tell him that we've got a country where he'll just fit in like a bung in a barrel. Tell him that religion is free to all there, and not a papist nearer than Baltimore or the Capuchins of the Penobscot. Tell him that if he wants to come, the *Golden Rod* is waiting with her anchor apeak and her cargo aboard. Tell him what you like, so long as you make him come."

" Then we must come at once," said De Catinat, as he listened to the cordial message which was conveyed to his uncle. " To-night the orders will be out, and to-morrow it may be too late."

" But my business ! " cried the merchant.

" Take what valuables you can and leave the rest. Better that than lose all, and liberty into the bargain."

And so at last it was arranged. That very night, within five minutes of the closing of the gates, there passed out of Paris a small party of five, three upon horseback, and two in a closed carriage which bore several weighty boxes upon the top. They were the first leaves flying before the hurricane, the earliest of that great multitude who were within the next few months to stream along every road which led from France, finding their journey's end too often in galley, dungeon and torture chamber, and yet flooding over the frontiers in numbers sufficient to change the industries and modify the characters of all the neighbouring peoples. Like the Israelites of old, they had been driven from their homes at the bidding of an angry king, who, even while he exiled them, threw every difficulty in the way of their departure. Like them, too, there were none of them who could hope to reach their promised land without grievous wanderings, penniless, friendless and destitute. What passages befell these pilgrims in their travels, what dangers they met and overcame in the land of the Swiss, on the Rhine, among the Walloons, in England, in Ireland, in Berlin, and even in far-off Russia, has still to be written. This one little group, however, whom we know, we may follow in their venturesome journey, and see the chances which befell them upon that great continent which had lain fallow for so long, sown only with the weeds of humanity, but which was now at last about to quicken into such glorious life.

PART II
IN THE NEW WORLD

24. *The Start of the* Golden Rod

THANKS to the early tidings which the guardsman had brought with him, his little party was now ahead of the news. As they passed through the village of Louvier in the early morning they caught a glimpse of a naked corpse upon a dunghill, and were told by a grinning watchman that it was that of a Huguenot who had died impenitent, but that was a common enough occurrence already and did not mean that there had been any change in the law. At Rouen all was quiet, and Captain Ephraim Savage before evening had brought both them and such property as they had saved aboard of his brigantine, the *Golden Rod*. It was but a little craft, some seventy tons burden, but at a time when so many were putting out to sea in open boats, preferring the wrath of Nature to that of the king, it was a refuge indeed. The same night the seaman drew up his anchor and began to slowly make his way down the winding river.

And very slow work it was. There was half a moon shining and a breeze from the east, but the stream writhed and twisted and turned until sometimes they seemed to be sailing up rather than down. In the long reaches they set the yard square and ran, but often they had to lower their two boats and warp her painfully along, Tomlinson of Salem, the mate, and six grave, tobacco-chewing, New England seamen with their broad palmetto hats, tugging and straining at the oars. Amos Green, De Catinat and

even the old merchant had to take their spell ere morning, when the sailors were needed aboard for the handling of the canvas. At last, however, with the early dawn the river broadened out and each bank trended away, leaving a long funnel-shaped estuary between. Ephraim Savage snuffed the air and paced the deck briskly with a twinkle in his keen grey eyes. The wind had fallen away, but there was still enough to drive them slowly upon their course.

" Where's the gal ? " he asked.

" She is in my cabin," said Amos Green. " I thought that maybe she could manage there until we got across."

" Where will you sleep yourself, then ? "

" Tut, a litter of spruce boughs and a sheet of birch bark over me have been enough all these years. What would I ask better than this deck of soft white pine, and my blanket ? "

" Very good. The old man and his nephew, him with the blue coat, can have the two empty bunks. But you must speak to that man, Amos. I'll have no philandering aboard my ship, lad—no whispering or cuddling or any such foolishness. Tell him that this ship is just a bit broke off from Boston, and he'll have to put up with Boston ways until he gets off her. They've been good enough for better men than him. You give me the French for ' no philandering,' and I'll bring him up with a round turn when he drifts."

" It's a pity we left so quick or they might have been married before we started. She's a good girl, Ephraim, and he is a fine man, for all that their ways are not the same as ours. They don't seem to take life so hard as we, and maybe they get more pleasure out of it."

" I never heard tell that we were put here to get pleasure out of it," said the old Puritan, shaking his head. " The valley of the shadow of death don't seem to me to be the kind o' name one would give to a playground. It is a trial and a chastening, that's what it is, the gall of bitterness and the bond of iniquity. We're bad from

709

the beginning, like a stream that runs from a tamarack swamp, and we've enough to do to get ourselves to rights without any fool's talk about pleasure."

" It seems to me to be all mixed up," said Amos, " like the fat and the lean in a bag of pemmican. Look at that sun just pushing its edge over the trees, and see the pink flush on the clouds and the river like a rosy ribbon behind us. It's mighty pretty to our eyes, and very pleasing to us, and it wouldn't be so to my mind if the Creator hadn't wanted it to be. Many a time when I have lain in the woods in the fall and smoked my pipe, and felt how good the tobacco was and how bright the yellow maples were, and the purple ash, and the red tupelo blazing among the bushwood, I've felt that the real fool's talk was with the man who could doubt that all this was meant to make the world happier for us."

" You've been thinking too much in them woods," said Ephraim Savage, gazing at him uneasily. " Don't let your sail be too great for your boat, lad, nor trust to your own wisdom. Your father was from the Bay, and you were raised from a stock that cast the dust of England from their feet rather than bow down to Baal. Keep a grip on the Word and don't think beyond it. But what is the matter with the old man ? He don't seem easy in his mind."

The old merchant had been leaning over the bulwarks looking back with a drawn face and weary eyes at the red curving track behind them which marked the path to Paris. Adèle had come up now, with not a thought to spare upon the dangers and troubles which lay in front of her as she chafed the old man's thin cold hands, and whispered words of love and comfort into his ears. But they had come to the point where the gentle still-flowing river began for the first time to throb to the beat of the sea. The old man gazed forward with horror at the bowsprit as he saw it rise slowly upwards into the air, and clung frantically at the rail as it seemed to slip away from beneath him.

" We are always in the hollow of God's hand," he

whispered, " but oh, Adèle, it is a dreadful thing to feel His fingers moving under us."

" Come with me, uncle," said De Catinat, passing his arm under that of the old man. " It is long since you have rested. And you, Adèle, I pray that you will go and sleep, my poor darling, for it has been a weary journey. Go now, to please me, and when you wake, both France and your troubles will lie behind you."

When father and daughter had left the deck, De Catinat made his way aft again to where Amos Green and the captain were standing.

" I am glad to get them below, Amos," said he, " for I fear that we may have trouble yet."

" And how ? "

" You see the white road which runs by the southern bank of the river. Twice within the last half-hour I have seen horsemen spurring for dear life along it. Where the spires and smoke are yonder is Honfleur, and thither it was that these men went. I know not who could ride so madly at such an hour unless they were the messengers of the king. Oh, see, there is a third one ! "

On the white band which wound among the green meadows a black dot could be seen which moved along with great rapidity, vanished behind a clump of trees and then reappeared again, making for the distant city. Captain Savage drew out his glass and gazed at the rider.

" Aye, aye," said he, as he snapped it up again. " It is a soldier sure enough. I can see the glint of the scabbard which he carries on his larboard side. I think we shall have more wind soon. With a breeze we can show our heels to anything in French waters, but a galley or an armed boat would overhaul us now."

De Catinat, who, though he could speak little English, had learned in America to understand it pretty well, looked anxiously at Amos Green. " I fear that we shall bring trouble on this good captain," said he, " and that the loss of his cargo and ship may be his reward for having befriended us. Ask him whether he would not prefer

to land us on the north bank. With our money we might make our way into the Lowlands."

Ephraim Savage looked at his passenger with eyes which had lost something of their sternness. " Young man," said he, " I see that you can understand something of my talk."

De Catinat nodded.

" I tell you then that I am a bad man to beat. Any man that was ever shipmates with me would tell you as much. I just jam my helm and keep my course as long as God will let me. D'ye see ? "

De Catinat again nodded, though in truth the seaman's metaphors left him with but a very general sense of his meaning.

" We're comin' abreast of that there town, and in ten minutes we shall know if there is any trouble waiting for us. But I'll tell you a story as we go that'll show you what kind o' man you've shipped with. It was ten years ago that I speak of, when I was in the *Speedwell*, sixty-ton brig, tradin' betwixt Boston and Jamestown, goin' south with lumber and skins and fixin's, d'ye see, and north again with tobacco and molasses. One night, blowin' half a gale from the south'ard, we ran on a reef two miles to the east of Cape May, and down we went with a hole in our bottom like as if she'd been spitted on the steeple o' one o' them Honfleur churches. Well, in the morning there I was washin' about, nigh out of sight of land, clingin' on to half the foreyard, without a sign either of my mates or of wreckage. I wasn't so cold, for it was early fall, and I could get three parts of my body on to the spar, but I was hungry and thirsty and bruised, so I just took in two holes of my waist-belt, and put up a hymn, and had a look round for what I could see. Well, I saw more than I cared for. Within five paces of me there was a great fish, as long pretty nigh as the spar that I was grippin'. It's a mighty pleasant thing to have your legs in the water and a beast like that all ready for a nibble at your toes."

" *Mon Dieu !* " cried the French soldier. " And he have not eat you ! "

Ephraim Savage's little eyes twinkled at the reminiscence.

" I ate him," said he.

" What ! " cried Amos.

" It's a mortal fact. I'd a jack-knife in my pocket, same as this one, and I kicked my legs to keep the brute off, and I whittled away at the spar until I'd got a good jagged bit off, sharp at each end, same as a nigger told me once down Delaware way. Then I waited for him, and stopped kicking, so he came at me like a hawk on a chick-a-dee. When he turned up his belly I jammed my left hand with the wood right into his great grinnin' mouth, and I let him have it with my knife between the gills. He tried to break away then, but I held on, d'ye see, though he took me so deep I thought I'd never come up again. I was nigh gone when we got to the surface, but he was floatin' with the white up, and twenty holes in his shirt front. Then I got back to my spar, for we'd gone a long fifty fathoms under water, and when I reached it I fainted dead away."

" And then ? "

" Well, when I came to, it was calm, and there was the dead shark floatin' beside me. I paddled my spar over to him and I got loose a few yards of halliard that were hangin' from one end of it. I made a clove-hitch round his tail, d'ye see, and got the end of it slung over the spar and fastened, so as I couldn't lose him. Then I set to work and I ate him in a week right up to his back fin, and I drank the rain that fell on my coat, and when I was picked up by the *Gracie* of Gloucester, I was that fat that I could scarce climb aboard. That's what Ephraim Savage means, my lad, when he says that he is a baddish man to beat."

Whilst the Puritan seaman had been detailing his reminiscence, his eye had kept wandering from the clouds to the flapping sails and back. Such wind as there was

came in little short puffs, and the canvas either drew full or was absolutely slack. The fleecy shreds of cloud above, however, travelled swiftly across the blue sky. It was on these that the captain fixed his gaze, and he watched them like a man who is working out a problem in his mind. They were abreast of Honfleur now, and about half a mile out from it. Several sloops and brigs were lying there in a cluster, and a whole fleet of brown-sailed fishing boats were tacking slowly in. Yet all was quiet on the curving quay and on the half-moon fort over which floated the white flag with the golden fleurs-de-lis. The port lay on their quarter now and they were drawing away more quickly as the breeze freshened. De Catinat glancing back had almost made up his mind that their fears were quite groundless when they were brought back in an instant and more urgently than ever.

Round the corner of the mole a great dark boat had dashed into view, ringed round with foam from her flying prow, and from the ten pairs of oars which swung from either side of her. A dainty white ensign drooped over her stern and in her bows the sun's light was caught by a heavy brass carronade. She was packed with men, and the gleam which twinkled every now and again from amongst them told that they were armed to the teeth. The captain brought his glass to bear upon them and whistled. Then he glanced up at the clouds once more.

" Thirty men," said he, " and they go three paces to our two. You, sir, take your blue coat off this deck or you'll bring trouble upon us. The Lord will look after His own if they'll only keep from foolishness. Get these hatches off, Tomlinson. So ! Where's Jim Sturt and Hiram Jefferson ? Let them stand by to clap them on again when I whistle. Starboard ! Starboard ! Keep her as full as she'll draw. Now, Amos, and you, Tomlinson, come here until I have a word with you."

The three stood in consultation upon the poop, glancing back at their pursuers. There could be no doubt that the wind was freshening ; it blew briskly in their faces

as they looked back, but it was not steady yet, and the boat was rapidly overhauling them. Already they could see the faces of the marines who sat in the stern, and the gleam of the lighted linstock which the gunner held in his hand.

" Holà ! " cried an officer in excellent English. " Lay her to or we fire ! "

" Who are you, and what do you want ? " shouted Ephraim Savage, in a voice that might have been heard from the bank.

" We come in the king's name, and we want a party of Huguenots from Paris who came on board of your vessel at Rouen."

" Brace back the foreyard and lay her to," shouted the captain. " Drop a ladder over the side there and look smart ! So ! Now we are ready for them."

The yard was swung round and the vessel lay quietly rising and falling on the waves. The boat dashed alongside, her brass cannon trained upon the brigantine, and her squad of marines with their fingers upon their triggers ready to open fire. They grinned and shrugged their shoulders when they saw that their sole opponents were three unarmed men upon the poop. The officer, a young active fellow with a bristling moustache, like the whiskers of a cat, was on deck in an instant with his drawn sword in his hand.

" Come up, two of you ! " he cried. " You stand here at the head of the ladder, sergeant. Throw up a rope and you can fix it to this stanchion. Keep awake down there and be all ready to fire ! You come with me, Corporal Lemoine. Who is captain of this ship ? "

" I am, sir," said Ephraim Savage submissively.

" You have three Huguenots aboard ? "

" Tut ! Tut ! Huguenots, are they ? I thought they were very anxious to get away, but as long as they paid their passage it was no business of mine. An old man, his daughter, and a young fellow about your age in some sort of livery."

" In uniform, sir ? The uniform of the king's guard. Those are the folk I have come for."

" And you wish to take them back ? '

" Most certainly."

" Poor folk ! I am sorry for them."

" And so am I, but orders are orders and must be done."

" Quite so. Well, the old man is in his bunk asleep. The maid is in a cabin below. And the other is sleeping down the hold there where we had to put him, for there is no room elsewhere."

" Sleeping, you say ? We had best surprise him."

" But think you that you dare do it alone ! He has no arms, it is true, but he is a well-grown young fellow. Will you not have twenty men up from the boat ? "

Some such thought had passed through the officer's head, but the captain's remark put him upon his mettle.

" Come with me, corporal," said he. " Down this ladder, you say ? "

" Yes, down the ladder and straight on. He lies between those two cloth bales." Ephraim Savage looked up with a smile playing about the corners of his grim mouth. The wind was whistling now in the rigging, and the stays of the mast were humming like two harp strings. Amos Green lounged beside the French sergeant who guarded the end of the rope ladder, while Tomlinson, the mate, stood with a bucket of water in his hand exchanging remarks in very bad French with the crew of the boat beneath him.

The officer made his way slowly down the ladder which led into the hold, and the corporal followed him, and had his chest level with the deck when the other had reached the bottom. It may have been something in Ephraim Savage's face, or it may have been the gloom around him which startled the young Frenchman, but a sudden suspicion flashed into his mind.

" Up again, corporal ! " he shouted, " I think that you are best at the top."

" And I think that you are best down below, my friend," said the Puritan, who gathered the officer's meaning from his gesture. Putting the sole of his boot against the man's chest he gave a shove which sent both him and the ladder crashing down on to the officer beneath him. As he did so he blew his whistle, and in a moment the hatch was back in its place and clamped down on each side with iron bars.

The sergeant had swung round at the sound of the crash, but Amos Green, who had waited for the movement, threw his arms about him and hurled him overboard into the sea. At the same instant the connecting rope was severed, the foreyard creaked back into position again, and the bucketful of salt water soused down over the gunner and his gun, putting out his linstock and wetting his priming. A shower of balls from the marines piped through the air or rapped up against the planks, but the boat was tossing and jerking in the short choppy waves and to aim was impossible. In vain the men tugged and strained at their oars while the gunner worked like a maniac to relight his linstock and to replace his priming. The boat had lost its weigh, while the brigantine was flying along now with every sail bulging and swelling to bursting-point. Crack ! went the carronade at last, and five little slits in the mainsail showed that her charge of grape had flown high. Her second shot left no trace behind it, and at the third she was at the limit of her range. Half an hour afterwards a little dark dot upon the horizon with a golden speck at one end of it was all that could be seen of the Honfleur guard-boat. Wider and wider grew the low-lying shores, broader and broader was the vast spread of blue waters ahead, the smoke of Havre lay like a little cloud upon the northern horizon, and Captain Ephraim Savage paced his deck with his face as grim as ever, but with a dancing light in his grey eyes.

" I knew that the Lord would look after His own," said he complacently. " We've got her beak straight now and

there's not as much as a dab of mud betwixt this and the three hills of Boston. You've had too much of these French wines of late, Amos, lad. Come down and try a real Boston brewing with a double stroke of malt in the mash tub."

25. *A Boat of the Dead*

FOR two days the *Golden Rod* lay becalmed close to the Cape La Hague, with the Breton coast extending along the whole of the southern horizon. On the third morning, however, came a sharp breeze, and they drew rapidly away from land, until it was but a vague dim line which blended with the cloud banks. Out there on the wide free ocean, with the wind on their cheeks and the salt spray pringling upon their lips, these hunted folk might well throw off their sorrows and believe that they had left for ever behind them all tokens of those strenuous men whose earnest piety had done more harm than frivolity and wickedness could have accomplished. And yet even now they could not shake off their traces, for the sin of the cottage is bounded by the cottage door, but that of the palace spreads its evil over land and sea.

" I am frightened about my father, Amory," said Adèle, as they stood together by the shrouds and looked back at the dim cloud upon the horizon which marked the position of that France which they were never to see again.

" But he is out of danger now."

" Out of danger from cruel laws, but I fear that he will never see the promised land."

" What do you mean, Adèle ? My uncle is hale and hearty."

" Ah, Amory, his very heart roots were fastened in the Rue St. Martin, and when they were torn his life was torn also. Paris and his business, they were the world to him."

" But he will accustom himself to this new life."

" If it only could be so ! But I fear, I fear, that he is over old for such a change. He says not a word of complaint. But I read upon his face that he is stricken to the heart. For hours together he will gaze back at France with the tears running silently down his cheeks. And his hair has turned from grey to white within the week."

De Catinat also had noticed that the gaunt old Huguenot had grown gaunter, that the lines upon his stern face were deeper, and that his head fell forward upon his breast as he walked. He was about, however, to suggest that the voyage might restore the merchant's health, when Adèle gave a cry of surprise and pointed out over the port quarter. So beautiful was she at the instant with her raven hair blown back by the wind, a glow of colour struck into her pale cheeks by the driving spray, her lips parted in her excitement and one white hand shading her eyes, that he stood beside her with all his thoughts bent upon her grace and her sweetness.

" Look ! " she cried. " There is something floating upon the sea. I saw it upon the crest of a wave."

He looked in the direction in which she pointed, but at first he saw nothing. The wind was still behind them, and a brisk sea was running of a deep rich green colour, with long creamy curling caps to the larger waves. The breeze would catch these foam-crests from time to time, and then there would be a sharp spatter upon the decks, with a salt smack upon the lips, and a pringling in the eyes. Suddenly as he gazed, however, something black was tilted up upon the sharp summit of one of the seas, and swooped out of view again upon the further side. It was so far from him that he could make nothing of it, but sharper eyes than his had caught a glance of it. Amos Green had seen the girl point and observed what it was which had attracted her attention.

" Captain Ephraim," cried he, " there's a boat on the starboard quarter."

The New England seaman whipped up his glass and steadied it upon the bulwark.

" Aye, it's a boat," said he, " but an empty one. Maybe it's been washed off from some ship, or gone adrift from shore. Put her hard down, Mr. Tomlinson, for it just so happens that I am in need of a boat at present."

Half a minute later the *Golden Rod* had swung round and was running swiftly down towards the black spot which still bobbed and danced upon the waves. As they neared her they could see that something was projecting over her side.

" It's a man's head ! " cried Amos Green.

But Ephraim Savage's grim face grew grimmer. " It's a man's foot," said he. " I think that you had best take the gal below to the cabin."

Amid a solemn hush they ran alongside this lonely craft which hung out so sinister a signal. Within ten yards of her the foreyard was hauled aback and they gazed down upon her terrible crew.

She was a little thirteen-foot cockle-shell, very broad for her length and so flat in the bottom that she had been meant evidently for river or lake work. Huddled together beneath the seats were three folk, a man in the dress of a respectable artisan, a woman of the same class, and a little child about a year old. The boat was half full of water and the woman and child were stretched with their faces downwards, the fair curls of the infant and the dark locks of the mother washing to and fro like water-weeds upon the surface. The man lay with a slate-coloured face, his chin cocking up towards the sky, his eyes turned upwards to the whites, and his mouth wide open showing a leathern crinkled tongue like a rotting leaf. In the bows, all huddled in a heap, and with a single paddle still grasped in his hand, there crouched a very small man clad in black, an open book lying across his face, and one stiff leg jutting upwards with the heel of the foot resting between the rowlocks. So this strange company swooped and tossed upon the long green Atlantic rollers.

A boat had been lowered by the *Golden Rod* and the unfortunates were soon conveyed upon deck. No particle of either food or drink was to be found, nor anything save the single paddle and the open Bible which lay across the small man's face. Man, woman and child had all been dead a day at the least, and so with the short prayers used upon the seas they were buried from the vessel's side. The small man had at first seemed also to be lifeless, but Amos had detected some slight flutter of his heart, and the faintest haze was left upon the watch glass which was held before his mouth. Wrapped in a dry blanket he was laid beside the mast and the mate forced a few drops of rum every few minutes between his lips until the little spark of life which still lingered in him might be fanned to a flame. Meanwhile Ephraim Savage had ordered up the two prisoners whom he had entrapped at Honfleur. Very foolish they looked as they stood blinking and winking in the daylight from which they had been so long cut off.

" Very sorry, captain," said the seaman, " but either you had to come with us, d'ye see, or we had to stay with you. They're waiting for me over at Boston, and in truth I really couldn't tarry."

The French soldier shrugged his shoulders, and looked around him with a lengthening face. He and his corporal were limp with sea-sickness, and as miserable as a Frenchman is when first he finds that France has vanished from his view.

" Which would you prefer, to go on with us to America, or go back to France ? "

" Back to France, if I can find my way. Oh, I must get to France again if only to have a word with that fool of a gunner."

" Well, we emptied a bucket of water over his linstock and priming, d'ye see, so maybe he did all he could. But there's France, where that thickening is over yonder."

" I see it ! I see it ! Ah, if my feet were only upon it once more."

" There is a boat beside us, and you may take it."

" My God, what happiness ! Corporal Lemoine, the boat ! Let us push off at once."

" But you need a few things first. Good Lord, who ever heard of a man pushing off like that ! Mr. Tomlinson, just sling a keg of water and a barrel of meat and of biscuit into this boat. Hiram Jefferson, bring two oars aft. It's a long pull with the wind in your teeth, but you'll be there by to-morrow night, and the weather is set fair."

The two Frenchmen were soon provided with all that they were likely to require and pushed off with a waving of hats and a shouting of *bon voyage*. The foreyard was swung round again and the *Golden Rod* turned her bowsprit for the west. For hours a glimpse could be caught of the boat, dwindling away on the wave-tops, until at last it vanished into the haze, and with it vanished the very last link which connected them with the great world which they were leaving behind them.

But whilst these things had been done, the senseless man beneath the mast had twitched his eyelids, had drawn a little gasping breath, and then finally had opened his eyes. His skin was like grey parchment drawn tightly over his bones, and the limbs which thrust out from his clothes were those of a sickly child. Yet, weak as he was, the large black eyes with which he looked about him were full of dignity and power. Old Catinat had come upon deck, and at the sight of the man and of his dress he had run forward, and had raised his head reverently and rested it in his own arms.

" He is one of the faithful," he cried, " he is one of our pastors. Ah, now indeed a blessing will be upon our journey ! "

But the man smiled gently and shook his head. " I fear that I may not come this journey with you," said he, " for the Lord has called me upon a further journey of my own. I have had my summons and I am ready. I am indeed the pastor of the temple at Isigny, and when we heard the orders of the wicked king, I and two of the

faithful with their little one put forth in the hope that we might come to England. But on the first day there came a wave which swept away one of our oars and all that was in the boat, our bread, our keg, and we were left with no hope save in Him. And then He began to call us to Him one at a time, first the child, and then the woman, and then the man, until I only am left, though I feel that my own time is not long. But since ye are also of the faithful, may I not serve you in any way before I go ? "

The merchant shook his head, and then suddenly a thought flashed upon him, and he ran with joy upon his face and whispered eagerly to Amos Green. Amos laughed, and strode across to the captain.

" It's time," said Ephraim Savage grimly.

Then the whisperers went to De Catinat. He sprang in the air and his eyes shone with delight. And then they went down to Adèle in her cabin, and she started and blushed, and turned her sweet face away, and patted her hair with her hands as woman will when a sudden call is made upon her. And so, since haste was needful, and since even there upon the lonely sea there was one coming who might at any moment snap their purpose, they found themselves in a few minutes, this gallant man and this pure woman, kneeling hand in hand before the dying pastor, who raised his thin arm feebly in benediction as he muttered the words which should make them for ever one.

Adèle had often pictured her wedding to herself, as what young girl has not ? Often in her dreams she had knelt before the altar with Amory in the temple of the Rue St. Martin. Or sometimes her fancy had taken her to some of those smaller churches in the provinces, those little refuges where a handful of believers gathered together, and it was there that her thoughts had placed the crowning act of a woman's life. But when had she thought of such a marriage as this with the white deck swaying beneath them, the ropes humming above, their only choristers the gulls which screamed around them,

and their wedding hymn the world-old anthem which is struck from the waves by the wind ? And when could she forget the scene ? The yellow masts and the bellying sails, the grey drawn face and the cracked lips of the castaway, her father's gaunt earnest features as he knelt to support the dying minister, De Catinat in his blue coat, already faded and weather-stained, Captain Savage with his wooden face turned towards the clouds, and Amos Green with his hands in his pockets and a quiet twinkle in his blue eyes ! Then behind all the lanky mate and the little group of New England seamen with their palmetto hats and their serious faces !

And so it was done amid kindly words in a harsh foreign tongue, and the shaking of rude hands hardened by the rope and the oar. De Catinat and his wife leaned together by the shrouds when all was over and watched the black side as it rose and fell, and the green water which raced past them.

" It is all so strange and so new," she said. " Our future seems as vague and dark as yonder cloud banks which gather in front of us."

" If it rest with me," he answered, " your future will be as merry and bright as the sunlight that glints on the crest of these waves. The country that drove us forth lies far behind us, but out there is another and a fairer country, and every breath of wind wafts us nearer to it. Freedom awaits us there, and we bear with us youth and love, and what could man or woman ask for more ? "

So they stood and talked while the shadows deepened into twilight and the first faint gleam of the stars broke out in the darkening heavens above them. But ere those stars had waned again one more toiler had found rest aboard the *Golden Rod*, and the scattered flock from Isigny had found their little pastor once more.

26. *The Last Port*

FOR three weeks the wind kept at east or north-east, always at a brisk breeze and freshening sometimes into half a gale. The *Golden Rod* sped merrily upon her way with every sail drawing, alow and aloft, so that by the end of the third week Amos and Ephraim Savage were reckoning out the hours before they would look upon their native land once more. To the old seaman who was used to meeting and to parting it was a small matter, but Amos, who had never been away before, was on fire with impatience, and would sit smoking for hours with his legs astride the shank of the bowsprit, staring ahead at the skyline, in the hope that his friend's reckoning had been wrong, and that at any moment he might see the beloved coast line looming up in front of him.

" It's no use, lad," said Captain Ephraim, laying his great red hand upon his shoulder. " They that go down to the sea in ships need a power of patience, and there's no good eatin' your heart out for what you can't get."

" There's a feel of home about the air, though," Amos answered. " It seems to whistle through your teeth with a bite to it that I never felt over yonder. Ah, it will take three months of the Mohawk Valley before I feel myself to rights."

" Well," said his friend, thrusting a plug of Trinidado tobacco into the corner of his cheek, " I've been on the sea since I had hair to my face, mostly in the coast trade, d'ye see, but over the water as well, as far as those navigation laws would let me. Except the two years that I came ashore for the King Philip business, when every man that could carry a gun was needed on the border, I've never been three casts of a biscuit from salt water, and I tell you that I never knew a better crossing than the one we have just made."

" Aye, we have come along like a buck before a forest

fire. But it is strange to me how you find your way so clearly out here with never track nor trail to guide you. It would puzzle me, Ephraim, to find America, to say nought of the Narrows of New York."

" I am somewhat too far to the north, Amos. We have been on or about the fiftieth since we sighted Cape La Hague. To-morrow we should make land, by my reckonin'."

" Ah, to-morrow! And what will it be? Mount Desert? Cape Cod? Long Island? "

" Nay, lad, we are in the latitude of the St. Lawrence, and are more like to see the Arcadia coast. Then with this wind a day should carry us south, or two at the most. A few more such voyages and I shall buy myself a fair brick house in Green Lane of North Boston, where I can look down on the bay, or on the Charles or the Mystic, and see the ships comin' and goin'. So I would end my life in peace and quiet."

All day Amos Green, in spite of his friend's assurance, strained his eyes in the fruitless search for land, and when at last the darkness fell he went below and laid out his fringed hunting tunic, his leather gaiters, and his raccoon-skin cap, which were very much more to his taste than the broadcloth coat in which the Dutch mercer of New York had clad him. De Catinat had also put on the dark coat of civil life, and he and Adèle were busy preparing all things for the old man who had fallen so weak that there was little which he could do for himself. A fiddle was screaming in the forecastle, and half the night through hoarse bursts of homely song mingled with the dash of the waves and the whistle of the wind, as the New England men in their own grave and stolid fashion made merry over their home-coming.

The mate's watch that night was from twelve to four, and the moon was shining brightly for the first hour of it. In the early morning, however, it clouded over, and the *Golden Rod* plunged into one of those dim clammy mists which lie on all that tract of ocean. So thick was it that

from the poop one could just make out the loom of the foresail, but could see nothing of the fore-topmast stay-sail or the jib. The wind was north-east with a very keen edge to it, and the dainty brigantine lay over, scudding along with her lee rails within hand's touch of the water. It had suddenly turned very cold—so cold that the mate stamped up and down the poop, and his four seamen shivered together under the shelter of the bulwarks. And then in a moment one of them was up, thrusting with his forefinger into the air and screaming, while a huge white wall sprang out of the darkness at the very end of the bowsprit and the ship struck with a force which snapped her two masts like dried reeds in a wind, and changed her in an instant to a crushed and shapeless heap of spars and wreckage.

The mate had shot the length of the poop at the shock, and had narrowly escaped from the falling mast, while of his four men two had been hurled through the huge gap which yawned in the bows, while a third had dashed his head to pieces against the stock of the anchor. Tomlinson staggered forwards to find the whole front part of the vessel driven inwards, and a single seaman sitting dazed amid splintered spars, flapping sails and writhing, lashing cordage. It was still as dark as pitch, and save the white crest of a leaping wave nothing was to be seen beyond the side of the vessel. The mate was peering round him in despair at the ruin which had come so suddenly upon them when he found Captain Ephraim at his elbow, half clad, but as wooden and as serene as ever.

" An iceberg," said he, sniffing at the chill air. " Did you not smell it, friend Tomlinson ? "

" Truly I found it cold, Captain Savage, but I set it down to the mist."

" There is a mist ever set around them, though the Lord in His wisdom knows best why, for it is a sore trial to poor sailor men. She makes water fast, Mr. Tomlinson. She is down by the bows already."

The other watch had swarmed upon deck and one of

them was measuring the well. " There is three feet of water," he cried, " and the pumps sucked dry yesterday at sundown."

" Hiram Jefferson and John Moreton to the pumps ! " cried the captain. " Mr. Tomlinson, clear away the long boat and let us see if we may set her right, though I fear that she is past mending."

" The long boat has stove two planks," cried a seaman.

" The jolly boat, then ? "

" She is in three pieces."

The mate tore his hair, but Ephraim Savage smiled like a man who is gently tickled by some coincidence.

" Where is Amos Green ? "

" Here, Captain Ephraim. What can I do ? "

" And I ? " asked De Catinat eagerly. Adèle and her father had been wrapped in mantles and placed for shelter in the lee of the round house.

" Tell him he can take his spell at the pumps," said the captain to Amos. " And you, Amos you are a handy man with a tool. Get into yonder longboat with a lantern and see if you cannot patch her up."

For half an hour Amos Green hammered and trimmed and caulked, while the sharp measured clanking of the pumps sounded above the dash of the seas. Slowly, very slowly the bows of the brigantine were settling down, and her stern cocking up.

" You've not much time, Amos, lad," said the captain quietly.

" She'll float now, though she's not quite water-tight."

" Very good. Lower away ! Keep up the pumpin' there ! Mr. Tomlinson, see that provisions and water are ready, as much as she will hold. Come with me, Hiram Jefferson."

The seaman and the captain swung themselves down into the tossing boat, the latter with a lantern strapped to his waist. Together they made their way until they were under her mangled bows. The captain shook his head when he saw the extent of the damage.

"Cut away the foresail and pass it over," said he.

Tomlinson and Amos Green cut away the lashings with their knives and lowered the corner of the sail. Captain Ephraim and the seaman seized it, and dragged it across the mouth of the huge gaping leak. As he stooped to do it, however, the ship heaved up upon a swell and the captain saw in the yellow light of his lantern sinuous black cracks which radiated away backwards from the central hole.

"How much in the well?" he asked.

"Five and a half feet."

"Then the ship is lost. I could put my finger between her planks as far as I can see back. Keep the pumps going there! Have you the food and water, Mr. Tomlinson?"

"Here, sir."

"Lower them over the bows. This boat cannot live more than an hour or two. Can you see anything of the berg?"

"The fog is lifting on the starboard quarter," cried one of the men. "Yes, there is the berg, quarter of a mile to leeward!"

The mist had thinned away suddenly, and the moon glimmered through once more upon the great lonely sea and the stricken ship. There, like a huge sail, was the monster piece of ice upon which they had shattered themselves, rocking slowly to and fro with the wash of the waves.

"You must make for her," said Captain Ephraim. "There is no other chance. Lower the gal over the bows! Well, then, her father first, if she likes it better. Tell them to sit still, Amos, and that the Lord will bear us up if we keep clear of foolishness. So! You're a brave lass for all your niminy-piminy lingo. Now the keg and the barrel, and all the wraps and cloaks you can find. Now the other man, the Frenchman. Aye, aye, passengers first and you have got to come. Now, Amos! Now the seamen, and you last, friend Tomlinson."

It was well that they had not very far to go, for the boat was weighed down almost to the edge, and it took the baling of two men to keep in check the water which leaked in between the shattered planks. When all were safely in their places, Captain Ephraim Savage swung himself aboard again, which was but too easy now that every minute brought the bows nearer to the water. He came back with a bundle of clothing which he threw into the boat.

" Push off ! " he cried.

" Jump in, then."

" Ephraim Savage goes down with his ship," said he quietly. " Friend Tomlinson, it is not my way to give my orders more than once. Push off, I say ! "

The mate thrust her out with a boat-hook. Amos and De Catinat gave a cry of dismay, but the stolid New Englanders settled down to their oars and pulled off for the iceberg.

" Amos ! Amos ! Will you suffer it ? " cried the guardsman in French. " My honour will not permit me to leave him thus. I should feel it a stain for ever."

" Tomlinson, you would not leave him ! Go on board and force him to come."

" The man is not living who could force him to do what he had no mind for."

" He may change his purpose."

" He never changes his purpose."

" But you cannot leave him, man ! You must at least lie by and pick him up."

" The boat leaks like a sieve," said the mate. " I will take her to the berg, leave you all there, if we can find footing, and go back for the captain. Put your heart into it, my lads, for the sooner we are there the sooner we shall get back."

But they had not taken fifty strokes before Adèle gave a sudden scream.

" My God ! " she cried, " the ship is going down ! "

She had settled lower and lower in the water, and sud-

denly with a sound of rending planks she thrust down her bows like a diving water-fowl, and her stern flew up into the air, and with a long sucking noise she shot down swifter and swifter until the leaping waves closed over her high poop lantern. With one impulse the boat swept round again and made backwards as fast as willing arms could pull it. But all was quiet at the scene of the disaster. Not even a fragment of wreckage was left upon the surface to show where the *Golden Rod* had found her last harbour. For a long quarter of an hour they pulled round and round in the moonlight, but not a glimpse could they see of the Puritan seaman, and at last, when in spite of the balers the water was washing round their ankles, they put her head about once more and made their way in silence and with heavy hearts to their dreary island of refuge.

Desolate as it was, it was their only hope now, for the leak was increasing and it was evident that the boat could not be kept afloat long. As they drew nearer they saw with dismay that the side which faced them was a solid wall of ice sixty feet high without a flaw or crevice in its whole extent. The berg was a large one, fifty paces at least each way, and there was a hope that the other side might be more favourable. Baling hard they paddled round the corner, but only to find themselves faced by another gloomy ice-crag. Again they went round, and again they found that the berg increased rather than diminished in height. There remained only one other side, and they knew as they rowed round to it that their lives hung upon the result, for the boat was almost settling down beneath them. They shot out from the shadow into the full moonlight and looked upon a sight which none of them would forget until their dying day.

The cliff which faced them was as precipitous as any of the others, and it glimmered and sparkled all over where the silver light fell upon the thousand facets of ice. Right in the centre, however, on a level with the water's edge

there was what appeared to be a huge hollowed-out cave which marked the spot where the *Golden Rod* had, in shattering herself, dislodged a huge boulder, and so amid her own ruin prepared a refuge for those who had trusted themselves to her. This cavern was of the richest emerald green, light and clear at the edges, but toning away into the deepest purples and blues at the back. But it was not the beauty of this grotto, nor was it the assurance of rescue which brought a cry of joy and of wonder from every lip, but it was that, seated upon an ice boulder and placidly smoking a long corn-cob pipe, there was perched in front of them no less a person than Captain Ephraim Savage of Boston. For a moment the castaways could almost have believed that it was his wraith, were wraiths ever seen in so homely an attitude, but the tones of his voice very soon showed that it was indeed he, and in no very Christian temper either.

" Friend Tomlinson," said he, " when I tell you to row for an iceberg I mean you to row right away there, d'ye see, and not to go philandering about over the ocean. It's not your fault that I am not froze, and so I would have been if I hadn't some dry tobacco and my tinder-box to keep myself warm."

Without stopping to answer his commander's reproaches the mate headed for the ledge, which had been cut into a slope by the bows of the brigantine, so that the boat was run up easily on to the ice. Captain Savage seized his dry clothes and vanished into the back of the cave, to return presently warmer in body, and more contented in mind. The long boat had been turned upside down for a seat, the gratings and thwarts taken out and covered with wraps to make a couch for the lady, and the head knocked out of the keg of biscuits.

" We were frightened for you, Ephraim," said Amos Green. " I had a heavy heart this night when I thought that I should never see you more."

" Tut, Amos, you should have known me better."

" But how come you here, captain ? " asked Tomlinson.

" I thought that maybe you had been taken down by the suck of the ship."

" And so I was. It is the third ship in which I have gone down, but they have never kept me down yet. I went deeper to-night than when the *Speedwell* sank, but not so deep as in the *Governor Winthrop*. When I came up I swam to the berg, found this nook, and crawled in. Glad I was to see you, for I feared that you had foundered."

" We put back to pick you up and we passed you in the darkness. And what should we do now ? "

" Rig up that boat-sail and make quarters for the gal. Then get our supper and such rest as we can, for there is nothing to be done to-night, and there may be much in the morning."

27. *A Dwindling Island*

AMOS GREEN was aroused in the morning by a hand upon his shoulder, and springing to his feet, found De Catinat standing beside him. The survivors of the crew were grouped about the upturned boat, slumbering heavily after their labours of the night. The red rim of the sun had just pushed itself above the water-line, and sky and sea were one blaze of scarlet and orange from the dazzling gold of the horizon to the lightest pink at the zenith. The first rays flashed directly into their cave, sparkling and glimmering upon the ice crystals and tinging the whole grotto with a rich warm light. Never was a fairy's palace more lovely than this floating refuge which Nature had provided for them.

But neither the American nor the Frenchman had time now to give a thought to the novelty and beauty of their situation. The latter's face was grave, and his friend read danger in his eyes.

" What is it, then ? "

" The berg. It is coming to pieces."

" Tut, man, it is as solid as an island."

" I have been watching it. You see that crack which extends backwards from the end of our grotto. Two hours ago I could scarce put my hand into it. Now I can slip through it with ease. I tell you that she is splitting across."

Amos Green walked to the end of the funnel-shaped recess and found, as his friend had said, that a green sinuous crack extended away backwards into the iceberg, caused either by the tossing of the waves, or by the terrific impact of their vessel. He roused Captain Ephraim and pointed out the danger to him.

" Well, if she springs a leak we are gone," said he. " She's been thawing pretty fast as it is."

They could see now that what had seemed in the moon-light to be smooth walls of ice were really furrowed and wrinkled like an old man's face by the streams of melted water which were continually running down them. The whole huge mass was brittle and honey-combed and rotten. Already they could hear all round them the ominous drip, drip, and the splash and tinkle of the little rivulets as they fell into the ocean.

" Hullo ! " cried Amos Green, " what's that ? "

" What then ? "

" Did you hear nothing ? "

" No."

" I could have sworn that I heard a voice."

" Impossible. We are all here."

" It must have been my fancy, then."

Captain Ephraim walked to the seaward face of the cave and swept the ocean with his eyes. The wind had quite fallen away now, and the sea stretched away to the eastward, smooth and unbroken save for a single great black spar which floated near the spot where the *Golden Rod* had foundered.

" We should lie in the track of some ships," said the captain thoughtfully. " There's the codders and the herring-busses. We're over far south for them, I reckon. But we can't be more'n two hundred mile from Port

Royal in Arcadia, and we're in the line of the St. Lawrence trade. If I had three white mountain pines, Amos, and a hundred yards of stout canvas I'd get up on the top of this thing, d'ye see, and I'd rig such a jury-mast as would send her humming into Boston Bay. Then I'd break her up and sell her for what she was worth, and turn a few pieces over the business. But she's a heavy old craft, and that's a fact, though even now she might do a knot or two an hour if she had a hurricane behind her. But what is it, Amos ? "

The young hunter was standing with his ear slanting, his head bent forwards, and his eyes glancing sideways, like a man who listens intently. He was about to answer when De Catinat gave a cry and pointed to the back of the cave.

" Look at the crack now."

It had widened by a foot since they had noticed it last, until it was now no longer a crack. It was a pass.

" Let us go through," said the captain.

" It can but come out on the other side."

" Then let us see the other side."

He led the way and the other two followed him. It was very dark as they advanced with high dripping ice walls on either side, and one little zigzagging slit of blue sky above their heads. Tripping and groping their way they stumbled along until suddenly the passage grew wider and opened out into a large square of flat ice. The berg was level in the centre and sloped upwards from that point to the high cliffs which bounded it on each side. In three directions this slope was very steep, but in one it slanted up quite gradually, and the constant thawing had grooved the surface with a thousand irregularities by which an active man could ascend. With one impulse they began all three to clamber up until a minute later they were standing not far from the edge of the summit, seventy feet above the sea, with a view which took in a good fifty miles of water. In all that fifty miles there was no sign of life, nothing but the endless glint of the sun upon the waves.

Captain Ephraim whistled. "We are out of luck," said he.

Amos Green looked about him with startled eyes. "I cannot understand it," said he. "I could have sworn —— By the eternal, listen to that!"

The clear call of a military bugle rang out in the morning air. With a cry of amazement they all three craned forward and peered over the edge.

A large ship was lying under the very shadow of the iceberg. They looked straight down upon her snow-white decks, fringed with shining brass cannon, and dotted with seamen. A little clump of soldiers stood upon the poop going through the manual exercise, and it was from them that the call had come which had sounded so unexpectedly in the ears of the castaways. Standing back from the edge they had not only looked over the topmasts of this welcome neighbour, but they had themselves been invisible from her decks. Now the discovery was mutual, as was shown by a chorus of shouts and cries from beneath them.

But the three did not wait an instant. Sliding and scrambling down the wet, slippery incline, they rushed shouting through the crack and into the cave where their comrades had just been startled by the bugle call while in the middle of their cheerless breakfast. A few hurried words and the leaky long boat had been launched, their possessions had been bundled in, and they were afloat once more. Pulling round a promontory of the berg, they found themselves under the stern of a fine corvette, the sides of which were lined with friendly faces, while from the peak there drooped a huge white banner mottled over with the golden lilies of France. In a very few minutes their boat had been hauled up and they found themselves on board the *St. Christophe* man-of-war, conveying Marquis de Denonville, the new Governor-General of Canada, to take over his duties.

28. *In the Pool of Quebec*

A SINGULAR colony it was of which the ship-wrecked party found themselves now to be members. The *St. Christophe* had left Rochelle three weeks before with four small consorts conveying five hundred soldiers to help the struggling colony on the St. Lawrence. The squadron had become separated, however, and the governor was pursuing his way alone in the hope of picking up the others in the river. Aboard he had a company of the regiment of Quercy, the staff of his own household, Saint Vallier, the new Bishop of Canada, with several of his attendants, three Recollet friars, and five Jesuits bound for the fatal Iroquois mission, half a dozen ladies on their way out to join their husbands, two Ursuline nuns, ten or twelve gallants whom love of adventure and the hope of bettering their fortunes had drawn across the seas, and lastly some twenty peasant maidens of Anjou who were secure of finding husbands waiting for them upon the beach, if only for the sake of the sheets, the pot, the tin plates and the kettle which the king would provide for each of his humble wards.

To add a handful of New England Independents, a Puritan of Boston, and three Huguenots to such a gathering, was indeed to bring fire-brand and powder-barrel together. And yet all aboard were so busy with their own concerns that the castaways were left very much to themselves. Thirty of the soldiers were down with fever and scurvy, and both priests and nuns were fully taken up in nursing them. Denonville, the governor, a pious-minded dragoon, walked the deck all day reading the Psalms of David, and sat up half the night with maps and charts laid out before him, planning out the destruction of the Iroquois who were ravaging his dominions. The gallants and the ladies flirted, the maidens of Anjou made eyes at the soldiers of Quercy and the bishop Saint Vallier read his offices and lectured his clergy. Ephraim

737

Savage used to stand all day glaring at the good man as he paced the deck with his red-edged missal in his hand, and muttering about the "abomination of desolation," but his little ways were put down to his exposure upon the iceberg, and to the fixed idea in the French mind that men of the Anglo-Saxon stock are not to be held accountable for their actions.

There was peace between England and France at present, though feeling ran high between Canada and New York, the French believing, and with some justice, that the English colonists were whooping on the demons who attacked them. Ephraim and his men were therefore received hospitably on board, though the ship was so crowded that they had to sleep wherever they could find cover and space for their bodies. The Catinats, too, had been treated in an even more kindly fashion, the weak old man and the beauty of his daughter arousing the interest of the governor himself. De Catinat had, during the voyage, exchanged his uniform for a plain sombre suit, so that, except for his military bearing, there was nothing to show that he was a fugitive from the army. Old Catinat was now so weak that he was past the answering of questions, his daughter was for ever at his side, and the soldier was diplomatist enough, after a training at Versailles, to say much without saying anything, and so their secret was still preserved. De Catinat had known what it was to be a Huguenot in Canada before the law was altered. He had no wish to try it after.

On the day after the rescue they sighted Cape Breton in the south, and soon running swiftly before an easterly wind, saw the loom of the east end of Anticosti. Then they sailed up the mighty river, though from mid-channel the banks upon either side were hardly to be seen. As the shores narrowed in, they saw the wild gorge of the Saguenay River upon the right, with the smoke from the little fishing and trading station of Tadousac streaming up above the pine trees. Naked Indians with their faces daubed with red clay, Algonquins and Abenakis, clustered

round the ship in their birchen canoes with fruit and
vegetables from the land which brought fresh life to the
scurvy-stricken soldiers. Thence the ship tacked on
up the river past Mal Bay, the Ravine of the Eboulements
and the Bay of St. Paul with its broad valley and wooded
mountains all in a blaze with their beautiful autumn dress,
their scarlets, their purples and their golds, from the
maple, the ash, the young oak and the saplings of the
birch. Amos Green, leaning on the bulwarks, stared
with longing eyes at these vast expanses of virgin woodland, hardly traversed save by an occasional wandering
savage, or hardy *coureur-de-bois*. Then the bold outline
of Cape Tourmente loomed up in front of them ; they
passed the rich placid meadows of Laval's seigneury of
Beaupré, and, skirting the settlements of the Island of
Orleans, they saw the broad pool stretch out in front of
them, the falls of Montmorenci, the high palisades of
Cape Levi, the cluster of vessels, and upon the right that
wonderful rock with its diadem of towers and its township
huddled round its base, the centre and stronghold of
French power in America. Cannon thundered from the
bastions above, and were echoed back by the warship,
while ensigns dipped, hats waved and a swarm of boats
and canoes shot out to welcome the new governor, and
to convey the soldiers and passengers to shore.

The old merchant had pined away since he had left
French soil, like a plant which has been plucked from its
roots. The shock of the shipwreck and the night spent
in their bleak refuge upon the iceberg had been too much
for his years and strength. Since they had been picked
up he had lain amid the scurvy-stricken soldiers with
hardly a sign of life save for his thin breathing and the
twitching of his scraggy throat. Now, however, at the
sound of the cannon and the shouting he opened his eyes,
and raised himself slowly and painfully upon his pillow.

" What is it, father ? What can we do for you ? "
cried Adèle. " We are in America, and here is Amory
and here am I, your children."

But the old man shook his head. " The Lord has brought me to the promised land, but He has not willed that I should enter into it," said he. " May His will be done, and blessed be His name for ever ! But at least I should wish, like Moses, to gaze upon it, if I cannot set foot upon it. Think you, Amory, that you could lend me your arm and lead me on to the deck ? "

" If I have another to help me," said De Catinat, and, ascending to the deck, he brought Amos Green back with him. " Now, father, if you will lay a hand upon the shoulder of each, you need scarce put your feet to the boards."

A minute later, the old merchant was on deck, and the two young men had seated him upon a coil of rope with his back against the mast, where he should be away from the crush. The soldiers were already crowding down into the boats, and all were so busy over their own affairs that they paid no heed to the little group of refugees who gathered round the stricken man. He turned his head painfully from side to side, but his eyes brightened as they fell upon the broad blue stretch of water, the flash of the distant falls, the high castle, and the long line of purple mountains away to the north-west.

" It is not like France," said he. " It is not green and peaceful and smiling, but it is grand and strong and stern like Him who made it. As I have weakened, Adèle, my soul has been less clogged by my body, and I have seen clearly much that has been dim to me. And it has seemed to me, my children, that all this country of America, not Canada alone, but the land where you were born also, Amos Green, and all that stretches away towards yonder setting sun, will be the best gift of God to man. For this has He held it concealed through all the ages, that now His own high purpose may be wrought upon it. For here is a land which is innocent, which has no past guilt to atone for, no feud, nor ill custom, nor evil of any kind. And as the years roll on all the weary and homeless ones, all who are stricken and landless and wronged, will turn

their faces to it, even as we have done. And hence will come a nation which will surely take all that is good and leave all that is bad, moulding and fashioning itself into the highest. Do I not see such a mighty people—a people who will care more to raise their lowest than to exalt their richest—who will understand that there is more bravery in peace than in war, who will see that all men are brothers, and whose hearts will not narrow themselves down to their own frontiers, but will warm in sympathy with every noble cause the whole world through ? That is what I see, Adèle, as I lie here beside a shore upon which I shall never set my feet, and I say to you that if you and Amory go to the building of such a nation then indeed your lives are not misspent. It will come, and when it comes, may God guard it, may God watch over it and direct it ! " His head had sunk gradually lower upon his breast and his lids had fallen slowly over his eyes which had been looking away out past Point Levi at the rolling woods and the far-off mountains. Adèle gave a quick cry of despair and threw her arms round the old man's neck.

" He is dying, Amory, he is dying ! " she cried.

A stern Franciscan friar, who had been telling his beads within a few paces of them, heard the cry and was beside them in an instant.

" He is indeed dying," he said, as he gazed down at the ashen face. " Has the old man had the sacraments of the Church ? "

" I do not think that he needs them," answered De Catinat evasively.

" Which of us do not need them, young man ! " said the friar sternly. " And how can a man hope for salvation without them ! I shall myself administer them without delay."

But the old Huguenot had opened his eyes, and with a last flicker of strength he pushed away the grey-hooded figure which bent over him.

" I left all that I love rather than yield to you," he

cried, " and think you that you can overcome me now ? "

The Franciscan started back at the words, and his hard suspicious eyes shot from De Catinat to the weeping girl.

" So ! " said he. " You are Huguenots, then ! "

" Hush ! Do not wrangle before a man who is dying ! " cried De Catinat in a voice as fierce as his own.

" Before a man who is dead," said Amos Green solemnly.

As he spoke the old man's face had relaxed, his thousand wrinkles had been smoothed suddenly out, as though an invisible hand had passed over them, and his head fell back against the mast. Adèle remained motionless with her arms still clasped round his neck and her cheek pressed against his shoulder. She had fainted.

De Catinat raised his wife and bore her down to the cabin of one of the ladies who had already shown them some kindness. Deaths were no new thing aboard the ship, for they had lost ten soldiers upon the outward passage, so that amid the joy and bustle of the disembarking there were few who had a thought to spare upon the dead pilgrim, and the less so when it was whispered abroad that he had been a Huguenot. A brief order was given that he should be buried in the river that very night, and then, save for a sailmaker who fastened the canvas round him, mankind had done its last for Theophile Catinat. With the survivors, however, it was different, and when the troops were all disembarked, they were mustered in a little group upon the deck, and an officer of the governor's suite decided upon what should be done with them. He was a portly, good-humoured, ruddy-cheeked man, but De Catinat saw with apprehension that the friar walked by his side as he advanced along the deck, and exchanged a few whispered remarks with him. There was a bitter smile upon the monk's dark face which boded little good for the heretics.

" It shall be seen to, good father, it shall be seen to," said the officer impatiently, in answer to one of these

whispered injunctions. " I am as zealous a servant of Holy Church as you are."

" I trust that you are, Monsieur de Bonneville. With so devout a governor as Monsieur de Denonville, it might be an ill thing even in this world for the officers of his household to be lax."

The soldier glanced angrily at his companion, for he saw the threat which lurked under the words.

" I would have you remember, father," said he, " that if faith is a virtue, charity is no less so." Then, speaking in English : " Which is Captain Savage ? "

" Ephraim Savage of Boston."

" And Master Amos Green ? "

" Amos Green of New York."

" And Master Tomlinson ? "

" John Tomlinson of Salem."

" And master mariners Hiram Jefferson, Joseph Cooper, Seek-grace Spaulding, and Paul Cushing, all of Massachusetts Bay ? "

" We are all here."

" It is the governor's orders that all whom I have named shall be conveyed at once to the trading brig *Hope*, which is yonder ship with the white paint line. She sails within the hour for the English provinces."

A buzz of joy broke from the castaway mariners at the prospect of being so speedily restored to their homes, and they hurried away to gather together the few possessions which they had saved from the wreck. The officer put his list in his pocket and stepped across to where De Catinat leaned moodily against the bulwarks.

" Surely you remember me," he said. " I could not forget your face, even though you have exchanged a blue coat for a black one."

De Catinat grasped the hand which was held out to him.

" I remember you well, De Bonneville, and the journey that we made together to Fort Frontenac, but it was not for me to claim your friendship, now that things have gone amiss with me."

" Tut, man, once my friend always my friend."

" I feared, too, that my acquaintance would do you little good with yonder dark-cowled friar who is glowering behind you."

" Well, well, you know how it is with us here. Frontenac could keep them in their place, but De la Barre was as clay in their hands, and this new one promises to follow in his steps. What with the Sulpitians at Montreal and the Jesuits here, we poor devils are between the upper and the nether stones. But I am grieved from my heart to give such a welcome as this to an old comrade, and still more to his wife."

" What is to be done, then ? "

" You are to be confined to the ship until she sails, which will be in a week at the furthest."

" And then ? "

" You are to be carried home in her, and handed over to the Governor of Rochelle to be sent back to Paris. Those are Monsieur de Denonville's orders, and if they be not carried out to the letter, then we shall have the whole hornet's nest about our ears."

De Catinat groaned as he listened. After all their strivings and trials and efforts, to return to Paris, the scorn of his enemies, and an object of pity to his friends, was too deep a humiliation. He flushed with shame at the very thought. To be led back like the home-sick peasant who has deserted from his regiment ! Better one spring into the broad blue river beneath him, were it not for little pale-faced Adèle who had none but him to look to. It was so tame ! So ignominious ! And yet in this floating prison, with a woman whose fate was linked with his own, what hope was there of escape ?

De Bonneville had left him, with a few blunt words of sympathy, but the friar still paced the deck with a furtive glance at him from time to time, and two soldiers who were stationed upon the poop passed and repassed within a few yards of him. They had orders evidently to mark his movements. Heart-sick he leaned over the side

watching the Indians in their paint and feathers shooting backwards and forwards in their canoes, and staring across at the town where the gaunt gable ends of houses and charred walls marked the effect of the terrible fire which a few years before had completely destroyed the lower part.

As he stood gazing, his attention was drawn away by the swish of oars, and a large boat full of men passed immediately underneath where he stood.

It held the New Englanders who were being conveyed to the ship which was to take them home. There were the four seamen huddled together, and there in the sheets were Captain Ephraim Savage and Amos Green, conversing together and pointing to the shipping. The grizzled face of the old Puritan and the bold features of the woodsman were turned more than once in his direction, but no word of farewell and no kindly wave of the hand came back to the lonely exile. They were so full of their own future and their own happiness that they had not a thought to spare upon his misery. He could have borne anything from his enemies, but this sudden neglect from his friends came too heavily after his other troubles. He stooped his face to his arms and burst in an instant into a passion of sobs. Before he raised his eyes again the brig had hoisted her anchor, and was tacking under full canvas out of the Quebec basin.

29. *The Voice at the Port-hole*

THAT night old Theophile Catinat was buried from the ship's side, his sole mourners the two who bore his own blood in their veins. The next day De Catinat spent upon deck, amid the bustle and confusion of the unlading, endeavouring to cheer Adèle by light chatter which came from a heavy heart. He pointed out to her the places which he had known so well, the citadel where he had been quartered, the college of the

Jesuits, the cathedral of Bishop Laval, the magazine of the old company, dismantled by the great fire, and the house of Aubert de la Chesnaye, the only private one which had remained standing in the lower part. From where they lay they could see not only the places of interest, but something also of that motley population which made the town so different to all others save only its younger sister, Montreal. Passing and repassing along the steep path with the picket fence which connected the two quarters they saw the whole panorama of Canadian life moving before their eyes, the soldiers with their slouched hats, their plumes and their bandoleers, habitants from the river *côtes* in their rude peasant dresses, little changed from their forefathers of Brittany or Normandy, and young rufflers from France or from the seigneuries, who cocked their hats and swaggered in what they thought to be the true Versailles fashion. There, too, might be seen little knots of the men of the woods, *coureurs-de-bois* or *voyageurs*, with leathern hunting tunics, fringed leggings and fur cap with eagle feather, who came back once a year to the cities, leaving their Indian wives and children in some up-country wigwam. Redskins, too, were there, leather-faced Algonquin fishers and hunters, wild Mic-macs from the east, and savage Abenakis from the south, while everywhere were the dark habits of the Franciscans, and the black cassocks and broad hats of the Recollets, and Jesuits, the moving spirits of the whole.

Such were the folk who crowded the streets of the capital of this strange offshoot of France which had been planted along the line of the great river, a thousand leagues from the parent country. And it was a singular settlement, the most singular perhaps that has ever been made. For a long twelve hundred miles it extended, from Tadousac in the east, away to the trading stations upon the borders of the great lakes, limiting itself for the most part to narrow cultivated strips upon the margins of the river, banked in behind by wild forests and un-explored mountains which for ever tempted the peasant

from his hoe and his plough to the freer life of the paddle and the musket. Thin scattered clearings, alternating with little palisaded clumps of log-hewn houses, marked the line where civilisation was forcing itself in upon the huge continent, and barely holding its own against the rigour of a northern climate and the ferocity of merciless enemies. The whole white population of this mighty district, including soldiers, priests and woodmen, with all women and children, was very far short of twenty thousand souls, and yet so great was their energy, and such the advantage of the central government under which they lived, that they had left their trace upon the whole continent. When the prosperous English settlers were content to live upon their acres, and when no axe had rung upon the farther side of the Alleghanies, the French had pushed their daring pioneers, some in the black robe of the missionary, and some in the fringed tunic of the hunter, to the uttermost ends of the continent. They had mapped out the lakes and had bartered with the fierce Sioux on the great plains where the wooden wigwam gave place to the hide tee-pee. Marquette had followed the Illinois down to the Mississippi, and had traced the course of the great river until, first of all white men, he looked upon the turbid flood of the rushing Missouri. La Salle had ventured even farther, had passed the Ohio, and had made his way to the Mexican Gulf, raising the French arms where the city of New Orleans was afterwards to stand. Others had pushed on to the Rocky Mountains, and to the huge wilderness of the north-west, preaching, bartering, cheating, baptising, swayed by many motives and holding only in common a courage which never faltered and a fertility of resource which took them in safety past every danger. Frenchmen were to the north of the British settlements, Frenchmen were to the west of them, and Frenchmen were to the south of them, and if all the continent is not now French, the fault assuredly did not rest with that iron race of early Canadians.

All this De Catinat explained to Adèle during the autumn day, trying to draw her thoughts away from the troubles of the past, and from the long dreary voyage which lay before her. She, fresh from the staid life of the Parisian street and from the tame scenery of the Seine, gazed with amazement at the river, the woods and the mountains, and clutched her husband's arm in horror when a canoeful of wild skin-clad Algonquins, their faces striped with white and red paint, came flying past with the foam dashing from their paddles. Again the river turned from blue to pink, again the old citadel was bathed in the evening glow, and again the two exiles descended to their cabins with cheering words for each other and heavy thoughts in their own hearts.

De Catinat's bunk was next to a port-hole, and it was his custom to keep this open, as the caboose was close to him in which the cooking was done for the crew, and the air was hot and heavy. That night he found it impossible to sleep, and he lay tossing under his blanket, thinking over every possible means by which they might be able to get away from this cursed ship. But even if they got away, where could they go to then? All Canada was sealed to them. The woods to the south were full of ferocious Indians. The English settlements would, it was true, grant them freedom to use their own religion, but what would his wife and he do, without a friend, strangers among folk who spoke another tongue? Had Amos Green remained true to them, then, indeed, all would have been well. But he had deserted them. Of course there was no reason why he should not. He was no blood relation of theirs. He had already benefited them many times. His own people and the life that he loved were waiting for him at home. Why should he linger here for the sake of folk whom he had known but a few months? It was not to be expected, and yet De Catinat could not realise it, could not understand it.

But what was that? Above the gentle lapping of the river he had suddenly heard a sharp clear "Hist!"

Perhaps it was some passing boatman or Indian. Then it came again, that eager, urgent summons. He sat up and stared about him. It certainly must have come from the open port-hole. He looked out, but only to see the broad basin, with the loom of the shipping, and the distant twinkle from the lights on Point Levi. As his head dropped back upon the pillow something fell upon his chest with a little tap, and rolling off, rattled along the boards. He sprang up, caught a lantern from a hook and flashed it upon the floor. There was the missile which had struck him—a little golden brooch. As he lifted it up and looked closer at it, a thrill passed through him. It had been his own, and he had given it to Amos Green upon the second day that he had met him, when they were starting together for Versailles.

This was a signal, then, and Amos Green had not deserted them after all. He dressed himself, all in a tremble with excitement, and went upon deck. It was pitch dark, and he could see no one, but the sound of regular footfalls somewhere in the fore part of the ship showed that the sentinels were still there. The guardsman walked over to the side and peered down into the darkness. He could see the loom of a boat.

" Who is there ? " he whispered.

" Is that you, De Catinat ? "

" Yes."

" We have come for you."

" God bless you, Amos."

" Is your wife there ? "

" No, but I can rouse her."

" Good ! But first catch this cord. Now pull up the ladder ! "

De Catinat gripped the line which was thrown to him, and on drawing it up found that it was attached to a rope ladder furnished at the top with two steel hooks to catch on to the bulwarks. He placed them in position, and then made his way very softly to the cabin amidships in the ladies' quarters which had been allotted to his wife.

She was the only woman aboard the ship now, so that he was able to tap at her door in safety, and to explain in a few words the need for haste and for secrecy. In ten minutes Adèle had dressed, and with her valuables in a little bundle, had slipped out from her cabin. Together they made their way upon deck once more and crept aft under the shadow of the bulwarks. They were almost there when De Catinat stopped suddenly and ground out an oath through his clenched teeth. Between them and the rope ladder there was standing in a dim patch of murky light the grim figure of a Franciscan friar. He was peering through the darkness, his heavy cowl shadowing his face, and he advanced slowly as if he had caught a glimpse of them. A lantern hung from the mizzen shrouds above him. He unfastened it and held it up to cast its light upon them.

But De Catinat was not a man with whom it was safe to trifle. His life had been one of quick resolve and prompt action. Was this vindictive friar at the last moment to stand between him and freedom ? It was a dangerous position to take. The guardsman pulled Adèle into the shadow of the mast, and then, as the monk advanced, he sprang out upon him and seized him by the gown. As he did so the other's cowl was pushed back, and instead of the harsh features of the ecclesiastic, De Catinat saw with amazement in the glimmer of the lantern the shrewd grey eyes and strong stern face of Ephraim Savage. At the same instant another figure appeared over the side, and the warm-hearted Frenchman threw himself into the arms of Amos Green.

" It's all right," said the young hunter, disengaging himself with some embarrassment from the other's embrace.

" We've got him in the boat with a buckskin glove jammed into his gullet ! "

" Who then ? "

" The man whose cloak Captain Ephraim there has put round him. He came on us when you were away rousing

your lady, but we got him to be quiet between us. Is the lady there ? "

" Here she is."

" As quick as you can, then, for someone may come along."

Adèle was helped over the side, and seated in the stern of a birch bark canoe. The three men unhooked the ladder, and swung themselves down by a rope, while two Indians, who held the paddles, pushed silently off from the ship's side, and shot swiftly up the stream. A minute later a dim loom behind them and the glimmer of two yellow lights was all that they could see of the *St. Christophe*.

" Take a paddle, Amos, and I'll take one," said Captain Savage, stripping off his monk's gown. " I felt safer in this on the deck of yon ship, but it don't help in a boat. I believe we might have fastened the hatches and taken her, brass guns and all, had we been so minded."

" And been hanged as pirates at the yard-arm next morning," said Amos. " I think we have done better to take the honey and leave the tree. I hope, madame, that all is well with you."

" Nay, I can hardly understand what has happened, or where we are."

" Nor can I, Amos."

" Did you not expect us to come back for you, then ? "

" I did not know what to expect."

" Well, now, but surely you could not think that we would leave you without a word."

" I confess that I was cut to the heart by it."

" I feared that you were when I looked at you with the tail of my eye, and saw you staring so blackly over the bulwarks at us. But if we had been seen talking or planning they would have been upon our trail at once. As it was they had not a thought of suspicion, save only this fellow whom we have in the bottom of the boat here."

" And what did you do ? "

" We left the brig last night, got ashore on the Beaupré

side, arranged for this canoe, and lay dark all day. Then to-night we got alongside and I roused you easily, for I knew where you slept. The friar nearly spoiled all when you were below, but we gagged him and passed him over the side. Ephraim popped on his gown so that he might go forward to help you without danger, for we were scared at the delay."

" Ah ! it is glorious to be free once more. What do I not owe you, Amos ? "

" Well, you looked after me when I was in your country, and I am going to look after you now."

" And where are we going ? "

" Ah ! there you have me. It is this way or none, for we can't get down to the sea. We must make our way over land as best we can, and we must leave a good stretch between Quebec citadel and us before the day breaks, for from what I hear they would rather have a Huguenot prisoner than an Iroquois sagamore. By the eternal, I cannot see why they should make such a fuss over how a man chooses to save his own soul, though here is old Ephraim just as fierce upon the other side, so all the folly is not one way."

" What are you saying about me ? " asked the seaman, pricking up his ears at the mention of his own name.

" Only that you are a good stiff old Protestant."

" Yes, thank God. My motto is freedom to conscience, d'ye see, except just for Quakers, and Papists, and—and I wouldn't stand Anne Hutchinsons and women testifying and suchlike foolishness."

Amos Green laughed. " The Almighty seems to pass it over, so why should you take it to heart ? " said he.

" Ah, you're young and callow yet. You'll live to know better. Why, I shall hear you saying a good word soon, even for such unclean spawn as this," prodding the prostate friar with the handle of his paddle.

" I daresay he's a good man, accordin' to his lights."

" And I daresay a shark is a good fish accordin' to its lights. No, lad, you won't mix up light and dark for me

in that sort of fashion. You may talk until you unship your jaw, d'ye see, but you will never talk a foul wind into a fair one. Pass over the pouch and the tinder-box, and maybe our friend here will take a turn at my paddle."

All night they toiled up the great river, straining every nerve to place themselves beyond the reach of pursuit. By keeping well into the southern bank, and so avoiding the force of the current, they sped swiftly along, for both Amos and De Catinat were practised hands with the paddle, and the two Indians worked as though they were wire and whipcord instead of flesh and blood. An utter silence reigned over all the broad stream, broken only by the lap-lap of the water against their curving bow, the whirring of the night hawk above them, and the sharp high barking of foxes away in the woods. When at last morning broke, and the black shaded imperceptibly into grey, they were far out of sight of the citadel and of all trace of man's handiwork. Virgin woods in their wonderful many-coloured autumn dress flowed right down to the river edge on either side and in the centre was a little island with a rim of yellow sand and an out-flame of scarlet tupelo and sumach in one bright tangle of colour in the centre.

" I've passed here before," said De Catinat. " I remember marking that great maple with the blaze on its trunk, when last I went with the governor to Montreal. That was in Frontenac's day, when the king was first and the bishop second."

The redskins, who had sat like terra-cotta figures without a trace of expression upon their set hard faces, pricked up their ears at the sound of that name.

" My brother has spoken of the great Onontio," said one of them, glancing round. " We have listened to the whistling of evil birds who tell us that he will never come back to his children across the seas."

" He is with the great white father," answered De Catinat. " I have myself seen him in his council, and

he will assuredly come across the great water if his people have need of him."

The Indian shook his shaven head.

" The rutting month is past, my brother," said he, speaking in broken French, " but ere the month of the bird laying has come there will be no white man upon this river save only behind stone walls."

" What, then ? We have heard little ! Have the Iroquois broken out so fiercely ? "

" My brother, they said that they would eat up the Hurons, and where are the Hurons now ? They turned their faces upon the Eries, and where are the Eries now ? They went westward against the Illinois, and who can find an Illinois village ? They raised the hatchet against the Andastes, and their name is blotted from the earth. And now they have danced a dance and sung a song which will bring little good to my white brothers."

" Where are they, then ? "

The Indian waved his hand along the whole southern and western horizon.

" Where are they not ? The woods are rustling with them. They are like a fire among dry grass, so swift and so terrible ! "

" On my life," said De Catinat, " if these devils are indeed unchained, they will need old Frontenac back if they are not to be swept into the river."

" Aye," said Amos, " I saw him once when I was brought before him with the others for trading on what he called French ground. His mouth set like a skunk trap and he looked at us as if he would have liked our scalps for his leggings. But I could see that he was a chief and a brave man."

" He was an enemy of the Church, and the right hand of the foul fiend in this country," said a voice from the bottom of the canoe.

It was the friar who had succeeded in getting rid of the buckskin glove and belt with which the two Americans had gagged him. He was lying huddled

up now, glaring savagely at the party with his fiery dark
eyes.

" His jaw-tackle has come adrift," said the seaman.
" Let me brace it up again."

" Nay, why should we take him farther ? " asked Amos.
" He is but weight for us to carry, and I cannot see that
we profit by his company. Let us put him out."

"Aye, sink or swim," cried old Ephraim with
enthusiasm.

" Nay, upon the bank."

" And have him maybe in front of us warning the black
jackets."

" On that island, then."

" Very good. He can hail the first of his folk who
pass."

They shot over to the island and landed the friar, who
said nothing, but cursed them with his eye. They left
with him a small supply of biscuit and of flour to last him
until he should be picked up. Then, having passed a
bend in the river, they ran their canoe ashore in a little
cove where the whortleberry and cranberry bushes grew
right down to the water's edge, and the sward was bright
with the white euphorbia, the blue gentian, and the purple
balm. There they laid out their small stock of provisions,
and ate a hearty breakfast while discussing what their
plans should be for the future.

30. *Inland Waters*

THEY were not badly provided for their journey.
The captain of the Gloucester brig in which the
Americans had started from Quebec knew Ephraim
Savage well, as who did not upon the New England
coast ? He had accepted his bill therefore at three
months' date, at as high a rate of interest as he could
screw out of him, and he had let him have in return three
excellent guns, a good supply of ammunition, and enough

money to provide for all his wants. In this way he had hired the canoe and the Indians, and had fitted her with meat and biscuit to last them for ten days at the least.

" It's like the breath of life to me to feel the heft of a gun and to smell the trees round me." said Amos. " Why, it cannot be more than a hundred leagues from here to Albany or Schenectady, right through the forest."

" Aye, lad, but how is the gal to walk a hundred leagues through a forest. No, no, let us keep water under our keel, and lean on the Lord."

" Then there is only one way for it. We must make the Richelieu River, and keep right along to Lake Champlain and Lake St. Sacrament. There we should be close by the headwaters of the Hudson."

" It is a dangerous road," said De Catinat, who understood the conversation of his companions, even when he was unable to join in it. " We should need to skirt the country of the Mohawks."

" It's the only way, I guess. It's that or nothing."

" And I have a friend upon the Richelieu River who, I am sure, would help us on our way," said De Catinat with a smile. " Adèle, you have heard me talk of Charles de la Noue, seigneur de Sainte Marie ? "

" He whom you used to call the Canadian duke, Amory ? "

" Precisely. His seigneury lies on the Richelieu, a little south of Fort St. Louis, and I am sure that he would speed us upon our way."

" Good ! " cried Amos. " If we have a friend there we shall do well. That clenches it, then, and we shall hold fast by the river. Let's get to our paddles, then, for that friar will make mischief for us if he can."

And so for a long week the little party toiled up the great water-way, keeping ever to the southern bank where there were fewer clearings. On both sides of the stream the woods were thick, but every here and there they would curve away, and a narrow strip of cultivated land would

skirt the bank with the yellow stubble to mark where the wheat had grown. Adèle looked with interest at the wooden houses with their jutting stories and quaint gable-ends, at the solid, stone-built manor-houses of the seigneurs, and at the mills in every hamlet, which served the double purpose of grinding flour, and of a loopholed place of retreat in case of attack. Horrible experience had taught the Canadians what the English settlers had yet to learn, that in a land of savages it is a folly to place isolated farm-houses in the centre of their own fields. The clearings then radiated out from the villages, and every cottage was built with an eye to the military necessities of the whole, so that the defence might make a stand at all points, and might finally centre upon the stone manor-house and the mill. Now at every bluff and hill near the villages might be seen the gleam of the muskets of the watchers, for it was known that the scalping parties of the Five Nations were out, and none could tell where the blow would fall, save that it must come where they were least prepared to meet it.

Indeed, at every step in this country, whether the traveller were on the St. Lawrence, or west upon the lakes, or down upon the banks of the Mississippi, or south in the country of the Cherokees and of the Creeks, he would still find the inhabitants in the same state of dreadful expectancy, and from the same cause. The Iroquois, as they were named by the French, or the Five Nations as they called themselves, hung like a cloud over the whole great continent. Their confederation was a natural one, for they were of the same stock and spoke the same language, and all attempts to separate them had been in vain. Mohawks, Cayugas, Onondagas, Oneidas and Senecas were each proud of their own totems and their own chiefs, but in war they were Iroquois, and the enemy of one was the enemy of all. Their numbers were small, for they were never able to put two thousand warriors in the field, and their country was limited, for their villages were scattered over the

tract which lies between Lake Champlain and Lake Ontario. But they were united, they were cunning, they were desperately brave and they were fiercely aggressive and energetic. Holding a central position they struck out upon each side in turn, never content with simply defeating an adversary but absolutely annihilating and destroying him, while holding all the others in check by their diplomacy. War was their business, and cruelty their amusement. One by one they had turned their arms against the various nations, until, for a space of over a thousand square miles, none existed save by sufferance. They had swept away Hurons and Huron missions in one fearful massacre. They had destroyed the tribes of the north-west, until even the distant Sacs and Foxes trembled at their name. They had scoured the whole country to westward until their scalping parties had come into touch with their kinsmen the Sioux, who were lords of the great plains, even as they were of the great forests. The New England Indians in the east, and the Shawnees and Delawares farther south, paid tribute to them, and the terror of their arms had extended over the borders of Maryland and Virginia. Never, perhaps, in the world's history has so small a body of men dominated so large a district and for so long a time.

For half a century these tribes had nursed a grudge towards the French since Champlain and some of his followers had taken part with their enemies against them. During all these years they had brooded in their forest villages, flashing out now and again in some border outrage, but waiting for the most part until their chance should come. And now it seemed to them that it had come. They had destroyed all the tribes who might have allied themselves with the white men. They had isolated them. They had supplied themselves with good guns and plenty of ammunition from the Dutch and English of New York. The long thin line of French settlements lay naked before them. They were gathered in the woods, like hounds in leash, waiting for the orders of

their chiefs, which should precipitate them with torch and with tomahawk upon the belt of villages.

Such was the situation as the little party of refugees paddled along the bank of the river, seeking the only path which could lead them to peace and to freedom. Yet it was, as they well knew, a dangerous road to follow. All down the Richelieu River were the outposts and block-houses of the French, for when the feudal system was grafted upon Canada the various seigneurs or native *noblesse* were assigned their estates in the positions which would be of most benefit to the settlement. Each seigneur with his tenants under him, trained as they were in the use of arms, formed a military force exactly as they had done in the Middle Ages, the farmer holding his fief upon condition that he mustered when called upon to do so. Hence the old officers of the regiment of Carignan and the more hardy of the settlers had been placed along the line of the Richelieu, which runs at right angles to the St. Lawrence towards the Mohawk country. The block-houses themselves might hold their own, but to the little party who had to travel down from one to the other the situation was full of deadly peril. It was true that the Iroquois were not at war with the English, but they would discriminate little when on the warpath, and the Americans, even had they wished to do so, could not separate their fate from that of their two French companions.

As they ascended the St. Lawrence they met many canoes coming down. Sometimes it was an officer or an official on his way to the capital from Three Rivers or Montreal, sometimes it was a load of skins, with Indians or *coureurs-de-bois* conveying them down to be shipped to Europe, and sometimes it was a small canoe which bore a sunburned grizzly-haired man, with rusty weather-stained black cassock, who zigzagged from bank to bank, stopping at every Indian hut upon his way. If aught were amiss with the Church in Canada the fault lay not with men like these village priests, who toiled and worked

and spent their very lives in bearing comfort and hope, and a little touch of refinement too, through all those wilds. More than once these wayfarers wished to have speech with the fugitives, but they pushed onwards, disregarding their signs and hails. From below nothing overtook them, for they paddled from early morning until late at night, drawing up the canoe when they halted, and building a fire of dry wood, for already the nip of the coming winter was in the air.

It was not only the people and their dwellings which were stretched out before the wondering eyes of the French girl as she sat day after day in the stern of the canoe. Her husband and Amos Green taught her also to take notice of the sights of the woodlands, and as they skirted the bank, they pointed out a thousand things which her own senses would never have discerned. Sometimes it was the furry face of a raccoon peeping out from some tree-cleft, or an otter swimming under the overhanging brushwood with the gleam of a white fish in its mouth. Or, perhaps, it was the wild cat crouching along a branch with its wicked yellow eyes fixed upon the squirrels which played at the farther end, or else with a scuttle and rush the Canadian porcupine would thrust its way among the yellow blossoms of the resin weed and the tangle of the whortleberry bushes. She learned, too, to recognise the pert sharp cry of the tiny chick-a-dee, the call of the bluebird, and the flash of its wings amid the foliage, the sweet chirpy note of the black and white bobolink, and the long-drawn mewing of the catbird. On the breast of the broad blue river, with Nature's sweet concert ever sounding from the bank, and with every colour that artist could devise spread out before her eyes on the foliage of the dying woods, the smile came back to her lips and her cheeks took a glow of health which France had never been able to give. De Catinat saw the change in her, but her presence weighed him down with fear, for he knew that while Nature had made these woods a heaven, man had changed it into a hell, and that

a nameless horror lurked behind all the beauty of the fading leaves and of the woodland flowers. Often as he lay at night beside the smouldering fire upon his couch of spruce boughs, and looked at the little figure muffled in the blanket and slumbering peacefully by his side, he felt that he had no right to expose her to such peril, and that in the morning they should turn the canoe eastward again and take what fate might bring them at Quebec. But ever with the daybreak there came the thought of the humiliation, the dreary homeward voyage, the separation which would await them in galley and dungeon, to turn him from his purpose.

On the seventh day they rested at a point but a few miles from the mouth of the Richelieu River, where a large blockhouse, Fort Richelieu, had been built by M. de Saurel. Once past this they had no great distance to go to reach the seigneury of De Catinat's friend of the *noblesse* who would help them upon their way. They had spent the night upon a little island in midstream, and at early dawn they were about to thrust the canoe out again from the sand-lined cove in which she lay, when Ephraim Savage growled in his throat and pointed out across the water.

A large canoe was coming up the river, flying along as quick as a dozen arms could drive it. In the stern sat a dark figure which bent forward with every swing of the paddles, as though consumed by eagerness to push on-wards. Even at that distance there was no mistaking it. It was the fanatical monk whom they had left behind them.

Concealed among the brushwood they watched their pursuers fly past and vanish round a curve in the stream. Then they looked at one another in perplexity.

" We'd have done better either to put him overboard or to take him as ballast," said Ephraim. " He's hull down in front of us now, and drawing full."

" Well, we can't take the back track anyhow," remarked Amos.

" And yet how can we go on ? " said De Catinat despondently. " This vindictive devil will give word at the fort and at every other point along the river. He has been back to Quebec. It is one of the governor's own canoes, and goes three paces to our two."

" Let me cipher it out." Amos Green sat on a fallen maple with his head sunk upon his hands. " Well," said he presently, " if it's no good going on, and no good going back, there's only one way, and that is to go to one side. That's so, Ephraim, is it not ? "

" Aye, aye, lad, if you can't run you must tack, but it seems shoal water on either bow."

" We can't go to the north, so it follows that we must go to the south."

" Leave the canoe ? "

" It's our only chance. We can cut through the woods and come out near this friendly house on the Richelieu. The friar will lose our trail then, and we'll have no more trouble with him, if he stays on the St. Lawrence."

" There's nothing else for it," said Captain Ephraim ruefully. " It's not my way to go by land if I can get by water, and I have not been a fathom deep in a wood since King Philip came down on the province, so you must lay the course and keep her straight, Amos."

" It is not far and it will not take us long. Let us get over to the southern bank and we shall make a start. If madame tires, De Catinat, we shall take turns to carry her."

" Ah, monsieur, you cannot think what a good walker I am. In this splendid air one might go on for ever."

" We will cross, then."

In a very few minutes they were at the other side and had landed at the edge of the forest. There the guns and ammunition were allotted to each man, and his share of the provisions and of the scanty baggage. Then having paid the Indians, and having instructed them to say nothing of their movements, they turned their backs upon the river and plunged into the silent woods.

31. *The Hairless Man*

ALL day they pushed on through the woodlands, walking in single file, Amos Green first, then the seaman, then the lady, and De Catinat bringing up the rear. The young woodsman advanced cautiously, seeing and hearing much that was lost to his companions, stopping continually and examining the signs of leaf and moss and twig. Their route lay for the most part through open glades amid a huge pine forest, with a green sward beneath their feet, made beautiful by the white euphorbia, the golden rod and the purple aster. Sometimes, however, the great trunks closed in upon them, and they had to grope their way in a dim twilight, or push a path through the tangled brushwood of green sassafras or scarlet sumach. And then again the woods would shred suddenly away in front of them, and they would skirt marshes, overgrown with wild rice and dotted with little dark clumps of alder bushes, or make their way past silent woodland lakes, all streaked and barred with the tree shadows which threw their crimsons and clarets and bronzes upon the fringe of the deep blue sheet of water. There were streams, too, some clear and rippling, where the trout flashed and the king-fisher gleamed, others dark and poisonous from the tamarack swamps, where the wanderers had to wade over their knees and carry Adèle in their arms. So all day they journeyed 'mid the great forests, with never a hint or token of their fellow-man.

But if man were absent, there was at least no want of life. It buzzed and chirped and chattered all round them from marsh and stream and brushwood. Sometimes it was the dun coat of a deer which glanced between the distant trunks, sometimes the badger which scuttled for its hole at their approach. Once the long in-toed track of a bear lay marked in the soft earth before them, and once Amos picked a great horn from amid the bushes which some moose had shed the month before. Little

763

red squirrels danced and clattered above their heads and every oak was a choir with a hundred tiny voices piping from the shadow of its foliage. As they passed the lakes the heavy grey stork flapped up in front of them, and they saw the wild duck whirring off in a long V against the blue sky, or heard the quavering cry of the loon from amid the reeds.

That night they slept in the woods, Amos Green lighting a dry wood fire in a thick copse where at a dozen paces it was invisible. A few drops of rain had fallen, so with the quick skill of the practised woodsman he made two little sheds of elm and basswood bark, one to shelter the two refugees, and the other for Ephraim and himself. He had shot a wild goose, and this, with the remains of their biscuit, served them both for supper and for breakfast. Next day at noon they passed a little clearing, in the centre of which were the charred embers of a fire. Amos spent half an hour in reading all that sticks and ground could tell him. Then, as they resumed their way, he explained to his companions that the fire had been lit three weeks before, that a white man and two Indians had camped there, that they had been journeying from west to east, and that one of the Indians had been a squaw. No other traces of their fellow-mortals did they come across, until late in the afternoon Amos halted suddenly in the heart of a thick grove, and raised his hand to his ear.

" Listen ! " he cried.

" I hear nothing," said Ephraim.

" Nor I," added De Catinat.

" Ah, but I do ! " cried Adèle gleefully. " It is a bell— and at the very time of day when bells all sound in Paris ! "

" You are right, madame. It is what they call the Angelus bell."

" Ah, yes, I hear it now ! " cried De Catinat. " It was drowned by the chirping of the birds. But whence comes a bell in the heart of a Canadian forest ? "

"We are near the settlements on the Richelieu. It must be the bell of the chapel at the fort."

"Fort St. Louis! Ah, then, we are no great way from my friend's seigneury."

"Then we may sleep there to-night, if you think that he is indeed to be trusted."

"Yes. He is a strange man, with ways of his own, but I would trust him with my life."

"Very good. We shall keep to the south of the fort and make for his house. But something is putting up the birds over yonder. Ah, I hear the sound of steps! Crouch down here among the sumach, until we see who it is who walks so boldly through the woods."

They stooped all four among the brushwood, peeping out between the tree trunks at a little glade towards which Amos was looking. For a long time the sound which the quick ears of the woodsman had detected was inaudible to the others, but at last they too heard the sharp snapping of twigs as someone forced his passage through the undergrowth. A moment later a man pushed his way into the open, whose appearance was so strange and so ill-suited to the spot, that even Amos gazed upon him with amazement.

He was a very small man, so dark and weather-stained that he might have passed for an Indian were it not that he walked and was clad as no Indian had ever been. He wore a broad-brimmed hat, frayed at the edges, and so discoloured that it was hard to say what its original tint had been. His dress was of skins rudely cut and dangling loosely from his body, and he wore the high boots of a dragoon, as tattered and stained as the rest of his raiment. On his back he bore a huge bundle of canvas with two long sticks projecting from it, and under each arm he carried what appeared to be a large square painting.

"He's no Injun," whispered Amos, "and he's no woodsman either. Blessed if I ever saw the match of him!"

" He's neither *voyageur*, nor soldier, nor *coureur-de-bois*," said De Catinat.

" 'Pears to me to have a jurymast rigged upon his back, and fore and main staysails set under each of his arms," said Captain Ephraim.

" Well, he seems to have no consorts, so we may hail him without fear."

They rose from their ambush, and as they did so the stranger caught sight of them. Instead of showing the uneasiness which any man might be expected to feel at suddenly finding himself in the presence of strangers in such a country he promptly altered his course and came towards them. As he crossed the glade, however, the sounds of the distant bell fell upon his ears, and he instantly whipped off his hat and sunk his head in prayer. A cry of horror rose, not only from Adèle but from every one of the party, at the sight which met their eyes.

The top of the man's head was gone. Not a vestige of hair or of white skin remained, but in place of it was a dreadful crinkled discoloured surface with a sharp red line running across his brow and round over his ears.

" By the eternal ! " cried Amos, " the man has lost his scalp ! "

" My God ! " said De Catinat. " Look at his hands ! "

He had raised them in prayer. Two or three little stumps projecting upwards showed where the fingers had been.

" I've seen some queer figureheads in my life, but never one like that," said Captain Ephraim.

It was indeed a most extraordinary face which con-fronted them as they advanced. It was that of a man who might have been of any age and of any nation, for the features were so distorted that nothing could be learned from them. One eyelid was drooping with a puckering and flatness which showed that the ball was gone. The other, however, shot as bright and merry and kindly a glance as ever came from a chosen favourite of fortune. His face was flecked over with peculiar brown spots

which had a most hideous appearance, and his nose had been burst and shattered by some terrific blow. And yet, in spite of this dreadful appearance, there was something so noble in the carriage of the man, in the pose of his head and in the expression which still hung, like the scent from a crushed flower, round his distorted features, that even the blunt Puritan seaman was awed by it.

"Good evening, my children," said the stranger, picking up his pictures again and advancing towards them. "I presume that you are from the fort, though I may be permitted to observe that the woods are not very safe for ladies at present."

"We are going to the manor-house of Charles de la Noue at Sainte Marie," said De Catinat, "and we hope soon to be in a place of safety. But I grieve, sir, to see how terribly you have been mishandled."

"Ah, you have observed my little injuries, then! They know no better, poor souls. They are but mischievous children—merry-hearted but mischievous. Tut, tut, it is laughable indeed that a man's vile body should ever clog his spirit, and yet here am I full of the will to push forward, and yet I must even seat myself on this log and rest myself, for the rogues have blown the calves of my legs off."

"My God! Blown them off! The devils!"

"Ah, but they are not to be blamed. No, no, it would be uncharitable to blame them. They are ignorant, poor folk, and the prince of darkness is behind them to urge them on. They sank little charges of powder into my legs and then they exploded them, which makes me a slower walker than ever, though I was never very brisk. 'The Snail' was what I was called at school in Tours, yes, and afterwards at the seminary I was always 'the Snail.'"

"Who are you, then, sir, and who is it who has used you so shamefully?" asked De Catinat.

"Oh, I am a very humble person. I am Ignatius Morat, of the Society of Jesus, and as to the people who

have used me a little roughly, why, if you are sent upon the Iroquois mission, of course you know what to expect. I have nothing at all to complain of. Why, they have used me very much better than they did Father Jogues, Father Brebœuf and a good many others whom I could mention. There were times, it is true, when I was quite hopeful of martyrdom, especially when they thought my tonsure was too small, which was their merry way of putting it. But I suppose I was not worthy of it ; indeed I know that I was not, so it only ended in just a little roughness."

" Where are you going, then ? " asked Amos, who had listened in amazement to the man's words.

" I am going to Quebec. You see I am such a useless person that, until I have seen the bishop, I can really do no good at all."

" You mean that you will resign your mission into the bishop's hands ? " said De Catinat.

" Oh, no. That would be quite the sort of thing which I should do if I were left to myself, for it is incredible how cowardly I am. You would not think it possible that a priest of God could be so frightened as I am sometimes. The mere sight of a fire makes me shrink all into myself ever since I went through the ordeal of the lighted pine splinters, which have left all these ugly stains upon my face. But then, of course, there is the Order to be thought of, and members of the Order do not leave their posts for trifling causes. But it is against the rules of Holy Church that a maimed man should perform the rites, and so, until I have seen the bishop and had his dispensation, I shall be even more useless than ever."

" And what will you do then ? "

" Oh, then, of course, I will go back to my flock."

" To the Iroquois ? "

" That is where I am stationed."

" Amos," said De Catinat, " I have spent my life among brave men, but I think that this is the bravest man that I have ever met ! "

" On my word," said Amos, " I have seen some good men, too, but never one that I thought was better than this. You are weary, father. Have some of our cold goose, and there is still a drop of cognac in my flask."

" Tut, tut, my son, if I take anything but the very simplest living it makes me so lazy that I become a snail indeed."

" But you have no gun and no food. How do you live ? "

" Oh, the good God has placed plenty of food in these forests for a traveller who dare not eat very much. I have had wild plums, and wild grapes, and nuts and cran-berries, and a nice little dish of *tripe-de-mére* from the rocks."

The woodsman made a wry face at the mention of this delicacy.

" I had as soon eat a pot of glue," said he. " But what is this which you carry on your back ? "

" It is my church. Ah, I have everything here, tent, altar, surplice, everything. I cannot venture to celebrate service myself without the dispensation, but surely this venerable man is himself in orders and will solemnise the most blessed function."

Amos with a sly twinkle of the eyes translated the pro-posal to Ephraim, who stood with his huge red hands clenched, mumbling about the saltless pottage of papacy. De Catinat replied briefly, however, that they were all of the laity, and that if they were to reach their destination before nightfall, it was necessary that they should push on.

" You are right, my son," said the little Jesuit. " These poor people have already left their villages and in a few days the woods will be full of them, though I do not think that any have crossed the Richelieu yet. There is one thing, however, which I would have you do for me."

" And what is that ? "

" It is but to remember that I have left with Father Lamberville at Onondaga the dictionary which I have made of the Iroquois and French languages. There also

769

is my account of the copper mines of the Great Lakes which I visited two years ago, and also an orrery which I have made to show the northern heavens with the stars of each month as they are seen from this meridian. If aught were to go amiss with Father Lamberville or with me—and we do not live very long on the Iroquois mission —it would be well that someone else should profit from my work."

" I will tell my friend to-night. But what are these great pictures, father, and why do you bear them through the wood ? " He turned them over as he spoke, and the whole party gathered round them, staring in amazement.

They were very rough daubs, crudely coloured and gaudy. In the first, a red man was reposing serenely upon what appeared to be a range of mountains, with a musical instrument in his hand, a crown upon his head, and a smile upon his face. In the second, a similar man was screaming at the pitch of his lungs, while half-a-dozen black creatures were battering him with poles and prodding him with lances.

" It is a damned soul and a saved soul," said Father Ignatius Morat, looking at his pictures with some satisfaction. " These are clouds upon which the blessed spirit reclines, basking in all the joys of paradise. It is well done, this picture, but it has no good effect, because there are no beaver in it and they have not painted in a tobacco-pipe. You see they have little reason, these poor folk, and so we have to teach them as best we can through their eyes and their foolish senses. This other is better. It has converted several squaws and more than one Indian. I shall not bring back the saved soul when I come in the spring, but I shall bring five damned souls, which will be one for each nation. We must fight Satan with such weapons as we can get, you see. And now, my children, if you must go, let me first call down a blessing upon you ! "

And then occurred a strange thing, for the beauty of this man's soul shone through all the wretched clouds of

sect, and, as he raised his hand to bless them, down went those Protestant knees to earth, and even old Ephraim found himself with a softened heart and a bent head listening to the half-understood words of this crippled, half-blinded little stranger.

" Farewell, then," said he, when they had risen. " May the sunshine of Sainte Eulalie be upon you, and may Sainte Anne of Beaupré shield you at the moment of your danger."

And so they left him, a grotesque and yet heroic figure staggering along through the woods with his tent, his pictures and his mutilation. If the Church of Rome should ever be wrecked it may come from her weakness in high places, where all Churches are at their weakest, or it may be because with what is very narrow she tries to explain that which is very broad, but assuredly it will never be through the fault of her rank and file, for never upon earth have men and women spent themselves more lavishly and more splendidly than in her service.

32. *The Lord of Sainte Marie*

LEAVING Fort St. Louis, whence the bells had sounded, upon their right, they pushed onwards as swiftly as they could, for the sun was so low in the heavens that the bushes in the clearings threw shadows like trees. Then suddenly as they peered in front of them between the trunks, the green of the sward turned to the blue of the water, and they saw a broad river running swiftly before them. In France it would have seemed a mighty stream, but, coming fresh from the vastness of the St. Lawrence, their eyes were used to great sheets of water. But Amos and De Catinat had both been upon the bosom of the Richelieu before, and their hearts bounded as they looked upon it, for they knew that this was the straight path which led them, the one to home, and the other to peace and freedom. A few

days' journeying down there, a few more along the lovely island-studded lakes of Champlain and Saint Sacrament, under the shadow of the tree-clad Adirondacks, and they would be at the headquarters of the Hudson, and their toils and their dangers be but a thing of gossip for the winter evenings.

Across the river was the terrible Iroquois country, and at two points they could see the smoke of fires curling up into the evening air. They had the Jesuit's word for it that none of the war-parties had crossed yet, so they followed the track which led down the eastern bank. As they pushed onwards, however, a stern military challenge suddenly brought them to a stand, and they saw the gleam of two musket barrels which covered them from a thicket overlooking the path.

" We are friends," cried De Catinat.

" Whence come you, then ? " asked an invisible sentinel.

" From Quebec."

" And whither are you going ? "

" To visit Monsieur Charles de la Noue, seigneur of Sainte Marie."

" Very good. It is quite safe, Du Lhut. They have a lady with them, too. I greet you, madame, in the name of my father."

Two men had emerged from the bushes, one of whom might have passed as a full-blooded Indian, had it not been for these courteous words which he uttered in excellent French. He was a tall, slight young man, very dark, with piercing black eyes, and a grim square relentless mouth which could only have come with Indian descent. His coarse flowing hair was gathered up into a scalp-lock, and the eagle feather which he wore in it was his only head-gear. A rude suit of fringed hide with cariboo-skin mocassins might have been the fellow to the one which Amos Green was wearing, but the gleam of a gold chain from his belt, the sparkle of a costly ring upon his finger, and the delicate richly-inlaid musket which he

carried, all gave a touch of grace to his equipment. A broad band of yellow ochre across his forehead and a tomahawk at his belt added to the strange inconsistency of his appearance.

The other was undoubtedly a pure Frenchman, elderly, dark and wiry, with a bristling black beard and a fierce eager face. He, too, was clad in hunter's dress, but he wore a gaudy striped sash round his waist into which a brace of long pistols had been thrust. His buckskin tunic had been ornamented over the front with dyed porcupine quills and Indian bead-work, while his leggings were scarlet with a fringe of raccoon tails hanging down from them. Leaning upon his long brown gun he stood watching the party, while his companion advanced towards them.

" You will excuse our precautions," said he. " We never know what device these rascals may adopt to entrap us. I fear, madame, that you have had a long and very tiring journey."

Poor Adèle, who had been famed for neatness even among housekeepers of the Rue St. Martin, hardly dared to look down at her own stained and tattered dress. Fatigue and danger she had endured with a smiling face, but her patience almost gave way at the thought of facing strangers in this attire.

" My mother will be very glad to welcome you, and to see to every want," said he quickly, as though he had read her thoughts. " But you, sir, I have surely seen you before."

" And I you," cried the guardsman. " My name is Amory de Catinat, once of the regiment of Picardy. Surely you are Achille de la Noue de Sainte Marie, whom I remember when you came with your father to the government *levées* at Quebec."

" Yes, it is I," the young man answered, holding out his hand and smiling in a somewhat constrained fashion. " I do not wonder that you should hesitate, for when you saw me last I was in a very different dress to this."

De Catinat did indeed remember him as one of the band of the young *noblesse* who used to come up to the capital once a year, where they inquired about the latest modes, chatted over the year-old gossip of Versailles, and for a few weeks at least lived a life which was in keeping with the traditions of their order. Very different was he now, with scalp-lock and war-paint, under the shadow of the great oaks, his musket in his hand and his tomahawk at his belt.

" We have one life for the forest and one for the cities," said he, " though indeed my good father will not have it so, and carries Versailles with him wherever he goes. You know him of old, monsieur, and I need not explain my words. But it is time for our relief, and so we may guide you home."

Two men in the rude dress of Canadian *censitaires* or farmers, but carrying their muskets in a fashion which told De Catinat's trained senses that they were disciplined soldiers, had suddenly appeared upon the scene. Young De la Noue gave them a few curt injunctions, and then accompanied the refugees along the path.

" You may not know my friend here," said he, pointing to the other sentinel, " but I am quite sure that his name is not unfamiliar to you. This is Greysolon du Lhut."

Both Amos and De Catinat looked with the deepest curiosity and interest at the famous leader of *coureurs-de-bois*, a man whose whole life had been spent in pushing westward, ever westward, saying little, writing nothing, but always the first wherever there was danger to meet or difficulty to overcome. It was not religion and it was not hope to gain which led him away into those western wildernesses, but pure love of nature and of adventure, with so little ambition that he had never cared to describe his own travels, and none knew where he had been or where he had stopped. For years he would vanish from the settlements away into the vast plains of the Dacotah, or into the huge wilderness of the north-west, and then

at last some day would walk back into Sault Ste. Marie, or any other outpost of civilisation, a little leaner, a little browner and as taciturn as ever. Indians from the furthest corners of the continent knew him as they knew their own sachem. He could raise tribes and bring a thousand painted cannibals to the help of the French who spoke a tongue which none knew, and came from the shores of rivers which no one else had visited. The most daring French explorers, when, after a thousand dangers, they had reached some country which they believed to be new, were as likely as not to find Du Lhut sitting by his camp fire there, some new squaw by his side, and his pipe between his teeth. Or again, when in doubt and danger, with no friends within a thousand miles, the traveller might suddenly meet this silent man, with one or two tattered wanderers of his own kidney, who would help him from his peril, and then vanish as unexpectedly as he came. Such was the man who now walked by their sides along the bank of the Richelieu, and both Amos and De Catinat knew that his presence there had a sinister meaning, and that the place which Greysolon du Lhut had chosen was the place where the danger threatened.

" What do you think of those fires over yonder, Du Lhut ? " asked young De la Noue.

The adventurer was stuffing his pipe with rank Indian tobacco which he pared from a plug with a scalping knife. He glanced over at the two little plumes of smoke which stood straight up against the red evening sky.

" I don't like them," said he.

" They are Iroquois, then ? "

" Yes."

" Well, at least it proves that they are on the other side of the river."

" It proves that they are on this side."

" What ! "

Du Lhut lit his pipe from a tinder paper. " The Iroquois are on this side," said he. " They crossed to the south of us."

" And you never told us. How do you know that they crossed, and why did you not tell us ? "

" I did not know until I saw the fires over yonder."

" And how did they tell you ? "

" Tut, an Indian papoose could have told," said Du Lhut impatiently. " Iroquois on the trail do nothing without an object. They have an object, then, in showing that smoke. If their war-parties were over yonder there would be no object. Therefore their braves must have crossed the river. And they could not get over to the north without being seen from the fort. They have got over on the south, then."

Amos nodded with intense appreciation. " That's it ! " said he, " that's Injun ways. I'll lay that he is right."

" Then they may be in the woods round us. We may be in danger," cried De la Noue.

Du Lhut nodded and sucked at his pipe.

De Catinat cast a glance round him at the grand tree trunks, the fading foliage, the smooth sward underneath with the long evening shadows barred across it. How difficult it was to realise that behind all this beauty there lurked a danger so deadly and horrible that a man alone might well shrink from it, far more one who had the woman whom he loved walking within hand's touch of him. It was with a long heart-felt sigh of relief that he saw a wall of stockade in the midst of a large clearing in front of him, with the stone manor-house rising above it. In a line from the stockade were a dozen cottages with cedar-shingled roofs turned up in the Norman fashion, in which dwelt the habitants under the protection of the seigneur's château—a strange little graft of the feudal system in the heart of an American forest. Above the main gate as they approached was a huge shield of wood with a coat of arms painted upon it, a silver ground with a chevron ermine between three coronets gules. At either corner a small brass cannon peeped through an embrasure. As they passed the gate the guard inside

closed it and placed the huge wooden bars into position.
A little crowd of men, women and children were gathered
round the door of the château, and a man appeared to
be seated on a high-backed chair upon the threshold.

"You know my father," said the young man with a
shrug of his shoulders. "He will have it that he has
never left his Norman castle, and that he is still the
Seigneur de la Noue, the greatest man within a day's ride
of Rouen, and of the richest blood of Normandy. He is
now taking his dues and his yearly oaths from his tenants,
and he would not think it becoming, if the governor
himself were to visit him, to pause in the middle of so
august a ceremony. But if it would interest you, you
may step this way and wait until he has finished. You,
madame, I will take at once to my mother, if you will be
so kind as to follow me."

The sight was, to the Americans at least, a novel one.
A triple row of men, women and children were standing
round in a semicircle, the men rough and sunburned, the
women homely and clean, with white caps upon their
heads, the children open-mouthed and round-eyed, awed
into an unusual quiet by the reverent bearing of their
elders. In the centre, on his high-backed carved chair,
there sat an elderly man very stiff and erect, with an
exceedingly solemn face. He was a fine figure of a man,
tall and broad, with large strong features, clean-shaven
and deeply-lined, a huge beak of a nose, and strong
shaggy eyebrows which arched right up to the great wig,
which he wore full and long as it had been worn in
France in his youth. On his wig was placed a white hat
cocked jauntily at one side with a red feather streaming
round it, and he wore a coat of cinnamon-coloured cloth
with silver at the neck and pockets, which was still very
handsome, though it bore signs of having been frayed
and mended more than once. This, with black velvet
knee breeches and high, well-polished boots, made a
costume such as De Catinat had never before seen in
the wilds of Canada.

As they watched, a rude husbandman walked forwards from the crowd, and kneeling down upon a square of carpet placed his hands between those of the seigneur.

" Monsieur de Sainte Marie, Monsieur de Sainte Marie, Monsieur de Sainte Marie," said he three times, " I bring you the faith and homage which I am bound to· bring you on account of my fief Herbert, which I hold as a man of faith of your seigneury."

" Be true, my son. Be valiant and true ! " said the old nobleman solemnly, and then with a sudden change of tone : " What in the name of the devil has your daughter got there ? "

A girl had advanced from the crowd with a large strip of bark in front of her on which was heaped a pile of dead fish.

" It is your eleventh fish which I am bound by my oath to render to you," said the *censitaire*. " There are seventy-three in the heap, and I have caught eight hundred in the month."

" *Peste !* " cried the nobleman. " Do you think, André Dubois, that I will disorder my health by eating three-and-seventy fish in this fashion ? Do you think that I and my body-servants and my personal retainers and the other members of my household have nothing to do but to eat your fish ! In future, you will pay your tribute not more than five at a time. Where is the major-domo ? Theuriet, remove the fish to our central store-house, and be careful that the smell does not penetrate to the blue tapestry chamber or to my lady's suite."

A man in very shabby black livery, all stained and faded, advanced with a large tin platter and carried off the pile of white fish. Then, as each of the tenants stepped forward to pay their old-world homage, they all left some share of their industry for their lord's maintenance. With some it was a bundle of wheat, with some a barrel of potatoes, while others had brought skins of deer or of beaver. All these were carried off by the major-domo, until each had paid his tribute, and the singular ceremony

was brought to a conclusion. As the seigneur rose, his son, who had returned, took De Catinat by the sleeve and led him through the throng.

" Father," said he, " this is Monsieur de Catinat, whom you may remember some years ago at Quebec."

The seigneur bowed with much condescension, and shook the guardsman by the hand.

" You are extremely welcome to my estates, both you and your body-servants——"

" They are my friends, monsieur. This is Monsieur Amos Green and Captain Ephraim Savage. My wife is travelling with me, but your courteous son has kindly taken her to your lady."

" I am honoured—honoured indeed ! " cried the old man, with a bow and a flourish. " I remember you very well, sir, for it is not so common to meet men of quality in this country. I remember your father also, for he served with me at Rocroy, though he was in the Foot, and I in the Red Dragoons of Grissot. Your arms are a martlet in fess upon a field azure, and now that I think of it, the second daughter of your great-grandfather married the son of one of the La Noues of Andelys, which is one of our cadet branches. Kinsman, you are welcome ! " He threw his arms suddenly round De Catinat and slapped him three times on the back.

The young guardsman was only too delighted to find himself admitted to such an intimacy.

" I will not intrude long upon your hospitality," said he. " We are journeying down to Lake Champlain, and we hope in a day or two to be ready to go on."

" A suite of rooms shall be laid at your disposal as long as you do me the honour to remain here. *Peste !* It is not every day that I can open my gates to a man with good blood in his veins ! Ah, sir, that is what I feel most in my exile, for who is there with whom I can talk as equal to equal ? There is the governor, the intendant, perhaps, one or two priests, three or four officers, but how many of the *noblesse ?* Scarcely one. They buy their titles over

here as they buy their pelts, and it is better to have a canoe-load of beaver skins than a pedigree from Roland. But I forget my duties. You are weary and hungry, you and your friends. Come up with me to the tapestried *salon*, and we shall see if my stewards can find anything for your refreshment. You play piquet, if I remember right ? Ah, my skill is leaving me, and I should be glad to try a hand with you."

The manor-house was high and strong, built of grey stone in a frame-work of wood. The large iron-clamped door through which they entered was pierced for musketry fire and led into a succession of cellars and store-houses in which the beets, carrots, potatoes, cabbages, cured meat, dried eels and other winter supplies were placed. A winding stone staircase led them through a huge kitchen, flagged and lofty, from which branched the rooms of the servants, or retainers as the old nobleman preferred to call them. Above this again was the principal suite, centring in the dining-hall with its huge fireplace and rude home-made furniture. Rich rugs formed of bear- or deer-skin were littered thickly over the brown-stained floor, and antlered heads bristled out from among the rows of muskets which were arranged along the wall. A broad rough-hewn maple table ran down the centre of this apartment, and on this there was soon set a venison pie, a side of calvered salmon and a huge cranberry tart, to which the hungry travellers did full justice. The seigneur explained that he had already supped, but having allowed himself to be persuaded into joining them, he ended by eating more than Ephraim Savage, drinking more than Du Lhut, and finally by singing a very amorous little French *chanson* with a tra-le-ra chorus, the words of which, fortunately for the peace of the company, were entirely unintelligible to the Bostonian.

" Madame is taking her refection in my lady's boudoir," he remarked, when the dishes had been removed. " You may bring up a bottle of Frontiniac from bin thirteen, Theuriet. Oh, you will see, gentlemen, that even in the

wilds we have a little, a very little, which is perhaps not altogether bad. And so you come from Versailles, De Catinat ? It was built since my day, but how I remember the old life of the court at St. Germain, before Louis turned serious ! Ah, what innocent happy days they were when Madame de Nevailles had to bar the windows of the maids of honour to keep out the king, and we all turned out eight deep on to the grass plot for our morning duel ! By Saint Denis, I have not quite forgotten the trick of the wrist yet, and, old as I am, I should be none the worse for a little breather." He strutted in his stately fashion over to where a rapier and dagger hung upon the wall, and began to make passes at the door, darting in and out, warding off imaginary blows with his poniard, and stamping his feet with little cries of " Punto ! reverso ! stoccata ! dritta ! mandritta ! " and all the jargon of the fencing schools. Finally he rejoined them, breathing heavily and with his wig awry.

" That was our old exercise," said he. " Doubtless you young bloods have improved upon it, and yet it was good enough for the Spaniards at Rocroy and at one or two other places which I could mention. But they still see life at the court, I understand. There are still love passages and blood lettings. How has Lauzun prospered in his wooing of Mademoiselle de Montpensier ? Was it proved that Madame de Clermont had bought a phial from Le Vie, the poison woman, two days before the soup disagreed so violently with monsieur ? What did the Duc de Biron do when his nephew ran away with the duchess ? Is it true that he raised his allowance to fifty thousand livres for having done it ? " Such were the two-year-old questions which had not been answered yet upon the banks of the Richelieu River. Long into the hours of the night, when his comrades were already snoring under their blankets, De Catinat, blinking and yawning, was still engaged in trying to satisfy the curiosity of the old courtier, and to bring him up to date in all the most minute gossip of Versailles.

33. *The Slaying of Brown Moose*

TWO days were spent by the travellers at the seigneury of Sainte Marie, and they would very willingly have spent longer, for the quarters were comfortable and the welcome warm, but already the reds of autumn were turning to brown, and they knew how suddenly the ice and snow come in those northern lands, and how impossible it would be to finish their journey if winter were once fairly upon them. The old nobleman had sent his scouts by land and by water, but there were no signs of the Iroquois upon the eastern banks, so that it was clear that Du Lhut had been mistaken. Over on the other side, however, the high grey plumes of smoke still streamed up above the trees as a sign that their enemies were not very far off. All day from the manorhouse windows and from the stockade they could see those danger signals which reminded them that a horrible death lurked ever at their elbow.

The refugees were rested now and refreshed, and of one mind about pushing on.

" If the snow comes, it will be a thousand times more dangerous," said Amos, " for we shall leave a track then that a papoose could follow."

" And why should we fear ? " urged old Ephraim. " Truly this is a desert of salt, even though it lead to the vale of Hinnom, but we shall be borne up against these sons of Jeroboam. Steer a straight course, lad, and jam your helm, for the pilot will see you safe."

" And I am not frightened, Amory, and I am quite rested now," said Adèle. " We shall be so much more happy when we are in the English Provinces, for even now, how do we know that that dreadful monk may not come with orders to drag us back to Quebec and Paris ? "

It was indeed very possible that the vindictive Franciscan, when satisfied that they had not ascended to

Montreal, or remained at Three Rivers, might seek them on the banks of the Richelieu. When De Catinat thought of how he passed them in his great canoe that morning, his eager face protruded, and his dark body swinging in time to the paddles, he felt that the danger which his wife suggested was not only possible but imminent. The seigneur was his friend, but the seigneur could not disobey the governor's order. A great hand, stretching all the way from Versailles, seemed to hang over them, even here in the heart of the virgin forest, ready to snatch them up and carry them back into degradation and misery. Better all the perils of the woods than that !

But the seigneur and his son, who knew nothing of their pressing reasons for haste, were strenuous in urging De Catinat the other way, and in this they were supported by the silent Du Lhut, whose few muttered words were always more weighty than the longest speech, for he never spoke save about that of which he was a master.

" You have seen my little place," said the old nobleman, with a wave of his beruffled ring-covered hand. " It is not what I should wish it, but such as it is, it is most heartily yours for the winter, if you and your comrades would honour me by remaining. As to madame, I doubt not that my own dame and she will find plenty to amuse and occupy them, which reminds me, De Catinat, that you have not yet been presented. Theuriet, go to your mistress and inform her that I request her to be so good as to come to us in the hall of the dais."

De Catinat was too seasoned to be easily startled, but he was somewhat taken aback when the lady, to whom the old nobleman always referred in terms of exaggerated respect, proved to be as like a full-blooded Indian squaw as the hall of the dais was to a French barn. She was dressed, it was true, in a bodice of scarlet taffeta with a black skirt, silver buckled shoes and a scented pomander ball dangling by a silver chain from her girdle, but her face was of the colour of the bark of the Scotch fir, while her strong nose and harsh mouth, with the two plaits of coarse

black hair which dangled down her back, left no possible doubt as to her origin.

" Allow me to present you, Monsieur de Catinat," said the Seigneur de Sainte Marie solemnly, " to my wife, Onega de la Noue de Sainte Marie, chatelaine by right of marriage to this seigneury, and also to the Château d'Andelys in Normandy, and to the estate of Varennes in Provence, while retaining in her own right the hereditary chieftainship on the distaff side of the nation of the Onondagas. My angel, I have been endeavouring to persuade our friends to remain with us at Sainte Marie instead of journeying on to Lake Champlain."

" At least leave your White Lily at Sainte Marie," said the dusky princess, speaking in excellent French, and clasping with her ruddy fingers the ivory hand of Adèle. " We will hold her safe for you until the ice softens, and the leaves and the partridge berries come once more. I know my people, monsieur, and I tell you that the woods are full of murder, and that it is not for nothing that the leaves are the colour of blood, for death lurks behind every tree."

De Catinat was more moved by the impressive manner of his hostess than by any of the other warnings which he had received. Surely she, if anyone, must be able to read the signs of the times.

" I know not what to do ! " he cried in despair. " I must go on, and yet how can I expose her to these perils ? I would fain stay the winter, but you must take my word for it, sir, that it is not possible."

" Du Lhut, you know how things should be ordered," said the seigneur. " What should you advise my friend to do, since he is so set upon getting to the English Provinces before the winter comes ? "

The dark, silent pioneer stroked his beard with his hand as he pondered over the question.

" There is but one way," said he at last, " though even in it there is danger. The woods are safer than the river, for the reeds are full of *cachèd* canoes. Five leagues from

here is the blockhouse of Poitou, and fifteen miles beyond, that of Auvergne. We will go to-morrow to Poitou through the woods and see if all be safe. I will go with you, and I give you my word that if the Iroquois are there, Greysolon du Lhut will know it. The lady we shall leave here, and if we find that all is safe we shall come back for her. Then in the same fashion we shall advance to Auvergne, and there you must wait until you hear where their war-parties are. It is in my mind that it will not be very long before we know."

" What ! You would part us ! " cried Adèle aghast.

" It is best, my sister," said Onega, passing her arm caressingly round her. " You cannot know the danger, but we know it and we will not let our White Lily run into it. You will stay here to gladden us, while the great chief Du Lhut, and the French soldier, your husband, and the old warrior who seems so wary, and the other chief with limbs like the wild deer, go forward through the woods and see that all is well before you venture."

And so it was at last agreed, and Adèle, still protesting, was consigned to the care of the lady of Sainte Marie, while De Catinat swore that without a pause he would return from Poitou to fetch her. The old nobleman and his son would fain have joined them in their adventure, but they had their own charge to watch and the lives of many in their keeping, while a small party were safer in the woods than a larger one would be. The seigneur provided them with a letter for De Lannes, the governor of the Poitou blockhouse, and so in the early dawn the four of them crept like shadows from the stockade-gate, amid the muttered good wishes of the guard within, and were lost in an instant in the blackness of the vast forest.

From La Noue to Poitou was but twelve miles down the river, but by the woodland route where creeks were to be crossed, reed-girt lakes to be avoided, and paths to be picked among swamps where the wild rice grew higher than their heads, the distance was more than doubled.

They walked in single file, Du Lhut leading, with the swift silent tread of some wild creature, his body bent forward, his gun ready in the bend of his arm, and his keen dark eyes shooting little glances to right and left, observing everything from the tiniest mark upon the ground or tree trunk to the motion of every beast and bird of the brushwood. De Catinat walked behind, then Ephraim Savage, and then Amos, all with their weapons ready and with every sense upon the alert. By midday they were more than half-way, and halted in a thicket for a scanty meal of bread and cheese, for Du Lhut would not permit them to light a fire.

" They have not come as far as this," he whispered, " and yet I am sure that they have crossed the river. Ah, Governor de la Barre did not know what he did when he stirred these men up, and this good dragoon whom the king has sent us now knows even less."

" I have seen them in peace," remarked Amos. " I have traded to Onondaga and to the country of the Senecas. I know them as fine hunters, and brave men."

" They are fine hunters, but the game that they hunt best are their fellow-men. I have myself led their scalping parties, and I have fought against them, and I tell you that when a general comes out from France who hardly knows enough to get the sun behind him in a fight, he will find that there is little credit to be gained from them. They talk of burning their villages ! It would be as wise to kick over the wasps' nest, and think that you have done with the wasps. You are from New England, monsieur ? "

" My comrade is from New England ; I am from New York."

" Ah, yes. I could see from your step and your eye that the woods were as a home to you. The New England man goes on the waters and he slays the cod with more pleasure than the cariboo. Perhaps that is why his face is so sad. I have been on the great water, and I remember that my face was sad also. There is little wind, and so

I think that we may light our pipes without danger. With a good breeze I have known a burning pipe fetch up a scalping party from two miles' distance, but the trees stop scent, and the Iroquois noses are less keen than the Sioux and the Dacotah. God help you, monsieur, if you should ever have an Indian war. It is bad for us, but it would be a thousand times worse for you."

" And why ? "

" Because we have fought the Indians from the first, and we have them always in our mind when we build. You see how along this river every house and every hamlet supports its neighbour ? But you, by Sainte Anne of Beaupré, it made my scalp tingle when I came on your frontiers and saw the lonely farm-houses and little clearings out in the woods with no help for twenty leagues around. An Indian war is a purgatory for Canada, but it would be a hell for the English Provinces ! "

" We are good friends with the Indians," said Amos. " We do not wish to conquer."

" Your people have a way of conquering although they say that they do not wish to do it," remarked Du Lhut, " Now, with us, we bang our drums, and wave our flags, and make a stir, but no very big thing has come of it yet. We have never had but two great men in Canada. One was Monsieur de la Salle who was shot last year by his own men down the great river, and the other, old Frontenac, will have to come back again if New France is not to be turned into a desert by the Five Nations. It would surprise me little if by this time two years the white and gold flag flew only over the rock of Quebec. But I see that you look at me impatiently, Monsieur de Catinat, and I know that you count the hours until we are back at Sainte Marie again. Forward, then, and may the second part of our journey be as peaceful as the first."

For an hour or more they picked their way through the woods, following in the steps of the old French pioneer. It was a lovely day with hardly a cloud in the heavens, and the sun streaming down through the thick

foliage covered the shaded sward with a delicate network of gold. Sometimes where the woods opened they came out into the pure sunlight, but only to pass into thick glades beyond, where a single ray, here and there, was all that could break its way through the vast leafy covering. It would have been beautiful, these sudden transitions from light to shade, but with the feeling of impending danger, and of a horror ever lurking in these shadows, the mind was tinged with awe rather than admiration. Silently, lightly, the four men picked their steps among the great tree trunks.

Suddenly Du Lhut dropped upon his knees and stooped his ear to the ground. He rose, shook his head, and walked on with a grave face, casting quick little glances into the shadows in every direction.

" Did you hear something ? " whispered Amos.

Du Lhut put his finger to his lips, and then in an instant was down again upon his face with his ear fixed to the ground. He sprang up with the look of a man who has heard what he expected to hear.

" Walk on," said he quietly, " and behave exactly as you have done all day."

" What is it, then ? "

" Indians."

" In front of us ? "

" No, behind us."

" What are they doing ? "

" They are following us."

" How many of them ? "

" Two, I think."

The friends glanced back involuntarily over their shoulders into the dense blackness of the forest. At one point a single broad shaft of light slid down between two pines and cast a golden blotch upon their track. Save for this one vivid spot all was sombre and silent.

" Do not look round," whispered Du Lhut sharply. " Walk on as before."

" Are they enemies ? "

" They are Iroquois."

" And pursuing us ? "

" No, we are now pursuing them."

" Shall we turn, then ? "

" No, they would vanish like shadows."

" How far off are they ? "

" About two hundred paces, I think."

" They cannot see us, then ? "

" I think not, but I cannot be sure.   They are following our trail, I think."

" What shall we do, then ? "

" Let us make a circle and get behind them."

Turning sharp to the left he led them in a long curve through the woods, hurrying swiftly and yet silently under the darkest shadows of the trees.   Then he turned again, and presently halted.

" This is our own track," said he.

" Aye, and two redskins have passed over it," cried Amos, bending down, and pointing to marks which were entirely invisible to Ephraim Savage or De Catinat.

" A full-grown warrior and a lad on his first war-path," said Du Lhut.   " They were moving fast, you see, for you can hardly see the heel marks of their mocassins. They walked one behind the other.   Now let us follow them as they followed us, and see if we have better luck."

He sped swiftly along the trail with his musket cocked in his hand, the others following hard upon his heels, but there was no sound, and no sign of life from the shadowy woods in front of them.   Suddenly Du Lhut stopped and grounded his weapon.

" They are still behind us," he said.

" Still behind us ? "

" Yes.   This is the point where we branched off. They have hesitated a moment, as you can see by their footmarks, and then they have followed on."

" If we go round again and quicken our pace we may overtake them."

" No, they are on their guard now. They must know that it could only be on their account that we went back on our tracks. Lie here behind the fallen log and we shall see if we can catch a glimpse of them."

A great rotten trunk, all green with mould and blotched with pink and purple fungi, lay to one side of where they stood. Behind this the Frenchman crouched, and his three companions followed his example, peering through the brushwood screen in front of them. Still the one broad sheet of sunshine poured down between the two pines, but all else was as dim and as silent as a vast cathedral with pillars of wood and roof of leaf. Not a branch that creaked, nor a twig that snapped, nor any sound at all save the sharp barking of a fox somewhere in the heart of the forest. A thrill of excitement ran through the nerves of De Catinat. It was like one of those games of hide-and-seek which the court used to play, when Louis was in a sportive mood, among the oaks and yew hedges of Versailles. But the forfeit there was a carved fan, or a box of bonbons, and here it was death.

Ten minutes passed and there was no sign of any living thing behind them.

" They are over in yonder thicket," whispered Du Lhut, nodding his head towards a dense clump of brushwood, two hundred paces away.

" Have you seen them ? "

" No."

" How do you know, then ? "

" I saw a squirrel come from his hole in the great white beech tree yonder. He scuttled back again as if something had scared him. From his hole he can see down into that brushwood."

" Do you think that they know that we are here ? "

" They cannot see us. But they are suspicious. They fear a trap."

" Shall we rush for the brushwood ? "

" They would pick two of us off, and be gone like

shadows through the woods. No, we had best go on our way."

" But they will follow us."

" I hardly think that they will. We are four and they are only two, and they know now that we are on our guard, and that we can pick up a trail as quickly as they can themselves. Get behind these trunks where they cannot see us. So ! Now stoop until you are past the belt of alder bushes. We must push on fast now, for where there are two Iroquois there are likely to be two hundred not very far off."

" Thank God that I did not bring Adèle ! " cried De Catinat.

" Yes, monsieur, it is well for a man to make a comrade of his wife, but not on the borders of the Iroquois country, nor of any other Indian country either."

" You do not take your own wife with you when you travel, then ? " asked the soldier.

" Yes, but I do not let her travel from village to village. She remains in the wigwam."

" Then you leave her behind ? "

" On the contrary, she is always there to welcome me. By Sainte Anne, I should be heavy-hearted if I came to any village between this and the Bluffs of the Illinois, and did not find my wife waiting to greet me."

" Then she must travel before you."

Du Lhut laughed heartily, without, however, emitting a sound.

" A fresh village, a fresh wife," said he. " But I never have more than one in each, for it is a shame for a Frenchman to set an evil example when the good fathers are spending their lives so freely in preaching virtue to them. Ah, here is the Ajidaumo Creek, where the Indians set the sturgeon nets. It is still seven miles to Poitou."

" We shall be there before nightfall, then ? "

" I think that we had best wait for nightfall before we make our way in. Since the Iroquois scouts are out as far as this, it is likely that they lie thick round Poitou, and we

may find the last step the worst unless we have a care, the more so if these two get in front if us to warn the others." He paused a moment with slanting head and sidelong ear. "By Sainte Anne," he muttered, "we have not shaken them off. They are still upon our trail!"

"You hear them?"

"Yes, they are no great way from us. They will find that they have followed us once too often this time. Now, I will show you a little bit of woodcraft which may be new to you. Slip off your mocassins, monsieur."

De Catinat pulled off his shoes as directed, and Du Lhut did the same.

"Put them on as if they were gloves," said the pioneer, and an instant later Ephraim Savage and Amos had their comrades' shoes upon their hands.

"You can sling your muskets over your back. So! Now down on all-fours, bending yourselves double, with your hands pressing hard upon the earth. That is excellent. Two men can leave the trail of four! Now come with me, monsieur."

He flitted from tree to tree on a line which was parallel to, but a few yards distant from, that of their comrades. Then suddenly he crouched behind a bush and pulled De Catinat down beside him.

"They must pass us in a few minutes," he whispered. "Do not fire if you can help it." Something gleamed in Du Lhut's hand, and his comrade, glancing down, saw that he had drawn a keen little tomahawk from his belt. Again the mad wild thrill ran through the soldier's blood, as he peered through the tangled branches and waited for whatever might come out of the dim silent aisles of tree-boles.

And suddenly he saw something move. It flitted like a shadow from one trunk to the other so swiftly that De Catinat could not have told whether it were beast or human. And then again he saw it, and yet again, sometimes one shadow, sometimes two shadows, silent, furtive, like the *loup-garou* with which his nurse had

scared him in his childhood. Then for a few moments all was still once more, and then in an instant there crept out from among the bushes the most terrible-looking creature that ever walked the earth, an Iroquois chief upon the war-trail.

He was a tall, powerful man, and his bristle of scalp-locks and eagle feathers made him look a giant in the dim light, for a good eight feet lay between his beaded mocassin and the topmost plume of his headgear. One side of his face was painted in soot, ochre and vermilion to resemble a dog, and the other half as a fowl, so that the front view was indescribably grotesque and strange. A belt of wampum was braced round his loin-cloth, and a dozen scalp-locks fluttered out as he moved from the fringe of his leggings. His head was sunk forward, his eyes gleamed with a sinister light, and his nostrils dilated and contracted like those of an excited animal. His gun was thrown forward, and he crept along with bended knees, peering, listening, pausing, hurrying on, a breathing image of caution. Two paces behind him walked a lad of fourteen, clad and armed in the same fashion, but without the painted face and without the horrid dried trophies upon the leggings. It was his first campaign, and already his eyes shone and his nostrils twitched with the same lust for murder which burned within his elder. So they advanced, silent, terrible, creeping out of the shadows of the wood as their race had come out of the shadows of history, with bodies of iron and tiger souls.

They were just abreast of the bush when something caught the eye of the younger warrior, some displaced twig or fluttering leaf, and he paused with suspicion in every feature. Another instant and he had warned his companion, but Du Lhut sprang out and buried his little hatchet in the skull of the older warrior. De Catinat heard a dull crash, as when an axe splinters its way into a rotten tree, and the man fell like a log, laughing horribly, and kicking and striking with his powerful limbs. The younger warrior sprang like a deer over his fallen comrade

and dashed on into the wood, but an instant later there was a gunshot among the trees in front, followed by a faint wailing cry.

" That is his death-whoop," said Du Lhut composedly. " It was a pity to fire, and yet it was better than letting him go."

As he spoke the two others came back, Ephraim ramming a fresh charge into his musket.

" Who was laughing ? " asked Amos.

" It was he," said Du Lhut, nodding towards the dying warrior, who lay with his head in a horrible puddle, and his grotesque features contorted into a fixed smile. " It's a custom they have when they get their death-blow. I've known a Seneca chief laugh for six hours on end at the torture-stake. Ah, he's gone ! "

As he spoke, the Indian gave a last spasm with his hands and feet, and lay rigid, grinning up at the slit of blue sky above him.

" He's a great chief," said Du Lhut. " He is Brown Moose of the Mohawks, and the other is his second son. We have drawn first blood, but I do not think that it will be the last, for the Iroquois do not allow their war-chiefs to die unavenged. He was a mighty fighter, as you may see by looking at his neck."

He wore a peculiar necklace which seemed to De Catinat to consist of blackened bean pods set upon a string. As he stooped over it he saw to his horror that they were not bean pods, but withered human fingers.

" They are all right fore-fingers," said Du Lhut, " so every one represents a life. There are forty-two in all. Eighteen are of men whom he has slain in battle, and the other twenty-four have been taken and tortured."

" How do you know that ? "

" Because only eighteen have their nails on. If the prisoner of an Iroquois be alive, he begins always by biting his nails off. You see that they are missing from four-and-twenty."

De Catinat shuddered. What demons were these

amongst whom an evil fate had drifted him ? And was it possible that his Adèle should fall into the hands of such fiends ? No, no, surely the good God, for whose sake they had suffered so much, would not permit such an infamy ! And yet as evil a fate had come upon other women as tender as Adèle—upon other men as loving as he. What hamlet was there in Canada which had not such stories in their record ? A vague horror seized him as he stood there. We know more of the future than we are willing to admit, away down in those dim recesses of the soul where there is no reason, but only instincts and impressions. Now some impending terror cast its cloud over him. The trees around with their great protruding limbs were like shadowy demons thrusting out their gaunt arms to seize him. The sweat burst from his forehead, and he leaned heavily upon his musket.

" By Sainte Eulalie," said Du Lhut, " for an old soldier you turn very pale, monsieur, at a little bloodshed."

" I am not well. I should be glad of a sup from your cognac bottle."

" Here it is, comrade, and welcome ! Well, I may as well have this fine scalp that we may have something to show for our walk." He held the Indian's head between his knees, and in an instant, with a sweep of his knife, had torn off the hideous dripping trophy.

" Let us go ! " cried De Catinat, turning away in disgust.

" Yes, we shall go. But I shall also have this wampum belt marked with the totem of the Bear. So ! And the gun too. Look at the ' London ' printed upon the lock. Ah, Monsieur Green, Monsieur Green, it is not hard to see where the enemies of France get their arms."

So at last they turned away, Du Lhut bearing his spoils, leaving the red grinning figure stretched under the silent trees. As they passed on they caught a glimpse of the lad lying doubled up among the bushes where he had fallen. The pioneer walked very swiftly until he came to a little stream which prattled down to the big river. Here he

slipped off his boots and leggings, and waded down it with his companions for half a mile or so.

" They will follow our tracks when they find him," said he, " but this will throw them off, for it is only on running water that an Iroquois can find no trace. And now we shall lie in this clump until nightfall, for we are little over a mile from Fort Poitou, and it is dangerous to go forward, for the ground becomes more open."

And so they remained concealed among the alders whilst the shadows turned from short to long, and the white drifting clouds above them were tinged with the pink of the setting sun. Du Lhut coiled himself into a ball with his pipe between his teeth and dropped into a light sleep, pricking up his ears and starting at the slightest sound from the woods around them. The two Americans whispered together for a long time, Ephraim telling some long story about the cruise of the brig *Industry*, bound to Jamestown for sugar and molasses, but at last the soothing hum of a gentle breeze through the branches lulled them off also, and they slept. De Catinat alone remained awake, his nerves still in a tingle from that strange sudden shadow which had fallen upon his soul. What could it mean ? Not surely that Adèle was in danger ? He had heard of such warnings, but had he not left her in safety behind cannons and stockades ? By the next evening at latest he would see her again. As he lay looking up through the tangle of copper leaves at the sky beyond, his mind drifted like the clouds above him and he was back once more in the jutting window in the Rue St. Martin, sitting on the broad *bancal*, with its Spanish leather covering, with the gilt wool-bale creaking outside, and his arm round shrinking, timid Adèle, she who had compared herself to a little mouse in an old house, and who yet had courage to stay by his side through all this wild journey. And then again he was back at Versailles. Once more he saw the brown eyes of the king, the fair bold face of De Montespan, the serene features of De Maintenon—once more he rode on

his midnight mission, was driven by the demon coachman, and sprang with Amos upon the scaffold to rescue
the most beautiful woman in France. So clear it was and
so vivid that it was with a start that he came suddenly to
himself, and found that the night was creeping on in an
American forest, and that Du Lhut had roused himself
and was ready for a start.

" Have you been awake ? " asked the pioneer.

" Yes."

" Have you heard anything ? "

" Nothing but the hooting of the owl."

" It seemed to me that in my sleep I heard a gunshot in
the distance."

" In your sleep ? "

" Yes, I hear as well asleep as awake and remember
what I hear. But now you must follow me close, and we
shall be in the fort soon."

" You have wonderful ears, indeed," said De Catinat,
as they picked their way through the tangled wood.
" How could you hear that these men were following us
to-day ? I could make out no sound when they were
within hand-touch of us."

" I did not hear them at first."

" You saw them ? "

" No, nor that either."

" Then how could you know that they were there ? "

" I heard a frightened jay flutter among the trees after
we were past it. Then ten minutes later I heard the
same thing. I knew then that there was someone on our
trail, and I listened."

" *Peste !* you are a woodsman indeed ! "

" I believe that these woods are swarming with Iroquois
although we have had the good fortune to miss them. So
great a chief as Brown Moose would not start on the path
with a small following nor for a small object. They must
mean mischief upon the Richelieu. You are not sorry
now that you did not bring madame ? "

" I thank God for it ! "

797

" The woods will not be safe, I fear, until the partridge berries are out once more. You must stay at Sainte Marie until then, unless the seigneur can spare men to guard you."

" I had rather stay there for ever than expose my wife to such devils."

" Aye, devils they are, if ever devils walked upon earth. You winced, monsieur, when I took Brown Moose's scalp, but when you have seen as much of the Indians as I have done your heart will be as hardened as mine. And now we are on the very borders of the clearing, and the block-house lies yonder among the clump of maples. They do not keep very good watch, for I have been expecting during these last ten minutes to hear the *qui vive*. You did not come as near to Sainte Marie unchallenged, and yet De Lannes is as old a soldier as La Noue. We can scarce see now, but yonder, near the river, is where he exercises his men."

" He does so now," said Amos. " I see a dozen of them drawn up in a line at their drill."

" No sentinels, and all the men at drill ! " cried Du Lhut in contempt. " It is as you say, however, for I can see them myself with their ranks open, and each as stiff and straight as a pine stump. One would think to see them stand so still that there was not an Indian nearer than Orange. We shall go across to them, and by Sainte Anne, I shall tell their commander what I think of his arrangements."

Du Lhut advanced from the bushes as he spoke, and the four men crossed the open ground in the direction of the line of men who waited silently for them in the dim twilight. They were within fifty paces, and yet none of them had raised hand or voice to challenge their approach. There was something uncanny in the silence, and a change came over Du Lhut's face as he peered in front of him. He craned his head round and looked up the river.

" My God ! " he screamed. " Look at the fort ! "

They had cleared the clump of trees, and the outline of

the blockhouse should have shown up in front of them. There was no sign of it. It was gone !

34. *The Men of Blood*

SO unexpected was the blow that even Du Lhut, hardened from his childhood to every shock and danger, stood shaken and dismayed. Then, with an oath, he ran at the top of his speed towards the line of figures, his companions following at his heels.

As they drew nearer they could see through the dusk that it was not indeed a line. A silent and motionless officer stood out some twenty paces in front of his silent and motionless men. Further, they could see that he wore a very high and singular head-dress. They were still rushing forward, breathless with apprehension, when to their horror this head-dress began to lengthen and broaden, and a great bird flapped heavily up and dropped down again on the nearest tree trunk. Then they knew that their worst fears were true, and that it was the garrison of Poitou which stood before them.

They were lashed to low posts with willow withies, some twenty of them, naked all, and twisted and screwed into every strange shape which an agonised body could assume. In front where the buzzard had perched was the grey-headed commandant with two cinders thrust into his sockets and his flesh hanging from him like a beggar's rags. Behind was the line of men, each with his legs charred off to the knees, and his body so haggled and scorched and burst that the willow bands alone seemed to hold it together. For a moment the four comrades stared in silent horror at the dreadful group. Then each acted as his nature bade him. De Catinat staggered up against a tree trunk and leaned his head upon his arm, deadly sick. Du Lhut fell down upon his knees and said something to heaven, with his two clenched hands shaking up at the darkening sky. Ephraim Savage examined the

priming of his gun with a tightened lip and a gleaming eye, while Amos Green, without a word, began to cast round in circles in search of a trail.

But Du Lhut was on his feet again in a moment, and running up and down like a sleuth-hound, noting a hundred things which even Amos would have overlooked. He circled round the bodies again and again. Then he ran a little way towards the edge of the woods, and then came back to the charred ruins of the blockhouse, from some of which a thin reek of smoke was still rising.

" There is no sign of the women and children," said he.

" My God ! There were women and children ? "

" They are keeping the children to burn at their leisure in their villages. The women they may torture or may adopt as the humour takes them. But what does the old man want ? "

" I want you to ask him, Amos," said the seaman, " why we are yawing and tacking here when we should be cracking on all sail to stand after them ? "

Du Lhut smiled and shook his head. " Your friend is a brave man," said he, " if he thinks that with four men we can follow a hundred and fifty."

" Tell him, Amos, that the Lord will bear us up," said the other excitedly. " Say that He will be with us against the children of Jeroboam, and we will cut them off utterly and they shall be destroyed. What is the French for ' slay and spare not ' ? I had as soon go about with my jaw braced up, as with folk who cannot understand a plain language."

But Du Lhut waved aside the seaman's suggestions. " We must have a care now," said he, " or we shall lose our own scalps, and be the cause of those at Sainte Marie losing theirs as well."

" Sainte Marie ! " cried De Catinat. " Is there then danger at Saint Marie ? "

" Aye, they are in the wolf's mouth now. This business was done last night. The place was stormed by a war-party of a hundred and fifty men. This morning

they left and went north upon foot. They have been *cachéd* among the woods all day between Poitou and Sainte Marie."

" Then we have come through them ? "

" Yes, we have come through them. They would keep their camp to-day and send out scouts. Brown Moose and his son were among them and struck our trail. To-night——"

" To-night they will attack Sainte Marie ! "

" It is possible. And yet with so small a party I should scarce have thought that they would have dared. Well, we can but hasten back as quickly as we can, and give them warning of what is hanging over them."

And so they turned for their weary backward journey, though their minds were too full to spare a thought upon the leagues which lay behind them or those which were before. Old Ephraim, less accustomed to walking than his younger comrades, was already limping and footsore, but, for all his age, he was as tough as hickory and full of endurance. Du Lhut took the lead again and they turned their faces once more towards the north.

The moon was shining brightly in the sky, but it was little aid to the travellers in the depths of the forest. Where it had been shadowy in the daytime it was now so absolutely dark that De Catinat could not see the tree trunks against which he brushed. Here and there they came upon an open glade bathed in the moonshine, or perhaps a thin shaft of silver light broke through between the branches, and cast a great white patch upon the ground, but Du Lhut preferred to avoid these more open spaces, and to skirt the glades rather than to cross them. The breeze had freshened a little and the whole air was filled with the rustle and sough of the leaves. Save for this dull never-ceasing sound all would have been silent had not the owl hooted sometimes from among the tree-tops, and the nightjar whirred above their heads.

Dark as it was Du Lhut walked as swiftly as during the sunlight, and never hesitated about the track. His com-

rades could see, however, that he was taking them a different way to that which they had gone in the morning, for twice they caught a sight of the glimmer of the broad river upon their left, while before they had only seen the streams which flowed into it. On the second occasion he pointed to where, on the farther side, they could see dark shadows flitting over the water.

" Iroquois canoes," he whispered. " There are ten of them with eight men in each. They are another party and they are also going north."

" How do you know that they are another party ? "

" Because we have crossed the trail of the first within the hour."

De Catinat was filled with amazement at this marvellous man who could hear in his sleep and could detect a trail when the very tree-trunks were invisible to ordinary eyes. Du Lhut halted a little to watch the canoes, and then turned his back to the river, and plunged into the woods once more. They had gone a mile or two when suddenly he came to a dead stop, snuffing at the air like a hound on a scent.

" I smell burning wood," said he. " There is a fire within a mile of us in that direction."

" I smell it too," said Amos. " Let us creep up that way and see their camp."

" Be careful, then," whispered Du Lhut, " for your lives may hang from a cracking twig."

They advanced very slowly and cautiously until suddenly the red flare of a leaping fire twinkled between the distant trunks. Still slipping through the brushwood they worked round until they had found a point from which they could see without a risk of being seen.

A great blaze of dry logs crackled and spurtled in the centre of a small clearing. The ruddy flames roared upwards, and the smoke spread out above it until it looked like a strange tree with grey foliage and trunk of fire. But no living being was in sight and the huge fire roared and swayed in absolute solitude in the midst of the silent

woodlands.   Nearer they crept and nearer, but there was no movement save the rush of the flames, and no sound but the snapping of the sticks.

" Shall we go up to it ? " whispered De Catinat.

The wary old pioneer shook his head.   " It may be a trap," said he.

" Or an abandoned camp ? "

" No, it has not been lit more than an hour."

" Besides, it is far too great for a camp fire," said Amos.

" What do you make of it ? " asked Du Lhut.

" A signal."

" Yes, I daresay that you are right.   This light is not a safe neighbour, so we shall edge away from it and then make a straight line for Sainte Marie."

The flames were soon but a twinkling point behind them, and at last vanished behind the trees.   Du Lhut pushed on rapidly until they came to the edge of a moonlit clearing.   He was about to skirt this, as he had done others, when suddenly he caught De Catinat by the shoulder and pushed him down behind a clump of sumach, while Amos did the same with Ephraim Savage.

A man was walking down the other side of the open space.   He had just emerged and was crossing it diagonally, making in the direction of the river.   His body was bent double, but as he came out from the shadow of the trees they could see that he was an Indian brave in full war-paint, with leggings, loin-cloth and musket.   Close at his heels came a second, and then a third and a fourth, on and on until it seemed as if the wood were full of men, and that the line would never come to an end.   They flitted past like shadows in the moonlight, in absolute silence, all crouching and running in the same swift stealthy fashion.   Last of all came a man in the fringed tunic of a hunter with a cap and feather upon his head.   He passed across like the others, and they vanished into the shadows as silently as they had appeared.   It was five minutes before Du Lhut thought it safe to rise from their shelter.

" By Saint Anne," he whispered, " did you count them ? "

" Three hundred and ninety-six," said Amos.

" I made it four hundred and two."

" And you thought that there were only a hundred and fifty of them ! " cried De Catinat.

" Ah, you do not understand. This is a fresh band. The others who took the blockhouse must be over there, for their trail lies between us and the river."

" They could not be the same," said Amos, " for there was not a fresh scalp among them."

Du Lhut gave the young hunter a glance of approval, " On my word," said he, " I did not know that your woodsmen are good as they seem to be. You have eyes, monsieur, and it may please you some day to remember that Greysolon du Lhut told you so."

Amos felt a flush of pride at these words from a man whose name was honoured wherever trader or trapper smoked round a camp fire. He was about to make some answer when a dreadful cry broke suddenly out of the woods, a horrible screech, as from someone who was goaded to the very last pitch of human misery. Again and again, as they stood with blanched cheeks in the darkness, they heard that awful cry swelling up from the night and ringing drearily through the forest.

" They are torturing the women," said Du Lhut. " Their camp lies over there."

" Can we do nothing to aid them ? " cried Amos.

" Aye, aye, lad," said the captain in English. " We can't pass distress signals without going out of our course. Let us put about and run down yonder."

" In that camp," said Du Lhut slowly, " there are now nearly six hundred warriors. We are four. What you say has no sense. Unless we warn them at Sainte Marie, these devils will lay some trap for them. Their parties are assembling by land and by water and there may be a thousand before daybreak. Our duty is to push on and give our warning."

804

" He speaks the truth," said Amos to Ephraim. " Nay, but you must not go alone ! " He seized the stout old seaman by the arm and held him by main force to prevent him from breaking off through the woods.

" There is one thing which we can do to spoil their night's amusement," said Du Lhut. " The woods are as dry as powder, and there has been no drop of rain for a long three months."

" Yes ? "

" And the wind blows straight for their camp, with the river on the other side of it."

" We should fire the woods ! "

" We cannot do better."

In an instant Du Lhut had scraped together a little bundle of dry twigs, and had heaped them up against a withered beech tree which was as dry as tinder. A stroke of flint and steel was enough to start a little smoulder of flame, which lengthened and spread until it was leaping along the white strips of hanging bark. A quarter of a mile farther on Du Lhut did the same again, and once more beyond that, until at three different points the forest was in a blaze. As they hurried onwards they could hear the dull roaring of the flames behind them, and at last, as they neared Sainte Marie, they could see, looking back, the long rolling wave of fire travelling ever westward towards the Richelieu, and flashing up into great spouts of flame as it licked up a clump of pines as if it were a bundle of faggots. Du Lhut chuckled in his silent way as he looked back at the long orange glare in the sky.

" They will need to swim for it, some of them," said he. " They have not canoes to take them all off. Ah, if I had but two hundred of my *coureurs-de-bois* on the river at the farther side of them not one would have got away."

" They had one who was dressed like a white man," remarked Amos.

" Aye, and the most deadly of the lot. His father was a Dutch trader, his mother an Iroquois, and he goes by the name of the Flemish Bastard. Ah, I know him

well, and I tell you that if they want a king in hell they will find one all ready in his wigwam. By Sainte Anne, I have a score to settle with him, and I may pay it before this business is over. Well, there are the lights of Sainte Marie shining down below there. I can understand that sigh of relief, monsieur, for, on my word, after what we found at Poitou I was uneasy myself until I should see them."

35. *The Tapping of Death*

DAY was just breaking as the four comrades entered the gate of the stockade, but early as it was the *censitaires* and their families were all afoot staring at the prodigious fire which raged to the south of them. De Catinat burst through the throng and rushed upstairs to Adèle, who had herself flown down to meet him, so that they met in each other's arms half way up the great stone staircase with a burst of those little inarticulate cries which are the true unwritten language of love. Together, with his arm round her, they ascended to the great hall where old De la Noue with his son were peering out of the window at the wonderful spectacle.

" Ah, monsieur," said the old nobleman with his courtly bow, " I am indeed rejoiced to see you safe under my roof again, not only for your own sake, but for that of madame's eyes, which, if she will permit an old man to say so, are much too pretty to spoil by straining them all day in the hopes of seeing someone coming out of the forest. You have done forty miles, Monsieur de Catinat, and are doubtless hungry and weary. When you are yourself again I must claim my revenge in piquet, for the cards lay against me the other night."

But Du Lhut had entered at De Catinat's heels with his tidings of disaster.

" You will have another game to play, Monsieur de Sainte Marie," said he. " There are six hundred

Iroquois in the woods and they are preparing to attack."

" Tut, tut, we cannot allow our arrangements to be altered by a handful of savages," said the seigneur. " I must apologise to you, my dear De Catinat, that you should be annoyed by such people while you are upon my estate. As regards the piquet, I cannot but think that your play from king and knave is more brilliant than safe. Now when I played piquet last with De Lannes of Poitou——"

" De Lannes of Poitou is dead, and all his people," said Du Lhut. " The blockhouse is a heap of smoking ashes."

The seigneur raised his eyebrows and took a pinch of snuff, tapping the lid of his little round gold box.

" I always told him that his fort would be taken unless he cleared away those maple trees which grew up to the very walls. They are all dead, you say ? "

" Every man."

" And the fort burned ? "

" Not a stick was left standing."

" Have you seen these rascals ? "

" We saw the trail of a hundred and fifty. Then there were a hundred in canoes, and a war-party of four hundred passed us under the Flemish Bastard. Their camp is five miles down the river, and there cannot be less than six hundred."

" You were fortunate in escaping them."

" But they were not so fortunate in escaping us. We killed Brown Moose and his son, and we fired the woods so as to drive them out of their camp."

" Excellent ! Excellent ! " said the seigneur, clapping gently with his dainty hands. " You have done very well indeed, Du Lhut ! You are, I presume, very tired ? "

" I am not often tired. I am quite ready to do the journey again."

" Then perhaps you would pick a few men and go back into the woods to see what these villains are doing ? "

" I shall be ready in five minutes."

" Perhaps you would like to go also, Achille ? "

His son's dark eyes and Indian face lit up with a fierce joy.

" Yes, I shall go also," he answered.

" Very good, and we shall make all ready in your absence. Madame, you will excuse these little annoyances which mar the pleasure of your visit. Next time that you do me the honour to come here I trust that we shall have cleared all these vermin from my estate. We have our advantages. The Richelieu is a better fish pond and these forests are a finer deer preserve than any of which the king can boast. But on the other hand we have, as you see, our little troubles. You will excuse me now, as there are one or two things which demand my attention. De Catinat, you are a tried soldier and I should be glad of your advice. Onega, give me my lace handkerchief and my cane of clouded amber, and take care of madame until her husband and I return."

It was bright daylight now, and the square enclosure within the stockade was filled with an anxious crowd who had just learned the evil tidings. Most of the *censitaires* were old soldiers and trappers who had served in many Indian wars, and whose swarthy faces and bold bearing told their own story. They were sons of a race which with better fortune or with worse has burned more powder than any other nation upon earth, and as they stood in little groups discussing the situation and examining their arms, a leader could have asked for no more hardy or more war-like following. The women, however, pale and breathless, were hurrying in from the outlying cottages, dragging their children with them, and bearing over their shoulders the more precious of their household goods. The confusion, the hurry, the cries of the children, the throwing down of bundles and the rushing back for more, contrasted sharply with the quiet and the beauty of the woods which encircled them, all bathed in the bright morning sunlight. It was strange to look upon the fairy loveliness of their many-tinted

foliage, and to know that the spirit of murder and cruelty was roaming unchained behind that lovely screen.

The scouting party under Du Lhut and Achille de la Noue had already left, and at the order of the seigneur the two gates were now secured with huge bars of oak fitted into iron staples on either side. The children were placed in the lower store-room with a few women to watch them, while the others were told off to attend to the fire buckets, and to reload the muskets. The men had been paraded, fifty-two of them in all, and they were divided into parties now for the defence of each part of the stockade. On one side it had been built up to within a few yards of the river, which not only relieved them from the defence of that face, but enabled them to get fresh water by throwing a bucket at the end of a rope from the stockade. The boats and canoes of Sainte Marie were drawn up on the bank just under the wall, and were precious now as offering a last means of escape should all else fail. The next fort, St. Louis, was but a few leagues up the river, and De la Noue had already sent a swift messenger to them with news of the danger. At least it would be a point on which they might retreat should the worst come to the worst.

And that the worst might come to the worst was very evident to so experienced a woodsman as Amos Green. He had left Ephraim Savage snoring in a deep sleep upon the floor, and was now walking round the defences with his pipe in his mouth, examining with a critical eye every detail in connection with them. The stockade was very strong, nine feet high and closely built of oak stakes which were thick enough to turn a bullet. Half way up it was loop-holed in long narrow slits for the fire of the defenders. But on the other hand the trees grew up to within a hundred yards of it, and formed a screen for the attack, while the garrison was so scanty that it could not spare more than twenty men at the utmost for each face. Amos knew how daring and dashing were the Iroquois warriors, how cunning and fertile of resource, and his face darkened as he thought of the young wife who had

come so far in their safe-keeping, and of the women and children whom he had seen crowding into the fort.

" Would it not be better if you could send them up the river ? " he suggested to the seigneur.

" I should very gladly do so, monsieur, and perhaps if we are all alive we may manage it to-night if the weather should be cloudy. But I cannot spare the men to guard them, and I cannot send them without a guard when we know that Iroquois canoes are on the river and their scouts are swarming on the banks."

" You are right. It would be madness."

" I have stationed you on this eastern face with your friends and with fifteen men. Monsieur de Catinat, will you command the party ? "

" Willingly."

" I will take the south face as it seems to be the point of danger. Du Lhut can take the north, and five men should be enough to watch the river side."

" Have we food and powder ? "

" I have flour and smoked eels enough to see this matter through. Poor fare, my dear sir, but I daresay you learned in Holland that a cup of ditch water after a brush may have a better smack than the blue-sealed Frontiniac which you helped me to finish the other night. As to powder, we have all our trading stores to draw upon."

" We have not time to clear any of these trees ? " asked the soldier.

" Impossible. They would make better shelter down than up."

" But at least I might clear that patch of brushwood round the birch sapling which lies between the east face and the edge of the forest. It is good cover for their skirmishers."

" Yes, that should be fired without delay."

" Nay, I think that I might do better," said Amos. " We might bait a trap for them there. Where is this powder of which you spoke ? "

" Theuriet, the major-domo, is giving out powder in the main store-house."

" Very good." Amos vanished upstairs, and returned with a large linen bag in his hand. This he filled with powder, and then, slinging it over his shoulder, he carried it out to the clump of bushes and placed it at the base of the sapling, cutting a strip out of the bark immediately above the spot. Then with a few leafy branches and fallen leaves he covered the powder bag very carefully over so that it looked like a little hillock of earth. Having arranged all to his satisfaction he returned, clambering over the stockade and dropping down upon the other side.

" I think that we are all ready for them now," said the seigneur. " I would that the women and children were in a safe place, but we may send them down the river to-night if all goes well. Has anyone heard anything of Du Lhut ? "

" Jean has the best ears of any of us, your excellency," said one man from beside the brass corner cannon. " He thought that he heard shots a few minutes ago."

" Then he has come into touch with them. Étienne, take ten men and go to the withered oak to cover them if they are retreating, but do not go another yard on any pretext. I am too short-handed already. Perhaps, De Catinat, you wish to sleep ? "

" No, I could not sleep."

" We can do no more down here. What do you say to a round or two of piquet ? A little turn of the cards will help us to pass the time."

They ascended to the upper hall where Adèle came and sat by her husband, while the swarthy Onega crouched by the window looking keenly out into the forest. De Catinat had little thought to spare upon the cards, as his mind wandered to the danger which threatened them and to the woman whose hand rested upon his own. The old nobleman, on the other hand, was engrossed by the play, and cursed under his breath, or chuckled and grinned as

the luck swayed one way or the other. Suddenly as they played there came two sharp raps from without.

" Someone is tapping," cried Adèle.

" It is death that is tapping," said the Indian woman at the window.

" Aye, aye, it was the patter of two spent balls against the woodwork. The wind is against our hearing the report. The cards are shuffled. It is my cut and your deal. The capot, I think, was mine."

" Men are rushing from the woods," cried Onega.

" Tut ! It grows serious ! " said the nobleman. " We can finish the game later. Remember that the deal lies with you. Let us see what it all means."

De Catinat had already rushed to the window. Du Lhut, young Achille de la Noue and eight of the covering party were running with their heads bent towards the stockade, the door of which had been opened to admit them. Here and there from behind the trees came little blue puffs of smoke, and one of the fugitives who wore white calico breeches began suddenly to hop instead of running and a red splotch showed upon the white cloth. Two others threw their arms round him and the three rushed in abreast while the gate swung into its place behind them. An instant later the brass cannon at the corner gave a flash and a roar while the whole outline of the wood was traced in a rolling cloud, and the shower of bullets rapped up against the wooden wall like sleet on a window.

36. *The Taking of the Stockade*

HAVING left Adèle to the care of her Indian hostess, and warned her for her life to keep from the windows, De Catinat seized his musket and rushed downstairs. As he passed a bullet came piping through one of the narrow embrasures and starred itself in a little blotch of lead upon the opposite wall.

The seigneur had already descended and was conversing with Du Lhut beside the door.

" A thousand of them, you say ? "

" Yes, we came on a fresh trail of a large war-party, three hundred at the least. They are all Mohawks and Cayugas with a sprinkling of Oneidas. We had a running fight for a few miles, and we have lost five men."

" All dead, I trust."

" I hope so, but we were hard pressed to keep from being cut off. Jean Mance is shot through the leg."

" I saw that he was hit."

" We had best have all ready to retire to the house if they carry the stockade. We can scarce hope to hold it when they are twenty to one."

" All is ready."

" And with our cannon we can keep their canoes from passing, so we might send our women away to-night."

" I had intended to do so. Will you take charge of the north side ? You might come across to me with ten of your men now, and I shall go back to you if they change their attack."

The firing came in one continuous rattle now from the edges of the wood, and the air was full of bullets. The assailants were all trained shots, men who lived by their guns, and to whom a shaking hand or a dim eye meant poverty and hunger. Every slit and crack and loop-hole was marked and a cap held above the stockade was blown in an instant from the gun barrel which supported it. On the other hand, the defenders were also skilled in Indian fighting, and wise in every trick and lure which could protect themselves or tempt their enemies to show. They kept well to the sides of the loop-holes, watching through little crevices of the wood, and firing swiftly when a chance offered. A red leg sticking straight up into the air from behind a log showed where one bullet at least had gone home, but there was little to aim at save a puff and flash from among the leaves, or the shadowy figure of a warrior seen for an instant as he darted from

one tree-trunk to the other. Seven of the Canadians had already been hit, but only three were mortally wounded, and the other four still kept manfully to their loop-holes, though one who had been struck through the jaw was spitting his teeth with his bullets down into his gun barrel. The women sat in a line upon the ground, beneath the level of the loop-holes, each with a saucerful of bullets and a canister of powder, passing up the loaded guns to the fighting men at the points where a quick fire was most needful.

At first the attack had been all upon the south face, but as fresh bodies of the Iroquois came up their line spread and lengthened until the whole east face was girt with fire, which gradually enveloped the north also. The fort was ringed in by a great loop of smoke, save only where the broad river flowed past them. Over near the further bank the canoes were lurking, and one, manned by ten warriors, attempted to pass up the stream, but a good shot from the brass gun dashed in her side and sank her, while a second of grape left only four of the swimmers whose high scalp-locks stood out above the water like the back-fins of some strange fish. On the inland side, however, the seigneur had ordered the cannon to be served no more, for the broad embrasures drew the enemy's fire, and of the men who had been struck half were among those who worked the guns.

The old nobleman strutted about with his white ruffles and his clouded cane behind the line of parched smoke-grimed men, tapping his snuff box, shooting out his little jests, and looking very much less concerned than he had done over his piquet.

" What do you think of it, Du Lhut ? " he asked.

" I think very badly of it. We are losing men much too fast."

" Well, my friend, what can you expect ? When a thousand muskets are all turned upon a little place like this, someone must suffer for it. Ah, my poor fellow, so you are done for too ! "

The man nearest him had suddenly fallen with a crash, lying quite still with his face in a platter of the sagamite which had been brought out by the women. Du Lhut glanced at him and then looked round.

" He is in a line with no loop-hole, and it took him in the shoulder," said he. " Where did it come from, then ? Ah, by Sainte Anne, look there ! " He pointed upwards to a little mist of smoke which hung round the summit of a high oak.

" The rascal overlooks the stockade. But the trunk is hardly thick enough to shield him at that height. This poor fellow will not need his musket again, and I see that it is ready primed." De la Noue laid down his cane, turned back his ruffles, picked up the dead man's gun, and fired at the lurking warrior. Two leaves fluttered out from the tree and a grinning vermilion face appeared for an instant with a yell of derision. Quick as a flash Du Lhut brought his musket to his shoulder and pulled the trigger. The man gave a tremendous spring and crashed down through the thick foliage. Some seventy or eighty feet below him a single stout branch shot out and on to this he fell with the sound of a great stone dropping into a bog, and hung there doubled over it, swinging slowly from side to side like a red rag, his scalp-lock streaming down between his feet. A shout of exultation rose from the Canadians at the sight, which was drowned in the murderous yell of the savages.

" His limbs twitch. He is not dead," cried De la Noue.

" Let him die there," said the old pioneer callously, ramming a fresh charge into his gun. " Ah, there is the grey hat again. It comes ever when I am unloaded."

" I saw a plumed hat among the brushwood."

" It is the Flemish Bastard. I had rather have his scalp than those of his hundred best warriors."

" Is he so brave, then ? "

" Yes, he is brave enough. There is no denying it, for how else could he be an Iroquois war-chief ? But he is clever and cunning, and cruel—— Ah, my God, if all the

815

stories told are true, his cruelty is past believing. I
should fear that my tongue would wither if I did but
name the things which this man has done. Ah, he is
there again."

The grey hat with the plume had shown itself once
more in a rift of the smoke. De la Noue and Du Lhut
both fired together, and the cap fluttered up into the air.
At the same instant the bushes parted and a tall warrior
sprang out into full view of the defenders. His face was
that of an Indian, but a shade or two lighter, and a pointed
black beard hung down over his hunting tunic. He
threw out his hands with a gesture of disdain, stood for
an instant looking steadfastly at the fort, and then sprang
back into cover amid a shower of bullets which chipped
away the twigs all round him.

" Yes, he is brave enough," Du Lhut repeated with an
oath. " Your *censitaires* have had their hoes in their
hands more often than their muskets, I should judge from
their shooting. But they seem to be drawing closer upon
the east face, and I think that they will make a rush there
before long."

The fire had indeed grown very much fiercer upon the
side which was defended by De Catinat, and it was plain
that the main force of the Iroquois were gathered at that
point. From every log, and trunk, and cleft, and bush
came the red flash with the grey halo, and the bullets sang
in a continuous stream through the loop-holes. Amos
had whittled a little hole for himself about a foot above
the ground, and lay upon his face loading and firing in his
own quiet methodical fashion. Beside him stood
Ephraim Savage, his mouth set grimly, his eyes flashing
from under his down-drawn brows, and his whole soul
absorbed in the smiting of the Amalekites. His hat was
gone, his grizzled hair flying in the breeze, great splotches
of powder mottled his mahogany face and a weal across
his right cheek showed where an Indian bullet had grazed
him. De Catinat was bearing himself like an experienced
soldier, walking up and down among his men with short

words of praise or of precept, those fire-words rough and blunt which bring a glow to the heart and a flush to the cheek. Seven of his men were down, but as the attack grew fiercer upon his side it slackened upon the others, and the seigneur with his son and Du Lhut brought ten men to reinforce him. De la Noue was holding out his snuff box to De Catinat when a shrill scream from behind them made them both look round. Onega the Indian wife was wringing her hands over the body of her son. A glance showed that the bullet had pierced his heart and that he was dead.

For an instant the old nobleman's thin face grew a shade paler, and the hand which held out the little gold box shook like a branch in the wind. Then he thrust it into his pocket again and mastered the spasm which had convulsed his features.

" The De la Noues always die upon the field of honour," he remarked. " I think that we should have some more men in the angle by the gun."

And now it became clear why it was that the Iroquois had chosen the eastern face for their main attack. It was there that the clump of cover lay midway between the edge of the forest and the stockade. A storming party could creep as far as that and gather there for the final rush. First one crouching warrior, and then a second and then a third darted across the little belt of open space, and threw themselves down among the bushes. The fourth was hit and lay with his back broken a few paces out from the edge of the wood, but a stream of warriors continued to venture the passage, until thirty-six had got across and the little patch of underwood was full of lurking savages. Amos Green's time had come.

From where he lay he could see the white patch where he had cut the bark from the birch sapling, and he knew that immediately underneath it lay the powder bag. He sighted the mark, and then slowly lowered his barrel until he had got to the base of the little trees as nearly as he could guess it among the tangle of bushes. The first

shot produced no result, however, and the second was aimed a foot lower. The bullet penetrated the bag and there was an explosion which shook the manor-house, and swayed the whole line of stout stockades as though they were corn-stalks in a breeze. Up to the highest summits of the trees went the huge column of blue smoke, and after the first roar there was a deathly silence which was broken by the patter and thud of falling bodies. Then came a wild cheer from the defenders, and a furious answering whoop from the Indians, while the fire from the woods burst out with greater fury than ever.

But the blow had been a heavy one. Of the thirty-six warriors, all picked for their valour, only four regained the shelter of the woods, and those so torn and shattered that they were spent men. Already the Indians had lost heavily, and this fresh disaster made them reconsider their plan of attack, for the Iroquois were as wary as they were brave, and he was esteemed the best war-chief who was most chary of the lives of his followers. Their fire gradually slackened, and at last, save for a dropping shot here and there, it died away altogether.

" Is it possible that they are going to abandon the attack ? " cried De Catinat joyously. " Amos, I believe that you have saved us."

But the wily Du Lhut shook his head. " A wolf would as soon leave a half-gnawed bone as an Iroquois such a prize as this."

" But they have lost heavily."

" Aye, but not so heavily as ourselves in proportion to our numbers. They have fifty out of a thousand, and we twenty out of threescore. No, no, they are holding a council, and we shall soon hear from them again. But it may be some hours first, and if you will take my advice you will have an hour's sleep, for you are not, as I can see by your eyes, as used to doing without it as I am, and there may be little rest for any of us this night."

De Catinat was indeed weary to the last pitch of human endurance. Amos Green and the seaman had already

wrapt themselves in their blankets and sunk to sleep under the shelter of the stockade. The soldier rushed upstairs to say a few words of comfort to the trembling Adèle, and then throwing himself down upon a couch he slept the dreamless sleep of an exhausted man. When at last he was roused by a fresh sputter of musketry fire from the woods the sun was already low in the heavens and the mellow light of evening tinged the bare walls of the room. He sprang from his couch, seized his musket and rushed downstairs. The defenders were gathered at their loopholes once more, while Du Lhut, the seigneur and Amos Green were whispering eagerly together. He noticed as he passed that Onega still sat crooning by the body of her son without having changed her position since morning.

" What is it, then ? Are they coming on ? " he asked.

" They are up to some devilry," said Du Lhut, peering out at the corner of the embrasure. " They are gathering thickly at the east fringe, and yet the firing comes from the south. It is not the Indian way to attack across the open, and yet if they think help is coming from the fort they might venture it."

" The wood in front of us is alive with them," said Amos. " They are as busy as beavers among the underwood."

" Perhaps they are going to attack from this side, and cover the attack by a fire from the flank."

" That is what I think," cried the seigneur. " Bring the spare guns up here and all the men except five for each side."

The words were hardly out of his mouth when a shrill yell burst from the wood, and in an instant a cloud of warriors dashed out and charged across the open, howling, springing and waving their guns or tomahawks in the air. With their painted faces, smeared and striped with every vivid colour, their streaming scalp-locks, their waving arms, their open mouths, and their writhings and contortions, no more fiendish crew ever burst into a sleeper's

nightmare. Some of those in front bore canoes between them, and as they reached the stockade they planted them against it and swarmed up them as if they had been scaling ladders. Others fired through the embrasures and loop-holes, the muzzles of their muskets touching those of the defenders, while others again sprang unaided on to the tops of the palisades and jumped fearlessly down upon the inner side. The Canadians, however, made such a resistance as might be expected from men who knew that no mercy awaited them. They fired whilst they had time to load, and then clubbing their muskets they smashed furiously at every red head which showed above the rails. The din within the stockade was infernal, the shouts and cries of the French, the whooping of the savages, and the terrified screaming of the frightened women blending into one dreadful uproar, above which could be heard the high shrill voice of the old seigneur imploring his *censitaires* to stand fast. With his rapier in his hand, his hat lost, his wig awry, and his dignity all thrown to the winds, the old nobleman showed them that day how a soldier of Rocroy could carry himself, and with Du Lhut, Amos, De Catinat and Ephraim Savage was ever in the forefront of the defence. So desperately did they fight, the sword and musket butt outreaching the tomahawk, that though at one time fifty Iroquois were over the palisades they had slain or driven back nearly all of them when a fresh wave burst suddenly over the south face which had been stripped of its defenders. Du Lhut saw in an instant that the enclosure was lost and that only one thing could save the house.

" Hold them for an instant," he screamed, and rushing at the brass gun he struck his flint and steel and fired it straight into the thick of the savages. Then as they re-coiled for an instant he stuck a nail into the touch-hole and drove it home with a blow from the butt of his gun. Darting across the yard he spiked the gun at the other corner, and was back at the door as the remnants of the garrison were hurled towards it by the rush of the assail-

ants. The Canadians darted in, and swung the ponderous mass of wood into position, breaking the leg of the foremost warrior who had striven to follow them. Then for an instant they had time for breathing and for council.

37. *The Coming of the Friar*

BUT their case was a very evil one. Had the guns been lost so that they might be turned upon the door, all further resistance would have been vain, but Du Lhut's presence of mind had saved them from that danger. The two guns upon the river face and the canoes were safe, for they were commanded by the windows of the house. But their numbers were terribly reduced and those who were left were weary and wounded and spent. Nineteen had gained the house, but one had been shot through the body and lay groaning in the hall, while a second had his shoulder cleft by a tomahawk and could no longer raise his musket. Du Lhut, De la Noue and De Catinat were uninjured, but Ephraim Savage had a bullet hole in his forearm, and Amos was bleeding from a cut upon the face. Of the others hardly one was without injury, and yet they had no time to think of their hurts, for the danger still pressed and they were lost unless they acted. A few shots from the barricaded windows sufficed to clear the enclosure, for it was all exposed to their aim, but on the other hand they had the shelter of the stockade now, and from the further side of it they kept up a fierce fire upon the windows. Half a dozen of the *censitaires* returned the fusillade, while the leaders consulted as to what had best be done.

" We have twenty-five women and fourteen children," said the seigneur. " I am sure that you will agree with me, gentlemen, that our first duty is towards them. Some of you, like myself, have lost sons or brothers this day. Let us at least save our wives and sisters."

" No Iroquois canoes have passed up the river," said

one of the Canadians. " If the women start in the darkness they can get away to the fort."

" By Saint Anne of Beaupré," exclaimed Du Lhut, " I think it would be well if you could get your men out of this also, for I cannot see how it is to be held until morning."

A murmur of assent broke from the other Canadians, but the old nobleman shook his bewigged head with decision.

" Tut ! Tut ! what nonsense is this ! " he cried. "Are we to abandon the manor-house of Sainte Marie to the first gang of savages who choose to make an attack upon it ? No, no, gentlemen, there are still nearly a score of us, and when the garrison learn that we are so pressed, which will be by to-morrow morning at the latest, they will certainly send us relief."

Du Lhut shook his head moodily.

" If you stand by the fort I will not desert you," said he, " and yet it is a pity to sacrifice brave men for nothing."

" The canoes will hardly hold the women and children as it is," cried Theuriet. " There are but two large and four small. There is not space for a single man."

" Then that decides it," said De Catinat. " But who are to row the women ? "

" It is but a few leagues with the current in their favour, and there are none of our women who do not know how to handle a paddle."

The Iroquois were very quiet now, and an occasional dropping shot from the trees or the stockade was the only sign of their presence. Their losses had been heavy, and they were either engaged in collecting their dead, or in holding a council as to their next move. The twilight was gathering in, and the sun had already sunk beneath the tree-tops. Leaving a watchman at each window the leaders went round to the back of the house where the canoes were lying upon the bank. There were no signs of the enemy upon the river to the north of them.

" We are in luck," said Amos. " The clouds are gathering and there will be little light."

" It is luck indeed, since the moon is only three days past the full," answered Du Lhut. " I wonder that the Iroquois have not cut us off upon the water, but it is likely that their canoes have gone south to bring up another war-party. They may be back soon, and we had best not lose a moment."

" In an hour it might be dark enough to start."

" I think that there is rain in those clouds, and that will make it darker still."

The women and children were assembled and their places in each boat were assigned to them. The wives of the *censitaires*, rough hardy women whose lives had been spent under the shadow of a constant danger, were for the most part quiet and collected, though a few of the younger ones whimpered a little. A woman is always braver when she has a child to draw her thoughts from herself, and each married woman had one now allotted to her as her own special charge until they should reach the fort. To Onega, the Indian wife of the seigneur, who was as wary and as experienced as a war sachem of her people, the command of the women was entrusted.

" It is not very far, Adèle," said De Catinat, as his wife clung to his arm. " You remember how we heard the Angelus bells as we journeyed through the woods. That was Fort St. Louis, and it is but a league or two."

" But I do not wish to leave you, Amory. We have been together in all our troubles. Oh, Amory, why should we be divided now ? "

" My dear love, you will tell them at the fort how things are with us, and they will bring us help."

" Let the others do that, and I will stay. I will not be useless, Amory. Onega has taught me to load a gun. I will not be afraid, indeed I will not, if you will only let me stay."

" You must not ask it, Adèle. It is impossible, child. I could not let you stay."

" But I feel so sure that it would be best."

The coarser reason of man has not yet learned to value those subtle instincts which guide a woman. De Catinat argued and exhorted until he had silenced if he had not convinced her.

" It is for my sake, dear. You do not know what a load it will be from my heart when I know that you are safe. And you need not be afraid for me. We can easily hold the place until morning. Then the people from the fort will come, for I hear that they have plenty of canoes, and we shall all meet again."

Adèle was silent, but her hands tightened upon his arm. Her husband was still endeavouring to reassure her when a groan burst from the watcher at the window which overlooked the stream.

" There is a canoe on the river to the north of us," he cried.

The besieged looked at each other in dismay. The Iroquois had then cut off their retreat after all.

" How many warriors are in it ? " asked the seigneur.

" I cannot see. The light is not very good, and it is in the shadow of the bank."

" Which way is it coming ? "

" It is coming this way. Ah, it shoots out into the open now, and I can see it. May the good Lord be praised ! A dozen candles shall burn in Quebec Cathedral if I live till next summer ! "

" What is it, then ? " cried De la Noue impatiently.

" It is not an Iroquois canoe. There is but one man in it. He is a Canadian."

" A Canadian ! " cried Du Lhut, springing up to the window. " Who but a madman would venture into such a hornet's nest alone ! Ah, yes, I can see him now. He keeps well out from the bank to avoid their fire. Now he is in mid-stream and he turns towards us. By my faith, it is not the first time that the good father has handled a paddle."

" It is a Jesuit ! " said one, craning his neck. " They are ever where there is most danger."

" No, I can see his capote," cried another. " It is a Franciscan friar ! "

An instant later there was the sound of a canoe grounding upon the pebbles, the door was unbarred, and a man strode in, attired in the long brown gown of the Franciscans. He cast a rapid glance around, and then, stepping up to De Catinat, laid his hand upon his shoulder.

" So, you have not escaped me ! " said he. " We have caught the evil seed before it has had time to root."

" What do you mean, father ? " asked the seigneur. " You have made some mistake. This is my good friend Amory de Catinat, of a noble French family."

" This is Amory de Catinat, the heretic and Huguenot," cried the monk. " I have followed him up the St. Lawrence, and I have followed him up the Richelieu, and I would have followed him to the world's end if I could but bring him back with me."

" Tut, father, your zeal carries you too far," said the seigneur. " Whither would you take my friend, then ? "

" He shall go back to France with his wife. There is no place in Canada for heretics."

Du Lhut burst out laughing. " By Sainte Anne, father," said he, " if you could take us all back to France at present we should be very much your debtors."

" And you will remember," said De la Noue sternly, " that you are under my roof and that you are speaking of my guest."

But the friar was not to be abashed by the frown of the old nobleman.

" Look at this," said he, whipping a paper out of his bosom. " It is signed by the governor, and calls upon you under pain of the king's displeasure to return this man to Quebec. Ah, monsieur, when you left me upon the island that morning you little thought that I would return to Quebec for this, and then hunt you down so many hundreds of miles of river. But I have you now,

and I shall never leave you until I see you on board the ship which will carry you and your wife back to France."

For all the bitter vindictiveness which gleamed in the monk's eyes, De Catinat could not but admire the energy and tenacity of the man.

" It seems to me, father, that you would have shone more as a soldier than as a follower of Christ," said he ; " but since you have followed us here, and since there is no getting away, we may settle this question at some later time."

But the two Americans were less inclined to take so peaceful a view. Ephraim Savage's beard bristled with anger, and he whispered something into Amos Green's ear."

" The captain and I could easily get rid of him," said the young woodsman, drawing De Catinat aside. " If he *will* cross our path he must pay for it."

" No, no, not for the world, Amos ! Let him alone. He does what he thinks to be his duty, though his faith is stronger than his charity, I think. But here comes the rain, and surely it is dark enough now for the boats."

A great brown cloud had overspread the heavens, and the night had fallen so rapidly that they could hardly see the gleam of the river in front of them. The savages in the woods and behind the captured stockade were quiet, save for an occasional shot, but the yells and whoops from the cottages of the *censitaires* showed that they were being plundered by their captors. Suddenly a dull red glow began to show above one of the roofs.

" They have set it on fire," cried Du Lhut. " The canoes must go at once, for the river will soon be as light as day. In ! In ! There is not an instant to lose ! "

There was no time for leave-taking. One impassioned kiss and Adèle was torn away and thrust into the smallest canoe, which she shared with Onega, two children and an unmarried girl. The others rushed into their places, and in a few moments they had pushed off and had vanished into the drift and the darkness. The great cloud had

broken and the rain pattered heavily upon the roof, and splashed upon their faces as they strained their eyes after the vanishing boats.

" Thank God for this storm ! " murmured Du Lhut. " It will prevent the cottages from blazing up too quickly."

But he had forgotten that though the roofs might be wet the interior was as dry as tinder. He had hardly spoken before a great yellow tongue of flame licked out of one of the windows, and again and again, until suddenly half of the roof fell in, and the cottage was blazing like a pitch-bucket. The flames hissed and sputtered in the pouring rain, but, fed from below, they grew still higher and fiercer, flashing redly upon the great trees, and turning their trunks to burnished brass. Their light made the enclosure and the manor-house as clear as day, and exposed the whole long stretch of the river. A fearful yell from the woods announced that the savages had seen the canoes, which were plainly visible from the windows not more than a quarter of a mile away.

" They are rushing through the woods. They are making for the water's edge," cried De Catinat.

" They have some canoes down there," said Du Lhut.

" But they must pass us ! " cried the Seigneur of Sainte Marie. " Get down to the cannon and see if you cannot stop them."

They had hardly reached the guns when the two large canoes filled with warriors shot out from among the reeds below the fort, and steering out into mid-stream began to paddle furiously after the fugitives.

" Jean, you are our best shot," cried De la Noue. " Lay for her as she passes the great pine tree. Lambert, do you take the other gun. The lives of all whom you love may hang upon the shot ! "

The two wrinkled old artillerymen glanced along their guns and waited for the canoes to come abreast of them. The fire still blazed higher and higher, and the broad river lay like a sheet of dull metal with two dark lines, which marked the canoes, sweeping swiftly down the centre.

One was fifty yards in front of the other, but in each the Indians were bending to their paddles and pulling frantically, while their comrades from the wooded shores whooped them on to fresh exertions. The fugitives had already disappeared round the bend of the river.

As the first canoe came abreast of the lower of the two guns, the Canadian made the sign of the cross over the touch-hole and fired. A cheer and then a groan went up from the eager watchers. The discharge had struck the surface close to the mark, and dashed such a shower of water over it that for an instant it looked as if it had been sunk. The next moment, however, the splash subsided and the canoe shot away uninjured save that one of the rowers had dropped his paddle while his head fell forward upon the back of the man in front of him. The second gunner sighted the same canoe as it came abreast of him but at the very instant when he stretched out his match to fire a bullet came humming from the stockade and he fell forward dead without a groan.

" This is work that I know something of, lad," said old Ephraim, springing suddenly forward. " But when I fire a gun I like to train it myself. Give me a help with the handspike and get her straight for the island. So ! A little lower for an even keel ! Now we have them ! " He clapped down his match and fired.

It was a beautiful shot. The whole charge took the canoe about six feet behind the bow, and doubled her up like an eggshell. Before the smoke had cleared she had foundered, and the second canoe had paused to pick up some of the wounded men. The others, as much at home in the water as in the woods, were already striking out for the shore.

" Quick ! quick ! " cried the seigneur. " Load the gun ! We may get the second one yet ! "

But it was not to be. Long before they could get it ready the Iroquois had picked up their wounded warriors, and were pulling madly up-stream once more. As they shot away the fire died suddenly down in the burning

cottages and the rain and the darkness closed in upon them.

" My God ! " cried De Catinat furiously, " they will be taken. Let us abandon this place, take a boat and follow them. Come ! Come ! Not an instant is to be lost ! "

" Monsieur, you go too far in your very natural anxiety," said the seigneur coldly. " I am not inclined to leave my post so easily ! "

" Ah, what is it ? Only wood and stone which can be built again. But to think of the women in the hands of these devils. Oh, I am going mad ! Come ! Come ! For Christ's sake come ! " His face was deadly pale, and he raved with his clenched hands in the air.

" I do not think that they will be caught," said Du Lhut, laying his hand soothingly upon his shoulder. " Do not fear. They had a long start and the women here can paddle as well as the men. Again, the Iroquois canoe was over-loaded at the start, and has the wounded men aboard as well now. Besides, these oak canoes of the Mohawks are not as swift as the Algonquin birch barks which we use. In any case it is impossible to follow, for we have no boat."

" There is one lying there."

" Ah, it will but hold a single man. It is that in which the friar came."

" Then I am going in that ! My place is with Adèle ! " He flung open the door, rushed out, and was about to push off the frail skiff, when someone sprang past him, and with a blow from a hatchet stove in the side of the boat.

" It is my boat," said the friar, throwing down the axe and folding his arms. " I can do what I like with it."

" You fiend ! You have ruined us ! "

" I have found you and you shall not escape me again."

The hot blood flushed to the soldier's head, and picking up the axe, he took a quick step forward. The light from the open door shone upon the grave, harsh face of the

friar, but not a muscle twitched nor a feature changed as he saw the axe whirl up in the hands of a furious man. He only signed himself with a cross, and muttered a Latin prayer under his breath. It was that composure which saved his life. De Catinat hurled down the axe again with a bitter curse, and was turning away from the shattered boat when in an instant, without a warning, the great door of the manor-house crashed inwards, and a flood of whooping savages burst into the house.

38. *The Dining Hall of Sainte Marie*

WHAT had occurred is easily explained. The watchers in the windows at the front found that it was more than flesh and blood could endure to remain waiting at their posts while the fates of their wives and children were being decided at the back. All was quiet at the stockade and the Indians appeared to be as absorbed as the Canadians in what was passing upon the river. One by one, therefore, the men on guard had crept away and had assembled at the back to cheer the seaman's shot and to groan as the remaining canoe sped like a bloodhound down the river in the wake of the fugitives. But the savages had one at their head who was as full of wiles and resource as Du Lhut himself. The Flemish Bastard had watched the house from behind the stockade as a dog watches a rat hole, and he had instantly discovered that the defenders had left their post. With a score of other warriors he raised a great log from the edge of the forest, and crossing the open space unchallenged, he and his men rushed it against the door with such violence as to crack the bar across and tear the wood from the hinges. The first intimation which the survivors had of the attack was the crash of the door, and the screams of two of the negligent watchmen who had been seized and scalped in the hall. The whole basement floor was in the hands of the Indians, and De

Catinat and his enemy the friar were cut off from the foot of the stairs.

Fortunately, however, the manor-houses of Canada were built with the one idea of defence against Indians, and even now there were hopes for the defenders. A wooden ladder which could be drawn up in case of need hung down from the upper windows to the ground upon the river side. De Catinat rushed round to this, followed by the friar. He felt about for the ladder in the darkness. It was gone.

Then indeed his heart sank in despair. Where could he fly to ? The boat was destroyed. The stockades lay between him and the forest, and they were in the hands of the Iroquois. Their yells were ringing in his ears. They had not seen him yet, but in a few minutes they must come upon him. Suddenly he heard a voice from somewhere in the darkness above him.

" Give me your gun, lad," it said. " I see the loom of some of the heathen down by the wall."

" It is I. It is I, Amos," cried De Catinat. " Down with the ladder or I am a dead man."

" Have a care. It may be a ruse," said the voice of Du Lhut.

" No, no, I'll answer for it," cried Amos, and an instant later down came the ladder. De Catinat and the friar rushed up it, and they hardly had their feet upon the rungs when a swarm of warriors burst out from the door and poured along the river bank. Two muskets flashed from above, something plopped like a salmon in the water, and next instant the two were among their comrades and the ladder had been drawn up once more.

But it was a very small band who now held the last point to which they could retreat. Only nine of them remained, the seigneur, Du Lhut, the two Americans, the friar, De Catinat, Theuriet the major-domo, and two of the *censitaires*. Wounded, parched and powder-blackened, they were still filled with the mad courage of desperate men who knew that death could not come in no

more terrible form than through surrender. The stone staircase ran straight up from the kitchen to the main hall, and the door, which had been barricaded across the lower part by two mattresses, commanded the whole flight. Hoarse whisperings and the click of the cocking of guns from below told that the Iroquois were mustering for a rush.

" Put the lantern by the door," said Du Lhut, " so that it may throw the light upon the stair. There is only room for three to fire, but you can all load and pass the guns. Monsieur Green, will you kneel with me, and you, Jean Duval ? If one of us is hit let another take his place at once. Now be ready, for they are coming ! "

As he spoke there was a shrill whistle from below, and in an instant the stair was filled with rushing red figures and waving weapons. Bang ! Bang ! Bang ! went the three guns, and then again and again Bang ! Bang ! Bang ! The smoke was so thick in the low-roofed room that they could hardly see to pass the muskets to the eager hands which grasped for them. But no Iroquois had reached the barricade, and there was no patter of their feet now upon the stair. Nothing but an angry snarling and an occasional groan from below. The marksmen were uninjured, but they ceased to fire and waited for the smoke to clear.

And when it cleared they saw how deadly their aim had been at those close quarters. Only nine shots had been fired, and seven Indians were littered up and down on the straight stone stair. Five of them lay motionless, but two tried to crawl slowly back to their friends. Du Lhut and the *censitaire* raised their muskets, and the two crippled men lay still.

" By Sainte Anne ! " said the old pioneer, as he rammed home another bullet. " If they have our scalps we have sold them at a great price. A hundred squaws will be howling in their villages when they hear of this day's work."

" Aye, they will not forget their welcome at Sainte

Marie," said the old nobleman. " I must again express my deep regret, my dear De Catinat, that you and your wife should have been put to such inconvenience when you have been good enough to visit me. I trust that she and the others are safe at the fort by this time."

" May God grant that they are ! Oh, I shall never have an easy moment until I see her once more."

" If they are safe we may expect help in the morning, if we can hold out so long. Chambly, the commandant, is not a man to leave a comrade at a pinch."

The cards were still laid out at one end of the table, with the tricks over-lapping each other as they had left them on the previous morning. But there was something else there of more interest to them, for the breakfast had not been cleared away, and they had been fighting all day with hardly bite or sup. Even when face to face with death Nature still cries out for her dues, and the hungry men turned savagely upon the loaf, the ham and the cold wild duck. A little cluster of wine bottles stood upon the buffet, and these had their necks knocked off, and were emptied down parched throats. Three men still took their turn, however, to hold the barricade, for they were not to be caught napping again. The yells and screeches of the savages came up to them as though all the wolves of the forest were cooped up in the basement, but the stair was deserted save for the seven motionless figures.

" They will not try to rush us again," said Du Lhut with confidence. " We have taught them too severe a lesson."

" They will set fire to the house."

" It will puzzle them to do that," said the major-domo. " It is solid stone, walls and stair, save only for a few beams of wood, very different from those other cottages."

" Hush ! " cried Amos Green, and raised his hand. The yells had died away and they heard the heavy thud of a mallet beating upon wood.

" What can it be ! "

" Some fresh devilry, no doubt."

" I regret to say, messieurs," observed the seigneur,

with no abatement of his courtly manner, " that it is my belief that they have learned a lesson from our young friend here, and that they are knocking out the heads of the powder-barrels in the store-room."

But Du Lhut shook his head at the suggestion. " It is not in a redskin to waste powder," said he. " It is a deal too precious for them to do that. Ah, listen to that ! "

The yellings and screechings had begun again, but there was a wilder, madder ring in their shrillness, and they were mingled with snatches of song and bursts of laughter.

" Ha ! It is the brandy casks which they have opened," cried Du Lhut. " They were bad before, but they will be fiends out of hell now."

As he spoke there came another burst of whoops and high above them a voice calling for mercy. With horror in their eyes the survivors glanced from one to the other. A heavy smell of burning flesh rose from below, and still that dreadful voice shrieking and pleading. Then slowly it quavered away and was silent for ever.

" Who was it ? " whispered De Catinat, his blood running cold in his veins.

" It was Jean Corbeil, I think."

" May God rest his soul ! His troubles are over. Would that we were as peaceful as he ! Ah, shoot him ! Shoot ! "

A man had suddenly sprung out at the foot of the stair and had swung his arm as though throwing something. It was the Flemish Bastard. Amos Green's musket flashed, but the savage had sprung back again as rapidly as he appeared. Something splashed down amongst them and rolled across the floor in the lamp-light.

" Down ! Down ! It is a bomb ! " cried De Catinat.

But it lay at Du Lhut's feet, and he had seen it clearly. He took a cloth from the table and dropped it over it.

" It is not a bomb," said he quietly, " and it *was* Jean Corbeil who died."

For four hours sounds of riot, of dancing and of revelling

rose up from the store-house, and the smell of the open brandy casks filled the whole air. More than once the savages quarrelled and fought among themselves, and it seemed as if they had forgotten their enemies above, but the besieged soon found that if they attempted to presume upon this they were as closely watched as ever. The major-domo, Theuriet, passing between a loop-hole and a light, was killed instantly by a bullet from the stockade, and both Amos and the old seigneur had narrow escapes until they blocked all the windows save that which over-looked the river. There was no danger from this one, and, as day was already breaking once more, one or other of the party was for ever straining their eyes down the stream in search of the expected succour.

Slowly the light crept up the eastern sky, a little line of pearl, then a band of pink, broadening, stretching, spread-ing, until it shot its warm colour across the heavens, tinging the edges of the drifting clouds. Over the wood-lands lay a thin grey vapour, the tops of the high oaks jutting out like dim islands from the sea of haze. Gradu-ally as the light increased the mist shredded off into little ragged wisps which thinned and drifted away, until at last, as the sun pushed its glowing edge over the eastern forests, it gleamed upon the reds and oranges and purples of the fading leaves, and upon the broad blue river which curled away to the northward. De Catinat, as he stood at the window looking out, was breathing in the healthy resinous scent of the trees, mingled with the damp heavy odour of the wet earth, when suddenly his eyes fell upon a dark spot upon the river to the north of them.

" There is a canoe coming down ! " he cried.

In an instant they had all rushed to the opening, but Du Lhut sprang after them, and pulled them angrily towards the door.

" Do you wish to die before your time ! " he cried.

" Aye, aye ! " said Captain Ephraim, who understood the gesture if not the words. " We must leave a watch

on deck. Amos, lad, lie here with me and be ready if they show."

The two Americans and the old pioneer held the barricade, while the eyes of all the others were turned upon the approaching boat. A groan broke suddenly from the only surviving *censitaire*.

" It is an Iroquois canoe ! " he cried.

" Impossible ! "

" Alas, your excellency, it is so, and it is the same one which passed us last night."

" Ah, then the women have escaped them."

" I trust so. But alas, seigneur, I fear that there are more in the canoe now than when they passed us."

The little group of survivors waited in breathless anxiety while the canoe sped swiftly up the river, with a line of foam on either side of her, and a long forked swirl in the waters behind. They could see that she appeared to be very crowded, but they remembered that the wounded of the other boat were aboard her. On she shot and on, until as she came abreast of the fort she swung round, and the rowers raised their paddles and burst into a shrill yell of derision. The stern of the canoe was turned towards them now, and they saw that two women were seated in it. Even at that distance there was no mistaking the sweet pale face, or the dark queenly one beside it. The one was Onega and the other was Adèle.

39. *The Two Swimmers*

CHARLES DE LA NOUE, Seigneur de Sainte Marie, was a hard and self-contained man, but a groan and a bitter curse burst from him when he saw his Indian wife in the hands of her kinsmen, from whom she could hope for little mercy. Yet even now his old-fashioned courtesy to his guest had made him turn to De Catinat with some words of sympathy, when there was a clatter of wood, something darkened the light

of the window, and the young soldier was gone. Without a word he had lowered the ladder and was clambering down it with frantic haste. Then as his feet touched the ground he signalled to his comrades to draw it up again and dashing into the river he swam towards the canoe. Without arms and without a plan he had but the one thought that his place was by the side of his wife in this, the hour of her danger. Fate should bring him what it brought her, and he swore to himself as he clove a way with his strong arms, that whether it were life or death they should still share it together.

But there was another whose view of duty led him from safety into the face of danger. All night the Franciscan had watched De Catinat as a miser watches his treasure, filled with the thought that this heretic was the one little seed which might spread and spread until it choked the chosen vineyard of the Church. Now when he saw him rush so suddenly down the ladder, every fear was banished from his mind save the overpowering one that he was about to lose his precious charge. He, too, clambered down at the very heels of his prisoner, and rushed into the stream not ten paces behind him.

And so the watchers at the window saw the strangest of sights. There, in mid-stream, lay the canoe, with a ring of dark warriors clustering in the stern, and the two women crouching in the midst of them. Swimming madly towards them was De Catinat, rising to the shoulders with the strength of every stroke, and behind him again was the tonsured head of the friar, with his brown capote and long trailing gown floating upon the surface of the water behind him. But in his zeal he had thought too little of his own powers. He was a good swimmer but he was weighted and hampered by his unwieldy clothes. Slower and slower grew his stroke, lower and lower his head, until at last with a great shriek of *In manus tuas, Domine !* he threw up his hands, and vanished in the swirl of the river. A minute later the watchers, hoarse with screaming to him to return, saw De Catinat pulled aboard the Iroquois

canoe, which was instantly turned, and continued its course up the river.

"My God!" cried Amos hoarsely. "They have taken him. He is lost!"

"I have seen some strange things in these forty years, but never the like of that!" said Du Lhut.

The seigneur took a little pinch of snuff from his gold box, and flicked the wandering grains from his shirt-front with his dainty lace handkerchief.

"Monsieur de Catinat has acted like a gentleman of France," said he. "If I could swim now as I did thirty years ago, I should be by his side."

Du Lhut glanced round him and shook his head. "We are only six now," said he. "I fear they are up to some devilry because they are so very still."

"They are leaving the house!" cried the *censitaire*, who was peeping through one of the side windows. "What can it mean? Holy Virgin, is it possible that we are saved? See how they throng through the trees. They are making for the canoe. Now they are waving their arms and pointing."

"There is the grey hat of that mongrel devil amongst them," said the captain. "I would try a shot upon him were it not a waste of powder and lead."

"I have hit the mark at as long a range," said Amos, pushing his long brown gun through a chink in the barricade which they had thrown across the lower half of the window. "I would give my next year's trade to bring him down."

"It is forty paces farther than my musket would carry," remarked Du Lhut, "but I have seen the English shoot a great way with those long guns."

Amos took a steady aim, resting his gun upon the window sill, and fired. A shout of delight burst from the little knot of survivors. The Flemish Bastard had fallen. But he was on his feet again in an instant and shook his hand defiantly at the window.

"Curse it!" cried Amos bitterly, in English. "I

have hit him with a spent ball. As well strike him with a pebble."

"Nay, curse not, Amos, lad, but try him again with another pinch of powder if your gun will stand it."

The woodsman thrust in a full charge, and chose a well-rounded bullet from his bag, but when he looked again both the Bastard and his warriors had disappeared. On the river the single Iroquois canoe which held the captives was speeding south as swiftly as twenty paddles could drive it, but save this one dark streak upon the blue stream, not a sign was to be seen of their enemies. They had vanished as if they had been an evil dream. There was the bullet-spotted stockade, the litter of dead bodies inside it, the burned and roofless cottages, but the silent woods lay gleaming in the morning sunshine as quiet and peaceful as if no hell-burst of fiends had ever broken out from them.

"By my faith, I believe that they have gone ! " cried the seigneur.

"Take care that it is not a ruse," said Du Lhut. "Why should they fly before six men when they have conquered sixty ? "

But the *censitaire* had looked out of the other window, and in an instant he was down upon his knees with his hands in the air, and his powder-blackened face turned upwards, pattering out prayers and thanksgivings. His five comrades rushed across the room and burst into a shriek of joy. The upper reach of the river was covered with a flotilla of canoes from which the sun struck quick flashes as it shone upon the musket barrels and trappings of the crews. Already they could see the white coats of the regulars, the brown tunics of the *coureurs-de-bois*, and the gaudy colours of the Hurons and Algonquins. On they swept, dotting the whole breadth of the river, and growing larger every instant, while far away on the southern bend, the Iroquois canoe was a mere moving dot which had shot away to the farther side and lost itself presently under the shadow of the trees. Another

minute and the survivors were out upon the bank, waving their caps in the air while the prows of the first of their rescuers were already grating upon the pebbles. In the stern of the very foremost canoe sat a wizened little man with a large brown wig, and a gilt-headed rapier laid across his knees. He sprang out as the keel touched bottom, splashing through the shallow water with his high leather boots, and rushing up to the seigneur, he flung himself into his arms.

" My dear Charles," he cried, " you have held your house like a hero. What, only six of you ! Tut, tut, this has been a bloody business ! "

" I knew that you would not desert a comrade, Chambly. We have saved the house but our losses have been terrible. My son is dead. My wife is in that Iroquois canoe in front of you."

The commandant of Fort St. Louis pressed his friend's hand in silent sympathy.

" The others arrived all safe," he said at last. " Only that one was taken, on account of the breaking of a paddle. Three were drowned and two captured. There was a French lady in it, I understand, as well as madame."

" Yes, and they have taken her husband as well."

" Ah, poor souls ! Well, if you are strong enough to join us, you and your friends, we shall follow after them without the loss of an instant. Ten of my men will remain to guard the house, and you can have their canoe. Jump in then, and forward, for life and death may hang upon our speed ! "

40. *The End*

THE Iroquois had not treated De Catinat harshly when they dragged him from the water into their canoe. So incomprehensible was it to them why any man should voluntarily leave a place of safety in order to put himself in their power that they could only set it

down to madness, a malady which inspires awe and respect among the Indians. They did not even tie his wrists, for why should he attempt to escape when he had come of his own free will ? Two warriors passed their hands over him, to be sure that he was unarmed, and he was then thrust down between the two women while the canoe darted in towards the bank to tell the others that the St. Louis garrison was coming up the stream. Then it steered out again, and made its way swiftly up the centre of the river. Adèle was deadly pale and her hand, as her husband laid his upon it, was as cold as marble.

" My darling," he whispered, " tell me that all is well with you—that you are unhurt ! "

" Oh, Amory, why did you come ? Why did you come, Amory ? Oh, I think I could have borne anything, but if they hurt you I could not bear that."

" How could I stay behind when I knew that you were in their hands ? I should have gone mad ! "

" Ah, it was my one consolation to think that you were safe."

" No, no, we have gone through so much together that we cannot part now. What is death, Adèle ? Why should we be afraid of it ? "

" I am not afraid of it."

" And I am not afraid of it. Things will come about as God wills it, and what He wills must in the end be the best. If we live, then we have this memory in common. If we die, then we go hand-in-hand into another life. Courage, my own, all will be well with us."

" Tell me, monsieur," said Onega, " is my lord still living ? "

" Yes, he is alive and well."

" It is good. He is a great chief, and I have never been sorry, not even now, that I have wedded with one who was not of my own people. But ah, my son ! Who shall give my son back to me ? He was like the young sapling, so straight and so strong ! Who could run with him, or leap with him, or swim with him ? Ere that sun shines

again we shall all be dead, and my heart is glad, for I shall see my boy once more."

The Iroquois paddles had bent to their work until a good ten miles lay between them and Sainte Marie. Then they ran the canoe into a little creek upon their own side of the river, and sprang out of her, dragging the prisoners after them. The canoe was carried on the shoulders of eight men some distance into the wood, where they concealed it between two fallen trees, heaping a litter of branches over it to screen it from view. Then, after a short council, they started through the forest walking in single file, with their three prisoners in the middle. There were fifteen warriors in all, eight in front and seven behind, all armed with muskets and as swift-footed as deer, so that escape was out of the question. They could but follow on, and wait in patience for whatever might befall them.

All day they pursued their dreary march, picking their way through vast morasses, skirting the borders of blue woodland lakes where the grey stork flapped heavily up from the reeds at their approach, or plunging into dark belts of woodland where it is always twilight, and where the falling of the wild chestnuts and the chatter of the squirrels a hundred feet above their heads were the only sounds which broke the silence. Onega had the endurance of the Indians themselves, but Adèle, in spite of her former journeys, was footsore and weary before evening. It was a relief to De Catinat, therefore, when the red glow of a great fire beat suddenly through the tree-trunks, and they came upon an Indian camp in which was assembled the greater part of the war-party which had been driven from Sainte Marie. Here, too, were a number of the squaws who had come from the Mohawk and Cayuga villages in order to be nearer to the warriors. Wigwams had been erected all round in a circle, and before each of them were the fires with kettles slung upon a tripod of sticks in which the evening meal was being cooked. In the centre of all was a very fierce fire which had been made of brushwood placed in a circle, so as to leave a clear

space of twelve feet in the middle. A pole stood up in the centre of this clearing, and something all mottled with red and black was tied up against it. De Catinat stepped swiftly in front of Adèle that she might not see the dreadful thing, but he was too late. She shuddered, and drew a quick breath between her pale lips, but no sound escaped her.

" They have begun already, then," said Onega composedly. " Well, it will be our turn next, and we shall show them that we know how to die."

" They have not ill-used us yet," said De Catinat. " Perhaps they will keep us for ransom or exchange."

The Indian woman shook her head. " Do not deceive yourself by any such hope," said she. " When they are as gentle as they have been with you it is ever a sign that you are reserved for the torture. Your wife will be married to one of their chiefs, but you and I must die, for you are a warrior, and I am too old for a squaw."

Married to an Iroquois ! Those dreadful words shot a pang through both their hearts which no thought of death could have done. De Catinat's head dropped forward upon his chest and he staggered and would have fallen had Adèle not caught him by the arm.

" Do not fear, dear Amory," she whispered. " Other things may happen, but not that, for I swear to you that I shall not survive you. No, it may be sin or it may not, but if death will not come to me, I will go to it."

De Catinat looked down at the gentle face which had set now into the hard lines of an immutable resolve. He knew that it would be as she had said, and that, come what might, that last outrage would not befall them. Could he ever have believed that the time would come when it would send a thrill of joy through his heart to know that his wife would die ?

As they entered the Iroquois village the squaws and warriors had rushed towards them, and they passed through a double line of hideous faces which jeered and jibed and howled at them as they passed. Their escort led them

through this rabble and conducted them to a hut which stood apart. It was empty, save for some willow fishing nets hanging at the side, and a heap of pumpkins stored in the corner.

" The chiefs will come and will decide upon what is to be done with us," said Onega. " Here they are coming now, and you will soon see that I am right, for I know the ways of my own people."

An instant later an old war-chief, accompanied by two younger braves and by the bearded half-Dutch Iroquois who had led the attack upon the manor-house, strolled over and stood in the doorway, looking in at the prisoners and shooting little guttural sentences at each other. The totems of the Hawk, the Wolf, the Bear and the Snake showed that they each represented one of the great families of the Nation. The Bastard was smoking a stone pipe, and yet it was he who talked the most, arguing apparently with one of the younger savages who seemed to come round at last to his opinion. Finally the old chief said a few short stern words, and the matter appeared to be settled.

" And you, you beldame," said the Bastard in French to the Iroquois woman, " you will have a lesson this night which will teach you to side against your own people."

" You half-bred mongrel," replied the fearless old woman, " you should take that hat from your head when you speak to one in whose veins runs the best blood of the Onondagas. You a warrior ? you who, with a thousand at your back, could not make your way into a little house with a few poor husbandmen within it ! It is no wonder that your father's people have cast you out ! Go back and work at the beads, or play at the game of plum stones, for some day in the woods you might meet with a man, and so bring disgrace upon the nation which has taken you in ! "

The evil face of the Bastard grew livid as he listened to the scornful words which were hissed at him by the captive. He strode across to her, and taking her hand he

thrust her forefinger into the burning bowl of his pipe.
She made no effort to remove it, but sat with a perfectly
set face for a minute or more, looking out through the
open door at the evening sunlight, and the little groups
of chattering Indians. He had watched her keenly in
the hope of hearing a cry, or seeing some spasm of agony
upon her face, but at last, with a curse, he dashed down
her hand and strode from the hut. She thrust her
charred finger into her bosom and laughed.

" He is a good-for-nought ! " she cried. " He does
not even know how to torture. Now, I could have got
a cry out of him. I am sure of it. But you—monsieur,
you are very white ! "

" It was the sight of such a hellish deed. Ah, if we
were but set face to face, I with my sword, he with what
weapon he chose, by God, he should pay for it with his
heart's blood."

The Indian woman seemed surprised. " It is strange
to me," she said, " that you should think of what befalls
me when you are yourselves under the same shadow.
But our fate will be as I said."

" Ah ! "

" You and I are to die at the stake. She is to be given
to the dog who has left us."

" Adèle ! Adèle ! What shall I do ! " He tore his
hair in his helplessness and distraction.

" No, no, fear not, Amory, for my heart will not
fail me. What is the pang of death if it binds us
together ? "

" The younger chief pleaded for you, saying that the
Mitche Manitou had stricken you with madness, as could
be seen by your swimming to their canoe, and that a
blight would fall upon the nation if you were led to the
stake. But this Bastard said that love came often like
madness among the pale faces, and that it was that alone
which had driven you. Then it was agreed that you
should die and that she should go to his wigwam, since
he had led the war-party. As for me, their hearts were

bitter against me, and I also am to die by the pine splinters."

De Catinat breathed a prayer that he might meet his fate like a soldier and a gentleman.

" When is it to be ? " he asked.

" Now ! At once ! They have gone to make all ready. But you have time yet, for I am to go first."

" Amory, Amory, could we not die together now ? " cried Adèle, throwing her arms round her husband. " If it be sin, it is surely a sin which will be forgiven us. Let us go, dear. Let us leave these dreadful people and this cruel world and turn where we shall find peace."

The Indian woman's eyes flashed with satisfaction.

" You have spoken well, White Lily," said she. " Why should you wait until it is their pleasure to pluck you. See, already the glare of their fire beats upon the tree-trunks, and you can hear the howlings of those who thirst for your blood. If you die by your own hands, they will be robbed of their spectacle, and their chief will have lost his bride. So you will be the victors in the end, and they the vanquished. You have said rightly, White Lily. There lies the only path for you ! "

" But how to take it ? "

Onega glanced keenly at the two warriors who stood as sentinels at the door of the hut. They had turned away, absorbed in the horrible preparations which were going on. Then she rummaged deeply within the folds of her loose gown and pulled out a small pistol with two brass barrels and double triggers in the form of winged dragons. It was only a toy to look at, all carved and scrolled and graven with the choicest work of the Paris gunsmith. For its beauty the seigneur had bought it at his last visit to Quebec, and yet it might be useful, too, and it was loaded in both barrels.

" I meant to use it on myself," said she, as she slipped it into the hand of De Catinat. " But now I am minded to show them that I can die as an Onondaga should die, and that I am worthy to have the blood of their chiefs in

my veins. Take it, for I swear that I will not use it myself, unless it be to fire both bullets into that Bastard's heart."

A flush of joy shot over De Catinat as his fingers closed round the pistol. Here was indeed a key to unlock the gates of peace. Adèle laid her cheek against his shoulder and laughed with pleasure.

" You will forgive me, dear," he whispered.

" Forgive you ! I bless you, and love you with my whole heart and soul. Clasp me close, darling, and say one prayer before you do it."

They had sunk on their knees together when three warriors entered the hut and said a few abrupt words to their country-woman. She rose with a smile.

" They are waiting for me," said she. " You shall see, White Lily, and you also, monsieur, how well I know what is due to my position. Farewell, and remember Onega ! "

She smiled again, and walked from the hut amidst the warriors with the quick firm step of a queen who sweeps to a throne.

" Now, Amory ! " whispered Adèle, closing her eyes, and nestling still closer to him.

He raised the pistol, and then, with a quick sudden intaking of the breath, he dropped it and knelt with glaring eyes looking up at a tree which faced the open door of the hut.

It was a beech tree, exceedingly old and gnarled, with its bark hanging down in strips and its whole trunk spotted with moss and mould. Some ten feet above the ground the main trunk divided into two, and in the fork thus formed a hand had suddenly appeared, a large reddish hand, which shook frantically from side to side in passionate dissuasion. The next instant, as the two captives still stared in amazement, the hand disappeared behind the trunk again and a face appeared in its place, which still shook from side to side as resolutely as its forerunner. It was impossible to mistake that mahogany, wrinkled skin, the huge bristling eyebrows, or the little

glistening eyes. It was Captain Ephraim Savage of Boston !

And even as they stared and wondered a sudden shrill whistle burst out from the depths of the forest, and in a moment every bush and thicket and patch of brushwood were spouting fire and smoke, while the snarl of the musketry ran round the whole glade, and the storm of bullets whizzed and pelted among the yelling savages. The Iroquois' sentinels had been drawn in by their blood-thirsty craving to see the prisoners die, and now the Canadians were upon them, and they were hemmed in by a ring of fire. First one way and then another they rushed, to be met always by the same blast of death, until finding at last some gap in the attack they streamed through, like sheep through a broken fence, and rushed madly away through the forest with the bullets of their pursuers still singing about their ears, until the whistle sounded again to recall the woodsmen from the chase.

But there was one savage who had found work to do before he fled. The Flemish Bastard had preferred his vengeance to his safety ! Rushing at Onega he buried his tomahawk in her brain, and then, yelling his war-cry, he waved the blood-stained weapon above his head, and flew into the hut where the prisoners still knelt. De Catinat saw him coming, and a mad joy glistened in his eyes. He rose to meet him, and as he rushed in he fired both barrels of his pistol into the Bastard's face. An instant later a swarm of Canadians had rushed over the writhing bodies, the captives felt warm friendly hands which grasped their own, and looking upon the smiling well-known faces of Amos Green, Savage and Du Lhut, they knew that peace had come to them at last.

And so the refugees came to the end of the toils of their journey, for that winter was spent by them in peace at Fort St. Louis, and in the spring, the Iroquois having carried the war to the Upper St. Lawrence, the travellers were able to descend into the English Provinces, and so to make their way down the Hudson to New York, where a

warm welcome awaited them from the family of Amos Green. The friendship between the two men was now so cemented together by common memories and common danger that they soon became partners in fur-trading, and the name of the Frenchman came at last to be as familiar in the mountains of Maine and on the slopes of the Alleghanies as it had once been in the *salons* and corridors of Versailles. In time De Catinat built a house on Staten Island, where many of his fellow-refugees had settled, and much of what he won from his fur-trading was spent in the endeavour to help his struggling Huguenot brothers. Amos Green had married a Dutch maiden of Schenectady, and as Adèle and she became inseparable friends, the marriage served to draw closer the ties of love which held the two families together.

As to Captain Ephraim Savage, he returned safely to his beloved Boston, where he fulfilled his ambition by building himself a fair brick house upon the rising ground in the northern part of the city, whence he could look down both upon the shipping in the river and the bay. There he lived, much respected by his townsfolk, who made him selectman and alderman, and gave him the command of a goodly ship when Sir William Phips made his attack upon Quebec, and found that the old Lion Frontenac was not to be driven from his lair. So, honoured by all, the old seaman lived to an age which carried him deep into the next century, when he could already see with his dim eyes something of the growing greatness of his country.

The manor-house of Sainte Marie was soon restored to its former prosperity, but its seigneur was from the day that he lost his wife and son a changed man. He grew leaner, fiercer, less human, for ever heading parties which made their way into the Iroquois woods and which outrivalled the savages themselves in the terrible nature of their deeds. A day came at last when he sallied out upon one of these expeditions, from which neither he nor any of his men ever returned. Many a terrible secret is hid

by those silent woods, and the fate of Charles de la Noue, Seigneur de Sainte Marie, is among them.

NOTE ON THE HUGUENOTS AND THEIR DISPERSION.

Towards the latter quarter of the seventeenth century there was hardly an important industry in France which was not controlled by the Huguenots, so that, numerous as they were, their importance was out of all proportion to their numbers. The cloth trade of the north and the south-east, the manufacture of serges and light stuffs in Languedoc, the linen trade of Normandy and Brittany, the silk and velvet industry of Tours and Lyons, the glass of Normandy, the paper of Auvergne and Angoumois, the jewellery of the Isle of France, the tan yards of Touraine, the iron and tin work of the Sedanais—all these were largely owned and managed by Huguenots. The numerous Saint days of the Catholic Calendar handicapped their rivals, and it was computed that the Protestant worked 310 days in the year to his fellow-countryman's 260.

A very large number of the Huguenot refugees were brought back, and the jails and galleys of France were crowded with them. One hundred thousand settled in Friesland and Holland, 25,000 in Switzerland, 75,000 in Germany and 50,000 in England. Some made their way even to the distant Cape of Good Hope, where they remained in the Paarl district.

In war, as in industry, the exiles were a source of strength to the countries which received them. Frenchmen drilled the Russian armies of Peter the Great, a Huguenot count became commander-in-chief in Denmark, and Schomberg led the army of Brandenburg, and afterwards that of England.

In England three Huguenot regiments were formed for the service of William. The exiles established themselves as silk workers in Spitalfields, cotton spinners at Bideford, tapestry weavers at Exeter, wool carders at Taunton, kersey makers at Norwich, weavers at Canterbury, hat makers at Wandsworth, sailcloth makers at Ipswich, workers in calico in Bromley, glass in Sussex, paper at Laverstock, cambric at Edinburgh.

Early Protestant refugees had taken refuge in America twenty years before the revocation, where they formed a colony at Staten Island. A body came to Boston in 1684, and were given 11,000 acres at Oxford, by order of the General Court at Massachusetts. In New York and Long Island colonies sprang up, and later in Virginia (the Monacan Settlement), in Maryland, and in South Carolina (French Santee and Orange Quarter).

NOTE ON THE FUTURE OF LOUIS, MADAME DE MAINTENON, AND MADAME DE MONTESPAN.

It has been left to our own century to clear the fair fame of Madame de Maintenon of all reproach, and to show her as what she was, a pure woman and a devoted wife. She has received little justice

from the memoir writers of the seventeenth century, most of whom, the Duc de St. Simon, for example, and the Princess Elizabeth of Bavaria, had their own private reasons for disliking her. An admirable epitome of her character and influence will be found in Dr. Dollinger's *Historical Studies*. She made Louis an excellent wife, waited upon him assiduously for thirty years of married life, influenced him constantly towards good—save only in the one instance of the Huguenots, and finally died very shortly after her husband.

Madame de Montespan lived in great magnificence after the triumph of her rival, and spent freely the vast sums which the king's generosity had furnished her with. Eventually, having exhausted all that this world could offer, she took to hair-shirts and nail-studded girdles, in the hope of securing a good position in the next. Her horror of death was excessive. In thunderstorms she sat with a little child in her lap in the hope that its innocence might shield her from the lightning. She slept always with her room ablaze with tapers, and with several women watching by the side of her couch. When at last the inevitable arrived she left her body for the family tomb, her heart to the convent of La Flèche, and her entrails to the priory of Menoux near Bourbon. These latter were thrust into a box and given to a peasant to convey to the priory. Curiosity induced him to look into the box upon the way, and, seeing the contents, he supposed himself to be the victim of a practical joke, and emptied them out into a ditch. A swineherd was passing at the moment with his pigs, and so it happened that, in the words of Mrs. Julia Pardoe, " in a few minutes the most filthy animals in creation had devoured portions of the remains of one of the haughtiest women who ever trod the earth."

Louis, after a reign of more than fifty years, which comprised the most brilliant epoch of French history, died at last in 1715 amidst the saddest surroundings.

One by one those whom he loved had preceded him to the grave, his brother, his son, the two sons of his son, their wives, and finally his favourite great-grandson, until he, the old dying monarch, with his rouge and his stays, was left with only a little infant in arms, the Duc D'Anjou, three generations away from him, to perpetuate his line. On 20th August, 1715, he was attacked by senile gangrene, which gradually spread up the leg until on the 30th it became fatal. His dying words were worthy of his better self. " Gentlemen, I desire your pardon for the bad example which I have set you. I have greatly to thank you for the manner in which you have served me, as well as for the attachment and fidelity which I have always experienced at your hands. I request from you the same zeal and fidelity for my grandson. Farewell, gentlemen. I feel that this parting has affected not only myself but you also. Forgive me ! I trust that you will sometimes think of me when I am gone."

RODNEY STONE

1. *Friar's Oak*

ON this, the first of January of the year 1851, the nineteenth century has reached its midway term, and many of us who shared its youth have already warnings which tell us that it has outworn us. We put our grizzled heads together, we older ones, and we talk of the great days that we have known ; but we find that when it is with our children that we talk it is a hard matter to make them understand. We and our fathers before us lived much the same life, but they with their railway trains and their steamboats belong to a different age. It is true that we can put history-books into their hands, and they can read from them of our weary struggle of two and twenty years with that great and evil man. They can learn how Freedom fled from the whole broad continent, and how Nelson's blood was shed, and Pitt's noble heart was broken in striving that she should not pass us for ever to take refuge with our brothers across the Atlantic. All this they can read, with the date of this treaty or that battle, but I do not know where they are to read of ourselves, of the folk we were, and the lives we led, and how the world seemed to our eyes when they were young as theirs are now.

If I take up my pen to tell you about this, you must not look for any story at my hands, for I was only in my earliest manhood when these things befell ; and although I saw something of the stories of other lives, I could scarce claim one of my own. It is the love of a woman that makes the story of a man, and many a year was to pass before I first looked into the eyes of the mother of my children. To us it seems but an affair of yesterday,

and yet those children can now reach the plums in the garden whilst we are seeking for a ladder, and where we once walked with their little hands in ours, we are glad now to lean upon their arms. But I shall speak of a time when the love of a mother was the only love I knew, and if you seek for something more, then it is not for you that I write. But if you would come out with me into that forgotten world ; if you would know Boy Jim and Champion Harrison ; if you would meet my father, one of Nelson's own men ; if you would catch a glimpse of that great seaman himself, and of George, afterwards the unworthy King of England ; if, above all, you would see my famous uncle, Sir Charles Tregellis, the King of the Bucks, and the great fighting men whose names are still household words amongst you, then give me your hand, and let us start.

But I must warn you also that, if you think you will find much that is of interest in your guide, you are destined to disappointment. When I look over my book-shelves, I can see that it is only the wise and witty and valiant who have ventured to write down their experiences. For my own part, if I were only assured that I was as clever and brave as the average man about me, I should be well satisfied. Men of their hands have thought well of my brains, and men of brains of my hands, and that is the best that I can say of myself. Save in the one matter of having an inborn readiness for music, so that the mastery of any instrument comes very easily and naturally to me, I cannot recall any single advantage which I can boast over my fellows. In all things I have been a half-way man, for I am of middle height, my eyes are neither blue nor grey, and my hair, before Nature dusted it with her powder, was betwixt flaxen and brown. I may, perhaps, claim this : that through life I have never felt a touch of jealousy as I have admired a better man than myself, and that I have always seen all things as they are, myself included, which should count in my favour now that I sit down in my mature age to write my

memories. With your permission, then, we will push my own personality as far as possible out of the picture. If you can conceive me as a thin and colourless cord upon which my would-be pearls are strung, you will be accepting me upon the terms which I should wish.

Our family, the Stones, have for many generations belonged to the Navy, and it has been a custom among us for the eldest son to take the name of his father's favourite commander. Thus we can trace our lineage back to old Vernon Stone, who commanded a high-sterned, peak-nosed, fifty-gun ship against the Dutch. Through Hawke Stone and Benbow Stone we came down to my father, Anson Stone, who in his turn christened me Rodney, at the parish church of St. Thomas at Portsmouth in the year of grace 1786.

Out of my window as I write I can see my own great lad in the garden, and if I were to call out " Nelson ! " you would see that I have been true to the traditions of our family.

My dear mother, the best that ever a man had, was the second daughter of the Reverend John Tregellis, Vicar of Milton, which is a small parish upon the borders of the marshes of Langstone. She came of a poor family, but one of some position, for her elder brother was the famous Sir Charles Tregellis, who, having inherited the money of a wealthy East Indian merchant, became in time the talk of the town and the very particular friend of the Prince of Wales. Of him I shall have more to say hereafter ; but you will note now that he was my own uncle, and brother to my mother.

I can remember her all through her beautiful life, for she was but a girl when she married, and little more when I can first recall her busy fingers and her gentle voice. I see her as a lively woman with kind, dove's eyes, somewhat short of stature it is true, but carrying herself very bravely. In my memories of those days she is clad always in some purple shimmering stuff, with a white kerchief round her long white neck, and I see her fingers

turning and darting as she works at her knitting. I see her again in her middle years, sweet and loving, planning, contriving, achieving, with the few shillings a day of a lieutenant's pay on which to support the cottage at Friar's Oak, and to keep a fair face to the world. And now, if I do but step into the parlour, I can see her once more, with over eighty years of saintly life behind her, silver-haired, placid-faced, with her dainty ribboned cap, her gold-rimmed glasses, and her woolly shawl with the blue border. I loved her young and I love her old, and when she goes she will take something with her which nothing in the world can ever make good to me again. You may have many friends, you who read this, and you may chance to marry more than once, but your mother is your first and your last. Cherish her, then, whilst you may, for the day will come when every hasty deed or heedless word will come back with its sting to hive in your own heart.

Such, then, was my mother ; and as to my father, I can describe him best when I come to the time when he returned to us from the Mediterranean. During all my childhood he was only a name to me, and a face in a miniature hung round my mother's neck. At first they told me he was fighting the French, and then after some years one heard less about the French and more about General Buonaparte. I remember the awe with which one day in Thomas Street, Portsmouth, I saw a print of the great Corsican in a bookseller's window. This, then, was the arch enemy with whom my father spent his life in terrible and ceaseless contest. To my childish imagination it was a personal affair, and I for ever saw my father and this clean-shaven, thin-lipped man swaying and reeling in a deadly, year-long grapple. It was not until I went to the Grammar School that I understood how many other little boys there were whose fathers were in the same case.

Only once in those long years did my father return home, which will show you what it meant to be the wife

of a sailor in those days. It was just after we had moved from Portsmouth to Friar's Oak, whither he came for a week before he set sail with Admiral Jervis to help him to turn his name into Lord St. Vincent. I remember that he frightened as well as fascinated me with his talk of battles, and I can recall as if it were yesterday the horror with which I gazed upon a spot of blood upon his shirt ruffle, which had come, as I have no doubt, from a mischance in shaving. At the time I never questioned that it had spurted from some stricken Frenchman or Spaniard, and I shrank from him in terror when he laid his horny hand upon my head. My mother wept bitterly when he was gone, but for my own part I was not sorry to see his blue back and white shorts going down the garden walk, for I felt, with the heedless selfishness of a child, that we were closer together, she and I, when we were alone.

I was in my eleventh year when we moved from Portsmouth to Friar's Oak, a little Sussex village to the north of Brighton, which was recommended to us by my uncle, Sir Charles Tregellis, one of whose grand friends, Lord Avon, had had his seat near there. The reason of our moving was that living was cheaper in the country, and that it was easier for my mother to keep up the appearance of a gentlewoman when away from the circle of those to whom she could not refuse hospitality. They were trying times those to all save the farmers, who made such profits that they could, as I have heard, afford to let half their land lie fallow, while living like gentlemen upon the rest. Wheat was at a hundred and ten shillings a quarter, and the quartern loaf at one and ninepence. Even in the quiet of the cottage of Friar's Oak we could scarce have lived, were it not that in the blockading squadron in which my father was stationed there was the occasional chance of a little prize-money. The line-of-battle ships themselves, tacking on and off outside Brest, could earn nothing save honour; but the frigates in attendance made prizes of many coasters, and these, as

is the rule of the service, were counted as belonging to the fleet, and their produce divided into head-money. In this manner my father was able to send home enough to keep the cottage and to pay for me at the day school of Mr. Joshua Allen, where for four years I learned all that he had to teach. It was at Allen's school that I first knew Jim Harrison, Boy Jim as he has always been called, the nephew of Champion Harrison of the village smithy. I can see him as he was in those days with great, floundering, half-formed limbs like a Newfoundland puppy, and a face that set every woman's head round as he passed her. It was in those days that we began our lifelong friendship, a friendship which still in our waning years binds us closely as two brothers. I taught him his exercises, for he never loved the sight of a book, and he in turn made me box and wrestle, tickle trout on the Adur, and snare rabbits on Ditchling Down, for his hands were as active as his brain was slow. He was two years my elder, however, so that, long before I had finished my schooling, he had gone to help his uncle at the smithy.

Friar's Oak is in a dip of the Downs, and the forty-third milestone between London and Brighton lies on the skirt of the village. It is but a small place, with an ivied church, a fine vicarage and a row of red-brick cottages each in its own little garden. At one end was the forge of Champion Harrison, with his house behind it, and at the other was Mr. Allen's school. The yellow cottage, standing back a little from the road, with its upper story bulging forward and a crisscross of black woodwork let into the plaster, is the one in which we lived. I do not know if it is still standing, but I should think it likely, for it was not a place much given to change.

Just opposite to us, at the other side of the broad, white road, was the Friar's Oak Inn, which was kept in my day by John Cummings, a man of excellent repute at home, but liable to strange outbreaks when he travelled, as will afterwards become apparent. Though there was a stream of traffic upon the road, the coaches from Brighton

were too fresh to stop, and those from London too eager
to reach their journey's end, so that if it had not been for
an occasional broken trace or loosened wheel, the landlord
would have had only the thirsty throats of the village to
trust to. Those were the days when the Prince of Wales
had just built his singular palace by the sea, and so from
May to September, which was the Brighton season, there
was never a day that from one to two hundred curricles,
chaises and phaetons did not rattle past our doors.
Many a summer evening have Boy Jim and I lain upon
the grass, watching all these grand folk, and cheering the
London coaches as they came roaring through the dust
clouds, leaders and wheelers stretched to their work, the
bugles screaming and the coachmen with their low-
crowned, curly-brimmed hats, and their faces as scarlet
as their coats. The passengers used to laugh when Boy
Jim shouted at them, but if they could have read his big
half-set limbs and his loose shoulders aright, they would
have looked a little harder at him, perhaps, and given him
back his cheer.

Boy Jim had never known a father or a mother, and his
whole life had been spent with his uncle, Champion
Harrison. Harrison was the Friar's Oak blacksmith,
and he had his nickname because he fought Tom Johnson
when he held the English belt, and would most certainly
have beaten him had the Bedfordshire magistrates not
appeared to break up the fight. For years there was no
such glutton to take punishment and no more finishing
hitter than Harrison, though he was always, as I understand, a slow one upon his feet. At last, in a fight with
Black Baruk the Jew, he finished the battle with such a
lashing hit that he not only knocked his opponent over
the inner ropes, but he left him betwixt life and death
for long three weeks. During all this time Harrison
lived half demented, expecting every hour to feel the
hand of a Bow Street runner upon his collar, and to be
tried for his life. This experience, with the prayers of
his wife, made him forswear the Ring for ever, and carry

his great muscles into the one trade in which they seemed to give him an advantage. There was a good business to be done at Friar's Oak from the passing traffic and the Sussex farmers, so that he soon became the richest of the villagers ; and he came to church on a Sunday with his wife and his nephew, looking as respectable a family man as one would wish to see.

He was not a tall man, not more than five feet seven inches, and it was often said that if he had had an extra inch of reach he would have been a match for Jackson or Belcher at their best. His chest was like a barrel, and his forearms were the most powerful that I have ever seen, with deep grooves between the smooth-swelling muscles like a piece of water-worn rock. In spite of his strength, however, he was of a slow, orderly and kindly disposition, so that there was no man more beloved over the whole country-side. His heavy, placid, clean-shaven face could set very sternly, as I have seen upon occasion ; but for me and every child in the village there was ever a smile upon his lips and a greeting in his eyes. There was not a beggar upon the country-side who did not know that his heart was as soft as his muscles were hard.

There was nothing that he liked to talk of more than his old battles, but he would stop if he saw his little wife coming, for the one great shadow in her life was the ever-present fear that some day he would throw down sledge and rasp and be off to the Ring once more. And you must be reminded here once for all that that former calling of his was by no means at that time in the debased condition to which it afterwards fell. Public opinion has gradually become opposed to it, for the reason that it came largely into the hands of rogues, and because it fostered ringside ruffianism. Even the honest and brave pugilist was found to draw villainy round him, just as the pure and noble racehorse does. For this reason the Ring is dying in England, and we may hope that when Caunt and Bendigo have passed away, they may have none to succeed them. But it was different in the days of which

I speak. Public opinion was then largely in its favour, and there were good reasons why it should be so. It was a time of war, when England, with an army and navy composed only of those who volunteered to fight because they had fighting blood in them, had to encounter, as they would now have to encounter, a power which could by despotic law turn every citizen into a soldier. If the people had not been full of this lust for combat, it is certain that England must have been overborne. And it was thought, and is, on the face of it, reasonable, that a struggle between two indomitable men, with thirty thousand to view it and three million to discuss it, did help to set a standard of hardihood and endurance. Brutal it was, no doubt, and its brutality is the end of it ; but it is not so brutal as war, which will survive it. Whether it is logical now to teach the people to be peaceful in an age when their very existence may come to depend upon their being warlike, is a question for wiser heads than mine. But that was what we thought of it in the days of your grandfathers, and that is why you might find statesmen and philanthropists like Windham, Fox and Althorp at the side of the Ring.

The mere fact that solid men should patronise it was enough in itself to prevent the villainy which afterwards crept in. For over twenty years, in the days of Jackson, Brain, Cribb, the Belchers, Pearce, Gully and the rest, the leaders of the Ring were men whose honesty was above suspicion ; and those were just the twenty years when the Ring may, as I have said, have served a national purpose. You have heard how Pearce saved the Bristol girl from the burning house, how Jackson won the respect and friendship of the best men of his age, and how Gully rose to a seat in the first Reformed Parliament. These were the men who set the standard, and their trade carried with it this obvious recommendation, that it is one in which no drunken or foul-living man could long succeed. There were exceptions among them, no doubt —bullies like Hickman and brutes like Berks ; in the

main, I say again that they were honest men, brave and enduring to an incredible degree, and a credit to the country which produced them. It was, as you will see, my fate to see something of them, and I speak of what I know.

In our own village, I can assure you that we were very proud of the presence of such a man as Champion Harrison, and if folks stayed at the inn they would walk down as far as the smithy just to have the sight of him. And he was worth seeing, too, especially on a winter's night when the red glare of the forge would beat upon his great muscles and upon the proud, hawk-face of Boy Jim as they heaved and swayed over some glowing plough coulter, framing themselves in sparks with every blow. He would strike once with his thirty-pound swing sledge, and Jim twice with his hand hammer; and the " Clunk —clink, clink! clunk—clink, clink! " would bring me flying down the village street, on the chance that, since they were both at the anvil, there might be a place for me at the bellows.

Only once during those village years can I remember Champion Harrison showing me for an instant the sort of man that he had been. It chanced one summer morning, when Boy Jim and I were standing by the smithy door, that there came a private coach from Brighton, with its four fresh horses, and its brass-work shining, flying along with such a merry rattle and jingling, that the Champion came running out with a half-fullered shoe in his tongs to have a look at it. A gentleman in a white coachman's cape—a Corinthian, as we would call him in those days—was driving, and half a dozen of his fellows, laughing and shouting, were on the top behind him. It may have been that the bulk of the smith caught his eye, and that he acted in pure wantonness, or it may possibly have been an accident, but, as he swung past, the twenty-foot thong of the driver's whip hissed round and we heard the sharp snap of it across Harrison's leather apron.

" Halloa, master ! " shouted the smith, looking after him. " You're not to be trusted on the box until you can handle your whip better'n that."

" What's that ? " cried the driver, pulling up his team.

" I bid you have a care, master, or there will be some one-eyed folk along the road you drive."

" Oh, you say that, do you ? " said the driver, putting his whip into its socket and pulling off his driving-gloves. " I'll have a little talk with you, my fine fellow."

The sporting gentlemen of those days were very fine boxers for the most part, for it was the mode to take a course of Mendoza, just as a few years afterwards there was no man about town who had not had the mufflers on with Jackson. Knowing their own prowess, they never refused the chance of a wayside adventure, and it was seldom indeed that the bargee or the navigator had much to boast of after a young blood had taken off his coat to him.

This one swung himself off the box-seat with the alacrity of a man who has no doubts about the upshot of the quarrel, and after hanging his caped coat upon the swingle-bar, he daintily turned up the ruffled cuffs of his white cambric shirt.

" I'll pay you for your advice, my man," said he.

I am sure that the men upon the coach knew who the burly smith was, and looked upon it as a prime joke to see their companion walk into such a trap. They roared with delight, and bellowed out scraps of advice to him.

" Knock some of the soot off him, Lord Frederick ! " they shouted. " Give the Johnny Raw his breakfast. Chuck him in among his own cinders ! Sharp's the word, or you'll see the back of him."

Encouraged by these cries, the young aristocrat advanced upon his man. The smith never moved, but his mouth set grim and hard, while his tufted brows came down over his keen, grey eyes. The tongs had fallen, and his hands were hanging free.

" Have a care, master," said he. " You'll get pepper if you don't."

Something in the assured voice, and something also in the quiet pose, warned the young lord of his danger. I saw him look hard at his antagonist, and as he did so, his hands and his jaw dropped together.

" By Gad ! " he cried, " it's Jack Harrison ! "

" My name, master ! "

" And I thought you were some Essex chaw-bacon ! Why, man, I haven't seen you since the day you nearly killed Black Baruk, and cost me a cool hundred by doing it."

How they roared on the coach.

" Smoked ! Smoked, by Gad ! " they yelled. " It's Jack Harrison the bruiser ! Lord Frederick was going to take on the ex-champion. Give him one on the apron, Fred, and see what happens."

But the driver had already climbed back into his perch, laughing as loudly as any of his companions.

" We'll let you off this time, Harrison," said he. " Are those your sons down there ? "

" This is my nephew, master."

" Here's a guinea for him ! He shall never say I robbed him of his uncle." And so, having turned the laugh in his favour by his merry way of taking it, he cracked his whip, and away they flew to make London under the five hours ; while Jack Harrison, with his half-fullered shoe in his hand, went whistling back to the forge.

2. *The Walker of Cliffe Royal*

SO much for Champion Harrison ! Now, I wish to say something more about Boy Jim, not only because he was the comrade of my youth, but because you will find as you go on that this book is his story rather than mine, and that there came a time when his name and his fame were in the mouths of all England. You will

bear with me, therefore, while I tell you of his character as it was in those days, and especially of one very singular adventure which neither of us is likely to forget.

It was strange to see Jim with his uncle and his aunt, for he seemed to be of another race and breed to them. Often I have watched them come up the aisle upon a Sunday, first the square, thick-set man, and then the little, worn, anxious-eyed woman, and last this glorious lad with his clear-cut face, his black curls and his step so springy and light that it seemed as if he were bound to earth by some lesser tie than the heavy-footed villagers round him. He had not yet attained his full six foot of stature, but no judge of a man (and every woman, at least, is one) could look at his perfect shoulders, his narrow loins, and his proud head that sat upon his neck like an eagle upon its perch, without feeling that sober joy which all that is beautiful in Nature gives to us—a vague self-content, as though in some way we also had a hand in the making of it.

But we are used to associate beauty with softness in a man. I do not know why they should be so coupled, and they never were with Jim. Of all men that I have known, he was the most iron-hard in body and in mind. Who was there among us who could walk with him, or run with him, or swim with him ? Who on all the country-side, save only Boy Jim, would have swung himself over Wolstonbury Cliff, and clambered down a hundred feet with the mother hawk flapping at his ears in the vain struggle to hold him from her nest ? He was but sixteen, with his gristle not yet all set into bone, when he fought and beat Gipsy Lee, of Burgess Hill, who called himself the " Cock of the South Downs." It was after this that Champion Harrison took his training as a boxer in hand.

" I'd rather you left millin' alone, Boy Jim," said he, " and so had the missus ; but if mill you must, it will not be my fault if you cannot hold up your hands to anything in the south country."

And it was not long before he made good his promise.

I have said already that Boy Jim had no love for his books, but by that I meant school-books, for when it came to the reading of romances or of anything which had a touch of gallantry or adventure, there was no tearing him away from it until it was finished. When such a book came into his hands, Friar's Oak and the smithy became a dream to him, and his life was spent out upon the ocean or wandering over the broad continents with his heroes. And he would draw me into his enthusiasms also, so that I was glad to play Friday to his Crusoe when he proclaimed that the Clump at Clayton was a desert island, and that we were cast upon it for a week. But when I found that we were actually to sleep out there without covering every night, and that he proposed that our food should be the sheep of the Downs (wild goats he called them) cooked upon a fire, which was to be made by the rubbing together of two sticks, my heart failed me, and on the very first night I crept away to my mother. But Jim stayed out there for the whole weary week—a wet week it was, too !—and came back at the end of it looking a deal wilder and dirtier than his hero does in the picture-books. It is well that he had only promised to stay a week, for, if it had been a month, he would have died of cold and hunger before his pride would have let him come home.

His pride !—that was the deepest thing in all Jim's nature. It is a mixed quality to my mind, half a virtue and half a vice : a virtue in holding a man out of the dirt ; a vice in making it hard for him to rise when once he has fallen. Jim was proud down to the very marrow of his bones. You remember the guinea that the young lord had thrown him from the box of the coach ? Two days later somebody picked it from the roadside mud. Jim only had seen where it had fallen, and he would not deign even to point it out to a beggar. Nor would he stoop to give a reason in such a case, but would answer all remonstrances with a curl of his lip and a flash of his dark eyes. Even at school he was the same, with such

a sense of his own dignity, that other folk had to think of it too. He might say, as he did say, that a right angle was a proper sort of angle, or put Panama in Sicily, but old Joshua Allen would as soon have thought of raising his cane against him as he would of letting me off if I had said as much. And so it was that, although Jim was the son of nobody, and I of a King's officer, it always seemed to me to have been a condescension on his part that he should have chosen me as his friend.

It was this pride of Boy Jim's which led to an adventure which makes me shiver now when I think of it.

It happened in the August of '99, or it may have been in the early days of September; but I remember that we heard the cuckoo in Patcham Wood, and that Jim said that perhaps it was the last of him. I was still at school, but Jim had left, he being nigh sixteen and I thirteen. It was my Saturday half-holiday, and we spent it, as we often did, out upon the Downs. Our favourite place was beyond Wolstonbury, where we could stretch ourselves upon the soft, springy, chalk grass among the plump little Southdown sheep, chatting with the shepherds, as they leaned upon their queer old Pyecombe crooks, made in the days when Sussex turned out more iron than all the counties of England.

It was there that we lay upon that glorious afternoon. If we chose to roll upon our right sides, the whole weald lay in front of us, with the North Downs curving away in olive-green folds, with here and there the snow-white rift of a chalk-pit; if we turned upon our left, we overlooked the huge blue stretch of the Channel. A convoy, as I can well remember, was coming up it that day, the timid flock of merchantmen in front; the frigates, like well-trained dogs, upon the skirts; and two burly drover line-of-battle ships rolling along behind them. My fancy was soaring out to my father upon the waters, when a word from Jim brought it back on to the grass like a broken-winged gull.

" Roddy," said he, " have you heard that Cliffe Royal is haunted ? "

Had I heard it ?   Of course I had heard it.   Who was there in all the Down country who had not heard of the Walker of Cliffe Royal ?

" Do you know the story of it, Roddy ? "

" Why," said I, with some pride, " I ought to know it, seeing that my mother's brother, Sir Charles Tregellis, was the nearest friend of Lord Avon, and was at this card-party when the thing happened.   I heard the vicar and my mother talking about it last week, and it was all so clear to me that I might have been there when the murder was done."

" It is a strange story," said Jim, thoughtfully ; " but when I asked my aunt about it, she would give me no answer ; and as to my uncle, he cut me short at the very mention of it."

" There is a good reason for that," said I ; " for Lord Avon was, as I have heard, your uncle's best friend ; and it is but natural that he would not wish to speak of his disgrace."

" Tell me the story, Roddy."

" It is an old one now—fourteen years old—and yet they have not got to the end of it.   There were four of them who had come down from London to spend a few days in Lord Avon's old house.   One was his own young brother, Captain Barrington ; another was his cousin, Sir Lothian Hume ; Sir Charles Tregellis, my uncle, was the third ; and Lord Avon the fourth.   They are fond of playing cards for money, these great people, and they played and played for two days and a night.   Lord Avon lost, and Sir Lothian lost, and my uncle lost, and Captain Barrington won until he could win no more.   He won their money, but above all he won papers from his elder brother which meant a great deal to him.   It was late on a Monday night that they stopped playing.   On the Tuesday morning Captain Barrington was found dead beside his bed with his throat cut."

" And Lord Avon did it ? "

" His papers were found burned in the grate, his wrist-band was clutched in the dead man's hand, and his knife lay beside the body."

" Did they hang him, then ? "

" They were too slow in laying hands upon him. He waited until he saw that they had brought it home to him, and then he fled. He has never been seen since, but it is said that he reached America."

" And the ghost walks ? "

" There are many who have seen it."

" Why is the house still empty ? "

" Because it is in the keeping of the law. Lord Avon had no children, and Sir Lothian Hume—the same who was at the card-party—is his nephew and heir. But he can touch nothing until he can prove Lord Avon to be dead."

Jim lay silent for a bit, plucking at the short grass with his fingers.

" Roddy," said he at last, " will you come with me to-night and look for the ghost ? "

It turned me cold, the very thought of it.

" My mother would not let me."

" Slip out when she's abed. I'll wait for you at the smithy."

" Cliffe Royal is locked."

" I'll open a window easy enough."

" I'm afraid, Jim."

" But you are not afraid if you are with me, Roddy. I'll promise you that no ghost shall hurt you."

So I gave him my word that I would come, and then all the rest of the day I went about the most sad-faced lad in Sussex. It was all very well for Boy Jim ! It was that pride of his which was taking him there. He would go because there was no one else on the country-side that would dare. But I had no pride of that sort. I was quite of the same way of thinking as the others, and would as soon have thought of passing my night at Jacob's gibbet

on Ditchling Common as in the haunted house of Cliffe Royal. Still, I could not bring myself to desert Jim ; and so, as I say, I slunk about the house with so pale and peaky a face that my dear mother would have it that I had been at the green apples, and sent me to bed early with a dish of camomile tea for my supper.

England went to rest betimes in those days, for there were few who could afford the price of candles. When I looked out of my window just after the clock had gone ten, there was not a light in the village save only at the inn. It was but a few feet from the ground, so I slipped out, and there was Jim waiting for me at the smithy corner. We crossed John's Common together, and so past Ridden's Farm, meeting only one or two riding officers upon the way. There was a brisk wind blowing, and the moon kept peeping through the rifts of the scud, so that our road was sometimes silver-clear, and sometimes so black that we found ourselves among the brambles and gorse-bushes which lined it. We came at last to the wooden gate with the high stone pillars by the roadside, and, looking through between the rails, we saw the long avenue of oaks, and at the end of this ill-boding tunnel, the pale face of the house glimmered in the moonshine.

That would have been enough for me, that one glimpse of it, and the sound of the night wind sighing and groaning among the branches. But Jim swung the gate open, and up we went, the gravel squeaking beneath our tread. It towered high, the old house, with many little windows in which the moon glinted, and with a strip of water running round three sides of it. The arched door stood right in the face of us, and on one side a lattice hung open upon its hinges.

" We're in luck, Roddy," whispered Jim. " Here's one of the windows open."

" Don't you think we've gone far enough, Jim ? " said I, with my teeth chattering.

" I'll lift you in first."

" No, no, I'll not go first."

" Then I will." He gripped the sill, and had his knee on it in an instant. " Now, Roddy, give me your hands." With a pull he had me up beside him, and a moment later we were both in the haunted house.

How hollow it sounded when we jumped down on to the wooden floor ! There was such a sudden boom and reverberation that we both stood silent for a moment. Then Jim burst out laughing.

" What an old drum of a place it is ! " he cried ; " we'll strike a light, Roddy, and see where we are."

He had brought a candle and a tinder-box in his pocket. When the flame burned up, we saw an arched stone roof above our heads, and broad deal shelves all round us covered with dusty dishes. It was the pantry.

" I'll show you round," said Jim, merrily ; and, pushing the door open, he led the way into the hall. I remember the high, oak-panelled walls, with the heads of deer jutting out, and a single white bust, which sent my heart into my mouth, in the corner. Many rooms opened out of this, and we wandered from one to the other—the kitchens, the still-room, the morning-room, the dining-room, all filled with the same choking smell of dust and of mildew.

" This is where they played the cards, Jim," said I, in a hushed voice. " It was on that very table."

" Why, here are the cards themselves ! " cried he ; and he pulled a brown towel from something in the centre of the sideboard. Sure enough it was a pile of playing-cards—forty packs, I should think, at the least—which had lain there ever since that tragic game which was played before I was born.

" I wonder whence that stairs leads ? " said Jim.

" Don't go up there, Jim ! " I cried, clutching at his arm. " That must lead to the room of the murder."

" How do you know that ? "

" The vicar said that they saw on the ceiling—— Oh, Jim, you can see it even now ! "

He held up his candle, and there was a great, dark smudge upon the white plaster above us.

" I believe you're right," said he ; " but anyhow I'm going to have a look at it."

" Don't, Jim, don't ! " I cried.

" Tut, Roddy ! you can stay here if you are afraid. I won't be more than a minute. There's no use going on a ghost hunt unless—— Great Lord, there's something coming down the stairs ! "

I heard it too—a shuffling footstep in the room above, and then a creak from the steps, and then another creak, and another. I saw Jim's face as if it had been carved out of ivory, with his parted lips and his staring eyes fixed upon the black square of the stair opening. He still held the light, but his fingers twitched, and with every twitch the shadows sprang from the walls to the ceiling. As to myself, my knees gave way under me, and I found myself on the floor crouching down behind Jim, with a scream frozen in my throat. And still the step came slowly from stair to stair.

Then, hardly daring to look and yet unable to turn away my eyes, I saw a figure dimly outlined in the corner upon which the stair opened. There was a silence in which I could hear my poor heart thumping, and then when I looked again the figure was gone, and the low creak, creak was heard once more upon the stairs. Jim sprang after it, and I was left half-fainting in the moon-light.

But it was not for long. He was down again in a minute, and, passing his hand under my arm, he half led and half carried me out of the house. It was not until we were in the fresh night air again that he opened his mouth.

" Can you stand, Roddy ? "

" Yes, but I'm shaking."

" So am I," said he, passing his hand over his forehead. " I ask your pardon, Roddy. I was a fool to bring you on such an errand. But I never believed in such things. I know better now."

" Could it have been a man, Jim ? " I asked, plucking up my courage now that I could hear the dogs barking on the farms.

" It was a spirit, Rodney."

" How do you know ? "

" Because I followed it, and saw it vanish into a wall, as easily as an eel into sand. Why, Roddy, what's amiss now ? "

My fears were all back upon me, and every nerve creeping with horror.

" Take me away, Jim ! Take me away ! " I cried.

I was glaring down the avenue, and his eyes followed mine. Amid the gloom of the oak trees something was coming towards us.

"Quiet, Roddy ! " whispered Jim. " By heavens, come what may, my arms are going round it this time."

We crouched as motionless as the trunks behind us. Heavy steps ploughed their way through the sift gravel, and a broad figure loomed upon us in the darkness.

Jim sprang upon it like a tiger.

" *You're* not a spirit, anyway ! " he cried.

The man gave a shout of surprise, and then a growl of rage.

" What the deuce ! " he roared, and then, " I'll break your neck if you don't let go."

The threat might not have loosened Jim's grip, but the voice did.

" Why, uncle ! " he cried.

" Well, I'm blessed if it isn't Boy Jim ! And what's this ? Why, it's young Master Rodney Stone, as I'm a living sinner ! What in the world are you two doing up at Cliffe Royal at this time of night ? "

We had all moved out into the moonlight, and there was Champion Harrison with a big bundle on his arm, and such a look of amazement upon his face as would have brought a smile back on to mine had my heart not still been cramped with fear.

" We're exploring," said Jim.

" Exploring, are you ? Well, I don't think you were meant to be Captain Cooks, either of you, for I never saw such a pair of peeled-turnip faces. Why, Jim, what are you afraid of ? "

" I'm not afraid, uncle. I never was afraid ; but spirits are new to me, and——"

" Spirits ? "

" I've been in Cliffe Royal, and we've seen the ghost."

The Champion gave a whistle.

" That's the game, is it ? " said he. " Did you have speech with it ? "

" It vanished first."

The Champion whistled once more.

" I've heard there is something of the sort up yonder," said he ; " but it's not a thing as I would advise you to meddle with. There's enough trouble with the folk of this world, Boy Jim, without going out of your way to mix up with those of another. As to young Master Rodney Stone, if his good mother saw that white face of his, she'd never let him come to the smithy more. Walk slowly on, and I'll see you back to Friar's Oak."

We had gone half a mile, perhaps, when the Champion overtook us, and I could not but observe that the bundle was no longer under his arm. We were nearly at the smithy before Jim asked the question which was already in my mind.

" What took *you* up to Cliffe Royal, uncle ? "

" Well, as a man gets on in years," said the Champion, " there's many a duty turns up that the likes of you have no idea of. When you're near forty yourself, you'll maybe know the truth of what I say."

So that was all we could draw from him ; but, young as I was, I had heard of coast smuggling and of packages carried to lonely places at night, so that from that time on, if I had heard that the preventives had made a capture, I was never easy until I saw the jolly face of Champion Harrison looking out of his smithy door.

3. *The Play-actress of Anstey Cross*

I HAVE told you something about Friar's Oak, and about the life that we led there. Now that my memory goes back to the old place it would gladly linger, for every thread which I draw from the skein of the past brings out half a dozen others that were entangled with it. I was in two minds when I began whether I had enough in me to make a book of, and now I know that I could write one about Friar's Oak alone, and the folk whom I knew in my childhood. They were hard and uncouth, some of them, I doubt not ; and yet, seen through the golden haze of time, they all seem sweet and lovable. There was our good vicar, Mr. Jefferson, who loved the whole world save only Mr. Slack, the Baptist minister of Clayton ; and there was kindly Mr. Slack, who was all men's brother save only of Mr. Jefferson, the vicar of Friar's Oak. Then there was Monsieur Rudin, the French Royalist refugee who lived over on the Pangdean road, and who, when the news of a victory came in, was convulsed with joy because we had beaten Buonaparte, and shaken with rage because we had beaten the French, so that after the Nile he wept for a whole day out of delight and then for another one out of fury, alternately clapping his hands and stamping his feet. Well I remember his thin, upright figure and the way in which he jauntily twirled his little cane ; for cold and hunger could not cast him down, though we knew that he had his share of both. Yet he was so proud and had such a grand manner of talking, that no one dared to offer him a cloak or a meal. I can see his face now, with a flush over each craggy cheek-bone when the butcher made him the present of some ribs of beef. He could not but take it, and yet whilst he was stalking off he threw a proud glance over his shoulder at the butcher, and he said, " Monsieur, I have a dog ! " Yet it was Monsieur Rudin and not his dog who looked plumper for a week to come.

Then I remember Mr. Paterson, the farmer, who was what you would now call a Radical, though at that time some called him a Priestley-ite, and some a Fox-ite, and nearly everybody a traitor. It certainly seemed to me, at the time, to be very wicked that a man should look glum when he heard of a British victory ; and when they burned his straw image at the gate of his farm, Boy Jim and I were among those who lent a hand. But we were bound to confess that he was game, though he might be a traitor, for down he came, striding into the midst of us with his brown coat and his buckled shoes, and the fire beating upon his grim, schoolmaster face. My word, how he rated us, and how glad we were at last to sneak quietly away.

" You livers of a lie ? ' said he. " You and those like you have been preaching peace for nigh two thousand years, and cutting throats the whole time. If the money that is lost in taking French lives were spent in saving English ones, you would have more right to burn candles in your windows. Who are you that dare to come here to insult a law-abiding man ? "

" We are the people of England ! " cried young Master Ovington, the son of the Tory Squire.

" You ! you horse-racing, cock-fighting ne'er-do-weel ! Do you presume to talk for the people of England ? They are a deep, strong, silent stream, and you are the scum, the bubbles, the poor, silly froth that floats upon the surface."

We thought him very wicked then, but, looking back, I am not sure that we were not very wicked ourselves.

And then there were the smugglers ! The Downs swarmed with them, for since there might be no lawful trade betwixt France and England, it had all to run in that channel. I have been up on St. John's Common upon a dark night, and, lying among the bracken, I have seen as many as seventy mules and a man at the head of each go flitting past me as silently as trout in a stream. Not one of them but bore its two ankers of the right

French cognac or its bale of silk of Lyons and lace of
Valenciennes. I knew Dan Scales, the head of them,
and I knew Tom Hislop, the riding officer, and I remember the night they met.

" Do you fight, Dan ? " asked Tom.

" Yes, Tom ; thou must fight for it."

On which Tom drew his pistol, and blew Dan's brains
out.

" It was a sad thing to do," he said afterwards, " but
I knew Dan was too good a man for me, for we tried it
out before."

It was Tom who paid a poet from Brighton to write
the lines for the tombstone, which we all thought were
very true and good, beginning—

> " Alas ! Swift flew the fatal lead
> Which piercéd through the young man's head.
> He instantly fell, resigned his breath,
> And closed his languid eyes in death."

There was more of it, and I dare say it is all still to be read
in Patcham Churchyard.

One day, about the time of our Cliffe Royal adventure,
I was seated in the cottage looking round at the curios
which my father had fastened on to the walls, and wishing,
like the lazy lad that I was, that Mr. Lilly had died before
ever he wrote his Latin grammar, when my mother, who
was sitting knitting in the window, gave a little cry of
surprise.

" Good gracious ! " she cried. " What a vulgar-look-
ing woman ! "

It was so rare to hear my mother say a hard word
against anybody (unless it were General Buonaparte)
that I was across the room and at the window in a jump.
A pony-chaise was coming slowly down the village street,
and in it was the queerest-looking person that I had ever
seen. She was very stout, with a face that was of so
dark a red that it shaded away into purple over the nose
and cheeks. She wore a great hat with a white curling

ostrich feather, and from under its brim her two bold, black eyes stared out with a look of anger and defiance as if to tell the folk that she thought less of them than they could do of her. She had some sort of scarlet pelisse with white swansdown about her neck, and she held the reins slack in her hands, while the pony wandered from side to side of the road as the fancy took him. Each time the chaise swayed, her head with the great hat swayed also, so that sometimes we saw the crown of it and sometimes the brim.

" What a dreadful sight ! " cried my mother.

" What is amiss with her, mother ? "

" Heaven forgive me if I misjudge her, Rodney, but I think that the unfortunate woman has been drinking."

" Why," I cried, " she has pulled the chaise up at the smithy. I'll find out all the news for you " ; and, catching up my cap, away I scampered.

Champion Harrison had been shoeing a horse at the forge door, and when I got into the street I could see him with the creature's hoof still under his arm, and the rasp in his hand, kneeling down amid the white parings. The woman was beckoning him from the chaise, and he staring up at her with the queerest expression upon his face. Presently he threw down his rasp and went across to her, standing by the wheel and shaking his head as he talked to her. For my part, I slipped into the smithy, where Boy Jim was finishing the shoe, and I watched the neatness of his work and the deft way in which he turned up the caulkens. When he had done with it he carried it out, and there was the strange woman still talking with his uncle.

" Is that he ? " I heard her ask.

Champion Harrison nodded.

She looked at Jim, and I never saw such eyes in a human head, so large, and black, and wonderful. Boy as I was, I knew that, in spite of that bloated face, this woman had once been very beautiful. She put out a hand, with all the fingers going as if she were playing

on the harpsichord, and she touched Jim on the shoulder.

"I hope—I hope you're well," she stammered.

"Very well, ma'am," said Jim, staring from her to his uncle.

"And happy too?"

"Yes, ma'am, I thank you."

"Nothing that you crave for?"

"Why, no, ma'am, I have all that I lack."

"That will do, Jim," said his uncle, in a stern voice. "Blow up the forge again, for that shoe wants re-heating."

But it seemed as if the woman had something else that she would say, for she was angry that he should be sent away. Her eyes gleamed, and her head tossed, while the smith with his two big hands outspread seemed to be soothing her as best he could. For a long time they whispered until at last she appeared to be satisfied.

"To-morrow, then?" she cried loud out.

"To-morrow," he answered.

"You keep your word and I'll keep mine," said she, and dropped the lash on the pony's back. The smith stood with the rasp in his hand, looking after her until she was just a little red spot on the white road. Then he turned, and I never saw his face so grave.

"Jim," said he, "that's Miss Hinton, who has come to live at The Maples, out Anstey Cross way. She's taken a kind of a fancy to you, Jim, and maybe she can help you on a bit. I promised her that you would go over and see her to-morrow."

"I don't want her help, uncle, and I don't want to see her."

"But I've promised, Jim, and you wouldn't make me out a liar. She does but want to talk with you, for it is a lonely life she leads."

"What would she want to talk with such as me about?"

"Why, I cannot say that, but she seemed very set upon it, and women have their fancies. There's young Master Stone here who wouldn't refuse to go and see a good

lady, I'll warrant, if he thought he might better his fortune by doing so."

" Well, uncle, I'll go if Roddy Stone will go with me," said Jim.

" Of course he'll go. Won't you, Master Rodney ? "

So it ended in my saying " yes," and back I went with all my news to my mother, who dearly loved a little bit of gossip. She shook her head when she heard where I was going, but she did not say nay, and so it was settled.

It was a good four miles of a walk, but when we reached it you would not wish to see a more cosy little house : all honeysuckle and creepers, with a wooden porch and lattice windows. A common-looking woman opened the door for us.

" Miss Hinton cannot see you," said she.

" But she asked us to come," said Jim.

" I can't help that," cried the woman, in a rude voice. " I tell you that she can't see you."

We stood irresolute for a minute.

" Maybe you would just tell her I am here," said Jim, at last.

" Tell her ! How am I to tell her when she couldn't so much as hear a pistol in her ears ? Try and tell her yourself, if you have a mind to."

She threw open a door as she spoke, and there, in a reclining chair at the further end of the room, we caught a glimpse of a figure all lumped together, huge and shapeless, with tails of black hair hanging down. The sound of dreadful, swine-like breathing fell upon our ears. It was but a glance, and then we were off hot-foot for home. As for me, I was so young that I was not sure whether this was funny or terrible ; but when I looked at Jim to see how he took it, he was looking quite white and ill.

" You'll not tell anyone, Roddy," said he.

" Not unless it's my mother."

" I won't even tell my uncle. I'll say she was ill, the poor lady ! It's enough that we should have seen her in

her shame, without its being the gossip of the village. It makes me feel sick and heavy at heart."

" She was so yesterday, Jim."

" Was she ? I never marked it. But I know that she has kind eyes and a kind heart, for I saw the one in the other when she looked at me. Maybe it's the want of a friend that has driven her to this."

It blighted his spirits for days, and when it had all gone from my mind it was brought back to me by his manner. But it was not to be our last memory of the lady with the scarlet pelisse, for before the week was out Jim came round to ask me if I would again go up with him.

" My uncle has had a letter," said he. " She would speak with me, and I would be easier if you came with me, Rod."

For me it was only a pleasure outing, but I could see, as we drew near the house, that Jim was troubling in his mind lest we should find that things were amiss. His fears were soon set at rest, however, for we had scarce clicked the garden gate before the woman was out of the door of the cottage and running down the path to meet us. She was so strange a figure, with some sort of purple wrapper on, and her big, flushed face smiling out of it, that I might, if I had been alone, have taken to my heels at the sight of her. Even Jim stopped for a moment as if he were not very sure of himself, but her hearty ways soon set us at our ease.

" It is indeed good of you to come and see an old, lonely woman," said she, " and I owe you an apology that I should give you a fruitless journey on Tuesday, but in a sense you were yourselves the cause of it, since the thought of your coming had excited me, and any excitement throws me into a nervous fever. My poor nerves ! You can see for yourselves how they serve me."

She held out her twitching hands as she spoke. Then she passed one of them through Jim's arm, and walked with him up the path.

" You must let me know you, and know you well,"
said she. " Your uncle and aunt are quite old acquaintances of mine, and though you cannot remember me, I
have held you in my arms when you were an infant. Tell
me, little man," she added, turning to me, " what do you
call your friend ? "

" Boy Jim, ma'am," said I.

" Then if you will not think me forward, I will call
you Boy Jim also. We elderly people have our privileges, you know. And now you shall come in with me,
and we will take a dish of tea together."

She led the way into a cosy room—the same which we
had caught a glimpse of when last we came—and there,
in the middle, was a table with white napery, and shining
glass, and gleaming china, and red-cheeked apples piled
upon a centre-dish, and a great plateful of smoking muffins
which the cross-faced maid had just carried in.   You can
think that we did justice to all the good things, and Miss
Hinton would ever keep pressing us to pass our cup and
to fill our plate. Twice during our meal she rose from
her chair and withdrew into a cupboard at the end of the
room, and each time I saw Jim's face cloud, for we heard
a gentle clink of glass against glass.

" Come now, little man," said she to me, when the
table had been cleared. " Why are you looking round
so much ? "

" Because there are so many pretty things upon the
walls."

" And which do you think the prettiest of them ? "

" Why, that ! " said I, pointing to a picture which hung
opposite to me.   It was of a tall and slender girl, with the
rosiest cheeks and the tenderest eyes—so daintily dressed,
too, that I had never seen anything more perfect.   She
had a posy of flowers in her hand and another one was lying
upon the planks of wood upon which she was standing.

" Oh, that's the prettiest, is it ? " said she, laughing.
" Well, now, walk up to it, and let us hear what is writ
beneath it."

I did as she asked, and read out : " Miss Polly Hinton, as ' Peggy,' in *The Country Wife*, played for her benefit at the Haymarket Theatre, September 14th, 1782."

" It's a play-actress," said I.

" Oh, you rude little boy, to say it in such a tone," said she ; " as if a play-actress wasn't as good as anyone else. Why, 'twas but the other day that the Duke of Clarence, who may come to call himself King of England, married Mrs. Jordan, who is herself only a play-actress. And whom think you that this one is ? "

She stood under the picture with her arms folded across her great body, and her big black eyes looking from one to the other of us.

" Why, where are your eyes ? " she cried at last. " *I* was Miss Polly Hinton of the Haymarket Theatre. And perhaps you never heard the name before ? "

We were compelled to confess that we never had. And the very name of play-actress had filled us both with a kind of vague horror, like the country-bred folk that we were. To us they were a class apart, to be hinted at rather than named, with the wrath of the Almighty hanging over them like a thundercloud. Indeed, His judgments seemed to be in visible operation before us when we looked upon what this woman was, and what she had been.

" Well," said she, laughing like one who is hurt, " you have no cause to say anything, for I read on your face what you have been taught to think of me. So this is the upbringing that you have had, Jim—to think evil of that which you do not understand ! I wish you had been in the theatre that very night with Prince Florizel and four Dukes in the boxes, and all the wits and macaronis of London rising at me in the pit. If Lord Avon had not given me a cast in his carriage, I had never got my flowers back to my lodgings in York Street, Westminster. And now two little country lads are sitting in judgment upon me ! "

Jim's pride brought a flush on to his cheeks, for he did

not like to be called a country lad, or to have it supposed that he was so far behind the grand folk in London.

" I have never been inside a play-house," said he ; " I know nothing of them."

" Nor I either."

" Well," said she, " I am not in voice, and it is ill to play in a little room with but two to listen, but you must conceive me to be the Queen of the Peruvians, who is exhorting her countrymen to rise up against the Spaniards, who are oppressing them."

And straightway that coarse, swollen woman became a queen—the grandest, haughtiest queen that you could dream of—and she turned upon us with such words of fire, such lightning eyes and sweeping of her white hand, that she held us spellbound in our chairs. Her voice was soft and sweet, and persuasive at the first, but louder it rang and louder as it spoke of wrongs and freedom and the joys of death in a good cause, until it thrilled into my every nerve, and I asked nothing more than to run out of the cottage and to die then and there in the cause of my country. And then in an instant she changed. She was a poor woman now, who had lost her only child, and who was bewailing it. Her voice was full of tears, and what she said was so simple, so true, that we both seemed to see the dead babe stretched there on the carpet before us, and we could have joined in with words of pity and grief. And then, before our cheeks were dry, she was back into her old self again.

" How like you that, then ? " she cried. " That was my way in the days when Sally Siddons would turn green at the name of Polly Hinton. It's a fine play, is *Pizarro*."

" And who wrote it, ma'am ? "

" Who wrote it ? I never heard. What matter who did the writing of it ! But there are some great lines for one who knows how they should be spoken."

" And you play no longer, ma'am ? "

" No, Jim, I left the boards when—when I was weary of them. But my heart goes back to them sometimes.

It seems to me there is no smell like that of the hot oil in the footlights and of the oranges in the pit. But you are sad, Jim."

" It was but the thought of that poor woman and her child."

" Tut, never think about her ! I will soon wipe her from your mind. This is ' Miss Priscilla Tomboy,' from *The Romp*. You must conceive that the mother is speaking, and that the forward young minx is answering."

And she began a scene between the two of them, so exact in voice and manner that it seemed to us as if there were really two folk before us : the stern old mother with her hand up like an ear-trumpet, and her flouncing, bouncing daughter. Her great figure danced about with a wonderful lightness, and she tossed her head and pouted her lips as she answered back to the old, bent figure that addressed her. Jim and I had forgotten our tears, and were holding our ribs before she came to the end of it.

" That is better," said she, smiling at our laughter. " I would not have you go back to Friar's Oak with long faces, or maybe they would not let you come to me again."

She vanished into her cupboard, and came out with a bottle and glass, which she placed upon the table.

" You are too young for strong waters," she said, " but this talking gives one a dryness, and——"

Then it was that Boy Jim did a wonderful thing. He rose from his chair, and he laid his hand upon the bottle.

" Don't ! " said he.

She looked him in the face, and I can still see those black eyes of hers softening before the gaze.

" Am I to have none ? "

" Please, don't."

With a quick movement she wrested the bottle out of his hand and raised it up so that for a moment it entered my head that she was about to drink it off. Then she flung it through the open lattice, and we heard the crash of it on the path outside.

" There, Jim ! " said she ; " does that satisfy you ?
It's long since anyone cared whether I drank or no."

" You are too good and kind for that," said he.

" Good ! " she cried. " Well, I love that you should
think me so. And it would make you happier if I kept
from the brandy, Jim ? Well, then, I'll make you a
promise, if you'll make me one in return."

" What's that, miss ? "

" No drop shall pass my lips, Jim, if you will swear,
wet or shine, blow or snow, to come up here twice in
every week, that I may see you and speak with you, for,
indeed, there are times when I am very lonesome."

So the promise was made, and very faithfully did Jim
keep it, for many a time when I have wanted him to go
fishing or rabbit-snaring, he has remembered that it was
his day for Miss Hinton, and has tramped off to Anstey
Cross. At first I think that she found her share of the
bargain hard to keep, and I have seen Jim come back with
a black face on him, as if things were going amiss. But
after a time the fight was won—as all fights are won if
one does but fight long enough—and in the year before
my father came back Miss Hinton had become another
woman. And it was not her ways only, but herself as
well, for from being the person that I have described, she
became in one twelvemonth as fine a looking lady as
there was in the whole country-side. Jim was prouder
of it by far than of anything he had had a hand in in his
life, but it was only to me that he ever spoke about it,
for he had that tenderness towards her that one has for
those whom one has helped. And she helped him also,
for by her talk of the world and of what she had seen, she
took his mind away from the Sussex country-side and
prepared it for a broader life beyond. So matters stood
between them at the time when peace was made and my
father came home from the sea.

4. *The Peace of Amiens*

MANY a woman's knee was on the ground, and many a woman's soul spent itself in joy and thankfulness when the news came with the fall of the leaf in 1801 that the preliminaries of peace had been settled. All England waved her gladness by day and twinkled it by night. Even in little Friar's Oak we had our flags flying bravely, and a candle in every window, with a big G.R. guttering in the wind over the door of the inn. Folk were weary of the war, for we had been at it for eight years, taking Holland, and Spain, and France each in turn and all together. All that we had learned during that time was that our little army was no match for the French on land, and that our large navy was more than a match for them upon the water. We had gained some credit, which we were sorely in need of after the American business ; and a few Colonies, which were welcome also for the same reason ; but our debt had gone on rising and our consols sinking, until even Pitt stood aghast. Still, if we had known that there never could be peace between Napoleon and ourselves, and that this was only the end of a round and not of the battle, we should have been better advised had we fought it out without a break. As it was, the French got back the twenty thousand good seamen whom we had captured, and a fine dance they led us with their Boulogne flotillas and fleets of invasion before we were able to catch them again.

My father, as I remember him best, was a tough, strong little man, of no great breadth, but solid and well put together. His face was burned of a reddish colour, as bright as a flower-pot, and in spite of his age (for he was only forty at the time of which I speak) it was shot with lines, which deepened if he were in any way perturbed, so that I have seen him turn on the instant from a youngish man to an elderly. His eyes especially were

889

meshed round with wrinkles, as is natural for one who had puckered them all his life in facing foul wind and bitter weather. These eyes were, perhaps, his strangest feature, for they were of a very clear and beautiful blue, which shone the brighter out of that ruddy setting. By nature he must have been a fair-skinned man, for his upper brow, where his cap came over it, was as white as mine, and his close-cropped hair was tawny.

He had served, as he was proud to say, in the last of our ships which had been chased out of the Mediterranean in '97, and in the first which had re-entered it in '98. He was under Miller, as third lieutenant of the *Theseus*, when our fleet, like a pack of eager foxhounds in a covert, was dashing from Sicily to Syria and back again to Naples, trying to pick up the lost scent. With the same good fighting man he served at the Nile, where the men of his command sponged and rammed and trained until, when the last tricolour had come down, they hove up the sheet anchor and fell dead asleep upon the top of each other under the capstan bars. Then, as a second lieutenant, he was in one of those grim three-deckers with powder-blackened hulls and crimson scupper-holes, their spare cables tied round their keels and over their bulwarks to hold them together, which carried the news into the Bay of Naples. From thence, as a reward for his services, he was transferred as first lieutenant to the *Aurora* frigate, engaged in cutting off supplies from Genoa, and in her he still remained until long after peace was declared.

How well I can remember his home-coming ! Though it is now eight-and forty years ago, it is clearer to me than the doings of last week, for the memory of an old man is like one of those glasses which show out what is at a distance and blur all that is near.

My mother had been in a tremble ever since the first rumour of the preliminaries came to our ears, for she knew that he might come as soon as his message. She said little, but she saddened my life by insisting that I

should be for ever clean and tidy. With every rumble of wheels, too, her eyes would glance towards the door, and her hands steal up to smooth her pretty black hair. She had embroidered a white " Welcome " upon a blue ground, with an anchor in red upon each side, and a border of laurel leaves ; and this was to hang upon the two lilac bushes which flanked the cottage door. He could not have left the Mediterranean before we had this finished, and every morning she looked to see if it were in its place and ready to be hanged.

But it was a weary time before the peace was ratified, and it was April of next year before our great day came round to us. It had been raining all morning, I remember—a soft spring rain, which sent up a rich smell from the brown earth and pattered pleasantly upon the budding chestnuts behind our cottage. The sun had shone out in the evening, and I had come down with my fishing-rod (for I had promised Boy Jim to go with him to the mill-stream), when what should I see but a post-chaise with two smoking horses at the gate, and there in the open door of it were my mother's black skirt and her little feet jutting out, with two blue arms for a waist-belt, and all the rest of her buried in the chaise. Away I ran for the motto, and I pinned it up on the bushes as we had agreed, but when I had finished there were the skirt and the feet and the blue arms just the same as before.

" Here's Rod," said my mother at last, struggling down on to the ground again. " Roddy, darling, here's your father ! "

I saw the red face and the kindly, light-blue eyes looking out at me.

" Why, Roddy, lad, you were but a child and we kissed good-bye when last we met ; but I suppose we must put you on a different rating now. I'm right glad from my heart to see you, dear lad ; and as to you, sweetheart——" The blue arms flew out and there were the skirt and the two feet fixed in the door again.

" Here are the folk coming, Anson," said my mother,

blushing. "Won't you get out and come in with us?"

And then suddenly it came home to us both that for all his cheery face he had never moved more than his arms, and that his leg was resting on the opposite seat of the chaise.

"Oh, Anson, Anson!" she cried.

"Tut, 'tis but the bone of my leg," said he, taking his knee between his hands and lifting it round. "I got it broke in the Bay, but the surgeon has fished it and spliced it, though it's a bit crank yet. Why, bless her kindly heart, if I haven't turned her from pink to white. You can see for yourself that it's nothing."

He sprang out as he spoke, and with one leg and a staff he hopped swiftly up the path, and under the laurel-bordered motto, and so over his own threshold for the first time for five years. When the post-boy and I had carried up the sea-chest and the two canvas bags, there he was sitting in his armchair by the window in his old weather-stained blue coat. My mother was weeping over his poor leg, and he patting her hair with one brown hand. His other he threw round my waist, and drew me to the side of his chair.

"Now that we have peace, I can lie up and refit until King George needs me again," said he. "'Twas a carronade that came adrift in the Bay when it was blowing a top-gallant breeze with a beam sea. Ere we could make it fast it had me jammed against the mast. Well, well," he added, looking round at the walls of the room, " here are all my old curios, the same as ever : the narwhal's horn from the Arctic, and the blowfish from the Moluccas, and the paddles from Fiji, and the picture of the *Ça Ira* with Lord Hotham in chase. And here you are, Mary, and you also, Roddy, and good luck to the carronade which has sent me into so snug a harbour without fear of sailing orders."

My mother had his long pipe and his tobacco all ready for him, so that he was able now to light it and to sit look-

ing from one of us to the other and then back again, as if he could never see enough of us. Young as I was, I could still understand that this was the moment which he had thought of during many a lonely watch, and that the expectation of it had cheered his heart in many a dark hour. Sometimes he would touch one of us with his hand, and sometimes the other, and so he sat, with his soul too satiated for words, whilst the shadows gathered in the little room and the lights of the inn windows glimmered through the gloom. And then, after my mother had lit our own lamp, she slipped suddenly down upon her knees, and he got one knee to the ground also, so that, hand-in-hand, they joined their thanks to Heaven for manifold mercies. When I look back at my parents as they were in those days, it is at that very moment that I can picture them most clearly : her sweet face with the wet shining upon her cheeks, and his blue eyes upturned to the smoke-blackened ceiling. I remember that he swayed his reeking pipe in the earnestness of his prayer, so that I was half tears and half smiles as I watched him.

" Roddy, lad," said he, after supper was over, " you're getting a man now, and I suppose you will go afloat like the rest of us. You're old enough to strap a dirk to your thigh."

" And leave me without a child as well as without a husband ! " cried my mother.

" Well, there's time enough yet," said he, " for they are more inclined to empty berths than to fill them, now that peace has come. But I've never tried what all this schooling has done for you, Rodney. You have had a great deal more than ever I had, but I dare say I can make shift to test it. Have you learned history ? "

" Yes, father," said I, with some confidence.

" Then how many sail of the line were at the Battle of Camperdown ? "

He shook his head gravely, when he found that I could not answer him.

" Why, there are men in the fleet who never had any

schooling at all who could tell you that we had seven 74's, seven 64's and two 50-gun ships in the action. There's a picture on the wall of the chase of the *Ça Ira*. Which were the ships that laid her aboard ? "

Again I had to confess that he had beaten me.

" Well, your dad can teach you something in history yet," he cried, looking in triumph at my mother. " Have you learned geography ? "

" Yes, father," said I, though with less confidence than before.

" Well, how far is it from Port Mahon to Algeçiras ? " I could only shake my head.

" If Ushant lay three leagues upon your starboard quarter, what would be your nearest English port ? " Again I had to give it up.

" Well, I don't see that your geography is much better than your history," said he. " You'd never get your certificate at this rate. Can you do addition ? Well, then, let us see if you can tot up my prize-money."

He shot a mischievous glance at my mother as he spoke, and she laid down her knitting on her lap and looked very earnestly at him.

" You never asked me about that, Mary," said he.

" The Mediterranean is not the station for it, Anson. I have heard you say that it is the Atlantic for prize-money, and the Mediterranean for honour."

" I had a share of both last cruise, which comes from changing a line-of-battleship for a frigate. Now, Rodney, there are two pounds in every hundred due to me when the prize-courts have done with them. When we were watching Massena, off Genoa, we got a matter of seventy schooners, brigs and tartans, with wine, food and powder. Lord Keith will want his finger in the pie, but that's for the Courts to settle. Put them at four pounds apiece to me, and what will the seventy bring ? "

" Two hundred and eighty pounds," I answered.

" Why, Anson, it is a fortune ! " cried my mother, clapping her hands.

" Try you again, Roddy ! " said he, shaking his pipe at me. " There was the *Xebec* frigate out of Barcelona with twenty thousand Spanish dollars aboard, which make four thousand of our pounds. Her hull should be worth another thousand. What's my share of that ? "

" A hundred pounds."

" Why, the purser couldn't work it out quicker," he cried in his delight. " Here's for you again ! We passed the Straits and worked up to the Azores, where we fell in with the *La Sabina* from the Mauritius with sugar and spices. Twelve hundred pounds she's worth to me, Mary, my darling, and never again shall you soil your pretty fingers, or pinch upon my beggarly pay."

My dear mother had borne her long struggle without a sign all these years, but now that she was so suddenly eased of it she fell sobbing upon his neck. It was a long time before my father had a thought to spare upon my examination in arithmetic.

" It's all in your lap, Mary," said he, dashing his own hand across his eyes. " By George, lass, when this leg of mine is sound we'll bear down for a spell to Brighton, and if there is a smarter frock than yours upon the Steyne, may I never tread a poop again. But how is it that you are so quick at figures, Rodney, when you know nothing of history or geography ? "

I tried to explain that addition was the same upon sea or land, but that history and geography were not.

" Well," he concluded, " you need figures to take a reckoning, and you need nothing else save what your mother wit will teach you. There never was one of our breed who did not take to salt water like a young gull. Lord Nelson has promised me a vacancy for you, and he'll be as good as his word."

So it was that my father came home to us, and a better or kinder no lad could wish for. Though my parents had been married so long, they had really seen very little of each other, and their affection was as warm and as fresh as if they were two newly-wedded lovers. I have learned

since that sailors can be coarse and foul, but never did I know it from my father ; for, although he had seen as much rough work as the wildest could wish for, he was always the same patient, good-humoured man, with a smile and a jolly word for all the village. He could suit himself to his company, too, for on the one hand he could take his wine with the vicar, or with Sir James Ovington, the squire of the parish ; while on the other he would sit by the hour amongst my humble friends down in the smithy, with Champion Harrison, Boy Jim and the rest of them, telling them such stories of Nelson and his men that I have seen the Champion knot his great hands together, while Jim's eyes have smouldered like the forge embers as he listened.

My father had been placed on half-pay, like so many others of the old war officers, and so, for nearly two years, he was able to remain with us. During all this time I can only once remember that there was the slightest disagreement between him and my mother. It chanced that I was the cause of it, and as great events sprang out of it, I must tell you how it came about. It was indeed the first of a series of events which affected not only my fortunes, but those of very much more important people.

The spring of 1803 was an early one, and the middle of April saw the leaves thick upon the chestnut trees. One evening we were all seated together over a dish of tea when we heard the scrunch of steps outside our door, and there was the postman with a letter in his hand.

" I think it is for me," said my mother, and sure enough it was addressed in the most beautiful writing to Mrs. Mary Stone, of Friar's Oak, and there was a red seal the size of a half-crown upon the outside of it with a flying dragon in the middle.

" Whom think you that it is from, Anson ? " she asked.

" I had hoped that it was from Lord Nelson," answered my father. " It is time the boy had his commission. But if it be for you, then it cannot be from anyone of much importance."

" Can it not ? " she cried, pretending to be offended.
" You will ask my pardon for that speech, sir, for it is
from no less a person than Sir Charles Tregellis, my own
brother."

My mother seemed to speak with a hushed voice when
she mentioned this wonderful brother of hers, and always
had done as long as I can remember, so that I had learned
also to have a subdued and reverent feeling when I heard
his name. And indeed it was no wonder, for that name
was never mentioned unless it were in connection with
something brilliant and extraordinary. Once we heard
that he was at Windsor with the King. Often he was
at Brighton with the Prince. Sometimes it was as a
sportsman that his reputation reached us, as when his
Meteor beat the Duke of Queensberry's Egham, at Newmarket, or when he brought Jim Belcher up from Bristol,
and sprang him upon the London Fancy. But usually
it was as the friend of the great, the arbiter of fashions,
the king of bucks and the best-dressed man in town, that
his reputation reached us. My father, however, did not
appear to be elated at my mother's triumphant rejoinder.

" Aye, and what does he want ? " asked he, in no very
amiable voice.

" I wrote to him, Anson, and told him that Rodney
was growing a man now, thinking, since he had no wife or
child of his own, he might be disposed to advance him."

" We can do very well without him," growled my
father. " He sheered off from us when the weather was
foul, and we have no need of him now that the sun is
shining."

" Nay, you misjudge him, Anson," said my mother,
warmly. " There is no one with a better heart than
Charles ; but his own life moves so smoothly that he
cannot understand that others may have trouble. During
all these years I have known that I had but to say the
word to receive as much as I wished from him."

" Thank God that you never had to stoop to it, Mary.
I want none of his help."

" But we must think of Rodney."

" Rodney has enough for his sea-chest and kit. He needs no more."

" But Charles has great power and influence in London. He could make Rodney known to all the great people. Surely you would not stand in the way of his advancement."

" Let us hear what he says, then," said my father ; and this was the letter which she read to him—

" 14, JERMYN STREET, ST. JAMES'S,
" *April* 15, 1803.

" MY DEAR SISTER MARY,

" In answer to your letter, I can assure you that you must not conceive me to be wanting in those finer feelings which are the chief adornment of humanity. It is true that for some years, absorbed as I have been in affairs of the highest importance, I have seldom taken a pen in hand, for which I can assure you that I have been reproached by many *des plus charmantes* of your charming sex. At the present moment I lie abed (having stayed late in order to pay a compliment to the Marchioness of Dover at her ball last night), and this is writ to my dictation by Ambrose, my clever rascal of a valet. I am interested to hear of my nephew Rodney (*Mon dieu, quel nom !*), and as I shall be on my way to visit the Prince at Brighton next week, I shall break my journey at Friar's Oak for the sake of seeing both you and him. Make my compliments to your husband.

" I am ever, my dear sister Mary,
" Your brother,
" CHARLES TREGELLIS."

" What do you think of that ? " cried my mother in triumph when she had finished.

" I think it is the letter of a fop," said my father, bluntly.

" You are too hard on him, Anson. You will think

better of him when you know him. But he says that he will be here next week, and this is Thursday, and the best curtains unhung, and no lavender in the sheets ! "

Away she bustled, half distracted, while my father sat moody, and his chin upon his hands, and I remained lost in wonder at the thought of this grand new relative from London, and of all that his coming might mean to us.

5. *Buck Tregellis*

NOW that I was in my seventeenth year, and had already some need for a razor, I had begun to weary of the narrow life of the village, and to long to see something of the great world beyond. The craving was all the stronger because I durst not speak openly about it, for the least hint of it brought the tears into my mother's eyes. But now there was the less reason that I should stay at home, since my father was at her side, and so my mind was all filled by this prospect of my uncle's visit, and of the chance that he might set my feet moving at last upon the road of life.

As you may think, it was towards my father's profession that my thoughts and my hopes turned, for from my childhood I have never seen the heave of the sea or tasted the salt upon my lips without feeling the blood of five generations of seamen thrill within my veins. And think of the challenge which was ever waving in those days before the eyes of a coast-living lad ! I had but to walk up to Wolstonbury in the war time to see the sails of the French chasse-marées and privateers. Again and again I have heard the roar of the guns coming from far out over the waters. Seamen would tell us how they had left London and been engaged ere nightfall, or sailed out of Portsmouth and been yard-arm to yard-arm before they had lost sight of St. Helen's light. It was this imminence of the danger which warmed our hearts to our sailors, and made us talk, round the winter fires, of our little Nelson, and

Cuddie Collingwood, and Johnnie Jarvis, and the rest of them, not as being great High Admirals with titles and dignities, but as good friends whom we loved and honoured above all others. What boy was there through the length and breath of Britain who did not long to be out with them under the red-cross flag ?

But now that peace had come, and the fleets which had swept the Channel and the Mediterranean were lying dismantled in our harbours, there was less to draw one's fancy seawards. It was London now of which I thought by day and brooded by night : the huge city, the home of the wise and the great, from which came this constant stream of carriages, and those crowds of dusty people who were for ever flashing past our window-pane. It was this one side of life which first presented itself to me, and so, as a boy, I used to picture the City as a gigantic stable with a huge huddle of coaches, which were for ever streaming off down the country roads. But, then, Champion Harrison told me how the fighting-men lived there, and my father how the heads of the Navy lived there, and my mother how her brother and his grand friends were there, until at last I was consumed with impatience to see this marvellous heart of England. This coming of my uncle, then, was the breaking of light through the darkness, though I hardly dared to hope that he would take me with him into those high circles in which he lived. My mother, however, had such confidence either in his good nature or in her own powers of persuasion, that she already began to make furtive preparations for my departure.

But if the narrowness of the village life chafed my easy spirit, it was a torture to the keen and ardent mind of Boy Jim. It was but a few days after the coming of my uncle's letter that we walked over the Downs together, and I had a peep of the bitterness of his heart.

" What is there for me to do, Rodney ? " he cried. " I forge a shoe, and I fuller it, and I clip it, and I caulken it, and I knock five holes in it, and there it is

finished. Then I do it again and again, and blow up the bellows and feed the forge, and rasp a hoof or two, and there is a day's work done, and every day the same as the other. Was it for this only, do you think, that I was born into the world ? "

I looked at him, his proud, eagle face, and his tall, sinewy figure, and I wondered whether in the whole land there was a finer, handsomer man.

" The Army or the Navy is the place for you, Jim," said I.

" That is very well," he cried. " If you go into the Navy, as you are likely to do, you go as an officer, and it is you who do the ordering. If I go in, it is as one who was born to receive orders."

" An officer gets his orders from those above him."

" But an officer does not have the lash hung over his head. I saw a poor fellow at the inn here—it was some years ago—who showed us his back in the tap-room, all cut into red diamonds with the boatswain's whip. ' Who ordered that ? ' I asked. ' The captain,' said he. ' And what would you have had if you had struck him dead ? ' said I. ' The yard-arm,' he answered. ' Then if I had been you that's where I should have been,' said I, and I spoke the truth. I can't help it, Rod ! There's something here in my heart, something that is as much a part of myself as this hand is, which holds me to it."

" I know that you are as proud as Lucifer," said I.

" It was born with me, Roddy, and I can't help it. Life would be easier if I could. I was made to be my own master, and there's only one place where I can hope to be so."

" Where is that, Jim ? "

" In London. Miss Hinton has told me of it, until I feel as if I could find my way through it from end to end. She loves to talk of it as well as I do to listen. I have it all laid out in my mind, and I can see where the playhouses are, and how the river runs, and where the King's house is, and the Prince's, and the place where

the fighting-men live. I could make my name known
in London."

" How ? "

" Never mind how, Rod. I could do it, and I will
do it, too. ' Wait ! ' says my uncle—' wait, and it will
all come right for you.' That is what he always says, and
my aunt the same. Why should I wait ? What am I
to wait for ? No, Roddy, I'll stay no longer eating my
heart out in this little village, but I'll leave my apron
behind me, and I'll seek my fortune in London, and when
I come back to Friar's Oak, it will be in such style as
that gentleman yonder."

He pointed as he spoke, and there was a high crimson
curricle coming down the London road, with two bay
mares harnessed tandem fashion before it. The reins
and fittings were of a light fawn colour, and the gentleman had a driving-coat to match, with a servant in dark
livery behind. They flashed past us in a rolling cloud of
dust, and I had just a glimpse of the pale, handsome face
of the master, and of the dark, shrivelled features of the
man. I should never have given them another thought
had it not chanced that when the village came into view
there was the curricle again, standing at the door of the
inn, and the grooms busy taking out the horses.

" Jim," I cried, " I believe it is my uncle ! " and taking
to my heels I ran for home at the top of my speed. At
the door was standing the dark-faced servant. He carried
a cushion, upon which lay a small and fluffy lapdog.

" You will excuse me, young sir," said he, in the suavest,
most soothing of voices, " but am I right in supposing that
this is the house of Lieutenant Stone ? In that case you
will, perhaps, do me the favour to hand to Mrs. Stone
this note which her brother, Sir Charles Tregellis, has
just committed to my care."

I was quite abashed by the man's flowery way of talking
—so unlike anything which I had ever heard. He had a
wizened face, and sharp little dark eyes, which took in
me and the house and my mother's startled face at the

window all in the instant. My parents were together, the two of them, in the sitting-room, and my mother read the note to us.

" My dear Mary," it ran, " I have stopped at the inn, because I am somewhat *ravagé* by the dust of your Sussex roads. A lavender-water bath may restore me to a condition in which I may fitly pay my compliments to a lady. Meantime, I send you Fidelio as a hostage. Pray give him a half-pint of warmish milk with six drops of pure brandy in it. A better or more faithful creature never lived. *Toujours à toi.*—Charles."

" Have him in ! Have him in ! " cried my father, heartily, running to the door. " Come in, Mr. Fidelio. Every man to his own taste, and six drops to the half-pint seems a sinful watering of grog—but if you like it so, you shall have it."

A smile flickered over the dark face of the servant, but his features reset themselves instantly into their usual mask of respectful observance.

" You are labouring under a slight error, sir, if you will permit me to say so. My name is Ambrose, and I have the honour to be the valet of Sir Charles Tregellis. This is Fidelio upon the cushion."

" Tut, the dog ! " cried my father, in disgust. " Heave him down by the fireside. Why should he have brandy, when many a Christian has to go without ? "

" Hush, Anson ! " said my mother, taking the cushion. " You will tell Sir Charles that his wishes shall be carried out, and that we shall expect him at his own convenience."

The man went off noiselessly and swiftly, but was back in a few minutes with a flat brown basket

" It is the refection, madam," said he. " Will you permit me to lay the table ? Sir Charles is accustomed to partake of certain dishes and to drink certain wines, so that we usually bring them with us when we visit." He opened the basket, and in a minute he had the table all shining with silver and glass, and studded with dainty

dishes. So quick and neat and silent was he in all he did, that my father was as taken with him as I was.

" You'd have made a right good foretopman if your heart is as stout as your fingers are quick," said he. " Did you never wish to have the honour of serving your country ? "

" It is my honour, sir, to serve Sir Charles Tregellis, and I desire no other master," he answered. " But I will convey his dressing-case from the inn, and then all will be ready."

He came back with a great silver-mounted box under his arms, and close at his heels was the gentleman whose coming had made such a disturbance.

My first impression of my uncle as he entered the room was that one of his eyes was swollen to the size of an apple. It caught the breath from my lips—that monstrous, glistening eye. But the next instant I perceived that he held a round glass in the front of it, which magnified it in this fashion. He looked at us each in turn, and then he bowed very gracefully to my mother, and kissed her upon either cheek.

" You will permit me to compliment you, my dear Mary," said he, in a voice which was the most mellow and beautiful that I have ever heard. " I can assure you that the country air has used you wondrous well, and that I shall be proud to see my pretty sister in the Mall. I am your servant, sir," he continued, holding out his hand to my father. " It was but last week that I had the honour of dining with my friend, Lord St. Vincent, and I took occasion to mention you to him. I may tell you that your name is not forgotten at the Admiralty, sir, and I hope that I may see you soon walking the poop of a 74-gun ship of your own. So this is my nephew, is it ? " He put a hand upon each of my shoulders in a very friendly way and looked me up and down.

" How old are you, nephew ? " he asked.

" Seventeen, sir."

" You look older. You look eighteen, at the least.

I find him very passable, Mary—very passable, indeed.
He has not the *bel* air, the *tournure*—in our uncouth
English we have no word for it. But he is as healthy as
a May-hedge in bloom."

So within a minute of his entering our door he had got
himself upon terms with all of us, and with so easy and
graceful a manner that it seemed as if he had known us
all for years. I had a good look at him now as he stood
upon the hearthrug, with my mother upon one side and
my father on the other. He was a very large man, with
noble shoulders, small waist, broad hips, well-turned legs,
and the smallest of hands and feet. His face was pale
and handsome, with a prominent chin, a jutting nose, and
large blue staring eyes, in which a sort of dancing, mischievous light was for ever playing. He wore a deep
brown coat with a collar as high as his ears and tails as low
as his knees. His black breeches and silk stockings ended
in very small pointed shoes, so highly polished that they
twinkled with every movement. His vest was of black
velvet, open at the top to show an embroidered shirt-front,
with a high, smooth, white cravat above it, which kept
his neck for ever on the stretch. He stood easily, with
one thumb in the arm-pit, and two fingers of the other
hand in his vest pocket. It made me proud as I watched
him to think that so magnificent a man, with such easy,
masterful ways, should be my own blood relation, and
I could see from my mother's eyes as they turned towards
him that the same thought was in her mind.

All this time Ambrose had been standing like a dark-
clothed, bronze-faced image by the door, with the big
silver-bound box under his arm. He stepped forward
now into the room.

" Shall I convey it to your bedchamber, Sir Charles ? "
he asked.

" Ah, pardon me, sister Mary," cried my uncle, " I am
old-fashioned enough to have principles—an anachronism,
I know, in this lax age. One of them is never to allow
my *batterie de toilette* out of my sight when I am travelling.

I cannot readily forget the agonies which I endured some years ago through neglecting this precaution. I will do Ambrose the justice to say that it was before he took charge of my affairs. I was compelled to wear the same ruffles upon two consecutive days. On the third morning my fellow was so affected by the sight of my condition, that he burst into tears and laid out a pair which he had stolen from me."

As he spoke his face was very grave, but the light in his eyes danced and gleamed. He handed his open snuff-box to my father, as Ambrose followed my mother out of the room.

" You number yourself in an illustrious company by dipping your finger and thumb into it," said he.

" Indeed, sir ! " said my father, shortly.

"You are free of my box, as being a relative by marriage. You are free also, nephew, and I pray you to take a pinch. It is the most intimate sign of my goodwill. Outside ourselves there are four, I think, who have had access to it—the Prince, of course ; Mr. Pitt ; Monsieur Otto, the French Ambassador ; and Lord Hawkesbury. I have sometimes thought that I was premature with Lord Hawkesbury."

" I am vastly honoured, sir," said my father, looking suspiciously at his guest from under his shaggy eyebrows, for with that grave face and those twinkling eyes it was hard to know how to take him.

" A woman, sir, has her love to bestow," said my uncle. " A man has his snuff-box. Neither is to be lightly offered. It is a lapse of taste ; nay, more, it is a breach of morals. Only the other day, as I was seated in Watier's, my box of prime macouba open upon the table beside me, an Irish bishop thrust in his intrusive fingers. ' Waiter,' I cried, ' my box has been soiled ! Remove it ! ' The man meant no insult, you understand, but that class of people must be kept in their proper sphere."

" A bishop ! " cried my father. " You draw your line very high, sir."

" Yes, sir," said my uncle ; " I wish no better epitaph upon my tombstone."

My mother had in the meanwhile descended, and we all drew up to the table.

" You will excuse my apparent grossness, Mary, in venturing to bring my own larder with me. Abernethy has me under his orders, and I must eschew your rich country dainties. A little white wine and a cold bird— it is as much as the niggardly Scotchman will allow me."

" We should have you on blockading service when the levanters are blowing," said my father. " Salt junk and weevilly biscuits, with a rib of a tough Barbary ox when the tenders come in. You would have your spare diet there, sir."

Straightway my uncle began to question him about the sea service, and for the whole meal my father was telling him of the Nile and of the Toulon blockade, and the siege of Genoa, and all that he had seen and done. But whenever he faltered for a word, my uncle always had it ready for him, and it was hard to say which knew most about the business.

" No, I read little or nothing," said he, when my father marvelled where he got his knowledge. " The fact is that I can hardly pick up a print without seeing some allusion to myself : ' Sir C. T. does this,' or ' Sir C. T. says the other,' so I take them no longer. But if a man is in my position all knowledge comes to him. The Duke of York tells me of the Army in the morning, and Lord Spencer chats with me of the Navy in the afternoon, and Dundas whispers me what is going forward in the Cabinet, so that I have little need of the *Times* or the *Morning Chronicle*."

This set him talking of the great world of London, telling my father about the men who were his masters at the Admiralty, and my mother about the beauties of the town, and the great ladies at Almack's, but all in the same light, fanciful way, so that one never knew whether to laugh or to take him gravely. I think it flattered him to

see the way in which we all three hung upon his words. Of some he thought highly and of some lowly, but he made no secret that the highest of all, and the one against whom all others should be measured, was Sir Charles Tregellis himself.

" As to the King," said he, " of course, I am *l'ami de famille* there ; and even with you I can scarce speak freely, as my relations are confidential."

" God bless him and keep him from ill ! " cried my father.

" It is pleasant to hear you say so," said my uncle. " One has to come into the country to hear honest loyalty, for a sneer and a gibe are more the fashions in town. The King is grateful to me for the interest which I have ever shown in his son. He likes to think that the Prince has a man of taste in his circle."

" And the Prince ? " asked my mother. " Is he well-favoured ? "

" He is a fine figure of a man. At a distance he has been mistaken for me. And he has some taste in dress, though he gets slovenly if I am too long away from him. I warrant you that I find a crease in his coat to-morrow."

We were all seated round the fire by this time, for the evening had turned chilly. The lamp was lighted, and so also was my father's pipe.

" I suppose," said he, " that this is your first visit to Friar's Oak ? "

My uncle's face turned suddenly very grave and stern.

" It is my first visit for many years," said he. " I was but one-and-twenty years of age when last I came here. I am not likely to forget it."

I knew that he spoke of his visit to Cliffe Royal at the time of the murder, and I saw by her face that my mother knew it also. My father, however, had either never heard of it, or had forgotten the circumstance.

" Was it at the inn you stayed ? " he asked.

" I stayed with the unfortunate Lord Avon. It was

the occasion when he was accused of slaying his younger brother and fled from the country."

We all fell silent, and my uncle leaned his chin upon his hand, looking thoughtfully into the fire. If I do but close my eyes now, I can see the light upon his proud, handsome face, and see also my dear father, concerned at having touched upon so terrible a memory, shooting little slanting glances at him betwixt the puffs of his pipe.

" I dare say that it has happened with you, sir," said my uncle at last, " that you have lost some dear messmate in battle or wreck, and that you have put him out of your mind in the routine of your daily life, until suddenly some word or some scene brings him back to your memory, and you find your sorrow as raw as upon the first day of your loss."

My father nodded.

" So it is with me to-night. I never formed a close friendship with a man—I say nothing of women—save only the once. That was with Lord Avon. We were of an age, he a few years perhaps my senior, but our tastes, our judgments and our characters were alike, save only that he had in him a touch of pride such as I have never known in any other man. Putting aside the little foibles of a rich young man of fashion, *les indiscrétions d'une jeunesse dorée*, I could have sworn that he was as good a man as I have ever known."

" How came he, then, to such a crime ? " asked my father.

My uncle shook his head.

" Many a time have I asked myself that question, and it comes home to me more to-night then ever."

All the jauntiness had gone out of his manner, and he had turned suddenly into a sad and serious man.

" Was it certain that he did it, Charles ? " asked my mother.

My uncle shrugged his shoulders.

" I wish I could think it were not so. I have thought sometimes that it was this very pride, turning suddenly

to madness, which drove him to it. You have heard how he returned the money which we had lost ? "

" Nay, I have heard nothing of it," my father answered.

" It is a very old story now, though we have not yet found an end to it. We had played for two days, the four of us : Lord Avon, his brother, Captain Barrington, Sir Lothian Hume and myself. Of the Captain I knew little, save that he was not of the best repute, and was deep in the hands of the Jews. Sir Lothian has made an evil name for himself since—'tis the same Sir Lothian who shot Lord Carton in the affair at Chalk Farm—but in those days there was nothing against him. The oldest of us was but twenty-four, and we gamed on, as I say, until the Captain had cleared the board. We were all hit, but our host far the hardest.

" That night—I tell you now what it would be a bitter thing for me to tell in a court of law—I was restless and sleepless, as often happens when a man has kept awake over long. My mind would dwell upon the fall of the cards, and I was tossing and turning in my bed, when suddenly a cry fell upon my ears, and then a second louder one, coming from the direction of Captain Barrington's room. Five minutes later I heard steps passing down the passage, and, without striking a light, I opened my door and peeped out, thinking that someone was taken unwell. There was Lord Avon walking towards me. In one hand he held a guttering candle and in the other a brown bag, which chinked as he moved. His face was all drawn and distorted—so much so that my question was frozen upon my lips. Before I could utter it he turned into his chamber and softly closed the door.

" Next morning I was awakened by finding him at my bedside.

" ' Charles,' said he, ' I cannot abide to think that you should have lost this money in my house. You will find it here upon your table.'

" It was in vain that I laughed at his squeamishness,

telling him that I should most certainly have claimed my money had I won, so that it would be strange indeed if I were not permitted to pay it when I lost.

" ' Neither I nor my brother will touch it,' said he. ' There it lies, and you may do what you like about it.'

" He would listen to no argument, but dashed out of the room like a madman. But perhaps these details are familiar to you, and God knows they are painful to me to tell."

My father was sitting with staring eyes, and his forgotten pipe reeking in his hand.

" Pray let us hear the end of it, sir," he cried.

" Well, then, I had finished my toilet in an hour or so—for I was less exigeant in those days than now—and I met Sir Lothian Hume at breakfast. His experience had been the same as my own, and he was eager to see Captain Barrington, and to ascertain why he had directed his brother to return the money to us. We were talking the matter over when suddenly I raised my eyes to the corner of the ceiling, and I saw—I saw——"

My uncle had turned quite pale with the vividness of the memory, and he passed his hand over his eyes.

" It was crimson," said he, with a shudder—" crimson with black cracks, and from every crack—but I will give you dreams, sister Mary. Suffice it that we rushed up the stair which led direct to the Captain's room, and there we found him lying with the bone gleaming white through his throat. A hunting-knife lay in the room— and the knife was Lord Avon's. A lace ruffle was found in the dead man's grasp—and the ruffle was Lord Avon's. Some papers were found charred in the grate—and the papers were Lord Avon's. Oh, my poor friend, in what moment of madness did you come to do such a deed ? "

The light had gone out of my uncle's eyes and the extravagance from his manner. His speech was clear and plain, with none of those strange London ways which had so amazed me. Here was a second uncle, a man of

heart and a man of brains, and I liked him better than the first.

" And what said Lord Avon ? " cried my father.

" He said nothing. He went about like one who walks in his sleep, with horror-stricken eyes. None dared arrest him until there should be due inquiry, but when the coroner's court brought wilful murder against him, the constables came for him in full cry. But they found him fled. There was a rumour that he had been seen in Westminster in the next week, and then that he had escaped for America, but nothing more is known. It will be a bright day for Sir Lothian Hume when they can prove him dead, for he is next of kin, and till then he can touch neither title nor estate."

The telling of this grim story had cast a chill upon all of us. My uncle held out his hands towards the blaze, and I noticed that they were as white as the ruffles which fringed them.

" I know not how things are at Cliffe Royal now," said he, thoughtfully. " It was not a cheery house, even before this shadow fell upon it. A fitter stage was never set forth for such a tragedy. But seventeen years have passed, and perhaps even that horrible ceiling——"

" It still bears the stain," said I.

I know not which of the three was the more astonished, for my mother had not heard of my adventures of the night. They never took their wondering eyes off me as I told my story, and my heart swelled with pride when my uncle said that we had carried ourselves well, and that he did not think that many of our age would have stood it as stoutly.

" But as to this ghost, it must have been the creature of your own minds," said he. " Imagination plays us strange tricks, and though I have as steady a nerve as a man might wish, I cannot answer for what I might see if I were to stand under that blood-stained ceiling at midnight."

" Uncle," said I, " I saw a figure as plainly as I

see that fire, and I heard the steps as clearly as I hear the crackle of the faggots. Besides, we could not both be deceived."

" There is truth in that," said he, thoughtfully. " You saw no features, you say ? "

" It was too dark."

" But only a figure ? "

" The dark outline of one."

" And it retreated up the stairs ? "

" Yes."

" And vanished into the wall ? "

" Yes."

" What part of the wall ? " cried a voice from behind us.

My mother screamed, and down came my father's pipe on to the hearthrug. I had sprung round with a catch of my breath, and there was the valet, Ambrose, his body in the shadow of the doorway, his dark face protruded into the light, and two burning eyes fixed upon mine.

" What the deuce is the meaning of this, sir ? " cried my uncle.

It was strange to see the gleam and passion fade out of the man's face, and the demure mask of the valet replace it. His eyes still smouldered, but his features regained their prim composure in an instant.

" I beg your pardon, Sir Charles," said he. " I had come in to ask you if you had any orders for me, and I did not like to interrupt the young gentleman's story. I am afraid that I have been somewhat carried away by it."

" I never knew you forget yourself before," said my uncle.

" You will, I am sure, forgive me, Sir Charles, if you will call to mind the relation in which I stood to Lord Avon." He spoke with some dignity of manner, and with a bow he left the room.

" We must make some little allowance," said my uncle, with a sudden return to his jaunty manner. " When a

man can brew a dish of chocolate, or tie a cravat, as Ambrose does, he may claim consideration. The fact is that the poor fellow was valet to Lord Avon, that he was at Cliffe Royal upon the fatal night of which I have spoken, and that he is most devoted to his old master. But my talk has been somewhat *triste*, sister Mary, and now we shall return, if you please, to the dresses of the Countess Lieven, and the gossip of St. James."

6. *On the Threshold*

MY father sent me to bed early that night, though I was very eager to stay up, for every word which this man said held my attention. His face, his manner, the large waves and sweeps of his white hands, his easy air of superiority, his fantastic fashion of talk, all filled me with interest and wonder. But, as I afterwards learned, their conversation was to be about myself and my own prospects, so I was despatched to my room, whence far into the night I could hear the deep growl of my father and the rich tones of my uncle, with an occasional gentle murmur from my mother, as they talked in the room beneath.

I had dropped asleep at last, when I was awakened suddenly by something wet being pressed against my face, and by two warm arms which were cast round me. My mother's cheek was against my own, and I could hear the click of her sobs, and feel her quiver and shake in the darkness. A faint light stole through the latticed window, and I could dimly see that she was in white, with her black hair loose upon her shoulders.

" You won't forget us, Roddy ? You won't forget us ? "

" Why, mother, what is it ? "

" Your uncle, Roddy—he is going to take you away from us."

" When, mother ? "

" To-morrow."

God forgive me, how my heart bounded for joy, when hers, which was within touch of it, was breaking with sorrow !

" Oh, mother ! " I cried. " To London ? "

" First to Brighton, that he may present you to the Prince. Next day to London, where you will meet the great people, Roddy, and learn to look down upon—to look down upon your poor, simple, old-fashioned father and mother."

I put my arms about her to console her, but she wept so that, for all my seventeen years and pride of manhood, it set me weeping also, and with such a hiccoughing noise, since I had not a woman's knack of quiet tears, that it finally turned her own grief to laughter.

" Charles would be flattered if he could see the gracious way in which we receive his kindness," said she. " Be still, Roddy dear, or you will certainly wake him."

" I'll not go if it is to grieve you," I cried.

" Nay, dear, you must go, for it may be the one great chance of your life. And think how proud it will make us all when we hear of you in the company of Charles's grand friends. But you will promise me not to gamble, Roddy ? You heard to-night of the dreadful things which come from it."

" I promise you, mother."

" And you will be careful of wine, Roddy ? You are young and unused to it."

" Yes, mother."

" And play-actresses also, Roddy. And you will not cast your underclothing until June is in. Young Master Overton came by his death through it. Think well of your dress, Roddy, so as to do your uncle credit, for it is the thing for which he is himself most famed. You have but to do what he will direct. But if there is a time when you are not meeting grand people, you can wear out your country things, for your brown coat is as good as new, and the blue one, if it were ironed and relined,

would take you through the summer. I have put out your Sunday clothes with the nankeen vest, since you are to see the Prince to-morrow, and you will wear your brown silk stockings and buckle shoes. Be guarded in crossing the London streets, for I am told that the hackney coaches are past all imagining. Fold your clothes when you go to bed, Roddy, and do not forget your evening prayers, for, oh, my dear boy, the days of temptation are at hand, when I will no longer be with you to help you."

So with advice and guidance both for this world and the next did my mother, with her soft, warm arms around me, prepare me for the great step which lay before me.

My uncle did not appear at breakfast in the morning, but Ambrose brewed him a dish of chocolate and took it to his room. When at last, about midday, he did descend, he was so fine with his curled hair, his shining teeth, his quizzing glass, his snow-white ruffles and his laughing eyes, that I could not take my gaze from him.

" Well, nephew," he cried, " what do you think of the prospect of coming to town with me ? "

" I thank you, sir, for the kind interest which you take in me," said I.

" But you must be a credit to me. My nephew must be of the best if he is to be in keeping with the rest of me."

" You'll find him a chip of good wood, sir," said my father.

" We must make him a polished chip before we have done with him. Your aim, my dear nephew, must always be to be in *bon ton*. It is not a case of wealth, you understand. Mere riches cannot do it. Golden Price has forty thousand a year, but his clothes are disastrous. I assure you that I saw him come down St. James's Street the other day, and I was so shocked at his appearance that I had to step into Vernet's for a glass of orange brandy. No, it is a question of natural taste, and of

following the advice and example of those who are more experienced than yourself."

" I fear, Charles, that Roddy's wardrobe is country-made," said my mother.

" We shall soon set that right when we get to town. We shall see what Stultz or Weston can do for him," my uncle answered. " We must keep him quiet until he has some clothes to wear."

This slight upon my best Sunday suit brought a flush to my mother's cheeks, which my uncle instantly observed, for he was quick in noticing trifles.

" The clothes are very well for Friar's Oak, sister Mary," said he. " And yet you can understand that they might seem *rococo* in the Mall. If you leave him in my hands I shall see to the matter."

" On how much, sir," asked my father, " can a young man dress in town ? "

" With prudence and reasonable care, a young man of fashion can dress upon eight hundred a year," my uncle answered.

I saw my poor father's face grow longer.

" I fear, sir, that Roddy must keep his country clothes," said he. " Even with my prize-money——"

" Tut, sir ! " cried my uncle. " I already owe Weston something over a thousand, so how can a few odd hundreds affect it ? If my nephew comes with me, my nephew is my care. The point is settled, and I must refuse to argue upon it." He waved his white hands as if to brush aside all opposition.

My parents tried to thank him, but he cut them short.

" By the way, now that I am in Friar's Oak, there is another small piece of business which I have to perform," said he. " I believe that there is a fighting-man named Harrison here, who at one time might have held the championship. In those days poor Avon and I were his principal backers. I should like to have a word with him."

You may think how proud I was to walk down the

village street with my magnificent relative, and to note out of the corner of my eye how the folk came to the doors and windows to see us pass. Champion Harrison was standing outside the smithy, and he pulled his cap off when he saw my uncle.

" God bless me, sir ! Who'd ha' thought of seein' you at Friar's Oak ? Why, Sir Charles, it brings old memories back to look at your face again."

" Glad to see you looking so fit, Harrison," said my uncle, running his eyes over him. " Why, with a week's training you would be as good a man as ever. I don't suppose you scale more than thirteen and a half ? "

" Thirteen ten, Sir Charles. I'm in my fortieth year, but I am sound in wind and limb, and if my old woman would have let me off my promise, I'd ha' had a try with some of these young ones before now. I hear that they've got some amazin' good stuff up from Bristol of late."

" Yes, the Bristol yellowman has been the winning colour of late. How d'ye do, Mrs. Harrison ? I don't suppose you remember me ? "

She had come out from the house, and I noticed that her worn face—on which some past terror seemed to have left its shadow—hardened into stern lines as she looked at my uncle.

" I remember you too well, Sir Charles Tregellis," said she. " I trust that you have not come here to-day to try to draw my husband back into the ways that he has forsaken."

" That's the way with her, Sir Charles," said Harrison, resting his great hand upon the woman's shoulder. " She's got my promise, and she holds me to it ! There was never a better or more hard-working wife, but she ain't what you'd call a patron of sport, and that's a fact."

" Sport ! " cried the woman, bitterly. " A fine sport for you, Sir Charles, with your pleasant twenty-mile drive into the country and your luncheon-basket and your wines, and so merrily back to London in the cool of the

evening, with a well-fought battle to talk over. Think of the sport that it was to me to sit through the long hours, listening for the wheels of the chaise which would bring my man back to me. Sometimes he could walk in, and sometimes he was led in, and sometimes he was carried in, and it was only by his clothes that I could know him——"

" Come, wifie," said Harrison, patting her on the shoulder. " I've been cut up in my time, but never as bad as that."

" And then to live for weeks afterwards with the fear that every knock at the door may be to tell us that the other is dead, and that my man may have to stand in the dock and take his trial for murder."

" No, she hasn't got a sportin' drop in her veins," said Harrison. " She'd never make a patron, never ! It's Black Baruk's business that did it, when we thought he'd napped it once too often. Well, she has my promise, and I'll never sling my hat over the ropes unless she gives me leave."

" You'll keep your hat on your head like an honest, God-fearing man, John," said his wife, turning back into the house.

" I wouldn't for the world say anything to make you change your resolutions," said my uncle. " At the same time, if you had wished to take a turn at the old sport, I had a good thing to put in your way."

" Well, it's no use, sir," said Harrison, " but I'd be glad to hear about it all the same."

" They have a very good bit of stuff at thirteen stone down Gloucester way. Wilson is his name, and they call him Crab on account of his style."

Harrison shook his head. " Never heard of him, sir."

" Very likely not, for he has never shown in the P.R. But they think great things of him in the West, and he can hold his own with either of the Belchers with the mufflers."

" Sparrin' ain't fightin'," said the smith.

"I am told that he had the best of it in a by-battle with Noah James, of Cheshire."

"There's no gamer man on the list, sir, than Noah James, the guardsman," said Harrison. "I saw him myself fight fifty rounds after his jaw had been cracked in three places. If Wilson could beat him, Wilson will go far."

"So they think in the West, and they mean to spring him on the London talent. Sir Lothian Hume is his patron, and to make a long story short, he lays me odds that I won't find a young one of his weight to meet him. I told him that I had not heard of any good young ones, but that I had an old one who had not put his foot into a ring for many years, who would make his man wish he had never come to London.

"'Young or old, under twenty or over thirty-five, you may bring whom you will at the weight, and I shall lay two to one on Wilson,' said he. I took him in thousands, and here I am."

"It won't do, Sir Charles," said the smith, shaking his head. "There's nothing would please me better, but you heard for yourself."

"Well, if you won't fight, Harrison, I must try to get some promising colt. I'd be glad of your advice in the matter. By the way, I take the chair at a supper of the Fancy at the Waggon and Horses in St. Martin's Lane next Friday. I should be very glad if you will make one of my guests. Halloa, who's this?" Up flew his glass to his eye.

Boy Jim had come out from the forge with his hammer in his hand. He had, I remember, a grey flannel shirt, which was open at the neck, and turned up at at the sleeves. My uncle ran his eyes over the fine lines of his magnificent figure with the glance of a connoisseur.

"That's my nephew, Sir Charles."

"Is he living with you?"

"His parents are dead."

"Has he ever been in London?"

" No, Sir Charles. He's been with me here since he was as high as that hammer."

My uncle turned to Boy Jim.

" I hear that you have never been in London," said he. " Your uncle is coming up to a supper which I am giving to the Fancy next Friday. Would you care to make one of us ? "

Boy Jim's dark eyes sparkled with pleasure.

" I should be glad to come, sir."

" No, no, Jim," cried the smith, abruptly. " I'm sorry to gainsay you, lad, but there are reasons why I had rather you stayed down here with your aunt."

" Tut, Harrison, let the lad come ! " cried my uncle.

" No, no, Sir Charles. It's dangerous company for a lad of his mettle. There's plenty for him to do when I'm away."

Poor Jim turned away with a clouded brow and strode into the smithy again. For my part, I slipped after him to try to console him, and to tell him all the wonderful changes which had come so suddenly into my life. But I had not got half through my story, and Jim, like the good fellow that he was, had just begun to forget his own troubles in his delight at my good fortune, when my uncle called to me from without. The curricle with its tandem mares was waiting for us outside the cottage, and Ambrose had placed the refection-basket, the lapdog and the precious toilet-box inside of it. He had himself climbed up behind, and I, after a hearty handshake from my father, and a last sobbing embrace from my mother, took my place beside my uncle in the front.

" Let go her head ! " cried he to the ostler, and with a snap, a crack and a jingle, away we went upon our journey.

Across all the years how clearly I can see that spring day, with the green English fields, the windy English sky, and the yellow, beetle-browed cottage in which I had grown from a child to a man. I see, too, the figures at the garden gate : my mother, with her face turned

away and her handkerchief waving ; my father, with his blue coat and his white shorts, leaning upon his stick with his hand shading his eyes as he peered after us. All the village was out to see young Roddy Stone go off with his grand relative from London to call upon the Prince in his own palace. The Harrisons were waving to me from the smithy, and John Cummings from the steps of the inn, and I saw Joshua Allen, my old schoolmaster, pointing me out to the people as if he were showing what came from his teaching. To make it complete, who should drive past just as we cleared the village but Miss Hinton, the play-actress, the pony and phaeton the same as when first I saw her, but she herself another woman ; and I thought to myself that if Boy Jim had done nothing but that one thing, he need not think that his youth had been wasted in the country. She was driving to see him, I have no doubt, for they were closer than ever, and she never looked up nor saw the hand that I waved to her. So as we took the curve of the road the little village vanished, and there in the dip of the Downs, past the spires of Patcham and of Preston, lay the broad blue sea and the grey houses of Brighton, with the strange Eastern domes and minarets of the Prince's Pavilion shooting out from the centre of it.

To every traveller it was a sight of beauty, but to me it was the world—the great wide free world—and my heart thrilled and fluttered as the young bird's may when it first hears the whirr of its own flight, and skims along with the blue heaven above it and the green fields beneath. The day may come when it may look back regretfully to the snug nest in the thorn-bush, but what does it reck of that when spring is in the air and youth in its blood, and the old hawk of trouble has not yet darkened the sunshine with the ill-boding shadow of its wings ?

7. *The Hope of England*

MY uncle drove for some time in silence, but I was conscious that his eye was always coming round to me, and I had an uneasy conviction that he was already beginning to ask himself whether he could make anything of me, or whether he had been betrayed into an indiscretion when he had allowed his sister to persuade him to show her son something of the grand world in which he lived.

" You sing, don't you, nephew ? " he asked, suddenly.

" Yes, sir, a little."

" A baritone, I should fancy ? "

" Yes, sir."

" And your mother tells me that you play the fiddle. These things will be of service to you with the Prince. Music runs in his family. Your education has been what you could get at a village school. Well, you are not examined in Greek roots in polite society, which is lucky for some of us. It is as well just to have a tag or two of Horace or Virgil : ' sub tegmine fagi,' or ' habet fœnum in cornu,' which gives a flavour to one's conversation like the touch of garlic in a salad. It is not *bon ton* to be learned, but it is a graceful thing to indicate that you have forgotten a good deal. Can you write verse ? "

" I fear not, sir."

" A small book of rhymes may be had for half a crown. Vers de Société are a great assistance to a young man. If you have the ladies on your side, it does not matter whom you have against you. You must learn to open a door, to enter a room, to present a snuff-box, raising the lid with the forefinger of the hand in which you hold it. You must acquire the bow for a man, with its necessary touch of dignity, and that for a lady, which cannot be too humble, and should still contain the least suspicion of abandon. You must cultivate a manner with women which shall be deprecating and yet audacious. Have you any eccentricity ? "

It made me laugh, the easy way in which he asked the question, as if it were a most natural thing to possess.

"You have a pleasant, catching laugh, at all events," said he. "But an eccentricity is very *bon ton* at present, and if you feel any leaning towards one, I should certainly advise you to let it run its course. Petersham would have remained a mere peer all his life had it not come out that he had a snuff-box for every day in the year, and that he had caught cold through a mistake of his valet, who sent him out on a bitter winter day with a thin Sèvres china box instead of a thick tortoise-shell. That brought him out of the ruck, you see, and people remember him. Even some small characteristic, such as having an apricot tart on your sideboard all the year round, or putting your candle out at night by stuffing it under your pillow, serves to separate you from your neighbour. In my own case, it is my precise judgment upon matters of dress and decorum which has placed me where I am. I do not profess to follow a law. I set one. For example, I am taking you to-day to see the Prince in a nankeen vest. What do you think will be the consequence of that?"

My fears told me that it might be my own very great discomfiture, but I did not say so.

"Why, the night coach will carry the news to London. It will be in Brookes's and White's to-morrow morning. Within a week St. James's Street and the Mall will be full of nankeen waistcoats. A most painful incident happened to me once. My cravat came undone in the street, and I actually walked from Carlton House to Watier's in Bruton Street with the two ends hanging loose. Do you suppose it shook my position? The same evening there were dozens of young bloods walking the streets of London with their cravats loose. If I had not rearranged mine there would not be one tied in the whole kingdom now, and a great art would have been prematurely lost. You have not yet begun to practise it?"

I confessed that I had not.

" You should begin now in your youth. I will myself teach you the *coup d'archet*. By using a few hours in each day, which would otherwise be wasted, you may hope to have excellent cravats in middle life. The whole knack lies in pointing your chin to the sky, and then arranging your folds by the gradual descent of your lower jaw."

When my uncle spoke like this there was always that dancing, mischievous light in his dark blue eyes, which showed me that this humour of his was a conscious eccentricity, depending, as I believe, upon a natural fastidiousness of taste, but wilfully driven to grotesque lengths for the very reason which made him recommend me also to develop some peculiarity of my own. When I thought of the way in which he had spoken of his unhappy friend, Lord Avon, upon the evening before, and of the emotion which he showed as he told the horrible story, I was glad to think that there was the heart of a man there, however much it might please him to conceal it.

And, as it happened, I was very soon to have another peep at it, for a most unexpected event befell us as we drew up in front of the Crown Hotel. A swarm of ostlers and grooms had rushed out to us, and my uncle, throwing down the reins, gathered Fidelio on his cushion from under the seat.

" Ambrose," he cried, " you may take Fidelio."

But there came no answer. The seat behind was unoccupied. Ambrose was gone.

We could hardly believe our eyes when we alighted and found that it was really so. He had most certainly taken his seat there at Friar's Oak, and from there on we had come without a break as fast as the mares could travel. Whither, then, could he have vanished to ?

" He's fallen off in a fit ! " cried my uncle. " I'd drive back, but the Prince is expecting us. Where's the landlord ? Here, Coppinger, send your best man back to Friar's Oak, as fast as his horse can go, to find news of my valet, Ambrose. See that no pains be spared.

Now, nephew, we shall lunch, and then go up to the Pavilion."

My uncle was much disturbed by the strange loss of his valet, the more so as it was his custom to go through a whole series of washings and changings after even the shortest journey. For my own part, mindful of my mother's advice, I carefully brushed the dust from my clothes and made myself as neat as possible. My heart was down in the soles of my little silver-buckled shoes now that I had the immediate prospect of meeting so great and terrible a person as the Prince of Wales. I had seen his flaring yellow barouche flying through Friar's Oak many a time, and had halloaed and waved my hat with the others as it passed, but never in my wildest dreams had it entered my head that I should ever be called upon to look him in the face and answer his questions. My mother had taught me to regard him with reverence, as one of those whom God had placed to rule over us ; but my uncle smiled when I told him of her teaching.

" You are old enough to see things as they are, nephew," said he, " and your knowledge of them is the badge that you are in that inner circle where I mean to place you. There is no one who knows the Prince better than I do, and there is no one who trusts him less. A stranger contradiction of qualities was never gathered under one hat. He is a man who is always in a hurry, and yet has never anything to do. He fusses about things with which he has no concern, and he neglects every obvious duty. He is generous to those who have no claim upon him, but he has ruined his tradesmen by refusing to pay his just debts. He is affectionate to casual acquaintances, but he dislikes his father, loathes his mother and is not on speaking terms with his wife. He claims to be the first gentleman of England, but the gentlemen of England have responded by blackballing his friends at their clubs, and by warning him off from Newmarket under suspicion of having tampered with a horse. He spends his day in

uttering noble sentiments, and contradicting them by ignoble actions. He tells stories of his own doings which are so grotesque that they can only be explained by the madness which runs in his blood. And yet, with all this, he can be courteous, dignified and kindly upon occasion, and I have seen an impulsive good-heartedness in the man which has made me overlook faults which come mainly from his being placed in a position which no one upon this earth was ever less fitted to fill. But this is between ourselves, nephew ; and now you will come with me and you will form an opinion for yourself."

It was but a short walk, and yet it took us some time, for my uncle stalked along with great dignity, his lace-bordered handkerchief in one hand, and his cane with the clouded amber head dangling from the other. Every one that we met seemed to know him, and their hats flew from their heads as we passed. He took little notice of these greetings, save to give a nod to one, or to slightly raise his forefinger to another. It chanced, however, that as we turned into the Pavilion Grounds, we met a magnificent team of four coal-black horses, driven by a rough-looking, middle-aged fellow in an old weather-stained cape. There was nothing that I could see to distinguish him from any professional driver, save that he was chatting very freely with a dainty little woman who was perched on the box beside him.

" Halloa, Charlie ! Good drive down ? " he cried.

My uncle bowed and smiled to the lady.

" Broke it at Friar's Oak," said he. " I've my light curricle and two new mares—half thoroughbred, half Cleveland bay."

" What d'you think of my team of blacks ? " asked the other.

" Yes, Sir Charles, what d'you think of them ? Ain't they damnation smart ? " cried the little woman.

" Plenty of power. Good horses for the Sussex clay. Too thick about the fetlocks for me. I like to travel."

" Travel ! " cried the woman, with extraordinary

vehemence. " Why, what the——" and she broke into such language as I had never heard from a man's lips before. " We'd start with our swingle-bars touching, and we'd have your dinner ordered, cooked, laid and eaten before you were there to claim it."

" By George, yes, Letty is right ! " cried the man. " D'you start to-morrow ? "

" Yes, Jack."

" Well, I'll make you an offer. Look ye here, Charlie ! I'll spring my cattle from the Castle Square at quarter before nine. You can follow as the clock strikes. I've double the horses and double the weight. If you so much as see me before we cross Westminster Bridge, I'll pay you a cool hundred. If not, it's my money—play or pay. Is it a match ? "

" Very good," said my uncle, and, raising his hat, he led the way into the grounds. As I followed, I saw the woman take the reins, while the man looked after us, and squirted a jet of tobacco-juice from between his teeth in coachman fashion.

" That's Sir John Lade," said my uncle, " one of the richest men and best whips in England. There isn't a professional on the road that can handle either his tongue or his ribbons better ; but his wife, Lady Letty, is his match with the one or the other."

" It was dreadful to hear her," said I.

" Oh, it's her eccentricity. We all have them ; and she amuses the Prince. Now, nephew, keep close at my elbow, and have your eyes open and your mouth shut."

Two lines of magnificent red and gold footmen who guarded the door bowed deeply as my uncle and I passed between them, he with his head in the air and a manner as if he entered into his own, whilst I tried to look assured, though my heart was beating thin and fast. Within there was a high and large hall, ornamented with Eastern decorations, which harmonised with the domes and min-arets of the exterior. A number of people were moving quietly about, forming into groups and whispering to

each other. One of these, a short, burly, red-faced man, full of fuss and self-importance, came hurrying up to my uncle.

" I have de goot news, Sir Charles," said he, sinking his voice as one who speaks of weighty measures. " *Es ist vollendet*—dat is, I have it at last thoroughly done."

" Well, serve it hot," said my uncle, coldly, " and see that the sauces are a little better than when last I dined at Carlton House."

" Ah, mine Gott, you tink I talk of de cuisine. It is de affair of de Prince dat I speak of. Dat is one little *vol-au-vent* dat is worth one hundred tousand pound. Ten per cent. and double to be repaid when de Royal pappa die. *Alles ist fertig*. Goldshmidt of de Hague have took it up, and de Dutch public has subscribe de money."

" God help the Dutch public ! " muttered my uncle, as the fat little man bustled off with his news to some newcomer. " That's the Prince's famous cook, nephew. He has not his equal in England for a *filet sauté aux champignons*. He manages his master's money affairs."

" The cook ! " I exclaimed, in bewilderment.

" You look surprised, nephew."

" I should have thought that some respectable banking firm——"

My uncle inclined his lips to my ear.

" No respectable house would touch them," he whispered. " Ah, Mellish, is the Prince within ? "

" In the private saloon, Sir Charles," said the gentleman addressed.

" Anyone with him ? "

" Sheridan and Francis. He said he expected you."

" Then we shall go through."

I followed him through the strangest succession of rooms, full of curious barbaric splendour which impressed me as being very rich and wonderful, though perhaps I should think differently now. Gold and scarlet in arabesque designs gleamed upon the walls, with gilt

dragons and monsters writhing along cornices and out of corners. Look where I would, on panel or ceiling, a score of mirrors flashed back the picture of the tall, proud, white-faced man, and the youth who walked so demurely at his elbow. Finally, a footman opened a door, and we found ourselves in the Prince's own private apartment.

Two gentlemen were lounging in a very easy fashion upon luxurious fauteuils at the further end of the room, and a third stood between them, his thick, well-formed legs somewhat apart and his hands clasped behind him. The sun was shining in upon them through a side-window, and I can see the three faces now—one in the dusk, one in the light, and one cut across by the shadow. Of those at the sides, I recall the reddish nose and dark, flashing eyes of the one, and the hard, austere face of the other, with the high coat-collars and many-wreathed cravats. These I took in at a glance, but it was upon the man in the centre that my gaze was fixed, for this I knew must be the Prince of Wales.

George was then in his forty-first year, and with the help of his tailor and his hairdresser, he might have passed as somewhat less. The sight of him put me at my ease, for he was a merry-looking man, handsome too in a portly, full-blooded way, with laughing eyes and pouting, sensitive lips. His nose was turned upwards, which increased the good-humoured effect of his countenance at the expense of its dignity. His cheeks were pale and sodden, like those of a man who lived too well and took too little exercise. He was dressed in a single-breasted black coat buttoned up, a pair of leather pantaloons stretched tightly across his broad thighs, polished Hessian boots, and a huge white neckcloth.

" Halloa, Tregellis ! " he cried, in the cheeriest fashion, as my uncle crossed the threshold, and then suddenly the smile faded from his face, and his eyes gleamed with resentment. " What the deuce is this ? " he shouted, angrily.

A thrill of fear passed through me as I thought that it was my appearance which had produced this outburst. But his eyes were gazing past us, and glancing round we saw that a man in a brown coat and scratch wig had followed so closely at our heels, that the footmen had let him pass under the impression that he was of our party. His face was very red, and the folded blue paper which he carried in his hand shook and crackled in his excitement.

" Why, it's Vuillamy, the furniture man," cried the Prince. " What, am I to be dunned in my own private room ? Where's Mellish ? Where's Townshend ? What the deuce is Tom Tring doing ? "

" I wouldn't have intruded, your Royal Highness, but I must have the money—or even a thousand on account would do."

" Must have it, must you, Vuillamy ? That's a fine word to use. I pay my debts in my own time, and I'm not to be bullied. Turn him out, footman ! Take him away ! "

" If I don't get it by Monday, I shall be in your papa's Bench," wailed the little man, and as the footman led him out we could hear him, amidst shouts of laughter, still protesting that he would wind up in " papa's Bench."

" That's the very place for a furniture man," said the man with the red nose.

" It should be the longest bench in the world, Sherry," answered the Prince, " for a good many of his subjects will want seats on it. Very glad to see you back, Tregellis, but you must really be more careful what you bring in upon your skirts. It was only yesterday that we had an infernal Dutchman here howling about some arrears of interest and the deuce knows what. ' My good fellow,' said I, ' as long as the Commons starve me, I have to starve you,' and so the matter ended."

" I think, sir, that the Commons would respond now if the matter were fairly put before them by Charlie Fox or myself," said Sheridan.

The Prince burst out against the Commons with an energy of hatred that one would scarce expect from that chubby, good-humoured face.

" Why, curse them ! " he cried. " After all their preaching and throwing my father's model life, as they called it, in my teeth, they had to pay *his* debts to the tune of nearly a million, whilst I can't get a hundred thousand out of them. And look at all they've done for my brothers ! York is Commander-in-Chief. Clarence is Admiral. What am I ? Colonel of a damned dragoon regiment under the orders of my own younger brother. It's my mother that's at the bottom of it all. She always tried to hold me back. But what's this you've brought, Tregellis, eh ? "

My uncle put his hand on my sleeve and led me forward.

" This is my sister's son, sir ; Rodney Stone by name," said he. " He is coming with me to London, and I thought it right to begin by presenting him to your Royal Highness."

" Quite right ! Quite right ! " said the Prince, with a good-natured smile, patting me in a friendly way upon the shoulder. " Is your mother living ? "

" Yes, sir," said I.

" If you are a good son to her you will never go wrong. And, mark my words, Mr. Rodney Stone, you should honour the King, love your country and uphold the glorious British Constitution."

When I thought of the energy with which he had just been cursing the House of Commons, I could scarce keep from smiling, and I saw Sheridan put his hand up to his lips.

" You have only to do this, to show a regard for your word, and to keep out of debt in order to ensure a happy and respected life. What is your father, Mr. Stone ? Royal Navy ! Well, it is a glorious service. I have had a touch of it myself. Did I ever tell you how we laid aboard the French sloop of war *Minerve*—hey, Tregellis ? "

" No, sir," said my uncle. Sheridan and Francis exchanged glances behind the Prince's back.

" She was flying her tricolour out there within sight of my pavilion windows. Never saw such monstrous impudence in my life ! It would take a man of less mettle than me to stand it. Out I went in my little cock-boat—you know my sixty-ton yawl, Charlie ?—with two four-pounders on each side, and a six-pounder in the bows."

" Well, sir ! Well, sir ! And what then, sir ? " cried Francis, who appeared to be an irascible, rough-tongued man.

" You will permit me to tell the story in my own way, Sir Philip," said the Prince, with dignity. " I was about to say that our metal was so light that I give you my word, gentlemen, that I carried my port broadside in one coat pocket, and my starboard in the other. Up we came to the big Frenchman, took her fire, and scraped the paint off her before we let drive. But it was no use. By George, gentlemen, our balls just stuck in her timbers like stones in a mud wall. She had her nettings up, but we scrambled aboard, and at it we went hammer and anvil. It was a sharp twenty minutes, but we beat her people down below, made the hatches fast on them, and towed her into Seaham. Surely you were with us, Sherry ? "

" I was in London at the time," said Sheridan, gravely.

" You can vouch for it, Francis ! "

" I can vouch to having heard your Highness tell the story."

" It was a rough little bit of cutlass and pistol work. But, for my own part, I like the rapier. It's a gentleman's weapon. You heard of my bout with the Chevalier d'Eon ? I had him at my sword-point for forty minutes at Angelo's. He was one of the best blades in Europe, but I was a little too supple in the wrist for him. ' I thank God there was a button on your Highness's foil,' said he, when we had finished our breather. By the way,

you're a bit of a duellist yourself, Tregellis. How often have you been out ? "

" I used to go when I needed exercise," said my uncle, carelessly. " But I have taken to tennis now instead. A painful incident happened the last time that I was out, and it sickened me of it."

" You killed your man—— ? "

" No, no, sir, it was worse than that. I had a coat that Weston has never equalled. To say that it fitted me is not to express it. It *was* me—like the hide on a horse. I've had sixty from him since, but he could never approach it. The sit of the collar brought tears into my eyes, sir, when first I saw it ; and as to the waist——"

" But the duel, Tregellis ! " cried the Prince.

" Well, sir, I wore it at the duel, like the thoughtless fool that I was. It was Major Hunter, of the Guards, with whom I had had a little *tracasserie*, because I hinted that he should not come into Brookes's smelling of the stables. I fired first, and missed. He fired, and I shrieked in despair. ' He's hit ! A surgeon ! A surgeon ! ' they cried. ' A tailor ! A tailor ! ' said I, for there was a double hole through the tails of my masterpiece. No, it was past all repair. You may laugh, sir, but I'll never see the like of it again."

I had seated myself on a settee in the corner, upon the Prince's invitation, and very glad I was to remain quiet and unnoticed, listening to the talk of these men. It was all in the same extravagant vein, garnished with many senseless oaths ; but I observed this difference, that, whereas my uncle and Sheridan had something of humour in their exaggeration, Francis tended always to ill-nature, and the Prince to self-glorification. Finally, the conversation turned to music—I am not sure that my uncle did not artfully bring it there, and the Prince, hearing from him of my tastes, would have it that I should then and there sit down at the wonderful little piano, all inlaid with mother-of-pearl, which stood in the corner, and play him the accompaniment to his song. It was called, as

I remember, " The Briton Conquers but to Save," and he rolled it out in a very fair bass voice, the others joining in the chorus, and clapping vigorously when he finished.

" Bravo, Mr. Stone ! " said he. " You have an excellent touch ; and I know what I am talking about when I speak of music. Cramer, of the Opera, said only the other day that he had rather hand his bâton to me than to any amateur in England. Halloa, it's Charlie Fox, by all that's wonderful ! "

He had run forward with much warmth, and was shaking the hand of a singular-looking person who had just entered the room. The new-comer was a stout, square-built man, plainly and almost carelessly dressed, with an uncouth manner and a rolling gait. His age might have been something over fifty, and his swarthy, harshly-featured face was already deeply lined either by his years or by his excesses. I have never seen a countenance in which the angel and the devil were more obviously wedded. Above, was the high, broad forehead of the philosopher, with keen, humorous eyes looking out from under thick, strong brows. Below, was the heavy jowl of the sensualist curving in a broad crease over his cravat. That brow was the brow of the public Charles Fox, the thinker, the philanthropist, the man who rallied and led the Liberal party during the twenty most hazardous years of its existence. That jaw was the jaw of the private Charles Fox, the gambler, the libertine, the drunkard. Yet to his sins he never added the crowning one of hypocrisy. His vices were as open as his virtues. In some quaint freak of Nature, two spirits seemed to have been joined in one body, and the same frame to contain the best and the worst man of his age.

" I've run down from Chertsey, sir, just to shake you by the hand, and to make sure that the Tories have not carried you off."

" Hang it, Charlie, you know that I sink or swim with my friends ! A Whig I started, and a Whig I shall remain."

I thought that I could read upon Fox's dark face that he was by no means so confident about the Prince's principles.

" Pitt has been at you, sir, I understand ? "

" Yes, confound him ! I hate the sight of that sharp-pointed snout of his, which he wants to be ever poking into my affairs. He and Addington have been boggling about the debts again. Why, look ye, Charlie, if Pitt held me in contempt he could not behave different."

I gathered from the smile which flitted over Sheridan's face that this was exactly what Pitt did do. But straightway they all plunged into politics, varied by the drinking of sweet maraschino, which a footman brought round upon a salver. The King, the Queen, the Lords and the Commons were each in succession cursed by the Prince, in spite of the excellent advice which he had given me about the British Constitution.

" Why, they allow me so little that I can't look after my own people. There are a dozen annuities to old servants and the like, and it's all I can do to scrape the money together to pay them. However, my "—he pulled himself up and coughed in a consequential way— " my financial agent has arranged for a loan, repayable upon the King's death. This liquor isn't good for either of us, Charlie. We're both getting monstrous stout."

" I can't get any exercise for the gout," said Fox.

" I am blooded fifty ounces a month, but the more I take the more I make. You wouldn't think, to look at us, Tregellis, that we could do what we have done. We've had some days and nights together, Charlie ! "

Fox smiled and shook his head.

" You remember how we posted to Newmarket before the races. We took a public coach, Tregellis, clapped the postilions into the rumble, and jumped on to their places. Charlie rode the leader and I the wheeler. One fellow wouldn't let us through his turnpike, and Charlie hopped off, and had his coat off in a minute. The fellow

thought he had to do with a fighting man, and soon cleared the way for us."

"By the way, sir, speaking of fighting men, I give a supper to the Fancy at the Waggon and Horses on Friday next," said my uncle. "If you should chance to be in town, they would think it a great honour if you should condescend to look in upon us."

"I've not seen a fight since I saw Tom Tyne, the tailor, kill Earl fourteen years ago. I swore off then, and you know me as a man of my word, Tregellis. Of course I've been at the ringside *incog.* many a time, but never as the Prince of Wales."

"We should be vastly honoured if you would come *incog.* to our supper, sir."

"Well, well, Sherry, make a note of it. We'll be at Carlton House on Friday. The Prince can't come, you know, Tregellis, but you might reserve a chair for the Earl of Chester."

"Sir, we shall be proud to see the Earl of Chester there," said my uncle.

"By the way, Tregellis," said Fox, "there's some rumour about your having a sporting bet with Sir Lothian Hume. What's the truth of it?"

"Only a small matter of a couple of thous. to a thou., he giving the odds. He has a fancy to this new Gloucester man, Crab Wilson, and I'm to find a man to beat him. Anything under twenty or over thirty-five, at or about thirteen stone."

"You take Charlie Fox's advice, then," cried the Prince. "When it comes to handicapping a horse, playing a hand, matching a cock or picking a man, he has the best judgment in England. Now, Charlie, whom have we upon the list who can beat Crab Wilson, of Gloucester?"

I was amazed at the interest and knowledge which all these great people showed about the Ring, for they not only had the deeds of the principal men of the time— Belcher, Mendoza, Jackson, or Dutch Sam—at their

fingers' ends, but there was no fighting man so obscure that they did not know the details of his deeds and prospects. The old ones and then the young were discussed—their weight, their gameness, their hitting power, and their constitution. Who, as he saw Sheridan and Fox eagerly arguing as to whether Caleb Baldwin, the Westminster costermonger, could hold his own with Isaac Bittoon, the Jew, would have guessed that the one was the deepest political philosopher in Europe, and that the other would be remembered as the author of the wittiest comedy and of the finest speech of his generation?

The name of Champion Harrison came very early into the discussion, and Fox, who had a high idea of Crab Wilson's powers, was of opinion that my uncle's only chance lay in the veteran taking the field again. "He may be slow on his pins, but he fights with his head, and he hits like the kick of a horse. When he finished Black Baruk the man flew across the outer ring as well as the inner, and fell among the spectators. If he isn't absolutely stale, Tregellis, he is your best chance."

My uncle shrugged his shoulders.

"If poor Avon were here we might do something with him, for he was Harrison's first patron, and the man was devoted to him. But his wife is too strong for me. And now, sir, I must leave you, for I have had the misfortune to-day to lose the best valet in England, and I must make inquiry for him. I thank your Royal Highness for your kindness in receiving my nephew in so gracious a fashion."

"Till Friday, then," said the Prince, holding out his hand. "I have to go up to town in any case, for there is a poor devil of an East India Company's officer who has written to me in his distress. If I can raise a few hundreds, I shall see him and set things right for him. Now, Mr. Stone, you have your life before you, and I hope it will be one which your uncle may be proud of. You will honour the King, and show respect for the Constitution, Mr. Stone. And, hark ye, you will avoid

debt, and bear in mind that your honour is a sacred thing."

So I carried away a last impression of his sensual, good-humoured face, his high cravat and his broad leather thighs. Again we passed the strange rooms, the gilded monsters, and the gorgeous footmen, and it was with relief that I found myself out in the open air once more, with the broad blue sea in front of us, and the fresh evening breeze upon our faces.

8. *The Brighton Road*

MY uncle and I were up betimes next morning, but he was much out of temper, for no news had been heard of his valet Ambrose. He had indeed become like one of those ants of which I have read, who are so accustomed to be fed by smaller ants that when they are left to themselves they die of hunger. It was only by the aid of a man whom the landlord procured, and of Fox's valet, who had been sent expressly across, that his toilet was at last performed.

" I must win this race, nephew," said he, when he had finished breakfast ; " I can't afford to be beat. Look out of the window and see if the Lades are there."

" I see a red four-in-hand in the square, and there is a crowd round it. Yes, I see the lady upon the box seat."

" Is our tandem out ? "

" It is at the door."

" Come, then, and you shall have such a drive as you never had before."

He stood at the door pulling on his long brown driving-gauntlets, and giving his orders to the ostlers.

" Every ounce will tell," said he. " We'll leave that dinner-basket behind. And you can keep my dog for me, Coppinger. You know him and understand him. Let him have his warm milk and curaçoa the same as

usual. Whoa, my darlings, you'll have your fill of it before you reach Westminster Bridge."

" Shall I put in the toilet-case ? " asked the landlord.

I saw the struggle upon my uncle's face, but he was true to his principles.

" Put it under the seat—the front seat," said he. " Nephew, you must keep your weight as far forward as possible. Can you do anything on a yard of tin ? Well, if you can't, we'll leave the trumpet. Buckle that girth up, Thomas. Have you greased the hubs, as I told you ? Well, jump up, nephew, and we'll see them off."

Quite a crowd had gathered in the Old Square : men and women, dark-coated tradesmen, bucks from the Prince's Court, and officers from Hove, all in a buzz of excitement ; for Sir John Lade and my uncle were two of the most famous whips of the time, and a match between them was a thing to talk of for many a long day.

" The Prince will be sorry to have missed the start," said my uncle. " He doesn't show before midday. Ah, Jack, good morning ! Your servant, madam ! It's a fine day for a little bit of waggoning."

As our tandem came alongside of the four-in-hand with the two bonny bay mares gleaming like shot-silk in the sunshine, a murmur of admiration rose from the crowd. My uncle, in his fawn-coloured driving-coat, with all his harness of the same tint, looked the ideal of a Corinthian whip ; while Sir John Lade, with his many-caped coat, his white hat, and his rough, weather-beaten face, might have taken his seat with a line of professionals upon any ale-house bench without anyone being able to pick him out as one of the wealthiest landowners in England. It was an age of eccentricity, but he had carried his peculiarities to a length which surprised even the out-and-outers by marrying the sweetheart of a famous highwayman when the gallows had come between her and her lover. She was perched by his side, looking very smart in a flowered bonnet and grey travelling-dress, while in front of them the four splendid coal-black

horses, with a flickering touch of gold upon their powerful well-curved quarters, were pawing the dust in their eagerness to be off.

"It's a hundred that you don't see us before Westminster with a quarter of an hour's start," said Sir John.

"I'll take you another hundred that we pass you," answered my uncle.

"Very good. Time's up. Good-bye!" He gave a *tchk* of the tongue, shook his reins, saluted with his whip, in true coachman's style, and away he went, taking the curve out of the square in a workmanlike fashion that fetched a cheer from the crowd. We heard the dwindling roar of the wheels upon the cobble-stones until they died away in the distance.

It seemed one of the longest quarters of an hour that I had ever known before the first stroke of nine boomed from the parish clock. For my part, I was fidgeting in my seat in my impatience, but my uncle's calm, pale face and large blue eyes were as tranquil and demure as those of the most unconcerned spectator. He was keenly on the alert, however, and it seemed to me that the stroke of the clock and the thong of his whip fell together—not in a blow, but in a sharp snap over the leader, which sent us flying with a jingle and a rattle upon our fifty miles' journey. I heard a roar from behind us, saw the gliding lines of windows with staring faces and waving handkerchiefs, and then we were off the stones and on to the good white road which curved away in front of us, with the sweep of the green downs upon either side.

I had been provided with shillings that the turnpike-gate might not stop us, but my uncle reined in the mares and took them at a very easy trot up all the heavy stretch which ends in Clayton Hill. He let them go then, and we flashed through Friar's Oak and across St. John's Common without more than catching a glimpse of the yellow cottage which contained all that I loved best. Never have I travelled at such a pace, and never have I felt such a sense of exhilaration from the rush of keen

upland air upon our faces, and from the sight of those two glorious creatures stretched to their utmost, with the roar of their hoofs and the rattle of our wheels as the light curricle bounded and swayed behind them.

" It's a long four miles up hill from here to Hand Cross," said my uncle, as we flew through Cuckfield.

I must ease them a bit, for I cannot afford to break the hearts of my cattle. They have the right blood in them, and they would gallop until they dropped if I were brute enough to let them. Stand up on the seat, nephew, and see if you can get a glimpse of them."

I stood up, steadying myself upon my uncle's shoulder, but though I could see for a mile, or perhaps a quarter more, there was not a sign of the four-in-hand.

" If he has sprung his cattle up all these hills they'll be spent ere they see Croydon," said he.

" They have four to two," said I.

" *J'en suis bien sûr*. Sir John's black strain makes a good, honest creature, but not fliers like these. There lies Cuckfield Place, where the towers are, yonder. Get your weight right forward on the splashboard now that we are going uphill, nephew. Look at the action of that leader : did ever you see anything more easy and more beautiful ? "

We were taking the hill at a quiet trot, but even so, we made the carrier, walking in the shadow of his huge, broad-wheeled, canvas-covered waggon, stare at us in amazement. Close to Hand Cross we passed the Royal Brighton stage, which had left at half-past seven, dragging heavily up the slope, and its passengers, toiling along through the dust behind, gave us a cheer as we whirled by. At Hand Cross we caught a glimpse of the old land-lord, hurrying out with his gin and his ginger-bread ; but the dip of the ground was downwards now, and away we flew as fast as eight gallant hoofs could take us.

" Do you drive, nephew ? "

" Very little, sir."

" There is no driving on the Brighton Road."

" How is that, sir ? "

" Too good a road, nephew. I have only to give them
their heads, and they will race me into Westminster. It
wasn't always so. When I was a very young man one
might learn to handle his twenty yards of tape here as
well as elsewhere. There's not much really good waggoning now south of Leicestershire. Show me a man who
can hit 'em and hold 'em on a Yorkshire dale-side, and
that's the man who comes from the right school."

We had raced over Crawley Down and into the broad
main street of Crawley village, flying between two country
waggons in a way which showed me that even now a
driver might do something on the road. With every
turn I peered ahead, looking for our opponents, but my
uncle seemed to concern himself very little about them,
and occupied himself in giving me advice, mixed up with
so many phrases of the craft, that it was all that I could
do to follow him.

" Keep a finger for each, or you will have your reins
clubbed," said he. " As to the whip, the less fanning
the better if you have willing cattle ; but when you want
to put a little life into a coach, see that you get your thong
on to the one that needs it, and don't let it fly round after
you've hit. I've seen a driver warm up the off-side passenger on the roof behind him every time he tried to cut his
off-side wheeler. I believe that is their dust over yonder."

A long stretch of road lay before us, barred with the
shadows of wayside trees. Through the green fields a
lazy blue river was drawing itself slowly along, passing
under a bridge in front of us. Beyond was a young fir
plantation, and over its olive line there rose a white whirl
which drifted swiftly, like a cloud-scud on a breezy day.

" Yes, yes, it's they ! " cried my uncle. " No one
else would travel as fast. Come, nephew, we're half
way when we cross the mole at Kimberham Bridge, and
we've done it in two hours and fourteen minutes. The
Prince drove to Carlton House with a three tandem in
four hours and a half. The first half is the worst half,

and we might cut his time if all goes well. We should make up between this and Reigate."

And we flew. The bay mares seemed to know what that white puff in front of us signified, and they stretched themselves like greyhounds. We passed a phaeton and pair London-bound, and we left it behind as if it had been standing still. Trees, gates, cottages went dancing by. We heard the folks shouting from the fields, under the impression that we were a runaway. Faster and faster yet they raced, the hoofs rattling like castanets, the yellow manes flying, the wheels buzzing and every joint and rivet creaking and groaning, while the curricle swung and swayed until I found myself clutching to the side-rail. My uncle eased them and glanced at his watch as we saw the grey tiles and dingy red houses of Reigate in the hollow beneath us.

" We did the last six well under twenty minutes," said he. " We've time in hand now, and a little water at the Red Lion will do them no harm. Red four-in-hand passed, ostler ? "

" Just gone, sir."

" Going hard ? "

" Galloping full split, sir ! Took the wheel off a butcher's cart at the corner of the High Street, and was out o' sight before the butcher's boy could see what had hurt him."

Z-z-z-z-ack ! went the long thong, and away we flew once more. It was market day at Redhill, and the road was crowded with carts of produce, droves of bullocks and farmers' gigs. It was a sight to see how my uncle threaded his way amongst them all. Through the market-place we dashed amidst the shouting of men, the screaming of women and the scuttling of poultry, and then we were out in the country again, with the long, steep incline of the Redhill Road before us. My uncle waved his whip in the air with a shrill view-halloa.

There was the dust-cloud rolling up the hill in front of us, and through it we had a shadowy peep of the backs

of our opponents, with a flash of brasswork and a gleam of scarlet.

"There's half the game won, nephew. Now we must pass them. Hark forrard, my beauties! By George, if Kitty isn't foundered!"

The leader had suddenly gone dead lame. In an instant we were both out of the curricle and on our knees beside her. It was but a stone, wedged between frog and shoe in the off fore-foot, but it was a minute or two before we could wrench it out. When we had re-gained our places the Lades were round the curve of the hill and out of sight.

"Bad luck!" growled my uncle. "But they can't get away from us!" For the first time he touched the mares up, for he had but cracked the whip over their heads before. "If we catch them in the next few miles we can spare them for the rest of the way."

They were beginning to show signs of exhaustion. Their breath came quick and hoarse, and their beautiful coats were matted with moisture. At the top of the hill, however, they settled down into their swing once more.

"Where on earth have they got to?" cried my uncle. "Can you make them out on the road, nephew?"

We could see a long white ribbon of it, all dotted with carts and waggons coming from Croydon to Redhill, but there was no sign of the big red four-in-hand.

"There they are! Stole away! Stole away!" he cried, wheeling the mares round into a side road which struck to the right out of that which we had travelled. "There they are, nephew! On the brow of the hill!"

Sure enough, on the rise of a curve upon our right the four-in-hand had appeared, the horses stretched to the utmost. Our mares laid themselves out gallantly, and the distance between us began slowly to decrease. I found that I could see the black band upon Sir John's white hat, then that I could count the folds of his cape; finally, that I could see the pretty features of his wife as she looked back at us.

"We're on the side road to Godstone and Warlingham," said my uncle. "I suppose he thought that he could make better time by getting out of the way of the market carts. But we've got the deuce of a hill to come down. You'll see some fun, nephew, or I am mistaken."

As he spoke I suddenly saw the wheels of the four-in-hand disappear, then the body of it, and then the two figures upon the box, as suddenly and abruptly as if it had bumped down the first three steps of some gigantic stairs. An instant later we had reached the same spot, and there was the road beneath us, steep and narrow, winding in long curves into the valley. The four-in-hand was swishing down it as hard as the horses could gallop.

"Thought so!" cried my uncle. "If he doesn't brake, why should I? Now, my darlings, one good spurt, and we'll show them the colour of our tailboard."

We shot over the brow and flew madly down the hill with the great red coach roaring and thundering before us. Already we were in her dust, so that we could see nothing but the dim scarlet blur in the heart of it, rocking and rolling, with its outline hardening at every stride. We could hear the crack of the whip in front of us, and the shrill voice of Lady Lade as she screamed to the horses. My uncle was very quiet, but when I glanced up at him I saw that his lips were set and his eyes shining, with just a little flush upon each pale cheek. There was no need to urge on the mares, for they were already flying at a pace which could neither be stopped nor controlled. Our leader's head came abreast of the off hind wheel, then of the off front one—then for a hundred yards we did not gain an inch, and then with a spurt the bay leader was neck to neck with the black wheeler, and our fore wheel within an inch of their hind one.

"Dusty work!" said my uncle, quietly.

"Fan 'em, Jack! Fan 'em!" shrieked the lady.

He sprang up and lashed at his horses.

"Look out, Tregellis!" he shouted. "There's a damnation spill coming for somebody."

We had got fairly abreast of them now, the rumps of the horses exactly a-line and the fore wheels whizzing together. There was not six inches to spare in the breadth of the road, and every instant I expected to feel the jar of a locking wheel. But now, as we came out from the dust, we could see what was ahead, and my uncle whistled between his teeth at the sight.

Two hundred yards or so in front of us there was a bridge, with wooden posts and rails upon either side. The road narrowed down at the point, so that it was obvious that the two carriages abreast could not possibly get over. One must give way to the other. Already our wheels were abreast of their wheelers.

" I lead ! " shouted my uncle. " You must pull them, Lade ! "

" Not I ! " he roared.

" No, by George ! " shrieked her ladyship. " Fan 'em, Jack ; keep on fanning 'em ! "

It seemed to me that we were all going to eternity together. But my uncle did the only thing that could have saved us. By a desperate effort we might just clear the coach before reaching the mouth of the bridge. He sprang up, and lashed right and left at the mares, who, maddened by the unaccustomed pain, hurled themselves on in a frenzy. Down we thundered together, all shouting, I believe, at the top of our voices in the madness of the moment ; but still we were drawing steadily away and we were almost clear of the leaders when we flew on to the bridge. I glanced back at the coach, and I saw Lady Lade, with her savage little white teeth clenched together, throw herself forward and tug with both hands at the off-side reins.

" Jam them, Jack ! " she cried. " Jam the —— before they can pass."

Had she done it an instant sooner we should have crashed against the wood-work, carried it away, and been hurled into the deep gully below. As it was, it was not the powerful haunch of the black leader which caught

947

our wheel, but the forequarter, which had not weight
enough to turn us from our course. I saw a red wet seam
gape suddenly through the black hair, and next instant
we were flying alone down the road, whilst the four-in-
hand had halted, and Sir John and his lady were down
in the road together tending to the wounded horse.

" Easy now, my beauties ! " cried my uncle, settling
down into his seat again, and looking back over his
shoulder. " I could not have believed that Sir John
Lade would have been guilty of such a trick as pulling
that leader across. I do not permit a *mauvaise plaisanterie*
of that sort. He shall hear from me to-night."

" It was the lady," said I.

My uncle's brow cleared, and he began to laugh.

" It was little Letty, was it ? " said he. " I might have
known it. There's a touch of the late lamented Sixteen-
string Jack about the trick. Well, it is only messages of
another kind that I send to a lady, so we'll just drive on
our way, nephew, and thank our stars that we bring whole
bones over the Thames."

We stopped at the Greyhound, at Croydon, where the
two good little mares were sponged and petted and fed,
after which, at an easier pace, we made our way through
Norbury and Streatham. At last the fields grew fewer
and the walls longer. The outlying villas closed up
thicker and thicker, until their shoulders met, and we
were driving between a double line of houses with garish
shops at the corners, and such a stream of traffic as I had
never seen, roaring down the centre. Then suddenly
we were on a broad bridge with a dark coffee-brown river
flowing sulkily beneath it, and bluff-bowed barges drifting
down upon its bosom. To right and left stretched a
broken, irregular line of many-coloured houses winding
along either bank as far as I could see.

" That's the House of Parliament, nephew," said my
uncle, pointing with his whip, " and the black towers
are Westminster Abbey. How do, your Grace ? How
do ? That's the Duke of Norfolk—the stout man in

blue upon the swish-tailed mare. Now we are in White-hall. There's the Treasury on the left, and the Horse Guards, and the Admiralty, where the stone dolphins are carved above the gate."

I had the idea, which a country-bred lad brings up with him, that London was merely a wilderness of houses, but I was astonished now to see the green slopes and the lovely spring trees showing between.

"Yes, those are the Privy Gardens," said my uncle, "and there is the window out of which Charles took his last step on to the scaffold. You wouldn't think the mares had come fifty miles, would you? See how *les petites chéries* step out for the credit of their master. Look at the barouche, with the sharp-featured man peeping out of the window. That's Pitt, going down to the House. We are coming into Pall Mall now, and this great building on the left is Carlton House, the Prince's Palace. There's St. James's, the big, dingy place with the clock, and the two red-coated sentries before it. And here's the famous street of the same name, nephew, which is the very centre of the world, and here's Jermyn Street opening out of it, and finally, here's my own little box, and we are well under the five hours from Brighton Old Square."

9. *Watier's*

MY uncle's house in Jermyn Street was quite a small one—five rooms and an attic. "A man-cook and a cottage," he said, "are all that a wise man requires." On the other hand, it was furnished with the neatness and taste which belonged to his character, so that his most luxurious friends found something in the tiny rooms which made them discontented with their own sumptuous mansions. Even the attic, which had been converted into my bedroom, was the most perfect little bijou attic that could possibly be imagined. Beautiful and valuable knick-knacks filled every corner of every

apartment, and the house had become a perfect miniature museum which would have delighted a virtuoso. My uncle explained the presence of all these pretty things with a shrug of his shoulders and a wave of his hands. " They are *des petites cadeaux*," said he, " but it would be an indiscretion for me to say more."

We found a note from Ambrose waiting for us which increased rather than explained the mystery of his disappearance.

" My dear Sir Charles Tregellis," it ran, " it will ever be a subject of regret to me that the force of circumstances should have compelled me to leave your service in so abrupt a fashion, but something occurred during our journey from Friar's Oak to Brighton which left me without any possible alternative. I trust, however, that my absence may prove to be but a temporary one. The isinglass recipe for the shirt-fronts is in the strong-box at Drummond's Bank.—Yours obediently, AMBROSE."

" Well, I suppose I must fill his place as best I can," said my uncle, moodily. " But how on earth could something have occurred to make him leave me at a time when we were going full-trot down hill in my curricle ? I shall never find his match again either for chocolate or cravats. *Je suis desolé !* But, now, nephew, we must send to Weston and have you fitted up. It is not for a gentleman to go to a shop, but for the shop to come to the gentleman. Until you have your clothes you must remain *en retraite*."

The measuring was a most solemn and serious function, though it was nothing to the trying-on two days later, when my uncle stood by in an agony of apprehension as each garment was adjusted, he and Weston arguing over every seam and lapel and skirt until I was dizzy with turning round in front of them. Then, just as I had hoped that all was settled, in came young Mr. Brummell, who promised to be an even greater exquisite than my uncle, and the whole matter had to be thrashed out between them. He was a good-sized man, this Brummell,

with a long, fair face, light brown hair and slight sandy side-whiskers. His manner was languid, his voice drawling, and while he eclipsed my uncle in the extravagance of his speech, he had not the air of manliness and decision which underlay all my kinsman's affectations.

" Why, George," cried my uncle, " I thought you were with your regiment."

" I've sent in my papers," drawled the other.

" I thought it would come to that."

" Yes. The Tenth was ordered to Manchester, and they could hardly expect me to go to a place like that. Besides, I found the major monstrous rude."

" How was that ? "

" He expected me to know about his absurd drill, Tregellis, and I had other things to think of, as you may suppose. I had no difficulty in taking my right place on parade, for there was a trooper with a red nose on a flea-bitten grey, and I had observed that my post was always immediately in front of him. This saved a great deal of trouble. The other day, however, when I came on parade, I galloped up one line and down the other, but the deuce a glimpse could I get of that long nose of his ! Then, just as I was at my wits' end, I caught sight of him, alone at one side ; so I formed up in front. It seems he had been put there to keep the ground, and the major so far forgot himself as to say that I knew nothing of my duties."

My uncle laughed, and Brummell looked me up and down with his large, intolerant eyes.

" These will do very passably," said he. " Buff and blue are always very gentlemanlike. But a sprigged waistcoat would have been better."

" I think not," said my uncle, warmly.

" My dear Tregellis, you are infallible upon a cravat, but you must allow me the right of my own judgment upon vests. I like it vastly as it stands, but a touch of red sprig would give it the finish that it needs."

They argued with many examples and analogies for a good ten minutes, revolving round me at the same time

with their heads on one side and their glasses to their eyes. It was a relief to me when they at last agreed upon a compromise.

" You must not let anything I have said shake your faith in Sir Charles's judgment, Mr. Stone," said Brummell, very earnestly.

I assured him that I should not.

" If you were my nephew, I should expect you to follow my taste. But you will cut a very good figure as it is. I had a young cousin who came up to town last year with a recommendation to my care. But he would take no advice. At the end of the second week I met him coming down St. James's Street in a snuff-coloured coat cut by a country tailor. He bowed to me. Of course I knew what was due to myself. I looked all round him, and there was an end to his career in town. You are from the country, Mr. Stone ? "

" From Sussex, sir."

" Sussex ! Why, that is where I send my washing to. There is an excellent clear-starcher living near Hayward's Heath. I send my shirts two at a time, for if you send more it excites the woman and diverts her attention. I cannot abide anything but country washing. But I should be vastly sorry to have to live there. What can a man find to do ? "

" You don't hunt, George ? "

" When I do, it's a woman. But surely you don't go to hounds, Charles ? "

" I was out with the Belvoir last winter."

" The Belvoir ! Did you hear how I smoked Rutland ? The story has been in the clubs this month past. I bet him that my bag would weigh more than his. He got three and a half brace, but I shot his liver-coloured pointer, so he had to pay. But as to hunting, what amusement can there be in flying about among a crowd of greasy, galloping farmers ? Every man to his own taste, but Brookes's window by day and a snug corner of the macao table at Watier's by night, give me all I want

for mind and body. You heard how I plucked Montague the brewer ?"

" I have been out of town."

" I had eight thousand from him at a sitting. 'I shall drink your beer in future, Mr. Brewer,' said I. 'Every blackguard in London does,' said he. It was monstrous impolite of him, but some people cannot lose with grace. Well, I am going down to Clarges Street to pay Jew King a little of my interest. Are you bound that way ? Well, good-bye, then ! I'll see you and your young friend at the club or in the Mall, no doubt," and he sauntered off upon his way.

" That young man is destined to take my place," said my uncle, gravely, when Brummell had departed. " He is quite young and of no descent, but he has made his way by his cool effrontery, his natural taste and his extravagance of speech. There is no man who can be impolite in so polished a fashion. He has a half-smile, and a way of raising his eyebrows, for which he will be shot one of these mornings. Already his opinion is quoted in the clubs as a rival to my own. Well, every man has his day, and when I am convinced that mine is past, St. James's Street shall know me no more, for it is not in my nature to be second to any man. But now, nephew, in that buff and blue suit you may pass anywhere ; so, if you please, we will step into my *vis-à-vis*, and I will show you something of the town.

How can I describe all that we saw and all that we did upon that lovely spring day ? To me it was as if I had been wafted to a fairy world, and my uncle might have been some benevolent enchanter in a high-collared, long-tailed coat, who was guiding me about in it. He showed me the West-end streets, with the bright carriages and the gaily dressed ladies and sombre-clad men, all crossing and hurrying and recrossing like an ants' nest when you turn it over with a stick. Never had I formed a conception of such endless banks of houses, and such a ceaseless

stream of life flowing between. Then we passed down
the Strand, where the crowd was thicker than ever, and
even penetrated beyond Temple Bar and into the City,
though my uncle begged me not to mention it, for he
would not wish it to be generally known. There I saw
the Exchange and the Bank and Lloyd's Coffee House,
with the brown-coated, sharp-faced merchants and the
hurrying clerks, the huge horses and the busy draymen.
It was a very different world this from that which we had
left in the West—a world of energy and of strength, where
there was no place for the listless and the idle. Young
as I was, I knew that it was here, in the forest of merchant
shipping, in the bales which swung up to the warehouse
windows, in the loaded waggons which roared over the
cobblestones, that the power of Britain lay. Here, in
the City of London, was the taproot from which Empire
and wealth and so many other fine leaves had sprouted.
Fashion and speech and manners may change, but the
spirit of enterprise within that square mile or two of land
must not change, for when it withers all that has grown
from it must wither also.

We lunched at Stephen's, the fashionable inn in Bond
Street, where I saw a line of tilburys and saddle-horses,
which stretched from the door to the further end of the
street. And thence we went to the Mall in St. James's
Park, and thence to Brookes's, the great Whig club, and
thence again to Watier's, where the men of fashion used
to gamble. Everywhere I met the same sort of men,
with their stiff figures and small waists, all showing the
utmost deference to my uncle, and for his sake an easy
tolerance of me. The talk was always such as I had
already heard at the Pavilion : talk of politics, talk of the
King's health, talk of the Prince's extravagance, of the
expected renewal of war, of horse-racing and of the Ring.
I saw, too, that eccentricity was, as my uncle had told me,
the fashion ; and if the folk upon the Continent look upon
us even to this day as being a nation of lunatics, it is no
doubt a tradition handed down from the time when the

only travellers whom they were likely to see were drawn from the class which I was now meeting.

It was an age of heroism and of folly. On the one hand soldiers, sailors and statesmen of the quality of Pitt, Nelson and afterwards Wellington, had been forced to the front by the imminent menace of Buonaparte. We were great in arms, and were soon also to be great in literature, for Scott and Byron were in their day the strongest forces in Europe. On the other hand, a touch of madness, real or assumed, was a passport through doors which were closed to wisdom and to virtue. The man who could enter a drawing-room walking upon his hands, the man who had filed his teeth that he might whistle like a coachman, the man who always spoke his thoughts aloud and so kept his guests in a quiver of apprehension, these were the people who found it easy to come to the front in London society. Nor could the heroism and the folly be kept apart, for there were few who could quite escape the contagion of the times. In an age when the Premier was a heavy drinker, the Leader of the Opposition a libertine, and the Prince of Wales a combination of the two, it was hard to know where to look for a man whose private and public characters were equally lofty. At the same time, with all its faults it was a *strong* age, and you will be fortunate if in your time the country produces five such names as Pitt, Fox, Scott, Nelson and Wellington.

It was in Watier's that night, seated by my uncle on one of the red velvet settees at the side of the room, that I had pointed out to me some of those singular characters whose fame and eccentricities are even now not wholly forgotten in the world. The long, many-pillared room, with its mirrors and chandeliers, was crowded with full-blooded, loud-voiced men-about-town, all in the same dark evening dress with white silk stockings, cambric shirt-fronts, and little, flat chapeau-bras under their arms.

" The acid-faced old gentleman with the thin legs is the Marquis of Queensberry," said my uncle. " His

chaise was driven nineteen miles in an hour in a match against the Count Taafe, and he sent a message fifty miles in thirty minutes by throwing it from hand to hand in a cricket-ball. The man he is talking to is Sir Charles Bunbury, of the Jockey Club, who had the Prince warned off the Heath at Newmarket on account of the in-and-out riding of Sam Chifney, his jockey. There's Captain Barclay going up to them now. He knows more about training than any man alive, and he has walked ninety miles in twenty-one hours. You have only to look at his calves to see that Nature built him for it. There's another walker there, the man with a flowered vest, standing near the fireplace. That is Buck Whalley, who walked to Jerusalem in a long blue coat, top-boots and buckskins."

" Why did he do that, sir ? " I asked, in astonishment. My uncle shrugged his shoulders.

" It was his humour," said he. " He walked into society through it, and that was better worth reaching than Jerusalem. There's Lord Petersham, the man with the beaky nose. He always rises at six in the evening, and he has laid down the finest cellar of snuff in Europe. It was he who ordered his valet to put half a dozen of sherry by his bed and call him the day after to-morrow. He's talking to Lord Panmure, who can take his six bottles of claret and argue with a bishop after it. The lean man with the weak knees is General Scott, who lives upon toast and water and has won £200,000 at whist. He is talking to young Lord Blandford, who gave £1800 for a Boccaccio the other day. Evening, Dudley ! "

" Evening, Tregellis ! " An elderly, vacant-looking man had stopped before us and was looking me up and down.

" Some young cub Charlie Tregellis has caught in the country," he murmured. " He doesn't look as if he would be much credit to him. Been out of town, Tregellis ? "

" For a few days."

" Hem ! " said the man, transferring his sleepy gaze

to my uncle. " He's looking pretty bad. He'll be going into the country feet foremost some of these days if he doesn't pull up ! " He nodded, and passed on.

" You mustn't look so mortified, nephew," said my uncle, smiling. " That's old Lord Dudley, and he has a trick of thinking aloud. People used to be offended, but they take no notice of him now. It was only last week, when he was dining at Lord Elgin's, that he apologised to the company for the shocking bad cooking. He thought he was at his own table, you see. It gives him a place of his own in society. That's Lord Harewood he has fastened on to now. Harewood's peculiarity is to mimic the Prince in everything. One day the Prince hid his queue behind the collar of his coat, so Harewood cut his off, thinking that they were going out of fashion. Here's Lumley, the ugly man. ' *L'homme laid* ' they called him in Paris. The other one is Lord Foley—they call him No. 11, on account of his thin legs."

" There is Mr. Brummell, sir," said I.

" Yes, he'll come to us presently. That young man has certainly a future before him. Do you observe the way in which he looks round the room from under his drooping eyelids, as though it were a condescension that he should have entered it ? Small conceits are intolerable, but when they are pushed to the uttermost they become respectable. How do, George ? "

" Have you heard about Vereker Merton ? " asked Brummell, strolling up with one or two other exquisites at his heels. " He has run away with his father's woman-cook, and actually married her."

" What did Lord Merton do ? "

" He congratulated him warmly, and confessed that he had always underrated his intelligence. He is to live with the young couple, and make a handsome allowance on condition that the bride sticks to her old duties. By the way, there was a rumour that you were about to marry, Tregellis."

" I think not," answered my uncle. " It would be a

mistake to overwhelm one by attentions which are a pleasure to many."

" My view, exactly, and very neatly expressed," cried Brummell. " Is it fair to break a dozen hearts in order to intoxicate one with rapture ? I'm off to the Continent next week."

" Bailiffs ? " asked one of his companions.

" Too bad, Pierrepoint. No, no ; it is pleasure and instruction combined. Besides, it is necessary to go to Paris for your little things, and if there is a chance of the war breaking out again, it would be well to lay in a supply."

" Quite right," said my uncle, who seemed to have made up his mind to outdo Brummell in extravagance. " I used to get my sulphur-coloured gloves from the Palais Royal. When the war broke out in '93 I was cut off from them for nine years. Had it not been for a lugger which I specially hired to smuggle them, I might have been reduced to English tan."

" The English are excellent at a flat-iron or a kitchen poker, but anything more delicate is beyond them."

" Our tailors are good," cried my uncle, " but our stuffs lack taste and variety. The war has made us more *rococo* than ever. It has cut us off from travel, and there is nothing to match travel for expanding the mind. Last year, for example, I came upon some new waistcoating in the Square of San Marco, at Venice. It was yellow, with the prettiest little twill of pink running through it. How could I have seen it had I not travelled ? I brought it back with me, and for a time it was all the rage."

" The Prince took it up."

" Yes, he usually follows my lead. We dressed so alike last year that we were frequently mistaken for each other. It tells against me, but so it was. He often complains that things do not look as well upon him as upon me, but how can I make the obvious reply ? By the way, George, I did not see you at the Marchioness of Dover's ball."

"Yes, I was there, and lingered for a quarter of an hour or so. I am surprised that you did not see me. I did not go past the doorway, however, for undue preference gives rise to jealousy."

"I went early," said my uncle, "for I had heard that there were to be some tolerable *débutantes*. It always pleases me vastly when I am able to pass a compliment to any of them. It has happened, but not often, for I keep to my own standard."

So they talked, these singular men, and I, looking from one to the other, could not imagine how they could help bursting out a-laughing in each other's faces. But on the contrary, their conversation was very grave, and filled out with many little bows, and opening and shutting of snuff-boxes, and flickings of laced handkerchiefs. Quite a crowd had gathered silently around, and I could see that the talk had been regarded as a contest between two men who were looked upon as rival arbiters of fashion. It was finished by the Marquis of Queensberry passing his arm through Brummell's and leading him off, while my uncle threw out his laced cambric shirt-front and shot his ruffles as if he were well satisfied with his share in the encounter. It is seven-and-forty years since I looked upon that circle of dandies, and where, now, are their dainty little hats, their wonderful waistcoats, and their boots, in which one could arrange one's cravat? They lived strange lives, these men, and they died strange deaths—some by their own hands, some as beggars, some in a debtor's gaol, some, like the most brilliant of them all, in a madhouse in a foreign land.

"There is the card-room, Rodney," said my uncle, as we passed an open door on our way out. Glancing in, I saw a line of little green baize tables with small groups of men sitting round, while at one side was a longer one, from which there came a continuous murmur of voices. "You may lose what you like in there, save only your nerve or your temper," my uncle continued. "Ah, Sir Lothian, I trust that the luck was with you?"

A tall, thin man, with a hard, austere face, had stepped out of the open doorway. His heavily thatched eyebrows covered quick, furtive grey eyes, and his gaunt features were hollowed at the cheek and temple like water-grooved flint. He was dressed entirely in black, and I noticed that his shoulders swayed a little as if he had been drinking.

" Lost like the deuce," he snapped.

" Dice ? "

" No, whist."

" You couldn't get very hard hit over that."

" Couldn't you ? " he snarled. " Play a hundred a trick and a thousand on the rub, losing steadily for five hours, and see what you think of it."

My uncle was evidently struck by the haggard look upon the other's face.

" I hope it's not very bad," he said.

" Bad enough. It won't bear talking about. By the way, Tregellis, have you got your man for this fight yet ? "

" No."

" You seem to be hanging in the wind a long time. It's play or pay, you know. I shall claim forfeit if you don't come to scratch."

" If you will name your day I shall produce my man, Sir Lothian," said my uncle, coldly.

" This day four weeks, if you like."

" Very good. The 18th of May."

" I hope to have changed my name by then ! "

" How is that ? " asked my uncle, in surprise.

" It is just possible that I may be Lord Avon."

" What, you have had some news ? " cried my uncle, and I noticed a tremor in his voice.

" I've had my agent over at Monte Video, and he believes he has proof that Avon died there. Anyhow, it is absurd to suppose that because a murderer chooses to fly from justice——"

" I won't have you use that word, Sir Lothian," cried my uncle, sharply.

"You were there as I was. You know that he was a murderer."

"I tell you that you shall not say so."

Sir Lothian's fierce little grey eyes had to lower themselves before the imperious anger which shone in my uncle's.

"Well, to let that point pass, it is monstrous to suppose that the title and the estates can remain hung up in this way for ever. I'm the heir, Tregellis, and I'm going to have my rights."

"I am, as you are aware, Lord Avon's dearest friend," said my uncle, sternly. "His disappearance has not affected my love for him, and until his fate is finally ascertained, I shall exert myself to see that *his* rights also are respected."

"His rights would be a long drop and a cracked spine," Sir Lothian answered, and then, changing his manner suddenly, he laid his hand upon my uncle's sleeve.

"Come, come, Tregellis, I was his friend as well as you," said he. "But we cannot alter the facts, and it is rather late in the day for us to fall out over them. Your invitation holds good for Friday night?"

"Certainly."

"I shall bring Crab Wilson with me, and finally arrange the conditions of our little wager."

"Very good, Sir Lothian. I shall hope to see you."

They bowed, and my uncle stood a little time looking after him as he made his way amidst the crowd.

"A good sportsman, nephew," said he. "A bold rider, the best pistol-shot in England, but . . . a dangerous man!"

10. *The Men of the Ring*

IT was at the end of my first week in London that my uncle gave a supper to the Fancy, as was usual for gentlemen of that time if they wished to figure before the public as Corinthians and patrons of sport.

He had invited not only the chief fighting men of the day, but also those men of fashion who were most interested in the Ring : Mr. Fletcher Reid, Lord Saye and Sele, Sir Lothian Hume, Sir John Lade, Colonel Montgomery, Sir Thomas Apreece, the Hon. Berkeley Craven and many more. The rumour that the Prince was to be present had already spread through the clubs, and invitations were eagerly sought after.

The Waggon and Horses was a well-known sporting house, with an old prize-fighter for landlord. And the arrangements were as primitive as the most Bohemian could wish. It was one of the many curious fashions which have now died out, that men who were *blasé* from luxury and high living seemed to find a fresh piquancy in life by descending to the lowest resorts, so that the night-houses and gambling dens in Covent Garden or the Haymarket often gathered illustrious company under their smoke-blackened ceilings. It was a change for them to turn their backs upon the cooking of Weltjie and of Ude, or the chambertin of old Q., and to dine upon a porter-house steak washed down by a pint of ale from a pewter pot.

A rough crowd had assembled in the street to see the fighting-men go in, and my uncle warned me to look to my pockets as we pushed our way through it. Within was a large room with faded red curtains, a sanded floor, and walls which were covered with prints of pugilists and race-horses. Brown liquor-stained tables were dotted about in it, and round one of these half a dozen formidable-looking men were seated, while one, the roughest of all, was perched upon the table itself, swinging his legs to and fro. A tray of small glasses and pewter mugs stood beside them.

" The boys were thirsty, sir, so I brought up some ale and some liptrap," whispered the landlord ; " I thought you would have no objection, sir."

" Quite right, Bob ! How are you all ? How are you, Maddox ? How are you, Baldwin ? Ah, Belcher, I am very glad to see you."

The fighting-men rose and took their hats off, except the fellow on the table, who continued to swing his legs and to look my uncle very coolly in the face.

" How are you, Berks ? "

" Pretty tidy. 'Ow are you ? "

" Say ' sir ' when you speak to a genelman," said Belcher, and with a sudden tilt of the table he sent Berks flying almost into my uncle's arms.

" See now, Jem, none o' that ! " said Berks, sulkily.

" I'll learn you manners, Joe, which is more than ever your father did. You're not drinkin' black-jack in a boozin' ken, but you are meetin' noble, slap-up Corinthians, and it's for you to behave as such."

" I've always been reckoned a genelmanlike sort of man," said Berks, thickly, " but if so be as I've said or done what I 'adn't ought to——"

" There, there, Berks, that's all right ! " cried my uncle, only too anxious to smooth things over and to prevent a quarrel at the outset of the evening. " Here are some more of our friends. How are you, Apreece ? How are you, Colonel ? Well, Jackson, you are looking vastly better. Good evening, Lade. I trust Lady Lade was none the worse for our pleasant drive. Ah, Mendoza, you look fit enough to throw your hat over the ropes this instant. Sir Lothian, I am glad to see you. You will find some old friends here."

Amid the stream of Corinthians and fighting-men who were thronging into the room I had caught a glimpse of the sturdy figure and broad, good-humoured face of Champion Harrison. The sight of him was like a whiff of South-Down air coming into that low-roofed, oil-smelling room, and I ran forward to shake him by the hand.

" Why, Master Rodney—or I should say Mr. Stone, I suppose—you've changed out of all knowledge. I can't hardly believe that it was really you that used to come down to blow the bellows when Boy Jim and I were at the anvil. Well, you are fine, to be sure ! "

" What's the news of Friar's Oak ? " I asked, eagerly.

" Your father was down to chat with me, Master Rodney, and he tells me that the war is going to break out again, and that he hopes to see you here in London before many days are past ; for he is coming up to see Lord Nelson and to make inquiry about a ship. Your mother is well, and I saw her in church on Sunday."

" And Boy Jim ? "

Champion Harrison's good-humoured face clouded over.

" He'd set his heart very much on comin' here to-night, but there were reasons why I didn't wish him to, and so there's a shadow betwixt us. It's the first that ever was, and I feel it, Master Rodney. Between ourselves, I have very good reason to wish him to stay with me, and I am sure that, with his high spirit and his ideas, he would never settle down again after once he had a taste o' London. I left him behind me with enough work to keep him busy until I get back to him."

A tall and beautifully proportioned man, very elegantly dressed, was strolling towards us. He stared in surprise and held out his hand to my companion.

" Why, Jack Harrison ! " he cried. " This is a resurrection. Where in the world did you come from ? "

" Glad to see you, Jackson," said my companion. " You look as well and as young as ever."

" Thank you, yes. I resigned the belt when I could get no one to fight me for it, and I took to teaching."

" I'm doing smith's work down Sussex way."

" I've often wondered why you never had a shy at my belt. I tell you honestly, between man and man, I'm very glad you didn't."

" Well, it's real good of you to say that, Jackson. I might ha' done it, perhaps, but the old woman was against it. She's been a good wife to me and I can't go against her. But I feel a bit lonesome here, for these boys are since my time."

" You could do some of them over now," said Jackson,

feeling my friend's upper arm. " No better bit of stuff was ever seen in a twenty-four-foot ring. It would be a rare treat to see you take some of these young ones on. Won't you let me spring you on them ? "

Harrison's eyes glistened at the idea, but he shook his head.

" It won't do, Jackson. My old woman holds my promise. That's Belcher, ain't it—the good-lookin' young chap with the flash coat ? "

" Yes, that's Jem. You've not seen him ! He's a jewel."

" So I've heard. Who's the youngster beside him ? He looks a tidy chap."

" That's a new man from the West. Crab Wilson's his name."

Harrison looked at him with interest. " I've heard of him," said he. " They are getting a match on for him, ain't they ? "

" Yes. Sir Lothian Hume, the thin-faced gentleman over yonder, has backed him against Sir Charles Tregellis's man. We're to hear about the match to-night, I understand. Jem Belcher thinks great things of Crab Wilson. There's Belcher's young brother, Tom. He's looking out for a match, too. They say he's quicker than Jem with the mufflers, but he can't hit as hard. I was speaking of your brother, Jem."

" The young 'un will make his way," said Belcher, who had come across to us. " He's more a sparrer than a fighter just at present, but when his gristle sets he'll take on anything on the list. Bristol's as full o' young fightin'-men now as a bin is of bottles. We've got two more comin' up—Gully and Pearce—who'll make yon London milling coves wish they was back in the west country again."

" Here's the Prince," said Jackson, as a hum and bustle rose from the door.

I saw George come bustling in, with a good-humoured smile upon his comely face. My uncle welcomed him, and led some of the Corinthians up to be presented.

" We'll have trouble, gov'nor," said Belcher to Jackson.
" Here's Joe Berks drinkin' gin out of a mug, and you
know what a swine he is when he's drunk."

" You must put a stopper on 'im, gov'nor," said
several of the other prize-fighters. " 'E ain't what you'd
call a charmer when 'e's sober, but there's no standing
'im when 'e's fresh."

Jackson, on account of his prowess and of the tact
which he possessed, had been chosen as general regulator
of the whole prize-fighting body, by whom he was usually
alluded to as the Commander-in-Chief. He and Belcher
went across now to the table upon which Berks was still
perched. The ruffian's face was already flushed, and his
eyes heavy and bloodshot.

" You must keep yourself in hand to-night, Berks,"
said Jackson. " The Prince is here, and——"

" I never set eyes on 'im yet," cried Berks, lurching off
the table. " Where is 'e, gov'nor ? Tell 'im Joe Berks
would like to do 'isself proud by shakin' 'im by the 'and."

" No, you don't, Joe," said Jackson, laying his hand
upon Berks's chest, as he tried to push his way through
the crowd. " You've got to keep your place, Joe, or we'll
put you where you can make all the noise you like."

" Where's that, gov'nor ? "

" Into the street, through the window. We're going
to have a peaceful evening, as Jem Belcher and I will show
you if you get up to any of your Whitechapel games."

" No 'arm, gov'nor," grumbled Berks. " I'm sure I've
always 'ad the name of bein' a very genelmanlike man."

" So I've always said, Joe Berks, and mind you prove
yourself such. But the supper is ready for us, and there's
the Prince and Lord Sele going in. Two and two, lads,
and don't forget whose company you are in."

The supper was laid in a large room, with Union Jacks
and mottoes hung thickly upon the walls. The tables
were arranged in three sides of a square, my uncle
occupying the centre of the principal one, with the
Prince upon his right and Lord Sele upon his left. By

his wise precaution the seats had been allotted beforehand so that the gentlemen might be scattered among the professionals and no risk run of two enemies finding themselves together, or a man who had been recently beaten falling into the company of his conqueror. For my own part, I had Champion Harrison upon one side of me and a stout, florid-faced man upon the other, who whispered to me that he was " Bill Warr, landlord of the One Tun public-house, of Jermyn Street, and one of the gamest men upon the list."

" It's my flesh that's beat me, sir," said he. " It creeps over me amazin' fast. I should fight at thirteen-eight, and 'ere I am nearly seventeen. It's the business that does it, what with lollin' about behind the bar all day, and bein' afraid to refuse a wet for fear of offendin' a customer. It's been the ruin of many a good fightin'-man before me."

" You should take to my job," said Harrison. " I'm a smith by trade, and I've not put on half a stone in fifteen years."

" Some take to one thing and some to another, but the most of us try to 'ave a bar-parlour of our own. There's Will Wood, that I beat in forty rounds in the thick of a snowstorm down Navestock way, 'e drives a 'ackney. Young Firby, the ruffian, 'e's a waiter now. Dick 'Umphries sells coals—'e was always of a genelmanly disposition. George Ingleston is a brewer's drayman. We all find our own cribs. But there's one thing you are saved by livin' in the country, and that is 'avin' the young Corinthians and bloods about town smackin' you eternally in the face."

This was the last inconvenience which I should have expected a famous prize-fighter to be subjected to, but several bull-faced fellows at the other side of the table nodded their concurrence.

" You're right, Bill," said one of them. " There's no one has had more trouble with them than I have. In they come of an evenin' into my bar, with the wine

in their heads. ' Are you Tom Owen, the bruiser ? '
says one o' them. ' At your service, sir,' says I. ' Take
that, then,' says he, and it's a clip on the nose, or a back-
handed slap across the chops as likely as not. Then they
can brag all their lives that they had hit Tom Owen."

" D'you draw their cork in return ? " asked Harrison.

" I argey it out with them. I say to them, ' Now,
gents, fightin' is my profession, and I don't fight for love
any more than a doctor doctors for love, or a butcher
gives away a loin chop. Put up a small purse, master,
and I'll do you over and proud. But don't expect that
you're goin' to come here and get glutted by a middle-
weight champion for nothing.' "

" That's my way, too, Tom," said my burly neighbour.
" If they put down a guinea on the counter—which they
do if they 'ave been drinkin' very 'eavy—I give them what
I think is about a guinea's worth and take the money."

" But if they don't ? "

" Why, then, it's a common assault, d'ye see, against
the body of 'is Majesty's liege, William Warr, and I 'as
'em before the beak next mornin', and it's a week or
twenty shillin's."

Meanwhile the supper was in full swing—one of those
solid and uncompromising meals which prevailed in the
days of your grandfathers, and which may explain to
some of you why you never set eyes upon that relative.

Great rounds of beef, saddles of mutton, smoking
tongues, veal and ham pies, turkeys and chickens and
geese, with every variety of vegetables, and a succession
of fiery cherries and heavy ales were the main staple of
the feast. It was the same meal and the same cooking
as their Norse or German ancestors might have sat down
to fourteen centuries before, and, indeed, as I looked
through the steam of the dishes at the lines of fierce and
rugged faces, and the mighty shoulders which rounded
themselves over the board, I could have imagined myself
at one of those old-world carousals of which I had read,
where the savage company gnawed the joints to the bone,

and then, with murderous horse-play, hurled the remains at their prisoners. Here and there the pale, aquiline features of a sporting Corinthian recalled rather the Norman type, but in the main these stolid, heavy-jowled faces, belonging to men whose whole life was a battle, were the nearest suggestion which we have had in modern times of those fierce pirates and rovers from whose loins we have sprung.

And yet, as I looked carefully from man to man in the line which faced me, I could see that the English, although they were ten to one, had not the game entirely to themselves, but that other races had shown that they could produce fighting-men worthy to rank with the best.

There were, it is true, no finer or braver men in the room than Jackson and Jem Belcher, the one with his magnificent figure, his small waist and Herculean shoulders ; the other as graceful as an old Grecian statue, with a head whose beauty many a sculptor had wished to copy, and with those long, delicate lines in shoulder and loins and limbs, which gave him the litheness and activity of a panther. Already, as I looked at him, it seemed to me that there was a shadow of tragedy upon his face, a forecast of the day then but a few months distant when a blow from a racquet ball darkened the sight of one eye for ever. Had he stopped there, with his unbeaten career behind him, then indeed the evening of his life might have been as glorious as its dawn. But his proud heart could not permit his title to be torn from him without a struggle. If even now you can read how the gallant fellow, unable with his one eye to judge his distances, fought for thirty-five minutes against his young and formidable opponent, and how, in the bitterness of defeat, he was heard only to express his sorrow for a friend who had backed him with all he possessed, and if you are not touched by the story there must be something wanting in you which should go to the making of a man.

But if there were no men at the tables who could have held their own against Jackson or Jem Belcher, there were

others of a different race and type who had qualities which made them dangerous bruisers. A little way down the room I saw the black face and woolly head of Bill Richmond, in a purple-and-gold footman's livery—destined to be the predecessor of Molineaux, Sutton, and all that line of black boxers who have shown that the muscular power and insensibility to pain which distinguish the African give him a peculiar advantage in the sports of the Ring. He could boast also of the higher honour of having been the first born American to win laurels in the British Ring. There also I saw the keen features of Dan Mendoza, the Jew, just retired from active work, and leaving behind him a reputation for elegance and perfect science which has, to this day, never been exceeded. The worst fault that the critics could find with him was that there was a want of power in his blows—a remark which certainly could not have been made about his neighbour, whose long face, curved nose, and dark, flashing eyes proclaimed him as a member of the same ancient race. This was the formidable Dutch Sam, who fought at nine stone six, and yet possessed such hitting powers, that his admirers, in after years, were willing to back him against the fourteen-stone Tom Cribb, if each were strapped a-straddle to a bench. Half a dozen other sallow Hebrew faces showed how energetically the Jews of Houndsditch and Whitechapel had taken to the sport of the land of their adoption, and that in this, as in more serious fields of human effort, they could hold their own with the best.

It was my neighbour Warr who very good-humouredly pointed out to me all these celebrities, the echoes of whose fame had been wafted down even to our little Sussex village.

" There's Andrew Gamble, the Irish champion," said he. " It was 'e that beat Noah James, the Guardsman, and was afterwards nearly killed by Jem Belcher, in the 'ollow of Wimbledon Common by Abbershaw's gibbet. The two that are next 'im are Irish also, Jack O'Donnell

and Bill Ryan. When you get a good Irishman you can't better 'em, but they're dreadful 'asty. That little cove with the leery face is Caleb Baldwin the Coster, 'im that they call the Pride of Westminster. 'E's but five foot seven, and nine stone five, but 'e's got the 'eart of a giant. 'E's never been beat, and there ain't a man within a stone of 'im that could beat 'im, except only Dutch Sam. There's George Maddox, too, another o' the same breed, and as good a man as ever pulled his coat off. The genelmanly man that eats with a fork, 'im what looks like a Corinthian, only that the bridge of 'is nose ain't quite as it ought to be, that's Dick 'Umphries, the same that was cock of the middle-weights until Mendoza cut his comb for 'im. You see the other with the grey 'ead and the scars on his face ? "

" Why, it's old Tom Faulkner the cricketer ! " cried Harrison, following the line of Bill Warr's stubby fore-finger. " He's the fastest bowler in the Midlands, and at his best there weren't many boxers in England that could stand up against him."

" You're right there, Jack 'Arrison. 'E was one of the three who came up to fight when the best men of Bir-mingham challenged the best men of London. 'E's an evergreen, is Tom. Why, he was turned five-and-fifty when he challenged and beat, after fifty minutes of it, Jack Thornhill, who was tough enough to take it out of many a youngster. It's better to give odds in weight than in years."

" Youth will be served," said a crooning voice from the other side of the table. " Aye, masters, youth will be served."

The man who had spoken was the most extraordinary of all the many curious figures in the room. He was very, very old, so old that he was past all comparison, and no one by looking at his mummy skin and fishlike eyes could give a guess at his years. A few scanty grey hairs still hung about his yellow scalp. As to his features, they were scarcely human in their disfigurement, for the deep

wrinkles and pouchings of extreme age had been added
to a face which had always been grotesquely ugly, and
had been crushed and smashed in addition by many a
blow. I had noticed this creature at the beginning of
the meal, leaning his chest against the edge of the
table as if its support was a welcome one, and feebly
picking at the food which was placed before him. Gradually, however, as his neighbours plied him with drink,
his shoulders grew squarer, his back stiffened, his eyes
brightened, and he looked about him, with an air of
surprise at first, as if he had no clear recollection of how
he came there, and afterwards with an expression of
deepening interest, as he listened, with his ear scooped
up in his hand, to the conversation around him.

"That's old Buckhorse," whispered Champion
Harrison. "He was just the same as that when I joined
the Ring twenty years ago. Time was when he was the
terror of London."

"'E was so," said Bill Warr. "'E would fight like
a stag, and 'e was that 'ard that 'e would let any swell
knock 'im down for 'alf-a-crown. 'E 'ad no face to spoil,
d'ye see, for 'e was always the ugliest man in England.
But 'e's been on the shelf now for near sixty years, and
it cost 'im many a beatin' before 'e could understand
that 'is strength was slippin' away from 'im."

"Youth will be served, masters," droned the old man,
shaking his head miserably.

"Fill up 'is glass," said Warr. "'Ere, Tom, give old
Buckhorse a sup o' liptrap. Warm his 'eart for 'im."

The old man poured a glass of neat gin down his
shrivelled throat, and the effect upon him was extraordinary. A light glimmered in each of his dull eyes, a
tinge of colour came into his wax-like cheeks, and,
opening his toothless mouth, he suddenly emitted a
peculiar, bell-like and most musical cry. A hoarse roar
of laughter from all the company answered it, and flushed
faces craned over each other to catch a glimpse of the
veteran.

" There's Buckhorse ! " they cried. " Buckhorse is comin' round again."

" You can laugh if you vill, masters," he cried, in his Lewkner Lane dialect, holding up his two thin, vein-covered hands. " It von't be long that you'll be able to see my crooks vich 'ave been on Figg's conk, and on Jack Broughton's, and on 'Arry Gray's, and many another good fightin' man that was millin' for a livin' before your fathers could eat pap."

The company laughed again, and encouraged the old man by half-derisive and half-affectionate cries.

" Let 'em 'ave it, Buckhorse ! Give it 'em straight ! Tell us how the millin' coves did it in your time."

The old gladiator looked round him in great contempt.

" Vy, from vot I see," he cried, in his high, broken treble, " there's some on you that ain't fit to flick a fly from a joint o' meat. You'd make werry good ladies' maids, the most of you, but you took the wrong turnin' ven you came into the Ring."

" Give 'im a wipe over the mouth," said a hoarse voice.

" Joe Berks," said Jackson, " I'd save the hangman the job of breaking your neck if His Royal Highness wasn't in the room."

" That's as it may be, guv'nor," said the half-drunken ruffian, staggering to his feet. " If I've said anything wot isn't genelmanlike——"

" Sit down, Berks ! " cried my uncle, with such a tone of command that the fellow collapsed into his chair.

" Vy, vitch of you would look Tom Slack in the face ? " piped the old fellow ; " or Jack Broughton ?—him vot told the old Dook of Cumberland that all he vanted vas to fight the King o' Proosia's guard, day by day, year in, year out, until 'e 'ad worked out the whole regiment of 'em—and the smallest of 'em six foot long. There's not more'n a few of you could 'it a dint in a pat o' butter, and if you gets a smack or two it's all over vith you. Vich among you could get up again after such a vipe as the Eytalian Gondoleery cove gave to Bob Vittaker ? "

" What was that, Buckhorse ? " cried several voices.

" 'E came over 'ere from voreign parts, and 'e was so broad 'e 'ad to come edgewise through the doors. 'E 'ad so, upon my davy ! 'E was that strong that wherever 'e 'it the bone had got to go ; and when 'e'd cracked a jaw or two it looked as though nothing in the country could stan' against him. So the King 'e sent one of his genelmen down to Figg and he said to him : ' 'Ere's a cove vot cracks a bone every time 'e lets vly, and it'll be little credit to the Lunnon boys if they lets 'im get avay vithout a vacking.' So Figg he ups, and he says, ' I do not know, master, but he may break one of 'is countrymen's jawbones vid 'is vist, but I'll bring 'im a Cockney lad and 'e shall not be able to break 'is jawbone with a sledge 'ammer.' I was with Figg in Slaughter's coffee-'ouse, as then vas, ven 'e says this to the King's genelman, and I goes so, I does ! " Again he emitted the curious bell-like cry, and again the Corinthians and the fighting-men laughed and applauded him.

" His Royal Highness—that is, the Earl of Chester— would be glad to hear the end of your story, Buckhorse," said my uncle, to whom the Prince had been whispering.

" Vell, your R'yal 'Ighness, it vas like this. Ven the day came round, all the volk came to Figg's Amphitheatre, the same that vos in Tottenham Court, an' Bob Vittaker 'e vos there, and the Eytalian Gondoleery cove 'e vas there, and all the purlitest, genteelest crowd that ever vos, twenty thousand of 'em, all sittin' with their 'eads like purtaties on a barrer, banked right up round the stage, and me there to pick up Bob, d'ye see, and Jack Figg 'imself just for fair play to do vot was right by the cove from voreign parts. They vas packed all round, the folks was, but down through the middle of 'em was a passage just so as the gentry could come through to their seats, and the stage it vas of wood, as the custom then vas, and a man's 'eight above the 'eads of the people. Vell, then, ven Bob was put up opposite this great Eytalian man I says ' Slap 'im in the vind, Bob,' 'cos I could see

vid 'alf an eye that he vas as puffy as a cheesecake ; so Bob he goes in, and as he comes the vorriner let 'im 'ave it amazin' on the conk. I 'eard the thump of it, and I kind o' velt somethin' vistle past me, but ven I looked there was the Eytalian a feelin' of 'is muscles in the middle o' the stage, and as to Bob, there vern't no sign of 'im at all no more'n if 'e'd never been."

His audience was riveted by the old prize-fighter's story. " Well," cried a dozen voices, " what then, Buckhorse : 'ad 'e swallowed 'im, or what ? "

" Vell, boys, that vas vat *I* wondered, when sudden I seed two legs a-stickin' up out o' the crowd a long vay off, just like these two vingers, d'ye see, and I knewed they vas Bob's legs, seein' that 'e 'ad kind o' yellow small clothes vid blue ribbons—vich blue vas 'is colour—at the knee. So they up-ended 'im, they did, an' they made a lane for 'im an' cheered 'im to give 'im 'eart, though 'e never lacked for that. At virst 'e vas that dazed that 'e didn't know if 'e vas in church or in 'Orsemonger Gaol ; but ven I'd bit 'is two ears 'e shook 'isself together. ' Ve'll try it again, Buck,' says 'e. ' The mark ! ' says I. And 'e vinked all that vas left o' one eye. So the Eytalian 'e lets swing again, but Bob 'e jumps inside an' lets 'im 'ave it plumb square on the meat safe as 'ard as ever the Lord would let 'im put it in."

" Well ? Well ? "

" Vell, the Eytalian 'e got a touch of the gurgles, an' 'e shut 'imself right up like a two-foot rule. Then 'e pulled 'imself straight, an' 'e gave the most awful Glory Allelujah screech as ever you 'eard. Off 'e jumps from the stage an' down the passage as 'ard as 'is 'oofs would carry 'im. Up jumps the 'ole crowd, and after 'im as 'ard as they could move for laughin'. They vas lyin' in the kennel three deep all down Tottenham Court Road vid their 'ands to their sides just vit to break themselves in two. Vell, ve chased 'im down 'Olburn, an' down Fleet Street, an' down Cheapside, an' past the 'Change, and on all the vay to Voppin', an' we only catched 'im in the

shippin' office, vere 'e vas askin' 'ow soon 'e could get a passage to voreign parts."

There was much laughter and clapping of glasses upon the table at the conclusion of old Buckhorse's story, and I saw the Prince of Wales hand something to the waiter, who brought it round and slipped it into the skinny hand of the veteran, who spat upon it before thrusting it into his pocket. The table had in the meanwhile been cleared, and was now studded with bottles and glasses, while long clay pipes and tobacco-boxes were handed round. My uncle never smoked, thinking that the habit might darken his teeth, but many of the Corinthians, and the Prince amongst the first of them, set the example of lighting up. All restraint had been done away with, and the prize-fighters, flushed with wine, roared across the tables to each other, or shouted their greetings to friends at the other end of the room. The amateurs, falling into the humour of their company, were hardly less noisy, and loudly debated the merits of the different men, criticising their styles of fighting before their faces, and making bets upon the results of future matches.

In the midst of the uproar there was an imperative rap upon the table, and my uncle rose to speak. As he stood with his pale, calm face and fine figure, I had never seen him to greater advantage, for he seemed, with all his elegance, to have a quiet air of domination amongst these fierce fellows, like a huntsman walking carelessly through a springing and yapping pack. He expressed his pleasure at seeing so many good sportsmen under one roof, and acknowledged the honour which had been done both to his guests and himself by the presence there that night of the illustrious personage whom he should refer to as the Earl of Chester. He was sorry that the season prevented him from placing game upon the table, but there was so much sitting round it that it would perhaps be hardly missed (cheers and laughter). The sports of the Ring had, in his opinion, tended to that contempt of pain and of danger which had contributed so much in

the past to the safety of the country, and which might, if what he heard was true, be very quickly needed once more. If an enemy landed upon our shores it was then that, with our small army, we should be forced to fall back upon native valour trained into hardihood by the practice and contemplation of manly sports. In time of peace also the rules of the Ring had been of service in enforcing the principles of fair play, and in turning public opinion against that use of the knife or of the boot which was so common in foreign countries. He begged, therefore, to drink " Success to the Fancy," coupled with the name of John Jackson, who might stand as a type of all that was most admirable in British boxing.

Jackson having replied with a readiness which many a public man might have envied, my uncle rose once more.

" We are here to-night," said he, " not only to celebrate the past glories of the prize-ring, but also to arrange some sport for the future. It should be easy, now that backers and fighting-men are gathered together under one roof, to come to terms with each other. I have myself set an example by making a match with Sir Lothian Hume, the terms of which will be communicated to you by that gentleman."

Sir Lothian rose with a paper in his hand.

" The terms, your Royal Highness and gentlemen, are briefly these," said he. " My man, Crab Wilson, of Gloucester, having never yet fought a prize battle, is prepared to meet, upon May the 18th of this year, any man of any weight who may be selected by Sir Charles Tregellis. Sir Charles Tregellis's selection is limited to men below twenty or above thirty-five years of age, so as to exclude Belcher and the other candidates for championship honours. The stakes are two thousand pounds against a thousand, two hundred to be paid by the winner to his man ; play or pay."

It was curious to see the intense gravity of them all, fighters and backers, as they bent their brows and weighed the conditions of the match.

" I am informed," said Sir John Lade, " that Crab Wilson's age is twenty-three, and that, although he has never fought a regular P.R. battle, he has none the less fought within ropes for a stake on many occasions."

" I've seen him half a dozen times at the least," said Belcher.

" It is precisely for that reason, Sir John, that I am laying odds of two to one in his favour."

" May I ask," said the Prince, " what the exact height and weight of Wilson may be ? "

" Five foot eleven and thirteen-ten, your Royal Highness."

" Long enough and heavy enough for anything on two legs," said Jackson, and the professionals all murmured their assent.

" Read the rules of the fight, Sir Lothian."

" The battle to take place on Tuesday, May the 18th, at the hour of ten in the morning, at a spot to be afterwards named. The ring to be twenty-foot square. Neither to fall without a knock-down blow, subject to the decision of the umpires. Three umpires to be chosen upon the ground, namely, two in ordinary and one in reference. Does that meet your wishes, Sir Charles ? "

My uncle bowed.

" Have you anything to say, Wilson ? "

The young pugilist, who had a curious, lanky figure, and a craggy, bony face, passed his fingers through his close-cropped hair.

" If you please, zir," said he, with a slight west-country burr, " a twenty-voot ring is too small for a thirteen-stone man."

There was another murmur of professional agreement.

" What would you have it, Wilson ? "

" Vour-an'-twenty, Sir Lothian."

" Have you any objection, Sir Charles ? "

" Not the slightest."

" Anything else, Wilson ? "

" If you please, zir, I'd like to know whom I'm vighting with."

" I understand that you have not publicly nominated your man, Sir Charles ? "

" I do not intend to do so until the very morning of the fight. I believe I have that right within the terms of our wager."

" Certainly, if you choose to exercise it."

" I do so intend. And I should be vastly pleased if Mr. Berkeley Craven will consent to be stake-holder."

That gentleman having willingly given his consent, the final formalities which led up to these humble tournaments were concluded.

And then, as these full-blooded, powerful men became heated with their wine, angry eyes began to glare across the table, and amid the grey swirls of tobacco-smoke the lamp-light gleamed upon the fierce, hawklike Jews, and the flushed, savage Saxons. The old quarrel as to whether Jackson had or had not committed a foul by seizing Mendoza by the hair on the occasion of their battle at Hornchurch, eight years before, came to the front once more. Dutch Sam hurled a shilling down upon the table, and offered to fight the Pride of Westminster for it if he ventured to say that Mendoza had been fairly beaten. Joe Berks, who had grown noisier and more quarrelsome as the evening went on, tried to clamber across the table, with horrible blasphemies, to come to blows with an old Jew named Fighting Yussef, who had plunged into the discussion. It needed very little more to finish the supper by a general and ferocious battle, and it was only the exertions of Jackson, Belcher, Harrison and others of the cooler and steadier men, which saved us from a riot.

And then, when at last this question was set aside, that of the rival claims to championships at different weights came on in its stead, and again angry words flew about and challenges were in the air. There was no exact limit between the light, middle and heavy-weights, and yet it would make a very great difference to the standing of a

boxer whether he should be regarded as the heaviest of the light-weights, or the lightest of the heavy-weights. One claimed to be ten-stone champion, another was ready to take on anything at eleven, but would not run to twelve, which would have brought the invincible Jem Belcher down upon him. Faulkner claimed to be champion of the seniors, and even old Buckhorse's curious call rang out above the tumult as he turned the whole company to laughter and good humour again by challenging anything over eighty and under seven stone.

But in spite of gleams of sunshine, there was thunder in the air, and Champion Harrison had just whispered in my ear that he was quite sure that we should never get through the night without trouble, and was advising me, if it got very bad, to take refuge under the table, when the landlord entered the room hurriedly and handed a note to my uncle.

He read it, and then passed it to the Prince, who returned it with raised eyebrows and a gesture of surprise. Then my uncle rose with the scrap of paper in his hand and a smile upon his lips.

" Gentlemen," said he, " there is a stranger waiting below who desires a fight to a finish with the best man in the room."

11. *The Fight in the Coach-house*

THE curt announcement was followed by a moment of silent surprise, and then by a general shout of laughter. There might be argument as to who was champion at each weight ; but there could be no question that all the champions of all the weights were seated round the tables. An audacious challenge which embraced them one and all, without regard to size or age, could hardly be regarded otherwise than as a joke— but it was a joke which might be a dear one for the joker.

" Is this genuine ? " asked my uncle.

" Yes, Sir Charles," answered the landlord ; " the man is waiting below."

" It's a kid ! " cried several of the fighting-men. " Some cove is a-gammonin' us."

" Don't you believe it," answered the landlord. " He's a real slap-up Corinthian, by his dress ; and he means what he says, or else I ain't no judge of a man."

My uncle whispered for a few moments with the Prince of Wales. " Well, gentlemen," said he, at last, " the night is still young, and if any of you should wish to show the company a little of your skill, you could not ask a better opportunity."

" What weight is he, Bill ? " asked Jem Belcher.

" He's close on six foot, and I should put him well into the thirteen stones when he's buffed."

" Heavy metal ! " cried Jackson. " Who takes him on ? "

They all wanted to, from nine-stone Dutch Sam up-wards. The air was filled with their hoarse shouts and their arguments why each should be the chosen one. To fight when they were flushed with wine and ripe for mischief—above all, to fight before so select a company with the Prince at the ringside, was a chance which did not often come in their way. Only Jackson, Belcher, Mendoza and one or two others of the senior and more famous men remained silent, thinking it beneath their dignity that they should condescend to so irregular a bye-battle.

" Well, you can't all fight him," remarked Jackson, when the babel had died away. " It's for the chairman to choose."

" Perhaps your Royal Highness has a preference," said my uncle.

" By Jove, I'd take him on myself if my position was different," said the Prince, whose face was growing redder and his eyes more glazed. " You've seen me with the mufflers, Jackson ! You know my form ! "

" I've seen your Royal Highness, and I have felt your Royal Highness," said the courtly Jackson.

" Perhaps Jem Belcher would give us an exhibition," said my uncle.

Belcher smiled and shook his handsome head.

" There's my brother Tom here has never been blooded in London yet, sir. He might make a fairer match of it."

" Give him over to me ! " roared Joe Berks. " I've been waitin' for a turn all evenin', an' I'll fight any man that tries to take my place. 'E's my meat, my masters. Leave 'im to me if you want to see 'ow a calf's 'ead should be dressed. If you put Tom Belcher before me I'll fight Tom Belcher, an' for that matter I'll fight Jem Belcher, or Bill Belcher, or any other Belcher that ever came out of Bristol."

It was clear that Berks had got to the stage when he must fight someone. His heavy face was gorged and the veins stood out on his low forehead, while his fierce grey eyes looked viciously from man to man in quest of a quarrel. His great red hands were bunched into huge, gnarled fists, and he shook one of them menacingly as his drunken gaze swept round the tables.

" I think you'll agree with me, gentlemen, that Joe Berks would be all the better for some fresh air and exercise," said my uncle. " With the concurrence of His Royal Highness and of the company, I shall select him as our champion on this occasion."

" You do me proud," cried the fellow, staggering to his feet and pulling at his coat. " If I don't glut him within the five minutes, may I never see Shropshire again."

" Wait a bit, Berks," cried several of the amateurs. " Where's it going to be held ? "

" Where you like, masters. I'll fight him in a sawpit, or on the outside of a coach if it please you. Put us toe to toe, and leave the rest with me."

" They can't fight here with all this litter," said my uncle. " Where shall it be ? "

" 'Pon my soul, Tregellis," cried the Prince, " I think our unknown friend might have a word to say upon that

matter. He'll be vastly ill-used if you don't let him have his own choice of conditions."

" You are right, sir. We must have him up."

" That's easy enough," said the landlord, " for here he comes through the doorway."

I glanced round and had a side view of a tall and well-dressed young man in a long, brown travelling coat and a black felt hat. The next instant he had turned and I had clutched with both my hands on to Champion Harrison's arm.

" Harrison ! " I gasped. " It's Boy Jim ! "

And yet somehow the possibility and even the probability of it had occurred to me from the beginning, and I believe that it had to Harrison also, for I had noticed that his face grew grave and troubled from the very moment that there was talk of the stranger below. Now, the instant that the buzz of surprise and admiration caused by Jim's face and figure had died away, Harrison was on his feet, gesticulating in his excitement.

" It's my nephew Jim, gentlemen," he cried. " He's not twenty yet, and it's no doing of mine that he should be here."

" Let him alone, Harrison," cried Jackson. " He's big enough to take care of himself."

" This matter has gone rather far," said my uncle. " I think, Harrison, that you are too good a sportsman to prevent your nephew from showing whether he takes after his uncle."

" It's very different from me," cried Harrison, in great distress. " But I'll tell you what I'll do, gentlemen. I never thought to stand up in a ring again, but I'll take on Joe Berks with pleasure, just to give a bit o' sport to this company."

Boy Jim stepped across and laid his hand upon the prize-fighter's shoulder.

" It must be so, uncle," I heard him whisper. " I am sorry to go against your wishes, but I have made up my mind, and I must carry it through."

Harrison shrugged his huge shoulders.

" Jim, Jim, you don't know what you are doing ! But I've heard you speak like that before, boy, and I know that it ends in your getting your way."

" I trust, Harrison, that your opposition is withdrawn ? " said my uncle.

" Can I not take his place ? "

" You would not have it said that I gave a challenge and let another carry it out?" whispered Jim. " This is my one chance. For Heaven's sake don't stand in my way."

The smith's broad and usually stolid face was all working with his conflicting emotions. At last he banged his fist down upon the table.

" It's no fault of mine ! " he cried. " It was to be and it is. Jim, boy, for the Lord's sake remember your distances, and stick to out-fightin' with a man that could give you a stone."

" I was sure that Harrison would not stand in the way of sport," said my uncle. " We are glad that you have stepped up, that we might consult you as to the arrangements for giving effect to your very sporting challenge."

" Whom am I to fight ? " asked Jim, looking round at the company, who were now all upon their feet.

" Young man, you'll know enough of who you 'ave to fight before you are through with it," cried Berks, lurching heavily through the crowd. " You'll need a friend to swear to you before I've finished, dy'e see ? "

Jim looked at him with disgust in every line of his face.

" Surely you are not going to set me to fight a drunken man ? " said he. " Where is Jem Belcher ? "

" My name, young man."

" I should be glad to try you, if I may."

" You must work up to me, my lad. You don't take a ladder at one jump, but you do it rung by rung. Show yourself to be a match for me, and I'll give you a turn."

" I'm much obliged to you."

" And I like the look of you, and wish you well," said Belcher, holding out his hand. They were not unlike

each other, either in face or figure, though the Bristol man was a few years the older, and a murmur of critical admiration was heard as the two tall, lithe figures, and keen, clean-cut faces were contrasted.

" Have you any choice where the fight takes place ? " asked my uncle.

" I am in your hands, sir," said Jim.

" Why not go round to the Fives Court ? " suggested Sir John Lade.

" Yes, let us go to the Fives Court."

But this did not at all suit the views of the landlord, who saw in this lucky incident a chance of reaping a fresh harvest from his spendthrift company.

" If it please you," he cried, " there is no need to go so far. My coach-house at the back of the yard is empty, and a better place for a mill you'll never find."

There was a general shout in favour of the coach-house, and those who were nearest the door began to slip through, in the hope of securing the best places. My stout neighbour, Bill Warr, pulled Harrison to one side.

" I'd stop it, if I were you," he whispered.

" I would if I could. It's no wish of mine that he should fight. But there's no turning him when once his mind is made up." All his own fights put together had never reduced the pugilist to such a state of agitation.

" Wait on 'im yourself, then, and chuck up the sponge when things begin to go wrong. You know Joe Berks's record ? "

" He's since my time."

" Well, 'e's a terror, that's all. It's only Belcher that can master 'im. You see the man for yourself, six foot, fourteen stone, and full of the devil. Belcher's beat 'im twice, but the second time 'e 'ad all 'is work to do it."

" Well, well, we've got to go through with it. You've not seen Boy Jim put his mawleys up, or maybe you'd think better of his chances. When he was short of sixteen he licked the Cock of the South Downs, and he's come on a long way since then."

The company was swarming through the door, and clattering down the stair, so we followed in the stream. A fine rain was falling, and the yellow lights from the windows glistened upon the wet cobblestones of the yard. How welcome was that breath of sweet, damp air after the fetid atmosphere of the supper-room. At the other end of the yard was an open door sharply outlined by the gleam of lanterns within, and through this they poured, amateurs and fighting-men jostling each other in their eagerness to get to the front. For my own part, being a smallish man, I should have seen nothing had I not found an upturned bucket in a corner, upon which I perched myself with the wall at my back.

It was a large room with a wooden floor and an open square in the ceiling, which was fringed with the heads of the ostlers and stable boys who were looking down from the harness-room above. A carriage-lamp was slung in each corner, and a very large stable-lantern hung from a rafter in the centre. A coil of rope had been brought in, and under the direction of Jackson four men had been stationed to hold it.

" What space do you give them ? " asked my uncle.

" Twenty-four, as they are both big ones, sir."

" Very good, and half-minutes between rounds, I suppose ? I'll umpire if Sir Lothian Hume will do the same, and you can hold the watch and referee, Jackson."

With great speed and exactness every preparation was rapidly made by these experienced men. Mendoza and Dutch Sam were commissioned to attend to Berks, while Belcher and Jack Harrison did the same for Boy Jim. Sponges, towels and some brandy in a bladder were passed over the heads of the crowd for the use of the seconds.

" Here's our man," cried Belcher. " Come along, Berks, or we'll go to fetch you."

Jim appeared in the ring stripped to the waist, with a coloured handkerchief tied round his middle. A shout of admiration came from the spectators as they looked upon the fine lines of his figure, and I found myself roaring

with the rest. His shoulders were sloping rather than bulky, and his chest was deep rather than broad, but the muscle was all in the right place, rippling down in long, low curves from neck to shoulder, and from shoulder to elbow. His work at the anvil had developed his arms to their utmost, and his healthy country living gave a sleek gloss to his ivory skin, which shone in the lamp-light. His expression was full of spirit and confidence, and he wore a grim sort of half-smile which I had seen many a time in our boyhood, and which meant, I knew, that his pride had set iron hard, and that his senses would fail him long before his courage.

Joe Berks in the meanwhile had swaggered in and stood with folded arms between his seconds in the opposite corner. His face had none of the eager alertness of his opponent, and his skin, of a dead white, with heavy folds about the chest and ribs, showed, even to my in-experienced eyes, that he was not a man who should fight without training. A life of toping and ease had left him flabby and gross. On the other hand, he was famous for his mettle and for his hitting power, so that, even in the face of the advantages of youth and condition, the betting was three to one in his favour. His heavy-jowled, clean-shaven face expressed ferocity as well as courage, and he stood with his small, blood-shot eyes fixed viciously upon Jim, and his lumpy shoulders stooping a little forwards, like a fierce hound straining on a leash.

The hubbub of the betting had risen until it drowned all other sounds, men shouting their opinions from one side of the coach-house to the other, and waving their hands to attract attention, or as a sign that they had accepted a wager. Sir John Lade, standing just in front of me, was roaring out the odds against Jim, and laying them freely with those who fancied the appearance of the unknown.

" I've seen Berks fight," said he to the Honourable Berkeley Craven. " No country hawbuck is going to knock out a man with such a record."

" He may be a country hawbuck," the other answered,
" but I have been reckoned a judge of anything either
on two legs or four, and I tell you, Sir John, that I never
saw a man who looked better bred in my life. Are you
still laying against him ? "

" Three to one."

" Have you once in hundreds."

" Very good, Craven ! There they go ! Berks !
Berks ! Bravo ! Berks ! Bravo ! I think, Craven, that
I shall trouble you for that hundred."

The two men had stood up to each other, Jim as light
upon his feet as a goat, with his left well out and his right
thrown across the lower part of his chest, while Berks
held both arms half extended and his feet almost level,
so that he might lead off with either side. For an instant
they looked each other over, and then Berks, ducking
his head and rushing in with a hand-over-hand style of
hitting, bored Jim down into his corner. It was a backward slip rather than a knock-down, but a thin trickle
of blood was seen at the corner of Jim's mouth. In an
instant the seconds had seized their men and carried
them back into their corners.

" Do you mind doubling our bets ? " said Berkeley
Craven, who was craning his neck to get a glimpse of Jim.

" Four to one on Berks ! Four to one on Berks ! "
cried the ringsiders.

" The odds have gone up, you see. Will you have
four to one in hundreds ? "

" Very good, Sir John."

" You seem to fancy him more for having been knocked
down."

" He was pushed down, but he stopped every blow,
and I liked the look on his face as he got up again."

" Well, it's the old stager for me. Here they come
again ! He's got a pretty style, and he covers his points
well, but it isn't the best looking that wins."

They were at it again, and I was jumping about upon
my bucket in my excitement. It was evident that Berks

meant to finish the battle off-hand, whilst Jim, with two of the most experienced men in England to advise him, was quite aware that his correct tactics were to allow the ruffian to expend his strength and wind in vain. There was something horrible in the ferocious energy of Berks's hitting, every blow fetching a grunt from him as he smashed it in, and after each I gazed at Jim, as I have gazed at a stranded vessel upon the Sussex beach, when wave after wave has roared over it, fearing each time that I should find it miserably mangled. But still the lamp-light shone upon the lad's clear, alert face, upon his well-opened eyes and his firm-set mouth, while the blows were taken upon his forearm or allowed, by a quick duck of the head, to whistle over his shoulder. But Berks was artful as well as violent. Gradually he worked Jim back into an angle of the ropes from which there was no escape, and then, when he had him fairly penned, he sprang upon him like a tiger. What happened was so quick that I cannot set its sequence down in words, but I saw Jim make a quick stoop under the swinging arms, and at the same instant I heard a sharp, ringing smack, and there was Jim dancing about in the middle of the ring, and Berks lying upon his side on the floor, with his hand to his eye.

How they roared! Prize-fighters, Corinthians, Prince, stable-boy and landlord were all shouting at the top of their lungs. Old Buckhorse was skipping about on a box beside me, shrieking out criticisms and advice in strange, obsolete ring-jargon, which no one could understand. His dull eyes were shining, his parchment face was quivering with excitement, and his strange musical call rang out above all the hubbub. The two men were hurried to their corners, one second sponging them down and the other flapping a towel in front of their faces, whilst they, with arms hanging down and legs extended, tried to draw all the air they could into their lungs in the brief space allowed them.

" Where's your country hawbuck now ? " cried

Craven, triumphantly. " Did ever you witness anything more masterly ? "

" He's no Johnny Raw, certainly," said Sir John, shaking his head. " What odds are you giving on Berks, Lord Sele ? "

" Two to one."

" I take you twice in hundreds."

" Here's Sir John Lade hedging ! " cried my uncle, smiling back at us over his shoulder.

" Time ! " said Jackson, and the two men sprang forward to the mark again.

This round was a good deal shorter than that which had preceded it. Berks's orders evidently were to close at any cost, and so make use of his extra weight and strength before the superior condition of his antagonist could have time to tell. On the other hand, Jim, after his experience in the last round, was less disposed to make any great exertion to keep him at arms' length. He led at Berks's head, as he came rushing in, and missed him, receiving a severe body blow in return, which left the imprint of four angry knuckles above his ribs. As they closed Jim caught his opponent's bullet head under his arm for an instant, and put a couple of half-arm blows in ; but the prize-fighter pulled him over by his weight, and the two fell panting side by side upon the ground. Jim sprang up, however, and walked over to his corner, while Berks, distressed by his evening's dissipation, leaned one arm upon Mendoza and the other upon Dutch Sam as he made for his seat.

" Bellows to mend ! " cried Jem Belcher. " Where's the four to one now ? "

" Give us time to get the lid off our pepper-box," said Mendoza. " We mean to make a night of it."

" Looks like it," said Jack Harrison. " He's shut one of his eyes already. Even money that my boy wins it ! "

" How much ? " asked several voices.

" Two pound four and threepence," cried Harrison, counting out all his worldly wealth.

" Time ! " said Jackson once more.

They were both at the mark in an instant, Jim as full of sprightly confidence as ever, and Berks with a fixed grin upon his bull-dog face and a most vicious gleam in the only eye which was of use to him. His half-minute had not enabled him to recover his breath, and his huge hairy chest was rising and falling with a quick, loud panting like a spent hound. " Go in, boy ! Bustle him ! " roared Harrison and Belcher. " Get your wind, Joe ; get your wind ! " cried the Jews. So now we had a reversal of tactics, for it was Jim who went in to hit with all the vigour of his young strength and unimpaired energy, while it was the savage Berks who was paying his debt to Nature for the many injuries which he had done her. He gasped, he gurgled, his face grew purple in his attempts to get his breath, while with his long left arm extended and his right thrown across, he tried to screen himself from the attack of his wiry antagonist. " Drop when he hits ! " cried Mendoza. " Drop and have a rest ! "

But there was no shyness or shiftiness about Berks's fighting. He was always a gallant ruffian, who disdained to go down before an antagonist as long as his legs would sustain him. He propped Jim off with his long arm, and though the lad sprang lightly round him looking for an opening, he was held off as if a forty-inch bar of iron were between them. Every instant now was in favour of Berks, and already his breathing was easier and the bluish tinge fading from his face. Jim knew that his chance of a speedy victory was slipping away from him, and he came back again and again as swift as a flash to the attack without being able to get past the passive defence of the trained fighting-man. It was at such a moment that ringcraft was needed, and luckily for Jim two masters of it were at his back.

" Get your left on his mark, boy," they shouted, " then go to his head with the right."

Jim heard and acted on the instant. Plunk ! came his

left just where his antagonist's ribs curved from his
breast-bone. The force of the blow was half broken by
Berks's elbow, but it served its purpose of bringing forward his head. Spank ! went the right, with the clear,
crisp sound of two billiard balls clapping together, and
Berks reeled, flung up his arms, spun round, and fell in
a huge, fleshy heap upon the floor. His seconds were
on him instantly, and propped him up in a sitting position,
his head rolling helplessly from one shoulder to the other,
and finally toppling backwards with his chin pointed to
the ceiling. Dutch Sam thrust the brandy-bladder between his teeth, while Mendoza shook him savagely and
howled insults in his ear, but neither the spirits nor the
sense of injury could break into that serene insensibility.
" Time ! " was duly called, and the Jews, seeing that the
affair was over, let their man's head fall back with a crack
upon the floor, and there he lay, his huge arms and legs
asprawl, whilst the Corinthians and fighting-men crowded
past him to shake the hand of his conqueror.

For my part, I tried also to press through the throng,
but it was no easy task for one of the smallest and weakest
men in the room. On all sides of me I heard a brisk
discussion from amateurs and professionals of Jim's
performance and of his prospects.

" He's the best bit of new stuff that I've seen since
Jem Belcher fought his first fight with Paddington Jones
at Wormwood Scrubbs four years ago last April," said
Berkeley Craven. " You'll see him with the belt round
his waist before he's five-and-twenty, or I am no judge
of a man."

" That handsome face of his has cost me a cool five
hundred," grumbled Sir John Lade. " Who'd have
thought he was such a punishing hitter ? "

" For all that," said another, " I am confident that if
Joe Berks had been sober he would have beaten him.
Besides, the lad was in training, and the other would
burst like an overdone potato if he were hit. I never
saw a man so soft, or with his wind in such condition.

Put the men in training, and it's a horse to a hen on the bruiser."

Some agreed with the last speaker and some were against him, so that a brisk argument was being carried on around me. In the midst of it the Prince took his departure, which was the signal for the greater part of the company to make for the door. In this way I was able at last to reach the corner where Jim had just finished his dressing, while Champion Harrison, with tears of joy still shining upon his cheeks, was helping him on with his overcoat.

" In four rounds ! " he kept repeating in a sort of an ecstasy. " Joe Berks in four rounds ! And it took Jem Belcher fourteen ! "

" Well, Roddy," cried Jim, holding out his hand, " I told you that I would come to London and make my name known."

" It was splendid, Jim ! "

" Dear old Roddy ! I saw your white face staring at me from the corner. You are not changed, for all your grand clothes and your London friends."

" It is you who are changed, Jim," said I ; " I hardly knew you when you came into the room."

" Nor I," cried the smith. " Where got you all these fine feathers, Jim ? Sure I am that it was not your aunt who helped you to the first step towards the prize-ring."

" Miss Hinton has been my friend—the best friend I ever had."

" Humph ! I thought as much," grumbled the smith. " Well, it is no doing of mine, Jim, and you must bear witness to that when we go home again. I don't know what—but, there, it is done, and it can't be helped. After all, she's—— Now, the deuce take my clumsy tongue ! "

I could not tell whether it was the wine which he had taken at supper or the excitement of Boy Jim's victory which was affecting Harrison, but his usually placid face wore a most disturbed expression, and his manner

seemed to betray an alternation of exultation and embarrassment. Jim looked curiously at him, wondering evidently what it was that lay behind these abrupt sentences and sudden silences. The coach-house had in the meantime been cleared ; Berks with many curses had staggered at last to his feet, and had gone off in company with two other bruisers, while Jem Belcher alone remained chatting very earnestly with my uncle.

" Very good, Belcher," I heard my uncle say.

" It would be a real pleasure to me to do it, sir," said the famous prize-fighter, as the two walked towards us.

" I wished to ask you, Jim Harrison, whether you would undertake to be my champion in the fight against Crab Wilson of Gloucester ? " said my uncle.

" That is what I want, Sir Charles—to have a chance of fighting my way upwards."

" There are heavy stakes upon the event—very heavy stakes," said my uncle. " You will receive two hundred pounds, if you win. Does that satisfy you ? "

" I shall fight for the honour, and because I wish to be thought worthy of being matched against Jem Belcher."

Belcher laughed good-humouredly.

" You are going the right way about it, lad," said he. " But you had a soft thing on to-night with a drunken man who was out of condition."

" I did not wish to fight him," said Jim, flushing.

" Oh, I know you have spirit enough to fight anything on two legs. I knew that the instant I clapped eyes on you ; but I want you to remember that when you fight Crab Wilson, you will fight the most promising man from the west, and that the best man of the west is likely to be the best man in England. He's as quick and as long in the reach as you are, and he'll train himself to the last half-ounce of tallow. I tell you this now, d'ye see, because if I'm to have the charge of you——"

" Charge of me ! "

" Yes," said my uncle. " Belcher has consented to train you for the coming battle if you are willing to enter."

" I am sure I am very much obliged to you," cried Jim, heartily. " Unless my uncle should wish to train me, there is no one I would rather have."

" Nay, Jim ; I'll stay with you a few days, but Belcher knows a deal more about training than I do. Where will the quarters be ? "

" I thought it would be handy for you if we fixed it at the George, at Crawley. Then, if we have choice of place, we might choose Crawley Down, for, except Molesey Hurst, and, maybe, Smitham Bottom, there isn't a spot in the country that would compare with it for a mill. Do you agree with that ? "

" With all my heart," said Jim.

" Then you're my man from this hour on, d'ye see ? " said Belcher. " Your food is mine, and your drink is mine, and your sleep is mine, and all you've to do is just what you are told. We haven't an hour to lose, for Wilson has been in half-training this month back. You saw his empty glass to-night."

" Jim's fit to fight for his life at the present moment," said Harrison. " But we'll both come down to Crawley to-morrow. So good night, Sir Charles."

" Good night, Roddy," said Jim. " You'll come down to Crawley and see me at my training quarters, will you not ? "

And I heartily promised that I would.

" You must be more careful, nephew," said my uncle, as we rattled home in his model *vis-à-vis*. " *En première jeunesse* one is a little inclined to be ruled by one's heart rather than by one's reason. Jim Harrison seems to be a most respectable young fellow, but after all he is a blacksmith's apprentice, and a candidate for the prize-ring. There is a vast gap between his position and that of my own blood relation, and you must let him feel that you are his superior."

" He is the oldest and dearest friend that I have in the world, sir," I answered. " We were boys together, and have never had a secret from each other. As to showing

him that I am his superior, I don't know how I can do that, for I know very well that he is mine."

"Hum!" said my uncle, drily, and it was the last word that he addressed to me that night.

12. *The Coffee-room of Fladong's*

SO Boy Jim went down to the George, at Crawley, under the charge of Jem Belcher and Champion Harrison, to train for his great fight with Crab Wilson, of Gloucester, whilst every club and bar parlour of London rang with the account of how he had appeared at a supper of Corinthians, and beaten the formidable Joe Berks in four rounds. I remembered that afternoon at Friar's Oak when Jim had told me that he would make his name known, and his words had come true sooner than he could have expected it, for, go where one might, one heard of nothing but the match between Sir Lothian Hume and Sir Charles Tregellis, and the points of the two probable combatants. The betting was still steadily in favour of Wilson, for he had a number of bye-battles to set against this single victory of Jim's, and it was thought by connoisseurs who had seen him spar that the singular defensive tactics which had given him his nickname would prove very puzzling to a raw antagonist. In height, strength and reputation for gameness there was very little to choose between them, but Wilson had been the more severely tested.

It was but a few days before the battle that my father made his promised visit to London. The seaman had no love of cities, and was happier wandering over the Downs, and turning his glass upon every topsail which showed above the horizon, than when finding his way among crowded streets, where, as he complained, it was impossible to keep a course by the sun, and hard enough by dead reckoning. Rumours of war were in the air, however, and it was necessary that he should use his

influence with Lord Nelson if a vacancy were to be found either for himself or for me.

My uncle had just set forth, as was his custom of an evening, clad in his green riding-frock, his plate buttons, his Cordovan boots and his round hat, to show himself upon his crop-tailed tit in the Mall. I had remained behind, for, indeed, I had already made up my mind that I had no calling for this fashionable life. These men, with their small waists, their gestures and their unnatural ways, had become wearisome to me, and even my uncle, with his cold and patronising manner, filled me with very mixed feelings. My thoughts were back in Sussex, and I was dreaming of the kindly, simple ways of the country, when there came a rat-tat at the knocker, the ring of a hearty voice, and there, in the doorway, was the smiling, weather-beaten face, with the puckered eyelids and the light blue eyes.

" Why, Roddy, you are grand indeed ! " he cried. " But I had rather see you with the King's blue coat upon your back than with all these frills and ruffles."

" And I had rather wear it, father."

" It warms my heart to hear you say so. Lord Nelson has promised me that he would find a berth for you, and to-morrow we shall seek him out and remind him of it. But where is your uncle ? "

" He is riding in the Mall."

A look of relief passed over my father's honest face, for he was never very easy in his brother-in-law's company. " I have been to the Admiralty," said he, " and I trust that I shall have a ship when war breaks out ; by all accounts it will not be long first. Lord St. Vincent told me so with his own lips. But I am at Fladong's, Rodney, where, if you will come and sup with me, you will see some of my messmates from the Mediterranean."

When you think that in the last year of the war we had 140,000 seamen and mariners afloat, commanded by 4,000 officers, and that half of these had been turned adrift when the Peace of Amiens laid their ships up in

the Hamoaze or Portsdown creek, you will understand that London, as well as the dockyard towns, was full of seafarers. You could not walk the streets without catching sight of the gipsy-faced, keen-eyed men whose plain clothes told of their thin purses as plainly as their listless air showed their weariness of a life of forced and unaccustomed inaction. Amid the dark streets and brick houses there was something out of place in their appearance, as when the sea-gulls, driven by stress of weather, are seen in the Midland shires. Yet while prize-courts procrastinated, or there was a chance of an appointment by showing their sunburned faces at the Admiralty, so long they would continue to pace with their quarter-deck strut down Whitehall, or to gather of an evening to discuss the events of the last war or chances of the next at Fladong's, in Oxford Street, which was reserved as entirely for the Navy as Slaughter's was for the Army, or Ibbetson's for the Church of England.

It did not surprise me, therefore, that we should find the large room in which we supped crowded with naval men, but I remember that what did cause me some astonishment was to observe that all these sailors, who had served under the most varying conditions in all quarters of the globe, from the Baltic to the East Indies, should have been moulded into so uniform a type that they were more like each other than brother is commonly to brother. The rules of the service ensured that every face should be clean-shaven, every head powdered, and every neck covered by the little queue of natural hair tied with a black silk ribbon. Biting winds and tropical suns had combined to darken them, whilst the habit of command and the menace of ever-recurring dangers had stamped them all with the same expression of authority and of alertness. There were some jovial faces amongst them, but the older officers, with their deep-lined cheeks and their masterful noses, were, for the most part, as austere as so many weather-beaten ascetics from the desert. Lonely watches, and a discipline which cut them

off from all companionship, had left their mark upon those Red Indian faces. For my part, I could hardly eat my supper for watching them. Young as I was, I knew that if there were any freedom left in Europe it was to these men that we owed it ; and I seemed to read upon their grim, harsh features the record of that long ten years of struggle which had swept the tricolour from the seas.

When we had finished our supper, my father led me into the great coffee-room, where a hundred or more officers may have been assembled, drinking their wine and smoking their long clay pipes, until the air was as thick as the main-deck in a close-fought action. As we entered we found ourselves face to face with an elderly officer who was coming out. He was a man with large, thoughtful eyes, and a full, placid face—such a face as one would expect from a philosopher and a philanthropist rather than from a fighting seaman.

" Here's Cuddie Collingwood," whispered my father.

" Halloa, Lieutenant Stone ! " cried the famous admiral very cheerily. " I have scarce caught a glimpse of you since you came aboard the *Excellent* after St. Vincent. You had the luck to be at the Nile also, I understand ? "

" I was third of the *Theseus*, under Miller, sir."

" It nearly broke my heart to have missed it. I have not yet outlived it. To think of such a gallant service, and I engaged in harassing the market-boats, the miserable cabbage-carriers of St. Luccars ! "

" Your plight was better than mine, Sir Cuthbert," said a voice from behind us, and a large man in the full uniform of a post-captain took a step forward to include himself in our circle. His mastiff face was heavy with emotion, and he shook his head miserably as he spoke.

" Yes, yes, Troubridge, I can understand and sympathise with your feelings."

" I passed through torment that night, Collingwood. It left a mark on me that I shall never lose until I go over the ship's side in a canvas cover. To have my beautiful *Culloden* laid on a sandbank just out of gunshot. To

hear and see the fight the whole night through, and never to pull a lanyard or take the tompions out of my guns. Twice I opened my pistol-case to blow out my brains, and it was but the thought that Nelson might have a use for me that held me back."

Collingwood shook the hand of the unfortunate captain.

" Admiral Nelson was not long in finding a use for you, Troubridge," said he. " We have all heard of your siege of Capua, and how you ran up your ship's guns without trenches or parallels, and fired point-blank through the embrasures."

The melancholy cleared away from the massive face of the big seaman, and his deep laughter filled the room.

" I'm not clever enough or slow enough for their Z-Z fashions," said he. " We got alongside and slapped it in through their port-holes until they struck their colours. But where have you been, Sir Cuthbert ? "

" With my wife and my two little lasses at Morpeth in the North Country. I have but seen them this once in ten years, and it may be ten more, for all I know, ere I see them again. I have been doing good work for the fleet up yonder."

" I had thought, sir, that it was inland," said my father.

Collingwood took a little black bag out of his pocket and shook it.

" Inland it is," said he, " and yet I have done good work for the fleet there. What do you suppose I hold in this bag ? "

" Bullets," said Troubridge.

" Something that a sailor needs even more than that," answered the admiral, and turning it over he tilted a pile of acorns on to his palm. " I carry them with me in my country walks, and where I see a fruitful nook I thrust one deep with the end of my cane. My oak trees may fight those rascals over the water when I am long forgotten. Do you know, lieutenant, how many oaks go to make an eighty-gun ship ? "

My father shook his head.

"Two thousand, no less. For every two-decked ship that carries the white ensign there is a grove the less in England. So how are our grandsons to beat the French if we do not give them the trees with which to build their ships?"

He replaced his bag in his pocket, and then, passing his arm through Troubridge's, they went through the door together.

"There's a man whose life might help you to trim your own course," said my father, as we took our seats at a vacant table. "He is ever the same quiet gentleman, with his thoughts busy for the comfort of his ship's company, and his heart with his wife and children whom he has so seldom seen. It is said in the fleet that an oath has never passed his lips, Rodney, though how he managed when he was first lieutenant of a raw crew is more than I can conceive. But they all love Cuddie, for they know he's an angel to fight. How d'ye do, Captain Foley? My respects, Sir Ed'ard! Why, if they could but press the company, they would man a corvette with flag officers.

"There's many a man here, Rodney," continued my father, as he glanced about him, "whose name may never find its way into any book save his own ship's log, but who in his own way has set as fine an example as any admiral of them all. We know them, and talk of them in the fleet, though they may never be bawled in the streets of London. There's as much seamanship and pluck in a good cutter action as in a line-o'-battleship fight, though you may not come by a title nor the thanks of Parliament for it. There's Hamilton, for example, the quiet, pale-faced man who is leaning against the pillar. It was he who, with six rowing-boats, cut out the 44-gun frigate *Hermione* from under the muzzles of two hundred shore-guns in the harbour of Puerto Cabello. No finer action was done in the whole war. There's Jaheel Brenton, with the whiskers. It was he who

attacked twelve Spanish gunboats in his one little brig, and made four of them strike to him. There's Walker, of the *Rose* cutter, who, with thirteen men, engaged three French privateers with crews of a hundred and forty-six. He sank one, captured one, and chased the third. How are you, Captain Ball ? I hope I see you well ? "

Two or three of my father's acquaintances who had been sitting close by drew up their chairs to us, and soon quite a circle had formed, all talking loudly and arguing upon sea matters, shaking their long, red-tipped pipes at each other as they spoke. My father whispered in my ear that his neighbour was Captain Foley, of the *Goliath*, who led the van at the Nile, and that the tall, thin, foxy-haired man opposite was Lord Cochrane, the most dashing frigate captain in the Service. Even at Friar's Oak we had heard how, in the little *Speedy*, of fourteen small guns with fifty-four men, he had carried by boarding the Spanish frigate *Gamo* with her crew of three hundred. It was easy to see that he was a quick, irascible, high-blooded man, for he was talking hotly about his grievances with a flush of anger upon his freckled cheeks.

" We shall never do any good upon the ocean until we have hanged the dockyard contractors," he cried. " I'd have a dead dockyard contractor as a figure-head for every first-rate in the fleet, and a provision dealer for every frigate. I know them with their puttied seams and their devil bolts, risking five hundred lives that they may steal a few pounds' worth of copper. What became of the *Chance*, and of the *Martin*, and of the *Orestes* ? They foundered at sea, and were never heard of more, and I say the crews of them were murdered men."

Lord Cochrane seemed to be expressing the views of all, for a murmur of assent, with a mutter of hearty, deep-sea curses, ran round the circle.

" Those rascals over yonder manage things better," said an old one-eyed captain, with the blue-and-white riband for St. Vincent peeping out of his third button-hole. " They sheer away their heads if they get up to

any foolery. Did ever a vessel come out of Toulon as my 38-gun frigate did from Plymouth last year, with her masts rolling about until her shrouds were like iron bars on one side and hanging in festoons upon the other ? The meanest sloop that ever sailed out of France would have overmatched her, and then it would be on me, and not on this Devonport bungler, that a court-martial would be called."

They loved to grumble, those old salts, for as soon as one had shot off his grievance his neighbour would follow with another, each more bitter than the last.

" Look at our sails ! " cried Captain Foley. " Put a French and a British ship at anchor together, and how can you tell which is which ? "

" Frenchy has his fore and maintop-gallant masts about equal," said my father.

" In the old ships, maybe, but how many of the new are laid down on the French model ? No, there's no way of telling them at anchor. But let them hoist sail, and how d'you tell them then ? "

" Frenchy has white sails," cried several.

" And ours are black and rotten. That's the difference. No wonder they outsail us when the wind can blow through our canvas."

" In the *Speedy*," said Cochrane, " the sailcloth was so thin that, when I made my observation, I always took my meridian through the foretopsail and my horizon through the foresail."

There was a general laugh at this, and then at it they all went again, letting off into speech all those weary broodings and silent troubles which had rankled during long years of service, for an iron discipline prevented them from speaking when their feet were upon their own quarter-decks. One told of his powder, six pounds of which were needed to throw a ball a thousand yards. Another cursed the Admiralty Courts, where a prize goes in as a full-rigged ship and comes out as a schooner. The old captain spoke of the promotions by Parliamentary

interest which had put many a youngster into the captain's cabin when he should have been in the gun-room. And then they came back to the difficulty of finding crews for their vessels, and they all together raised up their voices and wailed.

"What is the use of building fresh ships," cried Foley, "when even with a ten-pound bounty you can't man the ships that you have got?"

But Lord Cochrane was on the other side in this question.

"You'd have the men, sir, if you treated them well when you got them," said he. "Admiral Nelson can get his ships manned. So can Admiral Collingwood. Why? Because he has thought for the men, and so the men have thought for him. Let men and officers know and respect each other, and there's no difficulty in keeping a ship's company. It's the infernal plan of turning a crew over from ship to ship and leaving the officers behind that rots the Navy. But I have never found a difficulty, and I dare swear that if I hoist my pennant to-morrow I shall have all my old *Speedies* back, and as many volunteers as I care to take."

"That is very well, my lord," said the old captain, with some warmth; "when the Jacks hear that the *Speedy* took fifty vessels in thirteen months, they are sure to volunteer to serve with her commander. Every good cruiser can fill her complement quickly enough. But it is not the cruisers that fight the country's battles and blockade the enemy's ports. I say that all prize-money should be divided equally among the whole fleet, and until you have such a rule, the smartest men will always be found where they are of least service to anyone but themselves."

This speech produced a chorus of protests from the cruisers officers and a hearty agreement from the line-of-battleship men, who seemed to be in the majority in the circle which had gathered round. From the flushed faces and angry glances it was evident that the question

was one upon which there was strong feeling upon both sides.

"What the cruiser gets the cruiser earns," cried a frigate captain.

"Do you mean to say, sir," said Captain Foley, "that the duties of an officer upon a cruiser demand more care or higher professional ability than those of one who is employed upon blockade service, with a lee coast under him whenever the wind shifts to the west, and the topmasts of an enemy's squadron for ever in his sight?"

"I do not claim higher ability, sir."

"Then why should you claim higher pay? Can you deny that a seaman before the mast makes more in a fast frigate than a lieutenant can in a battle-ship?"

"It was only last year," said a very gentlemanly-looking officer, who might have passed for a buck upon town had his skin not been burned to copper in such sunshine as never bursts upon London—"it was only last year that I brought the old *Alexander* back from the Mediterranean, floating like an empty barrel and carrying nothing but honour for her cargo. In the Channel we fell in with the frigate *Minerva* from the Western Ocean, with her lee ports under water and her hatches bursting with the plunder which had been too valuable to trust to the prize crews. She had ingots of silver along her yards and bowsprit, and a bit of silver plate at the truck of the masts. My Jacks could have fired into her, and would, too, if they had not been held back. It made them mad to think of all they had done in the south, and then to see this saucy frigate flashing her money before their eyes."

"I cannot see their grievance, Captain Ball," said Cochrane.

"When you are promoted to a two-decker, my lord, it will possibly become clearer to you."

"You speak as if a cruiser had nothing to do but take prizes. If that is your view, you will permit me to say that you know very little of the matter. I have handled a sloop, a corvette and a frigate, and I have found a great

variety of duties in each of them. I have had to avoid the enemy's battle-ships and to fight his cruisers. I have had to chase and capture his privateers, and to cut them out when they run under his batteries. I have had to engage his forts, to take my men ashore, and to destroy his guns and his signal stations. All this, with convoying, reconnoitring, and risking one's own ship in order to gain a knowledge of the enemy's movements, comes under the duties of the commander of a cruiser. I make bold to say that the man who can carry these objects out with success has deserved better of the country than the officer of a battle-ship, tacking from Ushant to the Black Rocks and back again until she builds up a reef with her beef-bones."

" Sir," said the angry old sailor, " such an officer is at least in no danger of being mistaken for a privateersman."

" I am surprised, Captain Bulkeley," Cochrane retorted hotly, " that you should venture to couple the names of privateersman and King's officer."

There was mischief brewing among these hot-headed, short-spoken salts, but Captain Foley changed the subject to discuss the new ships which were being built in the French ports. It was of interest to me to hear these men, who were spending their lives in fighting against our neighbours, discussing their character and ways. You cannot conceive—you who live in times of peace and charity—how fierce the hatred was in England at that time against the French, and above all against their great leader. It was more than a mere prejudice or dislike. It was a deep, aggressive loathing of which you may even now form some conception if you examine the papers or caricatures of the day. The word " Frenchman " was hardly spoken without " rascal " or " scoundrel " slipping in before it. In all ranks of life and in every part of the country the feeling was the same. Even the Jacks aboard our ships fought with a viciousness against a French vessel which they would never show to Dane, Dutchman or Spaniard.

If you ask me now, after fifty years, why it was that there should have been this virulent feeling against them, so foreign to the easy-going and tolerant British nature, I would confess that I think the real reason was fear. Not fear of them individually, of course—our foulest detractors have never called us faint-hearted—but fear of their star, fear of their future, fear of the subtle brain whose plans always seemed to go aright, and of the heavy hand which had struck nation after nation to the ground. We were but a small country, with a population which, when the war began, was not much more than half that of France. And then, France had increased by leaps and bounds, reaching out to the north into Belgium and Holland, and to the south into Italy, whilst we were weakened by deep-lying disaffection among both Catholics and Presbyterians in Ireland. The danger was imminent and plain to the least thoughtful. One could not walk the Kent coast without seeing the beacons heaped up to tell the country of the enemy's landing, and if the sun were shining on the uplands near Boulogne, one might catch the flash of its gleam upon the bayonets of manœuvring veterans. No wonder that a fear of the French power lay deeply in the hearts of the most gallant men, and that fear should, as it always does, beget a bitter and rancorous hatred.

The seamen did not speak kindly then of their recent enemies. Their hearts loathed them, and in the fashion of our country their lips said what the heart felt. Of the French officers they could not have spoken with more chivalry, as of worthy foemen, but the nation was an abomination to them. The older men had fought against them in the American War, they had fought again for the last ten years, and the dearest wish of their hearts seemed to be that they might be called upon to do the same for the remainder of their days. Yet if I was surprised by the virulence of their animosity against the French, I was even more so to hear how highly they rated them as antagonists. The long succession of British

victories which had finally made the French take to their ports and resign the struggle in despair had given all of us the idea that for some reason a Briton on the water must, in the nature of things, always have the best of it against a Frenchman. But these men who had done the fighting did not think so. They were loud in their praise of their foemen's gallantry, and precise in their reasons for his defeat. They showed how the officers of the old French Navy had nearly all been aristocrats. How the Revolution had swept them out of their ships, and the force been left with insubordinate seamen and no competent leaders. This ill-directed fleet had been hustled into port by the pressure of the well-manned and well-commanded British, who had pinned them there ever since, so that they had never had an opportunity of learning seamanship. Their harbour drill and their harbour gunnery had been of no service when sails had to be trimmed and broadsides fired on the heave of an Atlantic swell. Let one of their frigates get to sea and have a couple of years' free run in which the crew might learn their duties, and then it would be a feather in the cap of a British officer if with a ship of equal force he could bring down her colours.

Such were the views of these experienced officers, fortified by many reminiscences and examples of French gallantry, such as the way in which the crew of the *L'Orient* had fought her quarter-deck guns when the main-deck was in a blaze beneath them, and when they must have known that they were standing over an exploding magazine. The general hope was that the West Indian expedition since the peace might have given many of their fleet an ocean training, and that they might be tempted out into mid-Channel if the war were to break out afresh. But would it break out afresh? We had spent gigantic sums and made enormous exertions to curb the power of Napoleon and to prevent him from becoming the universal despot of Europe. Would the Government try it again? Or were they appalled by

the gigantic load of debt which must bend the backs of many generations unborn? Pitt was there, and surely he was not a man to leave his work half done.

And then suddenly there was a bustle at the door. Amid the grey swirl of the tobacco-smoke I could catch a glimpse of a blue coat and gold epaulettes, with a crowd gathering thickly round them, while a hoarse murmur rose from the group which thickened into a deep-chested cheer. Everyone was on his feet, peering and asking each other what it might mean. And still the crowd seethed and the cheering swelled.

"What is it? What has happened?" cried a score of voices.

"Put him up! Hoist him up!" shouted somebody, and an instant later I saw Captain Troubridge appear above the shoulders of the crowd. His face was flushed, as if he were in wine, and he was waving what seemed to be a letter in the air. The cheering died away, and there was such a hush that I could hear the crackle of the paper in his hand.

"Great news, gentlemen!" he roared. "Glorious news! Rear-Admiral Collingwood has directed me to communicate it to you. The French Ambassador has received his papers to-night. Every ship on the list is to go into commission. Admiral Cornwallis is ordered out of Cawsand Bay to cruise off Ushant. A squadron is starting for the North Sea and another for the Irish Channel."

He may have had more to say, but his audience could wait no longer. How they shouted and stamped and raved in their delight! Harsh old flag-officers, grave post-captains, young lieutenants, all were roaring like schoolboys breaking up for the holidays. There was no thought now of those manifold and weary grievances to which I had listened. The foul weather was passed, and the landlocked sea-birds would be out on the foam once more. The rhythm of " God Save the King " swelled through the babel, and I heard the old lines sung in a

way that made you forget their bad rhymes and their bald sentiments. I trust that you will never hear them so sung, with tears upon rugged cheeks, and catchings of the breath from strong men. Dark days will have come again before you hear such a song or see such a sight as that. Let those talk of the phlegm of our countrymen who have never seen them when the lava crust of restraint is broken, and when for an instant the strong, enduring fires of the North glow upon the surface. I saw them then, and if I do not see them now, I am not so old or so foolish as to doubt that they are there.

13. *Lord Nelson*

MY father's appointment with Lord Nelson was an early one, and he was the more anxious to be punctual as he knew how much the Admiral's movements must be affected by the news which we had heard the night before. I had hardly breakfasted then, and my uncle had not rung for his chocolate, when he called for me at Jermyn Street. A walk of a few hundred yards brought us to the high building of discoloured brick in Piccadilly, which served the Hamiltons as a town house, and which Nelson used as his headquarters when business or pleasure called him from Merton. A footman answered our knock, and we were ushered into a large drawing-room with sombre furniture and melancholy curtains. My father sent in his name, and there we sat, looking at the white Italian statuettes in the corners, and the picture of Vesuvius and the Bay of Naples which hung over the harpsichord. I can remember that a black clock was ticking loudly upon the mantelpiece, and that every now and then, amid the rumble of the hackney coaches, we could hear boisterous laughter from some inner chamber.

When at last the door opened, both my father and I sprang to our feet, expecting to find ourselves face to

face with the greatest living Englishman. It was a very different person, however, who swept into the room.

She was a lady, tall, and, as it seemed to me, exceedingly beautiful, though, perhaps, one who was more experienced and more critical might have thought that her charm lay in the past rather than the present. Her queenly figure was moulded upon large and noble lines, while her face, though already tending to become somewhat heavy and coarse, was still remarkable for the brilliancy of the complexion, the beauty of the large, light blue eyes, and the tinge of the dark hair which curled over the low white forehead. She carried herself in the most stately fashion, so that as I looked at her majestic entrance, and at the pose which she struck as she glanced at my father, I was reminded of the Queen of the Peruvians as, in the person of Miss Polly Hinton, she incited Boy Jim and myself to insurrection.

" Lieutenant Anson Stone ? " she asked.

" Yes, your ladyship," answered my father.

" Ah," she cried, with an affected and exaggerated start, " you know me, then ? "

" I have seen your ladyship at Naples."

" Then you have doubtless seen my poor Sir William also—my poor, poor Sir William ! " She touched her dress with her white, ring-covered fingers, as if to draw our attention to the fact that she was in the deepest mourning.

" I heard of your ladyship's sad loss," said my father.

" We died together," she cried. " What can my life be now save a long-drawn living death ? "

She spoke in a beautiful, rich voice, with the most heart-broken thrill in it, but I could not conceal from myself that she appeared to be one of the most robust persons that I had ever seen, and I was surprised to notice that she shot arch little questioning glances at me, as if the admiration even of so insignificant a person were of some interest to her. My father, in his blunt, sailor fashion, tried to stammer out some commonplace

condolence, but her eyes swept past his rude, weather-beaten face to ask and re-ask what effect she had made upon me.

"There he hangs, the tutelary angel of this house," she cried, pointing with a grand sweeping gesture to a painting upon the wall, which represented a very thin-faced, high-nosed gentleman with several orders upon his coat. "But enough of my private sorrow!" She dashed invisible tears from her eyes. "You have come to see Lord Nelson. He bid me say that he would be with you in an instant. You have doubtless heard that hostilities are about to reopen?"

"We heard the news last night."

"Lord Nelson is under orders to take command of the Mediterranean Fleet. You can think at such a moment——. But, ah, is it not his lordship's step that I hear?"

My attention was so riveted by the lady's curious manner and by the gestures and attitudes with which she accompanied every remark, that I did not see the great admiral enter the room. When I turned he was standing close by my elbow, a small, brown man with the lithe, slim figure of a boy. He was not clad in uniform, but he wore a high-collared brown coat, with the right sleeve hanging limp and empty by his side. The expression of his face was, as I remember it, exceedingly sad and gentle, with the deep lines upon it which told of the chafing of his urgent and fiery soul. One eye was disfigured and sightless from a wound, but the other looked from my father to myself with the quickest and shrewdest of expressions. Indeed, his whole manner, with his short, sharp glance and the fine poise of the head, spoke of energy and alertness, so that he reminded me, if I may compare great things with small, of a well-bred fighting terrier, gentle and slim, but keen and ready for whatever chance might send.

"Why, Lieutenant Stone," said he, with great cordiality, holding out his left hand to my father, "I am very

glad to see you. London is full of Mediterranean men, but I trust that in a week there will not be an officer amongst you all with his feet on dry land."

" I had come to ask you, sir, if you could assist me to a ship."

" You shall have one, Stone, if my word goes for anything at the Admiralty. I shall want all my old Nile men at my back. I cannot promise you a first-rate, but at least it shall be a 64-gun ship, and I can tell you that there is much to be done with a handy, well-manned, well-found 64-gun ship."

" Who could doubt it who has heard of the *Agamemnon* ? " cried Lady Hamilton, and straightway she began to talk of the admiral and of his doings with such extravagance of praise and such a shower of compliments and of epithets, that my father and I did not know which way to look, feeling shame and sorrow for a man who was compelled to listen to such things said in his own presence. But when I ventured to glance at Lord Nelson, I found, to my surprise, that, far from showing any embarrassment, he was smiling with pleasure, as if this gross flattery of her ladyship's were the dearest thing in all the world to him.

" Come, come, my dear lady," said he, " you speak vastly beyond my merits " ; upon which encouragement she started again in a theatrical apostrophe to Britain's darling and Neptune's eldest son, which he endured with the same signs of gratitude and pleasure. That a man of the world, five-and-forty years of age, shrewd, honest, and acquainted with Courts, should be beguiled by such crude and coarse homage, amazed me, as it did all who knew him ; but you who have seen much of life do not need to be told how often the strongest and noblest nature has its one inexplicable weakness, showing up the more obviously in contrast to the rest, as the dark stain looks the fouler upon the whitest sheet.

" You are a sea-officer of my own heart, Stone," said he, when her ladyship had exhausted her panegyric.

" You are one of the old breed ! " He walked up and down with little, impatient steps as he talked, turning with a whisk upon his heel every now and then, as if some invisible rail had brought him up. " We are getting too fine for our work with these new-fangled epaulettes and quarter-deck trimmings. When I joined the Service, you would find a lieutenant gammoning and rigging his own bowsprit, or aloft, maybe, with a marlin-spike slung round his neck, showing an example to his men. Now, it's as much as he'll do to carry his own sextant up the companion. When could you join ? "

" To-night, my lord."

" Right, Stone, right ! That is the true spirit. They are working double tides in the yards, but I do not know when the ships will be ready. I hoist my flag on the *Victory* on Wednesday, and we sail at once."

" No, no ; not so soon ! She cannot be ready for sea," said Lady Hamilton, in a wailing voice, clasping her hands and turning up her eyes as she spoke.

" She must and she shall be ready," cried Nelson, with extraordinary vehemence. " By Heaven ! if the devil stands at the door, I sail on Wednesday. Who knows what these rascals may be doing in my absence ? It maddens me to think of the deviltries which they may be devising. At this very instant, dear lady, the Queen, *our* Queen, may be straining her eyes for the topsails of Nelson's ships."

Thinking, as I did, that he was speaking of our own old Queen Charlotte, I could make no meaning out of this ; but my father told me afterwards that both Nelson and Lady Hamilton had conceived an extraordinary affection for the Queen of Naples, and that it was the interests of her little kingdom which he had so strenuously at heart. It may have been my expression of bewilderment which attracted Nelson's attention to me, for he suddenly stopped in his quick quarter-deck walk and looked me up and down with a severe eye.

" Well, young gentleman ! " said he, sharply.

" This is my only son, sir," said my father. " It is my wish that he should join the Service, if a berth can be found for him ; for we have all been King's officers for many generations."

" So, you wish to come and have your bones broken ? " cried Nelson, roughly, looking with much disfavour at the fine clothes which had cost my uncle and Mr. Brummell such a debate. " You will have to change that grand coat for a tarry jacket if you serve under me, sir."

I was so embarrassed by the abruptness of his manner that I could but stammer out that I hoped I should do my duty, on which the stern mouth relaxed into a good-humoured smile, and he laid his little brown hand for an instant upon my shoulder.

" I dare say that you will do very well," said he. " I can see that you have the stuff in you. But do not imagine that it is a light service which you undertake, young gentleman, when you enter His Majesty's Navy. It is a hard profession. You hear of the few who succeed, but what do you know of the hundreds who never find their way ? Look at my own luck ! Out of 200 who were with me in the San Juan expedition, 145 died in a single night. I have been in 180 engagements, and I have, as you see, lost my eye and my arm, and been sorely wounded besides. It chanced that I came through, and here I am flying my admiral's flag ; but I remember many a man as good as me who did not come through. Yes," he added, as her ladyship broke in with a voluble protest, " many and many as good a man who has gone to the sharks or the land-crabs. But it is a useless sailor who does not risk himself every day, and the lives of all of us are in the hands of Him who best knows when to claim them."

For an instant, in his earnest gaze and reverent manner, we seemed to catch a glimpse of the deeper, truer Nelson, the man of the Eastern counties, steeped in the virile Puritanism which sent from that district the Ironsides to fashion England within, and the Pilgrim Fathers to spread

it without. Here was the Nelson who declared that he saw the hand of God pressing upon the French, and who waited on his knees in the cabin of his flag-ship while she bore down upon the enemy's line. There was a human tenderness, too, in his way of speaking of his dead comrades, which made me understand why it was that he was so beloved by all who served with him, for, iron-hard as he was as seaman and fighter, there ran through his complex nature a sweet and un-English power of affectionate emotion, showing itself in tears if he were moved, and in such tender impulses as led him afterwards to ask his flag-captain to kiss him as he lay dying in the cockpit of the *Victory*.

My father had risen to depart, but the admiral, with that kindliness which he ever showed to the young, and which had been momentarily chilled by the unfortunate splendour of my clothes, still paced up and down in front of us, shooting out crisp little sentences of exhortation and advice.

" It is ardour that we need in the Service, young gentleman," said he. " We need red-hot men who will never rest satisfied. We had them in the Mediterranean, and we shall have them again. There was a band of brothers ! When I was asked to recommend one for special service, I told the Admiralty they might take the names as they came, for the same spirit animated them all. Had we taken nineteen vessels, we should never have said it was well done while the twentieth sailed the seas. You know how it was with us, Stone. You are too old a Mediterranean man for me to tell you anything."

" I trust, my lord, that I shall be with you when next we meet them," said my father.

" Meet them we shall and must. By Heaven, I shall never rest until I have given them a shaking. The scoundrel Buonaparte wishes to humble us. Let him try, and God help the better cause ! "

He spoke with such extraordinary animation that the empty sleeve flapped about in the air, giving him the

strangest appearance. Seeing my eyes fixed upon it, he turned with a smile to my father.

" I can still work my fin, Stone," said he, putting his hand across to the stump of his arm. " What used they to say in the fleet about it ? "

" That it was a sign, sir, that it was a bad hour to cross your hawse."

" They knew me, the rascals. You can see, young gentleman, that not a scrap of the ardour with which I serve my country has been shot away. Some day you may find that you are flying your own flag, and when that time comes you may remember that my advice to an officer is that he should have nothing to do with tame, slow measures. Lay all your stake, and if you lose through no fault of your own, the country will find you another stake as large. Never mind manœuvres ! Go for them ! The only manœuvre you need is that which will place you alongside your enemy. Always fight, and you will always be right. Give not a thought to your own ease or your own life, for from the day that you draw the blue coat over your back you have no life of your own. It is the country's, to be most freely spent if the smallest gain can come from it. How is the wind this morning, Stone ? "

" East-south-east," my father answered readily.

" Then Cornwallis is, doubtless, keeping well up to Brest, though, for my own part, I had rather tempt them out into the open sea."

" That is what every officer and man in the fleet would prefer, your lordship," said my father.

" They do not love the blockading service, and it is little wonder, since neither money nor honour is to be gained at it. You can remember how it was in the winter months before Toulon, Stone, when we had neither firing, wine, beef, pork nor flour aboard the ships, nor a spare piece of rope, canvas or twine. We braced the old hulks with our spare cables, and God knows there was never a Levanter that I did not expect it to send us to

the bottom. But we held our grip all the same. Yet I fear that we do not get much credit for it here in England, Stone, where they light the windows for a great battle, but they do not understand that it is easier for us to fight the Nile six times over, than to keep our station all winter in the blockade. But I pray God that we may meet this new fleet of theirs and settle the matter by a pell-mell battle."

"May I be with you, my lord!" said my father, earnestly. "But we have already taken too much of your time, and so I beg to thank you for your kindness and to wish you good morning."

"Good morning, Stone!" said Nelson. "You shall have your ship, and if I can make this young gentleman one of my officers it shall be done. But I gather from his dress," he continued, running his eye over me, "that you have been more fortunate in prize-money than most of your comrades. For my own part, I never did nor could turn my thoughts to money-making."

My father explained that I had been under the charge of the famous Sir Charles Tregellis, who was my uncle, and with whom I was now residing.

"Then you need no help from me," said Nelson, with some bitterness. "If you have either guineas or interest you can climb over the heads of old sea-officers, though you may not know the poop from the galley, or a carronade from a long nine. Nevertheless—— But what the deuce have we here?"

The footman had suddenly precipitated himself into the room, but stood abashed before the fierce glare of the admiral's eye.

"Your lordship told me to rush to you if it should come," he explained, holding out a large blue envelope.

"By Heaven, it is my orders!" cried Nelson, snatching it up and fumbling with it in his awkward, one-handed attempt to break the seals. Lady Hamilton ran to his assistance, but no sooner had she glanced at the paper enclosed than she burst into a shrill scream, and throwing

up her hands and her eyes, she sank backwards in a swoon.
I could not but observe, however, that her fall was very
carefully executed, and that she was fortunate enough,
in spite of her insensibility, to arrange her drapery and
attitude into a graceful and classical design. But he,
the honest seaman, so incapable of deceit or affectation
that he could not suspect it in others, ran madly to the bell,
shouting for the maid, the doctor and the smelling-salts,
with incoherent words of grief, and such passionate terms
of emotion that my father thought it more discreet to
twitch me by the sleeve as a signal that we should steal
from the room. There we left him then in the dim-lit
London drawing-room, beside himself with pity for this
shallow and most artificial woman, while without, at the
edge of the Piccadilly curb, there stood the high dark
berline ready to start him upon that long journey which
was to end in his chase of the French fleet over seven
thousand miles of ocean, his meeting with it, his victory,
which confined Napoleon's ambition for ever to the land,
and his death, coming, as I would it might come to all
of us, at the crowning moment of his life.

14. *On the Road*

AND now the day of the great fight began to
approach. Even the imminent outbreak of war
and the renewed threats of Napoleon were
secondary things in the eyes of the sportsmen—and the
sportsmen in those days made a large half of the population. In the club of the patrician and the plebeian gin-
shop, in the coffee-house of the merchant or the barrack
of the soldier, in London or the provinces, the same
question was interesting the whole nation. Every west-
country coach brought up word of the fine condition of
Crab Wilson, who had returned to his own native air
for his training, and was known to be under the immediate
care of Captain Barclay, the expert. On the other hand,

although my uncle had not yet named his man, there was no doubt amongst the public that Jim was to be his nominee, and the report of his physique and of his performance found him many backers. On the whole, however, the betting was in favour of Wilson, for Bristol and the west country stood by him to a man, whilst London opinion was divided. Three to two were to be had on Wilson at any West End club two days before the battle.

I had twice been down to Crawley to see Jim in his training quarters, where I found him undergoing the severe regimen which was usual. From early dawn until nightfall he was running, jumping, striking a bladder which swung upon a bar, or sparring with his formidable trainer. His eyes shone and his skin glowed with exuberant health, and he was so confident of success that my own misgivings vanished as I watched his gallant bearing and listened to his quiet and cheerful words.

" But I wonder that you should come and see me now, Rodney," said he, when we parted, trying to laugh as he spoke. " I have become a bruiser and your uncle's paid man, whilst you are a Corinthian upon town. If you had not been the best and truest little gentleman in the world, you would have been my patron instead of my friend before now."

When I looked at this splendid fellow, with his high-bred, clean-cut face, and thought of the fine qualities and gentle, generous impulses which I knew to lie within him, it seemed so absurd that he should speak as though my friendship towards him were a condescension, that I could not help laughing aloud.

" That is all very well, Rodney," said he, looking hard into my eyes. " But what does your uncle think about it ? "

This was a poser, and I could only answer lamely enough that, much as I was indebted to my uncle, I had known Jim first, and that I was surely old enough to choose my own friends.

Jim's misgivings were so far correct that my uncle

did very strongly object to any intimacy between us; but there were so many other points in which he disapproved of my conduct, that it made the less difference. I fear that he was already disappointed in me. I would not develop an eccentricity, although he was good enough to point out several by which I might " come out of the ruck," as he expressed it, and so catch the attention of the strange world in which he lived.

" You are an active young fellow, nephew," said he. " Do you not think that you could engage to climb round the furniture of an ordinary room without setting foot upon the ground ? Some little *tour-de-force* of the sort is in excellent taste. There was a captain in the Guards who attained considerable social success by doing it for a small wager. Lady Lieven, who is exceedingly exigeant, used to invite him to her evenings merely that he might exhibit it."

I had to assure him that the feat would be beyond me.

" You are just a little *difficile*," said he, shrugging his shoulders. " As my nephew, you might have taken your position by perpetuating my own delicacy of taste. If you had made bad taste your enemy, the world of fashion would willingly have looked upon you as an arbiter by virtue of your family traditions, and you might without a struggle have stepped into the position to which this young upstart Brummell aspires. But you have no instinct in that direction. You are incapable of minute attention to detail. Look at your shoes ! Look at your cravat ! Look at your watch-chain ! Two links are enough to show. I *have* shown three, but it was an indiscretion. At this moment I can see no less than five of yours. I regret it, nephew, but I do not think that you are destined to attain that position which I have a right to expect from my blood relation."

" I am sorry to be a disappointment to you, sir," said I.

" It is your misfortune not to have come under my influence earlier," said he. " I might then have moulded you so as to have satisfied even my own aspirations. I

had a younger brother whose case was a similar one. I did what I could for him, but he would wear ribbons in his shoes, and he publicly mistook white Burgundy for Rhine wine. Eventually the poor fellow took to books, and lived and died in a country vicarage. He was a good man, but he was commonplace, and there is no place in society for commonplace people."

"Then I fear, sir, that there is none for me," said I. "But my father has every hope that Lord Nelson will find me a position in the fleet. If I have been a failure in town, I am none the less conscious of your kindness in trying to advance my interests, and I hope that, should I receive my commission, I may be a credit to you yet."

"It is possible that you may attain the very spot which I had marked out for you, but by another road," said my uncle. "There are many men in town, such as Lord St. Vincent, Lord Hood and others, who move in the most respectable circles, although they have nothing but their services in the Navy to recommend them."

It was on the afternoon of the day before the fight that this conversation took place between my uncle and myself in the dainty sanctum of his Jermyn Street house. He was clad, I remember, in his flowing brocade dressing-gown, as was his custom before he set off for his club, and his foot was extended upon a stool—for Abernethy had just been in to treat him for an incipient attack of the gout. It may have been the pain, or it may have been his disappointment at my career, but his manner was more testy than was usual with him, and I fear that there was something of a sneer in his smile as he spoke of my deficiencies. For my own part I was relieved at the explanation, for my father had left London in the full conviction that a vacancy would speedily be found for us both, and the one thing which had weighed upon my mind was that I might have found it hard to leave my uncle without interfering with the plans which he had formed. I was heart-weary of this empty life, for which I was so ill-fashioned, and weary also of that intolerant talk which

would make a coterie of frivolous women and foolish fops the central point of the universe. Something of my uncle's sneer may have flickered upon my lips as I heard him allude with supercilious surprise to the presence in those sacrosanct circles of the men who had stood between the country and destruction.

" By the way, nephew," said he, " gout or no gout, and whether Abernethy likes it or not, we must be down at Crawley to-night. The battle will take place upon Crawley Downs. Sir Lothian Hume and his man are at Reigate. I have reserved beds at the George for both of us. The crush will, it is said, exceed anything ever known. The smell of these country inns is always most offensive to me—*mais que voulez-vous?* Berkeley Craven was saying in the club last night that there is not a bed within twenty miles of Crawley which is not bespoke, and that they are charging three guineas for the night. I hope that your young friend, if I must describe him as such, will fulfil the promise which he has shown, for I have rather more upon the event than I care to lose. Sir Lothian has been plunging also—he made a single bye-bet of five thousand to three upon Wilson in Limmer's yesterday. From what I hear of his affairs it will be a serious matter for him if we should pull it off. Well, Lorimer ? "

" A person to see you, Sir Charles," said the new valet.

" You know that I never see anyone until my dressing is complete."

" He insists upon seeing you, sir. He pushed open the door."

" Pushed it open ! What d'you mean, Lorimer ? Why didn't you put him out ? "

A smile passed over the servant's face. At the same moment there came a deep voice from the passage.

" You show me in this instant, young man, d'ye 'ear ? Let me see your master, or it'll be the worse for you."

I thought that I had heard the voice before, but when, over the shoulder of the valet, I caught a glimpse of a

1023

large, fleshy bull-face, with a flattened Michael Angelo nose in the centre of it, I knew at once that it was my neighbour at the supper party.

" It's Warr, the prize-fighter, sir," said I.

" Yes, sir," said our visitor, pushing his huge form into the room. " It's Bill Warr, landlord of the One Tun public-'ouse, Jermyn Street, and the gamest man upon the list. There's only one thing that ever beat me, Sir Charles, and that was my flesh, which creeps over me that amazin' fast that I've always got four stone that 'as no business there. Why, sir, I've got enough to spare to make a feather-weight champion out of. You'd 'ardly think, to look at me, that even after Mendoza fought me I was able to jump the four-foot ropes at the ring-side just as light as a little kiddy ; but if I was to chuck my castor into the ring now I'd never get it till the wind blew it out again, for blow my dicky if I could climb after. My respec's to you, young sir, and I 'ope I see you well."

My uncle's face had expressed considerable disgust at this invasion of his privacy, but it was part of his position to be on good terms with the fighting-men, so he contented himself with asking curtly what business had brought him there. For answer the huge prize-fighter looked meaningly at the valet.

" It's important, Sir Charles, and between man and man," said he.

" You may go, Lorimer. Now, Warr, what is the matter ? "

The bruiser very calmly seated himself astride of a chair with his arms resting upon the back of it.

" I've got information, Sir Charles," said he.

" Well, what is it ? " cried my uncle, impatiently.

" Information of value."

" Out with it, then ! "

" Information that's worth money," said Warr, and pursed up his lips.

" I see. You want to be paid for what you know ? "

The prize-fighter smiled an affirmative.

"Well, I don't buy things on trust. You should know me better than to try on such a game with me."

"I know you for what you are, Sir Charles, and that is a noble, slap-up Corinthian. But if I was to use this against you, d'ye see, it would be worth 'undreds in my pocket. But my 'eart won't let me do it, for Bill Warr's always been on the side o' good sport and fair play. If I use it for you, then I expect that you won't see me the loser."

"You can do what you like," said my uncle. "If your news is of service to me, I shall know how to treat you."

"You can't say fairer than that. We'll let it stand there, gov'nor, and you'll do the 'andsome thing, as you 'ave always 'ad the name for doin'. Well, then, your man, Jim 'Arrison, fights Crab Wilson, of Gloucester, at Crawley Down to-morrow mornin' for a stake."

"What of that?"

"Did you 'appen to know what the bettin' was yesterday?"

"It was three to two on Wilson."

"Right you are, gov'nor. Three to two was offered in my own bar-parlour. D'you know what the bettin' is to-day?"

"I have not been out yet."

"Then I'll tell you. It's seven to one against your man."

"What?"

"Seven to one, gov'nor, no less."

"You're talking nonsense, Warr! How could the betting change from three to two to seven to one?"

"I've been to Tom Owen's, and I've been to the 'Ole in the Wall, and I've been to the Waggon and 'Orses, and you can get seven to one in any of them. There's tons of money being laid against your man. It's a 'orse to a 'en in every sportin' 'ouse and boozin' ken from 'ere to Stepney."

For a moment the expression upon my uncle's face made

1025

me realise that this match was really a serious matter to him. Then he shrugged his shoulders with an incredulous smile.

"All the worse for the fools who give the odds," said he. "My man is all right. You saw him yesterday, nephew?"

"He was all right yesterday, sir."

"If anything had gone wrong I should have heard."

"But perhaps," said Warr, "it 'as not gone wrong with 'im *yet*."

"What d'you mean?"

"I'll tell you what I mean, sir. You remember Berks? You know that 'e ain't to be overmuch depended on at any time, and that 'e 'ad a grudge against your man 'cause 'e laid 'im out in the coach-'ouse. Well, last night about ten o'clock in 'e comes into my bar, and the three bloodiest rogues in London at 'is 'eels. There was Red Ike, 'im that was warned off the Ring 'cause 'e fought a cross with Bittoon; and there was Fightin' Yussef, who would sell 'is mother for a seven-shillin'-bit; the third was Chris McCarthy, who is a fogle-snatcher by trade, with a pitch outside the 'Aymarket Theatre. You don't often see four such beauties together, and all with as much as they could carry, save only Chris, who is too leary a cove to drink when there's somethin' goin' forward. For my part, I showed 'em into the parlour, not 'cos they was worthy of it, but 'cos I knew right well they would start bashin' some of my customers, and maybe get my licence into trouble if I left 'em in the bar. I served 'em with drink, and stayed with 'em just to see that they didn't lay their 'ands on the stuffed parroquet and the pictures.

"Well, gov'nor, to cut it short, they began to talk about the fight, and they all laughed at the idea that young Jim 'Arrison could win it—all except Chris, and 'e kept a-nudging and a-twitchin' at the others until Joe Berks nearly gave him a wipe across the face for 'is trouble. I saw somethin' was in the wind, and it wasn't very 'ard to guess what it was—especially when Red Ike was ready to put up a fiver that Jim 'Arrison would never fight at all.

So I up to get another bottle of liptrap, and I slipped round to the shutter that we pass the liquor through from the private bar into the parlour. I drew it an inch open, and I might 'ave been at the table with them, I could 'ear every word that clearly.

"There was Chris McCarthy growlin' at them for not keepin' their tongues still, and there was Joe Berks swearin' that 'e would knock 'is face in if 'e dared give 'im any of 'is lip. So Chris 'e sort of argued with them, for 'e was frightened of Berks, and 'e put it to them whether they would be fit for the job in the mornin', and whether the gov'nor would pay the money if 'e found they 'ad been drinkin' and were not to be trusted. This struck them sober, all three, an' Fighting Yussef asked what time they were to start. Chris said that as long as they were at Crawley before the George shut up they could work it. 'It's poor pay for a chance of a rope,' said Red Ike. 'Rope be damned!' cried Chris, takin' a little loaded stick out of his side pocket. 'If three of you 'old him down and I break his arm-bone with this, we've earned our money, and we don't risk more'n six months' jug.' ''E'll fight,' said Berks. 'Well, it's the only fight 'e'll get,' answered Chris, and that was all I 'eard of it. This mornin' out I went, and I found as I told you afore that the money is goin' on to Wilson by the ton, and that no odds are too long for the layers. So it stands, gov'nor, and you know what the meanin' of it may be better than Bill Warr can tell you."

"Very good, Warr," said my uncle, rising. "I am very much obliged to you for telling me this, and I will see that you are not a loser by it. I put it down as the gossip of drunken ruffians, but none the less you have served me vastly by calling my attention to it. I suppose I shall see you at the Downs to-morrow?"

"Mr. Jackson 'as asked me to be one o' the beaters-out, sir."

"Very good. I hope that we shall have a fair and good fight. Good day to you, and thank you."

My uncle had preserved his jaunty demeanour as long as Warr was in the room, but the door had hardly closed upon him before he turned to me with a face which was more agitated than I had ever seen it.

" We must be off for Crawley at once, nephew," said he, ringing the bell. " There's not a moment to be lost. Lorimer, order the bays to be harnessed in the curricle. Put the toilet things in, and tell William to have it round at the door as soon as possible."

" I'll see to it, sir," said I, and away I ran to the mews in Little Ryder Street, where my uncle stabled his horses. The groom was away, and I had to send a lad in search of him, while with the help of the liveryman I dragged the curricle from the coach-house and brought the two mares out of their stalls. It was half an hour, or possibly three-quarters, before everything had been found, and Lorimer was already waiting in Jermyn Street with the inevitable baskets, whilst my uncle stood in the open door of his house, clad in his long fawn-coloured driving-coat with no sign upon his calm pale face of the tumult of impatience which must, I was sure, be raging within.

" We shall leave you, Lorimer," said he. " We might find it hard to get a bed for you. Keep at her head, William ! Jump in, nephew. Halloa, Warr, what is the matter now ? "

The prize-fighter was hastening towards us as fast as his bulk would allow.

" Just one word before you go, Sir Charles," he panted. " I've just 'eard in my taproom that the four men I spoke of left for Crawley at one o'clock."

" Very good, Warr," said my uncle, with his foot upon the step.

" And the odds 'ave risen to ten to one."

" Let go her head, William ! "

" Just one more word, gov'nor. You'll excuse the liberty, but if I was you I'd take my pistols with me."

" Thank you ; I have them."

The long thong cracked between the ears of the leader,

the groom sprang for the pavement, and Jermyn Street had changed for St. James's, and that again for Whitehall with a swiftness which showed that the gallant mares were as impatient as their master. It was half-past four by the Parliament clock as we flew on to Westminster Bridge. There was the flash of water beneath us, and then we were between those two long dun-coloured lines of houses which had been the avenue which had led us to London. My uncle sat with tightened lips and a brooding brow. We had reached Streatham before he broke the silence.

" I have a good deal at stake, nephew," said he.

" So have I, sir," I answered.

" You ! " he cried, in surprise.

" My friend, sir."

" Ah, yes, I had forgot. You have some eccentricities, after all, nephew. You are a faithful friend, which is a rare enough thing in our circles. I never had but one friend of my own position, and he—but you've heard me tell the story. I fear it will be dark before we reach Crawley."

" I fear that it will."

" In that case we may be too late."

" Pray God not, sir ! "

" We sit behind the best cattle in England, but I fear lest we find the roads blocked before we get to Crawley. Did you observe, nephew, that these four villains spoke in Warr's hearing of the master who was behind them, and who was paying them for their infamy ? Did you not understand that they were hired to cripple my man ? Who, then, could have hired them ? Who had an interest unless it was—— I know Sir Lothian Hume to be a desperate man. I know that he has had heavy card losses at Watier's and White's. I know also that he has much at stake upon this event, and that he has plunged upon it with a rashness which made his friends think that he had some private reason for being satisfied as to the result. By Heaven, it all hangs together. If it

should be so——!" He relapsed into silence, but I saw the same look of cold fierceness settle upon his features which I had marked there when he and Sir John Lade had raced wheel to wheel down the Godstone road.

The sun sank slowly towards the low Surrey hills, and the shadows crept steadily eastwards, but the whirr of the wheels and the roar of the hoofs never slackened. A fresh wind blew upon our faces, while the young leaves drooped motionless from the wayside branches. The golden edge of the sun was just sinking behind the oaks of Reigate Hill when the dripping mares drew up before the Crown at Redhill. The landlord, an old sports-man and ringsider, ran out to greet so well-known a Corinthian as Sir Charles Tregellis.

" You know Berks, the bruiser ? " asked my uncle.

" Yes, Sir Charles."

" Has he passed ? "

" Yes, Sir Charles. It may have been about four o'clock, though with this crowd of folk and carriages it's hard to swear to it. There was him, and Red Ike, and Fighting Yussef the Jew, and another, with a good bit of blood betwixt the shafts. They'd been driving her hard, too, for she was all in a lather."

" That's ugly, nephew," said my uncle, when we were flying onwards towards Reigate. " If they drove so hard, it looks as though they wished to get early to work."

" Jim and Belcher would surely be a match for the four of them," I suggested.

" If Belcher were with him I should have no fear. But you cannot tell what *diablerie* they may be up to. Let us only find him safe and sound, and I'll never lose sight of him until I see him in the ring. We'll sit up on guard with our pistols, nephew, and I only trust that these villains may be indiscreet enough to attempt it. But they must have been very sure of success before they put the odds up to such a figure, and it is that which alarms me."

" But surely they have nothing to win by such villainy,

sir ? If they were to hurt Jim Harrison the battle could not be fought, and the bets would not be decided."

" So it would be in an ordinary prize-battle, nephew ; and it is fortunate that it should be so, or the rascals who infest the Ring would soon make all sport impossible. But here it is different. On the terms of the wager I lose unless I can produce a man, within the prescribed ages, who can beat Crab Wilson. You must remember that I have never named my man. *C'est dommage*, but so it is ! We know who it is and so do our opponents, but the referees and stakeholder would take no notice of that. If we complain that Jim Harrison has been crippled, they would answer that they have no official knowledge that Jim Harrison was our nominee. It's play or pay, and the villains are taking advantage of it."

My uncle's fears as to our being blocked upon the road were only too well founded, for after we passed Reigate there was such a procession of every sort of vehicle, that I believe for the whole eight miles there was not a horse whose nose was further than a few feet from the back of the curricle or barouche in front. Every road leading from London, as well as those from Guildford in the west and Tunbridge in the east, had contributed its stream of four-in-hands, gigs and mounted sportsmen, until the whole broad Brighton highway was choked from ditch to ditch with a laughing, singing, shouting throng, all flowing in the same direction. No man who looked upon that motley crowd could deny that, for good or evil, the love of the Ring was confined to no class, but was a national peculiarity, deeply seated in the English nature, and a common heritage of the young aristocrat in his drag and of the rough costers sitting six deep in their pony cart. There I saw statesmen and soldiers, noblemen and lawyers, farmers and squires, with roughs of the East End and yokels of the shires, all toiling along with the prospect of a night of discomfort before them, on the chance of seeing a fight which might, for all that they knew, be decided in a .ing'e round. A more cheery

and hearty set of people could not be imagined, and the chaff flew about as thick as the dust clouds, while at every wayside inn the landlord and the drawers would be out with trays of foam-headed tankards to moisten those importunate throats. The ale-drinking, the rude good-fellowship, the heartiness, the laughter at discomforts, the craving to see the fight—all these may be set down as vulgar and trivial by those to whom they are distasteful ; but to me, listening to the far-off and uncertain echoes of our distant past, they seem to have been the very bones upon which much that is most solid and virile in this ancient race was moulded.

But, alas for our chance of hastening onwards ! Even my uncle's skill could not pick a passage through that moving mass. We could but fall into our places and be content to snail along from Reigate to Horley and on to Povey Cross and over Lowfield Heath, while day shaded away into twilight, and that deepened into night. At Kimberham Bridge the carriage-lamps were all lit, and it was wonderful, where the road curved downwards before us, to see this writhing serpent with the golden scales crawling before us in the darkness. And then, at last, we saw the formless mass of the huge Crawley elm looming before us in the gloom, and there was the broad village street with the glimmer of the cottage windows, and the high front of the old George Inn, glowing from every door and pane and crevice, in honour of the noble company who were to sleep within that night.

15. *Foul Play*

MY uncle's impatience would not suffer him to wait for the slow rotation which would bring us to the door, but he flung the reins and a crown-piece to one of the rough fellows who thronged the side-walk, and pushing his way vigorously through the crowd, he made for the entrance. As he came within the circle of

light thrown by the windows, a whisper ran round as to who this masterful gentleman with the pale face and the driving-coat might be, and a lane was formed to admit us. I had never before understood the popularity of my uncle in the sporting world, for the folk began to huzza as we passed with cries of " Hurrah for Buck Tregellis ! Good luck to you and your man, Sir Charles ! Clear a path for a bang-up noble Corinthian ! " whilst the landlord, attracted by the shouting, came running out to greet us.

" Good evening, Sir Charles ! " he cried. " I hope I see you well, sir, and I trust that you will find that your man does credit to the George."

" How is he ? " asked my uncle, quickly.

" Never better, sir. Looks a picture, he does—and fit to fight for a kingdom."

My uncle gave a sigh of relief.

" Where is he ? " he asked.

" He's gone to his room early, sir, seein' that he had some very partic'lar business to-morrow mornin'," said the landlord, grinning.

" Where is Belcher ? "

" Here he is, in the bar-parlour."

He opened a door as he spoke, and looking in we saw a score of well-dressed men, some of whose faces had become familiar to me during my short West End career, seated round a table upon which stood a steaming soup-tureen filled with punch. At the further end, very much at his ease amongst the aristocrats and exquisites who surrounded him, sat the Champion of England, his superb figure thrown back in his chair, a flush upon his handsome face, and a loose red handkerchief knotted carelessly round his throat in the picturesque fashion which was long known by his name. Half a century has passed since then, and I have seen my share of fine men. Perhaps it is because I am a slight creature myself, but it is my peculiarity that I had rather look upon a splendid man than upon any work of Nature. Yet during all that time I have never seen a finer man than Jem Belcher, and if I

wish to match him in my memory, I can only turn to that other Jim whose fate and fortunes I am trying to lay before you.

There was a shout of jovial greeting when my uncle's face was seen in the doorway.

" Come in, Tregellis ! " " We were expecting you ! " " There's a devilled bladebone ordered." " What's the latest from London ? " " What is the meaning of the long odds against your man ? " " Have the folk gone mad ? " " What the devil is it all about ? " They were all talking at once.

" Excuse me, gentlemen," my uncle answered. " I shall be happy to give you any information in my power a little later. I have a matter of some slight importance to decide. Belcher, I would have a word with you ! "

The Champion came out with us into the passage.

" Where is your man, Belcher ? "

" He has gone to his room, sir. I believe that he should have a clear twelve hours' sleep before fighting."

" What sort of day has he had ? "

" I did him lightly in the matter of exercise. Clubs, dumbbells, walking and a half-hour with the mufflers. He'll do us all proud, sir, or I'm a Dutchman ! But what in the world's amiss with the betting ? If I didn't know that he was as straight as a line, I'd ha' thought he was planning a cross and laying against himself."

" It's about that I've hurried down. I have good information, Belcher, that there has been a plot to cripple him, and that the rogues are so sure of success that they are prepared to lay anything against his appearance."

Belcher whistled between his teeth.

" I've seen no sign of anything of the kind, sir. No one has been near him or had speech with him, except only your nephew there and myself."

" Four villains, with Berks at their head, got the start of us by several hours. It was Warr who told me."

" What Bill Warr says is straight, and what Joe Berks does is crooked. Who were the others, sir ? "

" Red Ike, Fighting Yussef and Chris McCarthy."

" A pretty gang, too ! Well, sir, the lad is safe, but it would be as well, perhaps, for one or other of us to stay in his room with him. For my own part, as long as he's my charge I'm never very far away."

" It is a pity to wake him."

" He can hardly be asleep, with all this racket in the house. This way, sir, and down the passage ! "

We passed along the low-roofed, devious corridors of the old-fashioned inn to the back of the house.

" This is my room, sir," said Belcher, nodding to a door upon the right. " This one upon the left is his." He threw it open as he spoke. " Here's Sir Charles Tregellis come to see you, Jim," said he ; and then, " Good Lord, what is the meaning of this ? "

The little chamber lay before us brightly illuminated by a brass lamp which stood upon the table. The bedclothes had not been turned down, but there was an indentation upon the counterpane which showed that someone had lain there. One-half of the lattice window was swinging on its hinge and a cloth cap lying upon the table was the only sign of the occupant. My uncle looked round him and shook his head.

" It seems that we are too late," said he.

" That's his cap, sir. Where in the world can he have gone to with his head bare ? I thought he was safe in his bed an hour ago. Jim ! Jim ! " he shouted.

" He has certainly gone through the window," cried my uncle. " I believe these villains have enticed him out by some devilish device of their own. Hold the lamp, nephew. Ha ! I thought so. Here are his footmarks upon the flower-bed outside."

The landlord, and one or two of the Corinthians from the bar-parlour had followed us to the back of the house. Someone had opened the side door, and we found ourselves in the kitchen garden, where, clustering upon the gravel path, we were able to hold the lamp over the soft newly turned earth which lay between us and the window.

" That's his footmark ! " said Belcher. " He wore his running boots this evening, and you can see the nails. But what's this ? Someone else has been here."

" A woman ! " I cried.

" By Heaven, you're right, nephew," said my uncle.

Belcher gave a hearty curse.

" He never had a word to say to any girl in the village. I took partic'lar notice of that. And to think of them coming in like this at the last moment ! "

" It's clear as possible, Tregellis," said the Hon. Berkeley Craven, who was one of the company from the bar-parlour. " Whoever it was came outside the window and tapped. You see here, and here, the small feet have their toes to the house, while the others are all leading away. She came to summon him, and he followed her."

" That is perfectly certain," said my uncle. " There's not a moment to be lost. We must divide and search in different directions, unless we can get some clue as to where they have gone."

" There's only the one path out of the garden," cried the landlord, leading the way. " It opens out into this back lane, which leads up to the stables. The other end of the lane goes out into the side road."

The bright yellow glare from a stable lantern cut a ring suddenly from the darkness, and an ostler came lounging out of the yard.

" Who's that ? " cried the landlord.

" It's me, master ! Bill Shields."

" How long have you been there, Bill ? "

" Well, master, I've been in an' out of the stables this hour back. We can't pack in another 'orse, and there's no use tryin'. I daren't 'ardly give them their feed, for, if they was to thicken out just ever so little———"

" See here, Bill. Be careful how you answer, for a mistake may cost you your place. Have you seen any-one pass down the lane ? "

" There was a feller in a rabbit-skin cap some time ago. 'E was loiterin' about until I asked 'im what 'is

business was, for I didn't care about the looks of 'im, or the way that 'e was peepin' in at the windows. I turned the stable lantern on to 'im, but 'e ducked 'is face, an' I could only swear to 'is red 'ead."

I cast a quick glance at my uncle, and I saw that the shadow had deepened upon his face.

" What became of him ? " he asked.

" 'E slouched away, sir, an' I saw the last of 'im."

" You've seen no one else ? You didn't, for example, see a woman and a man pass down the lane together ? "

" No, sir."

" Or hear anything unusual ? "

" Why, now that you mention it, sir, I did 'ear somethin' ; but on a night like this, when all these London blades are in the village——"

" What was it, then ? " cried my uncle, impatiently.

" Well, sir, it was a kind of a cry out yonder as if someone 'ad got 'imself into trouble. I thought, maybe, two sparks were fightin', and I took no partic'lar notice."

" Where did it come from ? "

" From the side road, yonder."

" Was it distant ? "

" No, sir ; I should say it didn't come from more'n two hundred yards."

" A single cry ? "

" Well, it was a kind of screech, sir, and then I 'eard somebody drivin' very 'ard down the road. I remember thinking that it was strange that anyone should be driving away from Crawley on a great night like this."

My uncle seized the lantern from the fellow's hand, and we all trooped behind him down the lane. At the further end the road cut it across at right angles. Down this my uncle hastened, but his search was not a long one, for the glaring light fell suddenly upon something which brought a groan to my lips and a bitter curse to those of Jem Belcher. Along the white surface of the dusty highway there was drawn a long smear of crimson, while beside this ominous stain there lay a murderous little

pocket-bludgeon, such as Warr had described in the
morning.

16. *Crawley Downs*

ALL through that weary night my uncle and I,
with Belcher, Berkeley Craven and a dozen of the
Corinthians, searched the country-side for some
trace of our missing man, but save for that ill-boding
splash upon the road not the slightest clue could be
obtained as to what had befallen him. No one had seen
or heard anything of him, and the single cry in the night
of which the ostler told us was the only indication of the
tragedy which had taken place. In small parties we
scoured the country as far as East Grinstead and
Bletchingley, and the sun had been long over the horizon
before we found ourselves back at Crawley once more
with heavy hearts and tired feet. My uncle, who had
driven to Reigate in the hope of gaining some intelligence,
did not return until past seven o'clock, and a glance at
his face gave us the same black news which he gathered
from ours.

We held a council round our dismal breakfast-table,
to which Mr. Berkeley Craven was invited as a man of
sound wisdom and large experience in matters of sport.
Belcher was half frenzied by this sudden ending of all
the pains which he had taken in the training, and could
only rave out threats at Berks and his companions, with
terrible menaces as to what he would do when he met
them. My uncle sat grave and thoughtful, eating nothing
and drumming his fingers upon the table, while my heart
was heavy within me, and I could have sunk my face into
my hands and burst into tears as I thought how powerless
I was to aid my friend. Mr. Craven, a fresh-faced, alert
man of the world, was the only one of us who seemed to
preserve both his wits and his appetite.

" Let me see ! The fight was to be at ten, was it not ? "
he asked.

" It was to be."

" I dare say it will be, too. Never say die, Tregellis ! Your man has still three hours in which to come back."

My uncle shook his head.

" The villains have done their work too well for that, I fear," said he.

" Well, now, let us reason it out," said Berkeley Craven. " A woman comes and she coaxes this young man out of his room. Do you know any young woman who had an influence over him ? "

My uncle looked at me.

" No," said I. " I know of none."

" Well, we know that she came," said Berkeley Craven. " There can be no question as to that. She brought some piteous tale, no doubt, such as a gallant young man could hardly refuse to listen to. He fell into the trap, and allowed himself to be decoyed to the place where these rascals were waiting for him. We may take all that as proved, I should fancy, Tregellis."

" I see no better explanation," said my uncle.

" Well, then, it is obviously not the interest of these men to kill him. Warr heard them say as much. They could not make sure, perhaps, of doing so tough a young fellow an injury which would certainly prevent him from fighting. Even with a broken arm he might pull the fight off, as men have done before. There was too much money on for them to run any risks. They gave him a tap on the head, therefore, to prevent his making too much resistance, and they then drove him off to some farmhouse or stable, where they will hold him a prisoner until the time for the fight is over. I warrant that you see him before to-night as well as ever he was."

This theory sounded so reasonable that it seemed to lift a little of the weight from my heart, but I could see that from my uncle's point of view it was a poor consolation.

" I dare say you are right, Craven," said he.

" I am sure that I am."

" But it won't help us to win the fight."

" That's the point, sir," cried Belcher. " By the Lord, I wish they'd let me take his place, even with my left arm strapped behind me."

" I should advise you in any case to go to the ringside," said Craven. " You should hold on until the last moment in the hope of your man turning up."

" I shall certainly do so. And I shall protest against paying the wagers under such circumstances."

Craven shrugged his shoulders.

" You remember the conditions of the match," said he. " I fear it is pay or play. No doubt the point might be submitted to the referees, but I cannot doubt that they would have to give it against you."

We had sunk into a melancholy silence, when suddenly Belcher sprang up from the table.

" Hark ! " he cried. " Listen to that ! "

" What is it ? " we cried, all three.

" The betting ! Listen again ! "

Out of the babel of voices and roaring of wheels outside the window a single sentence struck sharply on our ears.

" Even money upon Sir Charles's nominee ! "

" Even money ! " cried my uncle. " It was seven to one against me, yesterday. What is the meaning of this ? "

" Even money either way," cried the voice again.

" There's somebody knows something," said Belcher, " and there's nobody has a better right to know what it is than we. Come on, sir, and we'll get to the bottom of it."

The village street was packed with people, for they had been sleeping twelve and fifteen in a room, whilst hundreds of gentlemen had spent the night in their carriages. So thick was the throng that it was no easy matter to get out of the George. A drunken man, snoring horribly in his breathing, was curled up in the passage, absolutely oblivious to the stream of people who flowed round and occasionally over him.

" What's the betting, boys ? " asked Belcher, from the steps.

" Even money, Jem," cried several voices.

" It was long odds on Wilson when last I heard."

" Yes ; but there came a man who laid freely the other way, and he started others taking the odds, until now you can get even money."

" Who started it ? "

" Why, that's he ! The man that lies drunk in the passage. He's been pouring it down like water ever since he drove in at six o'clock, so it's no wonder he's like that."

Belcher stooped down and turned over the man's inert head so as to show his features.

" He's a stranger to me, sir."

" And to me," added my uncle.

" But not to me," I cried. " It's John Cumming, the landlord of the inn at Friar's Oak. I've known him ever since I was a boy, and I can't be mistaken."

" Well, what the devil can *he* know about it ? " said Craven.

" Nothing at all, in all probability," answered my uncle. " He is backing young Jim because he knows him, and because he has more brandy than sense. His drunken confidence set others to do the same, and so the odds came down."

" He was as sober as a judge when he drove in here this morning," said the landlord. " He began backing Sir Charles's nominee from the moment he arrived. Some of the other boys took the office from him, and they very soon brought the odds down amongst them."

" I wish he had not brought himself down as well," said my uncle. " I beg that you will bring me a little lavender water, landlord, for the smell of this crowd is appalling. I suppose you could not get any sense from this drunken fellow, nephew, or find out what it is he knows."

It was in vain that I rocked him by the shoulder and

shouted his name in his ear. Nothing could break in upon that serene intoxication.

" Well, it's a unique situation as far as my experience goes," said Berkeley Craven. " Here we are within a couple of hours of the fight, and yet you don't know whether you have a man to represent you. I hope you don't stand to lose very much, Tregellis."

My uncle shrugged his shoulders carelessly, and took a pinch of his snuff with that inimitable sweeping gesture which no man has ever ventured to imitate.

" Pretty well, my boy ! " said he. " But it is time that we thought of going up to the Downs. This night journey has left me just a little *effleuré*, and I should like half an hour of privacy to arrange my toilet. If this is my last kick, it shall at least be with a well-brushed boot."

I have heard a traveller from the wilds of America say that he looked upon the Red Indian and the English gentleman as closely akin, citing the passion for sport, the aloofness and the suppression of the emotions in each. I thought of his words as I watched my uncle that morning, for I believe that no victim tied to the stake could have had a worse outlook before him. It was not merely that his own fortunes were largely at stake, but it was the dreadful position in which he would stand before this immense concourse of people, many of whom had put their money upon his judgment, if he should find himself at the last moment with an impotent excuse instead of a champion to put before them. What a situation for a man who prided himself upon his aplomb, and upon bringing all that he undertook to the very highest standard of success ! I, who knew him well, could tell from his wan cheeks and his restless fingers that he was at his wit's ends what to do ; but no stranger who observed his jaunty bearing, the flecking of his laced handkerchief, the handling of his quizzing glass, or the shooting of his ruffles, would ever have thought that this butterfly creature could have had a care upon earth.

It was close upon nine o'clock when we were ready to

start for the Downs, and by that time my uncle's curricle was almost the only vehicle left in the village street. The night before they had lain with their wheels interlocking and their shafts under each other's bodies, as thick as they could fit, from the old church to the Crawley Elm, spanning the road five-deep for a good half-mile in length. Now the grey village street lay before us almost deserted save by a few women and children. Men, horses, carriages—all were gone. My uncle drew on his driving gloves and arranged his costume with punctilious neatness ; but I observed that he glanced up and down the road with a haggard and yet expectant eye before he took his seat. I sat behind with Belcher, while the Hon. Berkeley Craven took the place beside him.

The road from Crawley curves gently upwards to the upland heather-clad plateau which extends for many miles in every direction. Strings of pedestrians, most of them so weary and dust-covered that it was evident that they had walked the thirty miles from London during the night, were plodding along by the sides of the road or trailing over the long mottled slopes of the moorland. A horseman, fantastically dressed in green and splendidly mounted, was waiting at the cross-roads, and as he spurred towards us I recognised the dark, handsome face and bold black eyes of Mendoza.

" I am waiting here to give the office, Sir Charles," said he. " It's down the Grinstead road, half a mile to the left."

" Very good," said my uncle, reining his mares round into the cross-road.

" You haven't got your man there," remarked Mendoza with something of suspicion in his manner.

" What the devil is that to you ? " cried Belcher, furiously.

" It's a good deal to all of us, for there are some funny stories about."

" You keep them to youi elf, then, or you may wish you had never heard th n.'

" All right, Jem ! Your breakfast don't seem to have agreed with you this morning."

" Have the others arrived ? " asked my uncle, carelessly.

" Not yet, Sir Charles. But Tom Oliver is there with the ropes and stakes. Jackson drove by just now, and most of the ring-keepers are up."

" We have still an hour," remarked my uncle, as he drove on. " It is possible that the others may be late, since they have to come from Reigate."

" You take it like a man, Tregellis," said Craven.

" We must keep a bold face and brazen it out until the last moment."

" Of course, sir," cried Belcher. " I'll never believe the betting would rise like that if somebody didn't know something. We'll hold on by our teeth and nails, Sir Charles, and see what comes of it."

We could hear a sound like the waves upon the beach, long before we came in sight of that mighty multitude, and then at last, on a sudden dip of the road, we saw it lying before us, a whirlpool of humanity with an open vortex in the centre. All round, the thousands of carriages and horses were dotted over the moor, and the slopes were gay with tents and booths. A spot had been chosen for the ring, where a great basin had been hollowed out in the ground, so that all round that natural amphitheatre a crowd of thirty thousand people could see very well what was going on in the centre. As we drove up a buzz of greeting came from the people upon the fringe which was nearest to us, spreading and spreading, until the whole multitude had joined in the acclamation. Then an instant later a second shout broke forth, beginning from the other side of the arena, and the faces which had been turned towards us whisked round, so that in a twinkling the whole foreground changed from white to dark.

" It's they. They are in time," said my uncle and Craven together.

Standing up on our curricle, we could see the cavalcade approaching over the Downs. In front came a huge yellow barouche, in which sat Sir Lothian Hume, Crab Wilson, and Captain Barclay, his trainer. The postilions were flying canary-yellow ribands from their caps, those being the colours under which Wilson was to fight. Behind the carriage there rode a hundred or more noblemen and gentlemen of the west country, and then a line of gigs, tilburies and carriages wound away down the Grinstead road as far as our eyes could follow it. The big barouche came lumbering over the sward in our direction until Sir Lothian Hume caught sight of us, when he shouted to his postilions to pull up.

" Good morning, Sir Charles," said he, springing out of the carriage. " I thought I knew your scarlet curricle. We have an excellent morning for the battle."

My uncle bowed coldly, and made no answer.

" I suppose that since we are all here we may begin at once," said Sir Lothian, taking no notice of the other's manner.

" We begin at ten o'clock. Not an instant before."

" Very good, if you prefer it. By the way, Sir Charles, where is your man ? "

" I would ask *you* that question, Sir Lothian," answered my uncle. " Where is my man ? "

A look of astonishment passed over Sir Lothian's features, which, if it were not real, was most admirably affected.

" What do you mean by asking me such a question ? "

" Because I wish to know."

" But how can I tell, and what business is it of mine ? "

" I have reason to believe that you have made it your business."

" If you would kindly put the matter a little more clearly there would be some possibility of my understanding you."

They were both very white and cold, formal and unimpassioned in their bearing but exchanging glances

which crossed like rapier blades. I thought of Sir Lothian's murderous repute as a duellist, and I trembled for my uncle.

"Now, sir, if you imagine that you have a grievance against me, you will oblige me vastly by putting it into words."

"I will," said my uncle. "There has been a conspiracy to maim or kidnap my man, and I have every reason to believe that you are privy to it."

An ugly sneer came over Sir Lothian's saturnine face.

"I see," said he. "Your man has not come on quite as well as you had expected in his training, and you are hard put to it to invent an excuse. Still, I should have thought that you might have found a more probable one, and one which would entail less serious consequences."

"Sir," answered my uncle, "you are a liar, but how great a liar you are nobody knows save yourself."

Sir Lothian's hollow cheeks grew white with passion, and I saw for an instant in his deep-set eyes such a glare as comes from the frenzied hound rearing and ramping at the end of its chain. Then, with an effort, he became the same cold, hard, self-contained man as ever.

"It does not become our position to quarrel like two yokels at a fair," said he; "we shall go further into the matter afterwards."

"I promise you that we shall," answered my uncle, grimly.

"Meanwhile, I hold you to the terms of your wager. Unless you produce your nominee within five-and-twenty minutes, I claim the match."

"Eight-and-twenty minutes," said my uncle, looking at his watch. "You may claim it then, but not an instant before."

He was admirable at that moment, for his manner was that of a man with all sorts of hidden resources, so that I could hardly make myself realise as I looked at him that our position was really as desperate as I knew it to be. In the meantime Berkeley Craven, who had been ex-

changing a few words with Sir Lothian Hume, came back to our side.

" I have been asked to be sole referee in this matter," said he. " Does that meet with your wishes, Sir Charles ? "

" I shall be vastly obliged to you, Craven, if you will undertake the duties."

" And Jackson has been suggested as timekeeper."

" I could not wish a better one."

" Very good. That is settled."

In the meantime the last of the carriages had come up, and the horses had all been picketed upon the moor. The stragglers who had dotted the grass had closed in until the huge crowd was one unit with a single mighty voice, which was already beginning to bellow its impatience. Looking round, there was hardly a moving object upon the whole vast expanse of green and purple down. A belated gig was coming at full gallop down the road which led from the south, and a few pedestrians were still trailing up from Crawley, but nowhere was there a sign of the missing man.

" The betting keeps up for all that," said Belcher. " I've just been to the ring-side, and it is still even."

" There's a place for you at the outer ropes, Sir Charles," said Craven.

" There is no sign of my man yet. I won't come in until he arrives."

" It is my duty to tell you that only ten minutes are left."

" I make it five," cried Sir Lothian Hume.

" That is a question which lies with the referee," said Craven, firmly. " My watch makes it ten minutes, and ten it must be."

" Here's Crab Wilson ! " cried Belcher, and at the same moment a shout like a thunderclap burst from the crowd. The west-countryman had emerged from his dressing-tent, followed by Dutch Sam and Tom Owen, who were acting as his seconds. He was nude to the

waist, with a pair of white calico drawers, white silk stockings, and running shoes. Round his middle was a canary-yellow sash, and dainty little ribbons of the same colour fluttered from the sides of his knees. He carried a high white hat in his hand, and running down the lane which had been kept open through the crowd to allow persons to reach the ring, he threw the hat high into the air, so that it fell within the staked enclosure. Then with a double spring he cleared the outer and inner line of rope, and stood with his arms folded in the centre.

I do not wonder that the people cheered. Even Belcher could not help joining in the general shout of applause. He was certainly a splendidly built young athlete, and one could not have wished to look upon a finer sight as his white skin, sleek and luminous as a panther's, gleamed in the light of the morning sun, with a beautiful liquid rippling of muscles at every movement. His arms were long and slingy, his shoulders loose and yet powerful, with the downward slant which is a surer index of power than squareness can be. He clasped his hands behind his head, threw them aloft, and swung them backwards, and at every movement some fresh expanse of his smooth, white skin became knobbed and gnarled with muscles, whilst a yell of admiration and delight from the crowd greeted each fresh exhibition. Then, folding his arms once more, he stood like a beautiful statue waiting for his antagonist.

Sir Lothian Hume had been looking impatiently at his watch, and now he shut it with a triumphant snap.

" Time's up ! " he cried. " The match is forfeit."

" Time is not up," said Craven.

" I have still five minutes." My uncle looked round with despairing eyes.

" Only three, Tregellis ! "

A deep angry murmur was rising from the crowd. " It's a cross ! It's a cross ! It's a fake ! " was the cry.

" Two minutes, Tregellis ! "

" Where's your man, Sir Charles ? Where's the man

that we have backed ? " Flushed faces began to crane over each other and angry eyes glared up at us.

" One more minute, Tregellis ! I am very sorry, but it will be my duty to declare it forfeit against you."

There was a sudden swirl in the crowd, a rush, a shout, and high up in the air there spun an old black hat, floating over the heads of the ring-siders and flickering down within the ropes.

" Saved, by the Lord ! " screamed Belcher.

" I rather fancy," said my uncle, calmly, " that this must be my man."

" Too late ! " cried Sir Lothian.

" No," answered the referee. " It was still twenty seconds to the hour. The fight will now proceed."

17. *The Ring-side*

OUT of the whole of that vast multitude I was one of the very few who had observed whence it was that this black hat, skimming so opportunely over the ropes, had come. I have already remarked that when we looked around us there had been a single gig travelling very rapidly upon the southern road. My uncle's eyes had rested upon it, but his attention had been drawn away by the discussion between Sir Lothian Hume and the referee upon the question of time. For my own part, I had been so struck by the furious manner in which these belated travellers were approaching, that I had continued to watch them with all sorts of vague hopes within me, which I did not dare to put into words for fear of adding to my uncle's disappointments. I had just made out that the gig contained a man and a woman, when suddenly I saw it swerve off the road, and come with a galloping horse and bounding wheels right across the moor, crashing through the gorse bushes, and sinking down to the hubs in the heather and bracken. As the driver pulled up his foam-spattered horse, he threw the

reins to his companion, sprang from his seat, butted furiously into the crowd, and then an instant afterwards up went the hat which told of his challenge and defiance.

" There is no hurry now, I presume, Craven," said my uncle, as coolly as if this sudden effect had been carefully devised by him.

" Now that your man has his hat in the ring you can take as much time as you like, Sir Charles."

" Your friend has certainly cut it rather fine, nephew."

" It is not Jim, sir," I whispered. " It is someone else."

My uncle's eyebrows betrayed his astonishment.

" Someone else ! " he ejaculated.

" And a good man too ! " roared Belcher, slapping his thigh with a crack like a pistol-shot. " Why, blow my dickey if it ain't old Jack Harrison himself ! "

Looking down at the crowd, we had seen the head and shoulders of a powerful and strenuous man moving slowly forward, and leaving behind him a long V-shaped ripple upon its surface like the wake of a swimming dog. Now, as he pushed his way through the looser fringe the head was raised, and there was the grinning, hardy face of the smith looking up at us. He had left his hat in the ring, and was enveloped in an overcoat with a blue bird's-eye handkerchief tied round his neck. As he emerged from the throng he let his great-coat fly loose, and showed that he was dressed in his full fighting kit—black drawers, chocolate stockings, and white shoes.

" I'm right sorry to be so late, Sir Charles," he cried. " I'd have been sooner, but it took me a little time to make it all straight with the missus. I couldn't convince her all at once, an' so I brought her with me, and we argued it out on the way."

Looking at the gig, I saw that it was indeed Mrs. Harrison who was seated in it. Sir Charles beckoned him up to the wheel of the curricle.

" What in the world brings you here, Harrison ? " he whispered. " I am as glad to see you as ever I was

to see a man in my life, but I confess that I did not expect you."

" Well, sir, you heard I was coming," said the smith.

" Indeed, I did not."

" Didn't you get a message, Sir Charles, from a man named Cumming, landlord of the Friar's Oak Inn? Mister Rodney there would know him."

" We saw him dead drunk at the George."

" There, now, if I wasn't afraid of it ! " cried Harrison, angrily. " He's always like that when he's excited, and I never saw a man more off his head than he was when he heard I was going to take this job over. He brought a bag of sovereigns up with him to back me with."

" That's how the betting got turned," said my uncle. " He found others to follow his lead, it appears."

" I was so afraid that he might get upon the drink that I made him promise to go straight to you, sir, the very instant he should arrive. He had a note to deliver."

" I understand that he reached the George at six, whilst I did not return from Reigate until after seven, by which time I have no doubt that he had drunk his message to me out of his head. But where is your nephew Jim, and how did you come to know that you would be needed ? "

" It is not his fault, I promise you, that you should be left in the lurch. As to me, I had my orders to take his place from the only man upon earth whose word I have never disobeyed."

" Yes, Sir Charles," said Mrs. Harrison, who had left the gig and approached us. " You can make the most of it this time, for never again shall you have my Jack— not if you were to go on your knees for him."

" She's not a patron of sport, and that's a fact," said the smith.

" Sport ! " she cried with shrill contempt and anger. " Tell me when all is over."

She hurried away, and I saw her afterwards seated amongst the bracken, her back turned towards the multi-

tude, and her hands over her ears, cowering and wincing in an agony of apprehension.

Whilst this hurried scene had been taking place, the crowd had become more and more tumultuous, partly from their impatience at the delay, and partly from their exuberant spirits at the unexpected chance of seeing so celebrated a fighting man as Harrison. His identity had already been noised abroad, and many an elderly connoisseur plucked his long net-purse out of his fob, in order to put a few guineas upon the man who would represent the school of the past against the present. The younger men were still in favour of the west-countryman, and small odds were to be had either way in proportion to the number of the supporters of each in the different parts of the crowd.

In the meantime Sir Lothian Hume had come bustling up to the Honourable Berkeley Craven, who was still standing near our curricle.

" I beg to lodge a formal protest against these proceedings," said he.

" On what grounds, sir ? "

" Because the man produced is not the original nominee of Sir Charles Tregellis."

" I never named one, as you are well aware," said my uncle.

" The betting has all been upon the understanding that young Jim Harrison was my man's opponent. Now, at the last moment, he is withdrawn and another and more formidable man put into his place."

" Sir Charles Tregellis is quite within his rights," said Craven, firmly. " He undertook to produce a man who should be within the age limits stipulated, and I understand that Harrison fulfils all the conditions. You are over five-and-thirty, Harrison ? "

" Forty-one next month, master."

" Very good. I direct that the fight proceed."

But, alas ! there was one authority which was higher even than that of the referee, and we were destined to an

experience which was the prelude, and sometimes the conclusion also, of many an old-time fight. Across the moor there had ridden a black-coated gentleman, with buff-topped hunting boots and a couple of grooms behind him, the little knot of horsemen showing up clearly upon the curving swells and then dipping down into the alternate hollows. Some of the more observant of the crowd had glanced suspiciously at this advancing figure, but the majority had not observed him at all until he reined up his horse upon a knoll which overlooked the amphitheatre, and in a stentorian voice announced that he represented the *Custos rotulorum* of His Majesty's county of Sussex, that he proclaimed this assembly to be gathered together for an illegal purpose, and that he was commissioned to disperse it by force, if necessary.

Never before had I understood that deep-seated fear and wholesome respect which many centuries of bludgeoning at the hands of the law had beaten into the fierce and turbulent natives of these islands. Here was a man with two attendants upon one side, and on the other thirty thousand very angry and disappointed people, many of them fighters by profession, and some from the roughest and most dangerous classes in the country. And yet it was the single man who appealed confidently to force, whilst the huge multitude swayed and murmured like a mutinous fierce-willed creature brought face to face with a power against which it knew that there was neither argument nor resistance. My uncle, however, with Berkeley Craven, Sir John Lade, and a dozen other lords and gentlemen, hurried across to the interrupter of the sport.

" I presume that you have a warrant, sir ? " said Craven.

" Yes, sir, I have a warrant."

" Then I have a legal right to inspect it."

The magistrate handed him a blue paper which the little knot of gentlemen clustered their heads over, for they were mostly magistrates themselves, and were

keenly alive to any possible flaw in the wording. At last Craven shrugged his shoulders, and handed it back.

" This seems to be correct, sir," said he.

" It is entirely correct," answered the magistrate, affably. " To prevent waste of your valuable time, gentlemen, I may say, once for all, that it is my unalterable determination that no fight shall, under any circumstances, be brought off in the county over which I have control, and I am prepared to follow you all day in order to prevent it."

To my inexperience this appeared to bring the whole matter to a conclusion, but I had underrated the foresight of those who arrange these affairs, and also the advantages which made Crawley Down so favourite a rendezvous. There was a hurried consultation between the principals, the backers, the referee and the time-keeper.

" It's seven miles to Hampshire border and about two to Surrey," said Jackson. The famous Master of the Ring was clad in honour of the occasion in a most resplendent scarlet coat worked in gold at the button-holes, a white stock, a looped hat with a broad black band, buff knee-breeches, white silk stockings and paste buckles —a costume which did justice to his magnificent figure, and especially to those famous " balustrade " calves which had helped him to be the finest runner and jumper as well as the most formidable pugilist in England. His hard, high-boned face, large piercing eyes, and immense physique made him a fitting leader for that rough and tumultuous body who had named him as their commander-in-chief.

" If I might venture to offer you a word of advice," said the affable official, " it would be to make for the Hampshire line, for Sir James Ford, on the Surrey border, has as great an objection to such assemblies as I have, whilst Mr. Merridew, of Long Hall, who is the Hampshire magistrate, has fewer scruples upon the point."

" Sir," said my uncle, raising his hat in his most

impressive manner, " I am infinitely obliged to you. With the referee's permission, there is nothing for it but to shift the stakes."

In an instant a scene of the wildest animation had set in. Tom Owen and his assistant, Fogo, with the help of the ring-keepers, plucked up the stakes and ropes, and carried them off across country. Crab Wilson was enveloped in greatcoats, and borne away in the barouche, whilst Champion Harrison took Mr. Craven's place in our curricle. Then off the huge crowd started, horsemen, vehicles and pedestrians, rolling slowly over the broad face of the moorland. The carriages rocked and pitched like boats in a seaway, as they lumbered along, fifty abreast, scrambling and lurching over everything which came in their way. Sometimes, with a snap and a thud, one axle would come to the ground, whilst a wheel reeled off amidst the tussocks of heather, and roars of delight greeted the owners as they looked ruefully at the ruin. Then as the gorse clumps grew thinner, and the sward more level, those on foot began to run, the riders struck in their spurs, the drivers cracked their whips, and away they all streamed in the maddest, wildest cross-country steeple-chase, the yellow barouche and the crimson curricle, which held the two champions, leading the van.

" What do you think of your chances, Harrison ? " I heard my uncle ask, as the two mares picked their way over the broken ground.

" It's my last fight, Sir Charles," said the smith. " You heard the missus say that if she let me off this time I was never to ask again. I must try and make it a good one."

" But your training ? "

" I'm always in training, sir. I work hard from morning to night, and I drink little else than water. I don't think that Captain Barclay can do much better with all his rules."

" He's rather long in the reach for you."

" I've fought and beat t em that were longer. If it

comes to a rally I should hold my own, and I should have the better of him at a throw."

"It's a match of youth against experience. Well, I would not hedge a guinea of my money. But, unless he was acting under force, I cannot forgive young Jim for having deserted me."

"He *was* acting under force, Sir Charles."

"You have seen him, then?"

"No, master, I have not seen him."

"You know where he is?"

"Well, it is not for me to say one way or the other. I can only tell you that he could not help himself. But here's the beak a-comin' for us again."

The ominous figure galloped up once more alongside of our curricle, but this time his mission was a more amiable one.

"My jurisdiction ends at that ditch, sir," said he. "I should fancy that you could hardly wish a better place for a mill than the sloping field beyond. I am quite sure that no one will interfere with you there."

His anxiety that the fight should be brought off was in such contrast to the zeal with which he had chased us from his county, that my uncle could not help remarking upon it.

"It is not for a magistrate to wink at the breaking of the law, sir," he answered. "But if my colleague of Hampshire has no scruples about its being brought off within his jurisdiction, I should very much like to see the fight," with which he spurred his horse up an adjacent knoll, from which he thought that he might gain the best view of the proceedings.

And now I had a view of all those points of etiquette and curious survivals of custom which are so recent, that we have not yet appreciated that they may some day be as interesting to the social historian as they then were to the sportsman. A dignity was given to the contest by a rigid code of ceremony, just as the clash of mail-clad knights was prefaced and adorned by the calling of the

heralds and the showing of blazoned shields. To many in those ancient days the tourney may have seemed a bloody and brutal ordeal, but we who look at it with ample perspective see that it was a rude but gallant preparation for the conditions of life in an iron age. And so also, when the Ring has become as extinct as the lists, we may understand that a broader philosophy would show that all things, which spring up so naturally and spontaneously, have a function to fulfil, and that it is a less evil that two men should, of their own free will, fight until they can fight no more, than that the standard of hardihood and endurance should run the slightest risk of being lowered in a nation which depends so largely upon the individual qualities of her citizens for her defence. Do away with war, if the cursed thing can by any wit of man be avoided, but until you see your way to that, have a care in meddling with those primitive qualities to which at any moment you may have to appeal for your own protection.

Tom Owen and his singular assistant, Fogo, who combined the functions of prize-fighter and of poet, though, fortunately for himself, he could use his fists better than his pen, soon had the ring arranged according to the rules then in vogue. The white wooden posts, each with the P.C. of the pugilistic club printed upon it, were so fixed as to leave a square of 24 feet within the roped enclosure. Outside this ring an outer one was pitched, eight feet separating the two. The inner was for the combatants and for their seconds, while in the outer there were places for the referee, the timekeeper, the backers, and a few select and fortunate individuals, of whom, through being in my uncle's company, I was one. Some twenty well-known prize-fighters, including my friend Bill Warr, Black Richmond, Maddox, The Pride of Westminster, Tom Belcher, Paddington Jones, Tough Tom Blake, Symonds the ruffian, Tyne the tailor and others, were stationed in the outer ring as beaters. These fellows all wore the high white hats which were at that

time much affected by the Fancy, and they were armed with horse-whips, silver-mounted, and each bearing the P.C. monogram. Did anyone, be it East End rough or West End patrician, intrude within the outer ropes, this corps of guardians neither argued nor expostulated, but they fell upon the offender and laced him with their whips until he escaped back out of the forbidden ground. Even with so formidable a guard and such fierce measures, the beaters-out, who had to check the forward heaves of a maddened, straining crowd, were often as exhausted at the end of a fight as the principals themselves. In the meantime they formed up in a line of sentinels, presenting under their row of white hats every type of fighting face, from the fresh boyish countenances of Tom Belcher, Jones, and the other younger recruits, to the scarred and mutilated visages of the veteran bruisers.

Whilst the business of the fixing of the stakes and the fastening of the ropes was going forward, I from my place of vantage could hear the talk of the crowd behind me, the front two rows of which were lying upon the grass, the next two kneeling, and the others standing, in serried ranks all up the side of the gently sloping hill, so that each line could just see over the shoulders of that which was in front. There were several, and those amongst the most experienced, who took the gloomiest view of Harrison's chances, and it made my heart heavy to overhear them.

" It's the old story over again," said one. " They won't bear in mind that youth will be served. They only learn wisdom when it's knocked into them."

" Aye, aye," responded another. " That's how Jack Slack thrashed Broughton, and I myself saw Hooper, the tinman, beat to pieces by the fighting oilman. They all come to it in time, and now it's Harrison's turn."

" Don't you be so sure about that ! " cried a third. " I've seen Jack Harrison fight five times, and I never yet saw him have the worst of it. He's a slaughterer, and so I tell you."

" He was, you mean."

" Well, I don't see no such difference as all that comes to, and I'm putting ten guineas on my opinion."

" Why," said a loud, consequential man from immediately behind me, speaking with a broad western burr, " vrom what I've zeen of this young Gloucester lad, I doan't think Harrison could have stood bevore him for ten rounds when he vas in his prime. I vas coming up in the Bristol coach yesterday, and the guard he told me that he had vifteen thousand pound in hard gold in the boot that had been zent up to back our man."

" They'll be in luck if they see their money again," said another. " Harrison's no lady's-maid fighter, and he's blood to the bone. He'd have a shy at it if his man was as big as Carlton House."

" Tut," answered the west-countryman. " It's only in Bristol and Gloucester that you can get men to beat Bristol and Gloucester."

" It's like your damned himpudence to say so," said an angry voice from the throng behind him. " There are six men in London that would hengage to walk round the best twelve that hever came from the west."

The proceedings might have opened by an impromptu bye-battle between the indignant cockney and the gentleman from Bristol, but a prolonged roar of applause broke in upon their altercation. It was caused by the appearance in the ring of Crab Wilson, followed by Dutch Sam and Mendoza carrying the basin, sponge, brandy-bladder and other badges of their office. As he entered Wilson pulled the canary-yellow handkerchief from his waist, and going to the corner post, he tied it to the top of it, where it remained fluttering in the breeze. He then took a bundle of smaller ribands of the same colour from his seconds, and walking round, he offered them to the noblemen and Corinthians at half-a-guinea apiece as souvenirs of the fight. His brisk trade was only brought to an end by the appearance of Harrison, who climbed in a very leisurely manner over the ropes, as

befitted his more mature years and less elastic joints. The yell which greeted him was even more enthusiastic than that which had heralded Wilson, and there was a louder ring of admiration in it, for the crowd had already had their opportunity of seeing Wilson's physique, whilst Harrison's was a surprise to them.

I had often looked upon the mighty arms and neck of the smith, but I had never before seen him stripped to the waist, or understood the marvellous symmetry of development which had made him in his youth the favourite model of the London sculptors. There was none of that white sleek skin and shimmering play of sinew which made Wilson a beautiful picture, but in its stead there was a rugged grandeur of knotted and tangled muscle, as though the roots of some old tree were writhing from breast to shoulder, and from shoulder to elbow. Even in repose the sun threw shadows from the curves of his skin, but when he exerted himself every muscle bunched itself up, distinct and hard, breaking his whole trunk into gnarled knots of sinew. His skin, on face and body, was darker and harsher than that of his youthful antagonist, but he looked tougher and harder, an effect which was increased by the sombre colour of his stockings and breeches. He entered the ring, sucking a lemon, with Jem Belcher and Caleb Baldwin, the coster, at his heels. Strolling across to the post, he tied his blue bird's-eye handkerchief over the west-countryman's yellow, and then walked to his opponent with his hand out.

" I hope I see you well, Wilson," said he.

" Pretty tidy, I thank you," answered the other. " We'll speak to each other in a different vashion, I 'spects, afore we part."

" But no ill-feeling," said the smith, and the two fighting men grinned at each other as they took their own corners.

" May I ask, Mr. Referee, whether these two men have been weighed ? " asked Sir Lothian Hume, standing up in the outer ring.

" Their weight has just been taken under my super-vision, sir," answered Mr. Craven. " Your man brought the scale down at thirteen-three, and Harrison at thirteen-eight."

" He's a fifteen stoner from the loins upwards," cried Dutch Sam from his corner.

" We'll get some of it off him before we finish."

" You'll get more off him than ever you bargained for," answered Jem Belcher, and the crowd laughed at the rough chaff.

18. *The Smith's Last Battle*

" CLEAR the outer ring ! " cried Jackson, standing up beside the ropes with a big silver watch in his hand.

" Ss-whack ! ss-whack ! ss-whack ! " went the horse-whips—for a number of the spectators, either driven onwards by the pressure behind or willing to risk some physical pain on the chance of getting a better view, had crept under the ropes and formed a ragged fringe within the outer ring. Now, amidst roars of laughter from the crowd and a shower of blows from the beaters-out, they dived madly back, with the ungainly haste of frightened sheep blundering through a gap in their hurdles. Their case was a hard one, for the folk in front refused to yield an inch of their places—but the arguments from the rear prevailed over everything else, and presently every frantic fugitive had been absorbed, whilst the beaters-out took their stands along the edge at regular intervals, with their whips held down by their thighs.

" Gentlemen," cried Jackson, again, " I am requested to inform you that Sir Charles Tregellis's nominee is Jack Harrison, fighting at thirteen-eight, and Sir Lothian Hume's is Crab Wilson, at thirteen-three. No person can be allowed at the inner ropes save the referee and the time-keeper. I have only to beg that, if the occasion

should require it, you will all give me your assistance to keep the ground clear, to prevent confusion and to have a fair fight. All ready ? "

" All ready ? " from both corners.

" Time ! "

There was a breathless hush as Harrison, Wilson, Belcher and Dutch Sam walked very briskly into the centre of the ring. The two men shook hands, whilst their seconds did the same, the four hands crossing each other. Then the seconds dropped back, and the two champions stood toe to toe, with their hands up.

It was a magnificent sight to anyone who had not lost his sense of appreciation of the noblest of all the works of Nature. Both men fulfilled that requisite of the powerful athlete that they should look larger without their clothes than with them. In Ring slang, they buffed well. And each showed up the other's points on account of the extreme contrast between them : the long, loose-limbed, deer-footed youngster, and the square-set, rugged veteran with his trunk like the stump of an oak. The betting began to rise upon the younger man from the instant that they were put face to face, for his advantages were obvious, whilst those qualities which had brought Harrison to the top in his youth were only a memory in the minds of the older men. All could see the three inches extra of height and two of reach which Wilson possessed, and a glance at the quick, cat-like motions of his feet, and the perfect poise of his body upon his legs, showed how swiftly he could spring either in or out from his slower adversary. But it took a subtler insight to read the grim smile which flickered over the smith's mouth, or the smouldering fire which shone in his grey eyes, and it was only the old-timers who knew that, with his mighty heart and his iron frame, he was a perilous man to lay odds against.

Wilson stood in the position from which he had derived his nickname, his left hand and left foot well to the front, his body sloped very far back from his loins, and his guard

thrown across his chest, but held well forward in a way which made him exceedingly hard to get at. The smith, on the other hand, assumed the obsolete attitude which Humphries and Mendoza introduced, but which had not for ten years been seen in a first-class battle. Both his knees were slightly bent, he stood square to his opponent, and his two big brown fists were held over his mark so that he could lead equally with either. Wilson's hands, which moved incessantly in and out, had been stained with some astringent juice with the purpose of preventing them from puffing, and so great was the contrast between them and his white fore-arms, that I imagined that he was wearing dark, close-fitting gloves until my uncle explained the matter in a whisper. So they stood in a quiver of eagerness and expectation, whilst that huge multitude hung so silently and breathlessly upon every motion that they might have believed themselves to be alone, man to man, in the centre of some primeval solitude.

It was evident from the beginning that Crab Wilson meant to throw no chance away, and that he would trust to his lightness of foot and quickness of hand until he should see something of the tactics of this rough-looking antagonist. He paced swiftly round several times, with little, elastic, menacing steps, whilst the smith pivoted slowly to correspond. Then, as Wilson took a backward step to induce Harrison to break his ground and follow him, the older man grinned and shook his head.

" You must come to me, lad," said he. " I'm too old to scamper round the ring after you. But we have the day before us, and I'll wait."

He may not have expected his invitation to be so promptly answered ; but in an instant, with a panther spring, the west-countryman was on him. Smack ! smack ! smack ! Thud ! thud ! The first three were on Harrison's face, the last two were heavy counters upon Wilson's body. Back danced the youngster, disengaging himself in beautiful style but with two angry red blotches

over the lower line of his ribs. " Blood for Wilson ! "
yelled the crowd, and as the smith faced round to follow
the movements of his nimble adversary, I saw with a thrill
that his chin was crimson and dripping. In came Wilson
again with a feint at the mark and a flush hit on Harrison's
cheek ; then, breaking the force of the smith's ponderous
right counter, he brought the round to a conclusion by
slipping down upon the grass.

" First knock-down for Harrison ! " roared a thousand
voices, for ten times as many pounds would change hands
upon the point.

" I appeal to the referee ! " cried Sir Lothian Hume.
" It was a slip, and not a knock-down."

" I give it a slip," said Berkeley Craven, and the men
walked to their corners, amidst a general shout of applause
for a spirited and well-contested opening round.
Harrison fumbled in his mouth with his finger and thumb,
and then with a sharp half-turn he wrenched out a tooth,
which he threw into the basin. " Quite like old times,"
said he to Belcher.

" Have a care, Jack ! " whispered the anxious second.
" You got rather more than you gave."

" Maybe I can carry more, too," said he serenely,
whilst Caleb Baldwin mopped the big sponge over his
face, and the shining bottom of the tin basin ceased
suddenly to glimmer through the water.

I could gather from the comments of the experienced
Corinthians around me, and from the remarks of the
crowd behind, that Harrison's chance was thought to
have been lessened by this round.

" I've seen his old faults, and I haven't seen his old
merits," said Sir John Lade, our opponent of the Brighton
Road. " He's as slow on his feet and with his guard as
ever. Wilson hit him as he liked."

" Wilson may hit him three times to his once, but his
one is worth Wilson's three," remarked my uncle. " He's
a natural fighter and the other an excellent sparrer, but
I don't hedge a guinea."

A sudden hush announced that the men were on their feet again, and so skilfully had the seconds done their work, that neither looked a jot the worse for what had passed. Wilson led viciously with his left, but mis-judged his distance, receiving a smashing counter on the mark in reply which sent him reeling and gasping to the ropes. " Hurrah for the old one ! " yelled the mob, and my uncle laughed and nudged Sir John Lade. The west-countryman smiled, and shook himself like a dog from the water as with a stealthy step he came back to the centre of the ring, where his man was still standing. Bang came Harrison's right upon the mark once more, but Crab broke the blow with his elbow, and jumped laughing away. Both men were a little winded, and their quick, high breathing, with the light patter of their feet as they danced round each other, blended into one continuous long-drawn sound. Two simultaneous exchanges with the left made a clap like a pistol-shot, and then as Harrison rushed in for a fall, Wilson slipped him, and over went my old friend upon his face, partly from the impetus of his own futile attack, and partly from a swinging half-arm blow which the west-countryman brought home upon his ear as he passed.

" Knock-down for Wilson," cried the referee, and the answering roar was like the broadside of a seventy-four. Up went hundreds of curly-brimmed Corinthian hats into the air, and the slope before us was a bank of flushed and yelling faces. My heart was cramped with my fears, and I winced at every blow, yet I was conscious also of an absolute fascination, with a wild thrill of fierce joy and a certain exultation in our common human nature which could rise above pain and fear in its straining after the very humblest form of fame.

Belcher and Baldwin had pounced upon their man, and had him up and in his corner in an instant, but, in spite of the coolness with which the hardy smith took his punishment, there was immense exultation amongst the west-countrymen.

" We've got him ! He's beat ! He's beat ! " shouted the two Jew seconds. " It's a hundred to a tizzy on Gloucester ! "

" Beat, is he ? " answered Belcher. " You'll need to. rent this field before you can beat him, for he'll stand a month of that kind of fly-flappin'." He was swinging a towel in front of Harrison as he spoke, whilst Baldwin mopped him with the sponge.

" How is it with you, Harrison ? " asked my uncle.

" Hearty as a buck, sir. It's as right as the day."

The cheery answer came with so merry a ring that the clouds cleared from my uncle's face.

" You should recommend your man to lead more, Tregellis," said Sir John Lade. " He'll never win it unless he leads."

" He knows more about the game than you or I do, Lade. I'll let him take his own way."

" The betting is three to one against him now," said a gentleman, whose grizzled moustache showed that he was an officer of the late war.

" Very true, General Fitzpatrick. But you'll observe that it is the raw young bloods who are giving the odds, and the Sheenies who are taking them. I still stick to my opinion."

The two men came briskly up to the scratch at the call of time, the smith a little lumpy on one side of his head, but with the same good-humoured and yet menacing smile upon his lips. As to Wilson, he was exactly as he had begun in appearance, but twice I saw him close his lips sharply as if he were in a sudden spasm of pain, and the blotches over his ribs were darkening from scarlet to a sullen purple. He held his guard somewhat lower to screen this vulnerable point, and he danced round his opponent with a lightness which showed that his wind had not been impaired by the body-blows, whilst the smith still adopted the impassive tactics with which he had commenced.

Many rumours had come up to us from the west as to

Crab Wilson's fine science and the quickness of his hitting, but the truth surpassed what had been expected of him. In this round and the two which followed he showed a swiftness and accuracy which old ring-siders declared that Mendoza in his prime had never surpassed. He was in and out like lightning, and his blows were heard and felt rather than seen. But Harrison still took them all with the same dogged smile, occasionally getting in a hard body-blow in return, for his adversary's height and his position combined to keep his face out of danger. At the end of the fifth round the odds were four to one, and the west-countrymen were riotous in their exultation.

" What think you now ? " cried the west-countryman behind me, and in his excitement he could get no further save to repeat over and over again, " What think you now ? " When in the sixth round the smith was peppered twice without getting in a counter, and had the worst of the fall as well, the fellow became inarticulate altogether, and could only huzza wildly in his delight. Sir Lothian Hume was smiling and nodding his head, whilst my uncle was coldly impassive, though I was sure that his heart was as heavy as mine.

" This won't do, Tregellis," said General Fitzpatrick. " My money is on the old one, but the other is the finer boxer."

" My man is *un peu passé*, but he will come through all right," answered my uncle.

I saw that both Belcher and Baldwin were looking grave, and I knew that we must have a change of some sort, or the old tale of youth and age would be told once more.

The seventh round, however, showed the reserve strength of the hardy old fighter, and lengthened the faces of those layers of odds who had imagined that the fight was practically over, and that a few finishing rounds would have given the smith his *coup-de-grâce*. It was clear when the two men faced each other that Wilson had made himself up for mischief and meant to force the fighting

and maintain the lead which he had gained, but that grey gleam was not quenched yet in the veteran's eyes, and still the same smile played over his grim face. He had become more jaunty, too, in the swing of his shoulders and the poise of his head, and it brought my confidence back to see the brisk way in which he squared up to his man.

Wilson led with his left, but was short, and he only just avoided a dangerous right-hander which whistled in at his ribs. " Bravo, old 'un, one of those will be a dose of laudanum if you get it home," cried Belcher. There was a pause of shuffling feet and hard breathing, broken by the thud of a tremendous body-blow from Wilson, which the smith stopped with the utmost coolness. Then again a few seconds of silent tension, when Wilson led viciously at the head, but Harrison took it on his forearm, smiling and nodding at his opponent. " Get the pepper-box open ! " yelled Mendoza, and Wilson sprang in to carry out his instructions, but was hit out again by a heavy drive on the chest. " Now's the time ! Follow it up ! " cried Belcher, and in rushed the smith, pelting in his half-arm blows, and taking the returns without a wince, until Crab Wilson went down exhausted in the corner. Both men had their marks to show, but Harrison had all the best of the rally, so it was our turn to throw our hats into the air and to shout ourselves hoarse, whilst the seconds clapped their man upon his broad back as they hurried him to his corner.

" What think you now ? " shouted all the neighbours of the west-countryman, repeating his own refrain.

" Why, Dutch Sam never put in a better rally," cried Sir John Lade. " What's the betting now, Sir Lothian ? "

" I have laid all that I intend ; but I don't think my man can lose it." For all that, the smile had faded from his face, and I observed that he glanced continually over his shoulder into the crowd behind him.

A sullen purple cloud had been drifting slowly up from the south-west—though I dare say that out of

thirty thousand folk there were very few who had spared the time or attention to mark it. Now it suddenly made its presence apparent by a few heavy drops of rain, thickening rapidly into a sharp shower, which filled the air with its hiss, and rattled noisily upon the high, hard hats of the Corinthians. Coat-collars were turned up and handkerchiefs tied round necks, whilst the skins of the two men glistened with the moisture as they stood up to each other once more. I noticed that Belcher whispered very earnestly into Harrison's ear as he rose from his knee, and that the smith nodded his head curtly, with the air of a man who understands and approves of his orders.

And what those orders were was instantly apparent. Harrison was to be turned from the defender into the attacker. The result of the rally in the last round had convinced his seconds that when it came to give-and-take hitting, their hardy and powerful man was likely to have the better of it. And then on the top of this came the rain. With the slippery grass the superior activity of Wilson would be neutralised, and he would find it harder to avoid the rushes of his opponent. It was in taking advantage of such circumstances that the art of ringcraft lay, and many a shrewd and vigilant second had won a losing battle for his man. " Go in, then ! Go in ! " whooped the two prize-fighters, while every backer in the crowd took up the roar.

And Harrison went in, in such fashion that no man who saw him do it will ever forget it. Crab Wilson, as game as a pebble, met him with a flush hit every time, but no human strength or human science seemed capable of stopping the terrible onslaught of this iron man. Round after round he scrambled his way in, slap-bang, right and left, every hit tremendously sent home. Sometimes he covered his own face with his left, and sometimes he disdained to use any guard at all, but his springing hits were irresistible. The rain lashed down upon them, pouring from their faces and running in crimson trickles

over their bodies, but neither gave any heed to it save to manœuvre always with the view of bringing it into each other's eyes. But round after round the west-country-man fell, and round after round the betting rose, until the odds were higher in our favour than ever they had been against us. With a sinking heart, filled with pity and admiration for these two gallant men, I longed that every bout might be the last, and yet the " Time ! " was hardly out of Jackson's mouth before they had both sprung from their seconds' knees, with laughter upon their mutilated faces and chaffing words upon their bleeding lips. It may have been a humble object-lesson, but I give you my word that many a time in my life I have braced myself to a hard task by the remembrance of that morning upon Crawley Downs, asking myself if my manhood were so weak that I would not do for my country, or for those whom I loved, as much as these two would endure for a paltry stake and for their own credit amongst their fellows. Such a spectacle may brutalise those who are brutal, but I say that there is a spiritual side to it also, and that the sight of the utmost human limit of endurance and courage is one which bears a lesson of its own.

But if the Ring can breed bright virtues, it is but a partisan who can deny that it can be the mother of black vices also, and we were destined that morning to have a sight of each. It so chanced that, as the battle went against his man, my eyes stole round very often to note the expression upon Sir Lothian Hume's face, for I knew how fearlessly he had laid the odds, and I understood that his fortunes as well as his champion were going down before the smashing blows of the old bruiser. The confident smile with which he had watched the opening rounds had long vanished from his lips, and his cheeks had turned of a sallow pallor, whilst his small, fierce grey eyes looked furtively from under his craggy brows, and more than once he burst into savage imprecations when Wilson was beaten to the ground. But especially I noticed that his chin was always coming round to his

shoulder, and that at the end of every round he sent keen little glances flying backwards into the crowd. For some time, amidst the immense hill-side of faces which banked themselves up on the slope behind us, I was unable to pick out the exact point at which his gaze was directed. But at last I succeeded in following it. A very tall man, who showed a pair of broad, bottle-green shoulders high above his neighbours, was looking very hard in our direction, and I assured myself that a quick exchange of almost imperceptible signals was going on between him and the Corinthian baronet. I became conscious, also, as I watched this stranger, that the cluster of men around him were the roughest elements of the whole assembly : fierce, vicious-looking fellows, with cruel debauched faces, who howled like a pack of wolves at every blow, and yelled execrations at Harrison whenever he walked across to his corner. So turbulent were they that I saw the ringkeepers whisper together and glance up in their direction, as if preparing for trouble in store, but none of them had realised how near it was to breaking out, or how dangerous it might prove.

Thirty rounds had been fought in an hour and twenty-five minutes, and the rain was pelting down harder than ever. A thick steam rose from the two fighters, and the ring was a pool of mud. Repeated falls had turned the men brown, with a horrible mottling of crimson blotches. Round after round had ended by Crab Wilson going down, and it was evident, even to my inexperienced eyes, that he was weakening rapidly. He leaned heavily upon the two Jews when they led him to his corner, and he reeled when their support was withdrawn. Yet his science had, through long practice, become an automatic thing with him so that he stopped and hit with less power, but with as great accuracy as ever. Even now a casual observer might have thought that he had the best of the battle, for the smith was far the more terribly marked, but there was a wild stare in the west-countryman's eyes, and a strange catch in his breathing, which told us that it is

not the most dangerous blow which shows upon the surface. A heavy cross-buttock at the end of the thirty-first round shook the breath from his body, and he came up for the thirty-second with the same jaunty gallantry as ever, but with the dazed expression of a man whose wind has been utterly smashed.

" He's got the roly-polies," cried Belcher. " You have it your own way now ! "

" I'll vight for a week yet," gasped Wilson.

" Damme, I like his style," cried Sir John Lade. " No shifting, nothing shy, no hugging nor hauling. It's a shame to let him fight. Take the brave fellow away ! "

" Take him away ! Take him away ! " echoed a hundred voices.

" I won't be taken away ! Who dares say so ? " cried Wilson, who was back, after another fall, upon his second's knee.

" His heart won't suffer him to cry ' Enough,' " said General Fitzpatrick. " As his patron, Sir Lothian, you should direct the sponge to be thrown up."

" You think he can't win it ? "

" He is hopelessly beat, sir."

" You don't know him. He's a glutton of the first water."

" A gamer man never pulled his shirt off ; but the other is too strong for him."

" Well, sir, I believe that he can fight another ten rounds." He half turned as he spoke, and I saw him throw up his left arm with a singular gesture into the air.

" Cut the ropes ! Fair play ! Wait till the rain stops ! " roared a stentorian voice behind me, and I saw that it came from the big man with the bottle-green coat. His cry was a signal, for, like a thunderclap, there came a hundred hoarse voices shouting together : " Fair play for Gloucester ! Break the ring ! Break the ring ! "

Jackson had called " Time," and the two mud-plastered men were already upon their feet, but the interest had suddenly changed from the fight to the

audience. A succession of heaves from the back of the crowd had sent a series of long ripples running through it, all the heads swaying rhythmically in the one direction like a wheatfield in a squall. With every impulsion the oscillation increased, those in front trying vainly to steady themselves against the rushes from behind, until suddenly there came a sharp snap, two white stakes with earth clinging to their points flew into the outer ring, and a spray of people, dashed from the solid wave behind, were thrown against the line of the beaters-out. Down came the long horse-whips, swayed by the most vigorous arms in England ; but the wincing and shouting victims had no sooner scrambled back a few yards from the merciless cuts, before a fresh charge from the rear hurled them once more into the arms of the prize-fighters. Many threw themselves down upon the turf and allowed successive waves to pass over their bodies, whilst others, driven wild by the blows, returned them with their hunting-crops and walking-canes. And then, as half the crowd strained to the left and half to the right to avoid the pressure from behind, the vast mass was suddenly reft in twain, and through the gap surged the rough fellows from behind, all armed with loaded sticks and yelling for " Fair play and Gloucester ! " Their determined rush carried the prize-fighters before them, the inner ropes snapped like threads, and in an instant the ring was a swirling, seething mass of figures, whips and sticks falling and clattering, whilst, face to face, in the middle of it all, so wedged that they could neither advance nor retreat, the smith and the west-countryman continued their long-drawn battle as oblivious of the chaos raging round them as two bull-dogs would have been who had got each other by the throat. The driving rain, the cursing and screams of pain, the swish of the blows, the yelling of orders and advice, the heavy smell of the damp cloth—every incident of that scene of my early youth comes back to me now in my old age as clearly as if it had been but yesterday.

It was not easy for us to observe anything at the time,

however, for we were ourselves in the midst of the frantic crowd, swaying about and carried occasionally quite off our feet, but endeavouring to keep our places behind Jackson and Berkeley Craven, who, with sticks and whips meeting over their heads, were still calling the rounds and superintending the fight.

" The ring's broken ! " shouted Sir Lothian Hume. " I appeal to the referee ! The fight is null and void."

" You villain ! " cried my uncle, hotly ; " this is your doing."

" You have already an account to answer for with me," said Hume, with his sinister sneer, and as he spoke he was swept by the rush of the crowd into my uncle's very arms. The two men's faces were not more than a few inches apart, and Sir Lothian's bold eyes had to sink before the imperious scorn which gleamed coldly in those of my uncle.

" We will settle our accounts, never fear, though I degrade myself in meeting such a blackleg. What is it, Craven ? "

" We shall have to declare a draw, Tregellis."

" My man has the fight in hand."

" I cannot help it. I cannot attend to my duties when every moment I am cut over with a whip or a stick."

Jackson suddenly made a wild dash into the crowd, but returned with empty hands and a rueful face.

" They've stolen my timekeeper's watch," he cried. " A little cove snatched it out of my hand."

My uncle clapped his hand to his fob.

" Mine has gone also ! " he cried.

" Draw it at once, or your man will get hurt," said Jackson, and we saw that as the undaunted smith stood up to Wilson for another round, a dozen rough fellows were clustering round him with bludgeons.

" Do you consent to a draw, Sir Lothian Hume ? "

" I do."

" And you, Sir Charles ? "

" Certainly not."

" The ring is gone."

" That is no fault of mine."

" Well, I see no help for it. As referee I order that the men be withdrawn, and that the stakes be returned to their owners."

" A draw ! A draw ! " shrieked everyone, and the crowd in an instant dispersed in every direction, the pedestrians running to get a good lead upon the London road, and the Corinthians in search of their horses and carriages. Harrison ran over to Wilson's corner and shook him by the hand.

" I hope I have not hurt you much."

" I'm hard put to it to stand. How are you ? "

" My head's singin' like a kettle. It was the rain that helped me."

" Yes, I thought I had you beat one time. I never wish a better battle."

" Nor me either. Good-bye."

And so those two brave-hearted fellows made their way amidst the yelping roughs, like two wounded lions amidst a pack of wolves and jackals. I say again that, if the Ring has fallen low, it is not in the main the fault of the men who have done the fighting, but it lies at the door of the vile crew of ring-side parasites and ruffians, who are as far below the honest pugilist as the welsher and the blackleg are below the noble racehorse which serves them as a pretext for their villainies.

19. *Cliffe Royal*

MY uncle was humanely anxious to get Harrison to bed as soon as possible, for the smith, although he laughed at his own injuries, had none the less been severely punished.

" Don't you dare ever to ask my leave to fight again, Jack Harrison," said his wife, as she looked ruefully at his battered face. " Why, it's worse than when you

beat Black Baruk ; and if it weren't for your topcoat, I couldn't swear you were the man who led me to the altar ! If the King of England ask you, I'll never let you do it more."

"Well, old lass, I give my davy that I never will. It's best that I leave fightin' before fightin' leaves me. He screwed up his face as he took a sup from Sir Charles's brandy flask. "It's fine liquor, sir, but it gets into my cut lips most cruel. Why, here's John Cummings, of the Friar's Oak Inn, as I'm a sinner, and seekin' for a mad doctor, to judge by the look of him ! "

It was certainly a most singular figure who was approaching us over the moor. With the flushed, dazed face of a man who is just recovering from recent intoxication, the landlord was tearing madly about, his hat gone, and his hair and beard flying in the wind. He ran in little zigzags from one knot of people to another, whilst his peculiar appearance drew a running fire of witticisms as he went, so that he reminded me irresistibly of a snipe skimming along through a line of guns. We saw him stop for an instant by the yellow barouche, and hand something to Sir Lothian Hume. Then on he came again, until at last, catching sight of us, he gave a cry of joy, and ran for us full speed with a note held out at arm's length.

"You're a nice cove, too, John Cummings," said Harrison, reproachfully. "Didn't I tell you not to let a drop pass your lips until you had given your message to Sir Charles ? "

"I ought to be pole-axed, I ought," he cried in bitter repentance. "I asked for you, Sir Charles, as I'm a livin' man, I did, but you weren't there, and what with bein' so pleased at gettin' such odds when I knew Harrison was goin' to fight, an' what with the landlord at the George wantin' me to try his own specials, I let my senses go clean away from me. And now it's only after the fight is over that I see you, Sir Charles, an' if you lay that whip over my back, it'_ only what I deserve."

But my uncle was paying no attention whatever to the voluble self-reproaches of the landlord.   He had opened the note, and was reading it with a slight raising of the eyebrows, which was almost the very highest note in his limited emotional gamut.

" What make you of this, nephew ? " he asked, handing it to me.

This was what I read—

" SIR CHARLES TREGELLIS,
     " For God's sake, come at once, when this reaches you, to Cliffe Royal, and tarry as little as possible upon the way.   You will see me there, and you will hear much which concerns you deeply.   I pray you to come as soon as may be ; and until then I remain him whom you knew as

" JAMES HARRISON."

" Well, nephew ? " asked my uncle.
" Why, sir, I cannot tell what it may mean."
" Who gave it to you, sirrah ? "
" It was young Jim Harrison himself, sir," said the landlord, " though indeed I scarce knew him at first, for he looked like his own ghost.   He was so eager that it should reach you that he would not leave me until the horse was harnessed and I started upon my way.   There was one note for you and one for Sir Lothian Hume, and I wish to God he had chosen a better messenger ! "

" This is a mystery indeed," said my uncle, bending his brows over the note.   " What should he be doing at that house of ill-omen ?   And why does he sign him-self ' him whom you knew as Jim Harrison ' ?   By what other style should I know him ?   Harrison, you can throw a light upon this.   You, Mrs. Harrison ; I see by your face that you understand it."

" Maybe we do, Sir Charles ; but we are plain folk, my Jack and I, and we go as far as we see our way, and when we don't see our way anv longer, we just stop..

We've been goin' this twenty year, but now we'll draw aside and let our betters get to the front ; so if you wish to find what that note means, I can only advise you to do what you are asked, and to drive over to Cliffe Royal, where you will find out."

My uncle put the note into his pocket.

" I don't move until I have seen you safely in the hands of the surgeon, Harrison."

" Never mind for me, sir. The missus and me can drive down to Crawley in the gig, and a yard of stickin' plaster and a raw steak will soon set me to rights."

But my uncle was by no means to be persuaded, and he drove the pair into Crawley, where the smith was left under the charge of his wife in the very best quarters which money could procure. Then, after a hasty luncheon, we turned the mares' heads for the south.

" This ends my connection with the Ring, nephew," said my uncle. " I perceive that there is no possible means by which it can be kept pure from roguery. I have been cheated and befooled ; but a man learns wisdom at last, and never again do I give countenance to a prize-fight."

Had I been older or he less formidable, I might have said what was in my heart, and begged him to give up other things also—to come out from those shallow circles in which he lived, and to find some work that was worthy of his strong brain and his good heart. But the thought had hardly formed itself in my mind before he had dropped his serious vein, and was chatting away about some new silver-mounted harness which he intended to spring upon the Mall, and about the match for a thousand guineas which he meant to make between his filly Ethelberta and Lord Doncaster's famous three-year-old Aurelius.

We had got as far as Whiteman's Green, which is rather more than midway between Crawley Down and Friar's Oak, when, looking backwards, I saw far down

the road the gleam of the sun upon a high yellow carriage. Sir Lothian Hume was following us.

" He has had the same summons as we, and is bound for the same destination," said my uncle, glancing over his shoulder at the distant barouche. " We are both wanted at Cliffe Royal—we, the two survivors of that black business. And it is Jim Harrison of all people who calls us there. Nephew, I have had an eventful life, but I feel as if the very strangest scene of it were waiting for me among those trees."

He whipped up the mares, and now from the curve of the road we could see the high dark pinnacles of the old Manor-house shooting up above the ancient oaks which ring it round. The sight of it, with its blood-stained and ghost-blasted reputation, would in itself have been enough to send a thrill through my nerves ; but when the words of my uncle made me suddenly realise that this strange summons was indeed for the two men who were concerned in that old-world tragedy, and that it was the playmate of my youth who had sent it, I caught my breath as I seemed vaguely to catch a glimpse of some portentous thing forming itself in front of us. The rusted gates between the crumbling heraldic pillars were folded back, and my uncle flicked the mares impatiently as we flew up the weed-grown avenue, until he pulled them on their haunches before the time-blotched steps. The front door was open, and Boy Jim was waiting there to meet us.

But it was a different Boy Jim from him whom I had known and loved. There was a change in him some-where, a change so marked that it was the first thing that I noticed, and yet so subtle that I could not put words to it. He was not better dressed than of old, for I well knew the old brown suit that he wore. He was not less comely, for his training had left him the very model of what a man should be. And yet there was a change, a touch of dignity in the expression, a suggestion of con-fidence in the bearing which seemed, now that it was

supplied, to be the one thing which had been needed to give him harmony and finish. Somehow, in spite of his prowess, his old school name of " Boy " had clung very naturally to him, until that instant when I saw him standing in his self-contained and magnificent manhood in the doorway of the ancient house. A woman stood beside him, her hand resting upon his shoulder, and I saw that it was Miss Hinton, of Anstey Cross.

" You remember me, Sir Charles Tregellis," said she, coming forward, as we sprang down from the curricle.

My uncle looked hard at her with a puzzled face.

" I do not think that I have the privilege, madame. And yet——"

" Polly Hinton, of the Haymarket. You surely cannot have forgotten Polly Hinton."

" Forgotten! Why, we have mourned for you in Fops' Alley for more years than I care to think of. But what in the name of wonder——"

" I was privately married, and I retired from the stage. I want you to forgive me for taking Jim away from you last night."

" It was you, then ? "

" I had a stronger claim even than you could have. You were his patron; I was his mother." She drew his head down to hers as she spoke, and there, with their cheeks together, were the two faces, the one stamped with the waning beauty of womanhood, the other with the waxing strength of man, and yet so alike in the dark eyes, the blue-black hair and the broad white brow, that I marvelled that I had never read her secret on the first days that I had seen them together. " Yes," she cried, " he is my own boy, and he saved me from what is worse than death, as your nephew Rodney could tell you. Yet my lips were sealed, and it was only last night that I could tell him that it was his mother whom he had brought back by his gentleness and his patience into the sweetness of life."

" Hush, mother! " said Jim, turning his lips to her

cheek. " There are some things which are between ourselves. But tell me, Sir Charles, how went the fight ? "

" Your uncle would have won it, but the roughs broke the ring."

" He is no uncle of mine, Sir Charles, but he has been the best and truest friend, both to me and to my father, that ever the world could offer. I only know one as true," he continued, taking me by the hand, " and dear old Rodney Stone is his name. But I trust he was not much hurt ? "

" A week or two will set him right. But I cannot pretend to understand how this matter stands, and you must allow me to say that I have not heard you advance anything yet which seems to me to justify you in abandoning your engagements at a moment's notice."

" Come in, Sir Charles, and I am convinced that you will acknowledge that I could not have done otherwise. But here, if I mistake not, is Sir Lothian Hume."

The yellow barouche had swung into the avenue, and a few moments later the weary, panting horses had pulled up behind our curricle. Sir Lothian sprang out, looking as black as a thunder-cloud.

" Stay where you are, Corcoran," said he ; and I caught a glimpse of a bottle-green coat which told me who was his travelling companion. " Well," he continued, looking round him with an insolent stare, " I should vastly like to know who has had the insolence to give me so pressing an invitation to visit my own house, and what in the devil you mean by daring to trespass upon my grounds ? "

" I promise you that you will understand this and a good deal more before we part, Sir Lothian," said Jim, with a curious smile playing over his face. " If you will follow me, I will endeavour to make it all clear to you."

With his mother's hand in his own, he led us into that ill-omened room where the cards were still heaped upon

the side-board, and the dark shadow lurked in the corner of the ceiling.

" Now, sirrah, your explanation ! " cried Sir Lothian, standing with his arms folded by the door.

" My first explanations I owe to you, Sir Charles," said Jim ; and as I listened to his voice and noted his manner, I could not but admire the effect which the company of her whom he now knew to be his mother had had upon a rude country lad. " I wish to tell you what occurred last night."

" I will tell it for you, Jim," said his mother. " You must know, Sir Charles, that though my son knew nothing of his parents, we were both alive, and had never lost sight of him. For my part, I let him have his own way in going to London and in taking up this challenge. It was only yesterday that it came to the ears of his father, who would have none of it. He was in the weakest health, and his wishes were not to be gainsayed. He ordered me to go at once and to bring his son to his side. I was at my wit's end, for I was sure that Jim would never come unless a substitute were provided for him. I went to the kind, good couple who had brought him up, and I told them how matters stood. Mrs. Harrison loved Jim as if he had been her own son, and her husband loved mine, so they came to my help, and may God bless them for their kindness to a distracted wife and mother ! Harrison would take Jim's place if Jim would go to his father. Then I drove to Crawley. I found out which was Jim's room, and I spoke to him through the window, for I was sure that those who had backed him would not let him go. I told him that I was his mother. I told him who was his father. I said that I had my phaeton ready, and that he might, for all I knew, be only in time to receive the dying blessing of that parent whom he had never known. Still the boy would not go until he had my assurance that Harrison would take his place."

" Why did he not leave a message with Belcher ? "

" My head was in a whirl, Sir Charles. To find a

father and a mother, a new name and a new rank in a few minutes might turn a stronger brain than ever mine was. My mother begged me to come with her, and I went. The phaeton was waiting, but we had scarcely started when some fellow seized the horse's head, and a couple of ruffians attacked us. One of them I beat over the head with the butt of the whip, so that he dropped the cudgel with which he was about to strike me ; then lashing the horse, I shook off the others and got safely away. I cannot imagine who they were or why they should molest me."

" Perhaps Sir Lothian Hume could tell you," said my uncle.

Our enemy said nothing ; but his little grey eyes slid round with a most murderous glance in our direction.

" After I had come here and seen my father I went down——"

My uncle stopped him with a cry of astonishment.

" What did you say, young man ? You came *here* and you saw your father—here at Cliffe Royal ? "

" Yes, sir."

My uncle had turned very pale.

" In God's name, then, tell us who your father is ! "

Jim made no answer save to point over our shoulders, and glancing round, we became aware that two people had entered the room through the door which led to the bedroom stair. The one I recognised in an instant. That impassive, mask-like face and demure manner could only belong to Ambrose, the former valet of my uncle. The other was a very different and even more singular figure. He was a tall man, clad in a dark dressing-gown, and leaning heavily upon a stick. His long, bloodless countenance was so thin and so white that it gave the strangest illusion of transparency. Only within the folds of a shroud have I ever seen so wan a face. The brindled hair and the rounded back gave the impression of advanced age, and it was only the dark brows and the bright alert eyes glancing out from beneath them which

made me doubt whether it was really an old man who stood before us.

There was an instant of silence, broken by a deep oath from Sir Lothian Hume.

" Lord Avon, by God ! " he cried.

" Very much at your service, gentlemen," answered the strange figure in the dressing-gown.

20. *Lord Avon*

MY uncle was an impassive man by nature, and had become more so by the tradition of the society in which he lived. He could have turned a card upon which his fortune depended without the twitch of a muscle, and I had seen him myself driving to imminent death on the Godstone Road with as calm a face as if he were out for his daily airing in the Mall. But now the shock which had come upon him was so great that he could only stand with white cheeks and staring, incredulous eyes. Twice I saw him open his lips, and twice he put his hand up to his throat, as though a barrier had risen betwixt himself and his utterance. Finally, he took a sudden little run forward with both his hands thrown out in greeting.

" Ned ! " he cried.

But the strange man who stood before him folded his arms over his breast.

" No, Charles," said he.

My uncle stopped and looked at him in amazement.

" Surely, Ned, you have a greeting for me after all these years ? "

" You believed me to have done this deed, Charles. I read it in your eyes and in your manner on that terrible morning. You never asked me for an explanation. You never considered how impossible such a crime must be for a man of my character. At the first breath of suspicion you, my intimate friend, the man who knew me best, set me down as a thief and a murderer."

" No, no, Ned."

" You did, Charles ; I read it in your eyes. And so it was that when I wished to leave that which was most precious to me in safe hands I had to pass you over and to place him in the charge of the one man who from the first never doubted my innocence. Better a thousand times that my son should be brought up in a humble station and in ignorance of his unfortunate father, than that he should learn to share the doubts and suspicions of his equals."

" Then he is really your son ! " cried my uncle, staring at Jim in amazement.

For answer the man stretched out his long withered arm, and placed a gaunt hand upon the shoulder of the actress, whilst she looked up at him with love in her eyes.

" I married, Charles, and I kept it secret from my friends, for I had chosen my wife outside our own circles. You know the foolish pride which has always been the strongest part of my nature. I could not bear to avow that which I had done. It was this neglect upon my part which led to an estrangement between us, and drove her into habits for which it is I who am to blame and not she. Yet on account of these same habits I took the child from her and gave her an allowance on condition that she did not interfere with it. I had feared that the boy might receive evil from her, and had never dreamed in my blindness that she might get good from him. But I have learned in my miserable life, Charles, that there is a power which fashions things for us, though we may strive to thwart it, and that we are in truth driven by an unseen current towards a certain goal, however much we may deceive ourselves into thinking that it is our own sails and oars which are speeding us upon our way."

My eyes had been upon the face of my uncle as he listened, but now as I turned them from him they fell once more upon the thin, wolfish face of Sir Lothian Hume. He stood near the window, his grey silhouette thrown up against the square of dusty glass ; and I have

never seen such a play of evil passions, of anger, of jealousy, of disappointed greed upon a human face before.

" Am I to understand," said he, in a loud, harsh voice, " that this young man claims to be the heir of the peerage of Avon ? "

" He is my lawful son."

" I knew you fairly well, sir, in our youth ; but you will allow me to observe that neither I nor any friend of yours ever heard of a wife or a son. I defy Sir Charles Tregellis to say that he ever dreamed that there was any heir except myself."

" I have already explained, Sir Lothian, why I kept my marriage secret."

" You have explained, sir ; but it is for others in another place to say if that explanation is satisfactory."

Two blazing dark eyes flashed out of the pale haggard face with as strange and sudden an effect as if a stream of light were to beat through the windows of a shattered and ruined house.

" You dare to doubt my word ? "

" I demand a proof."

" My word is proof to those who know me."

" Excuse me, Lord Avon ; but I know you, and I see no reason why I should accept your statement."

It was a brutal speech, and brutally delivered. Lord Avon staggered forward, and it was only his son on one side and his wife on the other who kept his quivering hands from the throat of his insulter. Sir Lothian recoiled from the pale fierce face with the black brows, but he still glared angrily about the room.

" A very pretty conspiracy this," he cried, " with a criminal, an actress and a prize-fighter all playing their parts. Sir Charles Tregellis, you shall hear from me again ! And you also, my lord ! " He turned upon his heel and strode from the room.

" He has gone to denounce me," said Lord Avon, a spasm of wounded pride distorting his features.

" Shall I bring him back ? " cried Boy Jim.

" No, no, let him go. It is as well, for I have already made up my mind that my duty to you, my son, outweighs that which I owe, and have at such bitter cost fulfilled, to my brother and my family."

" You did me an injustice, Ned," said my uncle, " if you thought that I had forgotten you, or that I had judged you unkindly. If ever I have thought that you had done this deed—and how could I doubt the evidence of my own eyes—I have always believed that it was at a time when your mind was unhinged, and when you knew no more of what you were about than the man who is walking in his sleep."

" What do you mean when you talk about the evidence of your own eyes ? " asked Lord Avon, looking hard at my uncle.

" I saw you, Ned, upon that accursed night."

" Saw me ? Where ? "

" In the passage."

" And doing what ? "

" You were coming from your brother's room. I had heard his voice raised in anger and pain only an instant before. You carried in your hand a bag full of money, and your face betrayed the utmost agitation. If you can but explain to me, Ned, how you came to be there, you will take from my heart a weight which has pressed upon it for all these years."

No one now would have recognised in my uncle the man who was the leader of all the fops of London. In the presence of this old friend and of the tragedy which girt him round, the veil of triviality and affectation had been rent, and I felt all my gratitude towards him deepening for the first time into affection whilst I watched his pale, anxious face, and the eager hope which shone on his eyes as he awaited his friend's explanation. Lord Avon sank his face in his hands and for a few moments there was silence in the dim grey room.

" I do not wonder now that you were shaken," said he at last. " My God, what a net was cast round me !

Had this vile charge been brought against me, you, my
dearest friend, would have been compelled to tear away
the last doubt as to my guilt.   And yet, in spite of what
you have seen, Charles, I am as innocent in the matter
as you are."

" I thank God that I hear you say so."

" But you are not satisfied, Charles.   I can read it on
your face.   You wish to know why an innocent man
should conceal himself for all these years."

" Your word is enough for me, Ned ; but the world
will wish this other question answered also."

" It was to save the family honour, Charles.   You
know how dear it was to me.   I could not clear myself
without proving my brother to have been guilty of the
foulest crime which a gentleman could commit.   For
eighteen years I have screened him at the expense of
everything which a man could sacrifice.   I have lived
a living death which has left me an old and shattered man
when I am but in my fortieth year.   But now when I am
faced with the alternative of telling the facts about my
brother, or of wronging my son, I can only act in one
fashion, and the more so since I have reason to hope that
a way may be found by which what I am now about to
disclose to you need never come to the public ear."

He rose from his chair, and leaning heavily upon his
two supporters, he tottered across the room to the dust-
covered sideboard.   There, in the centre of it, was lying
that ill-boding pile of time-stained, mildewed cards, just
as Boy Jim and I had seen them years before.   Lord
Avon turned them over with trembling fingers, and then
picking up half a dozen, he brought them to my uncle.

" Place your finger and thumb upon the left-hand
bottom corner of this card, Charles," said he.   " Pass
them lightly backwards and forwards, and tell me what
you feel."

" It has been pricked with a pin."

" Precisely.   What is the card ? "

My uncle turned it over.

" It is the king of clubs."

" Try the bottom corner of this one."

" It is quite smooth."

" And the card is ? "

" The three of spades."

" And this one ? "

" It has been pricked.   It is the ace of hearts."

Lord Avon hurled them down upon the floor.

" There you have the whole accursed story ! " he cried. " Need I go further where every word is an agony ? "

" I see something, but not all. You must continue, Ned."

The frail figure stiffened itself, as though he were visibly bracing himself for an effort.

" I will tell it you, then, once and for ever. Never again, I trust, will it be necessary for me to open my lips about the miserable business. You remember our game. You remember how we lost. You remember how you all retired, and left me sitting in this very room, and at that very table. Far from being tired, I was exceedingly wakeful, and I remained here for an hour or more thinking over the incidents of the game and the changes which it promised to bring about in my fortunes. I had, as you will recollect, lost heavily, and my only consolation was that my own brother had won. I knew that, owing to his reckless mode of life, he was firmly in the clutches of the Jews, and I hoped that that which had shaken my position might have the effect of restoring his. As I sat there, fingering the cards in an abstracted way, some chance led me to observe the small needle-pricks which you have just felt. I went over the packs, and found, to my unspeakable horror, that anyone who was in the secret could hold them in dealing in such a way as to be able to count the exact number of high cards which fell to each of his opponents. And then, with such a flush of shame and disgust as I had never known, I remember how my attention had been drawn to my brother's mode

of dealing, its slowness, and the way in which he held each card by the lower corner.

" I did not condemn him precipitately. I sat for a long time calling to mind every incident which could tell one way or the other. Alas ! it all went to confirm me in my first horrible suspicion, and to turn it into a certainty. My brother had ordered the packs from Ledbury's, in Bond Street. They had been for some hours in his chambers. He had played throughout with a decision which had surprised us at the time. Above all, I could not conceal from myself that his past life was not such as to make even so abominable a crime as this impossible to him. Tingling with anger and shame, I went straight up that stair, the cards in my hand, and I taxed him with this lowest and meanest of all the crimes to which a villain could descend.

" He had not retired to rest, and his ill-gotten gains were spread out upon the dressing-table. I hardly know what I said to him, but the facts were so deadly that he did not attempt to deny his guilt. You will remember, as the only mitigation of his crime, that he was not yet one and twenty years of age. My words overwhelmed him. He went on his knees to me, imploring me to spare him. I told him that out of consideration for our family I should make no public exposure of him, but that he must never again in his life lay his hand upon a card, and that the money which he had won must be returned next morning with an explanation. It would be social ruin, he protested. I answered that he must take the consequence of his own deed. Then and there I burned the papers which he had won from me and I replaced in a canvas bag which lay upon the table all the gold pieces. I would have left the room without another word, but he clung to me, and tore the ruffle from my wrist in his attempt to hold me back, and to prevail upon me to promise to say nothing to you or Sir Lothian Hume. It was his despairing cry, when he found that I was proof against all his entreaties, which reached your ears,

Charles, and caused you to open your chamber door and to see me as I returned to my room."

My uncle drew a long sigh of relief.

" Nothing could be clearer ! " he murmured.

" In the morning I came, as you remember, to your room, and I returned your money. I did the same to Sir Lothian Hume. I said nothing of my reasons for doing so, for I found that I could not bring myself to confess our disgrace to you. Then came the horrible discovery which has darkened my life, and which was as great a mystery to me as it has been to you. I saw that I was suspected, and I saw, also, that even if I were to clear myself, it could only be done by a public confession of the infamy of my brother. I shrank from it, Charles. Any personal suffering seemed to me to be better than to bring public shame upon a family which has held an untarnished record through so many centuries. I fled from my trial, therefore, and disappeared from the world.

" But, first of all, it was necessary that I should make arrangements for the wife and the son, of whose existence you and my other friends were ignorant. It is with shame, Mary, that I confess it, and I acknowledge to you that the blame of all the consequences rests with me rather than with you. At the time there were reasons, now happily long gone past, which made me determine that the son was better apart from the mother, whose absence at that age he would not miss. I would have taken you into my confidence, Charles, had it not been that your suspicions had wounded me deeply—for I did not at that time understand how strong the reasons were which had prejudiced you against me.

" On the evening after the tragedy I fled to London, and arranged that my wife should have a fitting allowance on condition that she did not interfere with the child. I had, as you remember, had much to do with Harrison, the prize-fighter, and I had often had occasion to admire his simple and honest nature. I took my boy to him now, and I found him, as I expected, incredulous as to

my guilt, and ready to assist me in any way. At his wife's entreaty he had just retired from the Ring, and was uncertain how he should employ himself. I was able to fit him up as a smith, on condition that he should ply his trade at the village of Friar's Oak. My agreement was that James was to be brought up as their nephew, and that he should know nothing of his unhappy parents.

"You will ask me why I selected Friar's Oak. It was because I had already chosen my place of concealment ; and if I could not see my boy, it was, at least, some consolation to know that he was near me. You are aware that this mansion is one of the oldest in England ; but you are not aware that it has been built with a very special eye to concealment, that there are no less than two habitable secret chambers, and that the outer or thicker walls are tunnelled into passages. The existence of these rooms has always been a family secret, though it was one which I valued so little that it was only the chance of my seldom using the house which had prevented me from pointing them out to some friend. Now I found that a secure retreat was provided for me in my extremity. I stole down to my own mansion, entered it at night, and leaving all that was dear to me behind, I crept like a rat behind the wainscot, to live out the remainder of my weary life in solitude and misery. In this worn face, Charles, and in this grizzled hair, you may read the diary of my most miserable existence.

"Once a week Harrison used to bring me up provisions, passing them through the pantry window, which I left open for the purpose. Sometimes I would steal out at night and walk under the stars once more, with the cool breeze upon my forehead ; but this I had at last to stop, for I was seen by the rustics, and rumours of a spirit at Cliffe Royal began to get about. One night two ghost-hunters——"

"It was I, father," cried Boy Jim ; "I and my friend, Rodney Stone."

"I know it was. Harrison told me so the same night.

I was proud, James, to see that you had the spirit of the Barringtons, and that I had an heir whose gallantry might redeem the family blot which I have striven so hard to cover over. Then came the day when your mother's kindness—her mistaken kindness—gave you the means of escaping to London."

" Ah, Edward," cried his wife, " if you had seen our boy, like a caged eagle, beating against the bars, you would have helped to give him even so short a flight as this."

" I do not blame you, Mary. It is possible that I should have done so. He went to London, and he tried to open a career for himself by his own strength and courage. How many of our ancestors have done the same, save only that a sword-hilt lay in their closed hands ; but of them all I do not know that any have carried themselves more gallantly ! "

" That I dare swear," said my uncle, heartily.

" And then, when Harrison at last returned, I learned that my son was actually matched to fight in a public prize-battle. That would not do, Charles ! It was one thing to fight as you and I have fought in our youth, and it was another to compete for a purse of gold."

" My dear friend, I would not for the world——"

" Of course you would not, Charles. You chose the best man, and how could you do otherwise ? But it would not do ! I determined that the time had come when I should reveal myself to my son, the more so as there were many signs that my most unnatural existence had seriously weakened my health. Chance, or shall I not rather say Providence, had at last made clear all that had been dark, and given me the means of establishing my innocence. My wife went yesterday to bring my boy at last to the side of his unfortunate father."

There was silence for some time, and then it was my uncle's voice which broke it.

" You've been the most ill-used man in the world, Ned," said he. " Please God we shall have many years

yet in which to make up to you for it. But, after all, it seems to me that we are as far as ever from learning how your unfortunate brother met his death."

" For eighteen years it was as much a mystery to me as to you, Charles. But now at last the guilt is manifest. Stand forward, Ambrose, and tell your story as frankly and as fully as you have told it to me."

21. *The Valet's Story*

THE valet had shrunk into the dark corner of the room, and had remained so motionless that we had forgotten his presence until, upon this appeal from his former master, he took a step forward into the light, turning his sallow face in our direction. His usually impassive features were in a state of painful agitation, and he spoke slowly and with hesitation, as though his trembling lips could hardly frame the words. And yet so strong is habit that, even in this extremity of emotion, he assumed the deferential air of the high-class valet, and his sentences formed themselves in the sonorous fashion which had struck my attention upon that first day when the curricle of my uncle had stopped outside my father's door.

" My Lady Avon and gentlemen," said he, " if I have sinned in this matter, and I freely confess that I have done so, I only know one way in which I can atone for it, and that is by making the full and complete confession which my noble master, Lord Avon, has demanded. I assure you, then, that what I am about to tell you, surprising as it may seem, is the absolute and undeniable truth concerning the mysterious death of Captain Barrington.

" It may seem impossible to you that one in my humble walk of life should bear a deadly and implacable hatred against a man in the position of Captain Barrington. You think that the gulf between us is too wide. I can

tell you, gentlemen, that the gulf which can be bridged by unlawful love can be spanned also by an unlawful hatred, and that upon the day when this young man stole from me all that made my life worth living, I vowed to Heaven that I should take from him that foul life of his, though the deed would cover but the tiniest fraction of the debt which he owed me. I see that you look askance at me, Sir Charles Tregellis, but you should pray to God, sir, that you may never have the chance of finding out what you would yourself be capable of in the same position."

It was a wonder to all of us to see this man's fiery nature breaking suddenly through the artificial constraints with which he held it in check. His short dark hair seemed to bristle upwards, his eyes glowed with the intensity of his passion, and his face expressed a malignity of hatred which neither the death of his enemy nor the lapse of years could mitigate. The demure servant was gone, and there stood in his place a deep and dangerous man, one who might be an ardent lover or a most vindictive foe.

" We were about to be married, she and I, when some black chance threw him across our path. I do not know by what base deceptions he lured her away from me. I have heard that she was only one of many, and that he was an adept at the art. It was done before ever I knew the danger, and she was left with her broken heart and her ruined life to return to that home into which she had brought disgrace and misery. I only saw her once. She told me that her seducer had burst out a-laughing when she had reproached him for his perfidy and I swore to her that his heart's blood should pay me for that laugh.

" I was a valet at the time, but I was not yet in the service of Lord Avon. I applied for and gained that position with the one idea that it might give me an opportunity of settling my accounts with his younger brother. And yet my chance was a terribly long time coming, for many months had passed before the visit to

Cliffe Royal gave me the opportunity which I longed for by day and dreamed of by night. When it did come, however, it came in a fashion which was more favourable to my plans than anything that I had ever ventured to hope for.

" Lord Avon was of opinion that no one but himself knew of the secret passages in Cliffe Royal. In this he was mistaken. I knew of them—or, at least, I knew enough of them to serve my purpose. I need not tell you how, one day, when preparing the chambers for the guests, an accidental pressure upon part of the fittings caused a panel to gape in the woodwork, and showed me a narrow opening in the wall. Making my way down this, I found that another panel led into a larger bedroom beyond. That was all I knew, but it was all that was needed for my purpose. The disposal of the rooms had been left in my hands, and I arranged that Captain Barrington should sleep in the larger and I in the smaller. I could come upon him when I wished, and no one would be the wiser.

" And then he arrived. How can I describe to you the fever of impatience in which I lived until the moment should come for which I had waited and planned. For a night and a day they gambled, and for a night and a day I counted the minutes which brought me nearer to my man. They might ring for fresh wine at what hour they liked, they always found me waiting and ready, so that this young captain hiccoughed out that I was the model of all valets. My master advised me to go to bed. He had noticed my flushed cheek and my bright eyes, and he set me down as being in a fever. So I was, but it was a fever which only one medicine could assuage.

" Then at last, very early in the morning, I heard them push back their chairs, and I knew that their game had at last come to an end. When I entered the room to receive my orders, I found that Captain Barrington had already stumbled off to bed. The others had also retired, and my master was sitting alone at the table, with his

empty bottle and the scattered cards in front of him. He ordered me angrily to my room, and this time I obeyed him.

" My first care was to provide myself with a weapon. I knew that if I were face to face with him I could tear his throat out, but I must so arrange that the fashion of his death should be a noiseless one. There was a hunting trophy in the hall, and from it I took a straight heavy knife which I sharpened upon my boot. Then I stole to my room, and sat waiting upon the side of my bed. I had made up my mind what I should do. There would be little satisfaction in killing him if he was not to know whose hand had struck the blow, or which of his sins it came to avenge. Could I but bind him and gag him in his drunken sleep, then a prick or two of my dagger would arouse him to listen to what I had to say to him. I pictured the look in his eyes as the haze of sleep cleared slowly away from them, the look of anger turning suddenly to stark horror as he understood who I was and what I had come for. It would be the supreme moment of my life.

" I waited as it seemed to me for at least an hour ; but I had no watch, and my impatience was such that I dare say it really was little more than a quarter of that time. Then I rose, removed my shoes, took my knife, and having opened the panel, slipped silently through. It was not more than thirty feet that I had to go, but I went inch by inch, for the old rotten boards snapped like breaking twigs if a sudden weight was placed upon them. It was, of course, pitch dark, and very, very slowly I felt my way along. At last I saw a yellow seam of light glimmering in front of me, and I knew that it came from the other panel. I was too soon, then, since he had not extinguished his candles. I had waited many months, and I could afford to wait another hour, for I did not wish to do anything precipitately or in a hurry.

" It was very necessary to move silently now, since I was within a few feet of my man, with only the thin

wooden partition between. Age had warped and cracked the boards, so that when I had at last very stealthily crept my way as far as the sliding panel, I found that I could, without any difficulty, see into the room. Captain Barrington was standing by the dressing-table with his coat and vest off. A large pile of sovereigns and several slips of paper were lying before him, and he was counting over his gambling gains. His face was flushed, and he was heavy from want of sleep and from wine. It rejoiced me to see it, for it meant that his slumber would be deep, and that all would be made easy for me.

" I was still watching him, when of a sudden I saw him start, and a terrible expression come upon his face. For an instant my heart stood still, for I feared that he had in some way divined my presence. And then I heard the voice of my master within. I could not see the door by which he had entered, nor could I see him where he stood, but I heard all that he had to say. As I watched the captain's face flush fiery red, and then turn to a livid white as he listened to those bitter words which told him of his infamy, my revenge was sweeter—far sweeter—than my most pleasant dreams had ever pictured it. I saw my master approach the dressing-table, hold the papers in the flame of the candle, throw their charred ashes into the grate, and sweep the golden pieces into a small brown canvas bag. Then, as he turned to leave the room, the captain seized him by the wrist, imploring him, by the memory of their mother, to have mercy upon him ; and I loved my master as I saw him drag his sleeve from the grasp of the clutching fingers, and leave the stricken wretch grovelling upon the floor.

" And now I was left with a difficult point to settle, for it was hard for me to say whether it was better that I should do that which I had come for, or whether, by holding this man's guilty secret, I might not have in my hand a keener and more deadly weapon than my master's hunting-knife. I was sure that Lord Avon could not and would not expose him. I knew your sense of family

pride too well, my lord, and I was certain that his secret was safe in your hands. But I both could and would ; and then, when his life had been blasted, and he had been hounded from his regiment and from his clubs, it would be time, perhaps, for me to deal in some other way with him."

" Ambrose, you are a black villain," said my uncle.

" We all have our own feelings, Sir Charles ; and you will permit me to say that a serving-man may resent an injury as much as a gentleman, though the redress of the duel is denied to him. But I am telling you frankly, at Lord Avon's request, all that I thought and did upon that night, and I shall continue to do so, even if I am not fortunate enough to win your approval.

" When Lord Avon had left him, the captain remained for some time in a kneeling attitude, with his face sunk upon a chair. Then he rose, and paced slowly up and down the room, his chin sunk upon his breast. Every now and then he would pluck at his hair, or shake his clenched hands in the air ; and I saw the moisture glisten upon his brow. For a time I lost sight of him, and I heard him opening drawer after drawer, as though he were in search of something. Then he stood over by his dressing-table again, with his back turned to me. His head was thrown a little back, and he had both hands up to the collar of his shirt, as though he were striving to undo it. And then there was a gush as if a ewer had been upset, and down he sank upon the ground, with his head in the corner, twisted round at so strange an angle to his shoulders that one glimpse of it told me that my man was slipping swiftly from the clutch in which I had fancied that I held him. I slid my panel, and was in the room in an instant. His eyelids still quivered, and it seemed to me, as my gaze met his glazing eyes, that I could read both recognition and surprise in them. I laid my knife upon the floor, and I stretched myself out beside him, that I might whisper in his ear one or two little things of which I wished to remind him ; but even as I did so, he gave a gasp and was gone.

" It is singular that I, who had never feared him in life, should be frightened at him now, and yet when I looked at him, and saw that all was motionless save the creeping stain upon the carpet, I was seized with a sudden foolish spasm of terror, and, catching up my knife, I fled swiftly and silently back to my own room, closing the panels behind me. It was only when I had reached it that I found that in my mad haste I had carried away, not the hunting-knife which I had taken with me, but the bloody razor which had dropped from the dead man's hand. This I concealed where no one has ever discovered it ; but my fears would not allow me to go back for the other, as I might perhaps have done, had I foreseen how terribly its presence might tell against my master. And that, Lady Avon and gentlemen, is an exact and honest account of how Captain Barrington came by his end."

" And how was it," asked my uncle, angrily, " that you have allowed an innocent man to be persecuted all these years, when a word from you might have saved him ? "

" Because I had every reason to believe, Sir Charles, that that would be most unwelcome to Lord Avon. How could I tell all this without revealing the family scandal which he was so anxious to conceal ? I confess that at the beginning I did not tell him what I had seen, and my excuse must be that he disappeared before I had time to determine what I should do. For many a year, however —ever since I have been in your service, Sir Charles— my conscience tormented me, and I swore that if ever I should find my old master, I should reveal everything to him. The chance of my overhearing a story told by young Mr. Stone here, which showed me that someone was using the secret chambers of Cliffe Royal, convinced me that Lord Avon was in hiding there, and I lost no time in seeking him out and offering to do him all the justice in my power."

" What he says is true," said his master ; " but it would have been strange indeed if I had hesitated to

sacrifice a frail life and failing health in a cause for which I freely surrendered all that youth had to offer. But new considerations have at last compelled me to alter my resolution. My son, through ignorance of his true position, was drifting into a course of life which accorded with his strength and his spirit, but not with the traditions of his house. Again, I reflected that many of those who knew my brother had passed away, that all the facts need not come out, and that my death whilst under the suspicion of such a crime would cast a deeper stain upon our name than the sin which he had so terribly expiated. For these reasons—— "

The tramp of several heavy footsteps reverberating through the old house broke in suddenly upon Lord Avon's words. His wan face turned even a shade greyer as he heard it, and he looked piteously to his wife and son.

" They will arrest me ! " he cried. " I must submit to the degradation of an arrest."

" This way, Sir James ; this way," said the harsh tones of Sir Lothian Hume from without.

" I do not need to be shown the way in a house where I have drunk many a bottle of good claret," cried a deep voice in reply ; and there in the doorway stood the broad figure of Squire Ovington in his buck-skins and top-boots, a riding-crop in his hand. Sir Lothian Hume was at his elbow, and I saw the faces of two country constables peeping over his shoulders.

" Lord Avon," said the squire, " as a magistrate of the county of Sussex, it is my duty to tell you that a warrant is held against you for the wilful murder of your brother, Captain Barrington, in the year 1786."

" I am ready to answer the charge."

" This I tell you as a magistrate. But as a man, and the Squire of Rougham Grange, I'm right glad to see you, Ned, and here's my hand on it, and never will I believe that a good Tory like yourself, and a man who could show his horse's tail to any field in the whole Down county, would ever be capabl of so vile an act."

" You do me justice, James," said Lord Avon, clasping the broad, brown hand which the country squire had held out to him. " I am as innocent as you are ; and I can prove it."

" Damned glad I am to hear it, Ned ! That is to say, Lord Avon, that any defence which you may have to make will be decided upon by your peers and by the laws of your country."

" Until which time," added Sir Lothian Hume, " a stout door and a good lock will be the best guarantee that Lord Avon will be there when called for."

The squire's weather-stained face flushed to a deeper red as he turned upon the Londoner.

" Are you the magistrate of a county, sir ? "

" I have not the honour, Sir James."

" Then how dare you advise a man who has sat on the bench for nigh twenty years ? When I am in doubt, sir, the law provides me with a clerk with whom I may confer, and I ask no other assistance."

" You take too high a tone in this matter, Sir James. I am not accustomed to be taken to task so sharply."

" Nor am I accustomed, sir, to be interfered with in my official duties. I speak as a magistrate, Sir Lothian, but I am always ready to sustain my opinions as a man."

Sir Lothian bowed.

" You will allow me to observe, sir, that I have personal interests of the highest importance involved in this matter. I have every reason to believe that there is a conspiracy afoot which will affect my position as heir to Lord Avon's titles and estates. I desire his safe custody in order that this matter may be cleared up, and I call upon you, as a magistrate, to execute your warrant."

" Plague take it, Ned ! " cried the squire, " I would that my clerk Johnson were here, for I would deal as kindly by you as the law allows ; and yet I am, as you hear, called upon to secure your person."

" Permit me to suggest, sir," said my uncle, " that

so long as he is under the personal supervision of the magistrate, he may be said to be under the care of the law, and that this condition will be fulfilled if he is under the roof of Rougham Grange."

" Nothing could be better," cried the squire, heartily. " You will stay with me, Ned, until this matter blows over. In other words, Lord Avon, I make myself responsible, as the representative of the law, that you are held in safe custody until your person may be required of me."

" Yours is a true heart, James."

" Tut, tut ! it is the due process of the law. I trust, Sir Lothian Hume, that you find nothing to object to in it ! "

Sir Lothian shrugged his shoulders, and looked blackly at the magistrate. Then he turned to my uncle.

" There is a small matter still open between us," said he. " Would you kindly give me the name of a friend ? Mr. Corcoran, who is outside in my barouche, would act for me, and we might meet to-morrow morning."

" With pleasure," answered my uncle. " I dare say your father would act for me, nephew ? Your friend may call upon Lieutenant Stone, of Friar's Oak, and the sooner the better."

And so this strange conference ended. As for me, I had sprung to the side of the old friend of my boyhood, and was trying to tell him my joy at his good fortune, and listening to his assurance that nothing that could ever befall him could weaken the love that he bore me. My uncle touched me on the shoulder, and we were about to leave, when Ambrose, whose bronze mask had been drawn down once more over his fiery passions, came demurely towards him.

" Beg your pardon, Sir Charles," said he ; " but it shocks me very much to see your cravat."

" You are right, Ambrose," my uncle answered. " Lorimer does his best, but I have never been able to fill your place."

"I should be proud to serve you, sir; but you must acknowledge that Lord Avon has the prior claim. If he will release me——"

"You may go, Ambrose; you may go!" cried Lord Avon. "You are an excellent servant, but your presence has become painful to me."

"Thank you, Ned," said my uncle. "But you must not leave me so suddenly again, Ambrose."

"Permit me to explain the reason, sir. I had determined to give you notice when we reached Brighton; but as we drove from the village that day, I caught a glimpse of a lady passing in a phaeton between whom and Lord Avon I was well aware there was a close intimacy, although I was not certain that she was actually his wife. Her presence there confirmed me in my opinion that he was in hiding at Cliffe Royal, and I dropped from your curricle and followed her at once, in order to lay the matter before her, and explain how very necessary it was that Lord Avon should see me."

"Well, I forgive you for your desertion, Ambrose," said my uncle; "and," he added, "I should be vastly obliged to you if you would rearrange my tie."

22. *The End*

SIR JAMES OVINGTON'S carriage was waiting without, and in it the Avon family, so tragically separated and so strangely reunited, were borne away to the squire's hospitable home. When they had gone, my uncle mounted his curricle, and drove Ambrose and myself to the village.

"We had best see your father at once, nephew," said he. "Sir Lothian and his man started some time ago. I should be sorry if there should be any hitch in our meeting."

For my part, I was thinking of our opponent's deadly reputation as a duellist, and I suppose that my features

must have betrayed my feelings, for my uncle began to laugh.

" Why, nephew," said he, " you look as if you were walking behind my coffin. It is not my first affair, and I dare bet that it will not be my last. When I fight near town I usually fire a hundred or so in Manton's back shop, but I dare say I can find my way to his waist-coat. But I confess that I am somewhat *accablé*, by all that has befallen us. To think of my dear old friend being not only alive, but innocent as well ! And that he should have such a strapping son and heir to carry on the race of Avon ! This will be the last blow to Hume, for I know that the Jews have given him rope on the score of his expectations. And you, Ambrose, that you should break out in such a way ! "

Of all the amazing things which had happened, this seemed to have impressed my uncle most, and he recurred to it again and again. That a man whom he had come to regard as a machine for tying cravats and brewing chocolate should suddenly develop fiery human passions was indeed a prodigy. If his silver razor-heater had taken to evil ways he could not have been more astounded.

We were still a hundred yards from the cottage when I saw the tall, green-coated Mr. Corcoran striding down the garden path. My father was waiting for us at the door with an expression of subdued delight upon his face.

" Happy to serve you in any way, Sir Charles," said he. " We've arranged it for to-morrow at seven on Ditchling Common."

" I wish these things could be brought off a little later in the day," said my uncle. " One has either to rise at a perfectly absurd hour, or else to neglect one's toilet."

" They are stopping across the road at the Friar's Oak inn, and if you would wish it later——"

" No, no ; I shall make the effort. Ambrose, you will bring up the *batterie de toilette* at five."

" I don't know whether you would care to use my barkers," said my father. " I've had 'em in fourteen

actions, and up to thirty yards you couldn't wish a better tool."

"Thank you, I have my duelling pistols under the seat. See that the triggers are oiled, Ambrose, for I love a light pull. Ah, sister Mary, I have brought your boy back to you, none the worse, I hope, for the dissipations of town."

I need not tell you how my dear mother wept over me and fondled me, for you who have mothers will know for yourselves, and you who have not will never understand how warm and snug the home nest can be. How I had chafed and longed for the wonders of town, and yet, now that I had seen more than my wildest dreams had ever deemed possible, my eyes had rested upon nothing which was so sweet and so restful as our own little sitting-room, with its terra-cotta-coloured walls, and those trifles which are so insignificant in themselves, and yet so rich in memories—the blow-fish from the Moluccas, the narwhal's horn from the Arctic, and the picture of the *Ça Ira*, with Lord Hotham in chase! How cheery, too, to see at one side of the shining grate my father with his pipe and his merry red face, and on the other my mother with her fingers ever turning and darting with her knitting-needles! As I looked at them I marvelled that I could ever have longed to leave them, or that I could bring myself to leave them again.

But leave them I must, and that speedily, as I learned amidst the boisterous congratulations of my father and the tears of my mother. He had himself been appointed to the *Cato*, 64, with post rank, whilst a note had come from Lord Nelson at Portsmouth to say that a vacancy was open for me if I should present myself at once.

"And your mother has your sea-chest all ready, my lad, and you can travel down with me to-morrow; for if you are to be one of Nelson's men, you must show him that you are worthy of it."

"All the Stones have been in the sea-service," said my mother, apologetically, t⸍ my uncle, "and it is a great

chance that he should enter under Lord Nelson's own patronage. But we can never forget your kindness, Charles, in showing our dear Rodney something of the world."

" On the contrary, sister Mary," said my uncle, graciously, " your son has been an excellent companion to me—so much so that I fear that I am open to the charge of having neglected my dear Fidelio. I trust that I bring him back somewhat more polished than I found him. It would be folly to call him *distingué*, but he is at least unobjectionable. Nature has denied him the highest gifts, and I find him adverse to employing the compensating advantages of art ; but, at least, I have shown him something of life, and I have taught him a few lessons in finesse and deportment which may appear to be wasted upon him at present, but which, none the less, may come back to him in his more mature years. If his career in town has been a disappointment to me, the reason lies mainly in the fact that I am foolish enough to measure others by the standard which I have myself set. I am well disposed towards him, however, and I consider him eminently adapted for the profession which he is about to adopt."

He held out his sacred snuff-box to me as he spoke, as a solemn pledge of his goodwill, and, as I look back at him, there is no moment at which I see him more plainly than that with the old mischievous light dancing once more in his large intolerant eyes, one thumb in the armpit of his vest, and the little shining box held out upon his snow-white palm. He was a type and leader of a strange breed of men which has vanished away from England— the full-blooded, virile buck, exquisite in his dress, narrow in his thoughts, coarse in his amusements and eccentric in his habits. They walk across the bright stage of English history with their finicky step, their preposterous cravats, their high collars, their dangling seals, and they vanish into those dark wings from which there is no return. The world has outgrown them, and

there is no place now for their strange fashions, their practical jokes, and carefully cultivated eccentricities. And yet behind this outer veiling of folly, with which they so carefully draped themselves, they were often men of strong character and robust personality. The languid loungers of St. James's were also the yachtsmen of the Solent, the fine riders of the shires, and the hardy fighters in many a wayside battle and many a morning frolic. Wellington picked his best officers from amongst them. They condescended occasionally to poetry or oratory ; and Byron, Charles James Fox, Sheridan and Castlereagh preserved some reputation amongst them, in spite of their publicity. I cannot think how the historian of the future can hope to understand them, when I, who knew one of them so well, and bore his blood in my veins, could never quite tell how much of him was real, and how much was due to the affectations which he had cultivated so long that they had ceased to deserve the name. Through the chinks of that armour of folly I have sometimes thought that I had caught a glimpse of a good and true man within, and it pleases me to hope that I was right.

It was destined that the exciting incidents of that day were even now not at an end. I had retired early to rest, but it was impossible for me to sleep, for my mind would turn to Boy Jim and to the extraordinary change in his position and prospects. I was still turning and tossing when I heard the sound of flying hoofs coming down the London Road, and immediately afterwards the grating of wheels as they pulled up in front of the inn. My window chanced to be open, for it was a fresh spring night, and I heard the creak of the inn door, and a voice asking whether Sir Lothian Hume was within. At the name I sprang from my bed, and I was in time to see three men, who had alighted from the carriage, file into the lighted hall. The two horses were left standing, with the glare of the open door falling upon their brown shoulders and patient heads.

Ten minutes may have passed, and then I heard the clatter of many steps, and a knot of men came clustering through the door.

"You need not employ violence," said a harsh clear voice. "On whose suit is it?"

"Several suits, sir. They 'eld over in the 'opes that you'd pull off the fight this mornin'. Total amounts is twelve thousand pound."

"Look here, my man, I have a very important appointment for seven o'clock to-morrow. I'll give you fifty pounds if you will leave me until then."

"Couldn't do it, sir, really. It's more than our places as sheriff's officers is worth."

In the yellow glare of the carriage-lamp I saw the baronet look up at our windows, and if hatred could have killed, his eyes would have been as deadly as his pistol.

"I can't mount the carriage unless you free my hands," said he.

"'Old 'ard, Bill, for 'e looks wicious. Let go o' one arm at a time! Ah, would you, then?"

"Corcoran! Corcoran!" screamed a voice, and I saw a plunge, a struggle and one frantic figure breaking its way from the rest. Then came a heavy blow, and down he fell in the middle of the moonlit road, flapping and jumping among the dust like a trout new landed.

"He's napped it this time! Get 'im by the wrists, Jim! Now, all together?"

He was hoisted up like a bag of flour, and fell with a brutal thud into the bottom of the carriage. The three men sprang in after him, a whip whistled in the darkness, and I had seen the last that I or anyone else, save some charitable visitor to a debtors' gaol, was ever again destined to see of Sir Lothian Hume, the once fashionable Corinthian.

Lord Avon lived for two years longer—long enough, with the help of Ambrose, to fully establish his innocence of the horrible crime, in the shadow of which he had lived

so long. What he could not clear away, however, was the effect of those years of morbid and unnatural life spent in the hidden chambers of the old house ; and it was only the devotion of his wife and of his son which kept the thin and flickering flame of his life alight. She whom I had known as the play-actress of Anstey Cross became the dowager Lady Avon ; whilst Boy Jim, as dear to me now as when we harried birds' nests and tickled trout together, is now Lord Avon, beloved by his tenantry, the finest sportsman and the most popular man from the north of the Weald to the Channel. He was married to the second daughter of Sir James Ovington ; and as I have seen three of his grandchildren within the week, I fancy that if any of Sir Lothian's descendants have their eye upon the property, they are likely to be as disappointed as their ancestor was before them. The old house of Cliffe Royal has been pulled down, owing to the terrible family associations which hung round it, and a beautiful modern building sprang up in its place. The lodge which stood by the Brighton Road was so dainty with its trellis-work and its rose bushes that I was not the only visitor who declared that I had rather be the owner of it than of the great house amongst the trees. There for many years in a happy and peaceful old age lived Jack Harrison and his wife, receiving back in the sunset of their lives the loving care which they had themselves bestowed. Never again did Champion Harrison throw his leg over the ropes of a twenty-four-foot ring ; but the story of the great battle between the smith and the west-countryman is still familiar to old ring-goers, and nothing pleased him better than to re-fight it all, round by round, as he sat in the sunshine under his rose-girt porch. But if he heard the tap of his wife's stick approaching him, his talk would break off at once into the garden and its prospects, for she was still haunted by the fear that he would some day go back to the Ring, and she never missed the old man for an hour without being convinced that he had hobbled off to wrest the belt from the latest upstart

champion. It was at his own very earnest request that they inscribed " He fought the good fight " upon his tombstone, and though I cannot doubt that he had Black Baruk and Crab Wilson in his mind when he asked it, yet none who knew him would grudge its spiritual meaning as a summing up of his clean and manly life.

Sir Charles Tregellis continued for some years to show his scarlet and gold at Newmarket, and his inimitable coats in St. James's. It was he who invented buttons and loops at the ends of dress pantaloons, and who broke fresh ground by his investigation of the comparative merits of isinglass and of starch in the preparation of shirt-fronts. There are old fops still lurking in the corners of Arthur's or of White's who can remember Tregellis's dictum, that a cravat should be so stiffened that three parts of the length could be raised by one corner, and the painful schism which followed when Lord Alvanley and his school contended that a half was sufficient. Then came the supremacy of Brummell, and the open breach upon the subject of velvet collars, in which the town followed the lead of the younger man. My uncle, who was not born to be second to anyone, retired instantly to St. Albans, and announced that he would make it the centre of fashion and of society, instead of degenerate London. It chanced, however, that the mayor and corporation waited upon him with an address of thanks for his good intentions towards the town, and that the burgesses, having ordered new coats from London for the occasion, were all arrayed in velvet collars, which so preyed upon my uncle's spirits that he took to his bed, and never showed his face in public again. His money, which had ruined what might have been a great life, was divided amongst many bequests, an annuity to his valet, Ambrose, being amongst them ; but enough has come to his sister, my dear mother, to help to make her old age as sunny and as pleasant as even I could wish.

And as for me—the poor string upon which these beads
1111

are strung—I dare scarce say another word about myself, lest this, which I had meant to be the last word of a chapter should grow into the first words of a new one. Had I not taken up my pen to tell you a story of the land, I might, perchance, have made a better one of the sea ; but the one frame cannot hold two opposite pictures. The day may come when I shall write down all that I remember of the greatest battle ever fought upon salt water, and how my father's gallant life was brought to an end as, with his paint rubbing against a French eighty-gun ship on one side and a Spanish seventy-four upon the other, he stood eating an apple in the break of his poop. I saw the smoke banks on that October evening swirl slowly up over the Atlantic swell, and rise, and rise, until they had shredded into thinnest air, and lost themselves in the infinite blue of heaven. And with them rose the cloud which had hung over the country ; and it also thinned and thinned, until God's own sun of peace and security was shining once more upon us, never more, we hope, to be bedimmed.

SIR ARTHUR CONAN DOYLE

THE HISTORICAL NOVELS

VOLUME TWO